OWARIMONOGATARI
End Tale
Part 03

NISIOISIN

Art by VOFAN

Translated by Ko Ransom

VERTICAL.

OWARIMONOGATARI, PART 03

First published in Japan in 2014 by
Kodansha Ltd., Tokyo.
Publication rights for this English edition
arranged through Kodansha Ltd., Tokyo.

Published by Vertical, an imprint of
Kodansha USA Publishing, LLC, 2020

ISBN 978-1-949980-22-6

Manufactured in the United States of America

First Edition

Second Printing

Kodansha USA Publishing, LLC
451 Park Avenue South, 7th Floor
New York, NY 10016

www.readvertical.com

CHAPTER FIVE
MAYOI HELL

MAYOI HACHIKUJI

001

I wouldn't mind dying if it meant seeing Mayoi Hachikuji again. Is that dire sentiment unexpected? Actually, I'm not exaggerating. I really was prepared, at one point, to surrender my life and immortality just to see that cheerful girl again—so why didn't I? I guess as much as or even more than I didn't mind dying, I wanted to live, and thought I had something I needed to accomplish. My family and girlfriend, saviors and buddies are the premise of that feeling, so if you told me it's terribly improper and imprudent to subject feelings to addition, subtraction, or proportions, you'd be quite right, I'd be left with no room for argument, but you see, people—or at least I—don't have the kind of self-control to become a martyr to a single emotion. Despite my tunnel vision and brooding, I'm easily distracted. Quick to go back on my words and bend my convictions—trying to gain the whole world and losing everything, that's me, Koyomi Araragi.

Not making friends.

Because it'd lower my intensity as a human.

It's with nostalgia that I look back on that line of mine, so weak I've become as a human. So damn feeble—weakest of all, I don't hate how feeble I am, and even find it charming.

How soft, and weak.

Annoying, yes.

But that's me, I can proclaim.

That's Koyomi Araragi, I do declare.

Not without—shame.

But I can insist on it—embarrassing to say.

Perhaps you find my weakness unforgivable—not dying, and feebly living on, makes me an inexcusable sinner.

Despite the hell of spring break.

I'm still alive, and it's not as if I don't notice the murderous stares—a certain transfer student, for instance, who stares at me with jet-black eyes, might say…

"You really are a fool."

Yeah, really.

Only death can cure stupidity.

At the same time, maybe it isn't so grave an illness if all it takes is dying.

002

"Ha-Hachikuji?"

"Yes."

"Hachikuji."

"The very same."

"Mayoi Hachikuji?"

"Hi—Mayoi Hachikuji, that's me."

"High Mayoi Hachikuji... Like a high elf to an elf? Are you some superior form of Hachikuji to the one I know?"

"Nope, just the regular Hachikuji. The common Mayoi Hachikuji you know well... High elf, in this day and age?"

"Mayoi Hachikuji Z?"

"No, I'm the unbranded Mayoi Hachikuji, I'm telling you. Nothing fancy, no pretension. Z? Well, since this is the final volume, I won't shy from being compared to Z-Ton of the trillion-degree fireballs."

"The most powerful monster in *Ultraman*? Shy from it, that's way too venerable a Z... Who wouldn't feel ashamed? Mayoi Hachikuji R."

"If it stands for Returns, then um, sure, absolutely."

"..."

...

No, hold on a second.

Stay calm.

No amateur calls—or rushing this.

Was there a single time in my life where rushing things turned out well? Hasn't it always ended horribly—premature celebrations followed by painful repercussions? Though I guess the painful repercussions came whether or not I rushed things (what kind of life is that?), you should always stay calm in the face of unexpected contingencies.

While it now seems like the distant past, spoken of only in legend, why not recall the time when Koyomi Araragi was called cool and handle this with steadfast composure?

You can do it.

That old self, bring him back.

Become me.

Yes, remember—what's my situation here, again? Even if it's going to be a sitcom, understand the situation before moving forward.

In other words, our usual *the story thus far.*

My name is Koyomi Araragi—not a nameless cat nor a weird bug who awoke in a futon, but a high school senior in a rural Japanese city.

Preparing to take entrance exams.

Yes, today, March thirteenth, was none other than exam day—hopefully a turning point in my life, after barely avoiding the cutoff score in the national admissions test and squeezing under the proverbial shutters as they fell.

Yet, considering who I was until not long ago, this itself is quite strange. Around this time last year, in March of my junior year, I never imagined I'd be trying to get into college. Actually, whether or not I'd be graduating at all was an earnest question.

Having entered Naoetsu High, a private prep school, thanks to a stroke of good or ill fortune, I fell behind and duly tumbled down what almost seemed like an established course, washing out and receiving one failing mark after the next—this was no mild slope but a double black diamond.

Or even a sheer drop.

A perfect instance of my *not understanding a thing,* as Sodachi Oikura might put it, but in any case, I thought that was where I'd made a wrong turn in life—how so careless. If I'd taken things as they came and moved on modestly, meekly, to a high school matching my academic level, you could say none of it would have ever happened.

What were my first and second years in high school like as these thoughts went through my head, you ask? I don't want to discuss the details, crucial opening flashback or not—please consult the previous volumes if you're curious.

I suppose what knocked me off my "washout" course, "the road to delinquency" according to a serious class president I know, were the events of precisely last March—I'm an accomplished lane weaver if I managed to drop out from dropping out.

Or maybe my car didn't have a steering wheel to begin with.

Right.

I met Tsubasa Hanekawa—a cat.

I met Shinobu Oshino—a vampire.

I met Hitagi Senjogahara—a crab.

I met Mayoi Hachijuji—a snail.

I met Suruga Kanbaru—a monkey.

I met Nadeko Sengoku—a snake.

And thus I, this me, the present me, accepted the yoke of studying for college exams—became me. An ideal rehabilitation of a delinquent high schooler, come to think of it, and you might say a stunning success on the part of Hanekawa, who'd declared around the end of spring break or on the first day back: *I'm gonna make sure you turn your life around.*

Expect no less of a class president among class presidents.

The gods' own elect.

Of course, if you said the achievement belonged to Tsubasa Hanekawa alone, she'd be madder than anyone—Senjogahara's downright devoted ministrations dramatically improved my academics (*ministration* better describes her meticulous care, *instruction* falling short for at least the latter half of it), while Shinobu and my little sisters propped me up through those tough times.

I'm not so petty, nor is my vision so tunneled, that I'd overlook them—or so I'd claim. Okay, as far as Kanbaru goes, I feel like all she ever did was distract me…

Still, during Sengoku's case.

When Sengoku's second serpent case saw me fail—and make a disastrous blunder of massive proportions, I could fight on without my spirit breaking thanks entirely to the support of those around me. I can't let myself forget that.

In the end, I may not have done any good.

But because they stood by me.

I was spared, if nothing else, the irreversible error of dying—making me who I am today.

I am here, now.

Heading out to my exams on March thirteenth.

...Hm?

Hold on, I'm forgetting something important—if I don't recall this, it's as if I didn't remember anything. Yup, on the way to the campus of my first-choice school, which had accepted my girlfriend Hitagi Senjogahara via recommendation and sans exams, I took a detour.

Nothing out of the ordinary, just the commonplace one for me lately; I'd been climbing a mountain like it was part of my daily routine about every day since February.

I wasn't trying to get into hiking—my physique had undergone a literally inhuman metamorphosis, and I didn't need any exercise to keep my body in its already-healthy condition.

Putting that aside in an act of escapism, it wasn't hiking that brought me day after day to an empty shrine at the summit of a small mountain in town.

A forgotten shrine that meant something to us.

I headed to Kita-Shirahebi Shrine—for a promised meeting. The wait was one-sided when I thought about it—I'd been stood up for nearly a month.

Right, that brings us to today.

March thirteenth—early in the morning.

While the person I waited for wasn't there, I faced the boss of the experts, Miss Izuko Gaen, who awaited me—

"..."

So now.

So now, why Hachikuji?

Miss Mayoi Hachikuji.

Try as I might to remember, no connection whatsoever to my current situation came to mind—the plot of *the story thus far* had a hole. I was meeting with Miss Gaen, so why Hachikuji all of a sudden?

I looked once more at the young girl before me.

I stared her at length.

A girl with a well-balanced pair of pigtails and a mature height for a fifth grader—her backpack so large it still seemed out of place—gazed at me with wide eyes and an innocuous smile.

No mistaking it.

No way to mistake it.

Up, down, left, right, however I looked at her, it was Mayoi Hachikuji.

The lost girl I met in that park last year on May fourteenth—with the exception of Tsubasa Hanekawa, there was nobody I was less likely to mistake for someone else.

I'm not exaggerating, even if Hachikuji had an identical twin or were a clone, I was confident I'd know.

"Ha ha ha. In other words, Mister Araragi, you could even find me in the opening of the anime's first season? Quite the *Where's Wally*."

"…"

Even this meta remark could only be Mayoi Hachikuji—but in that case, if so.

"Phew."

Geez, what a predicament.

Given this twist, I'm sure everyone expects Koyomi Araragi, reunited with his beloved Hachikuji not just for the first time in a while but after what seemed like a final parting, to jump for joy, sob tears of gratitude, shake with emotion, blabber confusedly and bustle triumphantly, and most of all, move in to hug her.

I'm sure that's what they expect.

Sigh, such weighty expectations.

My shoulders are gonna get dislodged.

Don't get me wrong, I get it.

I get them.

I freely admit, I can see it their way.

I'm hardly new to this industry, and I'd like to think, as a midcareer guy, that I get the drift of things—understandings, codes, that stuff. Don't get the wrong idea, but that said, I'm a high school senior now, who's about to graduate too—I'm not going to be moved to my core over every little development, you know?

I accept it, just like that, a total stranger to the kind of emotional instability that makes excessive use of "!" or "?!" or dashes as in "————————!"

In light novels of yore, this might be a scene featuring a huge font or bold text or something, but this is the twenty-first century, okay, and being somewhat precocious, I feel like I'm already living the twenty-second, the era of *Doraemon* and not *Astro Boy*.

Emotions? I've tucked them away in a fourth-dimensional pocket.

So if I were to go ahead and express my mood…

"Oh, it's Hachikuji."

That'd be it.

That and only that.

Maybe I'm cold, but facts are facts—whatever people are going to think of me, I just can't lie. Please, really, don't get the wrong idea though, it's not like I wasn't happy.

I never suggested that, did I.

Of course I was happy.

Yes, happy.

We were friends after all. If nothing more.

Yup, we did share some pleasant memories.

Like, erm, the time we had soft drinks together?

Vague as my recollection is.

Did she use to mangle my name?

I heard about that somewhere.

Bland exchanges, I must say now that I'm an adult, but fine, I enjoyed them to some degree at the time.

Seriously, when friends and acquaintances you parted ways with thinking you'd never meet them again—former friends and acquaintances as far as you're concerned—appear out of nowhere, how are you even supposed to react?

As a general, obvious rule.

Orthodoxly speaking, just orthodoxly.

I haven't ever transferred schools so this isn't firsthand, but don't those kids talk about how awkward it felt, say, when their transfer got postponed after a farewell party? Maybe this was similar.

Like in the final chapter of a kids' comic where the protagonist has to move and tells everyone, "So I guess this is it," only to move just one house over, their wacky adventures will continue or something?

Comic books get away with it, but you'd be flummoxed if it happened in real life. Where do you put those feelings when you've packed them up?

Or maybe it's like being left with an extra cardboard box after cleaning up a room—or putting a mechanical pencil back together and finding a piece still sitting there.

Where in your heart do you store it?

Those analogies capture how I felt.

Hachikuji, huh…

Wait, was that her name—Hachikuji?

I wasn't so sure about the first syllable there, and I couldn't trust my memory, not entirely—Mayoi, or Koyoi—on the issue of her given name. We'll say Mayoi Hachikuji for now—still.

They say when you attend an elementary school reunion as an adult and meet old friends, their impression can be so different that you go, *What the heck*. This might be a little different, but I dunno, it's more or less how I felt.

It was nobody's fault. You simply grow up.

I'd matured.

I guess the extraordinary emotional growth I'd experienced since that summer and our parting made a new man out of me who's nothing like my former self.

Right, that's how it shook out.

This disconnect, or discomfort, my stiff and halting demeanor upon our reunion, was simply inevitable.

Unavoidable in a creature that grows—the human being. People

17

change, cannot help but change.

Wouldn't it be creepy, in fact, if they stayed the same?

That carefree me, who took off like a rocket to tackle Hachikuji whenever I saw her in town, was no more. That guileless me—no more... To be honest, I don't understand why I did any of that, or what was so fun about it.

Spotting a girl, then dashing off to hug her?

A plain criminal!

Hard to believe I was once that person, but in a sense, that person just isn't me anymore—not Koyomi Araragi.

If that was Koyomi Araragi, then he died. He, if not God, is dead. The Koyomi Araragi who was better off dead in fact is. Rightly dead.

As for the reborn Koyomi Araragi, who faced a ten-year-old Mayoi Hachikuji, who hadn't grown the least bit since those days—a certain sense of disappointment visited me along with the joy of our reunion, I must admit.

Expecting an equal level of growth from her was absurd, certainly, but not maturing even a little in the half-year since our parting?

Demanding the same gusto of me despite this truth made no sense.

If I was supposed to engage in banter here as we used to, how could I hide my anxiety that we'd even hit it off, now that my vocabulary was inclined toward philosophy and ethics? I wasn't sure I could stoop properly to her jejune sensibilities.

Because stoop as I might, my mind, or spirit, had proceeded to such a sophisticated stage that the most vulgar topic I could think of to discuss was politics.

What level should I be aiming for?

The tragedy of mastery, so to speak—I was stumped as to what passed for general knowledge and common sense in our times.

Well, having said that.

Right, having said that (thank you for your patience).

According to my few tenuous strands of memories, Hachikuji had indeed done much—without her, without having met her, I wouldn't be me today, so I couldn't be callous with her.

Humanity, justice, courtesy, wisdom, fidelity, devotion, obedience.

Debts of gratitude must be repaid, and it's only natural to thank people who've aided you—it wouldn't do to say I didn't have a clue. Koyomi Araragi, now a mature individual, was obliged to match her level as best he could.

In that case, how felicitous.

As a rite.

As an initiation, as if I've returned to infancy, yes, like an uncle playing with his niece, I would repeat the act once more, one last time, with paternal generosity.

One last time, I mean it.

I had low expectations and desired nothing, but perhaps I'd discover something new in the process—um, how did this go again?

I only had a faint idea now, but no doubt I'd remember as I did it— not that it'd matter one bit if I didn't.

Yeah, let's just do it live.

Why practice?

On your marks. Phew, ready…

!! ?! !! ?! !! ?! !! ?! !! ?! !! ?! !! ?! !! ?! !! ?!

"Hachikuji———!"

!! ?! !! ?! !! ?! !! ?! !! ?! !! ?! !! ?! !! ?! !! ?!

I leapt toward her.

Leapt with a big, bold font.

Scattering countless exclamation points and question marks and throwing in some dashes.

"Eeeek!"

"Hachikujiiii! Hachikujiiii! Hachikujiiii!"

"Eeeek! Eeeek!"

"What're you doing here, what'd I do to deserve this?! No, forget why, you being here is enough for me, I can't even put it into words, aaa aaaaaaaaaaaaaaaaaaaaaaaaaaaaaaaaaaaaaahhh!"

"Eeeek! Eeeek! Eeeek!"

Hachikuji thrashed about.

I clung to her tight, moved to tears.

"Oh, the way you feel in my hands, the way you feel in my arms, the way you're just the right size to hold tight, it's the Hachikuji I know! Thank heaven! The more I rub my cheeks against yours, the more I know that it's you, Hachikuji! The more I lick you from head to toe, the more I know that it's you, Hachikuji! You can take a licking and keep on ticking, can't you, Hachikuji! These eyeballs, these lips, this nape, these collarbones, these breasts, these upper arms, these ribs, these thighs, these knee pits, these ankles! The way they feel, the way they taste, so Mayoi Hachikuji! How smooth you are, as if your every nook and cranny has been waxed down! I'm never letting you go, you're staying and won't get away, I'll keep on hugging you like this until I breathe my last! Imprisoned here, in my arms, for the rest of your days! Damn our bodies for getting in the way of our embrace! If we were both fluids, we could mix to our hearts' content! It's been so hard since we parted ways, I couldn't take it anymore! Let me vent, let me vent, heal me! C'mon, lemme touch you more hold you more lick you more!!"

"Eeeek! Eeeek! Eeeek! Eeeek!"

"Hey, stay still! You're making it harder for us to strip naked!"

"Eeeek! ...Graaah!"

She bit me.

As hard as a child could.

"Eeeek!"

It was my turn to scream—my arms came undone from the pain, all too soon after I'd sworn never to let her go, but now it was Hachikuji's teeth, lodged into my palm, that wouldn't let go.

Wouldn't let go? More like they were tearing through my skin!

Had she grown fangs or what?!

"Graaah! Graaah graaah graaah graaah graaah!"

"Ow ow ow ow ow! What're you doing, you stupid brat?!"

Yeah—the *ow*.

The *what're you doing* should have been her line.

In any case, leaving out all the details, for the first time in about six months—

My buddy Mayoi Hachikuji and I were impossibly reunited.

003

"All right…so, what's going on here?"

"Don't try to change the subject, Mister Pervert."

"Mister Pervert? Really, Hachikuji? How's that a slip of the tongue? It neither rhymes, nor has the right number of syllables. Has it been too long? Or did your inexhaustible vocabulary finally run dry?"

"My tongue didn't slip at all. It might not rhyme or have the same number of syllables, but you're Mister Pervert himself. Mister Araragi and Mister Pervert are identical."

"Heh. As harsh as ever, I see."

"You can't wrap all of that up with a cool line. Nothing's wrapped up here, look at my clothes."

Persistent!

I thought we ignored the previous chapter once we were in a new one? Ghost or not, she needed to follow the rules.

Yeah, hadn't breaking them mired her in a world of trouble—wasn't a quip I could make jokingly.

"Jokingly doesn't cut it, we have a case here. This is going to end up in court. Show some maturity for real, Mister Araragi. What do you think you're doing in the final volume's opening pages?"

"Oh, shut up. If you think a final volume has to start off melancholic, then you're badly mistaken."

Just not my style—a policy statement from Koyomi Araragi. We'll laugh and laugh until the bitter end.

"You're hopeless, Mister Araragi. Well…I guess it's very you. Wears me down, though."

Hachikuji shrugged and nodded.

She understood me.

And schooled me on how to wrap things up with a cool line.

It hadn't been too long, then—but now that we're in a new chapter, honestly, while I was elated to be reunited with her, logic be damned, I'd be lying if I said I didn't have any questions at all.

Logic has its own importance.

Why was Mayoi Hachikuji here?

Having passed on from the world and ascended to the next—what brought her to the grounds of Kita-Shirahebi Shrine? That was August twenty-third, and it was now March thirteenth, so—having said her final goodbyes to me six months and twenty-one days ago, to be exact, why was she back here?

To repeat, I was glad.

A bliss so supreme I almost didn't care—but coming back after all this time to tell me she hadn't passed on wasn't the sort of weirdness that I, for one, could accept.

How do I put it? Perhaps Miss Gaen, who'd given me advice back then, had taken some measure to safeguard Hachikuji—that's the kind of theory I could put together on the spot, but Mèmè Oshino, who acted like he saw through it all, was the expert who'd do something like that, while Miss Gaen seemed the least likely to resort to such plots and means.

She did scheme a lot, so it wouldn't be strange if she'd done something behind the scenes when Hachikuji passed on, given later developments—but I didn't see her as the type to plan such a surprise.

She was strict, or maybe realistic—looking back on him now, Oshino was something of a romantic, if a frivolous one, and operated in a somewhat different manner from Miss Gaen despite being her junior in college.

Which meant…what exactly?

I had to interpret this as the late Hachikuji returning to our world—yet, for all the various aberrations I'd encountered over the past year, I couldn't say on the spot if returning to our world after passing to the next was normal for them.

I mean, isn't it called passing on because you can't return? Because it's irreversible? But a priest who's renounced worldly pleasures can return to a secular life, and the *Obon* festival is all about welcoming back your ancestors... Even Senjogahara visited her father's hometown during Obon, didn't she?

True, Obon is in August, not March, but maybe my exam prep fell short and there's some annual event that takes place at this time of year.

So, was this okay?

Being reunited with Hachikuji like this?

This happy and convenient a turn—taking place in my life?

"..."

"Deep in thought, huh, Mister Araragi? I can only imagine...but while you were going berserk, you did mention that things have been tough for you since we said goodbye. Maybe you're having trouble trusting other human beings at the tender age of eighteen as a result."

Of course, I'm a ghost and aberration and no human, Hachikuji noted.

Hm. Her remark implied that she hadn't revived—though the feel of her skin just now made me think she might have.

Dead people don't come back to life, that piece of common sense still worked—I regained at least some degree of composure because right then, even that fact seemed to be standing on thin ice.

But wait.

Wait a sec—think back and remember.

I had to be forgetting a lot of things. It felt like I'd recalled various stuff but they weren't linking up; there was still a big disconnect between meeting up with Miss Gaen and being reunited with Hachikuji.

Miss Gaen safeguarding Hachikuji might be a delusional flight of fancy, but that lady must have had some sort of hand in this.

"Terrible, Mister Araragi. The pub dates have gotten a little spread out, but totally forgetting something like that being done to you is living your life a little too gracefully, don't you think?"

"…"

Leaving the meta comment aside…

If the current situation was Miss Gaen's doing, I couldn't just celebrate seeing Hachikuji again—as much as I wanted to, alas, I had to do more than that.

I had to make sense of this.

I looked up at the sky—where the sun climbed high.

Dazzled somewhat by its blazing rays—I realized I wouldn't make it to my exams in time, at the very least.

Late…was an understatement.

I didn't have to check my watch to know that I'd forfeited my seat— not tardy, but absent. What a royal waste of the grueling days I'd spent with Hanekawa and Senjogahara.

I felt drained, or maybe despondent…

Like I'd really messed this one up.

I didn't make it all the way to despair because, to be honest, some part of me wasn't surprised.

Yup.

Since saying goodbye to Hachikuji—I'd been through far too much.

Enough to have trust issues not just with humans, but everything.

Enough to believe nothing.

Maybe my heart had gone numb—to pain and to sorrow.

I guess it was still open to joy—but who knew for how much longer, if my pain poisoning continued.

Poisoned.

"You know… That's right. Ever since you went away, Shinobu's first thrall showed up, Oikura came back, all of that stuff happened with Sengoku at this shrine, I met Kaiki, I turned into a vampire all on my own, and I let Ononoki kill one of her parents… Right, I guess that happened at this shrine too. And it was also here that Miss Kagenui went missing. It's been one awful thing after the next… I've been panicking this whole time, and sure, some good things did happen, but not the kind of half-year you could expect to come out the other side of as a more mature person. I've taken nothing but steps back, in fact. I've been describing those two weeks of spring break as hell, but you know, the real hell might have been these last six months."

And it all started when I lost Hachikuji—my life had fallen into ruin like a home had lost its guardian spirit. I don't want to sound like I'm asking for more than my due, but if I was going to meet her again, I wish I'd been a version of me that could do so proudly.

In a different kind of situation.

As a different kind of me.

"You're wrong, Mister Araragi."

Then.

Hachikuji spoke.

"Wrong—Mister Araragi."

"Hm… Uhh, about what?"

"Mister All-too-lucky."

"A six-month hiatus might mean a six-month backlog of tongue slips, but I was talking about how incredibly unlucky I've been, so of all the ways your tongue might slip, why in such a merry and happy way? Mister Unlucky, at the very least. Also, my name is Araragi."

"I'm sorry. A slip of the tongue."

"No, you did it on purpose…"

"A quip from the stung."

"Or maybe not?!"

"A chip of the lip of the strip of the flip of the hip of the blip of the drip of the grip of the quip of the rip."

"You can say that without your tongue slipping?! I've heard of speaking in tongues, but that beats it!"

"I'm not trying to become a voice actress just for show."

"That was never part of your character, was it, now. Don't add things this late into the game."

"You're wrong, Mister Araragi," Hachikuji repeated.

Please just accept that it takes us a bit of time to get our conversations started.

"You're wrong."

"Wrong… About what? I got something wrong?"

Well, probably a lot of things.

Though not about wanting to be a different me if I was going to see her again.

"Oh, that's not where you're wrong, it's not about your feelings or anything sentimental—but something more real, or maybe material... Simply put, you're wrong about our location."

"Our location? What do you mean—"

"You keep on saying *this shrine*, but this isn't Kita-Shirahebi Shrine, Mister Araragi."

"What?"

Hearing this, I looked around.

Now that she mentioned it—I'd only been looking at Hachikuji and the sun, but now that she mentioned it.

We weren't at Kita-Shirahebi, or at the summit of a mountain.

This—was where Mayoi Hachikuji and I first met.

The plaza of that one park.

"Huh? Wait, huh?"

How could I not panic at this point?

Encountering Hachikuji was entirely impossible on its own, but I'd also moved without realizing it—and teleporting from Kita-Shirahebi Shrine to this park made me lose my calm.

All the cool-headedness I'd been working to regain.

Gone.

"Wh-What? How did I wake up in a totally different place? Hm? Did someone carry me here while I was asleep?"

Hachikuji? No, she couldn't have.

I'm hardly on the larger side, but I'm not so petite that an elementary schooler could carry me somewhere by herself.

From here, Kita-Shirahebi Shrine, to there, the park—no, the other way around, from there, Kita-Shirahebi Shrine, to here, the park—a pretty significant distance. Hachikuji couldn't carry me that far.

But if not Hachikuji...then Miss Gaen?

No, her doing that kind of physical labor? I guess that left Ononoki, working under her orders, as the only candidate?

She had the physical strength, no question.

Still, why?

"Why would Ononoki carry me to Namishiro Park?"

"You're also wrong about that, Mister Araragi."

"Huh? I must be wrong about all kinds of things... So, she didn't carry me? I suppose not..."

"Correct, it wasn't Miss Ononoki. Also, this isn't *Namishiro Park*."

"Oh, right. I still don't know how to read the name of this park... Huh? Hold on, Hachikuji. Do you actually know the correct reading? If it's not *Namishiro*, then what is it? *Rohaku?*"

"It isn't *Rohaku Park* either."

"?"

Neither Namishiro nor Rohaku?

Those seemed like the only options. How else would you read it?

The name of the park...no, that wasn't important.

"Wrong again—it's very important. To begin with, Mister Araragi, while it might look identical, which is to say it's been recreated here, strictly speaking this isn't the park where we first met."

"Huh?"

My confusion only grew.

What was the truth here?

Actually, being at the mercy of Hachikuji's statements was nothing new, but this was a little excessive—what was she trying to say?

If not that park, where were we?

What exactly was going on?

"Please calm down and listen, Mister Araragi," Hachikuji stated— almost like an able doctor telling her patient about an intractable disease he'd developed. "There seems to be a chance, or rather, it's clear you believe that I, after passing on to the next world, have returned to appear before you. But in truth, in reality, that's not so."

"What?"

"I haven't appeared before you—you appeared before me."

"Whaaat?"

"I'll be blunt. I was hoping you'd remember—but Mister Araragi, early in the morning on March thirteenth, you visited Kita-Shirahebi Shrine, where you met Miss Izuko Gaen."

And got killed.

Mayoi Hachikuji announced—*the truth.*

27

Her words made me remember.

On the grounds of the shrine—on the path to its sanctum.

Miss Gaen cut me into pieces—killed me.

The solution is for you to die, she had said. *Everything will be solved if you die—everything will come to an end.*

And with that, she sliced me up using the enchanted blade Kokorowatari.

The Aberration Slayer's very own.

I wasn't sure how Miss Gaen had come by the greatsword of a legendary vampire—or to go further back, the first thrall of a legendary vampire, but in any case.

Miss Gaen killed me.

Without mercy.

She slaughtered Koyomi Araragi.

And if this was the result—hm?

Wait, if I was here as a result—was I killed only to come back to life? Did I revive and appear before Hachikuji in the process?

Then I'd need to ask where she'd been—but no, that'd be the park, however you read its name.

"You've gotten so close, Mister Araragi. It'd be great for you to go all the way, but if the last volume is a little too thick, it'll seem like we're having trouble letting go. Let me wrap this up due to space concerns."

"Way too late to be saying that when there's already been a Part 1 and Part 2... I'd appreciate it, though. It's not like I'm invested in coming to an answer on my own."

"What an attitude in a student about to sit for his exams."

"Quickly abandoning problems you can't solve is an important part of being a good test-taker."

"Sounds like you're more interested in preparing for tests than studying for them. How lacking in ambition. Of course, they're assessing high schoolers in new ways now that they're abolishing the national entrance exam."

"Don't turn this into a discussion about testing. How 'bout you pick a different topic, like the situation I'm in right now."

"Fine, I'll stop picking at your wounds. You said trouble befell you since we parted ways. Knowing that you're only in for more pain at our reunion makes me feel so bad, I can't bear to look at you. If you've been visited by one tragedy after the next, and these past six months, not spring break, was the true hell for you, I feel terrible about piling onto that."

"Hold on, your preface is scaring me…"

"I should hope so."

Because this—Hachikuji said.

Mister Araragi, she said.

"Is hell."

"Excuse me?"

"The deepest hell among all—this is Avīci."

004

"Aaaaaaaaaaaaaaaaaaaaaaaaaaaaaaaaaaaaaaaaaaaaaagh!"

I screamed.

A shriek from the bottom of my heart.

"Hell?! Hell?! Avīci?!"

"Correct. The hell known as Avīci. Not Raurava, so would you be so kind as to stop yelling? You're being noisy."

"What, no! How could I not scream?! I feel like I'm in Maharaurava right now!"

"Again, you're in Avīci. You don't want to be criticized for misinforming people."

"Fine, but it's not helping me get it together!"

Hell? And Avīci, the deepest of them all?

A quick aside for some hell trivia (source: Tsubasa Hanekawa).

According to one school of thought, there are eight great hells, and the deeper you go, the crueler it gets. From top to bottom, these are 1: Sañjīva, the hell of revival, 2: Kālasūtra, the hell of black threads, 3: Saṃghāta, the hell of crushing, 4: Raurava, the hell of screams, 5: Mahāraurava, the hell of great screams, 6: Tapana, the hell of heating, 7: Pratāpana, the hell of great heating, and 8: Avīci, hell without interruption—for a total of eight great hells.

There are also eight cold hells, but I'm going to omit those—they say that Avīci, the deepest hell, involves more suffering than hells 1 through 7 combined, a true inferno.

Of all the sinners who fall into hell, only the worst make it all the way down. A top private institution among hells.

That is Avīci.

"And wait! I might not have led the most praiseworthy or extolled life and never saw myself as the kind of character who'd make it into heaven, but the lowest circle? No way! What did I do?! If it has to be hell, just let it be Sañjīva or so! How's this realistic?!"

"I'd say 'realistic' went poof the moment we started talking about hell."

She sounded upbeat.

Like she enjoyed my confusion—what a nasty personality. Well, they do say that seeing someone in the grip of panic sometimes make you more objective...

"We might be at the end here, Hachikuji, but this is absurd. Hell? Really? The world we live in has stuff like hell and the afterlife?"

"It'd be absurd not to assume there's a hell in a world with aberrations."

"..."

Shinobu once said something of that nature.

Time travel should be possible if aberrations exist—fine, hell was more plausible than warping through time.

But something about heaven and hell made them sound more fantastic than the occult. Maybe thanks to Japan's unique sense of religion, where all kinds of beliefs are muddled together...

"It's not uncommon," Hachikuji said. "Like characters not believing in fortune-telling when they're in a realm where magic is real. And this might be more of a balance issue in world building, but who'd eat meat in a world with talking animals?"

"I see what you're trying to say...but I'm still going to have trouble believing you if I'm told that I'm in hell. I mean..."

"You do stress out over the details, don't you? You need to take a more relaxed approach."

Sure, but...

You need to take a relaxed approach and accept being in hell?

"What you need to do is adapt to the situation and not shamelessly flail around in dismay. Be like a character in Izumi Kawahara's laid-back manga."

"Spare me your specific examples."

"What, are you a life-after-death denialist? After all those extravagant deaths of yours?"

"Well..."

True. Come to think of it, I couldn't be denying the idea of an afterlife when I recognized the existence of ghosts like Hachikuji and zombies like Ononoki.

Should I say a tacit understanding?

To be precise, regarding vampires, it seems more like they continue to live without dying rather than revive. You could explain that without the afterlife if you wanted...

"But," I said, "it'd really shake things up if death isn't the end..."

"Shake things up? How?"

"Well, take the meaning of life... It'd be nothing more than a warm-up. If there's an afterlife, whether that's heaven or hell, living with any kind of urgency seems a little pointless... It affects the austerity of life and death."

"Who cares if it isn't as austere? Or are you a fan of books where the author's all, *Trust me, I know how tough the world can be. Heh. That's why I'm writing this book. Heh.*"

"..."

What kind of book was that?

And what kind of description was that?

"Oh, you know the kind. People die left and right, the most terrible things happen to girls, you feel awful for the children, truly evil villains show up, and the world is cruel and unfair type thing."

"I get it, but 'type thing'? You're being so spiteful that I don't feel like arguing with you..."

"That was an academic classification, right?"

"No."

"I'm just saying, authors ought to depict sweet ideals, not the bitter truth. What's wrong about dreaming?"

"Said like an Izumi Kawahara fan."

"It's not too late—can we aim for that worldview too?"

"How?!"

It's way too late!

Not when there's only one book left!

And even if we had a hundred!

No matter how we hard we tried, we'd never arrive at that clean of a world!

"The line separating clean from not: whether a young girl like me is described as a sprite or as Lolita."

"That's where the line is?"

"We ought to build up from there. They're only going to get less permissive."

"Doesn't matter, this is the last volume. And anyway, let's examine this bit about me being in hell. Can we dig deeper here?"

"Tragically, Mister Araragi, there's nowhere deeper than this."

Right...

The lowest layer of hell, its deepest—Avīci.

"Actually, it's more ironic than tragic," I noted. "Araragi, Avīci... The first letters use the same character! I never even imagined it was foreshadowed from the very start. From birth, I mean."

"I do think that's a bit of a stretch..."

"They say that Avīci is covered in flames as far as the eye can see, so maybe my little sisters being called the Fire Sisters was foreshadowing too!"

Hm? But this park wasn't covered in flames or anything—and according to Hachikuji, it had been recreated here.

Why recreate the park in Avīci? What was the background there?

No, the question was more basic. If this was Avīci—I had one big question.

"A big question? Oh, you want to know why you've been sent this deep into hell. Um, you can figure that one out with a little thought."

"A little thought..."

Hm.

I needed to consult a few more entries in the dictionary that was Tsubasa Hanekawa.

Though Avīci is where those who committed the gravest sins are sent, what exactly were those again? Killing your parents or something?

I've been a pretty bad son, becoming a washout since entering high school and all, but I never killed my parents, or even thought about killing them...

"No, not that. You turned into a vampire, didn't you?"

"Huh?"

"You saved a vampire—and despite many other sins worth mentioning, that's the main one that brought you here. Of course you're going to hell for saving a demon."

Just like Taro Urashima was brought to the Dragon Palace at the bottom of the sea after saving a turtle—Hachikuji said, but that didn't sound like my situation at all. It didn't work as an example.

"This is completely off topic, but wouldn't it be interesting if we had a gender-swapped version of Urashima, a 'Hanako Urashima'? Then you'd get a handsome Dragon King in the fable."

"Don't take us off topic," I complained. "And Dragon King? Sounds tough."

Oh. So because I turned into a vampire...

I did remember now. Slaying a holy man was another way to end up in Avīci—even if I didn't kill them myself, I was indirectly involved in the deaths of Guillotine Cutter and Tadatsuru Teori, so maybe being sent this far down was justified in its own way.

Not that I wanted to think so...

"Agh. Whatever the reason, getting sent to hell is super depressing. It's like a total negation of everything I've done..."

"My condolences. I'm very sorry for your loss."

"..."

Well, putting aside feeling depressed.

My big question didn't have to do with any grave sin—we could put me aside.

It was Hachikuji.

The girl in front of me with whom I'd been reunited. Mayoi Hachikuji.

Sprite or Lolita aside, too—why was she here?

Wait, what?

No, really! Why was she here?!

"Why am I here?" Hachikuji had seemed to enjoy my confusion, but now she looked a little stuck, or maybe just stuck-up, at becoming the subject. "Well, you know. Because I was sent to hell."

Nonetheless, she hadn't so much as paused.

Like there was nothing serious about it.

But it didn't get more serious. *Because I was sent to hell.* What a joke! "Right? Ha ha!"

"That's not what I meant!"

"I was foreshadowing earlier when I brought up Z-Ton and his trillion-degree fireballs."

"If anything is a stretch, it's that! Whaaat?! You've gotta be kidding me! Seriously, you got sent down here after passing on in that moving of a way? What a waste! What are you even doing? How's that possible?!"

"Calling it impossible won't change the fact that I've been sent here. You're reacting as if a senior of yours who wanted to become a musician, and whom everyone loved to the point of giving him a send-off party, greets you as a hard-working businessman ten years later. Don't make his greeting stiff and awkward, okay?"

"That's a perfectly likely scenario compared to you being sent to hell! And what kind of business is this? What a career change, it's too steep a fall! Your selling point was your innocence and purity, and you're in hell? Did you commit some awful sin I don't know of when you were still alive?"

The eleven years she spent wandering the streets as a lost child shouldn't count—that was after she died, and you're only sent to hell based on the life you've lived.

How does a ten-year-old girl commit a sin so grave that she ends up in hell? No—but you'd be surprised by how minor, or rather, nonsensical the reason can be.

That tidbit is courtesy of Tsubasa Hanekawa too, of course.

"Well, it's technically a grave sin," Hachikuji tried to soothe me, "though I didn't know either until I ended up here. A child is sent to hell, no questions asked, if she dies before her parents."

"Oh…"

The ultimate act of disobedience.

Right, dying before your parents gets you sent to the Sanzu River, where you pile up stones to atone for your sin.

On Mother's Day, Hachikuji left her dad's home, alone, to meet her mom—and got run over and died before she arrived at her destination.

Whatever Mayoi Hachikuji's mother and father were up to now, they were alive at the time, eleven years ago. In other words, the daughter died before both her parents.

And so.

She was sent to hell—fell here.

"You've gotta be kidding me…"

That was all I could say.

I understood the reason but couldn't agree with the reasoning—how could I?

Society once saw children dying before their parents as an act of disobedience, and maybe some people still think so, but that mentality ignores how regretful the child must feel.

It wasn't as though Hachikuji wanted to die first—damning her to an afterlife of piling up stones was too severe a punishment…and even if she'd sinned, wouldn't her death be punishment enough—

"…"

"Hm? What's the matter, Mister Araragi?"

"Well, I was shaking with indignation over the absurdity of it… Yet my tragic fate as a master detective forced me to notice that something isn't quite right."

"How are you a master detective? Even when you seem to be solving mysteries, it's always someone else doing the actual solving for you."

Wow, harsh.

But true.

"So, what did you notice?"

"I already expressed my doubts when I heard that you were sent to hell after our moving farewell. Even if I were to back off by a trillion

37

degree—of deduction and not temperature—I still don't see how you committed a sin grave enough to end up here with me. You're supposed to be stacking up rocks in children's limbo, no?"

I didn't know much about the topic, but straining my memory to its fullest to conjure up relevant bits from Hanekawa, that seemed to be the case. Children's limbo, Sai-no-Kawara, was the riverbed of the Sanzu, a kind of entrance to hell.

There, children had to build stone towers for their parents; each time, a demon—not a vampire, but an *oni*—came to knock it down. A harsh sentence for children, yes, but Jizo Bosatsu, the Bodhisattva of deceased children, would eventually come to rescue them. A hell with a bailout mechanism, so to speak.

A hell on the mild side.

As gentle as a slap on the wrist compared to the cruelty of Sañjīva, where you spent an eternity suffering, slain by demons only to be revived again.

Perhaps not severe enough for the vampire Koyomi Araragi, who'd experienced dying and coming back to life plenty of times during his battles on earth—be that as it may, why was Mayoi Hachikuji in Avīci, for the lesser sin of dying before her parents?

"A very astute observation, Mister Araragi. Let alone a master detective, you're the reincarnation of Sherlock Holmes."

"Except I'm dead."

Not to mention, it wasn't *that* sharp.

Anyone would wonder—Tsubasa Hanekawa, the source of all my info, probably would have the moment she faced Hachikuji.

Not that Hanekawa would ever end up in hell, no matter what kinds of mistakes she made—but who knows? Hachikuji and I were here, no questions asked, so given all the trouble she got up to as Black Hanekawa, maybe the class president among class presidents didn't have a guaranteed ticket to heaven.

"Unless this Avīci stuff is just a mean joke on your part, and we're both in children's limbo for dying before our parents." Sure, it did seem to be a park, not a riverbed, but I wasn't seeing spires of flame, either.

"Stop trying to inch your way into a better situation every chance you get. Avīci is the hell you deserve to be in."

"When you're that emphatic about it, my downfall feels like it was a foregone conclusion..."

Tell me it wasn't.

How sad, if that's the series finale after nineteen volumes.

"Yes, Mister Araragi. That's right," Hachikuji doubled down. "I knew you'd land all the way down here—knew it in advance. It was a given. Which is why I left the riverbed where I belong and came here to receive you."

"To—receive me?"

"Yes. Like a welcoming ceremony. I wish I were waiting with a garland of flowers like in Hawaii. It was too much of a pain so I didn't bother."

"What a great attitude."

Not that I'd know how to respond if I were welcomed to hell that way. Presented with a garland of spider lilies, the flower of death, should I smile?

"I told them I needed to take the day off from stacking up stones because a friend of mine was here, then took off."

"It's that relaxed in children's limbo?!"

"Well, with all the people undergoing near-death experiences just dropping by, parts of the river are kind of like a tourist destination lately."

"Bullshit."

"I'm tight with the demons there. I get a free pass, they don't block me. Call it a killer pass."

"Could you not use your hell jokes on me? I haven't figured out the sense of humor down here just yet."

Not that I could tell where her joke started or ended—but I was intrigued that she knew in advance.

Of course, she couldn't have waited for me if she didn't before the fact... Before the fact?

"Yes," Hachikuji said. "It's not like I foresaw it—but I knew."

"You knew?"

"Yes. The fact that Miss Gaen would kill you, and that you'd end up here—I knew."

"You…knew…"

"Not me—the person who told me knew."

Everything, Hachikuji said, as if drawing on a memory.

Apparently, this person knows everything.

005

"Now that we're done giving detailed explanations about every last mystery, may we depart? Time to go, Mister Araragi."

"What? Where to..."

She hadn't explained every last mystery at all, and the explanations were so quick and rough that honestly, most of our conversation had been nothing more than small talk!

Someone needed to set up an explanation center.

"Oh, I can give you the details as we walk. We can't just sit around in this park talking forever—no need to sit in place the entire time, this isn't an anime commentary track. I'm originally a child, you know, and staying still goes against my nature."

"Hm... Willing as ever to cross over into any media you feel like. But yeah, I don't care where we discuss this."

"Didn't we use to talk on the road for the most part? You did lose both of your bicycles, but why not trek side by side with me for a change?"

For a change, or the first time in a while—that wasn't what I objected to. Of course we could talk as we walked, I was fine with it if she was...but where were we headed?

"Well, it seems you're a little out of position, so I'm correcting that and putting you back in it. Such is the role I've been assigned."

"Your role?"

"Heheh, call it another ironic twist of fate. I, whose former calling was to make people lose their way, am working as a guide."

I didn't take her meaning as she walked off, her large backpack swaying. If this was hell, or at least the afterlife (I couldn't let it go, thanks to my attachment to life or refusal to accept the situation), the girl before me had brought her favorite backpack down here.

I wasn't complaining, though, I didn't want to see her in a death shroud or anything—I was wearing my school uniform, too.

No trace of having been shredded.

Nor was my body sliced into ribbons—maybe only because I was in a hell where dying just meant reviving, and not because I was a vampire benefiting from the associated traits...

If I got a new set of clothes every time I died, hell was hard at work.

"Hm, but now that I mention it, Shinobu isn't with me. If I died, does that mean she actually regained her full vampiric nature?"

"Most likely. I think that was another one of her goals."

"Her?"

Repeating the word, I followed Hachikuji out of the park. Sidewalk, roadside trees, street, crossing, signal—I still saw the same town as always.

Not that I knew the area well enough to say so—but nothing seemed strange about it as a town.

Nothing about it was hellish.

If you pressed me—I guess it felt strange that there were no other pedestrians?

"At the entrance to Avīci, didn't people have to fall through flames for two thousand years? All the sinners are busy falling, and maybe that's why no one's arrived yet?"

Of course not.

I was here.

And couldn't have fallen faster than them, according to Newton's experiments.

"Yes, and you'll understand that part soon enough—I'll make sure you do. Don't worry, think of me as all-knowing and all-powerful. I've heard about most things from her."

"Again—who's this you're talking about?"

"Her august self."

"Yikes, what is she, the final boss?"

"Her Excellency."

"Why the period-drama affect? Who is this person—who knows everything?"

Well, I already knew by now.

If it wasn't Hanekawa, that left only one possibility—it had to be the big boss of the experts and the one who cut me into ribbons, Izuko Gaen.

But how did Miss Gaen contact Hachikuji, who'd ascended to the afterlife—or rather fallen into the depths of hell?

"An all-knowing, all-powerful ass in lion's skin, that's me."

"Nah, you can't bluff your way up that far. You do seem to know where we're going, Hachikuji, so start by telling me our destination. Your mother's place—couldn't be it."

"Right, and she appears to be alive and well. Her house was gone, but she'd simply moved. Thank goodness."

"…"

"Well, in terms of destinations, Mister Araragi, here's our designated goal: my job is to bring you back to life."

Putting you back in position was a figure of speech, I guess it's more like dislodging you from the correct position, Hachikuji added, just complicating things.

I didn't get it at all.

Then again, I hadn't understood much of anything lately—led to and fro by everyone, getting caught up in their affairs… I bet a slicker guy than me would have fared better.

"Bring me back to life… Wait, is that something I can do?"

"Of course. You're not just going to stay dead, are you?"

"But Miss Gaen…"

The solution is for you to die—she had said.

And since this was her, I believed it. Naturally I wasn't happy with it, and it made no sense, but whatever she was thinking, I could be certain of one thing. She acted in ways that, in her view, brought the greatest possible happiness to the greatest number of people—even if nothing could be less in my interest.

You could trust her on that.

Nor would she second-guess her own actions—if she thought killing me was the solution, she'd never take it back.

"Really, Mister Araragi, keep it together. It had to be this person's plan all along. To kill you, then have you come back to life."

"Kill me, then have me come back to life..."

All along?

What an unproductive plan.

That went beyond taking credit for solving a problem you created, it was like multiplying by two and then dividing by two—giving me a scare was all it accomplished.

Did she want to prove that hell existed?

Why now?

Even if that was it, she'd have known about it for a long time now—hm?

Did Hachikuji just say *this person*?

Rather than *she*?

...

Now I was splitting hairs.

"It isn't just multiplying by two and then dividing by two," Hachikuji continued, not engaging with my inner doubts—walking did seem to suit her better, and she was getting pretty talkative. "Subtraction's at play as well."

"Subtraction?"

"That, too, you'll understand soon enough."

"..."

Every crucial bit was being held back... As my guide, I guess Hachikuji had a proper procedure in mind, so I wasn't going to force the answers out of her.

The idea of coming back to life hardly left me cold, but I was letting a torrent of topics toss me about, entrusting myself to the flow, and not thinking clearly, focusing too much on Hachikuji—I don't know, the unvarnished truth is that words as potent as *come back to life* weren't ringing a bell for me.

"Is something the matter, Mister Araragi? Aren't you happy? You can return to being alive."

"Um, honestly, my brain hasn't gotten to that point. I'm having a hard time accepting that I'm dead, so I'm not in a place to wonder about not being dead..."

"Ha ha ha. Are we rehashing that discussion? Would a world where the dead come back alter the meaning of life?"

"That's not it."

Was it?

Nope, that wasn't it.

No, some part of me must have felt, *I can rest in peace now.* Though it did sound like a line out of a manga...

"Hm. I can sympathize. You've been battling, with your life on the line—they say gamblers who keep on winning actually have a subconscious desire to lose. Perhaps to bring balance to a life that's seen too much victory? I wouldn't mind believing that your relief was genuine and not affected."

"Why so condescending—"

"However, I doubt she is so generous that honesty suffices—this way," Hachikuji turned a corner.

As she did, the scene changed—well, the corner was a regular corner. I mean the color of the sky.

It should have been midday.

But the sky snapped to night—the streetlamps, just standing there until a moment ago, illuminated the darkened street as if they'd been doing so for some time.

"What? Did someone just cast Tick-Tock?"

"I wonder—oh, Mister Araragi. It appears as though someone's collapsed over there."

"Hm?"

Just as I was coping with the color shift in the heavens (we were supposed to be in hell, after all), Hachikuji spoke and pointed—looking in the direction of her finger, I saw why. Certainly, leaning against the streetlamp, lit as if in spotlight, was a person.

No, not certainly. Uncertainly.

And not a person, but a monster.

Collapsed there—covered in blood, in a pool of blood, was a vampire on the verge of death, her limbs severed.

A legendary vampire in a gruesome state.

The iron-blooded, hot-blooded, yet cold-blooded vampire—Kissshot Acerolaorion Heartunderblade.

006

"Shi-Shinobu!"

I ran to her side—no thought needed on my part. Rushed over as soon as I saw it. With neither the time nor the composure to consider why she was here, why our meeting during spring break was being recreated in hell—I just ran to her side.

What did I plan to do, I wonder? In retrospect.

In any case, in any event, I ran to her—and had no idea what to do next. Was I in my right mind?

Didn't I feel bitter regret for those past actions? I couldn't have forgotten—unthinkingly rescuing her then, lured in by her beauty, and about the tragedy that befell me as a result.

But all I could do was rush over—or more accurately, I tried to.

Our eyes met.

Or so it seemed, but that moment, a smile even more gruesome than her state spread across Kissshot Acerolaorion Heartunderblade's face—as she disappeared.

Vanished.

When she did—the darkness lifted as well, the sky that suddenly shifted suddenly shifting back. The foreboding night street seemingly arranged for her returned to being a plain, run-of-the-mill road.

"..."

A hallucination? An illusion? A mirage?

Doubtful—who needed them in hell?

Let alone the ghost of a vampire.

Had Miss Gaen gone on to use the enchanted blade Kokorowatari on Shinobu to put her in such a state? Except, true vampires wouldn't end up in hell. Maybe as a demon tormenting the damned, but...

What was that, then?

What did I just see?

"Did your body just move on its own, Mister Araragi?"

Hachikuji jogged over to catch up to me.

She didn't look too surprised by the strange occurrence—as if she'd foreseen it.

Foreseen it.

Or rather, she knew?

She'd been—told?

"Strange. You so regretted how you saved Miss Shinobu over spring break. Why do the exact same thing in an identical situation?"

"Because...well, um, my body moved on its own?" Although Hachikuji wasn't being openly critical, my reply sounded like an excuse. "R-Rushing over doesn't necessarily mean I'd save her like during spring break. Who knows, maybe I was trying to finish her off?"

"Even a child can see through that lie. Please don't forget that we're in hell. Around here, you get your tongue plucked out for lying," Hachikuji warned mischievously as she passed me—to lead me once more. I followed, flustered.

"Well, even if I wasn't going to finish her off..." Perhaps doing so meant helping that suicidal vampire noble—but even if I wasn't going to. "I do wonder what would've happened if I'd ignored Shinobu...if I'd run scared from a beautiful, blood-soaked woman. I see it play out in my dreams."

I never expected to see it play out in hell, though.

No chance in hell—but it was exactly where I chanced upon her.

"Come to think of it, by that point, Shinobu's first thrall had gathered as ash in my town—so who knows, maybe that armored warrior would have arisen to save his master as the three vampire hunters moved to kill her. Shinobu and the First, reunited for the first time in four hundred years…who parted ways with their relationship still in ruins, might have reconciled."

"That's what I'd call too good to be true."

"Yeah. And getting in the way of it—is an unbearable thought."

"This-a-way."

Hachikuji simply kept walking, and it was hard to tell if she'd heard my, shall we say, griping—not much of a guide given the origins of her character. Of course, I'd waddle along like a spot-billed duckling if it meant being brought back to life, but how could I get my bearings if she wasn't going to be a bit kinder as she led the way?

As proof of her ill-suitedness, she'd taken me through town and strayed into a nearly impossible location—a Naoetsu High building.

How do you proceed from a sidewalk straight into a school hallway? And wait—something was clearly strange.

This was more than being lost.

Sure, it was already strange the moment day flipped into night, but…

"So, Mister Araragi, the school where you take your classes—well, technically, a recreation. Even having wandered all over that town, this campus is like holy ground. Being at a high school is a first for me. Would the teachers get mad if they found me?"

"The trouble will be all mine if they see me walking around with a ten year old… My exams will be the least of my worries then."

I'd be looking at a battery of investigations, not examinations.

Heaven forbid.

That said, I wasn't running into any sinners or persecutors in this Avīci, so teachers seemed even less likely… But an abandoned hell?

Had the system changed? Was Avīci now a hell of solitary confinement? Regularly awful, but Hachikuji greeting me turned it into more of a paradise…

My perse-cute-or?

"But why was the street connected to a school hallway? I don't see the street we were on behind us, either. Just the usual school building…"

"Well, it's not a road unless it leads everywhere."

"Hm… But—"

"Oh, Mister Araragi. A perv. Be careful."

"A perv? Uh oh, Hachikuji. Quick, hide inside my clothes, that's to say behind me."

"I'm not sure that was a rephrasing."

We hastily slipped into a nearby classroom to avoid encountering this perv whom Hachikuji had spotted, but it was none other than me ambling in a school building I'd assumed was empty.

Koyomi Araragi.

A handsome youth, not any pervert.

Hachikuji had mistaken me for someone else.

Thinking that silly thought, I saw, walking next to me, another individual—Tsubasa Hanekawa.

First-gen, too. Tsubasa Hanekawa with glasses and braided hair.

Just one braid, as first-gen as you could get—single-braided Hane-kawa and I walking side by side at Naoetsu High never took place in reality, as far as I knew.

She wore her hair in two braids after spring break, then stopped wearing glasses and cut her hair short. What's more, it was a tiger-striped, black-and-white pattern now—but there was no mistaking her.

…And wait, hold on a sec.

Was that how smiley Koyomi Araragi looked talking to Tsubasa Hanekawa? I wanted to say I'd been striking a more manly look, but no.

They left my sight as I thought this—maybe they were headed to a classroom for a president-vice president meeting. To discuss the culture festival or something.

"Sure, you led a tumultuous life after you rescued Miss Shinobu—but coming to know Miss Hanekawa just before that was also signifi-cant. She's had a massive influence on you. What do you think about that?" Hachikuji asked abruptly.

The question came so unannounced that I couldn't process it for a moment. Excuse me? Are you saying—I'd be better off if I hadn't gotten to know Hanekawa?

"In hindsight, she made a mess of the situation with Miss Shinobu, didn't she? And quite terrible things happened to you over the course of your two encounters with Miss Black Hanekawa."

"…"

"If you'd never become friends with her, you wouldn't have been dragged into that long string of troubles—no one could blame you for feeling that way."

"Well, I won't deny that she's to blame for a lot. The girl who doesn't know everything, just what she knows, revealed so many truths that could've stayed hidden, and forgot so many truths that could've stayed remembered, sending me through reckless shortcuts and down impossible detours—but."

The question was liable to send me off into a fit of rage if anyone other than Hachikuji asked it, but since this was her, I could answer in a strangely serene, matter-of-fact way.

I wasn't sent anywhere. Persisting in the here and now, I answered—

"I'm still genuinely glad that I became friends with her."

"…"

"I'm beginning to get a vague idea about this walking side by side… So, what, do we need to follow them?"

"Hmm. There's no strict route, but sure, this way please. It's like *Alice in Wonderland* and I'm your White Rabbit."

"Wonderland, huh…"

For now, it did feel more like a wonderland than hell—not that I could say, with my shaky recollection of the original.

Hachikuji called it a recreation.

The park—and this Naoetsu High.

A recreation and vicarious experience.

From spring break to here—I followed Hachikuji out of the classroom, but Koyomi Araragi and Tsubasa Hanekawa were nowhere to be seen.

If we were going after them, we needed to go upstairs. Whatever the meeting was about, they were heading to our third-year class—I thought, and looked toward the staircase.

Then.

I saw a girl frozen in midair—posed like she was flying, but sure enough, there in stop motion was my girlfriend whom I knew so well.

"Senjogahara…"

"You could've not tried to catch her after she slipped—the choice wasn't as dire as saving a beautiful woman collapsed on the street, dying. Catching a falling person is just plain dangerous too—depending on how, the faller could get injured in addition to yourself. Miss Senjogahara weighed barely anything at the time, so I doubt she'd have suffered if you'd let her be. You know, the way small, light animals and bugs can fall from high places and somehow be fine."

"…"

"But you, Mister Araragi."

"If Senjogahara fell towards me? I'd catch her—every time."

She'd told me.

That she was glad it was me who'd caught her—and I felt the same way.

I was glad to be the one to catch her—only by chance, just by coincidence, but aren't those chance coincidences also called fate?

Duty, even?

"Hypothetically," Hachikuji said, climbing the stairs and glancing to the side, at Senjogahara, as she fell—or was in a bizarre state of motionless falling. As though the words meant nothing in particular. "If you hadn't caught Miss Senjogahara—she might've suffered minor injuries, but I doubt anything serious would have happened. She'd have continued to live her scornful life of defiant pride. That conman would come to this town a little later, correct?"

"You mean—Deishu Kaiki."

"Yes, a man with fateful ties to her. Perhaps they would have their destined showdown. As things stand, you prevented it during summer break…but I wonder, what might have happened if you hadn't gotten in the way, if her boyfriend hadn't butted in?"

"What would have happened?"

"Might they have gotten back together?"

Miss Senjogahara seems to be hiding it, but even you must have figured out that they once had something between them, Hachikuji said.

I followed after her and passed by Senjogahara.

Though motionless, her position was so precarious that I felt like grabbing and planting her down, but who knew. I might throw her off balance the moment I touched her…

"Their old flame may have been reignited then—life, love, it's all too much to know how to handle," commented Hachikuji.

"You, talking about love? Who's going to take you seriously?"

"Oh? You're interested in hearing my romantic history? Do you have any idea how precocious elementary schoolers are these days?"

"I don't want to know… About your romantic history, even less."

"What do you say, Mister Araragi? To the idea that you interfered with Miss Senjogahara's romance with the conman?"

"What do I have to say? What else but *hah, serves you right.*"

The situation with Kaiki was a little different from the one with the First.

Not that I could discuss it with Senjogahara…

"I'll admit, Kaiki helped me out with Sengoku…but that's separate. Completely separate. I can honestly say I wish I'd never met him."

"Ah. True, there are people like that in your life—you can't get along with every last person. Well, why don't we end by going over the name you just brought up, Miss Sengoku. Let's bon voyage."

"Let's bon voyage… I get what you're trying to say, but where do I even begin—hm? Wait, what about Kanbaru?"

"Excuse me?"

"You know, Kanbaru. Suruga Kanbaru."

I'd convinced myself that the packed itinerary starting from a park and heading to who-knows-where was a sort of hellish trial—my soul resting on a scale against opposing evidence.

Or maybe feathers, not evidence (source: Tsubasa Hanekawa).

I thought we'd be looking back at all of my conduct since spring break, or all that happened to me, everything that assaulted me since, in a kind of pilgrimage.

Kissshot Acerolaorion Heartunderblade during spring break, Tsubasa Hanekawa during Golden Week, Hitagi Senjogahara after the holidays…

I could understand skipping over Hachikuji since she was with me, but chronologically, Suruga Kanbaru came before Nadeko Sengoku.

This hell was silent for the time being because my sins were still being judged, and I wasn't undergoing the fiery torments that filled Avīci because my punishment was pending, or my case was ongoing—so went my arbitrary interpretation.

If it was correct, I'd fall through flames for two thousand years after this pilgrimage, so if it wasn't, I'd be totally fine with that...

"Oh, yes. Miss Kanbaru. She's a special case."

"A special case?"

"We're passing over her, or skipping her turn—her case is slightly different from everyone else's."

"It is?"

Wasn't that truer of Nadeko Sengoku, the individual she proposed we visit next?

Kanbaru and her aberrant left arm were on the standard side as far as aberrations go...

"Oh, no, this isn't about aberrational phenomena, Mister Araragi. The issue is their relationship to you—and in Miss Kanbaru's case, you couldn't help but get involved."

"...What does that mean?"

"Miss Kanbaru, with her characteristic assertiveness, decided to stalk you—and acted on her own initiative to kill you. You could be faced with that situation a thousand times, and your option would still be limited to taking appropriate measures."

Hachikuji sounded appalled, as if to say, *or could you have sat there and let her kill you?*

Hm, she had a point.

Even if stalking or coming to kill me didn't neatly summarize her behavior, minor initial choices in relationships with stronger communicators like Kanbaru, who come straight at you, probably don't make any difference down the line.

She held the reins.

Naturally, she wouldn't have stalked me if I hadn't started dating Senjogahara—and since I'd vowed to catch my girlfriend no matter how many times she slipped, you could say some sort of relationship with Kanbaru was as unavoidable as family ties.

In that sense, I understood ending with Sengoku—no point in visiting Karen or Tsukihi.

Even so, skipping Kanbaru after all that brouhaha was somehow hard to accept—it's not the exact same, but it felt like excluding an important friend without meaning to.

"Still, Miss Kanbaru's personality is unique in the Araragi harem. In fact, it's baffling that you get along so well. What could ever connect you, with your isolationist policy when it comes to people, and Miss Kanbaru, a human tax heaven?"

"Tax heaven…"

Paradise, huh?

At her core, though, Kanbaru isn't that much of a natural optimist—she has her own baggage. She carries it around with her.

Otherwise—why would she have wished upon a monkey?

"She had a unique upbringing too," I remarked.

"Did she?"

"Yeah. Didn't I tell you? Her parents eloped—and when they did…"

Kanbaru was raised as neither a Kanbaru nor a Gaen as a young child—she didn't know what family was, in the extended sense. Hence her estrangement from Miss Gaen, who was technically her aunt.

Miss Gaen had made no effort to reveal her identity even as she'd roped her older sister's daughter into her work last August.

"Hmm, how distressing. To have all of Miss Kanbaru's mental and physical strength, and not have life go the way you want—makes me wonder just how many people out there live as they wish."

"Who knows… Too heavy for a high schooler when we let it get that big. I'm sure everyone's stressed, though, to some degree."

Of course, that sentiment wasn't free of a desire akin to jealousy—wanting the winners to experience their fair share of suffering.

Still, how do you sympathize with: *Oh noes, I need to earn another ten billion yen but this isn't working. So cruel! I'm getting stressed out!*

"Well, aren't your own tribulations pretty luxurious too? Not all kids studying for college exams get the kind of fortunate, or exceptional, treatment that you enjoyed."

"You're right. I've got nothing to say in return."

"You can think about that once you've returned to life, though. You'll have plenty of time."

Hachikuji twirled around on the landing, then continued up to the next floor—or so I thought, but suddenly the stairs weren't Naoetsu High's, but rather…

On a steep mountain, surrounded by nature—steps I'd been climbing more often than those at school lately.

The long path snaking up toward Kita-Shirahebi Shrine.

This felt more like warping around than teleporting—as if space itself was twisted. The scene change wasn't traditional fantasy, but all-out phantasmagoric, but it no longer felt unusual to me.

I'd grown numb, or rather, acclimatized.

Acclimatizing to hell is a strange notion, I admit—but I did cross paths with Nadeko Sengoku on these stairs in June… If this wasn't some cosmic trial of my soul, my life was flashing before my eyes in my final moments after Miss Gaen cut me down.

Maybe I was just looking back—with regret.

…Yup.

Whether it was Shinobu, Hanekawa, or Senjogahara, not to mention Hachikuji, I'd take the same actions no matter how many times I found myself in the same situation—but I couldn't deny that maybe I could've done better.

"You did quite well, Mister Araragi. At least when it comes to me."

"That's comforting, thanks—but as far as Sengoku goes, I failed."

"You did. And how humiliating that your archnemesis, that conman of all people, cleaned up after you."

"Yeah, and so—"

So.

I continued to climb the stairs as I spoke—and sure enough, or as guaranteed in advance, Sengoku came walking down from the summit, as I thought she would.

Her hat pulled down deep to her eyes—a petite middle school girl wearing a fanny pack. With brisk steps, she hurried down the mountain as if running away—and in fact, that must have been her state of mind.

Run away.

She must have wanted to.

Of course, when I crossed paths with Nadeko Sengoku on the mountain—in reality, not in this recreation—I didn't recognize her.

Nor was I able to sense her pain.

If there's anything I wish I could've done better with Sengoku, that might be it...

"I wonder. I think the standard you're setting for yourself is a little too high. It's not as if you're omnipotent. Be more modest, like Miss Hanekawa."

"If I were as capable as her, I could afford to be ever humble—a guy like me is stuck wanting more."

"Miss Sengoku had a strained relationship with a friend back then, correct?"

"Yeah, that's what I heard. Even if that conman's bulk-sold 'charms' were at the root of it."

No...his charms were a minor detail. The roots ran deeper—

"Well," I continued, "if you can call someone who'd put a snake curse on you a friend. I forget who said it, maybe Oshino? *That's why I don't make friends.*"

"Quite the opinion itself—Miss Sengoku's case may have ended in failure, but don't elementary and middle school troubles usually turn into fond memories once you're an adult?"

"Dunno about that. I feel like nothing turns into an adult's baggage more than childhood memories. Maybe it's because I'm not an adult yet, but at least...my memories of not being better for Oikura back in elementary and middle school are nothing but painful."

"Miss Oikura."

"Oh... Right, Oikura started coming to school after we went our separate ways. You haven't heard? From 'her'?"

"Well, to some extent, but I never met Miss Oikura. I can't say I have a full understanding of the situation based on a game of telephone."

I just know the things that I know, Hachikuji said coolly. A line that would have landed if someone like Hanekawa had said it—regrettably, it just sounded pretentious coming from Hachikuji.

A game of telephone, though...

Would that be her wording if she'd heard it straight from Miss Gaen? I felt like it implied there was someone else in the chain. Was I reading too much between the lines?

"Actually, your home environment is rather unique too. I did hear about that. Your parents took in and sheltered misfortunate children, so you spent a good amount of time with them as an elementary schooler, et cetera. Perhaps that environment fostered the Fire Sisters' sense of justice, as well as your own."

"You know, I'm starting to think that maybe Sengoku played that kind of role in Tsukihi's life. I'm not saying there were any issues in Sengoku's family environment..."

"I don't know if any family is free of issues. Only they know about their home—I should let you know that any independent body would be creeped out by you and your little sisters."

"Could you not run an independent audit of my life? How about 'from an objective viewpoint'?"

As we shared this exchange, Sengoku passed all the way by us—but showed no signs of noticing us. It was of course a recreation, so maybe she couldn't see us—I forget, did she notice me when we crossed paths in reality? Even if she had, she wouldn't have said anything to me, given the situation. Especially since I was with Kanbaru...

In any case.

Not saying anything to Sengoku—made this another repeat of my actions. Later (the next day?), I'd see her in a bookstore, chase after her, then...

"Well, I might have failed with her, but I can't think of any better way I could've gone about it. Even if I was never directly harmed, it was an emergency."

"Yes, it was. If people could redo their lives from the start, maybe they'd just rehash their behavior again and again. With luck, I thought we might hop onto the time-loop-story bandwagon that's all the rage."

"I think that already passed."

"Booms are cyclical. If anything is a loop, that is. They do say that history repeats itself."

"We've been talking about me this whole time, but what about you?

In your case—if you could redo your life, where would you start?"

"Hard for me to say. I won't deny that I used to want to mend my parents' relationship. But when I think about it, I'm not sure how right it would be to reconcile two people who're on bad terms. Breaking up on a whim is sad, but so is making up on a whim."

"I don't think you could build any relationship if you saw things that way..."

"As their daughter, I want to complain to them that they shouldn't have gotten married in the first place if they were going to get divorced, but then, I wouldn't exist—I admit that's an extreme example."

"..."

"I guess you can only go to war with the army you have. What about you, Mister Araragi. You fought with everything you had in the moment and the circumstance—so maybe even in hindsight, you'd just keep on doing the same thing if events looped over and over."

Even if you didn't do the optimal thing every time, you surely did your best, she said.

"And...as far as Miss Sengoku's case goes, I do think that outside interference played a significant role. Blowback—might we say?"

"What? Outside interference? Blowback?"

"Right. You're unable to grasp that part well. Don't worry about it much, then. I'm only saying that extreme actions cause reactions."

"Hold on a second," I began to ask, curious. "Why are we still climbing this mountain? You said Sengoku was our last stop, and we've crossed paths with her. Shouldn't that bring this walking side by side to an end? Haven't we reached our mecca?"

"Oh, no. Didn't I tell you? The goal of Mayoi Hachikuji's Massive Hell-Cruise is to bring you back to life. We can't stop here—if anything, we were on a detour."

"A detour."

"We were lost, if you prefer."

"..."

"Don't worry. This is like a ceremony we need to carry out—initiation might be the better word."

"Bringing me back to life... I thought that was something you could only do with Yumewatari, the companion blade to Kokorowatari... Am I wrong?"

Kokorowatari, the enchanted blade Miss Gaen used to slice me up.

A blade that kills only aberrations, once wielded by an expert at slaying them—a blade to cut aberrations which should not, must not exist.

Paired with it was another enchanted blade, Yumewatari.

The Aberration Savior, though that's a bit of a stretch.

A second enchanted blade with the power to resurrect an aberration slain by Kokorowatari—was how Shinobu described it to me.

If Miss Gaen's scheme, the intent behind her uncharacteristic savagery, was to bring me back to life after killing me—I assumed the Aberration Savior was the only way.

My read didn't address the all-important question: how would she swing a blade that was supposedly engulfed by the Darkness four hundred years ago? Hm, did someone say something about that?

My memory was just so unclear...

"No, you're right. But that's a ceremony for the world of the living—hell has its own way of doing things."

"You're making this sound pretty cool..."

We were just on a walk.

We were taking a stroll together, that was it.

Walking with Hachikuji brought back such good memories that it was like walking on clouds, another world—I guess it was, since we were in hell.

This hardly felt like being in hell, though.

"It's fine, don't worry, Mister Araragi. There's no trial to best or barrier to overcome in order for you to come back to life. Nor any classic trick, like not being allowed to look back. Your resurrection is a guaranteed certainty, so relax and just get ready to go out there."

"..."

"Hm. Is something the matter? You look dissatisfied."

"Dissatisfied?"

More like gloomy.

Well, *dissatisfied* wasn't wrong—I felt that way too.

Because my dim, blurred memories started to coalesce as we climbed the stairs to Kita-Shirahebi—to early in the morning of March thirteenth, when Miss Gaen sliced me up.

The way things were going, did it mean I'd climb up to the shrine, find Miss Gaen waiting for me, be cut to pieces again, this time with the enchanted blade Yumewatari, to revive? Yeah, the thought of getting sliced up again wasn't exactly thrilling.

I had to wonder about hell's so-called way of doing things.

"Speaking of," Hachikuji said, "is Miss Ononoki doing well?"

"Hm."

"Is it because they're colleagues? That person didn't talk up Miss Ononoki, but during that business with the Darkness, Miss Ononoki helped me out big time. I was hoping to ask you about her when we met at last."

"Ononoki…"

Right, now that Hachikuji mentioned it.

They were only in contact for those few days when we faced the Darkness, but maybe journeys like those were a bonding experience. Or maybe, as aberrations of a similar age, they just clicked—either way, my impression was that they got along fairly well.

In contrast to the bad terms Shinobu and Ononoki were on.

That *shikigami* acts in pretty mysterious ways, so you can't let your guard down around her just because you're friends—I always forget because she's saved me so often, but she and I were at total odds when we first met.

Shinobu's continued animosity was actually the right stance.

I was the weird one, in effect living under the same roof regardless of our past—it was abnormal.

By all rights, I should be scolded.

"Well, she's been lively—though I guess she's dead. Maybe that isn't the right term… But in any case, she's doing well."

"Is that so. Having named her my successor, that's a relief to hear."

"Ononoki's your successor?"

"Yes. Officially approved."

You two must be having plenty of witty conversations, Hachikuji said—and maybe she meant it.

"During our treacherous journey, I asked her to take care of you in my place if the unthinkable happened to me."

"That's a surprise…"

Ononoki didn't have to listen to her request, but if it was valid, the shikigami was doing a better job than Hachikuji imagined.

And not just regarding our banter.

"But Ononoki isn't included in this Massive Hell-Cruise of yours?"

"There are time considerations at play here."

"That's why?"

"Yes. It was a difficult producorial call. I think it should be fine. She got so much attention in the anime."

"Can you really balance things out like that?"

Balance—I got hung up on the word as it left my mouth.

No, maybe not hung up. It was more like a flash of inspiration.

Lighting up a darkness that had lingered ever since Hachikuji told me about coming back to life—it had obscured my vision and senses even as we approached the end of our pilgrimage, even as we drew closer to my resurrection, that dawn of a new day. It became clear, so late it might not make a difference, as the word left my mouth.

Ah. That's what was weighing on my mind—balance.

"When you think about it, Mister Araragi, you really are lucky. You not only have a pretty girlfriend, a kind and wise friend, a talented junior, and two energetic little sisters—now you're also cohabitating with a reliable tween."

"…"

"A life anyone would envy. Lived in the lap of luxury. Someone in your position shouldn't be too self-deprecating—in excess, modesty turns to sarcasm, you know? It'd be like saying you want to die because you can't earn ten billion yen."

Was it so enviable to be living with Ononoki? But it was true that I was blessed in a host of ways.

That was exactly why, though.

I sought balance.

Emotional balance.

Who was it that first kept going on about balanced designs—Mèmè

Oshino? I'd been worried about that old bastard's negative influence on Hanekawa, who planned to roam the world, but maybe I'd been poisoned by his ideology too.

"The right thing..."

"Excuse me? What was that, Mister Araragi?"

"Oh, it's just that I remembered an argument I had with the Fire Sisters, with all their talk of justice—it came to me out of nowhere. Maybe it's because I'm in hell that I'm thinking of a topic I'd rather avoid."

"Hm. We'll be at the summit soon, so keep it short if you have something to say. This could be the last time we ever talk, after all."

"What..."

Then I'd rather talk about something else.

But the topic had come to me precisely because I was in hell. I'd wanted to ask for Hachikuji's opinion, and decided to continue.

"It's hard to do the right thing."

"Hard. What would it be in this case? Quite a lot of standards can determine what's right and what's not."

"In this case, a simple kind of rightness, so simple you don't even need to think about standards. It's so right that no one would ever disagree, but surprisingly, I sometimes can't bring it about, or realize it. No need to relativize—"

"Aha. This is like the discussion that at their core, humans are evil. I like talking about that kind of thing."

"No, I'm not trying for the kind of dialogue you get stuck in as an adolescent... How do I put it... It's not about evil, it's just that we're immature."

"Immature, you say."

"Maybe that's why people spend so much energy on Fire Sisters-like stuff. Okay, my sisters just go from one extreme to another, but don't a lot of people get more worked up about righting wrongs than doing the right thing?"

"Righting wrongs isn't doing the right thing?"

"They're similar on the surface, or maybe close but not quite the same—to correct my own error, so to speak, maybe the right word isn't *right* but *smite*."

"…"

That's confusing spoken out loud, Hachikuji opined with a vague expression—true, like her look, what I was saying was difficult to parse.

Not just my phrasing, but the point itself—I was talking about justice, evil, and right in a far from probing way. Maybe splashing around in the shallow end only made things harder.

"You mean people preferring to criticize the words and deeds of others who're trying to do the right thing, just finding fault instead?"

"Mm, I guess?"

Not exactly.

Though she was correct for the most part.

My key point was that righting wrongs makes people feel like they're doing the right thing—which is why distinguishing between the two can be so hard.

Not just for the person in question, but for everyone else. Even an independent body's judgment might fall short of the task…

"What do you think, Hachikuji?"

"What do I think? 'Boy, it's been a while since Mister Araragi has said something this misanthropic. The regular programming, is it? Glad he's okay,' is about it."

"I'm getting a little worried about your image of me…"

"If you're being critical, then allow me to point out this contradiction. Calling people out for mixing up 'righting wrongs' with 'doing the right thing' is just another instance of the same."

She'd complicated things.

What a tangled mess.

If she was right, then I was contradicting myself, grandly at that. Fortunately, that wasn't my point at all.

I wasn't being critical.

I was being supportive, if anything.

"If you keep on righting every wrong and stamp out every last mistake, are you going to be left with a pure, bright rightness? Maybe it'll be a pure, dark rightness, but anyway, if you boil it down, that's what I want to know."

"…"

"When you remained in the world of the living, Hachikuji, you were doing something wrong...or at least, something you weren't supposed to be doing. And like nature's providence came—"

The Darkness.

"You got burned—you nearly became a wandering soul, unable to pass on to heaven or hell."

"I nearly ceased to exist altogether. Yes, I was in danger there."

She sounded unmoved, but it was harrowing—so much so that she felt indebted to Ononoki.

"No, no, I'm grateful mainly because she let me ride on her shoulders so I could kiss you."

"Can't you show a little more tact?!"

I was trying to avoid the topic! I thought we had an unspoken agreement to just kind of gloss over it!

"You know what? It's a very Japanese way of thinking, that not failing is the easier way up the ladder to success than succeeding."

"..."

I'd say it's surprisingly global.

"You're preparing for college exams that grade you based on how many questions you get wrong. I can understand why you might be attracted to these ideas, and I myself wouldn't reject them outright. It's just that living your life that way means never getting what you really want."

"Never getting...what I really want?"

"You're assuming that someone is going to evaluate you. You'll only ever receive what others give you in that case. It isn't a bad thing, of course—but going about life that way, you'll never exceed yourself and your capabilities, which is what you've desired."

You have to make a lot of mistakes.

You have to fail a lot of times.

You have to try again, and again, and again.

You have to hesitate and get frustrated.

To go through round after round of trial and error.

And after all the blame and criticism—

"Only then can you succeed, wouldn't you say?"

"I wasn't...trying to put the spotlight on me. But maybe it is like that—no, that's how it should be."

"If you live your life only righting wrongs, then before you realize, you'll need other people and the world to be wrong—and frankly, that's a dangerous line of thinking. Nothing admirable about it."

"Hm..."

"You said this wasn't about you. In which case, who might you be speaking of?"

"..."

That was a hard one to answer.

The Fire Sisters, those defenders of justice? No, this discussion didn't even apply to them—nothing ran through their heads.

In that case, was I talking about Oshino?

The man who stressed balance, always mediating between right and wrong, good and evil, here and there—was I talking about a guy who declared that people just go and get saved on their own?

No, the person I had in mind.

That I wanted to discuss—was that girl.

The transfer student, his niece.

Ogi Oshino—I wanted to talk about her.

How odd that her name hadn't crossed my mind, that I didn't recall her—the most important individual in the second half of this year of my life.

Was she another exception in this pilgrimage? Hachikuji showed no signs of bringing up her name.

Of course, Ogi's stance toward me was very different from Senjogahara's or Hanekawa's. She had her way of appearing reserved even as she constantly pushed herself onto me. In that sense, maybe she was treated by this place like Kanbaru.

Similar to Kanbaru?

I'd never thought of it that way... Huh, so they were in the same category... Ogi might be glad to hear that since she'd called herself a devotee of Kanbaru's.

I considered bringing up that transfer student, and how I might do so, but I ran out of time before I could find the right words.

The stairs ended.

We walked under Kita-Shirahebi Shrine's *torii* gate.

As we did, a new scene—didn't appear before our eyes. Just Kita-Shirahebi Shrine.

The shrine before it was rebuilt, though.

In a state of crumbling disuse, disrepair, and decay—a forgotten place, a sorry sight. The grounds of a shrine you wouldn't recognize as such unless someone told you.

The same state as when Kanbaru and I first visited it together, though no snakes had been nailed to the surrounding trees.

The missing detail may have been a flaw, given that Sengoku had come down the stairs. Of course, crucified snakes aren't a pretty sight, so I felt only relief over that detail being omitted.

Even without it, because I'd gotten used to the current, restored—or more like freshly built from the ground up—Kita-Shirahebi Shrine, its decrepit state felt grisly enough.

My guard, down thanks to bantering with Hachikuji, went back up. The fact that we hadn't walked into another space or dimension seemed to indicate that we were at the end of the nonsensical route that began at the park.

Correcting what was out of position.

No, Hachikuji had been downright opaque—she was going to dislodge us from the correct position. Was she going to explain what she meant already?

Then.

Ahead of us on the shrine path.

In front of the collapsed shrine's sanctuary—around the offering box.

Someone was waiting for us.

Unlike the others—Shinobu and Senjogahara, Hanekawa and Sengoku—this person's eyes were trained on me, clearly awaiting me.

I did expect to see someone at the shrine—though maybe it was more premonition than expectation.

Or a case of déjà vu.

March thirteenth.

I'd climbed the stairs like this only to be sliced into pieces by Miss Gaen, who'd actually been lying in wait—but no, another part of me thought there might not be anyone.

Because when I tried to meet Miss Kagenui a month ago—when I tried to meet her as promised and visited our meeting spot, Kita-Shira-hebi Shrine, I got stood up.

Yozuru Kagenui.

That violent *onmyoji*—was still missing.

Ononoki never made any meaningful comment on the subject, which was normal given her personality—if she has a personality at all—but as someone who'd been left hanging by Miss Kagenui, and who'd taken in her shikigami, I couldn't help but worry about her safety.

Which is why.

I had a premonition that someone would be lying in wait at the shrine, even if it was just a set located in hell—and simultaneously a premonition that no one would be there. Having both premonitions meant that one of them would be right, but still.

I couldn't help but be shocked—I couldn't hold back my surprise at the identity of the individual waiting for us.

Sitting atop the elegant offering box, so twisted and creaking that it seemed ready to burst, was—neither Izuko Gaen nor Yozuru Kagenui.

Like them, an expert.

But an expert unlike them.

An expert who was dead.

A doll-user who'd been smashed dead to pieces.

Tadatsuru Teori.

"Hello—Araragi. I've been waiting."

007

"Wha…"

I unconsciously took a step back—nearly tumbling right down the stairs. If I'd gotten tangled up with Hachikuji, we might have swapped bodies along the way.

"Wh-Why are you here…"

He was supposed to be dead.

His body smacked by Yotsugi Ononoki's Unlimited Rulebook—earning him a death so complete that not a single chunk of his flesh remained in the world of the living.

I was shocked into silence.

When I thought about it, though, my reaction didn't make sense.

I was overreacting.

We were in hell.

He was dead, yes, but so was I. It was absolutely natural for him to be here—we were meeting again in the afterlife.

I did wonder why an expert like him was all the way down here in Avīci, but he was an outsider, excluded even from Miss Gaen's network… And personally, when I thought about what the guy did to Kanbaru, Tsukihi, and Karen, I couldn't help but think that Avīci was too lukewarm for him.

What was it, then?

Why did it feel wrong?

Being reunited with him felt wrong in an utterly different way from running into Hachikuji in the depths of hell—wrong, or like a puzzle piece fitting in a place you never expected, a strangely convincing (?) feeling…

No, ultimately, it didn't make any sense at all.

"Why that look, Araragi? I do appreciate how expressive you are… While a lot did happen between us, that was back when we were alive. Water under the bridge," Tadatsuru said breezily.

He seemed the most different from how I remembered him back when I was alive—given how tense the situation and circumstances were back then, maybe a different impression was inevitable, but wasn't our current predicament down in the depths of hell no less dire?

Why was he—oh.

That's what I wanted to know.

Why was he acting so *accustomed*?

In the world of the living, too, I'd met and faced off against him at Kita-Shirahebi (though it may have already been newly built)—but why did he seem so much more natural now as he sat there on the offering box? Not that it was a good idea, given how close it was to falling apart…

"Why don't the two of us get along? We've both been sent to hell, after all. Heh, just a little joke there," he said, relaxed enough to crack wise.

A joke? What did he mean, a joke?

What about his words just now were a joke?

How much of it was a joke?

Okay, everything he said sounded like a mean joke… He used to belong to the same university club as Oshino and Kaiki, so who knows, maybe he was endowed with a comedic mind.

I could do without his, here in hell—but as someone who'd conversed with Oshino and Kaiki, I knew I had nothing to gain by pressing him for details. I had to turn to the fifth grader standing by my side.

"Hey, Hachikuji."

"What might it be, Mister Aaaaagi?"

"I like the simplicity, but you shouldn't call people things that sound like hastily entered RPG hero names. My name is Araragi."

"I'm sorry. A slip of the tongue."

"No, you did it on purpose..."

"A skip from the young."

"Or maybe not?!"

"A slip of the slip."

"You're not putting any thought into that one either?! But tell me what's going on. Why is he here—why is Tadatsuru Teori there? You weren't calling this guy *she*, were you?"

"No, no, you were right, it's Miss Izuko Gaen. Don't worry, our hearts were one on that point."

"Then why?"

I looked at Tadatsuru again.

He almost seemed to be smiling on our conversation, or maybe my confusion. It was a look I didn't remember seeing on him before.

Just as Kaiki was an expert who acted only in the service of money, you could say Tadatsuru acted only in the service of "aesthetic curiosity." Was he finding beauty in my panic, Hachikuji's composure, and our interaction, or what?

"You were right to think that Miss Gaen was the august self. But—"

"There you go acting reverent again."

"The grand intent of her august self, or rather, intentions were conveyed to me by Mister Teori over there."

"C-Conveyed."

A game of telephone.

She'd used the phrase earlier—so that's what she meant?

Huh? That seemed a little... Did that timeline make sense? No, not just the timeline. This put a fundamental kink in all sorts of other lines.

Miss Gaen's network didn't include Tadatsuru, so why was he relaying her message to Hachikuji?

"Again, Araragi, why that look? I don't know everything, unlike my senior, and can't clear everything up for you, but at least I can give you a rundown of what I do understand. You may see us as alike, but I'm a bit more generous than Oshino or Kaiki—so long as my own interests aren't involved."

"Aren't they in this case?" Coming from Tadatsuru, his familiar, even accommodating tone only made me more suspicious—but I retook the step I'd ceded, as if to protect Hachikuji. "You're an expert who specializes in exterminating immortal aberrations—right? I'm unforgivable to you just by existing. You see me as something like a pest."

"A pest? You're being a little too self-deprecating there. But if you'll allow me, you're in the right ballpark—still, Araragi. If that's what's worrying you, there's no need to feel that way now."

"Huh?"

"Because *now*—there's nothing vampiric about you. In both senses."

You're a regular human. Thrown into hell. A regular human, Tadatsuru said.

"Any vampirism—has been *subtracted* from you."

"Subtracted…"

Ah… Now it made sense.

That's what Hachikuji meant earlier. Not just multiplication and division, but subtraction too was in play…

The value being subtracted—was my vampirism.

I, myself, didn't feel any different. Nothing about my body seemed off, back in the world of the living or in hell—but if there was no law condemning all aberrations to hell, it meant nothing about me was vampiric now.

So—I was human.

Nothing but human, no longer subject to extermination by the expert hand of Tadatsuru Teori—so that's what it was.

"…"

Of course, believing him, and carelessly approaching him, were a different matter.

While I didn't understand what was going on, I knew for sure that he'd harmed my junior and my little sisters—

"It's okay, Mister Araragi." Hachikuji patted me from behind as if to soothe me. "I understand how you feel, but stopping here gets in the way of my tour. Please keep going. This is necessary in bringing you back to life *as a human*."

"…"

"Otherwise, the subtraction will have been for nothing. I'd never be able to look Miss Ononoki in the eyes again."

Why bring her up now, I wondered—but realized that while Hachikuji and I got along as well as we did, she was at her core a fairly shy girl.

Tadatsuru Teori.

If we were just going to talk—then maybe it was okay?

Either way, I'd get nowhere acting so tense... Even putting aside the tour, I couldn't move forward unless I moved ahead.

"Stay behind me," I warned Hachikuji.

Still protecting her, I walked the shrine's path—come to think of it, a shrine in hell was yet another ridiculous setup.

If she'd come to get me at Tadatsuru's request, then my chivalry was a little pointless, but I just had to.

"It's almost like you're a prince, Araragi. Riding not a white horse but a white snake, given the god enshrined here."

Whether this was an attempt at wit or something else entirely, Hachikuji and I drew closer to him as he spoke.

In the meantime, I tried to recall more details about his profile. With my memory still fuzzy from the intense shock of being murdered, not to mention finding myself in hell, maybe it was futile—but I felt like I needed to remember what I could.

You go to war with the army you have.

That's how humans are.

Tadatsuru Teori, an expert doll-user.

Who incorporated origami into his job.

Digging into his roots, he was a college clubmate of Kaiki and Oshino—a member of the occult research club, which also included Yozuru Kagenui and a university-aged Izuko Gaen, who must have headed it.

And as students, they created the "doll" known as Yotsugi Ononoki.

Using the corpse of a human who'd lived for a hundred years, they gave form to a tween shikigami—and how did the story go? Did he and Miss Kagenui come to an impasse over who owned the familiar?

Tadatsuru would go on to part ways with Miss Gaen as well—while all of them followed their own paths as experts, only his headed in a different direction...

He and I met as something strange began taking place in my body—when I began to grow vampiric on my own, and not under Shinobu's influence...

After a fight, he was slain by the doll he created—you could call it chickens coming home to roost, but his death was so spectacular that words like "karma" didn't do it justice.

It was a Hindenburgian crash that could finish off even a vampire, lesser ones at least, which is why meeting him again felt so bewildering.

Now I knew what characters in manga and stuff meant by that oft-used line, *See you in hell!*

This goes without saying, but it doesn't feel too good when it actually happens to you.

Our reunion, however, was more complicated than mortal enemies meeting again in hell after their deaths—if Miss Gaen planned this, what was her intention, anyway?

Would the explanation he said he'd give me be honestly satisfying? You might be getting annoyed by now, but let me repeat, I was still plenty baffled that I was in hell.

Reluctant to speak with him up close, I stopped and maintained a distance of about five steps. Hachikuji halted too—seeing this, Tadatsuru began.

"Yotsugi—is she doing well? I hope killing me wasn't too traumatic for her."

"You're one of her birth parents, you should know the answer to that. She doesn't worry about anything—she just eats ice cream and stuff, like always."

"Yes, I'm sure. I am one of her birth parents, of course...one of her creators, so I know. But I ask out of affection, not to pry into her affairs—I always find myself worried about her, even when there's no need."

I never did apprise her of the circumstances, after all—said Tadatsuru.

The circumstances?

"What circumstances...are those?"

"Well. She doesn't need to be told, being a shikigami who simply follows orders. That's her strength—her advantage. The same goes for

Yozuru—though in that woman's case, she simply doesn't bother to consider the fine details. I suppose controlling the uncontrollable was where our senior was going to shine."

"...Are you not going to explain these circumstances?"

Though Tadatsuru Teori's demeanor was so proper that comparing him to someone as frivolous as Oshino was silly, my inability to read him did remind me of the Hawaiian-shirted expert.

I used to feel the same kind of constant irritation when I spoke with Oshino. We see the past through rose-colored glasses so I gave him high marks as an expert, but that particular memory was cast in the same harsh light.

"I will. If I don't hurry up and bring you back to life, Miss Gaen might lose her temper—she is a scary one when she's mad."

"..."

"To put it bluntly, the true role I'd been assigned *was precisely to be killed by Yotsugi in that way.*"

Tadatsuru looked as earnest as could be.

"Being killed by her so I could *come to hell first*—so that I may handle the preparations to bring you back to life. That was my job as an expert."

008

"Huh?"

For a moment, I didn't understand a word of it. A second passed, and then a minute, and I still didn't.

It must have taken me a full five minutes to comprehend his words—both he and Hachikuji waited patiently for my brain to crawl to that point.

I felt sorry for making them wait, but the only answer I could give with my boggled mind was, "Y-You're saying you pretended to die?"

That's it. Even I was disappointed in me.

It wasn't about pretending to be dead, we were in hell, nowhere you get by pretending.

But I want to say most people's answers would have resembled mine if their conclusion were to check out against common sense and past events. Few could have a conundrum of this caliber thrust before them and fire straight back with a brilliant response.

Hanekawa, maybe?

"Pretending to die—isn't quite it," Tadatsuru graded me dutifully.

Maybe this betrayed a nasty personality, but expecting anything else from Kaiki and Oshino's clubmate was its own reflection on yourself.

"I am, in fact, dead. But you aren't too far off the mark. I'm pretending to be dead in a sense—as if I've come across a bear."

"A…bear?"

"A bugbear, if you want. A devil," he quipped before continuing—maybe there was some deeper meaning, but he was easily over thirty if you did the math despite his youthful looks. Maybe it was nothing more than a pun.

A devil, though…

"Where should this explanation start—Oshino is glib, and Kaiki clever with his words, while I don't speak to people often. I was a lonely child who played with dolls."

"…"

"I'll try my best and pick a clear starting point. As a human, as an individual, I've been dead for quite some time," he divulged casually. Between his words and his tone, he certainly was a poor explainer if not exactly a poor speaker. It was kind of tragic if he'd become a doll-user because he always played with his dolls alone, but putting that aside—

"For quite some time? Um, what do you mean?"

"The me that Yotsugi killed was a *doll* I controlled—a substitute self, or perhaps body double you'd expect any doll-user to wield."

"…"

"Hm? I was bracing for more pointed questions from you around now, but you've gone silent. Conversations with people never go as well as those with figurines."

While playing alone with dolls and speaking to figurines were similar, they gave off very different impressions, but either way—I'd gone silent because I'd been left speechless.

If Tadatsuru thought I'd react promptly, I'm sorry, but he was overestimating me—faced with situations they never even imagined, people usually freeze up and can't say a word. That said, as a high school kid who loves manga, anime, TV shows, today's popular entertainment, I'd have no response or rebuttal if you called me a fool for not having imagined it at least.

A body-double doll.

A standard move for a doll-user.

Then he wasn't pretending to be dead—but had *pretended to be alive*?

To be alive, so that he could be killed?

"You said…Ononoki didn't know, right?" I asked.

"Correct. Not just her, Yozuru didn't, either—though in her case, she probably didn't bother trying to find out. Ever a seeker of intensity, she must not have been interested in shabby old me—what a sad romance it was."

"Romance…"

"Oh, forget it. It's in the past. Hearing an older guy reminisce and ramble on about his love life would only bore a youngster. As for Kaiki? He's a liar, after all, but I'd say the only ones who knew about my technique were—Miss Gaen and Mèmè Oshino."

"…"

Only a woman who knew everything—Miss Gaen.

And a man who acted like he saw through everything, Oshino.

Hearing their names, they did strike me as the type to notice details that people were trying to hide—but the question was *when he started* to harbor this secret.

The point wasn't unrelated to me. A fact that turned his position as an expert upside down, roots and all, it fundamentally changed the meaning of the night of February thirteenth, what happened exactly a month ago.

That kidnapping—that blackmail.

That battle, that calamity.

How did this rewrite it all?

"A doll destroyed a doll. That's all that happened—so, Araragi. I brought up Yotsugi, but if your indirect involvement in my death was weighing on you, go ahead and unburden yourself."

"It's not that simple…"

To be honest, I did feel that way, a little.

If all this was the whole point—then I wasn't just indirectly but directly involved in Tadatsuru's death. I'd be lying if I said that didn't weigh on me at all. Learning that it was a doll that had gotten smashed to pieces back then was poor comfort, but I did feel a little less tense.

It raised the question, however, of why he did what he did. I wanted to cross-examine him and point out that he'd ended up in hell anyway—and so the burden stayed on my shoulders.

"Then what was that farce for? What was the point? What were you trying to accomplish by abducting three people who're very important to me?"

"A farce, you say. I personally saw it as a tour de force." Tadatsuru smiled. "In a sense, you see, dying and coming back to life is my specialty. Even more than it is a vampire's."

"Specialty?"

"Not that I ever came back to life, strictly speaking. I simply possessed a doll and returned to the world of the living through a medium—my true body is always on this side."

This side.

Which, here in hell, meant the next life—our situation made demonstratives tricky, but he seemed far too familiar with this world...and what he just said had to be the main reason. If his true body was located here, that's where *this side* referred to.

"Oh, but know that I'm not a resident of Avīci. Being seen as someone who went to hell hurts worse than actually being in hell."

"Sure, I just had the same experience... In fact, it hasn't let up one bit."

"Normally, I live up in heaven, without a care in the world."

"..."

This instantly wiped out any guilt I might have felt over his death...

A child like Hachikuji getting sent to hell after passing on to the afterlife in a moving manner was quite a letdown, but the idea of enjoying the good life in heaven chipped away at my motivation to live in its own way.

I mean, why not hurry up and die rather than risk sinning throughout a poorly lived life... Not that I knew how serious Tadatsuru was being.

"Since when? When did you decide to kick back and retire—or I should say, how long have you been leading this lifestyle of traveling between this world and the other?"

"Call it labor, not a lifestyle," Tadatsuru answered. "Maybe migrant labor—or transmigratory labor. No, I was still a healthy soul in a healthy body back in college. A healthy human specimen. I became a doll-user after creating the doll known as Yotsugi, and after breaking away from the others."

"I'm not sure how much I should ask you about this since it sounds private... But was creating Ononoki, and Miss Kagenui ending up as her owner, your motive for becoming a doll-user?"

"Motive? You make it sound so criminal. To get to your point, though, it isn't far enough from the truth to call it a lie—in my telling of it, at least. Miss Gaen and Yozuru may have a differing opinion—oops."

Tadatsuru looked up at the sky.

This drew me into looking up as well, but I saw nothing in particular—the sky was just at the border between day and night, as dusk fell.

Not a single cloud, not a single bird.

I had no idea what Tadatsuru was looking at, but he seemed to have spotted something in the spotless sky. "*It seems we're being told to hurry—so I can't provide a full account of why I became a doll-user. You'll just have to wait for the theatrical spin-off,*" he said.

A spin-off is one thing, but really? A movie? Just how big of a prequel did he want?

"Allow me to give you a succinct explanation. If you're just dying to know more, then ask Miss Gaen once you're alive again—she knows everything, so she might even disclose more details than I could. Whether she will is another question, of course... I chose this path after college, but my old senior does look upon me with scorn. Things rarely went for me as I hoped, and my business never gained any traction. That's when I had a hasty thought—I see it as foolish now, but a sort of forbidden technique, if you would. A taboo amongst experts, or perhaps something closer to a curse."

"A curse..." I'd heard the word somewhere before.

"Maybe I should describe it as *transforming myself into an aberration*—the existence of Yotsugi Ononoki, the doll I created as a student, lay at the root naturally. Which is to say, I thought I might turn the corpse of Tadatsuru Teori into an aberration just as I'd done to her hundred-year-old cadaver."

I attempted to create a doll aberration called Tadatsuru Teori. A doll of myself—using my own corpse.

"And did you succeed?"

It seemed preposterous. If that was possible, you could gain undying, eternal youth. I was aware of the existence of immortality, given that I lived in a world that had formerly human vampires... Still, a human turning a human into an aberration was unbelievable.

What drove him to it? Aesthetic curiosity?

"I failed, and this is the result. Half-man, half-spirit, I wander between this world and the other—no, maybe I ought to say I'm stuck between this world and the other."

"Don't tell me you can't abide immortal aberrations because you resent that."

"I can't deny there's that element."

"You can't..."

"Is this where I make a joke about feeling out of my own element?" asked Hachikuji, from behind me.

That's what she says after staying quiet for all this time? She knew she didn't have to meet any wordplay-density quota, right? What a strong sense of duty, even here in hell.

"While I say I failed, I'm still able to live via my dolls—and since I was later successful in their mass production, in a sense I gained undying, eternal youth, and am an aberration. Like a doppelganger—or perhaps a half-a-ganger? I decided to make the most of my idiosyncratic nature as I applied myself to my profession."

"..."

And those idiosyncrasies permitted him to do as much as he did even outside of Miss Gaen's network... Was that the takeaway?

"And that's the story of Tadatsuru Teori... Is that good enough for you, Araragi? Or are you interested in hearing more?"

"Um..."

Honestly, I wasn't that interested, though I wouldn't say it to his face—he'd given me a suitable overview of his unique circumstances. Now it made sense.

I imagined there were other dramatic episodes, various twists and turns before he became a full-fledged doll-user, but my interest—my questions lay beyond that.

"Just to be sure, nothing serious happened to you even when Ono-noki blew you to smithereens?"

"I wouldn't say nothing serious. My dolls are a very serious matter to me, and I lost one—but in terms of my life, no, you needn't worry. I was half-dead to begin with."

"But why pretend to be dead..." Or rather, alive. Why that entire farce?

"Again, it wasn't a farce—neither Yozuru nor Yotsugi knew anything about it, after all. I would call it a live test performance, with no rehearsal. Let's go back to last month," Tadatsuru said, his eyes still turned upward. What was he seeing there, anyway? "I received a request for my services as an expert, Araragi, to resolve the anomalies occurring in your town."

He dove in with no introduction—or so it seemed, but I guess he was talking about it this entire time. He'd been waiting here to tell me—having asked Hachikuji to fetch me just so he could.

It wasn't to apologize for his long silence, or about what happened a month ago—and whatever ill will I felt toward him had waned significantly during our exchange.

"Anomalies occurring in my town... You mean Kita-Shirahebi Shrine and—no, that can't be it. That was solved already last month." To be precise, we hadn't solved it as much as returned it back to an unsolved state, but no need to nitpick.

"Yes. This request, simpler than that, painted you and the former Kissshot as my targets. Miss Gaen's network certified you as harmless, but that was none of my business—in fact, aberrations protected by her network ought to be my top priority. I should've moved against you even without a request."

"..."

Right, that was how it went.

He took my two little sisters and a junior hostage, an unimaginably cruel and villainous act, in order to come after me and Shinobu—he claimed it wasn't a farce, so I was on the edge of my seat as to why. A request, though, meant I'd had his motive right from the start.

If he was obligated to eliminate me and Shinobu after taking on a request, he was being perfectly honest in describing it as not a farce but a tour de force, a live test performance with no rehearsal—

"Yes, right. Exactly…" Tadatsuru nodded, unconcerned and unembarrassed. It almost felt like a magic show where you got to learn how the tricks were performed—okay, no real magician does that. "It'd be exactly right—*if someone hadn't acted first*. In fact, it would've been worse otherwise. Your little sisters and your junior might not have made it out in one piece…"

"Don't say stuff like that. You're scaring me."

"I'm the scared one here. Little did I know that Suruga Kanbaru was a Gaen daughter… I shudder to imagine what might have happened if I, in my ignorance, had harmed her. I'm glad I heard about it in advance."

"…?"

She indeed was Miss Gaen's neice—and he must not have known that when he kidnapped her, but shudder to imagine? Miss Gaen wasn't the type to dote on someone just because she was her niece. He did use the word *daughter*—was he afraid of Kanbaru's late mother?

"You heard about it in advance—and someone acted first—which almost makes it sound like Miss Gaen informed you prior to getting your request. About what was up in our town."

It seemed possible. Apparently, Miss Gaen coming forth and handling a job on her own was quite rare—but what she'd tried to do was something like pacify, or maybe govern our town… She'd even enlisted the help of Episode, a dangerous expert, so she might also have reached out to an old acquaintance outside of her network and spoken to Tadatsuru Teori—

"No, never. She and I are somewhat like odd bedfellows at the moment, but we only came into contact after I learned about the situation. The one to approach me—to act as a mediator between me and Gaen, was someone else."

A mediator.

I had a hunch when I heard that word. The kind that only someone studying for exams would have—but I felt certain for whatever reason. This hunch spoke a man's name to me with more eloquence than any well-reasoned theory…

"Oshino," I said without thinking. "Was the person who tipped you off in advance—who acted first...Mèmè Oshino?"

009

Of course, there were other possibilities.

Among people I knew who were aware of the situation, for example, Kaiki. I'd made a leap of logic based on a single word, but equating Oshino with mediation was going a little too far.

"Exactly," Tadatsuru replied nonetheless. "Right, that guy who acts like he sees through everything is an executive in Miss Gaen's network—so when he contacted me, an outsider, he seemed as free a spirit as ever. The word *executive* suits no one worse."

"…"

Likewise, calling Miss Gaen a *boss* didn't seem too fitting—an old acquaintance you just couldn't cut loose sounded more like it than any exaggerated title.

Oshino and Tadatsuru were old acquaintances too, whether they liked it or not. The folklorist might very well go meet the doll-user. As far as timing, it must have happened after Oshino left my town—I wondered what he told Tadatsuru.

A guy who acts like he sees through everything. In acting first, what might he do?

"He told me there was something I could do *because I didn't belong to our senior's network*. Very much in character for a guy who loves to resort to tricks that feel like cheating."

"…"

"By which I don't mean that he cuts corners because he's lazy. He does everything that can be done and takes out every insurance policy available, and as a result the majority of his endeavors come out to nothing. He's like a squanderer of wisdom, an anti-thrift expert. Getting me involved must have been like going beyond insurance in duplicate, a rare case even for him."

I sort of got that. Just in my own experience, he'd covered the possibility of me and Shinobu contacting him from another timeline—guessing on tests must be a foreign concept to him. Despite his frivolous demeanor, he was surprisingly diligent.

"But he doesn't spell things out fully and clearly," Tadatsuru said. "When he came to see me, he gave me the impression that he just wanted to chat with me. What a buffoon, is all I thought—I suppose his visit was nothing more than a precaution, originally."

"I have gripes of my own about the way Oshino likes to drop hints—but are you saying he sprinkled Kanbaru's background into your chat?"

Come to think of it, Oshino had been curious about her background—even he must have been surprised to encounter his college senior's niece.

He even made sure of Kanbaru's mother's name.

"Yep. And, Araragi. Your name came up too—or perhaps I should say your names."

"Our names? Me and…" Who? In this case, Shinobu?

"Which is why I grasped, or understood, a few things about this town before accepting my request. At the time, I had no idea what he was trying to say—but I think he was trying to promote just how *safe* you were."

"…"

"That's what he hinted. It wouldn't be worth wasting a doll on you two—that's what Oshino came to tell me. By the way, that's also when I learned he saw through my true identity. You know, in hindsight, it may have been a threat. As in, put a hand on my friends and I'll tell everyone what you are—a doll."

Tadatsuru gave a wry smile.

What could I say... I was at a loss for words—Oshino had made a move in anticipation of what was to come?

Our official "harmless" label only applied within their network, so he contacted outside parties to protect me and Shinobu. Perhaps he just saw it as proper aftercare, having been properly compensated for a job—but I was moved to hear about such thorough follow-up customer service.

Not something I could do, or did do—wait. Hold on a sec.

In the end, Tadatsuru still came to my town to exterminate me and Shinobu—hmm... Oshino had worked behind the scenes in advance, but the dots remained unconnected.

What happened after that?

"Well, it was insurance—again, most of what he said, he only insinuated, an unlit cigarette in his mouth. This is going to be my own interpretation, but if you're fine with that, then hearing me out should clear up most of your doubts—you should be able to return to life without any regrets."

"Without any regrets..."

"Think of my take as a souvenir," Tadatsuru said. "This was the case he made—'Koyomi Araragi and Shinobu Oshino. As a rule, they're harmless right now.'—'You don't have to act on it, they won't be a problem at all.' That isn't to say, though, that an exception to that rule couldn't occur—if Araragi conspires with Shinobu to become a vampire again and again.'"

" ... "

"In other words, the application Oshino filed to have you considered as harmless would no longer apply if you began heading down your own vampiric path, apart from your ties to the former Kissshot Acerolaorion Heartunderblade."

"That's..."

Exactly what happened to my body—I couldn't believe it.

The guy who acted like he saw through everything, Mèmè Oshino, predicted even this?

"As only one prediction of many, I believe. And it was a concrete fear of his, not some excessive precaution."

"A fear… He was afraid I'd unthinkingly overuse Shinobu's power? No…"

That wasn't it. If he feared that possibility, he wouldn't have left Shinobu in my hands and skipped town. In fact, I'd convinced myself it was because he trusted that wouldn't happen, because he believed in me, that he quietly took off to the next town without a word or even a goodbye.

"Yes. In which case, he feared a *situation where you'd have no choice*—I think that's why he came to visit me. It's not like he's capable of precognition. In fact, he must not have predicted many of the things that attacked your town after he left. Nor can we say for sure that he foresaw an outbreak of cases that'd force you to be reckless. But he did see how you wouldn't avoid being reckless if such cases did arise."

"Like that helps," I spat. I was hardly being gracious.

"A request could come my way were that to happen—that's what he told me. A request for my involvement. In *slaying a vampire*. In that event, he wanted me to get in touch with Miss Gaen, putting aside the years of ill will, tossing out that old bad blood, because she'd be waiting to hear from me. She couldn't make the first move given her position, he said. Not that I really understood him at the time…but that's exactly what ended up happening."

He might not be a precog, but that guy must have X-ray vision, the way he sees through things, Tadatsuru muttered. Although I owed Oshino a debt of gratitude, I couldn't agree more with the doll-user's sentiment.

"When I received nothing short of a request to slay the two of you, my blood ran cold. At the same time, though, I found it odd. If Oshino feared that eventuality, why hadn't he done something about it himself? A guy who says that people just go and get saved on their own, all but relying on an old friend? I was curious—which is why I played along. I contacted Miss Gaen."

Opening the curtain on the farce.

This was his explanation—I still didn't know what it meant.

010

I wasn't sure when Tadatsuru had lowered his gaze, but it lifted again—
like he was on the lookout for the first star in the night sky as the sun
continued to set and it grew darker. I followed suit and this time saw
clearly what he did.

No, *clearly* is an overstatement—it still looked dim to my eyes, but
it was clear what it was.

From the sky—or rather, from the heavens.

Came dangling a strand of string.

"Or a thread, Mister Araragi. It's here to collect you—which makes
it sound like it's bringing you to the world of the dead, but actually, it's
here from the world of the living," Hachikuji explained.

The world of the living... If it was a thread, it made me think more
of Akutagawa's short story about a spider's thread dangled down from
heaven by the Buddha.

Well, they say spider silk is tough enough even to be used in space, so
I didn't find it unreliable...but how did that story go? Was Kandata the
character's name? As he started climbing up the dangling spider's thread,
other sinners tried to make it to heaven with him, and when he told them
to get down, didn't the thread snap?

In that sense, the thread was a trial—especially if Miss Gaen was
doing the dangling.

"You really are running out of time. If you miss that thread, Mister Araragi, you'll burn in Avīci for eternity. An oni thwacking you with a giant knapsack."

"A giant knapsack? Isn't that you?"

"Excuse me. I meant to say with a giant club."

"Scary either way…" Or maybe cute as hell?

"So, Mister Teori, I'm sorry but can you stop with your story?"

"Hold on, Hachikuji, don't cut him off like that. Not when he's in the middle of what I need to hear. Tadatsuru, this thing you could do because you didn't belong to the network… You mean accepting the job to slay me and Shinobu—or pretending to."

I was jumping ahead in his story to get as much as possible out of him before the thread (?) from heaven reached the shrine. Not a very praiseworthy move as a listener, but a fortunate one, because the doll-user answered, "I suppose… I pretended to accept it, as I pretended to be alive. Not that I can say exactly what Oshino's intentions were."

So that's how it was.

He continued, "The fact that Yozuru Kagenui was considered uncontrollable despite being part of Miss Gaen's network was just perfect—she'd confront me with a merciless, ice-cold heart for my illegal act. So when your body started acting up, Miss Gaen *sent those two to work*—"

"…"

Even before I spoke to her about the strange phenomenon I was experiencing, namely my reflection disappearing, Miss Gaen had dispatched the onmyoji and her familiar—as if she'd foreseen things. Her seeming clairvoyance had sent chills down my spine back then, and I'd chalked it up to her "knowing everything"—but now that I was privy to the secret behind her trick, it was nothing special. That turn of events had been marked down in advance as part of her timeline.

Still, the timing being spot-on was very much like her…

"But why would you do it?" I asked Tadatsuru. "Couldn't you just turn down the request?"

"I had no reason to, and even if I did, it'd have just gone to another expert. Miss Gaen and I came to the conclusion that playing into the hands of our 'enemy' would be best."

"Y-Your enemy?" Not—client? The individual who came to him with the request to slay me and Shinobu. Wouldn't the two of us have been his enemy instead?

"Not necessarily. To say the least, Deishu Kaiki went missing in your town, and neither I nor Miss Gaen are so cold as to have not cared."

"Kaiki..."

Right, Miss Gaen had said some such thing—the info getting so complicated that she didn't know what the truth was...

I saw Kaiki as a guy who wouldn't stay dead even if you killed him, and his friends from college, Miss Gaen and Tadatsuru, must have felt that way more than I did... If the unthinkable had happened, they couldn't turn a blind eye.

"While I called it playing into the enemy's hands, it wasn't as if we knew what the plan was—we moved in order to find out. We also had to halt your ongoing transformation into a vampire. I could come to this side and guide you, but having played the part of a hated enemy, we needed to get Hachikuji over there to help out."

"And I did," she said. "Find me toward the end of the credits, under Cameo Appearances. Since I'd get to meet you again, I gladly waived my booking fee and gave it my all."

"Nothing would depress me more than you charging a booking fee to do this... That'd be worse than realizing I'm in hell."

For the time being, kill me to reset my body, then revive only the human part—so that's what was going on. They could've told me in advance, but if they didn't.

There must have been some reason.

Was that part of their strategy against the enemy? Hard to figure out from my position.

"If we killed you with the enchanted blade Kokorowatari and revived you with Yumewatari, you might just return as a vampire, and we'd be back where we started. That's why I, an expert, had to butt in and be ready for you in hell."

With this, Tadatsuru jumped down from the offering box—my eyes never left him, but a total change came over his outfit as he landed. On second thought, costume might be more apt—not only was his garb now as Japanese as it could be, it matched the occasion.

The vestments of a Shinto priest.

If having only a spiritual body meant instantly changing clothes when you felt like it, that seemed pretty handy—I wasn't jealous, but maybe *kicked back and retired* wasn't far off the mark.

"My former senior and I also agreed that fixing your issue was the only way to counter our enemy. How odd, given that I used to oppose her so vehemently, but let's simply praise Oshino's skill as a mediator."

"Were your doubts ever cleared up?" There were a lot of other things I wanted to ask him, but at the moment, this was foremost on my mind. "You had to go along with Oshino because you didn't know what his intentions were—that was the key, but did you ever reach a conclusion there?"

"I'm afraid not. I have a hypothesis, though—no, it'd be presumptuous to call it mine. This one, at least, is Miss Gaen's alone. Her guess as to why Oshino still refuses to show himself. Why he seems to have gone missing. Her thinking—is that it's for the same reason that Yozuru disappeared without a trace."

"…"

And what would that be?

Wasn't that a tautology? As good as saying nothing?

I knew very well that Miss Kagenui had vanished just like Oshino—hm? No, that wasn't it.

In that sense, Kaiki had disappeared too.

Instead of bringing him up as well, Tadatsuru treated Kaiki as an exception and didn't include him with the other two experts.

Did that provide a way out, or at least, did Miss Gaen see it that way? The solution she sought, when she didn't even know what she was up against…

"My thoughts and hers diverge on that point," Tadatsuru said. "Remember what I told you? Find Oshino. From the looks of it, you came up empty-handed."

"My friends are searching for him, though…"

Actually, only one still had the arsenal of means to find him: Hanekawa. Senjogahara and I had exhausted our connections—not only did we not know where he was and why, we didn't even know whether he was alive.

Only Hanekawa hadn't given up.

I'd seen it as impossible, but our only hope was that he was in fact overseas, where she'd gone looking for him...

"Then that line wasn't part of your performance. Even if the way you pretended to be killed by Ononoki was a farce."

"Not just that one line. Though only a doll died there, most of the things I said were the honest truth. Deception isn't my forte—I may be a doll-user, but feeling like a marionette and not calling my own shots is only humiliating. I felt like I'd been assigned an unpleasant role; the story was taking a twist that was altogether too neat. Of course, half of this was directed at Oshino and how he acts like he sees through everything."

"..."

"I do feel like apologizing to Yozuru, though. I played the role of the nasty villain, but she had to do the nasty work. Even she must've felt bad about using a shikigami to kill me—and feeling bad..." the priest trailed off.

I wasn't going to comment. Miss Kagenui's mindset was unfathomable to an inexperienced high schooler like me. Honestly, though, she might be even less bothered by it than Ononoki...

"May I tell them?" I asked Tadatsuru.

"Hm?"

"Ononoki...and Miss Kagenui, if we figure out her whereabouts. That you're a doll-user and didn't really die back there. That you pretended to die, or to be alive. I'm getting the sense you don't want too many people to know."

"True, but they'll find out anyway, now that this is happening. It's the right time for it, or rather, it's time for me to pay the piper. I'd appreciate it if you could apologize on my behalf."

"Don't be ridiculous."

Why should I apologize?

Say sorry for me—a common enough request that's unreasonable when you think about it.

Not gonna be his body double...

"If you want to apologize, do it yourself—even if you can't return to life, you can visit the land of the living through one of your dolls, right?"

"It's not that simple, unfortunately. Dying is a fairly grave offense, and getting sent to hell is only the start of it. Every crime is met with a punishment..."

"..."

His setup was more complicated than I'd imagined, then—letting a doll containing his ego get smashed wasn't exactly a painful decision for Tadatsuru, but obviously it hadn't been an easy one either.

"You're lucky because the enchanted blade Yumewatari can revive you immediately—Miss Gaen might have slaughtered you without a proper explanation, and as her junior, I must ask you to overlook that fact. It was more convenient to brief you in hell, you see..."

"Well, I'm used to being made a fool of without any kind of proper explanation. That's fine, but—"

"Don't worry," Tadatsuru cut me off, as if to erase any concerns I had before I could voice them. "Once you return to life, you won't face any more requests from Miss Gaen to help her with ridiculous jobs. Unless she lied to me about her aims, you'll have fulfilled your role by the time you come back to life as a human. Think of this trip through hell as a short-term hospital stay to excise your vampiric nature. I doubt even she would try to work you as you're convalescing. Her intent is to remove any concerns prior to the showdown with our enemy—though if you have to impute malice, she might be trying out that pair of enchanted blades."

"..."

I could see her wanting to do that... If Miss Gaen didn't have ulterior motives on at least that level, I'd be confused. Still, while Tadatsuru didn't totally fail to address my interrupted question, that hadn't been quite it.

Now down from the offering box, the priest continued at a relaxed pace toward the thread dangling from the heavens and stopped right below it.

Then beckoned me over.

"Let's get going, Mister Araragi," Hachikuji encouraged me as well—so I had to move. Yes, I had to, that's exactly how I felt.

The thread came so low that I could jump and grab it—or so I say, but if it wasn't a string, it wasn't a thread either.

A white snake.

A snake's tail dangled there.

...They wanted me to grab it?

At least it wasn't the head, and it did make sense—Kita-Shirahebi enshrined a white serpent, after all... A snake was more appropriate than a spider.

"What's the matter, Mister Araragi? You look scared. Is it because it's a snake?"

"I'd be lying if I said no... It's like a phobia at this point."

"If this is about what happened to Miss Sengoku, don't hate yourself too much." My phobia stemmed purely from being bitten countless times by poisonous snake fangs and hovering repeatedly on the brink of death—but Hachikuji waded into an even deeper part of my heart. "It was the aforementioned conman who saved Miss Sengoku's soul, but if he hadn't gotten involved, wouldn't you have saved her eventually? It might've taken a little more time, but I believe you would have."

"..."

"As far as that case goes, think of it as someone swooping in and taking the glory for himself—don't worry, I'll vouch for you. You're the best, Mister Araragi."

I never felt like I'd been competing with anyone, and it wasn't a question of winning or losing—of glory or anything, but hearing that from Hachikuji did help.

To the point I felt like I could even grab onto a snake.

I reached out—and held the white snake's tail.

It twitched.

The thing was alive?

"I'll back her up on that theory, Araragi. In fact, I'm sure our enemy wanted it—you spending a little more time, that is, rather than anything to do with Nadeko Sengoku herself. Perhaps my irregular turn only arrived because Kaiki's interference threw a wrench into the plan. You were originally supposed to spend more time in a drawn-out battle with

Nadeko Sengoku—becoming a vampire in order to save her. Oshino saw my deployment as an insurance policy. So it was for our enemy, too."

Tadatsuru was standing right next to me as he spoke, and it was unnerving on a whole new level.

"...By the way," I said to Hachikuji, "I still haven't asked you. Why was I off?"

"Excuse me?"

"You know, the reason you had to act as my guide. When I woke up in hell, I was in that park, even though Miss Gaen killed me at Kita-Shirahebi Shrine. You put me back in position—or dislodged me from the correct position. What's that about?"

"Hmm. We don't have any time, and I thought I needn't bother, but you're that curious?"

"I wouldn't go that far?"

Yeah, okay, I was only trying to drag this out.

I was putting off climbing up the white snake—and returning to life.

Postponing it as much as I could.

"Well, I'm curious, yes. Forget the stuff about being out of position. That got taken care of thanks to you—but tell me that park's name, if you say you know it. It's where we first met, but I still don't know how to pronounce it."

Namishiro? Rohaku?

I'd been told neither, but I honestly couldn't think of any other reading. It was too difficult even to appear on a Japanese test—if I really had to guess, maybe Robyaku or Namihaku...

"Shirohebi Park." It was Tadatsuru who answered. "Originally, it would be read Shirohebi."

"What? Shirohebi—as in 'white snake'?"

"Not the character we now use for serpents, but another with a common origin. More affiliated with water than pests, its modern meaning is *torrent*, as in a torrent of tears. Shirohebi was once the entire area's name—at some point, someone wrote it down incorrectly, resulting in the opaque characters."

Did that make sense? Maybe it did.

I didn't know about writing them wrong, but I could imagine mistaking one for the other. If I handwrote either to look it up in an electronic dictionary, the other one was similar enough to show up in the list of candidates.

The characters' order was flipped too, but that did happen from time to time in Japanese—to begin with, reading left-to-right was only a modern practice. Things could get jumbled as time passed. Shirohebi...

As in...

"Kita—Shirahebi Shrine."

"Mm-hm. Yes, it was the original location of Kita-Shirahebi Shrine—and why you were out of position. You've heard that the shrine had been moved...haven't you?"

"Oh, right." I forgot who'd told me, but yeah—and joining the two was a mistake, leading to distortion, or something?

"I'd call that an understatement—in essence, they brought a sea god to a mountain. Technically a lake, not the sea."

"A lake?"

"Like I said, at first it was written with a character associated with water."

That seemed good enough for him, but something else caught my attention—a lake. That sounded familiar, but before I could remember...

"Well then, Araragi, why don't we get going?" urged Tadatsuru. "Say hi to Miss Gaen for me—and to Yotsugi too. I'd never ask Yozuru, but be extra kind to Yotsugi, please, in my place."

"Sure, I understand," I agreed out of reflex, maybe too rashly given the nature of his request.

Then I worked up, at last, the nerve to confess what was really on my mind.

"I wonder, though—is it okay for someone like me to come back to life?"

011

"Hiya!"

A punch hit me.

Mayoi Hachikuji's punch.

Leaping into the air, a heroic jumping play from a dead standstill, still wearing her backpack, she struck my cheek with a closed fist.

Holding nothing back, she put a ridiculous amount of strength into it, despite being more or less an elementary schooler. Enough to send me flying, but I managed to cling on to the snake's tail, holding it tight reflexively to withstand the punch, wondering if it might tear—fortunately, it seemed to be elastic (?) and merely grew longer as I staggered back.

"That one was for me!" she declared as she landed.

For herself?

That was just called punching me.

Tadatsuru's eyes were opened wide—did he not know about her feisty side? Had she pulled the wool over his eyes?

"Hey...Hachikuji."

"Don't worry. My fist is fine."

She opened and closed it.

As if I was worried about that.

Sure, you could break your fingers punching someone that hard if you didn't know how to make a proper fist—but we were in hell.

All of us immortal.

Even I, the victim of her punch, didn't feel much pain in my cheek—in an environment where you could be beaten by metal clubs and come back to life, what was an elementary schooler's fist?

Still.

As clichéd as it might sound, her fist hit my heart harder than my body—my chest hurt far worse than my cheek.

"Then one for Miss Senjogahara, one for Miss Hanekawa, one for Miss Kanbaru, one for Miss Sengoku, one for your two little sisters, one for your parents, one for Miss Oikura, and one for Chiaraijima."

"I'm glad you care for Oikura when you didn't know about her until moments ago, but who was that last person?!"

"And one for Mister Oshino, and one for Mister Kaiki, and one for Miss Kagenui, and..." Hachikuji counted on her fingers—starting to ball her fist just as I thought it'd opened up.

And wait, even for Kaiki?

"As for Miss Ononoki, have her punch you herself once you're alive again."

"There'd be no trace left of me. She literally has bone-crushing strength."

"Is it okay for someone like you to come back to life? What kind of a line is that?" demanded Hachikuji, actually punching my stomach with the fist she'd made.

Whoomp, whoomp.

She did hold back a little this time...or maybe she only hit hard when it was for herself.

"You should be glad it was me who heard your whining. Miss Senjogahara would revert to her old self and treat you to a stationery storm."

"..."

Whoomp, whoomp, whoomp, whoomp.

Hachikuji pummeled me.

She got enough shots in to cover everyone, but I continued to take the punches.

"Miss Hanekawa...would let you fondle her breasts to inspire you, like always, but don't expect me to spoil you, Mister Araragi."

"Hold on. Like always? She's never done that… Could you not make it sound like a regular occurrence, for her sake and for mine?" Even if it almost happened once.

Finally stopping with her punches, Hachikuji said, "What's wrong, Mister Araragi? Spooked? Do you not want to return to life and have more trying experiences? Are you tired?"

Trying experiences… Of course I didn't want any.

Tadatsuru thought Miss Gaen wouldn't make any more absurd requests after I came back to life, but I found that hard to believe (she had a real knack for using people)—and even apart from her, all the things I needed to do once I was back was kind of depressing.

Including taking my entrance exams. Though I wouldn't make it in time even if I revived now, and all the knowledge I'd crammed into my head, all the memorization, must have been shot out the other side thanks to my sojourn in hell.

But that wasn't the issue.

I felt depressed, but not spooked—tired, true, but it wasn't even that.

"When you first came here," Hachikuji reminded me, "you did feel you could rest in peace now. Are you hoping you're done with bothersome tasks? Are you picking 'no' at the continue screen? Is credit feeding banned here?"

"No, but some taut thread in me snapped…" I glanced at the snake's tail still in my grip and gazed into the heavens it extended toward. I wasn't sure I could explain how I felt, but I'd give it my best. "…and part of me feels like I was able to die at last. Yeah, I'm a little hesitant to press continue. Like I've had enough, and am not hungry for more…" I learned that heaven and hell, the afterlife, exists, and while my understanding of the meaning of life wasn't shaken—

"In other words, Mister Araragi, you'd rather stay a ghost and settle into a position of watching over everyone?"

"Position… No, it's not like that at all."

"You're only saying this because you don't know how painful hell really is. I'd love for you to experience children's limbo for even a day, if we had the time. Being able to come back to life is quite fortunate."

"…"

Fortunate.

Yes, that was it. What I originally blurted out expressed my true feeling. It wasn't that I didn't want to return to life—I wasn't sure if it was okay for someone like me to be so fortunate.

Did I deserve it?

"How do I put it… Maybe I'm wondering if it's okay for me to come back to life when there are others who must deserve it more. It's not that I don't want to, but I feel like I'm jumping the line, or stealing someone's spot, or trashing the rules—cutting in when I shouldn't."

Like in my trip through hell so far.

Wouldn't it have been better for Seishiro Shishirui to save Shinobu?

For Hanekawa to save herself, through Black Hanekawa?

Senjogahara had Kaiki.

Despite Hachikuji's assurances, even Sengoku's case might have been just a quarrel between friends if I hadn't stuck my nose in. To say the least, leaving it to the Fire Sisters, girls her own age, might have been the better choice.

What Kanbaru might call playing second fiddle—I'd felt it keenly over the past six months.

Wasn't I the one taking unfair credit? "Pinch hitter" might be too harsh on myself, but a strong suspicion that it never needed to be me was ensconced in me.

You know what I think?

I still doubted I'd cede the role of being the one to save those girls—placed in the same situation, I'd surely want to be the lead violin or on the starting lineup. In which case I couldn't help but wonder if I shouldn't just stay the hell out of it, and stay in hell?

I'd been ready to sacrifice my life for a legendary vampire, after all.

And to die for Hanekawa's sake.

Senjogahara had turned over a new leaf—she'd be fine even if I died. Then…

Then knowing my place—like a good boy, shouldn't I just die here?

"You do," Hachikuji said. "You do deserve to come back to life.

You've at least earned that. Think of all you've done to earn it! And I know it all very well!"

"…"

"The half-year since we parted ways must have been tough, but it couldn't break Koyomi Araragi's spirit, could it? If not you, who ought to be coming back to life? You're the lead, hands down!"

If you keep on moaning, I'm gonna hate you—Hachikuji threatened, before taking a deep breath.

She was preparing for a long line. I steeled myself to hear her out—to accept her sermon, no matter how sharp or scathing.

"Listen, Mister Araragi. The Mister Araragi I know loved young girls, little girls, tween girls, the underside of skirts, girls' hips, big breasts, rough treatment, his bigger little sister, his littler little sister, MILFs, topless girls, volleyball shorts, school swimsuits, class presidents, tomboys, cat ears, athletic girls, bandaged girls, panties, eyeball licking, getting stepped on while groveling, dirty books, giving and receiving shoulder rides, being tyrannized by his girlfriend, cleaning up his junior's room, cutting girls' hair, taking baths together—"

"Hold on. Hold on, hold on, hold on, you've broken Koyomi Araragi's spirit clean in two."

Her logistics surpassed my expectations.

What a hopeless perv. The guy was better off dead.

Instead of cheering me on, she was making me want to stay in hell. Unless she turned it around at the end, I was going to have a hard time changing my mind after that onslaught.

I'm counting on ya, okay?

Or so I thought, but contrary to my hopes, Hachikuji capped off her long line with something of a fake-out—a simple, or from my perspective, an obvious liking. A natural preference.

"And living, didn't he?"

But—it worked.

A simple fact, spoken simply.

It was all I needed. It sufficed.

I'd forgotten because it was so obvious.

Being on the verge of death again and again—all those narrow escapes made me forget something I'd always felt.

I was glad to be alive.

Enough to keep on living, and not as a humble act—no matter how masochistic or miserable I tried to look.

"You're right… I can't cherish young girls unless I'm alive."

"Erm, that isn't what I wanted to say, you realize."

I'd creeped Hachikuji out.

Despite her whole speech.

But yes, maybe it was true.

There being a heaven and a hell—didn't annul the point of living.

"I was worried that life would have no meaning?" I marveled. "Just being alive had meaning. Loving life was enough, since I could come to love so many things, so many people."

"That's open to misunderstanding, given the context."

"Hmm."

I adjusted my grip on the snake's tail.

Held it with both hands.

I looked at Tadatsuru, whom we'd kept waiting all this time. "Please tell me that I don't have to climb all the way? I'm pretty sure I don't have that kind of upper body strength."

"Don't worry. Remember what I said? No trial stands between you and your resurrection. I just need to give the signal, and Miss Gaen will pull you right up. Just cling to that snake's tail and don't let go—you only have one chance, though. Be careful your hands don't carelessly slip."

"If they did?" I was holding on along the scales, so now that he mentioned it, it might be slippery…

"Who knows. I suppose you'd fall? For two thousand years, through flames—so hold on tight with both hands, and whatever happens, don't let go."

"Okay… Sorry for all the trouble, and thanks, Tadatsuru—Mister Tadatsuru."

"No need to be respectful after all this time. It's not as if I've relinquished my grudge against immortal aberrations. So long as you keep protecting Kissshot Acerolaorion Heartunderblade—you're my enemy."

"…"

Still, I said. "Thanks for everything this time around… I never imagined I'd get to speak with you like this. If we ever have the chance, I hope we can chat in a more relaxed setting."

"Sure, during a fight to the death."

"Yeah… Hachikuji," I said, turning toward her once again. "What're you going to do now?"

"Excuse me?" She tilted her head, baffled. "You're asking about me? This takes care of work, so once I see you off, I'm heading back to spending my days in children's limbo stacking rocks."

"Stacking rocks."

"Ha ha ha. Please, I don't need your sympathy. No, it isn't fun, and honestly I don't recall doing anything to deserve it. These rules about sin and punishment are far too inflexible, but then, I bear the guilt of having wandered for eleven years, even if that wasn't something I did during my time as a human. I'll accept my punishment to pay for that sin—and I'll pay up in full. Don't worry, Jizo will come save me soon enough and I'll transmigrate happily ever after."

Pay up… But Hachikuji's eleven years as a lost child wasn't supposed to be subject to judgment. In fact, weren't those years far more like hell to a ten-year-old girl than children's limbo?

"Perhaps I'll be reborn as the baby you have with Miss Senjogahara."

"That'd be a heavy one."

"Oh, how heavy? More than ten pounds?"

"I'm not talking about your weight as a newborn…"

"But if you die before I'm reborn, Mister Araragi, let's play again here."

"Could you not assume I'm being sent to hell?"

Now that I had been once, it seemed like a done deal—but maybe knowing that you were going to end up in hell was some sort of encouragement to go on living.

"Well then," Hachikuji waved. "If I could, I'd send you off with a kiss like last time, but I'm not tall enough without Miss Ononoki around."

"How about not saying that here…"

Just look at Tadatsuru's dubious stare. He was doubting my character.

Not to cover anything up, but after all that dallying, I found myself nudging him on.

"I'm good. Send it whenever. That signal of yours. Send me along."

"Yes. Perhaps you'd have liked to learn more, but ask Miss Gaen to fill you in once you're back. I'm starting the countdown, then—Ten. Nine."

He'd brought a wooden Shinto wand out from somewhere; maybe it was part of his costume change. Swinging it back and forth, he counted down the seconds.

That made it feel more like a reverse bungee than a spider's thread dangling from heaven—should I wrap the snake around my waist instead of holding onto it? But a countdown could be interpreted as a form of purification.

"Eight. Seven. Six. Five. Four. Three. Two. One… Ignition."

For whatever reason, the last part sounded like a rocket launch—in fact the approximate speed at which I was tugged straight into the air.

No kidding, my hands nearly slipped—as my feet left the ground.

It reminded me of Ononoki's Unlimited Rulebook. No, it was because I'd gotten used to her move to some degree that I could endure the shock of the liftoff.

I endured it.

And I think that's when my eyes met Hachikuji's.

"Ah."

She was seeing me off with a smile.

Satisfied, as though she'd accomplished something.

Her job. Wait—her job?

No booking fee, she'd told me.

Then word choice aside, she'd helped resuscitate me like this without any benefit to herself, despite not getting revived herself.

Right.

She said I deserved to be resurrected more than anyone else—and that's exactly what was happening, with her left by the wayside.

"H—"

Saying bye to Mayoi Hachikuji.

For how many times now?

"H—Hachikujiiiiii!"

The moment I had that thought, my legs moved.

Both of them.

Not with any profound understanding or sharp read—I certainly wasn't inspired by the story of the spider's thread and wasn't trying to turn it on its head.

If I have to say…

I had pretty long legs, that's all.

"What? Eek, eeeek!"

Hachikuji screamed.

You would too, young girl or not, if you found your torso in a surprise leg scissor—especially if you were also getting caught up in a reverse bungee jump toward the high heavens.

And so—it was with my legs wrapped around a pigtailed girl wearing a large backpack that I was pulled into the sky. Almost instantly, Kita-Shirahebi Shrine and our town came into view, as if on an airplane map.

"Oh, Araragi, one last thing!"

A voice from the distant surface down below.

Tadatsuru's—I couldn't see him anymore, but somehow his voice alone reached me. Either he could project at a superhuman level, or it was some sort of half-human, half-spirit technique.

"One last thing from me! The enemy who requested that I slay a vampiric you alongside Kissshot Acerolaorion Heartunderblade—let me be the one to give you the name!"

I heard it.

Grasping a white snake with both hands and hugging a young girl with both legs, I heard the name. Strangely reverberating as if through the Doppler effect.

"Ogi—Ogi Oshino—"

012

The epilogue, or maybe, the punch line of this story.

My hands were too occupied to do any punching, of course, and as for *epilogue*—when I came to at Kita-Shirahebi Shrine, the first thing I did was check my watch, and not even a minute had elapsed since I'd been sliced to pieces there by Miss Gaen.

March thirteenth.

Early morning, past seven.

"Really? You brought li'l Hachikuji back with you? What possessed you, her? Vastly exceeding my expectations as always, Koyomin. My plan was to have you stay out of the way if you managed to come back, so that you won't mess things up, but how can I not expect even more out of you now?"

I turned to face the familiar, aloof voice, and sure enough, it was the perpetrator of my murder, Izuko Gaen.

Yet her relaxed tone didn't reflect her state, which was far from halcyon—ten long claws, five from each hand, were to her neck.

Behind the smirking Miss Gaen, who sat cross-legged on the shrine stairs—prepared to rip out her windpipe at a moment's notice, was a tall and fair-skinned vampire.

With her blond hair and golden eyes, she was too beautiful for this world.

Long limbs extended from beneath her gorgeous dress.

An iron-blooded, hot-blooded, yet cold-blooded vampire.

The Aberration Slayer—a monster among monsters who had lived for six hundred years.

Kissshot Acerolaorion Heartunderblade—in her *complete form.*

"Koyomin, wanna start off by asking this scary, pretty lady to put her claws away? I had her stay my execution under the condition that I'd bring you back to life no matter what…"

But wow, I never imagined the girl would get this angry—Miss Gaen said, composed despite her life-or-death crisis.

Shinobu—should I be calling her that now? Anyway, Shinobu also looked at me now that I was up.

"Hey. My lord," she said with a supremely gruesome smile.

Right… If my vampiric nature had been fully "severed"—of course Shinobu Oshino would return to being a full vampire. We'd lost our link before, and we'd boosted our vampirism beyond the limit before—but seeing the complete Shinobu like this was impactful on another level.

This was no longer about our link via my shadow.

Our master-servant relationship itself had been severed.

She'd referred to me in the same way as always…but seeing Kissshot Acerolaorion Heartunderblade in her full form for just about the first time since spring break, I was quite nervous.

Nervous. Or maybe you could say tense.

"Ka—kakak. What, my lord? Why not play with my ribs as always?"

"No, that'd look way too weird…or rather, I don't recall ever—"

"Hmph. Well, it seems no pointless killing or futile tearing was necessary. 'Twas my first time witnessing Yumewatari in operation…"

With that.

Shinobu withdrew her hands from Miss Gaen's throat.

She'd planned on killing her if I hadn't come back to life… I really couldn't let her run rampant.

Shinobu then took long strides toward me—almost like a model on a catwalk, and in a way that emphasized her chest.

"Fool. How dare ye worry me," she said, patting my head and smushing my hair. It might have been her first time doing the head-patting…

"To think that after worrying me so, thou abducted a young girl from hell—'tis insane."

"N-No, I grabbed her instinctively…"

"Then thy instincts failed to counsel against grabbing a young girl more than anything in the world."

There was nothing I could say to that.

Then again, it wasn't grabbing but leg-scissoring, I thought, looking down at Hachikuji, who was still trapped tight. Apparently unable to endure the shock of the reverse bungee jump, she was out cold.

Weak as always in the face of adversity.

Or I should say, what've I done…

I'd brought her back from hell.

"Hey, Shinobu. This can't be good, right?"

"'Course not. But if thy plan is to turn thyself in, do it alone."

"Don't be so cold. And that's not what I mean. Won't this be enough for Hachikuji to activate the Darkness again?"

"I'm saying that was your highlight reel-worthy move, Koyomin."

With the two enchanted blades hanging from the belt on her waist—the look suited her, actually—Miss Gaen approached us.

"Originally, I'd sent you to the other side to remove your vampirism, to purge the seat of your disease, and nothing more, but thanks to this miracle of yours we'll enjoy an advantage in the battle ahead. The lost young girl—was a piece I wanted."

"…"

"Is 'a piece' rude? Don't get hung up on the word—call her a weapon then, a weapon in our fight. I could not thank you enough… Now that we're in this situation, I'm going to have to ask you, Koyomin, as well as the no-longer-former Kissshot Acerolaorion Heartunderblade, and Mayoi, of course, for just a little bit more help. For now, though," Miss Gaen said, "why don't you go take your entrance exams?"

"E-Entrance exams…" Did she expect me to leap back into regular life from a shrine that was host to a vampire, a little ghost girl, and an expert wielding two swords?

"It's a student's duty to study, after all. Get going, and you'll make it in time. Do your best."

"W-Well—yeah, of course."

I hadn't foreseen no time having passed at all on this side during my journey through hell... If I could still make it, there was only one thing to do: use every bit of academic ability drilled into me by Senjogahara and Hanekawa.

I couldn't say I was in good condition—

But you go to war with the army you have.

"I'll put you on it starting tomorrow, Koyomin—don't you worry, it'll be over by graduation day. We've got all the weapons we need. We were getting owned before today, but the preparations are in place at last. Let's end this, Koyomin—and what do you know, tomorrow's White Day. Perfect for ending this tale of a town a white snake once reigned over."

Miss Gaen spoke with an uncharacteristically aggressive smile on her lips.

"It's counterattack time, kiddos."

CHAPTER SIX
HITAGI RENDEZ-VOUS

HITAGI SENJOGAHARA

001

I love Hitagi Senjogahara. I can say that brazenly. Why? Because it's true. No other words needed, no other reasoning—the feeling's so clear it feels foolish to explain it in detail.

A year ago, though, the idea that I'd ever feel that way about anyone never crossed my mind—it would've been even harder to believe than the existence of vampires and hell. To go further, harder to tolerate.

The concept of a me in love with someone felt phonier than any urban legend.

Coming to like someone.

Loving someone—I was afraid of it.

At the risk of being misunderstood, you could even say I avoided putting myself in that situation. I'm still awful at building relationships with other people, but if we were to describe it as an intentional, continued avoidance of other human beings on my part, I'd done a pretty good job of it.

If you went on to ask why I was such a coward about love, that one's simple. I saw myself as precious—and feared no longer being that precious person.

I was afraid of changing.

And of being changed.

I think that's what it was—and still don't feel differently, I ought to let you know.

In my understanding, that's what it means to become involved with another human being—whether it's loving someone or hating someone.

Letting go of self-love is the condition.

Or else you won't love anyone but yourself.

Hitagi Senjogahara seems to believe this even more than I do—and I think that's fine.

Her love is probably…too heavy a thing to be directed at herself alone.

Splitting it with me seems just right.

If you aren't prepared to lift something on your own, you won't even with another person, they say, and her love needs to be shared with that understanding.

But that image makes me wonder.

I love Hitagi Senjogahara.

I can say it brazenly, but for all that I can.

Did my self-love abandon me somewhere along the way? Am I loving myself the way I love her?

Because if I'm not.

I might as well be dead.

002

"I'll go on a date."

So said Hitagi Senjogahara—okay, that's a pretty abrupt way to begin a story, and maybe you don't follow. Let me add a little more in the way of stage directions.

The date was March thirteenth.

In other words, the evening of the day I was doomed to an eternity in hell on account of my actions before immediately reviving on account of my doings—and also the evening after taking the entrance exams for my first-choice school in an exhausted condition (top condition, I'd insist if I were my little sister Karen) and coming out of it thinking, *At least I filled in the whole answer sheet!* Dead tired from my first time undergoing the rite since I got into Naoetsu High, I returned home so spent that being sent back to hell might have been preferable—to find Hitagi Senjogahara waiting in front of the Araragi residence.

My girlfriend.

By the way, it wasn't my first time seeing her that day—I'd been with her that morning too. Or rather, she escorted me to my first-choice school like a Secret Service agent so I wouldn't get caught up in any unnecessary trouble. She'd kept her right arm in her pocket the whole way, not because she carried a weapon there, I hope... Well, before she joined me as my bodyguard, I'd gotten caught up in the unthinkable bit of trouble that was being sliced to pieces by Miss Gaen, but thanks to Senjogahara's presence, or maybe not, I didn't get into any further trouble—as I said, I at least managed to fill in the whole answer sheet.

She, along with Hanekawa, had supported my studies for the last year or so, in fact. On a fundamental level, as someone whose catch-phrase used to be *I just need to graduate*, ninety percent of my motivation when it came to my exams was *attending the same college as my girlfriend Senjogahara*—it wouldn't be brown-nosing at all if I said I'd taken that test thanks to her.

So no matter how tired I felt, no matter how defeated my psyche, I planned to call her as soon as I got home—to my surprise, however, she was right there as if she'd anticipated my move, like she had a head start.

I learned later that she'd felt like Hachiko the faithful dog, but from my point of view, she was a bandit waiting to ambush me. I mean, what-ever your angle, the glare in her eyes was saying, "You're back, bastard," and not "Good job, Araragi!" You can't blame me if I faltered in front of my own home.

What could it be? Did she somehow find out that I'd gone to hell that morning? Did Miss Gaen tweet about it (I could see her having an account)? I hadn't told her because I didn't want her to worry, or rather because I knew it'd make her mad, and put it off to after my exams... Maybe her stern expression made sense. Finding out your boyfriend went to hell has to be pretty shocking.

I braced myself.

Just one more battle...

Determined, cautiously piecing together my plan to vindicate my-self, which is to say apologize, I approached Senjogahara, only for her to speak in a tone as stern as her expression.

What was once her standard tone, a flat delivery that knew neither intonation nor accent.

"I'll go on a date," she said.

I'd heard those words before.

Yes, the move she'd made back in June when we went on our first date—

"No, that's not it," she continued, which was again a perfect replay

122

as far as I remembered.

"I-It's not?" I replied, confused.

My reaction just as fresh and innocent.

How adorable, Araragi!

"Well," she said, "it's been so long since I had a proper appearance that I lost track of my personality."

"..."

Don't be sounding like Ononoki. That girl's a rare type of side character who loses track of her characterization even when she has plenty of appearances...

Which is better, I wonder—a side character with lots of screen time, or a principal character without any?

"What sort of person was I, again?"

"That line's a lot to take in..."

"I want to say a cool, beautiful woman who waves around staplers and paper cutters."

"If you're going that far back, I need to devise an approach and plan for a tougher trial than the exams I just took..."

Having mentioned them, I fully expected her to respond, "Oh, so how was it? Do you think you did well?"—since there'd be no point in beating myself up anymore, I'd answer "I did what I could" and thank her, or so the simulation in my mind went, but that wasn't the direction our conversation headed in.

She rephrased herself as if she didn't even know about my exams:

"Date me or else."

Her tone had changed—it was even more stern. She wasn't this tyrannical even back when she hadn't turned over a new leaf and was still a character who swung around staplers and paper cutters.

Date me or else?

That was just a threat.

"I-Isn't your characterization straying, Miss Senjogahara?"

"Tomorrow."

My retort, or my offer to interpret my girlfriend's bizarre and incomprehensible statement as a joke, my blurring of her wording, was flatly ignored and nullified.

Tomorrow, she said.

"Tomorrow, we'll make full use of the day on a half-year's worth of dates, Araragi—do you understand what I'm saying?"

"No, sorry, haven't got a clue…"

Despite being lovers, our minds were far from one—she was still a difficult individual and partner.

That did mean I never got tired of chatting with her, so maybe I should accept it with open arms. In certain tense situations, though, it was a negative and an accident risk.

"Then I'll provide commentary," she said, "like on the alternate audio track."

"…"

I didn't know much about those, having not been a part of many, but the word was that the audio commentary didn't do much to explain what's going on in the main story…

And in terms of commentary, right now I wanted some on those exam problems—but things hadn't cooled off to a point where I could ask her.

Though in fact, it felt ice cold.

It was March, but still chilly out…

Then Senjogahara continued as if she hadn't forgotten at all about my exams.

"First off, good job, Araragi," she appreciated my effort at last. But the appreciation seemed a bit sarcastic, almost as if she was mad… "You worked so hard that even if you're left empty-handed, you have nothing to be ashamed of. You've already succeeded."

"Could you not make it sound like it's a given that I won't make it in? That's consolation, not appreciation. Don't foreshadow a situation where I need to be soothed. I haven't said anything yet, have I? It's not over until the results are in."

"It's over already," she insisted.

She'd decided on a direction, and nothing I said could change our course—I guess I just had to sit back and watch.

When there's no point in saying anything, you should stay quiet.

"Your battle ends here."

"…"

"And so, after six months of self-control, I want us to begin dating anew. I'm spending all the points I've saved up. And what do you know, tomorrow is March fourteenth, White Day. The perfect special day for a date."

"…"

"Did you just think about how much you hate special days?"

How did she figure that out when I was silent? What a unilateral unspoken connection.

But with this, my frazzled mind finally caught a glimpse of her point—so that's what.

She hadn't blurted out anything outrageous—in fact, she'd petitioned me with a very proper request.

While doing so on the heels of my exams betrayed what you might call her unreconstructed agility—she was right, we'd been dating since last May, and we'd spent a lot of time together as home tutor and pupil or whatever, but only gone on a few dates you could actually call dates. Not only that, the majority were during first term, and to get into shocking specifics, we hadn't gone on a single one since I'd gotten serious about my exams. It wouldn't be an overstatement to say that after second term, we were quite the stoic couple for two high school students.

Yes, so despite spending a lot of time with her in her capacity as my tutor or what have you, whether at school or at home—we never once went somewhere to go have fun, on a trip, or the like.

I prepared for exams, and she instructed her pathetic boyfriend-cum-pupil, forcing us both to abstain—moreover, since the middle part of second term, Sengoku's case put both my life and Senjogahara's in extreme danger for an extended period of time, which wasn't conducive to seeking anything like a date.

As soon as the state of emergency lifted (thanks to a disagreeable conman), my body began growing vampiric on its own… The deluge of troubles had left me unable to come up for air; studying for exams had left me with no time to take a breather.

"Graduation is the day after tomorrow," Senjogahara said. "In other words, our glorious lives as high school students would come to an end having barely gone on any dates—isn't that sad?"

"Well, if you put it that way…"

"We had most of third term off from school, too. It went by so fast. I can see why they say that January jumps away, February flies, and March marches on."

"You're right. Third term did end in the blink of an eye."

"I can see why they say that April absconds, May makes a break, June jumps, July jogs, August ain't long, September stirs, October outruns, November is not long for this world, and December is like a sled pulled by reindeer."

"Hey, you cheated there at the end!"

"How will we ever tell the daughter we'll have one day that despite dating in high school, we graduated having barely done anything that lovers do?"

"That's a heavy question. A daughter?"

"Huh, you'd prefer a boy?"

"This isn't about gender."

"But I've already decided on a name."

"Now it's actually getting heavy…" So weighty, you'd never imagine she once struggled with having no weight at all. "You know, I think I'll ask. What's the name?"

"Tsubasa."

"Too heavy too heavy too heavy too heavy!"

And Hanekawa would agree! Cherish your friendship with other girls some other way!

"So," a nonchalant Senjogahara put us back on topic—a move that was so uniquely her. "We're spending all of tomorrow to have an entire half-year's worth of dates—an abridged edition, in other words. A recap episode of our time in high school."

"A recap episode…" How do you recap something that hasn't aired yet? I took her meaning, though. Simply put, now that my exams were done, she wanted to go on all the dates we'd missed, and why not do it tomorrow, on White Day.

"I've got the scoop, Araragi."

"…What?"

My *what* wasn't asking "what scoop?" so much as "what's with that phrasing," but Senjogahara seemed to interpret it as the former.

"It seems you're back in good health," she elaborated.

"Oh, er…"

It took me a moment, but not long, to understand what she meant: my transformation into a vampire, which should have been irreversible, and having returned as a human after going to hell.

I knew this, of course, since it was my own body.

But how did Senjogahara?

"Well, in the mirrors at the street corners and such as I walked you to the college campus, you had a reflection."

What a sharp girl.

I'd kept quiet about it, thinking I'd explain later. For her part, she hadn't said anything or grilled me because it wasn't appropriate when I was just about to take my exams—both of us were surprisingly considerate people.

"In other words, your outstanding problems, be it your exams or your body, have been taken care of. They've come to an end, right? Then there's no reason for you not to go on a date with me. There's no better time to resolve our undatedness."

"Undatedness…"

She had such a knack for coining and using awkward words.

Still, even if those two outstanding problems had come to an end… No. That was neither here nor there.

It wasn't about having no reason not to—I wanted to go on a date as much as she did. I'd been repressing myself despite being a healthy young high schooler and wanted to go on one asap.

Okay, if she actually asked to go right now, I might beg her to let me rest for the day (not only was I exhausted, I lacked any vampirism and my stamina recovery was notably sluggish—or rather, like a normal person's), but honestly, if it was tomorrow, which is to say after a good night's rest, I'd happily go anywhere with her.

There was Miss Gaen.

There was Miss Kagenui.

There was Hachikuji.

There was Kissshot Acerolaorion Heartunderblade.

And—there was *her*.

In fact, I had all sorts of concerns I needed to think about, and maybe I also needed to be acting like an exam-taker until I received my results, the way a school trip isn't over until you get home.

Still, I wanted to value our desire to do high school things while we were high schoolers. In which case, I couldn't stand around and hesitate forever—I needed to man up and respond to her feelings.

"And so, Araragi, you'll go on a date with me," Senjogahara propositioned once more, as if she'd finally remembered the correct phrasing—not that it was at all correct, but it reminded me of the days when we first started going out, and I felt a little high.

"If you don't go on a date with me, I'll bite off my own tongue as we speak."

"…"

Or a little down.

"You'll never be able to French kiss me again," she warned.

"That'd be the least of our worries if you bit your tongue off…"

Of course, it would've been my tongue being threatened in the past. When I thought of it that way, what a harmless cute thing Senjogahara had become.

Well, she'd done more than simply mellow out—I guess neither she nor I had stood still.

We needed to graduate.

To move forward.

I did hate arbitrary special days but would make an exception for tomorrow and not say that. It was likely to be my last date as a high school student, so I might as well allow myself to act like a high schooler.

"All right," I said. "It won't be a recap, we'll be capping it off—we're spending tomorrow to the fullest to have a half-year's worth of dates."

"Oh, sorry, I don't know about the fullest part. I have plans that night."

Slump—I almost did a pratfall.

"So let's start early in the morning and go to about the evening. Don't worry, I already have it all planned up here," Senjogahara said,

128

tapping her temple. The gesture made her look smart, but I felt a tinge of anxiety over a date mapped out by her.

I mean, the way our first date turned out... Still, I couldn't trample on her feelings by asking for an immediate review. I just had to hope she'd become harmless on this point too.

Okay. In that case, my plans for tomorrow night were good, too. Yup, I'd be sticking to them.

"Copy that, I hear you loud and clear. By the way," I threw out what I thought was a casual question, "what is it you need to do tomorrow night?"

"Well, it's White Day," she restated the obvious. "I'm having dinner with my dad."

"..."

Just another regrettably heavy reply from her that I needed to take in.

003

"A date? Tomorrow? Hold on, you need to report this kind of thing sooner. This is really sudden. I have plans of my own, okay? Oh, fine, I'll figure out a way to make some time. Anything for you, kind monster sir."

"Wait, why are you acting like you've been invited? What kind of position are you in, here?"

After seeing Senjogahara off, I at last entered the Araragi residence and dragged myself up to my room on the second floor only to find yet another individual waiting for me: the lodger and current freeloader in my home, Yotsugi Ononoki, the shikigami tween.

Being a doll, she was supposed to be staying under the guise of being my little sister's stuffed toy, but as of late she was moving around more or less for all to see. Today was no exception—she'd come on her own to my room and made herself comfortable on my bed, even reading a manga I'd bought before me.

Make some time? She looked like the world's most idle tween.

There was some strange woman outside the house, but I left her alone because it seemed like she was waiting for you, monstieur. Who was she? asked Ononoki, and I replied with the plain truth—but actually, if she saw a strange woman outside our home, the familiar should've checked it out, having been placed with me by her master Miss Kagenui to be my personal bodyguard.

In fact, I needed to tell Ononoki a lot of things—it didn't make sense to be leading off with a report that I'd booked a date.

What should I tell her, though, and how much? Miss Gaen didn't seem too interested in keeping me quiet, and Tadatsuru even wanted me to apologize to her in his place... But could it hinder whatever plans Miss Gaen was putting together if I revealed everything about my morning trip through hell? I couldn't let go of that concern, but I also felt that Ononoki needed to know about what happened with Tadatsuru, given her involvement. What to do...

"What's the matter, kind monster sir, monstieur for short? You're staring at my face. Are you admiring it? Do I look all dolled up? You know, being a doll and all."

"Well, it's just..." I made up my mind, then spoke before the tween could say anything too amusing. Even if it didn't clear things up, I needed to settle what I could before my date tomorrow. "Ononoki. I want to talk about something serious, is that okay?"

"I'm always serious. I've never talked about anything unserious. I'm so serious, they call me the brightest star."

Despite saying this with a deadpan look and tone, I picked up nothing earnest about her words, not to mention the disqualifying pun—it sounded like an utter lie anyway, but ignoring that, I briefly gave her the highlights of my adventure that morning, beginning with my trip to Kita-Shirahebi Shrine. I tried to be mindful of the fact that I'd be talking for way too long if I told her everything, but the story wrapped up quicker than I thought when I actually summarized it.

It felt like a two-thousand-year journey to me, but it did in fact all happen in a flash. Maybe that's how describing stuff goes—your emotional attachment to the events says nothing about their length.

"Huh."

On top of that, Ononoki barely reacted. What an unrewarding listener to recount your adventures to.

"You're telling stories to a stuffed toy and expecting it to be rewarding? My only reaction is annoyance that you got yourself in trouble as soon as I let you off the leash."

"Hold on, even hearing all that about Tadatsuru, one of your creators, doesn't do anything for you? He told me to say hi to you."

"Not in particular. I've told you, haven't I? Don't expect human emotions from me. Whether he was dead from the start, or immortal in a way, or a living doll, it doesn't change the meaning of what I did," Ononoki shrugged. "As in, what it means to you, monstieur."

"…"

"I'm sure you have your own thoughts on the matter, and maybe you feel redeemed. But if I had to come up with some sort of opinion… personally, I guess it just sounds fishy."

"Fishy? Like how?" I never quite agreed with the nuances of fishy (what's wrong with fish?) but of course knew they were negative. Ononoki's expressions were so deadpan, which is to say impossible to read, and conversing with her demanded a high level of communication skills.

"In no particular way. I just wonder how much of it went as Miss Gaen planned. Most of my dealings with her have been through Big Sis, so I've no clue how calculating she is or isn't… Maybe even bringing Hatchy back with you was part of her plan, and she only pretended to be surprised."

"Hatchy…" Why was everyone getting influenced by the audio commentary? Having fun behind my back, are you?

"Well, to be blunt, there's more audio commentaries at this point than books."

"Stop. No one asked you to be blunt."

"I don't believe in hell anyway… Are you sure it wasn't a hallucination you had while you were on the verge of death?"

"A hallucination? Like a near-death experience? But—"

"A hallucination Miss Gaen *made you have* or something. Kinda scary to think about."

"…"

It was kinda scary, true… But why was this doll going out of her way to scare me? Did she get a kick out of frightening me, or what?

"Come on," she said. "Frightened people are fun to watch, in general."

"You're terrible. Cut it out, you're gonna make me mad."

"Nothing's more fun than making people mad. So exciting. Whenever people lecture me it's like, whoa, this guy's so mad, he's totally lost control! I put on a meek look, but am all smiles inside."

"Well, I'm genuinely sorry I was about to get mad at you!"

Not that she ever looked meek or smiling.

Forget about deadpan, her expression was rigor mortis.

What a troublesome kid—though I was sure she'd only enjoy it if I looked troubled.

"Anyway," Ononoki said, "the flip side is that hearing that I might meet Tadatsuru again someday doesn't bother me. So thanks for the info."

"Oh… Well, that makes it feel worthwhile."

"You died for a noble cause."

"Now I'm not so sure."

"But that's not what matters to me," Ononoki changed the subject—and perhaps she was right. If we were going to talk about Tadatsuru, one of her creators, we also had to discuss another: Miss Kagenui, her master as a shikigami.

Whose whereabouts were currently unknown.

She wasn't even in hell—not that it helped brighten the mood, or so I assumed Ononoki felt. I was way off.

"Tell me more about Kissshot Acerolaorion Heartunderblade's complete recovery," Ononoki said. "The issue has a direct bearing on my safety."

"…"

"I bathed her in verbal abuse because she was a little girl, the dregs of her former self, but I need to change my tune drastically if she's complete again. Please teach me how to speak to others in a respectful manner, monstieur?"

A-ha!

Okay, she was right about the joys of watching someone fret—all the more so when it was a cheeky shikigami tween.

"Might your mistress Heartunderblade be listening to us now from your shadow?"

"I'm not sure that came out right."

She really didn't know how to address people with respect.

But she wanted to know if Shinobu was in my shadow—and minor linguistic errors are fine as long as you get your point across.

In other words, I was no longer preparing for exams.

"Nope, she isn't," I replied. Sure, I wanted to watch her fret for a little longer, but bullying her wouldn't get me anywhere. "Shinobu is with Miss Gaen, along with Hachikuji. They're having a meeting about what to do next, or maybe a discussion."

"Maybe a destination."

"Okay, now you're just getting the meaning of words wrong. Could you please keep your mistakes to respectful language?"

"I'm pretty sure I know what I'm talking about. They're talking about our fate."

"You mean our *destiny*." Or our *destino*, which can mean both—I learned that over the course of my exam prep, and it seemed useless at the time, but I guess not.

"I wonder what's next for us. You turned back into a regular boy at last, but are you gonna keep going? Even if you're dancing in the palm of Miss Gaen's hands?"

"Um, I don't think I gave a clear answer one way or another..."

But.

I felt like I couldn't stick my head in the sand and play dumb now—regardless of what happened next, I needed a helping hand from Miss Gaen to take care of Hachikuji and Shinobu's problems. And she didn't allow debts to remain unpaid—any reimbursement I could make now, I needed to attend to.

"And there's Miss Kagenui," I had no choice but to nervously bring up the name since Ononoki was refusing to.

I could be so considerate sometimes...

Yeah, I was showing consideration to a doll, but I couldn't remain indifferent about Miss Kagenui. In fact, I was most interested.

Yozuru Kagenui.

And—where was Mèmè Oshino?

"Well, isn't he just living like a vagrant as always? That's what I think," Ononoki said.

"I feel like the time to be that easygoing about his situation has passed… I mean, we've been looking and looking for him and still don't know where he is. You realize that Hanekawa, of all people, can't find him."

"Ah, yes. The girl who dozen snow everything."

"It's *doesn't know* everything."

"She's not a professional bounty hunter, okay? But how you view her is none of my business… As far as Big Sis goes, I assume she's off on a journey to perfect her martial skills."

And with that, Ononoki tried to go back to reading my manga.

She knew she couldn't end the conversation like that, right?

No one could be that *nil admirari*.

She'd grown way too uninterested the moment she learned that Shinobu wasn't present—but in her prime, Kissshot could travel anywhere in the world at a moment's notice, in essence teleporting for goodness' sake.

"Listen, I'm a free spirit," Ononoki said. "I can't do anything without instructions from Big Sis, so I can't help out with whatever you do next. Just keep that in mind."

"…"

Geez, I knew that without being told, why say it in such an aggravating way?

"But if you insist, I could join you on your date tomorrow."

"Why are you so interested in coming along? Stop trying to block the path of Cupid's arrows. This is going to be my first laidback episode in a while." Okay, I was hoping for one, but let's be real, it was going to be produced by Hitagi Senjogahara…

"Whaaat? But other people's dates are such a riot. Nothing dumber than someone else's romantic relationship."

"I can't lay into you because my little sisters are unmistakably to blame for your character just now…" Having yet another person in my life with that kind of a personality wasn't so much rough, as sad—how badly did I mess up as an older brother for them to turn out that way? Both of them, but the littler little sister, Ononoki's current owner, seemed to be getting worse by the day.

"I mean, isn't it amusing to watch people getting worked up about something that everyone else just finds hilarious? Nothing gets me more excited than that 'you might be serious about it, but you know I don't give a damn!' feeling."

"As someone tasked by Miss Kagenui with taking care of you, I'm starting to think I need to separate you from my sisters as soon as humanly possible... But Ononoki. Does a girl like you ever feel serious about anything?"

As an expert on immortal aberrations, Miss Kagenui approached their extermination with a pretty serious air. You might assume the same of Ononoki, who acted alongside her master, but that couldn't be what really motivated her when she was an immortal aberration herself.

In which case, what did make her serious?

"Isn't there anything you want to do, or want to have?" I asked.

"No way."

"How about just 'no'?"

"I'm just a combat machine that fights as Big Sis tells me to. Aren't you keenly aware of that already?" replied Ononoki, without even looking up from my manga. It really did feel like dealing with my little sisters... "You're asking a mug which makes it happier, coffee getting poured into it or tea."

"..."

Was it just me, or was she bad at coming up with examples? I got what she was saying, but it was a little confusing.

"Anyway, I'm immersing myself in the arts this time around, far away from your mundane affairs. Go ahead and dance away, monstieur. Whether it's on Miss Gaen's hand or someone else's."

"I'm not trying to drag you into it, personally..." But regarding a different matter, I indeed was curious—what her intentions were, or if dolls have no intentions, then what her function was. "In any case, Ononoki, what're you going to do if Miss Kagenui never comes back—if she never picks you up?"

The question was cruel in a way, and asking it did pain me. It had to be asked, though. Yet Ononoki herself, stone-faced, deadpanned, "In that case—I suppose I'll just have to spend the rest of my life here. If you get married and leave, I'll follow you, of course."

"You need to come up with a more realistic life plan than that. What do you mean, 'of course'?"

"Would you have preferred an 'or else'?"

She turned around threateningly, but her face remained blank—what a surreal image.

It was such a shame that she looked so emotionless even when she pulled off excellent reactions. Save the poker face for the poker table.

"My current mission is to monitor you, though... I can't leave you until it's rescinded. In other words, if Big Sis doesn't come back, you and I will be a couple for the rest of our lives."

"The rest of our lives?"

"Hey, could you not act so freaked out? I'm the one who's suffering thanks to this mission. I feel like I've been locked in a cage with a wild animal."

"I feel the exact same way... We're of like minds, huh?"

We needed Miss Kagenui to return as soon as possible—yeah, I couldn't hope for this situation to last forever. For the sake of my own future too.

"By the way, monstieur. By the by the way, monstieur. How did that test-taking business of yours go? I've been pretty concerned, you know."

"You have been? Me, I'm a little concerned by your condescending tone, but I guess I appreciate the concern?" After all, Senjogahara ended up leaving without so much as touching on my test performance, and I didn't know if that signaled trust. "Well, I did everything I could. I appreciate all the support you gave me."

She was the first person to hear these words from me for some reason, when it should have been Senjogahara and Hanekawa—but I guess Ononoki did feel concerned about me, a test-taker living under the same roof. I wasn't wrong to express my gratitude.

"You're welcome. Okay...in that case, why don't we get straight to checking your answers? Try telling me what kinds of questions you got. I'll double-check them for you."

"..."

As if she could.

Expertise was one thing, but sorry, academically she must be a twelve year old just like her appearance suggested.

"The material you were tested on won't stick with you unless you double-check your answers the same day."

"I bet that's just something you heard, don't pass it off as your own advice..."

"You need to start preparing for next year as soon as possible."

"You're also assuming I'll have to retake my exams."

She was getting in on this too?

I can take care of myself.

"But really, how did it go? Weren't you in pretty bad shape after going through a massive trip through hell in the morning?"

"I won't deny that, but we'll say it's a miracle that I managed to take them at all."

"You make it sound like the experience alone was worth it—you know they aren't free, right? Try not to cause too much trouble for your mom and dad."

"Scolding me on my parents' behalf? You? Anyway, I know it might sound like I'm bragging, but I feel pretty confident. Even outside of math, to some degree..."

"Hmm."

"Well, it'd be pretty awful if I came out empty-handed despite a setup as blessed as Senjogahara and Hanekawa looking after me... I feel like I did a good enough job not to get any mud on their faces."

"I have to say, though—mud wrestling is delightful. When do you get your results again? Before or after graduation?"

"After."

"Okay. Then maybe hurry up and go on that date. It'd be awkward if one of you didn't make it in."

Nah, that wasn't why Senjogahara picked tomorrow for our date...

"Oh, because it's White Day? You took an excuse like that at face value?"

"How's that an excuse? If anything, she's being sincere."

"True, any girl sincerely wants to be repaid threefold."

"Threefold? Oh. I guess that's the custom."

As someone who didn't care for special events, I didn't know much about the details of White Day—but yes, I'd received chocolates from Senjogahara a month ago, on Valentine's Day.

Threefold...

A pretty impressive interest rate for just a month when you thought about it, but if those were the rules, I wasn't flouting them—I didn't have that kind of spine. What did I need to buy to be ready for tomorrow, though?

"Remind me... Do I just need to give candy and marshmallows and stuff?"

"I'm fine with ice cream."

"You didn't give me any chocolate last month. Triple of nothing is still nothing."

"Are you sure? Have you proven it?"

"Um." When you phrased it that way, it was the math-lover's sad fate to feel momentarily uncertain.

Not that I needed to prove it. The answer was obviously zero.

"We're meeting tomorrow morning, so if I'm going to buy her something, I need to go shopping today... I'm really tired, though. I'd like to rest."

"Right. And I'm occupying your bed, you poor thing."

"Not an issue, I can always move you by force... What should I do, though—maybe I'll ask my little sisters?"

"Wouldn't they lack your heartfelt emotion? I think presents are something you need to pick yourself."

"Hm, can't argue with that..."

If anything, I should have prepared sooner for an important event like White Day, but it was Senjogahara who'd been telling me to give my undivided attention to test prep—she'd been freed after summer break, but I guess the last few months had been ascetic for her too.

It made me want to be that much more thoughtful about my return gift—let's see.

"I don't need to be so hung up on the candy part, right? This isn't Halloween."

"No, but be very hung up when it comes to ice cream. As opposed to frozen yogurt."

"That's just what you want."

"Can you believe that Haagen-Dazs is closing all its stores here? The cups are fine, but where am I going to get cones that taste that good?"

"I don't know... Somewhere that isn't Japan?"

By the way, how did Halloween suddenly become so ubiquitous in our country? Perhaps people like Oshino, who cared much more about those kinds of yearly rituals, saw it as a reason to celebrate.

In any case, asking Ononoki for advice didn't seem very productive, and I was beginning to wonder which of the forty-eight sumo techniques I should use to toss her off my bed, when she fell flat all of a sudden.

Letting go of the manga in her hands and slumping, sinking into the bed with her face down and limbs splayed, as if her batteries had run out.

Almost like an invisible enemy had landed a powerful shot to her chin—I'd been thinking sumo, but had she been boxing with an unseen foe?

No, of course not. As a shikigami aberration, her senses were hundreds of times sharper than a regular human's—which is to say my own at that moment in time. She simply noticed that someone was approaching the room before I ever could.

In other words, she'd entered stuffed-toy mode.

A moment later.

"Big brother!"

Kicking my door open and bursting into my room like some special-forces unit was—my littler little sister, in fact. Namely Tsukihi Araragi.

A girl with the longest of hair who was wearing Japanese clothes.

Her hair so terrifyingly long that she looked like a *yokai* after a bath—if she wasn't careful, she could trip on it.

"You took my doll out of my room again, didn't you?! Oh, there she is! I knew it! You need to stop going into other people's rooms without asking!" said the enraged girl, who'd just entered my room without asking—and while it's not like I never enter my little sisters' room without asking, in this case it was the doll who'd perpetrated an unauthorized entry.

As for Ononoki, she was committed to the stuffed-toy act.

She'd fallen to her face in a position that no body with a will could manage.

"You even put her on your bed? I hope you didn't do anything weird with my precious doll."

"You could say I was being hospitable..."

"I'm not big on stuffed animals, but I feel a sense of sympathy with that one for whatever reason. That's why I keep on telling you that you're not allowed to take her out of my room."

"Sympathy, huh?"

Then again, knowing something about my sister that she herself didn't, I had to admit that Tsukihi Araragi and Yotsugi Ononoki did have a connection. I could only praise my little sister's instincts if she felt that way about her doll.

Of course, though Tsukihi had forgotten about it, Ononoki had come to kill her once. If her instincts were going to kick into action, they needed to run in the opposite direction instead.

"Still, Tsukihi, if you're calling it yours and really care that much about this doll, why not give it a name?"

"Hm? Oh, no. If I gave her a name, I'd get attached to her and might hesitate when it's time to throw her away. If you feel sympathy for someone, what you need to be thinking about is what you'll do once that sympathy runs out."

"..."

I couldn't believe this little sister of mine...

Ononoki was expressionless to begin with, and now she was in stuffed-toy mode on top of that. I couldn't tell what went through her mind, but I thought she looked appalled by her owner Tsukihi's mindset.

I could've been projecting, of course...

"When that day comes, though," my sister offered, "I'd be happy to give her to you as a hand-me-down instead of throwing her out."

"A hand-me-down? You'd be handing her up to me..."

"So you were back," the recently irate Tsukihi observed, calm all of a sudden—the intensity of her mood swings gave her a one-of-a-kind personality... "Now that your exams are over, you can have all the fun you want! You're gonna be a college student starting next month! This calls for a celebration! I'll start getting ready for one! I'll get all the middle school girls in the area together for a party tonight!"

"How positive of you..."

Surprisingly enough, my little sister had more faith in my test-taking abilities than anyone else—but a party with every middle school girl in the area could wait, given the incalculable amount of damage it'd do to me in the off-chance that I didn't get in.

"And Karen's going to be a high schooler next month too. I'm going to feel left behind, all on my own. Maybe I'll go ahead and skip a grade!"

"Is it that easy to skip a grade?"

In fact, Japan didn't let you skip grades, as far as I knew.

Maybe with Tsukihi's academics, though.

"Joking aside, what do you say? Why don't we have a full day of fun tomorrow, celebrating you and Karen's start at new schools? It's been so long since we've done something like that with just the three of us."

"Hm. Not a bad suggestion, but sadly I have a prior engagement tomorrow." A prior engagement that had only come to be thirty minutes ago. "But if you want to do something this month, I wouldn't mind making some time."

I'd caught Ononoki's haughty speech.

The idea of speaking to Tsukihi in a way influenced by Ononoki, who herself was strongly influenced by Tsukihi, made for an Ouroboros-like image.

"Hey, you sound so relaxed now," she said nevertheless. "Until pretty recently, you'd punch your little sister if she came up and asked you to go play."

"I was that rough of a brother?!"

I didn't remember anything like that.

True, I wasn't on as bad of terms with my little sisters as I'd been in the past—perhaps both people and your relationships with others never stay the same?

Especially over the last year. So much had happened.

Yes—with Karen, and with Tsukihi.

Tsukihi in particular, during summer break...I thought as I turned

143

to Ononoki, but she lay there on the bed like a corpse.

Well, she actually was a corpse.

"Okay, then we'll go somewhere this month," Tsukihi said.

"Sure. I'll leave the planning up to you," I let the moment carry me away. Entrusting her with plans to have fun made me about as anxious as entrusting Senjogahara to come up with a date plan—there was something alike in the two, after all.

"Broadly speaking, which would you rather go to? The mountains or the sea?"

"I'd like to go to a mountain in the sea."

"What, like the Castle of the Undersea Devil?" she shot back, not missing a beat. "I see. But you're going on a date with Miss Senjogahara tomorrow? I'm so jealous, you're such a passionate couple. Me and Rosokuzawa have been dating so long that things between us have quieted down. I mean, I invited him to go somewhere on White Day and he ended up vaguely turning me down."

"…"

It seemed like only a matter of time before my little sister broke up with him. Vaguely? What a pathetic kid.

"Wait, did I ever say my plans were with Senjogahara?"

"You didn't have to. Plans on March fourteenth? It has to be either your girlfriend or Einstein."

"It'd be a huge deal if it was Einstein. People would start celebrating that on the fourteenth instead of White Day. Though I'd love to chat with him if we could…"

The story is that Einstein's last words were in German, and his nurse didn't understand what he said. I doubted the likes of me could keep up a conversation even if language wasn't a problem, though.

Thinking that Oikura's choice would probably be Euler, I continued, "Well, you're right. I guess I want you to tell me…to ask you what'd make you happy if you got it as a White Day gift."

"Some loving, caring cash."

"…"

Greedy little sister.

She wasn't any help. And it wasn't some appetizer of a joke preceding her real answer, but the main course itself, served from the heart, because Tsukihi switched topics.

"Okay, then. In that case, I'll pay Nadeko a visit tomorrow to see how she's doing. She's out of the hospital now, but still recovering at home. She said she'll start going to school once the new term starts. She must be lonely stuck at home all by herself, so I'll head over and make some noise!"

"You've been visiting her a lot, haven't you," I replied point-blank. It was my honest thought. "Frankly, I'm surprised. I knew you and Sengoku were friends, but I never thought you two were that close."

"You're wrong! We're best friends!"

Tsukihi snickered, showing no signs of being serious, but it seemed pretty clear that Sengoku had her to thank for somehow finding her way back into society after everything that happened.

The conman wasn't to thank for it. I of course hadn't done anything—unable to.

Impressive.

Then again, I suppose it wasn't for nothing that Tsukihi served as the brains of the Fire Sisters and had the support of all the area middle schoolers.

"She even told me a secret the other day."

"A secret? Like what?"

"I can't tell you, it's a secret."

"…"

"Listen, just leave Nadeko to me and go have a lovey-dovey time with Miss Senjogahara! I've got an airtight alibi for you!"

"Um, when did I ask for one?"

"Transfer trains multiple times!"

"A timetable-based alibi…"

What kind of a date was that? Maybe if you were a rail fan—not that I knew if Senjogahara was one.

"By the way, what's Karen doing tomorrow? With, um, what's-his-name."

"Mizudori."

"Right. Is she going on a date with what's-his-name?"

"You really have no interest at all in learning your sisters' boyfriends' names, do you? Mm, no, Karen said she'd be going to her dojo tomorrow. I guess to celebrate her graduation, rather than starting at her new school? Her master had a cool idea, and she's getting to go through a hundred-man *kumite*."

"Why on White Day..."

Romance was a foreign concept to both of my little sisters. They were making it seem like I was the only one floating in air.

Putting Karen aside, I admit it weighed on my conscience a bit that Tsukihi was visiting Sengoku...

"She's done a hundred-man kumite before," Tsukihi said, "but Karen wants to win every match this time around. If she does, she'll be granted a full-contact match with her master."

"Wow, she's been living a tale of her own..."

She ought to be the main character instead.

I felt like an improviser, the way I let my situation dictate my actions. Most of my story seemed ad-libbed.

"As the youngest sibling, it makes me proud that you and Karen are moving forward and growing, one step at a time," Tsukihi then said. "I guess I'm the only one who hasn't changed."

004

And so, the next day.

March fourteenth.

White Day, or Einstein Day.

The day of my last date as a high schooler.

Allow me to take this opportunity to make a note of something, since there just might be people who don't know this, or have forgotten. I was terribly anxious about Senjogahara's date plan because our first date, also planned by her, back in June, included the shocking element that was Daddy Senjogahara-as-chaperone.

Her excuse, or reason, was that Daddy could drive us promptly to that date's distant location, but I don't think I need to bother describing just how oppressive the enclosed space of an automobile felt as I sat there with my girlfriend and her father, who I was meeting for the first time. The three of us, all alone...

No, not just the three of us. At one point, I was left alone with just Daddy—chills still run down my spine when I think back to that.

Of course, that first date had good moments, and it was a positive memory overall. Still, I can't deny that it traumatized me in some way.

Senjogahara wouldn't recycle that plan, though. Even if she did spring the same surprise on me, I'd already met her father a number of times since then, going so far as to speak to him. I felt confident I'd be able to handle myself better.

Yes. I'd grown.

I hadn't been asleep in bed for the six months I'd been prohibited from going on dates—even if Daddy were to chaperone us again, even if Grandma and Grandpa came along to make it a family affair, I'd stay cool as a cucumber.

You're no match for me, Hitagi Senjogahara.

With that spirit in my heart, I arrived at the Tamikura Apartments, her residence, at nine in the morning on March fourteenth—I walked there, since both of my bikes had been totaled, and had left with a good bit of time to spare, but being on the lookout for Ononoki tailing me had slowed my journey.

The main event is only starting, so I'm skipping over everything that happened before my departure, but Karen left even earlier to get to her hundred-man kumite, while Tsukihi planned on visiting Sengoku in the afternoon.

The Araragi siblings were keeping busy today—in any case, I arrived at the Tamikura Apartments prepared, which is why I wasn't too shaken to see a car parked outside that I didn't recall seeing before.

Judging by its license plate, it was a rental.

"…"

I wasn't shaken, but it silenced me.

Sheesh, looks like another unusual date in store for me today, I thought as I braced anew. I'd accept it all, show my broadmindedness, and recaptivate my girlfriend after having showed her nothing but my lame side for a while.

Naturally, this was assuming that I'd ever captivated her in the first place, but I was gonna go ahead and make that assumption whatever lay in store for me. That said, I still couldn't begin to fathom why she'd asked for us to start seeing each other that day in that park…

Having passed by the 4WD without paying it any mind, which is to say pretending not to see it, I knocked on the second-floor door to Room 201, where the Senjogaharas lived.

"Welcome to a wonderful day."

Appearing with a mysterious and pretentious line, Senjogahara looked fairly dressed up—a fully coordinated outfit based around the color white. Though she'd taken the opportunity during summer break to change her hairstyle from long to short, a good amount of time had passed. It was the first time in a while I'd seen her wearing her hair braided.

A French braid, at that.

How fresh!

"I did this with Miss Hanekawa's old look in mind."

"Again, the way you express your friendship is a lot to handle…"

"I thought you might appreciate it, too, if I started looking more and more like her."

"As is your statement just now…"

I didn't want to think too much about it.

Her view of the world was too involved for me.

"I'd like to cut loose and enjoy today," she explained. "I want my remarks to create a sense of freedom, of there being no future."

"I'm fine with freedom, but the no future part? The future is exactly where we're trying to head next."

"Only if you're accepted, right? If not, there's a chance we'll be heading into the past."

"…"

Coming from someone who sailed right into college on a recommendation, her digs had a rich savor.

"What's the big deal?" she said. "We can only enjoy lighthearted gags about college exams for another few days, until the acceptance results are out."

"It'll be no laughing matter if I really got rejected. Forget about gags, I'd feel like puking."

"All right, time to go. I need to be back by seven tonight, I can't keep my dad waiting. We need to wrap this up, every second counts."

"Um, could you not treat your dinner with your dad as today's main event? Or you can, but just don't mention it."

"Hmph. Then why don't you shut me up with a kiss?"

"…"

Maybe I did need to shut her up.

Or so I thought, but reading into her words, I found a slight discrepancy with my current take on the situation—she needed to be back? He'd be waiting?

A ride in the car parked in front with Daddy Senjogahara—wasn't in store for us?

I'd even imagined a worst-case scenario: the three of us would go out during the day, and I'd have to leave on my own once it was time for dinner...but no?

Did the car parked outside have nothing to do with us? Did it belong to someone else living in these apartments? That did seem reasonable— but I was dealing with Hitagi Senjogahara here.

Though reformed, an unpredictable girl.

She shot past my worst-case scenario—coming out of her unit with car keys twirling around her fingertips.

Were we traveling in that 4WD after all? Who was going to sit behind the wheel, with those keys?

"Come on, ride shotgun," Senjogahara said, getting into the driver's seat.

The driver's seat.

Then she buckled up.

Ah, a fine demonstration of a driver respecting traffic rules—and well, since she had the keys, it was only natural for her to get in on the driver's side. No mystery there.

But! Even so!

"What? Whaat? Whaaat?! Hold-on-Gahara, wait wait wait wait. This is just a guess, but could it maybe, possibly, somehow be that you're going to be driving us today?! You'll be behind the wheel?! Hitagi Driver-Gahara?!"

"Yes," she simply nodded.

She clearly had no interest in prolonging this exchange, but I wouldn't have overreacted in the first place if that was enough to make me retreat with an *is that so, then please drive safe today.*

This was, in a way, more shocking than going to hell.

Her? Driving? I felt more prepared to accept her dad driving us than this!

"Why are you acting so agitated? I'm buckled in as you can see."

"Buckled in or bucking it out?"

I was so shaken that I was talking strange.

I could feel all my mental prep vanishing into thin air—no one else was in the car so we'd be the only ones for the date, but I found myself sincerely wishing that a third party would appear, which is to say a different driver.

"This is buck-crazy, your date plan is going on a drive without a license? You're joking, right? You're only trying to surprise me with this, and we're about to get out of the car, right?! It's just some sort of show of hospitality, a refreshing drink you've prepared for a guest? We're going to do as proper high school students do and get on the bus, yes?!"

"You know better than anyone how much I hate jokes, Araragi."

Um, no? I knew better than anyone how much she loved jokes—nasty ones in bad taste at that...

"And how very unpleasant of you to assume that I'll be driving without a license."

"What?"

"Ta-daaa."

And with that—she took a card out of her pocket.

Providing her own sound effects.

An object one would call a driver's license.

Hitagi Senjogahara.

Her name printed on it, alongside a photo of her face—and not an automatic transmission-only license, but a full one. A card signifying that its owner may drive on public streets in accordance with Japan's Road Traffic Act.

"Heh, surprised? While you were hard at work studying for your entrance exams, I was hard at work studying for the license test."

"..."

Was I surprised? Yes, yes indeed—it blew away every word I knew and every fact I'd stuffed into my brain over the course of my exam prep.

She'd been going for a driver's license?! And hiding it from me?!

"I passed on my first try," she boasted with a smug smile.

Praise me! Praise me, every inch of her body seemed to say—and as her boyfriend, I of course wanted to laud my girlfriend's achievements. Nor had I fought my battle against my exams alone. I wanted us to share our trials and tribulations, but unfortunately common sense came first.

Hold on, hold on, hold on! Not having a license was better in that case!

"D-D-Do you even know the school rules?" I asked her.

"Of course I do, I aced the written portion. Traffic is restricted around schools, namely school zones, during the mornings and afternoons."

"I'm not trying to test you on the Road Traffic Act!"

Those were the road rules.

Naoetsu High's school rules—or most prep schools, as far as I knew—strictly prohibited obtaining a driver's license.

As a high school senior born on July seventh, Senjogahara might already be eighteen, old enough to be granted a driver's license, but... that didn't mean she should do something as dangerous and nonsensical as getting one as a student.

Her recommendation-based university acceptance could be rescinded. In fact, an atrocity of this level jeopardized her graduation— I couldn't believe it. People out there really tried that? And one of those people was my girlfriend?

How do I put this? I know I've gone on about how she was reformed—but how do I put this, what can I say? She was a legit delinquent against whom I paled in comparison.

"Wow," I breathed. "You weren't kidding about the no future part... I might end up going to college all by myself now. I've gone all the way around and done a backflip to come to the point where I'm impressed by what you've done, but why would you ever do this?"

"We didn't have to go to school during third term, and I was just so bored that I didn't know what else to do?" replied Senjogahara, her head tilted.

My girlfriend was living proof that idle hands are the devil's workshop.

"And I thought I'd go ahead and get a license because you wouldn't be able to—though it seems that was an unnecessary concern."

"?"

I didn't quite understand what she was saying. I wouldn't be able to? How rude—I thought, but soon saw her point.

Not showing up in photographs, until just the other day, had been one symptom of my growing vampirism. Thus, I would never be issued a driver's license—and Senjogahara must have fretted over that fact in her own unique way.

In that sense, I couldn't scold her about her antics—wait, no, scratch that.

Emotional reasons didn't cut it.

Even when the emotion was love.

Getting a license as a high school student was still rash…putting a car before her courses, if it kept her from graduating.

"Don't worry," she said, "in that case I'll just break up with you and hang out with Kanbaru."

"Don't talk so casually about breaking up with me. And Kanbaru would be flabbergasted if that happened. You and her in the same year?"

"I think she'd simply be happy," Senjogahara said without a hint of remorse—she just wasn't going to feel any over this matter.

I needed to be the one to back down.

One more day until graduation… I just had to pray that our school didn't find out—and while I wasn't sure if it'd be possible after this start, I decided to focus on enjoying today.

That's also called not thinking, but there's a lot of thinking in this world that you'd rather not do.

"Don't forget to buckle up after all that talk about the rules, Araragi."

"Yeah, I know… I'm not brave enough to sit in a new driver's car without a seatbelt. I might be known as a raging bull, but even I feel like the China shop owner right now. In fact, I'd sit in a child seat if I could…"

A fresh concern crossed my mind.

"By the way, you're going to tell me where we're going in advance this time, right? It's not that I don't trust you, but if you want us to go somewhere far like that observatory again, I'm doing everything I can to stop you. I'm destroying that steering wheel."

"It'd be a problem if you did, since this is a rental car. Relax, I don't plan on going anywhere that far—and there'd be no point in going to an observatory during the day. Dude, you're dead."

"Excuse me?"

"I said use your head."

"…"

Her sense-of-freedom remarks could be pretty scary… It felt more like reckless abandon.

"So, where are we going? What's our *destino*?"

"A planetarium," Senjogahara told me flat out, when I thought she'd toy with me—well, I guess she couldn't hide it anymore because she was entering our destination into the car GPS.

"A planetarium?"

"Right. One of the world's many planetaria," she used a plural form that I never imagined I'd hear as she stepped on the gas.

And with that.

Our terrifying date drive began.

005

Though I said terrifying, fortunately Senjogahara was right to be proud of passing on her first try. There were no flaws in her technique—at least from my passenger-seat perspective.

No flaws.

Or maybe flawless—knowing Hanekawa messed up my judgment, not to mention my intense first impression of Senjogahara, but believe it or not, my girlfriend was a bit of a top-spec perfect superhuman herself.

Even the way she changed gears looked stylish.

Renting a car with a manual transmission felt like a sort of statement—and that seemed like the difference here between Hitagi Senjogahara and the humble and modest Hanekawa.

Speaking of skill and tact, I kept talking to her about the topic and learned that despite what she said, she'd at least prepared some countermeasures in case our school discovered her acquisition of a driver's license—in particular, she'd shield herself with a good cause if need be and tell them it was *to help her struggling family finances.*

Her willingness to use her own complexes to her advantage was, to be honest, something I admired…but what was I doing, being the one recaptivated here?

I didn't want to talk too much while she was driving, so I was quiet in the passenger's seat. Senjogahara, though, seemed to have no difficulty (ever a model student) talking while driving, and in fact she was the one to start speaking to me.

"It helps me relax, so if anything, I'd appreciate it if you talked to me, my dear Watson."

"Your dear Watson… I guess I'm sitting in your passenger seat, but I'd rather not be tasked with putting the tales of your adventures to paper. Nothing about you is Holmesian, anyway."

"True. Miss Hanekawa is Holmes, not me—by the by, she called me last night."

"What? Really?"

"Yes. Seems like she'll be able to make it back by graduation."

"Huh…"

Tsubasa Hanekawa.

A friend I shared in common with Senjogahara, currently roaming abroad—and though her mind was one of the best in the country, and in fact the world, she'd decided to go on a meandering trip after graduation rather than continue on to college with no set aim or purpose. Hence, she'd spent most of our third term, during which attendance wasn't mandatory for seniors at our school, diligently hunting down locations for her journey. Actually, she'd been gone from about halfway into second term.

Hunting down locations…

Her shaky plan for the future seemed like something put together by someone too smart for her own good. Perhaps it indicated an even more anarchic streak than Senjogahara's acquisition of a driver's license.

How ironic that I, the one supposed to be the biggest anarchist, found myself hewing to the proper path toward higher education.

Not sure who was being ironic there about what.

Hanekawa's trip was also of course a search for Mèmè Oshino, so in that sense she was traveling for my sake. This meant I, of all people, hadn't the words to stop her.

Still, Sengoku's case had somehow reached a solution, and so had my vampirism issue. You could say we didn't need to look for Oshino anymore…

Yet according to Tadatsuru.

Oshino would continue to be the key…

"Feels like it's been a while since I last saw Hanekawa," I said. "I haven't contacted her much since she's overseas and I didn't want to bother her, but she's been calling you and not me?"

What a shock. If she was coming back for graduation, she could have told me… I'd more or less assumed she wouldn't make it.

"You're right. I wonder why Miss Hanekawa didn't call you. Who knows, but I did assure her that I'd tell you."

"What other reason would there be?"

"Maybe I specifically asked her not to call you."

"You went that far? You were that specific about it? Why would you do that?"

"Don't worry. I told her that your vampirism's all better."

"I'm not worried, but I do feel like lecturing you now… I wanted to be the one to tell her. I'd have thanked her for helping me get through my exams, too."

"I didn't go so far as to thank her on your behalf, so let her know when you see her at graduation. Oh, right… She has bestowed upon me a message."

"Bestowed upon?"

Why so formal? Maybe Ononoki wasn't the only one who didn't know how and when to speak respectfully. Then again, you could credit Hanekawa with reforming Senjogahara's life as well as my own. She deserved so much respect from us, we could never show enough.

In my case, she may have replaced every element of my overall constitution—a pretty scary woman, in that sense. What kind of adult was she going to become?

"And what's this message?"

"She said she found Mister Oshino."

"Oh, huh… What?!"

For a moment there, it went in one ear then out the other.

Fortunately, I wasn't the one behind the wheel—I'm certain I would've caused a traffic accident had it been in my hands. Meanwhile, Senjogahara was nonchalant, still driving with only one hand on the steering—um, why hadn't she bothered telling me something that important yesterday?

Reporting is all about speed, isn't it?

"Seriously?" I said.

"Seriously. Well, to be exact, maybe she found the place where he's hiding out? I don't remember that well."

"I'm begging you, please remember. Do everything you can to."

And *hiding out*? Why was Senjogahara making him sound like a criminal... But in other words, Hanekawa hadn't discovered him yet, she'd only found his location—though that was already impressive enough.

"She said it was a tough call whether she could bring him back with her by graduation... There'd be nothing in particular for him to do even if she brought him back now, so she might not force him," Senjogahara relayed.

I'd yet to explain all of what happened the day before to Senjogahara—about my trip through hell, so maybe that was how she felt.

Perhaps I needed to explain at an early point during our date—though it did make me hesitate. How best to gently tell her that I was getting dragged into one of Miss Gaen's jobs yet again...

Oshino, of course, would never put it in such a self-victimizing way—I wasn't getting dragged into anything, I was at the center from the start.

But as Ononoki had pointed out, it was hard to tell whether Miss Gaen had planned on enlisting me from the start—and even she couldn't have predicted Hanekawa finding Oshino.

I wouldn't call it conflict, but there seemed to be a bit of tension in the air between Hanekawa and Miss Gaen—could this count as Hanekawa getting back at Miss Gaen?

That said, going by Senjogahara's words, it's not as if she'd seen Oshino—so it was still possible for her to be off the mark.

When I asked about this, Senjogahara answered, "You're right. It's not certain yet—but she said that after much reasoning, she narrowed down his location to two places."

"Two?"

"Yes—I didn't ask for details because I wasn't interested, but I think that's what she said."

"..."

Please, be more interested.

Come to think of it, though, Senjogahara hated personalities like Oshino's—maybe her apathetic stance was only natural, now that she thought he was no longer needed.

Two places... Where and where could they be?

If it was a tough call whether Hanekawa could bring him back by graduation, maybe it was because there were still two possible locations—and of course, both of them might be wrong.

"Much reasoning, huh? Yeah, she really is like some master detective."

Who didn't mind doing the legwork, either—a rarity these days.

"But she didn't say where these two places were?"

"She didn't. But don't get the wrong idea, Araragi. It's not because she was trying to act like some great detective. She tried to tell me like any normal person, but I said I wasn't interested and asked her not to."

"I can't help but wonder how Hanekawa reacted to that."

A master detective's greatest pleasure, thwarted like that. You called the wrong person, Hanekawa.

My reaction would've been superb—or maybe not, I might have acted a lot like Senjogahara thanks to how exhausted I was from the exams (and dealing with Ononoki)...

Being outside of Japan, she couldn't possibly know how they went, and maybe she'd decided not to call me out of consideration after Senjogahara asked her not to—which meant Hanekawa might mistakenly believe that I'd flunked them.

She was always surprisingly quick to jump to conclusions.

"What was it again?" Seeing just how down I was getting, my girlfriend used her notable memory to the fullest to recall Hanekawa's words, though only a small portion. "She said it was the other way around."

"The other way around?"

"Yes, her approach—she does like to leave so much implied and unspoken."

"Are you sure it wasn't because you weren't listening properly? I wonder what she could mean by that…"

Did she mean a situation where the solution was right under her nose the whole time, like in a mystery novel? Had she gone overseas to find Oshino when he was actually still in Japan? And he was near this town or something?

No, I couldn't imagine it being that simple.

I'd be mad if the man we'd searched so much for had been hiding out in our town—but in that case, Hanekawa would just need to come straight back. She wouldn't be in a dilemma where she didn't know if she'd make it in time for graduation.

"Miss Hanekawa also opined that…this was a paid man."

"Opined… And wait, a paid man?"

What did that even mean?

Hmm. I had a lot I needed to think about, I was still concerned, but there didn't seem to be anything I could do—I just had to trust in Hanekawa's self-reliance.

It might be best to keep it a secret from Miss Gaen, though.

Tsubasa Hanekawa, who doesn't know everything.

Izuko Gaen, who knows everything.

I might not know anything, but I at least knew those two. My decision for the time being was to minimize their contact as much as possible.

"As her friend, I guess I should be glad that the searching party didn't get lost too," I said. "I can't imagine that happening to Hanekawa, but you do worry about a girl traveling alone, you know?"

"Yes… By the way, Araragi. Do you know the ironclad rule for when you're a lost child?"

"When you're a lost child? Not for when you're looking for a lost child?" Though that wasn't how I'd describe Oshino and Miss Kagenui.

"Yes. Yet another suggestive remark on Miss Hanekawa's part…"

"You sure you aren't the reason why it sounded suggestive, and not definitive? Isn't the ironclad rule when you're lost to not move? That's how you keep your problems from cascading."

"Yes. That's what they say—but she mentioned that it's not that simple in real life. That it's actually faster to search for each other when you get split up."

"Really? Seems inefficient to me."

"It'd be horribly inefficient if you both searched at random—in reality, though, people don't meander around. You think about where the other person might be, which is to say you conjecture. In other words, you'll be shrinking the area of your search down to a small area, so it's faster if both of you move—or something like that."

It does assume that your reasoning about the other person's location is on the mark—Senjogahara said.

True. You could even say people get lost because they're incapable of doing just that—so was that what Hanekawa meant by a reverse approach?

Of course, this too was only conjecture.

Someone on my level could never catch up with Hanekawa's thinking no matter how much reasoning I did—so should I sit still and wait for Hanekawa to return by around graduation?

"What else did you two talk about? Did Hanekawa talk about anything other than Oshino?"

"We didn't get into too much detail because of the high phone bill—but I did discuss our date plan. I'll come clean and admit that a planetarium was Miss Hanekawa's idea."

"It was?"

"Yes. My plan was to go visit a volcanic crater."

"…"

It's not that I don't have any interest in volcanic craters, but I was grateful to Hanekawa… What kind of a ridiculous plan had this girl come up with?

"I didn't tell her about me driving because I thought she'd try to stop me."

"I wish you would've asked her about that one…"

"Miss Hanekawa told me about her favorite planetaria, so I chose one from the list. No need to worry, Araragi. Don't look so concerned, there won't be any big surprises waiting for you from here on out. I've been suitably censored by Miss Hanekawa."

Censored…

Not a word you wanted to hear in the context of a date, but knowing that Hanekawa had reviewed the plan brought me some small amount of comfort.

"She got pretty mad at me, and pretty depressed too. The angrier she got, the harder it became for me to tell her about the driver's license."

"I understand how you must have felt, but I feel like being on the receiving end of her anger there would've been the right thing for your own future..."

"I often go to planetaria, of course, so this doesn't feel too much like a special event to me. Still, going with you will be a nice twist."

"Hm... You say that, but isn't this still an uninteresting date for you, in that case?"

Kanbaru had mentioned enjoying planetariums. I wondered if the Valhalla Duo used to go have fun at them together...

"Well, when I go to a planetarium," Senjogahara said, "it tends to be less for fun and more in order to study—so I'd like to gaze out into artificial stars without any purpose in mind for a change. I wouldn't say I'm unenthused, so don't worry."

"In order to study? Oh, right. I guess you'd made the rather eccentric choice among students at our school to study planetary science as your science elective..."

I personally didn't even know what planetary science entailed... But it seemed that Senjoghara, who treasured her childhood memories of visiting observatories as a family, had a special attachment to celestial bodies. It's not as if I dislike talking about the stars, but I don't look up into the starry sky with the same kind of devotion as her...

"Yes, which is why my original idea for our date was to visit a volcanic crater. I wanted to observe the outcrops."

"What kind of an original idea is that? You just wanted to go study? I'd call that fieldwork. What kind of a date were you thinking of inviting me on fresh out of entrance exams?"

"It would be interesting, though. We may be on a proper and healthy date today thanks to Miss Hanekawa, but I can't deny that my curiosity is going unsatisfied. Considering that you find the greatest gratification in being dragged around and run ragged by me, is today becoming less stimulating for you?"

"Could you at least not say *gratification*?"

"Vivification?"

"That doesn't seem right either..."

"Capitulation?"

"You do sometimes make me feel like giving up..."

"But planetaria are often combined with science museums, including the one we're heading to today. In that sense, we could see it as us going there to study—it might be bad for your heart if we went cold turkey on studying. You might want to gradually cool down by coming into contact with some cutting-edge science at least."

"I never imagined it'd be bad for your heart to stop studying..."

This made Hanekawa's imprint on our plans for the day clear.

A science museum, a combination of study and play—going to one called into question the very idea of acting like high schoolers, but maybe it was an appropriate choice for people who were bad at having fun like me and Senjogahara.

With Senjogahara's unique twist added on top (driving a car), she didn't need to worry about the day not being stimulating enough. Even if I trusted her driving skills, just being in a new car can make you nervous.

"I don't normally go to science museums, so I'm looking forward to that part," she said. "I wonder what kinds of flying cars they'll have."

"You have high expectations of science museums..." Though flying cars do seem to exist. I continued, "Even if they don't fly, cars these days are pretty amazing. I don't know about this car, but some brake when they sense danger, or have sensors on all sides, or even drive themselves."

"Yes—they're already quite futuristic." *Like the Underwater Buggy*, she added utterly unnecessarily. The Castle of the Underwater Devil again... "The day might come when you just have to enter your destination into a navigation system for the car to take you there—and you only have to park and get started, just like planes that only require manual takeoff and landing."

"Data skills and parking skills, huh? It'd be nice if I didn't need to get a license. I'd like to step away from testing for a while..."

Not that I saw the law catching up to cars like that anytime soon.

Yes, that feeling of technological advancement surpassing human society.

Just like the way I don't know how to use a smartphone, cars—integrated collections of the latest technology—might become alien to me.

"What are you talking about? I do hope that you get your license over spring break. Next time around, I'd like you to drive me. After all, you finally show up in pictures."

"You want me to drive you when you can drive on your own, Miss Senjogahara?"

"As a girl, I can't help but dream about riding in my boyfriend's passenger seat," she responded with a somewhat maidenly remark. "I dream about it almost as much as I dream about having a reverse harem."

"That's a very girly dream in its own way, but I'm not sure if you can equate the two…"

"Drive me up to observe some outcroppings by a volcanic crater someday."

She may not have been joking, but at the same time, the way she sought my consent made it hard to reply, *Yeah, I'd love to…*

"I'm curious, Senjogahara. What do you learn in planetary science, anyway? It's not heavenly bodies all day, right?"

"To be exact, it's an earth science class. I guess you could say it's primarily about Earth as a celestial object—though my interest always tends to point toward the universe as a whole. My dream is to draw a complete map of the universe and be known as the second Tadataka Ino. That's what I'll be doing in college."

"Tadataka Ino… The first person to create a modern map of Japan."

"Sadly, they say he created it without knowing much about Hokkaido, but I won't cut any corners. I'll observe outcroppings along every last inch of space and map them."

"*Observe outcroppings* would be a gross understatement in that case."

Doesn't sound like any Tadataka I-know… Not that I thought Mr. Ino had cut any corners…

Still, I was hearing about this for the first time. My girlfriend wanted to become an astronaut? Did she mean it? It did sound like a throwaway quip.

"And wait, what is a map of the universe anyway? Do those exist? Are you talking about those diagrams you see of all the planets lined up around the sun?"

"No, those are just illustrations. I'm talking about a map that shows the entire universe... You wouldn't be too familiar with them unless you took planetary science."

"Yeah, I've never heard of one before."

"Most of the universe is empty space. Scattered within it are galaxies and gatherings of stars—you might have the vague idea that due to probability, stars are equally spread out through space, but that's not true. They clump up with one another and exist in unbalanced groupings. That's what a map of the universe depicts—heh. I wonder if stars prefer company, just like humans do."

"You can try to make it sound like there's a moral, but it's not going to make any sense to me when I haven't seen these maps."

"By the way, they aren't rectangular like world maps or country maps."

She explained that they're shaped like Japanese folding fans—which is to say, like *ogi*.

She said this undramatically.

Ogi.

Nor did I react to—that word.

006

"All right then, hello there, Araragi-senpai. It's me, Ogi Oshino. So, let's learn about constellations today," Ogi said with a smile. She used the laser pointer in her hand to make indications on a sky full of stars projected on a hemispheric dome. Though I found it suspicious that she, a first-year at Naoetsu High, soon to be second-year, would be working at this planetarium as an employee of its science museum, I soon realized I was in a dream.

Senjogahara had pulled off an impressive parallel parking job in the museum's lot without relying on any advanced automotive features, and we made it to the attached planetarium without incident, but my exhaustion from the previous day must have reared its head—I'd also woken up early. I realize it's wholly unbecoming for a boy on a date, but I must've nodded off in the structure's pitch darkness.

Since we were in a planetarium, you could say I'd nodded off into space—no, sorry, I continued to be sleepy in my dream and wasn't coming up with anything clever.

"Please don't fall asleep, Araragi-senpai. I'll throw my chalk at you if you do. And since I don't have any chalk, I'll throw my laser pointer at you if you do."

Please don't. I'd lose consciousness and wake up if she hit me with something like that...

"Ha haa. And then you'd have a thought once you wake up. Is the date you're on with Miss Senjogahara reality, or were those moments you spent cuddling with me just now the real world? Yes, it'd be what you'd call a butterfly dream, where you can't tell whether you're human or insect."

Even in dreams, Ogi still fired on all cylinders.

"Now then, let us deepen our insights."

If you asked me if this was dream or reality, it must have still been reality—they must have been discussing something similar in the real-world planetarium.

And because I could hear it in my shallow sleep, it affected my dream—well, in that case, Ogi's commentary might provide me with enough to at least think of an excuse for Senjogahara once I woke up.

"As you know, there are eighty-eight constellations visible in the sky from Earth—a fact you're familiar with thanks to *Saint Seiya*. Can you name them all?"

Come on, don't be ridiculous. All eighty-eight haven't even shown up in *Saint Seiya* yet.

"Indeed. And the southern constellations would be tough for someone living in Japan like yourself—though my rival Miss Hanekawa might just be looking at them from Australia or so right about now," Ogi said, sounding amused.

Despite her smile, she wasn't trying to hide anymore that Hanekawa was her rival.

"The constellations in the Southern Hemisphere really are interesting. They have so many you've never heard of. Like a chameleon."

A chameleon? Yeah, pretty amazing...

"As well as Pictor, an easel, and Vela, a ship's sail."

Ogi pointed at each constellation with her laser—like a regular navigator. Perhaps these kinds of lectures were always her strong point—perhaps she enjoyed explaining things to people.

But no, if this was a dream, it was just that I unconsciously thought those things about Ogi...

These unusual constellations—well, they would be commonplace in the Southern Hemisphere, but the names of these groupings of stars

I had little to no knowledge of came pouring forth from Ogi's mouth, until—

"Then there's Hydrus, the water snake," she said.

A water snake.

An aquatic—serpent.

"As opposed to Hydra, the sea snake—you do know about Hydra, don't you? It's the largest of all eighty-eight constellations."

The dome's starry sky underwent a total change.

Changing into a sky I'd seen before.

Ogi pointed to Hydra.

"The question of how one measures the size of a constellation is a difficult one, of course. It does start to fall apart once you look at them in three dimensions. Still, the presence of Hydra here does remind one of Kissshot Acerolaorion Heartunderblade, does it not?"

Descriptions of aberrations began mixing into her descriptions of the constellations.

I found it hard to believe this had any link to the real world—a planetarium attached to a science museum wouldn't casually bring up the name of the vampire I knew so well, the iron-blooded, hot-blooded, yet cold-blooded legend who'd returned to her full form the day before.

Was it another unconscious impression of Ogi? That she'd bring it up here? In that sense, you could say my dream's link to reality had only strengthened—

"And while we may call Hydra the sea serpent constellation, its classical name references the mythical beast—do you know about the Hydra? A monster that regenerates again and again, no matter how many times you cut at it. It wouldn't be an overstatement to call it immortal. Similar to the legend of the Yamata no Orochi in Japan—though it was the famed and heroic Heracles who rid the world of the Hydra, not Susano'o-no-Mikoto."

No matter how many of its heads Heracles cut off, the serpent continued to grow new ones from where they were severed—Ogi said.

Sounding amused.

Miss Kagenui was familiar with how to defeat immortal aberrations, but what exactly did the heroic Heracles do to slay the sea snake—to slay the Hydra? It can't be that the battle ended in vain without him ever defeating it.

"No, it's defeated in a very orthodox way. Though I doubt you could defeat Kissshot Acerolaorion Heartunderblade by doing this—he cut off each of the Hydra's nine heads in order, then burned the wounds with fire to block them off and prevent them from growing back. He cut off all of its heads one by one—and thus Heracles defeated the sea serpent."

An orthodox method indeed.

Burn the wounds with flame.

Ogi said it wouldn't work on Kissshot Acerolaorion Heartunderblade—and maybe it wouldn't, but using fire to burn a vampire did seem like a sound approach.

Immortal monsters.

Need to be fought with fire.

Just as I was sent to Avīci, the hell where nothing but flames surround you on every side…

"Perhaps only a legendary hero can defeat a legendary vampire—but I digress," Ogi continued. "When Heracles fought this sea snake, Cancer the crab attacked him as well, fighting on the side of the serpent and snipping at Heracles with its big claws."

Cancer—the crab?

"But the giant crab might as well have been a louse, not so much as tickling Heracles before being defeated in return. Crushed underfoot—and they say the impact turned the crab flat or something. Of course, the crab was praised for its heroism for facing Heracles, and a goddess placed it in the sky as a constellation, so that its name would be remembered."

Ogi pointed all around Cancer as she spoke.

One of the great things about planetariums must be their flexibility in situations like these—you can only see so many constellations in an actual starry sky, or over the course of a season, but the flip of a switch can show you anything you want, whether the south or north sky, summer or winter constellations, or the stars at dusk or dawn.

"Its attitude of taking on a frightful enemy with modest weapons is like Miss Senjogahara encapsulated—you ought to tell this story to her once you wake up and show her just how great of a boyfriend you are."

I didn't know about that last part...

The story was an interesting one, but Senjogahara wouldn't be happy to hear about a crab getting crushed underfoot...

I didn't know to what extent my dream and the real-life planetarium were connected, but if she was hearing this commentary on Cancer in the waking world, how did she feel? Not that she liked crabs or had any strong emotional attachment to them just because she'd been in the grips of a crab aberration.

But as someone born on July seventh.

Senjogahara—was a Cancer.

I would of course call it a stretch to read any sort of meaning into that—as far as I could recall, she'd never once allied herself with Kiss-shot Acerolaorion Heartunderblade...which is to say Shinobu Oshino.

In fact, Senjogahara had been the only one who didn't want to go looking for Shinobu when she went missing—her stance of disliking children remained the same, whether reformed or not.

Even if she were to come across Shinobu fighting for her life, I couldn't imagine Senjogahara risking a trampling just to lend her support...

"You're right—I'm not too familiar with the situation, but when Miss Senjogahara put herself on the line to protect you from Sengoku, she did so because it was you. The former Heartunderblade was just a bonus," Ogi nodded. "It is interesting to consider—who would win if the then-snake god, Nadeko Sengoku when she reigned over Kita-Shirahebi Shrine, faced off against the fully restored Kissshot Acerolaorion Heartunderblade. The odds are in favor of the Aberration Slayer, who has the power to end the entire world, but a snake god would be every bit as immortal—though this was a land and not sea serpent."

Snake vs. sea serpent.

A deeply poisonous scenario if they both possessed venom... While Ogi spoke of it like a dream matchup, I could only see it turning into a fruitless mudslinging match between immortals.

An eternal, snake-eat-snake competition.

"Indeed. And while it's not Hydra, Serpens is another constellation that symbolizes immortality—" Ogi said as the dome's night sky shifted again.

Her laser pointer indicated the constellation of Serpens.

"After all, it can be said to have a certain peculiarity that is unique among the eighty-eight. Do you know what it might be?"

I don't—

I replied.

Come to think of it, if this was a dream, it was odd for Ogi to be expounding facts that I didn't know—and the discussion seemed to be a little too much about aberrations to be something I was getting from the real-life planetarium by way of sleep learning.

Was that the talk we'd attended?

Serpens' characteristics—I couldn't see Ogi choosing planetary science as an elective, but did she still know the answer?

"I don't know anything," she said with a dark smile. "You're the one who knows. Really, you should be aware of it. See, just like this."

With that, the light from Ogi's laser pointer swung to both sides—from east to west, to use cardinal directions.

"Serpens exists while being divided into east and west, yet it's a single constellation. As a serpent—it's been *chopped in two*," she said. "It exists in separate parts, its upper half to the west, and its lower half to the east—which is to say that just by looking at it, you can tell it's immortal. Just think, it lives despite its body being split in two… Then again, it seems you often find your own body split in two."

Forget split in two, I was chopped to pieces just yesterday—but putting that aside, not only was this my first time hearing that Serpens existed in the sky as two disconnected pieces, the fact shocked me.

Why had it been placed there in the sky in that shape? Could there be another story behind it, just as for Cancer? Something like a legend of a snake being chopped in two, like the flattened crab—

"Yes," said Ogi, as if in reply. "In fact, another constellation exists in the sky between those two separated parts—and I'm certain you're familiar with this one. Ophiuchus."

The serpent-bearer.

Right, one of the thirteen constellations.

I vividly remembered the time when I discussed it with Kanbaru and she burst out laughing—in fact, the memory was still fresh. Kanbaru still brought it up as a way to annoy me.

"As a whole, the serpent-bearer is shown to hold the upper and lower parts of the snake in his left and right arms—to explain the detailed backstory in a mythical kind of way, it seems that the constellation of the serpent-bearer cut into Serpens' original location. Something I'm sure the serpent found quite annoying."

True, it made him seem more like someone who'd painted over and killed a serpent than someone bearing one.

But no, the serpent was immortal *because that wasn't enough to kill it*—a creature so mystical that it would be worshiped as a god.

A creature and a creeper.

In that sense, while I may have been in the dark about what made Serpens special, which is to say its division into east and west, I did know a little about the serpent-bearer—right, wasn't it supposed to be Asclepius, the great and famed doctor?

"That's right. I'd expect no less out of someone as learned as you," Ogi said with a tinge of sarcasm, but it seemed I wasn't mistaken. "While he may be called the serpent-bearer, if anything, you could say that Asclepius learned from the serpent—as he began down the path of medicine after witnessing the drama of a dying snake coming back to life."

Huh. I didn't know that part.

"But—this would come to haunt him as well. In a stroke of bad luck, you might say—or maybe he was crushed to death by his own talents. Asclepius' medical abilities grew and grew to the point where he could even bring the dead back to life. Reviving the dead is the ultimate form of regenerative medicine—but it was a step too far."

He went too far, Ogi repeated the essential point.

"He broke the rules. I guess you could say he violated a universal law... It earned him the anger of Hades, king of the underworld, who struck Asclepius with lightning and quite literally sent him into the heavens. Perhaps you could say that seeing an immortal snake is what caused him to lose his own life. It almost sounds like the fruit of knowledge..."

The fruit of knowledge.

Neither was exactly a happy outcome: being expelled from paradise, getting turned into a constellation…

In terms of what a doctor was for, however, I didn't see regenerative medicine as any kind of violation of a universal law—what could have made Hades, king of the underworld, so mad?

Then again, as someone who'd just managed to come back from hell, I did see aberrational and medical immortality as separate…

"Well, the underworld would empty out if every dead person came back to life—there wasn't anyone in your hell either, was there? But I wouldn't call it hell if it's abandoned, I'd call it a ghost town."

Sure, Asclepius, victim of that lightning bolt, might not have been immortal himself, but the act of bringing a human back to life—the act of mass-producing immortality is quite the sin.

Ogi then made another comment, as if it had just come to mind.

"Yotsugi Ononoki, too. She's someone who came back to life after death—but in retaliation, everyone involved in bringing her back was struck by a curse."

Huh? What was she talking about?

A curse?

I felt like Tadatsuru had mentioned Miss Kagenui not walking on the ground as being a kind of curse…

"You could of course debate which is worse, a lightning bolt or a curse—but it does make me wonder. What kind of punishment is going to come to Miss Gaen for bringing you back from hell? You may not be happy with the way things now stand, with you acting just as she wants, but keep in mind that it's not as if she's avoiding all risk herself."

Why would Ogi say that? Why was she defending Miss Gaen?

Asking that, of course, also forced me to wonder why Ogi knew about me going to hell and Miss Gaen bringing me back from it, but—

"Ha haa," Ogi laughed, putting the laser pointer back in her pocket—and ambling over to my seat.

She then tried to sit next to me.

In reality, the planetarium was a close to sold-out affair for the morning session, but I was its only visitor in this dream—yet despite it being empty, Ogi was trying to sit right next to me.

"Ogi. If you're going to sit, sit to my left."

"Why?"

"That's Senjogahara's seat."

"Oh? How romantic. No need to worry. I have no intention whatsoever of threatening the throne of the female lead. I think I could at least aim to become a little-sister character—but while Karen is one thing, I wouldn't want to have to compete against Tsukihi," Ogi said, sitting to my left as requested.

It seemed she was done with her time acting as a planetarium employee.

"By the way, what's your sign?"

Perhaps that's why she now came at me with what seemed more like plain small talk than any kind of celestial episode—and I admit, I have an easier time with more laidback topics.

"Hm... Um, I think it was either Taurus or Aries."

"How vague."

"That's how it is if you're not interested in horoscopes—I'm sure a surprising number of people out there don't know their blood type, either."

"Perhaps—do you not believe in fortune-telling much?"

"I don't know... I used to always be negative about it, but accepting the existence of aberrations and hell, while denying the existence of fortunes, seems inconsistent..."

"Ha haa. To compare your situation to a mystery novel, it'd be like a book that's okay with detectives who have superpowers but paradoxically refuses any supernatural phenomena."

Ogi and her mystery analogies—but maybe her example was the easiest to understand.

"Knowing you, I bet when you were sent to hell you started thinking about the meaning of life being lessened by the existence of a world after death. Am I right?"

"I didn't go that far, but...yes, I did think something similar. Still..."

"Yes, you were able to come back to life precisely because you didn't think that, no? Well, fools do tend to cling on to life. To me, it just looks like you glossing over one mistake with an even bigger mistake," Ogi said to my left as she looked up at the dome's projected sky. "Not a covering up of shame, but a covering up of your mistakes."

"…"

"Of course, it's this cover-up that must have led Miss Gaen to send me an invitation—an obvious trap, but one I can't help but react to. It's as if she's calling out to my very instincts. You can tell she's an expert by the way she's thought of so many things."

Ogi giggled.

In the most high-school girlish way.

But she—her true identity.

Was as Tadatsuru Teori said.

As he taught me in the depths of hell.

The client who had asked him to slay me and Shinobu—

"Araragi-senpai. What do you think being right means?"

Now the topic strayed entirely from the starry sky—

As Ogi asked me the question.

No, this was of course nothing more than a conversation in a dream. It wasn't as if I was really speaking with her—but what about the real her?

What did I know about Ogi Oshino?

Mèmè Oshino's niece.

A lineage of experts.

A transfer student introduced to me by Suruga Kanbaru—

"No need to give it too much serious thought. The meaning of being right changes all the time, after all. You can claim that justice always prevails all you want, but in truth, it does lose a lot of the time. That said, the idea that might makes right is shallower than you'd expect. It all gets tricky because we use grand words like *justice*—we might be better off with something like *justiness* instead."

I still didn't get what she was saying.

I don't normally live my life thinking about what's just or justy, what's wrong or mistaken—but I guess that's exactly why I was in my current predicament.

Had I never failed to focus on deciding what is right, or what is wise, or what is beautiful or cool this whole time, the situation wouldn't have gotten so complicated.

I didn't think of it as a better outcome.

But I also thought—what if it had been?

"It's hard to do the right thing," Ogi said. "In particular, it's very hard to *only do the right thing*—because doing the right thing means having to do things that are wrong, or not right, at the same time. Just flip through a newspaper and you'll see all the examples you want of people resorting to injustice in the pursuit of justice—to play off the idea that justice always wins out in the end, I guess I'm saying that in order to win, you also have to lose at some point. There's no such thing as a perfect record—"

Miss Gaen had said the same thing.

She'd compared it to the game of shogi—something about how even the greatest player can't win a match against the most rank beginner without losing at least one piece.

Of course, she cut me into pieces immediately after, so it made me think that I myself was the loss in her eyes…

"Which is why, in order to be just, you must avoid doing what is just. If doing the right thing means making mistakes, you can only end up even."

In that case, what were you supposed to do?

I certainly hadn't done everything right—but I was strongly attracted to what's right because of that.

Like Miss Kagenui, for example.

Or like the Fire Sisters.

I would be lying if I said I had no admiration whatsoever for people who believed in their own rightness and lived accordingly.

"Sure—but it's not as if Miss Kagenui and the Fire Sisters are *doing the right thing* when they put that way of life into practice, even if they call it justice. Instead of doing the right thing in order to be right—"

They right wrongs.

Adjust the unjust.

That's how they choose to live their lives.

What Ogi said was—an extension of the conversation I had in hell with Hachikuji.

An extension, and a case of extra innings.

"Or you could say that what they do—is smite, maybe upbraid. In other words, while the enemy of an enemy may not be an ally, becoming the enemy of evil does make you its antonym, appointing yourself as just. Though it does put you one wrong step away from a situation where you're simply complaining about what you find distasteful—it does allow you to get drunk off a sense of justice."

Drunk off a sense of justice, huh?

That if anything was the kind of thing I often said to the Fire Sisters...but it was true. Their acts of justice were often nothing more than eliminating "bad" guys, as best represented by that conman, or taking care of the aftermath of "bad" stuff.

Whether it was Karen or Tsukihi or Miss Kagenui, it would never cross my mind to describe their personalities as *just*—or *right*.

If anyone existed who was "right" in that sense, it was Tsubasa Hanekawa in her former days—which meant that Ogi was correct. Hanekawa had no choice but to create the aberration known as Black Hanekawa in order to maintain that sense of rightness.

In order to be right.

She had no choice but to make a mistake.

I may not have been able to right that wrong—in fact, I allowed Hanekawa's mistake to persist, which meant—that after all, I wasn't in the right back then.

As Ogi said.

"And I too seek the kind of rightness that comes from righting wrongs—my role is to eject those who break the rules."

Break the rules. Eject.

The words began to remind me of something—but I couldn't gather my thoughts, there in my dream.

They scattered—dispersed.

"Of course, I'm not a demon—neither a vampire nor one of hell's devils. I wouldn't eject someone over an illegal act, or two, and am prepared to hand out suspended sentences... The show's almost over. I think you ought to wake up."

Hearing this, I reflexively checked my watch.

I didn't know how reliable a wristwatch was in a dream, but indeed, nearly thirty minutes had passed since the beginning of the show.

"Miss Senjogahara will be disappointed in you if you're still dozing as the lights go up. She went to the trouble of putting this date together, so I wouldn't blame her if she dumped you for sleeping during it. So come on, now, let's wake up."

Ogi reached out to me and gave my body a gentle shake—she was pretty quick to make physical contact with me for a girl, but it was out of consideration. She only wanted to wake me up, so I wasn't going to lecture her.

"Enjoy the rest of your date with your lover—but, Araragi-senpai. Whenever you find yourself with time to kill, think about what being right means—and let's talk about it when we meet in the real world."

Okay, got it. If I remember after I wake up, of course—I answered her in my mind.

Then, as if to follow up—and while I expected no answer at all—I asked Ogi.

Still, what exactly are you, anyway?

"We'll discuss that too when we meet again. I had a lot of fun playing around with you for the past few months, but I'm sad to say that I don't exist in order to have fun. But if I were to say what I can here…"

I'm the cosmic rule.

Though Ogi's answer was calm and casual, it was also immense.

A map of the universe.

The shape of an *ogi*, a folding fan.

A pitch-dark void—an uneven galaxy.

"Don't think too much about that either. Now that you've been brought back from hell and are a full human being again, I may not have to involve myself with you too much—if everything goes well."

So please, don't fall for Miss Gaen's sweet talk, warned Ogi.

"I'm sincerely hoping that you'll make the right decision this time around when it comes to the now-whole Kissshot Acerolaorion Heartunderblade as well as Mayoi Hachikuji, who's made her way back to this world despite having passed on to the next one—who has strayed once more—and choose to abandon them."

007

I woke up.

I woke up?

Oh no, I'd dozed off—even if I was tired, and even if I was in an environment as cozy as a planetarium, who falls asleep during a date?

Me, of all people? Or rather—even by my standards, really?

I'd somehow managed to wake up right as the show came to an end, but I remembered nothing about any projections or starry skies displayed on the dome.

I'd fallen asleep and hadn't even dreamed.

How embarrassing.

What kind of approach did I need to take with Senjogahara, sitting to my right? Should I talk to her pretending I'd been awake the whole time, or should I be honest and tell her I'd nodded off, then apologize for ruining our first date in forever?

I turned to face her, still unable to make a decision—

"…"

Senjogahara was also sleeping.

She slept there in total silence.

The way she slept involved such a lack of vital reactions that I wondered for a moment if she might be dead… I guess I'd never seen her fully asleep—this was how she slept?

To be honest, it scared me.

Though nothing about her seemed like Sleeping Beauty or Snow White, a comparison with them could be drawn given how borderline comatose she appeared.

Wait, don't tell me she really was dead...

"Senjogahara?"

"I'm not sleeping."

Blink.

Both of her eyelids opened simultaneously without having betrayed the slightest sign of doing so.

It was more like an awakening than waking up.

Like a computer that boots in one second.

"I wasn't sleeping at all. I wasn't sleeping at all. I was just thinking with my eyes shut."

"..."

An artless excuse, but one that I started to believe when she said it with such a straight face.

Still, how shallow of a sleeper was she if whispering her name could wake her up?

Then again, considering her past experiences—and considering just how long she had to live with a constant threat looming over her, I could understand why she might have trouble kicking a habit of sleeping like some kind of wild animal.

"I'm sorry. To tell you the truth, I was asleep," Senjogahara now gave me an honest apology.

Perhaps she realized she wouldn't be able to make her excuse work—but apologizing at all showed how much more of an honest person she'd become.

She used to be the type to say she'd rather die than apologize.

No one needs a personality that strong.

I still can't believe that I agreed to start going out with her back in those days...

Anyway, it felt like my nap had been canceled out thanks to Senjogahara being asleep. I felt like thanking her, if anything...but it didn't feel right to let her be the only one afflicted with guilt, and to keep all my relief to myself.

"It's okay. I was sleeping a little too," I confessed. In fact I'd been sound asleep, but allow me that small flourish.

"Oh. I suppose we were both tired—going on a date the day after your exams was too much of a rush job, I guess," Senjogahara said as she stretched. Our seats hadn't been too comfortable or anything, and I did the same. "It's also because we're able to relax. Two of your problems were settled on the same day, your entrance exams and your vampiric body."

"Yeah, you're right."

My issues might have bothered her even more than they bothered me—now that I thought about it, I'd done nothing but worry her for the past six months.

What an awful boyfriend.

True, I caught Senjogahara when she slipped and fell from the stairs in May, and I played a role in resolving something that had plagued her for some time—and true, she must have felt grateful, but on the balance, I was the greater beneficiary by far.

I was the one who'd been repaid threefold.

Was there a couple any more poorly matched than us? I couldn't even start to pay her back with something like marshmallows.

"What should we do, Araragi? It'll ruin our plans, but do you want to give this another run if we were both asleep for it?"

"No..." I shook my head. "We'll have plenty more opportunities in the future, so some other time. Let's stick to your plan for today's date."

I tried to stress *in the future*—and while I don't know if this came across, Senjogahara said, "Right, it's not as if we're guaranteed to get tickets for the next show at this point," and stood right up. Briskly, like she hadn't been asleep until just now—I followed her lead, as if to learn from her example.

"So, what are the plans from here?"

"As I said in the car, we're going to learn about contemporary, cutting-edge science in the attached museum. While I don't know about flying cars, they do seem to have lots of different hands-on exhibits."

"Hm. Well, I guess I shouldn't lose interest in studying... It's something we'll have to keep on doing once we're in college."

"Yes. To become an astronaut," Senjogahara said with a smile.

Her smile was difficult to read. Still, even though I didn't know if I'd be accepted, I needed to start thinking about that kind of thing too once I finally became a college student.

That future thing.

College would be four years of trying to find out, because I'd enter not knowing what I wanted to do—but I knew I'd be able to describe the four years as something out of a dream, after spending a year nearly losing that future again and again.

"Do you have dreams for your future?" Senjogahara asked me as we left the planetarium, as if she'd read my mind—dreams for the future.

What an uncomfortable phrase.

"No, not really..."

"Like a job you're aspiring to."

"Can't say I do. I've never even wanted to become a baseball player growing up... I wasn't raised in an environment that made me aspire to work in any kind of profession."

"Well, your parents are in a pretty unique line of work—not that I'm one to talk... I would personally like it if you didn't take after Miss Hanekawa and try to become an expert in yokai extermination out of an admiration for Mister Oshino," Senjogahara stated, though in a reserved way.

I couldn't blame her.

She'd had five terrible experiences with so-called experts in the occult. Nothing could keep her from distrusting that whole endeavor.

Though her return to society was made possible in part by Oshino, that fact and her personal feelings must be two separate things.

"Sure, that's part of it, but I also find it hard to forgive Mister Oshino for being such a bad influence on my angel, Miss Hanekawa. I barely got to cuddle with her during the second half of this school year thanks to that location hunt or whatever she's on."

"..."

That hardly seemed fair.

And *my angel?*

Sure, Hanekawa's future plans did involve roaming the planet after graduation, but Oshino wasn't to blame for her going on a location hunt while still a student.

That was on someone else with the same surname: Ogi Oshino.

Everything that was happening—while not only Mèmè Oshino was away, but just as Tsubasa Hanekawa was as well.

That was now clear.

"Even if it's too late for Miss Hanekawa, I'd at least like to keep you from living that way."

"Well, I don't think I could."

My somewhat vague answer had to do with my suspicion that steering clear of aberrations for the rest of my life would be very difficult, or rather, absolutely impossible.

Given Shinobu Oshino.

I'd never cut ties with aberrations when I considered my relationship with her—even if it meant going to hell.

"I'd be fine with you not working at all, as long as you don't follow in his footsteps. I'll care for you for the rest of my life."

"Aren't people like that called spongers?"

"And I'll be known as a magnanimous woman."

"No, I'm pretty sure people wouldn't be so positive. They'll say I'm a no-good man and you're a no-good woman."

"Bring it on. A sponger and his sucked-dry woman. Seems like a perfect couple to me."

"Perfect in a very sad way…"

Made for each other, we'd deserve each other as well.

Hm.

Having (provisionally) completed my goal of making it through my entrance exams, there were many issues I needed to consider—it made me realize anew that life has lots of checkpoints but no finish line.

Which is exactly why it's so hard to always win in life. You have no choice but to lose at some point—hm? Where did that come from?

Was it something Miss Gaen said?

No, elsewhere. Like a dream I just had—but what kind of dream? Hadn't I not dreamed?

"We'll do a lap of the science museum, and then we'll have lunch. And while we won't be getting fast food, please think of it as just a light snack. A big lunch will interfere with my evening meal, you see," Senjogahara went back to explaining her plan for our date.

It was her father, let us note, that she'd be dining with... She was making lunch with her boyfriend a modest meal to better accommodate an event with Daddy, let us note.

Not that I could do anything to change her mind.

In fact, I needed to cheer her on.

During our first date in June, their relationship was still a rocky one. I wanted to be happy for her if it had improved so much, even if it meant putting up with a little bit of neglect.

Like Tsukihi had said the day before, I'd repaired my relationship with my little sisters, which hadn't been too great in the past, to the point where we could even go out on the town together. I saw this as a positive, and so I understood—just how valuable it is to have a family that gets along.

I wanted the same for Senjogahara.

She needed to value her ties to her father in particular since her mother was out of the picture—that said, I still found it a bit regrettable.

I can't be that understanding of a person.

I hoped our afternoon plans would be enough to make up for our perfunctory lunch—I felt ready to cause a ruckus and a scene if she said they were going to be just as light so she wouldn't be tired out by dinner.

Her professed desire to experience a high school-ish date while still a high schooler was no lie, though.

"Our morning plans were academic in focus, and now our afternoon plans, revolving around fun, await us," she explained. "We'll drive a bit over to town for some bowling and tea during the first half, then karaoke for the second."

"Whoa..." I was moved. Bowling was one thing, but karaoke felt so unlike her that she left me staggered.

"Yes. Well, I came up with the bowling, but I included karaoke on Miss Hanekawa's advice."

"Her advice."

"It seems that according to her, the two of you go to karaoke quite often? How should I describe it—as your girlfriend, I feel like I don't want to lose to Miss Hanekawa, even if it is her."

"…"

Not quite what you called taking someone's advice… How was I going to enjoy our karaoke session when that was her reason?

But I did want to hear Senjogahara sing. I'd allow it.

"And what's with the bowling? Are you…the bowling type?"

"I haven't been since I started high school, but I bowled a lot during middle school, with Kanbaru or celebrating with the track team. I used to carve out some artistic scores, so I felt like revisiting my roots for the first time in a while. What about you, Araragi?"

"Hm?"

"Bowling. What's your high score?"

"Oh, I'm a beginner when it comes to bowling. I don't think I've ever played before, in fact… I'd appreciate your instruction."

"Understood. So we agree? Loser gets punished?"

"You decided that after you found out I'm a beginner."

"Loser shows absolute submission to the winner's commands."

"That's way too harsh!"

To recap.

Her plan for our date seemed to be "Drive → Planetarium → Science Museum → Lunch (light meal) → Drive → Bowling → Move → Tea Time → Move → Karaoke → Disperse." A grueling schedule liable to fill you up, even if that meal was light.

"There were a lot of other places I wanted to go and things I wanted to do… Oh well. Love may be infinite, but time is finite," Senjogahara muttered, sounding dissatisfied with the tough schedule she'd put together herself, including dinner with her father after it all. "I guess it's fine… This may be our last date as high school students, but we can go on all the dates we want after this one. All the dates we want, every morning and every evening, from dawn to dusk. Isn't that right?"

"…"

When she worded it that way, there was only one possible answer.

"Yeah, that's right. Of course."

But I wasn't feeling as confident as I sounded—considering what came next.

When I considered Ogi Oshino.

Nothing was certain.

008

Despite the unbecoming blunder of sleeping in the planetarium, I made no major mistakes after that, and so we—or at least I was able to have a good time.

As far as the science museum goes, I honestly found it more interesting than I expected. It helped that my expected entertainment value was close to zero. The purpose of these facilities demanded that they feature more content for elementary and middle school students (or for families) than for high school students, which had made me nervous. Eighteen year olds like Senjogahara and me were at the most awkward age possible to enjoy it. However, and perhaps I ought to give credit to Hanekawa's advice contributing to our date schedule, the museum was pretty satisfying.

This made my nap in the planetarium all the more frustrating—but as far as that goes, it did allow me to see the rare and valuable sight that is Senjogahara's sleeping face. I decided to tell myself I'd seen a sight greater than any starry sky.

I wasn't off having a great time all on my own, of course. Senjogahara frolicked about as well—okay, maybe you can say she conducted herself just like the science nerd she was, but given how she never used to be open about herself, given how she'd never frolic in the presence of others or in public (or even with her boyfriend), the mere sight of her acting that way provided me with great joy.

"How about one more lap," she suggested quite seriously, her attitude nothing like it was in the planetarium, but I had to tell her no. Not treating her own date plan with due respect seemed like the inevitable drawback or natural flip side of a girl whose calling card was lightning-quick assessments and decisions.

Having fun in the moment and going with the flow was all well and good, but healthy young high schoolers spending the entire day in a science museum until it closed was just too wholesome for me, and I somehow managed to convince her out of that one.

She backed down when I used the day's now oft-repeated, or rather, all-powerful line: *We'll be able to do this as many more times as we want.*

Then, lunch.

She'd called it a light snack, so I kept the hurdles of my expectations low. That must have been her plan all along, though, as she took me to a place with a pretty nice atmosphere.

She said we wouldn't be getting fast food, and the only thing I could point out and jokingly complain about was that it was more of a cafe for women (their customers aside from me being all young ladies). The food tasted good, and it was even very reasonably priced.

If you're curious about any payments that took place during the date, we split them all right down the middle—and while part of me wondered if I should be paying for everything as a man, not just that day but in general (especially when I took her domestic situation into account), Senjogahara was the type of person with a strong aversion to receiving charity, no matter who it came from.

My guess is that this personality trait of hers had to do with a certain conman—perhaps she'd been influenced more deeply by that (mockery of an) expert than Hanekawa was by Oshino.

Though it'd have to be a case of learning from a good example of what not to do.

In any case, we split the payments, if not down to the last yen—well, she might have spent more in the end considering the costs for the rental car and gasoline.

The thought of this being an omen of sponging off of her someday does make me realize that I need to resolve to stay on my toes.

Nothing about Senjogahara seemed sucked dry yet, of course—in any case, while she seemed not to care about cafes and such, she was very much a connoisseur.

Then afternoon came.

The part revolving around fun.

The first half, bowling time—while I'd been terrified to learn that a bet was in place, to cut to the chase, I ended up winning.

"Damn you, Araragi... I can't believe you'd lie to me... You're no beginner at all," Senjogahara hurled complaints my way.

Even the resentment in her eyes was a heartwarming reminder, in its own way, of how rich her facial expressions had become (I was also re-minded of Ononoki's remark that nothing excited her more than seeing someone mad), but for the most part it just brought back scary memories.

It's not like I lied, though. I was a beginner—me being a bowling amateur was the honest truth, I just happened to win anyway. I mean, I'd have preferred to lose if she was going to glare at me like that.

I didn't need something like the right to boss her around.

In fact, Senjogahara only had herself to blame for the loss—it seems her memories had grown rose-tinted.

Artistic scores?

To put it in a somewhat harsher way, she'd only remembered the good parts.

Well, she did show some impressive skills from the first frame to the fifth. Pitching so perfect, I found it surprising that she hadn't brought her own ball.

I don't know exactly what the terms are, something about strikes or turkeys, but in any case, she kept on knocking down all ten pins at once, again and again, until about halfway through the game.

Wow, you're actually serious about this, I joked—and felt indulgent, ready to listen to an order or two in return for getting to see her beautiful form. As for me, I stayed in her shadow racking up a score neither good nor bad, neither impressive nor amusing, just a very average score.

Yet once the sixth frame started, something changed about the way she played—everything changed.

To put it simply, Hitagi Senjogahara's score from the sixth frame onward consisted of nothing but gutter balls.

Her throws were so tired that by the end I wondered if they'd make it to the end of the lane—yes.

In short, Senjogahara got tired.

Apparently her arm went numb.

A lack of endurance and stamina because of her background as a sprinter—must have been part of it, but the real problem must have been a lack of muscle.

Though she tried to put a clever spin on the situation by bowling with her left arm partway through, it wasn't a spin that helped the balls find their target.

And so, as the match progressed, my slowly but steadily growing score caught up, then ultimately overtook hers.

I guess you could say that I made a miracle happen.

Or that baseball doesn't have an exclusive patent on unscripted drama.

"Fine. I'll admit I lost."

Though Senjogahara displayed an unyielding competitiveness that made it clear she was once Kanbaru's direct senior, as a soon-to-be university student (so long as our school didn't find out about her license), she accepted defeat in the end.

"Give me whatever order you want. Come on, what kind of erotic demand are you going to make? My anticipation only grows."

She was being ridiculous. Out of curiosity, I asked her what kind of demand she had planned on making.

"Some kind of erotic demand, what else?!" she barked, seeming upset for whatever reason.

I had to point out that she was expecting the same outcome whoever won—and vaguely recalling that I'd been in a similar situation before, I decided my play would be to say we should walk to tea with our arms intertwined.

Ever after leaving the science museum, the word of the day seemed to be *wholesome*.

Tea time.

Or as they might say in Britain, afternoon tea.

I hate to describe it by price before anything, but it cost more than our lunch—maybe that's just how it goes, and that fact is why Senjogahara seemed to see it as the true main event.

As we elegantly sipped our tea and enjoyed fancy sweets, I took the opportunity to go over the previous day's events. I confessed to Senjogahara why my progressing vampiric transformation had come to a halt, why what should have been an irreversible forward march had become reversible.

There were of course parts I couldn't tell her, so I didn't disclose everything. Still, I shared with her whatever I could.

"Huh...I don't know whether to say it's surprising or typical Araragi behavior that you embarked on an adventure like that on the very morning of your exam...or maybe I should just ask what the hell you're doing."

As I feared, I'd mildly angered her.

Of course, no home tutor would be pleased to hear that her pupil had walked into a college exam with that carefree an attitude, but perhaps she had second thoughts about saying anything too harsh to someone who'd been sent to hell of all places just the day before.

"I'm sure that was very difficult for you," she said, keeping herself at that.

Not that I knew how to react to sympathy, either.

Also, I needed to tell her that it was too early to be using the past tense. It wasn't like everything had come to an end—while I didn't know the details of Miss Gaen's plan, I knew I'd have to play some sort of role.

"Yes, given your blond Lolita-slave and Hachikuji, that's probably true. Hachikuji in particular, since it sounds like she's Miss Gaen's de facto hostage."

I wasn't sure *hostage* was fair (not to mention *blond Lolita-slave*), but she was absolutely right.

It made total sense.

"And Araragi, if you looked at the situation as a balance sheet, you'd find yourself in the red. I suppose you do have to repay your debts... Just as I paid Mister Oshino his fee, however much I hated doing so."

Just how much did she hate him?

That had to be too much hate.

In fact, she seemed to hate him more than ever—had Hanekawa going on her location hunt left Senjogahara that lonely?

In which case, she formed a duo with Hanekawa at this point, not Kanbaru—what would you call that combination?

"But putting aside the issue of what you owe…there are some things I don't understand. What does this Miss Gaen want to do, anyway? What's the goal of her actions—is she doing this as part of a job?"

Pondering those questions left me at a loss for answers—it's not that I didn't have any, of course. I'd heard time and time again from both Miss Gaen and her associates about her goals, or rather, her sense of purpose.

It's just that it was so lofty.

Too lofty for people at my level to understand—to simplify, she must have plotted to subdue this aberration-filled town, but that almost made her sound like some champion of justice.

Justice.

Rightness.

And then you had what came from that rightness—mistakes.

Sacrifices.

Why did it seem like I'd talked about this recently? Super recently, at that…

"To speak from my experience of approaching every day from a risk-management perspective…there's nothing scarier in the world than someone whose goals you don't know," Senjogahara said. "As long as you have a clear view of someone's desires and ambitions, no matter how evil or powerful the person, you can start to come up with a plan."

Though maybe it just means she's an adult with a perspective that's different from little kids like us, she added, concerned.

She still worried about me.

The fact pained me.

Making her heart ache made mine ache as well. That said, I'd promised that I'd keep as few secrets as possible when it came to aberrations, so it wasn't as if I could hide anything from her.

I was causing her so much trouble all because she was going out with a guy like me—but putting it that way was so self-flagellating that it circled around to sounding like a persecution complex.

"I'm not sure what Miss Gaen is fighting against...but it might just be that she's fighting you, Araragi."

Hm? What could that mean?

"No, I'm not trying to tell you anything in particular. It's more like a hunch... I feel like your stance of only seeing what's in front of you can't avoid contradicting Miss Gaen's God's-eye view—or to use a somewhat harsher word, the two conflict."

I couldn't deny it when she worded it that way... Or rather, it had already played out in reality. I took up arms against Miss Gaen's plan to install Shinobu as the deity of the godless Kita-Shirahebi Shrine—causing Sengoku, an unrelated middle schooler, to get wrapped up in the situation. Were you to see this as a conflict between me and Miss Gaen, it'd be scored as a total loss for Koyomi Araragi. One where I ended up with my tail between my legs...

That said, if Miss Gaen was planning something like that again— if she was plotting to install the now-complete Kissshot Acerolaorion Heartunderblade in that shrine, I'd surely take up arms against her again.

It seemed very possible.

Kita-Shirahebi Shrine's predecessor had been located in that park, in an area then known as Shirohebi—in which case, the name meant *water snake*. And if *sea snake* meant the Hydra, all of this wasn't just suggestive or a coincidence, but history itself...

Which would mean.

Hm? Wait, when did I learn that sea snakes meant the Hydra? Weren't they totally different creatures? What was I talking about?

"Well, there's not much I can say on the subject since I'm on your side, Araragi. But to put it in an encouraging way, while most people tend to support an all-encompassing perspective like Miss Gaen's bird's-eye view, I believe humans need a short-term view of a situation just about as much—forgoing a meal today and wondering how to ring in next New Year's Day is nothing short of delusional, right?"

Her words were more consoling than encouraging, but hearing them did make me feel as though I could head into my confrontation with a confident, positive attitude—not that I had any idea who I'd be facing in this still-vague confrontation of mine.

"Now that we've savored our tea, why don't we move on to karaoke? Just to let you know in advance, I don't want you ordering any food. It'd detract from my date with my dad."

Her nighttime plans with her father had at last turned into a date— what kind of a double date was that? Actually, it felt more like a double booking at this point.

"I personally see it as a doubleheader."

Notwithstanding Senjogahara's baseball metaphor, unusual for a girl, we were headed not to the batting cages but a karaoke room.

I guess I'd yet to lose my innocent naïveté—I felt a little flustered being alone with Senjogahara in a small, dimly lit room, but shoving that feeling aside, I focused on her abilities as a vocalist. Incidentally, Hanekawa, a.k.a. the chairman of the world, was a ridiculously good singer.

She made me think I was listening to a CD.

Not only could she tackle her studies perfectly—she'd mastered recreation. I couldn't even go have fun with her if I didn't know what I was doing.

I didn't expect that level of singing from a regular date, though, and was sure that Senjogahara had been to karaoke with Hanekawa in the past. My girlfriend couldn't be thinking about competing with her...

Or so I carelessly thought, but it was of course Senjogahara who demanded concentration and preparation before anything involving fun. Operating the remote control with obvious inexperience, she set the karaoke machine to Score Mode.

Why corner herself like that?!

She wanted to get an objective number out of this!

The machine scores of people's singing and your impression of their skills were pretty disconnected, so I couldn't say for sure, but—I was still going to have a hard time covering for her if her results were poor.

As I thought this...

"We'll have a two-hour face-off. Whoever gets the lower overall score has to show absolute submission to the winner," she said, adding that condition into the mix again.

I see, it was you that I was confronting the whole time...

Did she always love competing this much? Or more importantly, had this girl not learned her lesson after our bowling match?

Though I could learn something from the way she threw caution to the wind, I also didn't know if you could call this a date when she was throwing down so many gauntlets.

I had the creeping suspicion that I was being used as a practice partner for her evening date with her dad... Still, I had to meet her attempt to avenge her earlier loss.

I really am weak when I feel obliged to someone. Or rather, where I have a weakness.

Maybe it was just the weakness of a fool in love.

"I'll bat first. You just sit there and listen," Senjogahara said as she took the mic.

Something about the way she looked reminded me of a person in the grips of desperation.

"What are you talking about, Araragi? I appreciate how you bravely accepted my challenge, but you're going to regret this. Just how many times do you think I've sung the anime's theme song?"

That only went for the anime version.

Unfortunately, it didn't count in print.

And it's not like they're going to animate all the way up to this volume.

As for her song selection, it told me she was serious—I won't give the name because it might cause problems, but in spite of all her bragging, it was easy to sing and presented no hurdles in terms of either key or tempo.

Just how much did she want me to show absolute obedience to her?

It even felt like she was channeling her frustration over losing at bowling—and the result of all this...

"82 points."

Was average.

Well, I'd never used the scoring mode at karaoke before, so I couldn't tell if 82 was an average score, a good score, or a bad score.

For the singer in question, though, apparently it was a hopeless result that left her astonished.

"No way...an 82? That's a failing grade. This is the first score I've gotten in the low eighties in my entire life."

Talk about a model student...

What kind of test could you fail with an 82?

"Is this how you felt through most of high school? This is how it feels to score in the low eighties... I can't believe it. I'd never understood you. I needed to be kinder to you. What horrible things I must have said to you."

She was saying horrible things to me now. Maybe the most horrible thing yet...

I'd rarely managed to score even in the low eighties for the majority of my time in high school. I'd gotten nothing but actual failing grades.

As you might expect, no aspect of her singing was worth needling her over in particular, the karaoke machine's mechanical scoring aside— her ability to neatly complete any task showed that she was a match for Hanekawa.

And I voiced precisely that observation.

"I didn't ask for your condolement," I got in return—an unexpected rejection.

Getting rejected with a word I didn't even know... Did it mean what I think it did?

She really was competitive—my turn came next, but I think we can skip over the details. Nothing is more pathetic than a guy talking about his singing chops, so I'll just present you with my score, the way the machine did.

82.

82 points.

There is a kind of richness to be found in getting a tied score as a young couple on a date, and perhaps some kind of heartwarming message... But when I tried to say something about that, Senjogahara's intense expression and grinding teeth kept any words from leaving my mouth.

She was way too competitive... Or maybe this wasn't about competition, and the simple fact that she'd gotten the same score as me, her pupil, irritated her.

Whatever the case, according to the machine we were evenly matched singing talents.

Not just during the first round, either. Though we didn't score clean ties in the second round and onward, we continued to get just about the same score again and again.

A hard-fought, competitive match if this was some kind of sport, but it was just a karaoke battle, only leaving you with—the despondent feeling of having won by a margin of error.

And so, as a result of margins of error.

I won yet again.

By a difference of three points—how close could you get?

"Impossible... How could I lose to you not once, but twice in one day?"

My girlfriend seemed to look down on me quite a bit—but that was to be expected when I'd always been showing her my pathetic side.

I offered to just call it a draw, but Senjogahara, competition personified, would not surrender her defeat.

"All right, give me whatever order you want," she said.

What integrity.

Well, she needed to know that nothing more than a fine line separated her integrity from reckless abandon...

"This must be my comeuppance for plotting something as underhanded as choosing to go first in the hopes that we'd run out of time during a round before you had a chance to sing," she casually revealed her dirty ruse.

Maybe that was really it.

The gods were watching—that was a shabby ruse for them to watch.

But if we're going to say that, there was no god in our town at the moment—in any case.

The time had come for our date to end. Our last date as high schoolers.

We'd competed twice in the afternoon, and I'd ended up with a two-win streak. There did seem to be a little bit of hostility in the air now, but it felt like we'd made progress in the sense that everything had gone according to plan. There was even a sense of accomplishment and satisfaction.

"Hold on a second, Araragi. Why are you acting like this is over? Don't wrap it all up. You haven't given me an order yet, have you? Make me show my absolute obedience."

...

Well, a promise was a promise. It'd be ridiculous to drag it out, anyway.

That said, the idea of searching my vocabulary to find a demand even more wholesome than walking arm in arm did seem pretty tough.

"What about a bridal carry until we get to the parking lot?" suggested the girlfriend needing to show her absolute obedience.

I had to wonder if this was another case of her getting the same thing whether she won or lost, but maybe it was an acceptable compromise.

"Just to make sure, you know I mean you holding me in a bridal carry, not me carrying you like some sort of princess, right?"

The other way around would make it a groomal carry or something. What a punishment that'd be—though a bridal carry was already punishment enough. However, I'd go along with it because I felt it'd do more damage to Senjogahara than to me.

"Just know that I'm going to kill you if you say I'm heavy."

It'd been so long since I last heard Senjogahara say the words *I'm going to kill you*...but it didn't make them any more romantic.

Her weight aside, I was a bit worried about my arm strength now that I'd lost all traces of my vampirism. It'd be a real problem if I dropped her, so I told her to put her arms around my neck. Then we traveled a few hundred yards to the parking lot in a bridal carry.

"Impressive, Araragi. I can tell you're used to picking up little girls."

That phrasing was going to give people the wrong idea.

Please stop.

"But if Shinobu is all big and busty now, it won't be easy for you to carry her on your back, in your arms, or atop your shoulders. You're going to need to train."

I really didn't see myself carrying around a fully recovered Shinobu... The mental image was a lot.

Chatting, subject to curious glances, the two of us arrived at the parking space where we'd parked our rental car for the afternoon—I at least got her to let me pay for parking.

"Phew. That was embarrassing," Senjogahara said as soon as she was in the driver's seat.

That was her impression of my bridal carry?

Not that I could do much but agree...

"I caught a glimpse of hell there."

She was going that far?

But I guess hell hadn't been as hellish.

There was nothing left to do but head back now—seeing Senjogahara drive made me feel like maybe I should get a license too, and not just because she'd told me to.

Of course, the joy she seemed to be feeling might not have come from driving, but from thoughts of her upcoming date with Daddy...

Well, even if you do have a license, you need a car before you can go out whenever you feel like it... I didn't know about going through the trouble of renting a car, either.

We just had to head back now—or so I say, but just in time, I remembered I had something I needed to tell her.

At first, I thought I needed to tell her at the start of the day, and it was in fact something I needed to tell her at the start of the day, but regrettably I'd lost my chance, overwhelmed by her acquisition of a driver's license.

She hadn't said anything, so the wicked notion that I might get away with not saying it did pass through my mind for a moment, but I of course couldn't do that.

"Senjogahara," I began abruptly, "there's something important I have to tell you."

"If you're going to ask me to marry you, my answer is sure."

"No, not that important. And that was way too ready of you. Actually, it's about reciprocating for those chocolates you gave me during Valentine's Day... I couldn't get anything for you." I'd run over different ways of putting it, but in the end, I just had to give her the honest truth. "I'm sorry, I didn't have time to get anything. I kept thinking about it until I realized I'd overthought it... I might have been able to get you some off-the-shelf marshmallows in time if I really tried, but I didn't know about that, either... And I kept overthinking things until I'd over-overthought them, and I was paralyzed..."

Finding an opening today and buying them seemed like an option, but no such luck—I shouldn't have expected any gaps when I was dealing with Senjogahara. The planetarium had offered an opportunity...but I was sleeping just like her then.

"So could you wait for another two or three days? I'll be sure to add interest."

"Oh, you were worrying yourself over something like that? Forget it. Interest? I know just how much you hate special days, Araragi." In contrast to my own tenseness, Senjogahara's response was muted. "It'd sound bad if I said I wasn't expecting anything, but it's not like I thought you had something for me. Spending a whole day on this date with me is enough. If you feel like giving me something, then give me something. It's not like I made you chocolates expecting anything in return."

Though I had trouble accepting this from someone as fussy about her debts as Senjogahara, maybe gifts weren't a part of that from the start.

"In fact, I was only able to build this relationship with you because you hate special days—remember? We started dating on Mother's Day."

"Oh, now that you mention it..."

I did remember. I also recalled that I'd gotten in a fight with my little sisters over whether or not I'd celebrate Mother's Day. I'd bolted out of our house.

I saw now how childish I'd been...but I happened to encounter Senjogahara in that park eventually.

And after that, she told me she liked me.

Oh.

It really was my dislike of Mother's Day that led to me dating Senjogahara—and I couldn't help but feel that relationships are such an odd thing.

To think that a fight with my little sisters would come to hold that much importance... Considering that I got along somewhat well with them now, I did sometimes look back in regret and wish that I'd started acting friendlier with them sooner. If I had, though, I wouldn't have run into Senjogahara, or even Hachikuji, that day...

How profoundly odd.

If mistakes were inevitable on an unyielding path of righteousness, were they also capable of leading to what's right?

...Had I also heard this line of thinking somewhere before?

"Don't worry, I'm not going to become the kind of annoying girl who demands that her boyfriend celebrate every special day... I'm the only one who needs to remember anniversaries, anyway. Like how you caught me on May eighth, and how I told you how I feel and started dating you on May fourteenth, and how we went on our first date and had our first kiss on June thirteenth, and how we had our first French kiss on..."

"I'd say you're being plenty annoying!"

Or just scary.

Of course, it may have had to do with her excellent memory instead.

"Sadly, even though we've been in the same class since our first year of high school, I don't remember my first impression of you... I do remember that you always got in fights with Miss Oikura. Do you know of any good way to alter my memories to say that I'd always had a crush on you? Maybe I should falsify my diary."

"I remember you during first year well... You were like a cloistered princess."

"What? Are you going to say you always had a crush on me?"

"I won't go that far..."

There's no way to change the past, so we'd have to rely that much more on our hopes for the future—but in any case, while I could deal with complaints or anger over not having a present ready for Senjogahara, I was just relieved that she didn't feel hurt.

"It's okay. I'm getting a White Day gift from my dad."

Those words gave me pause, but even so, I was glad we didn't seem to have a problem.

She said I could give her something if I felt like it, and of course I was going to feel like it. I appreciated this grace period—in fact, I'd also received chocolates from Hanekawa, as a friend, so I needed to think of what to get her as well. (Did you need to give friends three times as much back too?) If she'd be back by graduation, I needed to have Senjogahara's ready by then too. I'd called it a grace period, but it was just a day or two long at most.

"Mmh."

And then, the moment I relaxed.

Something seemed to come to Senjogahara—and she immediately stepped on the brakes and stopped the car on the side of the road. From the passenger's seat, though, I didn't know what it was, and gulped at the abrupt, surging twist.

"Araragi," Senjogahara said—her tone changed.

Deeper, deeper, deeper, deep.

I could sense none of the tolerance she'd been showing.

"I don't think I can forgive this."

"Huh?"

"To think you have nothing at all for your girlfriend on White Day, of all days, one of the three great lovers' days. I can't help but doubt your love."

"Huh? Whaa?"

"I've heard of men who stop caring about girls the moment they start dating, but I never imagined you were one of them. I'm so disappointed. I couldn't hide my dejection even if I wanted to. I'd been waiting all day to see just what kind of surprise you had for me, my heart pounding, fluttering, and trembling all at once, yet you hadn't prepared anything at all. It'd be generous to describe this as you giving me the slip. I'd convinced myself you'd at least give me a cabin cruiser."

"W-Wouldn't you say your expectations were a bit too mega-sized?"

"Ahh. Maybe I'll kill myself."

Senjogahara jokingly leaned against the steering wheel—she'd added so much flair to her performance that it just looked like a skit to me now...

I wanted to tell her to learn from Tadatsuru's example. He'd shown me what a true farce is.

What could have come to her to launch this one-woman sideshow? I wondered, but I certainly couldn't ignore it.

"S-Sorry, but that's why I'm apologizing," I had to respond. "Please don't kill yourself. O-Okay, then what'll it take for you to forgive me? I can't get you a pleasure boat, but if it's anything I can do..."

I of course couldn't help but find it strange that she'd flipped around on something she'd already forgiven, but when it came down to it, I was the one in the wrong here without a doubt. I had to take my lumps like a training dummy.

"Did you just say you'd do anything?" Senjogahara pounced.

Seizing on my words—as if I'd played right into her hand.

Why did she look the happiest I'd seen her all day... If this made her happier than anything, what exactly had we been doing today?

"Did you just say absolute submission?"

"N-No, I didn't say that?"

"..."

"I did. I did say it. Those were the exact words out of my mouth, absolute submission."

By the way, when Senjogahara was "..."-ing, she looked like she was going to cry. Her face was becoming so expressive, she'd be able to find work as a quick-change artist.

But now I understood, this was how desperate she was to force me into absolute submission—she'd used this opportunity to try whatever she'd been attempting during bowling and karaoke.

Maybe not the intertwined arms, but the bridal carry did seem like she'd gotten what she wanted, though... Did she really want to demand something from me so much that she was willing to go back on her forgiveness? What terrible tenacity.

Did she want to make some kind of erotic demand? No, looking back on it now, that must have been a spur-of-the-moment joke...

"I see. Yes, that's the kind of generous man I fell in love with. You've won my heart all over again."

"..."

It seemed that I'd managed to accomplish my goal of recaptivating my girlfriend's heart at the last possible moment. But I couldn't be mindlessly happy when these could be, well, my last moments...

"You don't even know what I'm going to request, and you still said you'd swear absolute obedience to it for the rest of your life."

"The rest of my life?!"

Didn't life-long absolute obedience go beyond the definition of a request? I'd call that signing myself into slavery, or maybe giving her carte blanche over my life, or whatever else you'd call giving Hitagi Senjogahara an unthinkable amount of control.

N-No. I was going to believe in her.

I would believe in Hitagi Senjogahara, my girlfriend.

Who wasn't the problematic person she once was.

She wouldn't ask for anything absurd! Though it was already pretty absurd if she wanted me to follow it for the rest of my life.

"Y-Yeah. The rest of my life. Okay. What do I need to do?"

"Call me by my name."

For the rest of your life, Senjogahara said—her expression changed. She simply blushed.

"I want you to use my name."

"What? I already do. I call you Senjogahara, don't I?"

"No, I mean my first name. Just my first name."

"..."

Her request.

It must've been something she couldn't make happen during our first date—and that she wanted to make happen while we were still high school students.

As boyfriend and girlfriend.

So that's why she set up punishments during bowling and karaoke. This was what she wanted.

Yes, it would become a high school regret.

Yes, it was embarrassing after all this time.

Something she could only say given the opportunity—absolute obedience for the rest of my life.

I'd keep calling her by her first name for the rest of my life.

I—I wanted to, just as much.

I wished for it just as much.

"Hitagi."

Thank you, Koyomi.
I didn't need to say another word for Hitagi to understand how I felt—and so she did the same for me.

009

The epilogue, or maybe, the punch line of this story.

I escorted Hitagi back to her home—or rather, I just sat in her passenger's seat, so I guess she was doing the escorting—before walking back to the Araragi residence in the now fully darkened night, only to experience déjà vu.

A feeling—that this had happened the day before, too.

To expand, a shadowy figure lay in wait for me in front of my home—it was too dark for me to make out the perp's identity, but it couldn't have been Hitagi, as we'd just parted ways.

Who could it be, I thought as I approached. Had Ononoki worried about me and come out? Or maybe it was my sisters? And then I saw.

The dark shadow—was Ogi Oshino.

It was Ogi.

"Hey there—I've been waiting for you. I've gotten tired of waiting for you. I've gotten tired just waiting for you," she said, sounding like her uncle—she was wearing the same easy, flippant smirk too. "How was it? Did you enjoy your last date with Miss Senjogahara? I did try to be considerate, and kept from forcing my way into the real world. I think that deserves some gratitude," she appended with a shrug.

"I am grateful…but why call that our last date? It was just our last date as high schoolers."

"Is it, now. Yes, that'd be nice—it'd be nice if you two had a future."

"…"

"Oh, don't get me wrong. I really do feel that way, you know. Please don't twist my words around. Despite all I am. It's just that I have these silly thoughts that there may be a number of factors that could call that into question—okay? Whatever happens, though, I can't imagine you having any regrets."

Ha haa, laughed Ogi.

And then.

"Hey, Araragi-senpai?" she continued. "There's one thing I wanted to ask you, just for reference—what are you planning on doing next?"

"What's that supposed to mean?"

"Well, exactly what I said. Don't overthink it. The question is a changed-around version of what being right means—or maybe a change-up, or maybe an extrapolation."

"An extra…"

"And I suppose a case of extra innings."

What does it mean to be right.

That's it. She'd asked me before—and told me we'd pick it back up when we met again.

Where could she have said that?

If not in the real world—then in a dream?

Or maybe in hell?

"Ogi. Did you try to get rid of me? Did you ask an expert to do something like that?"

"Oh, did someone tell you that? A groundless rumor like that? What a sad piece of misinformation—please allow me to explain myself. I would never do anything to harm you," Ogi replied, her voice calm, showing no signs of being shaken. "Remember what I said? I'm expecting you to make the right decision, and walk away and not fall for Miss Gaen's sweet talk."

"You did?"

Well, if she was saying she said it, she must have.

Even if she hadn't, my reply would be the same. I only had one answer to give her, whether it was right or wrong.

"But I can't—abandoning Shinobu and Hachikuji isn't a choice I can make. There's no room for choice, no room in my heart for that. I might not know what it means to be right, but I do know the path I need to take."

"I do wish you wouldn't rush to conclusions—but, well, I suppose so. I wasn't expecting a positive reply, I just thought I'd try asking. Still, it's disappointing," Ogi said, not sounding the least bit disappointed. "Personally, I'd ask you to bow out around now—would I be overstepping my boundaries if I insisted? Oh, by the way. May I correct you about something you might be getting wrong?"

"Something I'm getting wrong? Like...what?"

"*I'm not the Darkness.*"

"⁉"

I was surprised—but I think I managed to hide it.

I had trouble keeping my composure, though.

The shock came not so much from the words themselves but the fact that Ogi was speaking them.

This junior of mine had made plenty of borderline statements—but this one stepped right over the line.

Almost like a declaration of war, like a signal announcing the start of a battle.

Yet she showed no sign of realizing that she'd made an extraordinarily important statement.

"By the way," she changed the subject with ease. The way she switched topics was so skillful that I almost believed I'd misheard her earlier words. "Do you not have anything for me?"

"Hm? Uh...have any what?"

"Any White Day presents for me. I gave you chocolates, remember? Godivas."

"Godivas..."

Had she given me something that expensive?

I had no recollection, but if she said she did, I must have just forgotten about it—how pathetic of a boy was I to have forgotten?

"Ha haa. From the looks of it, you must not have anything for me—too bad," Ogi lamented, actually looking disappointed this time.

The sight made my heart ache.

"In that case, why don't I make a request of you instead, the way Miss Senjogahara did—what do you say?"

I didn't know how she'd learned about the agreement we'd made as a couple, but how could I say no? I couldn't make light of it, whatever it might be. If her request was for me to bow out, though, I of course intended to reject it flat-out.

But Ogi's request was of a different kind altogether—or maybe along the same line, but in the exact opposite direction.

"You may have no regrets now that you've gone to hell and on a date—but I still have one regret when it comes to this town."

"A regret?"

"A regret. Business left unfinished—that I was born in order to finish. I have a firm purpose, and a firm sense of purpose."

Surprising as that may be, Ogi said.

I listened in silence.

To her purpose. To her sense of purpose.

"I'm prepared to die to accomplish it—do you have a goal you'd be willing to die for? I do. Just one more. Which is why I have to accomplish it, whatever it takes—but that's why Izuko Gaen, the boss of all the experts, would pick this one place to lay a trap. Yes, I know. I know, and yet my only option is to set off this trap—I just have to suck it up and accept the counterattack."

"..."

"In other words, I'm about to go face-to-face and fight the lady who knows everything, no tricks involved—Araragi-senpai. Could you side with me when I do?"

Please save me, Ogi Oshino said with an innocuous smile.

CHAPTER SEVEN
OGI DARK

001

The present exists thanks to Ogi Oshino's presence—I, and we, have been able to make it to now because that enigmatic, unidentifiable mystery wrapped in a mystery stayed here in our town.

We have the present—as well as a future.

I'm sure the day will come when I'm able to see things that way— I can't yet, and I find it hard to believe that day will ever come when I consider what she did, what she carried out, but I'm certain that in the future, I will look back on her in that way.

That's the kind of person I am.

And that's who she is, too.

Ogi Oshino.

I'll remember her and think—she symbolized my youth.

Yes—I think the very first thing I'll recall when I reminisce about Koyomi Araragi during his high school days will not be Hitagi Senjogahara, nor Suruga Kanbaru, nor Shinobu Oshino or Mayoi Hachikuji, but Ogi Oshino's smile.

I had no idea what she was thinking.

What was so funny.

I didn't know her goals or her history.

The grinning girl's smile.

No, I already knew at that moment exactly why she always smiled so much—she must have been amused by my folly.

I was a great source of amusement, a fool who couldn't begin to see who she really was—in fact, it's hard not to smirk.

I find myself smiling.

I find myself bursting into laughter.

So maybe it was all a laughing matter in the end.

The way I spent my youth.

The way I spent my last year in high school.

The year that began with a chance encounter with a legendary vampire—that trying, tragic, painful, ugly, hopeless year that I'd look back on some day.

And talk about to someone, convey to everyone.

Tell the tale of.

As a laughing matter to be told with a smile, a shallow narrative of self-love—perhaps.

"Perhaps? I think we already know the answer to that—not that I know," I know Ogi would say. "It's you who knows—Araragi-senpai."

Yes.

I did know—I must have even known Ogi Oshino's true identity very well, from the very start.

Laughable, isn't it?

002

If I closed my eyes and thought back, I could recall many of the varied surreal images that I'd encountered over the past year—I don't plan to list them all out after we've come this far, but the sight I faced this night, which is to say the night of March fourteenth, after my date with Hitagi ended and the sun had set, could not be outdone by any of them as a summation of surreality.

I was in a park.

Yes—a park whose name I didn't know how to read for the longest time, which turned out to be not *Rohaku* or *Namishiro*, but *Shirohebi* due to misreadings and misprints throughout the years. I'd discovered it was Shirohebi Park a day ago, when I was in the depths of hell, but in any case, this sight was found in the park's plaza.

A game of baseball.

Or maybe I should call it a pretend game of baseball, since they were far from having enough people on each team—in any case, the roles of pitcher, batter, and catcher had been assigned as three individuals amused themselves by playing at baseball.

Baseball in the park.

That in itself could be called wholesome, but the characters at play and their tools made the scene surreal. A kind of surreality lacking in reality.

The pitcher was Miss Izuko Gaen.

A lady who despite donning a baseball cap-esque cap also wore loose and baggy clothing that seemed unsuited to any athletic endeavor. Someone with a thin body and, despite her youthful looks, a full-fledged adult you'd never expect to see playing innocently in a park.

The batter was Shinobu Oshino.

While it'd be one thing if she was playing in the little-girl form she'd taken until not long ago, she was now a woman of exceptional beauty, tall with long limbs and long blond hair, in a gorgeous dress, so dazzling she literally drew your eyes to her. What's more, she wore stiletto heels as she held a metal bat and waited on one leg for the ball to come, the very picture of a sewing machine on a dissecting table. So unbalanced it seemed like a dissecting table on a sewing machine.

I made one mistake there. A thoughtless mistake.

Not a bat. The long object she held in her hands as if she was going to row a boat with it was no metal bat—it was a Japanese greatsword.

A blade that even an amateur could tell was forged by a master.

Its name Kokorowatari, commonly known as the Aberration Slayer.

In that sense, she did appear to be a demon wielding a metal bat, but more the type you'd expect to see in hell—a genuine vampire who had regained her full nature, healthy in body and spirit this eve as she looked truly refreshed playing this night game.

That said, this king of the aberrations did appear to be fine the morning before on the grounds of Kita-Shirahebi shrine, so the noble and legendary and all-powerful vampire—the iron-blooded, hot-blooded, yet cold-blooded vampire in her complete form seemed to endure the sun's rays just fine so long as her defense was up.

"C'mon now, pitcher. You're looking scared to me."

The individual who pounded her mitt while for some reason aggressively heckling the pitcher, the position to whom she should have been playing the role of a loving wife, was the only one of the three whose age didn't make her out of place playing baseball in a park. A young girl, with pigtails—Mayoi Hachikuji.

She played catcher despite wearing a skirt, crouching down with her knees spread and showing the whole world her underwear.

How to explain it. Maybe her guard was too far down?

Seeing those panties brought me no joy at all.

In fact, in terms of bare fundamentals, she should have at least taken off her backpack when playing baseball—or maybe it was the backpack that allowed her to maintain her balance despite her unstable pose.

This sight was already as surreal as can be, but what made it super-surreal was the fact they used a rock of reasonable size as their ball.

A rock?

They were throwing rocks and hitting them with swords?

What kind of a baseball game was this?

I know that it's often described as a duel, but they were taking it too far.

As a common, upstanding citizen, I wanted to report this sight to the authorities the moment I saw it, but it involved people I knew—or rather, it consisted only of people I knew, so my plan was to pretend not to see it, turn around, and head back. I could even try to meet up with Senjogahara during her daddy date, but—

"Nope," the tween girl next to me said.

Ononoki stopped me—her fingers scissoring my sleeve. Stopped in such an adorable way, even someone as renowned for his bravery as myself couldn't help but halt.

To say nothing of the fact that Ononoki possessed great and powerful strength in spite of looking like a cute little doll. Even a scissoring of my clothes with her fingers had enough stopping power to make it feel like I'd been pinned to the ground by a stake.

"Aren't you settling this tonight?"

"Well, yeah…"

"I can't be of any help to you now that Big Sis is gone—but I will at least watch you fight, kind monster sir. So," said Ononoki, *Let's hurry up and join their circle.*

Though it seemed one would need extraordinary courage to join this circle, I couldn't cower, urged by a girl who appeared to be half my size, regardless of whatever resided in her.

I stepped on the field—or rather, into the park's plaza.

"Ah! Why, if 'tis not my master!"

Shinobu seemed to be the first to notice.

Beautiful, graceful, shining there in her elegance—this gorgeous blond woman with a perfect body who simply could not be captured in full by any number of flowery words gave me an innocent wave of her hand (well, of her sword) as she called to me, so of course I felt embarrassed, or rather, just flustered.

"How late ye are! How we've awaited thee—we were playing cricket courtesy of all the time we found on our hands!"

So it was cricket? The progenitor of baseball? You could say without exaggeration that I didn't know a thing about cricket as a sport.

"Ha!"Haha!"Hahahaha!" she laughed.

Shinobu came running over, held me up in her arms, and spun me around—kind of like a professional wrestler's giant swing, or even the way an adult would play with a child, but there existed such a difference in height between the two of us now that this was possible.

I had found our physiques reversed.

And aren't you in high spirits today, Miss Shinobu.

The last time I saw her this excited may have been back during spring break.

I recalled how that past excitement, too, expressed the joy of having regained her full abilities... It seemed that being complete is something to be happy about.

As Shinobu literally threw me around, Hachikuji and Ononoki looked on with choice expressions.

Me getting my just desserts, the sight of me being treated the way I always treated them, may have felt more pathetic than anything.

Maybe like the feeling of seeing someone scary with power over you kowtowing to someone even scarier with even more power? In that sense, though, this treatment may have been justifiable revenge from Shinobu's perspective.

An exhilarating tale of revenge.

To the point that I almost enjoyed it.

Of course, in some ways I couldn't even complain if she'd gone the full nine yards and carried me in her arms and on her back, considering the way I used to treat the young Shinobu.

Now that she'd returned to her full form, though, it seemed that her heart may have grown as big as the rest of her; she released me after having her fill.

Shinobu had mentioned earlier that her outward appearance affected her behavior, so as sad as it was for me, it seemed she couldn't talk to me the way she did while she was a little girl.

Then again, given that she now appeared to be twenty-seven years old, it'd be beyond ultra-surreal if she acted like that little girl.

That Shinobu was gone, but she now felt like a high-spirited cousin I was meeting during summer break.

"H-Hachikuji…"

Though fully toyed with, played with, and robbed of my balance, I still reached out to the young girl before me—but come to think of it, Hachikuji had passed out as soon as I kidnapped her out of hell, so this would in fact be the first time in six months that I was facing her in the real world.

I was very disappointed that I couldn't hug her like always thanks to the way the world spun around me.

"I think you did that more than enough back in hell, didn't you, Mister Dark-and-Stormy?"

"However cool that sounds, Hachikuji, don't make me sound like the opening of a Gothic novel. You'll give people the wrong idea. My name is Araragi."

"I'm sorry. A slip of the tongue."

"No, you're doing it on purpose…"

"A tip of the tongue."

"Or maybe not?!"

"A foul tip when she swung."

"I guess that's something you'd care about as a catcher, but still!"

Fortunately, our time apart seemed to have no effect at all on this interaction of ours.

Though we did also do this in hell.

"I thought you'd be close to out of ways your tongue could slip, but I guess there's more than expected…"

"I have to say, it really does hit home in a different way when it's

223

real-world."

"Could you not call the world of the living *real-world*?"

What was hell then, virtual reality?

Like the way you called a brick-and-mortar bookseller a *real book-store* these days?

I couldn't support it.

"It's nice to see you again as well, Miss Ononoki. Thank you for your earlier kindness."

"Yeah. I'm glad you're back," Ononoki said.

I didn't know what kind of position she took as she made this reply (even whether or not she was talking down to Hachikuji)—but right, it had also been a full half-year since the two had met like this.

Though I was ecstatic at the time over the tween girl, little girl, and young girl having assembled in one place (what kind of a person was I?), Shinobu had completed a sudden growth spurt, and looked different.

Speaking of which, though, I wondered—there was something I needed to check on. In fact, I should have checked the previous day.

I reached out toward Hachikuji's chest.

She ran away.

"What's wrong, Hachikuji?"

"I ought to be asking the same about your brain. Why were you so calmly attempting to grab a handful of my still-growing bosom?"

"No, I was just wondering how your body was doing—I grabbed you out of hell without thinking, but does that mean you're alive again like me? Or could it be that…"

"That's right, Koyomin. It could be."

From up on the pitcher's mound, Miss Gaen had been watching our little skit like an adult—not that she stood on any physically raised ground—but now she interrupted us.

Given her position, it felt like she'd picked me off.

"I'm sad to report that in Hachikuji's case, her body has been cremated, you see—heh, but she might be a nasty sight had she been buried. Like a zombie, or maybe a jiangshi—but in any case, she is now a ghost, just as she was when you first met her in this park."

A ghost.

She dropped the rock she held straight onto the ground as she said this.

"I made sure to take a close look into the situation today because of the possibility this raises. Around the time you and Miss Senjogahara were on your love-date, Koyomin."

"Love-date..."

What a way to put it.

It wasn't anything that saccharine, either.

It was a little more bloodcurdling than that. Bizarre would be another word.

Still, I understood—of course it wouldn't be that picture-perfect. Then again, depending on how you saw it, you could debate whether Hachikuji coming back to life was a good thing or a bad thing—she'd died eleven years ago, so even if she did return to life after all this time, she'd be just as lost in the world as she was as a ghost.

In fact, she may have had even fewer places to go had she come back to life and been bound to a physical body.

Still.

It was better than hell, right? I thought so but—

"Still, Hachikuji. I'm sorry," I bowed my head to her. Or maybe I should say I hung my head in shame. "I brought you back here without thinking—but now that I am thinking about it, I ruined the six months of work you did stacking rocks in children's limbo. Jizo or some other figure should've come and reincarnated you if you'd kept at it..."

And yet, I forced Hachikuji to escape all because I couldn't bear to see her like that—and yet, she would be the one paying any price for my actions, not me.

A punishment she wouldn't have even brought upon herself this time around.

"It's fine, Mister Araragi. There's no need for you to worry—I've already discussed that matter with Miss Gaen and come to a deal."

"A deal?"

With Miss Gaen?

Hearing this brought a wave of anxiety over me—making me look back at Miss Gaen, but she only shrugged, as if to play stupid.

"I'm not bothered in any way by you rescuing me," Hachikuji continued. "Hell was indeed hell. If I'm being honest with you, when I saw that thread of salvation dangling down from the heavens, I wanted to climb it so badly I even thought about pushing you aside."

"That's a pretty terrible thought you had."

Social climbers are bad enough, but that?

She must be joking, of course—I had trouble ridding myself of my guilty conscience even after hearing this.

"All right, we can cover that as well, so why don't we get this briefing started—Koyomin did show up, after all. Let's get through this fast, since we're going to wrap everything up today. So for now, Koyomin—do you think you could order your beautiful, all-grown-up slave to stop bullying my junior's shikigami?"

I looked over.

And found Shinobu Oshino throttling Yotsugi Ononoki for no discernible reason. For no good reason at all, in fact—just as Ononoki feared, Shinobu seemed to be in the midst of paying her back for the verbal abuse she'd suffered in the summer.

I take back my previous statement.

Whatever form she took, adult or complete, whatever the case, whatever the situation, my partner seemed to always have the same nasty personality.

003

While I guess it'd be an overstatement to call us bitter enemies brought together by fate, I couldn't help but feel that we were a ragtag bunch—still, you could also call our group an all-star cast, considering how incredible its members were. The unavoidable incohesive feeling among us, though, must have come from something between us—the way our differences contrasted so poorly.

Shinobu Oshino—a perfected legendary vampire who had flown in from overseas.

Mayoi Hachikuji—a ghost who'd returned from hell.

Yotsugi Ononoki—a shikigami of a corpse doll whose master had absconded.

Izuko Gaen—an expert aberration exterminator, and the big boss of those in her field.

Then there was me, Koyomi Araragi, former human, former vampire, and current human—it was hard to tell whether our interests lined up with one another or not, or whether we all acted with the same purpose, so I guess if you took an objective look at us, we were nothing but a bunch of weirdos gathered in a park.

"Don't worry, I haven't forgotten to put a barrier up. No outsiders will be able to enter. We've got this place to ourselves for the time being," Miss Gaen said with cheer.

A barrier, huh… I'd gotten pretty used to hearing that word.

We all moved from the plaza to the benches.

Miss Gaen sat Ononoki on her lap.

Her expressionless face made it hard to tell, but Ononoki did seem a bit uncomfortable—I wasn't sure whether or not dolls had feelings, but that feeling did come across to me.

As someone in a similar situation, sitting on the adult Shinobu's lap, her arms around me.

I could find no excuse to reject this position as I'd regrettably done the same thing to Shinobu countless times in the past. Still, being held on an older woman's lap when I was about to graduate high school did make me feel self-conscious, or embarrassed, or stop it Hachikuji I don't want you looking at me like that.

Shinobu had wrapped her arms around my torso like it was the most natural thing to do in the world, holding me tight and making sure she didn't drop me—her chin resting on top of my head.

Miss Gaen held Ononoki, Shinobu held me, and Hachikuji sat alone on the bench—there were only five of us, of course, so one would be left out by necessity if we formed two-person groups. I still wanted to place Hachikuji on the lap of my now-held body and hold her myself, but she may have been wary about that exact possibility, as she'd placed herself some distance away from me, in a position that my immobile self couldn't reach as if to say she welcomed being left out.

We were a strange enough group to begin with, but our arrangement was bizarre as well. I could see why Miss Gaen put a barrier up, because someone could have very easily called the authorities on us at first glance otherwise.

"Okay, then. Now I'm going to disclose the plan I've spent yesterday and today painstakingly putting together to all of you—and I'd appreciate it if you do as I say, but I of course won't force you to. There is something I want to check before that, though. Did you bring what I told you to bring, Koyomin?"

"I did. Still, this thing was yours to begin with, so I only wanted to return it to you… I don't know what you're thinking, but I want you to know that I didn't bring this thing here because I agree with whatever it is you are thinking," I said, taking out a long envelope and handing it to Miss Gaen—in fact, it was something I'd tried to rip up and throw away many times before, but couldn't. I didn't have the courage, and I doubt I had the skill.

Perhaps Shinobu could eat its contents, now that she was back to her full strength—but that too was a thought that inspired fear and trembling.

Because what the thing sealed.

Was—a god.

"Yes. That's fine with me, Koyomin. What I'm expecting from you is one of your miracles that not even reason can explain," the lady who knows everything said, as though she knew it all, and removed the contents of the envelope—a talisman.

A paper amulet with a snake drawn on it.

No plain amulet, as its effects had already been tested and proved— an all-powerful amulet that once took Nadeko Sengoku, an everyday middle schooler, and made her ascend into becoming a snake god.

A slip of paper entrusted to me by Miss Gaen immediately after the events following summer break. I'd failed to make full use of it.

It'd sound cooler if I said I didn't use it out of choice, but in reality, I got cold feet and was too afraid to use it.

"Yes, indeed—it's well preserved. It seems you took good care of it," Miss Gaen said, slipping the removed *ofuda* right into her pocket. She handled it roughly—without care. I guess she wouldn't be afraid of doing so as an expert, though... Wait, but shouldn't she be paying more respect to it as an expert?

I just couldn't understand her stance.

"Hmph," Shinobu breathed.

As if she felt somewhat disgusted—she'd suffered because of that amulet back when she had a child's body, and maybe she'd remembered those times.

Or so I thought, but that didn't seem to be the case.

"Really—'twas exactly as thou saidst. In fact, how could I not have noticed? It did take place quite far in the past, of course—and I did not want to recall it, either," she said, not making any sense to me.

It seemed that Hachikuji hadn't been the only one to *come to a deal* with Miss Gaen while I was off on my date with Senjogahara—I couldn't help but feel a little left out now.

So I was the one on the outside, not Hachikuji.

I wondered if Ononoki might be feeling the same way, but she remained expressionless, looking absentminded if anything.

Maybe she didn't care either way.

"No need for ye to fret—'tis not as though I've heard everything myself. Merely the essentials—and I decided to wait until we met before hearing this expert's detailed plans on what she will do next, in particular," Shinobu said, as if she'd sensed my alienation—regardless of the fact that our physical and spiritual link had been severed.

"That's right. And also, I was still piecing together my stratagems during the daytime, so I couldn't talk about them even if I'd wanted to—I only finished planning just now after hearing about the situation from Hachikuji and Shinobu."

I'm sorry to say I had trouble believing Miss Gaen—I even doubted whether this soon-to-be disclosed plan she'd *spent yesterday and today putting together* was even that.

At this point, I wouldn't have been surprised if she said this had been her plan ever since August—but who was making me think something like that? Ogi?

Ogi Oshino.

"Ogi Oshino," Miss Gaen began. "She is the enemy we will now face—the opponent we must fight. The target we must eliminate, and the object we must detest—right, Koyomin?"

"..."

Enemy. I couldn't help but feel uncomfortable when I heard her say the word out loud—I just couldn't get the image of her as one of my juniors out of my head.

Regardless of what Tadatsuru said.

And—whatever she herself said.

"Ye seem unsurprised. Had ye known from the start, after all?" Shinobu said as she held me tight from behind, but sadly she was off the mark here—and giving me too much credit. I'd never once doubted

Ogi.

But.

Just maybe, I had known.

I didn't know anything.

But maybe I knew about Ogi.

I thought this as I felt Shinobu at my back.

"..."

Ononoki maintained her silence.

Maybe she knew her place, held there on the lap of the woman who was her owner's senior, Miss Gaen, and was holding back...but that didn't seem to be in Ononoki's personality.

I could see her interrupting our conversation as she pleased wherever she was sitting, especially after all the influence the uninhibited characters who were my little sisters had on her.

"This is a very important point, though... We must not forget that the name Ogi Oshino is merely an expedient. The most haphazardly chosen of aliases—no, it wouldn't be accurate to call it an alias, but something like a user ID selected in order to avoid being bound by a name."

Bound by a name?

That was—something I'd heard before.

When Kissshot Acerolaorion Heartunderblade lost her existence as such—she had been given the new name of Shinobu Oshino, a name by which she was bound, or something. It did seem that this binding continued to be in effect even now that she'd regained her existence, though...

"You see, Ogi Oshino's true essence is found in that unknowability—the lone trait we could say she has is the way she loses her own identity... Well, even *she*, the pronoun we've been using here, doesn't have any true meaning to it."

"You almost sound like you know Ogi, Miss Gaen, but you've never actually met her before, right?" I asked.

A question I'd been wanting to ask.

Considering the chain of events until this point—and considering what Ogi had told me, there shouldn't have been any direct contact between the two.

Of course, as someone who knows everything, perhaps Miss Gaen should have been talking about Ogi in this way—but I couldn't help but feel a little disgusted to hear her talk about someone I knew as though she knew her better than I did.

I admit the feeling was closer to jealousy than anything.

"I haven't. Because she's been avoiding me—or for a better way to put it, those kinds of beings don't appear in front of people like me, who live their lives never digressing from their duty."

"...?"

"But while I haven't met her, *it's not as if I don't know her*—there are a lot of things I need to explain to you, Koyomin, this included, but why don't we start from the beginning? We don't have much time, and I'm only going to explain this once, so listen carefully."

Having said this much, Miss Gaen pulled out a smallish tablet. It seemed that as usual, she'd be writing on it as she explained this plan or whatever it was.

I recalled what happened in August.

That's when she told me about Shinobu's first thrall at Kita-Shira-hebi Shrine, right? But this lecture seemed like it would be even more complex, tricky, and grand.

"I'd like to make this discussion quick and head to our site asap. I do know that things rarely go as planned…but we do need to draw a line somewhere that we can make the standard."

"There's one thing I want to make sure of first. Or rather, something I want you to assure me of. Are you sure that Ogi is going to make her move tonight? No matter what kind of trap we set for Ogi, it won't matter unless she does, right?"

"She will. I wouldn't say I'm sure of it so much as it's a fact—tonight is the only night. If she doesn't move here, you could say that she isn't her. Though that would take care of the threat," Miss Gaen replied with confidence.

I didn't understand her grounds for saying so, which is to say that she hadn't told me anything essential at all, but her attitude was so commanding that I still didn't feel like pushing any further—it made me think that Miss Gaen's most outstanding feature wasn't the amount of knowledge or information she possessed, but rather this self-confidence.

A self-assuredness that overpowered any possibility of argument.

It sat in contrast with her relaxed demeanor.

…While I did try asking her, I already felt certain of it myself—I had this unshakable confidence that Ogi would move today, March fourteenth.

After all.

That's what she said she'd do.

Just now—before I came here, in front of the gate to the Araragi residence.

—Araragi-senpai.

—Could you side with me?

—Please save me.

"…"

"Hm? What's the matter, Koyomin? You look worried—no need to get so worked up, it's not like I'm going to talk about anything complicated. In fact, this ought to be an easy long passage for someone who just overcame his college entrance exams. I'm just trying to explain a convoluted situation in a clear way—I don't know about saying that we're checking each other's answers here, but it's like the reveal chapter of a mystery novel."

The reveal chapter of a mystery novel.

If anything—that was Ogi's role.

Or perhaps Tsubasa Hanekawa's, but she wasn't here—she didn't make it here in time for the big reveal.

She was already quite the master detective, having pinned down Mèmè Oshino's whereabouts—and perhaps the normal thing to do here would be to inform Miss Gaen of her junior's possible discovery, but I hesitated to do so for some reason.

Because I might give her false hope—or so my excuse went, but actually, I concealed the fact because I was cautious of her.

Though it's not like—I was trying to take Ogi's side or anything.

"All right," Miss Gaen said, then smiled.

The way a master detective would.

"Then why don't we begin with the relationship between this park and Kita-Shirahebi Shrine. With the genesis of our current tragedy. The tragedy that befell Shirohebi Shrine, Kita-Shirahebi Shrine's predecessor, *four hundred years ago*—"

004

"That said, Koyomin, you might know a little bit about this since you must have gotten a lecture from the very green Tadatsuru while in the depths of hell—or somewhere like it. Someone with good enough intuition should be able to arrive at the right answer after hearing nothing more than this park's official name.

"But we can't allow a conclusion made from a haphazard guess to turn into a mistake at a moment as critical as this one—so I'll be explaining this from the top. What I say here may seem to be unrelated to Ogi Oshino at times, but I want you to listen carefully since this is where everything began.

"Four hundred years ago.

"Tell me, what happened then?

"You can't be so dull that you'd even get this question wrong, Koyomin—yes, the date that the legendary vampire Kissshot Acerolaorion Heartunderblade arrived in Japan. Though it'd be a major event now, surely creating a major commotion at the airport, there were no airports in Japan then, I'm sad to report.

"But I don't say that as some sort of jokey metaphor—rather than use the ocean routes in that grand seafaring age, she arrived from afar by sky.

"You've already heard the circumstances from her own mouth—and we could have her explain it again since she's here with us, but I'm going to ask that you allow me to do the honors, given all the hard work I've put in. I'm sure it's not something that Shinobu—or rather, Miss Shinobu is very eager to do, either.

"To summarize… Kissshot Acerolaorion Heartunderblade, about two hundred years old at the time, went on a trip around the world out of boredom. I'm sure it had something to do with the fact that the two-hundred-year-mark or so is when immortal vampires tire most of life.

"The unusual thing about her was that she visited Antarctica as a part of this global trip—but this would also lead her down the path of destruction.

"This happened because nothing existed in Antarctica that could recognize the aberration she was. Aberrations can only exist by being recognized by humans, after all—so she couldn't exist for long on the massive uninhabited island that is Antarctica. Even Heartunderblade, however exceptional a vampire she may be, was no exception.

"So she panicked and escaped from Antarctica.

"She escaped with a super jump instant air dash.

"This is where the uncharacteristically flustered Heartunderblade flew into the air without thinking about her destination—I'm sure that she wouldn't have done anything so thoughtless in regular times, but it was an emergency involving her continued existence, after all. And even if she'd landed in the mouth of a volcano, it wouldn't have been much of a problem at all for someone like her with absolute immortality. Were you to compare it to something a human would do, it'd be like being flustered and walking barefoot to your front doorstep—or the opposite, walking back into your home without taking off your shoes in order to grab something you forgot. Nothing but a question of footing.

"At least, it should have been.

"No, in reality, that's what it was—but this would be more than a small splash for the place where she landed. Quite literally, the splash she created was stunning.

"There, in the country known as Japan.

"Stood a body of water in a provincial town.

"*She splashed down in the lake*—splashing it everywhere.

236

"It's incredible if you think about it in terms of probability. She'd essentially thrown a dart at a spinning globe, and not only did she happen to hit Japan, she landed right on a lake. The expectation would be for the dart to hit the ocean, and even if it did hit land, to hit a continent like the Americas or Eurasia.

"I guess you can just say she has great luck.

"That's Heartunderblade for you.

"To go further, that lake was no regular lake—what's incredible is that it was a sacred lake that had garnered the collective faith of the people of the area.

"A kind of Shinto shrine, if you want.

"She'd sent that splashing everywhere, so she'd created more than a little mess… She deserved more than divine punishment, and she would in fact face quite the punishment. That just shows you how well the world works.

"How balanced it stays.

"Heartunderblade jumped from Antarctica and flew halfway around the world like some sort of inter-continental ballistic missile only to land in a sacred lake—destroying it outright.

"Drying it out.

"She of course didn't suffer a scratch—and it would have healed in the blink of an eye even if she had, but as for the place where she landed, as for the impact zone, this was quite the problem—but, as I said just a moment ago, while the occult view of this mess she made would say she deserved punishment, she had in fact brought blessings to the area as well.

"The water of the lake that flew into the air as a result of her impact turned right into blessed rain that fell on the then drought-stricken area.

"This must have seemed like a miracle to the people there who worshiped the lake—a welcome rain that meant their daily and nightly prayers to their god had been answered. After all, there at the base of the dried-up lake appeared a beautiful blond woman.

"She appeared, or maybe she seemed born.

"And so, they thought of her as a manifestation of their god—which was hardly surprising.

"If anything, it'd be surprising if they didn't.

"As a result, the Western aberration that is a vampire—Kissshot Acerolaorion Heartunderblade, usurped their faith.

"Or you could say she scattered their god and took over its position.

"The shock is even greater when you consider that this means Heartunderblade had already slain a god before she was ever called the Aberration Slayer.

"You might be getting bored by now since this is your second time hearing this story, Koyomin, but is that how you've been reading this episode? That Heartunderblade had been treated like a god by accident, and that there was some god there that had been expelled from their seat?

"Come on, Miss Shinobu. There's no need to hold Koyomin that tight. He's nothing more than a delicate little human now. You'll tear his body in two if you squeeze him like that.

"I'm not criticizing you. This is just a story—of long before long, long ago. It'd be too late to try to say anything about it. If I did dare to say something, it'd be that you rejected becoming a god despite being treated like one... That your strong sense of self, something no aberration should have, made the situation worse.

"I do want to point out the fact you made the situation worse.

"And that you invited the Darkness in.

"As a result, Heartunderblade was chased from the land back once more to Antarctica... But we'll skip over what happened next.

"What we need to talk about right now is about the land whose god was scattered and whose false god was banished—in other words, we need to talk about the land with no god that had been created.

"Though blessed rains fell on the land, and rain continued to fall there thanks to their false god—that too disappeared, and the Darkness drastically reduced its population, and the land was devastated.

"But humans never stop growing in number, and have to live—they needed faith in order to live. No, you can't blame it on the era. We still need to believe in something to keep on living, don't we?

"Even I couldn't live without believing in something.

"So long as we're alive.

"So long as we live as humans, we have to believe in something or someone—whether that's god, common sense, devils, or uncommon sense is up to you, of course.

"I wonder what it is in your case.

"Now that you're familiar with aberrations, vampires, and even hell, what are you going to believe in as you keep living your life—what will you need to believe in to keep on living?

"In any case, as for the people who lost the lake they needed to worship, who'd lost their god—they needed to find a new god.

"No.

"They needed to create a new god.

"And so—they moved their shrine.

"They sealed the lake.

"And that's what sealed their fate.

"All this happened quite a long time ago, so this, if anything, is something I can't be certain of without the use of time travel…but it does seem the people of this land, having lost their faith and their population, decided to join a local indigenous faith to find a way to survive.

"This indigenous faith worshiped mountains, making it of a contrasting type to their former lake-based faith, in a way. If you'll allow me to irresponsibly drop in from the future to make an irresponsible criticism, they were trying to do something absurd by bringing the ways of their lake to the mountains. What kind of a grafting is that? Though almost all the citizens who had worshiped the lake, which is to say Heartunderblade, had been swallowed up by the Darkness.

"The lake had dried out by then.

"The people who moved the residence of their god must not have known the details—in a sense, that's when their traditions and their legends came to an end.

"An unsure next generation taking a faith—attempting to recreate a faith that seemed to have worked in the past. That's not something I can laugh at and call foolish.

"And it's not as if they were completely off the mark—they had the clamp needed to perform that grafting.

"A clamp.

"An axis—they had a thread that connected the mountain to the

239

lake.

"Or rather, not a thread, but something else long and winding.

"A serpent—a snake.

"To air it all out, just as Kissshot did to the lake, the actual form the god worshiped there took was a *water snake*—and the form taken by the god of the small indigenous faith in the mountains was a *mountain snake*.

"A water snake and a mountain snake.

"The snakes were connected.

"Are you familiar with the traditional saying and legend that the snake who lives a thousand years in the mountains and a thousand years in the seas will become a dragon? Well, strangely enough, that's the exact thing that happened here.

"This nearby indigenous religion was on the wane itself. As befitting of their god, taking in this new fold only meant creating a thin, long faith—it just didn't work. The graft wasn't meant to be.

"Like a puzzle piece that's been forced into a space just because the color looks right. While it may work at first glance, you can't deny that there's something warped about it.

"This twisted, unbalanced nature created a kind of air pocket. One that gathered what we'd call *bad things*. But while these side effects and reactions occurred, the faith did manage to squirm its way through the next four hundred years or so—while I've exaggerated and hyperbolized this story to make it sound as dramatic as possible, these kinds of minor errors do happen all the time.

"They're human acts, after all.

"Of course there will be mistakes.

"You can't disapprove of every single instance—if the mistake is not a lie, not a falsehood, then you ought to overlook it.

"To be more specific, while the Darkness did not forgive Heartunderblade for feigning to be a god, the connection of the lake to the mountain seems to have been beyond the scope of its duties.

"So.

"I could talk about the details of this forever. It's like an inexhaustible lake, but let's stop with the tales of old times here.

"What I'm trying to say, Koyomin, is that the remains of the lake that disappeared without a trace as a result of Shinobu's super jump instant air dash are located here, Shirohebi Park—and that the mountain shrine where they relocated the faith was Kita-Shirahebi Shrine."

005

Her wrap-up was so sudden that I thought for a moment I'd lost track of her story—but indeed, I had somewhat of a clue about this, having heard about it from Tadatsuru.

A snake's immortality.

It seemed only right for another immortal being, a vampire, to take over that faith—I even recalled hearing the legend of Hydra, the sea snake, regenerating itself again and again no matter how many times the heroic Heracles sliced through it.

It all checked out.

But.

It was also true that I had no idea how much Shinobu getting treated like a god, contrary to her wishes, had to do with Kita-Shirahebi Shrine—or rather, I had seen the two as separate, standalone stories until I heard what Tadatsuru had to say.

Because that meant Shinobu had already visited this town before, four hundred years ago—I'd never heard about that.

Had I not?

Really?

Hadn't I already heard that Shinobu's first thrall—Seishiro Shishirui—called *this place* home back in August?

If this was his home, that meant Shinobu had visited this area as well when she came to Japan four hundred years ago.

Yet she herself had never said anything like that, as far as I knew—I turned to face Shinobu, who held me in her arms, and this voluptuous woman looked at me with an expression now devoid of any childish innocence and—

"??"

Tilted her head to the side.

…Don't go tilting your head.

It just made her look stupid, like she still hadn't gotten rid of all her childishness.

She now appeared to be an adult, and she should have grown on the inside as well, but it seemed that your basic personality isn't that easy to change.

The child is mother of the woman, I suppose.

It might be especially true of her. She was capable of doing something as unbelievable as erasing her own memories (and still leaving them restorable), so it was possible for her not to remember any bad memories that she wished she could forget.

"By the way," Miss Gaen said, as if to add something extra. "The meager and dwindling Shirohebi Shrine-turned-Kita-Shirahebi Shrine managed to continue until it died out about fifteen years ago—we already talked about this before, right? That *he*, Miss Shinobu's first thrall…that *his* ashes managed to return home, eating up all the *bad things* that had gathered on the shrine's premises, god and all—that is when its replacement snake god died. Absorbed and acting to help his return. This too was a factor in what happened next, though."

"I understand what you're saying, but it's not that easy to swallow," I gave Miss Gaen my honest thoughts.

Actually, I wasn't confident that I knew what she was talking about—maybe I still didn't know anything.

It's not like I had any doubts.

If anything, it all seemed to line up.

It was just that the feeling of it all lining up was a restless, nauseous one—I felt repulsed, as though I was being made to dance in the palm of someone's hand.

Ononoki had said the same thing to me, but even if I was in the palm of someone's hand, whose palm was it? Miss Gaen's? Or Ogi's? Or someone else entirely?

"To guess at how you're feeling, you're looking at it the wrong way around. The way you see it, Heartunderblade having visited Japan and having come to the town you live in seems like too much of a coincidence to be true—but a neutral party like me sees this situation coming about as a plain old necessity *because* Heartunderblade had visited this place. Of course, we can't even be certain about that, either."

"..."

Had I heard that before as well?

Shinobu came to this town because she'd been summoned by the ashes of Seishiro Shishirui—which made it inevitable, and my meeting Shinobu here rather than someplace else was likewise inevitable.

The look of any town was bound to see a total change after four hundred years, so even if Shinobu wasn't so incurious, it'd be too much to expect her to notice this was the same place she once visited—there was no trace of the lake, after all.

"And it's because of this that once we took care of him, her thrall, I wanted to install Miss Shinobu as the new god of Kita-Shirahebi Shrine," Miss Gaen said, taking out the amulet she'd stuck into her pocket moments ago. "She'd been the one to replace the previously worshiped immortal water snake in the first place—so even in the sense of taking responsibility for that, she seemed to be the right woman for the job, or at least very suitable for it. In any case, the commotion in this town is never going to end until we fill in that air pocket. Mèmè just decided to put a lid on the garbage instead of taking it out, but as an expert who values prevention over investigation, I wanted to conduct some work on a more fundamental level. I wanted to contribute a pillar to the reconstruction of the fallen shrine—by placing in it a pillar of faith."

Though I was turned down, Miss Gaen said teasingly.

She acted like she was just teasing me, but it was still no laughing matter... I'd done an immeasurable amount of damage by refusing to allow her to turn Shinobu into a god.

"If you'd gone through and laid it all out like this from the start..."

I began to say, but even if she'd laid it all out, I doubt I'd have returned the favor by giving her Shinobu.

And not because Shinobu—wasn't cut out to be a god.

In fact, she had lived as a god in the past, though for only a short period of time, and as a false one. Still, you could say she had what it took.

I just didn't want to make Shinobu a god, that's all.

Restoring peace to the town would mean nothing if it meant having to make Shinobu into a god against her will—my selfish logic went.

And that selfish logic still applied.

Miss Gaen could lay it all out, but I would just pick up and go home—even after hearing her words now, I didn't want to make Shinobu swallow her amulet.

"Right, Koyomin?"

"But in that case, what are you going to do? Or...why bring this all up now? If you know that telling me won't do any good—"

"To put it plainly, because it'll do some good now—Koyomin. Why don't we take a quick break here and just state our opinions out loud?"

"Our opinions? State them?"

"You could say our goals, if you want. Or our sense of them."

"..."

I recalled what Hitagi said the day before.

That there's nothing scarier in the world than someone whose goals you don't know.

That described Izuko Gaen to a tee—but was she saying she'd come out and state those goals of hers?

I couldn't have asked for more—so much so that I felt wary. We weren't in opposition or anything, so why did our conversation have to take place on such pins and needles?

As far as I knew, Miss Gaen wasn't my enemy.

When I heard the explanation she gave next, though, I started to understand.

This was that explanation:

"I think that's where the two of us don't meet eye to eye—and it's not as if Miss Shinobu and Mayoi Hachikuji are on the same page, either. We're talking like this, face to face, but we aren't here to come to an agreement. I included you in this plan expecting one of those miracles that you cause…but I can't deny that you might bring about further disasters in the process. After all, when I left the question of what to do with Miss Shinobu, just li'l Shinobu at the time, in your hands, it seems like we ended up with an unrelated middle school girl getting turned into a god."

"…I can't argue with that."

In other words, it seemed Miss Gaen was the one who really wanted to know the goals, or the true intentions of an opaque character.

No, she knew everything, and that had to include something as simple as my true intentions—so she must have wanted to get me to say it.

What she must have wanted to say—is that I needed to live up to my words.

"Then I'll say it… My goal is to…"

But as I tried to put my thoughts into words, I had to confront my own goals. What would have to happen—to create an outcome I'd be happy with?

"For now… It has to do with Hachikuji and Shinobu's situations. Hachikuji, in particular. She might even get swallowed up by the Darkness if we don't do something—I wanted to ask you. Is it possible for someone to pass on to the afterlife twice?"

"It's not impossible, but she'd probably just end up in hell again, the way she did the first time. She may even have a charge of desertion added on top—Avīci might be taking it a little far, but I can't guarantee that she'd get off with just another trip to children's limbo."

What would satisfy you as far as that goes, asked Miss Gaen.

I of course couldn't abide Hachikuji getting sent down to hell again—it was beyond the pale, something I couldn't disagree with more. What then? Did I need to consider getting engulfed by the Darkness as a better outcome than going to hell? There didn't seem to be a path to satisfaction as far as this matter went…

"Well, as I told you already, I do have a plan in mind for Mayoi—so why don't you tell me your concerns about Miss Shinobu next? What exactly do you mean when you say you want to do something about her situation?"

"Well... You know, you see the way she is now," I said, pointing backwards at Shinobu.

The complete form of Shinobu Oshino. The way she is—the monster she is.

While I called her Shinobu Oshino, she was in fact now the iron-blooded, hot-blooded, yet cold-blooded vampire Kissshot Acerolaorion Heartunderblade herself.

Which meant losing her current certification as a harmless being—forcing her to once more face experts in the field of vampire slaying as she walked through a whirlwind of blood.

That—was not at all something desirable for this woman who'd grown suicidal after tiring of such a life...or so I'd decided for her on my own.

I didn't know how Shinobu felt about it, though.

Maybe she saw it as an improvement over living sealed inside my shadow as a little girl—in fact, it'd only be normal if she did.

She did seem to be in a good mood since returning to form.

At the same time, there was something perilous about it—after all, she did have a terrifying amount of influence in her full form. She could destroy the world in ten days.

Miss Gaen, at least, wouldn't overlook it.

And—the bigger problem than Miss Gaen would be Yozuru Kagenui, the master of Yotsugi Ononoki, that corpse doll she now held in her arms. There'd be nothing happy about the news to a woman who detested immortal aberrations—but wait.

She'd gone missing...

"I'm also worried about not knowing where Oshino and Miss Kagenui are," I said.

Though Hanekawa already seemed to have an idea as far as Oshino, I couldn't say the same about Miss Kagenui... The girl who only knew what she knew probably wouldn't be able to find a woman she'd never met.

"Would you not be able to start life as a college student with a fresh slate unless you cleared up those questions as well? Assuming you do get accepted. Only focused on what's right in front of you, just as always,"

Miss Gaen added with a laugh. "But I'm jealous. Jealous more than anything. I feel like I'm living my life pretty free, but I can't escape my position—so I can't say anything that free. My goal is to bring peace to this town. As I've said again and again, I want to bring stability to this spiritually disturbed town. Nothing more."

"…"

Her goal was so grand that it could seem devoid of any human emotion—but small minds cannot wrap themselves around the truly great—and Miss Gaen's words seemed to be proof of that.

Then again, after speaking with her for this long, even I started to get at least a glimpse of how she really felt—bringing stability to an entire town must have been on the small side as far as goals went for her.

"I mean, sure. I want the town I live in to be at peace, too, but…I'm not someone grand enough to set something that out as a goal for myself. Thinking about my friends and family is the most I can do."

"And I'm saying that's what poses a danger to me—but we can come to an agreement there. This time, at least."

"What do you mean?"

"You say you're worried about your friends and family, but you only ever care about others. We can come to an agreement here *because you don't pay any mind to yourself*," she said—she seemed relieved, but I didn't know what that relief meant.

Myself? I didn't have to worry about my body, now that I'd settled the issue of it growing vampiric…

"I know this might seem stubborn, but to stubbornly make sure—you don't oppose me subduing this town in general, do you? In fact, you'd help me out if the conditions are right, won't you?"

"Yeah, of course I would—"

"What about you, Miss Shinobu?" Though I was still mid-reply, Miss Gaen shifted her attention and spoke to the beautiful blond holding me in her arms, Shinobu Oshino. "What are your goals? What are you thinking right now, Miss Shinobu? What do you want to do?"

"I merely obey my master. If he tells me to cooperate with thee, then I shall—and if he tells me to oppose thee, then I shall," Shinobu answered without delay. She was certain. She didn't waver, the way

I did—but something about her...

"Something about you makes it seem like you're more loyal to Ko-yomin now that you're an adult, Miss Shinobu. Doesn't it? I can't say I expected this. The most likely outcome to me was that you'd slaughter him now that your link is severed, along with your master-servant relationship."

That was the most likely one?

I'm sure that meant Miss Gaen had put together some kind of way to prevent that from happening, but it was scary to hear her put it out there.

"Kakak. 'Tis not as though the relationship of master and servant exists only by way of blood—but anyway, expert. If ye would allow me to speak my own desires. If it were possible," Shinobu said.

Close to my ears.

"I'd much prefer it if ye could turn me back into a little girl."

006

It goes without saying that Mayoi Hachikuji and Yotsugi Ononoki had no goals of their own in this meeting—how could they? Hachikuji was an utter bystander, someone I'd dragged into the situation, if you wanted to put it that way, whom I'd brought with me from hell against her will. As far as Ononoki, forget about a doll like her having a sense of purpose, I didn't know if she sensed anything at all.

I suppose that as far as Hachikuji goes, you could say that I wanted to help her escape from her position between a rock and a hard place. It's not like she could go back to hell, but she couldn't stay either. She had nowhere to go.

Though I say this as if her problems had nothing to do with me, most of the responsibility for her situation did rest on my shoulders...

"So, now that we all know where we stand, let me explain what exactly we'll be doing next. The minimum required to fulfill your goals, Koyomin, and my goals, as well as Miss Shinobu's goals and Mayoi's goals all at the same time."

Miss Gaen said this as if she had some kind of fixed process in mind, but I found it hard to believe that any such requirements existed—though the way she said *minimum required* did make it seem like there may be more requirements out there...

"We have two minimum requirements. One is to install a new god at Kita-Shirahebi Shrine—the other is the elimination of Ogi Oshino."

Elimination.

Hearing the word said out loud so clearly made me a little bit nervous—I tried to be careful about not showing those nerves on my face, but Shinobu may have figured it out via osteophony as she held me in her arms.

Please save me.

Ogi's earlier words may have come across to her.

If we focused on Shinobu in this situation, though, the issue wasn't the second requirement. The first was the most pressing.

"Miss Gaen. If you're trying to say we should make Shinobu the god of the shrine, then—"

"Yes, that was the plan. That's why my original plan was to have you leave once you came back to life—but the situation changed when you brought Mayoi Hachikuji back from hell with you. There's no longer any need to install Miss Shinobu at Kita-Shirahebi Shrine, though this did come about half by force—because in a sense, an even more suitable substitute for a god than Miss Shinobu—no, because a *successor to a god* has appeared."

"A successor to a god?"

"I'm talking about Mayoi."

With that.

Miss Gaen pointed at the pigtailed girl who hadn't been participating much in the conversation—yet despite being pointed at, Hachikuji remained calm.

In other words.

They'd already—come to a deal.

But I was hearing this for the first time. Of course this shocked me—Hachikuji?

Mayoi Hachikuji—at that shrine?

"N-No! Th-That'd be even worse! I mean, Hachikuji is…"

"She's what?" urged Miss Gaen, but I had no words—I began knowing that we couldn't do it, that it was impossible, but pressed for a specific reason why we couldn't, why it was impossible, no answer came forth.

It was so unexpected that I'd reacted without thinking… Well, maybe I couldn't think of a reason to be against it, but I still couldn't think of a reason to be for it, either.

Not because I'd become overly conservative, afraid of losing anything—as far as I knew. Not because the experience of losing Hachikuji once had carved itself into me.

I didn't think Shinobu was too attached to Hachikuji, but in reality, this was a discussion about her potential successor.

It seemed she couldn't stay uninterested.

"The waif may be qualified," she inserted herself into the conversation, still concealing her stance on the matter. "We cannot deny that the lost girl has performed a miracle, having returned from hell."

That was true.

What's more of a miracle than resurrection? If the requirement to be a god is the performance of miracles, we could say that Hachikuji met it.

But in that case, I met the requirement as well, and so did Ononoki—not that I could ever imagine myself or Ononoki becoming a god, but the same went for Hachikuji...

"No, it's not the same," Miss Gaen said. "When it comes to Mayoi Hachikuji as compared to you or Yotsugi, while you did all come back to life, the conditions are different—you came back with a physical body, but she's a spirit."

"Are you saying you can't become a god if you have a physical body?"

"No. As we can see from Nadeko Sengoku. There are such things as gods incarnate—the difference here is that Mayoi will be swallowed up by the Darkness *unless she becomes a god.*"

Right.

She'd chosen to pass on to the afterlife in the first place because she'd been chased by the Darkness—and while it'd be one thing if she'd come back to life with a body, continuing to remain in our world as a spirit meant she'd inevitably find herself chased.

In other words, Miss Gaen said, there were three choices.

"1: Go back to hell. 2: Be engulfed by the Darkness. 3: Become a god—that's it. Okay, *become a god* is a little overblown. In reality, she's just changing jobs as an aberration. All aberrations are like gods. This also makes her situation different from deifying you or Yotsugi.

Enshrining her at Kita-Shirahebi Shrine—would permit Mayoi Hachi-kuji to continue existing in this world."

She'd receive citizenship. She'd receive residency, in other words.

"So for the most part, it'd be nothing but positive for little Hachi-kuji... She will of course have to do some work, but if she can manage the air pocket there, that'll be more than enough prevention. I wouldn't think of asking for anything more, I wouldn't demand anything unreasonable."

"That seems to be the case," Hachikuji said curtly.

From what her expression told me, she'd agreed to it on an informal basis and had no plans to change her opinion, either—and it'd be hard for me to complain if she felt fine with it.

In fact, if it worked, the idea did a perfect job of smoothing over my thoughtless deed, namely kidnapping Hachikuji out of hell. I ought to be grateful, and had no right to complain... Even then, I couldn't help but be the voice of prudence when it came to Hachikuji.

Maybe the concept of Hachikuji, the young girl, just didn't match up with the concept of god in my mind—oh, but speaking of not matching.

"B-But isn't that a shrine that worships snakes? Wouldn't it cause another distortion in the way of things if it housed Hachikuji, a snail aberration?"

"And that is the miracle so great that I can't even believe you made it happen by accident, Koyomin—without it, even I may not have thought of installing her as a god. Becoming Kita-Shirahebi Shrine's deity requires a reason, even if it's nothing more than a sophistic stretch—just as they brought the lake shrine to the mountains by way of a serpentine connection, or the way Heartunderblade claimed to be its false god by way of a shared immortality. We needed a reason on that level, or perhaps on an even higher one."

"R-Right? So—"

"Snails," Miss Gaen said. "They're backwards compatible with snakes."

"What?"

"Er, that wording might be too self-serving—but Koyomin, you must have heard of *sansukumi* before, right? It's hardly expert knowledge."

"Sansukumi?"

The original form of rock-paper-scissors?

The very basics of it, sure.

"With the snake, the frog—and the slug, right?"

The snake eats the frog, the frog eats the slug, and the slug feeds off the snake. It could also be used to describe a trilemma—a slug?

That sounded somehow familiar.

"Oh, right. *Namekuji tofu*—the Slug Tofu. The fake aberration Kaiki used on Sengoku…"

"That's right. *An aberration that's effective against snakes*—a slug."

Slugs and snails are closely related species, Miss Gaen added.

"Oh."

Right, what a blind spot—I should have realized what she was trying to say from the moment she brought up sansukumi. Snails have shells, while slugs don't—slugs are pretty much snails who've devolved their shells away.

In that case, far from having nothing to do with snakes.

Snails—could *suppress* snakes.

Instead of going wild like Sengoku, instead of being swallowed up by a snake, she could be the one to engulf the snake.

"I see. Call me Mayoi Namekuji," Hachikuji nodded along. The pun was almost too good to be true.

"Now, of course," Miss Gaen said, "it'd be best if a snake took over for a snake…but in a sense, this is even more ideal. In other words—we're spiraling around the solution the opposite way."

"…"

When she put it like that, even meeting Hachikuji at this park—the former site of Shirohebi Shrine, predecessor to Kita-Shirahebi—seemed fated. Though this too had to be a stretch.

Still, wasn't it a multitude of acrobatic stretches, one contortionist experience after the other, that brought us to where we were, by some sort of miracle?

"Speaking as an expert, if I had to point out a flaw, the *ji* in Hachikuji's name indicates a Buddhist temple, while she'd be residing in a Shinto shrine…but let's overlook that in the spirit of Shinto-Buddhist syncretism. It's not like we could change her name… Her family name was once Tsunade, *rope hand*, wasn't it."

Despite her laidback demeanor, Miss Gaen was surprisingly detail-oriented when it came to work—she must've turned over and thought through every side of any problem an amateur like me could come up with.

Also, she'd said *residing*—it would be Hachikuji's residence. The word choice was no doubt another attempt to persuade me, but how could I not be taken in?

Whether a shrine or a temple.

For Mayoi Hachikuji, lost on the streets for eleven years—treated to the mysterious misfortune of having to stack up stones by the side of a river—it was such a massive and clear saving grace to have a place she could call home, live in, return to.

Miss Gaen had framed it as a multiple-choice question with three answers, but there was no other choice.

Nor did we have time to search for a fourth. I could go on and on for as long as I wanted and nothing productive would come out of it—but.

"Are you really okay about this, Hachikuji?"

I had to make sure.

I'd been speaking with Miss Gaen this whole time and not asking Hachikuji herself—but I couldn't not ask.

"Yes, I am. A god—I feel like I'm walking on clouds."

In the lap and arms of a beautiful blond, my position may not have seemed the most serious in the world, but I'd tried to give my question some sincere weight; yet Hachikuji's response was light and offhanded.

Walking on clouds…

"I'm godly. A slip of the tongue."

"Stop it, you're making this sound like a joke. Don't take something as serious as this on as a joke."

"A posthumous two-rank promotion is nothing compared to this."

"Yeah, I'm pretty sure you don't get it…"

Her response was justifying my concern.

True, it's not like I got what was going on, but I knew of two examples where being trapped in that manner led to cruel situations.

Kissshot Acerolaorion Heartunderblade.

Nadeko Sengoku.

And frankly, I didn't want to add Mayoi Hachikuji to the list, no matter how much they told me there was no other solution.

"Oh, but I do," she still said, confident to the point of conceit.

"Are you sure? You understand the responsibility and meaning, the weight and role of becoming a god?"

"Well, no, those things, not at all."

"No?!"

"However," she perked up.

It was such a trademark Hachikuji smile.

"What I do understand is that it means I'll get to play with you."

007

Please don't think that my qualms vanished the moment I heard I'd be playing with Hachikuji. I'll admit, though, that I was stunned silent by her moving words.

Miss Gaen was not one to waste such opportunities.

"Anyway, we've cleared one of the hurdles. Mayoi Hachikuji just needs to swallow this amulet and Kita-Shirahebi Shrine's new god will be born," she proceeded to wrap up the discussion about the first requirement—um, wasn't she being too facile about an important point? "Ah, well, in Mayoi's case, maybe I should say *chew up and digest* rather than *swallow.*"

"My issue isn't with your precise wording..." I didn't want us to settle on a conclusion when the situation remained so hazy. At the same time, I knew that nothing could fully satisfy me here.

"If you want to let the Darkness swallow her up, I'll leave that decision to you, Koyomin—it's just a question of means to me. This is the one time where you can't take her place, though."

"Indeed...and while I will but do as ye conclude, surely 'twould weigh on thy conscience to have brought thy favorite child back from hell only to have her swallowed up by the Darkness," Shinobu chimed in, wrapping her legs around me in addition to her arms. It was as if she'd decided to sit cross-legged around my body, which was wanting in

259

manners for an adult—at least usually, but the pose looked handsome and cool when Shinobu did it, unfairly enough.

I bet I never looked that stylish holding her in my arms.

Anyway, being rebuked by her made it only harder for me to argue—in fact, I'd lost my grounds for objecting now. Shinobu and Sengoku had failed as gods for a reason, while the new unit had no short-comings according to the lecture of an expert, Miss Gaen.

"Yes, kind monster sir. Get your damn act together. You think whining and complaining about what other people want to do makes you so cool? Keep your mouth shut if you don't have an alternative. Is dragging down the doers all you can do?"

"Hold on, Ononoki. I can come up with plenty of arguments when it comes to you."

Such a nasty tone. She reminded me of an angry Tsukihi.

Mellowing a bit, she asked me, "Didn't we go over this more than enough in August?" With Miss Gaen's arms around her (looking like a ventriloquist dummy, given that she was a doll), Ononoki continued, "She could get swallowed up by the Darkness while we're squiggling and squabbling."

"Oh…by the way."

It wasn't so much Ononoki badmouthing me, but Miss Gaen, Shinobu, and her speaking in succession that made me come up with a rebuttal. Or rather, I'd been thinking about it for a while but hadn't had a good time to bring it up. I'd kept my earlier run-in with Ogi in front of my home secret, and kept quiet about it as a result, but maybe I should've informed everyone about it sooner.

If only to ascertain its veracity.

Though it was late in the game—no, maybe this was actually the best possible timing since Miss Gaen was trying to pivot to the second requirement, namely Ogi Oshino…

"Miss Gaen."

"What is it, Koyomin?"

"It's, um…about the Darkness. We might be terribly mistaken about something," I said, my voice subdued. "It could be that—*Ogi Oshino isn't the Darkness.*"

"I know."

An instant reply.

My subdued tone for naught.

I'd even used italics like a fool.

Instead of striking out swinging, I was getting called out on a bunted foul—did cricket have a similar rule?

"Get out of here."

This unpretentious expression of disbelief came from Ononoki. Since she and Miss Gaen didn't act as one, I suppose their views didn't always match up.

"Seriously? Damn. I'd been so convinced I foreshadowed all kinds of stuff assuming that was the case."

"…"

Who asked you to? Don't be foreshadowing like it's your mission, okay? What an annoying character trait, what an annoying character.

As for Shinobu, she stayed silent.

She seemed to belong to the camp who'd known… Maybe she wasn't saying anything out of caution to avoid revealing her position inadvertently.

Hachikuji, never knowing much about Ogi, who transferred into Naoetsu High after she'd passed on—sat there blankly like she didn't care either way.

"Why did you think Ogi Oshino is the Darkness in the first place?" Miss Gaen asked me.

"Well, I mean…"

"Oh, sorry, don't get me wrong, Koyomin. I wasn't trying to fault or laugh at you with that. If anything, it was only natural to think so," Miss Gaen said, quite naturally herself—as though this turn in our conversation had also been part of her calculations. But how could she predict this, too, without listening in on my earlier conversation with Ogi?

"Why was it natural…to think so?"

"I'll explain what I mean later," replied Miss Gaen, prioritizing her arrangements.

"What I need to know beforehand is—at what point you arrived at the notion. Depending on your answer, we might want to modify our measures... I have a pretty good idea, though."

"There was no specific point. Hearing and seeing how she spoke and acted, it just came to me... She was looking for Hachikuji and all. Then there's Sengoku, and Tadatsuru..."

And the very start of it, Ogi Oshino's initial case.

The chain of events surrounding Sodachi Oikura after I met the transfer student for the first time was—almost blatant, if you will.

No, but it wasn't through accumulating info that way, it was intuitive—just take her tar-black vibes.

The Darkness itself, wouldn't you say?

A deep darkness insisting on the rules.

An inky darkness revering balance.

"But if we're saying it was only natural for me to think so—was she actively trying to make me? To mislead me?"

It seemed possible. Ogi would do that. As nothing more than a prank, too.

Not that she'd ask Tadatsuru to hunt us down as a prank—

"Nope, that's not it." Miss Gaen shook her head at my assessment, however. Once again. "Well, actually, it might've been her own understanding at first—and she does continue to charge herself with that duty. Ogi Oshino may not be the Darkness itself, but is doing its work."

Bearing the same role, she rephrased.

"The same role as the Darkness..."

The "natural phenomenon" that once assaulted Kissshot Acerolaorion Heartunderblade, worshiped as a false god—and Mayoi Hachikuji, who stayed in this world despite losing her reason to exist.

The Darkness.

A.k.a. a black hole, dark matter—a phenomenon, or concept, that clamped down on aberrations that strayed from their path.

When it visited Hachikuji in August, I didn't have the time to think about it in depth, panic being my foremost reaction—but I did my best later and came to the conclusion that it was by no means a natural enemy, or the punitive body, of aberrations.

The rules of our world.

Like gravity or action-and-reaction, natural selection or survival of the fittest, math formulas or any of those kinds of laws—to be obeyed, and not to be defied, but without some sort of *thing* to the floating black thing.

Yes.

That's what I believed—until I met Ogi Oshino.

Who did exist.

And yet, mistaken as always, jumping to conclusions and spinning in place, I ended up as far off the mark as possible.

"Oh, don't be so down on yourself—what did I just tell you? Ogi Oshino took on the Darkness' role, so you weren't terribly off the mark thinking she was it. But to get everything straight just in case," Miss Gaen said, turning to Hachikuji, "the Darkness that might revisit this town if we left you in your current state, that we were fretting about earlier, is the genuine Darkness—which attacked Heartunderblade, and you in August. The authentic, veritable Darkness. Meanwhile, even if we enshrined you at Kita-Shirahebi and made you its god, you could still come under attack—from Ogi Oshino, in the role of the Darkness."

Miss Gaen turned from Hachikuji to me again, but stare at me though she might, this turn in the conversation was so sudden I couldn't react right away. The best I could do was echo her.

"We could enshrine her—and she'd attack?"

Huh?

Only after tracing the words did it sink in—and I had to wonder what the hell was going on. We'd been talking about enshrining and deifying her to stave off the Darkness, even though it hadn't been Miss Gaen's goal, but what was the point if Hachikuji was still going to be attacked?

What was it all for, then?

We wouldn't be able to play together—

"Well, that's why I said two minimum requirements—enshrining Mayoi as a god isn't enough *on its own*. That's half of it, but there's the other half: we aren't getting anywhere until we eliminate Ogi Oshino."

"You keep on using that word, *eliminate*..." I said, unable to take it anymore.

Maybe she was just using a customary term without meaning anything by it, but I had trouble putting up with such talk about my junior, a girl at that, even if she was opposed to us, whether or not she was the Darkness.

—Could you side with me?

—Please save me.

It wasn't that her plea swayed me. It was a matter of word choice.

"Could you please not?" I requested. "You're making it sound like Ogi's just some aberration."

"Well, but she is," came another immediate reply, "an *ordinary*— monster."

008

I realized that some time had passed.

I wasn't sure if this passage was also a part of Miss Gaen's plan. Although the situation steadily moved toward a resolution, and the truth was being revealed, I couldn't help but feel the opposite—that the situation was only deteriorating, the truth receding further into the depths.

A monster.

An ordinary—monster.

If we're going to nitpick, I don't think anything counts as ordinary once it's monstrous, but maybe the adjective was warranted amidst a grand assembly of irregularities: the complete form of legendary vampire Shinobu Oshino, man-made aberration Yotsugi Ononoki, and soon-to-be god Mayoi Hachikuji.

"Ogi's—an aberration?"

Well.

Once I heard the words out loud, maybe that wasn't so unnatural? Not that I had the right to say anything, having half-assumed that her true form was the Darkness...but her too-elusive appearances and disappearances did have a supernatural quality to them.

Since I'd already suspected that she was the Darkness, wondering if she was an aberration was hardly improper.

Monster... It felt like our tale was returning to its origins, after all this time.

Sure, you shouldn't forget your roots, but a monster, or an aberration, transferring into Naoetsu High? Going to school, taking classes, and studying?

"Hold on, Koyomin. It's not as if you've seen her going to school, taking classes, or studying—it's just that most of your contact with her is centered around school."

"…"

Fine, fine.

But wait, this called for a fundamental change in how I thought about the situation, and I needed to regain my composure. If I could, I'd go home, sleep on it, and come back—but knew that wasn't happening.

I tried to remember.

All of my exchanges with Ogi—but my memories didn't lead anywhere, I found no route to follow.

The harder I tried to recall them, the hazier they grew.

Not just now, either—this always happened with her. Speaking with Ogi muddled my memories. Remembering things I didn't want to remember, forgetting things I ought to be thinking about, finding memories that never existed planted in my mind.

Almost as if—some kind of supernatural force was involved, but…

"Even if Ogi is an aberration, isn't her identity too unclear? It's like we should just call her the Darkness and be done with it. What basis do you have for calling her a monster?"

"Well, what basis do you have for calling her *Ogi*?"

"?"

Did I sound too familiar calling her by her first name? Was I the one who needed to reconsider how I spoke about her, and to stop being so chummy—when it was clear that she was our opponent? That said, it's not like you can suddenly start calling someone by another name.

—Hitagi.

Ack. I remembered the night before, and felt more bashful than amused.

"What are you blushing for? Gross."

Ononoki never let a blunder like that get away from her. A nasty personality, through and through.

Come to think of it, calling the shikigami by her first name was odd, too...but that didn't seem to be Miss Gaen's point.

"You're calling her *Ogi* because she introduced herself as Ogi Oshino, and you just accepted it," the expert continued—loud and clear.

"...She gave me a fake name?"

"Nah, a false name, pseudonym—it wouldn't even qualify as those. It's as slapdash as a name can get, like something invented on the spot. What you should've done when she gave that name, Koyomin, was laugh. Me, I'd have burst out in hysterics."

"..."

So said Miss Gaen, but I had no clue what was so funny about the name. If she thought it was eccentric, what about Mèmè Oshino, who shared her surname? Not to mention Shinobu Oshino, whose given name deliberately repeated the first character of that surname? It was almost witty...

"Your instincts are uncharacteristically dull today, Mister Araragi," Hachikuji stepped in to take over the explaining duties. Who knew she saw me as a character with sharp instincts, but right, maybe I ought to have noticed a little sooner.

After all, she and I had been at each other's throats about names.

Still, calling me out when most of her info on Ogi came from our current discussion showed what a seasoned veteran Hachikuji was on the topic.

"My sense is that Miss Kanbaru introduced this Miss Ogi Oshino individual to you, correct? As a fan of the former star of the basketball team?"

"Yeah...that's how it happened."

"A fan. Like an *ogi*, a folding fan."

I almost passed out at how trivial it was.

Yes, nothing as grand as an alias—and more of a blithe user name, like *AAAA* or *CCCC* or *1234*, an offhanded, indifferent handle that I should have identified as a lie the moment I heard it.

The audacity of it, I guess, was nothing less than grand.

"But then what about her last name, Oshino... Oh, wait, the part about being his niece is a lie, too?"

"The situation is a little more complicated with the surname. Or maybe I should say roundabout... But yeah, she isn't his niece. If you ask me, having been his senior, he has no niece—I don't think. Mèmè's a living, breathing human being, so I'm sure he has relatives in the biological sense, but as far as I know, that junior of mine is all alone in this world," Miss Gaen declared.

"In that case, was she trying to gain our trust by claiming to be his niece? But why? What did she want so much that she'd come to us falsifying everything down to her background and the stuff she's made of?"

Aberrations.

There's a reason for every one.

Not intransigent like the Darkness.

So then, what necessity caused the aberration known as Ogi Oshino to appear at Naoetsu High—to throw my life into this much disarray?

"If Ogi Oshino isn't Ogi Oshino, what is that girl? What's—her true identity?"

I was being thoroughly disgraceful here, the type who knew only how to demand explanations, but I wasn't going to be told that she was an aberration and leave it at that.

Please, convince me.

"*Right now, her identity is the unidentifiable.* Which is why the way to eliminate her is clear... The original plan was for the enchanted blade Kokorowatari to do the job, though it wouldn't have been the appropriate method—more like expedient or rule-breaking. For an expert in my field, a greatsword that can slice up any aberration is a pretty big rules violation to begin with. What can you say, that's Kissshot Acerolaorion Heartunderblade's first thrall for you... How ironic that he was also the one to lead us to this twisted conclusion."

"Your plan was to kill Ogi with the Aberration Slayer?"

"Come on, don't glare at me like that—whose side are you on, anyway?"

It seemed to be a light-hearted quip, and not a knowing one, but her words made my heart leap. I felt like she'd pierced my strained nerves with needles.

Be that as it may, I couldn't reply without reservation that I was on Miss Gaen's side—even apart from that exchange with Ogi the night before.

"Cutting down an aberration with the Aberration Slayer. There shouldn't be anything contradictory about that—it's what an expert should do," Miss Gaen said.

"Is that why you made Kokorowatari?"

When she wielded the sword to slice me into pieces at the shrine, I wondered why it was in her possession, but by now the method of its creation was clear to me. The first thrall Seishiro Shishirui's armor—it had gone missing in August, and she'd reforged it.

I couldn't pinpoint the source of this reasoning, but I was certain. Had she already been planning to use it on Ogi?

That'd be ridiculous. Aberration or transfer student, Ogi appeared before us in October, and Miss Gaen shouldn't have had any reason to create the blade back in August.

At that point, Ogi hadn't done anything to merit elimination...

"Don't tell me that you *know everything* and made plans in your calendar in August to have this meeting today, on March fourteenth?"

"Of course not. School schedules don't matter to someone my age."

Her answer didn't line up with my question. I wasn't asking if she went by the calendar or academic year.

"Knowing everything," she continued, "is different from being able to predict things. As sad as it makes me to let a friend down, I'm not so transcendent that I could foresee every future twist and turn during the events in August. A common misconception, but I'm just omniscient, not omnipotent."

"But in that case—"

"I wasn't thinking of killing Ogi Oshino, but I'd anticipated her appearance. I thought it possible—which is why I gathered the First's armor. Just to prepare for the worst, of course."

"Hmph, so sayeth the looter of a fire scene. Little wonder I was left feeling hungry," Shinobu groused.

Every time she suddenly began speaking right next to my ear, I was jolted—and didn't know what to do about the warmth of her breaths.

"Oh, come on, Miss Shinobu, haven't I returned it to you?"

Judging by this response, the sword the legendary vampire had been using to play cricket earlier wasn't her own version, but rather the replica created by Miss Gaen.

Shinobu had swallowed it as always, prior to putting her arms around me, but this meant two enchanted blades were inside her—or maybe three, including the Yumewatari she must've received as part of the set?

"Because," Miss Gaen said, "I don't need it now. If I can get Koyomin's assistance, I don't have to resort to extreme measures—as an expert in eliminating yokai, I can rid us of Ogi Oshino through honest means and the standard method."

"What did you mean by anticipating her appearance?"

That intrigued me more than the precise nature of her honest means and standard method—if she'd anticipated Ogi's appearance, was that really any different from planning on killing her all along?

"Ah, that was just experience speaking—Ogi Oshino is a kind of aberration I've seen before... Maybe I wouldn't go that far, but *something similar.*"

So that's what she meant. She had a wealth of experience as the big boss of the experts in her field, and what would be a bolt from the blue for me was just another notch in her belt.

Or so I thought, but no.

"I encountered *it* back when I was in elementary school—so this case kind of takes me back, if you don't mind."

"In elementary school?" I couldn't picture her as a Lolita, but then, she couldn't always have been a big boss. Or the lady who knows everything.

"Yeah. To be specific, I wasn't the one to experience it, my older sister did—Toé Gaen. The mother of Suruga Kanbaru, whom you know so well."

As her little sister I had a front-row seat to her experience, and that might've been the origin of the rest of my life, Miss Gaen recollected with genuine nostalgia in her voice.

"My sister—came across an unidentifiable aberration... By the way, Koyomin. Just how much do you know about my older sister?"

"Um, no real details. Just that she left Kanbaru the Monkey's Paw, really…"

Kanbaru and I never really sweated the serious stuff and just talked about stupid things. Her mom eloped with the Kanbarus' only son, gave birth to Kanbaru, and later died in a traffic accident—was that how it went?

I'd heard vague facts but couldn't tell you what kind of person she actually was. Maybe her personality had been similar to Kanbaru's—not that I wanted to imagine it…

"'If you can't become medicine, then make yourself into poison. Or else you're nothing but plain water,'" Miss Gaen recited, adapting her voice. "She was the type to say something like that to her little sister. And well, honestly, I had trouble dealing with her."

Trouble dealing with family.

I felt as though I'd come in contact with Miss Gaen's human side for the first time—someone who'd speak such a line was kinda scary even to hear about. Yet just as I silently agreed with her…

"She was like you in a way, Koyomin," Miss Gaen showed just how smart I was for doing so. "Though my sister wasn't a demon, she was like a demon. I'm not saying she's like you because you were a bloodsucking demon, but even as an elementary schooler, I thought she was crazy. I knew all too well that she was a dangerous character. How do I put it? She wasn't a monster, but she was monstrous."

"…"

"Hard on herself, and hard on others. The more unforgiving she was, the better. That's the kind of person she was—well, ask Suruga for details next time you see her, if you get the chance. She was a child when she lost her mother, but she must've felt something of it, as her daughter—but I'm getting off topic. I'm not trying to explain my sister's personality to you here. Just saying that I associate you with her."

Hard on myself and hard on others?

Wait, that was my personality?

I'll admit I was tickled that Hachikuji had the most puzzled expression out of us all, but Miss Gaen spoke no more on the subject. Instead…

"Which is exactly why, Koyomin," she went on, "exactly why I anticipated that you might someday go down the same path—maybe I should say I feared it. From the time I worked with you in August, in fact. Sooner or later, you might be met with the same kind of aberration—and my fears hit the mark… That's why I always keep my guard up."

"Your guard, huh." My nerves would fray if I lived with my guard up that high all the time—but maybe keeping it so low had made my current predicament inevitable. "Just for reference, what did you do then? You didn't have Kokorowatari with you."

"Yeah, well, I took an orthodox approach. And I'd like to resume it now—you're going to do what my sister did, Koyomin."

"I am? Not you?"

"*You're the only one who can do it.*" Miss Gaen nodded forcefully. "There'd be no point in me doing it. Or Miss Shinobu—this method would be pointless for anyone else, even Mèmè or Yozuru. You're the only one who can do it, and you're the one who has to do it."

You have to do it. You and you alone, Miss Gaen said, emphasizing *alone*.

"Because people get saved on their own, or whatever?" I asked.

"That was Mèmè's policy, right? It's not mine, but…it does resonate in this case. Yes, you could say there's nothing at all I can do to help you."

"…"

Face off against Ogi, one-on-one, Miss Gaen seemed to be urging, but how could I react with anything but bewilderment to her springing that on me?

My duel against Seishiro Shishirui.

That, I understood—and I'd spent the last year facing off against all kinds, in lethal combat, again and again. I hate to brag, but the way I saw my situation, running through a hailstorm of bullets and making it out alive was no exaggeration. If I were to start the count with my spring-break death match with an earlier iteration of Kissshot Acerolaorion Heartunderblade, the bewitching beauty with her arms around me, fingers beginning to crawl along my ribs—I'd lose count by the time I reached the end of all the fatal encounters I'd endured.

But it was because of these experiences that I couldn't get my head around what Miss Gaen meant by facing off against Ogi—her words felt hollow, like a funny story whose punch line I couldn't make out.

Duel... Settle things... Lethal... All very impressive, but in this case quite devoid of substance.

"Huh. Would you compare it to being shown a five-minute anime short with a full-length opening and ending, Mister Araragi? Like the actual episode is only a minute long?"

"Please, Miss Hachikuji. Not right now."

A surprisingly lucid metaphor, but that's not what we were talking about.

My unease must have stemmed from the fact that whatever Ogi's identity, she didn't strike me as a fighting freshman. She was plenty mysterious, but cleaving a cute high school girl in half with a greatsword in order to dispatch her just seemed so criminal.

"Like I said," Miss Gaen corrected me, "we aren't relying on the sword. That plan is dead—we don't have to use it thanks to you. Even I'd hesitate to slice through anything in the shape of a high school girl, or really a human in general."

"..."

But you did. Despite my human shape, you mercilessly shredded me into so many pieces that I was no longer recognizable—at a shrine too, on holy ground, didn't you?

I couldn't tell whether she was trying to be clever or sincere, but no point in litigating the past now. I was curious as to why the old plan was dead *thanks to me*, but what I really needed to know was our operative plan, which I'd missed out on hearing. Especially if I had to carry it out on my own—there are things I can and cannot do, okay?

In fact, the list of things I could do was the shorter of the two. Even if she reminded me that she was hustling for the sake of Hachikuji and Shinobu, I couldn't agree to anything that rivaled using a greatsword to kill Ogi.

"I'm not asking you to do anything of the sort. In fact, it's as easy as can be. Anyone could, as far as doing it goes—it's just that you have to do it for it to be effective."

"This is starting to sound like a big deal. You're acting like it's nothing serious, but aren't you trying to trick me into doing something pretty tough?"

"What do you mean. We'll just have you do what my older sister did ten-plus years ago."

"Again, you're acting like it's no big deal, but you just told me how larger-than-life she was. Hard on herself, hard on others, like a demon—I can't imagine pulling off whatever this outrageous person did."

"Oh, no, in a way, it'd be easier for you than it was for my sister. After all, you're the kind of boy who'd throw his life away to save a vampire on the brink of death."

"…"

What did that have to do with this? Why bring up the time I helped Shinobu during spring break?

Was she going to tell me to save Ogi, another aberration, as I did back then? That was almost…

—Please save me.

The exact thing she'd begged for.

Miss Gaen would never go for that, though, having little to do with that sort of naïveté. I couldn't let her laidback, sisterly demeanor fool me.

Her policy as an expert was to seek only the optimal solution, to the point of severity.

True, from what I understood, she attended to Nadeko Sengoku's case when she became the god of Kita-Shirahebi Shrine, but that was only because Sengoku was deemed unfit.

"You see, at the end of the day, the threat of Ogi Oshino, the unidentified aberration—is that she's unidentified. Nothing else."

Miss Gaen opened her mouth again, to tell me what I needed to do.

"She'll crumble if you reveal that identity."

"Crumble?"

"You could also call it annihilation, in the particle physics sense—but what's important here is that she's a fake who's just pretending and falsifying herself. Believe it or not, she's a *big fat liar*. And when that lie is laid bare—I think Miss Shinobu and Mayoi know quite well what happens then."

They did.

And so did I.

"The Darkness—"

"—The Darkness—"

"—The Darkness."

The three of us spoke as one.

"Right. The Darkness consumes any aberration that misrepresents its nature—when she's misrepresenting herself to be the Darkness itself, all the more so. The punishment will be as harsh as it gets for her rules violation. She's reaping what she sowed, for all the ways she's behaved around you for the last six months, Koyomin. This time, she'll be on the receiving end of all the ferocity she lavished on you."

Miss Gaen smirked. Her expression was wicked, not befitting an amiable lady like her—but more than any sort of just desserts, it felt to me like the last act of a farce.

Like the end of a fairy tale.

Her identity is revealed.

And that alone would make Ogi Oshino's existence *come to an end*—if her core principle was unidentifiability, of course that would be her vulnerability.

"At the end of the day, that's what aberrations are—which is why I called her an *ordinary monster*. The first aberration you met, Koyomin, was the vampire noble Kissshot Acerolaorion Heartunderblade, and from there you experienced countless life-or-death battles and even met Yozuru Kagenui, an onmyoji with a nearly unmatched propensity for violence. That must've tainted your impression of aberrations—you see them as dangerous beings who must be fought, but at their most basic, they're just *metamorphoses*. Something transformed into what it is not, like foxes and tanuki in folklore. Reveal their true identity and they will vanish, like a bugbear in a closet. It's as simple as that."

"..."

"When science sheds light on an aberrational phenomenon, it becomes nothing more than a superstition, right? Same thing. We experts might look like walking antiques to young'uns these days like you, but really, our job is to investigate urban legends and dissect every little part of them, no matter how boorish or unromantic that may be, in order to nullify them. There are still things out there that science can't explain—isn't what I'm saying here. Our line of business is about reducing the number of things out there that science can't explain. We put food on the table by explaining the inexplicable in a way that anyone can understand. And in that sense, a profession like ours is going to vanish someday."

It's kind of like an octopus eating its own leg, Miss Gaen said self-mockingly—I recalled how Oshino also said early on that it's uncivilized to be solving matters violently all the time.

—What a violent line of thought, Araragi.

—Something good happen to you?

He said that too.

I see. To put it in a way that matched up with Miss Gaen's way of thinking, I wasn't going one-on-one against Ogi—this was a unilateral elimination.

As far as the taste the idea left in my mouth, though… It was about as bad as cleaving a high school girl in two with a greatsword. Yet as bad as the aftertaste might be, it seemed like the best and most optimal plan for resolving our town's situation.

"And is that how your sister got rid of an Ogi-like aberration—not the Darkness, but an imitation of it?"

"Yep, you got it. She was no expert, and she was about as old then as you are now, but she managed to figure a way out of her fix on her own. She really is—a strong person. Was a strong person," Miss Gaen corrected herself and used the past tense. "I guess that means being the strongest person is no match for a car crash. Did that upset you, Mayoi?"

"Well…I have to admit automobiles are convenient. Modern society wouldn't work without them," deadpanned Mayoi Hachikuji, the young girl who lost her life eleven years ago because she got run over crossing on a green light.

Deadpanned… But come on, be traumatized or something.

"Koyomin. You called it an imitation, just now, of the Darkness—and that's a perfect encapsulation, spur-of-the-moment or not. It's easy to understand, it's perfect. However. You'd be making a huge mistake if you also thought that it's somehow inferior. Being an imitation and not the real thing actually makes it more annoying than the genuine article—as my disgrace of a junior, the scam artist Deishu Kaiki would say, the fake is more real than the real deal, because it wills itself to be real."

"So, while the real Darkness wouldn't show up if we made Hachikuji the god of Kita-Shirahebi, the fake one, the imitation Darkness, might... Is that what you're saying?"

"Yup. The way I see it, an imitation Darkness is more dangerous than the Darkness itself, since *it would never allow for such an opportunistic, convenient solution—an answer that leaves everyone happy must be cheating.* That'd likely be her stance."

"..."

"One way or another, we need to settle this tonight. The elimination of Ogi Oshino, the second condition for fulfilling both my professional duties and your wishes—when I said the first condition would be nullified otherwise, that's what I meant."

—Please save me.

—Could you side with me?

—Please save me.

I couldn't help recalling those words, whatever her intentions were in speaking them.

Was she being sincere? Or were they the utterances of the unidentifiable, an imitation Darkness—either way, and even if she had ulterior motives, there seemed to be no way for me to honor her request.

Was I letting Miss Gaen talk me into a corner? Maybe I'd fallen for grownup rhetoric.

Whatever the case, an ending where Hachikuji was swallowed up.

More tragedy befalling those I held dear.

That—was something I couldn't ignore. Far too much had happened in the last half-year.

One way or another.

Whether I wanted to or not—I.

I needed to get rid of Ogi Oshino.

No matter what kind of smile she wore—I had to.

I glanced back at Shinobu. She looked back at me with silent gold eyes.

I once rejected Kissshot Acerolaorion Heartunderblade's plea.

Help me, she begged, and I answered—

I'm not helping you.

I couldn't be her answer.

And that'd be my response to Ogi, too.

"I understand, I won't help Ogi Oshino—so." I summoned all my determination. "So please, Miss Gaen, tell me. Who is Ogi Oshino, the mysterious transfer student?"

"That kid's true identity is…"

An immediate reply. To the bitter end—

Miss Gaen did know everything.

While I finally didn't know a thing.

009

Tsukihi Araragi is an aberration.

The youngest daughter of the Araragis, she'll soon be entering her third year of middle school. The strategist of the Fire Sisters, a girl who often changes her hairstyle—and a phoenix.

To classify her with more specificity, to give an exact classification based not in zoology but cryptozoology, a lesser cuckoo, the *Shidenotori*.

Said to travel between the land of the living and the land of the dead, the cuckoo could be called a symbol of immortality—in fact, Tsukihi Araragi is more of an immortal aberration than even a vampire.

More immortal than a vampire, more resurrected than a zombie, more eternal than a ghost—she can't succumb to sickness, poison, or accident.

Also utterly free of special abilities that come with aberrationhood, she'd live a human life, its course running without her ever noticing a thing, before being reborn into her next life like it's nothing.

Reincarnated.

They say that phoenixes resurrect from within flames, but in that sense, she's as plain an aberration as one could be, having nothing to do with such spectacles. Yet Tsukihi is, undeniably, an aberration, which is why an expert onmyoji, a native Japanese sorcerer, visited our town in August, to eliminate her.

Yozuru Kagenui.

Yotsugi Ononoki.

I still don't know how exactly that pair specializing in immortal aberrations intended to "eliminate" my sister, an aberration that just won't die—but to skip to the conclusion, they decided to overlook her.

Though that's another bit she doesn't know of.

She lives on as an aberration.

As a human too.

As a member of our family, because they let her get away—let her go on being Koyomi Araragi's little sister.

They *recognized* her.

And being recognized—is the duty of any aberration.

And there we have her, as she is now.

It is why Tsukihi Araragi is here on March fourteenth.

"See ya later!" she said, leaving home first thing in the afternoon, but the last to leave that day, which was a kind of first: her parents, both employed, gone to work like always; her brother, done with his exams, out on his last date as a high schooler with his girlfriend since shortly after breakfast; and her older sister, too, off in high spirits to face a hundred opponents in a kumite. Both of her siblings had left without her knowledge, but Tsukihi Araragi's uninhibited nature didn't pay close attention to every little thing they did.

If anything, the Araragi sibling whose activities were the most puzzling, that posed the greatest cause for concern, was the youngest of the three—notoriously dangerous, you never knew what she might do left to her own devices.

On this day too, already enjoying spring break, the girl had informed her family that her plans were to *visit her convalescing friend*, but in truth, it wasn't an accurate description of her plans.

She was lying.

Deceiving her family, without feeling particularly guilty about it.

That said, the broad strokes didn't contradict reality, since she headed to the Sengoku residence just as she'd told her brother—the home of Nadeko Sengoku, her friend from elementary school.

Although they'd gone their separate ways in middle school, they were once close enough to call each other by nicknames—and now, by way of Tsukihi's brother, their relationship had been restored.

She'd worried about her friend, who'd been spirited away for a few months at the end of the previous year, and even after the hospital discharged her, visited her often—ostensibly (Tsukihi of course didn't know that Nadeko hadn't just gotten spirited away but in fact had become a holy spirit herself). But there was no need to check up on a girl who had made a full recovery, at least not three times a week.

Going to meet Nadeko wasn't a lie, but it wasn't to care for her—Tsukihi visited the Sengoku residence on White Day to help her friend at a certain activity.

And this activity?

"Thank you, Tsukihi. Thanks to you I think I'll be able to finish by my deadline," Nadeko Sengoku told her, to which she replied, "Oh, it's nothing at all," there in Nadeko's room on the second floor of her home.

Facing a reading desk, Tsukihi filled in a manga manuscript's blacks with ink. Her temperament was so touchy she tended to snap when spoken to while busy, but she remained serene now.

Perhaps not because being thanked put her in a good mood, but simply happy to see the change in her friend—not too long ago, Nadeko's line in this situation would surely have been *I'm sorry*, not *Thank you*.

That feeble attitude had irritated Tsukihi.

Enough to want to throw a punch had they not been friends, or even more so since they were, but after getting spirited back, something about her childhood pal seemed a little different.

What could have happened?

Tsukihi Araragi did not ask this.

She did nothing so commonplace.

She focused only on the work before her—helping Nadeko Sengoku enter a manga manuscript for a newcomer's prize before its end-of-the-month deadline. In other words, acting as her assistant.

In the hospital room where Nadeko had stayed after getting spirited back, when Tsukihi was still checking on her health in earnest, she learned that her friend seemed to be interested in drawing manga.

She got mad at her friend for keeping it secret for so long—furious, in fact—but didn't mind at all when she was asked to go buy some supplies and help draw something.

One thing led to another, bringing us to this moment.

Nadeko Sengoku never expected Tsukihi Araragi, the strategist of the famed Fire Sisters who should have been quite busy in that capacity, to assist in manga-making so strenuously over such an extended period, and in that sense, might have felt like she'd gotten more than she bargained for.

Meanwhile, from Tsukihi's perspective, it was refreshing and fun to submit to the creative initiatives of Nadeko, who'd only cared for a lukewarm and cookie-cutter friendship until then.

Tsukihi had fun assisting Nadeko.

It wasn't as if checking up on her friend wasn't part of it, since Nadeko hadn't recovered to the point of returning to school (naturally, Tsukihi, head honcho of the area middle schoolers, knew of the troubles at her friend's Public MS 701). If the manga manuscript they now inked were any indication, however, she didn't need to worry.

Nadeko must have gotten over so much.

That was Tsukihi's impression.

Her friend's new hairstyle being one sign—before, which is to say ever since their time in elementary, Nadeko had tried to hide her face with grown-out bangs. More than just shy, or bashful, or even introverted, she'd seemed scared of people, but now she wore her hair extra-short.

She'd gone straight to a hairdresser after her hospital stay—the old her probably wouldn't have been able to at all. Nadeko Sengoku, who save for a lone instance had only ever gotten haircuts from her parents, stunned Tsukihi by asking for a rec.

Tsukihi had no reason to say no, in fact would get a referral bonus—but upon hearing the request (as she sat one seat over) for an extra-short haircut, even she worried that her friend had gone insane.

Well, Nadeko could make just about anything look good, so while her impression changed, it was hardly a disaster. Incomparably cuter, at least, than the time Tsukihi violently took to her bangs (said lone instance)—but then cuteness didn't seem to be what she was going for. She'd done it for the most logical of reasons: long hair got in the way of drawing manga.

Looking at her today, as she worked in her school track jacket that she didn't mind getting dirty with ink, she wasn't lying about the reason. Still, Tsukihi, picky about hairstyles, couldn't help but think that her friend's severed hair also spoke of a broken heart.

She only thought it, of course. She'd never say it, not even in her sleep. While Tsukihi's life philosophy was to come out and say anything and everything, she wasn't so insensitive.

"I don't really get this manga stuff."

This statement was just that, however.

"Nadeko, just how confident are you? Doesn't the winner get money or something?"

"Hmm, I don't know," her friend turned around and answered with a troubled smile—even this would've been obscured by her hair in the past. "I stopped thinking about things like confidence."

"Huh."

"Someone told me I might have the talent—but these things don't always go well even if you're talented."

"You'll never become a first-rate creator if you don't believe in your own talent. Because you won't have anything to fall back on to support you, when you run out of effort."

People who only work hard break down when they can't work hard anymore, Tsukihi rambled on. This surely would've made Nadeko retreat in the past, but she was different now.

"You say *believe,* but it's more like being tricked," she caught the ball tossed her way. "Becoming a manga artist is like winning the lottery, to borrow your expression."

"I said that? Still, why not. There wouldn't be any money to pay out to the winner if no one played." It was dubious whether this addressed what was being said—probably not—but Nadeko smiled nonetheless.

"I'm just doing what I want to do. Even if I look uncool or embarrassing. Aren't you the same way?"

Nadeko turned the question around on Tsukihi, who was the one at a loss for words—because surprisingly enough, she wasn't *doing what she wanted to do* as much as others thought.

Once again, she was candid.

"I don't really have things I want to do, goals and that sort of stuff. Maybe that's why I like rooting for other people like this. Even the Fire Sisters were more a support group for middle schoolers than defenders of justice at first."

"Really?" Nadeko seemed to find this strange. A facet of her friend that she hadn't really seen halted her pen for a moment. "From my point of view, I don't know anyone whose stance on life is as clear-cut as yours."

"Haha. I'm honored. Is it my birthday or something? Where are my candles, did they just melt away?" joked Tsukihi.

She used to refer to herself as Nadeko, she thought nostalgically. She vaguely remembered pointing this out to her friend, but when exactly had she made the leap to *me*?

"But I'm a little more nihilistic, or maybe self-destructive. I tend to let myself get dragged along by people who want to do something."

"Are you talking about Miss Karen…and Mister Koyomi?"

Nadeko had pronounced *Mister Koyomi* a little funny.

Funny. In an awkward manner.

But Tsukihi let it go.

Deciding that it was too soon to tease her.

"Yeah, I guess. And helping out with your job like this, I feel like I'm being dragged along by your motivation."

"Job…" Nadeko Sengoku blushed.

But of course she did. She was no machine, so even if she'd *gotten over things*, she hadn't ridden herself of all her bashfulness.

"It's not a job yet, though. Not even close," she said.

"Does someone like me have a future?" A weighty question, depending on the tone, here posed casually as Tsukihi's personality dictated. "I can do most things, but I almost don't want to do anything I can do. Doing something you can do is so boring! Since you can't leave it at that, I end up letting other people decide for me."

"But it's not like you don't want to do anything?" asked Nadeko, seeming to reference her past self—and once again going deeper than she would have before.

"No. I want to do something. I want to be active, and proactive.

That's why I do something if it interests me in the slightest. But I also get bored of everything right away—it all gets tedious. I don't really understand what kind of person I am. I don't know, it might be fine while I'm a young thing, but once I'm an adult I'm going to get snagged by some loser guy who talks about his boring dreams and end up in an awful place."

"What a realistic example..."

"I need to start thinking about my plans for the future, so that kind of thing won't happen. Karen's going to become a high schooler, and big brother's going to start college. I feel like now, when I'm being left behind for the second time in two years, the last time being back in sixth grade, is when I should decide what to do and who to become."

Like you, Nadeko, she added.

Just hearing you say that makes all my hard work feel worthwhile, Nadeko said and broke into a smile before going back to inking.

"I guess good things happen to people even if they can't find happiness—just as long as they're still alive."

"Hm. Yeah, you might be right."

Was she being consoled?

In the end, chatting thus, Tsukihi Araragi kept filling in blacks and even had dinner at her friend's home. It was fully night by the time she decided on her next workday (having promised to help until the manuscript was finished) and left the Sengoku residence.

"A-ha, could it be Araragi-senpai's little sister?"

Right after she left—as if to prey on her momentary uncertainty as to whether she should go straight home or take a detour, as if to blend into the dark of the night, and to slip through a crack in her mind, came this address.

From someone.

She looked over to find a high school-aged girl wearing the uniform of her brother's school and straddling a bicycle—eyes so glossily black you wondered for a moment if every streetlight in the vicinity had lost power.

A suspect smile plastered on her face.

A high school girl too young to be called bewitching but whose looks were anything but innocent, whose entire body seemed to exude an uncanny air.

In spite of her stylish bike, no one would ever term her healthy.

"*We met yesterday, too.* Hello."

"...Hello."

Had they?

Tsukihi wondered as she bobbed her head anyway. Her snap judgment was that she shouldn't be rude to an acquaintance of her brother's—and seeing this.

"My name's Ogi Oshino," the other girl introduced herself. "I hear about you all the time from your big brother—he says he's very proud of you. Gosh, I'm so jealous that you have a big bro like him."

"Uh huh..."

How were you to respond to such a greeting?

Also, her brother probably didn't say he was proud of her—Tsukihi Araragi was convinced that he wouldn't, even at gunpoint.

"It's late, I'll give you a ride. Hop on back," Ogi Oshino invited, pointing to the rear of her bike. Tsukihi was a bit surprised that anyone affable enough to casually offer to ride tandem with a stranger (or had they also met yesterday?) was friends with her brother.

The Sengoku and Araragi residences weren't so far away that a ride was warranted, but nor was refusing such a gesture, once made—so thought Tsukihi, ready to accept it gratefully, until she noticed that the rear area Ogi pointed to had no seat.

BMX bikes seat only one.

"Don't worry, I have pegs that let two people ride this," assured Ogi. She got off for a moment and swiftly rigged her bike so that it seated two—swiftly, skillfully. "Okay, all ready. C'mon, hop on. Put your hands on my shoulders to get some balance."

"I can balance myself without doing that."

"Ha haa. Don't be silly, how could you possibly—"

She could, though.

And she did.

Often overshadowed by the world-class core muscles of Karen, her sister a year older than her, Tsukihi's physical condition was nothing to scoff at. Standing on the pegs attached to the rear wheel and stretching her arms out to the side (her too-long hair wrapped around them so it wouldn't get caught in the wheels), she looked ready to guard Ogi's six.

Okay, more like just stand there.

It was very much like her to take an already risky situation, riding two to a bicycle, and make it even more dangerous for no good reason—but if the pilot was worried by the circus stunt taking place behind her, she didn't betray her alarm.

Tsukihi, herself, naturally enjoyed performing the trick, a believer in savoring fun to the fullest.

"My brother would love this bike!"

"Ah, right, he likes bicycles, now that you mention it—though it seems he lost both of his for certain reasons. Yes, you might say that's why I'm riding one."

"Hm? What do you mean?"

"No real meaning, more of a metaphor. Pay the right amount of attention to it, and maybe you'll be rewarded."

"Huh…"

"Was Sengoku doing well?" asked Ogi, apparently acquainted with not just her brother but Nadeko. Was she in the area to see how Nadeko was doing? Had Tsukihi cut in line somehow?

It was very much like her not to feel any kind of way about this.

Her moral code did include not cutting in line or skipping people's turns on purpose, but feeling bad over doing so by accident required a self-critical bent that she didn't possess.

"Maybe that's where you're different from your older brother."

"Hm? What?"

"Nothing. It's nothing. Anyway, Sengoku's condition. How did her bill of health look? Clean? Or was it a death certificate?"

"…I guess she's doing well."

She's doing great!

Tsukihi had nearly blurted that out, but her friend had yet to go back to school and needed an alibi.

A thoughtful girl, in that sense. Not just wise, but sly.

"She's not dead. Actually, she was deader before."

"Perhaps. Well, yes, no one's ever just cute—the way I see it, girls like her are cuter when they're not being cute," Ogi remarked, not making much sense. This bit of banter must have seemed perfectly logical to her because she continued without going into detail. "Good, good," she came to some understanding that was all her own. "So, for her, being a pretty girl was only ever self-harming—sad, no?"

"Sad? Aren't you lucky if you're cute?" questioned Tsukihi, innocently—maybe insensitively.

"Take how you don't get to choose what family you're born into. You might envy people born into class or wealth, but from their perspective, it's also a heavy burden to carry since day one—for instance, they might not be allowed to become manga artists, even if that's what they want. You'd call that unlucky, wouldn't you?" explained Ogi, but Tsukihi—or rather, a fourteen-year-old girl didn't seem to get it, and the older girl must have noticed. "It's not what you can do that decides your future, but what you can't do—because you won't know where to focus if there's too much you can do," she shifted the topic a little. "Thanks to a lifetime's worth of shame and other avenues getting cut off, Sengoku can now chase after her dream like mad—that's what I'm saying."

" ... "

"Cuteness must have been a chain holding her down, but it was also too precious a talent to cut loose—so drastic measures were needed."

"Drastic measures? What do you mean?"

"Who knows. Beats me."

Ogi held out her hands. In other words, took them off the steering.

Both riders of a bike seating two had both of their hands free—they were reaching for the freedom to cause a traffic accident.

"I don't know anything—it's Araragi-senpai who knows."

" ... "

"But maybe it wasn't about any drastic measure but learning from a bad example. Still, I feel bad for that conman...I didn't mean for it to go that far. Your brother might not forgive me, even if I showed remorse."

Ogi then put her hands back on the handlebars.

"It seems Sengoku wants to become a manga artist."

She began pedaling faster.

"Tsukihi Araragi. How do you want to become?"

"How?" Recalling her conversion with Nadeko about this, Tsukihi replied, "I don't have anything like that." Her friend was keeping her manga-drawing pretty secret, but she must've told this person? "If I'm having fun, then I'm fine. Maybe that'll keep going and be my future?"

"You might not know everything, but you can do everything. Omnipotent but not omniscient, you have too many choices, and your goals are scattered all over the place. That's why you're always content with the number-two spot. It's easiest for you to be pulled forward by someone else—but when it comes to your future..." Ogi said, like she knew all about her—how much had her brother told her? "It's just too grand and remote," she divulged with a smirk.

"...? Are you saying I'm depending too much on other people?" She let slide the comment about her future since it was just confusing—but the stuff about being number two and whatnot piqued her interest, and she wanted to dig deeper. Maybe it was just a continuation of the conversation back in Nadeko's room.

"I wonder. Considering how cuckoos lay their eggs in other birds' nests, I'd say parasitism more than dependence... Despite that nature, your personality is also kind of unique. Could it be your big brother's influence?"

"Cuckoos."

"Tsukihi. It's true that you're living your life thanks to other people's support—that they're giving you life. You could've died during summer break if not for your siblings' concern."

"...? Summer break?"

What could she mean?

Another metaphor?

"So, people can't live all on their own," Tsukihi interpreted it in her own way and reworded it as a cliché, but—

"People do live *all on their own*," Ogi quickly contradicted her. "The ones who can't—are monsters."

You and me for instance, Ogi Oshino appended—it made no sense to Tsukihi Araragi.

At first, she'd found it unusual that her brother had a friend like this girl, but now that they'd talked, she was the type, her mysteriousness would click with him.

"Wait, huh? Hold on, Miss Oshino—"

"Miss Ogi is fine."

"Miss Ogi, we're going in the wrong direction."

Her odd position as she rode tandem on the bike had made the scenery look different—or maybe not, maybe she'd just carelessly failed to notice until now, but at some point, they'd strayed far from the route between the Sengoku and Araragi residences.

It wasn't so far that their conversation could last this long—where were they now?

"Oops. Sorry, looks like I got lost—why don't I stop for a moment and look at a map on my phone."

Ogi hardly sounded embarrassed as she looked for a good place to park—and soon settled on a building and used her feet to brake in front of it.

The spot didn't seem remotely ideal to Tsukihi—the area was abandoned and untended, or maybe rundown was the better word. You only needed to glance at the building to tell that it was no longer in use. If her companion wasn't a girl, Tsukihi might have worried that she'd been abducted by a wicked scoundrel claiming to be her brother's friend (it'd be the scoundrel walking away the worse for wear in that case), but she felt no such danger as the girl fiddled with her smartphone. Instead, she looked up at the abandoned building with curiosity.

It wasn't worth more than a glance. Nor was it a place you'd ever come to, unless you were lost—her curiosity sedimented as soon as she had the thought, proving just how much this girl lived in the moment.

"Hm? Hold on."

But then she remembered something.

For some reason, she remembered seeing the abandoned building—even though it had to be her first time here, and her first time seeing it.

"Oh, right... Isn't this the building that burned down back in—was it August?"

She'd seen it in the news.

As a member of the Fire Sisters who tasked herself with maintaining

290

law and order in her town, she naturally came by such info—the case stuck out in her memory despite the many small fires breaking out at that time because it had been big enough to burn down an entire building.

Before it burned to the ground, and after it burned to the ground. She had looked at both pictures.

When she learned the facts of the case, it seemed like nothing more than a spontaneous fire, nothing as dangerous as arson or the like—still, the damage must have been massive. Not even a single pillar could have been left behind.

So then, why was a building that had burned down standing there majestically? Had it been rebuilt? No, why bother recreating an abandoned building?

"I figured out the way, Tsukihi. Don't worry, I won't get it wrong this time. Or maybe you'd like to try driving? This BMX bike is pretty exciting, it can even go backwards—hm? Hmmm? What seems to be the matter? Why are you looking up at such a plain, commonplace building?"

"Oh... It's just—"

Tsukihi explained. Ogi had only happened to get lost in the area and wouldn't have any answers as to why a building that should have burned down still existed. Tsukihi wanted to share her feelings nonetheless.

"Huh, how strange," commented Ogi. "I wonder if you could call this the ghost of a building. Why don't we try going inside?"

She was already chaining her bike to—and leaning it against (with no stand, the only option)—a nearby tree, and lost no time entering onto the grounds. She was so quick to act.

This girl was intrepid, unlike Tsukihi's brother, who overthought everything. Tsukihi wasn't the type to hesitate either, and rather than watch the girl walk off, followed right behind.

"Are you one of those abandoned building nerds, Miss Ogi?" she asked, inferring the possibility from the girl's light steps.

"No, ruins don't do much for me on their own. They scare me like they would any girl. But it's like my job to investigate suggestive places like these."

"Your job—you say." Echoing the word, Tsukihi recalled how it had made Nadeko self-conscious. Ogi couldn't be implying that it was some part-time gig, though.

"Yep."

With that, they stepped into the abandoned building. Technically speaking, this was trespassing, but the place was in such awful shape that it couldn't possibly have an owner or superintendent.

The footing couldn't be any worse, and no light could be expected given the time of day. They needed to be careful not to trip and fall, or else they could be seriously hurt.

"Looks like it used to be a school...er, a cram school," Tsukihi concluded, after carefully observing its interior—and climbing the stairs, as the elevator was of course broken.

"Hm, you're right. Bummer, by charging in head-first, we unveiled its true identity—and now that we know, it isn't the least bit scary." Ogi had never looked afraid but said this anyway as she turned the landing. Apparently, she wanted to begin her investigation with the top floor—the inverse of the theory that the most efficient way to look through drawers is to start with the bottom one. "That's how it is, you know? Whatever you're dealing with, the unidentified or unfamiliar is what's scary. People get anxious when they think about their future because they can't imagine their future selves. With a clear vision, you aren't afraid of growth."

"..."

"It's like Schrödinger's box. Open it, and it's just a plain box—of course you can't know if the cat in it is dead or alive when it's closed. The same goes for mystery fiction. You bite your nails and your heart pounds because you don't know who the culprit is. Once a mystery stops being a mystery and the list of suspects gets narrowed down to one—to be blunt, the book stops being interesting. Reveal scenes only need to be a line long, if you ask me."

Once their true identity is exposed, both the fear and the interest vanish—that's how it is, she summed up as she climbed, higher and higher.

Words of wisdom—her brother knew so many smart people. Despite this rare moment of honest respect, it was also Tsukihi Araragi's karma to begin nitpicking whenever she felt respectful.

"Is that really true?"

"Hm…what now, a rebuttal? I'd like to hear it. For my sake, and for yours."

"I wouldn't say a rebuttal…but while it might be true for detective novels, in real life doesn't it get scarier after the culprit is caught? Once they are, you know for sure that the person you found so frightening actually exists."

"Hm."

"Learning their identity kicks off its own story… I mean, doesn't the process after catching a criminal take longer than catching them? There's the trial, then there's imprisonment…"

She'd gotten a bit off track, but Ogi seemed to find this opinion novel, as the garrulous girl held her tongue for a moment.

Tsukihi continued, "And even if you call it a true identity, there's no guarantee that it's really true. Who knows, another twist could be waiting for you, to put it in detective-fiction terms."

"You might be right about that. I see, so there are true identities—and plain identities, which are only what they are. You got me there, I see you take after your brother."

I suppose that opinion was for your sake, and not mine, she remarked as she arrived at the top floor.

Having climbed four floors' worth of stairs, her breathing remained as calm as ever. The girl seemed to have good legs, but the same could be said of Tsukihi, who followed right behind.

She had health to spare—vitality, too.

Such was Tsukihi Araragi.

"People might accept your true identity, Tsukihi—or feel amused, but in my case I doubt it. *My true identity is—ugly.*"

"…?"

"Consider how we write that character: *saké* and *demon*. Not that the gods aren't just as fond of drowning in booze."

"The three strokes for 'water' in *saké* get left over when you combine the characters to form *ugly*, though."

"As they should. Signifying water—or a lake. Or maybe a sea snake."

This explanation only made things more confusing, and Tsukihi had to conclude that the girl had no interest in clarifying anything.

"Tsukihi," Ogi called to her, heading for the leftmost of the floor's three classrooms. "I'm afraid you have nothing you can call a future—forget not knowing what'll happen, you don't have any at all. No matter how many moments you cobble together in the present, they'll never add up to your future. All you have is an eternal present. Can you still—keep living in the now, not worrying about what's to come, never minding the future?"

"Yeah, probably," Tsukihi answered in a most casual manner, quite unsure of what the question meant. "I'm pretty good at living, so yeah."

"...It's wonderful you can say that. I envy you."

I envy you.

How was she supposed to respond to that, anyway? Ogi then put her hand on the door.

Turning its knob with grace.

She opened it with a smile.

"You're late, Ogi."

And—I spoke. Inside the now-open classroom, I stood from the chair where I'd been sitting and imitated the man she'd called her uncle.

"I've been waiting for you."

010

"Sorry, Tsukihi, but could you go back home on your own? Take my bike—I need to talk to your big brother about something very important. The combination on the chain is 1234," Ogi said, getting my sister to leave. The trivial combination seemed so her to me by this point.

We were now alone in the classroom.

I'd faced Oshino time and again in these ruins but never expected to be greeting someone in his position. Not to mention entering a burned-down abandoned cram school—a place you could also call the start of it all, which made putting an end to it all here almost too perfect.

Overdirected, even.

"Ogi. How did you create this abandoned building? The same way you recreated Year 1, Class 3 the first time we met?"

"No, the method is a little different—I had to put more into that. Meanwhile, this building just took the ability to generate matter. You know, like Kissshot Acerolaorion Heartunderblade—Shinobu Oshino does so often." Inspecting the tables lying around the classroom as she spoke, the germophobic girl selected a chair she deigned to sit in and dragged it up to me. "Not much care has been put into the details, so you can find rough edges all over the place, but it was a rush job. Please overlook them. Pray find warmth in the handmade feel of a papier-mâché structure... Ah, and speaking of Shinobu, what's she up

295

to? She should've regained her full powers, but she isn't with you? Is she lurking in your shadow?"

"Not yet. Restoring our link—binding us to each other again is something we agreed to put off until it's over."

"Huh." She sat down facing me, with her knees together and feet slightly apart. "Is that so—I was only asking if she's here, but I see. So Shinobu wants to go right back to where she started. And you—after going to hell and back to exorcise yourself, not only stopping your transformation into a vampire but becoming fully human again—want to become a mockery of a human of a pathetic excuse of a vampire again. How masochistic."

"What can I say. I love little girls," I replied. Thinking how meaningless our conversation was.

"You'd throw your life away for a little girl—you may have exorcised your demons, but couldn't do anything about the devil on your shoulder. Now, tell me, what will become of the young girl?"

"We make her into the god of Kita-Shirahebi Shrine—but that's also going to wait until it's over."

"Hm. Tying up every loose end into a nice little bow, I see. What to do with that shrine, that massive hole opened in this town, was a serious problem, but what a convenient solution."

"A problem—in other words, it was part of your job?"

"I suppose... I told you something of the sort, didn't I—but come on, why take every little thing so seriously?"

Ha haa, she laughed with cheer.

Her stance didn't seem to change in particular even now—the same Ogi Oshino as ever, her approach to life consistent from the time I first met her in October.

"Regarding your job—my little sister..." Wondering how I might segue into the topic, I gingerly touched on Tsukihi, who'd just left the scene. "Did you two have a nice fun talk?"

"We were only in the middle of talking—don't worry, I didn't get far enough to lay any trap. I had to leave my job halfway done, how disappointing."

"Was I wrong to interrupt?"

"You were right to. I was trying to do the right thing as well, but it ended as an attempt. In any case, it'd have been in vain. We exchanged a few words on the way, but she's a tough one. As overwhelming as you'd expect an undying bird to be. I have to wonder, how did Yozuru Kagenui plan on ridding the world of something with that much vitality?"

"Don't we get rid of monsters—by revealing their true nature?"

"What I'm saying is that you can't get rid of her even then, thanks to an older brother who knows her true nature and stubbornly loves her."

"…"

"Hm. Maybe that's why Yozuru Kagenui gave up on her—though *I can't see it going the same way for me.*"

"…"

"Am I wrong? You'll expose my true nature here and get rid of me. That's what's going to happen, right?" She stared at me, appraising me with her dark black eyes despite her defeatist words. "All in all, I did get pretty far—in fact, if failure was inevitable with Tsukihi, I left nothing undone even if it didn't all go right. Maybe my existence wasn't futile… Sorry, I hate to keep going back to this, but are you sure Shinobu Oshino isn't here?"

"She isn't."

"With Yotsugi Ononoki already neutralized…I'll skip over Mayoi Hachikuji if she hasn't been deified yet…but Izuko Gaen, the lynch pin, isn't here either?"

"Of course—" was a strange way to put it, but in any case, it was just me there. That's probably what Ogi wanted to make sure of. "Making this a one-on-one duel," I assured, my words insincere.

"Well, isn't that exciting."

Ogi broke into a big smile—I say so, but this was nothing new. She was always smiling.

I'd always thought of it as a show of composure, but for the first time I wondered if it brimmed with resignation.

Maybe, weary of the world and aware of its impermanence, hers was a poignant expression.

"What an honor it is to square off against the storied veteran Koyomi Araragi—my goodness. I was prepared to have Izuko Gaen get in my way, enchanted blade Kokorowatari in hand, in which case I'd have stood a chance of winning. I bet this is her secret to getting ahead in life, making her friends do the important stuff."

"I'm sure it's that too. But I think this is something I need to do myself. Something that only I can do, that I want to do alone."

"You want to, huh? Are you sure an adult didn't trick you into thinking that? Are you really working yourself to the bone for the sake of Shinobu and Hachikuji, or is it just inertia?" *What a fool*, mocked Ogi. "We tend to overvalue things that we nearly lost—but you'll never arrive at the future if you let nostalgia tie you down. Oh, by the way, I'm begging for my life here."

"…Begging for your life?"

"Don't you remember? I asked if you'd side with me. I asked you to save me—but I guess you callously rejected me. Maybe I wasn't charming enough."

She almost seemed to be having fun. Her amused air was kind of sad too now.

"It's the right choice, Araragi-senpai, right you are. Look at that, so you can do the right thing—though I wanted you to decline, unfortunately. Umm. Do you have any plans after this?"

"I told you. I'm putting Shinobu back in my shadow, and I'll watch over Hachikuji's apotheosis—there's a lot of other straightening-out to do, so I need to have a discussion with Miss Gaen."

"Oh. I was hoping we could go get food or something if you were free. Well, you seem quite busy, and I'm sure you don't want to be stuck here forever, so shall we bring things to an end?"

"Yeah, I think."

I didn't want to draw this out. That'd just be nasty. I needed to end her with one blow—with one word.

I couldn't side with her. I couldn't save her. If I could do her any favors, that was it.

"Ah, right, there's something I wanted to say, Araragi-senpai. About your entrance exams… You feel you did pretty well, but the section for your best subject, math? Partway through, you skipped a bubble and started filling them in for the wrong questions."

"What?!"

"After everything, you must've been flustered—my condolences. With an accident like that in your best subject, your odds are hopeless. Keep at it through next year," Ogi said meanly.

She'd landed a punch. At the same time, I took her encouragement at face value.

Because next year—did exist for me.

"Ogi. You're actually…"

I said it, thinking back to every last event since I'd encountered Ogi Oshino.

"You're actually me."

011

"That kid's true identity is Koyomi Araragi.

"This might be too extraordinary a claim to accept, Koyomin, and I'll of course explain in more detail. It's not too complicated of a situation, really—though the explanation might get a little complex.

"It's interlaced and entangled.

"I'll need to go step by step to untie it all.

"Because in trying to reveal her true identity, she herself seems interlaced and entangled—messy and mixed like a jumble of cords. Just as you consist of many influences, it'd be a little careless to say that her true identity is Koyomi Araragi, end of story.

"The quickest and easiest interpretation, though, would be…Ogi Oshino is an aberration brought into being by Koyomi Araragi.

"Just like my sister, Toé Gaen, made up the aberration called the Rainy Devil—but when I say made up, I don't mean it in the same way as making Yotsugi in college.

"If anything, it's closer to the way Tsubasa Hanekawa made up Black Hanekawa and the Tyrannical Tiger—which is why I'd been a little concerned about that in August. I could see it happening to you, someone who looks up to Tsubasa as a sort of mentor.

"Well, let's start with the precedent.

"With my older sister, even though it's my family's dirty laundry.

"I brought up the Rainy Devil without any explanation, but I'm sure you remember? The aberration that my sister's daughter, Suruga Kanbaru, my niece, wished upon? The proper name of that Monkey's Paw.

"Originally, though, it was neither a Monkey's Paw nor a Rainy Devil. It was by giving the thing an 'identity' as the Rainy Devil that my sister managed to mummify an unidentified aberration she'd birthed on her own.

"Originally, it was a less comprehensible aberrational phenomenon.

"A compendium of mysterious events.

"To keep it brief—my sister often misplaced things. All sorts of objects somehow went missing around her—frequently enough that even the grade schooler that I was thought she was awfully careless for someone so harsh.

"But she noticed a trend.

"Although she seemed to be losing various random stuff, they had one thing in common—everything that disappeared was a recreational or luxury item.

"Games, books, snacks, pagers. Clothes that weren't thrifty, bags on the expensive side, fashionable shoes. Simply put, items that weren't necessary, but desired—or that interfered with getting things done.

"The kind that strict parents might take away from their kids—it didn't take long for her to realize this. When she did, she also realized how these possessions were getting swallowed up into a black hole.

"They weren't getting lost, but being thrown away. The culprit was none other than my sister herself.

"Her heart, ever strict on herself, made up a Darkness that disallowed anything that wasn't right—or to be more accurate, something like the Darkness.

"She made it up to repress her adolescent, girlish feelings of wanting to play, fostered this aberration herself. I didn't really understand as a grade schooler and was baffled that she was staging it all, but looking back on it now, it's so typical of my strict older sister.

"An aberrational phenomenon of unknown origins, if you will.

"This unidentified aberration that Toé Gaen made up embodied her self-restraint—would be an unsatisfying ending, so we'll go into what happened next. While she might've been confused until this point, once she realized its identity, it was in her wheelhouse: cracking down on her unruly self-restraint, her mercilessness extending even to her own stern nature, she vanquished the imitation Darkness.

"She ditched her uncontrollable repression.

"She settled the situation by tidying it up as a Western aberration, the Rainy Devil—brought the tale to an end by giving her dark side a crybaby demon name.

"And lived happily ever after.

"That was a quick summary, but the black hole was threatening to swallow up her friends and then-boyfriend, and it could've gotten pretty bad had she not taken care of it—if you're interested, I can tell you the whole side story some other time.

"Passing down the mummified remains to her flesh-and-blood daughter like some family heirloom shows just how troublesome her personality was—but let's put that aside.

"The simple view, Koyomin, is that the Rainy Devil was to my sister what Ogi Oshino is to you.

"If you want, Ogi Oshino is—Koyomi Araragi's self-critical mind-set.

"Don't look so annoyed, I'm just telling the truth. Call me considerate for not saying self-negation.

"Doesn't a lot fall in place if you think about it that way? She knew every last thing about your concerns, your circumstances, and your relationships. The things you'd forgotten, concealed, wanted never to think about again—she knew all of that.

"While insisting she didn't know a thing.

"She knew everything about Koyomi Araragi.

"*You're the one who knows*—you only needed to take those suggestive words literally.

"And because she knew those things, she criticized you for them. Your lies, your deceptions, your vagaries, your ambiguities, your fence-sitting, your irresponsibility—she kept reprimanding you for them, asking if you were really okay with it all.

"That's what I mean by the real Darkness overlooking a convenient conclusion like Mayoi Hachikuji becoming a god, but not so the imitation Darkness. Your inability to accept a facile, forced solution to selfishly bringing Mayoi back from hell—your harshness on yourself would spur Ogi Oshino to act.

"Of course, like I said, she isn't just your self-criticism—that'd never yield an adorable junior, as you describe her.

"Remember? She's a mix.

"With a headache of a history.

"I'll try to be solemn during this one part, because the nice lady speaking to you right now isn't entirely free of blame.

"Wouldn't you say?

"Apart from outliers like Tsubasa Hanekawa and my sister, high schoolers don't give birth to aberrations every day.

"Just as Sengoku couldn't give birth to Mister Serpent, you see.

"In fact, it took a tangle of fate, a number of characters and unavoidable occurrences, for Ogi Oshino to be born—if even a single element had been missing, your last half-year as a high schooler might've been a little more cheerful.

"When it comes down to it, though, these are seeds that you sowed—and they were sown last August.

"That case where you and I formed a common front—its preliminaries.

"When Mayoi was attacked by the Darkness.

"Phase one was you *ending up learning* about the Darkness—a phenomenon that corrects mistakes.

"Bad is bad, wrong is wrong—an entity that *judges for us* in that way.

"Naturally, you couldn't abide a phenomenon that tried to swallow up your beloved Hachikuji—but at the same time, your strong self-punitive streak was drawn to this Darkness, which could discipline you for all your deceit, starting with the defanging of Kissshot Acerolaorion Heartunderblade.

"You can also look at it this way.

"If Mayoi Hachikuji is unpardonable—then how could I ever be pardoned?

"You wanted to be punished just as she was.

"If that was no good, then how is this good? If something's bad, so's everything else—wanting to condemn it all when just one detail is off, precisely because you yearn to protect everything you see.

"That feeling—*was planted*.

"Well, all of this is psychological.

"No matter how much you feel that way on the inside, not everyone is going to give birth to an aberration—but then, calling you an everyday high schooler would be a bit of a misnomer, Koyomin. You're a mockery of a human who keeps the shadow of a legendary vampire in his own.

"Now, phase two followed soon after, of course. I mean your duel with the first Aberration Slayer, the legendary vampire's first thrall. This is where I deserve the blame—Suruga.

"My niece got involved.

"During your first encounter with the First, he *energy-drained* Suruga's left arm, the Rainy Devil, didn't he?

"That *absorbed the effect* of the Monkey's Paw—though he must have had an affinity for it to begin with, since the First was something like a synthesis of all the aberrations in this town.

"But imagine if the First took in not just the Rainy Devil, but the pure essence of that unidentified thing that my sister made—no, I'm not getting off topic.

"I get how you see the First as your rival, but you and he are connected through Heartunderblade—Shinobu Oshino.

"In fact, Shinobu went and ate him. A part of my sister's estate made its way into you via Shinobu thanks to the food chain.

"A precedent—didn't I say?

"That's not all. If I'm the mainstay of the experts, he used to be the valve on the monster main. An 'unidentified' encompassing all the aberrational phenomena that occurred here along with their respective episodes was born as a result.

"Given her nature and origin, you're right that Ogi Oshino isn't a combat type—but she'd be quite adept at using, say, Heartunderblade's ability to generate matter.

"A hybrid monster that can rouse up just about any aberrational phenomenon—no reason to be embarrassed if you couldn't do a thing about her.

"Since she was born by way of the First, who was like the town's aberration itself, she was a true monster when it came to knowledge—though it took her quite a while to make full use of her abilities thanks to them being just so extraordinary.

"By the way, Mayoi already brought up Ogi's throwaway name and how it refers to being a Suruga Kanbaru fan, but we held off on her last name, Oshino, didn't we—now's the time to give you that explanation, Koyomin.

"Basically, it doesn't come from Mèmè Oshino, but rather, Shinobu Oshino. Considering how you two are inseparable, Ogi Oshino is like a collaboration between you and Shinobu.

"It would've been simpler if she'd gone with Ogi Araragi, but yeah, she wasn't going to be that transparent—as for claiming to be Mèmè's niece, I probably set a bad example in August when I claimed to be his little sister.

"Sorry.

"I thought I'd try apologizing.

"This is a small detail, but she must've introduced herself as a Suruga Kanbaru fan—as her junior—thanks to the element relating to Suruga's left arm.

"It was almost necessary.

"Suruga didn't know anything, of course.

"No way she could have—she barely knows anything about her own mother. Better that she doesn't—it's what my sister wanted as well.

"That's why I used a fake name and pretended to be Mèmè's little sister. I wasn't trying to play tricks on her, you know? It just ended up backfiring.

"No point in laboring over what's done—well, I'd love to be so glib, but we haven't actually gotten to anything special yet.

"Given how many times Shinobu showed off her matter-generation skill, it'd be 'okay' in a way if she'd tried to create an aberration or a high school girl.

"Compared to the examples I gave—Tsubasa Hanekawa's Black Hanekawa and Tyrannical Tiger—the logic is easier to understand since it's rooted in my sister's aberration. Likewise, Suruga manifested her own unconscious with the same Rainy Devil's left arm, and Nadeko Sengoku birthed a fantasy in herself, Mister Serpent, even if it didn't reach the level of an aberration.

"You didn't do anything that was especially weird. But uniquely, unlike those girls—uniquely like my sister—the aberration you created was *an aberration that attacked yourself*.

"It wasn't self-centered.

"It was self-critical—to the point you could call it, in a sense, auto-toxic.

"Regarding Sodachi Oikura's case.

"Regarding Mayoi Hachikuji's case.

"Regarding Nadeko Sengoku's case.

"Regarding Hitagi Senjogahara's case.

"Regarding Shinobu Oshino's case.

"Regarding Yotsugi Ononoki's case.

"Ogi Oshino blamed you tenaciously, dark rather than black—she kept on pushing you into a corner. Are you okay with that, can you forgive yourself, did you really solve it, isn't that all smoke and mirrors— she kept whispering into your ear.

"Not as a monologue, but as a dialogue.

"Nestling up close.

"…Putting it that way makes it seem like your conscience was trying to regulate you, and almost sounds praiseworthy. It must have been the same for my sister, but frankly, you're just going about your life making excuses to yourself. Bumbling around saving people, always offering aid as if you only existed to help others, hit a kind of limit and twisted your mind.

"That's nothing praiseworthy.

"To be blunt, it's a roundabout kind of self-harm.

"More than anything, you want to feel remorse, to be blamed. Ever since spring break, some part of your mind, or more like your entire body, felt like you weren't playing fair.

"You ended up saving Kissshot Acerolaorion Heartunderblade out of compassion—and sought to be punished for it.

"You formed a friendship with Tsubasa Hanekawa—and questioned your right to, since you couldn't respond to her feelings in kind.

"You rescued Hitagi Senjogahara from her longstanding distress—and wondered if going on to date her was taking advantage of her debt.

"You respect Suruga Kanbaru—and develop a complex because you could never live as sincerely as she does.

"You saved Nadeko Sengoku—but it wasn't just her that you really wanted to save then.

"You reconciled, little by little, with Shinobu Oshino—but is that forgivable? Speaking of forgiveness, the First was granted it in August by Shinobu—so aren't you petty for not granting it to her yet? Aren't you hoping to be just forgiven too?

"You pretend not to regret choosing a little girl over your girlfriend and your savior that one time, but aren't you carrying that baggage around with you?

"To begin with, isn't it cheating to make free use of immortality? Shouldn't you be punished?

"Aren't I—as terrible as it gets?

"According to Mayoi, you were mumbling about this stuff even in hell—and Ogi Oshino is the full and unfiltered expression of the critical eye you cast on yourself, a sort of Dark Koyomin. That's why she attended to it all, one by one, almost dutifully, with Sodachi Oikura's case as a blueprint—as if she was the Darkness.

"Moreover, as a spirit who's distinct from you, she's had dealings with others too. She's been working hard to create an environment where you'd be barraged with criticism.

"Mèmè Oshino and Yozuru Kagenui.

"And probably Deishu Kaiki, after he cleaned up Nadeko Sengoku's case.

"She *shut them out* of this town—because it goes without saying that their job as professionals got in the way of her own job.

"No, it wasn't too difficult. No different from what I've been doing to this park—you put a barrier in place.

"If she then makes them *lose their way*, we can't guide them to us—didn't the First cause an aberrational phenomenon that made you lose your way? In which case Ogi Oshino, with roots close to his, could do the same.

"So don't worry, Koyomin.

"Mèmè and Yozuru are probably fine.

"No guarantees about Kaiki, though, I don't understand the exact process in his case... Anyway, it seems you're concerned about them, but if they aren't here, it's only because you yourself refused the help of experts. While we might be in the dark about their whereabouts right now, once Ogi Oshino is defeated, we'll have no trouble finding them.

"Hm? Oh. I'm able to be here because I'm an expert of a superior caliber—just kidding.

"I committed the ultimate rules infraction when it comes to aberrations.

"I chopped through the barrier with the enchanted blade Kokorowatari to make my way in, how else—I forged the blade so I could cut down any imitation Darkness that came into existence, but it ended up serving an unexpected use.

"In fact, I'm only here now because I forged the blade in time—boy, was it close.

"Just like I predicted? Oh, no. Even if you begat an imitation Darkness, I thought it'd be a little smaller in scale—I guess I underestimated you in that sense.

"If I'd known, I'd have taken other measures, and sooner. We've been having to play defense instead.

"So many experts, against an amateur like you—take pride in that if you want.

"But only after we've eliminated Ogi Oshino.

"Your self-critical mindset is praiseworthy in certain situations, and maybe people could borrow a page from you—but not in a town without a god, no thanks, it's too destabilizing.

"Like I said yesterday, now that you're finished with your exams, I can't predict your moves at all—which means I can't predict what Ogi Oshino will do next, either.

"So we're setting a trap. A scheme to defeat her—to fence her in.

"Reading her next move while we still can, we'll lie in wait—I've already explained that part. If she's making a move, it'll be today.

"It'll be tonight.

"She, too, wants to avoid dealing with moves she can't predict—we should assume that her job's time limit is from now until they announce the test results, or until graduation.

"You get it, don't you?

"If she is Koyomi Araragi's self-critical mindset...if she surfaced as your guilt in face of the world, then she still has work to do.

"A job left undone.

"That's right. Tsukihi Araragi—your little sister.

"Your little sister, and not your little sister.

"An immortal aberration—the Shidenotori.

"She survives to this day, despite being Yozuru Kagenui and Yotsugi Ononoki's target, because you shamelessly and irrationally protect her—she survives mimicking a human, and a part of you, Koyomi Araragi, has to be wondering if that's fine.

"You don't hesitate to protect your little sister.

"But it's not as if you live by a clear philosophy that won't blame yourself for being unhesitant.

"So I'm going to use your sister as a decoy.

"The plan is to apprehend Ogi Oshino in the act of trying to do harm to your little sister, and to reveal the perp's true identity on the spot—to compare it to a mystery novel, as she loves to do, we have no evidence so we're going to have to catch her red-handed.

"Yep.

"That's right, no evidence—everything I said is nothing more than conjecture. It just bizarrely makes a mountain of sense. If you argued, 'No, that's impossible. I can't believe that she's me,' then there's nothing I could do to convince you otherwise.

"But you understand, right? You must know.

"Better than anyone—what she actually is. That's why you have to be the one to expose her.

"It won't work if it's me.

"If I'd gone ahead with my initial plan and forced Shinobu to become a god, I probably wouldn't enlist your help, but because you brought Mayoi back from hell with you, I can entrust you with ending this all and breathe easy.

"Breathe easy.

"Yes, I mean it—breathe easy.

"Koyomi Araragi, who's so harsh on himself that his self-criticism and self-negation birthed an aberration, can obviously defeat Koyomi Araragi, whom he hates so much.

"Win this battle against yourself.

"Easy, right? So far…

"For Kissshot Acerolaorion Heartunderblade's sake, for Tsubasa Hanekawa's sake, for Hitagi Senjogahara's sake, for Mayoi Hachikuji's sake, for Suruga Kanbaru's sake, for Nadeko Sengoku's sake, for Karen Araragi's sake, for Tsukihi Araragi's sake—going back to square one, for Sodachi Oikura's sake, you've gone to the brink of death and come back numerous times.

"Sacrificing yourself. Killing your self.

"Killing it continuously—until you landed yourself in hell.

"Koyomi Araragi, so selfless and altruistic that there must be something wrong with his head—should find defeating Ogi Oshino, none other than himself, easier than taking candy from a baby, from himself.

"You, who have been tossing your life away like a piece of trash for other people's sake, chucking any semblance of thought while you're at it, just need to do your thing here. Kill yourself without a thought.

"Commit self-harm. Commit suicide.

"Kill yourself for the sake of others.

"It's what you do every day.

"Nothing hard about it.

"Just kill yourself, show the spirit of self-sacrifice in your extreme but usual manner—what you're facing is no high school girl or junior, certainly no savior's niece, but yourself.

"So put an end to it.

"You end this, at your hand.

"That's how your—youth ends."

012

"You're actually me."

You're me.

Ogi Oshino—is Koyomi Araragi.

The moment I said it, rebuking her, *it* appeared.

I'd seen it before—but really, that's not the right word. Nothing more than a shade, a hole that sucked everything into itself, a lone, pitch black, darkness—nothing but darkness.

The Darkness.

Nothing was there.

A nihility, an absence.

So black, though, I couldn't call it emptiness.

Overwriting, blotting out the world's typos—a black, black blackness.

Black black.

Black—engulfing black.

"Well, that was fast. The main attraction, already on stage? Were the lies that serious, the crimes so grave?"

In contrast to my stunned state as I flashed back to my previous dramatic escape from it, Ogi was coolness itself—even smirking.

I knew this'd happen, of course. I'd been told.

If I exposed Ogi Oshino's true identity—which is to say, my own deceit, the Darkness would appear and swallow her up, according to Miss Gaen's plan.

I thought I was emotionally prepared, but the Darkness that I was facing once again had appeared with such astonishing abruptness.

"To think that I tried to play the part of *this*—I wasn't in my right mind, if I do say so myself. I imagined I was hewing to stricter standards than the real thing, but...not even close. It wasn't even a decent impression. I suppose being more unyielding than the world's rules, and dubbing myself the cosmic law, was unreasonable to begin with? I did hope to be dark matter."

I couldn't afford to take my eyes off the Darkness, which had entered the classroom with an impact that threw perspective out of the window, but Ogi had no problem looking away and faced me as she spoke.

Her composure seemed to imply—a critique of my own weakness, even now.

"Don't worry, I won't run or hide. I do love mystery novels, after all. Nothing more shameless than a culprit who doesn't know the score—in fact, I'm one of those old-fashioned readers who want it to end with the criminal's suicide."

"..."

"Oh, but cool and collected doesn't cut it either. It's a buzzkill in its own way, it just pisses me off, when they're calm even as they're confronted with the truth. Given that I'm about to disappear, I'm trembling on the inside. Annihilation, matter and anti-matter colliding. I'm trying to put up a bold front because you're watching, but I have to wonder, what's that like? Does it at least beat getting sent to hell?"

Ha haa, she laughed.

I was halfway out of my chair, but she showed no sign of standing up from hers.

"Suicide..." I began, my voice actually trembling. "But you knew this'd happen, didn't you? If you're me—that I'd be waiting here, having realized your true identity. So then why did you come? You could've dropped your criticism of Tsukihi's case and run away."

"Run away, like where? I just do what I need to do, even if it's pointless—remember? I'd leave some unfinished business behind, but no regrets. In that sense, it really is suicide," Ogi said with a beaming smile. "Sometimes you have to fight even if it's a losing battle. While we may never agree on anything, if you'll allow me something like my final words, I think I straightened your life out, in my own way. In a good way—though *life* might be going too far when I only spent a brief six months correcting a brief six months' worth of deeds. How about *youth*? Even if I didn't make yours any better, didn't I make it more just?"

"If this is what you call just, then I don't need my life to be just. Do you have any idea how much trouble you've caused?"

I'd resolved not to blame her—she'd done it all because of me—but the words slipped out of my mouth. I was being critical toward my self-criticism.

With the all-engulfing Darkness next to us, with nonexistence existing right there. With less than a minute left to exchange words with her.

"For Senjogahara, for Kanbaru, for Sengoku, for Hanekawa, for Shinobu, for Oshino, for Miss Kagenui, for Ononoki…for Kaiki—do you know how much trouble you've caused them? Do you have any idea just how much harm you've spread?"

"If they did suffer harm, it was nothing more than comeuppance," answered Ogi. "I didn't do anything—don't you know that yourself? Trouble, harm, misfortune, they aren't something you can come to terms with so easily. Even less so difficultly."

"But you can, if it's justice? You can neatly pack up what's right and wrong?"

"Impossible—which is exactly why I worked with you, as a team. Even if you can't determine what's right, can't you still decide which side is right?"

"…"

"Regarding Sodachi Oikura's case, I was wrong. Regarding Nadeko Sengoku's, I was right. Tadatsuru Teori's was maybe a dissatisfying draw—I knew he and Izuko Gaen were connected, believed a one-on-one match was winnable. Nor did the kind of rift I wanted between you and Yotsugi Ononoki ever materialize."

A match. That's how Ogi described it.

Okay… Then our face-off had begun as soon as we'd met—was every one of our conversations, and not just the three rounds she mentioned, a kind of duel?

A duel to test—not what's right, but which side is right.

That's what rightness meant to her…and maybe it was closer to justice than righting wrongs—however.

"What was the record in the end, then? Which of us ended up being right?"

"Since I'm about to be annihilated like this, I'd say you. Congratulations." With this, Ogi finally stood up from her chair. "What you've been doing wasn't wrong."

It was right.

Her saying so hardly made me feel any better. It was more like a fistful of salt in my wounds.

It was Ononoki who'd hit me where it hurt with her remark that I was seeking forgiveness by forgoing happiness. Since I was so pitiful, I ought to be beyond reproach—if that stance gave rise to Ogi, who'd unleashed so much fury, it put me deep in the wrong.

But maybe fury isn't correct—or right, when she'd been trying to pacify our town.

Just like Miss Gaen, in that they both sought to install a god at Kita-Shirahebi. Ogi's point of view was expansive, as if in reprimand of my inability to see past the end of my nose.

If she'd been righting my wrongs all this time, I needed to be thanking her—but I couldn't.

Even if this was goodbye, an eternal parting.

I couldn't allow myself to thank her—Koyomi Araragi and Ogi Oshino could only exist in opposition, critical of each other. We could only affirm our own existence by denying the other's.

And that existence would soon vanish. Go away—in atonement.

The imitation Darkness swallowed up by the Darkness.

"The end of youth, we might say. Or maybe of a tale. Well, nothing serious. It's not your life ending here, and nowhere near the end of the world. One of your many stories concludes, and it's not even the finale. *I'm glad I could disappear before you graduated,* great work," Ogi snuck in a mystifying bit—and dipped her head down in a bow. "Bye, Arara-gi-senpai."

"Bye, Ogi."

And now.

Ogi Oshino, who came on as Suruga Kanbaru's junior, threw my life into as much chaos as possible since second term, pulled strings behind the curtains all throughout town, crawled between the lines to dig up everything foreshadowed there, rehashed what had come to an end, demanded self-understanding and atonement, self-flagellation and silence, feared no opposition, flinched at no hostility, allowed nothing to slide with her sneering, unforgiving attitude, and forgave nobody.

Ogi Oshino, who appeared wherever I went, like my shadow—everywhere.

Her crime of self-falsification tried, her true identity exposed, like the many deceptions she herself had punished, Ogi Oshino, whom I could see anytime, would be swallowed up by the true Darkness, which virtually didn't exist, as though she never existed—leaving behind neither shape nor shadow, she'd vanish.

Her rightness and my wrongness.

My wrongness and her rightness—annihilating each other.

Done and gone, ceasing to exist.

All that she'd been up to was about to end.

So I'd say it again—I'd never allow words of gratitude to come out of my mouth, but I could at least see myself off with a recitation of my farewell.

Bye, Ogi.

Goodbye, my youth…

"*Nope, no can do!*"

I leapt.

Forcing my human body that dared not budge, using the strength in my human legs to stand from my chair, I put my mass to work like a human and ran like a human—in other words, as a plain human.

I leapt at Ogi and shoved her to the floor.

As if to dodge the Darkness, which was only inches away, I shoved a high school girl down on the cracked floor of an abandoned building.

317

I wasn't even sure if the Darkness had been moving, but it did pass over my head.

I—saved Ogi Oshino.

"A-Araragi-senpai?! Wh-What…"

For the first time.

For the first time now—Ogi let out what sounded like a panicked voice. No, thinking back, maybe this was the first time ever that I'd seen her truly shaken.

"What are you thinking?!"

Okay, maybe she was just angry.

But I couldn't respond to her anger—to her criticism. Not because I didn't know how to put my feelings into words.

I couldn't speak because I was in pain.

"…gh."

As if to dodge the Darkness, I'd said, but I hadn't actually—it had grazed my right arm.

A graze was all it needed to take the whole thing: my upper arm down was gone like it had never existed.

The bleeding wouldn't stop.

Naturally, it didn't regenerate.

I was nothing but human now.

The degree of pain probably wasn't too different from back when I was slightly vampiric, and I should've been used to it, in terms of tolerance—but the sense of loss was something else.

"Trying to save people when you aren't even immortal…" Ogi's indignation continued unabated. Still on the floor, she glared at me with her black eyes. "I-Is that who you are in the end? You throw your life away for others on a whim? You'd even save someone who only ever criticized you, who only ever attacked you? Why die here, what good will it do? Why save me here—you're wrong, after all. There's something wrong with you as a person. You're scum—"

"I wasn't trying to…" Despite everything growing hazy due to the blood loss, her rough dressing-down helped me hold on, and I replied haltingly, "…save people. I *saved myself* just now."

Miss Gaen had misjudged this one. The lady who knew everything was, how else to put it—wrong.

Hard on myself and hard on others? That wasn't me.

Self-sacrificing, self-critical, self-flagellating.

I, who couldn't stop throwing my life away for other people—self-centered for once.

Egotistically.

Saved myself.

Not caring what people wanted or how I looked, selfishly true to desire, to instinct—I saved myself.

Showing my true colors.

Self-staged, was what this was. Nothing more...

I'm hardly praiseworthy or great, and since I was such a weakling, if I didn't save myself—

I was going to die, wasn't I?

"Hitagi..." I said deliriously. "Hanekawa...Shinobu...Ononoki... saved me... They all saved me, so how can I not? How's that okay..."

"..."

Silently.

The ever-talkative girl silently and gently touched my wound—and the bleeding stopped. Using some aberration's power that she'd inherited, whether from Seishiro Shishirui or Toé Gaen I don't know, but anyway she stopped my bleeding.

Maybe this was pointless.

As pointless as shielding Ogi's body—we'd survived the initial strike, but now that I couldn't move, the Darkness might just swallow me up as well.

None of my muscles was responding to my will. Even if I reconsidered and chose to be strong and unforgiving, it'd be too late to abandon Ogi and run away—and I liked that it was too late. Getting swallowed up along with someone who'd worked so diligently on my behalf seemed like the least I could do.

"My goodness, Araragi-senpai. I was planning on offing myself, and now it's a double suicide. You do realize that I'm not a little girl?"

"Fine by me... You're still like a six-month-old...baby...aren't you."

According to Miss Gaen, defeating Ogi was easier than taking candy from a baby.

But you don't take candy from babies, you're supposed to protect them, like I was doing.

"If everything I've done so far wasn't some mistake, then I bet this isn't a mistake, either," I said. "I'm not doing things wrong."

Yes. Just as you're not.

Maybe it was because the bleeding had stopped—my words were miraculously clear. When Ogi heard them, that smile returned to her face.

No. This was another first.

It was a smile she'd never shown until now. A bit bashful, and somehow embarrassed, smile.

"You really are—such a fool."

"Not really."

Then.

I heard an unbelievable voice. Not mine or Ogi's, but a third party's—when I looked in its direction, which is to say at the door Ogi had opened to enter the classroom, I again couldn't believe who was standing there.

I thought Tsukihi had returned at first, but it was no one like my little sister, a middle-school girl who was adorable at least in appearance—a Hawaiian shirt.

A middle-aged dude in a Hawaiian shirt.

"It's nothing to sneeze at. You finally fought for yourself—I respect you, Araragi."

Easily, an unlit cigarette in his mouth.

Mèmè Oshino—uttered those words.

"…!"

I thought I was hallucinating, that on the verge of death, I was seeing the phantom of a man who couldn't be present. Yet under me, Ogi was looking in the same direction with a shocked expression, so it couldn't be a convenient delusion.

Well.

If Ogi and I were the same person, then surely, pushed to the limit, we could hallucinate the same thing—and witness a convenient mirage, like a party of travelers seeking out a desert oasis.

From behind the middle-aged delinquent, however, wobbled another figure, like a newborn fawn—or rather a dying fawn, with trembling legs. Spotting this second individual, I realized it was no convenient delusion or mirage but simply the result of honest effort.

Effort.

On the part of a girl with mottled hair who looked ready to fall flat on her pale face at any moment, bags carved so deep under her eyes that I could see them at my distance, her layers of clothes in utter disarray, just drained and depleted and dead on her feet in general—Tsubasa Hanekawa's outlandish effort.

"Ten all-nighters in a row was pushing it…"

She nevertheless wrung out her last bit of energy to force a victorious smile and point a provocative finger at Ogi, who lay under me.

"I win."

With that, Hanekawa collapsed.

So dramatically I thought she might've died—but she'd only fallen asleep.

"I don't believe it. Miss Hanekawa really brought him…from Antarctica. How did she even get there and back?" Ogi muttered in a feeble whisper I could barely make out—hm? Antarctica?

Antarctica, a frozen land that even an exceptional aberration at her full strength, Kissshot Acerolaorion Heartunderblade, could not tolerate and evacuated—*a place absolutely devoid of aberrations.*

In other words, a place absolutely no expert would visit.

Is that what she meant by…a reverse approach? We'd only searched places where Oshino might go, but should have tried places where he wouldn't, instead? Hiding a tree not in a forest but on the ocean floor—was legitimate. Yes, but it was human psychology to look for it in a forest. Who'd go dredge the ocean, other than Hanekawa…

I was speechless—she hadn't said *a paid man*, Hitagi.

Depaysement.

So Hanekawa's two possible locations had been Antarctica and its opposite, the North Pole... Beautifully winning that coin toss, she had tracked down Mèmè Oshino and, moreover, made it back to Japan with a day to spare.

"Her head's messed up."

This probably wasn't referring to the jumbled speckles of white and black—but Ogi Oshino admitting defeat to Tsubasa Hanekawa.

Come to think of it, Ogi had been wary of her from the start, which made total sense, since I knew better than anyone how incredible Hanekawa is. If Dark Koyomin was an answer to Black Hanekawa, no wonder they didn't get along.

Miss Gaen and Hachikuji's read on the name Ogi was that it played on *fan*—it seemed forced, and I realized belatedly that it wasn't just forced but tacked-on, a bit of misdirection to put it in mystery novel terms. Wasn't the point that you obtained Ogi by adding the character for *portal* on top of the *feather* in Hanekawa's name?

All that wariness, all the countermeasures did have an effect but could only buy time and got breached, futile in the final analysis—Tsubasa Hanekawa.

Just how Tsubasa Hanekawa was she?

"Araragi," Mèmè Oshino said with a grin, not so much as glancing at Hanekawa, who'd collapsed right next to him. "In an abandoned place like this... *What's the idea, shoving my cute li'l niece down to the floor*—so spirited, Araragi. Something good happen to you? You're acting awfully suspicious with a junior when you have a girlfriend."

What a ridiculous thing to say, look at the situation we're in, I nearly shot back as I always used to in this classroom, but before I could—it was gone.

Not Ogi's form. The Darkness.

The law of nature that seemed ready to engulf us at any moment vanished entirely—the existence, or nonexistence, we could neither see nor feel in the first place.

The Nothingness was no more.

"Ah..."

Niece? He just said that. About Ogi.

Mèmè Oshino said that.

In other words, he recognized her *as a relative*—meaning her *actual existence.*

Her presence was no longer a lie or fake.

Hence—the Darkness disappeared.

" "
"..."

Ogi could say nothing, dumbstruck.

Even Ogi Oshino, who acted like she saw through everything, must not have imagined being saved like this, not by someone whose return she thought she'd resisted by putting up a barrier, to keep her true identity under wraps.

But that's the kind of guy Mèmè Oshino is.

The original and progenitor—when it comes to acting like he sees through everything.

"You saved us there...Oshino," I thanked on behalf of the speechless Ogi—though speaking for her simply meant saying what I felt.

"It's not like I saved you. You just went and got saved on your own."

Well done.

When I heard those words.

I reached my breaking point and crumpled, no longer able to support my own weight—and Ogi, who had to bear all of it, groaned. *Geh*—the moan sounded real, with nothing cute about it, and perhaps proved her existence. She had substance.

Became real the moment her true identity was exposed.

Ogi Oshino became Ogi Oshino.

So ended my, Koyomi Araragi's, youth—a period when not caring for myself meant loving others, and even sacrificing myself to save someone made sense—that weak thin inebriation, that sweet deception came to an end.

But it was only the beginning of my bitter, gruesome, and evenly pitched battle against Ogi.

Neither brightly affirming myself, nor blindly negating myself.

I'd not stop thinking, and not be afraid to act; I'd not hesitate to try again, no matter how frustrating, scrutinizing my constant trials and errors, experiencing remorse and regret as if to split every hair, but taking on yet greater challenges and gambles; recouping every loss with three times the gains—an endless battle in pursuit of happiness, hereby begun in earnest.

013

The epilogue.

The following day, March fifteenth. The morning of my graduation ceremony.

Roused from bed by my little sisters Karen and Tsukihi as usual, I began walking to school for the last time—or rode my bike. Turning the pedals, yes sir, this feeling. It was the BMX Ogi had lent Tsukihi. Of course, I had to return the bike and could only use it today, but the comfort of riding one after so long was like a rich, ripe reward for making it to the future called today, to graduation.

If you're curious, when I saw Tsukihi in the morning, she'd forgotten about the reappearance of a cram school that should've burned down. Are you serious, I wondered, just how bad is your memory, but to be more precise, she seemed to have filed it away as "one of those mysterious things that happen in life."

I guess my littler little sister's days were more colored by trouble than I thought—maybe she couldn't be bothered about every low-risk event, and I was genuinely worried that starting next school year, she and Karen would be split between middle and high schools.

Despite my sweet dreams of finding my own lodgings in college, even of cohabiting with Hitagi, I couldn't leave home right away when I thought about my little sister.

What's more, her case, the phoenix, wasn't really solved.

And I doubted Hitagi would want to leave her father anyway—not to mention, all of this needed to wait until my exam results were out. In fact, if Ogi's talk about my answer sheet being a question off was true, leaving for college was a pipe dream. I could even see myself diving straight into a job hunt.

Then again, my parents might just kick me out of the house if I'd failed.

"By the way, Tsukihi, what was your wish? You know, with that hair?"

She'd started growing it out at some point, not that I was one to talk, so I brought it up as I was heading out.

A loose end that hadn't been tied up.

I'd heard a while back that she was growing it out as part of some kind of wish but realized she never told me what the wish was. If she was still growing it out, it must not have come true yet.

"Oh, right. I guess I can cut it already—I forgot I'd been making a wish to begin with."

"Now I really want to know just how bad your memory is."

"I actually made wishes about you getting into college, and about Nadeko—call it a pray-hair to the gods."

If they exist, I mean, qualified Tsukihi.

What? I had a sneaking suspicion it had to do with me, but Sengoku, too? As her older brother, I seriously needed to learn from her example when it came to friendship.

"Your exams are over one way or another, and Nadeko's doing better—yeah. Maybe there is a god."

"Yeah. Since yesterday."

"Hm?"

"It's nothing."

"Okay," Tsukihi said, easily convinced.

I was dropping a hint, did she just not care? How grand for a petite girl.

"Maybe I'll get a matching haircut with Nadeko once you find out you passed. Since the Fire Sisters are disbanding, maybe I'll team up with her next… And you, aren't you going to cut your hair?"

"Well, you know," I answered vaguely—touching the fang marks etched deep into the back of my neck, around my nape.

So the fate of her long grown-out hair depended on my test results—but I wasn't going to think about that today. Today was graduation.

I'd honestly considered dropping out at one point, but I'd made it. Right now, that alone was enough to fill my bosom.

…Oh, and I'd talked to Karen in the morning too.

Siblings talking a lot is a good thing.

"Big Brother, Big Brother. I can't canoodle with you after next month since I'll be a high schooler, so let's feed each other mouth-to-mouth one last time!"

"…"

I worried about this little sister too. Was she punch-drunk from her hundred-person sparring?

I'd never asked her if she beat all of them. I didn't want to be any more scared of her than I already was.

"Then afterwards, we can brush each other's teeth!"

"No, brush up on how people with brains act… Um, listen, Karen. Are you planning on fighting for justice even in high school—even after Tsuganoki Second's Fire Sisters disband?"

"Say no more!" she assured me, sticking out her noticeably larger breasts—I guess her chest was just as full as mine? Though I believe the expression she wanted was *needless to say*, not *say no more*…

If she cared, that is.

"Karen. In that case, pause to reflect here and try to sum up your three middle-school years. What did righteousness mean to you in the end?"

"Hrrm?"

"Righteousness. Justice. What is it?"

Doing the right thing? Righting wrongs? Perhaps deciding which side is right?

I tossed a question thrown my way by Ogi straight over to my little sister—cast it to the next generation.

I saw the Fire Sisters' justice as poetic justice, the defeating of bad guys, but wondered what they saw themselves as performing—and how she planned to proceed.

"Helping people."

Making no attempt to understand my question, Karen responded reflexively—a straightforward and easy-to-understand answer, hard to argue with, but just as hard to carry out. That was her answer.

"Oh," I said.

I climbed on a nearby chair, reached out my hand, and patted her head (can't reach without climbing one).

A submissive gesture for vampires, all it signified here was affection for my awful little sister.

"Well, why don't you start by helping yourself?"

You better.

That's how our conversation went—but whatever happened, my bigger little sister's high school life probably wouldn't suck like mine.

May Karen Araragi continue to be unbroken by righteousness...

So I happily creaked along, pedaling an unfamiliar bicycle, when a figure stood before me that I recognized at once—a pigtailed fifth grader wearing a large backpack.

Had I come up on her from behind, I might have spent another five pages pretending to hesitate, like a true virtuoso, before going to embrace her, but sadly she was facing me and walking in my direction.

Even I couldn't tackle that.

"Hey, Hachikuji," I called out to her like a normal person.

"Please don't speak to me," she said with a visible frown. "I'm a god now."

It went to her head! And she was back where she started!

"If you have to speak to me, bow twice, clap twice, bow one more time, then present me with an offering like you're supposed to for a god."

To begin with, Hachikuji didn't look any different even if she was a god—she wasn't wearing the garb of a shrine maiden or any traditional attire.

Maybe in the future, but I guess aberrations, like humans, don't change overnight. Only gradually.

"So why's a god wandering around town? Don't tell me you're lost."

"Don't be ridiculous. I'm on the side of saving the lost now, unironically at that."

"Who's being ridiculous? I gotta admit though, it's quite a promotion…"

"I'm taken aback that you'd call this wandering around. Observing the lowly creatures of the world below is one of the more trivial duties of a god."

"This god stuff has really gotten to your head. Don't change so much overnight. Gradual change, I was saying."

"Is your commencement ceremony being held today, Mister Araragi? I'd like to congratulate you on all your hard work," Hachikuji lauded me at last and bowed her head. "I'd love to attend and help you celebrate, but my divine presence could disturb the unwashed masses, so I abstain out of consideration."

"You know, no one's coming to worship at your shrine. This town is going to end up godless again."

"Ha ha ha. Don't say that. Come by whenever you'd like. All are free to worship at Kita-Shirahebi, do come over to play anytime."

"Sure. I'll come over—to play at your house."

"Yes, to my house," Hachikuji said and walked off in the direction I came from—she wasn't kidding as far as the bit about observing our town.

" … "

I saw her off.

Well, she wasn't the type to sit quietly at home. Interacting with her took me back but also seemed normal.

It was a normal that had required no small effort.

In any case, Miss Gaen's terribly reckless plan to deify Mayoi Hachikuji seemed to have worked out in the end—honestly, I'd had my doubts about such a forced solution, but you might say that's what the big boss of the experts was capable of.

"Capable? You mean you, Koyomin, because I sure didn't expect it to end this way. Please, I'm begging you, don't go around spreading stupid rumors that I was envisioning an ending this slapdash from the start," she'd told me the previous night.

Did she have to go that far?

"Seriously, I haven't been this shocked since I mentioned Nostradamus' prophecy just to pander to a kid and was told, 'I wasn't born yet in 1999'—guess I'm getting up there."

"I'm not seeing your point."

"There's no particular point. Just that we're living in a future that didn't end then."

"Okay...but Miss Gaen. A lot of the credit for getting to our slapdash ending should go to Hanekawa." I mean, if not for her, wouldn't Ogi and I have died in a double suicide? Nothing interesting about that end.

"Right, she does deserve my thanks for finding that amateurish junior of mine—I can only raise a white flag to her. What's really amazing isn't that she found him, but that she found him and brought him back."

"...Because she broke through the barrier? But it wouldn't affect Hanekawa, who's a resident of this town—the Lost Cow can't make you lose your way if you want to go home."

"No, that's not what I mean," Miss Gaen brushed my lay opinion aside with a shake of her head. "She managed to make him feel like it."

"..."

"As far as I know, Mèmè Oshino isn't the type to make a 'Special Cameo Appearance'—and when I say as far as I know, it's a fact... By the way, are you sure about this, Miss Shinobu?" she asked the golden-haired, golden-eyed babe (and not little girl) standing next to me. "If I'm being honest with you, your decision pleases me, as an expert, but your desire to be sealed in Koyomin's shadow again is one I have trouble understanding. If you have some kind of aim here, I'd like you to make it clear."

"I harbor none—is tiring of battle and wishing to be regarded once more as harmless so mystifying to an expert? I think not. Kakak!"

From little girl to bewitching woman. She now wanted to go back to being a little girl. Our link hadn't been restored yet, but as she answered with her gruesome smile, I could tell she wasn't lying.

"If my master, who fast removed all traces of vampirism from his form, doth protest against becoming a mockery of a human and of a vampire, I defer to his wishes of course—having healed his arm, I shall retreat to a mountain mayhap to live as a recluse."

"Like I'd ever let you," I spoke up before Miss Gaen could. "You know there aren't any Mister Donut branches in the mountains."

"True."

After this exchange—and naturally, after I vowed not to err and become a vampire again by offering excessive blood libations, or rather donations, my link to Shinobu was fixed for a third time. Kissshot Acerolaorion Heartunderblade, who hadn't enjoyed her full form since spring break, was sealed off in my shadow once more as Shinobu Oshino, a harmless eight-year-old kid.

During spring break, there was no choice—but this time was different.

Of her own will.

She sealed away her existence—and wasn't lying or faking it. She, who'd rejected godhood four hundred years ago, chose to be a little girl, four hundred years later.

Well, maybe there was no choice. At least, I didn't have any future that involved not living alongside Shinobu.

Not that we'd forgiven each other, needless to say—a time to forgive, and to forget, might come after four hundred years; for now, that's where our relationship stood, whether you call it collusion or caprice, custom or compromise.

"If you want to die tomorrow, I'm ready for my life to end tomorrow—if you care to live for today, then so will I."

"If ye were to die the day after tomorrow, I shall live until the day after that—to speak of thee to another. I shall speak, and they shall listen to the tale of my master."

I arrived at school.

I passed through the gates decorated for graduation and headed toward the bike racks—to find Tsubasa Hanekawa waiting there.

Maybe model students were exemplary in terms of stamina too. Outwardly, at least, she'd made a complete recovery from last night's state of exhaustion—even the bags under her eyes had vanished. I was impressed.

"Good morning, Araragi."

"Good morning, Hanekawa—so you made it to graduation. I thought you'd be dead all of today." Was *tough* even the right word? Who knew, maybe she was the most immortal of us all. "And you're in the bike lot because…"

"I was waiting for you, of course—there's a lot I want to talk to you about."

"Yeah?"

"I need to leave as soon as the ceremony is over, so I thought this would be the only time we could really talk."

"…"

What an active girl. If she was going to say that, I needed to talk to her too—about a mountain of things. Or rather, I wanted to compare answers with her.

"Do you have a plane to catch? Is that why you're leaving so soon?"

"Mm. Mmm. Well," Hanekawa demurred somewhat. She ran her fingers through her hair, now significantly longer since she cut it during first term—it wasn't speckled, of course, because she dyed it black for school. "In bringing Mister Oshino back from Antarctica, I kind of sold off my brain."

"You sold your brain…"

What the heck—that didn't sound safe, at all.

"Jet-setting, I guess you'd say?" she went on. "That's about the only way I could charter a fighter plane—don't worry. I sold it to a relatively scrupulous agency."

"…"

What kind of international adventure had she gone on, exactly?

But no surprise that she was outsized in the real world too.

It felt quite strange in the first place for her to be at school in a uniform—though this would be my last time seeing her in her school uniform.

I felt like I should ogle her when I thought about it that way.

Ogle, ogle.

"Don't make me knock you down."

"Yikes."

Was it overseas, too, where she acquired this level of defense?

If she'd learned how to fight, she was perfect at this point.

"Speaking of fighting," I said, "Miss Kagenui seems to be at the North Pole. It took Miss Gaen all of five minutes to find out after she learned Oshino's location."

"Oh—I decided to go with the continental choice out of a vague hunch, but I guess I wouldn't have been wrong if I'd chosen the North Pole," remarked Hanekawa, the tension seeming to leave her shoulders— that part really must have been a gamble.

If you were separating Oshino and Miss Kagenui, though, she had to be the one at the North Pole—she couldn't walk on the ground, after all. Ogi had no choice but to send her there where it was all icebergs and no ground.

"Ononoki wanted to go get her, but apparently Miss Kagenui is having a blast fighting polar bears, a training method I've heard of somewhere, and is fine for now," I told Hanekawa.

"What an incredible lady... I'm glad I didn't end up going there. Wait, then what about Ononoki? What's she doing now? Has she left our town, like Miss Gaen and Mister Oshino?"

I shook my head at the question. "She's still at my house."

"That's..."

Hanekawa had a subtle look on her face.

And I couldn't blame her.

I did realize that Ononoki's prediction that Miss Kagenui had gone off on a journey to better herself, while still wrong, wasn't too far off the mark. Maybe she'd come closest to the truth.

I hate admitting that.

"I guess it's more like Miss Gaen and Oshino left too suddenly— adults are always so busy," I said.

All too soon.

The way Miss Gaen took off with an "Alrighty, bye-bye" after installing Hachikuji as the god of Kita-Shirahebi and sealing Shinobu back into my shadow was one thing, but before I knew, Oshino had left without a word yet again—as if to disappear along with the ruins Ogi had created.

Truly like some mirage, he flat-out, flatly vanished.

Without the time to so much as reminisce before parting anew—but we'd been reunited after he'd gone all the way out to the South Pole, so I knew we'd meet again in the not-too-distant future.

Still, scramming before I could even thank him for everything, including the Tadatsuru business, was pretty unforgivable.

And in this way—whatever way this is—I gained custody of Ono-noki for the time being, pending the conclusion of Miss Kagenui's training. Assuming Miss Gaen hadn't just forgotten the familiar, maybe it meant continued surveillance.

I'm not complaining. I did mess up.

Personally, I felt like I'd cleaned things up, but not everyone out there would agree.

Least of all, her—myself.

"Adults... Aren't we also going to be adults starting tomorrow?" asked Hanekawa.

"Hitagi and I will still be students. You're the only one becoming an adult."

"Hitagi?" I thought I'd dished out a snappy line but had only slipped up, and Hanekawa latched onto my misstep gleefully. "Huh, I see. I see—while I was gone."

"Wait, wait, wait. Don't jump to any conclusions. It hasn't gone as far as you might be imagining."

"Good, good—I can leave with my mind at ease," Hanekawa said and started walking.

She'd wanted to talk to me before she left Japan again—was that it? She really cared about her friends...or just worried too much.

You could say she'd singlehandedly solved everything this time—indeed, everything since August. Forget about due credit, maybe it was all hers.

Exactly a year ago.

If I hadn't met Hanekawa then, what would my last year of high school have been like? I couldn't help but get sentimental.

Not making friends.

Because it'd lower my intensity as a human—leaving those words behind, I might've graduated alone, in silence (or failed to).

It might've been fine in its own way. But now, I could only picture this way.

"Oh...right."

"Hm? What's the matter, Araragi?"

"Well, I know it's a little late to bring it up, but I noticed something... The reason Miss Gaen was so sure Ogi would make a move on Tsukihi on March fourteenth."

Ogi had said it herself, too. She wanted to put an end to it before I graduated, the point, her read, being: before my youth ended.

While still in high school.

As much as Ogi needed an opening in my schedule, she also needed Tsukihi to show an opening...but my littler little sister is full of them. Surviving without doing a thing really makes her a phoenix.

As I headed to my classroom alongside Hanekawa—we ran into Hitagi Senjogahara by the building entrance. Catching sight of the two of us together, she grimaced for a second—no doubt because Hanekawa had managed to ambush me first.

Please, no odd battle between friends...so damn uncomfortable.

Sure, Hitagi had a stubborn complex when it came to her, but given how Hanekawa had soared to a height that neither of us could reach, curbing those feelings little by little would only be wise...

Not that I was one to talk—in spite of singing her praises, somewhere inside of me I too saw her as a rival in that I'd given birth to Ogi Oshino, who couldn't stand her.

"Good morning, Araragi."

"Oh? You don't call him Koyomi?" Hanekawa asked before I could reply. She'd gotten a little meaner after being knocked around by the world.

Maybe Hitagi thought resistance was futile. "Good morning, Koyomi," she corrected herself, cheeks mildly aflush. "And welcome back, Tsubasa."

While she was at it, she also first-named Hanekawa—who looked surprised but returned, like the genius she was, "Glad to be home,

335

Hitagi-chan."

Hitagi-chan…sounded so cute.

Probably because they'd be talking taking girl-to-girl in due course, Hanekawa didn't get into how she'd be leaving soon after the ceremony, and the three of us walked to our classroom.

The school's atmosphere felt different too—but that just had to be me.

"Koyomi. It seems like Kanbaru got us a graduation present."

"Oh, yeah? A present from Kanbaru? I'm worried."

"She wouldn't prepare a weird surprise for something like this, not even her. I did ask in so many words, and it seems to be a regular bouquet of flowers."

"Flowers, huh."

Hitagi was worried too if she bothered to ask—meanwhile, not putting any questions to me, as we conversed, was very much like her. No attempts to ferret out whatever happened last night or how we cleaned things up.

She waited for me to tell her.

It wouldn't put me in a flattering light, it wasn't anything I was eager to volunteer—but she needed to hear about everything.

I hoped it would come across as a funny story.

I hoped I could tell it to her with a smile.

"By the way, Araragi," Hanekawa said. "How many points short of a perfect score were you on your exams?"

"…"

Who asked such a question?

She meant it as a joke, of course.

I told her I seemed to have filled in the wrong bubbles by one question for math—and Hanekawa was pensive for a moment.

"I don't think so," she said. "I contacted Miss…someone who took the same college's math exam and already asked about the kinds of test questions you had. This wasn't the kind of answer sheet where you could lose your place."

She was way too proactive. Just how concerned was she about me, anyway?

But…not that kind of answer sheet?

True, I'd wondered how I could be off by one question when there hadn't been that many, but why would Ogi…

I'd assumed it was true since she said it.

"That is so Ogi's way of being mean," commented Hitagi. "I could never imagine you pranking anyone like that."

Was that right? No, she said it precisely because I never would—I'd burdened her with doing what I couldn't and wouldn't do.

All this time until now, and probably going forward.

I was reminded of Kanbaru, who'd gotten us flowers—Suruga Kanbaru, a distant, underlying cause of Ogi Oshino's birth, who had no direct knowledge of the Darkness but, compared to me, had far more of what it took to exert self-control.

Above all, a direct descendant of Toé Gaen—in some form, a disposition that gave birth to aberrations must have been passed down their lineage.

Which meant Kanbaru, too, might experience being in the throes of her youth.

Her own Ogi Oshino could appear before her—would I be able to support her when that happened?

Just as Hanekawa had done for me?

…Well, I'd just have to do my best.

I'm only me, after all.

Not just as Oshino, nor just as Hanekawa, but just as me, I'd lend my support.

So that someone could go and get saved on her own.

I thought these things like I'd come to a great understanding as I finished climbing the stairs, and just then, it happened.

I crossed paths with a girl—a student who descended the stairs without looking our way. A first-year, judging by the color of her scarf. She had to be here for our graduation ceremony, but why was a first-year in the third-year area?

The girl looked so pale, however, that it quashed any such questions—and her wobbling, unsteady gait got me worried about her mental state as much as her physical condition.

She looked drained.

Possessed.

At that notion—I stopped.

Hitagi and Hanekawa turned back to look at me and shrugged in resignation. Their movements synchronized, the best of friends.

"Go ahead."

They spoke in unison as well.

"Yeah. Could you pick up my diploma for me?"

See you, I said, handing my bag to Hitagi and leaping down the whole set of stairs I'd just climbed—in pursuit of the first-year student. With the eyes of the two girls watching me off at my back, I hit the landing, pivoted, and rushed down another set of stairs.

Searching where the girl might have gone, I ran through the first-year halls, past another student—who had pitch-black eyes.

Like darkness itself, she sneered.

And said, "You never change, do you, Araragi-senpai."

No.

I do.

But no matter how much I change, I'm going to be me.

"Long, long ago, in a distant land, was an odd fellow named Koyomi Araragi—aye, and is still."

Happily ever after, my shadow recited, running alongside me.

If the story continued, I couldn't wait to hear what happened next.

Afterword

So, people talk about *mistakes you can't live down,* but when you really think about it, what sort of fail can you live down? If you lose something or suffer a defeat, it's not as if some later accomplishment cancels it out—still, while a fail might never go away no matter how much regret or remorse you feel, it certainly seems possible to forget about it. In other words, *a mistake you can live down* implies a win big enough that lets you forget that earlier mistake, doesn't it? In success stories where a miserable past serves as a springboard, misery is by no means fueling happiness, but rather, perhaps, accumulating enough of a future lets the past be forgotten; conversely, you can accumulate enough misery to ruin a happy present, so actually I don't see much of a causal relationship between happiness and misery. Like, they aren't antonyms or anything. This is getting complicated, so to lay it out—or just to split hairs about success and failure, happiness and misery, as I see fit—it's not all a matter of mindset but instead simply a question of memory. That's to say, the most powerful ability we have as humans might be *forgetting.* Of course, as Koyomi Araragi, Hitagi Senjogahara, and Tsubasa Hanekawa proved over the course of a year in this story, or ten years in my reckoning, I think the ability shouldn't be spammed.

And so, this has been *End Tale* part three, the de facto final installment of the Final Season of the *MONOGATARI* series. Looking back, "Hitagi Crab" was published in the *Shosetsu Gendai* supplement *Mephisto*'s September 2005 issue—supposedly as a self-contained short story, but it's 2014 now and I'm still writing, so more than incredible, it's a plain shock. I imagine some folks have been reading along for ten years, while others read them all just yesterday, but it's thanks to all of you that I've been able to pen the *Monster, Wound, Fake, Cat Black/White, Dandy, Flower, Decoy, Demon, Love, Possession, Calendar,* and *End Tales* to finish the series. After this, we'll cutely publish *End Tale (Cont.),* an encore final installment of the Final Season, and wrap it up for real. Yes, cutely. And so, this has been *OWARIMONOGATARI Part 03,* "Chapter Five: Mayoi Hell," "Chapter Six: Hitagi Rendezvous," and "Chapter Seven: Ogi Dark."

The cover depicts Senjogahara with braids inside a planetarium.* It's fantastic. My thanks go out to VOFAN. Whatever I may forget, I'd never forget my gratitude as I continue to work my hardest.

Thank you very much for reading.

* Editor's Note: The art that has been included as an insert for this translation. In the previous paragraph, references to the original "seventeen volume" partitioning were omitted to reflect the larger count of the North American release—which also kicked off with *Wound* rather than *Monster* and rolled out over half the time.

NISIOISIN

BAKEMONOGATARI

OH!GREAT

ORIGINAL STORY:
NISIOISIN

ORIGINAL CHARACTER
DESIGN: VOFAN

One day, high-school student Koyomi Araragi catches a girl
named Hitagi Senjogahara when she trips.

But—much to his surprise—she doesn't weigh anything. At all.

She says an encounter with a so-called "crab" took away all her weight...

Monsters have been here since the beginning.
Always.
Everywhere.

VOLUMES 1-9 AVAILABLE NOW!

Seraph of the End

Guren Ichinose: Catastrophe at Sixteen

Story by Takaya Kagami
Art by Yamato Yamamoto

All 4 Volumes Available Now!

The apocalypse is not only near, but a certainty. Set before the event and the aftermath detailed by the hit manga, this stand-alone prequel light novel series chronicles the inexorable approach of the reign of vampires. At the center of this story arc are the trials of Guren Ichinose, who enters an academy for the insufferably privileged and hides his true strength even as he is trampled on.

And Don't Miss...
Guren Ichinose: Resurrection at Nineteen

Story by Takaya Kagami
Art by Yo Asami
Volumes 1-2 Available Now!

KOYOMIMONOGATARI

CALENDAR TALE

PART 02

NISIOISIN

VERTICAL.

KOYOMIMONOGATARI
Calendar Tale

Part 02

NISIOISIN

Art by VOFAN

Translated by Daniel Joseph

VERTICAL.

KOYOMIMONOGATARI, PART 02

© 2013 NISIOISIN
All rights reserved.

First published in Japan in 2013 by Kodansha Ltd., Tokyo.
Publication rights for this English edition arranged
through Kodansha Ltd., Tokyo.

Published by Vertical, an imprint of
Kodansha USA Publishing, LLC, 2019

ISBN 978-1-947194-69-4

Manufactured in the
United States of America

First Edition

Second Printing

Kodansha USA
    Publishing, LLC
451 Park Avenue South
7th Floor
New York, NY 10016

www.readvertical.com

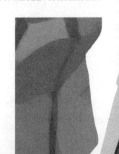

CHP SEVEN

KOYOMI
TEA

CHP EIGHT

KOYOMI
MOUNTAIN

CHP NINE

KOYOMI
TORUS

CHP TEN

KOYOMI
SEED

CHP ELEVEN

KOYOMI
NOTHING

CHP TWELVE

KOYOMI
DEAD

CHAPTER SEVEN
KOYOMI TEA

SUN	MON	TUE	WED	THU	FRI	SAT
1	2	3	4	5	6	7
8	9	10	11	12	13	14
15	16	17	18	19	20	21
22	23	24	25	26	27	28
29	30	31				

10
October

001

Tsukihi Araragi, the younger of my two little sisters, doesn't really give the impression of someone walking down a road—but when I say that, I'm not trying to evoke some cool sense of treading a path that is not a path or blazing new trails in life. How can I put this? It seems like she forges ahead lightly, airily, as if she's flying.

That's just my personal view as her big brother.

I wouldn't go so far as to call it a viewpoint.

Though I bet almost everyone who knows her thinks of her as being hard to pin down—as she floats about like a bird.

Hard to pin down, hard to figure out.

Everyone knows that birds can fly—but the fascinating thing is, apparently they were equipped with the capacity to fly even before they flew. They call that preadaptation.

Without the capacity they could never have flown, so it stands to reason. Still, it's strange when you think about it. Before birds branched off from reptiles, before they flew, they were already prepared to fly.

When you get right down to it, isn't that more like a dormant ability than evolution? Knowing that they'd soar through the skies someday, they steadily prepared themselves—evolution is supposed to be a process of natural selection via adapting to circumstance, but they foresaw the potential circumstance and adapted to it in advance.

That sort of canny shrewdness does remind me of my little sister. She may not have her feet planted firmly on the ground, but that only contributes to her birdlike quality.

Asking someone like her might be pointless, but I asked her anyway.

Tsukihi, how do you see the path you tread—even if her road isn't contiguous with the ground, the skies must have pathways too.

They must have tracks.

Even airplanes follow fixed courses at fixed times, traveling along predetermined flight paths—taking into consideration air resistance and the direction of the wind. So even Tsukihi, floating along like a cloud, had to have a path, or the concept of a path, that served as her compass, that she took to be her compass.

Hence my question.

However.

"There're no paths in the sky, big brother," answered Tsukihi. "Even if there were, I'd ignore them. I just can't do things the way they're supposed to be done."

My little sister was even more of a risk than I'd imagined.

If she was dead set on being a bird, not an airplane, then getting sucked into the engine of a jet and causing a major accident almost seemed like a certainty.

002

"Welcome home, big brother!"

"Hi, Tsukihi."

"Back early, huh? I've got goodies, you want some?"

"Goodies? Yeah, I'd love some."

"I've got tea, too."

"Well, aren't you thoughtful."

"I've got something I need to talk to you about, too."

"I'll have some of that as well…hey."

And so I was cajoled into listening to what Tsukihi had to say. Such a fluid delivery, truly a rare bird of a strategist—though this time I'd left myself wide open.

Always a mistake to be too amiable with my sister.

In any event, my defenses were down because I'd just gotten home from school, and Tsukihi ambushed me, one day in October.

Enjoying the tea and cakes she'd set out in our living room, I found myself lending an ear to her, like with Karen the previous month. Both of my little sisters were starting to communicate with me like they'd used to, which was in itself a welcome turn of events, and I'd be lying if I said it didn't make me happy, but it was also getting in the way of my exam prep.

Well.

It was hard to imagine that Tsukihi's issue would be as sensitive as Karen's and something I'd want to help out with. As far as I could tell, Karen was the driving force behind the Fire Sisters' game of defenders of justice, and Tsukihi was just along for the ride—I was pretty sure her problem was asinine.

No doubt we'd have it sorted out before the tea and cakes were even finished—the cakes were the real deal, she must've brought them home from the school tea ceremony club's supply.

Wondering if they could be lumped under the general heading of "sweets," I nonetheless ignored etiquette and started grabbing them and popping them into my mouth.

I say ignored, but damned if I know the proper etiquette.

"Okay, dear brother. My dear, dear brotherother."

"Keep it simple, stupid."

"I'm doubling the respect I'm showing you. So, about this thing."

"Keep it brief. I'll stay as long as these delightful cakes hold out. Now, can you put your big brother to good use?"

"Do you believe in ghosts?"

"Ghosts?"

If I have to say, I generally don't. They're just an excuse to disappear some donuts.

"Why, did you hear something from Sengoku?" I probed, not sure how candid I should be with my little sister.

Given her information network, keeping tabs on the happenings in this town over the past six months, regarding that swindler or anything else, wasn't all that hard. But how much of it would she swallow even if she found out about it?

The thing is, though in a different way than Karen, Tsukihi too is a realist—however birdlike, she wouldn't be gulled into believing in "charms" and what have you so easily.

"What does Nadeko have to do with anything? Sometimes I have no idea what you're on about, big brother."

Indeed, she cocked her head in confusion. That was comforting, but to keep her from realizing that it comforted me, I answered her question with a question. "Never mind. Why this sudden talk of ghosts, though? Is there one in the tea room at school or something?"

I had no basis for supposing there was, I was just continuing with the questions to distract her from the Sengoku thing—and simply combining her talk of "ghosts" with the cakes I assumed she'd brought from there.

It just so happened I was right on the money.

Let no one cast aspersions on my hunches. If only I could manifest my penetrating intuition on a scantron sheet—it never seems to work when I fill in the bubbles with wild guesses.

"Exactly, I'm impressed," confirmed Tsukihi.

"Huh? Exactly, like how?"

My pathetic response made it seem like I couldn't even remember what I'd just said. What a birdbrain, a fitting brother for Tsukihi.

Yours truly.

"Like, there's a ghost in the tearoom—" she said, twisting her pigtails, which she had for a month now, around her finger. I'd advised against the look, but she wasn't the type to listen to her big brother. "Or actually, there *was* a ghost in the tearoom."

"Actually?"

Once there's a ghost involved, we're miles away from *actual*, but I could check myself a little longer to see where this was going.

"And?" I prompted.

There were still plenty of cakes and tea, so I was ready and willing to stick with her story a little longer. Unlike Karen, Tsukihi was thankfully blessed with at least a modicum of conversational prowess—the act of listening itself was unlikely to be a source of stress.

"I just told you, there was a ghost."

"When you say 'there was'…what exactly do you mean? There were signs a ghost had been in the tearoom?"

"Signs, no…I couldn't tell you there was. There's no objective proof that *the girl* was there."

The girl? Oddly specific.

"Tsukihi, let me enlighten you about something. No proof means no ghost. Great, so it's settled. We'll use whatever time we have left for a nice chat."

"Hup!"

Tsukihi launched an attack at me, her older brother. Wielding a three-color retractable ballpoint pen that happened to be sitting on the table—she wasn't trained in any kind of combat technique, unlike Karen, and so had no compunction about bringing a weapon to a fight.

Just when Senjogahara finally gave up using office supplies as armaments… Tsukihi had a short fuse, but I was starting to suspect she was also the other kind of mad.

Truly terrifying.

To think that one phone call was all it'd take to cart off someone who lived under the same roof… Thankfully, primed by my long years of being her brother, I easily dodged the three-color clicky pen.

I used the boxing technique known as a sway. It'd never be of use to me in the future, and naturally, I want nothing to do with a future where I'd need it to be of use.

"Chat, my ass. I want to talk to you *about* something, not just talk to you."

"Okay, okay…whoa there. I get it, so stow that pen already."

"Stow? Which color?"

"All of them. Black, blue, and red, stow 'em all. So? What's the deal? There was a ghost in the tearoom, but there's no proof?"

"That's what I said. Weren't you listening?"

"You're the one who's not listening. No proof means no ghost, doesn't it." I didn't think it bore repeating, but my sagacious little sister was also stubborn, and maybe I just needed to say the same thing twice. "In fact, let me guess. You proved there was no ghost?"

"Wow. How did you know?"

Tsukihi was floored.

Her reaction was gratifying. Just a touch more and it would've seemed contrived, but if I may, my little sister is quite good at discerning where to draw that line.

"Well done, big brother, you're a genius!"

"I'm no genius, all it took was a little hard work."

By contrast, I tend to get carried away and step right over it.

Well, in this case, it was less about hard work and more about having accumulated XP as a big brother—I can sort of tell what she's likely to do.

You never know what she might be getting up to, but at the same time, I know how "you never know what she might be getting up to"— there's a high degree of randomness to her behavior, but I have some sense of its general orientation.

Thanks to that, I can apply the brakes… Karen's similar, but the problem with her is that her speed and power are of a different order of magnitude. I can try to stop her, but a "road closed" sign means nothing to her.

She blasts right through any roadblock.

True, Tsukihi might soar right over it—but that's what nets are for.

I bet the story went something like this:

Whether it was a so-called "school ghost story" or more like "the seven wonders of campus," rumors had sprung up about a spirit haunting the Tsuganoki Second Middle School tea ceremony club's venerable tearoom—and Tsukihi set out to investigate, probably as private citizen Araragi rather than as a member of the Fire Sisters.

And she resolved it.

"Resolved" might be the wrong word when the truth is that there was no "it"—but anyway, she gathered evidence and testimonies, and demonstrated that no spirit haunted the tearoom.

There is no ghost there, she concluded—more or less.

Through plain old intuition, or something sub-intuition, I'd hit upon the notion that a ghost lurked in the tearoom; meanwhile, on my honor as a big brother, the above conjecture must be more or less correct. That would also raise some questions, though.

If I was right, what the hell did Tsukihi want to discuss with me? Wasn't the issue—the case, already closed?

This "girl" doesn't exist—and never did.

That was the punch line.

We could call it a day with a simple: *Nice one, Tsukihi.*

Maybe she wanted me to lavish her with praise?

I'd feel awkward praising my little sister…yet if that was the right epilogue, well, I don't know about in ages past, but these days I had no real objection.

"Well done, Tsukihi, you're a genius!"

"You're missing the point. I've got a problem."

I thought she'd be as pleased as I was if I praised her in the same way, but nope—her face just clouded over.

"What should I do, big brother?"

"Hm? About what?"

"C'mon, like you said—I explained, logically, that there was no ghost… But nobody believes me."

Everyone.

Believes in the ghost instead—griped Tsukihi, sipping her tea.

003

There's a game called Square.

Well, it doesn't have much entertainment value, or as we'll see, it's a group activity that doesn't pass muster as a game—but it's famous, so I'm sure everyone will have heard of it, even if I don't go into it here. That said, it's kind of my job to go into stuff that everyone must have heard of, so here's a barebones description.

The field, or scene, is often a cabin on a snow-covered mountain during a blizzard—and the players are four stranded climbers.

The standard fare in that scenario is "Don't fall asleep, you'll die if you do!" as they slap your cheek—though there are various theories about whether you'd actually die. Some argue that it'd maintain your strength, and your life, by slowing down your metabolism—but anyway, Square is played under those circumstances, to keep from falling asleep.

Each person goes to stand in a different corner of the room—and the game begins. A goes to where B is standing, and taps B on the shoulder. This signals B to go to where C is standing and tap C on the shoulder. As you might expect, C then goes to where D is standing and taps D on the shoulder. Finally, D goes to tap A on the shoulder, and one circuit, or round, is complete, and we're back to the beginning.

Circling the room in this fashion, the quartet manage to stay awake until dawn, and that's that—okay, I'm sure I don't need to tell you that "that" is not in fact "that."

You see, when D finally goes to tap A on the shoulder, A isn't there—since at the outset, A went to where B was standing. D just heads to an empty corner, and the game would end right there, hence the lack of entertainment value.

Mysteriously, though, sometimes the game continues through the night without interruption. Or so they say.

For Square to work, you need five people for four corners, so at some point, a "fifth person" gets involved to help the stranded climbers stay awake. When morning finally comes, the survivors realize: *You can't play this game with only four. Who was the fifth person?*

It'd be uncouth of me to sneer that surely someone would've noticed sooner—I mean, however sleepy you are, notice it already—or to opine that if your goal is to kill time and stay awake, surely there are smarter ways. Understood as a ghost story, it's mysterious but not very scary, a kind of feel-good anecdote. After all, the "fifth person" saved the lives of the other four…

Not that Tsukihi played Square in the tearoom with her club-mates. From what I've heard of the kimono fashion show they put on for the culture festival, they seem pretty uninhibited, but I doubt tea ceremony aficionados would run around in circles in their sacred space.

I don't even remember where I first heard about Square, or from whom, but what Tsukihi said reminded me of that rumor of a ghost story.

The "fifth person."

Well, since there were currently seven people in the tea club, the "eighth person"—Eight is Great, as they say, though I don't think that's relevant here.

"Um, so you're saying there'd been sightings of this 'eighth person'? And you squashed the rumor?"

"I didn't squash anything. There wasn't any 'eighth person' to begin with—it was just a rumor that arose spontaneously. The idea that my stronghold was being fingered as the point of origin for such a weird-ass rumor stuck in my craw, so I decided to look into it, big brother."

"…"

Weird-ass, stuck in my craw—pretty rough choice of words… Talking with her one on one like this, I couldn't help but think that dealing with Karen, whose personality was super straightforward even if she seemed like the rough one at first glance, was so much easier.

"I'll spare you the details, but I logically refuted every single account of a sighting and every piece of circumstantial evidence that this rumor about an 'eighth member' was based on. Logically."

"Don't harp on the logically part. Makes it sound like a lie."

"Saying that it sounds like a lie makes you sound like an asshole," Tsukihi puffed out her cheeks. "When you eliminate the impossible, whatever remains is whatever remains when you eliminate the impossible."

"That's true, logically speaking, but…"

It also didn't mean anything, logical or not.

"But whether you were squashing a rumor or investigating it, why the whole brouhaha? People might start spreading rumors about your own behavior. You've got a real match-pump approach."

"Match-pump? Huh? What does that even mean?"

"Um…"

If you haven't put too much thought into it, being asked about your word choice can catch you off guard. In my case, since I don't have a particularly large vocabulary, I occasionally use expressions because I like the way they sound, without really understanding what they mean, which sometimes leads me to realize that I've been using them wrong.

In order to keep a smug look off my sister's face and maintain my dignity as her older brother, I had to give a proper explanation…

"'Match' as in a match you light a fire with. The kind you strike. The 'pump' is like a water pump—so 'match-pump' means you light something on fire and then put it out yourself."

"I understand the pump part, but what's a match?"

"…"

Are matches that obscure? Was it a generational thing?

I explained to her that it's like a lighter.

The mechanism is totally different, of course, but she'd get the general idea.

"Hmm… In other words, like Miss Hanekawa."

"No, in other words like you. Don't criticize Hanekawa."

"I'm not being critical. I'm being supportive, really supportive. I'm a real Hanekawa supporter, and a real me supporter too."

"I'm pretty sure you're the biggest you supporter around…"

"I'm so supportive I'm like Atlas. By match-pump approach, you mean I always take responsibility for my own actions, right?"

"…"

Tsukihi's one hell of a spin doctor, I'll give her that.

She was gonna need a different kind of doctor when I was through with her, though—and dammit, she ended up with a smug look on her face anyway.

If she always took responsibility for her own actions, why come to me for advice like this in the first place?

Wait…

No, Tsukihi's always dumping her difficulties, troubles, and disaster cleanup on me or whoever else, we're always wiping her ass for her, so in that sense she's in no way someone who takes responsibility for herself—but this time was different.

The story was already over.

This rumor of the "eighth member" of the tea ceremony club was already officially disproven thanks to Tsukihi's independent investigation—so the story was over.

The matter had been resolved.

The tale had ended.

She'd taken—full responsibility.

Nevertheless—she needed to talk to me.

"So here's the thing, big brother. The cute, cute, cute li'l sis character Tsukihi—"

"Nah, you're only a little sister character to me and Karen... To everyone else you're just some girl."

"What? I'm a sister to the masses."

"Just how many siblings have you got?"

Terrifying...

I'll never sleep again.

"Well, sure, it'd be scary if they were all like you and Karen. I'm sorry, but can you try and stay on track here, big brother? I'm trying to talk to you about something serious."

"Hmph." Her demeanor didn't exactly exude seriousness, given that her mouth was full of cake. "Fine. And what about this cute, cute, cute li'l sis character?"

"Yeah, so I went to all this trouble to disprove the existence of the 'eighth person,' but everyone just says, *Maybe. But who knows.*"

"..."

Who knows.

Ah. Not that their reaction even amounted to a conversation, but the nuance was clear—or rather, it was the non-conversation that bothered Tsukihi.

It was a thorn in her side.

"*You might be right, Tsukihi, logically that makes sense, but then again, maybe there was an 'eighth person'*—that's the kind of thing they're saying! The rumor hasn't gone away at all!"

Whether the first half was an imitation of someone or just an artist's rendering, the tone was poignant, and that just made the blast of indignation seem even harsher when she reverted to her usual mode.

Still as peaky as ever.

If even Senjogahara can turn over a new leaf, there's still hope...

"What do you think, big brother?"

Having surged to her feet in her indignation, she seemed to be over the peak of her peakiness. Cooling down just as quickly, Tsukihi resettled herself on the floor and asked me—

"What should I do?"

"What should you do?"

"What can anyone do in cases like these? How can I put it—I asserted the truth, and everyone got that it was true, so any opposition or argument is already over, but the situation hasn't changed one bit... The 'truth' is meaningless, ineffectual. What do I do then?"

"..."

The "truth" is meaningless.

Unfortunately, that happens all too often—something I've tried to drill into the skulls of these self-proclaimed defenders of justice, these merchants of truth. How I've grappled with trying to explain to the Fire Sisters (sometimes literally grappling with them) that justice and truth aren't some kind of magic-bullet trump card that'll always win over society at large...

Whether or not they ever got the message, in this instance we seemed to be dealing with something different.

Not a clash between two truths.

Nor the impotence of justice.

It was the sense that truth—that reason itself was being treated as if it didn't matter, and someone like Tsukihi couldn't stand the airiness.

Though she's as airy as they come.

"So by way of analogy, can we say—"

"No analogies," she objected.

"Just let me finish."

"This is my story, and honestly I'm not wild about getting lumped in with some random anecdote."

"You think I care?"

"I'm always kind of taken aback by it. Like, after I've gone out on a limb to express my individuality, whoever's listening goes, 'Yup, yup, happens all the time.' Maybe, but wouldn't the mature thing be to let it pass?"

"Yup, yup, happens all the time."

"Exactly!"

"So by way of analogy—when someone believes in blood-type divination, no amount of logical confutation will accomplish anything," I submitted, eschewing *who knows* in favor of an *easy there* to mollify Tsukihi's ire. Even without her complaint, it wasn't entirely clear that my analogy was a good one, but at least it was simple.

"I don't know what 'logical confutation' means, but yeah, I guess," Tsukihi conceded. "I've actually experienced that exact example. Once, I said to this person, 'The Japanese are the only ones who believe in blood-type divination,' only to be told, 'With that kind of logical mind, you must be Type A!'"

"That's kind of an extreme example…"

The logical extreme, you might say.

The "charms" the swindler spread around might also fall into that category—you know from the start that something's a "lie" but believe it anyway. Everyone has those kinds of inconsistencies in their lives to some degree.

It's not limited to the blood type thing.

For instance, I've gone to a shrine on New Year's Day to pray for health in the coming year—though I have no illusions that throwing a five-hundred-yen coin into the offertory box and pressing my palms together has any bearing on my health.

I'm not devout.

But I do make the pilgrimage—for instance.

"Tsukihi-chan thinks Type B gets the short end of the stick in those personality tests."

"Don't call yourself Tsukihi-chan. Are you a toddler?"

"You don't complain when Nadeko does it… Seriously though, I think there are tons of Type B and AB who're scarred by that personality test stuff. It really goes to show you how minorities get crapped on."

"Hunh, interesting." The whole thing would be a lot less popular if Type A got crapped on, that's for sure. "What's it called, labeling theory?

Personality classifications according to blood type get drummed into kids from a young age, so they end up growing into the personalities associated with the blood types."

"Nope, labeling theory is something else. It's seeing Type A people as embodying what we expect of a Type A personality. We start off knowing that someone is Type A, so they start to seem that way—it's like we're slapping them with a letter and not just a label."

"Hm… But the issue here isn't whether blood type actually determines anything about you. Most people don't really believe it, but they get a kick out of fortune telling and personality tests anyway—right? Not that it's a real issue…"

What it is—is entertainment.

It's like a game.

In which case, telling someone who enjoys it that *the Japanese are the only ones who believe in fortune telling by blood type* is totally uncool…or depending on how you look at it, harassment.

And it's not just blood type, it's probably the same with astrology, palm reading, all that stuff—I have a hard time believing that people actually base their life decisions on fortune telling the way rulers did in antiquity.

"Yeah. Same as with monsters and ghosts, and UFOs," Tsukihi said. "As you can see, I'm a rational girl, right? Endowed with an analytical mind and androgynous charms?"

"I'm not so sure about that last part."

"What does 'androgynous charm' even mean… At this point isn't that kind of an anachronism? Or is it just a question of anatomy? I'm a rational person," she continued after that digression, "so when I saw everyone losing it over a ghost, I automatically felt like I had to do something to calm everybody down. It seemed like they all wanted me to, and they even cooperated with my investigation, but when I actually came back with an answer, they just smirked at me, or tried not to laugh—or whatever."

"They didn't argue and heard you out—but kept right on clamoring about the 'eighth person'?"

"Bingo," Tsukihi said discontentedly.

Well, she wasn't androgynous, and judging from her usual peakiness, she wasn't too rational either, but I knew her well enough to know that that wouldn't sit well with her.

It wouldn't sit well.

That is, she couldn't sit back and let people completely ignore her endeavor—but mostly, she found it inexplicable.

Why? How?

After learning that they were mistaken—that they'd been incorrect, that it wasn't true, why would they refuse to revise their understanding of the situation? How could they keep on enjoying it without adjusting their attitude at all?

But the real problem was that while I totally got how Tsukihi's stance felt precarious, up in the air, in the face of her unyielding club-mates, I didn't know what I could do about it.

In actuality, this tale of an aberration—this ghost story had already been taken care of thanks to her own resourcefulness and talent.

She couldn't possibly be telling me to strong-arm the other six members of the Tsuganoki Second Middle tea ceremony club, though. My little sister Tsukihi Araragi might be prone to clubbing me over the head with unceremonious requests, but even she wouldn't go that far.

That'd be asking for trouble.

A high school senior busting into a middle school and childishly browbeating six students into submission… That would be as uncool as it gets, the very embodiment of harassment.

I'd be guaranteed a severe tongue-lashing, but Tsukihi's subsequent standing with the tea club would likely be the nadir of her young life. She'd go down in history as the li'l sis character with a monster brother rather than monster parents.

That'd be the end of the heroic tale of the Fire Sisters.

In which case, when she said she needed to talk to me, maybe she wasn't looking for answers and just wanted to gripe? If so, I'd already fulfilled my role...

If I tried to leave now, would she wield the point of that three-color pen at me again? *Wield* it in a manner unique to my little sister, and the old Senjogahara?

"Listen, Tsukihi," I decided to make my move and get to the point—not of the pen, mind you. I only fence with words. "What is it you want me to do?"

"Huh? What kind of a question is that, big brother, have you not been listening?"

"Oh, wipe that surprised look off your face...and that hostile tone of voice isn't going to get you anywhere, either."

"Hupp!"

She reprised her three-color ballpoint pen attack. I somehow managed to dodge it again, but my skin nearly ended up looking like a tricolor flag.

Well, given the way those pens are constructed, I guess it'd be impossible to get me with all three colors in one blow... Worried it might be dangerous to get up and leave without warning, I'd asked her straight out like that, but unfortunately I was painted into a corner, game-wise it was checkmate. It had been my fate to be attacked.

"Keep spouting bullshit, big brother, and you'll get the tricolor penalty."

"What is this, the French Revolution? No more beating around the bush, no more threats, just tell me straight out, Tsukihi. What is it you want me to do?"

"When you put it that way, I don't know what to say—but I'm asking for your opinion. I want to research the question. Do you believe in ghosts, big brother?"

We were back where we started.

I'd assumed that her question was just a conversation starter, a lead-in to the topic at hand, but apparently I was wrong.

In fact.

We'd started with the main event—there'd been plenty of threats and beating around the bush afterwards, but the topic at hand had been on the table right from the start.

The conversation began to get complicated when I accidentally hit on the specifics of the situation—but in essence her question was a simple one.

She was asking me where I stood.

This little sister of mine.

"Hm…"

Come to think of it, while I'd been turning the matter over in my mind, I had yet to voice any kind of answer to that simple question.

Because it was actually a hard question to answer.

I couldn't just blurt something out.

I could tell Tsukihi what she wanted to hear, of course, but someone might be listening—the walls have ears, the hills have eyes.

And in my shadow is a vampire.

"Come on, big brother. What's the holdup? It's a simple yes or no question."

"That's where you're wrong, Tsukihi. You'll find that in life, questions can't always be taken care of with a simple yes or no."

"Oh yeah? If you like, I can take care of you right now with a simple yes or no."

She had her tricolor ballpoint pen at the ready.

Or should I say guillotine?

Seemed like a preview of what might happen if she didn't like my answer…in which case the only option left to me was to tell her what she wanted to hear.

Hmmm.

Well, with the teacakes just about finished, and my teacup empty for ages, maybe I ought to shake my head no and take off.

I had plenty of studying to do, after all.

I answered Tsukihi's question.

"No. I don't believe in ghosts. You're right and the other members of your tea club are wrong, I guarantee it, so don't let it get to you. You know you're right, so stick to your guns, keep doing what you're doing."

In the ten-plus years since my little sister Tsukihi was born, I'd never said anything so supportive towards her, but I did now.

To which Tsukihi, or should I say Atlas, responded, "That's what I thought. But it still bothers me."

"…"

Not changing your tune, even when someone guarantees that you're right?

Not so different from those other people, are you?

004

Not so different.

Everyone has that side to them, of course—just as, in real life, questions can't always be taken care of with a simple yes or no, the reality of human sensibilities and emotions isn't always as simple as right or wrong.

People might be shown what's correct and what isn't and still opt for the latter knowing full well what they're doing.

And in the course of everyday life, sometimes you can't help but "worry about things that are pointless to worry about," as Tsukihi was currently in the process of discovering.

The advice I gave her basically amounted to embracing the idea that "there's no point in worrying about it, so don't"; while there might be someone somewhere in the world who can do that, it's basically impossible for the rest of us.

We regret things that are pointless to regret.

And we keep on saying things that are meaningless to say.

Human life boils down to that brand of hopeless monotony.

I recalled the matter Karen had come to me about the previous month—the inconspicuous old tree growing behind her dojo. Thinking back on it now, how many of the students actually thought the old tree was freaky, how many of them were actually frightened?

Them too.

They must've realized that their own reaction, *to hell with this old tree, cut it down*, was excessive and known they were over the line.

But that feeling had been unstoppable. It never stopped until it ground to a halt thanks to Hanekawa's proposal.

Changing how you feel.

Switching mental gears is no easy thing—it might even be utterly impossible.

"This might sound overblown," I said, "but it's really more common than you'd think. Take hyenas, for instance. We have a negative image of them, right? They can't seem to shake their reputation as cunning creatures that scavenge a lion's kill, snatching whatever carrion they can get. But hyenas actually do their own hunting, and if anything it's the male lions, with their big manes, that are often too lazy to hunt… Listen, I'm not trying to show off my knowledge of trivia here. I mean, this isn't trivia, it's the kind of thing that people who know stuff know without having to go to the trouble of looking it up, just common knowledge—and yet it doesn't make any inroads, doesn't ripple out into the general consciousness. Once a perception of something has taken root, once it's got a label slapped on it, that never goes away even after the truth comes out—people go on with their lives pretending that they don't know the truth, pretending that they don't know they're wrong. I wonder why."

"People avert their eyes from inconvenient truths, Araragi-senpai," answered Kanbaru-kohai.

The next day, at the Kanbaru residence.

To give a slightly more detailed description of the situation, the next day I went to Kanbaru's to clean her room, a kingdom descending anew into chaos that I was attempting to restore—and as always showing no inclination whatsoever to help, that was the answer she gave from the hallway.

"What was it called? Senjogahara-senpai told me about it... Something-bias. Even in emergencies, people refuse to accept inconvenient information and keep on telling themselves, *'I'll* be okay'..."

"Maybe this isn't the same? Since in this case, maintaining a belief in monsters—in the 'eighth person,' doesn't actually put the tea club members at ease or benefit them."

"But isn't believing in monsters even though it's illogical more fun than logically denying their existence? Sure, it's a bit different from people's views of hyenas...but don't you think that might be what's going on here?"

Kanbaru and I shared an understanding of so-called aberrations—of demons, and monkeys, and snakes—that Tsukihi lacked, so we were able to have a somewhat more in-depth discussion.

"What Senjogahara was talking about was probably normalcy bias."

"There you go again, calling her by her last name. There's no need to try and keep up appearances with me. Why don't you just call her Hitagin like always?"

"Not with other people... Wait, I never call her that!"

"Oops. It wasn't Hitagin? Was it Leggings?"

"Why'd I call her that when she doesn't wear leggings? Anyway, in terms of the fun factor—from what I understand the tea club members aren't enjoying this rumor about the 'eighth member' all that much."

"What exactly is the rumor? If Tsukihi's already dealt with the tale itself for this aberration, maybe there's no point in hearing it—but depending on the details, we might actually find a satisfactory explanation," Kanbaru suggested.

From the hallway.

Seriously, how did it make her feel...standing in the hallway with her arms folded watching her senpai clean her room?

Or maybe that kind of thing doesn't faze rich people. Seems like appropriate behavior for a monarch, sure.

"Araragi-senpai, what if it's like the case at Karen's dojo you were telling me about—the students were able to accept the tree once they

29

thought of it as a 'guardian deity,' right? Wasn't this 'eighth person' like that? The tea ceremony club's eighth member…turns out to be the god of the tea ceremony."

"The god of the tea ceremony…"

Who would that be?

Though I've heard of the god of tea, and maybe some tea-related apparitions.

"No, it isn't like that. Well, I only know a few tidbits, and I'm an outsider when it comes to their school so I can't say for certain, but as a ghost story I think this one falls under the creepy heading."

"Hmm. Give me the full rundown, then. I'm listening."

"…"

Getting a little imperious, aren't we?

Acting like she's the ace of the basketball team—come on, you're no longer an ace or a star. You're nothing but a popular girl!

Okay, I suppose that's reason enough to be imperious.

"Like I said, I only know a few tidbits so I can't give you the full rundown… But maybe a 'school ghost story' got adapted from its original form. Adapted, or applied to a tea ceremony club—"

"And what's the 'original' ghost story?"

"I think it's the kind where there's an extra classmate. Like, a class of thirty suddenly has thirty-one students… But you don't want to be the one to notice, because then you trade places with that person…and have to carry on as the unnoticed 'thirty-first student,' watching helplessly as the 'original thirty-first student' cozies up to all your former friends…"

"Hmm. The replacement type. Or is it the spirited-away type? Scary either way," commented Kanbaru, hardly sounding afraid—I mean, it's a "scary story," but not the kind that could scare a high school student. "So applying it to their own situation, they started to sense the presence of an 'eighth member'? In which case, maybe I was wrong."

"What kind of story did you think it was?"

"Well, even if it's not a 'guardian deity,' wouldn't some sort of leprechaun be pretty fitting? A traditional tearoom is a *zashiki* sitting

30

area, seems perfect for a Zashiki-warashi. And if the 'eighth member' was an aberration that brings good fortune, then no matter how logically Tsukihi refuted its existence, the others would want to keep on believing."

"True."

If it was a Zashiki-warashi... In that case, it wouldn't just be about the fun factor, since driving one out brings down ruin on your household—but that's not what we were dealing with.

In fact, the gist, or the highlights, or the "come-on" of this ghost story was that the eighth member might replace you, and that you yourself might vanish. You'd want to disprove it.

That'd benefit them more.

"In which case, this is something else Senjogahara-senpai told me about, but maybe we're dealing with deviance amplification rather than normalcy bias. If nine out of ten people agree about something, even if it's incorrect or irrational, it seems correct and rational and the tenth person appears to be wrong—maybe we should call it majority rule. It's hard to change your opinion in the face of that kind of pressure."

"Majority rule, huh..."

Senjogahara herself doesn't side with majorities, but maybe that's why she's so knowledgeable about the theories behind them. She stands apart from the illusion of consensus.

"Still," I said, "it's a little extreme—you'd think at least one other member would agree with Tsukihi."

That'd make things a lot easier. With seven members of the tea ceremony club, the majority rule stood at six against one.

Six against one, definitely not great odds—but if the ratio were five against two, she might have a fighting chance. If she could form a faction, it'd be harder for the group to ignore her.

If that wasn't enough, one more would certainly do it—four against three, that'd be a proper fair fight.

"Right now my little sister's in a pretty disadvantageous position because that ain't happening. It's stressing her out."

"What's her current mindset? We're not talking about the illusion of consensus…but it must be quite a burden. Is she starting to think maybe she should just go along with the others?"

"The fact that she isn't is what's so amazing about her." Or where she's biting Senjogahara's style—unlike my girlfriend, though, Tsukihi generally likes group activities. "She's like the poor man's Senjogahara."

"Don't call your own little sister a poor man's anything…"

"Anyway, the situation isn't as urgent as it was with Karen. Things aren't so severe that accepting or denying the existence of this 'eighth member' is going to be the end of the club, it's not going to destroy any friendships—it's just that she's hit a wall."

"A wall?"

"Tsukihi claims the mantle of a defender of justice, so an environment where people are ignoring what's right and true is uncomfortable for her—"

Although.

It wouldn't be comfortable for anyone…

"—but actually it's all too common for irrationality and illogic to rule for no good reason. Is Tsukihi still too young for that lesson?"

"Too young… We've been talking about Tsukihi and Karen this whole time, but what about you?"

"Hnh?"

"Whose side are you on this time?"

"This time it's not a question of allies and enemies… I took Karen's side, but that was, how can I put this, because things were moving in a bad direction. I did what little I could, though maybe it was too much."

"Hm. Except, that little push actually came from Hanekawa-senpai," Kanbaru reminded me. "Her travails never end, do they? Even in the second term. There was that thing with the tiger—"

"…"

"Well, it's a tad bit tough to tell from the tidbits you've told me, but nothing seems to be affected by believing in the 'eighth member' or affirming its existence—it's just about how people feel."

"Yup. About how people feel—but whatever else you might say, they're impressively strong-willed, my little sisters. Both of them. Not that I'm taking sides, but if it were me—if I were a member of the tea club, I'd totally cave and go along with everybody else."

"Heheh. It all becomes clear. The 'eighth member' was you all along, wasn't it, Araragi-senpai?"

"What the hell? Don't go confusing the issue. Anyway," I began to wrap things up.

Apologies to Tsukihi, but this was basically the stuff of idle chatter—it wasn't something I wanted to talk about forever, and I was anxious to move on to the next topic.

I said, "Experiencing that kind of nonsense builds character, it'll be useful for her down the line."

"Nonsense, huh? Tsukihi could not have been more sensible, though—which makes me want to take her side."

"When do you ever not want to take a cute girl's side, Kanbaru?"

"It's got nothing to do with cuteness. I mean, the other six club-mates might be cute, too."

" … "

What a thing to be considering.

This whole time, was she factoring in the other girls' looks?

"The question of who is cuter, Tsukihi or the others—the so-called Schrödinger's Pussycat," Kanbaru mused.

"'So-called'? Never even heard of it. Take your so-calling more seriously."

"But don't you feel the same way? You and me…" She looked first at her bandaged left arm—and then at my shadow, as I cleaned her room. "We know aberrations. We know nonsense—irrationality, absurdity. Which is exactly why I want to take Tsukihi's side in this. Your little sister, who'd try to deny the existence of aberrations—and martyr herself to reality."

" … "

"Oh, um, I hope it's clear I'm not trying to deny Shinobu's pride of

33

place? Her cuteness is indescribable. Truly, she is Schrödinger's Imp."

"Don't call her an imp. What kind of a 'truly' is that? Gimme something a little trulier."

"Trulier?"

"But sure—when you put it like that, I guess I agree, but still, there's nothing we can do, is there? There's nothing we can do for her, is there?"

"If you say it must be done, I'm ready and willing to storm the Tsuganoki Second Middle tea ceremony club."

"I'm not going to say that."

Kanbaru would have no problem arguing a bunch of middle school girls into submission...but that would clearly be going too far.

Was there no way to soothe Tsukihi's feelings?

Without going too far, in other words, peaceably?

"Well, there is a way."

"Huh?"

"If you're just looking to humor Tsukihi for now, Araragi-senpai, there's a way."

"That's not what I'm looking to do...but there is?"

"Uh huh. I mean, I'm with you, I agree that Tsukihi's too young to face this reality head on—though there's one little problem with my solution."

"A problem? That doesn't sound good... What's this problem?"

"Ultimately, it's going to involve fooling her. So, Araragi-senpai, do you have any objection to lying to your little sister?"

"Ha ha ha."

As if.

005

The epilogue, or maybe, the punch line of this story.

Well, since Tsukihi already took care of the aberration tale, this whole story has been a sort of epilogue—so maybe I should call it the bonus material.

I accepted Kanbaru's suggestion and persuaded Tsukihi—persuaded, or mollified, or something like that.

Why did the other members of the tea ceremony club—those other six girls, persist in believing in the "eighth member"? Even after the truth was clear, after they were shown reason, why did they let themselves be ruled by emotion and maintain their belief? Basically, *if I could explain that*, if I could rationalize their irrationality, Tsukihi would be satisfied.

So Kanbaru rationalized it: *they all believed in the "eighth member" for Tsukihi's sake.*

Just as she did the other day when she came to me for advice, Tsukihi often made free with the clubroom's supplies: the tea, the teacakes. Not that big of a deal, but strictly speaking, not aboveboard—if it became public, the club's activities might even be suspended again.

So everyone affirmed the existence of the "eighth person"—as a kind of camouflage for the liberties Tsukihi was taking.

That's how we rationalized it. By inventing this "eighth person," they could explain away the speed with which the supplies were dwindling.

Not that they contrived to get their stories straight beforehand, but to cover for Tsukihi, they all allowed this "eighth member" to join the club—

"So that's it! They did it for me!"

The dumbass fell for it in a split second.

"And there I was, boorishly blathering about how ghosts don't exist—when I was the one who was haunting them!"

Nice try.

Well, the truth was probably completely different—but even if this lie were the truth, Tsukihi was accommodating enough to go along with it.

"Okay, I'll buy it!"

I'll drink the Kool-Aid.

Or in this case, the tea.

And just like that, she seemed to forget about the whole thing.

"Hm," Kanbaru wondered when I reported this outcome. "The other members of the club, or you—who was Tsukihi buying it from?"

CHAPTER EIGHT
KOYOMI MOUNTAIN

SUN	MON	TUE	WED	THU	FRI	SAT
			1	2	3	4
5	6	7	8	9	10	11
12	13	14	15	16	17	18
19	20	21	22	23	24	25
26	27	28	29	30		

11
November

001

What would Ogi Oshino have to say about roads? I've yet to hear her, this niece of Mèmè Oshino's, say much of anything on the subject. Intersections and traffic lights, sure, but she's kept mum on the topic of roads themselves. Well, she may have made some offhand remark about them in the course of one of our idle chats, but if she did, I don't recall it. Her words have a strange way of disappearing from my memory—and not just her words: her behavior, her appearance, they're all difficult for me to retain.

Gone with the wind.

Just like a rumor after seventy-five days—everything pertaining to her vanishes as if it had never been there.

However.

We did have a conversation that I do remember, not about roads, not about roadways, but about road construction—it wasn't even all that recently, and yet I remember it like it was yesterday.

"Araragi-senpai—sorry if I sound political, but in our society, roads mainly seem to be a means of creating jobs and stimulating the economy, don't they…what with all the maintenance, repairs, and construction."

That's what she said.

She, Ogi Oshino—in an all-knowing tone that reminded me of her missing uncle.

A philosophical tone quite unlike what you'd expect from a high school student, and your junior to boot—though her resigned air did set it apart from Oshino's brand of incisiveness.

The desire to balance good and evil, positive and negative, light and dark, on the other hand—her insistence on maintaining neutrality, that was Oshino to a tee.

"Not so much a space for walking or running—the engineering project itself is what makes a road a road. In the modern world, the goal of roadways lies in the very act of opening up the path."

It's like living for the sake of being alive—she went on.

"Even if it's a road that not a single person will ever walk down. It doesn't matter, the act of creating a road where there wasn't one before is enough to give it meaning."

Building a road that no one will ever walk down.

Building a road that no one will use.

And then rebuilding it when it goes to seed or falls apart, as many times as is necessary, repairing it ad infinitum. Filling in every crack that opens, washing away whatever filth collects—maintaining it as a road.

"What do you think, Araragi-senpai? Do you think it's meaningless—to build a road that no one will walk down?"

To build a road that no one will walk down.

Such a road—do you think it's meaningless?

"Maybe you do at that—Araragi-senpai. After all, my uncle tells me you've got a tendency to look for too much meaning in everything. But I'm not saying that it's meaningless. I'm just saying that it's wrong."

Wrong.

Did she mean wrong as in different—or wrong as in mistaken? I couldn't tell, so I didn't answer her question and instead turned it around on her.

What.

Do you think?

Was it, or was it not, meaningless to build a road that no one will walk down? Grinning cheerfully, she—

Ogi Oshino was all too happy to answer my question.

Unfortunately, as to what that answer was—I have absolutely no recollection.

002

"Winter's really arrived, hasn't it—feels like it might start snowing at any moment," she remarked. "Even with all this talk about global warming, in the end, winter's as cold as ever—we'll never get eternal summer. What do you think?"

"I mean, it's certainly cold, but...I dunno. According to the weather report, it won't stay cold. The average temperature's rising, even for winter. Maybe with how much hotter it's been getting in summer, even if winter temperatures don't drop all that much, we just experience it relatively as being as cold as ever?"

"It all becomes clear. Wise words indeed, Araragi-senpai. No wonder my uncle took off his hat to you—"

"Just to set the record straight, your uncle never once took off his hat to me. He didn't even wear a hat..."

"Ha hah, it's only an expression. I think it came from a time when everyone wore hats and took them off when someone important passed by... By doing so you're acknowledging your inferiority, aren't you? It's like asking your opponent to play with a one-piece handicap in *shogi*.

And you're right, however much my dear uncle admired you, I don't suppose he saw you as his superior."

"…"

There's a mountain in my town, and at the top of that mountain is a shrine. I call it a mountain, but it's too small for anyone to care about climbing it, and I call it a shrine, but it's too dilapidated for anyone to go worship there.

Still and all, a mountain's a mountain, and a shrine's a shrine.

Early morning, November first.

A few hours before I had to be at school, Ogi and I were ascending that mountain together—headed for the shrine at the top.

When was the last time I'd climbed this mountain?

That time with Shinobu, maybe?

And before that—Kanbaru and Sengoku and I came up here together.

Ogi doesn't look all that buff, but she must have legs of iron because she was striding ahead of me, almost like a guide—with my vampiric power currently at a low ebb, I felt like she might leave me behind altogether.

"If my uncle ever used the expression 'a one-piece handicap' towards you, I'm afraid it would hurt both of your rankings—"

"Listen, Ogi. I really don't care what happens to our rankings… Come on, won't you tell me already? Why I'm out here on this trek with you?"

"Ugh, I've already explained it to you, haven't I?"

"…?"

Had she?

I guess it rang a—nah, while I was leaning into my role as a character with a hopeless weakness for girls of late, I doubted I'd let myself be dragged out to a deserted mountain without knowing a thing about why, without asking, just doing as I was told.

She must've given me a good reason.

It's just that I'd completely forgotten what it was—hmm, maybe I'd

44

better ease up on the exam prep? At last I was getting used to memorizing reign names, but I needed to keep my priorities straight. I couldn't fill my brain with school-related stuff at the cost of my regular memory.

Anyway, if she already explained it to me, I felt awkward asking her again at that point. I suppose I wanted to impress this junior of mine, whom I'd only just met—all the more so because she was Oshino's niece.

...

Wait.

How had I even met her in the first place?

"Sorry, Ogi, but—remind me how we met?"

If I was trying to impress my junior, asking such a basic question was probably the worst possible way to go about it, but it just kind of slipped out.

"Ha hah. You're spirited today, Araragi-senpai. Did something good happen to you?"

She'd replied without slackening her pace. When I looked at her feet, I saw that she hadn't even bothered to put on sneakers though we were climbing a steep mountain path.

She knew we would be, and yet she'd come so unprepared—maybe this didn't even qualify as mountainous terrain as far as Ogi was concerned.

She didn't look it, but was she the Patagonia type?

The path was in pretty rough shape...

"It was Kanbaru-senpai who introduced us. Don't you remember?"

"Yeah? Oh—now that you say it, that sounds right. Um, remind me, Ogi, are you a freshman on the basketball team or something?"

"You're full of questions today—are you that curious about me? I'm a bookworm, I'm not involved in sports at all."

"If you're a bookworm...how come you're so good at climbing mountains?"

"Because mountains are homes to the gods, I guess? Right in my wheelhouse, unworthy as I am."

I didn't take her meaning.

Despite the fact that I didn't, it was somehow convincing—the statement possessed a murky persuasiveness, and I couldn't press the point. In that regard, she was every inch Oshino's—that expert's niece.

I kept quiet and listened to what she had to say.

As she stayed one step ahead of me.

"Because, well, mountains are like aberrations themselves—my area of expertise, in other words. I understand why people feel inclined to establish shrines at their summits. Then again, Kita-Shirahebi Shrine and this mountain have absolutely nothing to do with each other. I suppose jamming two unrelated things together is bound to create discord—"

"Discord?"

"Ah, forget it. I said 'discord' because I couldn't think of a more appropriate word, but it isn't as drastic as all that. Usually, any mistakes in the initial configuration aren't hard to correct."

"Are you saying that when they built this shrine here way back when, someone made a mistake?"

"Even if they had, is what I'm saying. I'm talking about trying that idea on for size. A first fitting. What I'm saying, Araragi-senpai—is something like this, for instance. Right now you're feverishly devoting yourself to your exam prep because you want to go to the same school as your sweetheart, but say you and Ms. Senjogahara broke up. What would you do? Would you give up on your studies?"

"That's an unpleasant for instance…"

The way she bluntly made insensitive remarks in spite of her impeccable manner of speaking really jibed with the notion that she was Kanbaru's junior.

I frowned, but Ogi continued on without any indication that she cared—that is, she didn't even turn around. "I don't think you would. You might shoot for a different school, but I don't think you'd throw away these long months of hard work. Or rather, I don't think you could. Even if you blew it with your baby, I don't think you'd throw the baby out with the bathwater. Am I wrong?"

"You're implying that I made a mistake when I started going out with

Senjogahara. Ease up, Ogi."

"I'm afraid I can't. I'm not an easygoing person—as you can see. Though if I've offended you, I'm sorry. It's a purely hypothetical example anyway. I have faith that no what-if scenario can truly offend you, Araragi-senpai."

"…"

Well, taking her to task over every little analogy certainly wouldn't make me seem like a very tolerant senpai.

I assume the point Ogi was trying to make was that your original goal isn't the be-all-end-all—to borrow her analogy, it's true that I started my exam prep with the overriding goal of going to the same university as Senjogahara, but that doesn't mean that's still my only motivation.

Let's say.

It's an unthinkable "let's say," but even if things don't work out between me and Senjogahara—I'm not sure I could ditch out on the grudging enjoyment I've found in studying.

Partly because I'd hate to let all my hard work go to waste, as in the Concorde Effect, but that's definitely not the only reason.

"Hey, Ogi."

"What is it? Are you angry, after all? That's a real shame; I wasn't trying to make you angry. In fact, I spoke with the best of intentions."

"No, listen, I'm not angry…but what do you mean, the best of intentions? Uh, weren't we talking about mountains and shrines, rather than my exam prep? This mountain, and the shrine at the top of it? A mistake in the initial configuration—"

"Yes, true," said Ogi. "Only a malicious person would call it a mistake. Even if it was one, I think it's safe to declare the statute of limitations long past on that—"

Though the trend in society seems to be toward abolishing statutes of limitations for the worst crimes, she noted—and here my guide did stop walking, and turned around to face me.

"I've come to fix that mistake."

That's what she said.

Her putative reason for currently climbing this mountain—okay, sure, that did ring a bell.

I felt like I'd gotten a more detailed explanation, even.

It was precisely because I'd found her reason convincing that I was there with her, having eked out a moment's breathing room from my exam prep—and when I looked.

She hadn't stopped so she could turn and face me. She wasn't waiting for me because my pace was flagging. It appeared that we'd reached our destination.

Behind her stood a tumbledown torii.

Behind it, then, was a sacred path where neither worshippers, nor gods now, walked—and farther behind stood a crumbling shrine hall.

"…"

It wasn't anywhere close to time for a traditional New Year's visit, but at any event, our climb was at an end, and we arrived at that place of discord—at Kita-Shirahebi Shrine.

003

The subject of Kita-Shirahebi Shrine probably warrants a bit of extra explanation—fate has seen fit to bind me to the place in some strange way, as I've already mentioned, but above and beyond that, it's a spot that lately—since spring break, to be precise—has become one of the hottest in town.

Since spring break.

Since Shinobu Oshino, in other words—since the vampire.

It was about half a year ago that she came to our town. The arrival of a legendary vampire, a demon beautiful enough to send chills down your spine. And the day the iron-blooded, hot-blooded, yet cold-blooded vampire arrived—was a momentous one.

I don't just mean that it was momentous to me, nor is that some rhetorical flourish to indicate that the existence of vampires in the real world is itself momentous—the mere fact that such a mighty aberration was "on the move" was enough to be big news in *the industry.*

Maybe the analogy of a hurricane will make it clearer.

The category and trajectory, speed and scale of any given hurricane will dominate the news cycle for as long as it lasts. There's a wealth of meteorological information out there, a wealth of meteorological phenomena, but is there any other kind of "weather" to which we give categories and even names?

That's pretty much what it was.

Shinobu Oshino's—the former Kissshot Acerolaorion Heartunderblade's journey was in and of itself a type of disaster.

Which is why Oshino mobilized—and put everything he had into disaster recovery. During his time here, he did come off as a grubby expert, collecting local ghost stories, and urban legends and campfire tales, which is mostly how he makes his living, but he was also engaged in other work.

In fact, as far as it goes, I directly assisted him—first as a party involved in the vampire brouhaha, and then to repay my debt.

In order to return our spiritually disarrayed town to its normal state—it was terribly disarrayed by the coming of a legendary vampire—I was asked to help rectify the center of that spiritual disarray.

The center, or from what I heard.

More like an epicenter—and it was here, at Kita-Shirahebi Shrine.

People talk about urban air pockets, so borrowing that terminology, I guess you could call this place a rural air pocket: a gathering place for spiritual disarray, for all the "bad elements" that precede aberrations, but which can provide the raw material for their creation. A hangout, a haunt, you might say.

A dumping ground.

Not a blade of grass survives where a vampire passes—such seemed the fury with which Shinobu struck, but if only that had been true. Because lo and behold, the byproducts, the after-effects she left behind turned out to be a real pain in the neck.

Given the horrors, physical and mental, that I went through during those two short weeks when I myself was a vampire, I'm loath to admit it, but I can understand why those vampire-expurgation experts went a little overboard in their enthusiasm to exterminate Shinobu.

In point of fact, a friend of my sister's called Nadeko Sengoku went through a grievous experience thanks to the "bad elements" gathered at this shrine—you might even say that the swindler who was the original cause of that grievous experience was yet another "bad element" that had crawled out of the woodwork in response to the whole vampire brouhaha.

Well, maybe that has more to do with how I feel about him—but either way, Oshino made it clear that depending on how things went, depending on certain logistical niceties, Kita-Shirahebi Shrine could very well end up as ground zero for the outbreak of a Great Yokai War.

A Great Yokai War.

It sounds so fake, but it's no joke. Why dump into the lap of an ordinary high school student like me the job of nipping something like that in the bud? Either Oshino was living on the edge, or I couldn't clear my five-million-yen debt to him unless he gave me something really big to do.

To put it another way, it was a job worth five million yen.

"I wonder if the whole reason Kita-Shirahebi ended up as an anchor for 'bad elements' was that it was a ruined, overgrown shrine without a god—that it was empty?" I ruminated, feeling emotional as I cast my gaze over the abandoned shrine for the first time in a long time. The source of emotion wasn't the dilapidated state of the shrine itself, though, but rather my thoughts of Oshino. Maybe coming here with his niece had brought him closer to mind.

"An anchor, did you say? Ha hah," laughed Ogi. Lightheartedly—it was forced, out of keeping with the atmosphere of the abandoned shrine. "Well, I guess people need some kind of anchor in their lives—"

"Um, I'm not talking about people here, I'm talking about 'bad elements.'"

"Don't people also fall under that heading?"

"…"

Like swindlers, is that what she meant?

As Oshino's niece, maybe Ogi knew that con man—*I could bring him up,* I thought, wavering for a moment. If I did and she didn't know

51

what I was talking about, I'd have no choice but to tell her all about the bastard; if she did know him, and I got too worked up about it, that'd be just as unpleasant.

It'd be one thing if she brought it up, but for now I was going to hold off on broaching the subject of that swindler. I swallowed the words that had risen to my tongue.

And yet, something he had told me came to mind.

That in order to disseminate something—in order to make something go viral, first there has to be an empty space for it, and that emptiness is something you can "create"—

"…"

Hurricane Shinobu struck, making landfall with a rampaging fury.

Then hordes of "bad elements" massed in the emptied town as if they sought a feeding ground—at this shrine, which was emptiest of all.

And if my reading is correct (even if it doesn't deserve to be called a reading), it was "emptiest of all" because the shrine lay in ruins and the god was absent—

"…So where did the god go?"

"Did you say something, Araragi-senpai?"

"Forget it…"

I was thinking about this talisman I'd been entrusted with—that someone had forced on me, really. The truth is, I was at a loss as to what to do with it.

I'd been instructed to do something when even Shinobu couldn't—it was a talisman, so maybe I should present it as an offering somewhere?

I wanted to get rid of it, if possible.

"By the way, Araragi-senpai, isn't it kind of odd that we call anyone who visits a shrine a 'worshipper'? Most of them are probably just tourists."

"Hm? Oh… Well, I see what you're saying, but I can't think of a better word off the top of my head. So, Ogi. How exactly are you going to fix this discord? This mistake with the initial configuration that you mentioned—I'm guessing a serpent deity wasn't a fitting object of worship for a shrine founded on this mountain?"

"Fitting? You make it sound like we're talking about someone's outfit."

Ogi, the niece of an expert, casually strode straight down the middle of the ritual path. Even a greenhorn like me knows that the center is where the gods walk, and humans aren't supposed to tread there...but if no god lived here, then maybe it was no path at all.

Passing by the literally, not metaphorically empty hand-washing basin, she arrived at the shrine itself—and peered up at it.

"Hmm..." she muttered, "this is turning into a hassle—isn't it. Makes me want to turn around and go home. If I had a home to go to, that is."

"Huh? What about the Oshinos'?"

"Well, sure, there's the Oshinos' but—this...is a delicate balance. How could my uncle leave things in such a state and take off... Is this it?"

Ogi pointed at a talisman that had been pasted to the hall. I say *had been pasted*, but I was the one who pasted it there.

I came to the shrine for that purpose on Oshino's orders, accompanied by Kanbaru—and affixed it with essentially no knowledge of what I was doing, certainly in the dark about the talisman's spiritual purpose, so it was blasphemy in a way. But apparently the situation required that the thing be placed there not by an expert, but by someone like Kanbaru or myself, fully immersed in that other world and at the same time in the dark about it.

So it wasn't entirely out of kindness, in other words to help me repay my debt, that Oshino handed me an extraordinary job: climbing a mountain once for five million yen.

I'm sure this other talisman that's been entrusted to me serves a similar purpose—rather than being collateral for a loan, though, it's more like a bad debt...

"Yeah, that's the one," I replied. "Oshino sent me to put it there, back in..."

I'm pretty sure it had been June. Was it already over four months since then? It's not exactly something I view with nostalgia, but I'd been reunited with someone from my past, Nadeko Sengoku, thanks to the job Oshino gave me, so in that sense it meant something to me.

If it weren't for that chance reunion, we almost certainly wouldn't be hanging out now. Fate can be a funny thing.

And it's not just Sengoku—that goes for Hanekawa, and Senjogahara, and Hachikuji, and Kanbaru...

And Shinobu.

The vampire, too.

"Well, it's precarious, but I suppose you managed to maintain the balance—the air in the shrine grounds feels clear."

"Clear?"

"Yes. Hard to imagine it was a hangout for 'bad elements' to gather, if only temporarily."

"..."

If the grounds of this abandoned shrine were indeed "clear" at the moment, I had a sense of why that might be—obviously, since on the last day of summer vacation, Shinobu and I cleared them out ourselves.

Did I already tell Ogi?

"With this, we're good for the next hundred years or so—provided things stay as they are. We'll say it scattered nicely. It's not why I came here today, though..."

As she spoke, Ogi did something unbelievable. It was an inarguably bizarre act—true, no one had tended to the dilapidated shrine hall for who knows how long, but she suddenly began scaling its wall.

"Wh-What are you doing, Ogi?"

The actual feel I was going for was more of a shout: "What are you doing, Ogi?!" It can be hard to raise your voice when something happens, so it kind of ended up as a regular question.

I don't know if her claim to be a bookworm was serious or a joke or what, but in the blink of an eye, she clambered up onto the roof of the shrine like a wild animal.

Like a monkey, or a cat.

There may've been time to say something, but there wasn't time to stop her—it was quite a feat, and the fact that she was wearing restrictive clothing and the wrong shoes didn't hold her back one bit.

Just because she'd made it to the top didn't mean she was safe, though—at the risk of repeating myself, the shrine was dangerously dilapidated with the passage of time. It looked like one good gust of wind was all it would take.

The weight of a single person on the roof seemed like more than enough to flatten the building. If she were in an elevator, an alarm would be going off, one hundred percent.

But thanks to that derelict state, there were plenty of possible approaches to the ascent, the uneven surface providing plenty of hand- and footholds, which is maybe why Ogi was able to clamber up it like a jungle gym...

"What's wrong? Come on up here with me, please."

"No, um, I'm wearing a skirt today, so..."

As if.

Still, however devoted I may be to my juniors, I wasn't ready for something quite so audacious, or so active.

"I don't think I can do it."

"Sure you can. My oh my, I never thought I'd hear such pitiful words from the man they call the Rising Dragon of Naoetsu High."

"No one calls me that. What am I, a *shoryuken*?"

"Speaking of, I heard that Ryu from Street Fighter writes his name with the character for prosperity."

"Really? Not the one for dragon?"

"Nope. Ken does use the character for fist, though. At least, that was true back in the day, maybe it's changed at this point—which reminds me, Araragi-senpai," she said, not actually looking down at me from her perch atop the roof but gazing out over the entire town, though I wasn't sure how much of it you could see from up there. "This isn't about dragons, but snakes. Do you mind?"

"Go ahead... You wanna talk about the serpent deity you're trampling right now?"

"Serpent deities are the best example, sure, but even regular snakes are seen as sacred. Do you happen to know how that came about?"

"How snakes came to be seen as sacred?"

Hmm.

Well, they do engender a certain amount of dread, but it's true, there's nothing jarring about the idea of a "snake god"—why that might be, though, is something I've never really considered.

"They aren't useful like horses or cattle, say, and they aren't exactly woven into the fabric of our everyday lives—when some other reptile might have served, why do you think it's the snake?"

"Why?"

"Consider the signs of the Chinese zodiac. Mouse, ox, tiger, rabbit, dragon, snake—doesn't that sequence seem kind of unfair? Don't you think the dragon must be a tough act to follow, coming right before the snake like that? Though the snake might be able to eke out a laugh with a line about the dragon having bad breath or something."

"I'm pretty sure the Chinese zodiac isn't a comedy club—" I began, craning my neck towards the roof.

It's a surprisingly difficult angle at which to speak. Being looked down on by my junior didn't exactly make me want to jump for joy, at the very least.

"—but I give up. Why is it? Is there some particular source? A myth about a snake or something—"

"No, though of course there are myths involving snakes. A veritable mountain of them. But what I'm asking here is why snakes might be eligible for a leading role."

By *here*, did she mean the roof? I started thinking, or searching through my memory banks—Hanekawa or Oshino might have mentioned something.

"Wait, I've got it. Isn't it because the snake is a symbol of immortality, or regeneration?"

"Oops, the right answer, out of the blue," nodded Ogi. She didn't look down at me, so it was hard to know if she was actually nodding or just moving her head to scope out the scenery from a different angle. "I guess college hopefuls really are a breed apart."

"Well...thanks, but it's not like this subject is included in the national exam."

"They shed their skin as they grow—what's more, the skins they leave behind retain a clear, or you might say obvious shape, since snakes don't have any limbs to disrupt their evenness. And when you consider how stealthy snakes are, their shed skins might be easier to spot than the creatures themselves."

"..."

"And in an age when the study of biology wasn't as advanced as it is today, someone witnessing a snake molting—might well see it as sacred."

Immortality, regeneration.

And—divinity?

"But listen, Ogi. That's—"

"Yes, it is. Ecdysis is a physiological phenomenon that has nothing whatsoever to do with immortality. The exceptional vitality of snakes isn't particularly rooted in fact, either."

"It's like how people view hyenas?"

"Yes, indeed. Mistaken assumptions from the outset—yet it's impossible to rid snakes of their sacred image at this point, right? Even though—"

"..."

"Everyone learns about ecdysis in science class. There probably isn't a single person in modern Japanese society who doesn't know that snakes shed their skin, but nevertheless—somewhere deep down, everyone still holds snakes in some kind of awe. We unconsciously accept the term 'serpent deity' without a second thought—"

A mistake in the initial configuration.

No, not a mistake—it was just a different time.

"What's wrong, Araragi-senpai? Do you think it's boorish of me to explain away articles of faith through science? Am I being insensitive? But if you peruse the pages of history, you'll find countless examples of people being arbitrarily executed or irrationally punished because of groundless faith, a veritable mountain of them."

"Again with the veritable mountains…"

"If we should cut something loose, we ought to do so rationally—but no need to worry, it's exactly as I just described. However boorishly one tries to explain it away, faith, once engendered, won't be dispelled by reason or logic."

"…"

I already knew this story.

I heard it last month, from my sister.

She logically debunked the rumors of a ghost haunting the tearoom, the "eighth member" of the tea ceremony club—debunked it thoroughly, from top to bottom, leaving no stone unturned. Knowing how immature she can be, I don't even want to know how she went about it.

But in the end, it meant nothing.

The other members believed in the "eighth person" no matter what she said—and so within the confines of the club, it was Tsukihi who came across as the fringe loony.

"They say that faith can make even a sardine's head sacred—so why not a snake's discarded skin? That's just the way it goes, Araragi-senpai. A few hundred years of science aren't going to upend thousands, if not tens of thousands of years of instinct etched into our very bodies. That's people for you, always going with their gut. That's human society in a nutshell."

"But don't you think even that might change someday? If the scientific evidence mounts over hundreds or thousands of years, can't humanity start prizing truth over feeling?"

"Probably, given that much time."

Though I sincerely doubt human beings who prize truth over feeling could still be called "human"—qualified Ogi.

It seemed that way to me too.

That is.

I *felt* the same way.

"But the future can be considered in the future—after you're dead, Araragi-senpai, I'll go ahead and think about it."

Blithely tossing off this pronouncement about living longer, much longer, than me despite my tinge of vampirism, Ogi switched gears.

"The problem right now is what to do about this place, Kita-Shirahebi—where over a thousand years ago they enshrined a snake that lived for over a thousand years. Though you might just call it cleaning up after my uncle."

"What's that supposed to mean? In terms of keeping bad stuff from building up, that's already taken care of, isn't it?"

Wasn't that chapter over thanks to the "errand" Kanbaru and I ran?

"It isn't over. In fact, it's only just begun."

"You'd drop on me what's become a stock phrase…"

I wonder who said it first?

I'd like to know who came up with that line, same as with: *The real adventure starts now.*

"No, it really isn't over—because my uncle took a passive approach. He took care of the defense, but not the offense."

"Oshino's…not really the aggressive type, is he."

"Broadly speaking, my uncle succeeded in dealing with the fallout from Hurricane Kissshot Acerolaorion Heartunderblade striking this town. He prevented a Great Yokai War from breaking out, which was definitely an achievement, a great achievement for him as an expert. But was that enough? Personally, I think my uncle's too soft—he didn't take any steps to deal with the next Heartunderblade-level aberration that shows up, did he?"

"…"

The person who entrusted the talisman to me—had said something similar. Or rather, said it and then entrusted the talisman to me.

But…

"Now that security has been ensured for the time being, I think the next step is to do something about this place itself—without a hangout, the 'bad elements' won't have anywhere to hang out."

"Hmmm... Well, I see what you're saying. But doesn't that seem like too much for a private individual to handle? If this is about Oshino having to procure the funds to rebuild this shrine..."

"Funding alone isn't going to cut it. Ideally, this abandoned shrine would be rebuilt from the ground up and turned into a place where a ceaseless stream of faithful came to worship year in and year out... In other words, the cult of the serpent deity needs to be revived... Ha hah, but it's just as you say, Araragi-senpai, that's probably impossible for individuals..."

Just because it's impossible doesn't mean we can give up, though, continued Ogi. "We can't shirk our duty to correct what needs correcting—even if it's meaningless, and even if it's impossible. Don't you think it's wrong not to correct mistakes, even if doing so is meaningless?"

"Well, as someone who's constantly making mistakes in his exam-prep workbook, I have no choice but to answer that question with a yes. But the reality is that there are things we can and cannot do. Isn't that reality in its proper form? I can't get behind the idea that a world where anyone could do everything is proper."

"Nor can I. This is a question of will. A question of my determination to implement an offensive defense—ha hah, though 'offensive defense' makes my will seem pretty low-key. Um...should we get back to the topic at hand?"

"Was there ever one to get back to? I still don't have a clue what you're trying to tell me, Ogi. You said that the fact that this shrine is on this mountain involved a poorly balanced mistake in the initial configuration, but that of all things isn't something a high school girl like you could do anything about. It's not like we're going to move the shrine somewhere else at this point, after all this time."

"Yes, you're right," Ogi readily assented.

This sudden reversal was redolent of her uncle—the conversation never quite turned into an argument.

"Let me give you a little history lesson, Araragi-senpai. Originally, this shrine—Kita-Shirahebi was in another place altogether."

"Another place altogether?"

"Yes. It also had a different name back then—but it had to be moved for a reason, to this mountain. *It was jammed on here.* At the summit, where I'm standing now."

"…"

"If you want a slightly more in-depth explanation of what happened, at that time this mountain was considered highly sacred—and so the shrine was moved here to enjoy the benefits of its great spiritual power."

"When you say 'moved here'…you mean they established a branch shrine?"

"No, they moved the original shrine to this new location."

"You can do that? Okay, I don't know much about how shrines work…but aren't shrines and temples the kind of things that basically stay in one place?"

"Not necessarily. Sometimes they're forced to move by circumstances beyond their control, like hurricanes, for instance—but that's not what I want to talk about."

"Huh? Weren't you giving me a history lesson?"

"No, no, the history is irrelevant. I discussed it, but it wasn't what I wanted to discuss—there's just one question I want you to consider, Araragi-senpai. How did they, by which I mean the people involved with the shrine back when it was in a different location—at the time it had a different name as well, but for the sake of convenience and clarity let's call it the old Kita-Shirahebi Shrine—relocate it to the top of this mountain?"

"How? Well, whenever it was, we're talking about a super long time ago, right? Seems unlikely they had the technology to move the entire building as is—so I imagine they took it apart temporarily, then reassembled it at its new location. Smaller things like the offertory box they could probably bring as is…"

"Mm-hmm. This kind of structure is built without using a single nail—it's probably not all that troublesome to dismantle it. You know, the way you describe it makes it sound like a ship in a bottle. To get the ship through the narrow opening, you put the pieces in first and then assemble it on the inside… But a shrine wouldn't necessarily be easier to transport once you've taken it apart."

"Huh?"

"Look—back then, not even the road we took to get here existed."

As she said this, Ogi pointed beyond the torii to the steep mountain path, up which we'd climbed. Right, a steep mountain path. It seemed hard enough to get lumber and building materials up such a narrow, precipitous route—but even that wasn't there?

"Nope. It wasn't there. The steps weren't installed until after the war. Recently."

"I wouldn't call it recently…"

"In Kyoto, 'after the war' apparently means after the Onin War, over five hundred years ago…"

"Well, I never believed that story. That can't actually be true."

"Think about it. It has a certain logic. During a so-called world war, Kyoto emerged relatively unscathed from the bombings that decimated other major cities, so it doesn't make sense for them to use that conflict as their yardstick. In light of that, it's quite plausible for them to use the expression to refer to the Onin War."

"Interesting. Maybe you've got a point…" When I hear the phrase, it takes me a second to realize people aren't referring to the time since spring break, so I guess I get it. "Anyway, the stairway was constructed relatively recently."

"Yes. So to put it in ship-in-a-bottle terms, the neck of the bottle was abnormally long and twisted, you see?"

"In which case…isn't the conventional approach to clear a road and use that for transporting the building materials up the mountain? Once it was finished, the road would've fallen into disuse and ended up obscured by the trees and plants that regrew there. At least until the stairway was constructed…"

"That's right. Anytime you want to build something, you have to build a road first. From the Silk Road on down, you could say the history of humanity has been the history of roadways. From roadways, to shipping lanes, to flight paths—I suppose the next step will be pathways into space? That's still not the right answer, though."

"Huh? It's not?"

"No. As I told you a minute ago, this is a highly sacred mountain. That kind of large-scale construction would be out of the question. In the course of moving a shrine to the top of it, of course, a minimal amount of building would be inevitable, but doing everything possible to avoid harming the mountain was the humane route. Humane—or pious, I suppose."

"They didn't build a road?"

"Nope. Not an artificial one, anyway. Look, we came up that post-war stair, but if we plucked up our grit—we could've made it to the top without it, trekking through the foliage without the benefit of a real path, right?"

"…"

I wonder.

If we plucked up our grit, probably, but then I just don't have that much grit. Though it might be fine for a Patagonia type like Ogi…

Well, the grit of our forbearers was nothing to sneeze at.

Especially when it comes to architecture. They left behind all these unbelievable World Heritage treasures without recourse to Mister Bull-dozer or Miss Crane…

I said I couldn't necessarily get behind the idea of a world where absolutely anyone could do literally anything, and yet, once you ignore little things like human rights and labor conditions, people can probably accomplish just about anything.

But even so.

Even on those terms—how would you actualize this shrine's "move"?

I don't know anything about the mountain's great spiritual power at the time, but from a purely architectural standpoint, how would they have moved a building to such a wildly unfavorable location?

"Are you saying they used some otherworldly skill? Supernatural superpowers, or spiritual ones… That really would take some great spiritual power."

"No, nothing like that. Just plain old human ingenuity. As far as I'm concerned, nothing could be more annoying than that 'move'—in a way it was the whole reason I had to come here, to this town."

Kita-Shirahebi? What white snake of the north? she muttered.

As if something bad had happened to her—though her expression didn't change, she gave the shrine roof beneath her feet a gratuitous kick.

004

The epilogue, or maybe, the punch line of this story.

In a truly unexpected turn of events, the person who unraveled the mystery of Kita-Shirahebi Shrine, the relocation of what Ogi referred to as old Kita-Shirahebi Shrine, was none other than my little sister's friend Nadeko Sengoku.

"Piece of cake, Big Brother Koyomi." That night, for certain reasons, I'd hauled Nadeko Sengoku into the Araragi precinct for questioning, er, protective custody, and this is what she told me. "That's easy mode."

"Easy mode?"

No.

Whatever the answer turned out to be, transporting a building up to the top of a mountain wouldn't be a piece of cake, or easy mode—it wouldn't be a game at all.

But maybe it was precisely because Sengoku was a gamer, someone who could see it as a game, that the solution came to her so easily.

"Sounds like they didn't tackle any large-scale projects like building a paved road, but as far as I can tell from what you told me, Big Brother

Koyomi, they did at least a minimal amount of construction, right?"

"Huh? Yeah…"

Incidentally, I kept Ogi's name out of it when I asked Sengoku about this—not just her name but the very fact of her existence. Considering everything that'd been going on, I was somehow hesitant to introduce them to each other.

I can't deny that I was maybe being overly cautious.

Or reading too much into things, at any rate…

But Sengoku had a right to know what I'd learned about Kita-Shira-hebi Shrine—she was very much involved with that place, after all.

"So they did do a minimal amount of construction," she said.

"Meaning?"

"The people who did the construction, the people who were made to eff-eck-choo-eight it—"

Her manner of speaking somehow ended up like Karen's—why Karen's, and not Tsukihi's? Maybe it was a question of how influential they were or weren't. Karen influenced easily, and Tsukihi was easily influenced…

"—had to at least clear the land on top of the mountain, to create space to build the shrine, right?"

"Uh huh. Well, clearing the land to make space… I guess that's the minimal amount of construction? It's not like that kind of open space would occur naturally in the middle of the mountains."

"Yeah. And *they used the lumber they obtained to build the shrine.*"

Waste-free construction—Sengoku said.

Waste-free, minimal.

"Then they wouldn't need to haul lumber all the way up to the top, right? In other words, they wouldn't need to clear a path for that. They could just pluck up their grit and climb to the summit on whatever path, then lodge there while they were doing the actual construction."

"…"

Well, you wouldn't necessarily have to lodge there, but—huh. Since it's a mountain, you've got all the lumber you need without having to transport it from somewhere else.

A veritable mountain of it.

A while back, I employed a falsehood about trees in the back courtyard of Karen's dojo being used to build the dojo itself...but even if it was out of the question to harm such a sacred mountain for no good reason—using the lumber obtained from clearing a space for a shrine to build that very shrine was based in a spirit of keeping things local, or in contemporary terms, it was eco-friendly.

Such a simple answer was so clearly true once you heard it, there could be no other possibility—if the question Ogi posed had been, "How would you build a new shrine on top of a mountain with minimum harm done to the mountain itself?" it might've taken me a while, but I probably would've arrived at the same answer eventually.

But the question she posed had been...

"Hang on, though, Sengoku. We're talking about relocation, not new construction...'moving.' If you use new lumber to build a new shrine, then isn't that a different shrine?"

"They'd probably bring along their relish...I mean, their relic. But if you're taking the trouble of moving to a new place, don't you think you'd want a new building anyway?"

"..."

The ship of Theseus.

If its pieces are replaced in the course of repeated repairs until ultimately all the original parts are gone—can you still call it the same ship?

I think that's how that one went.

"So the building was completely replaced, switched out, and only the name was brought along—no, wait, the name was changed too. Speaking of which..."

Whatever else may change.

As long as the faith doesn't, then nothing has—just like how people's feelings don't change in the face of reason?

You can try to replace them, but they won't change.

Immutable—no, maybe that idea is exactly what Ogi saw as being problematic.

Since, if I was to believe her, relocating the shrine to the top of that mountain had been a mistake.

A mistake?

No—what matters is the balance.

Worshipping a god atop that mountain upset some kind of balance—

"Speaking of which, Big Brother Koyomi. Your quiz made me wonder."

"Um, it wasn't a quiz…"

"That shrine is all falling apart, but do you think they'll rebuild it at some point?"

"Rebuild…"

I hadn't thought about it—but if they did rebuild it.

Modern times being what they are, I doubt they'd use lumber from the site for the construction—and of course they'd clear a road up to the top.

That's how dilapidated the shrine was. Its reconstruction would be welcome—but in that case, what would happen to the balance Ogi was worried about?

If a shrine that already had no worshippers, that had no god, were to be rebuilt—renovated, just what new kind of faith would be born there?

No—not a new faith.

A continuation of an old one.

Whatever kind of logic you try to apply, whatever reason you employ.

Faiths, like aberrations—abide.

"It would be great if they rebuilt it," Sengoku said. "If they did, I bet it wouldn't be a hangout for 'bad elements' anymore. I bet by then, Mister Serpent—I mean the snake god would have returned to the shrine. Right, Big Brother Koyomi?"

"Oh… Yeah. That'd be really great."

Would it?

I had no way of knowing—but that's what I told Sengoku.

Either way, since a certain point in time, the balance in our town had gone into a one-way nosedive.

And I had a bad feeling about where things were headed.

No, it wasn't just a bad feeling—a real feeling.

The day when I would use, when I'd have no choice but to use, the talisman entrusted to me by Izuko Gaen was perhaps not so far off.

CHAPTER NINE
KOYOMI TORUS

SUN	MON	TUE	WED	THU	FRI	SAT
					1	2
3	4	5	6	7	8	9
10	11	12	13	14	15	16
17	18	19	20	21	22	23
24	25	26	27	28	29	30
31						

12
December

001

For Shinobu Oshino, to speak of a road was once to speak of the road at night. And, as supreme ruler of the darkest hours, the night road was the royal road—of the immortal king of aberrations.

That's all in the past now, of course—way in the past, and her current domain consists solely of my shadow, an area not even ten feet square. I'm pretty sure that's a source of a bit, or, a great deal of disgruntlement for Shinobu, but at present I've yet to receive any formal complaints regarding the matter.

For those possessed of an absolute confidence in themselves, maybe the amount of property they own isn't actually much of a problem—well, it might be a problem, but whatever problems might arise, whatever they might lack, as long as they have themselves they're able to deal with it.

Even if they should lose their power.

Even if they should lose that which defines them.

Even then—as long as they have themselves.

"Verily, the road at night be no cause for alarm to one such as I— 'tis rather the noonday road with its blazing orb hanging overhead that presents a danger."

She said this to me on the roof of that abandoned building—back when she was not a pseudo-vampire, not the dregs of a vampire nor the shadow of her former self, but a full-fledged vampire.

In other words, back when she was still the iron-blooded, hot-blooded, yet cold-blooded vampire known as Kissshot Acerolaorion Heartunderblade.

A vampire speaking of the risks of the noonday sun—well, yeah, almost too typical. While people like Mèmè Oshino and that triumvirate of vampire experts were certainly her enemies, never has she had a greater natural enemy than the sun.

So the fact that losing her power paradoxically meant she could now walk around in broad daylight must've been something of an unexpected windfall.

No.

To collect that windfall she'd had to give up something much greater, so it's probably a little weird to talk about it in such positive terms.

"And yet, on the night road, the next step is ever shrouded in darkness—an unseen path. Canst truly call a path unseen a path at all?"

She's said some such thing.

True, for a road to function as a road, it has to be clearly delineated—simply defining it isn't enough.

You know one when you see one seems like an appropriate requirement for a path—if someone told you afterwards that the ground you'd been traversing was in fact this or that road, it'd leave you cold, right?

To put it another way.

So long as you walk with your eyes closed, whatever path you may be on isn't functioning as one—it's just the ground.

It's not a road, no matter how unwavering it might be.

That's precisely why.

The streetlights come on at night.

So you don't lose sight of the road—

Or so you don't encounter aberrations.

"Hmph. Streetlights, thou sayest."

The night hath long since lost its darkness—came the vampire's irritated reply. Well, it's understandable that she'd be irritated, given that a reduction in darkness diminished her territory—it might not be a problem, but her domain was still being invaded.

The dark.

Darkness.

These things are never extinguished. In fact, extinguishment creates the dark and darkness. And yet.

"Of old, 'twas naught but the moon—that illumined the roads at night."

The perfect disc of the moon.

Unfortunately the moon wasn't full that night—nevertheless, she gazed with longing at the sky.

At the night sky, illuminating the night road.

002

"For reals?!" exclaimed Shinobu, all of a sudden—while I'd had months to get used to her constant use of the phrase, hearing it out of the blue like that still startled me.

It made me cower in confused terror.

The strength of the exclamation made me feel like I was being yelled at. It was clearly a contraction denoting "Is what you're saying really true?" but at this point, it had lost its original meaning, she'd lost sight of it, and she used it as if it meant hello.

Which made me want to ask her if she was for reals, or just prone to exaggeration.

It was December.

The end of the year—the month that my ancestors called "Tutor-Run."

I've heard it was because even sensei got so busy that they ran everywhere, but apparently that's just a folk etymology. I mean, it always made me think, *They run even when it's not the end of the year*, so when Hanekawa told me it was nothing more than folklore, I was plenty satisfied. But that being the case, I still have no idea as to its origins.

And I've never asked.

Maybe that lack of intellectual curiosity is just one of my many faults—but given that we say January jets, February flees, and March makes its getaway, the idea of December running doesn't seem far-fetched enough to warrant comment or question.

Well, regardless of whether or not teachers are busy in December, those of us preparing for our college entrance exams sure as hell are—the national was coming up next month already.

I had very little in the way of free time.

Though if we're being honest, I wasn't swamped solely because of my exam prep. In fact, I had so much to deal with that I would've loved to say forget it, I don't have time for exams, and ditch out on my studies altogether.

But that's easier said than done.

Because even when they know their death is at hand—even when the day of execution has been announced, the sentence handed down, human beings still have to keep on living right up to the bitter end.

To keep on going about their business.

Which is why I was, in fact, spending the day speeding down the home stretch towards my exams—but just as I decided to take a quick break to intake some sugar in between math and Japanese, Shinobu appeared.

With a *For reals?!*

"…Shinobu, 'sup."

That was all the greeting I could muster for the little blond girl who'd come flying out of my shadow to peer intently around the room like a hawk, or a demon.

Shinobu Oshino.

Vampire—ex-vampire.

The king of aberrations—who spends most of her time lurking in my shadow. She was at present a fallen queen, but her brazen attitude was still every inch that of a monarch.

And, since she was by nature a vampire, which is to say nocturnal, even though she'd lost her power, lost sight of her true essence, she basically spent the daylight hours snoozing in my shadow. Yet here she was, awake despite the fact that it was only three in the afternoon.

At this point she seemed less nocturnal or vampire than someone with an unstable lifestyle—what's next, is she gonna tell me mornings still count as nighttime?

Seriously, though, what the hell?

It wasn't the witching hour, it wasn't the dead of night, it was just snack time. She'd show up now?

"Morning."

"Morealsning?!" Shinobu returned my greeting, half-heartedly.

A mash-up of "morning" and "for reals," neologism in action... Things were going to get really out of hand with this verbal tic of hers if the variations started proliferating. And, after peering intently around the room, she finally looked in my direction—

"Mm," she noticed me. "So there thou art. Hmph, as they say, 'tis truly darkest beneath the lighthouse."

"Isn't that a good thing for you?" Pleased at having been inadvertently likened to a lighthouse, a symbol of height, I returned her stare. "Come on. You had trouble finding me?"

"Nay," Shinobu pointed at me.

No, not at me—at the tray in my hands.

"Be that the source of the odor?"

"Uh, yeah... I figured I should replenish my blood sugar while I was taking a break..."

Resting on the tray I brought up from the kitchen were a plate piled with snacks and a mug filled with black coffee... Did this girl really make the trip out of my shadow just for snack time?

Some vampire.

The behavior of the royal family is sullying the good name of aberrations everywhere.

"If there be no cake, I shall resign myself to eating bread. I have spoken."

"You'll ruin your body that way, you know."

"And yet, I am troubled by how best to treat sweet buns. Be they sweets or be they bread, I cannot say! Tell me, be they staple foods or snacks?"

"Sweet buns are snacks. You can rest easy."

"And yet sweetbreads are a fitting meal for a vampire indeed— kakak," Shinobu laughed gruesomely.

Well, the laugh itself was all very picturesque, but it seemed wildly out of place when we were discussing the ontology of dessert with a tray of sweets between us…

"Now, tell me of these snacks. Be they donuts? They must surely be donuts. There can be no doubt of it."

"Yeah… They're donuts all right."

I wasn't actually as tall as a lighthouse (obviously), but given that Shinobu was currently the height of a little girl, she couldn't see what was on the tray I was holding.

With those eyes full of delighted anticipation fixed on me, I was frankly at a loss for words. It's just, if I didn't properly explain what was going on, it could come back and bite me in the…

"Here's the thing, Shinobu. They're donuts, but—"

"Donuts, ye say! Superb!"

Shinobu reached up with both hands.

Just like a child.

It was impossible to detect in that action even a hint of the majesty she once possessed, when she seemed almost twice my height—even with both her hands stuck straight up in the air, she can hardly reach my chin these days.

"I had a premonition that today's sweets would be donuts! Such unerring intuition! Now then, my master, render those donuts unto me, and not a moment too soon!"

"If it were a moment too soon, it wouldn't be snack time yet… Anyway, listen for a second, Shinobu."

Stumped as to how to explain things to an enigmatic little girl who ordered her master to render something unto her, I decided that in this case a picture was indeed worth a thousand words. I squatted down to her eye-level and placed the tray in question on the floor.

"Wahoo! ...Hn?"

For an instant Shinobu's excitement reached fever pitch, but her expression quickly turned dubious. Her gaze was fixed on the five donuts arranged on the plate atop the tray.

"My lord."

"What?"

"What are these? Be they the new line from Mister Donut?"

"No, Shinobu. These are called handmade donuts."

"The new line from Mister Donut which they hath dubbed 'handmade donuts'?"

"Calling their new product 'handmade' would cast undue suspicion on all their other donuts. No, no. You must've still been asleep inside my shadow, but Senjogahara just dropped by with these donuts to support the troops."

"...?"

Shinobu looked completely uncomprehending. If this couldn't get across to her, what the hell good was our pairing?

"Look, I'm saying that she made these donuts in the kitchen at her house, then brought them over to keep me going while I study," I tried slightly altering the wording and explaining again—apparently it was going to require a great deal of patience and perseverance to make this clear to her.

That is, I'd known it was going to be like this, which was the whole reason I'd planned to eat them all while Shinobu was still asleep instead of saving them for later...

"Huh? Um, hang on a sec. I'm thinking."

"You're talking totally normally. What happened to your old-timey speech?"

Hang on a sec, she says.

Dress it up a little.

"Then, the *tsundere* maiden (18) who counteth herself thy lady love hath—"

"You can leave out the (18) part, (600)."

"I am but (598). I'll thank thee not to round up."

"Says someone who was rounding down for, how long?"

"The tsundere maiden (even the most horrible demons were once eighteen)—"

"She's not horrible, you can't say that about a person's girlfriend. Plus you're the only demon around here."

We weren't getting anywhere.

Maybe that was a sign of just how discombobulated Shinobu was—she wasn't being violent, but that might just be because she was still in shock. If so, I was scared of what lay in store for me. Beyond scared.

"The tsundere maiden hath wrought a counterfeit of Mister Donut? That will not stand, 'tis a crime."

"They're not counterfeit. They're normal, regular donuts. Homemade donuts, the kind which, let's get real, don't require all that much expertise."

If we were going to get even realer, these were donuts that even Senjogahara could make, but I preferred to avoid being so deprecating toward my own girlfriend if I could help it.

"I am yet mystified…"

Shinobu crossed her arms and stared down at the donuts on the plate like an inspector of some sort. Or maybe more like an executioner, her gaze was so intense.

She could bore a hole through you with that look—though, being donuts, they already had them.

"I understand this incident which hath transpired, and yet."

"Incident? It's not a crime, okay? My girlfriend just brought me some refreshments, don't talk about it like it's some historical affair. It's literally as banal as could be."

"Then, in order to bring donuts to bolster my lord's efforts, the tsundere counterfeiter independently developed donuts in her own domicile, rather than hieing herself to the Mister Donut Shinobu Branch?"

"Developed... Whatever, sure. I mean, your word choice is kind of off, but you've got the basic gist."

I'm not aware of a store called the Mister Donut Shinobu Branch, but since there's only one Mister Donut in our town, she must be referring to that favorite haunt of hers.

Though as far as she was concerned, it might be more accurate to call it her personal outlet than her favorite haunt...

"Wherefore?" asked Shinobu with a serious expression.

She looked at me with round eyes full of earnest wonder, as if she were asking me why babies were born or why people die, but she was just asking: *Why did Senjogahara make donuts at her own house instead of buying them at the store?*

"Um, I don't know how to answer that question... To encourage me while I'm studying for exams?"

And also probably to check on me, to make sure I was studying, to make sure I haven't harmed myself out of despair—though I was pretty sure the overriding goal was encouragement. But that wasn't what Shinobu was asking.

"I am telling thee 'tis the meaning I do not understand. What is the intention behind troubling thyself to produce that which can be bought?"

"'Intention' might be too strong a word..."

"Buying them would be cheaper, nay?"

"..."

I was getting lectured by an almost six-hundred-year-old vampire about thrift... From a cost performance standpoint, maybe she's right? If we're talking purely about the cost of the ingredients, then maybe homemade would be more economical, but when you factor in the time spent shopping and the hassle of making the donuts—Hitagi Senjogahara's labor costs, in other words—the view that "buying them would be cheaper" wasn't totally wrong...

Still, she just sounded like someone who sucked at household tasks...

"When they have a special offer, 'tis but a hundred yen a donut at Mister Donut. These five donuts would be but five hundred yen. Taxed, 'twould amount to naught but five hundred and twenty-five yen. Five hundred and twenty-five yen, well, verily doth it depend upon thy circumstances, but most would see that as a paltry sum, would they not? Miss Tsundere begrudges even such a meager expenditure?"

"She wasn't begrudging anything... In fact, she took the trouble to make these."

"And what I am asking thee is wherefore would she take that trouble."

Man, was she persistent.

No, calling it persistent makes it sound like a legitimate line of questioning—this was just stubbornness.

"Even should the tax increase to eight percent...let me see, five hundred times eight..."

She began calculating on her fingers.

Sure, eight percent isn't as easy to calculate as five percent, but I don't think you can do multiplication on your fingers anyway.

"Feh! I know not! Fie on thy stepwise consumption tax increases, I would have them raise it to ten percent directly!"

"Getting a little ahead of yourself there."

Sure, it would be a lot easier to calculate.

But I'd be the one paying it, not you.

Taking responsibility for Shinobu, practically speaking, meant providing for a whole other person for the rest of my life, I was beginning to realize.

"Anyway! Without tax 'tis but a single coin! Wherefore would she not pay! Wherefore would she try to pass off these self-serving donuts as our snack!"

Now she was just thinking about it minus my tax burden.

The consumption tax... Well, just because I've started not to ignore social studies doesn't mean I know enough about politics to comment, but that's one tax that seems inexplicable to me. A tax on consuming things… So then, living, just living, has to cost you?

"But when there isn't a special offer, one coin wouldn't be enough even without the tax."

"Yet do they not have special offers throughout most all the year? I have noted that 'tis in fact the periods without a special offer that seem few and far between."

"I mean, I don't think that's actually true, but…"

But it does seem like that donuttery, that famous chain, is having a hundred-yen sale every time I turn around. I'd be curious to tabulate the actual numbers.

"Speaking of, they were just having a half-off sale, weren't they…"

Hm.

Speaking of that *speaking of*, it used to be that every single time they'd have a hundred-yen sale, this vampire would whine *take me, take me* (to the point that we once had a chance encounter with the swindler), but she didn't say much of anything about this most recent half-off sale, did she?

"If they were half off," I went on, "a rough estimate would be, a little less than three hundred yen for five donuts?"

"Methinks a half-off sale is beyond the pale. I would that they cease selling themselves so cheaply," Shinobu said with heartfelt emotion.

So that's why she didn't press me to take her to the Mister Donut Shinobu Branch during the sale—it wasn't out of consideration for my studying needs or anything.

"Perhaps 'tis the way of Japan in this day and age to raise the tax while making things cheaper, but behold, I envision the day when that shall make its end. 'Tis needful that the people of this nation come to appreciate that 'the finer things are costly.'"

"Don't talk politics. And don't lament the state of the nation."

You're a little blond girl.

And a vampire.

"We must make the people realize that for such things to cost a pittance, so too must someone labor for a pittance."

"And what I'm saying is, forget a pittance, Senjogahara made these donuts for me for nothing."

"Eh? My lord, thou hast not paid her?"

"Who's ever heard of a girlfriend who demands money for bringing her boyfriend a treat?"

"Balderdash... That miser?"

"..."

Senjogahara didn't exactly have a great reputation.

Considering what happened last month, though, at this point Shinobu Oshino owed Senjogahara her life same as I did...not that this little girl seemed to feel any gratitude for it.

"Have a care, my lord. She may have put something in these donuts."

"Come on, what kind of a girlfriend do you think I have... If she did put something into them, it was most likely love."

"Last month thou didst experience firsthand the fact that cooked just so, even love may be transformed to poison, my lord."

Shinobu cautiously plucked one of the donuts off the plate with a dubious *hmm*.

Exactly the way you'd handle hazardous material.

I bridled at Senjogahara's home cooking being treated like that, but since I was well aware of the special place donuts occupied in Shinobu's heart, I had no choice but to overlook her behavior.

She felt about donuts the way Doraemon feels about *dorayaki*—I wonder when they first introduced that into the comic?

"Hrrm. Nothing abnormal about the texture. Though like as not that toxic wench's artifice would not reveal itself to the touch..."

"Toxic wench... She retired her acid tongue a while ago."

"Hath it not reemerged of late?"

With another *hmmmm*, Shinobu brought the donut right up to her face and inspected it. She seemed to be using her former-vampire eyesight to visually confirm that there were no abnormalities on its surface. The only thing she'd be able to see would be the sugar it was coated with...

"No, in fact she's been nothing but sweet lately, up to and including bringing me donuts like this."

"'Tis only to be expected. All are kind to those whose death draws near."

"Nobody's death is drawing near. I'll take care of it. Somehow. I'd stake my life on it."

"'Tis that very tendency to stake thy life so readily that hath brought thee to this pass. My master hath not a whit of introspection within him—hm."

Something in Shinobu's attitude changed.

That is, she maintained the same severe expression, but the intensity stepped up a notch.

"What of this hole?"

"The hole?"

"'Tis suspect. Like as not she hath used it to inject something into the donut."

So saying, Shinobu glared up at me—through the hole in the donut.

"...Come on, leave out the tired set-ups. Donuts have holes, that's the whole point."

"And why is that?"

"Huh?"

"Aye, till now I have accepted that such is their design, ne'er pondering deeply 'pon the matter, but...wherefore do donuts have holes? Is it not merely a waste of potential donut?"

This time she stuck her finger through the hole and started spinning the donut like a hula hoop.

Treating it so cavalierly just because it wasn't from Mister Donut—I wanted to tell her not to play with her food.

I may not be well-educated enough to know when Doraemon's love of dorayaki was introduced, but happily I did know why donuts have holes.

That is, I just found out today. Mere moments ago, in fact.

It was Senjogahara who told me, when she came to drop off the donuts—she was kind enough to lay it out for me when I displayed my ignorance by saying, *Man, you must be a real perfectionist to put the holes in them like this.*

Just to be clear, when I say she was kind enough, I don't mean that sarcastically. She really did explain it in a generous manner that was easy to understand.

"Shinobu. Donuts with holes in the middle like that are called torus donuts. The hole allows the heat to pass easily and evenly through the whole donut while it's frying."

"Thermal efficiency? Is that of what you speak?"

"Yeah, something like that. If there was no hole in the middle, the center wouldn't fry well. Which is why they remove it."

Remove might be the wrong word in terms of how they're prepared, but I was putting comprehensibility above all else.

"Ah...is that so?"

"Well? Are you impressed by my erudition?"

"So they call this shape a torus."

"That's the part you're impressed by?"

"What difference be there twixt a ring and a torus?"

"That's a question of volume... A three-dimensional form like a donut or a bagel is called a torus, whereas a ring just means a circle, I think, or...uh..."

"How now, my master. If canst not unravel such a trifling question, how wilt thou penetrate the exam put forth by the National Center?"

Nope.

This kind of question ain't gonna be on the national exam.

"I wonder, is the same true of the hole in a Baumkuchen?"

"No, when they cook a Baumkuchen they stick a pole through the center—Baumkuchen and donuts are made totally differently..."

"And what of donuts that have no holes? How are they fried? Hast said that the heat would not reach to the center. Even Mister Donut maketh many such donuts, yet 'tis not as if they remain uncooked. Thus is the hole not superfluous?"

"I think you're getting a little too deep into their structure... Don't lose sight of your original goal. Which was to inspect these particular donuts."

I looked at the clock. It was already 3:30.

My break was only supposed to be thirty minutes, so I'd already used up my allotment—it's not as if I didn't have some stoppage time factored in, but sadly my plan to enjoy a refined snack of donuts, replenish my blood sugar levels, and rest my mind seemed to have ended in failure.

Well.

Eating five donuts all by myself already seemed like a bit much in any case—so while it did change their purpose somewhat, I'd bring this scene to a close by providing Shinobu with enough donut to shut her up and stop her endless bellyaching.

"Shinobu. Enough with investigating the texture, it's driving me crazy, move on to the flavor already."

"Hm? Eh?"

"I'm saying the only way to find out if it's poisoned is to taste it for poison."

"Art thou telling me to serve as thy poison taster? How cruel my master is, to treat me as the canary in his coalmine! I am speechless!"

Even as she said this, Shinobu's expression relaxed.

In an instant she was all a-sparkle.

To put it in anime terms, the marks on her cheeks got more pronounced—her eyes were glittering.

"Being thus treated by thee suffuses me with warmth, my lord! Aye, like a well-fried donut!"

"Trying to make it clever just makes it more complicated... Now eat up. Eat up and shut up."

Hopefully she'd keep quiet at least while she was chewing the damn things—as her guardian I had no intention of teaching her that it's okay to talk with your mouth full.

I mean, even supposing Senjogahara had poisoned these donuts, these provisions for the troops, that wouldn't be an issue for Shinobu— sea bream even when it's gone bad, as the expression goes, likewise for a drained vampire.

Someone who could gobble up a pair of iron handcuffs without batting an eyelash wasn't going to die from a little thing like a poisoned donut.

"Now now, be not hasty, my lord. I warn thee, assume not that I shall eat anything so long as it may be called a donut. If thou thinkest one donut made by some nameless peasant can placate me, thou art gravely mistaken. If dost wish to slip the net of my investigation, wouldst do well to hie thee straightaway to yon Mister Donut Shinobu Branch and procure for me the new Pon de Ring Rare Choco Golden. Canst even believe it? The Pon de Ring Rare alone would be revolutionary, yet also have they made it in the form of a golden chocolate donut. How high might they fly, will they continue to heap glory upon glory? I have yet to taste the thing, but even as I envision it, 'tis as though the flavor fills my mouth. Aye, before all and sundry, surely I shall cry out at this donut of Japan *for reals?!*"

Cry out, she did.

Her cry cut off her discourse, so despite her earlier lamentations on the state of our economy, it came out sounding like a triumphant shout extolling our nation.

003

I should note at this point that my sweetheart Hitagi Senjogahara is anything but a good cook—or more accurately, she has somehow managed to live thus far without utilizing kitchens for the most part.

Her sickly elementary school years, her middle school years of relentless study, and her high school years spent in the clutches of an aberration—make no mistake, she was a model student throughout all of it, but she never seems to have gotten around to working on her cooking—though that said, or maybe nevertheless, now that her aberration problem has been dealt with for the moment, she seems to have carved out the space to pursue "everything else"—those fields that she had seen as extraneous; so while her progress may be baby steps, her skill in that regard does seem to be on an upward trajectory.

To be honest, the five donuts lined up on the plate were of wildly varying size and shape, diverse you might say, or uneven, or mismatched, a real motley crew. From their outward appearance it wasn't surprising that Shinobu might be wary of them, but when it came to their flavor, they apparently received a passing grade from the famous donut critic

Shinobu Oshino.

After all, she did cry out *for reals?!*

Cutting off her discourse.

If Mister Donut's "Pon de Ring Rare Choco Golden" (whose nature remains unfathomable to me, never having seen one) gets three Michelin stars, maybe this garnered at least one?

"The lass hath done it! I had ever thought that one day she might do something, but to think that today is that day!"

"I'm pretty sure that day was the second of last month, when she saved both our lives…"

"Hmm! I have yet to truly sink my teeth into the study of the donut, yet I know enough to hail this as a great achievement!"

"Seems like sinking your teeth into it would be the only way to go about it…"

Then again, she had sunk her teeth into no small number of donuts.

So it really had to be something special.

"'Tis well done! Summon Miss Tsundere! I would praise her in person!"

"Come on…'my compliments to the chef'?"

Since we were talking about donuts, strictly speaking maybe it was her compliments to the pastry chef.

Hmmm.

Well, naturally they weren't poisoned, but I'd accepted them to savor the sentiment more than the flavor, so I was genuinely pleased to see Shinobu, cream smeared all around her mouth, praising them to the skies like that.

Not that I'd done anything myself, of course.

"But, after having basically avoided contact with Senjogahara this whole time, you can't possibly feel compelled to face her because of some donuts."

"I wish to apologize to her for having called her Miss Tsundere heretofore. Even if I cannot yet call her Mister Donut, I think it meet to dub her Master Donut."

"That's a hell of a thing to dub someone…"

Isn't that a little over the top?

That's not just high praise, it feels like it's shading into sarcasm—given that Senjogahara was still at the "The adventure begins!" stage with cooking in general, it seemed frankly dubious for this deep-fried pastry alone to receive such a high evaluation.

People say that pastries are harder to make than anything on the menu of our so-called three square meals… You can't wing it with pastries, where the measurements and timing demand a level of precision far surpassing other kinds of cooking. Oh, hmm, could that be it?

I think I get it.

A convincing theory formed in my mind—knowing Senjogahara, something that demands precision might actually be easier for her. Relying on instructions and instruments instead of her own palate, she would be less likely to make a careless mistake. Maybe that was the logic here.

And with fried pastries you can't even taste them until they're basically done… Only the shape rested on the sensibilities of the chef, which explained the chaos in that department.

"…"

That was just according to logic.

Maybe the truth is that Senjogahara's distinctive palate and Shinobu's unique one just happened to line up.

Now I needed to taste my sweetheart's homemade donuts for myself—I thought, reaching out to take one.

But Shinobu snatched away the donut I had my eye on, along with the whole plate.

"…Hunh? What're you doing?"

"What art *thou* doing, my lord? The poison tasting is not yet complete."

"No, it is. You already went ahead and ate one, and you said it tasted good."

"'Tis yet too early to say. It could be a slow-acting poison. A slow-acting but mortal poison," Shinobu warned.

Her mouth was slathered with cream and sugar, but the words emanating from it were vigilant.

I thought about cleaning off those messy lips with a kiss.

Not that I actually did, mind you.

"Though it be safe for the moment, it might prove the type of poison to extend its malign influence to thy descendants, my lord."

"No, if Senjogahara poisoned me like that, she'd be screwing her own descendants."

"Pshaw, be not certain that thy house shall flourish with Miss Tsundere."

"..."

Well.

Given my current situation.

Maybe I ought to stop running away from reality and start considering how to save Senjogahara, even if I can't save myself.

As for Shinobu, though…it might come down to a double suicide.

"Hence I shall dig in my heels about continuing the poison inspection."

"Dig in your heels? Should that be head over heels?"

"Nay, leave the matter entirely in my hands! Four more samples for comparative analysis should be enough to yield the answer."

"Four? Shinobu-tan, from what I can see there are exactly four donuts left in the clip."

"Is that so? What a coincidence. Just what the doctor ordered."

"More like made to order. That's how you came up with that number. Now hand over the plate."

"Impossible. As thy valet, my lord, 'tis my duty to protect thee from even the most insignificant risk."

"You can't play the valet only when it suits you!"

Play the valet.

Hell of a ring to it, especially for something I came up with on the spot.

"Hand over the plate."

I tried saying it again, but Shinobu was clutching the plate to her and showed no signs of letting it go. Well, strictly speaking she wasn't clutching it to her—she was holding it loosely in one hand.

As a ruse, naturally.

One false move on my part could overturn the entire plate; she'd brought us to an obvious stalemate.

If I tried to take it by force, all four donuts would end up on the floor, and we'd be left with nothing—having lost her power as a vampire, all she could rely on was her wiles. Tough luck for me.

"This is my final warning. Shinobu. Hand over that plate right now."

"Kakak. Thou art a poor negotiator," she scoffed, her grip on the donuts precarious at best, "with thine uncompromising attitude, thy single-minded insistence: *give it to me, hand it over.* Is that not the very reason that the talisman entrusted to thee by the ringleader of those experts was stolen?"

"Urk."

I mean.

Absolutely.

But was that really something to be talking about in the same breath as this tug-of-war over some donuts? Consider the dire situation that I am in, that you are in—not to mention others around us who've gotten roped in thanks to the theft.

"If thou hadst acquitted thyself more admirably in that parley, we would not be in such grave circumstance. Thy level of introspection leaves much to be desired."

"…"

I feel like there's no arguing with anything anyone has to say to me about that case, but at the same time, you're the last person in the world I want to hear it from.

Sure, I was careless, but you were pretty goddamn careless yourself.

"Nay, I speak to thee in all earnestness." The little blond girl with a plate of donuts in one hand, who was apparently speaking to me in all earnestness, puffed out her chest and continued in a haughty tone. "In order that such a tragedy not befall thee a second time, my lord, I prithee take heed of the lessons learned from the accumulated days of thy life. Dost truly think that if thou canst not win me over here, 'tis still possible that ye might win over the snake god?"

"Nnnn…"

Well.

What can I say to that?

Obviously I'm going to try and avoid this tragedy—but if that's so obvious, then she's right, I'd better start thinking about what comes after.

Because if my subpar diplomacy really was to blame for the mess, that's a flaw I need to overcome. I'm not going to acquire Oshino's eloquence and skill at bridge-building negotiation overnight, of course—but if I can't do it overnight, all the more reason to work at it every day, like now…

"Nay, thy logic is skewed."

"Feh. You noticed?"

"Didst imagine I wouldn't?"

"Why should I need to be some master negotiator just to keep you from eating my donuts? Just give them to me. Give them back. If I insist on it, just hand them over. This is a purely private affair, it doesn't involve anyone but us."

"The matter of the snake god is also a private affair, though, is it not?"

"Last time I warned you, I told you that was it, but I'll say it just one more time out of the goodness of my heart. Out of single-minded insistence. Shinobu, hand over that plate."

"If 'tis naught but the plate thou desirest, then I have no objection."

"Naught but, my ass."

"Once poison hast ate, finish the plate, as they say. I shall eat the donuts, and my lord shall eat the plate. It seems a fair apportioning to me."

"Not only is it as unfair as it could get, you're still presuming that Senjogahara's donuts are poisoned. Cut the shit already."

We hadn't been on the same page for a while now. I figured our relationship would be a long one, but some intertribal barriers were proving more difficult to overcome than I'd expected.

Shinobu apparently felt the same way, because she made no attempt to hide a drawn-out sigh of discouragement.

She might as well have held up a sign that said, *I'm disappointed in you.*

Well, we were on the same page about that, at least, but most of the time it felt like we weren't even reading the same book.

"In my estimation, thou hadst already failed the moment didst reveal these donuts to me. Thou wouldst have done better to eat such as these before I could discover them. To eat them in secret without waking me. If hadst done so, this pointless trouble would have been avoided."

"You're the one causing this pointless trouble... Talk about a problem neighbor."

There was absolutely no way I was going to be eating these without being noticed by my neighbor, that is, by you down there in my shadow—what could I do, if the smell alone was enough to wake you up.

"Mm, in that case...before we work on thy negotiation skills, my lord, perhaps 'twould be best to polish thy flair for secrecy."

"Secrecy?"

"Aye, if hadst been more adept in secreting that talisman, 'twould never have reached the stage of negotiation, and we would not now be brought to such dire straits. 'Twas the fact that thou didst secrete the talisman in such an easily found place which gave rise to this tragedy."

"Uh...well, it's not like I can't see where you're coming from."

Maybe the whole problem is that I engage in this kind of discussion in the first place. Could my lack of skill at negotiation stem from the fact that I actually listen to what other people have to say?

"But you agree that finding a place to hide it was a problem, right? I mean, being handed that kind of, well, weapon..."

Handed.

Or more like backhanded.

"Letting it out of my sight was risky, but carrying it around with me was even riskier... Ultimately, I don't see what else I could've done but hide it in a place like that."

"Yet is that not why 'twas found so easily, o he who if he were a tarot card would be the Fool?"

"Why go to all the trouble of bringing the tarot card part into it? Calling me a plain old fool would be just as good."

Though it wouldn't be good.

You think a college hopeful is going to take that lying down?

"Were I a tarot card, wouldst be the Moon."

"No, I'm pretty sure the tarot deck already has the Devil or Death or something. Wouldn't that be more like a vampire?"

"I am the Moon. The proof lies in the fact that, had it been me, the talisman would have found a fitting hiding place. As would these donuts. Know thou, my lord, that thy present circumstance is entirely of thine own foolish making!"

"..."

Man, she pisses me off.

At the same time, if you can't turn a blind eye to your own shortcomings, maybe you don't survive as long as she has.

Last time she couldn't do it, she tried to kill herself, after all.

As for my present circumstances, even if we had to wait and see if our measures against the snake god would pay off—if I didn't resolve the donut issue soon, I was never going to get my exam prep back on track.

This was something of a critical moment.

"Go ahead and tell me then, Shinobu. Forget about the talisman for a sec—if it were you, how would you have kept the donuts secret?"

"'Tis difficult to put into words. Hm, easier said than done, they say, but aye, perhaps 'twould instead be easier in this instance to show thee than to tell thee of it. Avail me of but five minutes, and I shall make these donuts disappear from before thine eyes like magic. Thou shalt never find them."

"Five minutes... No, hang on, five minutes is plenty of time for you to eat four donuts. It's absolutely against the rules to eat them then say, 'Look, they're gone.'"

And of course it would be against the rules to hide them in my shadow—if I had that kind of method at my disposal, not only would I have been able to hide the talisman, you never would've known about these donuts.

"Kakak. Dost truly think I would be so duplicitous?"

"You? Definitely."

Holding Senjogahara's donuts hostage was already pretty underhanded.

"Perhaps I cannot keep all four from thee—but one or two, at least, I shall hide such that they never be found. What sayest thou, dost fancy a challenge? Canst find in five minutes that which I take five minutes to hide?"

"..."

"The rule shall be that any donuts thou dost not find, I may consume. Should my lord find all four, it shall be his right to eat all four."

"Hm..."

I wasn't wild about the idea of gambling for donuts that were mine to begin with, that is, if she didn't look like a little girl, I'd have an overwhelming urge to smack her...but in order to get back to my exam prep as soon as possible, I had no choice but to go along with it.

"All right, I'm in. But let me repeat, eating them doesn't count as hiding them, okay? You can't hide them in your stomach, okay?"

"Aye, aye, 'tis understood. Nor shall I hide them in my cleavage."

"You're a little girl, you don't have cleavage."

More likely she'd hide two by stuffing her bra with them—though that would still leave two more.

"If you tried it anyway, there would be the problem of how to recover them... I mean, if you eat them behind my back, it'll be too late no matter what I say."

"Thou hast too little faith in me."

"Right, here's what we'll do: I'm adding a rule that if you do something illegal, the punishment will be that I stick my hand down your throat and make you throw up."

"I shall break no rule, so thou mayest invent whatever punishment pleases thee, my lord, but dost intend to eat any donuts that I might throw up?"

She was acting horrified.

Don't look at me that way, I'm your partner in crime, we're in the same boat, our lives are inextricably linked.

"But Shinobu, there's one other problem. A practical problem, it's got nothing to do with preventing you from cheating."

"Namely?"

"You're bound to my shadow, right? So isn't it going to be pretty hard for you to hide something so it's hidden from me?"

Hide something so it's hidden is a weird phrase, but—when her only territory was my shadow, I didn't see how she could hide anything from me if I wasn't asleep. Even if I was asleep. There had been a period when our pairing, or tethering, had been severed, but...

"Well, I guess I can just close my eyes...for five minutes, or until you say you're ready."

"Nay, for if thou dost break thy promise and open thine eyes, the game is ruined. Thou wilt surely open them a little. Rejected. Dost the nincompoop think I have so much faith in him?"

"...Seeing as how up in arms you were about me doubting you a minute ago, don't you think you should take it down a notch?"

"As punishment for such a transgression I shall, let me see, I shall stick my hand into thine eye socket and gouge out thine eye."

"Take it down a notch!!"

"Well, if that be out of bounds, then there is nothing left but to employ a blindfold," said Shinobu Oshino, readily taking off her leggings.

004

The epilogue, or maybe, the punch line of this story.

"Huh? You're doing what, Araragi?"

"No, Hanekawa. The thing is…"

"Any way that anybody slices anything, this is no time for you to be doing that. How can you be playing around with Shinobu?"

"No, I mean, I totally agree, that's exactly what I thought—"

"You know perfectly well that you need to be studying for your exams right now, Araragi."

"…"

That's what you meant?

I mean, sure, that too, I guess.

"Using leggings as a blindfold? Pervert."

She let me have it, point blank.

Not gonna forget that one anytime soon.

"Let me explain, Hanekawa. It's not like I wanted to be blindfolded with leggings. Blindfolding me with leggings, stuffing leggings in my mouth, it was all Shinobu."

"In your mouth?"

"Slip of the tongue."

Should've left them stuffed in my mouth.

No?

"H-Hanekawa. I'm sure there's a whole heap of things you want to lecture me about, but international calls are expensive, aren't they? You probably can't—"

"Don't worry. I can."

"…? Oh, well, in that case there's something I want to ask you. Where do you think Shinobu hid the donut?"

"That's what you want to ask me? Not about my search for Mister Oshino?"

"We'll get to that later."

"Amazing. You're quite a guy."

"Ooh, appealing to my vanity, are we?"

"Your inability to recognize sarcasm is even more amazing."

"I found three of the donuts she hid, but I couldn't find the last one—we're talking about just my room. There are only so many places she could've hidden it."

"Hmmm."

"So all I can think of is that she ate it… Though given everything she said, I have a hard time believing she would've broken that rule."

"That does seem like the most likely possibility—but it sounds like you have faith that she wouldn't cheat. In which case I guess she must've gone with the second most likely possibility."

"The second most likely? You mean I overlooked something?"

"How come you have faith in Shinobu but not in yourself… If it's me, I'd say the likelihood that you've overlooked something in your own room is pretty low, Araragi."

"Wow. Your confidence in me is pretty high, Hanekawa!"

"A low likelihood isn't the same thing as high confidence."

"…"

Harsh.

Hanekawa is harsh on perverts… No, most people would be.

"Then what's this second most likely possibility?"

"What happened to the three donuts you did find, Araragi?"

"I ate them. That was the deal. Which means that me and Shinobu shared the donuts in a 3:2 ratio."

"Were they good?"

"Yeah, just like Shinobu said. Is that…important?"

"Nope, the flavor is irrelevant. I was just thinking how much I'd like to taste Senjogahara's handiwork as a pastry chef—4:1."

"Huh?"

"It's 4:1, the donut ratio. The sharing ratio. You ate four of them, Araragi."

"? No, I only ate three…"

"*The fourth donut was hidden inside one of the other three*—they say if you want to hide a tree, do it in the forest, but in this case, the tree was hidden inside another tree, so to speak."

"…"

"You said the donuts were all different sizes, right? Then she must've taken the smallest of the four remaining ones and hidden it inside the biggest one."

"Wha… But how? Hiding a tree inside another tree…"

"Hiding a tree inside another tree would be impossible without hollowing it out. But you could do it with a fried donut. Since the inside is soft, whatever the outside might be like. All it would take would be a good squeeze."

"Squeeze… B-But."

Sure, but.

"Even if the inside is soft, the outside is hard, okay? You'd know if someone tried that trick—"

"Not with a torus donut. Look, Araragi, after Shinobu ate the first one *her face was covered in cream*—isn't that what you said? Which means Senjogahara used whipped cream in the donuts. But since they were torus donuts, it's unlikely that the pastry was completely wrapped around the

103

filling like with curry bread, you know? Either the outside was decorated with cream, or the torus was split horizontally like a bagel and the cream was put in between the two halves. Either scenario would jibe with your testimony about the way Shinobu was holding the donut. The former clashes with your stated testimony that the outside was sprinkled with sugar, however, leaving us with only the latter possibility—"

"…"

Information leaking out of every word I said to her.

You're scary, Miss Hanekawa.

"And if it's the latter, then the donuts *were split from the start*, so there was no need for Shinobu to deal with the hard exterior at all. The cream probably acted as an adhesive once it was put inside the donut, I imagine? Though all that being said…there's no proof, is there. Since you ate the proof, Araragi."

In a certain sense, you could even say that Shinobu hid the donut in your *stomach*—finished Hanekawa.

Hm…

Is that why Shinobu wouldn't squeal about where she hid the last donut, no matter how much I grilled her? That would be hard to admit, wouldn't it, both that she had resorted to that kind of trickery to conceal Senjogahara's donut, and that she sat silently by and let me eat it as a means of destroying the evidence.

I unconsciously threw a look of reproach at my shadow, but I felt embarrassed. I'd gobbled up the double donut with gusto, not noticing any difference from the other two, never realizing the trick that had been played on me…

Maybe that was why Hanekawa asked me about the flavor—and not because she wanted to hear more about her friend Senjogahara's skill as a pastry chef.

I dunno, I was struck by the feeling that I needed to refine my own palate before I could say anything about Senjogahara's skill in the kitchen.

"Sorry, but…I think that's bullshit."

"Bullshit? How come, it's not like she broke the rules. Shinobu didn't eat the donut herself, after all."

"No, it's definitely bullshit—her goal was to eat the donuts, right? But if she set it up so that I would eat them, then everything's topsy-turvy. She didn't accomplish her goal at all—"

"That's the point, Araragi."

"Huh?"

"Abandoning your own interests, your own goals. Setting aside your personal judgment. In other words, being selfless, self-sacrificing. That's the point. That's what Shinobu was trying to teach you."

"The point...of negotiations? Of secrecy?"

"Of love."

CHAPTER TEN
KOYOMI SEED

SUN	MON	TUE	WED	THU	FRI	SAT
	1	2	3	4	5	6
7	8	9	10	11	12	13
14	15	16	17	18	19	20
21	22	23	24	25	26	27
28	29	30	31			

1

January

001

I wonder if Yotsugi Ononoki even makes a distinction between roads and everything else? I consistently have my doubts—she's bound by neither the forces of gravity, nor buoyancy, nor lift. The creatures known as human beings who're always bustling around her generally propel themselves by alternately moving one leg and then the other, and I can't help but think that Yotsugi Ononoki is simply emulating them when she does so herself.

At present the human race just so happens to have adopted perambulation as its primary form of locomotion, and she's just imitating them, no deeper meaning or consideration involved. If, for instance, crawling were to become the latest trend in human propulsion, Yotsugi Ononoki would probably start crawling around without a second thought.

According with reason holds no meaning for her—it's adapting to reality that's much more meaningful.

And that adaptation to reality is itself an absolutely goal-oriented way of life for a *shikigami* like Yotsugi Ononoki—then again, since she's an aberration who doesn't possess a lifeforce and can't be said to have a way of life in the first place, and is in fact relentlessly pursuing a goal she can never achieve, maybe it's more like a meaningless way of punishing herself.

"For me, the safest way to travel isn't walking along the ground or soaring through the sky—it's probably burrowing through the earth."

Some time or other.

When I was going along, being taken along, on a high-altitude trip fueled by her "Unlimited Rulebook"—it's really up to the observer whether to consider that mode of travel jumping or flying—she suddenly started explaining this to me.

In a monotone that sounded like a failed impersonation.

Lacking intonation.

Or even context.

"Tunneling through the earth like a mole—I think that's probably the safest way for me to travel."

Unless she was just making a groundless joke about *being* underground versus *going* underground, I couldn't even guess at what she was trying to say.

Safe.

Sure, being underground is probably safe.

Especially for someone like her, someone for whom battle is inevitable, an indispensable safety might well be found there.

There—beneath the earth.

She might find a safety that the surface doesn't afford her.

After all, in that kind of hermetically sealed environment there's no fear of a surprise attack, even from above—given the lack of obstructions in the sky, aerial movement naturally allows for the greatest velocity, but a lack of obstructions also means a lack of potential cover.

Which is why Yotsugi Ononoki said that subterranean travel was the safest—or so I thought, but she just quietly shook her head at my interpretation.

Shook her head expressionlessly.

And said in a monotone, "No. It's because there are no people around."

No people around.

There was no one for her to imitate, hence no one to be influenced by.

It was the one place she could really be herself.

002

"Oh. Kind monster sir. Monstieur for short. What a coincidence, running into you like this. Yaaay."

"…"

"Hey now, what's with the cold shoulder? That sort of behavior's no good for my moral education. How are you going to explain it to Big Sis if I end up as a delinquent, yaaay."

"…"

I turned on my heel and started back the way I'd come, but Ononoki zipped around in front of me so fast that she was just a blur, tenaciously maintaining her sideways peace sign like I was a television camera or something. This may not be a nice thing to say about a girl you're friends with, but the fact is that I had no patience for it right then.

Patently no patience.

Please don't misunderstand me.

It's not Ononoki that I had no patience for—sure, I couldn't hide the fact that I was a little fed up with her "yaaay sideways peace sign," wherever she might've picked it up, but my feelings towards Yotsugi Ononoki,

113

this shikigami aberration, this *tsukumogami* employed and commanded by an expert, were generally positive.

And the ignominious nicknames she gave me—kind monster sir, monstieur, and so forth—had to do with my vampiric nature. It wasn't that I treated her monstrously—be kind to young girls.

That's my motto.

And yet, if running into someone you don't want to run into at an inopportune time is the worst-case scenario, what do you call running into someone you do want to run into at an inopportune time? And the current time was, indeed, inopportune. My patience was exhausted.

Specifically.

It was the middle of January.

I was on my way home from the national exam—for the second day in a row, I had gone to the test center, filled up the scantron sheet, and taken the train back to my town.

Having walked Senjogahara to her place, I was now on my way home—and just about halfway between our houses, I bumped into this girl.

The timing seemed just a little too good, it felt like I'd been ambushed; but while I might have a reason to ambush Ononoki, I couldn't think of a good reason why she might ambush me, so it was probably just happenstance. No question about it.

"Hey, what're you doing, Monstieur?"

"Hm?"

"Hey, hello, over here," Ononoki beckoned with a twitch of her two fingers.

Or no, not beckoned—I'm pretty sure she was urging me to do *something* with that gesture, but body language is a means of linguistic expression that only works when it's based on a certain level of mutual comprehension.

Mutual comprehension is difficult with an aberration even at the best of times, and Ononoki lacks facial expressions in the bargain—to put it in kanji terms, she was a difficult and obscure character, not part of the

114

standard list.

In other words, unreadable.

"Yaaay."

"Come on, enough with the sideways peace sign. I have enough trouble reading it as it is, don't make it any more complicated."

"Oh man. Everyone and their mother gives me a hard time about my sideways peace sign."

"Everyone and their mother? Did someone besides me complain to you about it? Who was it?"

"That's a secret."

"A secret?"

"Obviously. Why would I tell you anything? Know your place."

"..."

What the hell.

Sure, I may've accidentally strayed into her private affairs, but why shut me down so forcefully...

"Let's get to know each other's places."

"Each other's? You and me? That's, well, that's a surprisingly ardent approach, but..."

"You see, this body language. This hand gesture," she started to explain, as if she thought we weren't going to get anywhere otherwise.

Well, I was the one thinking that.

But the gesture she now gesticulated struck me as completely different from her earlier body language... Was this doll just doing whatever popped into her head?

"Means 'I'm on a bit of a hunt for something, and if you happen to have the time, I wonder if you wouldn't mind helping me look for it, Monstieur.'"

"How would anyone know that?!"

You can't express such a complicated request with only two fingers! I'm not a telepath!

"Telepath? Don't you mean Derepath?"

"What does that even mean? Is it supposed to be a variation on tsundere?"

"So, what about it? Are you going to help me or not? Tell me now. If you don't want to help me, then hurry up and get out of my sight."

"…"

Her word choice…

Her tone…

Who the hell was giving this girl her moral education—though, the influence of others has a much more direct effect on Ononoki than it does on other aberrations.

She must be hanging out with the wrong crowd—this tween really embodies the expression "If you lie down with dogs, you'll get up with fleas."

For crying out loud, be a little choosier about your friends—not that I'm one to talk. I haven't exactly been hanging out with the best crowd myself lately.

"I'd love to help you, but…"

On a hunt, huh.

Did we really just happen to run into each other while Ononoki was out looking for something? Even so…

"I just finished my exam, and I'm wiped out—Senjogahara made me go over my answers with her at her house afterwards, and it got ugly."

That's what I meant by inopportune—it wasn't just an inopportune time to run into Yotsugi Ononoki, I didn't feel like running into anybody, didn't feel like talking to anybody at all.

What I needed to do was get myself home as quickly possible, review the questions I'd gotten wrong, and get a handle on the areas that were giving me trouble—I was in such a hurry that even stopping to talk with Ononoki for this long felt like I was wasting precious time, never mind going on some treasure hunt.

"Your exam? Ohhh. You mean that National Center Exam you were telling me about before. Back in my day, it was called the Common First-Stage Exam."

"Um, why's a tween spouting a stale line people of a certain age supply on cue?"

I really gotta find out whose influence this is.

"It used to be called 'First-Stage' but now it's 'Center'? What kind of a name change is that? It's a total turnaround. Maybe there was just some issue with the naming rights."

"That's some issue, in its own way!"

"They use that scantron sheet thing, right? I know all about that. Ahem. Yaaay."

" . . . "

Pretty impressive, except it was probably thanks to me. I seem to recall mentioning it when I was "telling her about it before."

"What's the big deal, then? The exam's over, right? Why are you acting like you're in such a rush? I don't have time for your *I'm so busy* routine, Monstieur."

"Um, I'm not doing any routine."

Or did I start acting that way without realizing it?

Reassuring myself that I hadn't, I said, "To put it bluntly, my scantron sheet results were pretty disgraceful. It's looking like I'm gonna need to give myself an extra boost from here on out."

"Hmmm... Well, that just goes to show what a warrior you are, Monstieur. No filling in the tough ones on a hunch for you. Me, I'd take a gamble on one-in-five odds, but you just leave that blank space pure and unsullied."

"'Fraid not."

Nothing upright and unsullied about me.

More like down and dirty.

How else would I be shamelessly going about my life after experiencing the kind of year I have?

"The thing is, my hunches are no good. Every single time I gambled on those one-in-five odds, I got it wrong."

"Yaaay. I mean, wow."

Her reaction and her catchphrase came out of order.

And what kind of a catchphrase is that, anyway?

"Amazing. I said one in five, but with a little bit of studying you should be able to reduce the odds to one in three or even one in two. What the hell have you been doing this past year to get them all wrong? You'd be better off dead."

" ... "

Why so harsh?

I should be asking *you* who the hell you've been hanging out with since the last time I saw you.

"This past year I've mainly been getting attacked by a vampire and beaten half to death by a cat, dealing with girls falling on me or losing her way, getting my ass kicked by a monkey, being enwrapped by a snake, and duped by a swindler, watching my little sisters become targets, traveling through time, getting attacked by darkness, and told that I only have six months left to live. When exactly should I have been studying? Dammit."

"I'm not saying you should have been studying, I'm saying you'd be better off dead."

"Don't you try and kill me, at least."

"I'm going to keep on berating you until you agree to help out with my search. I'm going to keep on telling you to drop dead."

"Don't. Because I won't feel like helping you."

"You won't?"

"Will I?"

"You're a will-I son of a bitch."

"Is that supposed to be like a wily son of a bitch? Clumsy, but fine, fine."

I raised my hands in surrender.

Unlike Ononoki's earlier gesture, this was the clearest possible body language.

"I give up, I'll help out, will-I-ngly. So this thing you're looking for. It's around here?"

"Who knows, it might not be."

" ... "

How irritating.

Not even a word of thanks?

True, it'd be more efficient to hurry up and locate whatever she was looking for as soon as possible then bid her a peaceable farewell, rather than stand around bandying words like this.

Instead of worrying later on about how things turned out for her, I could take care of this problem on the spot—that seemed like the best way to move ahead with my exam prep.

…

Wasn't precisely this sort of stopgap mentality whittling away all my study time, though? Like, *it'll be more efficient in the end if I clean my room before I start studying.*

Well, either way, that ship had sailed—it was too late to change my mind and just head home. To begin with, Ononoki had her "Unlimited Rulebook" as a last resort.

With that, it'd be a cinch to make me do anything she wanted—and submitting before the other person busts out the big guns is how you survive in this world.

A magic bullet against the big guns.

I guess that's not badass, no matter how badass I try to make it sound…

"Well, if you say it might not be around here, then we'll have to bear that in mind. So, what should I be looking for?"

"Hmm, good question."

"…"

"Yaaay."

"…Yaaay."

Just let me go home alreadaaay…

003

Ultimately, it came to pass that I joined Ononoki on her search still ignorant of what it was we were searching for—Nadeko Sengoku had looked for an "object of worship," but this was even more open-ended. How did I let myself get suckered into it? Yet I had, and that was that.

I couldn't get anything more out of her no matter how hard I pressed.

That is, Ononoki herself only seemed to have the vaguest idea—and tried to gloss over that point, but while we hadn't known each other for very long, we knew each other pretty well.

From her statement "Apparently it'll be instantly recognizable," I could see that someone else had ordered her to find this thing, and that she herself was operating on only the vaguest intel.

See, or rather, hear... An ordinary person, under ordinary circumstances, couldn't look for something based on information so vague it was accompanied by an "apparently," but I suppose it was more or less par for the course for a familiar.

A mission with an unknown objective, a search with an unknown target.

As an expendable asset belonging to an expert, maybe she wasn't permitted to question her owner—but anyway.

Despite not being owned by anyone or ordered not to ask questions, I ended up joining this ill-informed search party.

It was almost like I was a familiar myself—and I wasn't being used by an expert but by a shikigami, so go figure.

Where I stood, in this scenario.

"I'd pretty much finished a creep around this area—I was just thinking I should try looking somewhere else when I ran into you."

"I see... Too bad."

If I'd only taken the next train, I could've avoided this whole encounter? This just wasn't my day.

"Oh, and just to be clear, when I said 'a creep,' I wasn't talking about you, okay?"

"Why would you be?"

"As far as the search goes, the thing I want you to help me with..." she went on as if I hadn't said anything.

It's a breach of etiquette to play dumb and ignore a retort like that. Or maybe she never ratified that treaty? Or she wasn't talking about me, but she does think I'm a creep?

"Is expanding my field of vision."

"Your field of vision?"

"I hit a dead end—and started to think I needed to change my perspective."

"Well, I mean, start thinking whatever you want, but if it has something to do with me, could you clarify what it is you want me to do? Are you basically saying that when you're searching for something, the more eyes the better?"

"I wonder, what would be better?"

"Stop answering my questions like that. Setting my teeth on edge doesn't even begin to cover it."

"Oh? Then what is it setting? An event flag, like in a dating sim?"

"No flags are getting set with a girl as young as you."

"A flag is like a banner, right? So setting a flag means raising a banner...but is it a battle standard, or are we surrendering? Tough call."

"..."

This young shikigami, with her robotic thoughts and actions, occasionally, which is to say frequently, got her priorities backward. Not that I always made the right call when it came to my priorities, given that I was out here accompanying her on her treasure hunt when I absolutely needed to be studying, but one thing I could say for sure was that what this flag might or might not be signaling was pretty damn low on the list of priorities.

That's about as easy a call as they come.

"So yeah, basically, it's not about more eyes, instead I want to change my point of view. Since, as you can see, I started out as someone's cherished doll. I'm an ankle-biter."

"An ankle-biter."

"In other words, I don't have the requisite altitude to carry out a search like this. I mean, when you're looking for something in your room and you're stumped, you get up on a chair or a desk and scan the room, right? Tall people are at an advantage in searching for things."

"Hmm...from a perspective perspective, sure. If the thing you're looking for is hidden by something, it'll probably be easier to find with a bird's-eye view..."

Not always, though, of course.

There are places that are easier to burrow into if you're an ankle-biter—if you're small, and sometimes a low perspective is actually more advantageous.

Her owner must have tasked her with this search precisely because it required a low perspective—but having hit a dead end, I guess Ononoki decided she needed my help.

"Listen, though, Ononoki. It's true that I'm taller than you...but that's only relatively speaking. Objectively I'm not all that tall, you know?"

"Anyone can see that. Even someone as short as me. You're objectionably not very tall."

"Objectively, not objectionably."

"Objectively speaking, you're objectionable."

"Nope. That's just your point of view."

"My perspective is the whole problem. Sure, your height isn't going to make that much of a difference, Monsieur...but here's the thing. You're studying for your college entrance exams, so you must be familiar with the branch of mathematics known as addition?"

"You don't have to be studying for exams to be familiar with that branch of mathematics."

"Naturally, a mathematical girl like me knows about it too."

"Mathematical girl..."

Wasn't that the title of some ancient book on Japanese arithmetic?

Man, Japan is really something. Before we had magical girls we had mathematical girls—maybe the popular culture of this country really hasn't changed all that much since ancient times.

"I find that hard to believe about you, Ononoki..."

"Rude. Shall I prove it to you? I'll tell you what the largest prime number is."

"The second you said 'largest prime number,' what you proved is that you know zero about math."

"I'm the one who discovered the concept of zero."

"Shut up!"

"Right now we're talking about addition. We take my really short height, add your pretty short height to it, and abracadabra, aberrationcadabra, it becomes a really pretty tall height. About nine feet, specifically."

"..."

Thanks for rubbing it in about my height, but that aside—to put Ononoki's mechanical statement in terms that even someone of my limited linguistic skill could understand, she was in effect saying, "Let me ride on your shoulders."

The cherished dream of a cherished doll.

Well, even if nine feet was a bit of an overstatement, we'd definitely clear six, giving Ononoki a bird's-eye view that afforded a completely different perspective on her search—hmm, a tween girl shoulder ride event, huh?

That was not what I'd been after, and I had no illusions that an event could make up for my depressing exam results, but if it would get me home even one minute sooner, then I had no choice.

A flag had apparently been set whether I liked it or not, so to get out of that as well, I had no choice but to give this tween girl a ride on my shoulders.

Wait, hang on.

This wasn't a first, was it?

A shoulder ride event reminded me of this crazy occasion when I was the one getting the shoulder ride, if you can believe it—I ended up being the talk of the town for a while thanks to that.

What a sorry urban legend.

For someone who'd even been a vampire.

As a shikigami, Ononoki certainly had the strength to carry me on her shoulders, but in this case it was clearly better the other way around—there's a balance to everything. And it's only by preserving that balance that we can maintain the proper order of things.

But I was dealing with someone who lacked common sense.

In addition to common sense, Ononoki also lacked things like consideration, and humanity—probably best to make sure we were on the same page. In fact, I preferred to have it in writing, but...since there wasn't time for that, I'd have to make do with an oral response.

Either way, I was probably overthinking it.

Maybe thinking it over at all was a waste of effort—regrettably, however, Ononoki's reply was totally divorced from any human response I might've expected.

"Ononoki. There's something I need to know."

"Something you need to know? Uh-uh, if you want to know what it feels like to embrace me, you'll have to wait till after the mission's over."

"Enough with the jokes... For this addition you're talking about, it's cool if you ride on my shoulders, right? I know you've got superhuman strength, but I still think it would look better than doing it the other way around, yeah? Don't want to be too conspicuous, you know?"

"Somehow I get the sense that's not the only reason," Ononoki prefaced, making her seem suspiciously well-versed in human emotion despite being a shikigami, after which she continued, "but no, Monstieur."

"Huh? What'd you say?"

"No, Monster."

"Hey, what happened to the *u* and the *i*?"

"You and I are right here, so stop quibbling. Listen, Monstieur. I won't ride on your shoulders."

"Huh?"

"I won't squeeze your cranium with my thunder thighs."

"You can just leave it at 'I won't ride on your shoulders.' And when I ask you to repeat yourself, say the same thing again the second time."

"I won't ride on your shoulders, and you can't ride on mine. Think about it, the loss would be too great if we did it that way."

"Loss?"

"Whoever ended up on whoever's shoulders, it would involve sitting, right? We'd only be adding on that person's seated height. You may have a lot of confidence in your seated height, Monstieur, but your seated height plus inseam wouldn't be shorter than your seated height, would it?"

"How could that be true for anyone? My leg length isn't a negative number."

"I also discovered negative numbers."

"You'll get the Fields Medal for sure. Hell, they'll establish the Ononoki Medal."

"The Ononoki Medal. That's got a captivating ring to it."

"So by 'loss,' you meant that if one of us rode on the other's shoulders, we wouldn't be as tall as you hoped—but, still and all, Ononoki. That's an unavoidable loss. I don't see any way to get a higher perspective outside of, or above and beyond, a shoulder ride. Even if I held you up, at best you'd be at the same height as me."

"That's not holding me up, that's just holding me tight."

"Okay then, even if I tossed you upsy-daisy."

"I know I look like a little girl, Monstieur, but that doesn't mean I want to be treated like one… Seriously, it's simple. I just have to do the same thing I always do."

"Always do?"

"If I call it 'the thing she always makes me do,' does that help?"

"…?"

It didn't.

That is, I didn't want it to.

004

A few minutes later.

I stood looking out from a lofty vantage point.

That is, I was standing atop Ononoki—atop one of her fingers, which was thrust upward as if she was pointing at the heavens.

"…"

It's not totally clear to me what her primary role as the familiar of an expert really is—but the role she actually carries out in the course of her day-to-day duties seems largely to approximate that of a chauffeur.

Though obviously I don't mean that this tween girl actually drives a car—the expert who employs her "can't set foot on the ground," so instead, Ononoki ferries her employer around on her finger or her shoulders or her head.

Transporting someone around like a piece of luggage is impressive, and I've always been impressed by Ms. Expert's ability to be transported like that as well—but never in a million years did I think that I'd have the pleasure.

Okay, true…

This way there was no loss…

In fact, not an inch of my legs was wasted (whether or not I have confidence in their length is another story); moreover, the length of Ononoki's arm and finger were added in as well, so I was in fact looking down from a height of "about nine feet," as she had initially, and confoundingly, predicted.

That other time I'd "gotten" a shoulder ride, my perspective had been pretty damn high as well, but this was definitely higher—I mean, I could never be on the bottom of this particular arrangement…nor, ordinarily, on top either.

Balancing atop a single finger?

What was I, a basketball?

Not that I was being spun around, but as someone with a not particularly good sense of equilibrium, standing on her finger at all, however unsteadily, seemed entirely down to how good she was at adjusting the balance for me.

It was a bit like a ride, and while this wasn't the time or the place, I was enjoying this bit just a bit.

"When you carry her around, do you maintain the balance for her like this?"

"Nope, with her there's no need. She's got her own special riding style—though I do have to be extra careful not to make a mistake and dump her on the ground."

If I did, she'd be pissed off for real, said Ononoki.

"Pissed off for real, huh…"

For reals.

Shinobu slept through all of this, incidentally. Given how badly she and Ononoki get along, she may've been awake and just playing possum.

What sort of demon acts like a possum, though? Seems like an unbelievable step down for an aberration.

"I'd get the blame even if it was her own fault. There isn't much technique involved, but I do have to be really careful, it's pretty rough. It's so much more relaxing to carry you, Monsieur, since I know you won't complain at all."

"I hate to say it, Ononoki, since it makes me happy that you think so, but I'm not that easygoing."

In that sense, this was the perfect height.

It's not like I'd get off without a scratch if she dropped me, but as long as I didn't land on anything really terrible, it wouldn't be life-threatening, nor would I lose consciousness, so I'd be able to complain to Ononoki to my heart's content.

"…"

Speaking of dropping things.

"Listen, Ononoki. For now we'll continue the search in this configuration, but—"

"Man, you give up quick, Monsieur."

"I prefer to think that I'm just quick to move on."

"'If you can't figure out the solution, just leave the problem unsolved,' isn't that your catchphrase?"

"How is a guy like that going to pass any exams…"

Well.

Senjogahara did tell me that skipping problems you couldn't solve is an unavoidable technique for entrance exams—but Hanekawa advocates the prodigious technique of "solve the hard questions first, and the rest will be easy." A little too prodigious.

"This goes well beyond being conspicuous, so I'd like to find it as soon as possible…but since we're talking about finding something, does that mean that someone lost it somewhere?"

"Hm?"

"Come on, don't 'hm?' me, Ononoki. Are we looking for something that you…or that somebody, lost?"

"Good question. I'm a just-does-what-she's-told-to-do girl, so I just do what I'm told to do."

"If you're going to append a descriptor like that, at least make it easier to say. But when you're searching for something, it's usually something somebody lost, isn't it?"

"Not necessarily. You'll lose your balance for sure, almost necessarily, but maybe it isn't something that somebody lost."

"Don't even hint at such an inauspicious future."

"We could be looking for something that someone hid somewhere, or something that disappeared in some kind of accident. If you want to go around making assumptions about it, suit yourself, but can you not cause any confusion for the people on the ground with your hasty conclusions?"

"…"

Stern…

Like she even knew what we were looking for.

"You said that it'll be instantly recognizable, but does that go for me too? It must, since you've got me up on the watchtower here… If there's been some kind of misunderstanding, I'm sorry, but the drain on my vampiric skills has been pretty intense lately, so if you're counting on my aberrational vision, you're out of luck."

"It's fine. I'm not counting on anything from you."

"Then why the hell am I up here? Why are you carting me around like a portable shrine?"

"Right. The reason I'm kakakarting you around—"

"Ditch the pointless Shinobu imitation."

"…is that you can find it even without aberrational powers of vision. So make like a weather vane and look every which way, please."

"Can I assume it's on the ground?"

"Don't assume anything. Don't even think about anything. You just concentrate on keeping your eyes peeled."

"…"

How did I end up getting ordered around by a tween girl? When people are feeling emotionally vulnerable, I suppose they just opt for the path of least resistance.

Though it remained to be seen if getting ordered around by her actually fit that bill…

"Anyway, if you just inform me anytime anything catches your eye or seems weird, even if it isn't suspicious, that'll be sufficient."

"Sufficient, she says…"

Her character was all over the place, as usual.

How the hell can that violent onmyoji employ such an inconsistent shikigami—how does she control her?

By force, I guess?

That might shade into domestic violence territory, depending.

"Anything that catches my eye or seems weird…apart from our reflection in the traffic mirror at an intersection, I assume."

"If you want to be sarcastic, save it for later. Right now I'm busy."

"…"

Won't even make conversation with me, huh?

I wondered how she could qualify as busy when her only job was to hold me up, but apparently Ononoki was also scanning our surroundings while she supported me on one finger. She'd already searched this area once, but they say "search seven times before you blame someone else"— though that's a different type of admonition.

"It's not like I've got a ton of time myself," I griped.

"You talking about that 'six months left to live' thing?" asked Ononoki, still holding me up and not even pausing in her search—an intrusive remark, totally out of context. "Out of all the stuff you mentioned from this past year, that's the only one that's still unresolved, isn't it— your remaining days are marching right down the drain, aren't they. Is that why your exam results were so disgraceful?"

"…"

"Though I bet it's not your own life you're worried about, Monstieur—it's your wife, not your life."

"Don't try to squeeze in a pun while we're having a serious conversation."

"I'd rather you thought of it as a light jest."

"Don't try to squeeze in a light jest either."

"What? So you'd rather I squeezed you with my thunder thighs? I'm sorry, but my thighs aren't all that thunderous. I know you like 'em plump, I'm terribly sorry."

"I'll murder you," I threatened this tween girl. "And anyway, that's not what you should be apologizing about."

"Oh? You don't like 'em plump?"

"That's a whole other conversation. And while we're at it, Senjogahara's not my wife."

"Funny. I wasn't talking about Senjogahara."

"Huh? You weren't? Then did you mean Shinobu?"

"Nah, I was talking about Senjogahara."

"If you want to make light jests, be a little less heavy-handed as a conversationalist—and while we're at it, don't just call her 'Senjogahara.' You've never even met her, have you?"

"I never have, no," answered Ononoki, turning the corner.

Where the hell were we going? The exact opposite direction from my house… Was I even getting home before the day was out? Humans and aberrations have completely different senses of time and distance, after all…

Couldn't she at least tell me how large of an area we were searching? From her movements thus far, even that wasn't certain.

Not limited to this or any area.

Not that I was surprised, but the instructions the violent onmyoji gave Ononoki seemed pretty damn vague—though in light of an earlier case, maybe it wasn't the onmyoji that the shikigami was serving.

Particularly if it was the ringleader of those experts—

"How long was it again, Monstieur? The amount of time you've got left? Which ends first, your exam prep or your life?"

"That's a wonderfully indelicate question, thanks for that. Way to rub it in." Or maybe, to come right out with it. Because I have to say, that kind of candor felt better than weirdly dancing around the issue. "That's a tough one. The exams themselves end first. But the graduation ceremony comes before the exam results are announced."

"We could say you're lucky."

"Could we not?"

"Same goes for the intensity of the drain on your vampiric powers.

You're repeating the same futile effort, or even more, the same futile defeat, over and over again."

"It's not futile…"

But true, it hadn't been productive.

It'd even been counter-productive—maybe it was about time I rethought my strategy of charging in blindly as soon as I recovered.

"I'm not sure charging in blindly counts as a strategy," Ononoki shrugged.

Which very nearly made me topple off her finger.

"Nothing I can say to that…"

"I figured Big Sis was the only person who adopted that strategy."

"So does it count as a strategy or not?"

In her case, maybe it did…

Then again, the serpent deity isn't immortal, and she specializes in immortal aberrations, so it doesn't seem like her turn to take the stage—though the same's true for Ononoki.

Hm.

That reminds me, at some point someone told me that one of the reasons snakes became sacred was that the physiological phenomenon of ecdysis made them symbols of immortality—let me see, who did I hear that from again?

My memory's fuzzy, and I can't seem to connect the dots.

Been happening a lot lately.

Been pushing the exam prep a little too hard, I guess.

"Hanekawa's out trotting the globe looking for Oshino on my behalf—but unfortunately, she hasn't had any luck."

"Yeah. Big Brother Oshino—I haven't seen him in a while either."

"Hmmm…"

Seriously, where the hell could that dissolute bastard have gone?

Hanekawa went overseas, but I can't picture Oshino even having a passport…

"Hey, Monsieur. So what do you plan to do? If you want, I could always get in touch with Ms. Gaen for you like I did before, you know?"

"That's okay…"

Leaving aside why she was being so condescending, letting Ononoki rope that woman into this was right out. The whole situation came about in the first place because I'd done her a favor "as a friend"—no, scratch that, I really shouldn't be laying the blame for this at anyone else's feet.

But if you'll permit me to lay the blame at some*thing* else's feet—you could say the culprit was that talisman she entrusted me with.

The root of all evil.

"…Plus, I flouted her will by not using that talisman. I'm afraid I can't be looking to her for help."

"Well. As a friend, she might be surprisingly willing to listen to what you have to say?"

"I know she's not a bad person… She just expects a little too much from her friends in the way of payback."

Then again, with me and Senjogahara's lives on the line, maybe I should be willing to make any sacrifice—in this case, though, the price I have to pay might very well be Shinobu Oshino, at a minimum, and Nadeko Sengoku in the worst-case scenario.

I can't do that.

If I could make such a decision, I would never have ended up in this situation—I know full well that this is no time for rhetorical flourishes, but since cool-headed judgment was impossible at this point, the only strategy left to me was the heat of battle.

"Yeah, fair enough. That's Ms. Gaen for you, ask for a casual favor and later you'll pay for it in spades. If there's something you want to protect, maybe safest to leave her out of it."

"You said it…though I don't know about safest. My current sitch is about as unsafe as it gets."

"Though probably…the fact that there's been no contact from her end means that she has no desire to help you."

"Sounds like it's too much to ask, then."

"Maneuvering so that things seem like too much to ask is her strong suit."

"A little too shrewd for my taste."

"But isn't Big Brother Oshino the same way? Even if Miss Tsubasa of the Hanekawas found him, there's no guarantee he would help, is there? He'd say, 'Can't save, Missy, it takes a person on their own for saved' or something."

"Since when does Oshino speak such broken Japanese? What the hell kind of country has he been living in?"

"Listening to a conversation between me with my monotone and Big Brother Oshino with his broken Japanese would probably be intolerable."

"If you really think so, how 'bout you fix your monotone."

"It's unfixable," declared Ononoki.

It was a strangely firm declaration for the shikigami—her monotone was still monotone, but something felt kind of off about it.

I had to wonder.

Was her character shifting again?

"Anyway, you're not wrong, Oshino might say that—which is why Hanekawa's search is more for temporary peace of mind than anything. She's just doing it for me on the side while she does some location scouting."

Well, maybe not just on the side, but that was really all I could expect from her.

"Ultimately, it's up to me to take care of it somehow or other. I sowed the seed, I'll do something about it."

"If that's true, if you did sow the seed, then yeah, I guess it'd be up to you to do something about it."

"Hm? Are you saying someone else sowed it? No, I don't believe that for a second."

"Nor should you—since seeds are buried in the earth. Until they sprout, you don't even know they're there... But don't you think it's strange? How all this chaos has been centering around you, Monstieur, almost like it's maintaining the balance, almost like someone's got the answer sheet—"

"…"

"Even if it's true what they say, that once you encounter an aberration, you get drawn to them—it still seems like things are somehow balancing themselves out. I don't think you're so slow on the uptake that you wouldn't think it was unnatural."

"Oh, but I am. I'm constantly in over my head just trying to jerry-rig things—and I'm finally hitting my limit with that," I said.

Well, moping to a tween girl wasn't exactly a cool look, even if she was an aberration, and anyway, I shouldn't put Ononoki, who was ultimately on Ms. Gaen's side, in a difficult position, so maybe it was best to leave it at that.

With that in mind, I returned the conversation to our search.

"I don't see anything likely… Are you sure it's around here, Ononoki?"

"I don't need you to report that you don't see anything. Report back when you've found something."

"Geez…"

What an attitude to take with someone who's helping you search for something free of charge, spending his precious time in the bargain…

"Something instantly recognizable—I wonder what it is."

"Who knows, I can't even begin to guess… But Monsieur, I've got something of a *could be*."

"Oh yeah? What is it?"

"Something instantly recognizable to anyone—but which you lose sight of the moment you start searching. In other words," said Ononoki—looking up at me atop her finger. "A smile!"

She said it in a monotone.

With no expression whatsoever.

"…"

Okay, that definitely was something I wanted to find for her, and soon.

005

The epilogue, or maybe, the punch line of this story.

Though forget about a punch line, on this particular occasion nothing happened at all, I just went on a wild goose chase, standing on the finger of a tween girl. That's the whole story. Not even a run-of-the-mill mystery, let alone any tale of an aberration.

And though we wandered around town until night fell, we never found anything, our labors were fruitless, so there wasn't even a smile to be had—you could say that all that happened was that I went for a stroll with Ononoki.

"No luck, huh? Oh well. Bye-bye. Bye-byaaay."

And with that sideways peace sign, Ononoki headed off. She didn't seem particularly broken up about not finding what she was looking for—in fact, though she remained expressionless, she even had a vague air of satisfaction at having done a good day's work.

I wonder if she gets paid by the hour.

Gets paid the same whether she gets results or not... As far as I could tell, if nothing else, she didn't seem inclined in the slightest to put in any unpaid overtime.

Well, I guess a fee-for-service shikigami wouldn't really cut it.

Which is why, after being suddenly left in the lurch like that, I just headed home and went back to my exam prep as if nothing had happened—though having been mentally exhausted by the exam that afternoon and physically exhausted by helping Ononoki with her search, I got sleepy pretty early.

Headed home, messed around with a tween girl, got back to my house, went to bed?

Hey, wait a sec.

Don't you need an episode before you get to an epilogue? Isn't that kind of like playing Name That Tune, where you never get past the intro to the song? No surprise that I felt that way, but the person who gave me the answer to this answerless quiz was, if you can believe it, or you guessed it, or yet again, Tsubasa Hanekawa.

Really, I feel like Hanekawa's sleuthing percentage is a little too high, but I'd prefer if you chalked that up purely to her outstanding scholarly ability and intelligence. It's not just because I constantly rely on her to help me out or anything.

Though she didn't actually explain anything to me directly after my story was done—"Hmmm. You don't say. Is this really the time?" was all she said.

I didn't think that response was particularly unnatural—I just thought, *This isn't the time for that kind of thing, yeah,* since it wasn't the time for that kind of thing, and it wasn't unnatural.

In other words, I didn't notice.

Ononoki's thoughtfulness, and Hanekawa's thoughtfulness, and how they created a situation where it wasn't unnatural.

"What do you think is the hardest thing to find?"

It was some time later—

All the stuff with the snake god was over, but the next stuff had started, somewhere around then—Hanekawa asked me that question.

I mean, since she asked me out of the blue like that, at first I had no idea what she was trying to say.

"Huh? What are you talking about?"

"I'm talking about Ononoki, dummy—you've ended up cohabitating, right? So I thought maybe I should ask you. What do you think is the hardest thing to find?"

"The hardest thing to find…"

Rings a bell.

Reminds me of when Shinobu and I were playing hide the donut in my room—umm, should I answer based on that?

"Let's see, seems to me the hardest thing to find would be…"

"No, that question is just the warm up, how it seems to you and how you answer are irrelevant, Araragi."

"Irrelevant? Huh? Then what's the real question?"

"It's 'What do you think is the easiest thing to find?'"

"Now, that would have to be something 'instantly recognizable'…"

But what does that actually mean? When you think about it, pretty much anything becomes "instantly recognizable" as soon as you find it.

As long as the answer isn't "a smile," of course…

"No, no, Araragi, you can't let yourself get hung up on the 'instantly recognizable' part. I mean, it was a lie, after all."

"A lie?"

"Well, lie might be going too far. But Ononoki wasn't actually looking for anything. The hardest thing to find is, well, just that—*you can't find something that doesn't exist.*"

"…"

What?

Hang on a sec, I don't disagree…but why did she lie to me like that?

"Did she tell me a little white lie just so she could hang out with me?"

"Nope," Hanekawa flatly contradicted me.

A little too flatly.

"The answer to why she did it is 'the easiest thing to find'—of course, things that stand out are easy to find, but what stands out? Nothing does more than *someone who's looking for something*," she said. "Constantly stopping to peer at things, squatting down, standing on tiptoe—it all adds up to some pretty suspicious behavior. Getting out of control and yelling weird things or whatever is another story, sure—but standing on the finger of a girl who looks like a doll as you search for something is pretty much just as conspicuous."

"…"

Conspicuous—or even.

Ostentatious?

"In other words, Araragi, I imagine her intention was to make you conspicuous. So she ran you up the flagpole."

"Like a flag…"

I—set an event flag, or rather, I *was* an event flag?

What kind of a guy am I?

"B-But why would Ononoki want to make me conspicuous? Did she want to parade a moron who flubbed the national exam?"

"It's possible."

It's possible?

Come on, flatly contradict me already.

Now of all times.

"But not only that—you already know, don't you, Araragi? That there was someone in town back in January that you absolutely had to avoid running into?"

"…"

"*That you absolutely couldn't run into—and who definitely didn't want to run into you.*"

Though ultimately you did run into each other, continued Hanekawa.

"He was coming to town on a daily basis, so it wouldn't have been too surprising if you did cross paths—probably, Ononoki kept that from happening for you. By making you conspicuous, she made it easier for him to avoid you."

"Made me easy to find—*by making me hunt for something un-find-able…*"

So that I wouldn't have a chance encounter—with him.

142

With that swindler.

"…"

"Of course, there's no guarantee that he spotted you just because you were so conspicuous—so towering, but if he did, then he certainly would've avoided encountering you. Yotsugi probably just didn't want you to have to deal with any more anxiety than you already had on your plate. A situation where nothing happens, where there's no incident, nothing tale-worthy, is probably only going to happen thanks to someone's consideration for you."

Yotsugi Ononoki's consideration.

A consideration I hadn't even considered.

"Going on about how I'll take care of things and not even noticing that my peaceful life is being propped up by something—what a clown. No wonder that bastard always makes fun of me."

"Maybe so. It's true that people have to go and get saved on their own—but in reality, it's impossible to live life all on your own," Hanekawa riffed on Oshino's catchphrase. Perhaps it was an observation based on her experiences living overseas, even if she was still just location scouting. "You can't live all on your own, and even if you wanted to—everyone ends up benefitting from someone's good graces somehow. Eating, traveling, a change of clothes—even sleeping, probably. All of it's possible thanks to someone else."

"Well…yeah, totally. Though we go through our daily lives without ever being aware of it."

"We sure do. That inconspicuous consideration is probably the hardest thing to find," summed up Hanekawa.

Who knows how unpleasant that summary would've sounded in Ononoki's monotone, but coming from Hanekawa, it somehow wasn't grating—no.

Maybe it wouldn't have sounded unpleasant even coming from Ononoki.

It was that kind of feeling.

CHAPTER ELEVEN
KOYOMI NOTHING

SUN	MON	TUE	WED	THU	FRI	SAT
				1	2	3
4	5	6	7	8	9	10
11	12	13	14	15	16	17
18	19	20	21	22	23	24
25	26	27	28			

2
February

001

When I say that Yozuru Kagenui doesn't walk down any road, it's neither a metaphor nor some impressionistic, high-concept declaration—she literally never sets foot on the ground, every day of her life governed by that constraint.

Which, on its own, makes it sound like a children's game.

Living, proceeding, almost as if she were playing a one-woman game of king of the hill—where the ground is an ocean or the abyss, and you can only walk on raised things like stone steps or concrete walls. The first time I encountered her, she was standing on top of a mailbox.

Well, it might be a game if an elementary school student were the one doing it, but she's a grown woman, so it comes off as pretty damn eccentric—not to mention the fact that elementary school students can play that kind of game because they weigh so little, whereas it's actually pretty difficult for a grown-up. By now I'm sure I don't need to tell how impressive her physical prowess is, but I find myself wondering if that prowess might actually be the result of the daily conditioning this eccentricity affords her.

However you dress it up, though, eccentric is eccentric—a little too eccentric to touch upon, so I've never asked her about it directly.

But as far as I can tell from what I've picked up here and there in our conversations, and from a certain origami enthusiast, there does seem to be a real reason—or at least, it's clear she's not just doing it for the physical conditioning, nor as a game.

Of course, even if there is a reason, I doubt anyone could uphold such a norm without some real drive.

As her enemy.

Or as someone who's battled her head-on, battled and been driven through like that norm—well, well well well, I can safely say no one else is as scary as she is.

I've met quite a few experts in her field, Oshino included, but I have to say Yozuru Kagenui is the scariest of them all.

I'm terrified of her.

So much scarier than an aberration.

So much stronger than a demon.

An onmyoji who drives out aberrations by beating them up has to be rarer than an aberration—then again, it's precisely because she's that kind of person that her behavioral principle is so straightforward and easy to understand, while at the same time being irregular.

The randomness of never walking on the road is perhaps symbolic of her irregularity.

That reminds me, she told me once that she specializes in immortal aberrations because "with them, there's no such thing as going too far," but I wonder. Can I take those words at face value?

While her methodology may be easier to understand than Oshino's or Kaiki's, she's the most antisocial of the whole bunch, the biggest misfit—there's something I'd be curious to ask her, a human being who nonetheless dwells in a darkness darker than an aberration's.

And who doesn't walk on roads.

I want to ask her, *What is a road?*

I'm pretty sure she'd answer:

"Roads aren't the only places what are good for walking."

002

"Take that!"

"Gff!"

"And that! And that!"

"Gff! Gff!"

You might get the impression from these cute battle cries and grunts that the spectacle depicted here is nothing more than some friendly horseplay, but in fact they express an extraordinarily mild version of Ms. Kagenui beating the shit out of me. With a final "And that!" she released a back kick fit to tear off my entire flank—it felt as if a section of my torso popped out, like I was a Jenga tower or something, and I finally collapsed to the ground, ending our little back-and-forth.

"Well now, aren't you out of shape—when we had that little dust-up over the summer, I reckon you had a mite more backbone."

Not that I didn't smash that backbone to splinters—noted Ms. Kagenui, leaping through the air and landing on a brand-new stone lantern.

Landing atop a lantern at a sacred shrine seemed like blasphemy, but she'd probably be forgiven at a shrine like this, where no god was

151

currently present—though given that she couldn't set foot on the ground, she might've done the same thing even at a shrine where a god was in residence.

For my part, I was lying flat on my back in the center of the ceremonial path, so I was obstructing any right I might have had to criticize her.

"Gk…" I moaned. Every inch of my body felt bruised. "This is ridiculous… I thought we agreed that fighting was out of bounds this time…"

"'Fraid not. The only restriction was on meta jokes."

"Was that it? I really had the wrong impression…"

"That is, you were the one what invited a body here to fight, no?"

"Was I?"

I was.

I really had the wrong idea.

If you just heard that snippet, you might get the mistaken impression that I'm suicidal, but yes, on this particular occasion, I myself, of my own volition, asked Ms. Kagenui to spar with me—spar?

What, am I trying to become an MMA fighter or something?

And this wretched outcome—

"You know a body was going easy on you, right? Niiice and easy."

"Yeah, I'm aware of that…"

Couldn't she have gone a little easier on me, though? Niiicer and easier. Like a sponge filled with holes.

"I'm painfully aware of that…"

"By the by, what were you after? Challenging a body to a fight out of the blue like that."

"…"

I had assumed that since she knew the circumstances, she'd be able to guess without a full explanation and accept my reckless challenge on those grounds…but apparently, Ms. Kagenui had beaten the shit out of me for no particular reason, without knowing the reason.

She's really something.

That's not the kind of thing just anyone is capable of.

Since she was Oshino's classmate, I ended up unconsciously expecting her to be the "perceptive" type like him—but turns out she's nothing like Oshino, or Kaiki.

Easy to understand in a good sense.

And easy to understand in a bad sense.

Though I guess they do have something in common, insofar as there's nothing straightforward about dealing with any of them...

"Good question..."

February.

One day towards the end of February, I visited Kita-Shirahebi Shrine—that once-again-godless shrine where I'd almost died countless times, where there had recently been another casualty, was definitely not a place I went lightly, but this expert with whom I had business.

Ms. Kagenui, Ms. Yozuru Kagenui the violent onmyoji, had taken up residence there, so that day I had no choice.

Yes, just as Mèmè Oshino had lodged in the ruins of that erstwhile abandoned cram school while he was staying in town, Yozuru Kagenui was at present lodging at Kita-Shirahebi Shrine—which took a *you can't be serious* level of inner strength.

As an expert, she ought to know better than anyone what kind of a place that shrine is—I thought maybe she was there under orders from the ringleader of their little group of experts, but from what she said, it didn't sound like it.

Apparently, and this makes perfect sense to me, or seems natural, but those two don't exactly see eye to eye—even if she wasn't raising a flag of rebellion, the fact that she was living at the shrine was at least done somewhat out of spite.

Though—there was the thing with Tadatsuru.

So calling it spite might be going too far—but Ms. Kagenui herself must've had some level of self-awareness about it, because rather than making her shikigami Yotsugi Ononoki stay there with her, she put her in my home as a kind of precaution.

Putting a tween girl in my home...

As a precaution?!

"…"

Well, anyway.

To give an update, or, a simple summary of my present circumstances: Last summer a legendary vampire drank my blood, and if you can believe it, I turned into a vampire myself, after which I somehow managed to return to being human, though with some lingering vampirism in my body—if that was all, it wouldn't have been an impediment to me living life as a human being, but stupid me, I relied on that lingering vampirism to deal with the various difficulties that I encountered thereafter.

I don't think I was wrong to do so.

If I hadn't, I never would've been able to overcome those difficulties—and even my vampirism hadn't been enough to overcome that incident involving the serpent deity.

So I'd had no choice.

Even if I had known how it would turn out.

But I do have to pay the price.

The price for relying on the power of an aberration—on the power of darkness.

As I continued to flirt with the darkness of my own accord, as I continued to stray into the darkness, I was once again suffusing my body with darkness—of my own accord.

Concisely put, the fact that I was turning into a vampire became plainly apparent—it was a transformation I hadn't intended, and what's more, it's irreversible.

For now, I just don't appear in mirrors or photographs—right, just a small bug, but if I keep relying on my vampiric power, I'll start turning to ash under the sun's rays, I'll become unable to eat garlic, I'll melt at the touch of holy water.

In return I get absolute, awesome power—but I have no hope of continuing to be part of human society.

In other words, from here on out I can't rely any more on my vampiric nature, regardless of what I have to cope with—that's the long and the short of it.

"Which is why, now that things have kind of settled down for the moment, I was thinking maybe you could help me with some practice, Ms. Kagenui. I was thinking how great it would be if from now on, when I run into difficulties, I could deal with them as adroitly as you do, without resorting to my vampiric power—"

"A-ha," she clapped her hands.

Squatting there atop the stone lantern.

"So that's what you've got in mind. But I reckon you'd best forget it."

"Really?"

Had I best forget it?

I appreciated her candor, but then why the hell did she just...

"Firstly, my way o' doing things can't be learnt overnight, and secondly, it's not exactly the orthodox method among us experts. Not something I'm fixing to teach to a youngster."

"..."

Ms. Kagenui may not be in her teens, but I'm pretty sure she's still on the young side of things for her business.

And, just between you and me, part of the reason I wanted to learn her methodology was that she seems to employ the terribly simple and easy-to-understand negotiation tactic of "suppressing aberrations through violence"—though maybe it can't be learned overnight for that very reason.

The simplest things are always the most difficult.

It's the same with studying.

"And finally, if you're keen to learn my methods through actual combat like this," continued Ms. Kagenui, "you'll be dead before you learn them."

"..."

Yup.

That's a plenty good enough reason for me not to take her as my sensei.

The course fees are a little too steep.

I was completely helpless against her even in vampire mode, so I had no hope of matching her when I was mere flesh and blood—as I considered this, I finally got my breathing under control and stood up from where I lay sprawled out on my back.

Godless as the shrine might be, I still felt antsy lying around inside its precincts.

"Not exactly the time for this kind of thing, is it?" chided Ms. Kagenui. "The big exam must be coming up, everything you've been studying for—this ought to be the time for your, whatchamacallit, back-up-private-school exams."

"Unfortunately, my parents don't have such high hopes for me. The only exam I'm taking is for my first-choice school."

"Hmmm…takes a certain kind of grit, I'll give you that. Now, what'd I do when it came time for exams—can't recall anymore. Feels as though I just woke up one day and I was in college."

"I somehow doubt that…"

"Then I woke up one day, and I had graduated, then I woke up one day, and I was in this line of work—beating the daylights of anyone who rubbed me the wrong way."

"…"

If that's true, then she's a fucking prodigy.

When she says anyone who rubbed her the wrong way, I assume she's talking about aberrations…or is she including humans in that as well?

Hmmm.

I'd come to beg for instruction, but turns out she's really not the type of person I want to get too close to after all.

"It's no good to push myself too hard either, though, is it. At this point, things'll just turn out how they're going to turn out."

"Almost sounds like you're throwing in the towel. Eh, now that you've gotten a bit of an extension on your remaining days, s'pose a gap year might be looking A-OK to you."

"No, I'd really prefer to avoid that. For various reasons."

"All the more reason you shouldn't be up here at this godforsaken shrine trading punches with the likes of me," said Ms. Kagenui—what we were doing wasn't exactly trading punches, since I was the only one getting punched, but anyway, for once she sounded like a proper adult.

"Why do you reckon I had Yotsugi infiltrate your home? I was fixing to make things so you wouldn't be bothered by any aberrations, at least for a while."

"No, I understand that... It's just, being protected by little girls and tweens is a pretty sorry lifestyle."

"By little girl, you mean the former Kissshot, I take it? That's a six-hundred-year-old aberration you're talking about—and that tween, well, Yotsugi's a corpse doll tsukumogami."

"When you put it like that, I guess I've got some pretty amazing guardians..."

A life where nothing happens means someone's watching out for you. Was it Hanekawa who said that?

"Which is exactly why—*that one* can't act rashly."

"That one?"

"That one, or anyone—but enough about that. If you want to learn something from me, how's this: it's best not to overreach yourself. Not that there aren't some folk who've tried to do more or less the same, and not that I haven't acted the teacher on a whim now and again, but it's never once gone well." Ms. Kagenui cackled as she spoke—and trying to picture just exactly what she meant when she said, "it's never once gone well," it didn't seem like these disciples she'd taken on a whim had gotten off lightly...

Hm.

It seemed like a good idea, but maybe I'd jumped the gun—that is, maybe this was a lesson that I shouldn't act on impulse all the time. Though calling it a lesson puts me in mind of that swindler...

"Ms. Kagenui." Abandoning my vain notion of getting Ms. Kagenui to teach me, I asked her a question out of simple curiosity: "How did you get involved in this world?"

"Hmm? This world?"

"Well, I mean, aberrations, or tales of aberrations, that world..."

"To be honest, I'm not too keen on such distinctions—I just mess up anyone what sticks in my craw."

More or less the same thing she was saying before.

This struck me over the summer too, but seems like she operates on an even simpler behavioral principle than I suspected.

The dichotomy between justice and evil.

No, not justice—good?

Then again, if you ask the likes of Oshino, this world is overflowing with unpleasant goodness and insufferable justice—though that means there's an equal amount of eagerly anticipated and compelling evil.

Is Ms. Kagenui actually living on the straight and narrow in a world where nothing is straightforward?

"I reckon it all started back in kindergarten, when I slugged some uppity brat—though looking back on it now, perhaps that brat was possessed by some no-good something. This was in the days before I specialized in immortal aberrations, of course."

"Well, I would be surprised if you've been specializing in immortal aberrations since kindergarten…"

Ms. Kagenui's kindergarten days…

Something I absolutely can't imagine—I wonder if I could've even beaten her in a fight back then.

I wish nothing but happiness for that brat who got slugged by li'l miss Kagenui.

"And, you said the reason you choose to take on immortal aberrations now is that there's no such thing as going too far—right? Conversely, that must mean that you've gone too far on plenty of other occasions. Is that why you chose your particular specialty?"

"Well, I reckon it is—my, but you're full of questions. I don't suppose you're fixing to let me join this Araragi Harem or whatever that I've been hearing so much about?"

"…"

Why does she know about that?

About the Araragi Harem—no, I mean, no such tacky-ass organization exists. She must've heard about it from Ononoki.

What a blabbermouth.

The information leak's probably only getting worse since we've been living under the same roof—but maybe that's also a good thing?

Since it's definitely not a negative for me if Ms. Kagenui is kept abreast of the fact that Tsukihi is living a problem-free life.

"I'd love to be a big enough man someday to be able to make a pass at you—though forget about bigness, the way things are going, I'm gonna end up not being a person at all."

"And when that happens I'll kill you dead, don't you worry. Which is also why I've assigned Yotsugi to stick to you—I told her to show you no mercy if it seems you've strayed any further from the path of humanity."

"…"

The path of humanity, huh?

I felt as if I'd walked the path of human decency in my own way, so how the hell did it come to this?

And the idea that Ononoki was an assassin…

The unbelievable truth slid into focus.

No, upon reflection it made perfect sense, I just hadn't thought about it until she said it. It was easy to forget in the face of that adorable doll, but yes, Ononoki too was a professional who specialized in taking on "immortal aberrations."

Ha—Ms. Kagenui laughed.

Still and all.

"I reckon there's no need to be so negative—on account of if you can keep on with a normal day-to-day like this, you can live as a human being, no muss, no fuss."

"…Even without a reflection?"

"Not having a reflection isn't going to kill you. Turning to ash in the sunlight's a whole other kettle of fish—it'd be scary if you didn't know what was causing it, I reckon you might be crawling out of your skin, but you know perfectly well why it's happening. And as long as your vampir-ification doesn't cross the line, you're fine."

"Sure, I know all that, but—can I really live out the rest of my life like this without anything bad happening? It's only been a year since I heard of aberrations for the first time, and already so much has happened—"

"It's been mighty frequent indeed. That you've encountered trouble."

"..."

One of those mighty frequent troubles was with her and Ononoki, but I'm not complaining. Even now we definitely aren't what you'd call allies, but we've gotten to the point where she at least talks to me like this.

Giving me advice—is definitely not what was going on, but still.

"Well, no one lives out their whole life without some kind of trouble, do they? And yet most folk manage somehow, without becoming vampires—and without turning to heretics like me for help. They manage somehow or other, this, that, or the other way. To put it plainly, this awareness of aberrations and what not that you and I've ended up with makes us weak."

"Makes us—weak."

"We tremble in the face of the unknown, or we know that we can't know what'll happen. Or the unstable elements in our daily lives increase until we can't concentrate on daily life. I reckon Oshino had the same worry."

"Oshino…"

I can't really picture Oshino worrying about anything.

I always think of him as a slaphappy happy-go-lucky chappy, that is, I've never seen him ruminating or anything like that.

Though, hang on.

It's really just that I never imagined him that way—come to think of it, maybe his obsession with balance arose from his fear of the balance crumbling, of losing his neutrality.

Maybe he was afraid.

Pathologically afraid.

"Kaiki seems genuinely happy-go-lucky in that arena," I remarked. "He just does whatever the hell he feels like, without a thought for the balance of the natural world."

"Well, Kaiki doesn't even believe in aberrations—though you might say he's just protecting himself by adopting that stance. Hardly a lick of difference from Oshino's balance-driven stance, really."

Hardly a lick indeed.

Well, they did use to be friends back in the day—and while I'm the one who said it, there aren't many men less suited to the word "happy-go-lucky" than Kaiki.

Happy-go-lucky is more or less the opposite of ominous, after all.

"But it's impossible for folk like you and I to take such a stance, isn't it. Be it balance or denial or what have you."

"Impossible... How do you mean?"

"You yourself are something like an aberration—and me, I've got Yotsugi in my service."

And maybe we're more alike even than that, on account of you've got the former Kissshot in yours, Ms. Kagenui reminded me.

"Try as we might to maintain our balance, we lean toward the aberrations—we lean on aberrations. So any denial would be a denial of the truth of our own existences."

"..."

What can I say, hearing it like that made my head spin.

Talking about the two of us as if we had anything in common—the brazen and supremely self-confident Ms. Kagenui, who enacts her eccentricity of never setting foot on the ground with neither shyness nor showiness, unwavering and rooted in her convictions; and me, flailing this way and that every time something crops up, going whichever way the wind blows, like a kite will if you cut it free, or a kite not cut out for free will... But maybe it was precisely because I unconsciously sensed that commonality that I came to Kita-Shirahebi Shrine to seek her tutelage, to this place I really didn't want to come.

...Yeah.

Peppering Ms. Kagenui with so many questions like this, maybe it did seem like I was trying to persuade her to join the Araragi Harem—

not that there is such an organization—but in spite of all that, if there was just one thing I wanted to ask Ms. Kagenui, maybe that was it.

Not how to fight aberrations with my mortal body—nor how Ms. Kagenui got involved in their world—nor how often she'd "gone too far" in the past, nor even how she knew about the existence of the Araragi Harem.

What I wanted to ask her.

What I wanted to ask Yozuru Kagenui was—

"Hey, Ms. Kagenui."

"What is it?"

"What's the deal with you and Ononoki?"

003

The expert Yozuru Kagenui.

The shikigami aberration Yotsugi Ononoki.

At this point there's no need to reconfirm that the relationship between the two of them is that of an onmyoji and her familiar—the relationship between master and servant, between ruler and ruled. To Ms. Kagenui, Ononoki was property, a weapon to be used in the fight against aberrations, as well as a means of transportation.

If there's anything else I can add to that, it's that the corpse doll that provided the prototype for the tsukumogami Ononoki was apparently a sort of work of art, created in tandem by the Occult Research Club represented by Kagenui, Oshino, Kaiki, and Tadatsuru Teori, back in their college days—a work of art which Ms. Kagenui then took charge of, bringing us up to the present.

That much I know.

On the other hand, I only know that much—I have literally no idea why Ms. Kagenui and Ononoki have been acting in concert since then, after that point, up till now.

I mean, doesn't it seem like kind of a contradiction? Ms. Kagenui, who specializes in immortal aberrations and considers them contrary to the natural order of things, carries on the fight against them night and day, or maybe every night would be a better way of putting it—for her to employ none other than an immortal aberration as her vehicle, as her good right hand, a being with no lifeforce, who wouldn't even die if you smashed her into smithereens?

Isn't that—just as much of a contradiction as me living life alongside the very vampire I sealed away because I couldn't let her exist?

Isn't that exactly the same thing, exactly the same contradiction?

At some point I heard something about how Ms. Kagenui uses Ononoki as her stand-in to avoid getting too involved in the world of darkness—but using darkness as a buffer against darkness, yup, that's a contradiction.

I've tried to wrap my mind around it, but I've never come to any real conclusions—which is why I wanted to ask Ms. Kagenui directly.

Whatever the answer might be.

I had a feeling it might prove instructive down the line for me and Shinobu's relationship—because her host body inching ever closer to vampiredom was, naturally enough, also having an effect on Shinobu herself.

There was honestly no way of knowing for sure at this juncture whether that influence was positive or negative—but I wanted to hear what Ms. Kagenui had to say, to ensure I could make it a positive one.

An expert living alongside an aberration.

Maybe that was just my idealized image of her—though I assure you, it's not that I harbor some dreamy dream of becoming a half-human/half-fey expert, not at all.

"Me and Yotsugi?"

Asking about their relationship may have been kind of intrusive, but Ms. Kagenui didn't seem particularly put out, only surprised—if she was put out, she might put me out of my misery, so upon reflection I had risked my life by asking that question.

And her surprise seemed to be surprise that I was asking her after all this time—like, *We haven't already talked about that?* or *You haven't heard about it from someone else?*

"As you well know, we're master and s—onmyoji and shikigami."

"Were you about to say slave?"

"I was about to say serenade…"

"Master and Serenade?" Sounded like the title of a crappy musical maid anime. "No, I mean, of course I know you're onmyoji and shikigami…but look, Ononoki calls you 'Big Sis,' right?"

"That she does."

"So I just kind of wondered if you guys had a sisterly relationship."

"Well, when it comes to it, I reckon she calls most people big brother or big sister."

She calls Oshino "Big Brother Oshino," and she calls Kaiki "Big Brother Kaiki."

"'Course, she does call Ms. Gaen 'Ms. Gaen,' but she's an exception."

"I see—but."

Calling Kaiki "big brother"?

Bold…

"She calls you plain old 'Big Sis,' though. And me, she just calls 'kind monster sir,' or 'monstieur' for short."

I cannot *believe* that nickname has stuck.

"But you're the only one who's just 'Big Sis.'"

"Hmm."

Finally getting the point of my more or less pointless question—Ms. Kagenui lapsed into a pregnant silence. Or, I thought she lapsed into silence. I thought so, and in fact she did, but she did something else at the same time—she leapt from atop the stone lantern.

So suddenly that for a second I saw an afterimage, her motion faster than the human eye could follow—I say she leapt, but from my perspective it was more like she just vanished.

Which stands to reason.

Since the place she leapt to was the top of my head—she was squatting just like she'd been squatting on the stone lantern, but now on the crown of my head.

"Um, Ms. Kagenui?"

It had really bummed Shinobu out that time Ms. Kagenui had landed on her head, and now I understood: having someone sitting on your head really does carry a piquant feeling of defeat, distinct from simple humiliation...

And thus was Araragi awakened to a new fetish.

Then again, she was nullifying her weight as she had on that previous occasion, so it's not like she was a burden or anything...but isn't manipulating your weight usually a skill for aberrations, like Shinobu?

Ononoki just explained away this habit of Ms. Kagenui's with one word: "special"...

"An impressive reading—or intuition, maybe? I expect you must be acing the multiple-choice sections of your practice exams."

"Nice of you to say so, but it's just the opposite."

"Hmm. Well, I reckon getting them all wrong is just as amazing, statistically speaking."

"I don't need that kind of amazingness in my life."

"So, what do you think?"

"What do I think? Right, well, I'm really hoping your backstory is that the doll you and Oshino and Kaiki and Tadatsuru Teori used as the prototype, the model, for making Ononoki was fashioned out of the corpse of your actual little sister."

"I'll thank you kindly not to foist such a heavy past on a body."

She ground her heel into my head.

It hurt.

True, while pain is pain, I have to say I got off lightly given how horrible my hope, I mean my conjecture, had been.

"Well, you guys don't look like sisters anyway—though Ononoki has no facial expression, so it's kind of hard to tell. Since expressions are even more important than faces in determining whether people look alike—"

"Ha. If that's your deduction, you haven't a lick of intuition after all.

At this rate I'll warrant it's a sure thing you fail your entrance exam."

"I mean, Ononoki's origins and what not definitely won't be on the exam."

"Hm. Well, it's nothing what needs hiding, I might as well tell you, but—" Atop my head, Ms. Kagenui looked to be giving it some thought—she was on top of my head, so I couldn't actually see what she was doing. "—I dunno. Being asked all formal-like, it makes a body feel snooty. Not sure I want to tell you now."

"..."

Whaaat.

Since Ms. Kagenui was such a straight shooter, I'd been under the assumption (in addition to being under her) that she wouldn't try to extort money from me every time I asked a question, but I seemed to have accidentally brought out her contrary side.

Makes sense...

No way someone in the same cohort as Oshino and Kaiki would be a straight shooter through and through—not wanting to answer formal questions is an easy-to-understand disposition in its own way, though not an easy one to get along with.

If only I'd asked more casually.

If only I'd woven it in there with the rest of my barrage of questions—especially since she was all too happy to acquiesce to my request for a sparring match without even a guess as to the reason.

"So, you won't tell me?"

"I never said that. Nor do I have any intention of squeezing you for work or money in return, so don't you worry your pretty little head. By the by—how's about the rest of our battle?"

"Huh?"

The rest of our battle?

Don't be ridiculous.

Wasn't our battle already...

"What, are you saying that if I beat you, you'll tell me the truth about Ononoki? Because hold on a second there, that's crazy, by which I mean, batshit bonkers…"

I'd sooner pay Oshino five million yen, or let Kaiki fleece me for every last red cent—based on my experience over the summer, and my experience of this duel, I was dead sure that I could never beat her in a billion years.

A billion years.

Even a vampire can't live that long.

If I'm being honest, I did have a pretty strong interest in my house-mate Ononoki's origins, but I didn't want to know badly enough to throw my life away when it'd just been spared.

"Hold your horses, I wasn't fixing to suggest any such thing. I'd not demand that you do something no one else has ever accomplished."

"…"

Wait.

Was she lifetime undefeated?

When Shinobu and I challenged her, did she just let us off the hook?

What a precarious path I've been treading…

"Once is enough," said the lifetime-undefeated expert.

Still atop my head.

"If you go toe to toe with me—and hit me even once, I'll give you the skinny on Ononoki."

004

"And that's why it's your turn, Karen!"

"Um…what's why what's what?"

I thought I could win her over with enthusiasm, but apparently the magic formula "and that's why" doesn't work on Karen—after I got home.

I called her to my room and immediately got right to the heart of the matter. My other little sister Tsukihi was, at present, playing with Ononoki in the next room.

Ononoki was nothing more than a doll as far as Tsukihi was concerned, so the playing "with" takes on something of a different meaning, but either way, considering their relationship and how fate had brought them together, it was a pretty unsettling combination for a playdate.

I could've just asked Ononoki herself before bringing the matter to Karen, but it felt kind of against the rules to ask the chattel something that her owner wouldn't tell me.

This seemed like it might be a good time to apply my principle of not acting on impulse—in other words, questions should be asked of the people you should ask them of.

Though Ononoki (in her present character) was pretty uncooperative in her own way, so I didn't think she'd tell me even if I asked her...

Plus, someone whose "life began when Big Sis brought me back from the dead" might not even have a handle on the truth.

"It doesn't matter, Karen. There's a reason why I can't tell you the whole story, but there's this person who's as strong as a demon, who I'm basically helpless against, and I just want to land a single punch. Isn't there some good way of doing that?"

"What do you take me for, bro..." Karen looked dubious—and when I say dubious, I mean annoyed. "I'm a martial artist who follows the way of the martial arts. Even if I did know some method for exercising violence, I'd never teach it to a novice like you. Not based on such a half-assed explanation, anyway."

"Don't be like that. From now on, I'll fondle your boobies whenever you want."

"Yeah? I see. Well, in that case, I'm ready to entertain the not...on your life! I don't ever want you to fondle my boobies!"

She flew into a rage.

Man is she short-tempered.

As her older brother, it's very embarrassing.

"No, think about it, Karen. Which would you prefer: having your big brother fondle your boobies whenever you want, or having him fondle them whenever you don't want?"

"Hm? Oh, definitely when I do want! No contest! You really are smart, big brother!"

"..."

You really are stupid, Karen.

As her older brother, it's very worrisome.

"It's settled, then. I have a policy of not taking on disciples, but I'll make an exception for you, big brother. You can be my brotégé. Wait, did I say that right? Now I'm all confused!"

"It's *protégé*, obviously. Though I'm not talking about becoming your disciple... If it were you, what would you do? If you wanted to land a single punch on an opponent who's clearly stronger than you—what would you do?"

"Can't be done!" she answered peppily.

Why so peppy.

"No, seriously," she insisted. "I say this without knowing all the details, but judging from your request, landing even a single punch against that opponent is going to be tough, right? Landing any at all through their guard, let alone a clean hit, right?"

"Uh huh. Like I said, I'm helpless."

"If there's such a big gap in ability, you shouldn't fight. The true martial artist runs away from an opponent like that."

"..."

Karen's words were totally reasonable.

And yet, I've witnessed her rush in blindly millions of times against opponents she had no hope of beating—and every time, it's been do-or-die trying to restrain her. I mean that literally, if I didn't do, someone was going to die.

Do as I say and not as I do, but man, she really was dispensing advice she'd never be able to take herself.

"Then there's always the question of what'll happen afterwards, even if you do somehow land a punch. Like, if you land a lucky hit against an opponent whose superiority is clearly clear and they get pissed off, then what? They'll probably retaliate and beat the shit out of you."

"Hmm...you're definitely not wrong."

Even supposing I managed to land a blow on Ms. Kagenui by some fluke, she's not the type to clap me on the shoulder and say, "Nicely done!" More likely she'd say, "What the fuck!" and tear my arm off at the shoulder.

I only have the most general sense of Ms. Kagenui as a person...but somehow felt like the risk was too great for the information I was after. Yeah, scheming to try and hit her when she might not even keep her promise...

The wiser course of action might be to forget about going along with

Ms. Kagenui's suggestion, which was only a game to her anyway, and just beg her, groveling and scraping with my hands pressed together, to "forget about all that and tell meee!"...

Hm.

"Karen. What would you do? If there were someone you wanted to hit no matter what."

"Someone like you, you mean?"

"No, someone bad, like the polar opposite of me. If you were facing someone like that, who you knew you had no hope against, how would you approach it? Does anything strike you?"

"I told you. Nothing strikes me, and nothing's going to strike them, either. If anything, well, I'd say you should take the long view. Start training, so you can beat them somewhere down the line."

"Training..."

I was a little short on patience to take the long view...

I didn't care enough about learning about Ononoki's past to train to become a fighter—okay, the whole reason I went to see Ms. Kagenui in the first place was that I wanted to learn to fight with my mortal body, so there was a certain overall consistency there, but...

"Once you land a hit the battle's begun, so you have to go into it intending to win," Karen said. "A lethal blow would be another story—but if you're good enough that you can kill someone with one punch, then the fighting part shouldn't be a problem in the first place."

"Hmm, when you think about it like that, ultimately the martial arts are a set of skills for becoming stronger than your opponent, a technique for becoming stronger than the strong, rather than a way for the weak to defeat the strong—"

"My sensei always says that as long as you still think of the martial arts as a technique, you'll never become strong. And, well, that's the unavoidable reality, because in the end the mindset we seek in martial arts is that with great power comes great responsibility. Which is why I cleave to justice."

"And when someone shows up who you can't cleave with that

justice?"

"There's no one who can't be. My justice is a waterjet cutter!"

"You're a slippery one, aren't you…"

I thought you guys were the *Fire* Sisters.

Though lately my little sisters have been acting independently most of the time.

They're going to be in high school soon… Terrifying.

Then it struck me. Even if I got Karen to reveal the innermost mysteries of karate to me, there was definitely the danger that when I showcased them for Ms. Kagenui, she'd just beat the living shit out of me instead of telling me about Ononoki. But that assumed the kind of power gap, the kind of disparity that existed between me and Ms. Kagenui.

Did I necessarily have to be the one to hit her, though? No, I could bring in a ringer.

What if I got this waterjet cutter here to stand in for me—I couldn't let Ms. Kagenui get anywhere near Tsukihi, but she and Karen had somehow passed like ships in the night that one time.

In which case, how about.

"Hey, Karen."

"What is it, brother."

"Feel like fighting on my behalf?"

"Nope."

Didn't even have to think about it for a second.

"How could I beat an opponent that my big brother couldn't even touch?"

" … "

Your confidence in your big brother is frighteningly misplaced.

"I mean, from everything you've told me, big brother, there's some person who's going to answer some question for you if you can hit them, right?"

"Mm-hm, exactly. You're really on the ball, aren't you, Karen."

"Don't you think this person was just letting you down easy?"

" … "

"Like, you asked an impertinent question, didn't you? So don't you think this person was just putting you off without ruffling any feathers? I guess you could call it the ol' bait-and-switch... All of a sudden you're entirely focused on hitting your opponent instead of thinking about whether or not your question is going to get answered, right?"

"Damn..."

I was at a loss for words.

Loss in a very visceral sense, like the loss of a relative—it was such a shock that I felt like I might never speak another word for the rest of my life.

A loss so mournful that it seemed like the scene where I got my speech back should be the moving climax of the story—there were two reasons for this shock.

Well, the two reasons were virtually identical, but two big reasons above and beyond the shock of having fallen for that kind of bait-and-switch.

First, there was the embarrassment of having this pointed out to me by my little sister Karen Araragi, who I had heretofore thought was made entirely of muscle, right down to her brain, or even her soul—the shock of shame, in other words. Then there was the shock of having that casual, almost considerate bait-and-switch, almost like a magician's sleight of hand, pulled on me by none other than Ms. Kagenui.

To think that Yozuru Kagenui, a walking tempest who always tries to solve everything with violence, would do something like that—at some point I had likened Shinobu to a hurricane, but Ms. Kagenui was a calamity with the potential to do even more damage. That's how dangerous she was, and yet.

"..."

Well.

Maybe it was precisely because she was that kind of person that Karen had been able to see through the stratagem—

"I see...so that's Ms. Kagenui's version of acting like an adult..."

Unlike Oshino and Kaiki.

By turning my indiscreet question into a game, she wrapped things up without making them awkward—no.

Maybe my question had been so "intrusive" that instead of leaping straight into solving the situation with violence, she'd had to opt for that kind of street-smart "adult behavior."

"But if that's true, what am I supposed to do about it?" I asked Karen.

Thoroughly dispirited by my own rashness, that is, by the fact that I'd once again acted on impulse, I equally thoroughly put myself in Karen's hands.

At this point I idolized my little sister Karen as my savior.

"How the hell should I know? Figure it out for yourself."

" … "

My savior was cold.

"But yeah, if someone showed me that kind of consideration, forced that kind of consideration on me, I'd do my best not to embarrass her. At the very least, I'd try not to let it come out that I'd consulted my exemplary little sister about it and figured out that the whole challenge idea was just a pretext."

"Not sure who this exemplary sister you're talking about is, but well, yeah. It'd be pretty uncouth to point that out."

Pretending not to consider someone's casual consideration. Sounds like something Kanbaru would do.

Maybe that was what I needed to do at this point—but then, could I?

"If I pretend not to have considered it, I'm still headed for a showdown… In other words, I'm challenging her to a pointless fight I know I have no hope of winning, and I'm gonna get the shit beaten out of me…"

"Too bad. Go get the shit beaten out of you."

"You don't have any interest in keeping your big brother safe?"

"The only thing I'm interested in is keeping my big brother honest."

"What if he honestly doesn't want to get the shit beaten out of him?"

And my honesty aside, if I tried to hide my intention to return the favor—by which I mean Ms. Kagenui's casual consideration, I really was

175

going to need some kind of pretext when I faced her.

I couldn't rush blindly into battle without preparing some possible means of success; she'd suspect that I'd come intending to throw the match. But she also wasn't the type of person to just let it go if I gave up and said, *I've decided to forget about our challenge.*

Even if she were, I didn't want to embarrass her.

"..."

What a mind-fuck.

Did I actually have to figure out a way to try to land a blow, not in order to win—but to lose convincingly?

I had to come up with a way to win, but mustn't win that way? Why was I stuck doing all this cloak-and-dagger maneuvering?

It was like getting a question wrong on purpose to keep the class average from going up too much… If this was the price of acting on impulse, it was too steep for me.

"Looks like a body's come to the end of the line, as she would say."

"Your body's come to the end of the line? Wow, you mastered the martial arts just like that, big brother?"

What a dumbass.

And this dumbass was the one who'd pointed out how insensitive I'd been.

005

The epilogue, or maybe, the punch line of this story.

So how did I fix this blunder, you ask—how did I put together an ersatz strategy for victory?

Well, it was nothing to be proud of.

It's not like there's all that much variation in my patterns of thought and behavior—I decided to retread the way I took on Ms. Kagenui over summer break.

Even if it's a little late at this point, I'll give a quick summary for those of you who don't know what I'm talking about: One day over the summer, in order to challenge Ms. Kagenui, I let the legendary vampire Shinobu Oshino, or what's left of her anyway, drink my blood...thereby mutually raising our vampiric levels and strengthening myself (and her).

The thing is.

However much I may have raised my skill as a vampire, I was shockingly helpless in the face of Ms. Kagenui, specialist in immortal aberrations—nevertheless, that had been the best option available to me.

The worst, but at the same time, the best.

So if there were no restrictions, letting Shinobu drink even more of my blood and powering myself up to face Ms. Kagenui would be my "ace in the hole," a "no-brainer," an obvious choice for how to defeat her at this game she cooked up—but this time I couldn't use that plan as such.

I could no longer turn myself into a vampire—and Ms. Kagenui knew it. So if I pretended that I had, then yeah, it would only make the beating I received that much worse.

And anyway, if I gave any sign of becoming more vampiricized than I already was, as an expert—as an expert who takes down immortal aberrations in the name of justice, Ms. Kagenui would obliterate me without fail.

The fact that she let me go over summer break was nothing short of a miracle—since she's fundamentally not one for sob stories.

Since she's a pro.

So vampiricization was off the table, even as a strategy for losing— but the possibility of having Shinobu exercise her power on my behalf, well, that idea was alive and well.

Her power to manifest matter, specifically.

One of Shinobu's fabulous abilities (fabilities, I like to call them) is that she can completely ignore the laws of conservation, of energy and mass, to construct at will, out of shadows and darkness, anything that she's able to imagine—and so, on this occasion I had her make me a pistol.

A handgun.

A firearm.

Woo-hoo!

I don't care how strong Ms. Kagenui is. With a gun, beating her will be a cinch!

Yeah right.

I wouldn't even be able to beat her with a bazooka—a silver bullet might kill her if she were a vampire, but no matter what kind of bullet I used, nothing was going to penetrate Ms. Kagenui's defenses, let alone kill her.

I went with the gun idea in spite of all this for purely rhetorical reasons—"hit," she had said.

If I hit her even once—it would do.

So it shouldn't matter if I hit her with my fist, or with a bullet!

Exactly the kind of rash impulse a complete idiot like myself would act on—and crucially, it was one hundred percent destined to fail.

It was extremely convincing as bad ideas go—once I pulled the trigger, the bullet wouldn't even graze Ms. Kagenui.

A moronic high schooler with a moronic little sister played a game and lost—end of story. As a spur-of-the-moment response to her casual consideration…no, as a blunder in response to a mishap, I'd say it deserved a passing grade.

Which is how I ended up going to Kita-Shirahebi Shrine the next day with a pistol in my hand (a pretty strange pistol, since Shinobu had just kind of thrown together the design, somewhere between an automatic and a revolver).

It was pretty dangerous putting a pistol in the hands of a foolhardy guy like me, even if I do say so myself, but we'll leave that aside. I still wanted to know about the relationship between Yozuru Kagenui and Yotsugi Ononoki, that hadn't changed…but probably best to put that off a little longer until some other things were tidied up.

My not very reliable intuition, however—informed me that Ms. Kagenui's habit of never setting foot on the ground might have something to do with Ononoki.

Just as I paid dearly for having Shinobu by my side—couldn't I maybe ask her about that, at least?

If I could just find out that one thing.

I could settle down a tiny bit and face my exams—that was my thinking, anyway.

But when I arrived at the grounds of Kita-Shirahebi Shrine, I discovered that my not very reliable intuition had failed me again—though not on the subject of Ms. Kagenui and Ononoki's relationship.

"What the…"

The grounds of that shrine without a god.

That empty, forsaken hangout for aberrations—where just the building, just the facilities had been renewed.

Was deserted—the strongest woman I'd ever met, the lifetime-undefeated expert Yozuru Kagenui, was gone.

Vanished, without a trace.

"What the?"

Impossible, she'd never leave without saying some kind of goodbye—never mind leaving Ononoki behind.

"What the…"

To be continued.

CHAPTER TWELVE
KOYOMI   DEAD

SUN	MON	TUE	WED	THU	FRI	SAT
				1	2	3
4	5	6	7	8	9	10
11	12	13	14	15	16	17
18	19	20	21	22	23	24
25	26	27	28	29	30	31

3
March

001

I don't know what Izuko Gaen thinks about roads—that is to say, I don't know anything about her. I don't know anything about that woman who goes around brazenly pronouncing, pompously declaring that she knows everything—I know that she's Mèmè Oshino, Deishu Kaiki, and Yozuru Kagenui's "senpai," and that she's Suruga Kanbaru's "aunt," but that's about it. If you can call that level of knowledge "knowing" someone, then I guess I know pretty much everyone.

Then again, all it takes to become friends with someone in modern society is knowing their screen name and cell number, so in that sense she and I are perfectly well acquainted. And above all, Izuko Gaen does refer to me as her "friend."

Even though she doesn't really know me very well.

Or does she?

Maybe she knows me—the same way she knows everything?

If so—well, that wouldn't be all that surprising.

It wouldn't be a surprise if I took up a tiny micro-percent of her vast array of knowledge—but that would mean that she has a handle on me, which isn't necessarily a good feeling.

Because unlike Tsubasa Hanekawa, when she has a handle on something it's more like she has command of it—and that right there is the difference between Hanekawa, who "only knows what she knows," and Izuko Gaen, who "knows everything."

An analogy to shogi should make things clear.

I may have a basic knowledge of how the individual pieces move, of how I can move them—but Hanekawa understands the sum of her forces as an "army." That's having a handle on things—the ability to connect and synthesize knowledge.

The ability to link pieces of knowledge with one another.

That's what it means to be an intellectual.

You could also call it the difference between trivia and knowledge—but Izuko Gaen doesn't just understand her own forces, she understands the enemy's as well—though her view isn't so unilateral as to see the other camp as an enemy at all. She sees the pieces lined up on both sides of the board as a single collective "army"—a unified "unit."

And that's what it means to have command of something.

To have it in the palm of your hand.

To hold its fate in your hands.

In one sense that means that she's the kind of all-around shogi player who can sit on either side of the table, who can go first or second, and it doesn't matter—but being seen as "one of them" by someone like that goes beyond "not necessarily a good feeling," it's full-on creepy. Because even if she calls you a "friend," that only means that you're a five-sided piece with the word "friend" on it.

Friends can be useful.

The path of friendship has a certain utility.

That's all.

Which is to say, nothing more than that.

Then again, I don't know how the "friend" piece moves—

002

"The solution is for you to die."

"Huh?"

"Sacrifice your rook to strike at the king—is not what I mean, though."

"Huh? Huh?"

"Don't worry, it'll only hurt for an instant," Ms. Gaen said as she swung her sword.

I felt like I'd seen that sword before.

No, not quite—not at all. I'd never seen that particular sword before in my life, but it resembled one with which I was familiar.

Resembled?

That's not right either.

That makes it sound like the one I know is the real thing—but the sword I'd seen in the past, that I'd known in the past, that I'd cut and been cut with, that was the replica.

While the katana she was presently swinging—was the real deal.

A katana—known as the Aberration Slayer.

The Aberration Slayer.

The original Aberration Slayer, supposed to have vanished long, long ago.

That katana.

That real-deal katana—slashed through me.

Through my fingers, my wrists, my elbows, my biceps, my shoulders, my ankles, my shins, my knees, my thighs, my hips, my waist, my belly, my chest, my collarbones, my neck, my throat, my jaw, my nose, my eyes, my brain, my scalp—it cut all of them.

Into slices.

In an instant.

I tried to scream—but my mouth, my throat, my lungs, had all been sliced into rings like the kind you use for a ring toss.

The instant part hadn't been a lie, but Ms. Gaen had told one, and a whopper at that—because that sword moves so fast.

So blazingly fast.

That I didn't feel any pain at all.

003

Backtracking.

Backtracking in time—and going back up that mountain track.

Early on the morning of the thirteenth of March, the day of the entrance exam for the school I hoped to attend, I climbed the steps to Kita-Shirahebi Shrine where it sat atop the crest of the mountain—as had been my habit for the past month or so.

Habit.

Though if you do something every single day, maybe it's more of a routine?

Well, since I was basically hiking, or maybe trail-running, every day, it was good for my health—but the reason I stuck to my routine so readily, without even thinking about it, even on the day that was going to decide the course of my future, might actually be that I'm a diligent guy.

Being diligent isn't necessarily a virtue, though, and in this case maybe I just didn't know when to quit and got dragged along by force of habit...

In this case maybe my habit was a bad one—more vice than virtue.

In fact, Tsubasa Hanekawa, whose level of diligence, whose diligence strength, is much stronger than mine, had told me that there was no point in searching Kita-Shirahebi Shrine anymore, that if I was going to search I should do it someplace else—and Ononoki never even seemed concerned about it in the first place, but for me, it was one more thing I couldn't quit... Against my better judgment, or maybe just indifferent to it, I kept on going to Kita-Shirahebi Shrine every day.

Visiting the precincts of that shrine where there was no longer any god.

And of course no middle school girl.

And—no expert.

"Well, not knowing when to give up the ghost seems pretty natural for a vampire—"

Being immortal and all.

Though in my case I wasn't immortal, I just didn't have a reflection—an utterly useless, and in fact pretty annoying, undead trait to possess.

Anyway, that was about the size of things.

Yozuru Kagenui had vanished from Kita-Shirahebi Shrine—suddenly, without so much as a fare-thee-well, and in the blink of an eye just about an entire month had passed.

Without incident.

Uneventfully.

Under the circumstances, it seemed correct to assume that, having finished her business in this town and lacking a fixed abode to begin with, Ms. Kagenui—like Oshino—simply drifted on. But that wasn't the case.

No way.

No, unlike Oshino, Ms. Kagenui hadn't done any of the things she was here to do—though I say that based only on my own limited knowledge and narrow view of the situation, so maybe she had after all. Maybe she'd finished whatever she came to do... Knowing her, maybe she'd taken down some great evil in the course of that single night before she disappeared, but even if she had.

Ms. Kagenui—the onmyoji Yozuru Kagenui.

Would never leave her familiar Yotsugi Ononoki behind.

"Wouldn't she, though? Big Sis is pretty all over the place when it comes to that kind of thing. One time she left me in the bottom of a ravine in the middle of nowhere and forgot all about me."

Well.

Ononoki herself might say so…and I'm truly stumped as to how she could forget her at the bottom of a ravine, but…

"Even so, even if Big Sis would leave me at the bottom of a ravine, I don't think she'd leave me at your house, Monsieur…"

I was a little upset that my house was being compared unfavorably with a place as dangerous as the bottom of a ravine, but anyway, Ononoki had her doubts too.

Though she really didn't seem concerned.

True—for me it goes without saying, but even Ononoki wasn't enough of a badass to be in any position to be concerned about Ms. Kagenui.

Ms. Kagenui was, in a certain sense, a more fearsome person than either Oshino or Kaiki—probably the only individual in the world who could solve anything and everything through violence.

Why would someone like me be concerned about her? Could I be? Didn't she just leave on a whim? After all, all she did was break her promise to meet me at the shrine.

…And then never come back.

I'd tried telling myself this a million times in the ensuing month, but I didn't know when to quit, didn't know when to give up, didn't know when to sist and decease—and I ended up visiting the shrine every day. Almost like I was making a hundred-day pilgrimage.

"Wait, sist and decease doesn't sound right, now that I think about it…"

Uh oh.

Today's the exam, and I'm losing my confidence—well, anyway,

Senjogahara got recruited so she's all set for college, and she said she'd escort me to the campus for the exam, so I'd better get back down the mountain in time to meet up with her.

The fact that she thinks I need an escort means she doesn't have much faith in me, but thus spake Senjogahara: "Look, you know the expression 'the wayward dog will meet the rod'? Well, the wayward Araragi always seems to meet an aberration."

Wiser words were never spoken.

That's my sweetheart, always keeping her eye on the ball—and keeping an eye on me.

"Your scores are already good enough to pass, and as long as you can avoid missing the exam itself, campus life is within your reach."

That's what she said.

I didn't know how much to believe the part about being good enough to pass, but if she was more worried about me failing to take the exam than about how I'd do on it—I must've been responsible for leading a pretty irresponsible life.

Well.

Going mountain climbing on the morning of my exam *was* pretty damn irresponsible—

"And after the exam, it's finally graduation time, huh? Can't wait to see how this turns out," I muttered to myself as I climbed the now thoroughly familiar and not particularly burdensome steps. Shinobu was there inside my shadow, of course, but apparently she was pretending to have gone to bed early, so there was no reply—since Shinobu and I were together 24/7, strictly speaking I guess I never said anything just "to myself," but well, if she wasn't listening, then close enough.

Can't wait to see how this turns out—by no means implied some kind of rosy outlook for my future. When you get right down to it, the implication was more one of despair, that it might be impossible for me to lead anything like a normal campus life in the first place.

A campus life or any other kind of normal lifestyle, given my close association with an aberration, and being somewhat of an aberration myself—me, oh my.

It's not like I was relying on her, but in that regard it was pretty discouraging when Ms. Kagenui disappeared—it had been a real support to have her there to talk to when I realized that I, myself, was an aberration.

The fact that that support had been completely removed.

Was perhaps another reason I was making this daily pilgrimage—maybe I was just pretending to be worried about Ms. Kagenui, like it was no big deal, and really I was just worried about my own precious self.

It's not like she'd done much of anything about the transmogrification of my body, nor was she going to…but her oddly bold, supremely self-confident attitude was a comfort to be around—as one would expect of a self-proclaimed champion of justice, she never wavered.

There was some overlap with Karen in that regard—no, it was more than that.

In being constrained never to set foot on the ground thanks to some curse I don't know anything about, yet managing to keep her cool and live her life, Ms. Kagenui might've become a kind of role model to me—so if that "cool" could possibly come under threat, it was no wonder I was scared.

"Though…it's hard to imagine who, or what, could threaten her in the first place…and even supposing there was such a thing, there's still the question of why. Could it have something to do with everything that's going on?"

…

Everything that's going on—it was uncertain at present how applicable that phrase really was. Some might argue that the present tense, "going on"—should be replaced with the past tense.

In the month since Ms. Kagenui disappeared, at least, nothing—not a single mysterious thing, has gone on in this town.

A month passed uneventfully, without incident—that's not just a turn of phrase, it's a plain fact.

No aberrations.

And no Darkness.

No urban legends.

No word on the street.

No secondhand gossip.

And obviously no school ghost stories—none of it.

Nor had there been anything Oshino would've been interested in collecting if he'd still been here—nothing mysterious, nothing weird, nothing out of the ordinary.

As if it was all over.

It was as if it was all over.

"I guess if there's anything at all I can point to, it'd have to be the lingering mystery of why Ms. Kagenui went missing—"

And.

As I got to the top of the steps and went to pass under the torii at the entrance to Kita-Shirahebi Shrine—I saw her.

Standing within the grounds of the shrine.

Smack in the middle of the ceremonial path—striking no particular stance, and with no air of awe or reverence, on that path meant for the gods alone.

In her baggy clothes.

With her hat down over her face—her identity and age impossible to determine at a glance.

"...Ms. Gaen."

A month without incident.

A daily pilgrimage turned routine.

Well, it seemed like my hundred-day pilgrimage hadn't turned out to be such a colossal waste of time after all.

Something was about to happen.

Something decisive—or no.

Maybe something was about to stop happening.

004

"'Sup, Koyomin—g'morning," said Ms. Gaen.

Ms. Izuko Gaen.

Just a normal greeting, nothing out of the ordinary—I get the sense she greets people like that no matter where or when she runs into them, whether she's walking down the street or at a shrine on top of a mountain.

It's doubtful anything qualifies as a special location or special circumstance for her—for all I know, maybe nothing in this world is special to her.

Since if you know everything—then everything's the same, it's all blasé.

"Been a while—when did we last see each other? Oh yeah, that time in September, right? Heheh, though I've heard a thing or two about what you've been up to since then."

"...Good morning."

I gave a quick bob of my head.

Well, we'd been through a thing or two ourselves—but basically, I owed her a lot. Just as I did her junior, Oshino.

No.

It wasn't just about returning a favor or something. Insofar as I'd been pretty damn ungrateful—betrayed her, even—I owed her an even larger debt than I did Oshino. Even if I wouldn't go so far as to call it guilt, I can't deny that I felt awkward, or sheepish, around her.

So to be confronted by her like this, without warning—nope, couldn't look her in the eye.

By contrast, Ms. Gaen didn't seem to harbor any ill will whatsoever and was grinning same as she had been the last time we met—though her grin never slips even as she uses, abandons, and bleeds dry the people around her, so that part didn't make me feel any better.

And considering what happened to Sengoku and Hachikuji—Nadeko Sengoku and Mayoi Hachikuji, it wouldn't have been a surprise if I were angry at her...but some part of me knew that that anger would've been misplaced.

Part of me, but.

"Seems like you went through some serious shit—physically, I mean, Koyomin."

"No...I mean, it wasn't that serious."

"Heheh. Guess you're right, I mean, considering everything you've done, the crazy crisis you've been through, maybe your current physical situation...your state of health, isn't something to be all that worried about. I guess if anyone's situation is serious—"

Ms. Gaen looked behind her.

The only thing behind her at the moment was the brand spanking new shrine building—though it was just an empty structure, with nothing doing in the object-of-worship department.

In which sense, it wasn't all that different from that shed thing I'd made in class way back when—though the carpenters who built the shrine might be pretty offended by the comparison.

"It's Yozuru."

" ..."

"Yozuru Kagenui—my dear junior. The very idea that someone would go after her—I mean, this is unexpected. Even for me."

"I didn't think that was possible?"

Go after her.

I couldn't let that flagrant phrase go without some kind of reaction—but hearing the word "unexpected" come out of Ms. Gaen's mouth was way more startling.

No, not startling.

It just seemed like a lie.

"I thought you knew everything."

"Come on now, you going to be sarcastic towards a friend you haven't seen in so long? Koyomin. Nobody actually knows everything. That's just rhetoric. A bit of a bluff, to be honest—"

"…"

I couldn't get a read on her true intentions.

I also couldn't figure out what Oshino was thinking most of the time—and Kaiki and Ms. Kagenui were both somewhat unfathomable to me, but she really took the cake, as befitted their senpai.

No…

She was kind of, different, somehow.

Ms. Gaen was unreadable in a different way from Oshino and the rest of them—hers was not the same type of unreadability at all.

Even if I can't put it clearly into words, the junior class all had something in common—Mèmè Oshino, Deishu Kaiki, Yozuru Kagenui.

I didn't know what they were thinking.

And so—I couldn't read them.

But…with Ms. Gaen, it wasn't just that I didn't know what she was thinking—I didn't want to know.

And so—I couldn't read her.

I wouldn't read her.

I didn't want to read her—though I'm not saying I "didn't want to read her" because her mind was full of abominable malice or something.

On that score, it's Kaiki's mind I'd much prefer not to read—it's simply that the inside of Ms. Gaen's head is too convoluted and strange, and if I tried to get a read on it my own brain would blow a gasket.

Which is why.

I didn't want to read Izuko Gaen's true intentions: as a means of self-protection, so to speak—in the same way that no one would choose to take a punch from a heavyweight boxer if they didn't have to.

But…this was maybe a situation in which I did have to.

Coming here like this.

Coming personally to see me—since if she came to see me, there was something she needed to see me about at the very least.

Whatever the case, Ms. Gaen was lying in wait for me, taking it for granted that I'd come to the shrine regardless of the fact that it was the day of my exam, almost as if we shared a Google calendar or something—I would've felt much more at ease if she'd said "there's nothing I don't know" as usual, rather than informing me at this late date that "there are some things I don't know."

In fact…it freaked me out.

Rather than knowing there was something afoot in our little backwater that even Ms. Gaen didn't have a grasp on—I would so much rather believe that *that* part was just rhetorical, just a mean little joke among friends…or plain old humility.

Please let me believe that.

"Don't look at me like that. That's no way to look at a friend, Koyomin—when I say unexpected, well, when you roll a die with 1's on five sides and it comes up 6, that's unexpected, isn't it. You know perfectly well that it's statistically possible for it to come up 6…but one thing I do know is that it's hard for statistically unlikely things to happen."

" … "

"I never would've expected there to be someone who would take action against Yozuru Kagenui, violence personified—which is exactly why I sent her here to cope with the abnormal situation occurring in your body."

"Someone who would take action against her—is a phrase that doesn't sit well with me, I have to say."

In response to this doubt that I nervously, and (in my own way) cautiously raised, Ms. Gaen cocked her head with a theatrical *hm?*

"What do you mean, Koyomin?"

"No, uh…I'm very grateful and everything that you sent Ms. Kagenui here on my behalf."

Yes.

Grateful to the point that I should've thanked her for it the second I saw her—though, with the Ms. Kagenui in question missing at present, maybe I should've apologized instead.

The blame for the fact that Ms. Gaen's junior was currently M.I.A.— could certainly be laid at my feet. At least, if it weren't for me, I doubt Ms. Kagenui would've ever come to this town again.

But right now, more than apologies or gratitude.

I had questions.

"Hahaha, gimme a break, Koyomin. They say a hedge between keeps friendship green, but come on, you and I can dispense with the formalities. So, what do you mean?" Ms. Gaen danced around my words and repeated her question, totally focused on the topic at hand. It felt more like protocol than the art of conversation, though.

"Someone who would take action against her—seems out of line with my impression of Ms. Kagenui. I was just thinking that in her case, it'd have to be more like someone who would take her out."

"A-ha. Sounds like you've got absolute faith in Kagenui's strength— seeing as you've actually fought her, maybe you're in a position to raise that doubt. You recklessly challenged her over the summer, so in that sense, there was already someone who took action against her."

"…"

"Come now, you can't have forgotten about that—but I don't have quite as much faith in Kagenui's strength as you seem to. Another thing I know is that there's always someone better—or rather, that there are no absolutes when it comes to strength. Even if it's statistically unlikely—

you know?"

Ms. Gaen beckoned to me.

Beckoned?

What's the deal, I wondered, but it seemed like she simply didn't want to have a conversation with the torii between us.

I girded my loins and passed under it.

Was there someone stronger and more violent than Ms. Kagenui, or was there a way to render her strength ineffective? Ms. Gaen's words took on a different implication in each case, but regardless...

"Are you saying you can't believe anyone would take action against Ms. Kagenui given the risk?"

Yes.

I had my doubts on that score.

What would it take for someone to face off with Ms. Kagenui? To face off with violence personified—in my case, my little sister's life had been on the line.

That probably fell under Ms. Gaen's "statistically unlikely" clause... But that was maybe just down to a simple lack of prudence on my part, and I might've opted for a different strategy if I'd known what Ms. Kagenui was capable of. Be that as it may—without Shinobu, I never would've plucked up the courage to take on the violent onmyoji.

And the price I had to pay for relying on Shinobu like that was the loss of my humanity—my physical, if not my mental, humanity, anyway.

...

Yeah. Maybe what I should be trying to work out wasn't the reason someone had taken action against Ms. Kagenui—but the price this supposed someone had paid for doing so.

Someone.

Ms. Gaen used that word, which gave such specificity to its referent, as if it was a given—under normal circumstances, maybe it would just be a figure of speech, or an unimportant, even misleading statement, but since it was Ms. Gaen who said it, I didn't think so.

In other words, any hope that Ms. Kagenui had quit her HQ at the shrine of her own volition was hereby completely—thoroughly eliminated.

Someone—a word you usually use to describe a human being, but which you could also use to describe an aberration—or even something else.

Just what exactly was Ms. Gaen referring to—when she said "someone"?

"Well, as an expert who lives as she does, fighting as she does—there's no question she has a way of incurring people's enmity. But she doesn't invoke justice on a whim, or as an affectation. People may bear grudges against her, but I don't think anyone does so without justification."

"…"

As someone with not one but two little sisters who invoke justice on a whim, and as an affectation, that really made my ears burn, or it gave me heartburn.

"In other words, you think that Ms. Kagenui herself wasn't the source of the trouble."

"It's not a question of what I think, Koyomin, that's just the fact of the matter—by the way, how's Yotsugi?"

"Huh?"

She changed the subject so suddenly that I was taken off guard—but since it was Ms. Gaen doing it, it must've been a necessary protocol, had to be.

I answered her fully aware that it was dangerous to go along with someone's protocol when you didn't know where it was heading—or were unable to, not wanting to read her true intention. Obviously Ms. Kagenui was Ononoki's primary guardian, but in light of Ononoki's origin, Ms. Gaen was also one of her guardians, broadly speaking—and guardians have the right to know how their charges are doing.

"She's…doing well. Since she's totally expressionless, I don't actually know how she's feeling about this particular matter…but that girl knows Ms. Kagenui better than anyone. And she doesn't seem to be concerned—at the moment."

Judging that there was no need to provide detailed information on her fiendish desire for ice cream and so forth, I summarized Ononoki's status report as such.

I mean, I imagine that's what Ms. Gaen wanted to know.

"Yotsugi knows Kagenui better than anyone? Haha...seems like *you* don't know much of anything, Koyomin."

"Huh?"

"Well, as long as you aren't weirdly pretending to know all about Yotsugi the aberration, then it's all good—"

And incidentally, since I know everything, naturally I know about Yotsugi too, Ms. Gaen said—she's surprisingly self-congratulatory. Though when it comes to Ononoki, she's pretty much right on the money when she says I don't know a damn thing.

We've been living under the same roof for almost a month, but I don't know much about that little tween other than the fact that she likes ice cream. And that information is all but useless.

"Then again, given how your own transformation into an aberration is progressing, it's not like you wouldn't understand someone else just because they were an aberration—though some vision of mutual comprehension based solely on the fact you're both aberrations would be a fantasy."

"Uh huh... Well, Ononoki and Shinobu definitely don't see eye to eye..."

By virtue of which things are currently pretty tense in the Araragi room at the Araragi residence—at first it was constant fighting but now it's more like a cold war, with Ononoki doing her thing during the day and Shinobu remaining nocturnal, keeping out of each other's way and living a life of non-communication.

Honestly it was stressful, and you can imagine how little progress I was making with my exam prep lately—it was down to the wire.

"Not to mention the fact that Yotsugi's peculiar even among aberrations—being artificial and all."

"Artificial..."

"I imagine she was even totally calm when she confronted Tadatsuru, right? I tested her once—I made her fight Kagenui."

Ms. Gaen just tossed off this mind-blower like it was nothing.

"I wondered if she possessed anything like human compassion, you know? At the time I didn't think it was so unlikely that she might, but she attacked her 'Big Sis' without a moment's hesitation."

"..."

"The match itself ended with Kagenui victorious, though. It was just like her not to order Yotsugi to stop, even though she could've—oh, but don't worry, Koyomin. I'm not telling you this all of a sudden because I think Yotsugi Ononoki is the cause, the culprit, behind Kagenui's disappearance or anything."

Such a suspicion had only barely crossed the back of my mind, but Ms. Gaen quickly brushed it away—the combination of nonchalance and a zero tolerance for wasted action reminded me of the kind of shogi problems they set in the newspaper.

"Since she wouldn't make a move like that unless she was ordered to—unless she was directed to."

"Sure—I guess you're right."

The fact that she purposely phrased it that way, that she said Ononoki wouldn't *make a move*, demonstrated that Ms. Gaen wasn't completely denying her individuality, her free will—but looking back on how Ononoki had seemed when she confronted, when she took on Tadatsuru... Ms. Gaen definitely seemed to be onto something.

Just as Ononoki has no expression.

She has no emotion—and so, of course, no compassion.

"Then again, that's exactly why—Kagenui was removed."

"Uh...removed?"

I was getting fed up with reacting like that to every word Ms. Gaen said—I may not be able to read her intentions, but I'd rather retain my composure and dignity while I was facing her.

Was that impossible without the gravitas of, say, a Hanekawa? Though it beggars the imagination to try and picture the two of them

201

having a conversation.

"What do you mean, removed?"

"Like I said, Kagenui's disappearance has nothing to do with Kagenui herself, Koyomin—she was essentially unconnected to the series of stories that unfolded in this town. She almost got involved on account of your little sister, but that was avoided thanks to your efforts."

More declined than avoided, really, glossed Ms. Gaen. "Which is precisely why I sent her in this time...but I guess the problem was more deep-seated than I expected."

"Even if it was more—more deep-seated than you expected, I'm sure you *knew* about it?"

"Don't take it out on me, Koyomin—it's not like I'm not broken up too, my adorable junior was your collateral damage."

"..."

"Kagenui may have been collateral damage, but it was Kaiki who got entangled in it—I really do wonder what happened to him. There's a mess of intel, and I know all of it—but the problem is that it's probably all false. He probably spread most of that himself, though—a wayward junior is a senpai's woe. As for Oshino—haha."

Ms. Gaen started to say something about him, but lightly laughed it off. As far as I was concerned, there was nothing to laugh about—whether she was talking about Oshino, which goes without saying, or Ms. Kagenui, naturally, but even Kaiki.

"Hm? No, no, Kaiki gets what he deserves, so don't let that bother you—though given your nature, Koyomin, I imagine that's impossible. But really, don't let it bother you. Nor Oshino—but as far as Kagenui is concerned, let me make something clear right now, for the sake of the future. For the sake of your future, Koyomin, and that of this town."

"My...future?"

"Mm-hm. For your sake, now and to come. Though when it comes to the town...that's not all on you. The reason Kagenui was removed," said Ms. Gaen, "was simply that she was in the way—not Yozuru Kagenui herself, but her familiar Yotsugi Ononoki. The very Yotsugi Ononoki—

who's been installed by your side, Koyomin. Point is, in order to render that shikigami, that tsukumogami, that little doll, powerless and ineffectual, her master was dealt with. Yotsugi Ononoki, a shikigami who does exactly as directed, who only follows orders. If her master, the person at the top of the chain of command, is gone, then that dashing-look tween is nothing to fear—"

Dealt with.

That blunt expression—panicked me.

Pained me.

005

"Ms. Gaen...what do you mean, dealt with?"

"Dealt with. Though I doubt Kagenui, for her part, would feel things had been dealt with satisfactorily—well, strictly speaking she wasn't here on business, so it wouldn't be fair to take her to task for that."

By "here," I assume she meant both Kita-Shirahebi Shrine, and, in a broader sense, the town as a whole.

Ms. Kagenui's "business"—her business as an expert, had been about eighty percent wrapped up the moment she gave her opinion on my physical abnormality. The subsequent stuff with Tadatsuru was just something she might as well look into since she was already here, and staying in our town even afterwards was simply irregular.

"Private business, you might say—personal interest, not professional. Though curiosity...is not something that motivates her, is it. Well, there's no question that the presence of Tadatsuru, motivated as he is by aesthetic rather than intellectual curiosity, made her a little sentimental... There's no way she stayed here because she was worried about Yotsugi being at your house, Koyomin...or at least I'd like to think not."

That's what you'd like to think, huh?

Don't try to tell me it's "unlikely but conceivable," Ms. Gaen.

"Sending Yotsugi to your place kept things unpredictable, Koyomin, not to mention that, as a purely artificial aberration, she could protect you—but apparently there was someone who wouldn't stand for that."

"Wouldn't stand for it…"

Someone.

"Yet, *they* still couldn't take action against Yotsugi herself—because she's a purely artificial aberration. And so they took action against her master. The reason there was someone who took action against her—the reason someone took action against her, was this."

Someone.

Someone who wouldn't stand for it—someone who took action against her.

Ms. Gaen kept repeating these phrases—almost like she was trying to implant some kind of suggestion in me.

"We can divide the subsequent story into roughly two possible paths: Yotsugi is rendered powerless as planned, and remains by your side as a meaningless bodyguard—or she surprises us by awakening to her humanity and tries to protect your bonkers-ass self of her own free will, Koyomin…losing sight of her proper role as an aberration in the process."

"…"

"I don't need to tell you what happens if she loses sight of her role as an aberration, right, Koyomin? Since you've seen the consequences of that with your own two eyes—"

In that case.

Yotsugi Ononoki will no longer be a purely artificial aberration—and she'll become vulnerable to any action taken against her, she'll no longer be anything to fear.

Ms. Gaen concluded her lecture—once she explained it that way, I finally got it, and Ms. Kagenui's sudden disappearance also started to make its own kind of sense… Not to mention.

That business with Tadatsuru.

That time, too, there'd been two possible outcomes: I further vam-piricize myself in order to rescue the "hostages," or Ononoki comes out swinging to forestall that eventuality—and in so doing displays her full aberrationhood to me.

And with that display.

She destroys the relationship that might've been between us, or that might've grown between us—in the event, it was this latter option that occurred, but that's, how can I put this, that's just about my psychology.

My frame of mind.

Ms. Kagenui averted that state of affairs by having Ononoki come live with me—and that's exactly why this past month passed without incident, one might say.

But speaking of *exactly why*.

That's exactly why Ms. Kagenui was removed—thus transforming Ononoki into nothing more than a doll—by this "someone" Ms. Gaen keeps talking about.

…But I don't get it.

It doesn't quite add up for me—why the hell would anyone go that far? It's almost like they were trying to keep me from doing something… or to make me do something?

Either way, I don't like it.

Feeling like an attack could come at any moment—like they've rigged it so I stand alone.

Starts to make me wonder if the vampirization of my body, my trans-formation into an aberration, hadn't been planned all along—at the very least, the idea doesn't seem entirely delusional.

Since if it weren't for everything with Sengoku—and this shrine, I wouldn't have relied so heavily on Shinobu—and what about her?

Where does Shinobu stand in all this?

She's more of a bodyguard to me than Ononoki ever—oh, I see. Since I can't rely on Shinobu anymore without exacerbating my physical transformation into an aberration…in a certain sense, she's been ren-dered just as powerless as Ononoki.

Since the fact that I can't power myself up.

Means that Shinobu can't power herself up either.

At this point she's the dregs of an aberration, in the truest sense, a shadow of her former self. Just a little blond girl—she can't be my ace in the hole, or even her own.

Neither an ace in the hole nor a sword in the sheath—

"Is Miss Shinobu…"

She seemed to have picked up on the fact that I was thinking about Shinobu—or rather, Ms. Gaen had probably guided my thoughts in that direction.

In fact, she'd been periodically glancing away from me and down at my shadow.

"Fast asleep at the moment, Koyomin?"

"Yeah…lately she's been a total night owl."

I didn't say, *Because of Ononoki.* If anything, Shinobu was avoiding Ononoki more than the other way around—

"She's usually asleep around this time."

"Heheh. Well, I guess that's her version of setting her mind to something—actually bringing her lifestyle closer to her essential nature as an aberration, just in case? Then again, seeing as how she's barely an aberration anymore, seems pretty pointless…and it's not like that's going to allow you to become human again, Koyomin."

Seems like our Miss Shinobu is a real optimist, or should I say hopeful, or…clinging to hope, maybe—said Ms. Gaen. The way she said it sounded somehow sympathetic, but at the same time sober, as if she was just relating a factual truth.

As if she was just relating that Shinobu's actions and whatever passed for Shinobu's feelings were nothing more than a worthless waste of time—though even if that were so, I was in no position to give her a hard time about it, having totally failed to notice Shinobu's uncharacteristic hyper-vigilance on my behalf.

"Not only that—it's liable to get you into an even worse predicament than you're already in, Koyomin."

"Huh? An even worse predicament?"

"Heheh. Though it's not like the current Kissshot Acerolaorion Heartunderblade, being neither fully immortal nor fully a vampire, could guard you around the clock anyway—tough to prevent an assassination. To put it in shogi terms, that's as crazy as trying to achieve victory without losing a single piece. Even the greatest shogi player of all time playing against a child who doesn't understand the rules couldn't win a game of shogi without losing a single piece. Even a proud, compassionate commander is forced to sacrifice pieces—that's what we're dealing with here, Koyomin."

"Like, trying to protect a pawn and losing your king—that kind of thing?"

"Not necessarily a pawn. They say the fool prizes his rook over his king—but whether it's a rook or a bishop, or even a gold or silver general, sometimes you've got to sacrifice them. The king is the only piece that can never be sacrificed."

"…"

"Shogi's an amazing game when you think about it—even if you lose every piece on the board other than the king, you can still win as long as your king is alive. That's quite a balance for a game, don't you think? It's a good design. Or a good reflection of reality, maybe—now then, Koyomin. Do you think you're the king?"

Caught off guard by the question, I didn't have a chance to think at all before responding reflexively, "Oh, no—not a chance." Maybe I should've given a more considered answer, but I'm not nearly cheery enough to be able to call myself the king. Even if the vampire is the king of aberrations. "The king? That's absurd."

"That's what I thought, you're such a humble guy. And at the moment, there's no king in this town—you're not the king, and neither is Kissshot Acerolaorion Heartunderblade. And Nadeko Sengoku—"

Just as she'd done before.

Ms. Gaen turned and looked at the shrine building behind her.

"—is gone."

"…"

"Right now this town's throne is empty—which is causing certain inconveniences. In other words, it's like playing shogi without a king. Haha, I've heard of playing with a handicap of a rook and a bishop, but playing shogi with your king as a handicap is a rare bird. How would you even determine the winner?"

"In that case—no one would win, and no one would lose. Since there wouldn't be any parameters for determining victory or defeat—"

"Exactly, a situation where no one wins and no one loses. That's what you'd call anarchy… It's not like the king has to be the strongest piece, it just has to be there. As long it's there, the land is under control—even if that land is a battlefield."

"Comparing the town to a game of shogi isn't really enlightening me any. Let alone calling it a battlefield," I told her how I honestly felt.

Expressing how I honestly felt was apt to—no, I'm not sure that was how I honestly felt.

Maybe I just didn't want to be sure.

Vacancy.

I'm pretty sure it was—Kaiki who said something about the vacuum that precedes the chaos.

"Though that reminds me, Ms. Kagenui was talking about shogi as well…about how she and Kaiki and Oshino used to compose shogi problems for each other or something."

"Haha. Shogi problems are tough without a king as well."

"But with those, all you need is one king, right? It's okay if the other throne is empty—"

"There are dual-monarch shogi problems too, but that's neither here nor there."

Perhaps instinctively sensing danger, I'd tried to nudge the conversation away from the topic at hand—but Ms. Gaen brooked no such digressions.

"The shogi metaphor was just me being pretentious. I wasn't really trying to make it easier for you to understand," she said.

210

"…"

"And comparing the king to a god is, well, pretty customary—there's no god piece in shogi, after all. Now, if you'll allow me to continue with what I was saying, Oshino tried to spiritually stabilize this town without filling that vacancy—but I tried to put someone on the throne, even if it was just for show. I entrusted you with that task, Koyomin, and you failed. That's more or less how things went, right?"

"Well…I guess if you want a simple summary, that's about the size of it. But all the stuff that's been happening around me hasn't been quite so simple—"

"Not simple, no, but not complicated, either. Or maybe I should say, it didn't *end up complicated*. I thought putting Yotsugi by your side would make a good diversion if it went well—but it doesn't seem to have gone all that well. Kagenui's AWOL—Kaiki's in hiding—and no one knows where Oshino is. We're up against the wall, and the situation is untenable. So I had no choice but to act personally."

"By act, what do you…"

Ms. Gaen was not one to act unless it was absolutely necessary.

It was the same when she came to our town before.

The fact that she'd been waiting there for me—meant there was some reason she absolutely had to do so. There was no chance in hell she'd come just to give me a nice, thorough explanation of my town's current state of affairs.

Sure, I might be the kind of completely clueless guy someone would want to give a nice, thorough explanation to—but this particular person would never come all the way here just to do that.

"Casualties are mounting, Koyomin, and I want to put a lid on the situation. So maybe instead of act, I should say I had no choice but to put a stop to it. To stop you, in particular, from acting."

"Me? No, I mean…I have no intention of acting. And isn't that why Ms. Kagenui dispatched Ononoki to my place? As a bodyguard-slash… watchdog, or…"

"Yup. So even you managed to figure out that much, huh? But

Yotsugi can no longer carry out that task, Koyomin. Now that the chain of command has fallen apart, you know? If Yotsugi can no longer protect you—then she can't stop you, either. She's literally a puppet."

Uh oh, doesn't the character for puppet have the character for demon in it too?—Ms. Gaen said.

"So *you can act*. You can act, now—and there's no one to stop you. And unfortunately—when you act, *they act*."

"They?"

"You don't need to worry about who they are. 'Someone,' that's all." Ms. Gaen's words put the kibosh on my train of thought. Then she continued, "The problem is—that it's dangerous for you to act. Or rather, they're waiting for you to act—it's the kind of standoff where the first one to move loses. A dilemma of sorts."

"A dilemma…between what and what?"

"The solution is clear, though it will cause me a smidgen of heartache."

Solution?

Solution, to what?

Sure, all kinds of things had been going on around me—but ultimately, all that stuff got resolved.

Everyone who resolved those things was missing, and that was the problem, but—what action could I take?

"You worried about what it's the solution to? Well, that's got nothing to do with you anymore—"

Ms. Gaen moved.

One step, towards me.

She moved, came towards me—it must have been necessary, of course—but I didn't know why.

I still couldn't read her true intentions.

Right up to the end.

"It's the solution to the problem of the Darkness that's been coiled around this town for so long now—and the solution is for you to die."

"Huh?"

212

"Sacrifice your rook to strike at the king—is not what I mean, though."

"Huh? Huh?"

"Don't worry, it'll only hurt for an instant," Ms. Gaen said as she swung her sword.

I felt like I'd seen that sword before.

No, not quite—not at all. I'd never seen that particular sword before in my life, but it resembled one with which I was familiar.

Resembled?

That's not right either.

That makes it sound like the one I know is the real thing—the sword I'd seen in the past, that'd I'd known in the past, that I'd cut and been cut with, was the replica.

While the katana she was presently swinging—was the real deal.

A katana—known as the Aberration Slayer.

The Aberration Slayer.

The original Aberration Slayer, supposed to have vanished long, long ago.

That katana.

That real-deal katana—slashed through me.

Through my fingers, my wrists, my elbows, my biceps, my shoulders, my ankles, my shins, my knees, my thighs, my hips, my waist, my belly, my chest, my collarbones, my neck, my throat, my jaw, my nose, my eyes, my brain, my scalp—it cut all of them.

Into slices.

In an instant.

I tried to scream—but my mouth, my throat, my lungs, had all been sliced into rings like the kind you use for a ring toss.

The instant part hadn't been a lie, but Ms. Gaen had told one, and a whopper at that—because that sword moves so fast.

So blazingly fast.

That I didn't feel any pain at all.

"…"

The sword was just suddenly in her hand.

Why does she have the Aberration Slayer?

Without finding out—I was pulverized, and spread about the grounds of the shrine. *Hey, that reminds me, didn't Sengoku do this to a snake at some point—cut it into slices?*

With that recollection.

I, my various component parts, went flying every which way across the grounds.

"It's a shame it had to come to this. I really do feel that way. But I want you to understand that I waited until the last possible moment—I waited until the day of your exam. Once the exam was over, your constraints would've been lifted, and I couldn't be sure how you would act once you were liberated."

I felt like I could hear her voice, but that must've been a delusion—how could I hear it, when my auditory organs and the brain that received their signals had been slashed to ribbons?

"No need to worry that Kissshot Acerolaorion Heartunderblade will be restored after your death—maybe that just sounds like empty consolation, but I'll say it anyway. She's already seen that 'future'—that 'world' once before. So that action—that road is blocked. I don't think she could go on that kind of rampage even if she wanted to. There's no path for her to run amok, so even if she did—it'd be suicide."

A suicidal vampire.

Not sure what kind of existence that was for an aberration—at this point I'm not sure if it was appropriate or not—but even if it wasn't, maybe it didn't matter when you were dying anyway? Though it wasn't clear to me whether or not dying and getting swallowed up by the Darkness were the same thing.

"And this I can guarantee is not just empty consolation: I will personally take responsibility for minimizing the shock to your family and lover and friends when I tell them about your death."

Ah.

As long as Ms. Gaen takes responsibility—it's probably fine. Though that said—to devote the vast majority of my time to exam prep over the course of six whole months, and then see that come to nothing...that was a shame.

Just as Senjogahara had said, it wasn't the exam itself that was the real hurdle for a guy like me, it was getting myself to the exam in the first place—and in that, I hadn't made the grade.

So, like cherry blossoms, fell Koyomi Araragi.

006

The epilogue, or maybe, the punch line of this story.

Punch line?

I mean, isn't me getting sliced up and scattered across the ground in pieces already enough of a punch line?

"...Huh?"

I was alive.

I wasn't dead—the sun was directly overhead.

Which meant that six or so hours had passed, and it was already the middle of the day—instead of being sliced to ribbons, I was splayed out on my back beneath the rays of the noonday sun.

What the hell.

What's going on?

Ms. Gaen's gone.

Without a trace.

What's going on—didn't Ms. Gaen chop me into bits with the Aberration Slayer? Or did my vampiric immortality restore me from the brink of death? No, that's impossible, I didn't give Shinobu any of my blood to drink.

Ms. Gaen had aimed for a time when Shinobu would be asleep so as to prevent even an outside chance of that happening—but even if it had, if my body was possessed of enough immortality to restore itself after being chopped into such tiny pieces, I couldn't survive being out under the sun's rays like that.

It was almost as if—there was an *Aberration Savior* to go along with the Aberration Slayer.

What's happening here?

What the hell is happening—no.

What—*did Ms. Gaen do?*

"Ah, you awake?" A shadow fell over me as I lay there with my arms and legs splayed out, still totally confused. "Or did I wake up the sleeping child—Mister Rock-a-bye-baby?"

"Don't talk about me like I'm some kind of lullaby, my name is—Araragi," I spat out reflexively.

At the girl standing over me—a girl with pigtails and a giant backpack.

But the last bit caught in my throat.

Not that I'd forgotten my own name, of course—

"So it is. Sorry, slip of the tongue."

She grinned as she said this—showing me that sunny smile I had liked, had loved, so much.

That longed-for smile.

I had thought I would never see again—

"And, is the punch line that you failed the entrance exam because you didn't even make it to the test site, Mister Araragi?"

"Come on, it can't end with such a lame joke."

Afterword

The concept of "foreshadowing" is an important element in novels, and in particular mystery novels; to give a crude explanation, it's basically employed to make the reader think, "Oh, this is what that thing that time was all about!" But you know, it seems to me this sometimes happens in reality as well. *Thinking back on it, this is what was going on*; or, *looking back now, this is what that was*; or, *too late now, but this is what that was all about.* I imagine we've all had experiences like that, of reflecting on the past and realizing something along those lines. Which, how can I put this, seems like it's probably accompanied by a certain amount of regret most of the time—like, *if only I'd noticed earlier, this never would've happened*? If foreshadowing ends up making us think, "I should've noticed then" or "If I were more observant, I would've realized what was going on," then it makes a certain kind of inevitable sense that it would be accompanied by regret, but I wonder, is every recollection that makes us feel something akin to regret a product of foreshadowing? It certainly doesn't seem like it. If you're wondering whether an event in a novel that "in retrospect seems like foreshadowing" actually was fore-shadowing, you can ask the author, and if the author is an honest person then he or she might even tell you. But in real life there's no way of knowing. Human beings are prone to drawing all kinds of connections even where there are none, so depending on one's interpretation, just about anything might be seen as "foreshadowing." Not to bring up the whole "friend of a friend" thing, but there's a theory that everyone in the world is connected by no more than six degrees of separation. This would seem to suggest that we live in a surprisingly small world, but is a "relationship" separated by six degrees really worthy of the name? Can you really say you're connected to that other person? Can "a friend of a friend of a friend of a friend of a friend of a friend" really constitute some kind of foreshadowing in the tale of your life?

None of this foreshadows anything, of course, *KOYOMIMONO-GATARI* being the second installment in the Monogatari Series Final Season. Originally, *OWARIMONOGATARI: End Tale* was going to be second, but this one inserted itself between *TSUKIMONOGATARI* and *OWARIMONOGATARI* because, after so many years and so many books, I'd started to feel like a disconnect had developed between the current story and the beginning of the series, way back in *BAKEMO-NOGATARI*. I thus conceived the authorial desire to look back over this year in the life of Koyomi Araragi and company and reaffirm the connection. And so this has been *Calendar Tale*, a work that took me one hundred percent by surprise: "Koyomi Stone," "Koyomi Flower," "Koyomi Sand," "Koyomi Water," "Koyomi Wind," "Koyomi Tree," "Koyomi Tea," "Koyomi Mountain," "Koyomi Torus," "Koyomi Seed," "Koyomi Nothing," and "Koyomi Dead."

Since this ended up turning into a short story collection, VOFAN has provided us with a lot of illustrations. I'm very grateful. The final season will continue with *End Tale* and *End Tale (Cont.)*, so please stick around. Though who knows, something else might crop up in between, but we'll cross that bridge when we come to it.

NISIOISIN

KOYOMIMONOGATARI

CALENDAR TALE

PART 01

NISIOISIN

VERTICAL.

KOYOMIMONOGATARI
Calendar Tale

Part 01

NISIOISIN

Art by VOFAN

Translated by Daniel Joseph

VERTICAL.

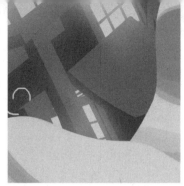

KOYOMIMONOGATARI, PART 01

First published in Japan in 2013 by Kodansha Ltd., Tokyo.
Publication rights for this English edition arranged
through Kodansha Ltd., Tokyo.

Published by Vertical, an imprint of Kodansha USA
Publishing, LLC, 2019

ISBN 978-1-947194-48-9

Manufactured in the
United States of America

First Edition

Second Printing

Kodansha USA
   Publishing, LLC
451 Park Avenue South
7th Floor
New York, NY 10016

www.readvertical.com

CHP ONE

KOYOMI
STONE

CHP TWO

KOYOMI
FLOWER

CHP THREE

KOYOMI
SAND

CHP FOUR

KOYOMI
WATER

CHP FIVE

KOYOMI
WIND

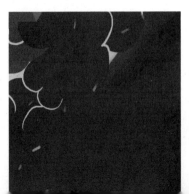

CHP SIX

KOYOMI
TREE

CHAPTER ONE
KOYOMI STONE

SUN	MON	TUE	WED	THU	FRI	SAT
						1
2	3	4	5	6	7	8
9	10	11	12	13	14	15
16	17	18	19	20	21	22
23	24	25	26	27	28	29
30						

4
April

001

You want to know how I was feeling about going to school back around the beginning of April, when I had just met Tsubasa Hanekawa, and we'd just been put in the same class? You want to know what I was feeling on the way to school, as I trod that path? Well, I wasn't feeling much of anything at all.

My feelings as I traveled that road.

Even the road itself, didn't seem concrete to me.

I couldn't find any concrete reason for going to school.

Get woken up by my little sisters, change into my school uniform, get on my bike, head to the out-of-my-league private prep school Naoetsu High—I'd been busy repeating that routine, that homework-like routine of busy work, for two years already, but I'd never once considered what that repetition meant, or didn't mean.

Or no, maybe I should say that I'd given up considering the question ages ago, because no matter how hard I thought about it, I was never going to find an answer.

But the same could be said of almost all the young men and women who have the honor of calling themselves high school students in this great nation of Japan, or I expect it could, so I wasn't actually the least bit special in that regard—the truth of the matter is that virtually all the young men and women who, despite having completed their compulsory education, continue to live the life of the high school student, who at least superficially "attend school of their own volition," can't even discern an abstract meaning in doing so, let alone a concrete one.

So it's perfectly understandable that the extremely small number of well-grounded students who do find a sense of fulfillment in their schooling would be left scratching their heads, dumbfounded by the fact that an outsider like me, who must seem to them like some kind of monstrous apparition, would still come to school every day.

Don't get me wrong, I'm not saying I'm dissatisfied.

When these sorts of thoughts pop into my head I do find it the tiniest bit disquieting, but no, I'm not dissatisfied—it's not like there's anything else I'd rather be doing, or even anything else I could be doing.

Me, I'm nothing—but precisely because I'm nothing.

The fact that I'm a high school student.

High school itself.

Provides me with the assurance that I'm me.

Especially, particularly, because over the spring break before the first term of my senior year—I went through hell.

I saw into the depths of a hell that could very well have made me forget I was a mere high school student, and put an end to my school career altogether.

It was a spring break that made me unpleasantly aware of the verity, the venerability, of banal aphorisms like *ordinary is happy* and *nothing beats an uneventful life*—and that assurance should've been a real life-saver for me. Nevertheless, as I rode along the road that April, I thought about how strange it was that I still blithely went to school as if bound by some hard-and-fast rule, as if it was normal—and that after class, I went home again the same way.

It's funny.

Having been through that kind of hell, you'd think I'd feel truly grateful for an ordinary life, that I would live each day as if it were my last—but the me that had returned from hell was still just regular old me. They say *danger past and god forgotten*, but I guess you forget hell, too, once it's past.

I asked Hanekawa about it once.

Asked her if the fact that I couldn't bring myself to feel grateful for the grace of everyday life meant that I was made of stone—and this is what she said.

What she told me, her face lit up by a wonderfully reassuring smile that, as always, made me wonder if she really did know everything.

"Of course you can't, Araragi. Because everyday life is something we take for granted. How can you take to heart something you take for granted? There's a road, and you walk down it, that's all. Take it from me."

002

"What? A rock?"

"Yup. A rock," she said.

"Do you mean...the kind you find by the side of the road? Or more like a precious stone?"

"Come on, I obviously don't mean a precious stone."

Sure, maybe it was obvious to her, but I had yet to learn what it was all about, so how was I supposed to know what was obvious and what wasn't?

The only thing that was obvious to me was that I had no idea what was going on.

But I wasn't about to let it stay that way—I have a low tolerance for confusion. I decided to try and piece together what was going on, piece by piece, step by step, from the beginning. Starting at the beginning is the basic principle of organization.

It was the eleventh of April, after school let out—no one else was in the classroom, and Hanekawa and I were having a meeting about the class get-together planned for the following week. The reason we were the ones holding it was that she was the class president, and I the vice president; you might expect the leader of each clique or their representatives to show their faces, but like clockwork, they all seemed to have found some other important business from which they simply couldn't tear themselves away.

Well, it may not have been an out-and-out lie that they had other things to do, but there was no question that the poor turnout was exacerbated by their faith in the fact that "everything will basically turn out fine if we just leave it all up to Hanekawa," which made her brilliance seem like something of a sin. And a grave sin at that.

Her brilliance, unhindered even by a burden as great as myself, unconsciously spoiled everyone around her—though I wasn't exactly upset about having a chance to be alone with Hanekawa.

Not that I had some kind of ulterior motive, it's just that since Naoetsu High is a prep school, pretty much all the third-years were studying for their college entrance exams; everyone was on edge. The mood was extremely volatile, like, *Is this any time to be throwing a party?* So it was a particularly uncomfortable atmosphere for a washout like myself.

In other words, it's less that I was happy to be alone with her and more that I was happy not to be around all those other anxious students—needless to say, since Hanekawa could've aced the entrance exam for any institution of higher learning anywhere in the world even if it were held the following day, she didn't share our classmates' bristling anxiety.

And also needless to say, given my total lack of inclination to prepare for exams, not to mention the fact that I wasn't even sure I was going to graduate, neither did I. So in that sense, you could say that the two people participating in that meeting were the two best candidates for the honor.

Given my general lack of enthusiasm for such things, though, if I'd had anything else important to do, I might very well have gone home too. Unfortunately, however, I was free. Terminally free. And sitting across from Hanekawa seemed slightly more likely to prolong my life than going home to fight with my sisters.

Anyway, during that meeting.

Or once it was basically wrapped up, really, while we were chatting about one thing and another, Hanekawa brought it up.

"A rock."

"…Okay, a rock. What about it?"

A rock.

Or was she saying "Iraq"?

Was she implying that I didn't know enough about international relations or something? We hadn't really been talking about anything that would flow naturally into a critique of my knowledge base. Our meeting had been perfectly genial up to that point.

"A rock, or…yeah," Hanekawa said.

It was rare, odd, for her to be so vague—or rather, it seemed as if she couldn't decide how to describe *it*.

She was unsure.

Not—unsure of her judgment.

We weren't yet at the stage to define *it*, or able to refer to *it*, so she just wasn't making a decision.

Which is why she vaguely said—a rock.

That was how it seemed to me, anyway.

"I guess if I had to call it something—then a stone statue."

"A stone statue?"

"Though it isn't really a statue."

"…"

"That's why I said *if I had to*—lemme think."

Heheh, giggled Hanekawa.

It was really cute, but in terms of a command, it was a laugh laughed to misdirect. I would've been perfectly willing to go along with her misdirection, but my interest in this "rock (or stone statue)" won out.

"C'mon, Hanekawa. What's the deal?"

"Oh, forget about it. I shouldn't ask other people about something I don't understand myself."

"Wise words. A little too wise."

That's exactly what you should ask other people about, that's the whole point.

Doesn't she know the saying *To ask is a moment's shame, not to ask, a*

13

lifetime's? Okay, I doubt I know any sayings Hanekawa doesn't.

"But, well, I was thinking—wasn't collecting this kind of story Mister Oshino's line of work?"

"This kind of story?"

"Urban legends. The word on the street. Secondhand gossip," Hanekawa said, counting on her fingers. "In which case, I thought he might also be interested in the Seven Wonders of the School."

"Seven Wonders? Huh?"

"No, no, there aren't really seven wonders, of course. But listen, isn't a school like a treasury of ghost stories? It was built over a cemetery, or it was hit with an air raid during the war, that kind of—"

"Wait, does Naoetsu High have that much history?"

"No, but…"

But what?

I mean, I don't know the pedigree of our school either—and upon reflection, it might be risky not to know the origins of your own school. Going every day to a place you don't really understand without really understanding your feelings about going there?

As if it were the most natural thing in the world?

That's—a little bit too little understanding.

"Phew, seems like the disgrace I bring to this school might be wonder number one…"

"Um, that doesn't sound cool at all," Hanekawa retorted.

And no, it didn't make me happy that she did.

Maybe she hadn't gotten the joke—but her serious bent didn't mean that she didn't have a sense of humor, in which case I guess it just wasn't funny. Forget about not being happy, it was kind of a shock.

Besides, would any guy on earth be happy to hear a girl say he wasn't cool?

"I wouldn't go so far as to call it disgrace, and anyway, putting it at number one seems weird."

Drop it already.

She was being more like a guidance counselor than a straight man.

Her position that everything in need of correction should be thoroughly corrected was, indeed, laudable, but I didn't particularly welcome being on the receiving end of it.

Didn't particularly welcome, or particularly unwelcomed, or just felt restless.

You might even say hopeless.

"The buildings themselves seem relatively new, so I don't think the school's been around since before the war or anything."

Was there a pamphlet or something that touted the year the school was founded? Seems like there would be, but if I ever saw one I don't remember... I would've just ignored a number like that anyway.

"There was another educational institution here before," Hanekawa enlightened me, "but it's been Naoetsu High School for eighteen years. It turns eighteen this year. About the same age as us."

"Wow, I would've expected it to be..."

Younger, I was going to say, but if it was the same age as me and Hanekawa, I guess it wasn't all that old.

But that's Hanekawa for you.

Unlike me, she had a firm handle on the history, the origins, of her school—I bet when she was in her last year of middle school and studying for the entrance exams, she looked into it because she wanted to know what kind of high school she'd be attending.

Then again, maybe she'd found out about it long before that, just a piece of common knowledge she'd picked up along the way—in either case, no one likes that kind of middle schooler.

"Hmm? What? Expected it to be..."

"Nothing. It's just such a half-assed number."

"Hahaha. Maybe. But you're right, I guess this school doesn't have quite enough history for there to be seven wonders—there don't seem to be any stories about students who died here or anything."

"Don't seem to be..."

That's.

Well, I wondered—something like a death. Not the kind of info you'd look for while you were studying for the entrance exam, let alone just a piece of common knowledge.

It wasn't anything you'd find out unless you really dug deep into the eighteen years of the school's history—

"In other words, how can I put this? Naoetsu High—doesn't have anything like a real ghost story."

"Hmm…yeah, I suppose I've never really heard one."

Then again, I was always decisively disconnected from the student circles in which such rumors circulated.

Partially because I was never interested in knowing any of the hot gossip about who was dating who, or who was getting into fights with who.

It wasn't my intention to be the standard bearer for some revolution against our information overload society, but it's true that I never wanted to play the town gossip or the town crier. That much is certainly true. I've wanted to live in isolation from anything that could be called news.

At the same time, I idolize Hanekawa for "knowing everything," so my attitude towards life is vaguely, you know, vague.

"Um, what were we talking about? Sorry, Hanekawa. My mind's been wandering a little too far, and I lost the thread…"

"Huh? C'mon, Araragi, I told you. It's this stone—"

"This stone that I have no clue about. Please, just start at the beginning."

"Aren't I?" asked Hanekawa, flabbergasted.

Well, sure, I bet she thought so—she thought she was explaining it clearly, from the beginning, and in fact it might've been perfectly clear to a good listener.

Unfortunately, I was the listener, and it was all Greek to me. You've got to adjust your conversation to the level of your interlocutor. As in crank it all the way down for me.

At the bare minimum, I wanted her to clarify whether we were talking about a stone or a ghost story.

"Mmm. Um, I guess it's…" Hanekawa responded in mild consternation in response to my demand, "a ghost story about a stone, yeah."

"?"

A ghost story about Estonia?

16

003

It wasn't a ghost story about Estonia. Or Iraq, for that matter.

If it were, then instead of being roundabout or giving me the run-around, she'd have gotten to the point right away.

A ghost story about a stone.

Yes.

But telling me it was a ghost story about a stone, being told that it was a ghost story about a stone, didn't advance the conversation—I remained, as ever, baffled.

However.

"Oh—"

After we had finished locking up the room and I had trailed Hanekawa out into the quad, however, we made some progress.

I say progress, but things only progressed in my own head—nothing actually moved.

The situation itself stood immobile, like a rock.

Since Hanekawa hadn't made her intentions clear to me, as I trailed after her I had to wonder if she was taking me to the garbage area on the other side of the quad, but our destination was in fact a flowerbed.

No.

A stone—in a flowerbed.

And that stone, too.

Stood immobile, like a rock.

"—I'm starting to get the picture. But…it's not really a 'rock' *or* a 'stone statue,' is it? I mean…"

I saw why her description had been so ambiguous—in the quad's flowerbed, maintained by god knows who, a flowerbed that mystified me, was the thing.

A rock.

A stone statue, if she had to call it something—but only because I'd pressed her, because she had to call it something, and it didn't resemble a "statue" at all.

It just sat there.

It was in and of itself nothing but a rock, but whether you had to or were pressed to, calling it a "stone statue" was not entirely without basis.

Because it was ensconced in a small shrine—ensconced it was, surrounded by dutiful offerings to boot.

"…"

No, "dutiful" might be a bit of an exaggeration. The arrangement of the offerings and the shrine's construction were both anything but—a better word might be haphazard, or even crude. It didn't seem like any sort of proper procedure had been followed, or rather, the whole thing seemed like some kid's art project, like the product of playing house.

"One kick is all it'd take to smash this shrine to pieces…"

"Where do you even get ideas like that, Araragi? Kicking a shrine…"

You'd be punished, Hanekawa warned.

Well, she was right—since spring break, my ideas were tinged with a touch more violence than before.

And, possible divine retribution aside, the shrine just looked to be some wooden boards held together with a few nails, so one kick probably would leave it in pieces, but the rock enshrined in it was another story.

A story where I'd probably break my foot.

It definitely wasn't big enough to be called a boulder, but nor was it small enough that you could just kick it out of the way.

I don't walk around with a tape measure in my pocket so I couldn't say precisely, but I'd estimate it was about the size of a rugby ball.

An uneven rugby ball—and a somewhat dirty one at that. Judging from its size, I gauged that it would be too heavy for Hanekawa, as a girl, to lift—but I didn't think that I, as a boy, could lift it either, so best not to rush into anything.

I didn't want to embarrass myself in front of Hanekawa.

A vain high school boy, that's me.

"Hanekawa. Is that the rock you were talking about?"

"Yup. That's it."

"Umm…"

With that confirmation, the conversation came to a grinding halt. But then, what was the appropriate question to ask to keep things going?

"…Were you the one who left these offerings here?"

"As if. I never bring sweets to school."

"Thought not…"

Our conversation had gotten derailed.

We seemed to be in sync but weren't.

But, well, whether she'd actually bring such things to school or not, the cheap sweets on the wooden altar, which was rustic, or obviously handmade like the shrine itself, hardly reflected her sensibilities.

I imagine she eats slightly classier snacks—and since she goes about life with a drive that must burn through a lot of blood sugar, I doubt she dislikes sweets altogether.

"At first, actually—well, you know how Mister Oshino really looked out for us over spring break? I was wondering if there was some way to repay him—"

"Repay him…"

Wait.

It was just me, not "us" that Oshino looked out for over spring break, plus he demanded a fee (five million yen total). It didn't add up for her to worry about "some way to repay him," but she was a girl who didn't add up when it came to stuff like that.

When you get right down to it, I ought to be thinking about repaying Hanekawa herself—and I definitely had been, which is why I'd agreed to take on the ill-fitting mantle of class vice president...and meekly followed her to the quad at this particular moment. That said, was there anything someone like me could do that could benefit her in the first place?

The thought left me feeling hollow.

Unaware, however, that I was thinking such thoughts—or well aware of it, for all I know—Hanekawa continued her explanation.

"—And Mister Oshino collects tales of aberrations, right? That's his real occupation or...his job, right?"

"His job? Does that guy even work? Now that you mention it, I do remember him saying something about collecting tales of aberrations, but...wouldn't that be more of a hobby?"

I doubted he had a goal in mind like putting together a book of them or giving a presentation at an academic conference. The guy just lived one day to the next, he didn't even have a permanent address...

"Collecting tales of aberrations can't possibly be lucrative. He's not exactly stimulating the economy."

"Working isn't about money, Araragi."

"..."

Heavy stuff.

What kind of high schooler was she? At the same time, maybe only a high schooler could go and say that. But this was Hanekawa, and I suspected she'd go on saying it even after joining the workforce.

"Getting back on topic. Hop! The point is, if there were anything like seven wonders, or a 'school ghost story' at Naoetsu High, we could tell Mister Oshino about it. As a thank you."

"Would it serve...as a thank you? I'm not trying to throw cold water on the thought itself...but the aberrations Oshino collects, aren't they more like the real deal? Vampires, for instance..."

"A 'school ghost story' can be the real deal. And in terms of name recognition, 'school ghost stories' are among the elite of the aberration world. There may not be all that many people who're familiar with the

Cackling Woman, but everyone knows Toilet Hanako, don't they?"

"Well, sure, if getting talked about is the barometer of aberration-hood, then name recognition would be important…" It's a cultural paradox, isn't it? Becoming too well-known can make something seem cheap or vulgar. It's a far cry from so-called sophistication, anyway. "It's by achieving widespread popular recognition that they become urban legends and secondhand gossip… Maybe it's just a matter of degree? Like, you know it when you see it…or there's no point in trading rumors once everyone knows about something?"

"But I don't think Mister Oshino cares about sophistication. Rumors are a kind of popular culture, after all."

"Hmmm. Maybe so, but I wonder. I know it's the thought that counts, but wouldn't Oshino just snort at a 'school ghost story'?"

"Mister Oshino isn't that kind of person."

"…"

To me he was precisely *that kind of person*, but apparently she felt differently.

"No, that's not what I mean. Listen, Hanekawa, what I'm trying to say is that I'm not sure Oshino is looking for something so well-known, with as much name recognition as a 'school ghost story'… If it's such common knowledge, maybe he already knows about it?"

"I wonder. He might, of course, but every school has its own variations on a 'school ghost story'—plus, once you're an adult, it's harder to waltz into a school. As far as tales of aberrations go, a school ghost story might be a difficult type for Mister Oshino to get his hands on."

"Difficult…"

Ah.

Sure—as a student I take going to school for granted, so it took me a minute to see what she meant. But yeah, a school might be a closed space, the hardest place there is to get into if you're a stranger, and moreover, an adult.

Particularly an adult like Oshino… Lacking anything resembling a steady job or a fixed abode, a guy like him might get nabbed the second he set foot on school grounds.

So if he wanted to take stock of any tales floating around the school, he'd have to interview the students individually, which would seem just as shady.

Since he wasn't with some TV show, even if he made a formal request he'd probably just get the door slammed in his face...

"I'm back on board. So you decided to investigate a 'school ghost story' with an eye to teaching him about it."

"That sounds so presumptuous—I would gift it to him. Maybe you're right, Araragi, maybe he wouldn't need it. Still, don't we want to do everything we can?"

"...No, I'm not that proactive about life."

Forget about doing everything you can, the guiding principle of my life is to do as little as possible.

Be that as it may, sighed Hanekawa. "It's like I said. I looked into it, but Naoetsu High doesn't have the history, and nothing like a ghost story has coalesced yet. 'Well, a swing and a miss,' I thought."

She sounded perfectly natural slipping the words "a swing and a miss" into conversation.

Tsubasa "Want to Do Everything We Can" Hanekawa must have swung and missed more times in her life than I could guess—but that hadn't broken her spirit, and she kept on "swinging and missing," as well as hitting the odd "home run," which I thought made her a real iconoclast.

Oshino had put it so well—what was it he'd said?

"But there was one thing that bothered me. Bothered me—or somehow, that I wanted to bother about."

"...You mean, this rock? Or stone statue, or whatever?" I asked, glancing at the thing again.

It still looked like an ordinary rock—and yet, with the little shrine over it and the offerings surrounding it, the stone did seem like it might be "graced" with wondrous spiritual power.

Like a stone statue carved into that particular shape.

Ah, and speaking of—wondrous spiritual power (I'm not at all knowledgeable about this stuff so maybe I'm speaking out of turn here), aren't there stories about stones that turn into protective amulets for their owners, "power stones" or something?

Though talking about "power stones" and "power spots" takes things in a bit of a different direction from tales of aberrations.

"Mm-hmm, yup. That's what I mean."

"So, while you were looking into all sorts of stuff, you came upon a mysterious rock way out in this quad's flowerbed—but you can't for the life of you figure out what's up with it, something like that?"

I tried to get everything I'd learned thus far straight in my mind. Organization isn't exactly my forte, but I don't do well with a chaotic mess, so I have a bad habit of wanting to sum everything up as simply as possible as soon as possible. Though I'm well aware that it's not the best way to arrive at the truth.

Hanekawa's ability to process information, on the other hand, was on a different order of magnitude—or was measured with entirely different units, so apparently she could cope with this level of chaos as if it were "perfectly well-ordered."

"That's not it," she unceremoniously, but gently, deflected my summary.

I had to wonder if her room was actually a total disaster. Well, not just hers, geniuses' rooms are always messy in the collective imagination.

A biased assumption, either way...

"In fact, I already knew this rock was here."

"You really do know everything."

"I don't know everything, I just know what I know. But," she added, "it didn't use to be like this."

"What didn't?"

"When I was a first-year—right after I started here, in other words? I did a general survey of the school."

"Why the hell would you..."

"Well, I wanted to see where I'd be spending the next three years of my life, I guess? Out of curiosity?"

"Curiosity..."

You're the curiosity here.

A model student's behavior was rife with mysteries. Her prodigious eccentricity went far beyond thoroughly researching Naoetsu High before taking its exam—which, admittedly, was just a figment of my imagination.

This was no time to be nattering on about such things, though.

"So two years ago, when you surveyed…or explored the school, this flowerbed didn't have any rock?"

"I never said that. Listen, okay? I'm saying it was here. I almost tripped over it, so I remember it clearly."

"Tripped? Seriously? You trip over things too?"

"What do you take me for, Araragi…"

Hanekawa looked fed up—no attempt to hide it.

The fact is that she hated being treated like a model student, or a superwoman.

"Yes, even I almost trip over things sometimes."

"I'm…surprised to hear that."

True, she'd tripped over a rock named Araragi and stumbled into something horrible over spring break, so maybe she wasn't so perfect after all.

Let us note, however, that she said *almost tripped*, meaning she didn't actually.

"But if it was here, what's the problem?"

"That's what I'm trying to tell you: it didn't use to be like this. The rock was here—but the shrine wasn't."

"?"

"Nor the offerings, nor the altar they're sitting on."

In other words, someone, continued Hanekawa.

"Someone, in the past two years, dolled up this rock like an icon—enshrining it."

"…"

004

That night.

I headed to a certain abandoned building.

The ruins of a cram school that had gone out of business a few years back—it had taken up the entire building so it must've been a sizable enough cram school, but unable to stand up to the furious onslaught of a major exam prep-chain that had moved in over by the station, it was forced to retreat, or to abscond under cover of darkness—you hear all kinds of stories, but who knows what really happened.

Well.

Hmmm.

In that sense, I was heading from a high school whose origins I didn't really have a handle on to an abandoned building whose origins I didn't really have a handle on. Even I'm a little shocked that I could tread such a vague path without any sense of danger whatsoever.

But, not being Tsubasa Hanekawa, I didn't want to know about any of it badly enough to do my homework.

"Hey, Araragi—I've been waiting for you."

Oshino.

Mèmè Oshino, Expert, greeted me with the same mock-innocent line as always—when I arrived at a certain classroom on the fourth floor.

There was a little blond girl in the corner, but I'll omit a description of her.

I informed Oshino of the situation.

I may have added a few dramatic flourishes.

"Hm. A stone, huh?" said Oshino—an older guy in a Hawaiian shirt. "Stones often become objects of worship, don't they—the power stones you mentioned are somewhat different, but you can lump them in."

"Huh…like precious stones taking on magical properties?"

"Maybe, though these days—in modern society, it tends to be their value and not their appearance that fascinates people—"

Oshino chuckled softly.

He always came off as totally flippant, which is honestly not a type I do well with.

But Mèmè Oshino wasn't just a flippant old fart—he was an old fart who had saved my life, my dignity, and my humanity.

Flippant though he most definitely was.

"You said it was about the size of a rugby ball, right, Araragi? So, which way was this rugby ball enshrined?"

"Which way?"

"Vertically? Horizontally? You said it was like a rugby ball, so I'm assuming it has a width and a height."

"Oh…"

A pretty detailed question, I thought, but on the flipside, I'd come in Hanekawa's stead to give a detailed explanation, so it was really an oversight on my part.

Maybe it would've been best if Hanekawa herself had come, but since it wasn't a crisis or an emergency, my conscience had prevailed against the idea of marching a youthful maiden around town in the middle of the night.

"It's kind of like a Jizo statue…and when you include the shrine, maybe it actually is patterned after one… Let's see. Was Jizo a Buddhist deity?"

"This Araragi kid really knows his stuff."

"You don't have to say it like that."

Not so naturally, anyway.

Though it was just a random fact I happened to have picked up, and the first and last I could muster on the subject.

I wasn't even sure what Jizo was the Buddhist deity *of*.

"Lemme see…the patron saint of travelers? No, wait, isn't there something about the Six Jizos? Hm, but Bamboo-Hat Jizo…"

The more I spoke, the more I seemed to be giving myself away.

"Ha hah. Well, in Japan, Jizo certainly has come to be conflated with the roadside gods that watch over travelers—though it'd be odd for it to be in a flowerbed."

For once, Oshino almost seemed to be giving me the benefit of the doubt and didn't make fun of me as I flailed helplessly.

"A stone statue," he continued. "Since you described it as a stone statue, I'm assuming it's got that sort of a shape? Meaning it's not just round, but carved into the shape of a person—"

"I dunno… Honestly, Hanekawa had already given me that impression, so I guess I sort of saw it that way… But if I'd just happened to see it as I passed by the flowerbed, without any preconceptions—I probably would've thought it was just some nondescript rock."

"A-ha."

"Or…" I shook my head at Oshino's smirking nod. "Maybe not—even if I hadn't been told about it, just passing by and seeing it ensconced in that wooden shrine, with that altar and everything, I might've thought it was carved like a statue—"

"The simulacrum phenomenon."

"Huh?"

"When people see something that resembles a face, they find a face in it—or a human form in a stain or dirt on the wall. As the old saying goes, the truth behind the ghost is withered grass."

"The truth behind the ghost—so I guess aberrations, and tales of aberrations, have something to do with this simu-whatever too?"

"No, that's a separate issue entirely. Not to mention, Araragi, even if the stone took the form of a statue, that doesn't mean someone carved it. It could've been naturally worn down by the elements until it ended up looking that way."

"The elements, huh."

"Would that be it? According to your story, two years ago your beloved friend saw the stone just lying around—has its shape changed at all?"

"She said it hasn't."

Ordinarily, even if you almost tripped over it, no ordinary person would remember a rock, or the shape of one, from two years ago, but in that regard Tsubasa Hanekawa is no ordinary person.

She'd told me that though the last couple of years had weathered the stone somewhat, it'd had that same rugby-ball shape.

In other words, even if someone had enshrined it during those two years, the main body—the stone itself, had remained unaltered.

"Hmm. And what's missy class president's take on it?"

"Her take, well—"

Oshino always calls Hanekawa "missy class president."

You'd think that since she hates being treated like a model student she wouldn't be thrilled about that nickname either, but for some reason, maybe because it's Oshino, she doesn't particularly seem to mind.

Incidentally, the one time I tried calling her "missy class president" as a joke, she really went ballistic on me. I wasn't sure I would ever recover.

"Hanekawa saw it when it wasn't enshrined, so at the time she seems to have thought it was just a rock. But now, she's researching our campus as a way to repay you, Oshino—and she noticed how something's happened to the rock she stumbled across two years ago. She found it really unsettling—or something."

"Unsettling," Oshino repeated the word back to me. "Sure, it must be unsettling when what used to be just a rock is sitting in some shrine—though I can't begin to guess, ha hah, if missy class president actually finds anything unsettling."

"This is no laughing matter."

Maybe the way Hanekawa talked about it made it seem that way, but—I dunno, some mysterious faith springing up on campus was thoroughly unsettling, and even if it weren't, we couldn't just let it go.

Even someone with as little school spirit as me felt that way.

"Well then, Araragi—seems like the first thing to do would be to investigate the origin of the sweets, but we're talking about missy class president here. Maybe she did that before she even talked to you?"

"..."

Acting like he saw through it all, that was Oshino.

For some reason it grated on me this was Hanekawa he was pretending to get; it was a strange feeling. *As if you know so much about someone you just met*—yet I myself had gotten to know her only a few days before him.

When you got right down to it, I didn't know a damn thing about her.

"Yeah," I said. "From the brand and time of purchase, calculated backward from the sell-by date, she nailed down which shops they could've been bought in and the students most likely to buy them—"

"A regular Sherlock Holmes. Did she make enquiries?"

"No, not yet, apparently."

"Maybe she felt like that would be rushing things?"

"No. She figured out that whoever left the offerings wasn't acting alone, an unspecified number of people seemingly left the sweets and whatever else at the shrine—in which case she needed to widen the scope of her investigation, and couldn't continue operating under the veil of secrecy."

"..."

"Which is why I'm here. You'd be interested in a story like this. She says it's her way of repaying you for looking out for us."

Judging that I'd more or less said what I needed to say, that was how I wrapped up my explanation.

Well, it was unclear if it was wrapped up, but in any case, it emphasized that I was there not to consult Oshino about a mysterious stone, but simply to do him the favor of delivering info about strange doings at our school.

If I didn't make that clear up front, my debts might balloon even further. True, since I already had no way of paying off the five million yen I currently owed him, maybe it didn't matter if I accrued more.

I've heard that once the amount you owe grows beyond a certain point, you start not to mind not being able to pay it off, or taking on even more debt, and not necessarily because you've gone to pieces. I felt like I was standing on the edge of that precipice—which meant I really couldn't afford to get any more bills.

Since I couldn't risk incurring one of Oshino's consultation fees, on this occasion I had no choice but to act slightly, or flagrantly, like I was doing him a favor.

"Ha hah," Oshino let out a forced laugh, as though my ulterior motive was obvious to him.

Hanekawa had mentioned the "Cackling Woman" to me, and I bet the monster had the same sort of laugh.

"Wh-What?" I put on a show of consternation. Or if he really had seen through my little ploy, it wasn't a show, and my consternation was genuine. "S-So something like a school ghost story holds no interest for an expert, huh? You prefer something a little more difficult, based on archival evidence or whatever?"

"No, no, missy class president was right on that score—even a jack-of-all-trades like myself has his strengths and weaknesses. It can be a hassle to get ahold of stories from inside a closed space like a school—I'm grateful for the offer."

"O-Of course."

"Nevertheless, Araragi. This is a favor from missy class president, not from you, so it by no means cancels your debt. I eagerly await your consideration in that regard."

"..."

Well.

At least I didn't incur any new debts. I guess that was all I could ask for.

I can't deny I'd had my hopes up, but this seemed like a good compromise.

30

"I'm not sure it qualifies as a tale of an aberration—ha hah, but it's a good story. Gotta be sure and write this one down."

"…Oshino. Just for my edification, I'd love to know what you ultimately plan to do with all these 'tales' you've been collecting."

"Hm?"

"Um, like, are you planning to put them in a book, or present them at a conference…or anything like that?"

There was no particular need for me to ask him about it right then, but I'd been wondering about it while I was talking with Hanekawa after school and I'd wanted to ask him if I had the chance.

At least to that extent, I was intrigued.

In other words, was this man, my savior so to speak, actually amassing aberrations as part of his occupation, or was he just insisting on calling his hobby "work" when he was actually unemployed…

"Ha hah. I'm not some sort of authority on aberrationology, so I don't have such lofty goals. I do sell the stories I collect to interested parties, though."

"Sell? And you get customers? They're just ghost stories."

"Says the guy who almost played the lead role in one?"

"Just curious, how much do you get for one?"

"Ha hah. I don't know about divulging my negotiated prices to a supplier."

"…"

If that was how he felt about it, what could I do but drop the subject, but charging me a fee for dealing with an aberration then turning around and selling the story to someone else did strike me as a pretty sweet business.

Is that what they call the middleman margin?

I'm sure it's not as sweet as it seems to a neophyte, of course…but either way, simply finding out that Oshino derived an income from his fieldwork was enough for me.

"But, do you really think someone'll buy this story?"

"Good question. I have one customer who'll take anything and everything—but lately *that one* seems to have started behaving erratically

31

again, and I get the feeling it'd be best to put a little distance between us. Not that I can go sell it to *him* instead..."

Oshino seemed to be thinking about how to monetize this, which seemed a little premature, like he was counting his chickens before they'd hatched.

A weird stone getting enshrined in a school flowerbed wasn't going to interest anyone—it quite literally wouldn't be worth the paper it was written on.

It'd take an expert to find an interesting way to spin it.

"So, what about it, Oshino?"

"Hnh? What about what?"

"That's not fair, I asked you first... As an expert, what do you think?"

Running through all the pertinent points, I tried again.

"What was seemingly just a hunk of rock two years ago has, two years later, become an object of worship for some part of the student body—for an unspecified number of people, it's become an aberration-y thing. Does that ever happen?"

"It's not uncommon for objects to become aberrations—after all, aberrations come into being according to some standard. And yet."

"Hm?"

"It's hard to say if it's worshipped because it's an aberration—or if it became an aberration because it was worshipped."

"Is it worshipped because it's an aberration, or is it an aberration because it's worshipped?"

I only intended to repeat Oshino's words back to him verbatim, but apparently I'd gotten something wrong.

"No, no," he corrected, "It's not 'is it an aberration because it's worshipped.' It's: 'Is it worshipped because it's an aberration, or did it become an aberration because it was worshipped.'"

"...? Sure, the wording and grammar might be a tiny bit different, but is it such an important difference that it's worth harping on?"

"In this case," said Oshino significantly. "But it's a little hard to know just from hearing the story. Think you can draw me a picture of it, Araragi?"

"Huh?"

"You heard me. If you came here straight from school, you must at least have a notebook and something to write with."

"I do, but..."

I'd never imagined I'd be asked to draw at that point. I was taken aback, but if that was what he wanted, I guess that was what he would get.

"To be honest, though, I'm not exactly artistically inclined. Even if I seem like I would be."

"They never taught you to draw in art class?"

"Naoetsu's a prep school, so they don't put a lot of emphasis on the arts. And I didn't take any art classes for my electives."

"Hmph... Well, just do your best."

"Roger."

I ran my mechanical pencil across the page of the notebook I'd taken out. I was relying on memory—if it was two years ago, I'd have to admit that I didn't remember, but it had only been a few hours. I might not be Hanekawa, but as a teenager and currently active high school student, my powers of recall could handle that much, at least.

"It's about like this."

"Nope, that's not gonna cut it."

Dismissed out of hand.

If I aspired to become an artist someday, that would've put an end to my dream.

Can't you say something nice, even if it's not true?

"Don't 'nope' me. I tried my hardest to draw it the way it is. Maybe the lines seem a little wobbly, but that's how the thing looks in real life."

"That's not what I meant. I need you to draw the shrine and altar, not just the stone itself."

"Hunh? But—"

"Just do it."

Urged to blindly forge ahead, I begrudgingly did as I was asked. Not like it was such a hassle to add in the shrine and altar—they weren't exactly the most complex structures.

I've been calling it a shrine because I don't know how else to describe it, but it couldn't have been simpler. That is, if it hadn't been held together with some nails, it would've been just a pile of toy blocks.

"Oh, that kind of shape? The shrine, I mean."

"Yeah, but..." I said once I'd finished drawing everything. I almost wanted to add in a background for kicks but decided not to push it. "In terms of the altar, its shape seemed totally unremarkable, like it was no more than a tiny desk to put offerings on, but the shrine's shape felt like it was based on something, if only clumsily."

Scrutinizing the notebook, which I'd handed over to him, Oshino responded, "Yeah?"

"Was it at a temple? Or had I seen it around a Jizo statue or some roadside god, I dunno...but I feel like the shrine's shape rings a bell."

"Hey, if you've got tidbits like that up your sleeve, you've gotta tell me up front—was that supposed to be some hidden-ball trick revealing your erudition?" asked Oshino, smirking.

Judging from his tone, he was mocking me, rather than scolding me.

"No, it was a vague notion, and it only came to the forefront of my mind when I drew it out like this. In that sense—"

I only remembered thanks to your bright idea to have me draw it, I almost said before cutting myself off in a fluster. If I started throwing around words like "thanks" and "bright idea," he could hit me up for money—not that I actually thought he was that much of a money-grubbing miser.

I just felt wary, since the subject of money had come up.

Anyway.

"Um, but, I can't specifically call anything to mind. It's more like I'd seen it somewhere, like it wasn't my first time ever... Can you tell, Oshino? If this shrine is modeled on some part of something—"

"No, I can't say I recognize it. But..."

After saying *but*, Oshino fell silent and handed the notebook back to me. I felt a certain sadness that the masterpiece I'd labored over had outlived its usefulness in a few short minutes, but we weren't critiquing my artistic skills.

34

"But what? Don't start saying something and clam up—if you've got an inkling, tell me already."

I'd meant to press him on the point calmly and rationally, but frustrated that my masterwork had been so useless, that he'd been such a dick about it after forcing a bad artist to draw, I ended up sounding a little heated.

But Oshino let my reaction roll off him like water off a duck's back and simply came back with, "Ha hah. You're spirited today, Araragi. Something good happen to you?" He added, "While we're at it, I'd like to hear what *you* think about it. Boy, would I ever like to hear the erudite Mister Araragi's opinion on the subject. What's your take on this particular matter?"

"What's my... Well, you said it yourself in passing. It might be a 'school ghost story,' but I'm not so sure it's about an aberration."

"A-ha. Meaning?"

"Well, this is a pretty boring, realistic interpretation, but I bet somebody, I don't know who but somebody, started worshipping some stone that had landed in the flowerbed as if it were a god—I mean, a shrine doesn't just appear out of thin air. A person's got to build it."

"A vampire, on the other hand, might be able to manifest one." Oshino turned his eyes to the little blond girl in the corner.

True, there were exceptions.

"But that shrine was obviously a human creation," I objected. "It seemed that way to me, anyway. Though I'm not a hundred-percent certain..."

"Hm."

"So in this case the somebody is plural, in other words an unspecified number of students started a little religion, or a faith group kind of a thing, and took that stone as their object of worship... Something like that?"

I wasn't expressing myself well, and it was hard to put into words what the relevant questions were in this case, but the idea that a bizarre faith had sprung up at my school was definitely unsettling.

Or flat-out frightening.

35

"People have freedom of religion, ya know. It's guaranteed by law," Oshino reminded me.

"Right, no question about that—in this case, though, it's clear from Hanekawa's testimony that two short years ago this now-deified stone was nothing but a lump of rock—doesn't that kind of give you the creeps?"

Unlike Naoetsu High, which had only been around for eighteen years, not long enough to develop a "school ghost story," this venerated stone had just been a rock sitting by the roadside up until a couple of years ago, and that was difficult for me to accept.

I think that's what it was.

"An aberration doesn't have to have a history or pedigree, though," answered Oshino, "since new aberrations are being born, being produced, all the time."

"When something creeps you out, it's because some kind of malign influence might be involved. That's my hunch, and I believe that's what Hanekawa's worried about. In other words, someone's knocked together this sham religion, fabricated this object of worship, and is taking a bunch of students for a ride—"

"For a ride? To rip them off for some cheap candy?"

"Well, I dunno."

"If someone was going to take them for a ride, you'd think they'd do a proper job of it—I haven't seen it for myself, Araragi, but as far as I can tell from your crude drawing, the construction of the shrine is itself quite crude. About as crude as the drawing."

"Oshino. I'm well aware of how bad I am at drawing, but it hurts my feelings to hear someone else say it, okay?" Don't make it sound like my crude drawing has made a crude shrine even cruder.

"Anyone who's trying to take them for a ride would build a more impressive shrine, don't you think? In order to fool people, work on the design—or so says a friend of mine."

"Like you have any friends."

"You're right. Maybe not a friend."

I was trying to get back at him by hurting his feelings, but not only did I fail, Oshino even smiled in apparent delight.

What the hell went on in his mind? It was a mystery.

"Not to mention, in that guy's case, it might've been just another lie," mused the expert. "Putting that aside, Araragi, how does it strike you?"

"Well, sure, I guess it makes perfect sense. If you were trying to take them for a ride, you wouldn't use such a childish shrine. If you can't build one yourself, you might outsource the construction. So then, is it a genuine religion? It's part of their creed that they have to build the shrine themselves, no matter how broke-ass it is? I know we have freedom of faith in this country, but all the same, founding a new religion at your school is kind of…"

And why would anyone want to worship a rock that was just sitting there like that? It would be one thing if it were some kind of precious stone… Then again, maybe it was some kind of insane power stone, and Hanekawa and I just couldn't pick up on it?

"You'd sense something from a power stone, wouldn't you, in your present condition—hmm. Okay, listen, Araragi. This is the message I want you to relay to missy class president. Knowing her, it'll tell her everything she needs to know."

Forget about the "school ghost story" angle for the moment, the ever-smirking Oshino advised—for some reason with an even jollier expression than usual.

"Now *try taking a look at the Naoetsu High curriculum.* The lot of the student is to study, after all."

005

The next morning.

In homeroom, when I told the overly sagacious Tsubasa Hanekawa what the all-seeing expert Mèmè Oshino had said, she paused a moment then went, "Ah," as though it indeed told her everything she needed to know.

What the hell was up with the both of them? It was scary.

Since the village idiot over here naturally didn't understand any of it, I did my best to avoid voicing such rude sentiments and simply asked, "What's it all mean?"

"Hm? Oh, no, just that I was jumping at shadows this time around—man, I really let you and Mister Oshino see an embarrassing side of myself. Not just a swing and a miss, a full-on strikeout."

"That still doesn't tell me anything... An embarrassing side of yourself? Did I miss something? Come on, what do you mean?"

"Nothing, really. This might sound like bullshit, but I had my doubts all along. If people were going to worship something, they'd do a better job of it—still, it was the very defectiveness of that half-assed object of worship and half-assed shrine that gave you the creeps and unsettled Mister Oshino, and that's what was worrying me. I'm glad it was a false alarm."

"Hanekawa, hang in there, I know you can find a way to explain it that even I can understand."

"Hang in there?" Our class president's face twisted into a wry smile. Apparently my wording had tickled her. "Listen, once all the evidence is neatly lined up, everything turns out to be totally fine. Up until now, you and I had both been focusing on the rock itself, right?"

"Huh? Oh, yeah…but what's there…apart from the rock?"

"The shrine. Focus on the shrine."

"The shrine?"

"Yes, the shrine. If we'd focused our attention on it instead, we never would've had to bother Mister Oshino."

Bother my ass, all he did was sit in an abandoned building and listen to me talk…

"Focus our attention on the shrine… Where does that get us? That raggedy-ass—"

"Okay, um, I'll put this as plainly as I can. I'm pretty sure the rock wasn't put in a shrine in order to be worshipped—it was chosen as *a thing to put in the shrine*."

"How's that different?"

"It's totally different. A shrine is only ever the container and not the object of worship—so at least, we can discount the possibility that there's some bizarre religion at the heart of all this."

"Still sounds the same to me. If there's no religion involved, doesn't that mean somebody was trying to pass off some sham religion—"

"No, that was our false assumption," Hanekawa said. "*Since that shrine wasn't originally built to be a shrine.*"

"…?"

"About the Naoetsu High curriculum—I don't have to look at it again to understand because I'd checked it out before I took our exams."

So she'd done that, after all.

Gives me the willies.

"Look, when we were first-years, we had to pick an art elective—I

40

took fine art, but they also offered calligraphy and technical arts, didn't they? Mister Oshino was specifically nudging me to consider the curriculum for the technical arts class."

"Technical arts?"

"Yup. You know, woodworking and stuff. And the curriculum for that class includes a *freestyle shed construction* project—something along those lines, anyway."

"…"

"I didn't actually take it so I can't say for sure, but I can only assume that the shrine in question was *a shed built for that class*."

"…"

"And judging from the workmanship, I'd say it was a reject—this is just a theory, mind you, but I think this is more or less how it went: Some student tried to build a shed for technical arts but botched it. Having built the thing in class, the student was instructed to take it home. It would just get thrown out once he or she got it home, though, so off this student went to the garbage area to surreptitiously get rid of it. And passed by the flowerbed on the way."

True enough.

There was a garbage area near the flowerbed.

A piece of junk that large wouldn't fit in the classroom trashcan, so the logical course of action was to take it outside and put it straight into the garbage.

"As our hypothetical student passed by, he or she laid eyes on the rock in question—or maybe tripped over it, like I almost did. Either way, finding this appropriately sized rock, the student figured that even a botched job might look surprisingly good with a rock in it…"

It wasn't that the rock looked like a stone statue—because it was inside a shrine.

It was that some scraps of wood looked like a shrine—because there was a rock in it.

Like the simulacrum phenomenon—or, not quite.

But a reject.

A botched job, ceased to be a botched job.

"So it was the opposite—the reverse," I managed to get out, in a trembling voice.

"Yup. Of course, it isn't any less crude, but at least it went from being a botched job bound for the dump to looking like a shrine—a shed, so the student just took off and left it there. Thus a stone statue worthy of worship was born."

"What about the altar...and the offerings of candy?"

"I assume the altar got there in more or less the same way. I don't know if it was for class or a club or what, but some other student must have 'botched' a project and figured it'd look like an altar if it were left in front of the shrine... As for the candy, I imagine either the gardener or some students passing by the flowerbed had some with them and left it there for no particular reason."

"...You mean they just kind of leave an offering because it seems like the thing to do, and not out of anything as overblown as faith?"

"An offering, or maybe they just left whatever candy they hadn't eaten during the day before going home... It was always a possibility, but if the stone isn't religious in origin, then that's the most likely scenario."

Right...

Cheap candy—not even loose change—has a strong "I chucked what was left over" vibe...

"I don't know who's in charge of the flowerbed," I said, "but wouldn't that person dispose of a shrine that suddenly showed up one day?"

"Nah, most people don't destroy something that looks like a shrine without a second thought. Why invite divine retribution."

"Fair enough..."

And after a while, they start to take its existence for "granted," I suppose.

They don't ask where it came from.

They take for granted—the "gratitude" they feel for its grace.

"..."

"Phew, I feel so much better!"

Hanekawa stretched happily.

For someone like her, "not understanding something" must be a source of stress, because she smiled as if she really did feel much better.

"I see… Something still doesn't sit right with me, or rather, I've got some feelings about that conclusion—"

"Forget about it. It's all thanks to you, Araragi."

"Huh? It is?"

"I mean, wouldn't you say Mister Oshino was only able to figure it out because you told him the shrine 'rings a bell'? Even he couldn't if he didn't base his judgment on the proper material—and how could he predict what the curriculum of a 'closed space' like a school might contain? It's not because it was modeled on something that you recognized it, it's because you'd made something like it yourself for class. The art elective you took was technical arts, wasn't it?"

"Well, yeah…that would be it."

I hadn't seen it at a temple or by the side of the road.

I'd seen it—in the school woodshop.

When Oshino demanded that I draw a picture of it, probably it was just to learn the shrine's shape—but witnessing my reaction when I *recalled as I drew*, he hit upon the truth. That was how it had gone.

That was how, but…

"Okay, case closed—wait, Araragi, where are you going? Class is about to start. Hey, c'mon, don't run in the halls—"

006

The epilogue, or maybe, the punch line of this story.

Paying no heed to Hanekawa's injunction, I ran down the hallway and out of the building towards the quad, to the flowerbed, and once there I picked up the shrine housing the rock that resembled a stone statue and smashed it on the ground.

"Huff, huff, huff, huff…"

I mean.

There was no point in smashing it at this point—but I couldn't help myself, I completely dismantled the shrine, reducing it to its constituent scraps of wood.

Even if I hadn't, the second it no longer surrounded the rock, it was nothing more than that—in any case, I carried the scraps over to the garbage area.

The completion of a trip begun two years earlier.

"…"

Yes.

Needless to say, I was the one who had built the shrine for woodworking two years earlier and left it in the flowerbed, more or less just as

Hanekawa surmised, instead of bringing it home.

The reason it rang a bell wasn't that I'd made something like it myself for class—I'd made *it* myself.

I'd completely forgotten about it.

Even if I couldn't remember things from two years back like Hanekawa could, this was pushing it. I'd said all kinds of horrible things about it, called it a crude, childish, raggedy-ass shrine, but it had been my own handiwork all along.

Now I understood Oshino's detestable little smile.

He must've been holding in a massive burst of laughter—Hanekawa might have shown us an embarrassing side, but it was nothing compared to me.

Happily, Hanekawa (who probably assumed that no one could forget, so completely, something that happened only two short years ago) didn't seem to have caught on yet...but I was so ashamed that I didn't feel like I'd ever be able to look her in the eye again.

That said, my attendance record was dangerously poor and she had ordered me to turn over a new leaf, so if school was about to start, I had no choice but to return to the classroom.

As I trudged away from the garbage area, I caught sight of the stone that up until recently had been ensconced in a shrine. Yup, now it just looked like a regular old rock.

Nothing but a rock.

Immobile.

The offerings of candy were still there, but that alone wasn't enough to make it look like a stone statue or an object of worship—if someone cleaned up the cheap candy, no one would ever leave another offering there again.

It made me feel a little guilty about having destroyed the shrine in the throes of my humiliation. Having built it myself, though, I knew better than anyone that absolutely no divine retribution would be forthcoming...

Yet I still felt a little bad for that rock. Thanks to my sheer laziness and shame at the thought of taking my failed creation home, it had been on a real rollercoaster ride, now worshipped as a god, now reduced to a regular old rock.

Apologizing to a rock is kind of weird, but... I entered the flowerbed and lifted the stone off the ground.

Is it worshipped because it's an aberration, or did it become an aberration because it was worshipped, Oshino had asked.

Undeniably, this rock had "gone" so far as to receive offerings, even if they were only cheap candy. Realizing how my unprincipled behavior might have turned it into an aberration made me feel even worse.

A stone we took for granted.

Became a statue whose grace we took to heart.

It could have turned into a graceless aberration—its origins no longer relevant.

Graceless or not, it would have come to be taken for granted.

That day could have arrived.

The thought struck me, and in turn, drove home another. Maybe I shouldn't be attending school without feeling much of anything.

If the teacher wasn't there yet when I got back to the classroom, I'd ask Hanekawa. Did my failure to be grateful for everyday life mean that I was like a stone, or that I was made of wood?

Though if stone can become statue—and wood a shrine, maybe it wasn't such a bad thing.

"Huh? What the...this rock."

And that's when I noticed.

It was the texture that did it, though I hadn't noticed two years earlier. No question about it, though, this texture, this feel.

"It's concrete?"

CHAPTER TWO
KOYOMI FLOWER

SUN	MON	TUE	WED	THU	FRI	SAT
	1	2	3	4	5	6
7	8	9	10	11	12	13
14	15	16	17	18	19	20
21	22	23	24	25	26	27
28	29	30	31			

5
May

001

I don't mean to sound like a whiner, but in early May, in other words around the beginning of Golden Week, when a strange fate bound me to Hitagi Senjogahara, I was both mentally and physically spent. Mentally and physically spent, or beaten to a pulp—at any rate, I was a mess.

Or should I say a bloody mess—such a mess that the idea of an ordinary life didn't even seem real to me anymore.

Only the deck separates us from hell—I believe fishermen on the high seas use that expression, but it seems like pretty much the same thing on land.

Only the ground separates us from hell.

I'd become painfully aware—how unreliable the ground we walk upon is, how fragile the Earth's crust, how easily it can give way.

I'd become aware of it along with the pain.

I had come to know how precariously balanced it all is—the road I blithely take to school, the road I blithely take home, how blithely it might all collapse.

Come to know?

Uh-uh.

I don't know anything—I don't mean to sound like Tsubasa Hanekawa, the girl with the mismatched wings, but I really only know what I know, and what I know is that I'm a fool.

Hitagi Senjogahara.

My classmate, who some kids called the Cloistered Princess, well, she knew how fragile everyday life could be long before I learned that lesson.

You could say she'd had no choice but to learn it from her life, her lifestyle. Even lending half an ear to the more restrained rumors I'd heard about the fraying tightrope of her life thus far was enough to scare me half out of my wits.

"To begin with, it's a mistake to imagine that there's a wall between the ordinary and the extraordinary—you have to distinguish between the two, of course, you can't go on living if you don't, but they're contiguous—here and there are connected," she said flatly, in an even, level tone devoid of emotion. "It's not a question of above or below—you don't fall from the ordinary into the extraordinary, and you don't crawl up out of the extraordinary to the ordinary. It's more like you're walking along and suddenly you're somewhere else, somewhere you don't recognize…"

Like straying from the path?

You're walking along the sidewalk when suddenly you realize that you've stepped out into the street without knowing it—her analogy made sense, more or less.

It's certainly true.

That if there were no guardrails or crosswalks, there'd be no distinction between the sidewalk and the street.

"Right. And before you know it you've been in an accident—though between the car and the pedestrian, who's to say which is ordinary and which is extraordinary. And there are things like your bicycle, Araragi, that blithely move between the street and the sidewalk…"

Strictly speaking, it contravenes the traffic laws to ride your bicycle on the sidewalk, but then again, from the cars' perspective it's a pain in the ass to have people riding in the street. Modern problems, right?

"Yup. In other words, you can still get into an 'accident' even if the ground you're walking on doesn't collapse, even if you keep to the straight

52

and narrow—and not because you've lost your footing and fallen from the ordinary into the extraordinary. But you know, Araragi," continued Senjogahara without much in the way of emotion. "Sometimes you fall from ordinary into ordinary. And sometimes you crawl up out of the extraordinary and find that wherever you are now is extraordinary too."

002

"Ah, that must be it. I've been feeling kind of nauseous, but now it makes sense, it's because I've been walking with you, Araragi."

"Wha?! You trying to breach my defenses with some inner monologue about an epiphany you supposedly just had?!"

May ninth.

Tuesday evening—I was on the way back from that ruined cram school with Hitagi Senjogahara. Like a proper gentleman, my intention was to escort the young lady to her door, but her attitude was intensely harsh and dreadfully prickly.

"What's that? You can't go around listening to other people's inner monologues, Araragi. Were you raised in a barn or something?"

"I didn't go anywhere, your shit-talking came to me!"

"Feh. And I meant it as a compliment."

"Don't start acting like some cynical character! I can give you the benefit of the doubt till the cows come home, but there's no way 'being with you makes me feel nauseous' could be a compliment!"

"I wonder, do you think it might be morning sickness?"

"So being with me makes you feel pregnant?!"

No.

That still didn't sound like a compliment.

"It was just a token of my desire to tout your manliness to the wider world."

"That's one hell of a negative campaign. That's only promoting my cons."

"But you know, Araragi, your own inner monologue's been making a real racket this whole time."

"Huh? That's odd, I could've sworn I was talking with you…"

Felt like I was taking a wound about once every five seconds.

What the hell was I chatting with?

A girl, or a sword?

"…"

Well.

Nevertheless, a thoroughly gentlemanly interpretation would be that this attitude of Hitagi Senjogahara's—of this classmate of mine—was understandable. I really did have to plumb the uttermost depths of gentlemanliness, but I managed to understand it.

She'd been in constant misery, after all—so miserable that she couldn't even experience misery.

Misery so constant that she wasn't even numb anymore, she'd become an addict.

The misery of illness.

She'd been constantly struggling with illness—and thanks to her accidental brush with me the previous day, a period had been put at the end of that sentence of struggle.

Though saying it was thanks to her brush with me sounds kind of self-aggrandizing. Even if she'd never met me, I'm sure she would've rescued herself from her own plight eventually—but that's neither here nor there.

With Oshino's help, we'd more or less taken care of her aberration-based malady—that had been just last night, and today we'd gone to see him again to tie up the loose ends, or to deal with the final cleanup, or to take care of the last few minor issues that had cropped up.

And now we were headed home.

For Senjogahara, it was all so new—it made sense that she couldn't just turn off this prickly personality, cultivated to combat her illness, like flipping a light switch. As her friend, I simply prayed that at some point her thorns would be blunted.

"But you know, they say that you really learn to feel grateful for good health when you recover from an illness, but after having been sick for so long, even 'walking along' like this feels totally novel to me."

"Hmm, I bet."

"I feel like I'm in a completely different world."

"A different world, huh?"

The part about walking feeling novel sounded like an exaggeration, but maybe that was her genuine impression after having been mired in fakeness.

Incidentally, I'd ridden my bike to the ruined cram school the night before, but that day I walked there and back with her. Circumstances—or inconveniences stemming from the previous night's resolution had ruled out my bike.

Happily, those inconveniences had been taken care of once and for all, so starting the next morning I'd be riding my beloved mountain bike around town again, the thought of which made me want to skip all the way home.

But I couldn't even imagine the lengths to which Senjogahara, walking along beside me, would go to mock me if I did, so I settled for walking.

"By the way, Araragi. Since by some miracle you're walking with a girl, how about you walk between her and the street. You really are a tactless piece of shit, aren't you?"

"..."

I didn't even have to skip for her to mock me.

She was right, though, I was being thoughtless, so I went around to stand on her left.

And I told myself, *What's this, she's trying to raise me to be a proper gentleman*, so it didn't even hurt my feelings.

"Do you mind not standing on my left? I see what you're up to, you're after my heart."

"..."

She'd set me up.

It was a little too predictable.

As her friend I'd wanted to pray for her thorns to be blunted, but never mind the prayer, the friend part was starting to come into question.

"You seem plenty lively," I said. "Maybe you don't need me to walk you all the way home. See you around..."

"What are you talking about? If you're going to walk me home, walk me all the way home. What if word got out that a boy only walked Hitagi Senjogahara partway home? My reputation as the Cloistered Princess would be ruined."

"Self-involved much?"

"If you bail on me here, I'll spread the rumor that you tried to kill me."

"I see you're not too worried about other people's reputations."

Plus, who the hell would believe it?

I'm not exactly renowned as an assassin.

"You don't have anyone to spread rumors to anyway."

"Don't worry, I'll just mutter endlessly to myself about it in our classroom and all around school."

"Hard not to worry about a girl like that."

I'll walk you home already, I shrugged.

I'd intended to do it out of the goodness of my heart, but it somehow ended up feeling more like an obligation—that was fine, though, it's not like I had anything else to do.

I didn't care to be "silenced" for saying the wrong thing like the day before—I'd already given her back the arsenal of office supplies I'd confiscated.

"Now then... What about it, I wonder."

"Hm? What about what?"

"Uhh, give me a second. I'll think of a way to put this that even Araragi will be able to understand."

"How about thinking of a way to put it that won't piss Araragi off instead."

"Look, Mister Oshino demanded a fee for this, right?"

"Oh. Yup."

One hundred thousand yen.

It might not be a huge sum in comparison to the five million that I owed him, but it was still a lot for a high school girl.

The thing that somehow felt worst about it was that one hundred thousand yen seemed calculated to be just within reach, even considering Senjogahara's family circumstances—it made you think *I'll work it out somehow.*

"Do you have any savings or anything?" I asked.

"None at all. In fact I'm in the red."

"Huh? Your parents would be one thing…but you, yourself? Not counting Oshino?"

"Uh huh. My team finished last year's pennant race with a four-game deficit."

"Do you own a professional baseball team or something?"

She was a multi-millionaire in that case.

Just pay off the hundred thousand right now.

Put it on your credit card.

But even if she didn't have other debts, I believed the part about not having any savings—in which case Senjogahara was going to have to find a way to save up a hundred thou.

"I guess I'll just have to get a part-time job at a fast food joint like Mister Oshino said."

"Well, he didn't say anything to either of us about a deadline, so I don't think you need to be too worried about coming up with a plan to get the money."

"Unlike you, Araragi, I try to be scrupulous about money."

"Don't just assume that I'm careless with it."

"If I'm going to default on my loans, I'll default on them properly, and if I'm going to pay them off, I'll pay them off properly."

"…"

Is there a proper protocol for defaulting on your loans?

In any case, I had a hard time picturing Senjogahara working part-time at a fast food joint...

"Hi, welcome. You're taking this to go?"

"Offer them the option to stay. Don't be so eager to send 'em on their way."

"Would you like *fries* with that?"

"Why say it like a native English speaker?"

"Would you like some *potato* with that?"

"Now it sounds like I'm going to get a raw potato..."

"Hmm. Sounds like I'm not cut out after all for a part-time jibe."

"If it's jibes we're talking about, you're cut out for overtime."

And then—something occurred to me.

Something I'd talked about with Hanekawa the previous month, about how Oshino's "line of work" was collecting tales of aberrations and selling them off for a pretty penny...

"Senjogahara. Do you know any scary stories or anything?"

"Sure, if you count walking with you like this."

"That doesn't count."

"Then no, I don't."

What a harpy.

I've heard of abusing the kindness of others, but being abused before you've even gotten the chance to be kind? A rare bird indeed.

I said, "Listen, I was just thinking. As an expert, Oshino's doing his part to collect tales of aberrations—so if you know any unusual ones, any rare urban legends or anything, you might be able to take care of your debt that way."

"Hmmm, like a barter, you mean. That's not a bad idea, Araragi, especially given that it came from you. I shall grant you my praise."

"..."

A simple thank you would've sufficed.

Of all possible expressions of thanks, "I shall grant you my praise" has to be the least gratifying to receive.

"Unfortunately, though, I don't know any above and beyond the one

I personally experienced."

"I don't think there's any above or beyond when it comes to aberrations."

"Ooh, thy words come from on high. Not for nothing has he associated with the king of aberrations, his esteemed lordship Araragi's pronouncement is precious, so very precious."

"Esteemed lordship…"

"Indeed, from the lofty perch whence his lordship condescends to view the world, all aberrations, all mysterious phenomena, must appear equal, but for a lowly worm like myself, crawling through the mire, the difference is quite pronounced, O Araragi the Great."

"O? The Great?"

Hmm, she was usually domineering, but this submissive act really worked for her…

"Greek mythology tells of Ajax the Great and Ajax the Lesser, but what a title to append to a person's name…" she observed. "I would never call anyone the Lesser."

"Sure, calling someone the Great is all well and good, but Lesser is just cruel."

"Isn't it, Araragi the Tiniest?"

"My name's one thing, but if you're talking about my height I must protest in the strongest possible terms!"

"What, should I call you The Grand Araragi, then? O Grand Araragi."

" … "

Obsequiousness suited her…

This could be a problem.

"Anyway, I don't know any tales of aberrations. I'm fundamentally no good with scary stories. Even worse than I am with mindless labor, so I guess I just need to find a part-time job."

"Hmmm… I mean, sure, do what you feel."

To me, scary stories seemed like nothing but her forte…or to be honest, I felt like my first encounter with her yesterday had been one hell of a "scary story" itself.

The Madness of the Stapler Lady.

Mightn't Oshino pay for that one?

To the tune of oh, say, around five million yen?

"You're thinking something rude, aren't you, Araragi."

"So pointlessly perceptive…"

I'm not even allowed to gripe in my own head?

She was a little too worried about unfavorable reviews.

"Let me make this clear, Araragi. No internal freedom is allowed within five hundred feet of me."

"Despotism."

"Your unfreedom of expression, unfreedom of faith, and unfreedom of thought are guaranteed."

"Tyranny."

With a surprisingly wide jurisdiction!

Quite an individual.

"Some call me the Red Queen."

"What, is this *Through the Looking Glass*?"

"Or they call me a red herring."

"Sounds fishy."

"Some also call me a red flag. A flaming red fake."

"What kind of an alias is that? It sounds cool, but it just means you're a pariah."

"Huh? Right, why am I such a pariah… Will my life play out okay?"

Suddenly ill at ease, Senjogahara halted and began to worry for real.

So emotionally unstable…

I'd been relatively serious about parting ways partway home, but it didn't seem like I could leave a girl like her alone on a public road. I figured it was my duty as a friend to see her all the way home. I mean, even if we weren't friends, it was my civic duty.

"This is bad, Araragi. I've got to start getting on people's good side. I'd hate being second only to you on the world's shit list."

"…Hey, do you want to be my friend, or not?"

"Of course I do. I want to be your *frenemy*."

"Isn't that a combination of 'friend' and 'enemy'?!"

"Yup. In other words, we'll be both friend and foe…"

"Wait, isn't a friend who's also your enemy just an enemy?!"

She was trying to make it sound like a healthy rivalry.

I so lacked any reason to compete with her.

"By the way, I can't stand people who go around saying 'OMG, I don't have any friends' but have friends they can say it to," she declared.

"…"

So narrow-minded.

A little too intolerant.

"Makes me want to teach them what it really means not to have any friends."

"It's fine, ease up. Now you've got me."

"Hmph."

Senjogahara looked at me.

And what a look it was.

Like her eyes might swallow me whole—I wondered, considering what I knew of her personality, if she also hated people who claimed to be her friend, like me?

Hmmm.

Maybe this wasn't going to go the way it did with Hanekawa…

"Feh. I suppose you're right," she said after what seemed like forever—without producing either stapler or box-cutter.

I was more relieved than I could ever remember being.

"I'll ease up this time, out of the goodness of my harp seal."

"Harp seal?"

"I thought turning a sentence ending into an animal might be cute."

"I can't get a read on your personality…"

A puzzling point.

Past the point of puzzling.

Then again, was this just her way of hiding her embarrassment? In which case, maybe there was some cuteness in there somewhere.

"A scary story, huh? I wish I did know one."

Even though she'd adopted the part-time job plan, she acted as if she wasn't done considering mine.

Though maybe that was still just her hiding her embarrassment.

"Of course we could always make one up," she concluded.

"Nope."

Not cute, after all.

How could she calmly discuss passing off some bullshit to my, to our, savior?

"Yeah, you're right... If I tried to cash in on a lie, I'd be no different from that low-life jerk."

"Huh? 'That' low-life jerk? Who do you mean?"

"Hm? Oh, sorry... Anytime I say 'low-life jerk' I mean you."

"Even in this context?!"

"Hey."

With that interjection, Senjogahara, who had come to a halt, suddenly started moving—not forwards, but sideways. In other words, she made to hop from the sidewalk into the street.

I couldn't begin to figure out why she tried to all of a sudden. Still, even though we hadn't known each other for very long, I was already somewhat accustomed to her erratic behavior after a couple of days together, and I reflexively blocked her movement.

By putting my arm around her shoulders.

I was blocking the momentum of another person's entire body, even if that person was a girl, so as you might expect I felt a real heft—unlike.

Unlike the day before, when I'd caught Senjogahara on the stairs...

"What."

"Huh?"

"Getting a little familiar, aren't you?"

"Oh, my bad," I said, removing my arm from her shoulder. "But you tried to jump out into the street..."

"What, you thought I was committing suicide? Impulsively?"

"Impulsively, or..."

Though I wasn't going to say so out loud, I didn't put it past her.

Her battle with illness may have ended, but I doubted her struggles were over—even apart from still having to go to the hospital for a thorough battery of follow-up tests.

64

"Don't worry, Araragi. Unlike you, with your regimen of offing yourself three times daily, at mealtimes, I'd never kill myself."

"I don't have a prescription for suicide, okay?"

"Wha? Then how come all the girls in our class call you Johnny Suicide?"

"Wha? The girls in our class all call me that?"

Way to make you feel suicidal.

I'm pretty sure she *was* lying this time, but it bothered me nonetheless. I'd have to check with Hanekawa later on...though she'd be taken aback if I asked her flat-out, *What do all the girls call me?*

"Fine, Johnny Suicide wants to know why you tried to jump out into the street."

"I wasn't jumping out into the street, I just wanted a better view of that."

"That?"

I looked in the direction Senjogahara was pointing, at the sidewalk on the other side of the street—and a telephone pole that stood there. Well, strictly speaking not the telephone pole itself, but something at its base.

At a bouquet of flowers.

A brand-new bouquet.

There wasn't a stand or anything, but that had to be...

"I couldn't tell from my angle, since it was behind the telephone pole—and I wanted to get a better view. Guess there must've been a car accident somewhere around here."

"Seems like it... Recently, you think?"

The road that ran from the cram school ruins to Senjogahara's house wasn't the one I usually took, it being outside my territory, so even if there'd been a car accident, or really any kind of accident, I just wouldn't know...

"Anyway, if you got hit by a car because you were distracted by the flowers, the person who died would never be able to rest in peace. You've gotta be more careful."

Sadly, you sometimes heard about follow-on victims—distracted by a "Frequent Accidents in This Vicinity" billboard, they end up in a head-on collision, that kind of thing.

"I made sure there were no cars coming. No need to worry, low-life jerk."

"When that's how you keep referring to a friend, how could I not worry?"

Plus, I call bullshit.

She'd been totally distracted by the flowers. Taken together with her slip-and-fall on the stairs the day before, maybe she actually was pretty careless.

High-strung and careless... What a terrible combination.

She'd finally recovered from her "illness" but could still wind up dead if I didn't attend to her—what was she, an endangered species? Perhaps seeing her all the way home didn't cut it, better make sure she got safely inside.

Hmmm, this new friend of mine was a real handful...

"I just remembered."

"Huh?" I cocked my head at Senjogahara's sudden statement. "You remembered what? My dignity? The proper way to apologize to me?"

"I can't remember something that never existed."

"Is that right."

"I remembered a 'scary story'—so Araragi."

"Yeah?"

"This is a command from Your Highness. Do what you gotta do."

"..."

What kind of princess talks like that?

003

Obeying Princess Senjogahara's command, early the following day, May tenth, I visited the rooftop of a school building at Naoetsu High.

Alone.

Given how things had unfolded, originally the plan was for her to accompany me, but unfortunately she was obliged to begin a period of regular hospital visits that very day.

So I, as her "friend," ended up acting on her behalf—or I guess, was just getting used, but I really didn't have any reason to refuse.

It's not like I had anything else to do.

"'Preciate it. If things go well, I'll show you my tits again."

"Keep 'em to yourself."

And "again" my ass.

Somewhere amid this back and forth I readily agreed, and found myself visiting the roof as Senjogahara had asked.

"The roof? Of which building?"

"Whichever. They were all *like that*."

That's what Senjogahara told me, so first I tried the roof of the building where my class was—though that makes it sound like I reached my destination by some legitimate means.

At Naoetsu High, however, the roofs are basically off-limits. The doors are kept locked, denying access to your average student, let alone your below-average one like me.

So how did I infiltrate the rooftop, how did I manage my illicit trespass? I went out the window of the top floor and crawled up the outside of the building, that's how.

One slip meant instant death.

I, myself, was hard pressed to understand why I was braving such dangers on behalf of a girl I'd only gotten to know the day before yesterday, but maybe I was just starved for something like a "favor to do for a friend."

Hrmm.

I'd already abandoned my belief that making friends would lower my intensity as a human, but confronted with this state of affairs, I had to admit I might not have been so far off the mark...

Let me note, for Senjogahara's honor, that I'm sure she wasn't expecting me to go to such great lengths.

Which is to say she'd suggested, "Ask your good friend Hanekawa. If she cooked up some reason to ask a teacher for the key to the roof, they'd happily give it to her."

Sure, most of the teachers would oblige, no matter how over the top the request was, if it came from a model student like Hanekawa—but I hesitated to bring it up to her. After Golden Week, I felt kind of awkward about asking her for anything.

Sure, it was a dangerous thing to do, and climbing up the outside of the school wasn't exactly my idea of a good time, but compared to the nightmare of Golden Week and the hell of spring break, it didn't strike me as all that risky.

So.

"Ah...it's true. Just as she said."

Once I'd clambered over the fence and had my feet planted on the tiles of the rooftop, I discovered that she hadn't been lying—did I think she had been? Well, yeah, I kinda thought she had been.

I mean, I'm sorry, but every other word out of that girl's mouth is a lie, I can't just blindly swallow everything she says.

Gotta keep your mouth shut and your eyes open, watch her like a hawk.

There, I got too preoccupied with having to watch her and put off explaining—I also didn't mention it earlier because I thought she might be lying—that what was "just as she said" about the roof of the school building was a bouquet of flowers.

A bouquet of flowers.

Someone had left a bunch of flowers wrapped in plastic by the fence—left, or offered, maybe?

Anyway.

There was a fresh bouquet on the rooftop, which was supposed to be off limits.

"…"

Apparently, when Senjogahara saw those newish flowers by the telephone pole the day before, she remembered this rooftop bouquet—which meant, conversely, that it had been such a trifling matter to her that she'd forgotten about it completely.

A trifling matter, easily forgotten and incidentally recalled.

And yet.

Trifling though it may have been—it also struck her as mysterious, I suppose.

"Hang on—how come you were up on the roof in the first place?"

The previous night.

Still thoroughly doubting her claim, I was questioning her so she'd back it up a little.

"How did you get onto the roof? It's off limits."

"I may not be Big Sis Hanekawa, but I'm a model student, too. I've got enough juice to wrangle the roof key out of a teacher with the right pretext."

"Maybe, but don't call her Big Sis Hanekawa."

"My, my. So you're the only one who gets to call her that?"

"I've never called her that."

Senjogahara suspects, for no good reason, that I have an unrequited crush on Hanekawa. I have no idea on what basis...

"All right, for now. We'll drop it. When, and why, did you go up to the roof? You spoke of a pretext, so it sounds like you weren't being entirely truthful with the teacher..."

"Whoa, lame. Mister detective, showing off his powers of deduction."

"..."

I guess I wasn't allowed to read too much into Senjogahara's words. She just lay into every single word I said. If I keep going at this rate this flashback is never going to end, so abridging those bits and getting to the meat of her story—

"When I matriculated at Naoetsu High, I had to consider my personal safety, okay? So I personally took considerable steps to safeguard it."

Leaving aside the half-assed wordplay, Senjogahara was so wary of other people that she'd even given a false address for the class directory.

Hanekawa had researched Naoetsu High before taking the entrance exam and after getting in; for reasons of her own, Senjogahara carried out an exhaustive study of where was safe and where was not, who was friend and who was foe.

We're not just talking about right after she enrolled. She undertook continual follow-up surveys for two years—she must've been aware of the little shrine in the quad that I'd recently destroyed but deemed it "safe" and not paid it too much mind.

And—she'd given the rooftop flowers a pass as well.

"It's no tale of an aberration, or a ghost story, but if you really think about it, isn't it mysterious?"

Yup.

It was mysterious.

Because, according to Hanekawa—

In the eighteen years of Naoetsu High's existence, there hadn't been a single incident like the death of a student—which meant.

This.

An offering of flowers, lain as if someone had jumped off the roof—was mysterious.

"…"

This wasn't like passersby leaving offerings of cheap sweets at some flimsy shrine. It felt formal...

I climbed up the ladder of the water tower on the roof, and from there I was able to confirm that the roofs of all the other school buildings—were also just as Senjogahara said.

A single bouquet of flowers lay on each and every roof. It was hard to say for sure at that distance, but as far as I could tell, the flowers seemed to be the same kind.

"…"

Hanekawa.

She'd wanted to repay Oshino with some "school ghost story," but despite her research, this had escaped her notice—probably because she only investigated the *legal* areas of the school, unlike Senjogahara.

So Hanekawa didn't know everything, after all...though in this case what was funny, or scary, was that Senjogahara did know.

"No one's ever committed suicide by jumping off a building at our school, but bouquets of flowers continue to be lain on all the roofs, quietly, anonymously, unbeknownst to anyone—might this story interest Mister Oshino?" said Senjogahara, as expressionlessly as ever. In the same level tone she speculated, "Should be worth around, say, a hundred and twenty thousand yen?"

"…"

She was angling for a twenty thousand-yen kickback.

Man, she was weird...

She was warped due to her illness, or aberration, or so I had assumed, and of course she was, but it seemed like she'd been weird even before any warping.

Senjogahara said she was called the Cloistered Princess thanks to an act she put on, but if she hadn't put on that act, I wonder what people would've called her...

Whatever.

I'd confirmed her story—my next move should be to report the whole thing to Oshino.

That sounds a little indifferent, like I wasn't particularly interested in this case, but in fact I was curious how Oshino might interpret it.

Floral memorials to non-existent suicides.

Bouquets.

Was there some clear objective, some design, behind them or—

"More importantly," I muttered.

From atop the water tower.

"How do I get back into the building…"

004

"Going up is easy, but coming back down is hard—ha hah. Just like life. So, Araragi, how did you actually get back down?"

Whether collecting tales of aberrations was his hobby or his job, Oshino seemed to love hearing tales of my blunders, and he listened to this one with glee.

I'd hurried over to the ruins of the abandoned cram school as soon as classes ended that day, not expecting my own foolishness to be the first thing on the agenda.

A little blond girl watched me sullenly from the corner—she didn't seem to think much of my stories, whether they were about aberrations or blunders.

I suppose no story involving me was pleasant for her to hear.

"Well, um, like anyone would, hanging in there like anyone would. I climbed over the fence and used my arms and legs to crawl down the wall and back in through the top-floor window I'd left open."

"Ha hah. Sounds like you definitely hung in there, Araragi. Feeling nostalgic for your vampiric power? With that you could've just jumped off the roof, easy breezy."

"Sure, but…nostalgic? Not a chance. Even the power of a pseudo-vampire is way too much for me."

"Hmm. Speaking of the power of a pseudo," Oshino said, indicating the girl in the corner, "come by sometime this weekend and give li'l Shinobu some blood, okay? If you don't, the kid'll croak."

"…Got it."

Right.

He'd given the little blond girl a name—Shinobu Oshino. Honestly, I still wasn't used to it—but I couldn't call her by her true name, so I just needed to adapt whether I liked it or not.

"Give, Shinobu, some blood," I recited.

Be that as it may, I'd been coming to these ruins a little too often since Golden Week—why was I wasting the precious, one-and-only springtime of my high school years hanging out with some tacky old geezer in an abandoned building?

He'd been staying here long enough to transition from a tacky old geezer into more of a grubby one…

"…"

That said.

I don't actually think of my high school years as a precious, one-and-only springtime—sure, it only happens once, and it is the springtime of my life, but precious?

One gust of wind and it's gone—one moment of uncertainty and poof, that's how light it seems to me.

The springtime of my life?

After spring—comes summer, that's all.

"So, what do you think, Oshino? Is that story worth a hundred and twenty––I mean a hundred thousand yen?"

"Mmmm…"

"Hey."

He was falling into his silent pondering routine, leaving me no choice but to press him for an answer.

"I mean, it doesn't have to be the full amount. If a hundred thousand is too much, how about eighty thousand, or fifty thousand, or—"

"…"

"T-Twenty thousand."

Damn, this ain't working, I thought as I haggled.

Oshino wasn't the kind of guy who gave much away in his face, but my intuition was telling me that, how do I put this, he wasn't biting.

He'd shown at least some interest in Hanekawa's story about the shrine—and might even have paid her for it if she'd asked—but this time around things seemed different.

"Do you have that missy's phone number or email address, Araragi?"

"No, I haven't asked for them," I answered his abrupt question honestly.

"Should've the other day. So you have no way of contacting her, then?"

"Uh…I meant to ask her sooner rather than later…"

No need to make me look stupid.

I'm just not used to stuff like exchanging phone numbers.

"Why do I need to contact her?"

"I wanted you to deliver this message: 'I regret to inform you that I cannot comply with your wishes, so please find another avenue for paying my fee'—"

"…"

Well, I had prepared myself for that, so it's not like I was surprised.

And that wasn't worth contacting her about—Senjogahara was already planning to get a part-time job to pay off the whole hundred thousand.

This was only ever the back-up plan…

I'd promised to let her know within the day if her long shot was worth anything. In other words, if she didn't hear from me, she wouldn't think anything of it and just start checking the help wanted listings for a part-time gig.

But, and I hadn't realized this until Oshino pointed it out, on the off chance that he was willing to pay for Senjogahara's story, not having her phone number meant having to go all the way to her apartment…

Which was crazy.

How mobile was I, unlike your typical high schooler these days—not that I'm claiming to be a typical high schooler by any means.

"Hmph. Well, the next time you see her at school, could you tell her formally?"

"Sure, but she'll be visiting the hospital for day treatment for a while, so I don't think she'll be at school… And when I do end up reporting back to her, she'll murder me if I don't give her a reason… Can't you tell me why this story isn't worth even a single yen?"

"I never said that. It's just that since I don't keep a ledger, I have to round off the small change or my accounting gets messed up."

"Small change…"

What did he consider small change?

Personally, I wouldn't call even a five hundred-yen coin change, but even if you did, getting rounded off felt harsher than simply being dismissed as worthless.

Totally inconsiderate…exactly the sort of thing the jerk would say. I was really glad Senjogahara wasn't there to hear it.

It might've turned into a battle to rival spring break and Golden Week.

Got to avoid that at all costs…

"Ha hah. You're spirited today, Araragi. Something good happen to you?"

"No, I dunno, I just want to be ready for anything, I guess…"

My response to Oshino's catchphrase couldn't but be sluggish as I mulled over what the future might hold. While he callously laughed off tales of my blunders, I guess he wasn't so inhuman as to laugh off my anxieties because he said, "Yeah? Yeah, makes sense. Ordinarily I would charge a consultation fee for this, but it's not like we're perfect strangers, you and me, so just this once I'll tell you something for nothing."

"…Thanks, you're a real life-saver."

I was trying to help him with his work, even if I had ulterior motives, so I wanted to object that I shouldn't be paying him in any case, but if it was going to be for free, we were all set.

However—"I'm not saving you. People just go and get saved on their

76

own," was how Oshino responded. "First off, as for the site of that traffic accident you two happened upon—there was a fatality there last month. A pedestrian who was crossing the street got hit by a kei truck."

"Wow...okay. You're really well informed."

"It's close by is all, and Araragi, it's to collect tales of aberrations, with or without your help, that I've been poking around here and there—of course I'm informed."

"I see..."

That "with or without your help" felt pretty alienating, but I guess it was true. And Oshino made a point of talking in a style that pushed people away.

Even though I'd figured as much, the fact that someone had been killed in an accident was grievously tragic—but since I had no idea who they were or where they'd lived, there was a limit to how much I could grieve for their tragedy.

My thoughts could never measure up to those of the bereaved family that I assume placed the bouquet of flowers there, but I offered up a silent prayer for the deceased.

"Well, I'm not a traffic accident investigator, so I didn't look into it all that carefully...but that spot's layout seems almost designed to cause accidents," Oshino continued his exposition. "Though, apparently, the pedestrian's own recklessness was at fault this time..."

I had to wonder if he ever showed any respect for the dead, but if we're addressing the humanity of it, maybe I just came off as a hypocrite.

"Even if that isn't the case, and even if we're not talking about fatalities, there've been a whole mess of single-vehicle accidents and minor collisions—supposedly."

"Hmm, Senjogahara nearly leapt out into the street right there herself." She told me she'd made sure it was safe, but most people said so in that situation. And probably even after getting in an accident. "Oh, but I guess in her case, she was distracted by the bouquet of flowers—and it wasn't the layout."

"Uh huh. That can happen too. I'm concerned in that regard, but we don't want to ignore the feelings of the bereaved family. Next time I go out, I'll just change the placement of the bouquet."

"Yeah, please do."

In fact, I should've done that myself the day before—in which case, what was I thinking, telling someone "please do" like that... Nothing at all, I have to admit.

Oshino was insensitive towards me, but he could be so attentive to these concerns...

"All that aside, let's get back to the matter at hand, Oshino."

"There's no matter to get back to. We haven't gotten off topic at all. Now then, the issue is that even though no one's committed suicide by jumping off of one of the school buildings—or accidentally fallen to their death, someone has nevertheless left a bouquet of flowers on the roof of every building at your school—yes?"

"Um... Y-Yeah. That's about the size of it."

That Johnny Suicide nickname Senjogahara tried to foist on me must've colored my thinking on the matter, because it had never occurred to me that someone could've fallen off the roof accidentally.

I could've fallen during my climb that morning, for instance...

"Well, whether or not anyone actually falls off of it, a roof is an accident waiting to happen, isn't it, Araragi? That's why it was off limits."

"Sure... At schools where it isn't, there's usually a ridiculously high fence. At Naoetsu High, though, it's low enough that I could climb over it from the outside."

"Indeed... Streets and schools are both prone to accidents and incidents—to put it plainly, I guess they're like the opposite of power spots?"

"You mean spiritually poor places? Let's see, I've heard about that stuff. Like how the northeast is called the demon's gate—"

I hustled, once again, to trot out half-remembered lore, but Oshino shut me down with a simple, "Nope, that's different."

He had no interest in cultivating my mind, did he?

What if I was filled with astounding potential?

For what, I'm not sure...

"There are, of course, spiritually poor places—I'm doing a little research on that subject even as we speak."

"?"

"No, forget it. It's still too early to talk to you about that, I shouldn't have said anything. *Now* let's get back to the matter at hand. We're losing precious time because you keep derailing the conversation."

"Come on, what's the rush…"

I sort of felt like he was giving me the runaround, but…fine. I wasn't interested in knowing the particulars of Oshino's work.

Though he definitely seemed to be settling in for a long stay in a town that he'd originally only come to because of a vampire.

"We're losing precious Times Square."

"…If you've got time to make terrible jokes, I think you can make time for my little digressions."

"That street isn't so bad, but as a drifter, I've found accident-prone setups all over the country. This footbridge blocks line of sight, that construction will make it impossible to see someone coming the other way— and then there are spots that are obvious choices for suicides. What they call suicide hotspots… But that has everything to do with the terrain or the surroundings, and spiritual factors are irrelevant."

"Huh, I guess I agree. Not what I'd expect an expert on aberrations to say, though."

"Well, I'm trying to counteract people's tendency to chalk up anything negative to aberrations. Ha hah," laughed Oshino.

Sounded commendable enough, but since taking on the negative aspects of society was part of their function, that threatened to turn into a chicken-or-egg argument…

"It's not like I think this particular case has anything to do with aberrations, Oshino. It's not a 'scary story,' or even a 'creepy story' like the one about that little shrine. Senjogahara herself had forgotten about it until yesterday, so it's no more than a slightly niggling…'mysterious story,' I guess."

"Are you saying it's *Slightly Mysterious?*"

"I mean, I wasn't trying to bring up Fujio Fujiko here."

But something like that, yeah.

On the level of *what the fuck?*

The ol' WTF.

"And like you said, the accident on that road probably wasn't the work of any aberration—nor was Senjogahara's attempt to leap out into it. That was just a question of the placement of the bouquet of flowers."

"Indeed," Oshino concurred. "The terrain or surroundings was the issue there, too, most likely—which is why I'm going to go change the position of that bouquet soon. Because, Araragi, *if an offering of flowers can invite accidents—don't you think the reverse might also be true?*"

005

The epilogue, or maybe, the punch line of this story.

Though this time around, the punch line didn't actually come until much later—the reason being that "satisfied" by what Oshino said, the sense of "mysteriousness" cleanly swept away, I never ended up reporting back to Senjogahara about it.

And Senjogahara, never hearing back from me, left it alone—I'd figured I could give her the full report next time I saw her, but the next time I saw her, namely Sunday, May fourteenth, things got pretty hairy and this business just kind of, if I may, got lost in the shuffle.

Senjogahara must have forgotten about it again.

And so did I.

It wasn't until the end of May that I remembered—

"I just remembered," I said, finally telling her about it. "Basically they were part of the school's *roof supervision* policy—those bouquets."

"Roof supervision?" she reacted as if she'd only remembered because I brought it up. But being the brainy lady she was, it all seemed to come back to her in an instant.

"Yeah, just like managing the keys and putting up the fence—though

81

compared to that, the bouquets seem more like they're for peace of mind, like a protective talisman or good-luck charm."

"How do bouquets—how does putting bouquets on the roof supervise anything? If it's supposed to be like a rooftop garden—it's in bad taste. Almost as bad as your fashion sense."

"There's no call to bring my fashion sense into this."

"What's with that uniform?"

"Whatever you may say about my civvies, how can you talk smack about my school uniform?! Are you trying to make an enemy of every single boy who goes to Naoetsu High?!"

"What do I have to fear from them as long as you're on my side, Araragi?"

"I'm on their side, dammit! Though it is in really poor taste, isn't it…"

"Thank you."

"I'm not talking about my uniform, I'm talking about the bouquets! It's a tasteless tactic—and I don't know who came up with it, but the bouquets, which basically say 'someone died here,' were in fact taking the place of a warning that 'this place is dangerous'…"

"Taking the place of a warning? Like 'Frequent Accident Zone Ahead'?"

"Yeah. Apparently, there are signs at suicide hotspots to try and dissuade people…though I've heard the same signs can also make them suicide hotspots in the first place. Anyway, someone must have decided that 'danger' signs are so ubiquitous that they've become ineffectual. It sends a pretty intense message, saying 'someone died here'—"

"…"

Although, distracted by a bouquet, Senjogahara had jumped out into the street—Oshino called it "the reverse," and the normal reaction to seeing one was to think, "There was an accident here, maybe this place is dangerous," and to be extra cautious.

The school put the bouquets there.

To arouse caution.

"Kind of like how people hang up the corpse of a crow to drive off other crows?" asked Senjogahara. "They see the corpse and are wary of getting too close? But does it really serve any purpose beyond being a good-luck charm? It'd be different if, say, instead of a bouquet of flowers, they left some person who died in an accident…"

"Where do you come up with such horrifying ideas, are you a demon? Oshino said it was for peace of mind, or just a little playful inventiveness. Keeping the doors locked and putting up a fence is really plenty to keep people from falling—though it's not a perfect defense. Since there are still students like you who lie their way up to the roof."

"Hold it, Araragi. I don't appreciate being called a liar. I've got a silver tongue, that's all."

"Don't you mean an acid one? That silver's gotta be pretty corroded by now. Listen, the point is, in the face of imperfect supervision, the school opted for a sort of protective charm to give them peace of mind— it's not like anyone's been leaving floral tributes for imaginary deaths."

"Hmm…"

Makes sense, said Senjogahara, seeming convinced.

I mean, once you hear that explanation it seems obvious, it's just common sense, no room for doubt.

Not at all mysterious.

Let alone aberrant.

The story held an unseemly interest—but to say the least, it wasn't the type Oshino was interested in collecting.

No wonder he thought it wasn't worth more than pocket change.

Maybe Hanekawa knew about it—even the truth behind it, which is exactly why she hadn't brought it to him.

"But that just creates another mystery, Araragi. How could Mister Oshino be so sure? Had he encountered a similar situation? How could he have come to such a firm conclusion based only on what you told him?"

"I wouldn't call it a conclusion, exactly…but look. You and I made the same mistake. Whether it's an accident or suicide, if someone falls to their death, the roof isn't where you'd leave a bouquet of flowers."

"Ah."

"You'd leave it on the ground, where the person landed."

With a car accident you obviously can't leave an offering of flowers smack dab in the middle of the road where the person actually died—but if someone died falling off a roof, you'd ordinarily leave the flowers on the ground. Of course—since that's where they died, not up on the roof.

"I see, we were thinking about it all wrong. Though anyone would've made the same mistake."

"Really covered for yourself quickly there…"

"It's meant to deter people from falling, even if it's no more than a good-luck charm, so whoever put it there had to choose the roof despite the logical inconsistency—although."

I guess they won't be doing that anymore—said Senjogahara, looking up at one of the roofs, which were currently being renovated: a towering new fence was being erected around the perimeter.

Yes.

The roof improvement project was what made me remember the whole incident in the first place. And I finally made my report to Senjogahara, almost twenty days late…but that didn't mean I felt relieved or that a weight was lifted from my shoulders.

In fact, I'd felt much more at ease when I'd let the whole thing slip my mind—the reason being that the project had been deemed necessary thanks to rumors about "a student climbing up the outside of the building and onto the roof."

The school probably never imagined anyone would be stupid enough to try and get onto the roof from the outside—and a bouquet of flowers wouldn't be terribly effective against such a trespasser.

The cost of erecting new fences.

A hell of a lot more than a hundred thousand yen.

And if it came out that I was the trespasser in question—they'd do a hell of a lot more than just expel me. Senjogahara, who had put me up to it, naturally wouldn't be spared, either…

"Araragi."

"I know, I know, this is our secret."

"No, secret isn't good enough."

"Then what do we do?"

84

"What we've been doing."

"What we've been doing?"

"We forget."

Though I've got to do something about the hundred thousand yen I owe Mister Oshino, before I forget—said Hitagi Senjogahara, in her usual level tone, devoid of any discernable emotion.

CHAPTER THREE
KOYOMI SAND

SUN	MON	TUE	WED	THU	FRI	SAT
				1	2	3
4	5	6	7	8	9	10
11	12	13	14	15	16	17
18	19	20	21	22	23	24
25	26	27	28	29	30	

6
June

001

I first became aware of Mayoi Hachikuji—we first became aware of each other—in a park with an unreadable name, but thereafter our encounters always took place out on the road.

She'd gotten lost on the way to visit her mother, which was also how she ended up in that park, so I thought she might have her own take on the subject of roads, and at some point I asked her about it.

How.

How do you view the roads you walk down—which is the same as asking, *How do you view your own life?*

Just to be clear, I didn't necessarily think I was in much of a position to be asking such a question—and I was well aware as I asked it that whatever thoughts and feelings lay behind the way she chose to live her life were inconsequential to me.

If calling them inconsequential sounds inconsiderate, all I really mean is that it's Hachikuji's business how she lives her life—and if that sounds like I'm giving you the business, then let me rephrase: I just think she's free to do as she pleases.

Even a friend.

Even a selfless, peerless friend like Hanekawa—has no right to meddle in how a person lives.

Though maybe in how a person dies…

"Roads," replied Hachikuji, "are just someplace to walk, as far as I'm concerned."

Uh-uh.

That's just the literal meaning of a road—I don't mean that, or I mean that too, but I was thinking about roads in a more conceptual sense.

"No, no, Mister Araragi. It's still the same. Roads are for walking." Hachikuji didn't budge in the face of my amended question. She just continued on with an amiable grin, as always. "A road, whatever road it might be, is a space that connects one place to another—wherever it begins, wherever it ends, that never changes. You wouldn't normally call a dead end a road, would you?"

In other words, continued Hachikuji.

"You can think, *What kind of road is this, anyway,* or *Where does this road lead to,* or *This road is unstable, it seems like it might collapse at any moment,* or *I'd like to be on a different road*—but there is one thing you mustn't do. The moment you break that taboo, the road ceases to be a road."

I asked Hachikuji, seasoned veteran of wandering lost, what this taboo act might be, and here's what she told me: "To stop walking."

Once you come to a stop, that place ceases to be a road.

002

"Oh, hello, Mister Enoughararaready."

"Come on, Hachikuji. Don't make it sound you're so fed up with our conversations that you've got tedium coming out your ears. My name is Araragi."

"My bad. A slip of the tongue."

"No it wasn't, you did it on purpose…"

"A tip of the slung."

"You telling me it wasn't on purpose?!"

Sometime in mid-June.

Right in the middle of the month.

I caught sight of Hachikuji while I was walking down the street as usual, and I addressed her just like always—and as usual, she mangled my name.

In a nasty way.

Enough already?

We haven't chatted enough for that. There's a chat deficit here.

Lemme chat with you some more.

"Please don't try to place the blame on me for mangling it. I was chatting away normally, but someone with an easily mangled name chanced to appear."

"Why are you separating your chatting from the fact of my appearance? They're inextricably linked. You didn't start chatting until after I showed up with my easily mangled name."

"And yet consider this, Mister Araragi. I frequently maul your name, but you've never once mangled mine. The situation here is that only your name is getting mauled. You're the one at fault here."

"Don't try to logic it into being my fault. There are a few steps missing from your reasoning. You're the one who mauls my name, so it's your fault."

"Well, you could certainly say that I maul so involved."

"Ha ha, very funny. You're the *only* one involved."

My mind flashed to how I might mangle Hachikuji's name—Hachikuji, Hachikuji, Hachikuji…

Dammit.

Pretty easy to say.

"So, Mister Araragi."

Switching gears.

Hachikuji asked me, "Where're you headed today?"

"As you can see, I'm off to school. I told you the other day, didn't I? I've class-changed from a worthless washout to a responsible high school student. So I'm going to school."

"Irresponsible students go to school too, though, don't they."

"Listen, Hachikuji. Don't underestimate my previous irresponsibility. Where do you think I was going these past two years while I was pretending to go to school?"

"Where were you going?"

"Shopping, at the mall."

"Pretty weak irresponsibility…"

"And since I didn't have any money, I was only window shopping."

"Are you an adult girl?"

Well. Leaving aside how weird the turn of phrase "adult girl" is, I must admit that in retrospect my behavior was puzzling.

I ran the risk of getting caught by a truant officer because I wanted to look at the shop windows so badly?

My experiences from that period didn't teach me a damn thing... They weren't beneficial to my life in any way.

"..."

But I don't think that was the point, I think I just didn't want to go to school back then—and being at home was rough, too.

So I was probably happy to be literally anywhere else—that alone must have made me feel like I'd been rescued.

From what, I have no idea.

But like I'd been rescued.

"Phew... My, my. What an airy way of escaping from reality. Surface-to-air evasion, I'd call it. I've always known you were hopeless, Mister Araragi, but I never imagined you were so hopeless."

"Hey, that's kind of harsh."

"Would you like me to call you Mister Sohopeless from now on?"

"Don't do me any favors! You're mangling my name so badly they'll have to identify it from dental records!"

"Not exactly a name to leave for posterity, though, is it?"

"I'm not interested in going down in history, but even if I were, I sure as hell wouldn't want it to be as Mister Sohopeless!"

Well.

"Surface-to-air evasion" just made it confusing, but an airy way of escaping from reality? She hit the nail on the head there—how can I put this, if I'd gone on like that, things might've gotten pretty bad by now.

A lot worse.

Than simply straying from the path...

In which case, meeting Hanekawa over spring break, meeting Shinobu.

Meeting Senjogahara—might have been a huge turning point in my life.

"Hmm, you may be right," Hachikuji conceded. "Walking down the road also means meeting people."

"Whoa. Did you just say something positive, Hachikuji?"

"Yes I did. It's true, meeting those people might have been the halfway point in your life."

"No, a turning point, not a halfway point! I'm too young to be over the hill!"

"Well, they say geniuses and fools die young."

"You're clearly lumping me in with the fools! Halfway point, my ass! I'm eighteen, which means I'd die when I'm thirty-six!"

"Hm, that was unexpected. Who knew you could do arithmetic."

"J-Just how incompetent do you think I am?"

Don't you know math is my forte?

It's the sole basis for my class-change from washout to college hopeful, the only guiding light.

"But you know, Mister Araragi. Mathematical aptitude or lack thereof aside, isn't it kind of amazing that everyone can do multiplication and division? Everybody ends up more or less getting the hang of it, but it's actually pretty advanced stuff."

"Now that you mention it...yeah, for sure. I don't know who decided it, or when, but whoever decided that kids would learn their times tables in second grade is kinda impressive."

In which case, maybe it isn't such a bad idea to teach kids in our country English when they're little.

"Well, before I can tackle my college entrance exams I've got to graduate from high school first. I may have told you this before, but that's why I'm still showing up for school. Impressive, huh? As impressive as whoever decided to teach kids multiplication in second grade."

"But everybody goes to school..."

"By virtue of which, Hachikuji, I don't have time to talk with you."

I'd been pushing my bicycle along as I walked in step with Hachikuji, but now I re-straddled it. My school-commuter granny bike. Then again, my non-commuter mountain bike got smashed to bits in an unforeseen accident the previous month, so the prefix "school-commuter" was no longer really necessary.

When you think about it, it's kind of odd to call it a granny bike when the rider isn't a granny... And why shouldn't grandma these days

94

ride, say, a monster bike?

"Fare thee well," I bade. "Be not downhearted. When you wish to see me again, I shall appear before you once more like a knight in shining armor."

"So this is goodbye forever?"

"What do you mean! Wish for it, already! To see me again!"

"I'll wince for it, maybe," Hachikuji said disgustedly.

Making no attempt to hide how put off she was that I'd put on airs.

Being loathed by a child can deal massive damage, and when I tried to start riding away, I missed the pedal completely.

Having blown my chance at a smooth exit, I thought—*Hmm, gotta turn this into some kind of opportunity. Was there something I wanted to tell Hachikuji?*

A-ha.

Got it.

I hadn't told her about that yet.

"Hey, Hachikuji."

"What is it, Mister Remainder-of-1."

"Remainder-of-1? What the hell is that, did you get my name wrong again? Or did you just divide 3 by 2?"

"Oh, don't worry, this time it wasn't a slip of the tongue. It's your new nickname, since you're the one who's most likely to be left over anytime people are picking teams."

"Most likely to be left over…"

Why does everyone and their mother want to give me these horrible nicknames?

"There's something I have to tell you," I forged ahead.

"What is it?"

"Oshino," I said. "Mèmè Oshino—that middle-aged expert, your benefactor. He left town."

It was just the other day.

He took off as suddenly as he'd shown up, and probably in some other town now, he was collecting tales of aberrations as he'd done here— while also looking after this or that hopeless guy, the kind who exist everywhere, in other words someone like me.

"I see… That was pretty abrupt, huh?"

"Well, yeah, it was definitely abrupt. He was a rootless vagabond to begin with, so from his perspective maybe he stayed here for a long time—oh, right, you never actually met him face to face, maybe you don't care that much… But it's not like you guys weren't connected. I figured I ought to tell you."

"Please, I do care. You can't even hold a candle to how much gratitude I feel towards that man."

"Being grateful is all very well, but do it without snubbing me along the way. I'm immensely grateful to him, too."

"No matter how much gratitude we express for Mister Moshino, it would never be enough."

"Moshino? If you're so grateful to him, don't make him sound like a phone booth where you can make wishes."

"If we're talking Moshimo Boxes, he's more like Doraemon's little sister Dorami's. All decked out."

"Decked out… Sheesh."

"Huh, so in any case, Mister Oshino's gone." Hachikuji must have said "Moshino" on purpose (not that it isn't on purpose when she mangles my name) because now she spoke his name normally, and nodded. "That spells trouble, though, doesn't it, Mister Araragi. How will you ever subsist without him?"

"Um, it's not like I'll be sleeping on the street just because Oshino left?!"

He hadn't been providing for me, or anything.

Sure, I may have leaned a little too hard on him regarding aberration-related matters—from now I was on my own.

We.

We had to walk our own road—standing on our own feet.

"Well, we might not end up homeless, but we'll miss him. Oh, but Mister Araragi, if he's gone, what about that issue?"

"That issue? Which issue?"

"Aaalways playing innocent. Aaalways getting up on your high horse. Aaalways keeping me on the edge of my seat. You're one hell of a teaaase."

"I can't even guess what kind of character you're trying to be…"

She rarely followed up with anything good when she was like this, and was preparing me for it—what was it this time?

"Oh, should I just leave it alone? Did I perhaps bring up a taboo subject? Am I touching on the dirty secrets of the Araragi industry?"

"The Araragi industry? What sort of insular field is that, I don't form such a thing. Come on, Hachikuji, out with it. This is unlike you."

"I'm not going to let anyone from the Araragi industry tell me what I'm like."

"Whether or not I should be defining what you're like is a fair question, but I'm not someone from the Araragi industry, okay? I'm Araragi, period."

"Ugh, this is what I'm talking about, this."

Hachikuji made a loop with her thumb and forefinger.

Good!

A-OK!

If that wasn't what she meant, she was making the sign for money.

"…?"

Well, I was pretty sure that's what her sudden gesture meant, but I still couldn't figure out what she was getting at. I didn't have any money (in either sense) coming to her…

Or did I need to cough up some dough to get her to talk with me? Did this grade-school girl operate like a hostess bar?

I needed to think twice about initiating a conversation with her?

"Uh oh," she said, "a flat reaction."

"No, I really don't see what you're getting at…"

"Ah, maybe I should put it this way then." Hachikuji dropped her candid hand gesture, and assuming the proper posture, spoke with proper etiquette. "Congratulations on skipping out on your five-million-yen bill."

"I didn't skip out on it!"

Ah.

Got it—there we go.

I had told Hachikuji before about how I owed Oshino five million yen—told her about it, or consulted her about it.

Maybe it's not the best idea to consult elementary school kids about your debts, but I wanted my relationship with Hachikuji to be one where I could talk to her about anything—and yet, I hadn't shared how things had turned out.

In other words, I hadn't found the chance to tell her that taking over an aberration-handling job from Oshino...or having the whole thing dumped in my lap happily resulted in the cancellation of my debt—I had to admit, having consulted her about it, I was amiss not to have informed her of the outcome.

But, believe it or not, Hachikuji's take was that Oshino had left town without getting his money from me.

Quite the idiosyncratic interpretation.

And how far-fetched—did she really think I was the kind of guy who'd skip out on a debt?

"Listen good, Hachikuji. I'm a guy who pays his debts."

"Well... That's a good attitude, but it's pretty standard."

What a normal reaction, after all that.

"I mean, don't borrow money you can't repay, right?"

"Wrong, Hachikuji. Debt essentially makes the world go round. Individuals and corporations are all smothered in debt. Credit cards, loans, collateral, all of them involve borrowing money from someone and then working your ass off to pay it back. How much debt do you think Japan carries?"

"When you put it that way, sure... But then the world is a sad place, isn't it?"

"It's not sad. Because a debt is basically just a promise. There's the trust that in the future, sometime in the future, you'll pay it back from the money you earn. In other words, it's the future and promises and trust that make the world go round."

"You make it sound so good..."

"Mm-hmm."

In between the future and promises and trust are dire straits, filled to the brim with human misery, but that's a secret.

It had been my lot until the other day.

If you include that, I guess it's the future and promises and trust and secrets that make the world go round—by the by, Senjogahara also took care of the fee she owed Oshino.

Unlike me, she ultimately paid it off with cash, not work—or out of the pocket money she received for helping her father out with his work, in lieu of a regular part-time gig.

I just kind of let it pass at the time, but exactly what sort of help do you perform to earn a hundred thousand yen in such a short time?

"Anyway, I took care of the money I owed Oshino. I'm squeaky clean, totally debt-free."

"A filthy mind in a squeaky-clean body, huh?"

"Nope, not filthy, my mind is not filthy. I believe in Santa Claus and everything."

"You do?"

"Yeah. He still brings me presents every year."

"You still get presents from Santa Claus even though you're in high school…"

"How do you like that, a squeaky-clean mind in a squeaky-clean body. The only other debt I have left is the three thousand yen I borrowed from my little sister."

"Three thousand yen? Pay it back already, please."

"It's my personal policy not to return something that doesn't need returning, even if it's just an email."

"No wonder you don't have any friends…"

I thought you were a guy who pays his debts, Hachikuji lamented with an exaggerated sigh.

Now that she mentioned it, I did vaguely recall having said something of the sort, but my conversations with Hachikuji are mostly about the vibe, so please understand that something said on one page is forgotten by the bottom of the next.

"I see," she said. "Either way, glad to hear the money's been paid back. Hmm, I'm a little disappointed."

"Huh? Why? You're disappointed about me paying Oshino back? Do you want me to be the kind of character who's always up to his ears in debt? Are you after my land or something?"

"And exactly where is this land, Mister Araragi? No—look, you said it yourself at some point."

"At some point? When?"

"When you were being stalked by your speedy junior. When you came to consult me—about owing Mister Oshino so much money and what to do about it. And while we were talking, you said something about how if you didn't have the scratch, you might be able to give him a rare aberration tale or something in place of money—didn't you?"

"Oh. I said all that?"

Well, I must have.

Back then, I was flustered because that "speedy junior" was stalking me, and to be honest my memory of the period is pretty unclear… But I do remember consulting Hachikuji about my debt, so it wouldn't be surprising if I'd said all that.

Though I very much doubt I used the word "scratch"…

"In other words," commented Hachikuji, "it would be like two CCG players exchanging rare cards."

"Well, that childish analogy may be all very well for an elementary school student, but it's somewhat divorced from reality…"

If we had to put it in terms of CCGs, it'd be like trading a rare card for cash, so her analogy wasn't particularly appropriate.

Nor was it something that kids should be doing at home.

"So ever since then, Mister Araragi, your humble servant has been keeping an eye out during her travels for any story that might fit the bill and be of help to you. 'Tales of aberrations' or 'ghost stories' or what have you."

"R-Really? Y-You've been doing that? For me?"

I was moved.

Moved by the friendship of Mayoi Hachikuji.

Who would have thought this girl in the prime of her cheekiness worried about my debts and tried to help me pay them back?

I had misjudged her.

I'd assumed she was just one more person who couldn't stand me…
This fifth grader was a wonder.

"Such an industrious spouse!"

"That's a strange way to put it, Mister Araragi."

"Such an industrial space!"

"I wasn't planning on getting involved in factory production for your
sake, Mister Araragi—but in any event, I've been conducting this secret
activity on your behalf. Now that it's come to nothing, though, I'm kind
of disappointed."

"Yeah…stands to reason."

"My disappointment is on par with the Three Great Disappointing
Landmarks of Japan."

"It can't be that bad. And what the hell are you even talking about?"

"Famous landmarks that aren't as disappointing as you thought they
would be, which is itself a disappointment."

Ah well, said Hachikuji.

"I went to all this trouble to find a story, but now my plan to sell it to
you for an astronomical sum is ruined."

"Plan?! Astronomical sum?! Y-You weren't just going to give it to me?!
It wasn't a present for Mister Araragi?!"

"Not a chance," she said, sounding vexed. "What 'present for Mister
Araragi'? Stick to getting your presents from Santa Claus, thank you very
much. If I were to give you something, it'd be a presentation on how to
be a stand-up guy."

"A harsh one, I bet…"

Wait, this was vaguely terrifying, when I thought about it.

So basically, she'd been trying to sell me an aberration tale… If she'd
been roaming the town since then on that mission, the girl's obsession
with money was not to be taken lightly.

On a mission? More like on commission.

No, maybe it wasn't about the money. Had this girl just been looking
forward to driving me even deeper into debt?

What a close call.

Good thing I got a handy job from Oshino before that could happen.

"Ouch," she said, "seriously, I'm in a pickle here. I laid out a ton of money on spec for this. What am I going to do with this aberration tale I hunted down so I could flip it to you, Mister Araragi?"

"Don't ask me."

Here we were feeling the effects of Oshino's disappearance. If he were still in town, we could probably have gotten at least a little something for the aberration tale Hachikuji had found, even though I'd already paid him back what I owed. But with Oshino's Aberration Mart closed for business, there was no one in town who'd be interested in doing business around urban legends and the word on the street.

Hmmm.

Market speculation isn't a game for greenhorns... A cautionary tale.

"Mister Araragiiii, I won't ask for five million, just buy it pleeease. Go ahead, drive a hard bargaaain. Do you really want to make me feel like I've done all that work for nothing? For another obedient child to disappear from this world, replaced by a jaded kid?"

"I don't care if you're jaded or not. The second you tried to sell your friend a ghost story, you were already plenty jaded."

Although.

Her faux-nefarious, or flagrantly nefarious speech aside, it wasn't an out-and-out lie that Hachikuji had gone to some trouble on my behalf, so maybe I shouldn't let her feel like it was all a waste of time.

It'd be detrimental to her upbringing, sure, but if she internalized the lesson that "any more work I do on Mister Araragi's behalf will also be pointless," my prospects might also be somewhat dimmed.

This kid might come in handy for me somewhere down the line, so going easy on her right now might actually be a good move.

"Uh oh, are you concocting some devious scheme, Mister Araragi?"

"Excuse me? I'm just continuing to be moved by your friendship."

"You're certainly being moved for a long time... Got stuck on the *moved* setting, huh. Are you emotionally unbalanced, Mister Araragi?"

"By the by, how much were you hoping to get for it, Ebenezer

Hachikuji?"

"Fifty yen would be plenty."

"That's a steal!"

I was sure she'd try to haggle for more.

Maybe I was getting the friend discount?

"No, the story was never worth more than that in the first place."

"You were trying to pass off a fifty-yen story on your friend for five million?!"

That's not a friend, not even close!!

That's a sucker!!

"Gimme a break, Hachikuji… We don't want people thinking that conning me is as easy as taking candy from a baby."

"Babies shouldn't have any in the first place, they might choke."

"Isn't that sweet. The candy I mean, not you."

I felt around in my pocket and took out a fifty-yen coin that happened to be there. If it had been a hundred-yen coin, I would've said keep the change, but tough luck, Mayoi Hachikuji.

"So, what's the story? Let's hear it."

"Right. Um, it's a story about sand."

"Sand?"

"Right. Well sand or—oh, but before I get to that, may I ask you something?"

"Hm? What."

"It's about Mister Oshino taking off… Now that he's left the cram school, what's become of this vampire I keep hearing rumors about? This newfound lost child, Miss Shinobu Oshino? I doubt Mister Oshino took her along with him…"

"Ah, well, she's—"

I looked down at my shadow as I spoke.

My deep, dark, pitch-black shadow.

"Sorry, if I stay to hear your story, I'm already barely going to slip in under the bell as it is."

I'll tell you next time, I dodged.

003

Hachikuji had said "sand," but more specifically it was a "sandbox"—the sandbox in a certain small park.

It wasn't the same one where I'd first encountered Hachikuji. True, apart from parks where I'd played as a child, they all pretty much seemed the same to me. But unlike the one where I'd met Hachikuji, the one with the name I couldn't read, the smallish grounds of this park were packed with a wide variety of playground equipment including a seesaw, a jungle gym, and monkey bars.

And of course, a sandbox.

It was at the bottom of the slide—though the slide was just a slide, and the sandbox was, in that sense, nothing but an ordinary sandbox, nothing strange or clever about its construction.

That only went for the design of this sandbox, however—there was definitely, as Hachikuji had said, something abnormal about the *sand*.

An abnormal phenomenon.

A bizarre phenomenon.

That may sound like an exaggeration—but if you'd suddenly been shown this in the middle of the night, if you'd witnessed it, I guarantee you'd be shaken up.

"Yeah, I was all shook up," Hachikuji had said. "Or do I mean shook down."

"Someone robbed you?"

"I shook it off."

"You should've been shaking in your boots."

Sandwiched though it'd been between our playful banter—Hachikuji's explanation had been, largely, clear and comprehensible. She has yet to contract Senjogahara's disease of feeling the need to attack me with literally every other word.

Though she's bound to catch it before long...

Once they've taken hold, diseases like that are almost impossible to fully cure, so prevention is the key.

The first bell had already rung by the time she'd finished telling her story, but I'd managed to slip into the classroom before the final bell. After that I lived the life of the diligent student for six hours or so, and after *that*, on the way home from studying for finals at Senjogahara's house, I headed to the park that Hachikuji had told me about.

It was nighttime.

The dead of night, you might say.

Hachikuji didn't actually know the name of the park, and I didn't see anything like a sign when I entered—still, as soon as I saw the sandbox in question, there was no longer any doubt in my mind that she'd meant this park. Like they say, seeing is believing.

It was obvious at a glance.

That this was the sandbox.

"Seeing is believing, but I can't be leaving just yet..."

Despite the darkness, I had my vampiric sight, or its after-effects—and they were serving me well now. It was as if I'd been fitted with a high-res night vision scope.

As far as I could tell from looking through it—some kind of "picture" had been drawn on the surface.

Had been drawn, or.

Had emerged.

106

I don't know, this might sound ironic, coming from someone who was only seeing it thanks to the after-effects of being a vampire—but it looked downright demonic.

A monstrous portrait.

As if the sand itself—were an aberration.

"What was it that Oshino said...the simulacrum phenomenon? How people can end up seeing human faces in anything..."

Sure, I got that.

But what about when it's a demon's face instead of a human's? Well, okay, spirit photography, provided it's not done with CG, is mostly some incidental combination of light and shadow, or haze, or dirt, which just ends up looking "that way"... Hachikuji had been walking around looking for a bizarre and mysterious phenomenon to sell me—and under those circumstances you might very well see something mysterious in the topography of a perfectly normal sandbox.

Perhaps, having heard her story, I had a preconceived notion of what I'd find—and ended up getting the same impression.

The stone statue back in April.

The bouquets back in May.

They'd been more or less like that—so it made sense to suspect this, too, was such a case. But only if Hachikuji and I had at least seen the sandbox on the same day.

This wasn't a stone statue or a bouquet of flowers.

Each individual grain of sand may have solid form, but sand as a whole is a shifting mass—was it really possible for us to see the same "demonic face" on different days?

Not to mention sweet nothings written by lovers on the beach, basically all it takes is a gust of wind for sand to change its shape. That's why sandboxes are great places for kids to play.

Surely, in the almost half a month between when Hachikuji saw this demon "drawn" on the surface and today, when I came to check it out, a parade of kids had played in this sandbox.

Making mountains, tunneling through those mountains, digging holes...or perhaps calling on all the skill at their command to construct a castle.

Could a sandbox, having undergone all that—really display an identical aspect to me as it had to her? It meant that whatever changes had been wrought upon it, however much it had been moved around and turned over, the sand contained in this sandbox—shifted back into a demon.

A remonstrating monster.

As if the sand had—a will of its own.

"Was there any kind of sand aberration? The Sand-Throwing Hag? Though in that case the hag is the monster, not the sand..."

He wasn't a monster, but I did recall a relevant superman from the *Kinnikuman* manga called Sunshine—even so, I very much doubted this sand was about to take on human form and suddenly attack me.

And yet, I'd almost died twice at the hands of aberrations recently... The mere thought set off alarm bells.

"..."

Well.

Having confirmed that the info Hachikuji sold me for fifty yen wasn't bogus, what now? Not that I came here just out of curiosity.

If there really was a threat, I couldn't just leave it alone, if for no other reason than that it was in a public park—it was the kind of thing that doesn't bother you if you don't know about it, but now that I did, I could spare at least a little time to look into it. Ridding myself of a bizarre worry simply by stopping by on my walk home from Senjogahara's for a few minutes would be a dream come true.

...Maybe not a dream come true.

Man, my vocabulary is pretty weak.

Anyway, unlike my disagreeable little sisters, I'm not the kind of person who goes around intentionally looking for trouble, but when trouble sideswipes me, I can't just let it be.

Such a dicey, or...

Enigmatic sandbox which, worst case scenario, might curse the children who play in it, was no laughing matter—if I were going to look into it, I'd better do it right away.

Though a high schooler playing in a sandbox in a deserted public park at a time that could be called "the dead of night" might seem even dodgier than an aberration.

"That said...it's probably just someone's idea of a prank. Someone like, for instance, a high schooler playing in a sandbox in a deserted park in the dead of night."

When I actually put it into words, this supposed prankster struck me as a pretty far-fetched character, but if you left out the high schooler part, it didn't seem like an impossible explanation. In fact, it seemed pretty plausible. Drawing a face on the surface of the sandbox to scare away kids who were trying to play there...or no, maybe it wasn't a prank.

Maybe it was the work of their so-called guardians.

Some parents don't want their children playing in places like sandboxes, where their clothes and hands will get dirty. Maybe they made this "drawing" to keep their kids away from the sandbox, to scare them, to frighten them off... And even if they weren't so high-strung, there was always the possibility that it was just a question of supervising the park at night.

Like how Naoetsu High put bouquets on the roofs—to keep people away...nope.

I promised Senjogahara I'd forget about that whole thing. I shouldn't be remembering it here.

That aside, chances were this was a man-made phenomenon—not to parrot Oshino's oft-stated frustration with everyone blaming aberrations every time something goes wrong, but when something does happen, it makes the most sense to accept whatever explanation seems to be, on the whole, most likely.

When something goes down, blaming humans rather than aberrations will yield a much higher success rate—though coming from someone who's still saddled with the after-effects of having been a vampire, that sounds somehow supercilious, or weirdly pompous, or just unconvincing.

After all, ever since Hachikuji had told me, I'd harbored my fair share of doubts about this "sand," even before getting here.

"Now then..."

With that, I got into the sandbox. For a moment I debated taking off my shoes, but I'm pretty sure there's no rule about having to go barefoot in the sandbox.

Mmmm.

My investigation had a serious goal, but my inner child couldn't help being stimulated... Since the beginning of middle school—or even the last year of elementary school, boxes of sand have essentially only been for doing the long jump, not for playing.

This return to childhood made me want to try sliding down the slide into the sandbox, but that was taking the merrymaking too far.

I could think of excuses for investigating a sandbox, but it'd be a catastrophe if anyone saw me swooshing down into it.

Why were you doing that?! they'd ask.

It was an aberration, an aberration made me do it! I'd answer.

And in that case, it wouldn't be the police station they would haul me off to...

"...Hm."

I squatted in the center and gingerly scooped up some sand. The demonic face had gotten messed up the moment I set foot in the sandbox, but now I helped it along further.

I called it investigating, but I was destroying the object of study. Then again, I couldn't hope to match Oshino's armchair omniscience.

Carrying out any kind of Nondestructive Examination was off the table.

In detective novels, they always say that preserving the scene exactly as it was is fundamental to investigations, but a layman can't be expected to do it without disturbing things...

"Seems like normal sand. True, I'm no expert when it comes to sand..."

Ordinary sand from a sandbox in a public park.

In fact, thanks to me "playing in the sand" under the guise of an investigation, the "demonic face" or whatever had disappeared without a trace—and was failing, of course, to revert to its original form in an instant, or anything like that.

"…"

As a test, I formed a small mound.

I thought maybe if I played in the sandbox like a child, there'd be some sort of "reaction"—but there wasn't.

A shabby little mound of sand took shape, that's all.

After a minute or so lost in thought, I knocked it over and smoothed it back the way it had been. Then, brushing the sand off my hands, I stepped out of the sandbox—and once outside, I noticed that even though I hadn't played, er, investigated all that vigorously, my shoes were filled with sand.

Not just sand, anything made up of tiny grains will get in every-where, no matter what you do… Taking off my shoes, I shook them one at a time, dumping the sand back into the sandbox.

Thanks to my vigorous trampling, it looked like an ordinary sand-box—but once I saw it in that state, I realized just how difficult it was to recreate that "demon."

Even making a little mound was harder than I thought—never mind making, transforming, the whole sandbox into a face, demonic or other-wise. You needed to be able to grasp the whole sandbox as a canvas, or…

To put it simply, it required some modicum of painterly ability. Though I guess it was three-dimensional, so a sculptor-ly ability?

At any rate, it was an impossible task for a guy like me who couldn't even construct a decent shed. Perhaps one of the parents, or pranksters, who lived nearby had a flair for the fine arts…

Actually, was it done as an art project in the first place? Maybe it wasn't just here, maybe the sandboxes in all the parks, up to and includ-ing Unpronounceable Park, were inscribed with similar pieces of art. The sandbox would be an odd medium to choose, but that very transience might make it art—I didn't get that way of thinking, but I did get that it existed. About as well as I got writing sweet nothings amid the breakers at the seashore, at least…

Although it was night, I cast a shadow in the moonlight. I looked at that shadow—just a shadow, and muttered, "Well, if I can play in this

111

sandbox without incident, vampiric after-effects and all—then it seems like there's no urgent issue here."

I couldn't help sounding like I was looking for reassurance. I knew perfectly well there'd be no reaction, but I just had to.

Even knowing there'd be no response, I'd continue addressing my shadow anyway.

"Honestly, it doesn't speak highly of whoever's doing it—whether it's a prank, or art, or a parent over-parenting, but I don't think I need to intervene, or interfere. It's not like I can get involved at the drop of a hat every time there's an aberration, so the work of a human being?"

With that, I put the park in my rearview mirror.

Calling it a mistake might be a little too hard on myself—but if there was a mistake I made here, it was assuming that if something wasn't the work of an aberration, it had to be a man-made phenomenon—and conversely, that if something wasn't a man-made phenomenon, it had to be the work of an aberration.

If this assumption had reached Oshino's ears—I'm sure he would've laughed it off, as always.

Though.

Who knows—maybe he would've scolded me.

004

"Tut!"

"..."

Oshino may or may not have scolded me, but Hanekawa did, unambiguously.

Tut!

I hadn't been scolded in that way since kindergarten... It happened right after I got home from the park.

I got a phone call from Hanekawa.

Currently, not one but two model students, Senjogahara and Hanekawa, were helping me with my studies, which made me extremely lucky. Since Senjogahara had been on duty that day and our work had been successfully concluded, I had no idea why Hanekawa was calling me—but ignoring a call from my great benefactor was hardly an option, so I answered it.

"Hello?"

"Hey, Araragi? Sorry for calling so late—it's just, something's been on my mind. Is now an okay time?"

"Sure, now's fine..."

Actually, I wanted to wash off the dirt from the sandbox, but I'm not enough of a clean freak to put off Hanekawa in favor of a shower.

"I just received Senjogahara's regular report…"

"Regular report?! What the hell?!"

It sounded terrifying!

Wait, so, after our study sessions, Senjogahara reported to Hanekawa about how it went? A debriefing about whether or not I was studying properly?

Gaaah…

A serious lack of faith…

"Oh, no, this wasn't for the Araragi Rehabilitation Program, it had more to do with the Senjogahara Rehabilitation Program—but forget about it."

"Um, is that really a *forget about it* kind of an it?"

"In any case, I happened to catch that you were planning to investigate the sand at a certain park on your way home, Araragi… You finished with that? I tried to call when you'd be done."

"…"

Her ears are a little too sharp, and her timing was dead on. And she doesn't beat around the bush. If it were me, I would've waited until tomorrow—we'd see each other at school.

Frankly, I didn't think it was worth telling Hanekawa—though I was perfectly willing to, if she wanted to hear about it.

I'm not Hachikuji, so I didn't demand money for the story, of course. Compared to Hanekawa's free tutoring, it barely amounted to anything.

I reported the findings of my sandbox investigation.

I didn't embellish the story much, but I did leave out the reawakening of my inner child and my desire to slide down the slide. No harm done by a few small omissions.

Whether or not I left my inner child out of it, Hanekawa treated me very much like a little kid when she scolded:

"Tut!"

Scolded, or reprimanded, maybe.

What's she think I am?

"No good, Araragi."

"Huh? Sure, I know I'm no good, but you'd just come out and say so? Sugarcoat it."

"No, I wasn't saying 'no-good Araragi'—what you did was no good…"

Your persecution complex is in overdrive, she accused.

Sure, fair enough.

Though maybe it was more of an inferiority complex than a persecution complex.

"But what do you mean, what I did was no good? What's bothering you, anyway? You said you had something on your mind…"

"Yeah. I figured you'd take care of things, so I thought I'd settle for an after-action report."

"After-action report…"

Who the hell was she, receiving reports from Senjogahara, receiving reports from me.

Our commanding officer or something?

"Wait, then what did I do wrong? I'm pretty sure I did just about everything I could. I envisioned the worst-case scenario, and performed a scrupulous investigation, okay?"

"Mm-hmm, you sure did. Playing in the sand, building a mound."

"…"

I'd left that out of it…

Had something in my "report" tipped her off? Apparently, since she sounded so sure of it.

Once again, talking to her is freaky.

I feel like she sees through me, though from a different angle than Oshino.

"Mm. Mmmm, you've overlooked something important, Araragi. You made an erroneous assumption."

"Assumption?"

"You're assuming the sandbox case has to be either the work of an aberration—or a man-made phenomenon. Correct?"

"Yeah, now that you mention, I guess I am, but…what, is there

115

another possibility?"

Hanekawa hadn't even seen the sand arranged in the shape of a demonic face with her own eyes, she'd only heard about it from Senjogahara, so how could she talk like she knew exactly what was going on—and Senjogahara had only heard an incredulous version of Hachikuji's fifty-yen tale from me, before I'd even seen the real thing. As with the reawakening of my inner child—how could Hanekawa be so sure?

"There is. Another possibility. A third possibility."

"Damn, there is? You really do know everything, don't you?"

Ordinarily I say this line with a sense of admiration, but I can't deny that just this once there was a little bit of irony mixed in there as well.

Despite my shameful pettiness, Hanekawa treated me to her usual response. "I don't know everything, I just know what I know."

This left me feeling utterly benign and coolheaded—which is no great feat, I have to admit. Hanekawa had me eating out of her hand.

Maybe it was thanks to the Rehabilitation Program or whatever.

"A third option… Neither the work of an aberration nor the work of a human being, so, um… Let's see." I thought it over inside my newly cooled head. It felt somehow like an extension of my exam prep. "Well, a process of elimination just leaves something like a natural phenomenon, I guess… Maybe the air flow in the park and the position of the slide are such that a face could form by happenstance…"

I said this exactly as it occurred to me, but even as I was saying it, I knew it was nonsense.

Or rather, the nature-as-culprit theory was pretty much the first one you'd consider, and just as quickly, dismiss—a crevice between two buildings was one thing, but no way the wind would be uniform in an open, unobstructed space like a park.

Even supposing the shape didn't form all the time, Hachikuji and I had visited the park on totally random days—hard to believe the parameters just so happened to line up perfectly.

I'd only said it as conversation filler, and I girded my loins for Hanekawa's cursory dismissal.

Perhaps another *Tut!*

Was I making a foolish remark on purpose, hoping for another one of those? I want to believe that I'm not that big of a fool—but if I was, my faint hopes were about to be dashed.

"Bingo, sounds like you're on the right track, Araragi. No need for me to get involved, then."

"Huh? No, hang on, you can't just bail on me like that. Don't back out now. It's still your job to explain to me what that actually means."

"Why's it my job..."

"I mean, a natural phenomenon? The sand just happened to end up that way because of the wind or whatever? Impossible—"

Even as I spoke, I thought: *This is what they mean by "better left unsaid."* Hanekawa not picking up on a problem, when I did? Maybe it's just my inferiority complex talking again, but...

No, putting that aside.

Even if the "demonic form" were the result of a natural phenomenon, the most placid "solution" here, why would Hanekawa want to scold me for dismissing the possibility out of hand and making my assumption?

Could the Rehabilitation Program really be that strict? Was it a Spartan style of education that punished even the slightest moment of carelessness?

That was my fear, but it was misguided.

Because Hanekawa was quite justified in scolding me.

"Come on, Araragi. Wind and rain aren't the only natural phenomena."

"Huh?"

005

The epilogue, or maybe, the punch line of this story.

After that I returned to the park to confirm the "solution" Hanekawa suggested—and obviously, I mean this goes without saying, but her deduction was right on the money.

"Listen, Araragi. You keep saying that you checked out the sandbox—but it was just the sand you checked out, wasn't it?" That's what she said. "A sandbox—also includes the *container* the sand is in."

The container?

Even after she said it, it didn't click right away—and this usually ends up driven to the periphery of our thoughts on the subject, but of course, in order to keep it from mixing with the soil around it, the "sand" in a "sandbox," unlike the sand on a beach, is surrounded by a container that is, for lack of a better analogy, like a swimming pool that's been partially buried in the ground.

If you kept digging down into a sandbox, at some point you would reach the "bottom"—but a sandbox is surprisingly deep, so children sometimes believe that it's bottomless or that it simply melds into the soil around them.

That's how sandboxes are generally constructed, anyway, and once it's pointed out—or once you think about it for a second, it all makes sense.

"So Araragi, if you're investigating a sandbox but didn't investigate the box itself, it doesn't really count as investigating the sandbox. And—" Hanekawa's tone became somewhat severe. "Sand is heavy."

Even sand with nothing unusual about it.

That's what she said—which is how I found myself at the sandbox in question, digging a hole with a shovel I'd brought.

Digging hurriedly, but cautiously.

And at last, after an excavation of about two feet, I reached the bottom.

Where—there was an enormous crack.

An enormous.

Crack.

"…"

Now it all made sense.

Because the bottom of the "sandbox" was ruptured, probably from a combination of age and the weight of the sand (as Hanekawa had pointed out), the surface settled into *that shape*—appeared to be the solution to the mystery.

Just as water conforms to the shape of a vessel, so too does sand—though it takes much longer and the process is less obvious than it is with water.

Which is why the sand didn't "revert" immediately after children played there, or immediately after I kicked it all over the place in the course of my investigation—but it would "revert" over time.

Almost as if it had a will of its own.

Taking on a shape that reflected the topography of the bottom of its container.

And, as predicted, the demonic form was probably pure happenstance—thanks to the simulacrum phenomenon or what, I don't know.

But it was just as Hanekawa said—the deterioration of the container, and the weight of the sand, being neither man-made nor aberration-related, were indeed natural phenomena, yet not at all placid ones.

The most placid solution, this was not—far from it.

Natural phenomena, though not wind and rain.

Up to this point, it's natural phenomena—and it would be natural phenomena *from here on out* as well.

As of now, those phenomena's effect was limited to a strange pattern appearing on the surface of the sand, but if the fissure in the container continued to grow, then the sandbox really might become bottomless—sand and earth mingling until they turned into quicksand, or to the point of liquification...not on a scale that would pose a problem for an adult, perhaps, but one that might prove fatal for any children playing in the sandbox.

Who might be swallowed up.

As if by a bottomless swamp.

Even if that was the worst-case scenario, playing in a sandbox whose container was broken was a dangerous thing to do—dangerous enough that at this point, it was a race against time.

Which is why Hanekawa had scolded me.

"So, for now...a call to the management company that oversees the park?"

No, it was probably the town that oversaw the park, not a private company... Well, if I contacted the all-knowing Hanekawa, she could tell me.

Then at last we'd be leaving this case behind.

But seriously... I thought, looking at the hole I had dug. *Maybe that whole debate misses the mark. Aberrations are more frightening than human beings, human beings are more frightening than aberrations—that debate entirely missed the mark.*

More frightening and less placid than human agency or any aberration...is nature.

As scary as a demon, as scary as people.

CHAPTER FOUR
KOYOMI WATER

SUN	MON	TUE	WED	THU	FRI	SAT
						1
2	3	4	5	6	7	8
9	10	11	12	13	14	15
16	17	18	19	20	21	22
23	24	25	26	27	28	29
30	31					

7
July

001

I bet Suruga Kanbaru thinks of a road as a place for running rather than walking—given that she runs full-tilt down whatever road she's on, no matter the circumstances, regardless of wind or weather. In fact, this junior of mine seems to have a hard time even slowing down, let alone proceeding at anything like a leisurely pace.

A hard time, yeah.

Hardly her forte.

But even though she's always hoofing it at top speed, maybe it's not so much that a fast pace is her specialty, especially, but rather that a slow pace is so difficult for her to maintain that it's out of her hands—though not so difficult that she's bound hand and foot.

In fact, Kanbaru, who has no qualms about embarking on a wild goose chase, probably never even considers taking a leisurely stroll—anyway, a road.

Not trod but raced down.

Ever since she became a star, garnering the attention of the entire school—and even now, having lost none of her luster even after quitting the basketball team, Kanbaru has been in possession of a roadmap depicting an altogether different route from my own.

"Hm. A road—isn't how I think of it, Araragi-senpai."

This was her response when I broached the subject one time. As always, she looked directly at me when she spoke.

"When running is a part of everyday life like it is for me, the place where you run isn't a road, it's a track."

A track?

Sure, that's definitely what you'd call the "road" where the runners run in track-and-field—for a guy like me, though, whose everyday life does not involve running, for whom running is a big deal, calling it a "track" didn't sit well.

How can I put this?

Doesn't "track" strongly suggest an absolute, fixed route from which you can't deviate?

"What? I'm surprised at you, Araragi-senpai. Even when it means 'street,' a road is still fixed, something you can't deviate from. If you just up and move into the next lane, you'll cause an accident. Changing lanes is never a simple matter, no matter what road you're on."

True.

"Street" or "track," it's merely a question of context, nothing more than semantics.

In practice, whether you're running or walking.

Whether it's a street or a track, a road is a road.

People talk about a life where "the roadmap is already laid out for you," but since everyone is traveling down the road of life, we're all following some set of rules.

Obeying some set of traffic regulations.

It's not so easy to drop out of the race—to deviate from the fixed path. Changing lanes is all well and good, but you have to be careful, or you might drive straight off a cliff.

And there's always the possibility of a head-on collision.

So we have no choice but to keep chugging along down the road.

"Well, that said," qualified Kanbaru, "dropping out isn't actually all that hard—the truth is, even if you don't stray out of your lane, you can still drop out. Going full-tilt down the road, down the track, is certainly 'chugging along,' but it doesn't necessarily mean you're 'moving forward'—people can 'chug along backwards' too."

They can and do, she said.

"Because every route comes with an escape route."

002

"Kanbaru. Hey, jackass, you haven't been listening to a word I say."

"What? Araragi-senpai, as your junior it makes my heart go pitter-pat to hear you call me 'jackass,' but it's also upsetting to have such a charge leveled at me. The very idea that I, Suruga Kanbaru, hailed as the world's greatest devotee of the world's greatest Araragi-senpai, could possibly not listen to what he has to say is completely out of the question. A total fantasy. Get a grip, Araragi-senpai. Do you have any idea how much consternation you could cause with such careless remarks?"

"No remark of mine could cause the slightest consternation, even if I wanted it to. And no one's hailing you for that, trust me. Listen, Kanbaru. Out of consideration for you as my junior, I'll repeat what I said, since you were most definitely not listening. I'm gonna repeat after me."

One day in July.

I was standing in a hallway of Kanbaru's house—a Japanese-style home, which I was visiting on my day off. To be precise, I had no choice but to stand in the hallway, like I was being punished for arriving late to school.

Naturally I'd done no such thing; I'd shown up at her house on time, at the appointed hour.

I was forced to stand there because I simply couldn't enter the room to which she'd led me—so to be precise, I wasn't standing in the hallway so much as I was standing aghast in the hallway.

"All right, Kanbaru. Listen good."

"I already am. I never miss a single word that comes from the wise lips of the great orator Araragi-senpai. My only fear is that I'll become so overcome with emotion at what I hear that I'll faint."

"…I asked you to take me to your room."

Choosing for the moment to ignore her tiresome habit of putting me on a pedestal, I pointed at the room—through the open sliding door, at the interior.

"I never asked you to take me to the storage."

Messy.

Didn't even begin to describe the room's interior—to put it simply, it wasn't just cluttered horizontally, but cluttered vertically. No, like I said, it was more than messy—it was chock full. The total chaos in the room wasn't just a question of area, we're taking about volume here…

"Storage? How rude. There are some things that even Araragi-senpai shouldn't say." Kanbaru grinned smugly. "Though that doesn't happen to be one of them."

"So you don't mind having your room described that way…"

Well, to be honest, I did hold back in calling it the storage—my actual inclination was to call it a trash compactor.

I was starting to wonder if a place like the Kanbaru residence might actually have a trash compactor in it.

Or maybe it was more like a junkyard—piles of scrap metal towering menacingly overhead…

The room somehow seemed to be maintaining this precarious, not to say miraculous, state of balance, but if I impatiently stamped my foot, there might just be a teensy-weensy little avalanche out into the hall—where I therefore continued to stand aghast, not moving a muscle.

"…"

Suruga Kanbaru.

My strange bond with the former ace of the Naoetsu High basketball team, a second-year, had begun at the end of May—she'd been cronies with Senjogahara back in middle school, which also helped bring us closer together.

Our relationship isn't actually so simple that such a simple explanation could explain it, though—if I can expand on the subject a little without derailing the story, she also got involved with an aberration, same as me, or more than me—and the vestiges of that remain in her left arm.

Wrapped up in a bandage.

Hidden under a bandage.

That said, if you forget about all that stuff, or even if you don't, at this point Suruga Kanbaru had become my darling junior. Though for someone with no redeeming qualities, a total washout like myself, to refer to a superstar athlete (even a retired one) as "darling" might be overstepping my bounds...

The superlative athlete part aside, however, she was also an undeniably debauched and undisciplined woman.

For example, as we're seeing, Suruga Kanbaru "didn't pick up after herself"—the unvarnished truth is that she was a "slob."

A chaoslob.

The first time I was shown into her room, I looked to the heavens for strength and promised that I'd find a time to come back and do a thorough cleanup. It hadn't been all that long ago, but now that I'd found that time and actually come to clean up, the room was in such a state that I couldn't even see the ceiling, let alone the heavens.

I'm no slouch when it comes to cleaning and organizing, in fact I can't relax unless things are nice and orderly, but to be honest, in this case I didn't even know where to begin.

I was frankly at a loss as to how to restore order to this storage of a room—the garbage bags I'd brought from home seemed laughably insufficient.

Ten 45-gallon bags.

What could I possibly accomplish with them? They'd be no use at all. What I needed wasn't garbage bags but cardboard boxes. Though if it was cardboard boxes I wanted, this storage seemed a likely enough place to find some…

"Keheheh. So, how will Araragi-senpai go about cleaning up this room? Show me what you've got."

"Get off your high horse."

"High? Not at all. More like subterranean."

"Terrifying. A voice from underground telling me to 'show me what you've got'… Sounds like the series is heading into a whole new stage. Listen, you knew I was coming to clean up, so you crammed your room full of all the trash from every other room in the house just to fuck with me, didn't you?"

One way to take care of the housekeeping, I guess.

Consolidate all the boxes and useless crap in one room, then clean all the other rooms one at a time. Seems kind of inefficient, like it'd end up requiring twice as much effort, but it would lower the difficulty level of the actual cleaning.

"What a thing to say, Araragi-senpai. Now you're just showering me with accusations. Though I'm overjoyed to be showered with anything by you, be it praise."

"I'd feel so stupid praising such a girl…"

"This is the only room I've got. I'm not the kind of spoiled rich kid who's always been allowed multiple rooms. This is my one and only room."

"Yeah? Well, thank god for small favors."

"Yup. Just as Araragi-senpai is my one and only senpai."

"That's a lot of pressure!"

What about Senjogahara!

How can you call someone you only met a couple of months ago your only senpai in the world? I haven't done anything to deserve that from you, and I probably never will.

"Wait a minute, though…I mean, it doesn't make sense. With your room like this, where the hell do you sleep?"

"Here in my room, where else?" Kanbaru cocked her head, puzzled. "The only places I would lay my head are this room, Senjogahara-senpai's lap, and your outstretched arm, Araragi-senpai."

"I don't know about Senjogahara's lap, but my arm's no pillow, and this room seems like a no-go too... You can't even get inside, can you?"

"An amateur like yourself might think so," Kanbaru casually insulted her honored senpai—I'd love to learn to be so insensitive, even if it's from my junior.

Well, if she wanted to call me an amateur, I'd ask her to spell it out for me. I'm certainly not an expert—in anything.

"Okay then, let's hear it. How do you manage to sleep in this room?"

The renowned polymath and genius Leonardo da Vinci is said to have slept standing up—shocking if true, but did Kanbaru do something along those lines? She was something of a genius when it came to sports, at least...and yet, it seemed impossible for anyone, even a genius, to so much as stand up in that room, let alone sleep...

"Heheheh. Now I've seen everything, Araragi-senpai. I never expected to live long enough to see the day when I could be the one to teach *you* something."

"You're only seventeen, plus we haven't even known each other for a hundred days..."

She was already seeing the day, more like.

"Now quit putting on airs and tell me already. How do you sleep? If the punch line is that you sleep in the hall, I'm gonna kick your ass."

"I wish that *was* the punch line. Boy, I'd love to get my ass kicked by you. I'd love to get a hall-slam instead of a wall-slam from you."

"What's a hall-slam?"

I mean, I get slamming your hand against a wall, like in a rom-com...

Geez.

We'd been talking all this time, and I still hadn't set foot inside Kanbaru's room.

We're going to run out of tape before the intro's even over.

"Are we talking about breakfast at Denny's or something? A fluffy, buttermilk hall with two eggs, sausage *and* bacon on the side?"

"Hm. Well, anything's possible, I guess there could be a hallway you'd want to slather with maple syrup, but… Let's see, you were asking how I sleep, right? Okay, Araragi-senpai. Please, look. See that opening over there?"

Kanbaru pointed into her room.

Sure enough, there was an opening, or a cave dug out of the sheer cliff face…a kind of air pocket, I guess you might say, created by the precarious balance of the piled boxes.

"Sure, but what about it? You can't possibly be telling me that you sleep in that crevice like a mole or something."

"Oh, but I can. If I get a running start in the hallway and do a Fosbury flop, I can get myself in there."

Kanbaru puffed out her chest like she was proud. Arching her back like she was doing a Fosbury flop… But leaping backwards into a place like that rather than a mattress or a sandbox could cause the kind of grievous injury that would require immediate medical attention…

No need to bend over backwards just to sleep in your room.

If it's that much of a pain in the ass, sleep in the hall.

"No, no, Araragi-senpai. The speed with which you come to conclusions is one of your many virtues, but it does sometimes invite lapses in judgment."

"I don't need any friendly advice from you, Kanbaru. My only lapse in judgment was agreeing to clean up this room. Well? So it's comfy, your little cave?"

"It's comfy."

"Even if you don't hurt yourself, it doesn't seem like a pleasant place to sleep. Seems like your body'd be stiff as all hell by the time you woke up. You may not know this, Kanbaru, but sleeping is a biological necessity whose general purpose is to rest the mind and body."

"I know that. Sure, it may not be the most cushiony place to sleep, but it fits me perfectly, like a sleeping bag, so it's surprisingly comfy."

"Really…"

"It can't compare with Senjogahara-senpai's lap, of course, but it's certainly comfier than your arm."

"Hold on just a second there! First let me state unambiguously that

134

I've never once offered you my arm as a pillow, before retorting that being told a mountain of garbage is more comfortable than my arm is beyond dismaying!"

"Boy, you're rolling up your sleeves to yell at me? No need to get so up in arms over an arm pillow."

"Wipe that smile off your face and quit talking nonsense!"

To begin with, I hadn't rolled up my sleeves.

I was wearing short sleeves. It was July, the middle of summer. There was nothing to roll up in the first place.

"Well, I may have slightly overstated the case."

"You've never not overstated the case. Everything you say is an exaggeration. So? What case specifically did you overstate?"

"It's true that a mountain of garbage is more comfortable than your arm, but…"

"…"

She wasn't retracting that part.

She also admitted it was a mountain of garbage…

"But that comfort is a double-edged sword. Since that cave fits my body so perfectly, there isn't room for someone else to share it with me," Kanbaru said achingly.

Aching in both senses.

"If only you could sleep beside me in my cave, Araragi-senpai, it would outstrip Senjogahara-senpai's lap—the perfect bed, perfected at last!"

"Take it down a notch!"

"I should have pointed this out sooner, but as you said earlier sleeping is a biological necessity undertaken to rest the mind and body, and in terms of physical needs, 'sleeping'—"

"Dirty jokes prohibited!"

The banter had run its course.

Having bided my time, I girded my loins, so to speak, and finally turned my hand to cleaning Suruga Kanbaru's room.

003

Upon reflection, I had in fact done some light organization the first time I visited Kanbaru's room—if I hadn't, there wouldn't even have been anywhere to step.

That time, it felt like it'd be dangerous to go barefoot in there—like a minefield. Whether it's rooms or thought processes, I know I'm more of a neat freak than most boys, but any human being confronted by that room would've been moved to do something about it.

Anyway, what I'm trying to say is that I underestimated the situation and assumed today's task wouldn't be so hard, having completed the preliminary preparations a couple of months ago.

If Kanbaru was neither fucking with me nor testing my mettle, then a certain lassitude born of the expectation that "Araragi-senpai will clean it up for me" was probably to blame for the fact that her room had ended up in this ignominious state in barely over a month.

And so as her senpai, as a senpai who should provide guidance to his juniors, the ethical and moral choice may have been to turn right back around and go home without lifting a finger to clean her room. But that's life for you, we all make mistakes.

It's a lot harder to stop doing something than it is to start.

I didn't want to disappoint Kanbaru, but more importantly, I couldn't let her go on living in a little cavern inside a mountain of trash. Also, her room's initial overwhelming state simply stimulated my desire to clean up, just as it had the month before last.

While I had recoiled in horror, if I turned tail, Koyomi Araragi's name would be mud.

The cleanup took hours—it's no exaggeration that I started around noon, and night had fallen by the time I was finished. Ultimately, though, I did manage to clear out some breathing room.

"Frankly, I think some well-placed explosives might've been quicker..."

"Hahaha," Kanbaru laughed cheerfully. "Hold off on the explosives, please. The house is made of wood, the whole thing'd be blown to bits."

What's so goddamn funny?

Just FYI, she didn't help out with the cleanup one bit—only the bare minimum, telling me what was trash and what wasn't from the sidelines.

Anyone observing us during those hours would've been convinced that she was the senpai—and that a junior had come over to help her move.

Compelled to do so under great duress.

"I'm pretty sure your grandparents would happily give me permission to carry out a bombing raid to get this mess cleaned up."

"You just don't get it. You have no idea how precious those books are."

"They're the first to go."

First or not, it was a holiday so there was no trash pickup. All I could do was tie up all the unwanted crap with string or whatever and leave it in the courtyard—nothing to do but pray that it didn't rain before trash day.

I wonder if I should help take out their trash as well...though maybe that was over the line, don't want to get *too* involved in another family's affairs.

"Anyway...good work, Kanbaru," I said.

138

To be honest, I was the only one who'd done any work at all, be it good or bad, but I couldn't come up with anything else. "We did it!" didn't seem quite right either...

And if I'm being generous, I can see how watching someone else clean up for that long might constitute work in its own way.

Me, I hate it when someone else cleans my room...but with Kanbaru, who knows. Maybe she loved every minute of it.

I really don't get this girl's character at all.

Seriously, what's her deal?

"Okay, I'm headed home. It's already completely dark out—no need to overstay my welcome."

"Hold it right there, Araragi-senpai, young man."

"I'm sorry, but that's just not the kind of thing you say to your senpai."

She speaks in such a robust and cheerful manner that it's hard to tell, but apart from calling me her dear senior, she doesn't have time for actual polite speech.

"Do you really think I'd let an esteemed senpai just clean my room and go home, especially when that senpai is you, finest of them all?"

"'Let'? Exactly what are you planning to do to me?!"

"Why be so alarmed..."

What do you take me for, Kanbaru said, pouting.

Why be pouting?

She'd given me plenty of reason to be alarmed.

"I just wanted to serve you some tea. Uh-uh, tea won't cut it. A little supper, Araragi-senpai."

"Supper? Oh, you mean dinner? No, I'm fine. I'm pretty sure they've got dinner waiting for me at home."

"I can't allow that. You're not permitted to be fine."

"Wha? I can't be fine without someone's permission? My junior's?"

"Understand that until you've eaten my grandmother's home-cooked supper, you won't be leaving this mansion."

"Is that a threat?"

And what the hell, her grandmother's home cooking?

A little supper, she says, but she's not even going to make it herself... though any way you slice it, Kanbaru doesn't seem like the type to be any good at cooking.

Her grandmother made the lunch she gave me that other time, too.

While cooking and cleaning may both come under the heading of housework, they are not, of course, directly linked. Still, someone skilled at cooking would, at the very least, be unable to remain impassive in the face of a room in such a disastrous state.

They say the kitchen is the baseline for household mess, and once that starts to go, it's all over...

"Heh. Or will you try and force your way out? Go ahead, try it. I wonder, though, do you have the agility to best me?"

Kanbaru spread her arms wide and stood on the threshold.

As if she was taking a defensive stance in a basketball game—clueless about proper etiquette in a traditional Japanese home. Didn't she know it was rude to stand there?

"Come on, come at me. I may be retired, but my defense hasn't gotten so lax that I'll let an amateur like you get by me."

"Um, I'm not coming at anyone, okay?"

And you know, for someone who respects me, she seems a bit too committed to calling me an amateur.

It would've been one thing if I were vampiricized from giving Shinobu some of my blood, but since I wasn't, I didn't have a snowball's chance in hell of breaking through her defense.

Seemed like my only option was to go along quietly.

Well, I wouldn't be much of a senpai if I brushed off the kindness... or the gratitude of my junior.

To be honest, having consistently refused to participate in clubs or sports since middle school, I was unaccustomed to the very experience of being treated like a senpai and didn't know how you acted like one in the first place... I couldn't gauge the distance between us very well.

I guess I'd ask Senjogahara next time I saw her.

Was it okay to spend my entire day off cleaning my junior's room, and then to get treated to dinner by way of thanks? Or was that a no-go?

That one doted on Kanbaru like a pet cat, though. I might not get a straight answer...

"Okay, okay. You win, Kanbaru, you got me. I give up."

"You can't throw in the towel yet. You've still got an opening, this is no time to give up."

"Just what exactly do you want me to do?"

"Grapple with me."

"I thought you were on the basketball team, not the sumo team..."

If I lost a sumo bout to a girl, and to my junior no less, my name really would be mud. So taking her pep talk, with due respect, as just that, talk—

"I'll stay for dinner, then," I relented. "I just need to call my folks."

"Hm, if that's how you feel, I suppose I have no objection," answered Kanbaru, sounding strangely magnanimous.

She hadn't gotten to grapple with me but seemed pleased that everything had, on the whole, gone according to her wishes—and if my junior's day off had been a satisfying one, well then I couldn't be happier.

Let's leave it at that.

"Now then, Araragi-senpai. Before you take your seat at the supper table."

"Hm?"

"Go take a bath. You can't show up to our dining room like that, you look filthy."

004

Even I know that you don't call the place where you eat in a traditional Japanese home a "dining room," but since I have no earthly idea what you do call it, I decided to refrain from pointing that out.

And, regardless of the nature of our relationship, Kanbaru was absolutely right that it would be bad manners to show up at dinner completely covered in dust from a day of intensive cleaning, so I was actually grateful that she'd said something.

I had very nearly behaved most indelicately in someone else's home—but at the same time, I would never have conceived of using the bath at that someone's home, so you can imagine my consternation as I sat there in the tub.

Consternation, or...

A feeling of immorality, maybe?

I felt like I was transgressing some deep-seated taboo... It was a cypress bath, I think, a splendid bath commensurate with their splendid home. The bathroom was big enough that it wouldn't have been out of place in a modest inn, and getting to take a bath in there felt like more than ample repayment for the day's hard work.

"..."

But it still felt odd.

Submerged up to my neck, enjoying a relaxing soak at the home of a junior I didn't know *that* well...

Even Senjogahara, whose sensibilities were a little off, would opt for "not" if I asked her whether or not this was okay.

Though if I actually brought it up she'd probably kill me.

Death by office supply.

Rubbed out by an erasable ballpoint pen—though I wasn't sure exactly how that would work.

I took a look at the waterproof clock, which was somewhat incongruous with the cypress bath—or conversely, which served as a reminder that this was a private home and not an inn. I wasn't so much worried about the hour as I was pondering how long I had until this "supper."

It seemed like Kanbaru hadn't planned to host a dinner party for me, she'd just hit on the idea in the moment and gotten her grandmother's permission after the fact.

It must've been a real hassle for her grandmother to suddenly be making dinner for me as well—I'm sure she thought I was an overweening senpai—but she must be a kindhearted woman because she apparently gave the okay.

I'm very grateful. That is, terribly sorry.

"...Dammit, I can't relax."

There was plenty of room to stretch out, the water was the perfect temperature, that was all great. I have no intention of retracting my earlier statement that this was more than ample repayment for my hard work. When it comes to someone else's shampoo and conditioner and soap, however, I can't relax.

Man, am I uptight.

Well.

I'll get out as soon as I'm all warmed up, I told myself, but that was when a sound came from the changing room.

A sound, by which I mean a voice.

"Hm?! What's this?! The door won't open?! It's locked?! What's going

144

on, Araragi-senpai, are you all right?! I'll save you!!"

"…"

Someone was frantically rattling the door handle—a hoodlum was attempting to break into the changing room.

"Open this door! Come out with your hands up! This is your last warning!"

"…"

Or maybe it was the police?

"I am Suruga Kanbaru, Araragi-senpai's sex slave! My signature move is the triangle jump!"

"…"

Nope, a hoodlum.

"Why won't this open? I guess I've got no choice, I'll be back in a sec with that stick the S.W.A.T. team uses for breaking down doors!"

"Enough already! And don't bring something if you don't even know what it's called!"

Though.

It's not like I know either.

"Oh, what's this, you're unharmed, Araragi-senpai…"

After my retort the violent banging finally ceased. She sounded sincerely concerned for my wellbeing—though that doesn't excuse her initial attempt to break into the changing room.

I'd shouted from inside the bath; my voice as it echoed off the walls was kind of unsettling, but I needed to talk loud enough for my voice to reach her through two doors, across the changing room.

For her part, Kanbaru always spoke in a voice that was plenty loud enough to carry that far.

"You gave me quite a scare, Araragi-senpai… I was really worried you were being held captive in there."

"You're pretty much the only person in the world who'd hold me captive."

"I don't think so. There's always Senjogahara-senpai."

"Hahaha, not a chance. Whatever else she might do, Senjogahara wouldn't go that far."

"But, how come the door won't open?"

"Because I locked it, obviously."

She acted surprised, or maybe she really was surprised, but Kanbaru barging in while you were in the bath was a probable scenario for anyone who knew her.

Locking the door was a natural precaution.

"Locked… There's a lock on the changing-room door?"

Kanbaru seemed genuinely taken aback.

It's your house, how can you not know that?

"I mean, when I take baths, I just leave the changing-room door open…"

"That's leaving yourself a little too open, don't you think? Though it's fundamentally up to you how you want to behave in your own home."

That is.

I was the one who was buck-naked in someone else's home, even if I was in the bath.

"There seems to be some sort of misunderstanding here, Araragi-senpai, so allow me to clear it up. I only came because I wanted to get into the bath with you."

"Nope, no misunderstanding. Nothing to clear up."

"I misspoke. I only wanted to wash your clothes for you while you were in the bath, Araragi-senpai. My conscience is clean."

"…"

Her conscience could use a bath.

And even if she was telling the truth, I had a hard time believing that the person who was responsible for the room that had made my clothes so filthy was any good at doing laundry… She could very well be even worse at it than cooking.

"What? I'm a jock, I've been playing sports my whole life, so I've always done tons of laundry. You might even call it my forte."

"Mm…that's a fair point. Still, if you wash my clothes I won't have anything to wear."

"Just come out naked then, it's fine."

"It's not fine. I don't have that much confidence in my body."

"If you like, in addition to your clothes, I can wash your body for you. From in front and behind!"

"..."

The sound-only aspect really amplified this girl's perviness. And the fact that I was buck-naked only served to double my, what would you call it, visceral sense of impending danger.

"I'm saying that in return for cleaning my room, I want to clean your body, Araragi-senpai!"

"You should worry about getting your mind clean first. How can it be so filthy when you're using such a great bath every day?"

"Heheh. Well, I can't deny that it's a great bath. I'm sure it'd just be off-putting if I pretended to be humble about it."

She only hears the positive parts.

I could see her proud smile in my mind's eye.

Then again, it was definitely a bath to be proud of...

"It's not just the bath, though, the water itself is great too, isn't it? We pass the water up from the well in the garden and then heat it. It may not be from a natural hot spring, but it's deepsomething water full of somethingium."

"What the hell is that supposed to mean... If you're so proud of it, at least learn the proper terms."

Was it like mineral water or something?

Well water isn't necessarily mineral water—but oddly enough, once she'd said that, I started to feel like the water filling the cypress tub really was special.

Hmmm.

Well water, huh?

"Oh, speaking of which, Araragi-senpai."

"What is it, Kanbaru-kohai?"

"That water has something of a past, you know?"

"Something overcast? Listen, you're the only thing around here that's dreary."

"Not something overcast, something of a past."

"Oh yeah?"

Well, either way, she really was something—but well water with "something of a past"? What was that supposed to mean? Sure, it passes up the well, but what past?

"What kind of a past are we talking about?"

"My, my, interested are we?"

"I don't know about interested…"

When someone brings up something like that, how else do you respond? Though if there was a story behind the water I was currently immersed in, I certainly wanted to hear it.

Purely out of curiosity.

"Okay, fine, I'm interested in this so-called past. Why not? And by the way, right now you're being something of a pest."

"It's a story about my father."

"Wow, your fath…"

Er.

Kanbaru threw it into the conversation so naturally that I almost didn't think anything of it, but her father, yeah, passed away many years ago—not just her father, but her mother too, together.

In a—car accident.

Which is why Kanbaru lives with her grandparents. Their only son was Kanbaru's father.

" … "

"Naturally, my father bathed in that bath—not just the bath, but the well water too—daily."

Not knowing how to respond to this, I fell silent, but Kanbaru just went on telling me this story about her father from the far side of two intervening doors.

She must've accepted his passing as a fact of life by now—in which case handling the subject with kid gloves might be rude, or from Kanbaru's perspective, vexing.

Which is why I responded, "Hmm… Daily, huh?"

"Yup. Since he used it all the time, I guess my father didn't treat the water as anything to be particularly grateful for…"

"Well, stands to reason…"

As someone who lives in a regular house, I was jealous that they had a well at all—or at least, I thought it was cool. But if you had one in your yard your whole life, of course you wouldn't be grateful. It's just there.

"But from the time he was a little kid—once in a blue moon, something caught his attention while he was taking a bath."

"Caught his attention?"

"A certain phenomenon—might be a better way to put it."

Not quite aberration-related, but a mysterious phenomenon, Kanbaru elaborated.

"Not quite aberration-level—but mysterious? That's awfully, or very, specific."

I tensed up somewhat in the tub.

I mean, if the well water involved an aberration in some way, that could spell big trouble—even apart from the fact that I was personally submerged in it at that very moment, using water with that kind of a past on a daily basis didn't seem like a great idea.

"I'm telling you, Araragi-senpai—it's not aberration-related. It doesn't involve aberrations."

"Right…"

Non-aberration-related, aberration-unrelated?

A mysterious phenomenon that doesn't involve aberrations? Actually, I guess they're a dime a dozen.

Man-made phenomena.

Or natural phenomena.

Such things were eminently possible—the question was how dangerous they might be.

In other words, just because it wasn't aberration-related didn't guarantee that this thing Kanbaru was telling me about was safe.

"Sure, but the monkey aberration that you wished on was left to you by your parents, so—no, was it just your mother?"

"Yup, it was my mother. Your memory is remarkable, Araragi-senpai, not that I'm surprised."

"Being complimented after I had to correct myself just makes me feel shitty, actually…"

"Back in the day, I thought 'remark' meant 'mark again.'"

"Truly remarkable."

Toé Gaen.

I think that was it, or that's how my decidedly unremarkable memory remembers it—Suruga Kanbaru's deceased mother's name.

I don't think she ever told me her father's name...and now seemed like an awkward time to be asking her.

"So, what was this mysterious phenomenon that didn't involve any aberration? What are we dealing with here, Kanbaru? Depending on your answer, I might need to get out of this bath sooner rather than later..."

"No need to be on edge, Araragi-senpai. Don't worry, it's not a scary story. It's not a ghost story or anything."

"Not a ghost story—"

Hearing that didn't put my mind at ease.

I still had the lingering influence of an aberration in my body, after all—supposing, and I know this might seem like a wild thought, but supposing the well was filled with holy water or something, my body might just melt.

But Kanbaru also had an aberration lingering in her body, so if she could bathe without incident then there was nothing to worry about—except she's a raging masochist, and she might enjoy the pain from her body melting a little bit.

"..."

What a caveat: *except she's a raging masochist.*

One hell of an aberration.

Truly abnormal and irrational.

Able to be doubted again.

"Sure, if you want to get out, I won't stop you. And if you want to come out of the changing room naked, I won't stop you either."

"Do stop me."

"But first, Araragi-senpai, I want you to look at the surface of the water you're in."

"?"

I didn't know what she was up to, but I reflexively did as Kanbaru said—not that I had to do much, since most of my body was immersed and the water was already taking up most of my field of vision.

"I looked. It's a little late to be asking this, but…what's up with the water?"

"It's not the water."

"Huh? What is it, then? I guess for baths you call it *oyu* instead of water, but—"

"No, no, that's not what I meant. Look, I already told you, it's not the water that I want you to look at."

It's the surface of the water, she reminded me.

The surface?

005

This little tidbit shocked me when I first heard it—but apparently the concept of "oyu" doesn't exist in English. Or rather, there isn't a separate word for it—the distinction between "oyu" and water is expressed as "hot water" and "cold water," and they're basically treated as the same thing.

It's inconceivable to me as someone raised in Japan not to have a distinct word for "oyu," but from a foreign perspective maybe the ambiguity of our word for water—"mizu"—is itself troubling. We make a distinction between "oyu" and "mizu," but at the same time "oyu" *is* "mizu"—and while "mizu" refers to H_2O, it can also refer to liquids in general.

No, forget about troubling, when you really think about it, that's downright disturbing.

Anyway—Mademoiselle Hitagi Senjogahara, who shared that disturbing truth with me, also told me to *Drop dead.*

"Dead. Dead. Dead. Dead. Dead. Dead. Dead."

"…"

Eek.

She's terrifying whether it's sound-only or the full sensory experience… She starts out cranked to the max, so it doesn't make much of a difference anyway.

I very nearly dropped my cell phone but somehow hung on and said, "I-I can't die yet. We've only just fallen for each other. We've only just started going out. I want to go on so many more dates with you. It would be too painful to let go of life at this point."

"Well now. That's a very nice thing to say. Fine, you don't have to die yet."

"…"

You're too soft, Miss Senjogahara.

Tell me to drop dead at least a couple more times.

Actually, she could quit being so open about her murderous desires if she was just going to back off at the drop of a hat—but whatever.

"In any case," I returned to the topic at hand, "I ended up going over to Kanbaru's today to clean up."

Ultimately I got out of the bath and partook of Kanbaru's reward, namely the supper party that she held for me. By the time we were done eating it was quite late, and they were about to lay out a bed for me, but on that, at least, I held firm—and somehow made it home before the clock struck midnight.

I got a lecture from my little sisters for staying out so late.

Usually when they lecture me it unfolds into a bloody civil war, but luckily for them I was too tired this time.

The bath had done a fair job of washing away the fatigue of cleaning Kanbaru's room, but I was worn out from the tension of the supper that followed.

So ignoring my little sisters, I headed to my room—intending to fall asleep right away.

When I went to plug in my cell phone, however, I saw that I'd gotten an email and not noticed. An email from Senjogahara.

I could ignore my sisters, but not an email from her. Because she's scary—partly, but we've been going out since the month before last, so even if she weren't, I wouldn't just ignore her.

Given the time, I figured it was a good-night message, but judging from the subject line "I hear you were in Kanbaru's room," it had more to do with surveillance.

There was nothing in the body.

Even the way she used email was scary...

Maybe it was a good-night-forever message.

And so I ended up calling Senjogahara and giving a detailed report of the day's activities—faithfully and accurately.

It'd be terrifying if I got caught in a lie, and there was a dreadfully open line of communication through the mental hotline that connected the newly reborn Valhalla Duo, so any lie would most definitely be detected. In that sense maybe they should've been called the Valhalie-Duotector.

I was thoroughly whipped.

No, forget about whipped, I was downtrodden. They were walking all over me—Kanbaru treated me as a headrest, and Senjogahara treated me as a doormat. I didn't have one iota of dignity left.

I oughta left my dignity in a safe-deposit box.

I wanted to ask Hanekawa to save me, but if Senjogahara was monitoring me, Hanekawa was supervising me; if she wasn't already riding to the rescue, then she had no intention of saving me this time, whether I asked her to or not.

While I hadn't told Senjogahara that I was going to Kanbaru's house to clean (hence Kanbaru's report to her), I had duly informed Hanekawa in advance—yikes...

Seriously, what the hell has happened to my life?

Zero free will.

I have to wonder, my decision to buckle down and study so that I could go to the same college as Senjogahara—was it really my own?

"Going to clean your junior's room for her... Well, aren't you the helpful one, Araragi—taking a bath though, that's over the line. I think you really ought to drop dead."

"Don't think that."

"It's better than thinking 'I'm going to kill you,' isn't it?"

"..."

Sure, but.

"So, Araragi. What did you make of Kanbaru's story?"

"Hm?"

"The story—*not the water, look at the surface*, that one."

"Oh, right..." I nodded.

My intention was to tell her what had happened faithfully and accurately, so I included the story as well, but not said anything about what I made of it.

"Yeah, I mean, it's definitely a weird story. Or maybe not weird? I guess I should call it a romantic story—since Kanbaru's father saw *the face of his future wife* on the surface."

That was the story.

From the time he was little, Kanbaru's father had seen the figure of an unfamiliar woman when he bathed in that cypress tub—not always, mind you, only occasionally, but either way, the woman with whom he'd elope one day was reflected for him there on the surface.

He didn't pay it much mind since it was clearly some sort of illusion, and at some point he stopped seeing it. What, if anything, the illusion meant kept on tugging at some corner of his mind, however—so he had quite a shock the first time he laid eyes on Kanbaru's mother, on Toé Gaen, in other words.

Almost as if.

They'd been destined to meet.

"Sounds like the kind of charm girls would be into," I said. "Wasn't there one like that, where you'd fill the sink with water, and it would reflect the face of your future husband or something?"

The story was about Kanbaru's dad, so instead of a girl I ended up picturing a man in the prime of life, but the story took place when he was a kid, plus, they got married quite young, so it didn't feel that off.

Romantic.

You could call it that, sure.

From the smattering of knowledge I'd acquired as a high school student just dipping his toes into the world of exam prep, a liquid surface could function as a sort of screen... But in that case, seeing his "soul mate," or even just "the face of someone he'd meet in the future," was pretty crazy.

This wasn't like the sandbox.

Water is, of course, even more protean than sand—and while the cypress tub may have been an antique, there was of course nothing funny going on with the bottom of it.

"Hm," said Senjogahara. "So when you looked at the surface of the water like Kanbaru asked, who did you see reflected there? Me? Or me? Or was it me?"

"Ugh!"

"Hanekawa? Kanbaru? Li'l Hachikuji?"

"You're scaring me!"

I was quaking with fear.

"I didn't see anyone... The only thing I saw was a normal reflection of my own face."

"Wha? Are you trying to tell me that your soul mate is your precious self?"

"Oh shut up. What do you mean, my precious self?"

She always maintained such a level tone, why was this the only time she managed to sound properly surprised?

"There was a story like that, wasn't there? A myth where a guy was so enamored of his own reflection that he drowned himself... What was it again?"

"You know perfectly well. You're just trying to get me to say that I'm a narcissist."

"Here's another story. Once there was a dog that was carrying some meat in his mouth. When he saw his own reflection in the river, he wanted the meat that was 'in' the water too. So he started barking, and when he did the meat in his mouth fell into the river and was washed away... That kind of foolishness is what they call Araragism."

"That's not a word! Don't try to make me the gold standard for foolishness. Anyway, the water just looked like regular water to me. And the surface seemed totally normal too."

"Hmmm. So even though you're a vampire, surfaces reflect your image."

"No, I'm not a vampire anymore... I just have some lingering after-effects. My reflection appears in regular old mirrors too."

"That reminds me, don't they say vampires can't cross rivers and can't swim and stuff like that? Are you able to swim, Araragi?"

"Hm? Well, I haven't tried, but...I wonder. I probably can, right?"

What about Shinobu, though?

While she was a little girl, her vampiric level seemed higher than mine... I got the sense that she was at the mercy of her identity.

"Well, whether or not an aberration was involved, it's still a pretty strange story," I said. "It'd be one thing if it were her mother, but her father..."

Not like I know all about her mother, but the simple fact that she'd bequeathed the "monkey" to Kanbaru suggested she had some connection to *all that*.

Especially considering how Kanbaru's seemingly sound grandparents despised her even before she stole their only son from them.

"It seems more like a curse than a charm," commented Senjogahara. "Sending your image to your soul mate."

"You make it sound so scary. What are you trying to make Kanbaru's mother out to be?"

"Juuust—" Senjogahara said in a playful tone. No, her tone was totally flat, only the stretched-out vowel was playful. "Kidding, hellooo."

"...Right, of course you are."

"I'd already heard that story from Kanbaru, though."

"Huh?"

Just gonna drop that into the conversation, eh?

How about a "the fact is" at the beginning there or something?

"What. It's not like I told you I hadn't heard it. Me and Kanbaru go way back, of course I know about stuff like that. Seeing as you only just met her, if you knew something about her that I didn't, that's what would be shocking."

"..."

As far as I could tell from this defense, she'd heard the story back in middle school, not after the recent rebirth of the Valhalla Duo.

"I didn't mean any harm. I just wanted to savor how ridiculous you were, proudly relating to me this story you'd heard from Kanbaru."

"That's the cruelest thing I've ever heard…"

So damn cruel, even when she didn't mean any harm? What kind of a person was she?

"Well, the truth is that I'd heard it but totally forgotten about it. I remembered partway through. Like, *oh yeah, that rings a bell*—then again, back when I was the one getting invited to Kanbaru's house and being allowed to use the bath and stuff, I was a good kid, so I never said anything uncouth."

"Huh?"

Um, uncouth?

What's she talking about?

"Of course, unlike you I did share the tub with Kanbaru. Heheh, jealous, aren't you?"

"That's not what I want to ask about…"

Senjogahara and Kanbaru in the bath together?

Not jealous at all, more like scared.

Don't wanna go anywhere near that.

"…What do you mean, you didn't say anything uncouth?"

"I'm telling you I had a good personality at the time. In other words, I wasn't a low-down, twisted, unpleasant woman like I am now."

I gasped. A little *too* self-aware, aren't we…

Heedless of my reaction, Senjogahara went on. "I'm saying that I didn't boorishly offer my analysis of a love story that was romantic, and not a tale of an aberration—"

006

The epilogue, or maybe, the punch line of this story.

We don't need to fall back on the Greek myth of Narcissus to say that people love themselves—in a biological sense in addition to self-love or self-infatuation.

They do so out of an instinctual hereditary drive to pass on their genes to future generations.

People hold themselves in high esteem, they idealize themselves.

Senjogahara was the one who said this.

"Huh? What? So, are you trying to tell me Kanbaru's father thought his own reflection in the bathwater was his 'soul mate'? I mean, come on, that...can't be."

"Why not?"

"Because it's idiotic."

"Exactly, it's an idiotic story. And pointing that out is like calling Kanbaru's father an idiot, so I didn't tell Kanbaru. I wouldn't say something that harsh even now, so of course I wouldn't when I was in middle school."

"...That's on the level of the fable you told about the dog. He'd realize. How could anyone in the world not recognize his or her own face?"

"No one in the world knows it that intimately. The face you see in the mirror is flipped left to right. In photographs and videos, the colors and sense of depth are completely different. We ourselves are actually the ones who're least familiar with the us that people see."

"That's not what we're talking about here…"

"For example, Araragi, people from other families all look alike, right? But the members of those families don't think so. You and your sisters look disturbingly alike, but I bet you don't think you look all that similar."

"Disturbingly? Thanks for that…though I guess I see what you mean. But aren't you just saying that it's easier to tell people apart if you're used to seeing them, than if you're not? Like how a counterfeit might fool a layman, but an expert would be able to tell the difference—"

"Yeah. Well, no, but it'll do."

"No? Whatever, anyone looking at a face reflected in the water would at least be able to tell if it's their own."

"Not really. In a mirror, maybe—but…"

"…"

"A watery surface is moving, sparkling, it's blurry—it's not the same as looking in a mirror. You've heard of the uncanny valley, right? How with CG or robots or whatever, the more humanlike you make them look, the less human they seem—the dissimilarity actually becomes more distinct, and they start to seem creepier. I think you'll agree that my metaphor is more accurate."

"The uncanny valley…"

"They also say that once you cross the uncanny valley, the feeling of intimacy grows by leaps and bounds. Though I've heard incest and hating your kin are rooted in the same sort of reasons. The point is, your own image, reflected on water, *can not look like you*—they make mirrors that are rigged so the reflection isn't flipped left to right, but apparently most people who look in them think: *That's not me.* And they say people experience a similar disconnect when they see the reflection of a close

162

friend or relative."

"…So he didn't perceive the self he saw reflected in the bathwater as himself because it wasn't the 'self' he took for granted from constantly seeing it in the mirror?"

"Yes. And if he only saw it occasionally, mightn't that blurry self look like a girl?"

"I mean…that's possible, I guess, since when you're a little kid the difference between genders is a lot less obvious—it's a fine answer if we're talking about the kind of charms or fortune-telling that girls are into, but once you're a grownup, or once you've reached a certain level of discernment, you'd realize what was going on."

"And he did. Which is why he stopped seeing her at a certain point."

"…"

"But it's another question entirely whether you connect that to recollections of seeing such a thing in the past. Her father must've retained his memory of discerning someone's image in the water."

"…And thought that it was his 'soul mate'? That's a hell of an assumption—though I guess the dad we're talking about here is Kanbaru's dad."

"You've got it backwards. He met someone who seemed like his 'soul mate,' and she reminded him of the reflection he'd seen in the water all those years ago."

"Hm? Oh, I get it… Yeah, you must be right, for a third party discussing this in hindsight, the cause and effect are backwards…but that's not how he felt. As far as he knew, he finally found the answer to a puzzle from his childhood."

"Love aside, we tend to seek out people like ourselves, so…"

So.

Senjogahara left off there. Instead—

"This is all just my interpretation, of course," she summed it up.

That summation may have been her way of hiding her embarrassment—or of apologizing for being unable to swallow a romantic story without analyzing it first.

There was no way of knowing the truth.

It was just her interpretation, not the solution—she'd said accordingly.

Kanbaru and her father saw it one way, and she saw it another way, that was all. Senjogahara had decided that Papa Kanbaru's interpretation was "unlikely," or even "impossible," but conversely he might think her quibbling explanation was "unlikely" or "impossible."

And the fact that Kanbaru's father had only ever seen "her" in that bath—in that well water, in other words—could lend credence to the idea that there really was something mysterious about the water itself.

Senjogahara would likely dismiss the specificity of the location with an interpretation like a greater chance for tricks of the light. And I have to say I'm with her—I'm also the type who can't accept romantic notions at face value, who needs to nitpick them all the way down the line. So I wasn't inclined to say anything uncouth, to use her word, about her take on it.

In that regard.

Maybe Senjogahara and I were a couple of peas in a pod—a couple, and peas in a pod.

"Well, goodbye. Good night. See you at school tomorrow."

Was not how Senjogahara signed off.

"If you say one wrong word to Kanbaru, I'll kill you. I'll never forgive you. Even if it was a slip of the tongue, you'd be better off killing yourself before tomorrow morning."

Then my girlfriend hung up.

I seriously don't get her, I thought as I placed a second call, this time to Kanbaru, figuring that it was still probably just early enough.

The pretext for the call was to report that I'd gotten home safely, but the truth was that there was also something I wanted to ask her—believe me, I had no intention of saying one wrong word.

I didn't particularly feel like killing myself before dawn.

"Hey, Kanbaru. I meant to ask—what about you? When you look into that bathwater, what do you see?"

The reason I asked: If her father's interpretation was correct, then Kanbaru would see her future mate reflected there. If Senjogahara's inter-

164

pretation was correct, however, what my junior saw reflected there might be—

Her mother.

Toé Gaen.

Kanbaru might see her—just like her father had. In the rippling image of herself reflected on the surface, she might well see the mother whose blood ran in her veins. The mother who'd had such an enormous influence on my junior's life, who affected her even now through that left arm—but then, I have no idea which of her parents she resembles more, so for all I knew it could be her father she saw there. Depending on the movement of the water, she might even see both of them.

Mom and dad.

She might even see—the two of them there together.

And if so—that really was romantic, in its own way. Her departed parents, together, reunited in her eyes...

"Hm? Oh. I see my own boobs, of course. Which are reaaally sexy, if I do say so myself, I spend the entire time I'm in the bath staring at them. The contrast with my abs is reaaally evocative, and I oversoak myself on a nightly basis sitting there captivated by the sight. To be honest, nothing else enters my eyes. But, why do you ask, Araragi-senpai—"

I hung up.

CHAPTER FIVE
KOYOMI WIND

SUN	MON	TUE	WED	THU	FRI	SAT
		1	2	3	4	5
6	7	8	9	10	11	12
13	14	15	16	17	18	19
20	21	22	23	24	25	26
27	28	29	30	31		

8
August

001

What does Nadeko Sengoku, a girl in her second year of middle school, think about roads? Does she even think about them at all? I'm forced to conclude that she probably doesn't. I'm just making an assumption, of course, and depending on how you look at it, that might be a very rude thing to say. But a girl who always keeps her head down, who goes through life with eyes downcast, doesn't see the road; the only thing she sees is her own two feet.

She's a shoegazer.

I'm not saying that's a bad thing.

Please don't misunderstand, I'm not trying to be critical—having walked, sometimes even run through life with my eyes completely shut, how could someone like me, with quite literally no foresight, take issue with Sengoku, who has lived with her eyes fixed on her feet by hook or by crook, or rather, head-on without a wayward glance?

As someone who avoids looking at any part of himself, feet included, and who as a result lost sight of himself completely, I should be praising rather than criticizing Sengoku and her perpetually downturned gaze.

Step.

By step.

Always staring down at her feet—at her shoes, regardless of where she's coming from or where she's going. In a sense, in every sense, that's a grueling life.

Life can be like that.

Life is like that.

It's not for you or me to dismiss—at least, to dismiss out of hand.

Still, while hers may be a life, is she walking the path of humanity? Sengoku, who doesn't know what path she's following, who doesn't even know the name of the road she's on, has nothing to say about humanity.

The more important, the most important thing I want to point out about the way Nadeko Sengoku goes through life, however, is that if you live your life with your head down—

If you're always focused on your feet, then you might manage to avoid falling, or tripping, or straying from the path—but you can't avoid running into things unless you watch where you're going.

And there's this, which may not be all that important, but talk of humanity aside—when you take the low road.

The path of the snake, as in a real snake.

There are no feet in sight.

0 0 2

"P-Pardon me for intruding, Big Brother Koyomi."

"Oh, it's you. Thanks for coming by, Sengoku. C'mon in."

"I-It is an intrusion, isn't it, Nadeko'll just head home."

"You can't leave, you just got here!"

"G-G-Goodbye. It's been fun."

"Not yet it hasn't?!"

"It…it was the greatest day ever."

"You get that much of a kick out of taking off your shoes in our front hall?! Have you found the secret to happiness?!"

One day in early August—during summer break.

A day when a case involving a certain swindler had been settled for the moment, and my little sister's friend Nadeko Sengoku had come by the house—as promised.

The excuse was that I'd gotten intel on the swindler from Sengoku, and now I was going to give her the rundown on what'd happened along with a proper thank you.

The correct thing probably would've been for me to go to her house to express my gratitude—but when I went to hang out over there last month, despite the fact that we had a great time playing The Game of Life, things eventually got weird and I ended up kind of fleeing from Sengoku's mother, so I didn't really have a strong inclination to head that way again.

Animal instinct, perhaps.

Or aberrational instinct.

Which is why I called Sengoku up and invited her over to our house—I thought about meeting her on the road and giving her an escort back, but, "That's, okay," was the response I got.

I mean, she'd come over to our place with Kanbaru month before last, so she knew where it was—and she used to come over all the time to see my sister when they were in elementary school anyway.

If she could get here on her own, no need to be overbearing—spare the road and spoil the child, as they say.

Nevertheless, Sengoku isn't the most reliable kid, so I was a little anxious that she wouldn't show up at the appointed hour, and if she didn't I had every intention of pulling out all the stops to find her—but the doorbell rang at precisely the appointed time.

She was so punctual that it almost seemed like she'd been waiting outside the gate monitoring the atomic clock or something—she didn't have a cell phone, though, so that wasn't possible.

Maybe she'd synchronized her watch with it before she left the house—well, no, I guess no one's that anal.

Every single one of Sengoku's phone calls is precisely at the top of the hour in my cell's log, but that's obviously just a coincidence too.

"Anyway, come in. It's fine, I cleaned my room and everything."

"Ah, o-okay…"

"Everything's set, so we can party all night!"

"E-Eek."

I'd meant this as a joke to make her feel more relaxed, since she seemed anxious about being at my house despite knowing me for so long, but she'd taken it literally and shrunk back in terror. She was quaking in her boots.

Hmmm.

Then again, in the six months since our reunion, I'd never really seen Sengoku not panic-stricken.

Sengoku = panic-stricken.

This was her personality, so maybe there was nothing I could do about it—I guess I just needed to keep a close watch over her from here on out.

When I'd been the one darkening her door, she'd had her bangs pulled up with a hair band, but today, perhaps because she'd walked here, she was in her default mode, bangs down over her face.

I couldn't even get a glimpse of her expression.

So to be perfectly honest, I had no idea what she was really feeling.

From the looks of it, she was being bashful, or maybe reserved, but it was equally possible that she was just repulsed.

If she felt at a loss, like she couldn't refuse the persistent invitations of her friend's older brother and ended up somewhere she didn't want to be, I couldn't feel worse, that is, what a big misunderstanding...

I want to believe that wasn't what was going on.

If she'd only be a little more frank, it would make everything okay—seriously, even just one percent as frank as Kanbaru.

Just when Senjogahara's acid tongue, or dispiritingly acrimonious disposition, was showing signs of mellowing—promising to go into remission after the con-man case, I just couldn't face being hated by my little sister's friend.

It would interfere with, impede, my exam prep.

"C'mon, get those shoes off already. Come in already."

"R-Right. Okay. Off they come. Whatever you say. Anything at all."

"..."

How so timid...

If she hated me, I suppose there was nothing I could do about it, but could she please not bring undue suspicion on me with her antics?

Anyway, whether she was being bashful, or watchful, or just plain waffling, Sengoku somehow made it across the threshold—and followed me right on up to the second floor.

"Tsukihi was supposed to be here too...but apparently she's still stuck mopping up."

"M-Mopping up? After what?"

"That swindler, obviously—not like I know what that actually means. Yeah, I have no idea what Karen or Tsukihi is thinking—"

Nor what Sengoku is.

I just don't understand how middle school girls think, I guess—though that's a real can of worms. How can you ever really know what anyone else is thinking?

Even Shinobu, with our link and everything—I can't say I understand her.

"W-Wow. It's true. It's a party, you're throwing Nadeko a party."

At long last, after a whole stack of waffling—it took us thirty minutes to go a distance of not even thirty steps—Sengoku finally started to sound happy and excited when she got to my room.

Though it was less about the room and more about the snacks and juice spread out on the floor.

It was pretty modest as parties go, and there wasn't any surprise element—in fact, the warm welcome I'd received at Sengoku's house the other day had been a few notches more lavish—but I was just glad that it made her happy.

Though it was actually my sister who'd done all the preparation for this "party," not me... It was after she'd put the finishing touches on it that she'd gone out to "mop up after that swindler."

Part of me hated her thoroughness, but maybe it was only to be expected from someone who'd become the boss of all the middle school girls in the area.

Show Nadeko the same good time I would, Tsukihi had directed me—quite the direction, when it came from your own little sister.

"Wh-Whoa, popcorn. Nice! Let's stuff our faces full of popcorn... Nadeko's gonna pack it in till she can't breathe. Then swallow it without chewing."

"You'll die."

"Dreamy."

Sengoku squatted down, sounding entranced.

I was a little surprised anyone could be so happy about snacks... Maybe she wasn't allowed to eat sweets at home?

Given how cloyingly sweet her parents were to her...

It was surprising indeed.

Hup, Sengoku plopped down on a cushion and started taking off her socks. Both left and right. Apparently she wanted to be barefoot—and she was, before I could finish the thought.

She carefully folded her socks and laid them next to her.

"..."

She took off her socks almost like people take off their hats indoors, but...huh? Hang on, I dunno. I dunno I dunno. Is there some rule of etiquette that you take off your socks when you're in someone else's room?

I had very little experience being in other people's rooms, so it didn't help much by way of comparison...

I was always only going to Senjogahara's or Kanbaru's room...and in Kanbaru's case, never mind socks, you could get hurt if you went in there without work boots.

"Y-You said Tsukihi had gone out..." It was clearly taking Sengoku everything she had to restrain an overwhelming urge to go buck wild on the smorgasbord of snacks laid out before her. Somehow managing to set aside her desire to shove her face full of popcorn at the earliest possible opportunity, she asked, "What about Karen?"

"Her too. They're a set, a package deal."

True, the difference in size made it hard to bundle them together, so they might not be easy to sell as a set... What to do with them?

Nothing, some people would say, it just wasn't something you did to your little sisters.

"Y-Your good parents?"

"Well, that's a very polite way of putting it... No, my good parents are also out, that is, at work. Holidays, summer break—their jobs don't have anything to do with those things. By which I mean they don't have any of those things."

"R-Really... Th-Then it's just the two of us today, Big Brother Koyomi."

"Hm? Well, since you put it that way, yeah, it's just the two of us. Something wrong with that?"

"Of course not. Teeheeheeheehee," Sengoku giggled adorably.

Finally.

Huh, I guess she was so tense because she was worried about my parents—other people's parents are definitely a source of tension, that's for sure.

I'd had a hell of a time with Senjogahara's dad, and even if we don't bring that in, I did run away from Sengoku's mother. And while I'm totally used to it now, to the point that I'll go hang out with them even when Kanbaru isn't there, at first her grandparents made me nervous too.

"Well, first off, welcome, Sengoku."

I poured juice into the two glasses I'd set out, and handing one to Sengoku, we started off with a toast.

"Y-Yeah! Nadeko is welcome, Big Brother Koyomi! Cheers! Happy birthday!"

"…"

My birthday's in April.

003

"I see… It's all taken care of. Nice, phew."

Naturally, I couldn't share everything about what had happened with the swindler, but as we ate our snacks and drank our juice, I told Sengoku everything she needed to know.

It seemed to give her peace of mind.

She was relieved—that is, it was probably a real load off her mind. Which made sense, seeing as her involvement with the case had gone one step further, one step deeper than any of the other middle school girls who were affected.

Thanks to Oshino—and also thanks very much to Kanbaru—she hadn't gotten sucked in any further than that, but I'm sure she hadn't been able to rest easy until just now.

"Maybe not 'all'—from my perspective it's got kind of a bitter aftertaste, it's gray—or something," I mused. "It's a hazy, or a middle-of-the-road resolution."

"But nothing else bad is going to happen?"

"Right… In that sense, I guess it can't be beat."

Though I wasn't sure if it couldn't be beat, or if we just couldn't beat it.

Not sure in the slightest.

This might be a pessimistic attitude, or a straight-up negative one depending on how you look at it, but either way, in so far as things weren't going to get any worse, a resolution was a resolution.

No, a resolution is a resolution, full stop—my little sisters got too big for their britches and got caught with their pants down, but I was never involved in the first place. Why should the peanut gallery have anything to say about it?

No one likes a backseat driver.

Holding this little victory celebration might've been ridiculous, when you get right down to it, but ignoring that little quibble—just that loathsome swindler leaving our town called for a toast, for me personally.

We'd made him promise never to show his face in our town again—so "when you get right down to it," that alone was reason enough to throw one hell of a party.

"You said Tsukihi and Karen are 'mopping up,' but...hashtag how do you think it's going?"

"Hashtag?"

Were we on Twitter?

I'd associated her more with Twister than Twitter...

"Oh, sorry," Sengoku corrected herself, "how do you think it's going?"

"Who knows."

I felt bad giving such a lackluster response after making her go to the trouble of correcting herself, but "who knows" was the only answer I could muster—since unlike my little sisters, I wasn't tapped into the middle school girl network.

Thinking about it that way really threw the peculiarity of what that swindler had done, had tried to do, into stark relief... Seriously, it gave me the creeps.

Intentionally spreading charms.

Curses.

Aberrations—

"Hmm…do you think Tsukihi's mop-up involves rooting out those aberrations one by one?"

"No…I think that might be impossible. If I had to guess, I'd say she's probably trying to comfort the victims, something along those lines—though maybe she's trying to do some of that too."

Trying to, maybe, but I think that'd be beyond her. At that point you're completely in the realm of information warfare. That'd be too much to handle, even for the strategist of the Fire Sisters—no, saying "even for the strategist of the Fire Sisters" begs the question of just how formidable the Fire Sisters are in the first place.

"Th-The Fire Sisters are awesome, Big Brother Koyomi. Maybe it's hard to tell because you're family, but they're really, really, really awesome."

"Oh yeah?"

"Really, realty awesome."

"Realty?"

Even if you took her words with a grain of salt, or with a whole handful, someone as quiet and modest as Sengoku insisting so firmly made me wonder if it might not be true after all.

Maybe the Fire Sisters were awesome.

"They are! So awesome that Nadeko gets to be the big man on campus just because we're friends!"

"Do you really act like the big man?"

Not a chance.

For this tiny little girl to be the big man…

"N-No," *ahem*, Sengoku cleared her throat.

Even that was cute.

"But seriously, no exaggeration, being friends with the Fire Sisters means Nadeko's got enough influence to rake in some money."

"Sounds like the wrong kind of influence…"

That's exactly how swindlers are born.

Were my siblings being used to pitch fraudulent investment schemes or something? I've heard it said that too much justice breeds crime, and maybe the Fire Sisters had reached that point.

Though I'm sure nothing could be further from their intentions…

"Speaking of which, an imitation group called the Cold Sisters debuted recently."

"That's a pretty obvious fake."

Well, if you ask me, my sisters are the fakes—or no, that'd be going too far. To me, they'll always be the kind of slovenly little sisters who strut around the house naked, but to Sengoku they're old friends, and nothing's going to change that. I'm sure she's not interested in hearing them slandered, even by a member of their own family.

"*Doki doki! Fire Sisters* also came out."

"That just sounds like a special, to fill the gap between seasons."

That or a whole new show.

Huh, so my sisters aired their final episode without my knowing it…

"Now, whether my sisters can handle it or not, rumors only last for seventy-five days, as the saying goes. I think the right way to handle the ghost stories that swindler spread around town is to leave things alone, watch and wait, not do anything rash."

"It's all so complex… Do you think there's anything Nadeko can do? To help Tsukihi and Karen… Actually, Nadeko was hoping to talk to them about that today."

"If there's something you can do, it's to bounce back from that snake case and stand on your own two feet, I think—though I'm not sure things will ever go back to the way they were."

"…That makes it sound like Nadeko was standing to begin with. But it feels like Nadeko was crawling even before that. Slithering along the ground, like a snake…" she brooded. Then, with a sudden "A…awawa," she grabbed a handful of popcorn and crammed it into her mouth. Just like she'd said she wanted to earlier.

Like a squirrel—or very much like a snake.

Though she didn't swallow it whole. She munched it to bits.

"Wh-What the hell," I said, thinking at the same time how cute everything she did was.

Munch munch, munch, she finished eating the popcorn before answering, "Um, lessee, Big Brother Koyomi. In Nadeko's case it's clear,

180

but how did Mister Swindler…"

It was charmingly typical of her to say "Mister" Swindler, but as someone who'd actually met and spoken with "Mister" Swindler, it rubbed me the wrong way, somewhat.

I'd have told anyone but Sengoku never to call that bastard "mister" again.

"How did he spread those rumors?"

"Hunh?"

"Those rumors, or charms, or ghost stories…that occult stuff… How—"

"Oh, well, it was like a get-rich-quick scheme—he spread free trial charms around the middle school girl community, then waited in the wings to sell them charms that actually cost money…"

Come to think of it, it was such a current sales philosophy.

Give out the basic version for free, then sell the optional add-ons… He was right on trend, just as you'd expect from a man who'd devoted his life to the career of a con man.

Nah.

Being a con man wasn't a career, it was a crime.

"No, no, Big Brother Koyomi. Nadeko is asking 'how,' not 'how come'…"

"Hm? You want to know more about his methods, not his goal? His methods—" I started out like she was asking something obvious, ready to launch into a big lecture on the subject as her dependable "big brother" if that was what she wanted. When I actually tried, though, nothing came out.

Oops.

Methods?

He spread rumors targeted at middle school girls, vaguely speaking… But yeah, seriously, how do you go about doing that?

As an expert, Oshino made his living collecting tales of aberrations— urban legends, the word on the street, secondhand gossip; that's what he came to this town to gather, and then he left.

Whether that actually constitutes a profession is another question entirely, and we'll leave it aside once again, but in some sense it's straightforward—what he does is put out his net and catch whatever rumors are floating around, whatever stories are circulating.

He's in the position of observer, poacher, recorder, you might say—in other words, he's on the listening end of things, so it might not be easy, but it's still the kind of thing anyone could do, at least to some extent.

You can go out and hear the stories for yourself, you can opt to go more contemporary and search for them on the internet—there are plenty of methods available.

But what about the opposite?

Urban legends, the word on the street, secondhand gossip.

What about spreading them rather than collecting them?

As the teller, not the listener—what would your methods actually be?

As transmitter rather than receiver.

And if you're not just transmitting but also controlling the subsequent course of the transmission—we're getting into seriously difficult territory.

Setting a trap instead of a net—how would you go about it?

"Sengoku. You tried to deal with it yourself, didn't you? The rumor, the ghost story that the swindler put about."

A snake.

A snake aberration.

"Y-Yeah. But it didn't go so well."

"Doesn't matter if you succeeded or not—you tried to use something you found in a book, right? Rather than buy anything from him."

I'm pretty sure that was the case.

No doubt about it, really, since I'd seen Sengoku from behind at the bookstore, doing research—everything about that swindler's grand plan was abominable, but nevertheless, if there was one saving grace.

If I had to find one saving grace, it'd be the fact that she'd avoided direct contact with him. If that bad omen personified, if he even was a person, had laid eyes on Nadeko Sengoku, who looked even more helpless than a chihuahua, she would never have come out of it unscathed.

Even Karen had such a terrible time of it.

If it were Sengoku...

"Y-Yeah. Come to think of it, Nadeko probably could've gotten in touch with Mister Swindler with a little effort... If only we'd met up," she said bravely, "Nadeko could've tied him up and handed him over to the police."

"No chance," I let a typical retort slip out.

That aside—it wasn't as if finding out now helped in any way, and Sengoku probably wasn't asking me for any pressing reason, but I'd be lying if I said my curiosity wasn't piqued.

That swindler.

How had he spread those rumors?

"Who did everyone hear them from in the first place? It wasn't from the swindler—himself?"

"As far as Nadeko knows, how people answered when Tsukihi asked around was—a whisper on the wind."

"..."

The wind?

004

"Urban legends are a kind of folklore...the kind of thing that happened to 'a friend of a friend.' But if you actually try to find that 'friend of a friend,' you'll come up empty—"

On the subject of the swindler himself, I had nothing more to tell Sengoku—that is, nothing more that I was able to tell her, so I decided to pass the time with a discussion of this new topic until Tsukihi and Karen got home.

Calling it a discussion might be a bit of an exaggeration, since it was just for fun—I had no illusions that it would prove useful down the line.

But leaving aside the rumors disseminated by that swindler for a moment, I was pretty sure I remembered something similar from back during spring break.

It was already months ago—at the time I wasn't studying for exams yet, nor had I had any dealings with aberrations. But the very first time I talked with Hanekawa, before we were even in the same class, she told me a rumor that was going around about a "vampire."

A blond vampire.

An iron-blooded, hot-blooded, yet cold-blooded vampire.

Overpoweringly beautiful—and as I recall, that rumor, too, spread mostly among girls.

The charms cooked up by that swindler and the rumor of the "vampire" were alike in that regard.

It didn't necessarily mean they had some common denominator, though. Maybe girls—that is, females, just like to gossip more than males do.

I've heard that it's women who create the trends at any given moment—so isn't it possible that folklore, too, comes out of such a community? It would explain why that swindler chose to target girls.

"Though maybe this kind of 'talk' is a type of rumor as well...since there are girls like you, Sengoku, who are outside the rumor mill, and I heard about the vampire even though I'm a boy."

"Totally. So instead of a narrow focus, Big Brother Koyomi, we should question the question of how rumors spread more generally, more broadly."

"Yeah, you're right." *Question the question* sounded pretty odd, but Sengoku seemed to be as linguistically hopeless as myself, so I let it go. This was no time to be pedantic about semantics. "The process by which rumors spread—or should I say the process by which rumors *are* spread? How did that swindler make it happen..."

The propagation of urban legends.

The spread of secondhand gossip.

"...The thing is, if he could wrap his head around something like that, I feel like he wouldn't have to stoop to something with as poor a cost performance index as swindling."

"Not everyone is motivated by cost performance, though, are they, Big Brother Koyomi? Nadeko never actually met him, so it's hard to say... but from everything you've said, it seems like he's the kind of person who just enjoys deceiving people."

"Well, you're right about that..."

But I don't think it's even a question of whether or not he enjoys it.

It seems more pathological or...like it's his karma or something.

So maybe swindling wasn't a career he chose of his own free will—

maybe it was the only path open to him.

Which means that he's a victim too—is something I would never think, though, not ever.

He's a perpetrator any way you slice it.

I mean, come on.

"Maybe we need to think of making trends and making a profit from trends as two separate things," I suggested. "That swindler said himself that this time around he'd failed..."

Is it basically a question of getting out while the market is still good? Duping people with baseless rumors and turning a profit off it are two different things—yeah, if we were going to have this discussion, that's the first thing we needed to recognize.

"After all, we're not trying to deduce the method for starting a trend, and to unravel the mystery of a swindler's methods, in order to get rich quick."

"Wha?" Sengoku looked startled, then tried to salvage the situation by saying, "Oh, uh, uh huh. Right. Of course not."

...She'd been hoping to get rich quick.

Well, that in and of itself wasn't something to reprimand her for. As long as it's obtained by legitimate means, there's nothing to criticize about making money, or making money your goal—though as a high school senior who'd shouldered a five-million-yen debt, I didn't know about getting too engrossed in it.

"But, Big Brother Koyomi. If someone did figure out how to intentionally create rumors, or trends...if they had that kind of artificial know-how, that'd be pretty awesome. It'd be the discovery of the century. They could create a social phenomenon."

"Well, personally, I have no desire to create a social phenomenon... Although we're trying to think this through, it's not even clear that you really could artificially generate ghost stories or urban legends or trends."

"B-But, Nadeko's heard about that happening. Like, they decide next year's popular fashions at meetings a whole year earlier."

"Yeah, I've heard that too. But I've also heard that the fashions they come up with at those meetings don't necessarily take off…" That seems like precisely the kind of thing Oshino could elucidate for us clearly and succinctly; there really are organizations that are trying to create trends, even if they aren't swindlers. "But that's neither here nor there. First maybe we should try and define the object of our discussion: a fad, in other words."

Right, even if this was just for fun, I'd be lying if I said I didn't harbor a faint hope that it might come in handy if someone like that swindler showed up to menace our town again.

If you know your enemy and know yourself—as Sun Tzu said.

Either way, the difference between baseless rumors and urban legends kind of escapes me—you can't distinguish between them on the basis of which are true and which are false, for instance, because they're all false.

Reality is inherently a mixture of truth and fiction.

"A definition, huh? Does hearing it from 'a friend of a friend' count as one? Since we're talking about a whisper on the wind—"

"But 'a friend of a friend' is hard to define. And something you hear from 'a friend of a friend' is actually just something you hear from your friend—in which case it's a game of telephone…"

And so our conference began in earnest.

It wasn't a meeting to decide next year's fashions, nothing nearly so serious, but I still cleared away the snacks and set up the table because I thought it might create a certain atmosphere.

I opened a notebook and took out a pen—it felt like we were about to start a study session. Though any conference that Sengoku and I were holding would be over in a heartbeat if Hanekawa were present.

"I guess maybe the first definition should be 'something you end up knowing without knowing it.' In other words, something that you learn even though you make no active effort to obtain the information…"

"Totally. The 'charms' that went around school were like that too. Everyone was doing them before you knew it…almost like it was contagious."

"Contagious…"

188

"But that makes it sound like the flu or something."

"Actually, *influenza* originally meant something like 'outbreak,' didn't it? So given that these things spread like a pandemic, it makes sense to think of them the same way. Hmm…"

In which case, can we define a rumor as "something infectious"? You can hazard a guess, but it's difficult to pin down exactly who you were infected by…and by the time you realize what's going on, you've already got the symptoms.

A whisper on the wind, well put.

Though it might be more of a tickle in the throat.

"If that's the case, then what that swindler did to this town was almost like a kind of bioterrorism. I remember hearing something at some point about the three principles of infectious diseases…"

Umm, I tried to recall them.

Of course the person I'd heard this from was Hanekawa— almost all of my knowledge comes from her or Senjogahara.

"Oh wow, what are they? These three pillars."

"No, I think the three pillars are friendship, effort, and victory, but—umm."

The three principles of infectious diseases.

Or the three principles of pandemics.

"① Rapid rate of infection. ② Wide scope of infection. ③ Resistant to countermeasures—I'm pretty sure that was it. Seems like you could apply these three principles to rumors just as easily."

"Kind of like weapon speed, range, and power?" Sengoku offered.

That's right, I forgot she was a gamer.

"Nadeko more or less understands speed and range…but what does 'resistant to countermeasures' mean, Big Brother Koyomi?"

"Well, just what it sounds like—once the infection starts, once it starts to spread, it can't be stopped. Or really I should say, 'It can't be stopped easily'…"

"But rumors only last for seventy-five days, right?"

"Yeah. But that also means you've got to resign yourself to them until seventy-five days have passed—"

Even the Fire Sisters had found themselves playing catch-up. And they still weren't caught up—in the end, the only real way to stop an outbreak or an epidemic is prevention, to stop it before it starts.

"I see..." Sengoku nodded solemnly.

In her own way she was doing everything she could to contribute to the proper atmosphere of a meeting. Adorable, but it wasn't working. I couldn't rid myself of the sense that she was "playing make-believe."

Maybe the same was true for me...

"That goes for a naturally occurring rumor as much as it does for an artificial one like the ones the swindler created—I have a hard time believing that his plan included getting the 'charms' he'd unleashed back under control again..."

Even if things had turned out well for him, he'd probably meant to go as big as he could and then skip town without worrying about what happened afterwards.

A real scorched-earth policy...

"With Mister Swindler, the speed of infection was amazing... Those 'charms' worked their magic in just a few months."

"The scope, too... An entire town."

And the frightening part is that it was all done by just one person.

It's not praiseworthy, and I have no desire to praise him, but damn, that swindler is really something.

"So taking those principles as the basic requirements...let's think of a method that fulfills all three. Come on, there's nothing he can do that we can't."

Okay, I guess there are.

But it didn't cost me anything to say it.

Then again, there's no such thing as a free lunch.

"Sengoku. If it were you, for instance, what would you do? Say... if you were going to try and popularize something like an aberration tale. If you were going to do it intentionally."

"Hmmm... It's kind of hard for Nadeko to see what creating a fad actually requires..." After considering it, she continued, "But it seems like the easiest and quickest thing would be to 'make something that's

190

already popular even more popular.'"

Damn.

Kind of hard for her to see what it actually required? She'd just come up with a surprisingly actual methodology—hitting the nail on the head, in fact.

"If there's already some sort of foundation, something to build on, then the trail is already blazed for you... Maybe like how, neurologically speaking, once a synaptic connection has been made, it becomes easier for subsequent electrical impulses to travel the same route?" We probably could've done without the neuroscience analogy, but I was showing off for Sengoku. I wanted to try and sound intellectual. Whether or not I succeeded is another question. "There are plenty of variations, like 're-popularizing something that used to be popular'... With ghost stories, for instance, they say the same tropes come back again in ten- or hundred-year cycles... You're totally right, that would be the easiest and quickest way to do it."

"Y-You think?"

Embarrassed Sengoku.

Embarrassengoku.

Disgustingly cute.

"Ehehe."

"But while you might be able to create a trend that way, you wouldn't be able to create the trend you want...which is fine if your only goal is to create *some* trend."

"Oh...sorry."

"Um, it's nothing to apologize for..."

This girl apologizes compulsively.

She hadn't apologized yet today, and I figured she might make it to the end, but uh-uh, no dice.

I hate constantly using that unpleasant swindler as an example, but if he wanted to popularize tales of aberrations as efficiently as possible, it would've made sense to disseminate the "vampire" story. It had already infected the girls once, so the foundation was laid.

If he didn't, it was because he didn't see the benefit—*"vampires" aren't a moneymaker,* he must've judged.

"I wonder if the vampire rumors made the rounds over spring break—that is, *made the rounds so easily,* because vampires are already such a familiar concept," I said.

"Totally. Every single person in Japan knows about them... TV, manga, movies...and video games too. Vampires are always being shoved down our throats. Maybe instead of something that 'used to be popular,' they're just part of the culture now..."

"Hmm. Part of the culture..."

Well.

It's the way of the world that the things we take for granted suddenly go out of fashion, but the object of our current discussion was the rise of trends, not their decline.

"It's definitely easier for well-known things...that is, things with a certain brand recognition, to become a fad. But something that already has that foundation might deviate from our definition of going viral— since it wouldn't need that explosive infectiousness. Let's forget about making something famous even more famous, what about the know-how to make something unknown famous for the first time?"

"Uh... In that case, there's TV, and the...what do you call it."

"Mass media?"

Introducing something to the public through TV, newspapers, magazines, that's definitely a common way of spreading these infections.

"Ah, that's it. Mass media. Publicity, or advertising."

"Advertising, yeah...but even if it's not an ad, whenever the media introduces anything, fiction or nonfiction, there's some awareness of trying to 'spread' or 'popularize' it."

There must be.

It wouldn't make any sense to present something to the public at large with no intention of popularizing it. People who succeed often say, "I never expected everyone to be so into it," but they're either being humble or humblebragging.

"Still," noted Sengoku, "isn't that kind of related to what we were saying before? Something that's advertised on TV or in the newspaper is probably already famous to some degree, isn't it?"

"Hmmm...you may be right."

If the media's role is to facilitate the transition from "people in the know knowing about it" to "everyone knowing about it," then there has to be a prior stage. It's a different story if you've got the media in your pocket, of course...but I refuse to believe that swindler's got such substantial political pull.

He's like Oshino, not the type to throw in with any kind of organization.

"If we think of the mass media as a certain kind of authority, then relying on an authority is one way of disseminating a trend... In school terms, that intermediary would be the teachers, or the class president..."

"Totally. If Nadeko wanted to spread some kind of rumor... Considering, what is it, cost performance? Nadeko would probably go through Tsukihi. She's a big name with all the middle school girls, she's the boss, so if you spread a rumor to her—that might be even more effective than telling the story to a hundred other people. Assuming Tsukihi actually spreads it around for you—she's got tight lips."

"She sure does—she didn't even crack under torture."

"T-Torture?"

"Oh nothing," I waved it off.

Anyway, Tsukihi's tight-lippedness was well documented—if we're comparing rumors to viruses, she's got one hell of an immune system.

Not only did she not fall victim to that swindler, she tried to drive him out—even if a rumor is resistant to countermeasures, you can always cut off the source of infection.

"I guess if you want to popularize something with the general public, you can turn a personality into a billboard..."

"By personality, you mean celebrity, right? Yeah, the forefront of any trend... But does that mean intentionally creating a trend is always gonna involve jumping on some kind of bandwagon?" Sengoku sounded kind of disappointed—she wasn't displaying it openly, but it definitely seemed like she was losing interest.

Well, it indeed was a terribly boring conclusion, maybe not for a jaded high schooler like me, but certainly for a naive middle schooler like Sengoku.

"What sells sells because it sells"—that may be the watchword of the business world, but it sure as hell wasn't interesting.

It isn't necessarily true that good things become popular.

Bad money drives out good—but if that's the reality, let's hear it for the ideal.

"...I don't think that swindler uses the kind of methods we're talking about, though. I'm sure he understands them, of course... Still, I can't imagine him having direct contact with important people. In fact, they must be exactly the ones to whom he contrives for things to be transmitted from 'a friend of a friend.'"

"..."

"If I were in his position..." Not a hypothetical I wanted to consider, but I'd just have to grin and bear it. "I don't think I'd want to get anywhere near someone like that. Tsukihi's name just came up as an example, but in the end he made contact with Karen and avoided Tsukihi completely—"

"Is that...because important people are also dangerous?"

"Uh huh. How can I put this? It feels like a contradiction...but the ideal virus popularizes itself on its own, without any fancy footwork on your part, no need for any advertising or publicity or marketing."

"Yeah...but isn't hoping for a virus to popularize itself like standing around waiting for lightning to strike? That's not artificial, it's just a natural occurrence... At that point, aren't you just counting on chance?"

"In which case..."

In which case, maybe that swindler's methodology was of the "throw some mud at the wall and see what sticks" variety: simultaneously start circulating a whole bunch of aberration tales, or charms, that you want to popularize, that you want to disseminate—and statistically speaking, one of them will catch on.

Maybe he left it up to chance.

The invisible hand of god...

"But—I wonder if that guy would rely on chance for laying the groundwork, for the preliminary arrangements for a swindle. Well, okay, maybe we should wrap up that part of the discussion for today... Our conclusion for now is: thorough dissemination, and throwing mud at the wall to see what sticks..."

"'Kay."

"Next let's turn to the content of those trends. Leaving aside what someone might want to popularize, what would be easy to popularize?"

Easy to popularize.

Highly contagious—easy to spread.

"When you want to popularize something, whether it's a rumor or a ghost story, or a product, it's important to package it in a form that makes your job easier. With ghost stories, for instance, 'scary' ones spread more readily...right?"

"But they won't catch on if they're 'too scary.' You have to adjust the scariness to the right level, so they're not too intense, and people want to tell them..."

"Hm."

So you needed to draw a line, like the one between horror films and splatter films? They can't be too extreme, or excessive, in other words.

"In every period there are things that come into fashion and things that go out of fashion, and while unexpected things do become popular sometimes, I bet if you investigated those unpredictable trends, you'd find that they have a surprising amount of overlap."

"Like the three principles of pandemics?"

"This time I think it really is more like the three pillars—with the caveat that there will always be exceptions to the rule..." This was something that Senjogahara, not Hanekawa, had told me. The phrasing was somewhat different, but I relayed the gist of it: "Easy to comprehend, easy to obtain, easy to share—I guess."

"Comprehend, obtain, share?"

"Easy to comprehend, well, I think that one's easy to understand even without an explanation. Something that involves a complicated, confusing procedure won't spread readily. I think we can safely say that approaching something with the idea that 'it's fine if only the people who get it get it' isn't going to make anything go viral—"

Conversely, if you want to popularize something complicated, or a complicated configuration, you have to come up with a way to get that across—to make it clear. Alternately, it becomes essential that people be able to use it as-is, without understanding its underlying complexity.

TVs, cell phones, and computers, for instance—most people use them constantly without ever understanding how they work...

"What about easy to obtain?"

"In a word, I guess that means affordable...though it's not only a question of price. For example, a diamond is a rare gemstone, so regardless of how cheap it becomes, it won't be easy to obtain. And the last one, easy to share, means that it's easy for everyone to enjoy together—however great something is, if anyone ends up monopolizing it, it won't spread any further. Something that's set up to reward you for sharing your work or your impressions with other people will become a trend much more easily—or be much easier to mold into a trend."

In that regard, the "charms" the swindler spread around were totally on point. I already touched on his *first one's free* M.O., but that must've been why he homed in on "charms" that hinged on human relationships.

Human relationships.

A trend—calculated to debase human relationships.

Another example of bad money driving out good...

"Because a fad means people are getting crazy—even if it's understood as 'staying one step ahead'... Still," I conceded, "if we're bound by these basic principles, we're diverging once again from our original objective of popularizing something in particular."

"I see, something besides the thing you were trying to popularize might take off, but it's just impossible to control which way the wind blows? All you can do is trust in heaven?"

Whichever way the wind blows—is that how it is? asked Sengoku.

"..."

Was that it?

No, I don't buy it.

196

That swindler, Deishu Kaiki, leaving the swindles by which he makes his living up to divine providence—just didn't jibe with my understanding of how he went about things. No way he was going to clasp the invisible hand of god—or even the hand of the devil.

005

The epilogue, or maybe, the punch line of this story.

In the end, we never decided what kind of methods that swindler had used to popularize his "charms" within the middle school girl community—and in that sense, our meeting ended fruitlessly. I suppose it was still a little early for Sengoku to take on a subject like the state of trends in modern society.

While we were still chatting, Karen and Tsukihi came home, and the meeting came to a close—then the four of us hung out for the first time in ages. Actually, Karen, who was a year ahead, hadn't really hung out with Sengoku back in elementary school, so it might have been the first time that particular quartet had been assembled.

Sengoku's shyness skill was operating at maximum capacity, though it was canceled out by Karen's amiable-to-a-fault interpersonal skills—but anyway.

It wasn't until a little later that I found out the truth about that swindler's methods—specifically, it was the middle of August.

August fourteenth.

And how did it happen? I met with the man himself—met with him the way someone meets with an accident.

Having promised never to return to our town a second time, he'd "returned for his first time." Gimme a break and fuck off already.

The main topic on that occasion was a couple of his fellow experts—but in the course of the conversation, I asked him about it.

"Hm," he said. "The ability to know which way the wind is blowing, the ability to control the wind—nope, that's beyond me. Granted, that might also be a lie."

"..."

Can't trust this guy even an inch.

Maybe it was stupid to even ask, I was thinking, but then he went on. "If you ask me, though, something like the ability to know which way the wind is blowing isn't particularly important. Because the most conducive environment for a pandemic is a state of calm."

"C-Calm?"

"That's the vital thing for causing a pandemic in my opinion, Araragi."

"By 'calm' you mean like—the absence of wind?"

"*While one thing is popular, another thing can't be*—strictly speaking, I suppose you could say that even if something else tried to break through, it wouldn't be able to... So if I wanted to popularize something specific, I'd be sure to choose the right time and place even if I couldn't choose the target."

"..."

"Rumors last for seventy-five days—then for those seventy-five days, you have to give up on creating a trend. Take this town. I wouldn't have been able to do anything over spring break because rumors of a 'vampire' had captured everyone's imagination. No sense in trying to take on an overwhelming number-one smash—and when I say overwhelming, I mean the virus would've overwhelmed any other virus. So once that rumor had run its course—I injected my own into the empty space, the hungry space, it had left behind."

It seemed so obvious once he said it.

In other words, a pandemic will break out where there's a vacuum—

or is more likely to do so, anyway.

"Ghost stories and the word on the street, urban legends—and baseless rumors, they all run rampant when people are emotionally distraught. Which is the same as saying when people have nothing anchoring their lives. A trendless time, in other words—now Araragi. What kind of person do you think a swindler targets, who's the mark? Think about it."

"Th-Think about it? That's not something I want to think about."

"Humor me."

"Nothing funny about that question. Anyway…rich people, I guess? Don't you go after the wealthy?"

"Just what an upstanding person would think. But satisfied people are surprisingly hard to deceive—people who have financial leeway also have emotional leeway. So swindlers target those who're unsatisfied with their lot, who don't have that room to breathe."

"Which is why you set your sights on middle school girls the last time you were here?"

Or.

Going further back—on Senjogahara's family, while they were agonizing over their daughter's illness.

"That's right. A mind filled with anxiety is a mind ripe for deception. Because that person doesn't have the leeway to worry about whether you're lying to them or not," pontificated the swindler, without any hint of remorse. "You were saying that in preparation for my con, I popularized 'charms' that would debase human relationships—but in fact it was just the opposite. Their relationships were already debased, so they jumped all over my 'charms.'"

A state of calm is not necessarily a state of asepsis.

In fact, a virus with the potential to cause an explosive pandemic is always lying dormant just below the surface—said the swindler.

"Are you saying—it was their own fault they got duped?"

"When you put it like that, it makes me not want to put it like that. How about we just blame it on the zeitgeist? If you want to understand the kind of chaotic situation that makes you wonder, 'Why is this even popular?' or 'How did that get so popular?' it's really the vacuum that precedes the chaos you should be thinking about."

"The vacuum—"

"The darkness, you might say. So let me give you a piece of advice: if 'something inexplicable' becomes trendy—keep an eye on the zeitgeist. Keep an eye on the very ground beneath your feet. Assume that something is fucked—assume that the situation is critical. Whether it's a human scheme or a natural occurrence—it's happening because you live in an age enveloped by darkness."

"Enveloped by—darkness."

"The circumstances that make it easy for a fad to break out are pretty much the same as those that make it easy for a riot to break out—when there's no stable footing, you end up getting swept up by the tide. Ah, but there's no easier time to be a guy like me," Kaiki observed, ominously, before continuing, "Now, Araragi. Having taught you such an important trade secret, I must demand an additional fee from you."

"…"

I'd already paid this guy for information about a certain two-man cell of experts—but because I'd foolishly asked a question, some kind of option had kicked in.

"I know you've got your emergency fund in the inside pocket of your jacket."

He'd seen right through me.

Hmm.

The wind isn't blowing my way today.

CHAPTER SIX
KOYOMI TREE

SUN	MON	TUE	WED	THU	FRI	SAT
					1	2
3	4	5	6	7	8	9
10	11	12	13	14	15	16
17	18	19	20	21	22	23
24	25	26	27	28	29	30

September

001

There's no question that the path Karen Araragi treads, the path of karate, is a steep and severe one. But for a slacker like myself, the very idea of having such a clear path laid out before me is enviable. If it were anyone but my little sister, I would be eyeing her jealously; since it's my little sister, however, I just avert my eyes awkwardly. Nevertheless, I'd be lying if I said I never tried to imagine just what it would feel like, what it would be like, to walk unfalteringly down a ramrod straight one-way street, a highway even, laid out before me with no twists or turns, no need for a map.

To know I was striding down the right road.

Both feet firmly on the ground.

Proceeding step by steady step every day.

The journey of a thousand miles begins with a single step—and on a journey of a hundred miles, ninety miles is only halfway. In a world where darkness is always one step ahead of you, it's an untold blessing just to be able to see the path you travel down, even if it's a path without an end.

Darkness.

The Darkness.

For her there's no such thing.

I said I'd be jealous if it were anyone but my little sister, but by the same token, if it weren't my little sister, I might fall in love with that level of humanity—and yet, the kind of life she lives always comes with a disclaimer.

Precisely because her path is so clearly laid out before her—think how shocking it would be to lose sight of it. I can't help envisioning that horrible eventuality as well.

I've asked her.

If you were in a situation where you had to give up karate, what would you do?

A situation where she had to give it up.

A situation where she had to give up.

Where she had to leave that path—that highway down which she walks.

I really wasn't scheming to upset my sister by bringing up this statistically improbable, exceptional eventuality—I'm not such a mean person. I was only trying to show my concern for her by mulling over my misgivings about a real possibility.

And it is a very real possibility.

When you train morning, noon, and night in a combat sport like karate, there's always the possibility of sustaining a grievous, career-ending injury—or the love of your life might implore you to give up such a dangerous activity. Maybe you end up in a position where you have to focus all your attention on your studies—however clear the road before you, however well-maintained and spectacular, there's always the chance of mechanical trouble.

With the engine, or the electrical system.

There's potential trouble everywhere—however bright the path, however dazzlingly the sun shines down upon it, that doesn't necessarily mean the future is bright.

The Darkness isn't only ahead.

It can also be—inside.

If you stalled out on your path—what would you do?

You find yourself in a pickle sooner or later.

But Karen's unruffled, confident response was simply, "You're wrong, big brother. Because wherever I drop is the finish line. Getting to the point where I can't go any further *is* the goal."

To walk until you drop, without ever stalling out.

In other words, she expressed a fierce determination to forge ahead until she fell.

002

"This is the tree, big brother," said Karen—pointing to a tree behind the dojo where she had led me. Hanekawa probably could've identified the variety at a single glance, but unfortunately I'm ill-versed in both horticulture and forestry, so "tree" is the best I can do.

Whether "ill-versed" is a generally accepted opposite for the idiomatic term "well-versed" is a whole other question—the only other thing I can say about it is that it was old and almost totally leafless.

"This tree, huh?" was my initial response to Karen's words—I didn't know how else to react. "Well—it's definitely a tree. It's...slenderer than I expected. From what you told me, I was envisioning something a little sturdier..."

"I didn't say anything like that."

"But this is the tree that's in your way?"

"I didn't say anything like that either, that's horrible. It's all them others who are treating this tree like it's in the way—I'm its ally."

"Uh huh..."

All them others struck me as an unexpectedly pungent phrase.

I also found myself wondering if trees really have allies and enemies, but that aside, it seemed clear that Karen, my bigger little sister, had a tremendous amount of empathy for this tree.

Empathy.

My richly sentimental little sisters, in particular this older one, had a tendency to pour their excess emotions into literally anything—so if you didn't watch what you said, they could end up casually throwing their support behind anything or anyone.

Which is precisely why, as one wing (?) of the Fire Sisters, this kid reigned over the middle schoolers by popular writ—but one false move and that personality could also prove terribly precarious.

So I never take anything she says at face value. I always have to listen with a cool head—as I pondered this, I reappraised the tree that stood there before me.

"…"

Late September.

I had come along with my little sister Karen Araragi to the town dojo where she trains—a privately owned dojo where they teach karate. A dojo run by a "master" of practical combat karate, where for many years already Karen had been devoting herself to her training.

The melee skills she cultivated there had been demonstrated to her older brother on many occasions, and in that sense I couldn't set foot in that place without a certain bitterness… But under the circumstances, I had no choice.

That is, setting aside my bitterness for a moment, I was definitely interested in darkening the dojo's door at least once—because I had a hankering to meet the person whom Karen, the same Karen who turned up her nose at any kind of etiquette or manners, called "sensei," to find out just what kind of a person this sensei might be.

Half because I wanted to say thanks for taking such good care of Karen, and half because I wanted to complain, *What the hell kind of skills are you teaching my little sister?*

So after an hour and a half, my heart pounding, I reached the dojo that Karen could dash to in just under an hour. But unfortunately the sensei wasn't in.

"This isn't what I was promised."

"What? I never said aaanything about introducing you to my sensei. Or did I? When? What second of what minute of what hour of what day of what month? How many revolutions of the Earth are we talking about?"

"…"

Shaddup.

If she weren't my little sister, I'd smack her one. No, it's because she was my little sister that I wanted to smack her for being so immature.

"Karen, the only reason I don't smack you right now is that you're stronger than me!"

"How can my own big brother say something so pathetic?"

She looked sad.

I hate that even more than when she looks disgusted.

"Well, I've wanted to introduce the big brother I'm so proud of to my sensei for a long time, too. I thought today would be a perfect opportunity, since there are no classes at the dojo…but nobody's home."

"I mean, it's pretty normal for people to go out on their days off… Wait, did you even make an appointment?"

"Me and my sensei are on the same wavelength, we don't need appointments or Apollos or anything."

"First of all, I don't think too many relationships require spaceships, and second of all, judging from how things have turned out, we very much did need an appointment."

"Gyahahah, that's all over my head."

Despite the fact that I'd taken the time to lay it all out clearly, and in numerical order no less, Karen just laughed it off and lightly vaulted over the gate.

When I say gate, though, I'm not talking about your garden-variety garden gate. The dojo had a gate like the kind in front of a certain kind of house: impressive, or imposing, or really huge, but Karen took off like a ninja and leapt clean over it.

Damn, she doesn't even need CG.

It made me want to market her as the antithesis of today's movie industry—while I was thinking this over, she opened the gate from the inside.

"Okay big brother, c'mon in, this way."

"What are you, a ninja, a phantom thief? You can't just go in there when nobody's home."

I never thought I'd have to explain such a basic concept to a defender of justice like my little sister, but Karen didn't seem phased. In fact she seemed proud. "Don't underestimate the trust between me and my sensei, big brother. I always come and go as I please like this, and it's never been an issue."

"That's unheard of, you're just a disciple…"

That's it.

Next time I'm coming to the dojo with our parents instead. To formally apologize.

"Oh, come on. It's not like I'm going into the house. Just the dojo, and really just the backyard."

"That's all very well, but…"

"Don't be such a stick in the mud. You've got to be more flexible. I can help you with that, if you want. We can do our daily stretches together from now on."

"If I did the kind of stretches you do, I'd break every bone in my body. It'd be more like splatter than stretch."

"Tra la la."

She practically skipped towards the dojo—I followed after her, thinking how much I envied her seemingly carefree life, and she introduced me to the "tree" in question.

"But even if it's slenderer than I expected, a tree's a tree—it's got such presence," I said.

Looking up again at the problematic tree—though of course Karen said there was no problem at all—I asked, "Are you sure? That up until now—no one noticed this tree was here?"

003

Allow me to rewind the story a little further.

There I was in my bedroom, studying for exams—it was the end of September, the final stretch, and I must say that my feverish zeal was a fearsome thing indeed.

I was so intensely devoted to the pursuit of knowledge that no one could even get near me, but Karen just waltzed up and plunked her breasts down on top of my head.

"Heyyy, big brotherrr. It's your beloved boobies, big brotherrr."

"..."

The big brother comes off looking bad, and the little sister comes off looking stupid.

It wasn't like this back in April or May.

How did it come to this...when did we start coming off like this? I'd always endeavored to be an exemplary brother to my little sisters.

"What is it. What do you need, Karen?"

"A fine question. But not the pertinent one."

What an irritating attitude. She's as flighty as a feather.

"The correct question would be, 'When should we go?'"

213

"You make it sound like I've agreed to go somewhere with you. To begin with, it'd be so wrong if we could communicate like that, like we were psychics. Now get your enormous boobs off my head and answer my question already. What do you need?"

"Let's see, what do I need? The truth is, I think you already know what I need, big brother."

"Okay. Don't tell me what you need. Just remove your enormous boobs, that's plenty. The boobs, if you please."

"Fine. I'll back off this time."

She backed off.

Well, I say enormous, but they weren't Hanekawa-caliber, and if you factored in height relative to size, the comparison wasn't even worth making.

"Okay. Now that you've had your fill of touching your little sister's boobies, big brother, will you listen to what I have to say? Since I laid my boobies by your ear, won't you lend it to me in return?"

"I don't know what Tsukihi's been telling you, but this time I'm utterly not to blame, okay? You unilaterally laid those balloons on me, okay?"

"Unilaterally? I'm shocked to hear you say that. Just as some people's hearts accept God's grace, your head accepted Karen's boobies."

"I've had enough of your made-up sayings."

Apparently I was going to have to call a halt to my exam prep—what can you do? I don't know what she wanted my ear for, but it looked like I had no choice but to lend it.

I mean, since the incident with the swindler back in July, she'd stopped bottling things up (let alone going on the rampage) and learned how to ask her older brother for advice like a proper little sister, that was an improvement, right?

"So. Let's hear it."

"You want to hear it? Guess I've got no-o-o choice then," Karen said smugly.

Not the kind of attitude you'd expect from someone who was asking for advice, but since she could beat me up, I decided to overlook that.

214

"The fact is, I need your help. Save me, big brother."

Not quite what I was expecting from someone who was acting so big, but she was so physically large that even if she acted small, it wouldn't make much of a difference.

"Save you? Heheh. Would you look at that. Listen, Karen, people can't save other people. People just go and get saved on their own."

"Quit talking that nonsense or I'll pound you."

She brushed me off…

That is, I had a brush with death.

Well, not like it wasn't my own fault for espousing a philosophy that wasn't even mine, but why's my little sister have to crack down on me like that?

"I'm telling you to cut the shit and give me some advice, dumbass. You cruising for a bruising?"

She started cracking the knuckles on both fists.

This was more than a crackdown, she was going to stamp me out.

I was about to be shut up. Permanently.

In a last-ditch effort to demonstrate my dignity as a big brother, I said, "Understood, I'll give it. I'll give it, so hurry up and talk. Chop chop."

"Ehehe, whoopee, score!"

She got all childlike and innocent all of a sudden. It was like riding a rollercoaster.

"Thanks, big brother, that makes me so happy! I'll give you a peek at my boobies while we talk to say thank you! Peek! Peek!"

"…"

Looks like we've got a feral little sister in the house.

With a sister like her, I'll probably fail my exams no matter how hard I study. They say it's always those closest to you who trip you up in the end…

"Hey, big brother! You can stroke these legs while you listen! Aren't they shapely!"

"Sure, if toothpick is a shape. And there will be no stroking. Now if you don't want to turn me into the silent type, hurry up and tell me what it is you want my advice about."

"It's a tree," she said abruptly.

A total non-sequitur.

That is, she didn't telegraph the topic at all—which I'm sure is a fearsome skill to wield in combat, but in conversation it just makes you a bad conversationalist.

It made me keenly aware of the difference between the art of war and the art of conversation.

But if I didn't get the conversation back on track, I could end up with a different kind of keen sensation, so I nodded soberly. "Ah, a tree, you say? I see, I see."

I was appeasing my little sister.

I'm the kind of guy who can make the tough decisions…like not hesitating to be obsequious towards my little sister in the service of my goal—however I dress it up, though, in this case my goal was *I don't want my little sister to hit me.*

The A of Araragi also stands for Appease!

"But of course, makes perfect sense. Who else would you talk to about a tree but me."

"Thunderbolt Punch!"

I got hit anyway.

She may be an idiot, but I guess she still picked up on the fact that I was making an idiot out of her.

"The Thunderbolt Punch, a strike employing the power of static electricity!"

"That clearly employed the power of your muscles!"

"A tree was discovered at the dojo, and everyone's treating it like it's in the way. So I want to save it. But I don't have the power to, so please big brother, do something. I know you'll be able to do something. I believe in you. Now show me that you can live up to my expectations. Show me."

"…?"

As I recall, "speak like water running down a board" was an idiom originally used for describing the fluid speech of silent film narrators, but the way Karen embodied it felt more like a cold shower.

Transmit failure, I'm not getting any of this…

"Come on. Don't you get it? Man, you're slow on the uptake, big brother. If you can't get motivated without seeing some titties, just say so already."

"What do you take your own brother for, the Turtle Hermit?"

"Ahaha. If only my big brother was Master Roshi, that would be amazing. Though I guess Master Roshi minus his strength would be kind of like you."

"If you took away the Turtle Hermit's strength, what would that leave?"

"A turtle?"

"I'll take the hermit!"

Still, a big brother who can't understand what his little sister's talking about would be pitiful, so I decided to make an effort to make sense of her story.

"A tree was discovered at the dojo… You mean like some timber, to use for breaking?"

"No. What a horrible thing to say. Want me to rearrange your face for you?"

"Who's being horrible here? As if I'd let you rearrange it."

"Let's see, so there's the dojo, right? Like so."

Karen started explaining with motions and gesticulations. But it's hard to imagine how gesticulations could help in explaining the existence of a dojo, and indeed, I didn't understand her explanation at all.

Fine.

Forget the details, for now let's focus on the big picture.

I don't know about the "like so" part, but basically there's a dojo? And that dojo is the practical combat dojo you attend?

With you so far.

"The dojo's been around for fifty years. It's a big, beautiful /an-tee-duh-loo-vee-un/ dojo."

"Seemed like 'antediluvian' wasn't spelled out just now. You don't know how, do you? Well, whatever. So, what's wrong with the dojo?"

"Nothing's wrong with the dojo."

"I'm sorry?"

What the heck? I was quickly starting to suspect that asking my advice was merely a pretext for disrupting my exam prep…

"It's 'round back of the dojo."

"'Round back?"

"'Round back, not a roundhouse."

"I wasn't confused. I don't exactly have roundhouses on my mind all the time."

"Back in the day I used to think the Round House must be an awesome school of martial arts or something. A warrior clan like the Tairas or Minamotos. I was so disappointed to find out it was just a single move… but watch out, big brother, watch out, don't derail the conversation. We're talking 'round back here, not a roundhouse."

"You're the only one who's mixed up."

She's the worst explainer.

I started to wish she would draw me a picture instead.

"By back I mean backyard. There's a courtyard behind the dojo. And that's where the tree was discovered."

"Yeah, but this 'discovered' part is the part I really don't get… Are you basically saying some lumber was lying on the ground in the courtyard behind the dojo?"

"You don't understand a thing, do you, big brother? That's not what I'm saying at all. All you ever think about is boobies, so that's how you start to see the world. That's how you see your own little sister."

"No, I don't, and never mind what goes on in there the rest of the time, right now I'm just worried about you."

"Yeah? Thanks for worrying about me, big brother!"

She turned cute all of a sudden.

She only hears the good parts.

"It's not lumber. It's not for breaking. It's a living tree. Roots in the ground and everything."

"Hunh?"

"No good? You still don't get it?"

"No. I think I get it, but…"

By getting it, I no longer got it.

Or it got harder to get.

I'd gotten the vague impression she was telling me that one day some mysterious lumber had been on the ground in the backyard of the dojo—had been put there, or brought there—but a living tree? With roots in the ground?

"Let me get this straight, Karen."

"Ha, no need."

"Indulge me. So you're saying that there's a tree growing in the backyard of the dojo you go to...but you never noticed it before now?"

"It wasn't just me. It's not like someone else would ever notice something I didn't, right?"

"Wrong, but that's some serious self-confidence you've got there."

"It was everyone. Including my sensei, who owns the place. We only just now noticed that there's a tree there—and we don't only practice inside the dojo, you know, we train outside too."

"Uh huh... Sure, outdoor karate practice seems reasonable."

But if they were training out in the courtyard—the story was getting stranger and stranger.

This courtyard had been getting plenty of use all along—and yet no one had ever noticed this tree growing there?

"And then recently, I found it. 'What's this? Have you always been here, o honored tree?' I said."

"Huh? You can talk formally?"

"Don't act so surprised, of course I can. With those who deserve it. Seems pretty basic."

"But you've never once with me."

"Didn't I just say, who deserve it?"

She doesn't beat around the bush, my little sister.

Does she think her big brother's feelings can't get hurt?

"Karen, you don't have to be formal with me, but try talking that way to your big brother to see how it feels."

"Even though I won't mean it? Um, 'O honored brother, would you care to look upon my humble boobies?'"

"I would not. Fine. Continue the story."

"'What's this? Have you always been here, o honored boobies?' I said."

"You're getting mixed up again. If there were heretofore unnoticed boobies in the courtyard, that would be a big deal."

"A tree was a big deal too. I mean, no one'd ever noticed. It was higgledy-piggledy, everyone was like, *Huh? What's this doing here? Did someone plant this here in the middle of the night?*"

"..."

"'Higgledy-piggledy' sounds like the name of a sausage-maker, doesn't it? Hilda the Pig Lady."

"Just because I'm not talking doesn't mean I'm bored, no need to force yourself to say something funny."

"Seems like their sausages would be the best. Or not the wurst, anyway."

"Maybe it's your turn to try not talking! Um, so, what was it actually like? Was there anything left?"

"Huh? Oh, no, big brother, I haven't actually eaten there. No leftovers, sorry."

"I'm not asking about the sausages. I'm asking if there was any trace left of someone coming into the courtyard in the middle of the night and planting that tree. That's a big operation, examining the dirt around it ought to tell you something."

"Yup. I'm sure it would even tell you something, big brother."

"Are you asking me for help, or mocking me? Which is it?"

"I'm mocking you while asking you for help."

"Don't try to be clever."

"There was no trace of anything like that. It was firmly rooted. No evidence of any digging or planting. Of course neither the sensei nor any of the pupils are experts on soil or trees, so I can't be perfectly, a hundred-percent certain, but as far as anyone can tell, the tree seems to have been there for ages. It's an /an-tee-duh-loo-vee-un/ tree, seems like it's been growing there for decades and decades."

"Hmmm..."

Not only does she not know how to spell "antediluvian," she seems to think it's just a synonym for "old."

How can she possibly get such good grades?

She must've figured out how to game the system.

"But that's...kind of scary. A tree no one ever noticed, growing in a courtyard that everyone uses all the time for training and whatever else—"

"That's the thing, big brother!"

Karen slapped the floor.

With a smack.

What's she trying to do to my floorboards?

"That's what everybody says! What, are you on their side too, big brother?!"

"No, no, I'm on your side, of course." I instantly tried to appease my little sister. I seemed to be making a habit of it; this big brother really doesn't have any dignity, does he... "And? What exactly are they saying, Karen?"

"Everybody, they keep saying that the tree is scary. Scary, or freaky. Of course our sensei isn't saying anything like that, but all my insufficiently disciplined senpai and kohai are, they're spooked."

"..."

Lumping her senpai in with her kohai. Even supposing she spoke formally towards anyone besides her sensei, it's gotta be a pretty exclusive group...

"Freaky, huh? Even if that's going too far, it's not like I can't understand where they're coming from."

I'm not sure this is a fitting analogy, but wouldn't it be like cleaning your room and finding a book on your bookshelf that you didn't remember ever seeing before?

A book you didn't remember buying, didn't remember reading.

Sitting on the shelf as if it had been there all along—even if it wasn't freaky, it'd be a little unsettling.

"I see. So you're on their side, after all. You're one of them."

"One of them? You keep talking about *them*, but I've never even met a single one of these people..."

"How can you side with people you've never even met! I'm the one you should believe! Are you really going to listen to a perfect stranger over me?"

She was getting really worked up.

A scary little sister. And even stupider than she is scary.

What could be worse than a scary, stupid little sister?

Maybe this is asking too much, but how about you try being just a tiny bit moé.

"At least hear me out! Can't you treat us evenly, even?"

"Okay, okay. I'll even be even. So, you're saying you don't feel that way?"

"Huh? About what?" Karen looked blank. "Um, what were we talking about again?"

"Don't get sidetracked. You're losing the thread of your own story. You didn't feel like it was freaky that there was a tree you'd never noticed before growing in the courtyard?"

"Nope. Sure, I was shocked, but I wasn't spooked. I always order gizzard when I have yakitori, so I have a lot of grit."

"That's not how it works, and I think courage is associated with the heart."

"That's fine. I usually order that too."

Now that you mention it, the girl does go for the innards.

"In fact, when I first noticed it I felt ashamed to call myself a martial artist. So ashamed I considered suicide."

"Sounds like you don't have the mental fortitude to be a martial artist…"

"I hoped everyone else would feel the same about it, but apparently they didn't."

Completely ignoring my dig, Karen continued with an uncharacteristically forlorn look in her eye. No, not just uncharacteristic. She's not the kind of person who ever has that look in her eye. Which meant—this must've been a greater shock to her than I'd thought.

"And because they're scared—they're talking about cutting it down."

004

And that's how I ended up 'round back of the dojo.

Led there by the arm.

I don't mean that metaphorically, we really did go the whole way arm in arm.

I'd be delighted to seem like a guy out for a companionable jaunt with his little sister, but the reality is that people probably thought I was the younger sibling. Karen's so much taller than me.

And while we're at it, the arm in arm part was "to keep me from running away before we got there," so the truth is that it wasn't particularly "companionable" either.

Well.

There is precedent for me breaking my promise to Karen and running off, so I can understand why she felt that way, but for once I had no thought of running away.

Given how emotional and quick to judge she is, I took her story with a grain of salt—but to be honest, this story of a "tree that existed without anyone noticing it" piqued my interest.

…It had nothing to do with avoiding my exam prep, of course.

"Hmm…"

As I'd told Karen, the tree was a lot smaller than I'd imagined—even so, and even though it was an aged tree, it seemed highly unlikely that it could've been there without anyone noticing.

It seemed unlikely—but apparently that's what happened, so what can I say? If Karen had been the only one claiming this, I would've said my little sister was oblivious and that'd be the end of it (okay, maybe not?), but with the other pupils and even the master of the dojo all corroborating her story…

"So you were the first one to notice it? This tree?"

"I sure was. Praise me, praaaise me. Pat my head, paaat it."

"I'm sorry to say you're too tall, I can't reach."

"I'm not that huge…"

"So when everyone is training in the courtyard, you stand closest to this tree, right? Don't you think it was just that no one could see the tree because you were in the way?"

"I'm telling you, I'm not that huge."

Karen went and actually stood in front of the tree.

Some portion of the trunk was hidden, of course, but it's not like I couldn't see the tree—obviously, since it was at least ten feet tall.

There wasn't a single leaf or fruit or anything—whether it was just that the season had passed, or whether the tree had run out of the requisite life force to produce such things, I couldn't say… But judging from its height, I would've expected it to be visible even from outside the walls.

I asked Karen about this.

Shaking her head, she replied, "Dunno. I take a different route. Maybe I saw it…but I was never aware of it."

"There you go… I mean, most people don't go around peering at the trees in other people's yards, right?"

"Yeah. And I think the same is basically true even when you're inside the yard itself, or in the middle of training. So maybe we just never noticed it. But doesn't that mean it was just our own negligence?" As she said this, Karen turned around and touched the tree. "We never noticed this tree thanks to our own negligence—we weren't kind enough to

224

notice it, and now that we've noticed it we say that *it's* freaky and ought to be cut down? Isn't that fucked up?"

"Well..."

To be perfectly honest, I could see where the people who said it "ought to be cut down" were coming from. But at the same time, it was only natural for Karen to think the whole thing was "fucked up"—whether or not it actually was "fucked up" is another question, all I'm saying is it was only natural for Karen to think so.

Both sides' opinions were valid.

As a disinterested third party, I could only say that I understood where everyone was coming from—but the important thing here was that I wasn't a disinterested third party.

There's a time and a place, of course.

But at that time, and in that place, all I could be was Karen's big brother—that's all I wanted to be.

"Okay then. It seems like you were telling the truth this time, so I'll help you."

"What the hell, big brother, are you saying you didn't believe me? How rude, when have I ever lied to you?"

"Including only the clearly verifiable instances, you've lied to me on 293 occasions. The first time was when you were two years old and had broken one of my toys."

"I don't know whether to say you've got an amazing memory, a small mind, or a short stature..."

"Leave my stature out of it."

Anyway, let's get down to business.

Needless to say, we were currently trespassing on someone else's property—for Karen this was evidently a *mi casa es su casa* situation, but this was my first visit to the home of someone who I didn't know from a hole in the ground.

I could not have been more antsy.

"In other words—you want to figure out some way to keep the tree from being cut down, right?"

"Yeah. With your political pull, big brother, I know you'll manage something."

"I wouldn't count on my political pull."

"I have an even more shameless request... 'Keeping the tree from being cut down' makes it sound like it'd be okay if we found some way of moving it somewhere else. But that's off the table."

"Off the table..."

Dial back the language when you're asking for help, okay?

Why the hell are you saying that to me like it's some kind of rule, or a condition of my contract?

"It'd feel like we were driving this tree out of its home, and I couldn't stand that. Which is why I ask that you find a way for it to stay here like this forever."

"Forever, huh..."

The tree seemed like it was going to die of its own accord in the not too distant future, so the "forever" part honestly seemed a bit difficult... though likewise, moving a tree that old somewhere else was probably worse than difficult.

If we were to preserve the tree, it seemed like it was going to have to be done there—whether or not I had the political pull.

"From what you said, your sensei doesn't think this tree is freaky."

"Are you kidding my? It's me sensei we're talking about."

"That didn't come out right, did it?"

"Are you kidding me? It's my sensei we're talking about."

"Geez, saying it with the same gusto like you never messed up. In that case, though...can't you just ask your sensei to talk to the students who're so freaked out about it?"

"It's not that easy! Sensei certainly isn't freaked out by the tree, but that's only because to a martial artist, trees are just something to be kicked over."

"..."

That's nuts.

Kicking over trees instead of cutting them down?

Faced with someone like that, I guess Karen couldn't simply come out and say she felt sorry for the tree—

226

"If this tree were gone, there'd be more room for training. So freaky or not, I think sensei would secretly be glad to see it go. But it's not like I haven't already pled my case. I managed to get the tree a temporary reprieve."

"Is that so?"

"Just because I came to you, big brother, doesn't mean I didn't go to my sensei first."

"Is that so…"

"But it's impossible to stop all the other disciples. They're all pretty cocky and won't just quietly follow sensei's orders."

"Hmmm… In that case, what if you tried to convince them as their fellow karate student instead of your sensei handing down an order?"

"No good. Otherwise I would've done it already and not have bowed my head to you, big brother, I seriously hated having to."

"Seriously hated, huh…"

The hurts just keep on coming from this little sister of mine.

Like she's trying to gradually wear down my health bar.

"At the same time, if I can convince the others, I bet I can convince my sensei—that is, sensei said as much."

"A-ha…"

"To be exact, what sensei said was, 'If you can beat the shit out of all the other disciples and change their minds, I don't mind leaving the tree alone. For your sake, I'll suppress my desire to kick it over.' But I really don't want to beat the shit out of all the other disciples."

"…"

Seemed like her sensei erred a little too far on the side of practical combat.

And the fact that Karen said she didn't "want to" rather than "couldn't" was terrifying… Though if they went by majority rule, she would get pwned, so maybe her sensei was considering her feelings in a way.

The courtyard belonged to the dojo, so it was up to the sensei what happened to the tree—yup, Karen was a cherished disciple.

"And my cherished little sister… If that's how it is, the obvious course of action would be to try and convince each of the other pupils one by one..."

Cocky.

I'm not sure exactly what Karen meant by that, but if every one of them was a seasoned combatant, convincing them one by one didn't seem like it'd be an easy task.

Instead of dealing with them one at a time—the best solution would be to come up with a "principle" that could convince all of them at once.

I touched the aged tree as Karen was doing—and it felt real, in a way that didn't come across when you were simply looking at it.

It made me think, *This is a living thing.*

It wasn't just Karen, anyone might've been opposed to "killing" it simply because it'd started to wither...or simply because no one had been aware of it before.

Putting aside whether or not I agreed.

"If nothing else, we've got to get rid of this preconception that the tree is freaky. In other words—if we can prove that it's not an aberration, or an apparition, or some kind of evil spirit, but just a regular old plant..."

"Right. If only we can set those scaredy-cats' minds at ease."

"..."

It might not be so easy to convince those "scaredy-cats" with such a hostile attitude...

"Yeah? Fine, let me rephrase that. Chickens, not scaredy-cats."

"Still only sensing hostility. You've got to be buddy-buddy with them."

"It's not like we're not buddies. I usually have the utmost respect for my fellow fighters. But in this case they're chicken. A bunch of Chicken Littles, running around like chickens with their heads cut off. But mark my words, their actions will come home to roost."

"Uh huh... Anyway."

Naturally, it wouldn't be too hard to prove that the tree was just a plain old tree—we could verify it by taking a cell sample. No exaggeration, we could end the whole business with a little trip to the school science lab.

228

But I didn't think that was what Karen was after—and I didn't think it'd make the "chickens" back down.

Scientific inquiry doesn't necessarily do anything to dispel a visceral doubt—saying the tree had been falsely accused might be putting it a little forcefully, but establishing its innocence was a bit of a Devil's Proof...

I knew.

I knew that this was just a plain old tree and not an aberration—but there was absolutely no way for me to get that across to someone else...

And when you get right down to it, even my sense of things isn't always correct. It'd be the Vampire's Proof, not the Devil's Proof—still, if push came to shove, I could get Shinobu to confirm it.

"Karen. Can you think of a reason why no one noticed this tree all those years? Doesn't it seem a little much to ascribe it entirely to the greenness of some karate students?"

"Not at all."

"I see..."

If that was how she felt then so be it, but if we could only "cook up" some kind of reason, something that made sense, it seemed like we might be able to convince the other students.

I say "cook up" like I'm some sort of swindler because when you really think about it, we could probably chalk up the fact that no one ever spotted this tree to simple negligence—if not greenness.

No, maybe negligence was overstating the case, too.

But it's only natural for there to be trees in a certain type of courtyard—Kanbaru's house has them, for instance, and since it's a pretty standard scenic option for a house with this kind of vibe, you don't end up really paying it any mind.

It was neither negligence nor greenness.

It's just that nobody paid any attention to the presence of the tree—until Karen "pointed it out," and then it was suddenly thrust into the forefront of everyone's mind.

Which is probably...precisely why Karen felt responsible for an old tree growing in somebody else's courtyard, even if that person is her sensei.

"So, what did Tsukihi say about it?"

"Hm?"

"Don't play dumb with me. There's no way you consulted me without consulting Tsukihi first—what did the Fire Sisters' strategist have to say?"

"Oh. She told me about Washington."

"...The city?"

"The president."

"..."

I assumed she meant the story about how George Washington, first president of the United States of America, cut down a cherry tree...

"D-Dare I ask why she brought up that story?"

"She said, *Can't you just break it and apologize?*"

"..."

Sounds like Tsukihi when she has no interest in what you're saying...

My littler little sister Tsukihi loves to stick her nose into other people's troubles, but is the flipside of that her utter lack of interest in her own family's troubles?

"I'm afraid she wasn't actually listening to anything you had to say. What would you be apologizing for? What misdeed?"

"She was saying that regardless of what you have or haven't done, whether you're in the wrong or not, if something happens, just apologize."

"Tsukihi's entire life philosophy laid bare..."

Though in this case, Karen would probably be a hero if she broke it—seeing as that's what everyone including her sensei was hoping for.

I was reminded afresh of Karen's inner strength—sticking to her own opinion even when everyone around her, her erstwhile comrades no less, all saw it differently.

I, at least, wasn't possessed of the mental fortitude to brave friction and conflict when victory promised no concrete advantage or benefit.

That alone.

That alone was enough to make me want to help her out, just this once—oops, that makes it sound like I care about my little sister.

Let's call it an opportunity for me to put Karen in my debt.

"Heheheh."

"What's with the evil look?"

"Karen. How much time have we got to play with?"

"Almost none. Even tomorrow might be too late. We're up against the possibility that someone'll try and knock it over sometime today."

"Gosh, at least use a saw."

Anyway, not much time.

Almost none, or none.

Even if we did have some time, it would be of the essence—I had to assume that all the other disciples came and went as freely as Karen, so it was entirely possible one of them might go rogue. And seemingly every last one of them could topple the tree without using any tools—

"Then I know what to do. Karen, you can rely on your reliable brother."

"Really? Then as thanks I'll let you do whatever you please with my boobies."

"I don't want you to think that I was motivated by that reward, so I will not do whatever I please."

"Playing hard to get, huh. Why, you…"

"How about I do whatever I displease."

"Whatever you displease?! What are you planning to do to my boobies?! Anyway, big brother, what are you going to do?"

"Heh. Trust me."

005

"Please, Hanekawa!"

"You're just unloading it on me?"

That night, I called Hanekawa. I'd decided to give her a full rundown on the old tree and Karen's dojo, and to ask for the benefit of her wisdom.

"I did everything I could, but I hit a wall. Please, do something for Karen. Help me, Hanekawa, you're my only hope."

"Aren't you giving up a little too easily?"

I heard her sigh.

Lately Hanekawa had stopped even trying to hide her disappointment in me.

"Please. I'll do whatever I please with your boobies if you do."

"My boobies are my own, thank you very much...but fine. For Karen's sake, not yours, Araragi. If I think of it that way, I can find the motivation."

"So, what do you think?"

"Hm? Hmm? About what?"

"I mean, first off I'd like to hear your thoughts on the matter—who are you with, Karen or everybody else?"

"Karen, of course. You can't just dispose of a living tree for no good reason. You don't agree, Araragi?"

"Let's see…that's my gut feeling, but if I were actually involved, who knows—I probably would've gone along with everyone else's opinion, whatever my own feeling might've been."

"And there you go."

"Hnh?"

"That's how everyone besides Karen must have felt—what I mean is, I don't think the majority of them actually want to dispose of the tree like you and your sister think they do. If you can just get the opinion leaders to change their minds, everything'll be taken care of."

"Hmm…"

Hanekawa's done it again.

My faith in her is not misplaced.

"And I think you were exactly right about the reason no one noticed that tree up until now, Araragi—it wasn't a question of noticing or not noticing, it was just that nobody was really aware of it. But once it's on your mind, it's really on your mind—it ends up catching your eye more than it would otherwise. Like your bed head, Araragi."

"Like my bed head, huh…"

If it's catching your eye, say something.

At the time, I mean.

"When you learn a new word, it starts cropping up everywhere—that sort of thing?"

"Yeah, I suppose so," Hanekawa said. "Or like how nobody remembers every single shop on a street even if it's one they walk down all the time."

"Except for you."

"Ahaha, as if," Hanekawa laughed.

To cover up the truth, probably.

"This goes back to what we were talking about earlier, but I wonder if some of the disciples at the dojo actually *had* noticed the tree before. But once everyone started talking about the 'tree no one had noticed,' they felt like they couldn't speak up. Doesn't that seem possible?"

"Like they didn't want to spoil the mood? Definitely seems possible."

"But even if that explains the phenomenon itself, we still need to figure out how to spin it. It's only natural for people to see it as a mysterious phenomenon, as a mysterious tree."

"I mean, this confluence of coincidences might get passed down to future generations as the tale of an aberration. Who knows what kinds of stories get popular, or how…"

We can theorize about it.

But a theory is just that.

It can never be anything more.

"Just to be clear, Araragi, there's a pandemic of panic sweeping the dojo now, right?"

"Panic is kind of an exaggeration…but yeah, there's something of an outbreak."

"So we just need to bring that to an end."

"Hm? Well, sure. But countermeasures are ineffective against pandemics, aren't they? That's the whole problem."

"No, that's not necessarily true. There is a way to stop a pandemic."

"Huh?"

"A way to stop one, or a way for one to stop—"

I guess this time there's nothing for it.

Hanekawa made it sound like she'd prefer it to be otherwise—and once I'd heard the "wisdom" she was about to share, I understood why.

This time, even I couldn't bring myself to say—*you know everything, don't you.*

006

The epilogue, or maybe, the punch line of this story.

Well, the fact that I didn't set Hanekawa up for her usual catchphrase is already a hell of a twist ending, but anyway, here's what happened. Cutting straight to the conclusion, the old tree Karen wanted to protect didn't get chopped down.

And naturally I don't mean that it got punched or kicked over, either—it's alive and well even as we speak. I can't guarantee it'll be there forever—but for now, it does seem to have weathered the storm.

As for what we did:

"A pandemic or a panic will come to an end—when it gets to where it's going."

It'll stop when it reaches its goal.

Basically, when any kind of virus has spread so widely that it can't spread any further, there's nothing else for it to infect, so the outbreak ends of its own accord.

That's how the food chain remains stable—though in this case, of course, we couldn't actually let it get to where it was going since "the end of the line" for this particular pandemic was the old tree's disposal.

"So what we have to do is *move* the goal posts—at this stage, every-one thinks the tree is 'freaky,' right? Or one step up, 'scary'—that's where the general awareness level is at, right? 'Freaked out,' 'terrified'—we just have to move them one stage further up the ladder. That's where we need to put the goal."

"One stage further…"

"Which would be awe, I guess?"

Awe. Not just fear.

Fearful—reverence.

The next day, this is what Karen told her fellow disciples.

That aged tree was like the ones used in the construction of our sacred dojo—and apparently it was planted in the rear courtyard as the dojo's guardian deity.

Which explains—the mysterious phenomenon we all experienced.

That was how she explained it to them.

That was how she spun it to them.

"Having watched unseen over the disciples of this dojo for many decades, a god of the martial arts finally revealed itself, its energy expend-ed. To cut it down would be unthinkable—"

She adopted Hanekawa's fairy tale pretty much as-is—Karen, of course, isn't the kind of person who'd lie to anyone except her big broth-er, so first I had to dupe her.

She also isn't the type to believe in aberrations, but a few months previously she'd experienced some weird shit, and apparently the spiritual frame story of an "invisible martial arts guardian deity" was relatively easy for her, as a martial artist, to accept.

As for the other students of the dojo, including the ones who'd only been swept along—"the truth of the matter" had been brought to light without negating their opinions and feelings, it even extrapolated from them, so that was the end of the line for the panic, or to put it another way, nothing more happened.

And—

If that was the truth, they'd never dream of harming the tree.

This fiction was not going to fool Karen's sensei, the master of the

238

dojo, of course. It stands to reason, though there's no way of knowing for sure, that the lumber used to build the dojo didn't come from the same kind of tree as our aged friend.

"But I somehow doubt that'll come up—their sensei won't want to spoil the mood. After all, Karen will have convinced everyone like she promised."

Apparently, that was indeed how it went.

I guess Hanekawa's view that the sensei, who had a dojo to run, wasn't foolish enough to rekindle a panic that had finally abated, was on point—and so.

For the moment, the tree's life has been prolonged—Karen, taking responsibility, protected this tree she had "found."

"I do feel bad about lying, though…"

Having leaned on Hanekawa's wisdom, I was in no position to bolster her spirits when she said this, but I couldn't help trying to console her.

"It wasn't necessarily a lie."

"Hunh?"

"For all we know, that tree might be an aberration. I don't know if it's a guardian deity, but…maybe it was an aberration that no one was aware of because it was hiding its presence all along. And the dojo being built from the same kind of wood isn't out of the question. It's statistically possible."

"Haha. Sure, a statistically negligible possibility."

"Statistically negligible possibilities are still possible. And…"

Well.

Even if I meant it by way of consolation, the next thing I said might've gone too far.

"Thanks to the way we spun it, that tree might actually have become an aberration. One to watch over the disciples as they train."

TSUKIMONOGATARI

POSSESSION TALE

NISIOISIN

VERTICAL.

TSUKIMONOGATARI
Possession Tale

NISIOISIN

Art by VOFAN

Translated by Daniel Joseph

VERTICAL.

TSUKIMONOGATARI

© 2012 NISIOISIN
All rights reserved.

First published in Japan in 2012
by Kodansha Ltd., Tokyo.
Publication rights for this English edition
arranged through Kodansha Ltd., Tokyo.

Published by Vertical, an imprint of Kodansha
USA Publishing, LLC, 2019

ISBN 978-1-947194-47-2

Manufactured in the United States of America

First Edition

Third Printing

Kodansha USA Publishing, LLC
451 Park Avenue South, 7th Floor
New York, NY 10016

www.readvertical.com

CHAPTER BODY

YOTSUGI DOLL

CHAPTER BODY
YOTSUGI DOLL

001

Yotsugi Ononoki is a doll. To put it another way, she's not human. Not a person, not a living being, not a part of the natural world—that's Yotsugi Ononoki, a *tsukumogami* possession employed as a *shikigami* familiar.

Though to all appearances she's just an adorable tween.

This expressionless child, who delights all and sundry with her eccentricities, is in truth an aberration, an apparition, a monster, one of the endless varieties of ghosts 'n goblins with which nature abounds.

For which reason.

She's hopelessly incompatible with human society.

"Nay, truth to tell, my lord, 'tis not so—not that lass," came Shinobu's response. From within my shadow. "For she springs originally from a human corpse, and is a doll—a creation patterned after humankind. An imitation of a person."

Then.

Then does that mean she's trying to be, or become, human? But when I voiced this question, Shinobu informed me that I was still off the mark.

To be patterned.

Proves you aren't trying to be it.

It's only a means for mingling with human society—for making her compatible—and not a means for assimilation.

"However skillful thou mayst become in a foreign tongue, however much dost study it and speak it like 'twere thine own, 'tis only ever for the sake of communicating with the people of a foreign land, and thou mayst not wish to become their countryman—'tis much the same. She was made in the image of humankind, but not for the sake of being human or becoming human. 'Twas for being with humans."

Not to be, nor to become.

To be with.

That foreign language analogy really did the job—well, bringing other countries into the mix makes it all terribly global, but framing it in terms of other cultures does put us back in the realm of everyday conversation for me, or for anyone, I bet.

In order to forge a positive relationship with someone from another culture, you've got to see through the eyes of that culture—when in Rome, as they say.

"Come, my lord. Hast thou never considered why aberrations, why monstrous beings of legend, wear the aspects of human beings or of animals—to wit, why the form of the unreal is founded in reality?"

I never had.

I mean, can't we just say that our imagination has its limits? We can't picture, can't visualize, things that *aren't*, so we *fashion* them by spicing up things that *are*.

Take Shinobu Oshino's base form, Kissshot Acerolaorion Heartunderblade, for instance—though a vampire, a beautiful demon, she was ultimately modeled on a human being.

When she sprouted wings, they were a bat's.

When she bared her fangs, they were a wolf's.

Though she embodied the unreal and surreal as a vampire, substantially she was an assemblage of realistic elements—no more than an idealization.

A beauty that no painting can capture isn't going to be captured in a painting.

A beauty that our eyes can't behold isn't going to be beheld by our eyes.

To resort to another linguistic analogy, people can only relate reality using the words available to them—however inexpressible the reality, however inexhaustible the dream, in the end we have to rely on our voices and our pens.

Expressing with words.

Exhausting them.

But we can't just say that, I suppose. Aberrations, whose appearances are modeled on, and dictated by, the limits of our imagination aren't going to take it lying down. Sure, they're unstable, they change their appearance depending on the observer and transform depending on their surroundings, but I bet they desire a fixed form.

So I couldn't say anything—certainly not to the aberration right there in front of me, Shinobu, a former vampire who now looked like an eight-year-old blonde of all things.

Having read my thoughts, and for that reason not touching on the matter, she said, "All in all, 'tis because people exist, because they are, that aberrations are too. Which meanest not the latter are dependent upon the former—'tis simply that if none observe, none are observed either."

I had to wonder.

I assumed she was talking about the so-called Observer Effect, but this sounded different—it was something else, not some theory, but more emotional and sentimental, so to speak.

"Every presence, every act, requireth a witness lest it be devoid of meaning. Untold, any tale of heroes or of aberrations may as well have ne'er been." Shinobu seemed to be reflecting on her own experiences. "I have been called a legendary vampire—but if those legends did not exist, 'twould be as if I were no vampire at all. An aberration that goes unheralded is not worthy of the name."

Weird tales—must be weird in the telling, she remarked.

"Though 'tis less mine own thinking or values than that execrable Aloha shirt's, ultimately an aberration is a deep attachment."

Deep attachment—feeling.

Like empathizing with a doll? You could say that's how tsukumogami, or more generally the spirit of not being wasteful, the *mottainai obake,* is born.

They say the belief that gods reside in everything, that there are eight million of them, is native to Japan, but empathizing with something that isn't human, be it living or inanimate, isn't unique to one culture.

Which is why tales of aberrations are told throughout the world.

Told—by humans.

It was a pretty convincing argument, or rather, an argument I had no choice but to be convinced by, as someone who's spoken of so many aberrations.

And told their tales.

Of a vampire.

Of a cat.

Of a crab.

Of a snail.

Of a monkey.

Of a snake.

Of a bee.

Of a phoenix.

As someone who has, I had no choice but to be convinced.

And now I'm about to speak again, of a doll this time, but I have the sneaking feeling that I've been telling too many tales.

Urban legend, word on the street, or secondhand gossip, it's all just idle chatter if you speak of it too much. It ceases to be eerie, or alarming—when I think back to the beginning of second term and the bizarre "Darkness," or to the matter of Nadeko Sengoku's godly serpent-god from around New Year's, I have to ask how long this is going to continue, and feel a little exhausted. Since my tricks are starting not to work on these aberrations that keep coming out of the woodwork, I'm kind of sinking into despair—though that feeling is a luxury.

Forever, is how long.

Our world doesn't afford that luxury, I ought to have known by now—but it's a little too late for ought's.

Every tale comes to an end.

My, my, I guess the crazy times weren't quite over yet—even that refrain has its limits.

Because the story I'm about to tell you about a doll is also the story of how I "learned that"—learned it, whether I liked it or not.

So this is the beginning of the end.

The tale of how I, the human being called Koyomi Araragi—began to end.

002

"Rise and shine, big brother!"

"Come on, you can't sleep all day!"

That morning I developed a sudden philosophical interest on the issue of alarm clocks. To be frank, I dislike the term *alarm clock* almost as much as the existence of the things themselves. I've never liked them. At all. In fact, they disgust me. I've never liked them for a single moment. I feel a singular, momentous disdain for alarm clocks.

But as to why I dislike them so much, the answer is guaranteed to come out sounding like some kind of Zen exercise. Do I hate them for being alarm clocks, are they alarm clocks because I hate them, or are they hate clocks because I alarm them? While the unvarnished truth is that I've wished for every single alarm clock in the world to go to hell, I don't believe that everything that goes to hell must be an alarm clock. That thought never even crossed my mind. If that proposition were true, wouldn't it mean that I myself am an alarm clock, since I'm almost certainly headed for hell?

You, yourself, being an alarm clock—who'd ever want to grapple with that fear?

There is one proposition that I *have* considered, however, and I'd love to run it by you. I need to run it by you. It inevitably arises when I consider the question of why I, or in fact, probably everyone in the world, or at least most people, the vast majority of the majority anyway, loathe and abhor alarm clocks as if they've wronged our loved ones. Perhaps it's not a proposition but the proper position—I honestly feel sheepish about describing my own realization as if it's some kind of grand discovery, but anyway, maybe people find alarm clocks so difficult to like because the words *clock* and *alarm* together sound too much like *lukewarm*.

Something that's not hot enough.

Something you took the trouble to heat up that went and cooled down.

All for naught, a wasted effort.

That act, which even smacks of a blasphemous revolt against the law of entropy, shares something with the irritation of being jolted from sleep, and this is why I, we, why all the world holds such a deep hatred for alarm clocks—I call it the Nuance Proposition. And it doesn't end there; I propose that similar words end up with similar implications and drag similar emotional responses along behind them. I can give you any number of examples. Take Bruce Lee and *brûlée*. I think we can all agree that they share the quality of being awesome.

But even putting aside the veracity of the Nuance Proposition, it must be noted that there are some minor issues with its application to our hatred of alarm clocks. First of all, as I've discussed at length, it's an affliction shared by humanity the world over, whereas the likeness between the *clock-alarm* combo and *lukewarm* is specific to one language, unfortunately rendering the proposition's use as the sole expositor of the phenomenon somewhat vexed. I haven't thoroughly examined the literature on the subject, but nonetheless suspect that the alarm clock predates modern English. It calls for a trial translation of both phrases into, say, ancient Greek, but a second piece of counter-evidence frees us from that need.

This second point is a so-called *irrefutable rebuttal*, and thus not really the second but the ultimate piece of counter-evidence: even if we limit the field of inquiry to languages where the two phrases are indeed similar, the average person probably learns the term *alarm clock* prior to *lukewarm*.

That's some counter-evidence.

You might say irrefutable.

Upon reflection, I myself feel unclear to this day about the precise meaning of *lukewarm*. Luke, warm. From the word itself I can just about grasp that something has been at least partially warmed, but any request for a concise definition would be greeted with grave silence on my part. I would remain as silent as the grave. In fact, if we refuse to let go of the Nuance Proposition, perhaps what we're really talking about here is *alarm clock* having a negative influence on *lukewarm* rather than the other way around.

Still, I hate alarm clocks.

A wise man once said there's no accounting for taste, some people have a taste for accounting—which is all well and good, but it's equally true that no one wants to feel like the kind of nobody whose preferences are based on nothing. Everybody wants to be a somebody. Surely I am no snob to want to ascribe a reason to them, for the sake of my own worth, even if it requires straining interpretation.

And I trust we can also agree that it is because I'm not a snob that I'm about to lead the discussion into even more profound territory. "I am not unthinking, therefore I am unthinkable"—well put, or actually it's me putting it like some maxim, I must be the first person in human history to put down those cryptic (or crappy) words. All thinkers must of course recognize the debt they owe to their predecessors, but you don't get to blame them for your stupidity.

Anyway, back to alarm clocks.

Alarm clocks, for waking up.

I'm not sure how this could have happened, but I somehow forgot to explain the second law of the Nuance Proposition: the appearance clause, which goes beyond the way it sounds. Words with similar appearances provide similar sensations, and what's similar is assumed to be the same. If the first hypothesis is auditory, then this second is visual.

Take for example *E* and *F*. They don't sound a thing alike, but because their shape is ninety-percent similar, the nuance we derive must be similarly similar. *I* and *L* would of course provide an equally valid demonstration of this principle.

And from this we can derive the similarity between a lack of self-awareness and a clock of self-awakeness—it'd be no surprise if some people deemed them equivalent, synonymous. Leaving aside the initial *c*, a little bit of pressure turns an *a* into an *o*, and surely no one will dispute that with the addition of a small line or two, *r* becomes *k*.

In which case a lack of self-awareness and a clock of self-awakeness are the same thing.

Even if they're not identical, they're nearly identical. No evidence has yet been offered to refute this.

And the word, or rather phrase, or maybe I should call it a line… Anyway, whatever you call it, however you put it, "a lack of self-awareness" does not carry a positive implication.

They say it's not about what was said but who said it, and they've said it so many times that I'm sick of hearing it, but no matter who utters the phrase "a lack of self-awareness"—no matter who told you that—it's uniformly and fundamentally a rebuke, or dare I say an insult.

You're not very self-aware, huh?

Not too self-aware, are ya, buddy.

No one would take such a remark as a compliment—even if it were said affectionately by one's teacher or master, even knowing it was said with one's best interests at heart, there's not a person on earth whose feelings wouldn't be at least a bit hurt.

The notion that this antipathy might be connected to our negative emotions toward alarm clocks is both logically and intellectually compelling, and as far as I'm concerned it leaves no room for argument. Alarm clocks are themselves manifestations of a lack of self-awareness, so to speak.

If I am hesitant to present this theory in academic circles, it is by no means because I have reservations about accepting the concomitant honor and prestige, but rather for the two reasons outlined above. In other words, the congruence between a lack of self-awareness and a clock of self-awakeness is once again a phenomenon specific to one language, and while I cannot make such an extreme pronouncement as I did regarding *lukewarm*, people learning about their own lack of self-awareness before learning about alarm clocks strikes me as a contradiction.

Leaving aside our vocabularies, or our order of linguistic acquisition, it makes some kind of intuitive sense that a person wouldn't be scolded for a lack of self-awareness before "waking up" from some kind of standby state. It seems slightly foolish to rely on gut feelings in the course of our reasoning, and yet intuition can prove to be a surprisingly reliable tool.

When people say, "I have a bad feeling about this," for instance, they're often correct. Because, alas, we can say with certainty that there's no such thing as a life, or even a day, when not a single bad thing happens. Not a single such day in our entire lives. And that's why it's much more auspicious to blatantly disregard this fact and declare first thing in the morning, in the way of autosuggestion, "Seems like something good will happen again today!" Just tell yourself, "I've got a good feeling about this," whether or not you do. Because there's also no such thing as a life, or a day, when not a single good thing happens—in fact, if you've woken up in circumstances where you can still make that statement, you're having a pretty good day. In

19

any event, trust your instincts. In fact, alarm clocks and a lack of self-awareness having precious little to do with each other is something you might realize quite well without having to think about it, even if you can't explain why.

Let us forget about the Nuance Proposition for now, if we may.

It was a bad joke, okay?

Like waking up on the wrong side of the bed.

If seeking things that are like an alarm clock is a futile endeavor, just as seeking people who are like ourselves often is, might we not instead consider the thing itself? They say like attracts like, but if we interpret this as friendship, or fellow feeling, then it's hard to imagine an alarm clock having any friends, or fellows. Hence, it is only in speaking about the alarm clock as a unique entity in the world, a unique concept, that we can discover the true nature of our loathing. It is only in so doing that the man can become the master.

Alarm clock, alarm clock, alarm clock.

Mclockalar.

If you repeat the words it starts to sound like *mackerel*, at which a thoroughly average Japanese person like myself can't help but be reminded of breakfast. A joyful association, but we've decided for the time being to dispense with associations, so I won't say any more on the subject.

Here's the real issue.

The term in question is *alarm clock*, but what *alarm* means in this instance is *cause to wake up*—it is thus a clock that causes a target, the person sleeping next to it, instantiated in this case as *me*, to wake up. That's the definition of an alarm clock, or its raison d'être to put it in slightly exaggerated terms. If it didn't cause me to wake up, it'd be an un-alarming clock.

Which is hard to say.

And now we come to it.

It is without a doubt due to the maddening pushiness of the word *alarm* itself that I, that we loathe alarms clocks so much. People, left alone, generally tend to wake up, and I do feel a Luddite-like antipathy toward the very idea of relying on a machine, but all of this begs the fundamental question of why we have to wake up in the first place.

Not waking up means dreaming. Waking up means abandoning our dreams, which doesn't leave a particularly good impression. Not particularly good, or not to mince words, bad. It would be appropriate to call it the embodiment of heinousness.

Recessions, economic slumps, an uncertain future.

Precisely because we live in a world that is hostile to dreams, shouldn't at least nighttime offer a space for them? The behavior of alarm clocks, who so churlishly upend this (and yes, I will anthropomorphize them with a "who") is unforgivable. We all learn the truth of this world at some point. Why rouse sleeping children from their dreams?

I'd rather not wake up, thank you very much.

Nor waken, awaken, or be woken.

People like to say "bright and early," but if it's so goddamned early, how about you let me sleep a little longer? Forget *early*, how about we go for *just right*. If you were nice enough to say *good night* to me before I went to bed, then let me get a good night's sleep! To be perfectly honest, when someone who wished me a good night gives me the bright-and-early treatment the next morning, I feel somewhat betrayed.

Betrayal is tragic.

To begin with, it's been proven that needing to wake up just because it's morning is hopelessly outdated. History has proven this. Humanity has become nocturnal, as is evident from the mostly late-night broadcast times of anime, Japan's proudest international cultural export. Even biologists will recognize the ironclad fact in the not too distant future; it is no joke. Study and construction work are also carried out late at night. In becoming nocturnal, humanity is poised to evolve further. In time, the significations of the Moon and the Sun may become reversed. Indeed, morning is when people should sleep, and alarm clocks, who wake people up in the morning, indeed must be called works of fiendish deviltry for obstructing our evolution.

I get it.

I get why people want to depend on alarm clocks, their functionality—but now is when we summon the courage to wean ourselves from that function. A time for clean breaks is at hand.

Can't we just stop worrying about the whole "waking up" thing? A life of loafing is at least good for a laugh. In fact, isn't a life that isn't laughable kind of lame?

Why not go through life looking at smiling faces everywhere you go?

So this is what we should say to alarm clocks.

With gratitude, not animus.

"Thank you. And good night."

"Wake up already!!"

"Wake up already!!"

Punched. Kicked.

Jabbed. Head-butted.

And right where it counts. It'd take too long to enumerate the many vital areas of the human body targeted by these attacks, so I'll leave that to your imagination and simply state that they were only the most critical. Were I not to make this clear, my blinding agony and the ensuing developments would make less sense.

"What a long excuse for not wanting to get up, big brother."

"And we're not some clock, we're your sisters. Your alarm sisters."

So said Karen Araragi and Tsukihi Araragi, my two little sisters, as they stood planted on either side of my bed like the vajra kings. I don't mean this metaphorically, it's not a rhetorical analogy to spice up the narrative, they really were expressing their fuming discontent by striking the alpha-and-omega poses of statues flanking a temple gate.

Karen, with her mouth open.

And Tsukihi, mouth closed.

Cool.

I hope they make figurines of them like that.

"So what? According to the Nuance Proposition of Professor Me, similar words can be deemed identical."

"Boy let me tell ya, 'sister' and 'clock' ain't similar at all," Karen kicked me in Kansai-ben. Not only was her intonation off, since she has no ties to the region whatsoever, but the *boy let me tell ya* came out sounding liked *boiled meathead.*

Sounds like quite a recipe.

And Tsukihi added, "I've heard of a grandfather clock, but…"

That seemed less like a retort than a quibble, but from it I derived the (leap of) logic for my next idea.

"I've got it! We'll sell merchandise called 'Sisterclock.' Karen the big hand and Tsukihi the little hand. Wakes you up in the morning with the voices of Ms. Kitamura and Ms. Eguchi."

"Hey, keep their names out of it."

"The anime's already over, big brother. No more tie-in products."

"Oh…"

How sad.

Such a sad fact.

But sad as it might be, it was a reality that I needed to accept.

Though judging from how they woke me up in the anime version's style, Karen and Tsukihi were clinging to the past in their own way.

"Urr~~~~r."

This wasn't me confronting that shocking reality; talking with my sisters, I had woken up, sobered up, perked up somewhat and stretched out from that curled-up ball of blinding agony. On all fours, looking like some sexy cat. Koyomi Araragi's cougar pose isn't something I want you to try and picture.

"All right, I'm up. I've regained consciousness." I faced my Sisterclock, sorry, sisters. "What century is it?"

"Nah. Quit pretending you just woke up from cryosleep."

"You haven't been asleep long enough for it to be a new century."

A twin-engine retort, surround sound—a comedy trio with two straight men, or rather women, is pretty rare, I think?

Wanting another taste of the rare experience, I kept going. I threw them a softball.

"If they've woken me up, does that mean they've found the cure?"

"As if you're somebody they'd freeze until they found one."

"They'll never develop a medicine that can help you, big brother."

Nice.

Karen was in an unfortunate position, though, stopping at an inoffensive jibe against her older brother while Tsukihi lay into me with no respect.

"Is the nuclear war over?" I asked next.

"What's unclear? It's not over."

"Huh?!"

Tsukihi was startled by Karen's line.

I take it back.

When Karen bombed she dragged her little sister down with her, a truly unfortunate position for Tsukihi.

"Hmm...but I think this could work. Coming up next episode: The Three Araragis."

"We told you, big brother, the anime run is over. And that means no more previews of the next episode."

"No more promotional videos, either."

Relentless.

No more PVs either, huh?

"Damn... Looks like we're back to square one. Starting over from scratch, with the bare essentials."

The "bare" bit might make Kanbaru happy, but we had to adopt that mindset.

Starting over from scratch.

If we gave it our all, maybe we'd grace your screens again.

"In which case, Karen, give me the time of day."

"One, two, three, four, five, six...hnh?"

For a second it seemed like she was on board with my *rakugo* allusion, but middle schoolers these days don't know the original well enough, and she trailed off midway.

Once again Tsukihi was forced to pass.

The dual-straight-women setup didn't stand a chance, after all.

I gave up on trying to elicit a reply from them and looked at the clocks sitting in my room. Yes, plural. There are four—though none with an alarm function.

I did use to have an alarm clock, until Karen punched right through it with her fist of righteousness and enlightened me that, hot damn, steel can give as easily as newspaper.

Spake the master: "It's our duty to get our big brother out of bed, no machine will take that away from us!"

It was an odd character trait for a little sister.

My Little Sister Is a Luddite.

Waking me up every morning at the same time means having to wake up even earlier, which wasn't easy. Why would you take it upon yourself like it's your mission in life?

Let's see... Right.

Pretty sure this has been going on since middle school.

They wake me up like this ever since I started middle school... but why? Why do they wake me up?

Is it to recapture some kind of lost familial bond? If so, when was it lost?

With that long-overdue question in the back of my mind, I confirmed, having just woken up, that it was six o'clock. Confirmed that the big hand and the little hand formed a 180-degree angle.

No way it could be evening, so it followed that it was six in the morning—and since I hadn't been in cryosleep, today's date was...

"February—thirteenth?"

I said it out loud.

Mine is a room with four clocks but no calendar.

I know, I know, how could I be named *Koyomi* and not have my namesake in my room, but I don't let my name dictate my lifestyle.

After all, what's in a name?

"The day before Valentine's Day. Hey, sisters o' mine, have you finished shopping for all the chocolate you're going to give me?"

"Aaagh," Tsukihi let out a cry of disgust in response to my charming little witticism. She looked at me like I was a vase of dead flowers. "What a disappointing big brother... Brazenly demanding chocolate from your little sisters is just too disappointing. Are you even human? Are you humanity's final stage?"

"What the hell are you talking about? It's only kind of disappointing."

"You've finally maxed out on your disappointing. That was something that should never be said. Poor big brother. The whole girlfriend thing must be a lie too. Ms. Senjogahara is some extra you hired for a thousand yen an hour."

"Don't call Senjogahara an extra. Money doesn't motivate that woman," I protested, but upon reflection, she's pretty hung up on money. A thousand yen an hour would definitely get her moving. Like lightning. Tsukihi, who clearly knew this, wore a triumphant smile. As if to say, *He claims to be her boyfriend but doesn't know shit about her.*

Well.

Maybe I don't know anything.

Maybe I'm profoundly ignorant.

Even if I put that aside, though, ever since I introduced my sisters to Senjogahara, they've been thick as thieves—especially Tsukihi, who really jibes with her personality-wise.

Under the circumstances, the chocolate they apparently hadn't bought for me might be prepped and waiting for Senjogahara.

"Interesting... So the plan is to focus more on the *yuri* stuff, huh? That shows some business acumen."

"What're you talking about, big brother? *Yuri*? Is that someone's name? Plus, if it's about business acumen, pivoting toward BL would be a better idea."

Tsukihi was cooking up some fiendish scheme.

As befits the brains of the Fire Sisters.

Maybe even overcooking it.

"Come on, big brother," Karen taunted, "this is no time for you to be worrying about Valentine's Day. Is it? Is it? You like that?"

She started stomping me. I remained in my sexy cat pose—or was continuing my morning calisthenics routine, so she was grinding her heel into my back as she spoke.

"Only one more month until your college entrance exams. You realize that, right? Do you realize that if you don't realize that, you'd be better off dead? I'll kill you myself."

"What? You've got no right to talk to me like that, let alone kill me?"

Though that said, it was indeed exactly one month until March thirteenth, the day when Koyomi Araragi would at last face his college entrance exams.

Happily, I hadn't been culled by the national exam right out of the gate—considering what was going on at the time, it was nothing short of a miraculous outcome. Though I prefer to think of it as the outcome of my hard work. In either case, it was a close shave as these things go, of course, and when I took a step back, it regrettably seemed like I'd raised the bar for myself...

"Fer chrissakes, this is why you'll never be anything but trash," Karen said, crossing her arms.

What a word to use—you see it often in manga and whatnot, but rarely hear people in real life call another living, breathing person *trash*.

"You can't even see what you have to do. You can't see even a month down the line, all you can see is tomorrow, whatever's staring you right in the face. Your eyes are closed, squeezed shut, you've got no prospects for the future. You plan to live like that? You're in such a sorry state, you probably couldn't even manage to off yourself. And even if you do get into college, what then? Just thinking about it kills me. It's quite an achievement to hand me my ass like that, goodwill handassador."

"Goodwill handassador..."

I think I might be the only person on earth to have been abused in that particular fashion. We were both third-years, the difference between middle and high school notwithstanding, but Lady Karen, who was in an escalator system and didn't need to do any studying to speak of to get into a high school, was having a grand old time looking down on me.

She already did, purely in terms of height (and unbelievably, the girl was still growing! She wasn't just taller than me, she was on her way to being taller than everyone), but looking down on me metaphorically as well?

This went well past giving me a complex and ended up being kind of pleasurable. Trampled upon by my towering little sister, who'd also stomp my whole approach to life into the ground. With my youngest sister watching, no less...

"Now, get up and get studying. Put a little pressure on yourself."

"It's definitely time for a little pressure, but I don't know about putting myself in a corner... If you aren't careful, you might get held back too. You sure you should be worrying about me?"

I twisted myself and, in my new posture, grabbed hold of the foot that was grinding into me. This goes without saying given her height, but Karen's feet are pretty huge. Almost too huge to wrangle, even with both hands.

"There! I'm gonna tickle you. How's that!"

"Hahaha, it won't work. I've been training, so the skin on the soles of my feet is nice and thick."

"There! Then I'm licking you. How's that!"

"Hiiiik!"

To protect our privacy as siblings, I won't reveal if I managed to lick her foot before she could pull it away, but in any case, she did withdraw it. I was granted freedom of action, and got out of bed.

At this point I was well and truly awake.

Fully and completely.

I'm a weak-willed person who falls back to sleep if I'm not careful, but thanks to the interference of my little sisters, I completely missed my second window for a snooze. My kindly wake-up crew seemed to have noticed because Karen nodded in satisfaction.

"Our work here is done."

From her airs you'd think she'd accomplished a momentous task when all she'd done was wake up her big brother.

Karen has impressive powers of self-affirmation.

"'Kay then, I'm gonna go running. I'm going 'na run. Make sure a bath is ready for me. A scalding one. Wanna come with me, big brother?"

"You know I can't keep up with you. Running means a hundred-meter dash to you—and for the length of a marathon, 42.195 kilometers. Get Kanbaru to go with you."

"I actually cross paths with her sometimes this time of day."

"Oh yeah?"

Come to think of it, my dearly beloved junior does two ten-kilometer dashes every morning, doesn't she? Not quite a marathon, but almost half of one. So statistically, it would make sense for her to cross paths with Karen... They're different types so maybe it's like comparing apples and oranges, but which of them wins out in the stamina department?

"So long, big brother. I'm sure you'll be terribly lonely while I'm gone, but see you again at the breakfast table. If I don't, you're going to be tried in absentia."

"What the hell for?"

Well.

A few things did come to mind.

I'd be lucky if I end up dressed like an inmate rather than some bagged game.

"Bye now, Pops big bro!"

With this parting line, which I could at least tell was an impression, though the resemblance to Lupin the Third was so faint it could have just been a coincidence, Karen left at a run. Whether it's jogging or a hundred-meter dash or a marathon, I'm pretty sure she's the only person who gets up a head of steam while she's still inside the house.

She's the jersey girl, after all, so she doesn't even need to change.

I considered coining a term, *jerl*, but doubted it'd catch on.

"Her hair's gotten long," Tsukihi said, watching Karen depart, and now alone with me in my room. "Super long, really. I was pretty surprised when she severed her ponytail over the summer. But it's pretty much grown back now. Super back, really. When kids grow fast, I guess their hair grows fast too?"

"Yeah, seems like it…"

Severed made it sound like it was a lizard's tail or something, which was a little scary but not inaccurate, and either way, Karen's ponytail had recovered well enough. Even if it wasn't exactly the same, it was long enough to be pulled into a short tail.

"Though it doesn't grow as fast as yours, kiddo."

"Or yours, kiddo," countered Tsukihi.

"Don't call me kiddo, kiddo."

It was immature of me to invoke my authority as a big brother, but in any case, Tsukihi's hair and my own were bizarrely long now.

She'd always been fickle about her hairstyle, but whatever she was thinking or feeling, for a while now she'd been letting her hair grow and grow—it was almost long enough to reach down to her ankles because she wore it straight.

Combined with her taste for traditional Japanese clothes, she looked like some lady ninja who used her hair as a weapon. *Kunoichi*

Tsukihi.

Tsukikage.

As for me myself, I'd originally grown out my hair to hide my "neck," but approximately a year after the events of that hellish spring break, it was pretty damn long even if it wasn't down to my ankles. The tips brushed the middle of my back, and I could probably sport a ponytail that rivaled Karen's old one.

After putting off the matter over and over again—*I'll cut it next time, I'll cut it tomorrow, I'll cut it at some point so no need to do it today*—it had gotten pretty crazy.

Batshit.

"Never mind me, big brother, don't you think you should cut your hair before exam time? It won't make a great impression in interviews."

"What interviews? There aren't any for college entrance exams. It's not a part-time job. Though I guess there is the impression you make on the examiner. Dammit, yeah, there's that. I'm not even growing it out because I want to. In fact I'd like to cut it, but this is how I look in the photo I submitted with my application form, and if I cut it now they might not recognize me," I said, touching my relatively bedhead-free hair. "I'll cut it off after exams. The whole mop of it."

"Makes me feel hot just looking at it, even though it's winter."

"Look who's talking. Yours isn't hair, it's a trench coat...hmm."

I reached out and mussed her hair for no particular reason. So much hair. It's no good blaming things on other people, but I dunno, Tsukihi's being that long must have numbed my senses. It's like that thing, that optical illusion where you put two lines next to each other and try to tell which one's longer.

Okay, her hair was easily twice as long...

"All right...guess I'll go get the bath ready for Karen," I said. "Up with the sun, giving up my precious time, I'll spur on these old bones to go prepare her bath."

31

"I'm sure she's grateful, but not as full of greatness as you are, big brother."

"While she's been tempering her body like it's a katana, I keenly observe that she doesn't seem to have joined any school clubs."

Karen Araragi is a karate girl.

Nowadays they're called *karate dames* (nowadays?).

So you'd think she'd be a member of the karate club, or some other athletic club... As someone who'd never had a lick of interest in what my little sisters did, I'd hardly wondered or even conceived of the question, but now all of a sudden it was on my mind.

"Karen can't join any clubs. Geez, big brother, you really don't know anything, do you? Do you?"

Tsukihi looked smug.

She was a kind person insofar as she liked to tell you things you didn't know, but despite that caveat, her attitude was unpleasant.

Well, she always rubbed me the wrong way, and afterwards I would beat her black and blue, but first I wanted to know why Karen couldn't join any clubs. What was the deal?

"Why can't Karen join any clubs? This is totally the first I've heard of it. That's no good, I need to know everything about my sisters. Has she been blacklisted? It couldn't possibly be because she's too busy with the Fire Sisters."

If that was it, I'd have to put the kibosh on their activities right away. It'd be a splendid excuse.

"No, no. It's a rule at her dojo. The students there are forbidden from participating in clubs. Because they're a combat-oriented school. Because they're an ultra combat-oriented school. Because they're a school. Because."

"...? I don't really get it?" I cocked my head. "You're my little sister too, so explain it in a way your big brother can understand, fool. You Le Fou."

"That's a hell of an attitude... My attitude is horrible too, but yours is the worst. It's horribly horrible. Unreal. Just listen for once, okay? If you've attained a belt in a martial art or have a pro boxing license, don't they say it's like you're carrying a deadly weapon? This is the same."

"Ah... I guess they do say that."

Hmmm.

I've also heard that's just a rumor, but I understood why Karen couldn't join any clubs. Basically it was against the rules of her dojo.

A combat-oriented school.

An ultra combat-oriented school.

It wasn't at all clear to me what that all-too-vague expression really meant, but having personally experienced the karate techniques at our sister's disposal, I was prepared to agree. If Karen employed them in society at large, the whole power balance was liable to crumble.

For my part, at least, I didn't want to face an opponent who could pierce a magazine with her fingertips—the only people who would were probably those with the same skill, in other words her dojo mates.

"But now that you mention it, I did hear something about that. I forgot because I don't give a shit about my little sisters."

"Really? After all that?"

"And now I remember...I've been wanting to meet her sensei. Got to tie up those loose plot threads. I'm pretty sure that's the last of them, too."

"I'm pretty sure you're dead wrong..."

"But it kind of feels like a waste, doesn't it? It's kind of, what, a shame for Karen's strength, the power of that body, her physical might, not to be shared openly and to stay buried amidst the Fire Sisters' illegal activities."

"Our activities aren't illegal," Tsukihi insisted, but I ignored her.

They weren't treated as crimes only because the two of them were still in middle school. The activities themselves by and large exceeded the bounds of anything that could be called lawful.

They were out of bounds.

Not to mention, what they exacted wasn't even justice in my view, but there was no exhausting that argument with my sisters; even if I exhausted my strength the argument wouldn't be, so I decided to let it go at that.

But even if I benevolently let them ramble on about justice and the significance of their work and blah blah blah, the Fire Sisters business got me in a complaining mood.

"You don't think it's a shame, Tsukihi? For Karen's abilities to remain hidden?"

"Nya?"

"That girl's got talent coming out of her ears, no question, even if she's not up to my level. Look, don't you think that deserves to be in the spotlight? I don't want her to be held back by her dojo or the Fire Sisters, she should be going for Olympic owwww!"

Tsukihi had stepped on my foot.

And not in a cute way, she'd crushed the nail of my little toe with her heel. A surgical strike, dead on target. "Crushed" is neither excessive nor exaggerated, but the truth—she split my toenail, for crying out loud.

"What the hell?!"

"Huh? You were being annoying, big brother…" She looked at me blankly, her sudden flare of emotion seemingly already cooled. She wasn't regretting her own behavior one bit. "No one, not even our big brother, can be allowed to annul the bond of the Fire Sisters."

"Wha… You were considering disbanding the Fire Sisters yourself, weren't you? Didn't you say you'd invite me to a farewell party chock full of middle school girls?"

"Hearing someone else say it makes me angry." At least she was honest, this hazardous, dangerous little sister of mine. "The Olympics? They make me sick. The same stale thing over and over again, every time."

"Tradition isn't stale. Don't call a festival held once every four years stale. Don't be giving it a thumbs-down. Who do you think you are, anyway?"

"Anyway, Karen will retire from the Fire Sisters someday, but I don't need my big brother to tell me that," Tsukihi said, this time with total composure. A tough nut to crack, how vexing. "All kinds of stuff will happen when she goes to high school. All kinks of kinds. Her environment will change. I still don't think she'll give up the dojo. She's so besotted with her sensei, and all."

"Huh…"

Funny.

Hearing that my little sister was besotted with a stranger I didn't know anything about was sort of unsettling. Tying up loose plot threads aside, I needed to check out this sensei. For my own peace of mind.

"And I bet they won't let Karen go that easily, either," Tsukihi predicted. "Her sensei has an even higher estimation of our sister's physical abilities than you do."

"Pardon me? An even higher estimation, you say? Bullshit, this so-called sensei doesn't know a damn thing about the delicate softness of Karen's tongue."

"Um, probably not… And how do you know how soft her tongue is?" Tsukihi glared at me. "Why are you even familiar with the charms of Karen's oral cavity?"

"Mrgh."

Yikes, time to retreat.

She had me there.

Either way, it was all just idle chatter, and I had no illusions about settling Karen's future in the course of a morning's trifling chat. Just learning that Tsukihi was still ready and willing to disband the Fire Sisters, that she hadn't forgotten that conversation, was more than enough to satisfy me.

Well, I didn't know how my exams would fall out, or maybe fall flat, but either way, there was no question that before too long my environment was going to change even more than Karen's.

But before that happened.

I was, in fact, not totally devoid of a brotherly desire to set Karen and Tsukihi on something like the right path—because yes, it was about time.

For the Fire Sisters to wake up.

For me to.

003

Whether out of kindness or out of habit, or maybe a desire to harass and feel superior to their older brother, or for no reason at all, my two wretched little sisters Karen and Tsukihi Araragi, known to the world as the Tsuganoki Second Middle Fire Sisters, wake me up every morning. They wake me up in the morning like I walk the night. They wake me up regardless of whether it's a weekday or a Sunday or a holiday, almost like it's their occupation, like their life depends on it.

Sure, there have been times when I lashed out at them in annoyance (mostly when I was a freshman, I think), but on this one point they remained undaunted. Whatever horrid miseries I might treat them to, whatever silent treatment, still they woke me up. It bordered on obsession.

Lately, though, by which I mean for a while now, I'd been studying for my college entrance exams, which sometimes kept me up late into the night, and on such occasions I was grateful for their morning "wake-up call"—honestly I'm grateful even now. In fact, when I think back, I should always have been grateful.

And now I'm even grown up enough to admit it.

It's just that as a high school senior in my last term, I didn't really need to show up at school anymore, which meant that there was no need for me to wake up so early... A consistent amount of sleep was necessary to maintain both my performance and my health, but no need to be so hung up on waking up early per se. Considering that I'd been receiving their constant blessing for the past six months or so, however, I couldn't really tell them to get lost. I mean, even if I did tell them to get lost they definitely wouldn't, and it's not just about exam prep. Since it was the Fire Sisters whom I have to thank for rescuing me from the peril of potentially not graduating due to the number of absences, tardies, and early departures I racked up during the second half of my first year and the beginning of my second, I really couldn't tell them to get lost. Leaving aside justice and all that, their unswerving dedication to waking me up constituted a meritorious service I could not ignore.

Without question, I owe Tsubasa Hanekawa and Hitagi Senjogahara for my scholastic improvement on the road to entrance exams, but equally indisputably, Karen and Tsukihi Araragi are to thank for supporting me on the road to graduation—and it's only human nature to want to repay that debt in some small way.

Only human.

Just to be clear, it has nothing to do with me being into my little sisters.

That kind of thing only exists in manga (how many times now have I said that?).

In fact it's what they call "the reciprocity principle" in psychology—that's definitely what it is. Apparently, human beings have this "quirk" of wanting to repay a person from whom they've received some kind of favor.

Take this fact in isolation, and you might get the impression that human beings are a fair species, that they possess a spirit of fairness, but reality isn't so pretty. Basically, people just "feel shitty when they owe somebody something."

People want that free and clear feeling of paying back a debt, or of feeling superior by paying it back and then some—that seems to be the gist of it.

Which is exactly why I felt it was about time I repaid my debt to Karen and Tsukihi after six months—no, six years of being woken up by them.

As an older brother.

Out of consideration for their futures—

"Karen's got her strength and her looks, though, so even if I don't give it too much attention, she'll make something of herself... I can leave her alone and she'll be somebody, but..." I grumbled as I went downstairs.

The walls have ears, the doors have eyes, and the shadows have vampires in them.

I couldn't be sure no one was eavesdropping on me so I didn't finish my thought, but yeah, I was worried about Tsukihi.

Tsukihi Araragi.

I'm genuinely worried about her future.

I have to care.

I have to be careful.

I can't even imagine what she'll be up to this time next year... The wheels are always turning in that head of hers, but she's always turning them for the wrong reasons.

Just spinning her wheels.

It was only thanks to managing the unmanageable mayhem of the Fire Sisters' brawn, that is, the over-engineered weapon of mass destruction known as Karen Araragi, that Tsukihi Araragi paradoxically, or passably, functioned as the Fire Sisters' brains... But with the impending increase in her level of independence, I couldn't imagine what kind of schemes she'd concoct—or rather I didn't want to think about it.

Sure, how she lives her life is her own business, but it's also human nature for me to want to avoid any kind of situation where I would end up mobbed by reporters.

Yes.

Taking all of these things into consideration, my first priority as I faced the prospect of graduation was, it goes without saying, completing my exam prep, but the second was rehabilitating my little sisters, particularly Tsukihi.

I hadn't discussed it yet with my parents, but if I got into college I'd probably be leaving home—and if I did, I couldn't bear to leave behind two little sisters like them.

It'd be irresponsible of their big brother, wouldn't it?

Maybe of any human being.

To repeat, I could care less what happens to those two. They can go ahead and live whatever kind of life they please, but I'm going to do what I need to do to avoid any sort of blame down the line.

So, for the time being, I began that day by running a morning bath for Karen, who would inevitably return home drenched in sweat.

I felt triumphant at the prospect of being able to say: *No way, I'm not irresponsible, I never shirked my responsibilities, I mean look, I drew a bath for her and everything.*

Keheheh.

A hot bath, just the way she likes it, how about that.

But my pseudo-villainous attempt at kindness backfired because the scalding temperature Karen prefers is how I like it too. As I cleaned the room and prepared all the amenities, I got the urge to take a bath myself.

Some of you might wonder what's up with a guy who takes a bath in the morning even when he hasn't gone for a run, but they say a person releases a full cup of sweat during the night. Jogger or not, there's nothing wrong with taking a bath in the morning. And it wasn't just that particular day; while I was studying for exams I often took a shower in the morning to clear my head after I woke (was woken) up.

"…"

Consider this.

The warlords of the Warring States period employed cadres of poison tasters. As a result, the food was all cold by the time it reached the warlord's mouth, but this serves to illustrate how precious his life was. Our anecdote might be apt to elicit laughter at the expense of the poor warlords, whose overabundance of caution meant they never had tasty meals, but that's totally wrongheaded, that's merely the condescending attitude of a peaceful age. Some poison tasters must have made the ultimate sacrifice, which goes to show just how many more lives were riding on the shoulders of the soldiers' commander, on his wellbeing.

Upon reflection, didn't this mean that if I really wanted to look out for Karen, if I really cared about her welfare and her future, I shouldn't let her take a bath without getting in first and ensuring that there was no danger?

From what I've heard, the bathroom is where the most fatal accidents occur in the supposed safety of our homes, so before letting my sister enter that danger zone when she was back from her run, I needed to confirm its security. I had to taste the bath for poison, so to speak. I had no choice.

And so I decided to get into the bath.

I decided to take a nice, hot bath.

Damn, it's hard being a big brother, forced to take baths against my will for my little sister's sake—but as I quickly began to shed my clothes in the changing room.

"Oh."

Tsukihi appeared.

And she was only half-dressed. In other words, she was half-naked. She must have shed her *yukata* in the hall before coming into the changing room. Which she did all the time. Just disrobed wherever

41

she pleased. The easy-on-easy-off aspect of traditional Japanese clothing was to blame. And naturally, she never picked up after herself (I did, mostly).

Fixing me with her severest glare, the half-naked Tsukihi accused, "You're the first! I mean, the worst! You said you were getting a bath ready for Karen but want to get in ahead of her! You're the worst, the worst, the worst, the worst!"

"Um, given your state of undress, I can only surmise that you had exactly the same intention…"

In fact, since she was hoping to hijack a bath that she hadn't even prepared, that I had prepared for Karen, who was the real villain here? Trying to scold me about it on top of that—I was seriously concerned about her future.

How had she made it through fourteen years unscathed with her sorry excuse for a personality?

In any case, Tsukihi had a strong metabolism, which meant she sweated easily. She took a bath every chance she got, kind of like Shizuka, to put it in *Doraemon* terms.

She wasn't about to let this opportunity pass her by.

How shrewd of her.

How shrewd and rude.

"Just stand aside, big brother. I'm getting into that bath, and no one's going to get in my way, brother or not."

"What a line. You're willing to fracture our family over who takes the first bath, and a morning bath at that…"

Frightening.

My sister lived entirely in the moment, didn't she?

"But I've already gotten completely into the bath-time mindset," she said. "My body may be out here, but my spirit is already in there."

"Oh, shut up. The tub's still only half full."

"Don't forget to add my volume to it."

"Like that's something to brag about."

Yet I, myself, was too deep into the bath-time mindset at that point to yield my turn. Well, my heart may not have been in the tub like Tsukihi's, my body and spirit were still there in that changing room, but surrendering the bath without a fight just because my little sister told me to would be a stain upon the honor of big brothers everywhere.

Shoving her out of the way so I could be first might in fact be appropriate, but the alternative was unacceptable. It could only be described as a dereliction of my duty as a big brother.

So I puffed out my chest (I was shirtless by then, incidentally. It was a half-naked sibling standoff) and gave Tsukihi an ultimatum.

"Little sister, if you're determined to get into that bathroom, you'll have to take me down firwatchit!"

I barely managed to dodge the shampoo bottle that she unhesitatingly hurled at me. The cheeky little middle schooler apparently brought her own shampoo. She was at least classier than Karen, who'd happily wash her hair with a bar of soap, but a truly classy person doesn't throw (with a spin, no less) shampoo bottles at other people's faces.

"Tsk."

And classy people don't click their tongues.

But man, was she a frightening little sister.

What was she thinking? Or was she not thinking at all?

"What the hell?! Someone could get hurt!"

"You told me to take you down."

"No, no, I meant mentally. Physically, you don't take me down, you respect me and kneel before me."

"You're a pain in the ass," Tsukihi said, closing the door behind her. She didn't actually lock it, but her meaning was clear: *I'm not budging from this spot no matter what.* And she started forward to reclaim her personal bottle of shampoo, which had landed behind me.

And what's more, that motion flowed naturally into a nonchalant attempt to slip past me into the bathroom, so I rushed to block her.

Putting my body on the line, like a real man. Protecting the door to the bathroom as if it hid a gaggle of wounded children.

"You shall not palookout!"

This time she went for the eye-gouge.

An attack the old Senjogahara would have gone for (and did).

At least in Senjogahara's case she was so stubbornly combative because of all the issues she was dealing with. Tsukihi just wanted to get into the bathroom.

"Enough already, big brother, don't get heated. Heating up the bath was enough, your work here is done."

"That's an unspeakable line."

"Move."

"No."

There was no point in being so stubborn, but what kept me standing there was my pride as an older brother, my not wanting to bow before or fall behind my little sister.

Or you could say I was frozen with terror.

I mean, Tsukihi was glaring at me for real.

She wasn't a *yandere*, but still over yonder in the psycho ward.

When you take away the sweet *dere* part, all you're left with is the pathology.

"I'm the one who heated up this water, so the first bath is mine by right."

"I allowed you to heat it up for me, and you should be satisfied with your lot."

Our arguments ran perfectly parallel, never intersecting.

Which is to say it didn't even constitute an argument.

We weren't engaging with each other at all; if anything, the first engagement was yet to come, as in a battle.

Somewhere along the line, the premise that I'd prepared the bath for Karen had gotten lost.

In fact, the very existence of Karen, off happily running along somewhere, had vanished from our minds.

While she was enjoying the refreshing morning breeze, an in-

44

ternecine family struggle was unfolding, a sordid sibling rivalry that perhaps rendered her the real winner among the three Araragi children.

Sooner or later, that very Karen would come home from her run and appear in that changing room, ready to cleanse the sweat from her body—she would waltz in there drenched in sweat, dripping with perspiration.

And in that three-way contest, the winner would undoubtedly be her. Circumstantially speaking, she would obviously arrive plenty sweaty enough to warrant a bath by anyone's standards, and if it came to blows, Tsukihi and I combined couldn't beat her even if she had one hand tied behind her back.

Indeed, Tsukihi and I were at this impasse because our combat levels were more or less evenly matched. Naturally, I was a boy and had a boy's strength, but Tsukihi had a crazy streak that I lacked. The craziness to unhesitatingly go for the vitals.

In other words, it was a stalemate.

I couldn't but envision a future where Karen came in and snatched the prize out from under us while we maintained that equilibrium—and I'm sure Tsukihi saw it too.

My little sister wasn't so oblivious to her actions' consequences that she'd overlook that eventuality—okay, she was oblivious, but her wheels turned quickly. I bet she arrived at that conclusion well before I did. It's just that her emotional brakes were shot, by virtue of which she was only able to deal with the situation on a par with me, who had only just realized the danger.

"All right then, big brother. We'll meet in the middle."

"Meet in the middle?"

A compromise?

Ah ha.

A proposal worthy of a strategist.

They say war is customarily conducted with a middle ground in mind.

But in this case, what middle ground—what point of compromise could exist between us? The right to take the first bath was a one-of-a-kind item, so to speak, and the competition for it a zero-sum game. One person wins, the other loses. So I didn't see any room for compromise, anything to compromise on.

But I underestimated Tsukihi.

Not for nothing had she managed to become the idol of every middle schooler in town despite her boundlessly irritating personality. The Fire Sisters' brains proposed a plan that no ordinary strategist could have conceived of.

"Let's meet in the middle and go in together."

004

We met in the middle.

Somehow I ended up going into the bathroom with Tsukihi.

"Why…"

How come?

How did it come to this?

You could say it was thanks to our mutual stubbornness.

You could. I don't want to, but you could.

"Whaaat? You don't want to? Why, does your little sister's naked body make you think dirty thoughts? No waaay! Baths are for getting clean, big brother."

Maybe it's because I was bamboozled by those words. But in the first place, Tsukihi must have offered her compromise on the assumption that I'd lose my nerve and slink out of the changing room with my tail between my legs.

And precisely because I knew she made that assumption, there was no way I was going to slink out of that changing room. Instead I threw down the gauntlet and said, "What, are you all talk, you little brat? Time to put your money where your mouth is. Or don't you have the guts to go into the bathroom with me, you chickenshit."

And now here we were.

All in and going all the way.

Me and Tsukihi, brother and sister, seated side by side in the bathroom washing our long hair. I took this rare opportunity to try out Tsukihi's shampoo, and what do you know, the lather really did feel different.

"…"

"…"

The thing is.

Here's the thing.

Getting two, more or less grown-up siblings into the bathroom together was ten times tougher than I imagined… The room isn't as big as it is in the anime, I mean, it's just the regular size of a bathroom in a normal family home, so with two teenagers in there, it was pretty cramped.

Like, while we were washing our hair we kept banging elbows.

"Big brother."

"What is it, little sister?"

"Say something. This is more awkward than I thought it'd be."

"Yeah…"

You're not wrong, but you don't have to come right out and say it.

Though it takes a certain burden off me if you're the one to bring it up.

It wasn't going to do much for the narrative either if that silence went on forever.

Every once in a while you hear some media personality tell a funny story on television or the radio about being in the bathroom with their parents as a grown woman, but you don't hear much about siblings doing it, it just doesn't happen.

In that sense, Tsukihi and I were delivering a rare piece of reportage in the present progressive, but did anyone ask for rare?

More like well-done.

If it was so awkward, you'd think I might say, "I'm going to get out first, take your time," or that she would say, "I'm about done. Excuse me, big brother," but then this was me and Tsukihi.

On the contrary, I tragically blurted out, "If it's so awkward then get the hell out, Tsukihi. You're just fronting anyway. If you're pissed off at yourself for saying what you said, you shouldn't have said it to begin with."

"You're the one who's pissing in the wind, big brother. All I meant was that it's awkward looking at your scrawny body. I'm cool as a cucumber about being in the bathroom with you. So cool I'm positively frigid."

That was our lamentable exchange.

Someone, please, put us out of our misery.

"Scrawny? I resent that, I'm a lean, mean beefcake machine."

"A lean, mean beefcake machine? Did you mean to say a tee-ny-weeny beanpole machine?"

"Hey, that's out of order. But listen, Tsukihi, I might consider getting out if you tell me that's what you really want."

"I really, really, really, really want you not to get out," Tsukihi brushed off the concession I had finally forced myself to offer.

What the hell was wrong with her?

She lived just to be stubborn.

"Are you already clean, big brother? Or do you want to get out so soon because you're still feeling dirty?"

"Again? You're going to recycle that joke? When *you're* the one who's so fascinated by *my* body? What you really want is to touch these washboard abs, I bet."

"No I don't, why would I want to touch abs divided into eight like that?"

"You counted them! You counted my abdominal muscles. You're giving them the eye, aren't you?"

"*You're* the one who's eyeing your little sister's boobs, big

49

brother."

"Yeah right. It's not like I've never seen them before."

"Isn't that a little weird? A big brother who's seeing his little sister's boobs *not* for the first time?"

"I'm all about them, I know all about those two hunks of meat."

"Don't call them hunks of meat. Don't talk about a woman's chest like you're at a butcher shop."

"Psh. You don't have anything to worry about with those melons."

I must have been rattled by the situation after all, though, because as soon as I said this I realized I'd lost track of what "melons" meant as slang. Did it refer to big breasts or small breasts?

Judging from the huge grin on Tsukihi's face, probably the former. Dammit, I might as well have sent her a fruit basket along with that one. Or maybe it was just a case of sour grapes.

Not that I know what *it* is here.

"Though the fact is," I regrouped.

Again.

"You and Karen happily flounce down the hall half-naked during summer time. Forget half-naked, you've got a three-quarters-naked lifestyle. Nudity is one of your essential biogenic needs. So being in the bathroom together is no big thing at all. If there's a problem, it's just that we're a little too close together."

"That's exactly the problem. That's exactly the big problem, isn't it, big brother? If you came this close to me in the hall in the summertime, you'd get a taste of my elbow."

"Elbow…" So realistic an attack—in fact our elbows were already touching.

"I'd elbow you even if I were fully dressed."

"Aren't you being a little harsh towards your older brother? But dammit, it really is narrow in here…narrow like a certain someone's mind. Tsukihi, hurry up and finish washing your hair already. I guess I have no choice, I'll cede the right to be first into the tub."

The whole point of the Battle for the First Bath became unclear if I gave up now, but it wasn't about that anymore.

Forget about the bath or being first, simply feeling superior to Tsukihi, my impudent little middle school brat of a sister Tsukihi Araragi, was my goal now. Bringing her to heel.

I wanted to make the girl who, I'm pretty sure, never once thanked me for anything in her life, say: *Thank you, big brother.*

I wanted to make her express her gratitude to me verbally.

But the more I pressed, the more she resisted. That's Tsukihi for you.

Or rather, her mindset might have been similar to my own here.

"Feh. Shouldn't you be the one, big brother? I'd sooner cede it to you than let you cede it to me. It's a cedar tub, after all."

"Cedar? Isn't it plastic? Quit screwing around and get in there like I told you."

"And I told you that I don't want to."

"Gaaa!"

"Grrr!"

When a battle of wills goes sub-verbal, you know it's all over.

The end of the world.

Our quarrel descended into a fierce clashing of elbows, our elbows as we both washed our hair clashing like sabers—thankfully we were side by side and both facing front, but at this rate we were going to end up six-pack to boobs.

The awkwardness was quelled somewhat by our loud dispute, but the fundamental problem hadn't been dealt with.

This was a wildly immoral, or maybe just plain old distasteful situation.

But here again came clever Tsukihi to the rescue—her wheels really do turn faster than mine.

The plan she proposed: "Listen, big brother, let's wash our hair one at a time. We each have too much hair for us to do it side by side, it's inefficient. Uneconomical."

51

"I'm pretty sure economics has nothing to do with washing your hair…"

But she was absolutely right in terms of efficiency.

Even she could be right once in a while.

We were using good shampoo and everything, but doing it this way was killing its cost-performance index. Not to mention, the stress was liable to make our hair start falling out.

"But Tsukihi, if side by side is no good, what do we do? When you say we'll wash our hair one at a time, what exactly are you envisioning, logistically speaking?"

"This!!"

Tsukihi leapt up energetically and got behind me. Her tendency to become enthused without warning, written or otherwise, was another element of her peakiness. Her emotions constantly going from positive to negative to hot to cold also made her nothing but a completely unpredictable pain in the ass, but in any event, she got behind me and thrust her hands into my soapy hair.

"I'm going to wash your hair for you!!"

"That…"

This *that* was of course an abbreviated form of the expression of surprise *that's crazy*, but at the same time, of *that answers my question*. She was right that trying to wash our hair at the same time in such a confined space was tricky, but if we washed each other's hair, we'd fit into place like puzzle pieces.

It was like two hostages abducted and stuffed together in a small room, with their hands tied behind their backs, having a hard time untying their own bonds but undoing them with surprising ease once they put themselves back to back.

A real paradigm shift.

Like the Copernican Revolution.

I had to doff my chapeau to Tsukihi, she'd won this round. But… "What's a *chapeau*, anyway?"

"It's a hat, isn't it? That you use to hide the bedhead on your absurdly long hair."

"Stop making things up. I never wore a hat to hide my bedhead."

"Well, I have."

"Don't tip your hand, I don't want to know your style tips."

"Scrub-a-dub-duuub," Tsukihi added sound effects as she lathered up my hair.

She made it seem like they were coming from my head—either she was a fool or she was making a fool out of me, and I almost told her to quit it, but no point in getting myself all in a lather. I gritted my teeth and let it happen.

Mature amid the moisture, humility in the humidity.

"Hmm. I'm feeling oddly superior washing someone's hair, I like it. Literally holding someone's most vital organ in your hands is so pleasurable. Holding their life in your hands. Now I know how a hairdresser feels."

"Don't go around acting like you understand other people's feelings, and stop talking such horseshit. Hairdressers don't think about stuff like that."

"But if this were a barbershop, you'd get a shave. I'd shave your face with a straight razor, right? Now that's absolutely a dominance relationship."

"A dominance relationship, or…"

A relationship based on trust, more like.

But regardless of how she said it, I got what she was saying.

The reverse was also true.

Although holding my life in her hands was an exaggerated way of putting it, trusting someone else with your head and body can be a very pleasurable experience, depending on the context. In the course of our daily lives, we unconsciously guard ourselves against everyone and everything around us—turning off that security system once in a while might carry with it a certain feeling of liberation.

That comes with the caveat that the other person will do you no harm, of course… But a theory that trust is important in interper-

53

sonal relationships because it's connected to a feeling of liberation, or even of pleasure, might hold water.

Then again, my despicable little sister (where's this justice you supposedly defend?) saw that relationship of trust as dominance.

Though it's basically true.

Basically true, and basic psychology.

Since total domination of someone, their total reliance on you, is liberating and pleasant—though I've gotten somewhat off track here, and to sum up what was really going on, my little sister was just washing my hair in the morning.

"Hunh," she grunted.

"What's wrong, Shampoocifer?"

"Don't address your little sister like she's the devil! I haven't made you sign anything in exchange of washing your head, have I? Anyway, with my hands on your head like this, giving it a scrub scrub and a rub rub, I'm surprised how teeny-weeny it is."

"Says the littler little sister."

"Yeah right. We're almost the same height now. I feel like I've really been growing."

"How tall do the two of you plan on getting, anyway..."

"Not that I want to get as tall as Karen. Seems tough to be that size. But we're sisters, and I guess I can't help but keep growing, same as Karen. Actually, we were about the same height back in elementary school."

"..."

It was terrifying to contemplate.

Both sisters, taller than me, their older brother... To hell with an older brother's authority and dignity.

My head wouldn't be the only teeny-weeny thing.

"But maybe there's hope," I said. "The hope that I, the older brother, will get as big as Karen yet lies dormant at the bottom of that Pandora's Box."

"I hate to rain on your parade, but you'd better rein in those hopes. Your reign as the tallest one in the family is over for good."

"Don't crush my dreams with a triple homophone, Tsukihi, don't dump out Pandora's Box. Because I'm warning you, if you ever get taller than me, I'll make you a head shorter again even if it means I have to lop off your feet."

"That's horrifying. That amounts to a death threat."

"Ridiculous. Can't you divine the brotherly compassion in my threat, you little turd? I could've said I'd make you a foot shorter by lopping off your head."

"You could've, my ass."

She twisted my neck.

I'd forgotten that she held my life in her hands.

"C'mon, I'll preserve your severed feet in my room," I offered.

"You keep getting more grotesque. Extra grotesque."

"Extra, huh?"

"The fact is if I stood my hair straight up, I could crush you and even Karen right now. It'd be a landslide."

"If you stood all that hair on end, you'd look like a monster. It'd take some serious gel. But your hair's about as long as your body, so it's a simple calculation: you'd be twice as tall, right?"

"Yup."

"I'd say *so long* to a little sister like that."

"Hm? Did you say something?"

"You heard me fine!"

Even if she didn't stand it on end, with hair down to her ankles she looked every inch, every foot, every mile a monster. While I've seen illustrations of girls with hair like that in manga, it'd be genuinely scary in real life.

But its fear factor aside, I'd witnessed any number of epic fails where Tsukihi tripped over her own hair.

Don't fail in front of someone preparing for exams! Such bad luck...

I definitely found myself thinking *just cut it already*, but I'm sure she simply hadn't found the right opportunity, same as me.

"At the risk of repeating myself, though, your hair grows insanely fast."

"Not as fast as yours, big brother. Not nearly. You only started growing it this year, there's no way it could grow that much normally. What's your secret?"

"There's no secret to growing out your hair. It's just... My metabolism might be even better than yours."

To be precise.

My metabolism—sped up after spring break.

"Okay, let's stand it up," Tsukihi said, beginning to play with my hair.

Making shapes with the foam and molding it to look like Astro Boy's.

"Awesome. Astro Bro. Super Sibling."

"Trying to make me sound like a Super Saiyan."

"Rinse time!" Tsukihi grabbed the handheld showerhead and flushed all the shampoo out of my hair. And she didn't neglect to throw in a little head massage, like a real hairdresser.

Maybe all that time spent at the salon, back when she was constantly changing her hairstyle, had rubbed off on her.

Next came the conditioner.

This was from Tsukihi's private stash as well.

Though when I think about it, she'd only be able to wash all that hair about three times before the bottle was empty... Her metabolism might've been good, but it got terrible mileage.

"Ooh, this conditioner is like wax, so now we can really shape your hair. Teehee, it's like you've got a pompadour!"

"Hey, quit playing around with my head... In fact, quit doing everything you're doing."

Not that I could see what was going on up there.

Something dreadful, I was pretty sure.

"Heheh. Now I'll wash your body for you." Paying no heed to

anything I said, Tsukihi picked up the family bottle of body soap that's always in the bathroom. Squirting out an appropriate amount and working it into a lather, she suddenly exclaimed, "Oh! Big brother, big brother!"

"Why the hell are you shouting like you clearly must've figured out something."

"A hilarious gag just came to me."

"As if. You're setting me on edge."

The adjective *hilarious* doesn't sound right with the term *gag* in the first place. That might come off kind of insulting to people who stake their livelihood on them, but gags are fundamentally more about the energy of the delivery than about actually being funny.

"C'mon, c'mon, look over here, look over here."

"What is it?"

I turned my head and looked over my shoulder like she asked me to.

In other words, without a shred of embarrassment or anything else, my little sister was demanding that I look at her naked... The way she'd said it was so natural that, naturally, I obeyed, but was that okay?

It was not.

It was not, not, not okay.

My little sister was posing naked for me.

Sitting with her knees up and both hands clasped behind her head. And—with the body soap she'd lathered up so thoroughly in her palms dolloped across her chest, her crotch, and her thighs.

"I call it, *The Metropolitan Ordinance*."

"Yikes!"

Leave out the satire!

In a panic I grabbed the hand basin, scooped some water out of the tub, and splashed it on her. Off came the soap bubbles. That might be even worse Metropolitan Ordinance-wise, but contriving to hide the naughty bits is much more objectionable in this sort of situation, in my humble opinion.

Full frontal is more wholesome, and more artistic.

"What are you dooooing?!" she complained.

"What are *you* doing, you mean!"

"Wait...maybe sticking up my hands and calling it *The Skytree* is better, less direct?"

Tsukihi adopted just such a pose.

She'd said something back in the changing room about her volume, and it did seem like she'd been working on her weight, but the reality is that she just wasn't prone to plumpness. So when she stretched her body vertically like that, her ribs were clearly visible, and she did look kind of like the Skytree.

"But if you're really going for the Skytree, you should stick your hair up. It's supposedly over six hundred meters tall."

"Yaaaah. Though my hair won't actually reach that high. In which case, maybe Karen should be the one to do it."

"Hmm..."

In fact, Karen might manage to be convincing.

However.

"Tsukihi, actually, Karen's boobies are just as enormous as you'd expect for someone of her height, and on a tower, that sort of uneven surface spells danger—!"

Tsukihi unleashed a kick at me there in the danger zone of the bathroom, if you can believe it. And a high kick to boot, aimed at my throat. Her retorts, a.k.a. her attacks, are unleashed silently and without warning, making them truly murderous.

"Quit critiquing your little sisters' boobs. No side-by-side comparisons!"

"Huh. I guess you're right. My bad. But even if it was my bad, you're crazy if you think I'm going to apologize so easily."

"That's a hell of an attitude... Listen, I'm going to wash your body now, so face that way. Scrub-a-dub-duuub."

"That sound effect makes you sound a lot more childish than

you think... Come up with something that makes you seem a little more cultured."

"Fine, *abababa*."

"Is that a Ryunosuke Akutagawa reference??"

Though that story title kind of wrecks the image of him as a literary giant.

At least, it's not very refined.

"Was that the right number of *ba*'s?" I asked.

"Of course. Of course it was. Look it up if you want to," came Tsukihi's supremely self-confident reply from over my shoulder, as she poured water down my back.

But it was unusual for her self-confidence to match the facts, which is to say she had a tendency to act self-confident only when she wasn't, so her attitude suggested a high probability that she'd gotten it wrong.

"Ababababa. Abababababa. Abababababababaaaa!"

And indeed, while she scrubbed my back, Tsukihi tried to hedge her bets by saying it a bunch more times with varying numbers of *ba*'s.

"At any rate, don't be such a slacker," I scolded. "Don't wash me with your hand like that, use that sponge and put a little elbow grease into it."

"But scrubbing with your hand lets you really clean all the hard-to-reach spots. And using grease when I'm trying to get you clean? Wait, hang on a sec, is being touched by your little sister getting you all hot and bothered, big brother? You naughty boy, I'll never let you live this one down!"

"Just watching your thrilling, moment-to-moment, stopgap way of life bothers me plenty..."

"Teeheehee, I'll wash between your toes for you. Think you can stay calm?"

"Thrilling..."

For better or for worse (mostly for worse), she only thinks about the immediate situation.

She only brings her smarts to bear on what just happened and what's just about to happen.

It felt pointless to try and tell her to consider her future, to focus on what was coming a little further down the line... You know what they say, you can lead a horse to water, but you can't make it drink. Or, given that she was already perfectly aware of anything I might say to her, maybe this was about beating a dead one. Even Karen, a runaway train who never thought anything through, had slightly better prospects.

But I'm sure Tsukihi didn't want to hear that from a guy who hadn't even tried to get out of ending up in the bathroom with his little sister... Hmmm.

"Okay, all clean! Sparkling! Like you've been shellacked! Switch!"

"Switch?"

"Duh. It's your turn to wash my hair now, obviously."

"Grk... You set me up, you bastard."

A reciprocity clause.

Sure, maybe it should've been obvious, maybe it was inevitable, but having it dropped on me after the fact filled me with a sense of defeat. Refusing, though, meant promptly exiting the bathroom, so I had no choice but to fall in line with Tsukihi's scheme and wash her hair.

Dammit.

Forced to wash my little sister's hair—how humiliating... I considered a plot to pay her back by doing it with body soap, but the bottle might get shoved down my throat if she found out, so I let that one go.

It would be too pitiful, on both our accounts.

Nothing for it, I'd wash my little sister's hair like a mature adult.

And so we switched spots.

On the surface, abandoning our attempts to wash in tandem and washing each other's hair one at a time instead was paying off—but in reality not so much. For two people with hair as long as ours to shampoo in succession took a commensurately long time, and as a result neither of us had managed to make it into the tub, when competing to be the first one in there was the whole reason we were sharing the room.

We weren't just washing each other's hair, we were getting in it.

I'm sure there's some perfect aphorism to describe our predicament, but it's not coming to me.

"But maaan, you really do have a shit ton of hair, Tsukihi... Actually hefting it like this, you know, it's almost more like cloth than hair."

"Cloth?"

"Cloth for a kimono. It weighs a ton. It's super heavy, maybe it's all the water it's soaking up."

"Oh."

"What?"

"I figured it out, little Tsukihi figured it all out. Lately I keep thinking I've been getting fat, but no matter how much I diet I haven't been able to lose any weight. It was my hair all along."

"Now I see...that you're a complete idiot. Gimme a break and cut it already. Though I'm sure you just haven't found a chance. Well, I'll cut it for you right now, if you want. I'll snip it all off for you. Come on, it's not like it's the first time I've cut a girl's hair."

"I don't know the details, but that's a hell of a backstory they've given you... No, leave it alone. Leave it leave it leave it. Because I'm making a wish with it."

"A wish?"

"Not a *whish*, got it? A *wish*."

"Yeah, I get it..."

What was this all about?

So it wasn't that she just hadn't found a chance, she had a real reason for letting her hair grow that long? Unexpected. That someone like Tsukihi Araragi, who lives only in the present, would do something so forward-looking.

True, given that she used to change her hairstyle every month, I probably should've realized something was up the second she started letting it grow out.

A shameful failing as an older brother.

"Huh, okay. Well, what are you wishing for? Spill it."

"Not a chance. I can't. If I tell you, my wish won't be granted."

"Oh yeah? I guess they do say wishes won't come true if you tell them to other people... But it's fine, don't be such a stickler, your older brother's a special case. Tell me."

"You don't get to act like a big brother only at times like this."

"Hmmm. In any case, look at all this hair..."

I'd given it a shot, but the truth was that I wasn't all that interested in why she was growing out her hair, so I returned my focus to the hair itself.

Crap.

There was so much hair I couldn't even work up a lather.

No scrub-a-dub-dub sound effect.

I couldn't bear it if that got ascribed to a lack of skill on my part—I never had much of a way with shampoo to begin with, but what a sorry situation for an older brother to find himself in, after Tsukihi managed to work up such a lather.

On behalf of the older brothers of the world, I couldn't let my position slip any further.

"Looks like there's not enough shampoo... You want to talk about uneconomical, this hair is it. Your special shampoo is a terrible waste. Though I guess since you don't have to go to the salon, maybe you actually come out ahead. With a little pocket money, even."

"But I do go to the salon."

"What?"

"Unlike you, I'm not just letting my hair grow wild... I have to keep the ends even and stuff."

"Really, when no one ends up giving a stuff about your hair?"

"Don't get snippy. Your words cut deep. Don't forget, it was the repetition of cruel words like those that gave birth to me and Karen's twisted brand of justice."

"You're calling your own justice twisted?"

Oh.

When I added about twice as much shampoo, even Tsukihi's ginormous mane started to lather up nicely. It also looked like she had even more hair than she already did.

"Heeheehee. Latherrr, more latherrr. This is actually fun, a guy could get used to washing people's hair. I have to say, makes even a cool guy like me feel all bubbly."

"You're having to say it? Sounds like you're going to pop."

"Makes me wanna bury myself in all this hair. To be bound hand and foot in your hair."

"That's a little too kinky. I'd flee this bathroom at top speed. I'd be willing to accept defeat."

"You washed my body with your hands and fingers; I want to wash your body with this hair."

"Don't, you'll damage it. I'll end up with a ton of split ends. Just its length makes it a lot more susceptible to wear and tear. If you're going to do it, at least use your own hair."

"I bet if you wrapped yourself in all this hair, you could walk down the street totally naked. No one would know."

"And why would li'l miss Tsukihi ever want to walk down the street naked?"

"Hmmm."

As I was washing her hair, it just naturally transitioned into a head rub. I was massaging her scalp. Now I understood what she meant about holding someone's life in your hands. Now I saw why she liked it.

It does give you a full-on sense of superiority.

"It's amazing feeling so above you like this... Straight up amazing, it's the tops. Like your head might come right off if I gave it a little twist."

"That hadn't occurred to me."

"Rubbing your head gets me even more excited than fondling boobs."

"That's scary. And rude."

"Fondle fondle fondle fondle."

"Keep your perverse feelings out of my head rub. Or at least cap the sound effect at *scrub-a-dub-dub*. Sad as I am to admit, though the shampooing wasn't much to speak of, this head massage is actually pro-quality pleasant."

"Mm-hmm," I replied smugly.

Then again, that didn't seem like a skill with broader applications. No matter how things shake out, I doubt a future as a hairstylist is waiting for me.

And I can't think of any other line of work where you rub other people's heads.

"Okay, time for the condition...er?"

"What's wrong, big brother?"

"There's not nearly enough. Mister Conditioner is nearly empty."

"Whaaat?!"

Tsukihi flipped out.

You might even say she was flippant.

Well actually, you can't.

She flipped out—but whatever amount the bottle still contained had been used up by none other than Tsukihi, to wash my hair. It wasn't something I, the beneficiary, should blithely say, but I said it anyway: "Your fault." Easily, unambiguously: "You should've checked first."

"I don't care whose fault it is. I think we can all agree that what's important here is that my hair is going to be a mess? That PreCure is going to die?"

"PreCure is going to die? That *is* a big deal."

For a moment I couldn't figure out what she'd meant to say, but

64

it had to be *cuticle*. Not even close! But then, there was a character called Cure Cool or something, wasn't there…

"In any case," I said, "the point is that *Smile PreCure!* was a good show."

"That wasn't the point at all?"

"The theme was smiling, so all the heroines did their best to keep smiling even when they wanted to cry. It was awesome."

"I don't want to hear about your fetishes, big brother. I don't care about your smile fetish. Just let a smile be a smile."

"Then there's Kenji Miyazawa."

"What? Quit changing the subject."

"Kenji Miyazawa asked his students what the longest word in the English language was, and the answer was 'smiles.' Because there's a mile between the first *s* and the second one."

"So true. I hope he got some good smileage out of it, too. Pretty funny guy, this Miyazawa-san."

"Don't call our great poet 'Miyazawa-san.' Show some respect."

"I said 'san,' didn't I?"

"Which oddly sounds too familiar… It's strange, huh, that adding 'san' sometimes feels more intimate, not less."

"Definitely. With Miyazawa-san, dropping the honorific actually feels more respectful. What's that all about… Seems like it'd be interesting to try and figure out the criteria for that."

"Maybe, but it might just have to do with whether or not you know them personally, and whether or not they're still alive…" As I said this, I turned on the showerhead and rinsed the lather out of Tsukihi's hair. "Okay, all finished. Now let's wash that body. With your hair."

"Were you even listening?" Tsukihi's temper flared and she blurted out the first retort that came to her: "What are you trying to do to this hair of hair? Ruin it?!"

"Hair of hair?"

"Head of hair!! Mane! My beautiful tresses!" she shrieked in my face.

Her delivery lacked a certain je ne sais quoi, was wanting in panache.

"But what choice do we have," I demanded to know. "We're out of conditioner, and I want to wash your body with your own hair."

"The second one is just your preference! We definitely have a choice!"

"Hmph. Well, when you put it like that, I can't deny it. You're a perspicacious one, I'll give you that. Tsukihercule Poirot."

"Just put something on it! Anything!"

"Hm. That gives me an idea."

I removed the cap of the virtually empty conditioner bottle and used the showerhead to spray in a small amount of hot water.

Then, replacing the cap, I shook the bottle, for all the world like a classy bartender. To get it properly mixed.

In my mind I was wearing a vest.

"What're you doing, big brother?"

"Well, the bottle may be 'empty,' but there's got to be some conditioner still stuck to the walls, and watering it down should supplement it enough to cover your hair just this once."

"Stop it, that's something a poor person would do."

"A poor person?!"

To hear that kind of bourgeois talk coming from my own sister... I was shocked. I couldn't believe my ears, when had she become so arrogant? But then I realized she'd always been that way. No doubt about it.

I guess anyone could have inferred that aspect of her since she'd gotten an obviously expensive conditioner to use just for herself.

"I'd rather let my hair take its course, and end up looking like a Super Saiyan, than act like a pauper," she sniffed. "I'm me, after all."

"Hrmm."

My little sister, soon to be a middle school third-year, had gotten a Super Saiyan confused with a Great Ape. Stands to reason that kind of game of telephone would happen across the generations.

But then again, there's Dragonball GT, where Super Saiyans can achieve a further transformation thanks to the power of the moon. So maybe she was just an obsessively knowledgeable Dragonball fanatic.

"The stuff's going to mix with the water that's already been absorbed by your hair, so it's just a question of timing," I reasoned with her.

"Don't call my fancy conditioner 'stuff.' Don't talk about my 'ditioner that way."

"Look, it's not as watered down as you think. I just added a few air bubbles, it's a fantastic conditioner. 'Ditioner."

I took off the cap again and squirted some of the hot water/conditioner mixture into my hand to show her. She knit her eyebrows as she peered at it, then hung her head and said, "I suppose I have no choice. I'll let you save face this time, big brother."

The hanging her head part was purely physical, though; she was just trying to make it easier for me to apply the conditioner.

Putting up her hair, or putting up with her, I resumed my task.

I'd hoped to get enough for one go-around by diluting the conditioner, but it was easier said than done, given the full shock of Tsukihi's hair—I had to be very careful about how I applied what I had.

I had to be deliberate beyond deliberate.

Deliberate like a lacquerware artisan applying gold leaf.

"Hrmm... Hey, Tsukihi. I don't mean to nag, and I don't know what your wish is all about, but how about at least cutting your bangs?"

"If I'm half-hearted about it, the ends would poke me in the eyes. And no matter how tenderly you care for it, there's no way to achieve hair that doesn't hurt when it gets in your eye."

"I see..."

I didn't.

"But that kind of question is a boomerang, big brother, you know? Your bangs are plenty long too, so right back at you."

"For some reason mine don't bother me."

"Speaking of bangs," Tsukihi said suddenly—as I massaged her scalp—"Nadeko's out of the hospital."

"Yeah? Glad to hear it."

"Hm? You're not as excited as I expected. I thought you'd do a little dance of glee." Tsukihi turned around a little to look at me. Her expression was sincere. "A naked dance of glee."

"As if."

"I thought it'd be a cinch to get you to do a naked dance. I specifically waited until we were in the bathroom to tell you and everything."

"Don't add some frivolous rider to such a serious subject."

"Yessir. Anyway, she's out."

"Huh."

Huh.

What else could I say? What else did I have the right to say?

I was certainly glad she was out of the hospital, though.

Not that I could ever face Sengoku again—

But I was glad anyway.

Somehow I was able to be.

"Big brother?"

"What?"

"Owowowowowowowowow. Are you ow trying ow to crush my ow head ow like a vice owowow?"

"Oh, sorry, sorry. I guess I was overdoing it."

"You probably don't want to hear this from me, which is exactly why I'm going to say it, but haven't you taken on too much? You *are* overdoing it. Nadeko wasn't your responsibility or your problem."

Tsukihi was talking like she knew it all, but in fact she didn't know the truth about Nadeko Sengoku and her mysterious disappearance for the past few months.

While I wouldn't say my sister wasn't involved in any way, it was hard to say she was—which is exactly why she could say something about it, I guess.

She could say something.

That I didn't want to hear.

"It's fine," she said. "Nadeko's been a lot livelier lately. She's cheered up some, gotten more optimistic."

"Really... That's great."

"She even laughs sometimes."

"That's...even better."

Things really were looking up.

To the point that I didn't need to worry anymore about not seeing that face, that smile, ever again.

"You should go see her sometime. She's laid up at home, and you'll be busy with exam prep for a while so it might be tough..."

Tsukihi said this in all innocence, knowing nothing—if she'd been speaking with full knowledge of the situation, it would've been scathingly ironic. But, for better or for worse, Tsukihi Araragi is a frank, straightforward person, so I can't imagine her saying something like that on purpose.

And yet there was something that still concerned me.

Concerned me—so much I was still something of a wreck.

It was impossible for me not to worry—about what Nadeko Sengoku might have told Tsukihi Araragi regarding Koyomi Araragi.

It wasn't a question of a lack of closure.

But the word *regret* didn't even begin to cover it—

"Still, Nadeko talked a *ton* of shit about you, big brother. What did you do to her, anyway?"

"Seriously?!"

"What? No, I was kidding."

"..."

Some joke.

The timing was positively scary.

Almost like it was guided by a divine hand.

"Right, well—I suppose that problem remains," I muttered.

Nadeko Sengoku had left the shrine—and her "disappearance" had come to an end, which was of course a good thing, a fabulous thing, but that good, fabulous thing also meant that the town was spiritually unstable again.

That was the problem I was referring to.

I didn't know all the particulars in perfect detail myself—but in any event, Kita-Shirahebi Shrine was once again a hollow vacuum.

Not resolving that issue or at least trying to do something about it meant endless trouble for our town—and I had to admit that I was reluctant to move away and leave my little sisters behind with the problem as it stood.

Even if I couldn't fully solve the problem.

I at least needed to bring things back into balance—

"Balance? That's not really my job, though, is it…"

Job.

I'd thought I'd muttered the words under my breath, but as if she'd heard my whole inner monologue, Tsukihi responded, "It's not your job."

My heart skipped a beat. Was it synchronicity, or a psychic connection between siblings? No, it seemed to be nothing more than a coincidence since Tsukihi continued, "You're taking on too much, big brother," returning to her previous topic. "You can't fix everything on your own. Some things you've just got to let go of, some things you've got to leave be. Know your limitations, it's okay to let other people handle things sometimes, you know? You're too concerned about Nadeko, about Karen, and about me too."

"…"

Huh.

So that's what she wanted to tell me?

And she hadn't just picked up on it because I'd brought up Karen's abilities, she seemed to have sensed it for a while.

Sensed that I was using graduation, and my exams as a chance.

To take care of a bunch of things—to solve them, to settle some accounts.

That I was trying to wrap up some things.

Things that I'd let go.

Things that I'd fudged.

"We—or I'll just speak for myself, I, will manage somehow. After Karen graduates and I'm alone at the middle school, I know I'll feel off balance, but I'll manage somehow, in my own way. So you don't need to worry, okay? It's fine, everything's A-OK. And Karen'll manage too, of course. We'll all manage somehow. Even Nadeko. So for now, you should just focus on the exams staring you in the face."

"…"

Just moments ago, I'd wanted to admonish my little sister for only paying attention to what was right in front of her, to get her to think more about her future. For her to tell me to focus on the now—what could I say?

It wasn't funny.

But it didn't piss me off, either, didn't make me want to throw it back in her face—I definitely *was* taking on too much, and couldn't fix everything on my own.

There were limits to what I could do.

In fact, there were things I hadn't been able to fix.

With Hachikuji.

With Sengoku.

Nothing would have gotten done without help from the experts. In fact, was there a single goddamn thing this past year that I'd managed to fix on my own?

When I tried to count them, there was nothing to count.

Even with my exams, and the graduation on which they hinged, I hadn't gotten anywhere on my own. So yes, she was right, I'd taken on too much. She was absolutely right.

I'd spouted some line about the duties of an older brother.

But sensing your duty doesn't necessarily mean being able to carry it out—there are times when you have to get help from someone else, times when you have to leave it to someone else.

Tying up every loose end by the time I graduated, by the time I left town, might be inherently impossible—but that didn't mean I could be irresponsible and just neglect everything.

It isn't good to take on too much.

But there are things you have to do.

And things that you have to try to do, even if you know you can't.

"So how *are* things going with your exam prep, big brother? One month to go, think you'll manage?"

"I...think so, I guess," was the only reply I could give.

Even if I didn't think I'd manage, that was the only reply I could give.

A lamentable attempt at autosuggestion.

Senjogahara had been recruited, and there was no question about where she was going to college. So all I could do was try and follow her—too late at this point to even shoot for a backup, it'd be impossible.

Here I was, not taking even a single backup exam in an ultimate display of manliness—though actually it was only because my parents didn't have much faith in me and hadn't been willing to shell out more in the way of exorbitant exam fees.

"Okay," my sister said, "then listen to me when I tell you that this isn't the time to be taking more on, you moron. It's crunch time. I'm giving you good advice here, big brother. Given the circumstances, is this any time to be giving your little sister a sponge bath?"

"Well, on that score, I'm not trying to shoulder some kind of responsibility, I'm not appointing myself to some role, I'm not helping you with your bath... I'm not lathering you up and fondling you."

"The fundamental problem remains, though. Taking turns

washing each other solved the issue of how small the bathroom is—but not of how small the bathtub is."

"You're absolutely right… The tub's size makes it hard enough to enact the idea of cozy co-existence with a little girl, let alone a middle schooler."

"A little girl?"

"Nothing. *Obliviate.*"

Ultimately I decided against using the showerhead and took the washbasin, like I'd done earlier when Tsukihi tried out her horrifying gag, to scoop water from the bathtub-which-was-kind-of-small-to-share-with-a-middle-schooler, this time dumping it over her head from behind.

I contrived this rough-and-ready method of flushing it all out at once instead of relying on the shower's water pressure since that conditioner clung tenaciously to hair.

"Aaagh!"

It was so gratifying to hear this cry of apparent pleasure from my client that I doused her two more times, on the house.

"Aaagh! Aaagh aaagh aaagh!"

She seemed to be enjoying it.

"Aaagh! Do it again!"

A little too much.

If I complied with her request, complied a little too much, there wouldn't be enough hot water left in the tub, so I stopped there and reached for the showerhead, intending to use that to finish the job.

And as I did.

I froze.

There was a full-length mirror on the wall by where we'd been shampooing each other's hair, but up until then, up until that very second, it had been all fogged up and beaded with water so that nothing could be reflected there, and nothing had been—yet as I was dumping all that water from the washbasin over Tsukihi's head, the spray had splashed forcefully onto the mirror as well.

73

As a result, the moisture covering it was momentarily washed away, and reflected there was Tsukihi's naked body as she sat facing the mirror—a simple natural phenomenon. Perfectly natural.

But there was also something unnatural.

No.

Supernatural.

My figure, that of Koyomi Araragi, which should have been standing there behind Tsukihi—was nowhere to be seen.

I had no reflection.

Just like—the immortal aberration we call a vampire.

005

The nail on my pinky toe that Tsukihi had crushed earlier in my room was still split—still miserably, painfully split. Which meant that, at present, I was not in vampiric form. And yet, I had no reflection—how was I to interpret this?

Whatever the answer, it was at the very least not a phenomenon I could approach with a cool head.

Because this was happening for the first time since I'd become a vampire over spring break—but maybe bringing up all this stuff out of the blue will make you think I've finally lost my marbles, things having been weird ever since I went into the bathroom with my little sister. So let me give a brief explanation.

Over spring break I was attacked by someone—by something. By a vampire.

A vampire beautiful enough to freeze your blood.

I was attacked by the iron-blooded, hot-blooded, yet cold-blooded vampire—Kissshot Acerolaorion Heartunderblade.

She sank her teeth into my neck, clung there like a leech.

She possessed me utterly.

And she sucked me dry, of all the blood, all the spirit I possessed.

She wrung out my very being.

Then hung me out to dry as the vampire I'd become.

"Become."

I had mutated—into an aberration.

That was the end of Koyomi Araragi the human being, and the beginning of Koyomi Araragi the vampire—and those two weeks of spring break were hell on earth.

Fourteen ghastly days.

The upshot is that, as you can see, in the end I became human again—there were some lingering side effects, but I went from being a demon to being a person once more.

What I had to give up in return was not insignificant, the price I had to pay was a heavy one indeed, but at any rate—if nothing else, at least I became human again.

Happily, proudly.

I revere Tsubasa Hanekawa like a second mother, like my own personal Mother Teresa, because of the debt I owe her for saving me back then—but if I start in on that story we'll be here all night, so shameful as it is, I'm going to skip that part for the moment.

The hell came to an end.

It came to an end after fourteen days.

Or I thought it had, anyway.

Of course I'm not trying to say that everything was wrapped up tight with a neat little bow on top, that there were no hard feelings and no more troubles waiting for me down the line. My experiences over that spring break became the catalyst for a catalogue of catastrophes—but at least that single issue, of me personally becoming a vampire, well, that at least I thought had been sorted out.

I thought I'd become human again—but if I had.

Then why the hell didn't I have a reflection?

Isn't the lack of a reflection one of the primary characteristics of a vampire? Immortality, drinking blood, turning into a shadow, turning into mist, shapeshifting, flying, using bats as servants.

And.

No reflection.

Not appearing in mirrors.

That made it seem like I wasn't a misbegotten, half-assed vampire—but the real deal.

Wasn't that the inescapable conclusion?

"…"

"What's wrong, big brother?"

I'd fallen silent without realizing it, and naturally enough, when I clammed up all of a sudden, Tsukihi sensed that something was wrong and nonchalantly turned to face me—with her eyes still closed, since I'd just been dumping buckets of water over her head, which meant she'd yet to notice my lack of a reflection.

It would be a disaster if she ever did.

So I took Tsukihi's face, turned towards me as it was, in both hands and held it there.

Not massaging it.

Holding it firmly in place.

Reflected in the mirror beyond her, needless to say, was just her body. Just the nakedness of her developing body. My reflection, which should have been visible beside her nakedness, was nowhere in evidence.

The wall of the bathroom was reflected instead as if nothing stood there—just the towels on the towel rack affixed to the wall.

Nothing else.

No one else.

"Wh-What are you doing, big brother?" asked Tsukihi in consternation.

And consternation seems like the reasonable reaction if your big brother grips you by the head when you idly turn around. However fast the wheels in there might turn, no other spin you could put on that turn of events.

Well, if your wheels turn quickly enough, apparently there's one conclusion that might, in its own way, present itself—

"I see. It's okay, big brother, go ahead," Tsukihi said, gently closing her eyes and puckering her lips.

How is that okay?! would ordinarily have been my comeback, but under the circumstances I had no choice. The time had finally come to bring to bear on my little sister the ol' act—by now so routine a part of Koyomi Araragi that it has been granted citizenship—of *silencing her with a kiss.* I squared myself.

"There—"

Now that I'd made up my mind, I didn't hesitate (since this wasn't a first, scarily enough) and moved to steal a kiss from my little sister, four years my junior. But at that moment fate intervened.

The work of the Skytree, perhaps.

"Phew! Man, am I sweaty! Thanks for getting the bath ready, big brother! I'll come say a proper thank-you afterwards—"

With that, the door to the bathroom banged open and a jockish girl whose high-rise, I mean, height rose to almost six feet traipsed in buck naked and covered in sweat, clutching a towel in one hand. It was Karen Araragi.

"—The fuck are you trying to pull!"

As befits a hand-to-hand combat specialist.

She was freer of hesitation than I was.

The second she appeared she unleashed a spontaneous spinning jump-kick perfectly geared to the cramped bathroom and sent both me and Tsukihi flying into the tub.

In other words, the first bath was a cozy shared affair, after all. Tsukihi's mental wheels may spin faster, but Karen spins faster in the body department—uh huh, yeah.

Then the three Araragi siblings, Tsukihi and Karen and I, all got to know one another a little better as we took a bath together for the first time in forever—is not what happened next. Karen just threw me out.

No, this is about a big brother's duty, compunction, point of honor, pride, story development—I attempted logical counterarguments, but she expelled me. "Are you a moron?! Use your common sense! Use your lack of common sense!"

Use your lack of common sense.

That little nugget of constructive criticism fit me like a glove.

Well, the older brother who'd been expelled from the bathroom was pathetically tragic in his own way, but compared to the girl who had to stay and get a serious earful from her older sister, I'd say he got off pretty light.

Speaking as a brother, it was truly painful to leave Tsukihi alone at the mercy of an enraged Karen, but well, I had my own issues, and it was actually a favorable outcome to be driven out into the hallway where there were no mirrors.

No, forget favorable.

Things were pretty goddamn unfavorable for me at the moment—

"Hey, Shinobu. Shinobu. Shinobu, are you awake? C'mon, wake up, Shinobu, I need you."

Alone in my room, I checked the mirror in futile desperation, but no reflection in that one either, so I leaned in close to where my shadow fell on the carpet and called for Shinobu.

Shinobu being Shinobu Oshino.

The merest specter of she who was once the vampire Kissshot Acerolaorion Heartunderblade, the one who attacked me over spring break—now a little girl.

An eight-year-old.

In other words, she was, in her own way, no longer a vampire—but now, as I was now mysteriously manifesting the "symptoms" of a vampire, I feared that *something was happening* to her as well.

Well, it was a totally realistic fear—since whatever else was going on, our souls were paired.

Shinobu and I were like a single entity.

The pseudo-vampire hidden in my shadow.

She who dwells in the shadows—Shinobu Oshino.

"Shinobu! Shinobu!"

Gave no response at all.

Unable to determine whether this lack of response was basically a holdover from the nocturnal habits of her vampire days or the result of *something happening*, my distress continued to mount.

Shinobu.

What's wrong, Shinobu.

"Rise and shine, Shinobu! Come on, you can't sleep all day!"

For no particular reason I tried imitating my little sisters, but as I feared, I got no reaction. Here I was, unexpectedly learning first-hand the hardships those two endure in trying to get their sleepyhead brother out of bed.

Vowing to leave off manufacturing weird excuses in my head and to leap out of bed awake and refreshed from tomorrow on, I continued calling into my shadow.

"Shinobuuu! I've got donuts, Shinobuuu! Your beloved Mister Donuuut! Golden Chocolaaaate!"

"For reals?!"

A little blond girl, making her entrance accompanied by this recycled line.

Casually, guilelessly.

When she appeared she had her fist in the air for no apparent reason, like a lively character from an old anime. Since I was leaning in close over my shadow, the pose became an uppercut to the jaw, and I tumbled over backwards.

Like a dead bug.

"The Golden! Where be the Golden Chocolate, my lord?! If thou hast played me false, shalt die for it, I shall tear out thy carotid artery!"

" . . . "

My head hurt from banging it against the floor when I fell over backwards, but that was the least of my worries, since Shinobu herself was about to kill me.

Her lively energy was seemingly enough to keep her from feeling the damage she should have experienced through our link.

At least nothing appeared—nothing disappeared to be out of the ordinary with Shinobu. Consoling myself with this fact, whilst simultaneously dealing with the fresh anxiety of being excoriated and possibly slain by Shinobu, I raised my torso off the floor and said, "Something's horribly wrong, Shinobu! I don't appear in the mirror!"

"What sayest thou? Speakest of the tale of Snow White? Fair ye may be, my lord, but sadly not fairest of them all, methinks."

Shinobu's gaze darted about the room as she said this.

I'd hoped that raising my voice would force her into following my script, but it didn't seem to have worked. I'm pretty sure the only reason her gaze was darting about the room was because she was looking for donuts.

Don't tell anyone, but it made me surprisingly happy that she called me "fair," even if she was just bullshitting.

"..."

Shinobu's glance ceased its darting.

Having likely ascertained that she wouldn't find any donuts no matter where she looked, she fixed me with an icy glare.

Terrifying.

Terrifying enough to make me stop worrying about that piddling no reflection thing.

Is that any way to look at your "lord and master"?

"Heed these words, my lord. Art thou aware?"

"Of wh-what?"

"That in this world there be lies which may be told, and lies which must ne'er be. Lies which concern not the immortal soul fall into the former camp, whilst those which do fall into the latter."

"Get real, the only thing you're worried about are lies that concern donuts, right?!"

What, is your immortal soul a donut?! Complete with a void in the center?!

"'Tis just so…" said Shinobu, moving languidly—and laughing gruesomely.

Don't bust out your signature expression for this!

"This place be devoid of donuts… Devoid of donuts, as unto the center of a donut itself. Wherefore I shall pierce thee bodily and make a donut of thee, my lord!"

"The Donut Effect!"

Joking aside, Shinobu really did come at me, but ever since spring break she had lost almost all of her vampiric power, and her attack was nothing more than the pretty little Bodyattack you would expect from an eight-year-old. I simply caught her in a gentle bear hug. A simple display of my hugging prowess.

Still, my blood ran cold for a moment.

Her expression, at least, was deadly serious.

"Ahh. To be so embraced by thee, my lord, I feel my anger cooling even now."

"You're too soft on your lord."

While not being turned into a donut was certainly something of a relief, at the same time it engendered another feeling quite apart from that.

You see, up to that point, whenever the physical and mental "after-effects" of having been a vampire—my symptoms—grew stronger, Shinobu's vampiric "nature"—her symptoms—grew stronger in direct proportion.

At present, however, Shinobu's vampiric power remained lost despite the fact that I was in vampire mode, me and me alone—this had never happened before.

No, it wasn't just—that it had never happened before.

It was something that could never happen, no matter what.

Wasn't it?

Never—under any circumstances.

"Shinobu. Please listen."

"Mmm. If thou dost not embrace me further, I shall pay thee no heeeed."

"Listen!"

You can't always let your body rule your mind!

You're a little girl, for crying out loud!

I summed up that morning's events from the time my sisters woke me up—or no, I didn't sum anything up. I went on and on, blah blah blah, telling her every single thing in excruciating detail.

As she listened, Shinobu's face indeed underwent a transformation from soft and sweet to something much more serious. Seemingly the gravity of my predicament had gotten through to her.

"...And that's what happened."

"Hmm. I see," Shinobu nodded. "At long last thy relationship with thine own sisters hath crossed a certain line."

"Nope, that's not the important bit!"

"It may not be important, but 'tis most serious indeed. How wilt thou fix this mess thou hast made? Or hast thou already given up hope of further anime adaptations?"

"Shinobu, please, work with me here. We can talk about my sisters later. I'm seriously confused right now—it's the first time this has ever happened," I implored her, my tone becoming more and more frantic. "I mean, it's really tough not having a reflection. How can I put this, it really hits me where it hurts."

"Indeed? And yet a mirror is naught but a reflector of light."

Shinobu, for whom it was probably the most obvious and banal thing in the world not to have a reflection, wasn't sharing my agitation. She just gazed blankly back at me. I don't think she meant it maliciously, but I couldn't help feeling frustrated by her lackadaisical response.

I wanted to get us on the same page, but how to do it?

Without my having to do anything, however, Shinobu received the wireless signal of my angst, if not my thoughts, through our soul linkage. With a light shrug she said, "What," finally seeming ready to engage with me, "hast my lord turned without giving me to drink of his blood?"

"Yeah, that's it, that's what I'm trying to tell you...or no, not quite. Here, look at the nail on my pinky toe. It's split, right?"

"Aye. Didst say 'twas crushed by thy sister."

"If it hasn't healed, then we can assume I'm not in vampire form right now."

"Aha," said Shinobu, taking hold of the ankle I had proffered for inspection and roughly rolling around the toe in question like it was a perfectly natural thing to do.

"Owowowow!"

"Calm thyself. 'Tis distracting."

"...!"

I didn't think she could possibly be doing it just to mess with me, so I looked on silently as this scene, ripe with a certain kind of sadism, unfolded—I endured the pain as I waited for the results of Shinobu's "examination."

"Hmm. I see."

"Y-You figured it out?"

"'Tis hard to say—nay, I discerned what is afoot, but cannot for the life of me determine why it should be so—"

How vague.

Not that I'd had my hopes up.

From her reply, it didn't sound like she'd actually figured anything out—the matter would go no further than a little girl torturing my toe, and I wasn't about to let that happen. The only thing that would go down was my favorability rating.

"What the hell, Shinobu. If it's hard to say, forget about that part and just tell me what you discerned, and in a way I can understand."

"Aye, so I shall—but first, my lord," said Shinobu. "Clothe thyself."

006

"Cutting to the chase, my lord, thou art most definitely a vampire at present—just as thou didst suspect. Lacking a reflection is a purely vampiric phenomenon, it has naught to do with any other sort of aberration," Shinobu explained. As she'd commanded, I was dressed in whatever clothes had been lying around. What had been lying around, or hanging on the wall, getting aired out, was my school uniform, which I wasn't wearing lately since I wasn't going to school.

You might call my look Naked Uniform.

Sexy? No?

"A vampiric phenomenon... But Shinobu, see for yourself, my toenail."

"Quit thrusting it at me. I shall only torture thy foot once a day."

"That's not what I'm asking for, is it? It's not like I enjoyed it, did I?"

"'Tis I who ought to say, *see for thyself*." And she did as much. "Thy toe. 'Tis healed."

"Huh?"

Hearing this, I grabbed my foot and peered intently at it—I had to force myself into a kind of yoga pose, but anyway, I examined the toe in question.

The nail was split, and there were traces of blood—no, it didn't look healed to me at all.

"That is naught but a superficial view—internally, 'tis quite another matter."

"Internally?"

"I was not there to witness the scene with mine own eyes, so I cannot be sure, but I have reason to believe that when thy sister didst stomp upon thy foot, the bones of that toe were well and truly broken."

"Broken?"

She really did crush it!

Super painful, right?!

What the hell was that hair-washing devil thinking?!

"Calm thyself. 'Twas naught but an infinitesimal fracture."

"An infinitesimal fracture…"

What the hell is that?

An infinitesimally small fracture?

Or does it mean the entire bone was fractured into infinitesimally small pieces?

Because the latter sounded hard to bounce back from…

"When I perpetrated my torture…er, palpitated thy toe, it felt as if the bone had been broken but had since set—which is to say, 'tis healed. Even if not entirely."

"I see…"

Come to think of it, Senjogahara or somebody was telling me about that.

About banging your pinky toe on the corner of the dresser and curling up in pain—it might sound like just a funny story, but in fact a lot of the time people shatter the bone in their toe like that. Because a broken pinky toe doesn't actually affect your life all that much on a practical level, it often heals up without the person ever realizing it had been broken—something like that, anyway?

Incidentally, when I tried out the "banging your pinky toe on a corner" subject on Hanekawa, her only response was, "Huh? I've never banged my pinky toe on a corner." That aside, if what Shinobu said was true, it all added up.

Which reminds me, by which I mean, now that she'd said it, the excruciating pain from when it happened had vanished without a trace—interesting.

So this—was a form of healing as well?

"But it's totally different from my impression of how a vampire's body heals…"

"Thy impression."

"Yeah."

To be honest, I'm loath to compare it to spring break, when I was transformed into a full-on vampire—but back then, if my arm, or leg, or even head got blown off, it'd heal a second later.

No, the already overblown phrase "a second later" doesn't even cover it.

If a part of my body was destroyed, it regenerated simultaneously—is, I think, closer to the truth. Hard to believe if you haven't seen it with your own eyes.

But it's true. I know because I didn't just see it, I experienced it, experienced it personally—the vampiric healing factor is, how can I put this, a bat-shit crazy, fucked up, out of control, jaw-dropping thing.

Or at least I'd thought it was.

"Hmm…thou hast the right of it. But 'tis also true that no human being could heal a fractured bone in a mere hour."

"Yeah…"

Though with Karen, all bets were off.

Not to mention Karen's sensei.

Though never having met her sensei, I'm really just speculating on that one.

"Then I shall perform a simple test for thee. Proffer me thine arm."

"Like this?"

"Scratch!"

Accompanied by this sound effect (?), Shinobu scratched my arm. Like a cat.

In a feat of bodily manipulation, she'd suddenly extended her fingernails into sharpened claws.

"Owww that—doesn't hurt?"

"I should think not. I merely grazed thy skin." Shinobu flashed her claws for me to see. "'Tis the same level of damage as scraping the inside of thy cheek for a scientific experiment."

"How does a vampire know anything about scientific experiments?"

"I have lived lo these five hundred years."

It was more like six hundred, actually.

Not that I was going to hassle her about fudging her age.

It's bad manners to talk about a woman's age.

Not sure about an aberration's, though.

"Okay, so you scraped my arm, now what?"

"Observe."

"Hm?"

Unbelievably.

Or should I say inevitably?

The wound on my arm where Shinobu had scratched me vanished—well, it was never exactly a wound, but any sign of it vanished without a trace.

"Look there. Thy body hath healed itself."

"Mm-hmm…no question about it."

Somehow the unimpressive healing of that unimpressive wound didn't sweep away all my misgivings, but there was no question that my healing factor, my physical regeneration, was somewhat enhanced.

"Nay, I know thy mind is not fully at ease, my lord, but be wary—I advise thee to draw those curtains closed. For should a vampire with such a meager healing ability be exposed to sunlight, he would be reduced to ash without even catching flame."

"Oh, uh huh…"

Shinobu's dire words filled me with dread. I rose, and contorting my body to keep it out of the sun's rays, closed the curtains. This naturally made the room pretty dim, so I turned on the light.

"'Tis merely a precaution… 'Tis possible, nay probable, that ye might walk openly beneath the sun in safety. Simply because thou hast manifested some ability to heal meanest not that thou art fully become a vampire once more, my lord. Here now, say *eee*."

"Hm?"

"Say *eee*."

She said it so childishly that I failed to take her meaning, but the second time, Shinobu just did it for me—it was super cute—spreading my lips apart on the side like I was saying, "*eee*."

Okay, it wasn't that cute.

Holding my lips in that position, Shinobu inspected the area closely, then concluded with, "Aye. For now, at least, thou hast not grown fangs."

"Really?"

"Aye. If thou believest me not, look in the mirror."

"But the whole point is that I don't have a reflection!"

"Ah, of course."

Heh, a smile rose to Shinobu's face.

Gimme a break.

On purpose or not, it was pretty annoying.

But also super cute.

"Then touch it and see," she suggested.

"Like this?"

"Who told thee to touch mine chest? I'm talking about thine

own tooth."

"Yes, ma'am."

Her cool reaction made me feel like a plain old pervert. No, regardless of her reaction, I was a plain old pervert.

"Mm-hmm."

"And?"

"It's hard, feels normal."

"'Tis not a question of texture."

Shinobu didn't seem too impressed that I'd remembered to throw in a nice little joke even at a time like this. "Well, it isn't pointed. My teeth are definitely regular teeth—and very fine teeth at that, if I do say so myself. Let's see, what other vampiric phenomena can we check for right now…"

"Why not try eating garlic for thy morning meal?"

"I don't want to have such an intense breakfast… Wait, but if that tested positive, wouldn't I just keel over and die?"

"Like as not."

"I'm not liking like as not."

It was no joke.

Sure, I was living a life where I might die at any moment, but I could never face my parents if I died just because I ate some garlic. Nor could I face Senjogahara. And not because of the garlic breath.

"Such experiments can be left for another day. At present, 'tis the most dire of scenarios to which we ought turn our minds, my lord—'tis not a reality that thou might wish to face, but in my judgment, thou art at present a half-baked vampire. If thou canst," and here Shinobu's tone turned serious, "I ask that thou dost trust my judgment. Lest we waste time in pointless investigations."

"Okay. I'll trust you."

Which didn't mean that my misgivings had vanished.

While my toe and skin had indeed healed, neither one seemed like an impossible occurrence, which meant that the only phenomenon of note, and my predicament at the moment, was "lacking a reflection."

Definitely insufficient evidence to say that I was a vampire, or at least, it would be a premature conclusion—Mèmè Oshino, the expert, might even call it imprudent and rash—but.

But nonetheless.

I trusted Shinobu.

I'm embarrassed even to say it, I can't believe I'm putting it in print, but it felt only right.

"Then it's really you I'm worried about. Are you okay? Nothing's happening with your body?"

"Nay. And judging from mine earlier inability to pierce thy body, my lord, my power hath not returned—"

Wait a minute, she really tried to put a hole in me?

Not a shred of mutual trust to be found in that thought.

"And what is more, our link is born purely of the drinking of blood—save for if I should bite thy neck whilst half-asleep and drink thy blood, no connection should be possible."

"Well, I never wanted to say so, but I've always thought that seemed like a strong possibility."

"Impertinent lout. Never in all my five hundred years have I been half-asleep."

"Oh really…"

I let that one pass.

If further investigations were a waste of time, using that time for our comedy routine definitely was too. Just this once, we had to abandon the stance that the idle banter was the real point of these books.

What mattered now was whether there'd been some change in Shinobu's body.

"Shinobu, first things first, take off your clothes. So I can take a look."

"What dost thou intend with me?"

"I want to torture your little girl feet."

"Thy sisters have not crushed them."

"Shit…useless little sisters. They couldn't even manage to give her a little wound like that?"

"I have ne'er even crossed swords with my lord's sisters, but… That's it," said Shinobu, clapping her hands.

The kind of clap where you slap your fist with your open palm.

"I know who to ask."

"Huh? Who?"

"Well, 'tis certain that some manner of change hath been wrought upon thy body, my lord—and if that change is, as I suspect, some manner of vampiric phenomenon, 'twould be best to consult an expert."

Her arms crossed, Shinobu sounded strangely reluctant.

At least it didn't seem like the attitude of someone who'd just been struck by a brilliant idea.

"By an expert…do you mean Oshino? Mèmè Oshino—but we don't even know where to find him."

"Nay, I suspect this is outside that brat's ken—for had he harbored apprehensions that such might befall thee, he would most certainly have shared them with me."

Shinobu wasn't overly fond of Mèmè Oshino, the parent whose last name she bore, the master who had bound her with that name, but judging from what she just said, it wasn't like she didn't recognize his competence.

At least, she recognized that he wouldn't skip town—if he knew there was still some kind of crisis lying in wait for me.

In other words, in Shinobu's considered opinion, this situation was beyond Oshino's control.

And of course I had no objection to that opinion. I agreed wholeheartedly.

"I know not how to grapple with thy circumstance, my lord. Which means that neither would it profit us to turn to that Aloha brat for aid, even if we knew where to find him. He is naught but useless grime upon my boot heel."

"…"

She recognized his competence, but apparently that was it. I guess she still hated him.

Fair enough, but…

"Then who are you talking about? Who's this person you think we should ask?"

"Thou knowest full well. When I say 'who' with such a nuance, 'tis clear of whom I speak," Shinobu replied with real revulsion.

Far more revulsion even than when she spoke of Oshino, who was one of the main causes, one of the architects of her transformation from a bewitching beauty into a helpless little girl.

"I speak of *Yotsugi Ononoki*."

007

My first encounter with Yotsugi Ononoki came over summer break—thinking back on that "incident," I have to be honest, she didn't make a very good impression on me.

To put it plainly, we were enemies.

What I mean when I say "encounter" is that we fought.

It made sense that Shinobu seemed unhappy about her own suggestion—because she and Ononoki had an honest-to-god duel to the death that time. Or no, maybe it wasn't a duel to the death for Shinobu—but let's leave that aside for now.

Yotsugi Ononoki.

Was an expert—and an expert specializing in immortal aberrations, including vampires, in fact.

"Ononoki, huh... But strictly speaking, Ononoki isn't an expert, is she? It's Yozuru Kagenui, who employs her as a *shikigami*, who deploys her as a familiar, who's the expert, right?"

It's unclear whether I understood that part correctly, but I'm pretty sure that was the deal. I somehow kept running into Ononoki since that incident over summer break, and our relationship had moved away from straightforward hostility—though her master Ms. Kagenui remained very much my enemy.

I'd heard rumors, but we hadn't come face to face.

It was Shinobu who faced off against Ononoki.

And it was me who faced off against Ms. Kagenui—in a one-sided massacre. She ran roughshod all over me, but let's leave that aside as well.

Yotsugi Ononoki and—Yozuru Kagenui, huh?

"Okay... Well, it's definitely a good idea. Though it's a real shame I can't say so with a smile on my face."

"Indeed."

Shinobu's feelings seemed similarly complicated.

Something seemed to be rankling her.

An expert who specialized in immortal aberrations was, when you get right down to it, fundamentally her enemy—so was it any wonder?

Then again, during that summer break both Shinobu and I were nothing more than "former" vampires, having already lost our immortality, so they let us off the hook—what was it they said, something about us being certified harmless?

I said, "Ononoki is one thing... But Ms. Kagenui, well, you know what kind of person she is, what kind of expert she is. If she found out I was manifesting symptoms of vampirism, you know she'd be eager to take me out."

"To that too, I say indeed—indeed, what else could I? And yet, it cannot be that those two solve anything and everything by violent means. In fact, is not their central task, their bread and butter, ye might say, to keep the peasantry from transforming into immortal aberrations and the like?"

"Uh huh... But either way, their services won't come for free. It's their job, after all."

Not gonna be cheap.

Gonna be pricey as hell.

Oshino had asked for five million yen—thinking back on it now, what the hell was he doing demanding that much money of a high school student?

"At least, Ms. Kagenui and Ononoki aren't like Dramaturgy and those other guys... I'm pretty sure they aren't."

If they were, we'd be in trouble.

Because once I'd become a vampire over spring break, "those three" did their level best to take me out—me, and I was just Shinobu's victim. Shoot first and ask questions later. Though I guess that makes sense, since once you narrow down the field even further from immortal aberrations to "vampire specialist," you had to start viewing all vampires as uniformly evil.

"Ms. Kagenui..." I muttered. "You're right. You're absolutely right. She's without a doubt the 'strongest' person I've ever met, and I'm sure if we could sidestep our past hostilities and get her to step over to our side, she'd make for a reliable ally."

Karen once said that Yozuru Kagenui "might just about be a match for my sensei"—at that point I could only guess at how strong Karen's sensei was from the many anecdotes she'd told me, but it struck me that her statement really said something about Yozuru Kagenui, that expert who avoids treading on the ground at all costs.

"When you get right down to it, Ononoki herself is something of an immortal aberration—"

"A zombie, more like. A corpse *tsukumogami*. Or to put it plainly, more a doll than aught else."

"A doll..."

Yup.

That was about the size of things.

"Being a shikigami as she is. Though she be most free for a shikigami... 'Tis surely thanks to the nature of her master."

As onmyoji are somewhat out of fashion of late, Shinobu added—though I doubted it had anything to do with what was trendy at the moment.

A shikigami's level of freedom, I mean.

"So, what wilt thou, my lord?"

"Good question…"

If you removed my personal feelings—if you removed the resentment, of course, and the fear, the chattering teeth, going to them for help was an excellent idea. It almost seemed like a made-to-order model solution.

But at the same time, like I said, those two—or really just Ms. Kagenui, to be honest, had an extremely dangerous disposition, and she had *what it took* to back it up.

To the point that even that most ominous of ominous villains, the swindler Deishu Kaiki, openly hated dealing with her—probably because that silver-tongued devil knows better than anyone the privileges enjoyed by those who can solve things with violence.

One wrong word and instead of helping me she might just take me out—though if that's as far as it went, I guess that would be my just deserts. If things really went south and we rehashed the events of the summer—

"But, or, hang on a sec, Shinobu."

"Aye?"

"I don't even know how to get ahold of those two."

"Whaaat?"

Shinobu turned an accusing glare at me.

Seriously, those eyes really are something.

"Kagenui aside, ye joined forces with that Ononoki time and time again—and yet, thou art ignorant? Why did ye not ask for her digits?"

"Vampires don't say 'digits.'"

It lacked dignity.

Way too contemporary.

It was like Oshino using email.

"No, I mean, Ononoki just isn't the kind of character who'd be walking around with a cell phone… I feel like she said something about not having one even for emergencies. Aberrations seem fundamentally unsuited to a technological civilization in the first place, don't you think?"

"Is she really such a delicate flower? Hmmm. Then our situation is a difficult one indeed. If we cannot reach her by telephone, is there some other means we might employ?"

"I wonder…"

I wondered.

Modern society's headlong rush towards increased connectivity, in the form of cell phones and email and whatever else, made it increasingly difficult to get in touch with people who chose not to rely on such tools.

Or maybe we just surrendered to convenience and let those skills atrophy.

It would've made things a lot easier if something like Monster Mail actually existed, but it didn't, so—yup, it seemed like getting in touch with Ms. Kagenui and Ononoki would be just as tough as finding Oshino, now that he'd skipped town.

"What of Kaiki? Could we not contact him? Mayhap he could put us in touch with Kagenui."

"You can't be serious."

I knew how sour my expression was even without a mirror, a reflection. Sure, that swindler was more cell phone-savvy than your average youth—but he'd used that savvy to pull a massive, outrageous con on the people of this town.

"Well…yeah. Though I obviously don't have Kaiki's digits, there's a good possibility that Senjogahara would know how to get in touch with him, even if she didn't have them either… But that's a last resort, or a resort I wouldn't even use as my last, Miss Shinobu."

"Refrain from calling me 'Miss.' And wipe that pathetic look from thy countenance, 'twas clearly said in jest."

However, noted Shinobu, "that leaves but one candidate."

"It does? Who else is left? Oh, you mean Hanekawa?"

"That lass is indeed sagacious, but she is no expert—'tis rather *Gaen* to whom I refer."

"Gaen."

"*Izukogaen*. Is she not the ringleader of these experts?"

"Izuko Gaen…"

Right.

Now that Shinobu brought her up, I realized she was the first person we should've thought of—Oshino and Kaiki, and even Ms. Kagenui, referred fondly (?) to her as "Gaen-senpai." An expert among experts.

And very much their ringleader.

She'd saved my skin before, and we'd also joined forces—and she carried plenty of telecom devices. It seemed like she carried five or six of the things in her pockets, from feature phones to smart phones.

And I felt like I had maybe gotten the number for one of them—

"I wonder, though. I find myself feeling more and more reluctant to ask her for help… Ms. Gaen's a good person in her own way, but…"

I.

I know everything—she's the type who can make a declaration like that with a straight face and no hint of shame, and rashly relying on her for help could lead me to a horrible end.

If Ms. Kagenui was scary for being so violent, and Kaiki for being so ominous, then Ms. Gaen—

Scared me by being too clever.

"Indeed, 'twould be no surprise for one who seemeth to know everything as she does to know a way to tackle the problem which now besets thee, and yet I cannot council thee to rely directly upon her. Even if 'twas not said in jest, 'twas nonetheless said merely to try the idea on for size. Therefore the most amenable option available to us at present is to send word to Gaen and ask to be put in touch with Kagenui after all."

"…"

After giving it some thought, I said, "Okay, I've got no objections," and reached out for my cell phone where it was plugged into the charger. "*Domo arigato*, Shinobu."

"'Tis not a question of thanks. 'Tis a question of donuts."

I guess she bore a grudge.

Her love of donuts was just too deep.

Not just deep, almost dark.

I picked up my cell phone.

"Mm—"

Mm?

When the display came up, I turned pale. That may sound like an exaggeration for literary effect, but psychologically it was entirely accurate. And it might sound contradictory, but I felt like I'd been headed off at the pass by someone I'd been chasing after furiously.

There was a message in my inbox.

The phone number itself I didn't recognize, but the body of the message went like this:

Go to the arcade in the department store by the station

Fourth floor

7 p.m. tonight

I've arranged for you to meet Yotsugi there.

Please repay this favor with your friendship at some point in the future.

Your friend

Izuko Gaen

"…"

Speaking with the forced composure of hindsight, maybe it shouldn't have been much of a surprise. Knowing Izuko Gaen's sui generis character and generally peculiar characterization, maybe I shouldn't have been surprised.

Since "heading people off at the pass" was her credo.

If—Oshino was the kind of guy who saw right through you.

Then—Ms. Gaen saw inside you.

She was penetrating.

She perceived exactly what my situation was—and knew exactly what to do about it. She must have.

"Nay, my lord. My lord my lord. Attempt not to force a rational explanation upon this. 'Tis merely creepy, this message which smacks of such omniscience. Seemeth it not almost as if she hath heard the very words of our conversation?"

"I'm doing my best to come to a realistic understanding of this bizarre occurrence, but don't you go getting all realistic on me…"

I was terrified by the nonchalant request that I pay her back with my friendship, but at the same time, a path had opened before me— apparently, if I went to the department store by the station at seven o'clock that evening, Ononoki would be there waiting for me.

I hadn't seen Ononoki…for about a month, maybe?

So it was not like I hadn't seen her in a long time, but back then, things had been in crisis mode with Sengoku, and it was all lost in the maelstrom.

Then again, I was in one now—though I was "merely" dealing with my lack of a reflection this time.

"Oh yeah, I have to tell Senjogahara… We promised each other not to keep secrets when it came to aberrations."

"That promise hath been broken not a few times."

"Shut up… There are some things you can't say no matter what, even if you don't mean to keep them secret. But this is something I can't not tell her—"

I didn't want to worry her unnecessarily.

Was honestly how I felt—but then, this "I didn't want to worry her unnecessarily" business often ended up becoming a source of worry for her.

"As for Hanekawa…I guess I won't tell her yet. And even though Ms. Gaen's involved, or precisely because she's involved, it's probably best not to tell Kanbaru either."

"Indeed. On the occasion of thy previous alliance with her, Madam Ringleader desired to keep her true identity from her own niece—which might even turn out to be her weak point."

"Quit looking for people's weak points."

"The wench might become a foe at any moment. Discerning her weak point could save us from hardship later on."

"That's my point! It's precisely because she might become an enemy at any time that I don't want you to do anything inflammatory, like, oh, search for her weak point. We definitely want to keep her on our side."

"Aha, I see thy point."

I checked the screen of my phone one more time.

Reread the message.

I was apprehensive that another penetrating message from Ms. Gaen might've appeared right then, but it hadn't—maybe I didn't need to be so scared?

Either way, the arrival of this lifesaver of a message was a positive development for me.

However frightening.

It was a positive development.

She was a terrifyingly pragmatic person—a nightmarish realist, so if there was nothing to be done about my current situation, she wouldn't have sent me the message. The fact that Ms. Gaen was putting me in touch with Ononoki meant that there had to be some means of solving my problem.

That was what I thought.

Though maybe I just wanted to think it.

And as I was thinking that despite the early hour, I should call Senjogahara, whose path to higher education was already set in stone, and who was consequently spending her days loafing since she didn't have to go to school anymore—

"Biiig brotherrrr!" the door to my room flew open and Tsukihi barged in.

It's not that she didn't knock, but her knock was so violent that it was part and parcel with the "flew open" bit.

"What the hell do you think you're doing, running away and leaving me behind like that?! Do you have any idea how badly Karen thrashed me after you left?!"

Maybe because she was so incensed, Tsukihi busted into my room in nothing but a bath towel. It was only wrapped around her waist, leaving her upper body completely exposed.

A hell of a fashion statement. A little too cutting edge.

Shinobu was used to my sisters barging into my room like that, so she dove instantly back into my shadow.

"What the? Why are the curtains drawn, big brother? You becoming a shut-in? Or were you planning to go back to sleep? As if I'd let that happen!"

"No no no. The sunlight was just too bright."

There was no way I could properly explain, so I just told her a little white lie—not that she bought it or anything, but nor did I think she was in a place to really get into it with me about my curtains being closed.

As I expected, Tsukihi let it drop, with a satisfied *hunfnyaan*...

Hunfnyaan? What even is that?

What a way to express your satisfaction.

"Anyway, big brother, you owe me an apology. Come on, apologize. Apologize with words. Apologize out loud. Say you're sorry. Admit your mistake and apologize to me."

"Look at the attitude on you... Fine, come a little closer."

"Oh? You're going to apologize to me? O ho ho, fine by me."

The topless girl with the towel around her waist trotted towards me. What was it about my little sister that made her so surprisingly unseemly even though all that was going on was that she was fresh out of the bath?

I embraced that unseemly little sister.

Tightly.

"Hunfnyaan?!" Tsukihi shrieked in surprise—no, was it surprise, satisfaction, or something else? I wish she'd hurry up and standardize that one already.

Her character was too peaky *and* too vague.

"What kind of an apology is this?! What culture says sorry like this? In what country do they express their regret by embracing a naked woman?"

"The naked part isn't my fault," I whispered.

Into her ear.

I guess we really were the same height now, given that I could whisper directly into her ear as we embraced without having to lower my head at all.

"Just let your big brother make one request."

"What? You're going to ask for something instead of apologizing? You really are perverted... Look down your shirt and spell attic!"

That wasn't how it was supposed to go.

My melons gaffe notwithstanding.

"Just consider yourself lucky that what I want entails a request, and not a demand."

"Did you say 'Wanton Tale'?"

"Tsukihi, listen, okay? I want you and Karen to stay at Kanbaru's place tonight."

"Huh?"

Tsukihi looked taken aback like I'd just said something totally nonsensical—no, from her perspective I *had* said something totally nonsensical, so her reaction was right on the money.

"What's going on?"

"Don't ask me why. Please don't ask. I'll talk to Kanbaru and Karen about it too, so just do it... Please."

The home of Suruga Kanbaru, daughter of Izuko Gaen's older sister Toé Gaen—the safest place I could think of on the spur of the moment.

Ononoki was one thing, but if I was going to make contact with

Ms. Kagenui—I had to get Tsukihi far away, at least from our house.

If I didn't.

It would be summer break all over again.

"Hmph," grumbled Tsukihi.

Judging from how she didn't say *hunfnyaan*, she was going along grudgingly. "Fine. And if I do, it'll be okay?"

"Yeah. If you'll do it, I'll apologize."

Still embracing her, I said in the present tense, not the past tense: "Sorry I'm doing this to you."

But I really blew it.

I was a fool.

Because given what was to come—I should've apologized for something else entirely.

008

Night fell.

By "night," I mean the time after the sun goes down.

Until which point I spent the entire day inside.

Thank goodness school was out for the moment—if I missed any more days, I actually wouldn't be able to graduate. And it was also fortunate that I was studying for exams, and barely hanging on by the skin of my teeth at that—since no one thought it strange that I spent the entire day holed up in my room studying with the curtains closed. Nor would they invite me to go outside.

Once the sun went down and I'd eaten dinner with the whole family, I left the house—I used to have two bicycles, but I lost both of them in what you could call self-inflicted accidents, and they were now just a fond memory. Putting it that way really doesn't sit right with me, but—but basically, what can you call dealing with such aberration-ness, such "darkness"-ness, other than self-inflicted, a self-fulfilling prophecy?

And so I walked.

To the station.

After I had left the house and walked for a while, there was suddenly a little blond girl beside me—Tsubasa Hanekawa once said that I looked like I was on *Gmen '75* when I walked, and having Shinobu by my side definitely gave me that kind of reassurance.

"Sorry about this. Thanks for coming with me."

"I am not doing it for thee. We have ever shared a common destiny, we merely act as though 'twere otherwise."

"Guess you're right."

I lifted Shinobu off the ground where she was walking beside me and put her on my shoulders. I figured it'd be tough on a little girl to trek all the way to the station and was being considerate in my own way.

Man, was she light.

Like she was made of paper.

But even if she'd become almost entirely human, there was no partner I'd rather have by my side.

"As a precaution in the face of the two we go to meet, wilt thou not make me a vampire? If ye let me drink only as much as would be taken for a blood test, we can at least flee should dire circumstance arise."

"Ummm... But if I make you a vampire, then I'll become vampirified as well, and my current symptoms will become indistinguishable from everything else... I might not be able to get an accurate 'diagnosis.' Plus, Ms. Gaen's message only said that Ononoki would be waiting for us, she never actually said anything about Ms. Kagenui being there as well..."

"Didst bid farewell to thy lady?"

"No, I didn't bid her farewell..."

But I'd gotten in touch with Senjogahara.

And after her instantaneous response of *I'm coming too*, it had been a backbreaking labor to convince her otherwise.

I definitely don't think I was just being selfish in not wanting to let her meet that onmyoji & shikigami duo.

"To be honest, though, talking to her did make me feel a little better."

"Hmm. Because—in comparison to her former ailment of weightlessness, thine own lack of a reflection is in fact of no great concern? My lord."

"Umm, that wasn't exactly it..."

Though maybe that was exactly it.

"I think it was more because Senjogahara gave me a bunch of advice—and also helped me confirm a bunch of details. Like what happens if I look in the mirror with clothes on."

"Hmmm..."

"When I tried it, turned out my clothes were just floating there in the reflection, so it seems like I have to do everything in my power not to get near a mirror. She also told me to watch out for cars. If I don't appear in their side-view and rearview mirrors, the chances of my getting hit increase drastically."

"The lass truly doth take note of the smallest details... How cautiously she must have lived these two years gone."

Saying this, Shinobu threw her arms around my head. Being as small as she was, embracing my head like that was enough to completely fill her arms.

Just as I was wondering what she was doing, she announced, "I shall sleep a bit more. Wake me when we encounter Ononoki." And just like that she closed her eyes, her breathing slowing until it was clear that she was asleep. The thought did cross my mind that if she was going to sleep, she could do it in my shadow, but maybe she figured that with what was coming, events could turn on a dime. Sleeping outside would cut out the time it'd take her to emerge from my shadow.

That very morning Tsukihi had likened holding someone's head in your hands to holding their life in your hands, but maybe by embracing my head like that, Shinobu was actually protecting my life with her hands.

"Now then…"

I've heard that in order to develop a refined posture, aristocratic young women practiced walking with a cup of water balanced on their head, and this was something close to that: don't spill the water, don't wake Shinobu.

And so, walking with my most refined posture, I arrived at my destination, the department store near the station, at 6:55 p.m., just before the appointed time—though depending on how long the elevator took, I might actually end up being a little late.

Picking up my pace, I entered the building.

I thought maybe it'd be faster to take the escalator or run up the stairs… Running up the escalators would be quickest, but they're not for running.

So I chose the stairs.

Not that you're supposed to run up the stairs either, but I couldn't keep Ononoki waiting. I'd probably be out of breath after racing all the way up to the fourth floor—but while some people might be taken aback if the person they were waiting for showed up all out of breath, that wasn't a concern with Ononoki.

She would let it go expressionlessly as always, guaranteed.

"She said the arcade, right? The arcade, the arcade… Is there even an arcade here?"

Wait, it was ringing a bell.

A while back Kanbaru was telling me about this game Love and Berry that she was addicted to, and I could swear she said it was this department store where she played it…

I arrived at the fourth floor and began wandering around with that recollection in mind—and hit pay dirt almost immediately.

Since it was in a department store, though, it was tiny, just a place for parents to put their kids while they shopped, patterned after an arcade but really an arcade in name only. In that sense you could say it was a fitting place for a rendezvous with Ononoki. Plus it wouldn't be weird to have a little girl like my partner Shinobu with me.

"Hunh? She's not here."

I got there at seven sharp, but not only was Ononoki not there, there wasn't a soul in sight.

"Of all the... Empty. I did exactly like Ms. Gaen said, followed her instructions to the letter..."

I started to worry that maybe Ononoki had gotten into some kind of trouble, but that somewhat paranoid concern vanished when my eyes fell upon the game next to a Love and Berry-like cabinet.

It was what they call a UFO Catcher.

The kind made famous by *Toy Story*.

Though they would probably be famous even without *Toy Story*.

The kind where you put in a coin, move the arm, and try to pick up the prize—and, all alone, inside the glass case.

Was Ononoki.

Her legs splayed out in front of her, like a doll.

Not even a twitch of movement, like a doll.

"..."

Huh?

Wait, it *was* Ononoki...wasn't it?

It had to be Ononoki, didn't it?

How did she end up as the prize inside a crane game? I wondered, approaching the machine.

Easy now. I was trying not to transmit my impatience to Shinobu who slept atop my shoulders. Easy does it now.

"Ononoki?"

I tried rapping on the glass, but no response.

No response.

No expression, no emotion.

It was weird, she looked like a real figurine.

No, a figurine is an imitation of the human figure, so maybe calling something a *real figurine* is itself weird. Plus, Ononoki was always expressionless and emotionless and unresponsive, so her lack of response didn't prove anything.

"Yotsugi? Yo-o-otsugi-i-i!"

No response.

"Yotsy!"

No response.

Hmmm, maybe they'd just produced a figure of her and I'd missed it somehow... But this was life size.

Big enough that if we were talking Ichiban Kuji Premium, it'd be the Last One Prize... It seemed like there was nothing for me to do but play the game.

I took my wallet out of my pocket. I didn't think I'd be able to do it with only a hundred yen, so maybe a five-hundred...

Nope, don't have any. Okay, gotta break a thousand.

I went over to the change machine to break a one thousand-yen bill into ten one hundred-yen coins, and then hurried back over to the UFO Catcher.

Since there was no one else around, maybe I was just being overly anxious, but with this kind of machine you hear stories all the time about people poaching your prize while you're running to get more change.

"Though I've never really played this kind of prize-type game myself... I wonder how it works."

I should've brought Kanbaru after all.

Despite being a wildly talented athlete, she was deep into this kind of stuff—a perfect superwoman in a totally different sense than Hanekawa.

Musing about that, I inserted one of my newly changed coins into the cabinet. It wasn't crunch time yet, but the department store did close at eight.

I didn't imagine it'd take me an hour to get the prize, but still, no sense in dilly-dallying.

"Let's see... First move the arm sideways with the ① button, then forward with the ② button... Mm-hmm. Got it. The rules aren't too complicated. Awright then, let's give it a shot."

Apparently you started it by pressing the ① button.

I sent the crane arm flying over to where it could pick up Ono-noki's body—

Hm, I think that's a little too far. That's not gonna cut it, glad I noticed. Now, how do I bring it back?

Just a slight adjustment… Wait, you can't make adjustments?

I couldn't find a button anywhere with a reverse arrow on it…

Feeling abashed, I pressed the ② button—I'd blown it that time, but now that I knew there was no reverse button, I wasn't going to repeat the same mistake twice.

Definitely seemed like the strategy was to stop the arm a little bit before the prize, then inch your way towards it—WTF? As soon as I took my hand off the button, the arm started to drop!

No, not there! Not there, I'm aiming for deeper in!

But my internal screams did nothing to control the arm, and it came up empty, tracing a path back along the route of my failure almost as if it was mocking me.

"Thou art an abject bungler, my lord."

"Hmph. So you're awake, huh, Shinobu?"

"'Tis the jangling of that obnoxious background music… My lord's head is indeed a comfortable pillow, yet the constant racket renders it inferior to my usual place of repose."

Did she mean my shadow?

Treating someone's head and shadow as nothing more than beds… She might have lost her vampiric power, but her haughtiness still knew no bounds.

"But have a care, my lord. Approach not too closely unto the glass."

"Huh?"

"'Tis reflective."

Ah, in an excess of enthusiasm I'd sidled right up to the glass and was virtually pressed against it, and the light would cause me to be reflected there.

No—would cause everything but me to be reflected there.

Just my clothes would be reflected.

"Hm? Shinobu, you've got a totally normal reflection... Maybe not normal, since it looks like you're floating in midair, but is it because you've lost your vampire powers?"

"At present 'tis so. But at the height of my powers, I could give myself a reflection whenever I so chose. No weakness is truly a weakness for one such as I."

"…"

But of course.

The legend herself.

She left me speechless—but at that point, I should have picked up on what her words implied. True, I guess even if I'd picked up on "it" then, the timing wouldn't have changed anything.

"It."

By which I mean the difference between us as vampires.

Anyway, time for my second attempt.

"So basically, I only get one shot at going sideways and one shot at going forward?"

"Aye, 'tis so. Though 'tis written plainly enough, if thou wouldst only read the explanation."

"I've always been hopeless at reading the instructions... Not that it matters."

With any game, you've got to learn by doing.

I pressed the ① button with the utmost deliberation.

I backed away from the glass slightly so I wouldn't be reflected there, so what wasn't being reflected wouldn't be reflected there. But if I backed up too much my sense of distance would be off—I adjusted my position until I was standing in the right spot, or at least a spot that I judged to be the right one, and released the button.

Yup, right there. No question.

"Heheh, I think I might have a gift for crane games."

"Methinks 'tis too early to say, but even were it so, how might such a talent stand thee in good stead in the future?"

"I'll become the mysterious old man who wins stuffed animals for little children in arcades."

"Mayhap a little too mysterious."

As the words *Is that a sufficient future for thee, my lord?* floated down from above, I pressed the ② button. This wasn't some RPG, and I didn't have time to mess around.

"Okay, right there!"

With the split-second timing of a god among master swordsmen, I released the button. The claws began to descend precisely where I wanted it, directly above Ononoki's head.

"Hey! Look, Shinobu!"

"I am looking… However, should it descend as such…"

"Hm?"

Before Shinobu could finish, the wide-open claws struck Ononoki, or her figure—legs splayed out in front of her—directly on the noggin.

With a dull thud.

I unconsciously released a sighing "Ah…"

Dealt an overhead attack, the figure of Ononoki crumpled, her upper body losing its equilibrium and teetering before finally falling backwards. In other words, she ended up flat on her back in the glass case and was staring upwards with her arms and legs spread wide.

Her expression changed not at all.

I could observe no physical response.

She remained expressionless when the crane struck her, when she toppled over—well, since she was always expressionless, you could say like her usual self, but this expressionlessness really made me wonder if the prize in the game might not be a doll made to look like Yotsugi Ononoki, after all.

"'Tis not a question of her expression, her movements be utterly like unto those of a marionette…a doll. She made not the least

117

movement to ready herself for the coming impact."

"Uh huh... Ms. Gaen couldn't possibly be messing with us... could she? I didn't think she was that kind of person, it's not like she said, 'There's a doll that looks like Ononoki in this department store.' Man, that would piss me off. If all I get after blowing this wad of cash is a stupid doll...guess I'll have no choice but to snuggle up with it when I sleep."

"While 'tis true that mine own sense of money is a spot spotty, methinks thou canst not term a few hundred yen a wad of cash, my lord. Get thyself a clue. Truly, thou shalt end up as a mysterious old man who wins stuffed animals from crane games for little children."

"You're right. I've got to do whatever I can to avoid that fate, even if I'm the one who brought it up in the first place..."

Putting that aside.

And while I may have already become an extremely mysterious teenager with a little blond girl sitting on my shoulders, racing the clock in a closing department store to try and win a life-size doll of a young girl from a crane game, definitely putting that aside as well.

My second attempt had ended in failure—all I'd done was knock Ononoki down so she was splayed out flat—and the crane arm had returned to its original position. Third time's the charm?

"Well, at least that blunder wasn't a waste... I've learned something. Seems like it's not as simple as just positioning the arm directly above the prize. You've got to consider the way the claws move too. I bet not a lot of people realize that."

"Would not those of superior intuition realize it before they even made their first attempt?"

"Don't you think the computer should just make those adjustments for you?"

"What would be the point of such a forgiving prize game?"

"Before, it would've been best to drop it around her thighs, but with the position she's in now...her waist would be best, I guess. If

118

I can hook her waist with a claw, I should pick her right up."

"I wonder, be the arm powerful enough for that?"

"GO!"

I went.

I inserted the coin and started moving the arm—aiming for Ononoki's waist. If everything went according to plan, the crane would pick Ononoki up by the waist, pull her up, raise her up, and provide the perfect angle for me to get a full view of the contents of her skirt.

I was planning to fine-tune my own position in addition to the crane arm's, but in the end, my aim was thwarted.

The arm did begin to lift Ononoki by the waist, but her mass wrenched the claw open, and she fell back into her original spot—this time on her side.

And the arm returned to its original position.

"This arm's got no strength at all!"

"Did I not tell thee? I believe I did. Thou shouldst heed my advice."

"Sure, yeah, that's true, but…"

I was all out of protestations.

Apparently I sucked at UFO Catchers (I take back everything I said), so maybe I should let Shinobu do it for me?

No, she was more of an armchair quarterback…

"Still, the crane just let Ononoki drop without even putting up a fight! It's too weak! It didn't even get her off the ground for a second!"

"Mayhap the screws are loose. Though that too may simply be a question of the generosity of the house, or lack thereof. The power of the arm is in truth theirs to dictate as they see fit."

"You can't be serious… That's not fair."

What the hell was I going to do?

The game was rigged against the player.

The only thing I could control was the movement of the arm—and that incompletely, while the house had full hegemony over the arm's power. I was helpless.

"Nay, my lord—while 'tis true that the claws' power to close, hold, and lift be paltry, there is yet one thing the house cannot control."

"Yeah? And what's that?"

"The power of the arm as it falls—its descending force. Erst struck Ononoki from above, did thee not? And that had, if nothing else, the requisite force to alter the lass's position."

"...And?"

"Ergo—" Shinobu pointed by way of explanation, "just as one might use a stick to push a rock into a river, thou canst use the arm to trundle Ononoki over to the hole without ever raising her up."

"..."

That might be a "feasible" strategy for a UFO Catcher, but Shinobu's phrasing made it a cheat without an ounce of affection for the doll in question.

Trundle.

"Well, I guess that's the only hope we've got left...but I've only got seven coins left. I wonder if seven'll do it?"

"My lord. By the by."

"What is it?"

"It appears thou mayest play four times if dost insert three coins at once."

"Why didn't you say so sooner?!"

The battle certainly didn't get any easier from there on out. We'd figured out a back door, but of course things didn't go according to plan, and time and again the arm banged ineffectually against Ononoki's body.

Her lack of reaction was somehow painful to look at.

It was just too pitiful.

Even when I did succeed, the distance she moved was so incremental that it was extremely unlikely I could pull it off with the coins, the credits, I had remaining—seven coins meant nine plays.

120

My coffers were slowly but steadily dwindling.

Trundling towards oblivion.

"Hrk… What am I gonna do when these credits are gone…"

"Change another thousand-yen bill. Thou art carrying that much, art thou not?"

"What's with the lukewarm comeback? Heat things up for me, like in an arcade manga in *CoroCoro Comics*."

"Dost such manga still exist?"

And while this banter was going on—at last.

At last, with my final credit, I succeeded in using the arm to nudge Ononoki into the hole—she landed in the retrieval drawer with a thud. It was more than just a dull sound, though, it sounded like something somewhere in there broke.

"I did it, Shinobu!" I pumped my fist, pretending I hadn't heard that sound. "It's a happy ending!"

"Why do I feel as though our original goal hath been forgot…"

"Original goal? Wasn't our original goal to get Ononoki?"

"Nay."

"That's ridiculous. What higher goal could there be in this world than to win a tween girl?"

"If that is all thou desirest, my lord, then there, take the lassy and go. 'Tis nigh on the time for this store to close its doors."

She was right.

I'd thought we had plenty of leeway, but all of a sudden it was past 7:45—any second now they were going to start playing "Auld Lang Syne" over the speakers.

Obviously *not* having forgotten my original goal—of dealing with the mysterious phenomenon afflicting my body—I moved to retrieve Ononoki. I mean, whether or not I'd forgotten, either way we weren't going to get anywhere unless I got her out of there.

I pulled the handle on the drawer.

"Mph… It's stuck, I can't get it open."

"Grit thy teeth and pull with all thy might. She may lose an arm or a leg, perhaps, but even so."

"You think I can just ignore that 'perhaps'?"

Ononoki, probably a little too big for the opening, had gotten hung up... If this was an ordinary prize, I could just call over an employee, but that didn't seem like such a good idea if it was the real Ononoki.

Jiggling the handle back and forth, I pulled the drawer out little by little—kind of like sifting flour into cake batter.

That's purely a metaphor, I've never actually baked a cake before—but nonetheless, my stratagem worked, and I was able to get the thing open.

Ononoki was stuffed in there in a crumpled heap—like one of those sponges that regain their shape when you add hot water.

"Yo-o-otsugi," I tried calling to her.

Like I was on a children's television program, for some reason.

...No reply.

The expression *like a dead body* was a little too fitting for Yotsugi Ononoki given that she'd been made from a corpse, but there you go.

"What took you so long?"

Finally she replied.

In a placid, emotionless voice that reminded me of the way Hitagi Senjogahara used to be—though it differed from Senjogahara's voice in being totally mechanical, artificial in every way.

"How long could it possibly take to win me? You suck at games."

"And you've got a big mouth for a doll..." I said, pulling Ononoki out and flipping up her skirt to make sure everything underneath was okay.

"Chop."

Ononoki's karate chop came down on the back of my neck.

And it was a backhand, like in tennis. A chop that wove skillfully between Shinobu's legs.

"Don't get fresh, kind monster sir. Monstieur."

"No no no, I was just wondering what's going on under the skirts of beautiful girl figurines like this one. I just thought I'd check."

"If that's your excuse, at least get it out there before I've spoken. While there's still the possibility that I'm just a common doll." This fierce retort was delivered in an endlessly placid voice—a monotone so unnatural it was almost like it was processed. "That is, I'm not just a common doll—but I am a doll. An uncommon doll, dolled up to look like a real person."

"..."

"Yaaay," she flashed a sudden sideways peace sign.

A sideways peace sign that said, *To hell with the flow of this conversation.* Her pose was ludicrously, lethally cute, but her expression was expressionless, totally unconcerned, and totally unchanged from when she was in the glass case. The gap was surreal.

Not gap moé, surreal moé.

"Anyway, haven't seen you in a while, monsieur."

"Don't call me that."

"Haven't seen you in a while either, sis," Ononoki said, raising her gaze from my face to the space above my head—where I imagine it came to rest on the little blond girl riding on my shoulders.

"Address me not as sis. What meanest thou, what thinkest thou our relationship to be?"

"My apologies. I'm not ashamed to admit that I forgot what our relationship was like, Ma'am Vampire."

"'Tis more like it, thou forgetful lout," spat Shinobu.

I guess that first impression had been seriously negative, and Shinobu's attitude towards Ononoki was severe—the little girl really knew how to hold a grudge.

While we're on the subject, the tween girl standing before me didn't hold onto much of anything. That is, her character was unstable. I knew as much from the time we'd spent together up to that point, but—her personality was totally indefinite.

Blurry as all hell.

Although she did have something approaching a characterization every time I saw her—or it appeared that way, anyway, but it could diffuse at a moment's notice, evaporate like mist, and transform into something else entirely.

Which in a sense just marked her as an aberration, and maybe *blurry* wasn't a very precise way to describe her.

Now then.

What the hell kind of character was she at the moment? Seemed like she had an acid tongue, or a bad attitude...

"Ah. I don't suppose, Ononoki. Miss Yotsugi Ononoki."

"What is it, monstieur. Kind monster monstieur."

"Too much monster."

"Aren't you playing *Dr. Kawashima's Monstrous Training*?"

"Since I'm studying for exams I do have an interest in the game, but forget the monster connection. Don't connect us. Anyway, I don't suppose," I brought the conversation back around.

To my baseless supposition.

"That you've seen Deishu Kaiki recently?"

"I haaave," Ononoki replied with a calm nod.

Interesting...

Ms. Kagenui had told me that the "ki" in "Ononoki" came from Kaiki—from that ominous swindler's name.

This was apparently because he'd had a hand in her "production," but I didn't know much more than that.

So my conjecture had been more or less pure guesswork. But, to my surprise, bingo.

Not that it was a bingo I was pleased by.

Quite the opposite.

That swindler, exerting his malign influence on this innocent young girl.

"Well, fine. I'll let that go for now."

Influence was nothing but influence, after all.

Even a malign influence was still just influence.

Light-years better than the man himself.

"Haven't seen you in—it actually hasn't been that long, has it, Ononoki."

"You're right. How long's it been, I wonder. And since the three of us were all together—oh, yeah, when snail girl—"

"..."

"Hm?" Ononoki cocked her head.

Not in response to her own insensitive words, seemingly—but that time, that time that brought together the little girl and the young girl and the tween girl, was definitely very memorable.

In various senses.

In many senses—in every sense.

Very memorable indeed.

"Well, we've got a lot to talk about. We've got a lot to talk a lot about, but this is no time for chitchat, is it, monsieur. I'm not here to hang out with my friend this time, I'm here on business. I'd forgotten, sorry sorry sorry."

"Ononoki."

I was secretly thrilled that Ononoki casually made it clear she thought of me as a friend, but it pretty much turned to ashes in my mouth with that last "I'd forgotten."

I guess I'm a forgettable friend, I thought—but it was definitely true that this time around, we weren't just hanging out and eating ice cream together.

To the outside observer, a teenager standing in the arcade at a department store with a little girl and tween girl probably appeared to be their babysitter (god help me if it looked like anything else), but that wasn't the case.

I was there to ask this girl.

To save me.

This expert—this expert's familiar.

This tsukumogami, Yotsugi Ononoki.

"So, Ononoki."

"What is it, what is it? Yaaay."

Even with Kaiki's influence, her absurdly sunny disposition remained relatively intact, making Ononoki's personality even more frustratingly complicated and strange, but I aimed my words between the spread fingers of that sideways peace sign. "There are two things I want to ask you."

"Ask me anything. I want to answer my most favorite monstieur's questions even if he doesn't ask them."

"…"

I hated to think that this part of her personality might derive from Deishu Kaiki…but it was the kind of frivolous thing he might very well say.

The same line could have a completely different effect coming from this lovely young girl's lips rather than from that ominous man in his funerary suit, though.

There would be nothing charming about Kaiki saying it…

"Ononoki, why were you inside the UFO Catcher?"

"I was waiting for you. We had an appointment. Isn't it common practice for businesspeople to arrive five minutes early?"

"Well…"

"Or are you an advocate of Hakata time?"

Hakata time refers to being slightly late for an appointment (apparently).

"Or heading a little further south, do you hold to Okinawa time?"

Okinawa time refers to being very late for an appointment (apparently).

"Sorry, monstieur, I don't mean to brag, but I was here fifteen minutes early. Big Sis is like a drill sergeant when it comes to practical life skills."

"Practical life skills…"

What I'd wanted to know was how she got inside that glass case (and furthermore, why she thought it was a good idea to wait for me inside a UFO Catcher), but before I could get an answer, the words "Big Sis" forced me to move on to my second question.

My second question.

Big Sis.

"Ms. Kagenui, she—" As I spoke, my glance darted casually all around. "Isn't here, is she? In other words, you're alone, right, Ononoki?"

"Nope," she said, pointing her finger at me.

Why's she pointing at me, I wondered, but her finger arced smoothly upward—to indicate Shinobu.

Which raised the question *why's she pointing at Shinobu*, but Ononoki wasn't pointing at her either.

That finger.

That finger, the vehicle for Ononoki's finishing move "Unlimited Rulebook" and therefore potentially a most lethal weapon, wasn't pointing at me, or at Shinobu—but even further above us.

Further above us.

Above us?

But there's just empty space above Shinobu—I thought as I raised my eyes. The human body isn't constructed so that you can look directly upwards, but it can look "almost directly up," which in this case was enough.

Shinobu Oshino, riding on the shoulders of Koyomi Araragi.

A vampire, riding on the shoulders of a human.

And above them both—her.

Yozuru Kagenui.

The latter-day, ultra-violent onmyoji.

Standing on one leg atop Shinobu's blond mane.

Ms. Kagenui hadn't even bothered to take her shoes off.

"Make yerselves at home."

You're welcome.

009

Shinobu might have lost her power, she might have become a little girl, but in spite of it all she was still proud of her blond hair, and having it trod upon so rudely must have been quite a shock because she ended up sequestering herself inside my shadow.

You could also say that by ditching me like that she was abandoning her role as my buddy, or bodyguard, which would be inexcusable behavior for my trusted partner, but when I considered what a shock it must have been, I didn't have the heart to blame her for it.

Shinobu had been interposed between us, but even if she hadn't been, I'm not so fragile that I'd feel insulted by a woman standing on my head. Nevertheless, the fact is that I was startled—the fact is that I was so startled I jumped.

I'd shot up, shrieking *gaaah*, but Ms. Kagenui's balance hadn't been thrown off in the slightest, she'd remained perched atop Shinobu's head with a composed look, not moving a muscle—

But hang on, she didn't weigh a thing.

It was like she was floating.

Not like when I say, *Shinobu's so tiny, she's light as a feather*—nor like Senjogahara, when she'd been stripped of her weight—it just seemed like Ms. Kagenui didn't weigh anything at all. This might not be a particularly apt metaphor, but it was like physically experiencing trompe-l'œil.

If Shinobu was made of paper.

Ms. Kagenui was a paper balloon.

Maybe as a master of the martial arts she can erase her weight by shifting her center of gravity—indeed a match for Karen's sensei, I thought, trying to force the situation to make sense, but it felt too illogical.

The reasoning was unreasonable, unremittingly unrealistic.

Well.

This was an illogical person I was dealing with.

Despite being more human than anyone—

She was more un-human than anyone.

"First off, mightn't we up stakes and take ourselves someplace else, young man—seems this department store's fixing to close. And darn if I don't have just the place. The ruins of that cram school where you and I had a ball slaughtering each other—"

She didn't seem to be psyching herself up or prettying things up as she said this in her Kyoto dialect—even the disturbing part about "slaughtering each other" came out of her mouth as naturally as could be.

I guess that's how it must be for her...

That's how it is.

Just another day.

Good enough for me, I decided to go along with her suggestion. Having a conversation about aberration-related phenomena after hours in a department store seemed somehow unappealing—it would be a hell of a setting for a ghost story. But the security guard would be coming around, so we couldn't stay there either way. Well, I imagine Ononoki and Ms. Kagenui could, but...

I preferred to avoid a fight scene.

It would be an unmitigated disaster if this turned into a battle. I'd much prefer if we could figure things out calmly and maturely, without incident indecent or otherwise.

That sentiment, that laudable sentiment, might have gone to shit the second the pair showed up, but—anyway.

We left the department store arcade and headed to that ruined cram school so redolent with memories.

That ruined cram school.

The adjective "ruined" had taken on a slightly different nuance after summer break—before, the spot had been occupied by "an abandoned building that used to be a cram school," still standing even if it was totally rundown (it was inside that abandoned building that Ms. Kagenui and I, and Shinobu and Ononoki, had done battle); but at the end of August, it had burned to the ground, and been reduced to ashes, leaving no trace behind, not even a ruin—so at present, it was what you might call a vacant lot.

Empty land with a "No Trespassing" sign.

Either way, though, visiting that place at night was not for the faint of heart. That much, at least, hadn't changed—but it was also still devoid of human activity and remained a good location for a confidential conversation.

On the way there, I sized up Ms. Kagenui as she walked ahead of me—or didn't walk, didn't set foot on the ground; she rode the whole way on Ononoki's shoulders.

When you were little, didn't you play that game on the way to school where you pretend that "the ground is an ocean, and if you step on it you'll drown"—and the one rule is that you have to stay on top of walls or benches or whatever?

I didn't know why she did it (I was pretty sure she didn't really believe she'd drown), but Ms. Kagenui absolutely would not set foot on the ground—the first time I met her, she was standing on top of a mailbox.

At that moment she was riding on Ononoki's shoulders—not the way I'd been carrying Shinobu a little earlier, but standing dexterously on tiptoe astride them.

When I saw it for the first time over the summer, I was floored by Ononoki's inhuman strength, but having now personally experienced Ms. Kagenui's ability to nullify her weight, I realized she was the extraordinary one. Granted, Ononoki was by no means ordinary herself, but—that said.

Whatever impression it might leave me with and however it worked, aside from her decidedly oddball habit of "taking the high road," which was pretty much impossible to leave aside, the impression I got of Yozuru Kagenui was the same one I'd gotten when I first met her: that of "an attractive woman who was my elder."

Like a dignified teacher.

Or a diligent businesswoman.

At least, she didn't appear to be of the same ilk as the middle-aged man in the Hawaiian shirt and the ominous guy in the funerary suit—she didn't look at all like she would've been friends with them in college.

She didn't, but strictly in terms of dangerousness, she far outstripped either Oshino or Kaiki—far transcended them. Unlike Oshino, who was open to conversation, and Kaiki, whose attention could be bought, there was no dealing with Ms. Kagenui.

And that made her more trouble than any aberration or anyone else—which was precisely why she was an aberration-slaying, aberration-employing onmyoji, I imagine.

The fact that her very appearance on the scene could drive the former Kissshot Acerolaorion Heartunderblade, once the king of aberrations even if she had lost her power, into hiding so easily, so disappointingly quickly—forcing her back into my shadow, spoke to the extent of Ms. Kagenui's true power.

Shinobu was the Aberration Slayer.

But Ms. Kagenui was an expert, known as the Aberration

Roller—and specialized in immortal aberrations.

"I—" I began when we reached the vacant land, er, wasteland where the ruins of the cram school had been. There'd been an awkward lack of conversation on the way there. Though maybe I was the only one who found the total silence awkward. "—bid you welcome. You. To my place. Ms. Kagenui."

"Mm-hmm. Kakakak."

Her policy of "taking the high road" seemed to allow walking inside buildings (the floor isn't the ground), but this was just a wasteland, very much the ground, so while she stopped, she didn't alight from Ononoki's shoulders, and when she responded she did so from that position.

Ms. Kagenui herself had suggested this place for our talk, and I figured it had probably been her idea of a "fair suggestion"—conducting our consultation in an open space where she couldn't touch the ground created a "difficult combat environment" for her, so there'd be no sudden eruptions of violence—though if push came to shove, it seemed like that ball was entirely in her court.

Or maybe I was just overthinking it.

But this lady—

"I go wherever I please, my young friend—where I please throughout Japan or this here entire world of ours. Slaying immortal aberrations, as is my wont."

"…"

Yup.

All this lady wanted to do was kill immortal aberrations.

I didn't understand why, I didn't know why, and in fact I didn't even know if there was a reason in the first place, but Yozuru Kagenui hated immortal aberrations with a passion—despised them.

So consulting with her on this matter was extremely risky, even if I kept various aspects of the situation to myself—she'd come to see me personally, but I'd have felt much more at ease if she'd just sent Ononoki to act as a kind of carrier pigeon.

133

It's a sad fact, though, that human beings know the things they hate better than the things they love, which meant that at the moment, whatever form this might take, Ms. Kagenui was unmistakably the most appropriate and logical choice for a consultation.

She of all people could do something.

About my unnatural transformation into a vampire.

Naturally I had high expectations.

"Though of course I'm here now because Gaen-senpai was keen I should come—you've caught her fancy something fierce, I reckon, young man. What'd you do?"

"Nothing...worth mentioning. I haven't done anything, or, I don't remember doing anything. In fact, it's more like she did a bunch of things to, I mean, for me..."

No good.

I sounded way too nervous.

I was obviously on my guard—that is, I was shaking in my boots.

Over summer break, Ms. Kagenui had beaten the living shit out of me right here, though at a different altitude, and I guess my body hadn't forgotten.

Well, since I was asking her for help, I was in no position to be anything but humble towards her, whether I dragged our past enmity into the present or not...

"Hmm... Well, fair enough, I reckon. No need to fuss ourselves over it. You have yourself whatever relationship with Gaen-senpai your little heart desires. And yet, a body—never mind." Ms. Kagenui gave a little shake of her head.

Like she was about to say something but thought better of it.

Or like she cut herself off?

"Enough of that, I'll not speak on it any further. Whatever plans Gaen-senpai may have, whatever her motives—a body's just keen to slay immortal aberrations. So long as I'm allowed that, I reckon I've no complaints."

"..."

I doubt she was going to say anything good, but it always nags at me when someone breaks off in mid-sentence, you know?

"Well then? What seems to be the trouble? I find I've yet to hear the whole story—I heard tell of an immortal aberration in these parts, so I just dropped everything and hightailed it here."

"Oh…"

She was operating on some seriously vague information.

To put it another way, this lady seriously wanted to kill some immortal aberrations—she seemed less like an expert and more like an executioner.

Though when it comes to facing a vampire—just like with that trio of specialists—maybe that's only proper.

But this was really going to make things tough, just like it had been with those three.

"It'll take a long time to explain everything…or maybe not actually all that long, but can I ask you something first?"

"Anything you please," Ms. Kagenui said with seeming satisfaction, her overwhelming gaze pouring down on me from on high. Just the difference engendered by Ononoki's height was enough for it to feel plenty oppressive, and I was like a deer in the headlights.

I had half a mind to call for Shinobu and cajole her into coming out of my shadow so I could make myself taller than Ms. Kagenui, but I gave up on the idea. I could see at a glance that even if I stood on Shinobu's head, I wouldn't measure up to Ms. Kagenui.

"You and Ononoki are, well, experts?"

"I reckon we are. Though strictly speaking, it's me that's the expert, and Ononoki here is a shikigami, my subordinate, you might say."

"Which means that you have—a price, don't you?"

A price.

Oshino used to talk about it all the time.

Not that he was an extreme miser like Kaiki, but when it came to the price of his labor, Oshino was severe, or you could say he lacked a spirit of volunteerism, or maybe that he was a stickler—he pretty much never did anything for free.

Ms. Gaen wasn't after money per se, but she demanded payment in kind, which was an even more troublesome bargain than money—and this time was no exception. Her price was returning the favor—a price of some sort or another was the rule in their business, as far as I could tell.

And if it was a rule, I assumed that even the iconoclastic Yozuru Kagenui would abide by it.

"I won't beat around the bush... How much will you need? To be frank, I don't have all that much money."

"Eh? I've no use for filthy lucre, what's more trouble than it's worth. I reckon I'm no good with such fiddly calculations. It don't make no nevermind to me, so get on with your jawing."

"..."

Total anarchy!

What the hell kind of attitude was that?!

Even an easy-breezy lifestyle has its limits!

Not having to pay was a godsend for a student like me (whatever Shinobu might say, using up a thousand yen on the UFO Catcher was a hard blow), but danger lurked in that unsociability, and I didn't want to accidentally get too close.

It wasn't that she had no material desires.

She was wearing classy clothes, after all.

Ms. Gaen's payment in kind was plenty frightening, but this "make no nevermind" attitude was frightening in its incomprehensibility. Kaiki's obsession with money was "insufferable," but insufferable was something I could wrap my head around—this was simply "inscrutable."

Insufferable, and inscrutable—similar according to the Nuance Proposition, but...

"Young man, seems as though you've been spending a good deal of time with Yotsugi here, which is plenty good enough for me. But if that won't do for you, then, well, I'd reckon it a kindness if you treated her to some ice cream again next time round."

"Häagen-Dazs." Ononoki had remained silent up to this point, but here she unexpectedly joined in—no need for her to give in to her desires quite so fully, but yeah, when you just come right out and say it like that, it's clear as day. Easy to get.

Made me want to throw in a Klondike Bar along with the Häagen-Dazs.

I wonder, though.

In that sense, Ms. Kagenui's "desire" seemed to me like nothing but the overt bloodlust of wanting to kill immortal aberrations—which was maybe what freaked me out.

"Do you also have a favorite food or anything, Ms. Kagenui? If you do—"

"I don't. So long as it's edible, I'm not fussed about it."

"…"

There was no way in, that is, she acted disinterested in a way that made me think, *She really isn't interested in anything but "that," is she.*

When most people say they don't have any preferences when it comes to food, you'll turn up an ingredient they really like or a something that puts them off if you hassle them about it long enough, but Ms. Kagenui's curt response gave no such impression, not even a crumb.

Ultimately, she was "scary" not because she was violent or hard to talk to—it struck me at that moment that it was because she lacked the little things that make people human.

Un-human—was that it?

In which case, closing the distance through small talk or attempts to create a friendly atmosphere would be totally futile with her… Sure, not paying a price, not needing to, made me feel ill at ease, but forcing money on someone who didn't want it would be no less weird.

Deciding that my malaise was a personal problem that I would just have to deal with (along with treating Ononoki to some Häagen-Dazs sometime. And I'm not talking about a cup, but a cone), I broached the real subject with Ms. Kagenui.

"It's mirrors."

"Huh?"

"Mirrors—there's no reflection. Of me. In them."

"..."

From that point on, Ms. Kagenui listened to what I had to say without giving any polite encouragement, but also without making fun of me, basically with a serious expression—she heard me out about my half-baked transformation into a vampire that didn't correlate to Shinobu Oshino.

The Aberration Roller was totally absorbed.

"Now I've got the picture," she nodded, after I finally finished speaking. "Your sister. Your little sister. Sounds like she's fit as a fiddle. Tsukihi Araragi, little Tsukihi."

"Uh, no, that's not the point…"

"After listening to you jaw on about all that, how could a body not be concerned about your deviant bath time with little sis? That's one long bath, I reckon."

But that aside, said Ms. Kagenui, changing the subject even as she jabbed me where it hurt.

It seemed that even she couldn't resist quipping about The Battle for the First Bath, but apparently her interests really were confined to immortal aberrations, because she changed the subject almost immediately.

"I'm fixing to ask a few questions, that all right with you?"

"Please do. Ask me anything at all."

"Just answer best you can remember. When was the last time you reckon you saw your reflection in a mirror?"

"?"

"Listen here, there was likely a mirror in the changing room—when you stripped down to your skivvies out there, did you have a reflection? And in the bathroom itself, surely the mirror wasn't fogged up right from the get-go. What about when you first got in there? When you were giving your sister a pompadour, for instance, you reckon there was anything then? Or if you don't remember that too well, how's about before bed last night? When you were brushing your teeth, or—"

"..."

Now that she was asking these questions, I realized I should've thought of them right away. I was so fixated on the mysterious phenomenon of my lack of reflection—that I hadn't thought about when in the world, when in hell it had started.

Even if I was panicking, that was still pretty negligent of me.

I searched my memory.

I searched—but came up empty. Humans take "having a reflection" for granted, after all, so we don't pay it any mind.

Even if we're aware of it in the moment, it's not going to form a lasting memory—though of course, if I hadn't had a reflection while I was brushing my teeth the night before, you'd think I would have noticed then and there. I figured we could say I'd still had a reflection at that point.

And probably also when I undressed in the changing room—if I hadn't had a reflection then, I would've noticed. So, I guess.

"We should assume that the last time I had a reflection was right before it happened...I think. Before the mirror got fogged up... So I think the moment in question was the first time I didn't have a reflection."

"Hmm...your toenails."

"I'm sorry?"

"Your nails. Let's see 'em."

I let my hands droop like a ghost's and displayed them to Ms. Kagenui—who grimaced in displeasure and said, "Your *toe*nails."

Oh right.

Why would Ms. Kagenui be interested in my nail art?

139

They weren't even decorated in the first place.

That being said, I honestly didn't know how to show her my toenail when I was standing in the middle of a vacant lot and she was up in the air on the shoulders of a tween girl.

Well, nothing for it but to improvise since I didn't have time for a rehearsal… I took off my sneaker, removed my sock, balled the sock up and put it into the shoe—then, taking a pose like the Y balance in rhythmic gymnastics, I extended my foot towards Ms. Kagenui.

"That's just about the strangest pose I've ever laid eyes on."

What's that supposed to mean, you're the one who asked me!

But before I could even think that, Ms. Kagenui grabbed hold of the foot I'd raised partway off the ground (I hadn't actually made it to a full Y balance. I'm not that flexible) and pulled it close to her face—I thought I was going to go head over heels, which is to say I almost did go head over heels, but Ms. Kagenui kept that from happening, by brute force.

In other words, she was able to support my entire body weight simply by holding my ankle with one of her hands—just how strong was she?

Maybe they hadn't exaggerated her brutality in the anime after all.

"Mirrors—"

"I'm sorry?"

"It's plenty frightening not to have a reflection—sure enough it is, but there's an aberration what *only* appears in mirrors as well, I reckon."

"Ah…you're right."

I couldn't bring a name to mind—but I did recall hearing about ghosts that only appear in mirrors, evil spirits that live in mirrors, aberrations that are themselves mirrors.

There were too many to count.

I don't think that had anything directly to do with the matter at hand, though, I imagine Ms. Kagenui just brought it up to fill the time while she was examining my toenail.

"What'd that child—that vampire, the former Kissshot Acerolaorion Heartunderblade, have to say about this here toe?"

"Let's see... That little girl, who's sulking now thanks to you... said there'd been an infinitesimal fracture that slowly sealed from the inside out, and that the bone was fully healed—that was this morning's diagnosis."

"Was it now? This morning, eh? Well, take a looksee."

"Sorr...eeeeee?"

Ms. Kagenui pulled my leg up even further and shoved the nail right up to my face. My stance was now well past a Y balance, and more like an I balance.

Yes, it hurt.

The joints in my crotch groaned.

Or maybe it was just my voice I was hearing.

"See there. All better."

"..."

To be frank, the pose was neither stable nor settled enough for me to ascertain the state of something as small as my pinky toenail, but when I forced my eyes up to look at it, sure enough, it seemed to be just as she said. The split in the nail had repaired itself, and the scab was gone.

This may sound a bit overblown when all we're talking about is a pinky toenail, but—it was definitely a full recovery.

Yes, as though...as though a vampiric healing factor was in effect.

"It's hard to tell from a purely external examination whether or not a fracture has healed, but we don't need an X-ray to see that the nail, at least, is back to normal... And it's definitely out of the question for a nail to repair itself like this in just one day," I summed up the situation for everyone's benefit, recapping the parts that added up, and the parts that didn't. "But the weird thing is, Ms. Kagenui—when I was putting on my socks to leave the house, my toe wasn't in nearly such good shape. It was pretty much like it'd been this morning when Shinobu made her diagnosis… Superficially, at least, it hadn't gotten better at all."

"The reason's obvious, oblivious monstieur." This response came not from Ms. Kagenui but from below her, from Ononoki. She extended one finger (probably just out of habit, but knowing the power inherent in that finger made it a terrifying gesture) and pointed at the sky.

At the sky—the night sky.

The dark night sky, the sun having already set.

"Oh, I get it. A vampire's power gets stronger at night—"

"And you've probably gotten plenty of moonlight. Moonbathing, not sunbathing, salves a vampire's wounds. Yaaay."

The instant she said *yaaay* she got a kick from Ms. Kagenui. It was a violent form of discipline, but I can't say I didn't see where she was coming from.

Not that I'm in much of a position to talk, being partially to blame for that *yaaay*.

"So that means Shinobu's diagnosis was right. Her deduction that I'm currently in vampire form means…"

It wasn't just regular healing, it was creature-of-the-night healing—vampire healing, in other words. No question about it.

"Well, I'll not render judgment quite yet, I reckon—not having seen the original wound and all. Here now, Yotsugi."

"What is it, Big Sis?"

"Take a gander." With that Ms. Kagenui tugged me around by my ankle once more—not back to my original position, but to an angle slightly lower than that of a Y balance, somewhere in the neighborhood of ninety to a hundred degrees.

And just like that she jammed my bare foot up to Ononoki's face. Right up to it. She pushed the sole of my foot onto the tween girl's face and rubbed it around, which was pretty kinky in its own way.

I wondered what the onmyoji was doing, if it was to please me or something, but then Ms. Kagenui instructed her familiar to "investigate."

"Okay, okay." With this somewhat recalcitrant response, Ononoki took my ankle from Ms. Kagenui—come on, guys, my leg isn't a relay baton.

Realistically, having it held by Ononoki instead of Kagenui should've been scarier, beyond scary in fact, but at that moment I was somewhat relieved that the baton had passed.

My relief only lasted a few seconds, though, really just the time it took for Ms. Kagenui to pass me off to Ononoki, who quickly put my toe into her mouth like a pacifier. This made even an inveterate veteran like myself quake with fear.

Shinobu tortuously torturing my foot was one thing, but putting it in your mouth and sucking on it? That was something else entirely.

It didn't even tickle.

"It's crunchy."

"Hey, no teeth! No biting, no biting!"

"Don't get so cranky, it's just a pinky toe."

"Cranky—!"

Sensing imminent, potentially fatal danger, I pulled away my leg—while Ms. Kagenui's hold had been so tight that my leg probably would've torn right off, Ononoki, despite holding it with both arms, was so intent on sucking on my toe that I was able to extract myself easily.

"What d'you reckon, Yotsugi?"

"Results pending."

"Well then, Araragi, my boy. While Yotsugi's processing the flavor of your foot, how's about we move on to the next step? Your hand, if you please."

"My hand?"

"Uh huh, just make believe I'm a fortune teller."

I'd mistakenly offered her my hands when she wanted to see my toenail, couldn't she just have checked then? Proper sequence is crucial, was that it? Actually, Oshino might have said something along those lines at one point.

Ms. Kagenui's *next step*, however, didn't refer to any crucial sequence.

It was probably about time to stop assuming that she and Oshino had anything in common.

I put out my hand like she asked.

And she took hold of it gently, softly, indeed much like a fortune teller would—so much so, in fact, that I wondered if she actually *was* going to read my palm, like maybe my palm could elucidate everything about my current situation. But that wasn't what was going on.

"And a-one, and a-two."

Ms. Kagenui took my outstretched hand and held my index and middle fingers. Then she bent them back to an untenable angle. So it wasn't my fingers that she'd counted…

"G…Gyaaaaaaaaaaaaaaaaaaaaaaaaaaaaaaaaaaaaaaaaaaaaaaaaaaaaaaaa aaaaaaaaaaaaaaaaaaaaaaaaaaaaaaaaaaaaaaaaaaaaaaaaaaaaaaaaaaaaaaaaa aaaaaaaaaaaaaaaaaaaaaaaaaaaaaaaaaaaaaaaaaaaaaaaaaaa!"

"What a ruckus, I do declare. Well, I've put up a barrier around the place, so you can writhe and scream all you like, it won't make a lick of difference."

When?

It didn't seem like she'd had an opportunity to put up a barrier, but I guess that's the kind of skill you should expect from a disciple (?) of Ms. Gaen's. Not that I had the leeway to be impressed.

I couldn't even work up the energy to ask what she meant by a barrier.

Now, since I've been wounded so many times, and who even knows how many times I've died, you'd think I'd be accustomed to pain. But pain isn't something you ever get accustomed to. When a vampire's wound heals, it "goes back to the way it was," just like for a normal person; when you break a bone, it's not like it gets stronger than it was originally.

So I didn't hold back. I collapsed and, just as Ms. Kagenui had offered, writhed screaming on the ground.

"Owwwwwwwwwwwwwwwwwwwwwwwwwwwwww! Wh-Wh-What are you doing, Ms. Kagenui! You can't suddenly owowowow—"

"Now this won't do at all. Don't *only* writhe around down there—turn your mind to healing those fingers for a spell. Believe that they'll heal. This is a test of your healing ability."

"T-Test?"

So then—

This act of violence, this unforgivable brutality, was just Ms. Kagenui's version of Shinobu scratching me with her claws—just a trial of my body's ability to heal itself?

Fine, I saw how this step couldn't come first, but hold on a goddamn second.

She was more ferocious than any aberration.

"You've got to put your mind to the grindstone. Think of your fingers healing, conceive of it. Look here, those fingers are on your right hand, aren't they? And the way I broke them, the way they broke, it'll take them plenty more than a few piddling months to heal. You won't be able to get back to a little thing called exam prep with fingers like that, now, will you, unless you heal them yourself."

"Guh…"

Not exactly the best motivation.

In fact, broken fingers were a great excuse *not* to study—*well, I'm injured, nothing I can do about it.*

Never underestimate a high school student's desire to slack off.

Plus, without a better motivation for wanting to heal my broken fingers ASAP—I could die from the pain. Maybe broken fingers didn't kill you, but the pain was killing me.

I mean, the fucking color they were turning.

What did you do to them, Ms. Kagenui?

Forget a few months, these fingers wouldn't heal in a lifetime.

"G...uuuuuuuuuuuuuuuuuuuuuuuuuuuuuuuuuuuuuuuuuuuuuuuuu uuuuuuuuuuuuuuuuuuuh!"

Think about it.

Think, think, think.

Picture it with everything you've got.

If these fingers don't heal. If these fingers don't heal. If these fingers don't heal. If these fingers don't heal. If these fingers don't heal. If these fingers don't heal.

"If these fingers don't heal...I won't be able to fondle Hanekawa's breasts!"

Well.

Even if they healed, I still wouldn't get to.

Apparently, though, this incentive was more than adequate; it was perfect. My two fingers, which had turned a blackish purple thanks to internal hemorrhaging, healed instantaneously—went back to normal.

"Just how pubescent are you?" Ms. Kagenui said, smiling despite her words.

Wasn't she a broadminded sis. Not even appalled.

"But thank you kindly for demonstrating your healing factor, your manner of regenerating. Now, Yotsugi, a body's keen to hear the results of your inspection."

"Results still pending...I'm about 84 percent done. I've got the basic picture, though. Big Sis Shinobu's interpretation that he's become a vampire is probably correct. But..."

"But?"

Thanks for the worrisome conjunction.

"But—no, I can't say the rest."

"Hey, you're making me worry," I butted in. "Why're you acting like that?"

"For my part, I'd rather talk to your parents first if possible."

"..."

146

Ononoki was as expressionless as a doll, as a corpse, so it was always impossible to tell if she was being serious, but I really hoped this was a joke.

I felt like I was being sentenced.

"So...that's a joke, right, Ononoki? You're kidding," I tried to confirm.

"Um, the bit about your parents, yes... But maybe you'd better call Big Sis Shinobu. Get her out of her hidey-hole in your shadow. I'd like to get that demon's opinion on this one."

"I reckon that's a good idea," seconded Ms. Kagenui. "If I ruffled her feathers by standing on her head earlier, I'll happily apologize, so come now, young man, summon the former Kissshot Acerolaorion Heartunderblade."

"Okay..."

That all made good sense. I had some things I wanted to ask my buddy as well, so I had no reason to refuse their request. But then, I'd already used up my trump card that morning.

If I lured her out with fictitious donuts twice in one day, I really might end up donutized—when night fell, she would've regained some of her power, maybe enough to put a hole in me if she wanted.

Therefore.

"I'm sorry, Ms. Kagenui, but if I'm going to do that, do you mind if I make a quick run to Mister Donut first?"

"What in tarnation?!"

A comeback in Kansai dialect!

Now, that was a treat.

"Don't waste my time, young man, call her out of there lickety-split. I'll not wait around. If it seems like it's fixing to take too long, I might just stick my hand into your shadow and pull her out like some intestines."

"Like some intestines?"

Was that a common figure of speech to go with "pull out"?

"I'm of a mind to rip that whole head of blond hair out at the—

hm?"

Before Ms. Kagenui could complete whatever disturbing thought she was about to express, Shinobu Oshino finally appeared from within my shadow. Good timing, almost as if she'd heard what Ms. Kagenui was saying.

Unlike this morning when she popped out all lively with her fist in the air, this time she rose out solemnly with great pomp and circumstance. She'd even revamped her outfit into some kind of classy dress.

Her eyes seemed puffy, and knowing her as I did, I wanted to ask her if she'd been crying herself a river in there, but as she made her entrance, arms folded, her chin thrust high in the air so she could look down her nose at us, that gruesome smile plastered on her face, there was no way I could rib her about it.

"Ah, the former Heartunderblade. Sorry 'bout having the audacity to stand on your head earlier and all."

"..."

"..."

"..."

Man, could she not read a room.

Some grown-up.

Sorry 'bout? Come on. And she didn't seem the least bit contrite... This is just a guess, but I bet Ms. Kagenui never once in her life admitted that she was wrong.

"K...Kakak."

Nevertheless, Shinobu did her best to laugh.

Such courage, it brought tears to your eyes.

"Kakak. It seems as though thine investigation of my master hath reached its conclusion. Ye have my thanks for carrying it out in my stead. I suppose 'tis true what they say, that to everything there is a season, if even ones such as you can be of use to my lord."

"Hahaha, my apologies. Truly, for having driven you to such ludicrously untoward posturing. That was never my intent. Your head

148

simply seemed a likely place to come in for a landing."

"…"

Enough already.

Daring to read other people's minds when you can't even read the room.

Seemed a likely place to come in for a landing… This was probably the first time in her almost six hundred years that someone had made that particular remark to Shinobu, and there was no question that it was an almost unthinkable insult.

"Ka…kak."

And yet she laughed. What backbone. Or she'd missed her chance to back down, more like.

"W-Watch thy tongue, human—an expert ye may be, and an expert in immortal aberrations at that, but do not for a moment think that means thou knowest aught of me. Forget not, the only reason I have not slain thee on the spot is so that thou might help resolve this physical malady that besets my lord and master. Kakak."

"Which is exactly why I'm apologizing to you, for stepping on your head and all. For someone so short, you sure are long on pride. Come on, now, let's bury the hatchet. You nightwalkers are such gloomy folk. I'm real sorry, I'll be sure never to step on your head again."

"…"

Gritting her teeth, Shinobu finally fell silent.

This was where I put on the brakes, worried that she might stay silent for months like she did last time. "Stop it, Ms. Kagenui, please."

At this, Ms. Kagenui looked stunned—apparently, she hadn't been trying to be mean and just didn't have a clue. What an unpleasant person.

Everyone—and I mean everyone, even Kaiki—disliked her.

"You too, Shinobu, let it drop. No sense in opening up old wounds."

"Y-Yet…"

Don't clutch my sleeve with those tear-filled eyes.

It's simply too pathetic. And adorably sympathetic.

"You bravely volunteered your own head," I told her, "to protect mine from the tread of Ms. Kagenui's feet. That was a selfless act of devotion and personal sacrifice. You can rest easy, your pride is intact, okay?"

"Huh? Oh, aye! 'Twas just as thou sayest, I protected thee, my lord. I am badass indeed!"

Her mood improved in an instant—pathetic, adorable, but also a pain in the ass and kind of a dodo.

"I can't believe I lost to her..." muttered Ononoki, but Shinobu seemed to be on cloud nine and didn't hear her. Thank God for small favors. Favors both large and small aside, everyone besides Ms. Kagenui was having a shitty time.

"Well now," she said, "we have all the players, we have all the information—time for all the answers, I reckon. It won't do to leave the readers with a mystery, so let's get to the solution, shall we? Time to solve the riddle."

"Solve the riddle..."

Something about her words bothered me.

My lack of a reflection wasn't a riddle, it was just something that was happening...

"Excellent. Proceed," urged Shinobu.

Her mood improved, she seemed to be feeling generous—well, she'd tasted the humiliation of being stepped on, but I imagine that the erstwhile king of aberrations still had so much self-confidence, not to say self-conceit, that Ms. Kagenui and Ononoki had nothing on her. Whether or not her self-image held water was a different question.

"Koyomi Araragi—kind monster sir," Ononoki began. "You are, at present—or in the present progressive, *turning into a vampire* little by little by little. That's, well, the situation."

"Turning into a vampire..."

"From human to vampire, little by little. I believe it's what biologists call metamorphosis, Latin *mutatis*, Japanese *hentai*. Hmm, only too appropriate for you, monstieur."

"…"

Was I supposed to laugh?

Not on your life.

My turn to be expressionless.

But it didn't come as a surprise, Shinobu's inspection that morning having already told me as much, and Ms. Kagenui's inspection (if that's what you want to call that outburst of violence) having just confirmed it.

"Turning into a vampire… Mm-hmm."

"How now, young man. You don't seem particularly put out."

"Well, I've become a vampire so many times at this point… I'm obviously not going to be as freaked out as I was the first time, over spring break. I don't want to brag in front of experts like yourselves, but I've had more on my plate over the past year than you might think…"

The past few months in particular had been pretty extreme.

The stuff with Hachikuji, the stuff with Sengoku—

And.

That transfer student.

"I'm sure you have," Ononoki agreed.

In an insinuating tone.

"You held that plate out like a moron."

"What?"

"Nothing," the familiar shook her head.

Her barb, loaded with a scathing sarcasm that could only have come from Kaiki, was too indirect, too roundabout, for me to understand what she was getting at.

When I said I didn't want to brag, was I actually bragging? Had an expert been offended by the remarks of a noob who was still in high school? No, Ononoki wasn't the type.

Whatever the case, the fact that her personality was different every time we met made her tricky to deal with. It's hard to get accustomed to such a mercurial character.

"Don't be so harsh on the boy, Yotsugi. I'll not deny the young man here may have behaved moronically, but I reckon some part of that responsibility lies with us," Ms. Kagenui covered for me, if that's what she was doing, for whatever reason—okay, fine, I have no clue what she was pulling there.

Suddenly I realized it was past nine o'clock.

Sure, everything had taken a while, but our meeting had been set for seven.

Could we get to it already?

"As for why you're metamorphosing, monstieur. As for why the hentai is being perverted into a vampire…"

Not gonna let that one drop, huh?

What's the deal, got a bone to pick with me?

"It has nothing to do with your interrelationship with the former Kissshot Acerolaorion Heartunderblade—I think you probably already knew that, but it's important enough that it bears repeating."

"Nothing to do with Shinobu…but can I really be turning into a vampire independent of the fact that she used to be one?"

"You can. There's one last thing I want to clarify. Sis," Ononoki turned to Shinobu, "do you really not have some inkling? Of why— this is happening to kind monster sir, your lord, your master?"

Shinobu seemed displeased. "Had I, I would not stoop to asking the likes of thee for aid."

"And Oshino never said a word about it?" asked Ms. Kagenui.

"Nay. 'Tis true that I cannot recall everything he spoke of— most of it washed over me like a cool breeze, but had he touched on something of such dire import, I would remember."

"I reckon you would," Ms. Kagenui took Shinobu's somewhat cocky remark in stride. "Yes indeedy, I reckon even Oshino missed this one. It was irregular, or, an oversight. If he'd known things were going to go this way, he'd never have let such misgivings go unheeded."

"An oversight? Oshino? Is that even possible? How can that be, how can a guy who acted like he saw through everything—"

An oversight.

Just thinking about it freaked me out.

"He didn't really," Ms. Kagenui corrected me. "And for what it's worth, he might see through to the truth of the matter but not take care of it for you. He's like Gaen-senpai in that way. Strict, or businesslike when it comes to that sort of thing, wont to operate solely on the basis of profit and loss. If'n you ask me, even a capricious contrarian like Kaiki at least has a little more warmth to him."

"..."

I had some reservations about calling it "warmth," but true, while a pain in the ass about money, Kaiki's petty accounting was also very human.

"Still and all, I reckon this time around it was nothing but a plain old oversight—in other words, it was opaque to Mister All-Seeing, to Mèmè Oshino."

"Opaque—to Oshino."

Saying those words out loud made me realize just how anomalous they felt. Maybe it was plausible to Ms. Kagenui, who'd known Oshino since college and seen her share of his failures, but to me, after everything he'd done for me this year—after watching him "see through" everything time and time again, it sounded like a bad joke.

A bad joke. A bad reality.

A bad—paranormal phenomenon.

"Isn't that a big deal? Something that's never happened before is happening in my body—something unprecedented, something that my accumulated experience is useless in dealing with—"

"Keep your shirt on. It's certainly unusual, that much is true. For Oshino's predictions and judgments to be wrong, I mean—but still, young man, it's a hoot to see you so shocked by it."

"A h-hoot?"

I guess from Ms. Kagenui's perspective as a fellow specialist and old friend of Oshino's, my level of shock seemed pretty ridiculous—no need to come right out and say it, though.

It hurt my feelings.

Man is she oblivious, I started to think, but apparently that wasn't what was going on since Ms. Kagenui went on to say:

"But the fact that this particular matter was opaque to Oshino was entirely your fault."

"…? Huh?"

I was shocked again, if you want to talk about shocked, but more than that, I was bewildered.

I simply didn't understand what she meant, but if she was saying that Koyomi Araragi was opaque to Mèmè Oshino, that was impossible.

I was like a flimsy piece of tracing paper to him—so transparent you could see right through to the other side.

I had always been the insubstantial, weak Koyomi Araragi to him.

Always and forever, consistently—I had never once stymied his predictions. I'm not like Hanekawa. And not even she threw him off all the time—

"Please tell me what you mean, Ms. Kagenui. How did I throw Oshino off his game? I think you must be wrong about that… But if something of the sort happened—I need to know."

"I'll let you know the moment I do. That's what I've come here to find out—but one thing's certain, there's trouble brewing. We could very well—that is, if things keep on this way…"

Me and Yotsugi here. We might have no choice but to kill you, she stated.

She did so without lowering her voice or changing her tone perceptibly, as though it was just part of the natural flow of the conversation.

"…"

"No choice but to kill you—if things go south, that is. Now then, young man. It's easy as pie to see why your body's metamorphosing into a vampire's—why you're clearly headed in that direction. Honestly, it doesn't take an expert, it's so simple you should've figured it out all by your lonesome."

You could've been self-aware enough to awake to the reality, she chided.

"What, do you mean?"

"You turned into a vampire *too much.*"

Ms. Kagenui said this in, you guessed it, the exact same tone—and from there, Ononoki took over, you guessed it, expressionlessly, speaking in her overwhelmingly placid voice.

"You just kept piling more on your plate—you moron. In the course of solving all those problems, you relied too much on your power as a vampire, and so, irrespective of the former Heartunderblade, your immortal soul inexorably ended up *approaching* vampiredom."

"Approaching—"

"You've been literally transforming yourself into a vampire."

010

It may be a little late at this point to insert "the story so far." It feels like I missed the window, and frankly it's a total embarrassment as a narrator—but if I'm going to explain everything in proper sequence, it's got to be now or never.

Where to begin? I guess it's got to be spring break—that hellish spring break.

Or no, strictly speaking, just before it started?

That bloodsucking spring when I was attacked by a vampire, when I became a vampire—up until then I had somehow managed to make my way down the road of humanity, sometimes unsteady on my feet, sometimes going off course of course, but that spring I strayed entirely.

That was about a year ago.

Once I became a vampire, it was neither a kinslaying vampire nor a half-vampire nor a vampire-hunting spec ops team who saved me—but a heaven-sent class president with braids and glasses, and an older guy in a Hawaiian shirt.

And I became human once more, a demon no longer.

Give or take a few lingering after-effects.

And they all lived happily ever after.

Except when they didn't.

I've already told you all of this, so let's skip ahead a month—to Golden Week. The end of April and into the beginning of May—a nightmare. Tsubasa Hanekawa, who'd played a central role in restoring my humanity, was bewitched by a cat.

It took more than a spritz of water in the face to repel that malicious, murderous feline assault on Hanekawa—on the world itself. I did it by exploiting my vampiric power.

The might of a vampire.

I employed the vampiric strength that I lost over spring break, which you'd think I would've abhorred, that power I risked my life to escape, and defeated the cat—well, temporarily sealed it away, anyway.

Incidentally, I regained my vampiric power by giving my blood to Shinobu. By letting the little girl bite me in the neck. It all comes down to this. At the time, Shinobu was not yet bound in my shadow, so I had to give her blood at regular intervals, but on that occasion I let her exceed her usual dosage—and so was able to turn into a vampire, or more precisely, a thrall of the Aberration Slayer.

I was able to—for better or for worse.

But then, during the subsequent school term—when Oshino was still around, in other words—the only time I really used my vampiric power was that time with Kanbaru, the thing with her and the monkey.

With Senjogahara, who met a crab.

With Hachikuji, waylaid by a snail.

With Sengoku, entangled by a snake.

Not to mention the second time Hanekawa was bewitched by the cat—on each occasion I dealt with the aberration-related phenomenon in question solely as a human being.

If Ononoki was right and I in fact leaned too hard on my power as a vampire, it had to be later on—like when Karen Araragi was stung by a bee.

When she was stung by a bee thanks to Kaiki's scheming—I used my vampiric healing factor to absorb some of the blistering fever that wracked her body.

And then it was Tsukihi's turn.

The matter both concerning and involving Tsukihi—it was Obon, and that was when it came to blows with Ms. Kagenui and Ononoki. In order to battle the Aberration Roller, slayer of immortal aberrations, I transformed myself into an immortal aberration. A vampire.

To tell the truth, even having commandeered the strength of a vampire, I was no match for Ms. Kagenui—but regardless, that must've been the inflection point.

When I stopped being human.

And began metamorphosing into a vampire.

A rapid-fire series of aberration-related phenomena cropped up since the last day of summer break and throughout second term—and each time, to deal with them, I turned into an immortal vampire.

I got used to using my vampiric power, relying on my vampiric power, wielding my vampiric power to deal with these unreliable and unwieldy aberration-related phenomena—sometimes I even used it to deal with other things.

I leaned on it most heavily when Sengoku was entangled by a snake for the second time—no, when she was the one who entangled the snake.

That was when it really started.

I wanted to save Sengoku.

So I turned into a vampire almost every day hoping to resolve the situation—which wasn't very effective as it turned out, and in fact effectively one hundred percent counter-productive, but anyway, that went on for a month, two months.

And that brings us to the present moment.

The present situation.

The present phenomenon.

"Basically, monstieur, you spent too much time as an immortal aberration. You overdid it, blithely bouncing back and forth like that. I imagine that as far as you were aware, you weren't 'overdoing' anything, let alone 'blithely,' but still…" said Ononoki.

I sensed something like sympathy in her tone, but that had to be my own self-serving imagination—she was speaking in her quiet, placid voice like always.

Placid, and expressionless.

"No…I did do it blithely."

I had to admit it.

I had to acknowledge it.

It wasn't the first time someone pointed this out to me—Senjogahara and Hanekawa and others from the female camp had warned that I was blithely over-relying on my power as an immortal ever since Oshino's disappearance.

Not that I was self-aware about it.

But it was definitely true that any reluctance I'd once felt about using my vampiric power—about becoming immortal, had slowly but surely faded. Not only that, but I felt a strange sense of connection every time I used my vampiric power to fight alongside a reinvigorated Shinobu.

Euphoria?

Well, there was certainly some of that.

Of course there was.

Anyone with a pulse would feel the same way.

Any average high school student who got to wield a power that transcends the human realm, transcends human knowledge, and denies the thrill of it would be full of it—as would anyone who denies getting lost in all that power.

"So you're saying that because I borrowed Shinobu's strength too frequently, I myself fully transformed into a vampire? But I was being so careful to avoid that!"

Oshino had cautioned me over and over again, after all: to maintain Shinobu's existence in this world, I had to keep giving her my blood in perpetuity, but I also needed to be super-careful about the dosage.

He strictly enjoined me that if I gave her too much, if I let her drink too much blood, Shinobu would become an aberration once again—the aberration-slaying king of aberrations.

At the same time.

He enjoined me (just as strictly) that I would transform into a vampire as well. So even when I let Shinobu drink my blood so I could fight, I never once exceeded the proper threshold—at least I didn't think I did.

"You're not listening, it's not about your relationship with Big Sis Shinobu. It's totally unrelated to you giving her your blood. Well, it's indirectly related, of course, but…the why and how and who-drank-your-blood of your transformations into a vampire isn't really the issue. Until now you've been 'metamorphosing' by borrowing Big Sis Shinobu's power, but it would've been the same if you'd borrowed from a different vampire each time."

"…"

"Let me give it to you straight, monstieur. I'll put it as plainly as I can. It's not that you became a vampire too often, it's that you became too comfortable about becoming one. You got too used to using the power. You got too good at it—at this point you could become a vampire even without Shinobu."

"Wait."

Wait a sec.

I couldn't keep up—no, that wasn't true, I was keeping up, or in fact, I'd finished the upkeep on my mental filing cabinet a while ago. I was convinced. So if this were somebody else's problem, I would've totally agreed with her here. I'd probably have praised her to the skies: *Great deduction, Ononoki.*

But this was *my* problem.

No matter how true, if it was also tragic, if it was also a failure I didn't want to acknowledge—I couldn't swallow it just like that.

"But Ononoki. Is it…is it really that easy to become a vampire? You just do it too much, get too used to doing it, and then you've done it?"

"Dance with the devil, and you'll become the devil—play with a demon, and you'll become a demon. And you really took the initiative playing that game."

"I…didn't feel like I was playing."

"Of course you didn't, young man, that's just a manner of speaking. You were dead serious. I reckon I can vouch for that myself, having battled you in your vampire form. Otherwise, a body wouldn't have backed off," Ms. Kagenui, silent all this time, finally interjected.

Well, Ononoki was only ever acting as her mouthpiece anyway, and as her familiar the opinions she expressed were most likely hers *and* Ms. Kagenui's, there being no difference between the two.

"Or maybe I ought to say you were seriously off your rocker. It might sound strange for me to go around jawing about what's normal, but normal sure as shooting doesn't include becoming a monster to protect your little sister."

"…"

"Listen, young man, this might seem to you like it's coming out of left field, but it's not as uncommon as all that—it's not easy, but it's not all that uncommon either. There are even those among us experts what end up becoming aberrations themselves. It's a particularly marked tendency among my closest colleagues, by which I mean onmyoji. Which is why, to avoid it," Ms. Kagenui's gaze dropped to Ononoki beneath her feet.

A chilly gaze, her eyes cold.

"I employ this here stand-in."

"…"

"That's how dangerous facing an aberration head-on can be—Oshino must've told you? That once you've dealt with an aberration, you're much more liable to get drawn in again."

He did tell me that, yes.

But what he didn't tell me...

"If I transformed into a vampire too often, I'd end up as one myself—that, he never mentioned."

"Because he failed to see it. What kind of a person you are, I mean. That was where he miscalculated. No, maybe never calculated at all—can't miscalculate if you never calculated in the first place. Sure enough, that's why I say it was an oversight. He never predicted that you, young man, would transform into a vampire so frequently in such a short span."

"That..."

That definitely wasn't a miscalculation—nor was it an oversight. Uh-uh.

That was an error in judgment.

"So you're saying...I betrayed Oshino's faith in me? Is that what it boils down to? He never expected me to do it. To keep on borrowing the power of an immortal aberration so blithely—to rely too much on a vampire—"

Shinobu.

He entrusted the former Kissshot Acerolaorion Heartunderblade to me, entrusted her to my shadow, and I betrayed that trust.

I couldn't live up to his expectations.

Shinobu's power, Shinobu's existence.

I used them like convenient tools—and that was something not even he could've *seen.*

Which is why he never informed me of *this possibility.*

Nor did he inform—Shinobu.

He almost certainly.

Thought it'd be *rude.*

"..."

"'Course, we can only guess at what Oshino's intentions might've been—for all we know, he just plumb forgot. And what about this, young man: supposing he'd told you about *this possibility*, would you have shrunk from making use of the vampire's power? Even if you'd known it would cost you your humanity, you'd've done it anyway, no?"

Words of comfort.

Were something I'd never expect to hear from Ms. Kagenui. She was too violent, too careless, too oblivious. Probably she was just thinking out loud.

There's really no way of knowing what I would've done.

If I'd known beforehand, maybe I could've done something about it, or maybe I'd have been well and truly scared off.

"So you're saying the reason my healing factor is so slow...or that I have a healing factor at all, even if it's non-existent compared to when I was Shinobu's thrall over spring break, the fact that I have some level of immortality, is proof that my transformation into a vampire is unconnected to Shinobu? In other words, I'm not transforming into Shinobu's thrall, but into my own brand—my own breed of vampire."

"That's about the size of it. Though, typologically speaking, I reckon you'd be treated as a natural vampire."

"There are two types of vampires, monstieur. Two breeds. Natural vampires, and human beings who become vampires after being bitten by one—it might seem like you belong in the latter category, but as it happens you're classified as the former. Someone who transforms into a vampire, who becomes one, is a natural vampire."

"I don't really understand that reasoning..."

I never really understood what I was told over spring break either, but this seemed even more confusing.

Or rather, viewing vampires as organisms and trying to understand their ecology already seemed outside the framework of human understanding.

"Seems like the incident involving the serpent deity was the biggest problem—you really, really, really, really, really overdid it there, monstieur—you turned into a vampire almost every day. 'High frequency' doesn't even begin to cover it. You spent more time as a vampire than you did as a human during that period, didn't you?"

"Sure…"

It was my fault that Sengoku had done that—that she ended up like that. Or I felt responsible, at least—so that's why.

That's why.

"I think I've got some kind of grasp of the situation. I wouldn't call it a firm grip, but…what do I do, Ononoki?"

"Do about what?" she threw the question back to me so ingenuously that I fell silent for a moment—and a bad feeling washed over me, but I quickly dispelled it, interpreting her response as a request to be more specific. I rephrased my question.

"What do I do to become human again?"

When was it?

It must've been over spring break that I'd asked Shinobu more or less the same question—what had her answer been?

Whatever, that was the past.

How she answered back then was irrelevant—what I needed to know.

And the one thing I knew I didn't want to hear—was Ononoki's hopeless reply.

"Kind monster sir," she said.

Like a doll, looking at me with those doll's eyes.

Without hesitation or consideration.

"There's no way to fix this."

011

No way to fix it.

No way back.

It struck me as odd that when I heard Ononoki's cruel pronouncement, when I heard that hopeless answer condemning me to my fate—I accepted it readily.

I accepted it.

Without shock or consternation.

Her answer touched something in me.

Something deep inside of me.

Or no, maybe not quite—it's not like it was totally unsurprising. It was definitely not what I thought she was going to say. But it was the kind of surprise you feel when you happen to put a piece of a jigsaw puzzle in exactly the right place, or when you open a dictionary to precisely the page you're looking for. I was startled by how "right" it felt.

"I see..." I nodded.

The one most likely to mock this response, in all its stiff-upper-lip gallantry, was none other than me. *Who're you trying to impress?* I wanted to ask.

Like when someone gets hit by a car and says, *I'm fine.*

"So that's the deal, huh? Well, there it is, then."

"I expected you'd be a mite more upset about it," Ms. Kagenui, eyeing me doubtfully, said from atop Ononoki's shoulders. "We're still inside the barrier, you know. You don't want to roll around on the ground for a spell and bawl your eyes out? Wail your frustrations at the heavens? Go on, I'll pretend I didn't hear nor see a blessed thing."

"No... Well."

When you stopped to think about it, this wasn't a question of a mere broken finger—I'd been informed that I was dropping out of the human race, never to return. I wasn't just losing some part of myself, I was losing my very humanity, so there'd be no shame in rolling around on the ground and crying for a while.

And yet.

I felt absolutely no need to do so.

"What can I say. It's like, *There you go. Guess that makes sense.*"

"..."

"I mean, I've been really reckless these past six months. It was the same when we fought each other... I was turning myself into a vampire like it was nothing, like I was drinking an energy drink or something, relying on the power of an immortal to battle aberrations. And the retribution for that..."

Retribution?

That's what I said, but somehow it didn't sound right.

Why, I couldn't say...or no, it sounded wrong because there was a better word for it.

It wasn't retribution.

The price.

"I had to pay some kind of price."

Yes, a price.

I'd been cooking the books, and the secret finally came out—that morning it finally came out, finally came into view (or, not).

That's all. No biggie.

I was actually surprised it'd taken so long.

I was just paying interest—on all the bills that had come due recently.

I was just settling the accounts for all my shenanigans.

No—

This was the last installment, the final payment.

Last year was over, even according to the traditional calendar—and Koyomi Araragi needed to wrap up his fiscal year.

That's all there was to it.

"Price, right," repeated Ms. Kagenui disinterestedly. Her expression suggested that maybe she'd wanted to watch me writhe around on the ground for her sadistic delectation. "Well, what else could you expect, throwing around all that power willy-nilly—no choice but to accept it, I reckon. Not that that ever-so-enlightened attitude of yours will do a lick of good. Still and all, I reckon you haven't lost your humanity just yet."

"What…do you mean?"

"There's no way to reverse the process, no way to fix it, but there's a way to keep your transformation into a vampire from progressing." Ms. Kagenui prompted Ononoki, seemingly telling her to pick up the thread of the explanation. As onmyoji and shikigami, they really seemed to have some kind of psychic link.

"Okay. So, there is a method, monstieur."

"By a 'method' you mean a way not to lose any more of my humanity?"

"Well, yeah… Yeah. We'll have to conduct a thorough, by-the-book examination to find out how vampiricized you are, kind monster sir, and how much of your humanity you retain. But either way, there's a way for you to maintain the current status quo, whatever that turns out to be."

"..."

I didn't ask right away what this method might be because I somehow felt like that'd be greedy.

Like it'd be shady, as if I were trying to default on my loans—sure, I'd talked like I was at peace with it, but ultimately, given my predicament, I had to find out what this method was, if there really was one.

"So what is it, Ononoki? What's the method?"

"Mmmm... Maybe 'method' wasn't the best way to describe it, since it doesn't really involve you doing anything. In other words," continued Ononoki, "You just have to stop using your vampiric power."

"..."

"You can keep feeding Big Sis Shinobu, of course—using your shadow as a battery charger like you've been doing should be fine. If that's as far as it goes, then there's no problem. But you've got to keep an even keel, and of course you've got to avoid actually transforming into a vampire. No matter what."

"Stop using my vampiric power..."

Definitely not what you'd call a method.

It didn't even require any action on my part.

Though that didn't mean it would be easy.

If anything, it sounded like a detox program—would it be that easy to wean myself off of vampiric immortality, given how handy it'd been?

And there was no question that, having so fecklessly immersed myself in the world of aberrations, I'd continue to be involved with them, to get sucked into their orbit.

Even now they were dragging me down.

"Supposing," I sprang a totally unnecessary question on Ononoki for the sake of confirmation. "Supposing from now on—I kept on using the power of immortality every time I had to deal with an aberration, what'd happen to me then?"

"You know what would happen—don't make me say it, not to a friend. You'd edge closer and closer to being a vampire. I can't say for sure how many more chances you've got—but you definitely have less wiggle room than you think, monstieur."

"I'm not thinking about wiggle room or more chances or anything, that would be too optimistic, but…"

But.

Supposing there was something—something I absolutely had to do, while I was still human, while I could still maintain my humanity, that required the power of a vampire.

Could I—really refrain from using it?

I couldn't help but envision such a scenario.

But Ms. Kagenui's next words wiped such visions from my mind. "Best not to speak any more on it, best not to think any more on it. I declared this to you before…and it was a declaration of war: if you transform into an immortal aberration even once more, even one more iota, it will be my professional duty to kill you. I will have no choice but to slay you. Even now you're on the brink of vampiredom—you might call your current status 'a somewhat vampiric human being,' but if that balance should tip any further… Need I say more?"

"…"

I'd been able to get a grasp on my current situation thanks to Ms. Gaen so swiftly dispatching Ms. Kagenui and Ononoki to meet me—but while that was an expression of Ms. Gaen's kindness and goodwill, it was also her way of driving the point home.

That's the kind of person she was.

She dispatched Ms. Kagenui knowing that the onmyoji was not only knowledgeable about all things immortally aberrant but also inordinately obsessed with destroying them.

The harsh reality was that Ms. Gaen had dispatched Ms. Kagenui under the assumption that if my transformation into a vampire exceeded the limits of what Ms. Kagenui felt she could let slide—she would exterminate me right then and there. Naturally, I wanted to believe that Ms. Gaen deemed that unlikely, but...

"Just so's you know, I've let you and the former Heartunderblade go on account of Oshino requesting that I certify you as harmless—but as it stands, you're right on the line. One step over, young man—or even if I just get the notion one day, I'm liable to put you down."

"..."

If she just got the notion, huh...

"*One more time should be fine, I'll make an exception just this once*—you start thinking like that, slipping back into the occasional transformation, and you'll be in my crosshairs just like that. Or, no. No no no. I'll act the second I judge you to lack the proper self-control. Though if you're apt to step out of line sooner or later, I reckon the proper thing might just be to take care of business right here and now."

"Do so and I shall slay thee on the spot, Madam Expert."

Shinobu broke her long silence then—in contrast with Ms. Kagenui's somewhat indifferent attitude and Ononoki's expressionlessness, she was brimming with fearsome emotion.

Animosity spilling over the sides of the words she unleashed.

"Should my lord and master die, or be slain, then would I be released from my bondage—and with my full power returned to me, I too would become thy target."

"So you would. Yes, you would indeed. And you and I would come to blows, then, I reckon—your harmless certification being revoked at that point and all."

Ms. Kagenui returned Shinobu's murderous stare without an ounce of fear; in fact, she was smiling. While they may have been at odds over summer break, the two never actually fought one another—which of them would win such a battle was anybody's guess.

The standoff dragged on for a while, the tension so thick I couldn't even speak, but eventually Ononoki dispelled it with the reasonable question, "Aren't we getting a little ahead of ourselves, Big Sis? Big

Sis Shinobu? What's the point of getting heated about it now?"

Speaking up in that situation, interjecting that aloof if reasonable question, had to be Kaiki's influence—and I felt a grudging sense of gratitude towards him.

If they started fighting it out at that moment, I'd have absolutely no way of stopping them without using my vampiric power.

Though I probably wouldn't be able to stop them even then...

"Sorry, kind monster sir. As you can see, my Big Sis is surprisingly quick-tempered, quick to jump to conclusions, and quick to tire of long-term talk. So even though she's older, you can't expect her to take you under her wing. That is, I hope not taking you under her wing is as far as it goes. And that's why I have a favor to ask of you, kind monster sir. As a friend...I want you to promise me right here and now that you will never, ever, ever use your vampiric power again—I want you to swear that no matter what hardships you face, you'll act without recourse to the power of immortality. That you'll live out the rest of your life as a human being."

I want you to swear. To live a human life, Ononoki summed up placidly.

"..."

"I'm a shikigami, after all. If Big Sis ordered me to, I'd have no choice but to fight, even if it was against you, monstieur—I have my personal feelings, but that's as far as it goes. That's how I was made."

"Ononoki..."

"You've already had a healthy dose of immortality, isn't that enough? Take my word for it as a corpse, immortality isn't all it's cracked up to be...even if you take us out of the equation. As it is, you're teetering on the edge, but you're still human...or you can pass for human, anyway."

Pass for human.

What a choice of words.

Coming from a doll who herself was only passing for human.

"No reflection, slightly accelerated healing—if that's all it is, you should be able to pull it off. Think of your formerly weightless girl-friend, or your friend with the monkey's arm—for now, you can just go back to studying for exams. Let's see, I imagine if you don't show up in mirrors you won't show up in photographs either, but...you already took your picture for the application, right?"

"Yeah."

The one with the long hair.

"Then you're fine," said Ononoki.

I couldn't fathom what basis she had for saying anything was fine... Plus, if I did get into college I'd have to take a photo for my student ID, but whatever, it was a nice thing to say.

A nice promise—she couldn't keep.

"I think I get the idea, Ononoki...Ms. Kagenui. I understand. I swear, I will never again borrow, use, or exploit the power of a vampire to face off against an aberration—if I do have to deal with an aberration in the future, I'll face it as a human being, using human ingenuity instead of vampiric power. Does that work for you?"

"Yes indeed, that'll do just fine," replied Ms. Kagenui. "If you can do that for me, I reckon it'll save me a lot of professional trouble. And it'll save your life, and the former Heartunderblade's."

"Kind of a lightly taken vow," Ononoki muttered under her breath, just when Ms. Kagenui and I somehow managed to arrive at an understanding.

What a nasty thing to say.

Something a nasty person would say.

Then again, lightly taken? Maybe so. I wasn't confident that I'd keep that promise if push came to shove.

In the end, no matter what vows I took—if, for instance, Sen-jogahara or Hanekawa was about to die before my very eyes and I could prevent it by transforming into a vampire, I'm pretty sure there'd be no question. I wouldn't think about the cost of my action, I'd just be lost in it.

174

That's the kind of guy Koyomi Araragi is.

I still felt that way after everything I'd learned, and regretted, and knowing full well how that pesky character trait of mine invited any number of crises in the past—even death wouldn't cure me of my recklessness, or make me wreck less stuff.

Even not dying wouldn't cure me—alas.

That said, however, my agreement with Ms. Kagenui wasn't just an expedient to escape her threats of violence.

Even if I harbored doubts about myself in my heart of hearts, I don't have the nerves of steel it takes to bullshit such a vicious opponent.

My nerves are probably more like rusty tin.

Which meant that I needed to come up with a way of dealing with aberrations that didn't involve transforming into a vampire—even if we weren't talking about aberrations, I had to figure out how to prevent situations like Senjogahara or Hanekawa's hypothetically imminent demise from cropping up in the first place.

Yes, prevention.

Prevention was the key—consider the situation from every angle, and prevent it. It was my failure to do precisely this that had landed me in the soup, but I could use my failure, my not being reflected in mirrors, as food for thought, a recipe for self-reflection. At least it was me and not someone else whose goose was cooked.

Well.

Ononoki was absolutely right that, compared to Senjogahara's old affliction and Kanbaru's arm—not having a reflection was more like a party trick.

So relax.

I mean, I should be thankful it was a vampire.

What if it had been a gorgon? That would've been terrible.

Then I'd have turned to stone when I looked in the mirror.

"Why force yourself to be so positive..." murmured Ms. Kagenui. "That optimism will just turn to ashes in your mouth. When

175

you wake up tomorrow, I reckon you'll find yourself in hell."

"What a nasty thing to say…the both of you, nothing but nasty things to say. Is that what you call informed consent? And don't worry, my little sisters put on a big show of waking me up every morning, so I won't have time to get depressed about it… Well, Ms. Kagenui, Ononoki. Thanks for all your help."

"And you, thank you kindly—no, wait a sec!" Ms. Kagenui wasn't playful enough to suddenly throw in a joke like that, so she must've just slipped for a second there. "I'm still fixing to examine your body—thoroughly."

"Is that so?"

"Of course. You may still be more human than not, but are you willing to die just because you ate some garlic by accident? I reckon the sun won't reduce you to ash this time of year, but I can't be sure about the dog days of summer. Think of the future, if you want to take a holiday to some tropical island in your old age, your nice tan skin might go up in flames."

"The UV index affects a vampire's sensitivity to the sun?"

First I'd heard of it.

Global warming was going to wipe out vampires once and for all…

"Figuring out what you can do and what you can't, what's okay and what's not, where the borderline is, and where the foul lines are—that'll make the rest of your life a whole lot easier. That's just my advice, though, my work as an expert is done here for the moment."

"I see…"

It sounded terrible.

That is, I was already fed up just thinking about it—I wasn't as strong-willed as Senjogahara. To live a life like that, a partner's… Shinobu's cooperation would be indispensable.

I needed someone to smack me every time I screwed up.

Seemed like Senjogahara's experience would be instructive—

but when I looked at my partner Shinobu, she had her arms crossed, and if she didn't seem displeased, she didn't seem convinced either.

"Um...Shinobu."

"What."

Uh oh.

Not trying to hide her feelings.

Zero effort at keeping up appearances.

Then again, it was hard to tell what she was feeling in the first place...though whatever it was, it definitely wasn't good.

"This'll probably be inconvenient for you too, so...sorry."

"'Tis not something to apologize for. I tire of telling thee this, my lord, but we share a common destiny, our lots are cast together—the fact that we are thus united at all is itself a miraculously convenient plot device, and for that alone 'tis meet that some price be paid as thou hast said."

'Tis no impediment nor inconvenience to me, Shinobu maintained, suddenly defiant—but she was absolutely right.

Then what was she so unhappy about? Perhaps for Shinobu Oshino, the formerly immortal king of aberrations, simply getting advice from this expert, her natural enemy the Aberration Roller, was unbearable enough. Even if she hadn't stood on her head.

"And I'm assuming we can't put it off until tomorrow?"

"No. No indeed, with your vampiric level at its highest here under the moonlight, we ought to be able to reckon the limit precisely. Not that I think it likely, but there's an outside chance that if we wait until tomorrow, you'll up and evaporate with the first rays of the sun. And I imagine you wouldn't be too keen on that, now, would you. If we work through the night we should be able to learn most everything we need to know."

"Don't worry, monstieur. I'll be the one to carry out the bulk of the examination... I'll be diligent, and gentlemanly. No sneak-attacks like when Big Sis broke your fingers."

"..."

I hadn't even considered that last possibility, but now that she'd brought it up, I was suddenly a little afraid of a full examination... And did Ononoki being the examiner put my mind at ease? If you turned her words around it sounded like she was announcing that she *would* break my bones, just not in a sneak attack.

Hang on.

Maybe she was going to perform the service—I mean the examination, by licking my entire body like she sucked on my toe?

I was starting to look forward to it.

"What are you grinning about, monstieur... It's creepy."

I don't know if it was Kaiki's influence or if she'd have said it anyway, but such a straight rejection was surprisingly hurtful.

I did hate Kaiki after all.

"Well, I'm keen to get started—you don't need to call home or anything?" asked Ms. Kagenui.

"No, it's fine. My parents pretty much leave me to my own devices. Plus my hard-to-please, hardly pleasing little sisters are at a pajama party tonight."

I'd sent them to Kanbaru's to protect them (Tsukihi in particular) but suddenly had the feeling that I'd done Suruga Kanbaru a huge favor.

Pajama party or no, Kanbaru always sleeps naked. I wanted to believe she wouldn't do that with my little sisters there...

"Hmm, fine and dandy, then. I'll just give Gaen-senpai a holler and tell her it was nothing big."

"..."

Right, nothing big.

Nothing at all.

A perfectly natural attitude for someone like Ms. Kagenui, who was constantly facing off against immortal aberrations, but it was also perfectly true—for me as well.

This was perfectly ordinary.

Compared to the months Nadeko Sengoku had lost.

This was nothing at all.

"Yotsugi. Cell phone."

"Yes, Sis."

Ononoki produced a cell phone—a smart phone—from who knows where, and handed it to Ms. Kagenui. Ononoki, a smart phone? I was taken aback. Though from their exchange I gathered that it was Ms. Kagenui's, and she was just making her familiar carry it.

Since she constantly needed to navigate difficult terrain, Ms. Kagenui probably did her best to travel as lightly as possible... Maybe she gave it all to Ononoki to carry, her wallet, her cell phone, everything.

"Too bad I didn't get to slaughter you, but having caught you just before you blossomed into an immortal aberration, I'm fully satisfied with my day's work—hmmhmhmm," Ms. Kagenui remarked as she typed on her cell phone, humming here and there—she was most likely composing a report for Ms. Gaen, but unlike Shinobu, Ms. Kagenui seemed to be in very high spirits indeed. I trembled in horror at her boundlessly disturbing disappointment at not getting to kill me, but as far as I could tell from her expression, she wasn't actually that disappointed.

Did catching people before they blossomed into immortal aberrations—having managed to—really make her that happy?

"Hey, Ms. Kagenui."

"What can I do you for?"

"Um... Let's see, actually I wanted to ask you this over the summer as well, but...why are you so set on killing immortal aberrations?"

"Sorry?" Her hand stopped typing mid-message.

I asked knowing that I might be stepping into taboo territory, but all she did was ask me to repeat myself. Like she was so wrapped up in composing her message that she heard me, but not really.

"What was that, young man?"

"I was just… I was just asking why you're so intent on killing immortal aberrations… As a field of aberration specialization, that's quite specific, isn't it?"

"Hm? Maybe it is at that. But I don't really think of it that way. Seeing as most aberrations, monsters that is, are already dead. Isn't that right, Yotsugi?"

"Sure…though the standard is pretty ambiguous, monstieur. Depending on how you interpret immortality, you could even say that Big Sis is a general practitioner."

"…"

Well.

Sure, fair enough.

Since the one saying so, her familiar, was a corpse tsukumogami, an immortal aberration you might expect to be a target for Ms. Kagenui in the first place. Because of that contradiction, or failure even, maybe her area of expertise was surprisingly fuzzy.

Intuitive, so to speak.

And it was Kaiki, of all people, who'd described Ms. Kagenui and Ononoki's specialty as "narrow"—maybe I'd made a real fool of myself taking what he said at face value.

I was mortified.

"The fact is, I'm not the only expert who specializes in immortal aberrations—though it's true enough that there's only one other who's as keen as I am to kill them, no matter what the cost."

"So there's someone else, huh?"

Somehow that didn't sit well with me.

As someone she'd tried to kill—as an immortal aberration she'd tried to roll, with that ferocious fanaticism—*no matter what the cost.*

"Keheh, that someone else is a bit of a recluse, though, so don't fret about it, young man—even went astray from Ms. Gaen's group, that one, a real stray dog," said Ms. Kagenui. "No need to take that into account. As to why a body specializes in immortal aberrations, well, it's because no matter how much you smash them or how hard you hit them, you can never go too far—hm? Don't I recall telling you this before?"

"Yeah, I've definitely heard that part before, but..."

But I didn't think that could be the only reason.

Did she really set herself against all immortal aberrations—for that reason alone? It seemed like an all-too-perilous way of life...

She was a street-fighting woman, maybe that was reason enough?

Like she was intentionally selecting the highest difficulty level or something—though other than the bigger of my little sisters, I've only ever encountered that kind of character in boys' manga.

"What, young man? You hankering for the spinoff about how I got started down this path?"

"No no no, I'm not such a nosey parker... It's just, to be honest, I'm bothered by how much it bothers me. Oshino was the first one of you I met, and his area of expertise barely seemed to amount to anything... But ultimately I guess the same is true of you and Kaiki, and Ms. Gaen too."

"What're you on about? You ought to be more worried about Yotsugi's reasons than mine, anyway."

"Huh?"

The thrust of my question suddenly deflected, I turned towards Ononoki—but she was just looking at me, expressionless as always.

Blankly, vacantly.

Looking at no longer fully human me.

"Ms. Kagenui, what do you mean—"

"Hm?"

Apparently her smart phone vibrated as I was about to pursue the matter. She'd gotten a call while she was still in the middle of composing that message to Ms. Gaen.

Ms. Kagenui checked the screen, which I couldn't see from where I was standing, and scowled—then pressed the button to pick up the call.

"Hello, Kagenui speaking," she answered like nothing was going on.

Well, it's not like it was such a race against time at this point, so I wasn't particularly worried about being interrupted.

What did worry me, though, was Ms. Kagenui's ebullient mood souring somewhat.

Her expression changed visibly.

"Uh huh... Hang on a minute. Hang on. I was just now telling the young man about... That can't be. Senpai, that's just too awful—"

Senpai?

Senpai—there's only one person in the world Ms. Kagenui calls senpai, so that meant she was talking to Ms. Gaen, Izuko Gaen. In which case her change of expression made sense. Even Ms. Kagenui had trouble with Ms. Gaen's unique brand of "presumptuousness."

For my part, my first reaction was that you'd expect no less—to call just as there was a break in our conversation, in fact just as Ms. Kagenui was composing a message to her—you'd expect no less of Ms. Gaen, and yet—

Something, somehow, seemed strange...

"Uh huh... Uh huh. But right now, Tadatsuru... Really? Okay. I'll let Araragi know—that's all we *can* do right now, I reckon. And we're okay as is? Just keep going with the flow?"

Mm-hmm, mm-hmm, Ms. Kagenui nodded two or three times, then said, "Goodbye," and hung up. She did know how to say a proper farewell, I thought to myself.

It was, frankly speaking, no time for such frivolous thoughts—but I had a bad habit of comparing Ms. Kagenui and Kaiki, and Ms. Gaen, to Oshino.

"Young man. The worst news has come at the worst time."

"Huh? Th-That call was from Ms. Gaen, though, wasn't it?"

No.

There was no doubt about that—but hang on, Ms. Kagenui hadn't told the other person a thing about the current situation, that is to say about my condition.

In other words, she hadn't delivered any of the report that she'd been preparing, that she'd been composing in written form—which meant, naturally, that the conversation had been about something Ms. Gaen had on her mind.

And that conversation concerned this "worst news"?

In which case, why would this be the "worst time"? To begin with, any time you get the worst news, whenever it is, that moment, that *right now* automatically becomes the worst time, doesn't it?

"I'll lend you Yotsugi for a spell. Now hurry, there's not a moment to lose."

"Hurry...to where?"

"To Suruga Kanbaru's house. To the house where Gaen-senpai's sister Toé's daughter lives—hurry up and go find your little sisters," Ms. Kagenui said with a sharp glare, her tone sharp—altogether sharply. "Though they may not actually be there anymore."

012

Yotsugi Ononoki's finishing move.

The finishing move of the shikigami employed by expert and violent onmyoji Yozuru Kagenui was known as the "Unlimited Rulebook" (rules consisting mostly of exceptions)—I don't know the origin of that bizarre name, but this no ifs, ands, or buts secret technique involved instantly and explosively enlarging one part of the body to attack the target, an extremely up-close-and-personal melee offense of unlimited power incongruous with Ononoki's outward appearance.

Though even if it didn't seem appropriate for a tween girl, it was appropriate enough for Ms. Kagenui's shikigami... The amazing thing about the move was that it was possible to use it for defense as well as offense. Well, defense might not be the proper term—more like evasive action.

If need be, one could use the reaction, the recoil from instantly and explosively enlarging one's body to travel at high speed in any direction—forward or backward or right or left, even up. If you could stand on the ceiling, I imagine it would be possible to use it to travel straight down as well.

So really you could just call it "movement" instead of "evasive action."

To put it in RPG terms, it was simultaneously both a ranged attack and a movement spell—what I'm getting at, in other words, is that even as the crow flies it was a fair distance to Kanbaru's house from the vacant land, er, wasteland where the ruins of the cram school had formerly stood, but with Ononoki's power, we could make the trip in just a few seconds.

Shinobu, however, grumbled, "At the height of my power, I too could accomplish such a feat."

Which was an understatement, to say the least. At the height of her power, when she was known as a legendary vampire, Shinobu could circle the globe seven and a half times in a single second. But unfortunately, she was at present not a legendary vampire at the height of her powers, but an eight-year-old girl at the nadir of her powers, so she was forced to sink into my shadow and ride along.

I wrapped my arms tight around Ononoki's waist, squeezed my eyes shut, and seconds later—I was standing in front of Kanbaru's night-enshrouded home.

"Shall we, kind monster sir?"

"No…hang on…a sec…please."

Ononoki was definitely a pro; she was ready for action the second we landed, but the pertinent question was whether or not I was up to it. And I wasn't.

It stood to reason. We'd taken an aerial shortcut, blasting off like a rocket, but the motion itself wasn't the problem; I was in no shape to handle the changes in atmospheric pressure and oxygen level.

I was dizzy, and couldn't catch my breath.

Altitude sickness mode, I was surprised I didn't pass out.

Though I guess I should've been glad just to arrive in one piece.

It probably would've been even worse if I wasn't already partially vampirified—though if it'd been through Shinobu's power instead of my own like the last time I experienced this kind of movement, the whole thing would've been no big deal.

"…Urk."

Yup.

At the time I hadn't thought I was relying so flagrantly on that power, which is to say I'd suffered from a certain lack of self-awareness, but now that I'd been told all of a sudden that I could never use it again—I was painfully aware of what I had lost.

Even though it didn't actually mean that I'd lost anything, and in fact, I'd been steadily losing some vital part of my humanity every time I did it.

"You okay, kind monster sir?"

Ononoki hurried over to me, seeming totally unconcerned.

Being a corpse and all, differences in air pressure or the oxygen level naturally had no effect on her.

"Do you need me to give you mouth-to-mouth?"

"Um… I'm in no condition for that kind of joke right now…"

Hmm.

I hate to say it, but if I, Koyomi Araragi, was in no condition for *that kind of joke*, then I must've been in terrible shape indeed.

But I couldn't huddle there forever—no point in staying hunched over on the ground. Whatever my condition, this was no time for huddling or hunching.

"Shinobu… Sorry, but let me lean on you."

"If it must be so," she replied, appearing from where she lurked in my shadow.

Sinuously.

I started to wonder where she'd been while Ononoki and I were gliding through the sky, since I wasn't casting even the faintest shadow on the ground while we were airborne; as I considered such trivial questions, Shinobu threw my arm around her neck and propped me up.

It was night, so her little girl's body had that much strength, at least.

A little-girl power character and a tween-girl power character.

"Now...Ononoki. I'm sorry but I've got another job for you."

"You're a real taskmaster. Giving me plenty to do, aren't you, kind monster sir. Well, we've got Big Sis's approval this time, so I'll help out any way I can. But won't it kill you if we jump that high again?"

"No no no, no one's saying anything about that... Listen, Kanbaru doesn't live alone, you get me?"

Her place is a bit of a mansion.

A real mansion, in the traditional style.

It's surrounded by a high wall, and you can tell at a glance that they're a wealthy family—there's even a grand gate. You can't see it from outside, but they've also got a stately rock garden with a koi pond and everything. What do you call that kind of garden, *karesansui* or something?

Whatever, the point is, it's sprawling.

Sprawlingly sprawling.

Maybe that's not the appropriate term to use for such a noble home, but sprawling is the only word I can come up with—and the only people who live there are Suruga and her grandparents, just the three of them with all that space.

So what, you say? Well, if we attempted a frontal assault through the front gate and ran into her grandmother or grandfather, it'd definitely count as trespassing—and while marching up to the front door and ringing the doorbell merited some small measure of consideration, it was a tough sell at that hour. Such boorishness would be just as bad as trespassing.

So I hoped to find a shortcut to Kanbaru's room that avoided both the front door and an affront to her family—and shortcuts were Ononoki's specialty.

I wasn't envisioning jumping thousands of feet through the air, I figured we could just leap the wall encircling the mansion.

"Well...we didn't end up having time for the test, but how vampiricized do you think you are right now, kind monster sir? You've got a healing factor, though it seems to be incredibly weak, but what about your physical strength—it's nighttime, don't you think if you really put your mind to it, you could jump over this wall?"

"It has nothing to do with whether or not I put my mind to it. There's bound to be an alarm on a place like this. If I blew it and accidentally touched the wall or something, I'd set it off."

"So what if you did... If what Ms. Kagenui, or really Ms. Gaen, said was true, then the inside of this house is already a warzone, or the aftermath of one anyway. It's a totally appropriate time for alarms to be going off."

"..."

No.

Ononoki was talking like she knew what was going on—*if what Ms. Gaen said was true*—but unless she really, literally had a telepathic connection with Ms. Kagenui, I didn't think she actually had a grasp on what was going on at the Kanbaru residence. So how could she talk so confidently about it?

And yet Ms. Kagenui had been very persistent—*Hurry up already, you'll find out when you get there*, so...

It didn't seem like she'd said "there's not a moment to lose" just to encourage us to hurry, she meant it literally—she didn't even take the time to explain the situation properly.

I imagine she hadn't accompanied us because, however un-human her violent capabilities, her body couldn't withstand the shortcut. Though the fact that she used Google Maps to show Ononoki the location of Kanbaru's house was a pretty contemporary, that is, an all-too-human form of wisdom.

"Okay. Hold tight, monstieur."

"Uh huh."

"And it's not that kind of joke."

"Any way you want it."

"You too, Big Sis Shinobu."

"I decline to hold tight to the likes of thee," Shinobu brushed away Ononoki's offer and sunk into my shadow. My partner's determination to be hostile to Ononoki was unrelentingly deep-seated.

"Ready for takeoff."

"Do it."

"*Unlimited Rulebook.*"

I felt like she didn't need to be quite so diligent about announcing the name of the skill, since if she made a little jump like that at full power she'd almost certainly overshoot the mark—but I didn't even get a chance to finish this train of thought before Ononoki and I had successfully infiltrated the Kanbaru family's courtyard.

Just like Lupin the Third.

"Just like Lupin the Third," said Ononoki.

Boy are we in sync, I thought. But when she added, "I mean, it's like we're sneaking into some little cutie-pie's boudoir," I was instead floored by our low synchronization rate.

How could we have such different images of Lupin the Third?

"Not sure how I feel about the term 'little cutie-pie'... Plus I don't think Lupin the Third does that nowadays. Anyway, we've got to hurry to Kanbaru's room. *Su casa es mi casa.*"

I may have been overstating the case, but I was confident that I knew Kanbaru's bedroom better than she did.

I was confident that I knew it inside and out.

After all, despite the fact that it was exam-prep season, despite the fact that it was crunch time, I still came to tidy up Kanbaru's room twice a month. Her room was a smorgasbord of mess, like it had a rewind function so that no matter how much cleaning I did it was buried in crap again in short order. I knew where every single thing in that room was.

I'd sent my two little sisters to Kanbaru's place largely because I'd been there just the other day to clean her room. Under normal conditions, I'd never have let my adorable little sisters anywhere near it—not without a lifeguard. They'd drown in garbage.

With my arm still over Ononoki's shoulder, I tiptoed across the grounds—thanks to her unexpected and unwelcome comment, I felt like I actually was sneaking into my junior's boudoir, but anyway, I took off my shoes and stepped into the hallway—the security in these old Japanese manors was far too lax. They ought to do something about it, I thought, conveniently disregarding the fact that I was the one breaking in.

I carefully slid open the screen to Kanbaru's room.

Well, not so carefully, more like *to hell with it*, but—sure enough!

" ... "

There was nothing there worthy of a *sure enough*.

What an anticlimax.

It was just as Ms. Kagenui said—we'd only gone there to confirm her suspicions, pretty much. Kanbaru's room was like an empty husk, nothing there but two vacant futons lined up side by side.

"It's weird that there aren't three, though," I muttered.

Why only two futons for three people?

What exactly had been going on here?

It's not like I didn't have my suspicions, I had plenty of them and they were massive, but in any case, now was the time for action—even though it seemed deserted, I crept into the room, careful not to make a sound.

And checked the futons.

Feels like a cliché from a detective show, but they were still warm.

They can't have got far may or may not have been the appropriate follow-up, but someone had definitely been lying on these futons until very recently—next I smelled the pillows. The pillow on one of the futons bore the lingering scent of Karen and Tsukihi, while the pillow on the other bore the lingering scent of Kanbaru—all three of them had been there until very recently indeed.

It did comfort me somewhat that the combination had been

Kanbaru on one and Karen + Tsukihi on the other—and then I saw it.

As I gazed all around the room, I saw something that hadn't been there the other day when I came to clean.

"…"

A paper crane.

Since Kanbaru's room was in the Japanese style, it had a grand *tokonoma* alcove—usually heaped with drifts of garbage. But in the spic-and-span alcove, which, if I may be permitted a small toot on my own horn, was only empty because I'd taken the trouble to clear it out, sat a paper crane, like a traditional decoration.

A paper crane is, it goes without saying, a representative form of origami—I bet there's not a single Japanese person who's never folded one, and yet.

And yet—a paper crane?

"What is it, kind monster sir?"

"Look at this."

Ononoki came up beside me and I pointed at my discovery— maybe I was being overly cautious, but I didn't want to be too hasty about touching it.

"…"

"You're probably thinking, *It's nothing but a paper crane, what's the big deal*, but Kanbaru's not the type of person to decorate her room with something like this. That's not the type of person she is. I mean, she doesn't have an inkling about decorating the tokonoma in the first place, she just thinks of it as a convenient place to put stuff. A stack of pervy books would be one thing, but something as refined as this?"

"Yeah, refined," echoed Ononoki, shaking her head—expressionlessly, which really made her seem like a doll.

The kind with a spring in its neck, that wobbles when you touch it.

I seriously wanted to touch it.

"It certainly is a ve-ry fine example—anyway, go on, monstieur, pick it up."

"Huh? But…what if it's some kind of clue?"

"It's okay, kind monster sir, if it's what I think it is—me, I'm a shikigami, or a corpse, so if I touched it I'm pretty sure nothing would happen, but you're still human…"

"All right."

That *still* bothered me, but this was no time for a Q&A—with Kanbaru and my sisters missing, nothing had changed. It was a race against time, there wasn't a moment to lose.

I picked up the paper crane.

Treating it as if it were some kind of explosive device—

A small, perfectly white paper crane.

"Ick!!"

I shrieked—not in surprise, but because it freaked me out.

The second I picked it up—I don't want there to be any misunderstanding, I'm honestly just putting the facts down on paper here exactly as they occurred—the lone paper crane suddenly became a string of a thousand.

It was like—a string of cranes had been planted in the floor of the alcove, and the single visible one was the bud, so that when I pulled it up I uprooted the whole thing.

A string of paper cranes.

Pretty banal, really, something everybody's familiar with—mostly as something you make for a friend or family member who's in the hospital. Coming out of nowhere, appearing suddenly and unexpectedly like that, though, it almost made me piss my pants.

I think it's one of the elemental fears of humankind—a dense swarm of tiny things wriggling around is creepy, even if they're inorganic.

Maybe it's even more basic than that, and we're just scared of anything innumerable—but anyway, I trembled at their abundance. I didn't let go of the one I was holding, at least.

"H-Hey, Ononoki—"

"Just as I thought."

"J-Just as you thought? If this is what you were expecting, why the hell didn't you warn me—that it was going to turn into a whole string of them!"

"Well, I wondered if you'd be startled."

"…"

I was doubly infuriated by the thought that I had Kaiki to thank for this aspect of her personality.

What if my shriek had woken up Kanbaru's grandparents? No, I mean, really.

Under the circumstances, they'd think I was a kidnapper.

There was no way I'd be able to talk my way out of this one.

Still holding the string of cranes out before me like a lantern, I turned to Ononoki.

"Well? *What* was just as you expected?"

"I know who's behind this. An acquaintance of Big Sis's and mine. This is a message—in Lupin the Third terms, it's like a calling card, advance notice of a crime."

"A calling card… Wait, is this a kidnapping then? Yeah, it's been carried out—"

Or no?

Maybe the kidnapping itself wasn't the point, maybe there was something else—though that didn't provide any consolation, nor alter the fact that Kanbaru, Karen, and Tsukihi were gone.

But—a calling card?

"That bastard loves this kind of parlor trick—he loves to scare people with malicious little pranks. Unbelievable, what a creep. But at least this time it's blatantly obvious why the message was delivered in the form of a crane."

"It…is?"

"It's a bird," Ononoki explained. "The shape of a bird—a phoenix. In other words, this flock of cranes, birds who are said to live

194

for a thousand years, implies your sister Tsukihi."

"Hunh?"

"Come on, monstieur. We've succeeded in our reconnaissance mission, our work here is done. Let's head back to Big Sis—we need her to analyze that string of cranes. If our acquaintance is involved, I'm honestly not sure how involved Big Sis is going to want to get… but I'm pretty sure she'll help that much, at least."

013

"Tadatsuru Teori—puppeteer," said Ms. Kagenui.

It didn't require much effort to discern the unmistakable feelings of antipathy, not to say animosity, Ms. Kagenui felt towards this individual.

She was visibly aggravated.

"Tadatsuru?"

She'd spoken the name when she was talking to Ms. Gaen on the phone earlier, hadn't she? But at the time, I hadn't realized it was a person's name—

In the end, Ononoki and I hadn't found anything other than the "calling card," so with it in hand we turned around and headed right back to the vacant land, er, wasteland where the ruins of the cram school had stood.

"Um," I started to tell Ms. Kagenui about what we'd found—my junior and my two little sisters had disappeared almost as if they'd vanished into thin air, the futons still warm—but she cut me off.

"No need."

It seemed like she grasped everything her familiar was doing if she put her mind to it, so maybe she just understood what was going on without my needing to explain.

I hadn't imagined that Ononoki's every experience might be getting transmitted to Ms. Kagenui...

Did they have an actual telepathic connection, even if it was a one-way street?

That'd be a hell of a thing.

Thinking back, there might've been a few shady moments I'd rather Ms. Kagenui didn't know about, but all I could do was comfort myself with the thought that she couldn't have the full picture. I didn't want to deal with any more stress than I already had to.

Well, even if she'd gotten an indirect grasp of the situation through her familiar's eyes, seeing something in person was different, so I went to hand over the string of cranes I was holding.

Ms. Kagenui just glanced at it, though, and made no move to take it—almost like she'd seen something unclean.

Assuming that thing wasn't me—it was the cranes she loathed.

Then she'd said:

Tadatsuru Teori.

Puppeteer.

"Tadatsuru, you say..." I was studying for my college entrance exams, aspiring to attend a national university—and anyway, math had always been my strongest subject.

Tadatsuru, Yozuru, Yotsugi—sine, cosine, cotangent.

Each of their names was an alternate reading of a trigonometric function. Which naturally made me curious to triangulate some kind of connection between Ms. Kagenui and Ononoki—and that puppeteer...

Seemed like there had to be some kind of common denominator.

But judging from Ms. Kagenui's brusque manner, it felt intrusive to ask...or rather, given the current emergency, I'd rather not take the time to ask if I could get away with it.

All I wanted was to find out where Kanbaru and Karen and Tsukihi were.

That was my overriding priority.

"Hm?"

"I just..."

"Tadatsuru is a puppeteer and, well, an expert—an expert of sorts who specializes in immortal aberrations, just like yours truly. I reckon I already told you that."

She put extra oomph into the *just like yours truly*, but I was pretty sure it was *not* because she wanted to emphasize that fact.

In fact, it sounded like her tone had become more emphatic in spite of herself, because she couldn't stand it—she just couldn't say it calmly.

But asking about that felt intrusive too.

I didn't feel like I could point it out.

It's not like I wasn't interested—in what kind of relationship Ms. Kagenui had with this Tadatsuru person, and I might need to know at some point—but given the current vibe, I couldn't come right out and ask her.

"When you say you already told me that," I began cautiously.

Although Ms. Kagenui was a violent person, I didn't think she was the type to make sparks fly for no reason, and maybe I didn't need to be so cautious. Nevertheless, I couldn't help but be on my guard. I was terrified that she might fly into a rage.

"You mean that this person—is the stray expert, right? A stray dog, the lone wolf who doesn't belong to Ms. Gaen's faction—"

"If you don't," said Ononoki.

Interrupting me.

Incidentally, it seemed that the entire time Ononoki had been gone, Ms. Kagenui had been standing on top of a rock (I had a hard time seeing the distinction between that rock and the ground, but I'm sure there was one). Now she was back on Ononoki's shoulders.

"If you don't belong to Ms. Gaen's faction, then you essentially don't belong, period…since what Ms. Gaen has is less of a faction and more of a network. In other words, Tadatsuru is like an off-line computer."

"Yotsugi. No need to tell him anything irrelevant," Ms. Kagenui reproved her familiar.

I wasn't sure which part of that could possibly be "irrelevant"— but I felt like that piece of intel sufficed to give me a sense of just how exceptional this Tadatsuru Teori was.

Even Mèmè Oshino and Deishu Kaiki, misfits to the end, were part of Ms. Gaen's faction—network. Those two, those two were.

But Tadatsuru.

Wasn't.

In which case, I couldn't even begin to imagine how stray this dog was—and when I forced myself, all I could envision was someone too outsized for words like *eccentric* or *ominous*. He loomed large, and I started to get scared.

"So you're saying that an expert who specializes in immortal aberrations—is the one who abducted my sisters and my friend? Then, his goal is…"

This was a kidnapping.

It was easy to get distracted thanks to the involvement of aberrations and experts, but this was a clear case of kidnapping—it certainly wasn't some spiriting-away. Depending on the facts, depending on how they unfolded, we'd need to alert the police post-haste.

No, it was ninety-nine percent clear that we needed to, but on the off chance that we'd be devising another solution ourselves…

"What, Ms. Kagenui? What does—Tadatsuru Teori want?"

"I reckon I ought to call Gaen-senpai before I answer—a body's subjectivity can muddy the waters, after all. Subjectivity, or personal feelings. What I can tell you is that our boy Tadatsuru…" Whereupon Ms. Kagenui described Tadatsuru Teori in what actually seemed to me a very detached way. It seemed like a real rarity for a straight shooter like Ms. Kagenui—"has a tendency to let his personal enmi-

200

ties guide his actions, so his professional work is weak. By virtue of which, the present situation isn't as hopeless as you might imagine, young man. But..."

"But?"

"I want to make it absolutely clear to you that in this situation, as always, you mustn't fall back on your vampiric power. Let's get that straight before you find out what's going on and fly off the handle."

"..."

So was she anticipating a situation that would make me fly off the handle? While I may not be quick-tempered, I am quick to jump to conclusions, and I was ready to fly off the handle right then and there—but because I was dealing with Ms. Kagenui, a violent onmyoji who was itching to shut me up with one blow from her fist, I somehow managed to retain my composure.

"I understand that," I managed to respond. "If I keep on transforming into a vampire—not having a reflection will be the least of my worries. I get it already."

"Do you really, though? I declined to bring it up when we were jawing earlier, but—it isn't just you. Who can't transform into a vampire, I mean," reminded Ms. Kagenui, looking down at my feet.

It was night, and the moonlight wasn't that bright, so my shadow was hard to see unless you really strained your eyes—but I guess an expert like her could even see Shinobu Oshino where she lurked in my shadow.

Could stare at her.

"The former Heartunderblade mustn't transform into a vampire, either."

"..."

"Stands to reason, I reckon. That's the inevitable logical conclusion, isn't it? The soul linkage between you and the former Heartunderblade is a geometric progression—so if you don't transform into a vampire, the former Heartunderblade can't regain the power what she's lost. Your companion must henceforth remain an eight-year-old girl in perpetuity."

It occurred to me that, depending on how you looked at it, that might not be such bad news, but of course it was. Shinobu being stuck as an eight-year-old girl might be an even bigger problem than my own inability to transform into a vampire.

"Yup…" I tried to nod along as if I was already well aware of that, but I'm not sure I pulled it off. It was just as she'd said, of course, I didn't need to be told that it was the inevitable logical conclusion, and it would've been weird if I'd been surprised when Ms. Kagenui pointed it out—but even though I felt like I had a handle on it, however tenuous, "discouraged" doesn't even begin to cover how I felt, confronted with the naked truth like that.

Discouragement, yeah, that was what I felt more keenly than anything.

It made me realize just how much I'd been counting on Shinobu—unconsciously. I realized just how much I'd been counting on the power and battle prowess that Shinobu—that Kissshot Acerolaorion Heartunderblade regained when she drank my blood, even if it was only a fraction of her true strength.

Yes.

Finally, ultimately, I guess what I'd been relying on wasn't my own strength as a vampire, but Shinobu's—or more than that, maybe I had just been counting on my partner Shinobu Oshino.

The things I'd taken for granted.

And in so doing lost, and betrayed—

"It's kind of funny, though, isn't it?"

"Hmm? What is, young man?"

"Well, over spring break I'd wanted to seal away Shinobu's power—and yet, suddenly, I was using that power to deal with all sorts of problems."

I joined Ms. Kagenui in looking down at my shadow. Despite the fact that it was my own shadow, unlike Ms. Kagenui I couldn't discern anything within it. Though I'm pretty sure Shinobu was in there. And would stay in there.

"How can I put this… The power that I thought I was using only as a last resort, as an underhanded makeshift means of getting me through this or that situation, the temporary power that I thought I was just borrowing—suddenly I was exploiting it as though it were my own, without a second thought… Maybe this divine punishment was only to be expected."

"Divine punishment?"

It was Ononoki who reacted to my words.

Yotsugi Ononoki.

"I wonder—you're obviously reaping what you've sown, kind monster sir, but I'm not sure that it's divine punishment."

"…? What do you mean?"

"Well now," Ms. Kagenui took over for Ononoki, "I reckon she's saying the timing is a little too good for it to be divine punishment—and when the timing is too good, assuming it's not simply a coincidence, more often than not it's been orchestrated that way."

It's the work of people, not gods.

"For your sisters and your friend to be abducted by an acquaintance of ours on the very day your reflection ceases to be, the day your vampirification exceeds the limits of your humanity, so to speak—now that's just a little too much of a coincidence."

"…"

Well.

It's not like that didn't make sense—it rang a distant bell, in fact.

Hadn't Deishu Kaiki once said something similar to me? Oh yeah, it was the first time Ms. Kagenui and Ononoki came to town. Over the summer, on Obon.

He said something like, "Coincidences are generally a product of malice"—but then again, in that case it was Deishu Kaiki himself who was the malicious source.

I said, "It hasn't been all that uncommon for my bills to come due all at once these days—I mean, lately it's been nothing but, endlessly paying for my own tomfoolery. All the stuff that's been piling up, the stuff I've been putting on the shelf, has come crashing down on me at the same time—"

"Been brought crashing down, more like, wouldn't you say? Like a game of Jenga. At least according to what I hear from Gaen-senpai—and from Yotsugi here."

"..."

By what she heard from Ononoki, did Ms. Kagenui mean that thing with the "Darkness"—or the thing with Mayoi Hachikuji? Now *that* was the ultimate example of something I put on the shelf.

And the ultimate example of something that came crashing down.

"Can I ask you something, Ms. Kagenui?"

"What is it."

"It's... This might sound strange, but is this Tadatsuru Teori guy the kind of righteous person or whatever whose ideology won't allow for any indiscretions or iniquities? Who believes that there's a proper form to the world, and that the world ought to be in that proper form—that just as the Earth turns on its axis, so too should the globe inscribe an ellipsis through the cosmos, that kind of thing?"

"Ideology? Ha—"

What a hoot, replied Ms. Kagenui.

Though she wasn't smiling at all, not even a tiny bit.

She wore the most serious expression imaginable.

"He's utterly divorced from such things. And by *such things* I mean anything like righteousness, or a proper form. Not only that, he's utterly divorced from anything resembling an ideology at all. Enmity doesn't constitute an ideology, does it? Other than our mutual focus on immortal aberrations, he and I have nothing whatsoever in common."

"..."

That almost made it sound like her own violence stemmed from some kind of ideology, but if I brought that up now the argument might go on forever, so I decided to keep things on the subject of Tadatsuru Teori for the time being.

Though all I really wanted to know was Tadatsuru's stance on aberrations—because if he was anything like that "Darkness," that black hole swallowing up all errors—then my friend and my little sisters, or at least two out of the three, were in real trouble. They were in for a rectification of all their indiscretions, all their monkey business.

The thought made my blood boil, and I wanted to pour all that boiling-hot blood down Shinobu's throat, to mobilize all my heightened senses and search for the girls.

If I did, I could have them safe and sound in a few hours at most—I don't know.

The idea was massively appealing, but the immediate presence of Ms. Kagenui and Ononoki, very much not my sworn allies, was a reliable deterrent.

Calm down.

That'd be the wrong move.

That'd be like taking out another loan to repay your current one—then I'd really be in hot water, like I was trying to keep a failing business afloat once all its liquid assets had dried up. Acquiring power came with a price, which lent a certain sense of self-sacrifice to that course of action, and as long as I was the only sacrificial victim, it felt like it was worth a shot—but it wasn't that simple.

I had to keep in mind, I had to be clearly, overtly self-aware.

That if I ceased to exist, if this human being ceased to exist, there were people who would feel a deep sense of loss, if nothing else—I.

Needed to be thoroughly aware of that.

I needed to realize that.

If I became blinded by that spirit of self-sacrifice in the course of this rescue mission because I didn't care what happened to me, I'd be depriving them of the part of themselves that I represented—I'd be tearing off one of their limbs, almost.

If push came to shove, it still might come down to that.

But it wasn't time to make that decision yet.

"Supposing Tadatsuru did have something like an ideology, it would have to be based on—aesthetic curiosity, I reckon. Though I'm a mite hesitant to apply the word 'aesthetic' to that man."

"Hunh?"

Aesthetic curiosity?

Not a phrase I was used to hearing.

Intellectual curiosity, maybe, but—

"He's possessed of the sense that *it's precisely what God did* not *create that is beautiful*—that the existence of aberrations created by humankind is beautiful. He fancies himself an artist. That's his failing."

"…"

Fancies himself an artist.

She—didn't mean it in a positive way, did she?

"I'm keen to take on immortal aberrations because, as you've seen for yourself, I despise them for their wickedness—but from what I've heard, Tadatsuru is the exact opposite."

"The exact opposite…"

"He loves them for their beauty."

I may not be the most perceptive guy, but even I could tell that the preface, or the obviously unnecessary annotation, *from what I've heard*, was a lie. And Ms. Kagenui didn't even try to pretend that it wasn't. But by lying about how close she and Tadatsuru were, she was indicating that she didn't care to divulge the truth.

"Even if it's not an ideology, though, he is very particular, so your sisters and your friend are still safe. Safer than they'd be if I was gunning for them, at any rate."

"Well, that's not saying a whole…"

I trailed off because it seemed like finishing that sentence might deprive me of any modicum of safety I might have enjoyed until then.

"But if he possesses this sense of the aesthetic worth of aberrations, why does he take them on? I guess it's not the same as being the Aberration Roller or the Aberration Slayer, but in the end, isn't he still exterminating aberrations?"

"His position is more like Oshino's, I reckon. Rather than exterminating aberrations, he makes his living as an intermediary or…a neutral mediator, I suppose? An art dealer understands the value of art and appreciates its beauty, but buys and sells it with plain old money. It's like that."

"…"

An art dealer isn't an art collector, was that it? Or maybe was it more like the contradiction inherent in an animal lover working at a zoo, where they lock animals in cages?

Actually, I didn't think that was a contradiction.

People who love to read books become writers—and if you really think about it, that's a grand contradiction, but the world is founded on such contradictions, it's positively foundering in them, so contradictions become normalized until finally they aren't contradictions anymore.

Then again, if you ask me, although on the surface the old chestnut about the unbeatable spear and the unbeatable shield seems like a clear example of a paradox, the underlying assumption is a little bit strange.

The unbeatable spear. The unbeatable shield.

Either one is already a contradiction in terms—because the moment a decidedly not unbeatable human being is wielding something, it stops being unbeatable.

Like how I couldn't get a handle on Shinobu's vampiric power—and ended up overindulging.

Like how I betrayed Oshino's expectations, betrayed his faith in me—and ended up losing my humanity.

It's based on the assumption of a human being who'd be unbeatable even without those things—and no such person exists. They do not exist.

"Sounds like this expert Tadatsuru is the perfect opponent for me to face as I am now."

"…"

My potentially masochistic-sounding line apparently didn't sit well with Ms. Kagenui, who, after a pause, said, "Don't wallow in it."

She abandoned her usual Kansai dialect and said this with something closer to the intonation of standard Japanese.

"That's not power. That's self-infatuation."

"Self-infatuation…"

Infatuated—with myself.

Even if it wasn't self-sacrifice…

"Don't wallow in the tragedy of the situation, you hear? The long and the short of it is that your sisters and your friend were kidnapped by some mysterious fool, nothing more. In regard to that, at least, you are one hundred percent the aggrieved party. If by some one-in-a-million chance you actually invited something like divine punishment, it was for pushing it until you lost your humanity. It has nothing to do with the fact that those three were targeted. Isn't that so, Yotsugi."

"Yup, it is."

For some reason Ms. Kagenui wanted Ononoki to back her up on that point, and the shikigami nodded meaningfully.

It seemed weird to seek approval from your own familiar, and it was also weird that the response seemed so pregnant with meaning.

Then again, their relationship was just kind of weird—to the point that it struck me as the real paradox here.

"Well then," I said, "no choice but to save those three girls who have nothing to do with it…for me, anyway. Whatever else happens. Ms. Kagenui, you…"

Man, it was hard to say.

A terribly brazen request—but I had to ask. For my own sake as well, so I wouldn't get lost in myself and wallow in self-sacrifice or self-infatuation.

"Will you help me? In this, we might say, dramatic rescue?"

"I will, since Gaen-senpai told me to—I'll take the liberty of going along with her wishes. But let's get one thing straight: I can't involve myself directly. My power is exclusively geared for defeating immortal aberrations, so it's no good against a human being."

"..."

"Don't look at me like that, young man. However aggravating Tadatsuru may be, I reckon you're more my enemy than he is. So don't look at me like that—I'll let you keep borrowing Yotsugi—and I'll lend you my wisdom as well. Anyhoo, the first thing we need to do is take a looksee at those cranes. If they *are* a message, I reckon they're a message for you."

"For me?"

"I can't say for sure how thoroughly he understands the situation, but—Tadatsuru's ultimate target is definitely you."

"Me? No, wait, Tadatsuru's target—"

"You, and the former Heartunderblade. The harmless certification that Oshino requested for you is only good within Gaen-senpai's network, it has no currency with an outsider like Tadatsuru."

Then this really couldn't have come at a worse time—someone gunning for me and Shinobu, just when we'd lost the ability to fight.

Artificially.

Intentionally.

Maliciously—bad timing.

"So if that hypothesis is correct, Kanbaru and my sisters are being held as hostages, to be used against me."

"That's about the size of it. And if the real target is the two of you, then I reckon those girls are even more likely to be safe. For now, anyway."

Somehow that didn't make me feel one iota better.

That is, all it did was make me more impatient.

I was worried about my sisters, of course, but I also felt super-guilty about Kanbaru—I sent my sisters to her house because

I thought it would be a safe zone, since she was related to Ms. Gaen, related to her by blood. But now I'd gotten her mixed up in this. If nothing else, I should at least have explained to her what was going on. Why the hell didn't I?

True, while Kanbaru may not be an immortal aberration, an aberration had taken up residence in her left arm, so she could conceivably find herself in an expert's crosshairs… Given the timing of her abduction, however, it seemed much more likely she'd been taken hostage because of me.

"Well, this is no time to stand around jawing. First off, let's see those cranes. If there's no message there, I reckon that changes things." And with that, after refusing to take them from me the entire time, Ms. Kagenui finally accepted Tadatsuru's cranes.

014

How well do people know their own towns? Like, if you asked people how well they know the town they live in, I imagine that most of them would say—*well, I may not know it like the back of my hand, but I've got a pretty good sense of it.*

That's how I'd respond, at least.

I live there, after all; at the very least I wouldn't say, *I don't know anything, I don't know a thing about it, what in the world does* town *even mean*—I couldn't feign that much ignorance, and the fact is that I do have a pretty good sense of it.

And yet, maybe it depends on how you define "town." One short year ago, I didn't know about that cram school building—I had absolutely no idea it existed until Shinobu brought me there.

Nor did I know about Kita-Shirahebi Shrine.

I knew nothing about that ophiolatrous shrine.

That forgotten shrine, bound so deeply to snakes, and to a serpent aberration—and to Nadeko Sengoku, until I visited it with Kanbaru at Oshino's behest.

"I don't know everything, I just know what I know"—class president Tsubasa Hanekawa's catch phrase. Hitagi Senjogahara, approaching this from the standpoint of set theory, says she's just telling it like it is, but if you understand Hanekawa's statement as a kind of reminder, a self-admonition, the implications go beyond "just telling it like it is."

In other words, human beings.

Can be self-aware about the boundaries of what they know— however, they can't always and in every circumstance be self-aware about the boundaries of what they don't know.

By way of example, I can state with certainty that I don't know French—no question about it. This is an example of "knowing" what I "don't know."

But let's say there's a country somewhere that I don't know about because I'm a lazy student and I'm weak in world history, and a language that's only ever spoken in this country (call it "Araragino-speakese"). Naturally, I wouldn't know that language—but wouldn't even know that I didn't, because I wouldn't even know that it existed.

Even a student as lazy as me has heard people talk about the wisdom of realizing your own ignorance. It's the Socratic Paradox: "I know that I know nothing." But it's virtually impossible to articulate the actuality of this aphorism.

Probatio diabolica, the so-called Devil's Proof. If some stubborn middle schooler pressed Socrates, *Do you really know everything that you don't know?* he'd have to admit defeat—though of course, I'm pretty sure they didn't have middle schoolers in Ancient Greece.

Now, what was I talking about?

Oh yeah.

About how maybe people don't actually know anything about the things they think they know—because they don't know what they don't know. And about how maybe some chance encounter is what it takes for them to realize what they don't know.

Hanekawa might put it like this: "I don't know anything about what I don't know."

If you know what you don't know, then maybe you can learn about it, but if you don't know what you don't know, then you can't act to remedy the situation—now I've gotten myself all confused, but anyway.

The message contained in the string of cranes that Tadatsuru Teori left in Suruga Kanbaru's alcove indicated that the appointed place was Kita-Shirahebi Shrine—apparently the message employed some kind of code used between experts, so that no matter how smart you are, you can't figure it out unless you know the keyword.

I'm only going to reveal the bare minimum about how Ms. Kagenui deciphered it, though, out of consideration for everything she did on my behalf.

First she performed the maddening task of unfolding all the cranes one by one—flattening them back out into simple sheets of origami paper, an unproductive activity if there ever was one, never mind that there were a thousand of them.

Given the scale of the endeavor, it seemed like I could've helped, and I even offered to, but she refused me flatly, and rather impolitely at that. Ms. Kagenui seemed to be the kind of person you encounter in school sometimes, you know the type, who hates being helped no matter how banal the task—in fact, Senjogahara used to be exactly that type. And it's easy enough for a person like me to understand not wanting someone to throw off your rhythm, even if it's less efficient.

Though given the circumstances, it made me antsy to watch someone doing something so obviously inefficient—as luck would have it, Ms. Kagenui was at least adroit at it. She briskly unfolded the origami cranes with an almost mesmerizing dexterity. To the point that it actually did seem more efficient for her to do it without my help, after all.

The majority of the one thousand unfolded sheets of origami paper (and there really were a thousand. Exactly one thousand. Usually a string of a thousand cranes is only about half that) were just that, sheets of origami paper.

No, majority isn't the right word; nine hundred ninety-nine of the thousand cranes were plain old origami paper, plain old paper cranes.

But the other crane.

The other sheet of paper.

Had a message written on the back in felt-tip pen—and deciphering this message, which looked to me like nothing more than a hasty scrawl, yielded: Kita-Shirahebi Shrine.

"Seems like there'd be no way for an ordinary person to even realize that this message was here... Leaving a code on one paper crane among a thousand, it's so inefficient it makes my head spin..."

"Now, that there is precisely the warped aesthetic sense I'm talking about—it's a question of patience. The pursuit of efficiency alone is hollow, and it ain't no picnic to make one of these, a string of cranes."

Tadatsuru made these all himself, finished Ms. Kagenui, sounding protective of Tadatsuru Teori for the first time—probably completing the task had relaxed her, or she'd let her guard down a little in the glow of accomplishment she felt for unfolding a thousand paper cranes. She's human after all, I thought to myself.

"It doesn't say anything about a time?"

"'Fraid not. Just a place. But I reckon it's got to be tonight—otherwise the police would be apt to get involved. Three young fillies getting kidnapped is clearly a criminal matter."

"What would Tadatsuru do then?"

"*What*, meaning?"

"Um...meaning, in that case, what would Tadatsuru do to my sisters and my friend?"

"Well."

One short word.

But that one word was more than enough.

"The one thing I can say for sure is that Tadatsuru knows I'm here—knows I've come to this town. Because otherwise he wouldn't have used a code that only other experts would understand, an inefficient means of communication that you, young man, wouldn't even have known to look for."

"O-Oh yeah. Of course. You're right, of course."

It had taken me a while to get there, but once she said it, it was obvious. If I'd been alone, I would've just picked up the crane and jumped when it became a string of a thousand, and that would've been the end of it.

If Ononoki hadn't been there to tell me it was an "advance notice," I might have let my anger take over and crumpled the whole thing up into a ball.

Folding a thousand paper cranes was hardly worth it for Tadatsuru if the objective was just to startle me.

Interesting.

That meant that just as Ms. Kagenui already knew about Tadatsuru from Ms. Gaen, Tadatsuru somehow knew that Ms. Kagenui was here in town, and probably also that she was accompanied by her constant companion, Ononoki.

In which case.

"Hm? So is this Tadatsuru calling me out knowing full well that you two are my sort-of allies? Knowing who you are, he's antagonizing you? No way. Would anyone really do that?"

"Come now, young man, how dangerous do you think we are?"

Well, incredibly.

More than anyone else in the world.

Was not something I was about to say.

That would've been like sticking out my head so someone could chop it off.

"I've told you a thousand times, I use violence only in the service of slaying immortal aberrations—never against human beings. Generally speaking."

"*Generally speaking*? That's a terrifying caveat… But how do you plan to apply that? Oh, wait, is that what you're saying? That even if Tadatsuru antagonizes you, he has absolutely nothing to worry about?"

"I wouldn't say that, monsieur. Since I don't operate under the same constraints as Big Sis," Ononoki interjected as placidly as ever, "I'll fucking blow Tadatsuru to smithereens."

"Watch your language." From atop Ononoki's shoulders, Ms. Kagenui kicked her in the head. Again with the violence. But then, Ononoki's an immortal aberration, so maybe it was okay? "Say, *I'll respectfully encourage him to become smithereens.*"

"Come on, who's ever heard of such a genteel character," muttered Ononoki, before turning to look at me. "Listen, monsieur. It's not like little old me doesn't have some small connection to your sisters. So you can count on my complete cooperation—provided that you under no condition commandeer Big Sis Shinobu's power, of course."

"I intend to abide by that condition, sure...but why go to the trouble of bringing it up again right now?"

Did she have so little faith in me?

Well, I didn't have much faith in myself either, but it was a straight-up shock that a character as ingenuous, as unworldly, by which I mean as gullible as Ononoki, wouldn't have faith in me.

"It's obvious, isn't it? It's because I have no faith in your powers of restraint or self-control... And the truth is, I don't relish the thought of Big Sis and me having to fight you and the former Heartunderblade because you turned into a vampire, a full vampire."

"..."

She threw that in without changing her intonation at all, so it took me a minute to understand that all she meant was, *I don't want to be your enemy.*

And while it may have been no more than Ononoki's personal take...it was really heartening that someone would say that to me under those circumstances.

What the hell was wrong with me? I found it so heartening that I wanted to cry.

"Then again, I can only assume Tadatsuru has taken precautions against me. Taken every precaution he can. Originally—"

"No need to finish that sentence, Yotsugi. Sometimes it's easier to keep it on the need-to-know. Anyway, we know where he is, and we know where he's coming from—nothing to do now but act." Ms. Kagenui, having cut off whatever Ononoki was about to say, looked at the watch on her left wrist. The band was a slender chain. I'm relatively conscious of the fact that I wear a watch, so I end up being conscious of other people's watches as well… In any case, apparently it indicated that it was "after one in the morning. We'd best have this settled before daybreak—any way you slice it. In other words, young man, your mission, should you choose to accept it, is to have your two little sisters and your friend, Gaen-senpai's niece, back home and snug in their beds before daybreak."

Hmm.

Summed up like that, it all seemed so simple—and even "better" than its simplicity was the fact that the mission didn't include an obligation to defeat or even fight Tadatsuru Teori—in other words, it was feasible for us to come up with a plan to outwit Tadatsuru and get the hostages back without bloodshed.

Not just feasible, that was the whole idea.

That was what we needed to do.

Since I couldn't currently use my vampiric power—the whole idea was for me to face my travails using only human ingenuity.

To do my part as a human being.

"But once they're back home and snug in their beds, I can't just leave them with the traumatic memory of being assaulted in their sleep and getting kidnapped by some stranger."

"Then make them forget. I reckon five or six blows to the head should do the trick."

"…"

Jesus, lady.

Well, Tsukihi had no memories of a similar experience she'd had over the summer…but I had to wonder.

Would it go that smoothly this time around?

No, I could worry about that later—first I had to weather tonight's storm, or there'd be nothing to worry about to begin with.

Given how meticulously our opponent had prepared that code, not to mention all those cranes, that would be no mean feat—but I had to do it. I had to, because I was a person.

Because I was a human being.

"Okay, Ononoki. I'm sorry to ask, but do you think we can take another hop to Kira-Shirahebi Shrine? It's located…"

It wasn't going to be so easy to look up that spot up in the mountains on a smart phone, and we needed to be pretty precise in our landing point, so it was going to be tough, but considering how little time we had and how long it would take to get there otherwise, we had no choice but to travel to our appointed meeting under Ononoki's steam.

With that in mind I started explaining where the shrine was, but Ms. Kagenui cut in. "You might as well stop right there. Tadatsuru sent us this message knowing full well that Yotsugi is here, so approaching from above is out. An aerial assault what comes from the clear blue sky'll leave you too exposed, it'll be over before it starts."

What would be over and why wasn't clear to me—what, were we going to be picked off by anti-aircraft fire? However, she was definitely correct that if we wanted to catch him unawares, arriving at the appointed location from the open sky (the fact that it was night notwithstanding) was not the most advisable strategy.

"Fine, then Ononoki can jump to somewhere near the mountain, and we go on foot the rest of the way…"

Going mountain climbing with Ononoki again?

We had a strange habit of getting lost in the mountains together. Maybe we should join Wandervogel?

"I'll take the normal route," Ms. Kagenui declared, "and join up with you by and by—but don't delay on my account, start the rescue operation when you see fit. Act on your own judgment. Even once I'm there, I probably won't be able to help out the team anyway."

"…"

No, probably not.

Plus, if we waited for Ms. "can't touch the ground" Kagenui to get there, the sun might come up already.

"Roger. Okay then," I said, putting my arms around Ononoki's waist.

It occurred to me each time I did that it must be kind of an indecent sight.

"By the way, Ononoki. Do you think you might be able to keep to a lower altitude? Just a teensy-weensy bit?"

"Can't do a lower altitude," Ononoki said.

Expressionlessly.

"But I can do a lower velocity. Want me to?"

"No." With my face buried in her side and my arms wrapped around her in a bear hug, I shook my head. "That's okay. Blast off!"

015

"Well—what took you so long, Araragi-senpai? My dear Araragi-senpai. I was getting tired of waiting for you."

As Ononoki and I alit from the sky at the foot of the mountain beneath Kita-Shirahebi Shrine, who should be crouching there by the red light at the intersection of the road and the footpath, bip-booping away on her cell phone (I guess she had never changed the factory settings, so the typing sounds were still enabled), but Ogi Oshino.

Ogi Oshino.

She was a freshman who'd transferred to Naoetsu High at the end of last year.

I had no idea how much she meant it when she said, *I was getting tired of waiting for you*—I wasn't even sure what she really meant by it in the first place. But a glance at the screen of her cell phone showed that Ogi wasn't texting away like your average high school girl. Instead, she seemed to be reading an e-book.

Man, people use their cell phones for literally everything these days.

It was no time to start quibbling about why the nickname for smart phone is *sumaho* and not *sumafo*—plus people don't even say smart phone anymore, lately they call them smart devices or whatever.

But maybe it's actually a pretty good idea to start making smartphone screens large enough for e-books—readers care about what kind of tool they use to read "works" that are, ultimately, only data, and when it comes to hardware, familiarity's more important than portability.

"Ogi, hey…"

I released my grip on Ononoki's waist and, getting her to stay there, trotted over to my junior.

Given the current situation, I didn't have time to stand around shooting the breeze, but I couldn't just breeze right by the "I was getting tired of waiting for you" part.

Especially not when it was Ogi Oshino who said it.

Mèmè Oshino's niece.

"It's dangerous for a high school girl to be out here alone this time of night. Always living on the edge, huh? Come on, I'll get you home."

"Hahaha, the same way you just arrived, Araragi-senpai? In a single bound? I'm all set, thanks. Not that I have a home to go to anyway—forget about that, totally didn't mean it, and you're in a hurry anyway, aren't you, Araragi-senpai? I just wanted to give you some words of encouragement on your way to the front lines and have been waiting here since morning."

"Since morning?"

Morning.

This morning it was still up in the air whether I had a reflection or not—well, she was probably just kidding like always. It was obviously one of Ogi's inflammatory jokes. She loved throwing people off balance with a steady stream of flamboyantly outlandish and bizarre humor.

Even if it wasn't since morning, though—she'd probably been there since around seven in the evening. That was the kind of kid she was.

The kind of niece.

Who put people off balance even without making jokes.

As a firm believer in the Nuance Proposition, I assumed that all nieces were also nice, but I guess she was the exception that proved the rule.

"Huh? What happened to your little blond loli slave? I never see you without her. Seems odd, according to your character background, you can't accomplish much of anything without her, Araragi-senpai."

"I didn't use to think that was true," I answered. Honestly. "But yeah, I do now. That's how our characters were written. And you know what? I'm not ashamed of it—nothing wrong with getting a little help from your friends."

"But you overdid it, didn't you? My uncle kept telling you, didn't he? Let's see…what was it again? You know, that catch phrase my uncle is always spouting, um…that one, that one, that one, that one."

There was no way she'd forgotten it.

Nonetheless, Ogi seemed to want to hear it from my lips.

With her train of thought so obvious, so transparent, I actually felt less reluctant to get on board than I would've otherwise. Though maybe she was just taking me for a ride.

"*People can't save other people. I can't save you. You'll just have to go and get saved on your own, Araragi*—something like that, anyway."

"Oh right, right, that's the one. How could I forget. I'm so scatterbrained, forgetting my own uncle's catch phrase."

"Yeah, your uncle's catch phrase. Not mine," I said. "Which is why I feel astonishingly unrepentant about it—*I messed up, I was rash, I should have thought things through, I should have been more prudent*, I don't think any of those things. At all. Though I do feel bad about betraying your uncle's expectations and his faith in me,

Ogi, and honestly I don't know what to say... You know, maybe I did mess up, maybe I was rash, maybe I should have thought things through and been more prudent, but even so—that is, even if I'd known ahead of time, I'm almost positive I would've done exactly the same thing. As Ms. Kagenui said—it's certainly not Oshino's fault for not telling me."

I was intentionally leaving out the most important part.

But I assumed that Ogi already knew everything—she knew my situation, knew the trouble I was in—knew why I didn't regret it. I was pretty sure she did, anyway.

She knew, but was purposely making me go to the trouble of telling her about it—playing with me, you could say.

Outwardly she didn't resemble Oshino, but personality-wise she was the spitting image of that Hawaiian shirt-wearing bastard—though for some reason Hanekawa said they were "nothing alike."

"Absolutely. Even if you'd known, you would've done the same thing, Araragi-senpai—which is the whole point."

"What do you mean, the whole point?"

"I mean the whole point, no more, no less. Which is to say, I'm only here like this, as me, because that aspect of you is so alluring—I think you're the kind of person who's capable, you know, of distorting things."

"Distorting *what* things?"

"I mean, all kinds of things. All kinds of things that aren't supposed to be. And I hate it when things are distorted—or should I say I love it when they're fair and balanced? I want to put things right, is what I'm trying to say."

"..."

To put things right—to put everything in order.

?

"It makes me feel good to put things right—though it seems like you prefer it when things feel a tiny bit bad, Araragi-senpai."

"I don't think you'd get on very well with Hanekawa. We hate

224

those most similar to us, or whatever... She believes so strongly, almost pathologically, that everything 'has to be put right.' Twice as much as anybody else."

"How much is twice as much in cat terms?" asked Ogi, then peered past me at Ononoki, who stood waiting like a doll just as I'd told her to. Still looking at the familiar, Ogi continued, "And here you are, getting a little help from your friend even as we speak. A friend or—tween girl? That's the term you use, right? Asking a teensy little girl like her for help is pitiful."

"Yeah...maybe you're right. Maybe it is pitiful. But you just saw for yourself, the girl is no ordinary—"

"I'm well aware. I've heard about her before."

"?"

Had I told her?

I guess I must've.

But then why call her a teensy little girl, in that case? Talking with Ogi always made me feel like I was lost in the clouds.

Like the conversation would never end, or like I'd never find a place to land.

Not that finding a place to land meant the conversation would end.

What did she know, and what didn't she—and how much had I told her?

"So does having a not-ordinary tween girl on your side make you feel like you've got an army at your back, Araragi-senpai? Well done, tonight'll be another easy victory."

"Easy victory... How dare you. Have you forgotten that until recently I was making the pilgrimage up this very path to Kita-Shi-rahebi Shrine almost every day, and every single time the tables were turned and I barely survived?"

"Yeah? I guess I must've forgotten. I only ever remember the cool things about you, Araragi-senpai."

Ogi played dumb.

That certainly reminded me of her uncle.

Still, I was worried about her future—about what that kind of attitude would do to her future, about whether she had a future at all.

Like I was about Tsukihi.

"Nope, no good," I said. "Maybe I do worry too much about other people—like, what am I doing worrying about other people when I can't even watch out for myself? So see you around, Ogi. At school, I guess."

"But you won't come to school anymore, Araragi-senpai."

Her words stopped me cold.

How can I put this, I felt like I'd been gently but firmly informed that I'd never again return to the familiar halls of Naoetsu High.

But I was reading into it too much, of course, and Ogi continued, "It sucks, why do seniors get to stop coming to school, what kind of a system is that? I wish they'd consider us sad and lonely underclassmen who're feeling left behind. Though it's not like you're banned from attending school, Araragi-senpai, so please come back. Your adorable kohai here is oh so sad and lonely."

"Yeah...well, sorry for ditching you. But with my grades, I have no choice, I have to shut myself up at home and study."

Sounding disappointed, Ogi replied, "Do you really though? It's not just me who's lonely, you know, Kanbaru-senpai's lonely too. I wonder what she's up to right about now."

"Who knows," I said, waving to Ogi as I turned away—though to be honest, I did want to walk her home. "See you around."

"You've really grown up, Araragi-senpai. Don't you think so too?"

"..."

I don't know if she hadn't heard my goodbye or if she'd just ignored it, but Ogi kept on talking even after I turned my back.

"You've really become an adult these past few months, don't you think? You've become very mature. You don't get worked up as easily as you used to. A while back, there's no way you could've stayed so calm in this situation, don't you agree?"

"…"

"I mean look, over spring break, when you thought you'd never become human again, you shut yourself up in the P.E. storage shed and cried. So how come you can keep your cool now? Do you think all the experiences you've had this past year helped you grow, that you've grown up thanks to everything you've had to give up, thanks to the prices you paid? Since you learned the hard way that all your tricks, your games, your workarounds won't get you anywhere? Boy, what a treat. To get to watch someone grow up right. I much prefer a bildungsroman to a success story. There's nothing like watching people learn from their mistakes, and grow through their failures."

"…"

"You failed with Hachikuji and Sengoku, Araragi-senpai, but if that helped you grow, then don't you feel like it was worth it? Ultimately, no one can protect everything or get everything they want, so when you can't get the things you want, when you can't protect the things you love, what's important is how you process that experience. Or I guess people just have certain expectations of how you'll behave in that kind of situation. Life never goes as planned, so on the occasions when it doesn't, what's important is how you avoid being crushed by that, how you turn it into a springboard—right?"

"Maybe so."

It may very well be so.

That my accumulated experiences—my accumulated failures—have matured me. That they've turned me into an adult. In that sense, maybe humans do learn more from failure than from success, from a bildungsroman than from a success-roman.

Maybe, maybe, maybe.

But.

"But even so, Ogi. I refuse to believe that failure and misfortune, sacrifice and sadness, are 'good things'—once you start believing that, you're screwed."

"…"

"I'd always rather mature through success. Duh," I said, returning to where Ononoki stood.

I couldn't waste any more time, and while it was undeniably an abrupt cliffhanger on which to end our conversation, well, we'd see each other again soon.

Whatever happened.

I was pretty sure we'd have to see each other again.

And I doubt the conversation was as much of a cliffhanger as it seemed to me. Since Ogi Oshino saw through you, just like her uncle.

016

"You know, I bet that kid is the one pulling the strings, kind monster sir, the mastermind who hired Tadatsuru to do some aberration elimination, the last boss who's amusing herself by tormenting you," Ononoki opined calmly as we hiked up the mountain path—though when I say mountain path, in fact when I say path, I'm unfortunately not referring to the familiar stairway up to Kita-Shirahebi Shrine.

Having given up on a direct descent from the sky to avoid being seen, what was the point of then approaching via the usual, well-known route—via that stairway on which I had once passed Sengoku? Well, Shinobu probably would've wanted to go that way even knowing that it might be a trap, but at the moment she was recharging her batteries in my shadow, and anyway, I no longer had the power to back up such a bold and brazen approach.

In order to get the drop on Tadatsuru—to take him by surprise, we kept hidden by taking a path that wasn't a path.

Compared to the mountain paths I once trod with Ononoki, and Hachikuji, this was nothing to speak of—or so I told myself, but no matter how much I tried to bolster my spirits, a mountain path at night is straight-up dangerous. Dangerous and scary.

I mean, you had to watch out for snakes on this mountain even in the middle of winter.

Speaking of which, I know the shrine's name is Kita-Shirahebi because Hanekawa told me so, but what's the mountain itself called, I wonder? Never occurred to me to ask.

Hmm.

Is this realization that I don't know something the wisdom of knowing my own ignorance?

"Hm? What did you say, Ononoki?"

"Oh nothing—just a half-baked prediction. Even supposing it were true, what would her motive be? Though I guess she said it herself: she wants to put things right—but what does that even mean? What is right, anyway? I'm an aberration, a shikigami, a corpse, a tsukumogami—that's probably more than enough to qualify me as wrong. It's all smoke and mirrors anyway, I'm just finagling my way through life—or death, I guess, using every trick in the book. But even if I'm an extreme example, isn't the same more or less true of human beings too?"

"…"

"Like, just for instance, kind monster sir—you've fought in the past to protect Tsukihi…right? You fought desperately to protect her secret—but I wonder, did you actually pull it off?"

"What are you trying to say? That I fought for no reason?"

"No, not at all—not at all. I'm just wondering if there really is such a thing as a secret in the first place, a secret that nobody knows. Whether it's really possible for Tsukihi's parents and sister, her classmates and seniors and juniors, in other words for all the people around her, not to know the truth."

"Are you saying I risked my life to protect an open secret?"

If so, that would make me the biggest clown of them all—and yet I couldn't come up with anything to refute Ononoki's theory, at least not right then.

But yes.

It was definitely absurd to imagine that I was the only one who knew my little sister's secret—even if no one knew the truth, the whole truth, how could Tsukihi keep such a massive secret from *everyone* else? It seemed impossible that no one would know.

In fact, it was much more realistic to imagine that everyone knew—but wasn't saying anything.

"I shouldn't let that discourage me, though—because then I'm not alone, then everybody's out to protect Tsukihi."

That thought gave me a thought.

A pretty shameless thought.

That if everyone found out about my situation—maybe they'd protect me as well.

That was probably aiming a little high.

"Listen, I'm just spit-balling, all I'm saying is that maybe it's possible," qualified Ononoki. "At the end of the day, even though everyone's pretty glum, they do their best to seem glib—just enough to make everything seem right with a world where everything really isn't. Just enough to make it seem like there's some kind of order to the universe, to their lives."

"You make it sound like the world is made of papier-mâché."

"More like the painted backdrop to a play—or maybe just a giant international expo. Same goes for Tadatsuru, I bet."

" ... "

"Do you want to hear about him?" asked Ononoki.

Incidentally, our marching order was her in front, trailblazing a path through the trees, and me following behind on the path she created, like a total loser.

Totally reliant on her.

They say snakes bite the second person that comes through, so it's not like I had it easy. But when it came to the requisite power to forge a path up a mountain, I couldn't hold a candle to Ononoki. I had no choice but to follow after her like a loser. How have the mighty fallen. Pitiful, just like Ogi said.

"To be perfectly honest, no, I don't."

"Really? Even though he's abducted three of your dearest people?"

"Yup. For me, the ideal course of events is that we take this Tadatsuru by surprise, snatch the three hostages from under his nose, and come back down the mountain without him ever seeing us or finding out that we were there. Conversely, nothing could make me happier than to get this over with without ever seeing Tadatsuru's face, hearing him speak, or generally knowing anything about him whatsoever."

"That would be wonderful. That would definitely be ideal, tonight, in light of our plight. But that'll just get us through tonight's plight; it won't actually resolve anything. What do they call that—a game of fox and mouse, of tanuki and mouse…"

"A game of cat and mouse."

"Right. That's the one. A game of cat and mouse…an endless string of fruitless battles. Doesn't feel like much of a game, honestly. Though I bet a cat would have a lot of fun with an endless string."

Ononoki unconsciously darted glances in every direction—maybe all this talk of animals made her feel like they were out there somewhere, close by. Not that I'd ever heard anything about foxes or tanuki or even cats on that mountain.

It felt like literally anything could appear out of that darkness, though—who knew it would be so hard to walk at night when you couldn't see in the dark?

It took all my concentration just to keep from tripping.

And I was covered in cuts… Would little wounds like that heal right away, given my current state?

"So I think you're going to have to 'convince' Tadatsuru like you've done in the past—face him, talk it over with him, and make him give it up."

"You might be right…but talking it over isn't actually such a mature solution. Lately I've been thinking that hashing it out is no different from fighting it out, it's just another form of violence. Which is why, to tell the truth, after we recover the hostages I want to shut myself up in my room and let you or Ms. Gaen or Ms. Kagenui take care of the rest."

"That really is the unvarnished truth, isn't it? It makes me happy that you can be so honest with me. Well, it seems like Ms. Gaen is working to protect you, monsieur…this time, anyway. She really seems to have taken a shine to you. Or maybe she feels responsible, in her own way."

"Responsible? For what?"

"Well, I bet she's super-conscious of failing to prevent what happened to Nadeko Sengoku… Ms. Gaen's not the type to regret it, but maybe she's trying to make amends for it. Since the thing with Nadeko Sengoku has been one of the main drivers of your precipitous descent into vampiredom these past few months."

"But that was just a matter of time anyway. Just a question of whether it'd happen sooner or later—even without the whole Sengoku thing, other problems would've cropped up. I would've borrowed Shinobu's power to deal with each of them, gotten complacent about wielding the unbridled fury of my vampiric power, gotten carried away—and lost my humanity. Am I wrong?"

"You're not wrong. Which is why you've got to stop now. Now's the time to give it up. Now that you can see—or, not see, the reflection of your actions, this is your golden opportunity. You said it yourself, monsieur: you probably wouldn't have stopped until these symptoms manifested anyway—but still, I want you to listen to me. I don't want to intrude on your view of life, or death, monsieur, I don't want to trample all over them in muddy shoes, but right now you don't know enough about Tadatsuru. Since whatever happens, I doubt you'll get out of this without exchanging at least a few words with him."

"…"

"Big Sis didn't seem like she wanted me to blab about this to you, she even stopped me from telling you about it earlier, but fortunately Big Sis isn't here right now."

"Wait, hang on a sec, Ononoki. Since you're a shikigami and she's your master, won't anything you do be transmitted straight to her?"

"It sure will."

"Then we're S.O.L., aren't we?"

"She can't hit me if she isn't here."

Ononoki, bloodied but unbowed.

In this age of telecommunications, where people can stay constantly connected regardless of distance, I was envious of her attitude.

Up to and including her indifference to the fact that Ms. Kagenui would probably just hit her later on.

"Tadatsuru, well, it's definitely true that he specializes in immortal aberrations same as Big Sis, but the nuance of 'immortal aberrations' is slightly different for each of them. Slightly, but clearly. Big Sis specializes in immortal but still-living aberrations—because you can't kill something that isn't alive. Tadatsuru primarily deals with dead aberrations. That's the source of the disconnect between them."

"Living immortality and dead immortality? I think I heard something about that somewhere before. The difference between ghosts and zombies or something…"

"Tadatsuru's love is reserved for life in the form of unliving dolls—originally, anyway. But that alone doesn't pay the bills, so he isn't too hung up on it, he does all kinds of odd jobs."

"Yeah, makes sense…totally makes sense. Otherwise, why would he come after a living immortal aberration like me?"

"I'm an artificial aberration, myself."

"…"

I couldn't immediately muster a response to Ononoki suddenly bringing up the subject of her own origins like that.

"It was Ms. Gaen who drafted the plan, just as you'd expect from Izuko Gaen, but it was Big Sis and Deishu Kaiki, along with Mèmè Oshino and Tadatsuru Teori, who carried out the actual creation—I guess it started as a summer research project for a bunch of college students with too much time on their hands, in the beginning of the beginning."

Though that beginning is too far back to have anything to do with me—noted Ononoki. "An artificial tsukumogami—made from the corpse of someone who lived for a hundred years."

"Hunh? I don't get it. I knew Kaiki was involved in your creation, but doesn't that mean Tadatsuru was part of Ms. Gaen's group too?"

"Back then even Ms. Gaen was just a college student. A regular old college student. She wasn't the leader of that faction or group or whatever yet. Though I don't think she thinks of herself that way even now… People just drift apart over time, even if there's no specific falling out. That's how it goes, right?"

Is that how it goes?

Well, the old me might have readily answered yes, but at this point I didn't want to believe it.

I didn't want people, didn't want groups of people, to drift apart.

But even if I didn't want to admit it, I knew somewhere deep inside—deep down in my core, that it was probably true.

Once I graduated from high school and moved away—the relationships I have would change.

And we'd probably drift apart.

"The reason Big Sis and Tadatsuru have bad blood, the reason they still have something like a feud going, the reason Big Sis maintains her unpraiseworthy attitude—I'm the source of all of it. It's a struggle over ownership of this shikigami, of me."

"…"

"Kaiki was the first to renounce his claim, followed by Mèmè Oshino, but…I'll skip that part. Different people have different takes on that part of the story. There are three sides to every story, you know. The me at the beginning and the me now aren't the same aberration anyway."

"Hmm…that definitely sounds complicated. But basically, you're saying that Ms. Kagenui and Tadatsuru ended up fighting over you, and Ms. Kagenui won, like in the Judgment of Solomon."

Though if we're going to liken it to the Judgment of Solomon, it seems highly likely that Ms. Kagenui would've won the tug of war and gotten Ononoki by sheer strength alone. In which case Tadatsuru would have a legitimate gripe.

In any case, a friendship ending over who got to keep a doll reminded me of kids playing house, and it seemed really childish.

"Actually." Ononoki, however, refuted my admittedly very rude surmise regarding Ms. Kagenui, even though I hadn't actually said it out loud. "I picked Big Sis."

"…"

"She tried to push me on Tadatsuru, but—in the end she agreed to take me. Ever since then, she and Tadatsuru have been estranged. Not that they were ever the best of friends, but that was the decisive split…not that a stray like Tadatsuru has much in the way of close friends to begin with."

Just Mèmè Oshino, I guess—if anyone—added Ononoki. That took me by surprise.

The idea of Oshino being close with someone had never occurred to me. He seemed like the kind of guy who didn't have friends—not that I was anyone to talk.

And yet, Mèmè Oshino.

Seemed like the kind of guy who'd intentionally distance himself from anyone who got too close—and *that* I couldn't relate to at all, so maybe I *was* someone to talk.

He was a natural-born hermit—who sucked at goodbyes.

"What I'm getting at—the reason I brought this up so suddenly, monsieur. Is the worst-case scenario," Ononoki said. "The worst-case scenario, where you end up getting into it with Tadatsuru but are no match for him, and Big Sis isn't there in time, the hostages are in mortal peril, you're in mortal peril—when every other option is off the table, when there's nothing to be done about it, I'm almost positive that if I offered myself in return for your lives, Tadatsuru would accept. That's what I wanted to say."

"…"

"He still desires me. I'm pretty sure that's why Big Sis lent me to you—whoa."

Ononoki never looked back at me during this speech, she just went on and on, up and up, walking towards the summit, but as she was saying that last part I grabbed the hem of her longish frilly skirt and lifted it up.

Whoa.

That's what kind of panties Ononoki wears?

That's going to be a real problem when they make a figurine out of her.

"What do you think you're doing, monstieur."

"People who say stupid things get stupid things done to them— heheh. There's no way I'd ever offer you up just to save my hide. I'll thank you not to sell me so short."

"And I'll thank you not to look under my skirt."

"And Ms. Kagenui," I said, reining in Ononoki by her skirt, "didn't lend you to me with that in mind. Obviously, it's because she knew she could trust you with an undependable guy like me. Don't you think?"

"The kind of guy who goes around peeking under tween girls' skirts."

"Come on, I made a good point, so let's forget about the peeking under your skirt part."

"You want me to forget about it? Then let go. If you think I'm as shameless as a doll, you're very much mistaken."

I was?

That sucked, it was Ononoki's shamelessness that I was into…
But then, someone who isn't shameless seeming shameless thanks
to her expressionless face might be even more moé…

With these thoughts in mind, I tugged harder on Ononoki's
skirt and pulled her towards me. With her power, she could've just
planted her feet and dragged me towards her instead, but she didn't
offer any resistance, obligingly walking backwards.

"Ononoki, if we're going to come up with something resembling
a plan of attack, this is it: I'll be the decoy, and while I draw Tadatsuru's attention, you take the opportunity to rescue the hostages. After
you've got them, use 'Unlimited Rulebook' to get as far away as you
can, doesn't matter where—leave me behind at the shrine and split,
in low gear. Some of the girls may pass out from the abrupt shift in
elevation, but at this point we don't have any other choice. I don't
think any of them will die."

"And if they die, they die. Got it."

"No, it wasn't meant to be a callous remark. If they die, do
everything in your power to bring them back to life."

Well, Karen and Kanbaru had extraordinary cardiopulmonary
systems, so I didn't think it would be any worse for them than it was
for me. Which left Tsukihi—and Tsukihi was Tsukihi, so…

"But if it comes to that, what will you do, monstieur? If I leave
you there alone…though I guess there'll be two of you, if we include
the former Heartunderblade. But anyway, I'm your muscle, if I leave
you alone at the shrine with Tadatsuru, what'll you do?"

"I'll be fine. I've got my secret technique: The Kowtow."

"You'd be better off keeping that one secret forever."

Ononoki sighed, still facing forward. I would've liked her to turn
and face me for the sigh, at least, but even without seeing her face I
knew it was expressionless, so it didn't hinder the conversation any.

"A little kowtowing isn't going to work on Tadatsuru. Getting
other people to bow down to him is basically his hobby."

"Sounds like a hell of a guy…but even a guy like that has probably never met someone whose hobby is bowing down to other people."

"I'm glad you're so pleased with yourself..." Ononoki shrugged her shoulders. It was weird, she actually seemed more emotive when you couldn't see her face. "If you're thinking that a sincere—a sincerely sincere apology is going to get you off the hook, monsieur, I'll tell you right now that you're being too optimistic. Sure, Big Sis decided to let you off the hook for the time being, even though you're well on your way to becoming an immortal aberration, but that was only ever her own provisional standard. By Tadatsuru's, even if you're not a vampire right now, the fact that you've ever been one is enough to make you a target."

"Right, the harmless certification carries no weight with him, is that it?"

"More like the harmless certification might work against you. Precisely because no one within Ms. Gaen's network will touch you, he might feel like he's *got* to do it—he's probably chomping at the bit."

"..."

What, like vigilante justice or something?

If so, then I'd really been cast as the villain here.

"Plus, even if your pathetic pleas for mercy convince him not to kill you, never forget that a little girl who used to be a vampire is lurking in your shadow as we speak. On the one in a million, one in a trillion chance that he lets you live, there's no way he'll do the same for Big Sis Shinobu. Absolutely no way. There's another route, though. If you offer up the aberration formerly known as Kissshot Acerolaorion Heartunderblade to Tadatsuru, he might spare you and only you."

"That's never gonna happen, Ononoki, though I might offer myself up for her sake," I said.

In fact, the proposal might have made me grab her by her lapels if I hadn't been prevented from doing so by the fact that my hand was busy holding up her skirt—that, of all things, was out of the question.

"Didn't think so. I wouldn't expect you to offer her if you wouldn't even offer me." Ononoki seemed to have already known what the answer would be when she suggested it, and backed off readily. "But here's the thing, monstieur. You're still talking the same way you always have—you haven't grown up at all. Retaking the three hostages safely, without offering him Shinobu or me, and saving yourself in the bargain—that's nuts. It's like dining and dashing at a fancy restaurant."

"..."

"Everyone's got to pay the appropriate price for their actions— right? Like how you paid for your overreliance on the immortal power of a vampire with your very *humanity*. As long as you don't learn that lesson, monstieur, you're going to keep skipping out on the bill until finally you lose everything."

Weighty words.

Beyond weighty, with the way things were going for me.

"And yet it's hard to take you seriously," I said, "when your panties are showing like that."

"The fact that my panties are showing is one hundred percent your fault, monstieur."

"Don't go blaming everything on me."

"Who else should I blame it on... Though maybe it'd be boring if you became a real adult. Listen, monstieur. If that's how you feel, then I have an alternate plan."

"Alternate plan?"

"No way I'm going to let you be a decoy. Actually, if you want to that badly, I won't stop you, but—if we can get close enough without being detected, how 'bout I go in all Unlimited Rulebooks blazing. A surprise attack. If I can take out Tadatsuru, then we can rescue the three hostages at our leisure."

"Umm..." It did seem like a foolproof plan.

Much like my strategy, it didn't involve talking with him and left no room for bargaining, but her way everything would be settled in an instant.

Even if Tadatsuru had some countermeasures in place against Ononoki, there was no way they could stand up to a surprise attack.

But...

"What'll happen to Tadatsuru? Will he get off with just a flesh wound?"

"He'll die."

"No shit!"

"No good, huh? But he's the kind of guy who kidnaps young girls. I feel like getting blown to smithereens is no more than he deserves."

"No...it's just no good. It's no good, and it's going too far. That would be murder. If we did that—then I'd really lose my humanity."

Lose my humanity, I said to Ononoki—recalling as I did what Oshino once told me.

"A murderer continues to be a human being, though," the familiar disagreed. "Well, I'm not against your pacifist worldview, and anyway, it's needed. I'm happy to hear you say that."

"Hm?"

"I said I'm happy to hear you say that. Listen, monstieur. Do you think you could let go of my skirt already? It's getting chilly down there, I'm worried I'm going to catch cold."

"Catch cold? Can that even happen to a tsukumogami, a shikigami like you?"

"No, but I feel like it's going to. If you want to talk about catching or not catching, though, I'm catching plenty of creepy vibes from you standing there clutching at my skirt for so long, monstieur."

"Oh."

Once she said it, I definitely, or finally caught on to how creepy I was being, and I let go of her skirt and stopped to take a breath.

But.

In retrospect, I really shouldn't have let go of Ononoki's skirt—I absolutely shouldn't have.

I shouldn't have let go no matter what she said.

Because, with Kaiki's influence so strong.

No, you know—forget about that.

Regardless of Kaiki's influence, it would've been easy to figure out what Ononoki was going to do if I'd only thought about it—but I didn't, I just let go of Ononoki's skirt like she asked me to.

017

And finally, just a little bit more commentary on Kita-Shirahebi.

As the sole shrine in town, it was supposedly responsible for maintaining the spiritual stability of the whole area—what "spiritual stability" means is completely opaque to a layman like myself, I can't even begin to guess, but my provisional understanding is that it functioned to keep aberrations and apparitions and so forth from "running amok."

But Kita-Shirahebi gradually lost its ability to carry out that function—people's faith diminished with the passage of time, and the shrine became an empty husk. Plunging headlong into ruination, it was essentially abandoned, becoming instead a kind of spiritual air pocket.

When I first visited the shrine—or its ruins, on instructions from Oshino, even the torii gate seemed likely to collapse at any moment.

The phrase *I can't bear to look* seemed coined for the place.

Forget about maintaining spiritual stability, already a hangout for aberrations by then, it was throwing the surrounding area into spiritual disarray—and the town itself, a ruined shrine sitting at its core, threatened to fall into spiritual disarray as a result.

And what caused all this? Yes, the arrival of the aberration now residing in my shadow: Kissshot Acerolaorion Heartunderblade.

She came from overseas, so maybe emigration is a better word?

Anyway, the arrival of the king of aberrations, the iron-blooded, hot-blooded, yet cold-blooded vampire known as the Aberration Slayer, threw the town into chaos—shook things up like a patch of heavy turbulence. And apparently the center of the chaos was the dysfunctional shrine.

Oshino entrusted me with the duty of sealing up that chaos—and I went there bearing a talisman that was, upon reflection, a total mystery to me, its true nature a little too murky.

I had no real idea how effective the talisman had been, but Oshino assured me that I'd prevented a Great Yokai War—the problem.

The problem came later.

Later, this abandoned shrine was restored—a lowly high school student like yours truly wasn't privy to the kinds of political dealings involved in that process, of course, but in any event, the main hall was rebuilt.

And a new deity was enshrined there.

Originally Shinobu had been scheduled to take up that responsibility, with some implication that she'd be taking responsibility for what she'd wrought, but things didn't go according to plan—which was mostly my fault, I was eventually informed.

And the town was in fact peaceful while the newbie god resided at the shrine—it seems to me. If you define peace as a lack of serious incidents, then sure, it was definitely peaceful. But in the past month, thanks to the meddling of a certain swindler, that god got demoted back to the mortal realm.

All that remained was a nice, new building.

And at last, I arrived at this shrine that was an empty husk once again, this holy ground devoid of a god—after a long and arduous trek up the mountain.

The plan was to approach from the back, but staying on course when you're traversing a mountain forest is no walk in the park, and we chanced upon the summit from a completely different angle.

Specifically, at an angle that was almost perpendicular to the main hall.

If this were a normal hike, haphazard wouldn't even begin to describe it—it was a disastrous flub that warranted turning around and marching straight back down the mountain. But in fact, arriving at the grounds from that angle had its benefits.

Ononoki and I were afforded a perfect side view of the building—and could get a sense of the situation right off the bat.

I, or at least I as I was then, couldn't see very well in the dark, and my vision was somewhat indistinct in the black of the night. But right up until that moment we'd been walking through a forest where I couldn't even see my own feet, so when we emerged onto the shrine grounds and the sky opened up above us, unobstructed by overhanging trees, the visibility was excellent. Felt excellent.

"Is that…Tadatsuru?"

Tadatsuru Teori? The puppeteer—expert? I asked, peering at Ononoki.

"Yup," she affirmed. "Though his hair was different last time I saw him."

"Hmmm…"

This person.

This Tadatsuru Teori—was seated blasphemously upon the shrine's offertory box. And what's more he was sitting cross-legged. What's even more, he was shamelessly folding little men out of origami, the kind with the separate trousers. It was blasphemous, but it also seemed so bold that a god might lose the urge to mete out divine punishment and just tell him *I admire your pluck.* It was so naughty, who wouldn't want to let it slide?

Though of course.

Kita-Shirahebi Shrine found itself without a god at the moment, once again.

Tadatsuru folded the origami men.

Adding the trousers, and then slipping them into the offertory box.

One after another.

I had no idea why he was doing that, and even if the gods didn't punish him, the current shrine attendant was probably going to be pissed off.

"Do you think he's using that as a way of marking time? Like, when the offertory box is full, time's up…"

"Bingo. You know, you're pretty sharp, kind monster sir. Yes, you're looking at one of the corollaries to the law of sines: Tadatsuru's Origami Clock."

"Tadatsuru's… I don't remember them assigning that in trigonometry class. Sounds kinda cool, but…"

I wonder if Yozuru had to cosign the patent application? Okay, enough of my tangents.

This was unexpected…or I guess I just hadn't given it any thought, but Tadatsuru Teori turned out to be a fragile-looking young man.

I'd assumed he'd be the same age as Oshino and Ms. Kagenui, or "thirtysomething" as we put it these days, but he certainly seemed younger than that.

His skin was so pale that I wondered if he was ill, and he was dressed in a plainly cut, plainly colored outfit. If Kaiki was dressed for a funeral, Tadatsuru was dressed like the deceased.

"Does he always look like that?"

"No," said Ononoki. "I think he used to dress more fashionably… …, but no one keeps the same hairstyle or has the same taste in clothes forever."

"Hmm, I suppose you're right."

"Especially a natty dresser like Tadatsuru."

"…"

That burial shroud he was wearing didn't exactly scream good taste—even if it wasn't as bad as Kaiki's funerary suit.

Could that be why Ononoki seemed a little perplexed?

Though speaking of, Oshino showed up for a ceremony there once wearing a Shinto priest's outfit, so maybe that's what was going on. It was a shrine, after all. All the same, I could understand if I was the one wearing a burial shroud, but why Tadatsuru?

He continued to fold little origami men.

And to slip them into the offertory box.

One after another.

I whispered, "No saying when that offertory box is going to be full…but we should assume it could be time's up at any moment. We took too long climbing up here, and it's already almost dawn. We don't have time to waste watching and waiting."

"Almost dawn, huh? But that's actually a good thing for you, isn't it, monsieur? They say the darkest hour is before the dawn, so even though ghosts are supposed to appear when the night's deepest, maybe this is vampire time."

"Well, there you go."

"The candle burns brightest just before it goes out."

"I don't think I like that metaphor."

Plus, I didn't need to be reminded of my little sister's boyfriend. What kind of a name was "Rosokuzawa" anyway? *Candledale*? Weird.

"But all I've got vampire-wise right now is the lack of a reflection, right? I guess I've also got enough of a healing factor that I can cure my wounds by thinking of Hanekawa's breasts."

"I don't want to count that among the powers of the noble vampire, but…yeah. Ironically, the more your immortal nature waxes, the more squarely you fall within Tadatsuru's field of specialization," Ononoki observed, her tone quite sarcastic.

Well, maybe not her tone, given her usual placidity, but she sounded plenty sarcastic.

What, should I have said something about *her* breasts instead? Girls were such a pain. Or maybe boys were just stupid.

"Okay, then what field is he bad at?"

"Good question—straight-up violence, I guess. Humans who wield mystical powers can be surprisingly weak in the face of regular old power. Come on, monsieur. The darkest hour may be before the dawn, but since we can't see when that Origami Clock is going to strike the hour, we should act now. If we're not going with any of the plans I proposed, I assume we're going with your penny-ante decoy strategy?"

"That's what I had in mind."

Her calling it penny-ante did wonders for my morale, but anyway.

"Okay," she went on, "I'm going to circle around to the spot where we originally intended to come out. Then I search the hall where we assume the three girls are being held, and I grab them and use Unlimited Rulebook to get out as fast as possible—sound good?"

"Yeah, sounds good."

"This is basically my first time meeting your sisters and Kanbaru, so if they resist, is it okay for me to shut them up?"

"Of course. Well, as long as you don't mean once and for all," I added just to be on the safe side. "How long do you think it'll take you to march around to the back?"

"Not long, since I'll be on my own. The only reason it took us forever to get here was because I had you underfoot, monsieur."

"Underfoot…"

"Or should I say underskirt? Literally." If she was going to abuse that adverb, she could've just stuck with *underfoot*, but whatever. "If the girls aren't inside the hall, though, that changes things—if I have to search the grounds, it'll take time. Be prepared to keep Tadatsuru talking for at least five minutes. If you haven't seen me take off like a rocket by then, if you don't see a reverse shooting star rising from the earth into the heavens, then they weren't in the hall."

" … "

"I'll search the grounds then, but at that point we'll have to assume the hostages aren't here, that they're confined elsewhere…in which case I'll swoop in, sweep you up, and take off."

"Huh, how come? If they're not here, shouldn't we make Tadatsuru tell us where they're being held?"

"No. Because if they're not here, Tadatsuru's unilateral demand for a parley was made under false pretenses—an inexcusable breach of the rules for an expert. Totally unconventional."

"Unconventional…"

"In other words, he will have done us a favor, monstieur. A big favor, enough for us to send him a thank-you note. Because if it's no holds barred, then Ms. Gaen will give us her full cooperation—since, as you know, she makes maintaining order within our professional sphere her top priority. Tadatsuru may not be part of her network, but she'd never allow such barbarism."

"I see. Well, knowing Ms. Gaen, that sounds about right, but…"

"Mm-hmm. Tadatsuru is well aware of all that, so I doubt he'd do anything to offend Ms. Gaen's principles. He wouldn't do anything to invite her wrath."

"But he's already abducted her lovely niece."

"Since Suruga's last name isn't Gaen, he probably isn't even aware of that. He doesn't even know she's got a monkey's arm. And, well, would her estranged niece's kidnapping even make Ms. Gaen…"

Ononoki didn't finish her sentence, and didn't need to. Ms. Gaen had plenty of goodwill to go around, but that goodwill was a little too good, there was something inorganic and desiccated about it.

Not to say she was cold, but somewhere in there, the thermostat was set too low.

She saw goodwill as a commodity.

Maybe I'm the unfeeling one, saying these things after all she's done for me, but that's my honest opinion.

"So I guess they must be inside the hall," I concluded. "Doesn't seem like there's anywhere else around here you could safely hide three fresh-faced maidens."

You could hide them in the dense undergrowth, but they'd be in danger of being bitten by snakes. That didn't qualify as safe.

"I agree. Okay, commence operations. Monstieur, use your Idle Banter skill to hold Tadatsuru's attention for a full five minutes if you can."

Idle Banter skill? What the hell?

Before I could unleash that retort on Ononoki, she disappeared into the trees. Now I could no longer stay hidden—time to make myself known to Tadatsuru so the shikigami could search the hall.

"My lord."

A voice, from within my shadow.

Shinobu.

"I must warn thee—I value thy life vastly more than I do those of the three abductees, and what's more, I have no particular stake in thee continuing to live it as a human being."

"…"

"Nor, my lord, would it be unwelcome to me if thou didst become a vampire. I shall do my utmost to abide by thy will, of course, but if such should become impossible, I shall not hesitate. If thou shouldst fail in thine effort to buy time and thus become imperiled by this Tadatsuru lout, in that instant shall I drink of thy blood. Should I have to pin thee down by force, still will I taste of it. I shall make thee a vampire, I shall make thee immortal, I shall make thee fight, and I shall make thee victorious."

Though I too will gladly fight, of course, empowered as I will then be, Shinobu footnoted.

"'Tis no concern of mine if thou shouldst lose the last vestiges of thy humanity as a result. No concern at all."

"…"

I nodded.

Got it.

Coming at that moment, it struck me as an effective threat—or maybe as more of a pep talk. I felt like I had to buy that time with my idle banter no matter what.

Even if I refuse to call it a skill.

I *had* spent many long hours idly chatting with all kinds of people—and I'd do my best to have an enjoyable chat with the expert in question as well.

Emerging from the underbrush, I said, "You looking for me? Well, here I am!"

Every guy's got to deliver a line like that at least once in his life.

018

"Hey. Or—well, hey."

This was Tadatsuru's somewhat lackluster greeting as we stood facing each other for the first time. You could hear the lack of enthusiasm in his voice, and he didn't seem particularly surprised to see me emerge suddenly from the forest. I felt like I'd wasted my big line.

His attitude was so, what's the word…apathetic that it seemed like even if I'd appeared from the sky clutching Ononoki, or marched right up the stairs and under the torii, his reaction would've been the same.

No, it wasn't just apathy.

It seemed more like the despondence of a sick man.

"You're…Koyomi Araragi, right?"

"Yeah…I am. I'm Koyomi Araragi," I replied, sauntering towards him, taking time to consider what would be an ideal distance for conversation.

Obviously it would be hard to talk if we were too far apart, but if I got too close it might put him on his guard. Getting too close could invite an attack. Slightly farther away than what seemed like the appropriate distance would be the actual appropriate distance.

"And…you must be Tadatsuru Teori."

"Must I? I suppose I must… I don't know who else I'd be. You the only person, Koyomi Araragi?"

"See for yourself."

It pained me to lie, but Ononoki was presently engaged in a separate activity, and Shinobu was presently submerged in my shadow, nowhere to be seen, so technically it wasn't a lie.

And, for the time being, at least.

I could still consider myself a person.

"Indeed… So how's Yozuru? I guess climbing a mountain would be a real hassle for someone cursed never to set foot on the ground—even if she ran through the treetops like a ninja, it'd probably take her at least another hour to get here…"

Cursed?

Cursed—never to set foot on the ground?

Huh?

Ms. Kagenui wasn't doing it by choice?

"When you say cursed—"

As I spoke, I got close enough to peek into the offertory box where Tadatsuru sat, legs crossed. Well, you could only see inside it from directly above, but the arms of the origami men were *overflowing* a tiny bit from within.

Uh oh… What did that mean? We hadn't been able to tell from farther away, but the Origami Clock was just about full up. What a close shave. If I'd chatted with Ogi any longer, the clock would've struck the appointed hour.

Tadatsuru had stopped folding the figures once I'd appeared… but man, the guy was an origami speed demon.

Maybe the thousand cranes had been prepared ahead of time to be left in Kanbaru's room, but as for these paper men, he must've folded them all right here for the clock system to function…and he'd

254

filled the offertory box in only a few hours.

It hadn't seemed like he was folding them *that* quickly, but…

"—What do you mean? Ms. Kagenui is cursed?"

"She carries a curse, and so do I. A children's game of a curse never to set foot on the ground, for the rest of our lives."

"You too?"

Well, true.

Sitting on the offertory box meant he wasn't standing on the ground. And even after I showed up, he didn't get down to approach me or anything.

Just like Ms. Kagenui.

And yet—

"Since we're at a shrine," explained Tadatsuru, "it might be easiest to compare it to the prohibition against walking down the center of the path to the hall…I guess. Ah, but calling it a curse might just be my persecution complex talking. I'm sure the person who laid it on us would call it a simple balancing of accounts. Yozuru and I got too big for our britches, and this is the price we had to pay—the cost of our actions."

"Like…"

Like, for instance, how I didn't have a reflection anymore because I abused my power as an immortal aberration—that kind of price? The price…forced out of me for going too far—if so.

Then this man.

And Ms. Kagenui… What did they go after—that was so out of their league?

No, hang on.

Didn't I just hear *that story*? And if that was the cause—

"No, this is all wrong," Tadatsuru said, shaking his head.

As though he'd suddenly noticed something.

"I didn't do this because I wanted to chat with you—I abducted those near and dear to you because you're an aberration, and I wanted to get rid of you."

"Well, fair enough... I didn't come here because I wanted to talk with you either."

Even as I said this, I panicked at the abrupt turn the conversation was taking.

In fact, I'd come for precisely that purpose—to keep Tadatsuru busy while Ononoki located and rescued the three girls.

If I had my druthers, I wanted to hear more about this "curse."

How far along the way was she?

How much time had passed?

Dammit, Ononoki had asked me to buy her five minutes, but I hadn't checked my watch before the conversation—I had no idea how long I'd been talking with Tadatsuru.

Two minutes, maybe?

No, that was too generous—wishful thinking. But had one minute passed, at least? Please say yes.

"Why don't you release the hostages? They've got nothing to do with this."

"Nothing to do with it? Come on, you know that's bullshit. Those precious girls of yours, especially that young lady Tsukihi—no."

I'd hoped to buy a little more time with what seemed like the standard template for these situations, but Tadatsuru nipped that in the bud as well, shaking his head once more.

"No, this isn't right, either."

"...?"

"Listen, Araragi, there's something I want to ask you. May I? I promise I'm not just trying to buy time—" What was the guy thinking, what did he mean by that? Seriously, what was he *thinking*—I was the one trying to buy time here.

Ah, okay, maybe he was talking about morning—about buying time until the sun came up? That would make sense. The darkest hour may be before the dawn, but once dawn comes, it's morning. And once morning came, I'd be a whole lot weaker—no, wait a second.

It was more complicated than that.

How much did Tadatsuru know at that point?

Ms. Kagenui and Ononoki and I had talked about suspiciously good timing, about how contrived coincidences are the product of malice—but how much did Tadatsuru know about the timing of all this to begin with?

Did he know—that I had lost my reflection? Or was he under the mistaken impression—that I'd powered up by letting Shinobu suck my blood? Which was it?

Even if he knew that I'd been talking to Ms. Kagenui, did he have a handle on why?

Ouch, why hadn't I thought this over more and analyzed it beforehand? If he didn't know anything about it, I might've fought him, bluffing that I was at full power.

Could it still work?

Though my entrance had been too pedestrian to lend itself to that particular change of plans... Maybe I could ad-lib it somehow?

"What is it you want to ask me?" Whatever the case, Tadatsuru broaching a new topic was more than I could've hoped for, so I responded as calmly and steadily as possible. "Sorry to say there are some questions I can answer, and some I can't."

I tried throwing that *tsundere* line into the mix, but felt surprisingly embarrassed right away.

Tadatsuru didn't comment on it, though, and with a look of feigned innocence, he asked, "What the hell am I doing here?"

That's what he asked me.

"...?"

Huh? I'm sorry?

I wanted to drag out the conversation as much as possible regardless of what he asked me, like the parents of a kidnapped child in a crime drama who get a phone call from the culprits, but clammed up when this question came at me out of left field—even though that was the one thing I absolutely needed to avoid doing.

What the hell am I doing here?

Tadatsuru didn't say another word.

Didn't say another word to me as I stood there in silence.

I didn't say anything either, so the silence dragged out.

I was going to have to be the one to break it.

"What does that mean? Isn't it obvious what you're doing here? Or no, if we're going to split hairs, I don't actually know what you're doing over there. There are plenty of possibilities, plenty of potential scenarios. So that's not a question I can answer. But how can you not know yourself?"

As I spoke, I started to get heated.

Maybe it was proof that Ononoki was right, that I wasn't as grown up as Ogi thought I was.

Whether that was a good thing or a bad thing, I didn't know—

"You're the one who took the initiative to kidnap my little sisters, the wild one *and* the worrisome one, not to mention my friend, and boy is she a handful—and now you're just sitting over there like that. Give up the innocent act, okay? Let them go right now—"

Shut up. Stop talking like that.

Your interlocutor has gone to the trouble of sidetracking the conversation, but all impatient, you're going to force him to get down to business? What the hell happened to your world-renowned Idle Banter skill?

Settle down.

You've already lost enough of your humanity—

That you can't rely on your vampiric power anymore.

"Oh, right. Right, right—I'm the one," said Tadatsuru.

Like he was sick.

"I'm the criminal here."

" . . . "

"If it's bothering you that I'm sitting, I'm happy to stand up—

but listen, Araragi. I'll still be in the dark, whether I'm sitting or standing. Even if I stand up, I won't be able to stand it. Not knowing why I'm here, I mean."

"What..."

What was he saying—was he making fun of me? But I refrained from voicing my uncertainty. Tadatsuru's expression was too serious, he seemed too genuinely worried, for me to say that—for me to get angry about being mocked.

He was troubled.

Like a philosopher.

Like a pessimist.

Or maybe it would be more accurate to say, like he was worn out—it seemed like he hadn't slept in days. It couldn't possibly be from the origami, so what had made him so tired?

So thoroughly exhausted—like a dead man?

"I don't understand. I really don't understand. I don't," he complained.

"What don't you understand? What do you mean by that? You think you can rattle me with all this cryptic muttering? Listen—"

I sounded pissed off, but also started to think this could be pretty great. I crossed my fingers, even. If Tadatsuru, an expert, was this wary of me, it meant he had the wrong idea—he'd misjudged the measly human being called me.

I said, "I don't really know the particulars so maybe I'm speaking out of turn, but the only reason you're here is to exterminate me. Right?"

"Right," he agreed readily. "But I don't understand."

"What don't you?!" my voice finally cracked into a shout.

"Why I would exterminate you."

My confusion just kept mounting—I mean, if anything was obvious, it was that, wasn't it? Ms. Kagenui had explained at length why Tadatsuru would exterminate me—

"I'm an expert, that much at least is certain. An expert who specializes in immortal aberrations—and a stray, an outlaw among outlaws, an expert who cares nothing for certifications of harmlessness, who acts on enmity not ideology, but who possesses a fully developed aesthetic sense, if nothing else. In other words, Araragi, you might say I'm the perfect choice to be cast opposite an exception like yourself."

"..."

"Yes, *cast*—I can't help but feel like someone else has cast me in this little drama. I'm simply the perfect choice to be here, now, to fight you, so I can't help but feel like I've been selected for the role. Like I'm here to meet the exigencies of the situation. No, not just me, Yozuru, and Yotsugi—"

His muttering seemed directed at himself, and I couldn't catch his mood. Talk about incomprehension.

Someone tell me what the hell this guy's going on about.

No.

If I forced myself to think about it, it wasn't such a mystery.

That is, when I looked at it in the light of my own sense of unease—wasn't he describing exactly what I'd been feeling about *this*?

The timing.

The timing was too perfect, which meant it couldn't be worse—wasn't that how I'd been thinking about this suspiciously neat, made-to-order sequence of events?

The terrible timing of an expert who specializes in immortal aberrations kidnapping my little sisters on the very day that I lose my reflection—that twist of fate was a little too perfect to be ascribed to coincidence.

Coincidences are generally a product of malice, and I'd taken the source to be Tadatsuru, Tadatsuru Teori himself. I'd vaguely assumed so—and yet.

If he was experiencing the same sense of unease, then where was the malice coming from?

Whose malice was it?

"Tadatsuru. You're an expert—whatever else you may be, you're an expert, not a hunter. In other words, you did this because a client hired you, right?"

I said this recalling Ononoki's theory that Ogi was the mastermind who'd hired Tadatsuru. Well, it made sense. I was there because Tadatsuru had summoned me, but he was there because someone, whoever, had hired him—

"A client. Yes, there's a client involved, of course there is. But the reason for hiring me seemed like a put-up job as well—in fact, it's as if things have been arranged *just so*, in just the right way. The client could very well have been an actor meant to produce the right plot developments, to create precisely this scene."

"…"

"They say the gods don't gamble, but I feel like someone's been tossing me around the craps table—using my idiosyncrasies, my proclivities, as the raw materials for something. Don't you feel it too, Araragi? Aren't you standing there because you *had no other choice*, because you were compelled, even?"

That's how I feel, at any rate, confessed Tadatsuru.

Gloomily.

Gloominess fit this slender man like a glove.

But his speech didn't suit the occasion, and he failed to convince me. Obviously, I mean cut the crap.

"No other choice? What the hell, you trying to tell me you abducted people who're dear to me because you had no other choice?!"

"Even this. Aren't you angry right now because you're supposed to be? Anger, to go along with the part you've been assigned—how are we any different? We're both just doing what we're meant to be doing. In the places we've been put, in the roles we've been assigned. No ad-libbing allowed."

"What're you talking about… Is this some *all the world's a stage* crap? Keep your clever Shakespeare—"

"The world isn't a stage. But that doesn't mean that people don't love a good story. Yes...people crave drama, don't they? Almost like their bodies crave nutrition. But this drama seems too perfect, too labored—it's hard for me to get into the spirit of the thing. Feels like the fix is in. There's nothing worse than contrived drama."

"What are you trying to say? I don't get it, I really don't—I mean, what is it you want from me?"

"What do I want from you?"

"You've taken hostages. So you must have a demand. Do you want me to meekly submit to my own destruction? Are you saying you'll let them go then?"

It was my job to buy time, so up to that point I'd avoided bringing up the subject of the hostages' wellbeing—avoided confirming that they were safe, but I'd reached the end of that particular rope. I couldn't wait any longer.

The thought that this baffling guy held their lives in his hands was enough to make every hair on my body stand on end.

"Sorry to say I'm not such a coward... If I were the kind of person who would use those girls as a threat rather than a bargaining chip, if I were that aesthetically bankrupt, I'm sure I wouldn't have been cast in this role."

Since Gaen-senpai wouldn't let that slide, he finished.

Gaen-senpai... He called her "senpai."

Despite the fact that he was a stray, not part of her network—of course, the term's sense was arbitrary. Maybe he'd just meant it ironically. But wasn't "senpai" a word people basically used to express some kind of devotion?

"Araragi. Find Oshino," Tadatsuru said.

Out of the blue, without preamble.

"If we can get him involved—I'm certain he can bring some balance to this tale. Not as part of the cast, not as anybody's pawn, but as a neutral party. He's the only one who can do it. Seems like Kaiki did manage to derail things, and thanks to him this shrine is empty again, but he's too much of a contrarian. He's all too proper about being improper—he's so contrarian that he's straightforward. Which is why it's got to be Oshino."

"We've already looked everywhere for Oshino."

I still couldn't get a read on Tadatsuru's intentions—but I wasn't lying. Back when everything was going down with Sengoku, we searched high and low for that Aloha-shirted bastard. Hanekawa even took the search global.

But we didn't come up with even a single clue.

He'd dropped off the face of the earth, like maybe he was dead or something.

"No, we would've had a better chance of finding a clue if he actually were dead... I see, Tadatsuru. Seems like you're friends with Oshino. That's what I heard, anyway. So, by any chance, do you know where he is?"

"If I knew, I wouldn't be here—I wouldn't have had to do this. I wouldn't have had to..."

Do what's right and proper.

Or be right and proper.

With those words, Tadatsuru Teori's motionless hands began to move again, folding little origami men. His dexterity was astounding. While I was considering how to respond, he also finished making the pants for the first one.

And slipped the assembled piece into the offertory box.

It—didn't go all the way in.

It stuck partway out of the box.

The Origami Clock was full to the brim.

"Well, shall we get started? Though really, we're finishing up."

Tadatsuru Teori stood.

Astride the offertory box—sitting cross-legged on it had seemed pretty disrespectful, but now as he unfurled his rangy frame to its full height, it didn't even seem that way anymore. It wasn't disrespectful or blasphemous, it was simply—a person standing on top of an offertory box.

He didn't seem like anything.

But a regular human being.

"Phew…"

Tadatsuru had a piece of origami ready in each hand.

Already folded, each in the shape of a shuriken—were those his weapons?

Well, aren't we refined.

Guess I blew it, I thought to myself.

I felt like we'd had a pretty wide-ranging conversation—definitely wouldn't have been surprised if five minutes had passed, but I hadn't seen Ononoki blast off through the roof of the shrine. There was no way I could have missed it—and since the hall wasn't particularly large, were the girls not inside after all?

Whatever the case, I'd bought all the time I could.

It was time to get started.

I wasn't sure what to do—should I at least lead him on a merry chase around the grounds?

Even if I was done for, I hoped Shinobu could get away, but she herself had nixed that idea…

"Tadatsuru. Wait. Listen to—"

"Can't wait any longer. I'm fed up."

My vain protestations had no effect on Tadatsuru, who spread his arms wide as he spoke. Spread his arms? What was he doing, why would he leave himself so thoroughly open to attack?

Was he luring me in?

If he was, then sadly I lacked the means to take him up on it…

"I'm fed up—with being positioned like a chess piece, moved like a chess piece, and used as a chess piece. *I don't want to help turn you into a vampire*," he went on, an agonized look on his face.

Those words weren't directed at me—what was directed at me was the advice he'd given me before, which he dispensed again now.

"Araragi. Find Oshino. If you don't, then you'll just have to be *proper*. And gain only to lose."

"Tadatsuru, if you're trying to tell me something, could you come out and say it? I'm dumb as a brick, beat around the bush like that and I'll never get it. If there's something you want to ask of me—"

If that was the real reason.

That you took those hostages—then go ahead.

"Just ask it."

"I don't want anything from you. You're—a human being."

"…"

"But I do have a favor to ask—of *you*," Tadatsuru said, smiling. Faintly—ever so faintly.

A masochistic smile that didn't suit his slender frame, that hardly went with it.

"I'm begging you, have mercy on me—and show no mercy," he said quietly.

Ever so calmly, spreading his arms wide.

Leaving his back completely undefended.

"And while I'm at it, I've got another favor to ask. A once-in-a-lifetime request, so please, hear me out. Seems like you've stopped saying it, I guess you started to feel embarrassed or something, but I want to hear that line one more time before the end. I always liked how you, usually so expressionless, tried to be expressive with that line…"

"*Understood.*"

The voice came from behind the offertory box.

From within the shrine hall.

"*Unlimited Rulebook*—he said with a dashing look."

She showed no mercy—which was itself a mercy.

I doubt he even had time to feel any pain.

Yotsugi Ononoki's pointer finger, massively enlarged, smashed through the doors of the shrine and pierced Tadatsuru Teori's body.

265

No.

Blew it to smithereens.

His slender form, like a withered branch, funeral shroud and all—evaporated despite the absence of great heat, like a vampire exposed to direct sunlight.

Not even a drop of blood was spilt.

A human being vaporized by a blunt-force trauma—a most bizarre paranormal phenomenon, aberrational, no doubt.

The sight of Ononoki, lingering expressionlessly in the hall.

Her pointer finger still extended, drove that point home.

A proper application—of the shikigami's secret technique.

"Oh…uh."

What happened?

I was perplexed at how Tadatsuru Teori's body had vanished, almost as if the whole thing was a conjuring trick, but I knew perfectly well what had transpired; it was clear to me, I simply didn't want to understand.

Ononoki ruthlessly said it anyway.

"I killed him."

"…"

"I hit him with maximum force, at point-blank range—you don't need to worry, monstieur, it was my act and mine alone. Even if you'd told me not to, I would've disobeyed you."

"Wh—"

Why did you kill him? was what I wanted to ask, but my mind went blank and I couldn't—no, that wasn't it, the reason was clear.

It was to protect me.

It was to protect the hostages.

I had no right to be outraged—

"Wrong, kind monster sir. I'm sure there was a way to protect you, and to rescue them, without killing him. But I killed him anyway," said Ononoki. Expressionlessly. "Because I'm a monster."

"Ononoki…"

"Don't end up this way, monstieur. If you ever live up to that nickname—you're done as a human."

019

The epilogue, or maybe, the punch line of this story.

The next morning, I woke up to my two little sisters Karen and Tsukihi kicking my ass out of bed—nah, I'd put them back into their futon at Kanbaru's house where they belonged.

And of course I put Kanbaru into the other one. The other one, I made very sure of that.

No matter how thoroughly we searched the shrine afterwards, we couldn't find the trio—it didn't seem like Ononoki had planned to do what she ended up doing. She'd searched for the three girls, just as she'd said she would, just as we'd planned, just as we'd arranged.

But they weren't there.

Karen Araragi, Tsukihi Araragi, and Suruga Kanbaru weren't being held captive in the shrine hall, contrary to our expectations—but neither were they secreted in a thicket somewhere in the forest. As I'd predicted, no one with any decency would confine three girls to those dangerous, snake-infested mountain woods.

Though no one with any decency would have kidnapped them in

the first place—let alone hidden them *in the offertory box.*

Yes, the three had been folded up and stuffed into the offertory box—no wonder the paper men were already spilling out of it. The Origami Clock had been padded from the start.

Much like the time I'd been folded up by Ms. Kagenui, the girls had been carefully folded up into the offertory box—and put to sleep.

Put to sleep.

In other words they were unconscious, but even the heaviest sleeper in the world would wake up if they were snatched out of bed, transported there, and folded up, so something special must have been done to sedate them—to my relief.

Because that meant the girls had been able to finish out the night happily dreaming away, none the wiser. Whatever had been done to them, I didn't think they'd be able to take the change in pressure if we flew home on Ononoki Air, so we took the stairs. I carried Tsukihi on my back, while Ononoki took Karen and Kanbaru.

Ms. Kagenui joined up with us partway down—though she was standing on a tree branch, so "joined" might not be the right word.

She really was running through the treetops...

I had to admit it seemed fun, but it did change my view somewhat to know that she was doing it because she was cursed and not because she wanted to. Ms. Kagenui, however, seemed unaware that I'd found out and just asked Ononoki bluntly, "Did you do it?"

Ononoki's response was equally curt: "Uh huh." And that was all.

She'd done it.

That was all—and in fact, that *was* all that had happened.

After shamelessly lying that she couldn't "do any heavy lifting," Ms. Kagenui headed on up to the summit—there was neither hide nor hair left of Tadatsuru, but as the shikigami's master, there must've been some mopping up left to do.

Surely she wasn't running away because she didn't want to carry someone on her back.

Afterwards, I parted ways with Ononoki in front of the Araragi residence—the sun had risen, but its dazzling morning rays hadn't vaporized me.

"Well, that's a relief, isn't it, kind monster sir. Looks like your body can still withstand the light of day. I guess you belong where the sun shines, for the time being."

That was all Ononoki said before she set off on foot toward the mountain. To return to her master, I imagine. It was probably out of consideration for me that she didn't use *Unlimited Rulebook* to fly there.

I missed my chance to express my gratitude to Ononoki—she'd saved my life, and I should've at least thanked her.

But I hadn't been able to say anything.

I couldn't thank a killer.

And I couldn't rebuke a savior.

I obviously didn't feel like I could, but if I'd been able to rebuke her for killing Tadatsuru—I probably would've felt a lot better.

Still, how could I?

There was no way.

Having allowed Shinobu into my shadow—as a person, where would I get off criticizing Ononoki?

Being a monster, she'd killed someone.

That was all.

Somehow, though—I felt like I wouldn't see Ononoki again. I asked myself what kind of tale this had been, this tale where Tadatsuru had been cast in a "role," and the answer seemed to be that it had been a didactic one, told to make me see an adorable pet doll called Yotsugi Ononoki as a murderous monster.

And because, even if I understood this intellectually, I couldn't overcome my instinctive revulsion, it was a tale that changed my view of her irreparably.

Somehow or other, through this and that.

Whatever finagling and tricks may have been involved.

Yotsugi Ononoki and I had ended up as okay friends, and opening up a rift between us must have been the very goal—of that "Darkness."

Mayoi Hachikuji.

Nadeko Sengoku.

And now Yotsugi Ononoki—I'd become estranged from all of them.

Tadatsuru hadn't resisted sacrificing himself—in fact he'd thrown himself, resignedly, on the funeral pyre.

That's what happened.

And so.

"Here you go. Your Valentine's Day chocolate."

After I finished my morning studies, I went to Tamikura Apartments to have Senjogahara help me with my exam prep, but the moment I arrived she shoved a chocolate into my mouth.

"How is it? Do you like? Is it good? C'mon, Koyokoyo, is it good?" beamed Senjogahara.

Seeing her smile, it sank in that today was Valentine's Day. I'd remembered yesterday, but realized as I chewed that with everything happening since then, I'd completely forgotten.

"Uh huh, it's good."

"Heehee. Yessss!" she exclaimed, pumping her fist.

A year ago she wouldn't have pumped her fist even if you put a gun to her head. What a difference.

But I guess I had changed too. Until a year ago I'd hated special occasions like Valentine's or Mother's Day, or at least they'd been tough for me—this was no longer true, and insofar as human beings are social animals, such a change might be termed, well, *growing up.*

What I needed to share with Senjogahara that day, however, wasn't that sort of change, but the other thing, which you'd be hard pressed to call growing up.

"Come on in, Koyokoyo, there's more where that came from."

"More, huh..."

I started wondering what Shinobu, obsessed as she was with Golden Chocolate donuts, thought about actual chocolates, but I remembered what I needed to tell Senjogahara, and it dragged me back down to earth. I hated to ruin her effervescent mood.

It'd be better to bring it up before we started studying, so when she brought me some tea, I said, "Listen, Senjogahara."

"Mm-hmm."

She listened to everything I had to say—the only thing I had told her thus far was that I didn't have a reflection, so she was hearing the rest of it for the first time—and then she nodded.

Her high spirits indeed departed, but she didn't receive the news as pessimistically as I'd feared. "So, what's the problem with not having a reflection for the rest of your life?" she asked.

"I don't know, I mean... Won't it be really conspicuous? What if people notice?"

"If that's as far as it goes, it doesn't seem so bad. As long as you're reflected in my eyes, who cares about mirrors?"

"..."

I wasn't sure if that was a good line, but at least she was trying to be kind and comforting.

"Though...you *are* going to have to think about the future, that's for sure. If it really is irreversible, I mean. I assume you've already talked to Hanekawa about it?"

"I wouldn't do that before I talked to you. And actually, I wouldn't know what to say... I don't want her to think I'm a fool... Plus, I don't know what's going to happen to me from here on out. Right now I'm just down one reflection, but there isn't any guarantee it'll stay that way. Even if I don't let Shinobu drink my blood, something else might upset the equilibrium."

"Was their expert diagnosis dubious? Do you want to get a second opinion?"

"No, it's how I go about my life that's dubious. I'll go through with the entrance exams, of course... But never knowing how long

I'll be able to maintain a normal life and the good old days is all that I'm sure of."

"Good old days," Senjogahara repeated back to me. "Listen, Araragi. About Kaiki."

"Hunh?" Hearing the name out of nowhere made me jump. If nothing else, it was the first time she ever brought him up to me of her own accord.

"Kaiki was the kind of guy who'd say stuff like that to sound cool. He tended to dismiss things like stability or a quiet life—he never expected life or relationships to stay as they were. Maybe he just hated feeling like he was settling down. And I was stupid enough to think that his attitude was cool—but if that's cool, then I'm glad you're uncool."

"…"

"Don't you think Hanekawa would say the same now? She hasn't been telling you to behave and act proper as much as she used to. She, too—"

This was some point my girlfriend wanted to make badly enough that she was bringing up Hanekawa and even Kaiki, but I'm not sure I understood her.

However.

It got across to me that Senjogahara was trying to get something across to me. That much at least.

I understood.

"Speaking of Hanekawa," I said, "what do you think she's up to today?"

"I dunno… Still on the hunt for Mister Oshino, I bet. It seems like there are certain circumstances only she grasps."

"Find Oshino… That's what Tadatsuru said, maybe it'd be best to talk to Hanekawa about that as well."

There were certain things that only she knew, no doubt.

No mistake about that.

So whatever else was going on, I had to talk with her—however angry with me she might be when I did.

"So I think I'd better talk to her right away, maybe I'll even see her on my way home today."

"Sure. Then I have a favor to ask," Senjogahara said. "Do it tomorrow. Please."

She asked this with a smile, but I don't know, her tone was unexpectedly forceful and compelling, which got across to me too, so I did as she requested and went straight home after we were done studying.

The shoes in the entryway suggested that Karen and Tsukihi were already home from school. They must've gone straight there from Kanbaru's, and well, I'd yet to speak to my sisters since yesterday. So even though their faces were the last thing I wanted to see right after I got home, I thought I'd better check on them—there was a slim chance they might remember last night's events in some kind of middle ground between dream and reality.

"Hey, Karen-chan, Tsukihi-chan."

Calling out both their names like that for the first time in ages, I threw open the door to their room without so much as knocking—and froze.

They were most definitely home.

But behind the pair (who were in the middle of changing out of their uniforms) and propped up on their bunk bed, sat a doll.

An expressionless doll in a frilly skirt.

By which I mean Ononoki.

"Gwa!"

Pratfalling halfway ass over tit, I pushed my way past my shrieking sisters and dashed to where Ononoki was sitting.

"What do you think you're doing?"

"Your sisters won me from the UFO Catcher." I'd asked my question in a hushed voice, and she responded the same way. "Tsukihi is way better at it than you, kind monster sir. It only took her three coins to win me."

"Who cares, that's not the point…"

"The point of this whole thing was to create a rift between you and me, monstieur…so it's Ms. Gaen and Big Sis's judgment that we should defy that plan. They said that until this town is stabilized, I should stick even closer to you than before."

So I'm going to be imposing on your hospitality for a while, Ononoki declared calmly—she calmly, placidly, expressionlessly informed me that she'd be staying in my sisters' room from now on.

"W-Wait a second, you can't be serious!"

"What do you think you're doing, big brother? Quit talking to the doll that *I* won with *my* skill and *my* money."

"Yeah, big brother. For crying out loud, when are you gonna grow up?"

"…"

I shook Ononoki's shoulder as my little sisters showered me with abuse, but she was already back to putting on her doll act.

True, it wasn't exactly an act.

I swear I heard a voice from my shadow say, *Thou hast to be kidding me*—and so.

My, my…

I guess the crazy days weren't quite over yet.

Afterword

They say that "he who laughs last, laughs best," but to me that just seems to mean "never laugh, because you won't be last." And they say that "fortune favors a home filled with laughter," but the road home can be paved with misfortune for those who laugh before they get there. They also say, "demons laugh when we plan for the future," but those demons aren't necessarily the ones laughing last, and they themselves are often laughed at for their own lack of foresight. "He who laughs at a penny will someday cry over one"? Seems like that just amounts to "he who laughs first cries in the end." What the hell is my point, you ask? It's that whether we're talking about an individual life or the entire world, ultimately we don't know how things are going to shake out. Stability, unending peace and quiet, unending hell, these things are all pretty untenable, as it turns out. Then again, there's no guarantee that the duration of "unending" won't be longer than a human life. We don't know what's going to happen tomorrow, and we don't know what's not going to happen tomorrow. Yesterday's pleasure causes today's hell, and today's hell produces tomorrow's heaven. That just keeps on happening, doesn't it? When is *last*, anyway? "All's well that ends well," that's like saying the result is all that matters. The proverb is hardly funny.

And so here we are, the fourteenth volume in the *Monogatari* series. This particular tale starred the expressionless and unlaughing

Miss Yotsugi. Fourteen volumes. Feels kind of excessive, but in the beginning, of course, I hadn't planned for the series to run so long. That is, I hadn't even planned for it to be a series at all. It really snuck up on me! Well, you might wonder, *How could he not realize what was happening*, but I honestly didn't. I still feel like everything's exactly the same as it was when I wrote the first short story, *Hitagi Crab*, but that's ridiculous of course. Generally speaking, consistency and a lack of change are two different things, and I'd like to learn to recognize the difference. I want writing a fourteenth installment to offer its own excitement, just as writing the first one. And of course, I hope there'll be a certain excitement in bringing the series to an end. With that in mind, then, it's time for Koyomi Araragi to pay the piper, and this has been a novel one hundred percent endward bound, *TSUKIMONOGATARI* "Chapter Body: Yotsugi Doll."

She appeared first in the anime, but the cover of this novel is the first time Yotsugi Ononoki has been visually rendered for the books. Thank you very much, Mr. VOFAN. The only books left to go now are *End Tale* and *End Tale (Cont.)*, so please stay with me for the Final Season, kicked off by this installment and featuring the tale's concluding trilogy.*

* The next installment turned out to be the unmentioned *KOYOMIMONOGATARI*, which Vertical will be publishing in two volumes due to its length. In the above, the original's mention of a "thirteenth" installment has been emended to "fourteenth" since the translated edition split *BAKEMONOGATARI* into three rather than two parts.

NISIOISIN

SEASON ONE BOX SET
ISBN 978-1-947194-39-7
$105.65 US | 137.65 CAN

SEASON ONE NOW AVAILABLE

KIZUMONOGATARI
WOUND TALE

BAKEMONOGATARI PARTS 1-3
MONSTER TALE

AS A BOX SET!

NISEMONOGATARI PARTS 1&2
FAKE TALE

NEKOMONOGATARI
CAT TALE (BLACK)

SEASON TWO BOX SET
ISBN 978-1-949980-06-6
$95.70 US | 125.70 CAN

AND DON'T MISS OUT ON

**NEKOMONOGATARI
CAT TALE (WHITE)**

**KABUKIMONOGATARI
DANDY TALE**

**HANAMONOGATARI
FLOWER TALE**

THE SECOND SEASON!

**OTORIMONOGATARI
DECOY TALE**

**ONIMONOGATARI
DEMON TALE**

**KOIMONOGATARI
LOVE TALE**

A SWASHBUCKLING SERIES FROM NISIOISIN!

SWORD TALE

刀語
KATANA
GATARI

HARDCOVER / 3-IN-1 OMNIBUS / ART BY TAKE

KATANAGATARI BRINGS TO LIFE A SWORDLESS 'SWORDS-MAN' AND A SELF-DESCRIBED 'SCHEMER' WHO EMBARK ON A QUEST TO OBTAIN TWELVE PECULIAR MASTERPIECE BLADES.
BRIMMING WITH ACTION, ROMANCE, AND UNEXPECTED WISDOM AND SHOT THROUGH WITH NINJAS, SAMURAIS, AND SECRET MOVES, SWORD TALE IS A MUST-READ FOR ANY FAN OF THE AUTHOR.

ALL FOUR PARTS AVAILABLE NOW!

JOIN THE CLUB

The Dark Star that Shines for You Alone

Ten years ago, Mayumi Dojima saw a star...and she's been searching for it ever since. The mysterious organization that solves (and causes?) all the problems at Yubiwa Academy—the *Pretty Boy Detective Club* is on the case! Five beautiful youths, each more eccentric than the last, united only by their devotion to the aesthetics of mystery-solving. Together they find much, much more than they bargained for.

A new series from the inimitable NISIOISIN!

The Swindler, the Vanishing Man, and the Pretty Boys

The Pretty Boy in the Attic

AVAILABLE NOW!

BAKEMONOGATARI

OH!GREAT

ORIGINAL STORY:
NISIOISIN

ORIGINAL CHARACTER
DESIGN: VOFAN

One day, high-school student Koyomi Araragi catches a girl named Hitagi Senjogahara when she trips.

But—much to his surprise—she doesn't weigh anything. At all.

She says an encounter with a so-called "crab" took away all her weight...

Monsters have been here since the beginning.

Always.

Everywhere.

VOLUMES 1-9 AVAILABLE NOW!

Story by NISIOISIN
Retold by Mitsuru Hattori

imperfect Girl

Legendary novelist NISIOISIN partners up with
Mitsuru Hattori (SANKAREA) in this graphic
novel adaptation of one of NISIOISIN's mystery
novels.

An aspiring novelist witnesses a tragic death, but
that is only the beginning of what will become
a string of traumatic events involving a lonely
elementary school girl.

All 3 Volumes Available!

ZOKU
OWARIMONOGATARI
END TALE (CONT.)
NISIOISIN

VERTICAL.

ZOKU OWARIMONOGATARI
End Tale (Cont.)

NISIOISIN

Art by VOFAN

Translated by Ko Ransom

VERTICAL.

CHAPTER FINAL KOYOMI REVERSE

ZOKU OWARIMONOGATARI

© 2014 NISIOISIN
All rights reserved.

First published in Japan in 2014 by
Kodansha Ltd., Tokyo.
Publication rights for this English edition
arranged through Kodansha Ltd., Tokyo.

Published by Vertical, an imprint of
Kodansha USA Publishing, LLC, 2020

ISBN 978-1-949980-44-8

Manufactured in the United States of America

First Edition

Second Printing

Kodansha USA Publishing, LLC
451 Park Avenue South, 7th Floor
New York, NY 10016

www.readvertical.com

CHAPTER FINAL
KOYOMI REVERSE

MAYOI

HACHIKUJI

001

As you are all aware, Koyomi Araragi's tale has come to an end. There's nothing in particular to add. Much was resolved, and much wasn't. Some matters were put off, but that doesn't change the fact that a stopping point was reached. Just as every beam of light casts a shadow, every beginning has an end. And because there's an end, there's also a new beginning—though a shadow doesn't necessarily mean the presence of light. Or should we say darkness, rather than shadow? Either way, if it's dark beyond the tip of your nose, then that's already darkness.

Still, the way of the world is that endings are far harder than beginnings, and what was begun with ease calls for no small amount of effort to end. For example, as I wrestled to end the many tales that began when I casually saved a vampire on the verge of death, I thought I might die too—in fact, did die a number of times. I couldn't say I acted wisely by any means, nor that I brought it all to a tidy conclusion, but yeah, I can say with certainty that a period in Koyomi Araragi's life came to a close.

I made many mistakes, but that alone is no mistake.

I made no mistake.

And so, what'll begin here is a continuation of the end.

A worldview that wasn't supposed to be. An impossible future.

Shinobu Oshino, the husk of a vampire.

Tsubasa Hanekawa, the class president bewitched by a cat.

Hitagi Senjogahara, the girl caught in a crab's claws.

Mayoi Hachikuji, the ghost led astray by a snail.

Suruga Kanbaru, the junior who wished upon a monkey.

Nadeko Sengoku, the snake enwrapped by a snake, who swallowed a snake.

Karen Araragi, the little sister stung by a bee.

Tsukihi Araragi, the literal phoenix.

Yotsugi Ononoki, the corpse doll.

Sodachi Oikura, the returned childhood friend.

All the experts: Mèmè Oshino, the wandering older dude; Deishu Kaiki, the conman; Yozuru Kagenui, the violent *onmyoji*; Izuko Gaen, the big boss; Tadatsuru Teori, the doll-user.

And Ogi Oshino.

This is their tale—continued.

Call it a free gift if you want, but let's not make light of it—people learn more from defeat than from victory, don't they.

So.

I'll try and take it—as a teachable moment.

002

The next day, I was roused from bed—but not by my little sisters Karen and Tsukihi.

My lovable siblings had warned me:

"You're not in high school anymore. You need to wake up on your own starting tomorrow, okay?"

"Uh huh, Karen's exactly right!"

These were pronouncements that should've been made before I moved on to middle school, at the latest. I found it rather mysterious that Tsukihi was behaving like Karen's lackey, but whatever the case, the next day.

In other words this morning, I woke up on my own—I'd been up late the previous night, and I didn't need to wake up early anymore, so I'd slept in for the first time in a while.

Now, this felt strange.

Not so much because my little sisters didn't come wake me up—but that was part of it, and I knew the exact reason for my odd feeling.

"Oh...right," I muttered absentmindedly.

The words pregnant with emotion—oh, right.

Starting today, I was no longer a senior at Naoetsu High—an

evident, or self-evident fact that still felt more bizarre than any of the mysterious and unfathomable tales of aberrations I'd experienced.

So strange I almost had trouble accepting it.

Speaking of moving on to middle school, or even the time I moved on from it—from Public MS #701 to Naoetsu Private High School—I'd felt no such discomfort whatsoever. Had my time as a student at Naoetsu left that deep of an impression on me?

Especially my final year. The very last one.

It began with a hellish spring break and ended all the way in actual hell. What's more, I survived it all, came out alive, and miraculously graduated, and was ruminating on it now—no, wait, it wasn't such a pretty and emotive reaction.

If we're going to say that a lot happened, a lot happened to me during middle school too. Even elementary was no walk in the park—after recalling my past shenanigans with Oikura, so many connected traumas had come back to me that it felt like I was drowning in a sea of regret every night.

Splashing and gasping for air. Like I was going to suffocate underwater.

If I was going to feel moved about being alive today, I ought to feel moved about being alive yesterday, too—not that anyone, teens included, can live every day moved to their core.

That much sentiment would kill even a vampire.

First off, I hadn't attended the graduation ceremony held at Naoetsu High's gymnasium the day before. Boycotting a commemorative ceremony that marked the end of my high school days makes me sound like quite an anarchist, with my juniors looking up to me, but pair it with the graceful groveling I performed on all fours in the teachers' room later, and it'd be enough to throw water on the flames of a century-long love.

I don't know if I should be sharing this, but at the last moment my alma mater became a forbidden place I never wanted to visit again.

What kind of legend was I leaving behind?

Could I have wound things up in any worse of a way?

I felt like winding a rope around my neck, if anything.

It'd be odd to say that's why—it'd sound like sour grapes, but I'm still saying it—frankly that's why graduating and not being a high schooler anymore was leaving me cold. The most I felt was relief that my little sisters wouldn't be reviving me each morning.

You've served your purpose, my little sisters!

I generally tried my hardest to act cool and wasn't going to let some commencement ceremony make me tear up or gird up—I'd rather get on all fours and grovel. The one clear difference between this graduation and all the graduations before it, though, was not knowing what followed.

A total mystery.

When I graduated elementary, I knew I'd be proceeding normally to #701, and when I graduated at #701, I'd already been accepted by my (then-)dream school, Naoetsu High—in other words, my graduations so far had meant a simple change in title.

A transposition if you want, a mere transfer.

But not this time.

I'd graduated from Naoetsu High but had no idea what would become of me—honestly, at that moment, on March sixteenth, I didn't know if I'd been accepted by my first-choice college.

What came next wasn't settled. My future was uncertain.

True, the same goes for everyone, of course, but having taken these titles for granted, as naturally appearing alongside or together with my name, I was flummoxed when it vanished just as naturally.

Something was off. Stripped of my title, I was nothing. My plain self.

Not a high school student. Not someone preparing for exams.

13

Not a college student, not a rejected applicant.

Not a member of the labor force.

Plain, unbranded Koyomi Araragi—they say you only appreciate how valuable something is after it's gone, but I never imagined losing your guaranteed status in a highly developed modern society would be so disorienting.

To be blunt, I didn't even like Naoetsu High while I was enrolled there. I'd been ready to drop out. Looking back on it, I still couldn't say I led a fulfilling life as a high schooler, not even out of insincere politeness—finally losing the title was so strangely liberating.

Liberating and disorienting.

To make a Kanbaru-like comparison, I was walking down the street butt naked—like oh, I'm nothing but me now.

I should be me no matter how much I dress up, change, or grow—Koyomi Araragi should be just Koyomi Araragi, but part of you seems to be shaped by your surroundings and environment, whether you like it or not.

If a policeman stopped me now for questioning, how should I answer—nah.

My own thoughts made me snicker.

It was funny how funny I felt.

Yeah, maybe I was just getting emotional about graduating from high school—embarrassed and ashamed, loath to admit this bit of childishness, I'd begun splitting a whole head's worth of hairs, that's all. That, or the stress of waiting for my college results was too much, and I was escaping reality by focusing on something other than what was really on my mind—I guess I was able to look at myself pretty objectively these days.

It'd be so presumptuous of me to agonize over a loss of identity, anyway—consider the goddess, scratch that, Hanekawa, who gallantly ventured out into the world as her very own self the day we graduated.

Forget about police questioning, she'd be traveling where militaries might want to have a word with her (why, Hanekawa?). In the end I clung onto her and tried to stop her with tears in my eyes (not exaggerating for effect, I seriously cried) instead of seeing her off with a smile; she was the one with a beaming face as she left on her journey.

She deflected me with ease. Dodged me like it was nothing.

No point going out of my way to feel even lonelier, but eventually, the time she spent in high school with me and Hitagi would become insignificant to her.

That's how I feel. Keenly.

Meanwhile, we'll probably never meet someone as talented as Hanekawa again. *Miss Hanekawa is the real deal. She's made from different stuff than us,* Hitagi once told me, I forget when, and I was beginning to understand what she meant.

Different stuff. Or maybe different tales. In any case, different.

But I couldn't keep whining either, not when my complex about her had given the final stages of my high school life a terrible paint job—if I woke up feeling funny, I had to wipe that feeling away. Maybe I needed to wash my face.

I couldn't waste today—fortunately it was still before noon, even though my sisters hadn't woken me up and I'd let myself sleep in, (literally) unconsciously.

I understand that adults in their prime fire themselves up with the notion that if their life is a day long, they aren't even to noon. For me, it wasn't even noon in the real world—freed from exam prep or not, Koyomi Araragi was too young to be sitting around absently staring at the lawn and sipping tea (should go without saying).

Time to get active.

Why not enjoy my title-less self for a few days? It'd be over in the blink of an eye in retrospect—and if the police pulled me over for questioning, I'd tell them:

"Koyomi Araragi here. Just the man you see."

...It'd probably get me taken downtown.

Maybe they'd call for backup. Maybe they'd surround me.

Thinking such thoughts, I realized leaving the house would be a place to start—it was past breakfast time anyway, and I couldn't borrow the BMX forever, so biking with no particular destination in mind sounded like a plan—and changed out of my pajamas.

I nearly put on my uniform out of habit, please excuse my error as a cute little quirk—wearing the jeans I'd lent Hanekawa back in August, perhaps to share in the good fortunes of the *real deal* who was standing on foreign soil by now, I passed my arms through the sleeves of a shirt.

This seemed to focus my attention at once, and I left my room—my parents would have left for work at this hour, but I wondered what my little sisters were up to.

They were on vacation as well... I thought about peeking into their room before heading down the stairs but decided against it at the last moment.

I wasn't being childish and sulking because they hadn't woken me up. They weren't grade schoolers anymore, either. I was the one who needed to figure out the right distance between us.

Pulling away from them after finally settling our differences and carrying on proper conversations again was a little sad, but older brothers and little sisters are fated to grow apart.

My plan was to stay at home for a little while even if I got accepted into college, but the idea of leaving made me feel a step closer to adulthood than them. I had to encourage them to become self-reliant—or maybe self-supporting. They needed to be able to live without me.

...It did feel like that wouldn't be a problem for them.

In fact, Karen, who'd be starting high school in a month, increasingly acted like a big sister (maybe Tsukihi was behaving like a toady in response, though that was just canceling out her sister's progress). Judging that I didn't need to worry—I ignored their room and walked downstairs.

By the way, there was another person, or rather, body in my little sisters' room, an expressionless and hard-to-define doll that dared freeload there, but I ignored her on a far more fundamental level.

If I exchanged words with that tween, she might end up joining me on my bike ride—best not to offer the kid the chance. Then again, I suppose it was her job since she'd technically been tasked with observing me.

All the more reason for me to tiptoe away from home, and in fact that was the manner in which I headed to the bathroom.

Making sure no one was in the bath (Karen could totally be washing off her sweat after a morning jog), I washed my face. Getting dressed had awakened me, but splashing cold water on my face was really refreshing, a jolt signaling that something new was to come—yeah, I'm a simple man.

I hadn't cut my hair once since spring break, and it'd grown a good bit too long after a year. Wet from the collateral damage of my face-washing, it could even use a hair dryer. When you're washing your face, you gotta be bold, man.

"Phew!"

And so.

I faced forward—and looked into the bathroom sink mirror.

There I was. Koyomi Araragi.

There, laterally inverted and reflected in the mirror, was Koyomi Araragi—which might sound obvious, but until just the other day it wasn't a given.

I should've been sick and tired of seeing my face, but hadn't scrutinized it in a while.

Stuff happened—and I, Koyomi Araragi, had been left without a reflection after February. When I faced a mirror, just the background was reflected, like some sort of special effect (chroma keying, was it?).

Like some vampire of legend.

I didn't appear in mirrors.

How did the story behind the word *narcissist* go, again? Wasn't a youth so enraptured by his own reflection in a spring that he fell in and drowned? Well, I fixed my eyes on that mirror like I never learned the moral.

Gazing.

They say what's essential isn't visible, but the practical thought struck me that the visible can be essential too.

"Hm?"

Still, I had all the opportunities in the world from now on to see this particular face, and whatever unavoidable circumstances may have been involved, a boy graduating from high school, barely post-adolescent, looking at his reflection forever wasn't very cool (if that doll saw me now, she'd be set for material for the rest of my life). I took my eyes off of myself.

But.

My self in the mirror—didn't take my eyes off of me.

"Um...what?"

Lo and behold. As a result of my training, did my movements now exceed the speed of light, leaving my reflection in the dust? I was flummoxed, but this wasn't the case.

I hadn't been training to begin with, and even if some dormant power in me had suddenly awakened, my reflection still didn't trace my movements on second glance.

It didn't reflect me; I wasn't reflected.

It only gazed at me, its eyes fixed on me.

I was looking at me through the mirror. The eyes almost seemed...

I reached a hand toward the surface without meaning to— what an idiot, what was I trying to check? As if the mirror might be a windowpane, and the person I took to be me was outside.

A twin brother? At this point? Were we fluffing up my back-story after all this time? Anyone would call that a stretch—far too after the fact. And anyway, that might work as a trick in a mystery novel, but people don't mistake windows for mirrors in real life.

In fact, it wasn't a windowpane installed there above the sink. Obviously enough—but after touching it, I couldn't call it a mirror, either.

Because—*bloop.*

My finger *broke into* its surface.

Broke in—or *sunk* in, maybe.

Like into some kind of spring—no.

A swamp.

"Shi-Shinobu!" I yelled down at my feet, but it was too late.

The mirror.

The face, the plane of what seemed like a mirror until moments ago, now an unknown substance, was stained purple, and—

003

Stained purple—and I was there in the bathroom.

There in the usual Araragi residence bathroom—having fallen on my butt.

"...Huh?"

Huh?

I stood right up and looked at the mirror, only to find a plain mirror, nothing particularly strange about it—reflecting nothing unusual as it reflected my usual self. I was properly mirrored, and it traced my movements.

An undeniable mirror.

I tried darting around, but it kept up with me—and naturally wasn't stained purple, either. What kind of mirror took on such a color? No matter how I much gazed at it or rubbed it, it was just a plain old mirror.

Wasn't there some phenomenon where if you keep on projecting the same photo onto a screen with an overhead projector, the kind you'd find in a school's AV room, the emitted light gets burned on and doesn't vanish even after you turn the power off? Could what just took place be similar?

Maybe I was just seeing things.

A waking dream? I might hallucinate Hanekawa, but would I really hallucinate me?

Who knew, contrary to my belief that I'd woken myself up by washing my face, maybe I was still half asleep—thinking so, I decided to finish the job and washed my face again, carefully.

Yes, with some refreshing cold water—but no.

That's what I tried to do, but I must've turned the wrong handle on the faucet because I ended up washing my face with scalding water. I accidentally put myself in a variety-show scenario, but it did even more to wake me up than if I'd used cold water, so it was an acceptable outcome.

Hm.

Looking up again, I still found nothing but a plain mirror— the mirror was a mirror, and just a mirror. I'd panicked like I'd encountered yet another aberrational phenomenon, but I suppose such dramatic occurrences aren't common.

I had to admit it felt somehow anticlimactic, or even the slightest bit disappointing, but now that I'd brought an end to my involvement with Ogi, I did want to live in peace for at least a short while.

I'd called out for Shinobu for no good reason, but it looked like I hadn't woken up the nocturnal girl, fortunately. No reaction came from my shadow.

Well, that was good to know. There was no telling how many donuts I'd have to treat the spoilt little girl to if I'd summoned her for no good reason. She was a reliable little girl but came at a high price.

Yes, I'd only seen a shadow and mistaken it for a ghost.

Actually, forget about shadows. How hopeless was I to let my own reflection scare me? While Koyomi Araragi may have spent a year fighting tooth and nail against countless aberrations, he was indeed but a shadow of his former self.

Appalled and disgusted, I picked up a towel and began drying down my hair—my self in the mirror moved in the exact same way, of course, and as he reached out for the hairdryer in the drawer with his left hand, me with my right...

"Oh, Koyomi. You're up."

A voice came from the bath—followed by the sound of the door opening.

It was Karen, the older of my two little sisters.

Huh?

I thought I'd checked before washing my face, but I guess she'd been bathing—where had she hidden that big body of hers? Our bath is of a very standard size, unlike in the anime—had she dived underwater or what?

I take back my earlier statement, she's always going to be a child. I turned to face her, but then...

"Hm?"

I was left at a loss for words—no, maybe it all made sense now. Maybe you could say in *that* case, of course she could've hidden, not just in the tub but anywhere in the room. Karen Araragi, my little sister who'd long outgrown her big brother in height, approaching six feet and still growing.

Karen Araragi's head—was far below mine.

"Hand me my towel, big bro."

While I was speechless, Karen simply had nothing special to say as she pointed at a bath towel atop a shelf—her finger hardly making it up to my face.

She could've reached it if she stood on her tiptoes, but she always knew how to make work for my idle hands—okay, it's an exaggeration that her head was far below mine, but still.

Was she even five foot tall?

She was shorter than Tsukihi... Maybe about Sengoku's height?

"What's the matter, big bro? Is there something on my face?"

Suspicious at last about the way I was sizing her up, she twisted

23

her fresh-from-the-bath body.

"Uh, no," I said, not sure how to reply. I handed her the towel for the time being.

"Tdɐnɹ≳!"

Karen took it and began wiping herself down but finished in no time given how little surface area she had.

"Hɐnb mɘ my qɐnɟiɘƨ ɐnb dɹɐ."

"S-Sure," her big brother obeyed like some kind of servant.

I might have continued to if she asked me to dress her next, but I couldn't stay confused forever.

"Um, Karen...right?" I asked as I handed the girl her underwear.

"Uɳ, χuqƧ I'm Kɐɹɘn. Wɳo ɘlƨɘ woulb I dɘƧ" she answered as if I was making no sense—Karen Araragi.

Yes. Of course.

I could never mistake a member of my family even after a height or size change, but fully acknowledging that fact—if I may, while teenagers get taller, it's highly uncommon for them to get shorter.

Overnight too.

"..."

Not even Karen ordered me to put the bra on her, and as I watched her do it herself, I came upon an awful possibility. Wasn't she about this height back in elementary?

An elementary-aged Karen had—no, no.

Ridiculous. Impossible.

Where was the demand for a lolita Karen?

A child forever, literally? That role belonged to someone, but not her.

As that thought went through my head, I asked, my voice nonchalant: "Karen, how old are you turning next birthday again?"

She fastened the hook of her bra and looked at me, her eyes expecting a birthday present (my aching heart).

"Sixteen," she replied.

Hm. I wasn't dealing with lolita-Karen, after all. Then again, she didn't start wearing a bra until middle school, and while her height was one thing, her legs and torso hadn't filled out like this during elementary. I'd guessed the answer to my question even before I asked, but it did away with the awful possibility of another godforsaken time warp.

Good.

You only need to experience something as absurd as time travel once in your lifetime—in fact, once is once too often. In terms of absurdities, though, my tall little sister shrinking overnight by about a foot rivalled traveling through time.

It wasn't right, no matter how you looked at it.

Oshino had warned me countless times about blaming everything on aberrations. Although I'd faced this side of myself and reflected on it not long ago, might my little sister be the victim of some urban legend? I hesitated to give voice to the thought.

"?"

Since my perplexed look seemed to be perplexing her in turn, she wasn't seeing things the same way... Though I was no longer speechless, I realized I mustn't speak carelessly—Karen didn't know she'd suffered from an aberration even last time around with that bee. She hadn't begun to notice that the Araragi residence was quietly turning into a haunted house, and I wanted her mind and spirit to remain in good health—but did anything like that exist?

An aberration that makes you shorter...

The scariest *yokai* in the world for a short guy like me, but when you think about it, is it really so scary? I've heard of monsters that grow larger like the *mikoshi-nyudo*, but...

"Big bro, what're your plans for today? Going on a date with Miss Senjogahara?"

"N-No, it's not like I have any... I was thinking of maybe

going for a bike ride on my own."

"Huh. Tsukihi and I are gonna go shopping. We're preparing for the start of the disbanding of the club or."

"A-Ah...you really are disbanding, then. Right, at long last you'll be a high schooler, in its full glory, huh?"

"Yeah. Well, I'm more worried about whether Tsukihi's deal is than my own—seems she has a lot to think about."

"Oh..."

I did wonder (in a bad way) about these things to *think about*, but it seemed like we were able to conduct a proper conversation.

Didn't someone say that you don't need to be too scared of aberrations if you can communicate with them?

It did also seem like Karen's voice was somehow flipped around, but maybe that was my imagination. Maybe it was echoing since we were near the bath.

How does a voice get flipped around, anyway?

How do you even express that?

"Well. Actually, you need to leave. Your little sister is in her underwear right now," Karen said after all this time.

Just as she finished putting on her panties.

Perhaps this was her complex, maidenly heart talking; she was fine being seen naked, but not in her underwear. I felt relieved, though—I'd started to wonder how much longer I was going to be there.

Yeah, sure—acting calm, I exited the bathroom.

I'd failed to dry my hair but was no longer in a place to be concerned about that. I climbed straight up the stairs and, without even knocking, opened the door to my little sisters' room that I'd ignored moments ago.

"Ah, big bro! So you're up."

"Do you two think I'm Sleeping Beauty or something?"

Tsukihi Araragi, who had immediately reacted in the same way as Karen—was no one but Tsukihi Araragi.

26

Tsukihi-chan.

Well, I guess Karen was also no one but Karen, but at least Tsukihi hadn't gotten any taller or shorter.

No deviations in her elevation. Normal sized. A 1:1 scale Tsukihi Araragi.

Even her hair was down to her ankles just like the day before—Karen said they were about to go shopping, but Tsukihi still had on the yukata she wore around home.

"What is it? Do you want me to praise you for waking up on your own?"

She laughed, and nothing about her struck me as unusual—if I wanted to nitpick, her voice did sound a little strange, but that had to be my paranoia. If you asked me how exactly, I didn't have a clue.

"Hey, Tsukihi? Is there something a little weird with Karen? I saw her just now in the bathroom—"

"Oh, that's both? I'm next! You know how sweaty I get, morning bath is a must," Tsukihi said, neither listening to a word I said nor answering my question (instead answering a question I hadn't asked) as she passed by me—but no, judging by this line, she hadn't found Karen's height to be strange in the least. She couldn't have gone to bed and gotten up in the same room without noticing…so then, had my eyes fooled me?

Had the steam from the bath refracted the light to make her look shorter or something? If I wanted a logical explanation, sure, but that was such a stretch.

I couldn't come to a logical understanding. Or to any understanding at all.

"Tsu-Tsukihi?" I stopped my sister reflexively.

"Hm? What is it?"

She paused in the hallway and looked back at me, but I didn't know what to say.

Hasn't Karen gotten shorter somehow? Even shorter than you.

Maybe that's what I needed to ask, but she'd doubt my sanity if it was just a misunderstanding on my part.

And so, "You're wearing your yukata wrong again," I pointed out in my desperation.

"Oh? Am I? I always forget which side is supposed to go over the other or what it means I'm messed up—well, it doesn't really matter at all if it's off."

She started undoing her *obi* in spite of the distance that remained between her and the bath as she descended the stairs—how much of a tomboy was she, anyway?

There'd been a change in her attitude lately according to Karen, but I couldn't detect any kind of growth or shift given the way she acted.

Right as I had the unsettling thought that maybe it would've been nice if Ogi had done something about just her...

"Kind monster dink," a voice came from the stuffed doll adorning a corner of my little sisters' now-empty room.

Yotsugi Ononoki—it goes without saying.

The corpse doll. The parting gift left behind by the experts.

"You dip off so much more toward the diap nob edam and emuno tzal gniwodahseroł hcum os... saw tub, seires tho rof tniop sroppirg taen yrterp a ekil mees ti pets or even sis gib ebil desruc yldesoppus—iroeT TsolabazTz dnuora gnikław tzul sih to tsor tho rof tho dnuorg tho no toot... ftamron ekil sesimerq s'enituz taht?"

" ... "

Ononoki seemed the same as ever, making this meta statement the moment Tsukihi left—but something was very different about her tone.

It wasn't her usual monotone.

And—she didn't have on the blank expression she always wore.

Yotsugi Ononoki, the rigor-mortised corpse doll.

Said it with a dashing look, of all things.

004

When I tied things together by explaining that Tadatsuru walked around like normal at the shrine because we were in hell, and that was fine because what happens in the world after death is no longer the rest of your life, Ononoki said, "You're pretty good at maintaining consistency. Fine, I won't keep dodging you about that. Out of pity, I'm directing for you, so keep on with that dink to edit this time around as well." Her look remained dashing, and her appearance had changed too.

She'd always been made to wear a draped skirt that didn't suit her, but today she modeled a pair of pants that reminded me of her master (or "Big Sis" as Ononoki called her), and they fit her surprisingly well. While you could chalk this up to Tsukihi, a good dresser herself, forcing Ononoki to change clothes, the dress-up-doll explanation didn't address her tone or expression.

Don't tell me her head could be swapped out like some kind of action figure.

She wasn't getting off her high horse and continued to nitpick, "Also, I think it's a little difficult to figure out how that final scene is supposed to tie into it or... Flower Tale..."

I walked outside, leaving her behind. Maybe I needed to be

questioning her instead, since she had as many nits to be picked as Karen, but her dashing look was kind of unbelievably irritating, and to be honest, I left home to avoid getting into a fight.

I thought an expressionless character showing an expressive expression for the first time might be charming, but real life didn't follow such dramaturgical rules.

It wasn't like my conversation with Karen had gone well either. Asking someone experiencing an irregularity to account for her situation wasn't going to yield a desirable answer—whether or not she was an expert on aberrations like Ononoki.

I went outside instead of back to my room because my shadow would be more distinct there at this hour. Shinobu didn't wake up earlier when I called for her in the bathroom, and I was glad about it then.

I had no choice but to rely on her powers now, though—on the knowledge of the aberration-slaying vampire who resided in my shadow.

More precisely, a husk of a vampire. The dregs of an iron-blooded, hot-blooded, yet cold-blooded vampire—the former Kissshot Acerolaorion Heartunderblade, whose current name, Shinobu Oshino, I called again, and loudly.

It did feel pretty contradictory to walk out under the sun to summon a vampire (another nit Ononoki would pick at viciously, I'm sure), but in any case, I called out to my shadow.

Yet no reply came—no response.

It seemed she'd fallen into a very deep sleep, though I couldn't blame her.

I'd asked the little girl for way too much the day before when I skipped graduation, and I'd constantly been relying on her until just a day before that as well—there weren't many events in my life I didn't rely on her for. I'd caused her a lot of trouble, so of course she'd be slumbering deep enough to require more than a poke to wake up since things had finally come to a stopping point, or maybe a breather today.

I had no choice but to rely on her but could only yell at my own shadow right outside my house for so long, considering how it looked... I did also want to let her, my precious partner, rest.

At the same time, when there was no guarantee that she hadn't been affected by this sudden change besetting my home, how could I wait until she woke up?

Was Shinobu not responding because something weird happened to her, just like with Karen and Ononoki? If that was why, how could I take it easy and wait until the cows came home? I'm no cattle rancher. Good things might come to those who wait, but that's not what I needed at the moment. Sure, maybe I was worrying too much, given that Tsukihi hadn't been affected at all.

In light of all this, I thought, *Then what about me?* As far as I could tell from the way I felt and what I saw in the mirror, there seemed to be nothing wrong with me, but what could be less reliable in a situation like this than a self-administered check?

Karen and Ononoki didn't seem to find their changes odd— zero reported symptoms. If anything, they all but told me they'd always been this short, that their dashing look always had pissed me off this much.

Maybe something about me changed overnight, and I just hadn't noticed. My suspicions threatened to be boundless once I got going.

Had I lost not just the title of high school student but something more important without ever noticing? Should I be taller, for instance, or more muscular or broad-shouldered, or smarter? Possible.

Quite possible.

I might even have been Tsubasa Hanekawa until yesterday... Okay, if I were her yesterday, I wouldn't have committed a huge blunder like turning into Koyomi Araragi today. I could rule that one out, at least.

There's of course Gregor Samsa, who woke up to discover he wasn't just someone else, but a bug... By the way, speaking of Franz Kafka, the author of *The Metamorphosis*, according to his bio he asked his best friend to dispose of his novels posthumously. The friend went against his wishes and released them, thanks to which the author is famous today.

Could you really call someone like that your best friend? After learning about Kafka's apparently difficult personality, though, I began thinking that "please dispose of my novels" might have also meant "but, well, you know." If this friend understood the subtext, then he was a true friend indeed.

A regular Pythias.

In any case, while there's an argument to be had about *The Metamorphosis* thematizing how wonderful and adorable little sisters are (please don't have it), this wasn't language arts class— wait, does foreign literature even go under language arts?

No good, I couldn't focus my thoughts.

Proof of my confusion—maybe I needed to go back inside and ask Ononoki, an expert, for her opinion despite everything. Between that enraging dashing look and her arrogant tone, though, I wasn't confident that me and my lack of maturity could stand her for too long.

Graduating high school hadn't made me that much of an adult.

Somehow, her expressionless face and flat tone had done a good job of neutralizing her character and let her settle into the position of *quirky girl*. Once she stepped up to operate on the same level as everyone else, the girl just had a nasty personality...

And anyway, I probably couldn't expect a satisfying answer from Ononoki when it was clear as day that something about her was off—physician, heal thyself.

That said, Oshino and Miss Gaen were no longer in town, and as for Miss Kagenui, she was at the North Pole—I couldn't rely on any experts.

Strictly speaking, I suspected the phone number Miss Gaen had given me still worked, but if the lady who "knew everything" hadn't called me, it probably meant I needed to do something about this on my own—not to mention, once you rashly asked her for help, she had a track record of demanding compensation so ridiculous you had to wonder out loud if she was being serious.

Leaning on a certain friend of mine who may not know everything but did know what she knew seemed like an option, but the thought of calling her when she was overseas gave me pause.

Not in the sense that it'd run up my phone bill. I didn't even know if whatever country Hanekawa was in right now had cell service.

In which case, I had no choice but to wait until night when Shinobu would be active again. Yup, I needed to wait for the aberration-slaying girl, to whom Oshino had imparted some amount of expert knowledge through special tutoring sessions, unless I was going to turn to the gods.

"Hm? Oh, right," I realized at this late stage. She was no expert, nor did I expect her to have any expert knowledge, but there was a god in this town now, wasn't there?

Yes, the grand deity known as Mayoi Hachikuji—okay, maybe not a grand deity, but the young ghost girl who'd been newly deified at Kita-Shirahebi Shrine to quell the strange happenings in town. She must've received some schooling from Miss Gaen before being placed atop that mountain to watch over us all.

Maybe she knew something.

Actually, these abnormalities could be a kind of side effect of turning her into a god half by force—an accidental solution owing to an impulsive act on my part, it had seemed like a sharp idea. Thinking about it with a calmer head though, deifying a young girl who'd been sent to hell sounded like a stretch even for an empty shrine.

Hachikuji becoming a god and Karen getting shorter, or Ononoki starting to have expressions, had no clear causal link. The reason might be entirely different, but since I had no clues at the moment, talking to her was worth the trouble.

Abnormalities aside, I wanted to tease the young girl at Kita-Shirahebi for her divine antics. And scold her if she was getting carried away.

As a friend, of course!

Oddly enough, I now had a destination for my bike ride—and no sooner than I'd decided, I straddled the BMX I still had on loan from Ogi and began pedaling toward the mountain that the shrine presides over. While I wouldn't be able to go up it on a bike (well, maybe on a BMX, since they say it can climb stairs, but not with my skills...), I'd still get to the entrance faster despite the slopes.

Or so I thought, but either I got flustered or wasn't used to a BMX, not to mention the several-month gap in my riding career—because it took me longer than I expected. Was it a lie that you never forget how to ride a bike?

I nearly tipped over again and again and got lost too. I hadn't heard about any barrier being placed on the mountain, but maybe, as someone with an aberrational nature, I was being prevented from approaching the shrine, holy ground where a god had alighted.

If that was the case, I couldn't just drop by casually. Since a vampire dwelled in my shadow, maybe it was to be expected, but being kept out of holy ground is pretty depressing...

I thought this as I chained up the now-parked bike (who knew how gleefully Ogi would browbeat me if I let it get stolen) and began up the familiar mountain path, which I could honestly say was much easier than half a year ago thanks to my trips up and down it. Not a game trail, but a me trail. By the time I finished my hike and passed through the *torii* gate, the sun was directly overhead.

In other words, it was noon—the time of day when aberrations seemed least likely to appear, but then not every aberration is nocturnal.

No one was on the well-kept grounds of Kita-Shirahebi, rebuilt last year. Not many people would visit a location as secluded as this, god or no. We needed to come up with something for the shrine to be worshiped again... There was probably nothing I could do, but given the events that led to Hachikuji becoming a god, I wanted to help in some way.

Maybe they could try selling *omikuji* fortunes.

Hachikuji omikuji—I liked how that sounded.

So what if it sounds good, you may ask, but it'd matter to Hachikuji.

I ought to broach the subject with her after discussing my issue—but then the all-important factor, Mayoi Hachikuji, wasn't even around... Maybe she was inside the hall? I'd met her in town only yesterday, so maybe she was out there observing, or just talking a walk? Something about a god who liked going out on the town seemed to lack gravitas, or to be too footloose...

"Hachikujiiii? Hello-o-o?" I called out from in front of the offering box. Even if she was inside, I couldn't just barge in. Maybe I shouldn't be scared when I had an aberration living in my shadow, but I still hesitated, fearing the divine punishment that would surely come. If Hachikuji was delivering it, not only would she not go easy on me, she'd be merciless.

Ah, right—how about putting some money in the offering box? Thinking back to when we first met, her reaction to hard cash was anything but cold... Heheh, it's not every day you come up with a novel idea like summoning a god with an offering.

How I've grown. Apparently, an unpleasant conman had visited this shrine on a regular basis since New Year's, but what set us apart was that only I had these dazzlingly original ideas...

With that pleasing thought, I took out my wallet. Having grabbed it as I left home and stuffed it in my pocket, I didn't know how much money I had...but yeah, this was a shrine.

The standard good-luck offering of a five-yen coin ought to do.

Alas, I happened to be out of five-yen coins—but did find four one-yen coins, which might serve as a suitable substitute. Four or *shi* is considered unlucky, given that it's homophonous with the word for death in Japanese, but maybe it was fine because it also alliterated with *shojo*, girl? The greater number of coins made you feel like you're getting more, yes?

I felt for a moment like I might be messing up, but pluckily refusing to be distracted by any figment of the imagination, I tossed the four coins into the offering box—then gave two bows, two claps, and one bow, or whatever. I'd been taught what to do but couldn't remember, so I bowed my own way to get across at least the sentiment and rang the bell extra hard.

Nothing in particular happened.

Nothing like the shrine's door opening and a god storming out—I almost wanted a refund but didn't even have anyone to complain to.

Was she really taking a walk? She wasn't the type to sit still, whether she'd ascended to godhood or descended to hell—my only option now would be to climb down the mountain and wander aimlessly around town.

Mildly despondent, I thought maybe I ought to see it as a good thing that she was being her active self even after becoming a god, and began to turn back when—

"Awɐwɐɡiiiii!"

Someone grabbed me from behind, tackling me. Not remotely ready for this full-body attack, I fell to the ground and panicked, only to be locked in a submission hold.

"Eeeek!" I shrieked, but the maneuver was in place before I knew it—what were these moves, military combatives? Every joint in my body had been locked into place.

I could neither resist nor run.

My opponent seemed to be about my size but was on a different level in terms of proficiency. I couldn't find any opening I could use to move—the submission hold affected my entire body as though I'd been vacuum-packed.

"You came to visit me! I'm so happy!!"

"Eeeek!"

No, forget about the joint lock. It was just creepy how my assailant didn't hold back and glued fast until our cheeks rubbed, which is why I screamed. I felt like a slug was crawling along my body.

Wh-Who was it? What was it? What exactly was going on?

Paying no mind to my utter confusion, the criminal—I see nothing wrong with using that word here—pressed our bodies together even more tightly.

"I'm so happy, I'm so happy, I'm so happy!! Aww, I was so lonely! I don't mind having a dog, but I didn't get any visitors at all! I felt like giving up on the whole dog thing and climbing down the mountain... C'mon, lady! Come closer and let me love you and lick you more!"

"Eeeek! Eeeek!"

"Hey, stop doing violent things lady! [tsut the violence! Yeah,] I'll be everything to you when I take it all away from you!"

"Eeeek!"

Wait... Lady?

My ears picked up this scrap of a word, and I tried to look behind me—only my eyes moved since my neck was locked too—but indeed, the perp who'd shoved me onto these holy grounds, and who was wound around my body, was a woman.

She had to be pretty muscular to have the strength, but actually, I did sense a kind of smoothness and softness as well—even if I was in pain more than anything else.

...Hold on, I knew this person.

"Graaah!"

"Aiə!"

Biting the earlobe in front of my face finally made her get away with a (feminine) cry—and stand slim and tall.

Her hair gathered together in the back, her balanced features betraying none of the perversion she'd been guilty of—yes.

I'd met this person before.

I'd met her before—in a different timeline.

"M-Miss...Mayoi Hachikuji?"

"Yes," she replied with a smile, her arms crossed as if to emphasize her developed bust. "Miss Mayoi Hachikuji, twenty-one years old."

005

I think this goes without saying.

But the Mayoi I knew was a ten-year-old little girl, not a twenty-one-year-old pervert—excuse me, lady.

Yet the young woman standing in front of me was Mayoi Hachikuji—and I knew this to be true.

She'd lost her life in a traffic accident nearly a dozen years ago, *but if she'd avoided that accident*—she'd have turned out like this lady.

I'd seen her thriving and surviving even in a world that had fallen into ruin—though her airs then seemed a little different (or rather, her personality had undergone a total change). But if we were to go by simple appearances, this was exactly how she looked.

"What is it, Awawagi? Why're you looking at me with so much passion in your eyes? Stop it, you know I'm everyone's big sister. I'm not going to do your dna stuff alone, okay?"

"First off, please stop calling me Awawagi."

Umm.

I put my mind to work—or at least put my hands to my head.

I'd started to get an idea of what was going on but was having trouble making sense of it all... The change to Karen's body, the change in Ononoki's personality, and now Hachikuji… In other words, this problem extended beyond the Araragi residence, to *the entire world*… But then what about Tsukihi?

Nothing had changed about her. Or maybe I just didn't notice?

"Araragi." Hachikuji…no, Miss Hachikuji spoke my name, this time in a slightly different tone. "You seem kind of serious today. You know I'm always here to listen if anything's worrying you."

"…"

This made me certain I was dealing with Hachikuji—as soon as she treated me with kindness, I felt like relying on her.

But just as I couldn't rely on Ononoki, I doubted I could get anything useful out of Hachikuji, given that she herself had changed…

At the same time, if a change had come upon the entire world, it didn't matter who I talked to, it'd be true of everyone—maybe that even included Shinobu, once she woke up at night.

In that case, I needed to ratchet up my readiness another notch.

"There's something I was hoping to check with you, if that's all right," I said. It did feel a little odd to be speaking politely to Hachikuji, but what choice did I have? I had to mind my tone with a twenty-one year old. "You're a…god, yes? Miss Mayoi."

"Uh huh, I am. Why ask that now? You made me into a god, interrogated yeah—yeah you already forgot?"

"…"

We were on the same page there. The details didn't seem to have changed much, either.

Which meant that this Miss Hachikuji was an aberration, and not alive—come to think of it, the parallel world where she survived to twenty-one instead of dying at ten was in exchange for a world in ruins.

40

Judging from the scenery as I rode toward this mountain, my town was fine—I'd had the same fear facing the shortened Karen, but it seemed I could count out a scenario where I was back in that other timeline.

But even if she was divine, there was the precedent set by Sengoku. Miss Hachikuji could be a god incarnate, or a living god, and not necessarily dead.

Hmmm.

I couldn't just ask her to her face if she was alive… She seemed to be, going by how her body felt as she held me (not to mention having bitten her earlobe), but even when she was a little ghost girl, I could touch her like normal, so that wasn't a valid criterion.

"Яɘɒllʏ, Aгɒгɒgi. Wdɒ1'ƨ ɘdı mɒ11ɘ1? Dib ʏou gгɒɓɘ ʏouг own uwo ɿuoʏ bib ?ɿɘ11ɒm ɘdı ƨ'1ɒdW .igɒɿɒɿA ,ʏllɒɘЯ ɘ11ɘ1ɔ .ɘ1ɘ1ɘ ,1ɒdT ?ƨmɒxɘ ɿuoʏ bɘdmob uoʏ ɘƨilɒɘ1 1ɒdı bnɒ gniʞ-1ɒ1 nI .1ɒdı ɘƨɒɔ ɿuoʏ gib ƨiƨ lliw ob ɘvɘɿʏ1ding ɘdƨ nɒɔ 10 mɒʞu oʏ 1ɒdı .lɘɘl bɘ11ɘ1"

"No, that's not it… Um…"

Then, after all my hesitation.

I ended up revealing everything to Miss Hachikuji, everything being all the abnormalities since the morning: Karen's body, Ononoki's expression and tone (also, I keep forgetting, but her clothes were a little different too)—and her own transformation from the Hachikuji I knew.

The fact that Shinobu didn't wake up even when I called.

Though perhaps unrelated, I also threw in the weird sense I got from my reflection in the mirror when I washed my face—I thought it might help gauge my mental state.

…The whole situation seemed kind of serious to me, but when I talked about it out loud, it sounded so comical, or just all in my head.

If I were told such a frivolous story, at least, I might dismiss it as "the sort of thing that happens when you're a teen"—what was it called again, jamais vu? The feeling that you're learning about something for the first time when in fact you've long known it to be true. Maybe Karen was always that tall, and Ononoki always that kind of character.

Even with Hachikuji, was I just under the impression she was ten, when she was actually twenty-one? Well, that was true, in a sense.

What about Shinobu? Once, she didn't come out of my shadow no matter how many times I called, but our link had been severed by the Darkness. Did it stay severed ever since or something?

That definitely made me too careless for my own good and also counted as its own kind of bad news. But even if it wasn't déjà vu or jamais vu, there remained a logical explanation for my predicament.

A way to make sense of the nonsensical situation.

The hypothesis was no less hard for me to accept—or believe, but nonetheless.

"Huh. Araragi…"

Nonetheless, having heard me out, Miss Hachikuji began speaking with a troubled expression (which made her look surprisingly intelligent).

"Sorry, that's right, that your little sister, Karen, got shorter. Expressionless Ononoki turned expressive—and the former Expressionless Ononoki now answered to Hachikuji, while I'll, you weren't watching, Hachikuji turned into Big sis Mayoi?"

"Y-Yes… That's it."

"So—everyone's been reversed in some way. Can we say that, right?"

"Reversed… Um."

Could we?

No—putting aside Shinobu (who could just be asleep), it wasn't *everyone* when nothing had changed about Tsukihi, who wasn't "reversed" or anything. That bit made the situation that

42

much trickier…

"You're right. We can think about that later, but wasn't Tsu-kihi wearing her yukata backwards?"

"Backwards? Oh."

The left side of her yukata over the right.

That's how it looked—and I let her know, because that's how you dress the dead.

I'd sort of sneered, thinking that she didn't know how to wear traditional clothes despite loving them so much, but if that was the change that overtook her…

It was the easiest to understand, in a way.

Reversed, or maybe inverted?

Inverted—*as if I'd seen her in a mirror.*

Not a delusion, but a reflection.

Left switched places with right. It also explained Shinobu's stubborn silence—*vampires aren't reflected in mirrors,* after all.

Something that I'd experienced myself recently—in other words.

"In other words, Araragi. It's not that everyone changed, or rather—it's just that you've changed. It's just that you see it over on this side," Miss Hachikuji declared.

A divine revelation.

"You're inside a mirror now."

"…!"

Faced head-on with a conclusion I'd quietly arrived at a while ago, I couldn't help but blurt out—

"A-Are we sure that lukewarm of a setup will do?!"

006

Lukewarm or not, whether it did it or not, this setup—or rather fact was something I needed to accept.

Having been told this, I took a look at the gate to find that it said "Ʞi̱ʁ-Ƨdiɿɛʜɘdi Ƨdɿinɘ." Left and right were indeed inverted. I wasn't going to fish them out to check, but when I'd thrown my offering into the box, something had felt wrong—I suspected that left and right had been flipped for the number on the coins.

As for my difficulties riding the BMX to the mountain, the bike's structure had been mirrored—the left brake controlling the front wheel and the right brake controlling the rear more than sufficed to make it a new experience, and if the town had been flipped around as well, that explained how I'd gotten lost. Of course, hearing it from Mayoi Hachikuji, the once-lost girl, felt backwards in its own way.

I confused hot for cold when I washed my face because the handles had switched places... And everyone's voice sounded somehow reverberant—or reversed, for the same reason.

Right. In hindsight there'd been hints all over the place, and as a professed fan of *Doraemon: Nobita and the Steel Troops*, about a mirror world, I should've noticed sooner.

An upside-down world.

Karen, Ononoki, Hachikuji—were inverted here.

I also needed to accept that Shinobu wasn't in my shadow. Vampires, who aren't reflected in mirrors, didn't exist in this world.

It was a world with a different worldview.

I still didn't get what was up with Tsukihi. She'd only worn her yukata in the wrong order.

"B-But," I objected, "going from my big all-out fight with Ogi, which had me going to hell and back, to something this lukewarm..."

"I think it's fine," Miss Hachikuji answered with an encouraging smile. "Chilled-out mascot characters have been all the rage, so what's wrong with a chilled-out world? A churld."

She was trying to encourage me...but "churld"?

It sounded so lame.

If you're curious, Miss Hachikuji's line here and the ones that follow were all still reversed. I concede that it's hard to read, so I'm using my narrator privileges to translate them.

"Ogi, huh," she muttered meaningfully but continued with a shrug. "I got carried away and said you're 'inside a mirror'—but I don't know. For us, *this* is the normal world, and *that* side is in a mirror, to match your perception. If you'll allow me to spin this, I don't think it's as lukewarm as you think. Aren't you in a pretty bad spot?"

Her assurance that it wasn't lukewarm freaked me out just as much. "Wh-What do you mean?"

"There's no way for you to return to what you'd call your original world, is there?"

"..."

A way to return?

Ah. Distracted by the lukewarm setup, I hadn't gotten around to wondering about that. If I was in another world, then I had to go on to return to my world—how?

The Araragi residence's bathroom mirror.

If I'd been pulled into "this side" when I touched it, returning from there seemed like a possibility. But right after I sensed something was off, I checked it myself—and found it to be a plain mirror.

Or found it had returned to being a plain mirror—I couldn't come and go between worlds simply by touching its surface.

Had a temporarily opened gate been closed, or was it a one-way path? I started to fret.

I was no Hanekawa, but I'd been stranded alone in a foreign country—even at a sunny tourist destination, being in another culture can be unsettling.

Yes, this reminded me of how I'd been sent to different realms, whether by traveling through time or by going to hell. The very rules of the world were different...

A world with different rules.

People I was familiar with becoming different made this more than a matter of, say, just trying to stay calm. The fact that Karen was shorter than me, for example, scrambled one of the factors that defined me (my complex over being outgrown by my sister) and messed with my ability to maintain my ego and sense of self.

...I guess I wasn't unhappy about getting to meet the grown-up Mayoi Hachikuji again, even if it was under these circumstances—then.

"Hup."

Then Miss Hachikuji pulled me close, not with another rough hug, but gently, as if to embrace my head.

"It's okay, it's okay. No need for you to be so scared. You're okay, Araragi, I promise."

Based on nothing, but it's also a divine pronouncement, assured Miss Hachikuji, patting my head repeatedly.

I felt embarrassed, almost as if I was being nursed, and wanted to pull myself free—I was too old to be comforted like this, I'd just graduated from high school a day ago—but reconsidered and let her have her way with me.

This was another world, even a kind of illusion reflected in a mirror, but that's how much seeing a grown Hachikuji meant to me. I was like a kid brother for this twenty-one year old, but having known her ten-year-old self best, it felt like seeing a daughter grow up.

In that sense, we were on totally different emotional pages, but even the ten-year-old Hachikuji had always comforted me, saved me. This wasn't much of a change.

"Still, what to do?" Miss Hachikuji freed me at last and began wandering around the shrine grounds—a little too restlessly for a goddess. Circling around with me as her focal point, she asked without slowing her pace: "You traveled back in time by eleven years once, to rescue me from my traffic accident. Remind me, how did you go there, and how did you get back?"

Her history, the tragedy eleven years ago and such, seemed not to have changed—I guess this Miss Hachikuji died back then, too?

By the way, if we're being precise, traveling eleven years into the past to rescue her was a reason we made up after the fact, after we ended up in the wrong year by accident. We were just trying to go back by about a day so I could do my summer homework—but I saw no need to go out of my way to correct her.

"How? Well, we used this shrine's torii as a gate...not that there was any deep meaning to it..."

Shinobu had used the spiritual energy gathered at the then-abandoned Kita-Shirahebi to open a gate—precipitating a major incident that would ensnare the whole town, but that had nothing to do with time travel.

"Hmm..." Miss Mayoi said, looking pensive.

Given my first impression, I couldn't help but see her as a

mischievous young woman. Sinking into thought like this for my sake, however, did quite a lot to affect me and win my trust—so there was a connection between her and the Hachikuji that I met in a ruined world.

"In that case, couldn't you go home if you made another one of those gates? I'm not sure the same logic applies, of course."

"Er, that's not really…" I started to convey the obvious fact that Shinobu, not I, had summoned the gate, and that we were now in a mirror.

But did Shinobu Oshino, or the former Kissshot Acerolaorion Heartunderblade, ever exist here in the first place? Even if I mentioned her to Miss Hachikuji, wouldn't her reaction be, *Who're you talking about?*

But then, she'd brought up Shinobu a moment ago: *the former Kissshot Acerolaorion Heartunderblade*, though it was a little standoffish of Miss Hachikuji to call her that.

Hm—the more I thought about it, the more it threatened to turn into a wholesale rejection of the life I'd been living. This was hardly a lukewarm twist.

If Shinobu didn't exist, though, would I have met Hachikuji at that park? How were those loose ends tied up?

"*The loose ends,*" Miss Hachikuji said as if she'd read my mind, "*must not matter—in this case.*"

"…"

"In this case—which is to say, this world. There are no paradoxes in a mirror world—or maybe I should say everything is a paradox here. That's how logic works, right?"

The word *logic* coming from Hachikuji's mouth felt like its own paradox, but she continued.

"Just as taking a true statement like 'Araragi is a pedophile' and flipping it around makes it false—'pedophiles are Araragi,' or 'you aren't a pedophile if you're not Araragi'—paradoxes and contradictions can exist here. There must be some propositions

49

that hold up even if you turn them on their head, so 'everything is a paradox' is an overstatement, but I'd imagine a great number of things here will feel 'inconsistent' to you since you came from a world that acts as the standard."

For instance, I don't realize it myself, but don't you see me as a pretty contradictory presence to begin with? asked Miss Hachikuji.

And I had to agree.

If she'd grown to be twenty-one, she'd lived until that age, but the accident eleven years ago also seemed to have happened. Even if she was a living god, we shouldn't have ever met, but she knew who I was.

The young woman was a walking mess of contradictions.

She was all loose ends.

And yet—her existence was undeniable.

Still, what kind of an example was that?

You aren't a pedophile if you're not Araragi—really?

"A world where loose ends are just fine," she said. "Considering how you've solved many cases by making ends meet by hook or by crook... Sounds like a cruel world for you—far from lukewarm. Haha!"

"..."

Perhaps she meant to buck me up with that cheerful laugh, but her analysis was plenty cruel on its own.

Given how little information I still had, I didn't know how meaningful it'd be to piece together a hypothesis, but if I were to: I looked at that mirror in the morning—and the "world" reflected at that point, when my movements didn't match up, got reversed, but not all of history up until then?

"Maybe. After all, I know about Miss Shinobu Oshino, the former Kissshot Acerolaorion Heartunderblade. *At the same time, I know that vampires don't exist in this world.* I don't find it strange that I'm talking about her and seem to be familiar with the name of a non-existent aberration. I accept the contradiction without a second thought, like how I might claim that life should be treasured and still eat meat every day—neither is a lie."

"..."

A world where contradictions were fine.

A dream scenario for a novelist. Not being needled with points like the ones Ononoki raised—but it also seemed tough.

What was it called again? The Ozma Problem?

How explaining the difference between left and right to an alien would be difficult, verbally, or something—but just as perfect spheres don't exist, probably nothing has perfect bilateral symmetry, so the world I knew and the mirrored land I now inhabited would conflict at every turn...

"No, Araragi, I don't think that's necessarily true. It's not that everything is upside down—though you could also say that makes the situation all the more troublesome."

"What do you mean?"

"Take Karen. If everything about her was reversed, she wouldn't be your little sister, she'd be your big sister or your little brother—she may have appeared from the bath when she shouldn't have been there because that part of her had been reversed, but getting out of the bath and wiping your body dry with a towel is the most proper thing in the world. If we were to be strict about it and reverse even that, she'd need to soak herself in a towel before splashing herself with water."

"I don't know if she'd need to..."

That'd be beyond bizarre.

Even I wouldn't have been able to keep my cool in that case—and would've questioned Karen's sanity.

Not everything had been reversed. So then, *what* had been?

I couldn't comprehend the standard when it came to things getting flipped around—considering the reversal of the bicycle's structure, the placement of the faucet handles, and letters in this world, the scenery did all seem to be reversed. Its denizens, on the other hand…

"The fact that there's been no change to your other little sister, Tsukihi, does seem key—I wonder about knowledge. Hey, Araragi, what's one plus one?"

"Should I answer using the decimal system? Or in binary?"

"Stop being clever and just answer me, kid," threatened Miss Hachikuji. A lady who was my senior—but she followed up with a gentle admonishment: "It's a serious question, so could you give me a serious reply?"

The emotional turbulence made me queasy.

With the ten-year-old Hachikuji, my light jab would have kicked off a three-hour conversation, but I guess it was natural for this lady to have left behind what you might call the Hachikuji-ness of the Hachikuji I knew, now that she was eleven years older—she didn't mangle my name even once.

If anything, I'd tried to mangle her earlobe.

While I felt a tinge of sadness, I'd be worried if she was still acting that way at twenty-one, so I accepted it.

"…"

But no, maybe this was a part of her personality that had been flipped around—the more I thought about it, the deeper I sank into the quicksand.

"Two. One plus one is two," I gave a straightforward answer anyway, as embarrassing as it was.

"Hm. Okay, then what's 100 minus 50?"

"50."

"What's 9 times 7, and 9 divided by 3?"

"63 and 3."

She tested me on the four basic arithmetical operations, one at a time.

Those laws were the same wherever you were, though… At least, they seemed to be in this mirrored land. And so—

"Okay. I'll ask non-arithmetic questions too," Big Sis Mayoi said.

"Bring it on."

"Maybe I should start with science."

"Sure thing."

"What is the biological species name of a seahorse?"

"Why would I know that?" Something a little more general, please?

"What's the largest star in the solar system?"

"Saturn."

"Is that so. Here, it's the Sun."

"Don't ask me trick questions!"

"Excuse me? Is that how you speak to an older person? This is for your sake, you know."

"…"

Awkward…

I actually knew that trick question and the correct answer. I'd replied with the ten-year-old Hachikuji in mind, but our banter wasn't going anywhere. It made me realize just how important age differences are when you're conversing.

"Also," she said, "if you're going to fall for it, the answer in this world is Jupiter."

"Oh, right!"

I'd fallen for it on purpose but mistaken it wrong. I didn't need to wait for my test results at this point, I knew my fate. It sapped my motivation to return to my world—not that I wanted to make this realm of contradictions my final resting place.

That said, as I confirmed more things with Hachikuji, this world didn't seem too different, in terms of knowledge and common sense—even idioms like *right-hand man* and *out of left field* weren't flipped around.

Even if most people were left-handed from my point of view, the logic here meant that they were called *right-handed*—hmm, this really was the Ozma Problem.

"Well," I said, "I guess I'm lucky that causality, or the overall laws of nature, aren't flipped around. How would I plan any course of action if my predictions and reasoning of X causing Y to happen had been turned upside down too?"

"Don't let your guard down. It's only true for what we talked about just now—but then, being too cautious might be *counter*productive in its own way," Big Sis Mayoi warned, touching my hair.

She didn't know how to keep her hands to herself. As a healthy young man, I was sort of tickled.

"Well, to summarize, it looks like there's only one way for you to get back to your world."

"Just one? You sure narrowed that down quick."

I wished she'd range a little further when it came to my options, but you can only ask a god for so much.

In fact, I was shamelessly receiving her divine favor for an offering of just four yen. I'd best shut up and listen with humility.

While I was perplexed after getting lost in another world all of a sudden, I was also enjoying this, improperly enough. Another world or not, it was Hachikuji's first job as a freshly appointed (freshly anointed?) god. Listen with humility, humbly watch her work her magic.

So...how's Miss Hachikuji gonna save me here?!

Perhaps to punish my mindset—Mèmè Oshino, who held that people just went and got saved on their own, would have sneered at me—the deity said, "Just get the former Kissshot Acerolaorion Heartunderblade to open up a gate."

"..."

"What's with the dissatisfied look? Wasn't that Aberration Slayer a broken, anything-goes character? She should at least be able to create an opening in and out of this mirrored land."

"Er, when you put it that way, I guess she could, but..."

I wasn't sure.

There are theories that time travel is physically possible with a massive amount of energy...or so I've heard, but traveling between entire worlds fell outside the purview of physics classes.

I suppose it was possible, if time travel were a type of travel between worlds, or for that noble king of aberrations, the exceptional aberrational existence—at her peak.

Practically Majin Buu, the way she could do anything.

But not now, when she was a little girl—and even if we could address that, "Shinobu doesn't exist in this world, though," I reiterated—stating her absence. "Vampires can't in a land of mirrors. Maybe you're assuming that a thrall might do the same, but I'm telling you, I can't. My being here means our link is as close to severed as it can get. Think of me as a plain human now that I've been separated from Shinobu, just like back in hell."

"I'd never expect something so unreasonable—only the former Kissshot Acerolaorion Heartunderblade could open a gate."

Her tongue really didn't slip, did it? Even when she was saying that whole name. "B-But like I've been trying to tell you, Shinobu's not on this side of—"

"Even if she's not on *this side*, she can open it from the *other side*," the god suggested. "If she's not here, it means she's there. And if you've been separated, isn't the legendary lady free from her bindings and back in peak form?"

"..."

A brilliant, unimpeachable plan—would be going too far.

There were details that needed filling in, but it was indeed a neat and clearheaded approach that I hadn't thought of myself. She'd responded solidly to my plea.

Geez, look at her.

I didn't have anything to worry about. She was doing just fine as a god.

"Ha ha ha, call it *The Only Neat Thing to Do*. One of science fiction's three greatest cool titles."

Not that I've read it, she added flippantly—in a faint echo of the eleven-year-younger Hachikuji.

"…Can I ask what the other two are?"

"*The Moon Is a Harsh Mistress* and *Do Androids Dream of Electric Sheep?* Neither of which I've read."

"You haven't read any of them…"

Read them already.

Putting aside whether this setup was more science fiction or fantasy, there was now a ray of hope—I'd get Shinobu to open a gate from the other side.

Having been left behind, she'd figure out in no time that I'd gotten wrapped up in some sort of anomaly. Even if a vampire couldn't enter this land of mirrors, she'd be able to open a gate if she'd returned to her peak condition.

I'd been causing her nothing but trouble lately, forcing her to become big, then small, then big all over again—but the question was how I might convey the plan when she inhabited a different world.

Maybe I needed to go home and start banging on that mirror? Did I just have to knock?

No, it had gone back to being a regular surface, and even if there were something to the mirror, Shinobu might not be standing in front of it… If she'd regained her full powers, she wouldn't show in it and wouldn't go out of her way to look in any—unless she'd heard my voice calling out to her right before I was sucked in.

Still, she was tired from all this getting bigger and smaller lately…so I might not have done enough to wake her up. If she'd woken up to find me missing all of a sudden, she'd simply be confused. She wouldn't possibly imagine that I'd become Araragi Through the Looking-Glass (doesn't roll off the tongue, does it).

Having been too powerful, she wasn't the intellectual type, and living for centuries had worn down her mind. This state of affairs would only make her panic, and she might not be able to trace my steps—this was bad.

"If you wrote a letter and left it on your desk, wouldn't it show up on the other side?"

"No, it doesn't seem like acts in the other world and this one are linked. Just a single moment got sliced out..."

In that case—why did the Araragi residence's bathroom mirror turn into a gate to another world at that moment? Was there some kind of reason?

There's a reason for every aberration, the experts say, but it happened so abruptly that I couldn't see the need. It seemed more like a random supernatural phenomenon—I'd been spirited away, if you would.

It did seem ironic that I was asking a god for help if they spirited me away... So, how to contact Shinobu. If only I could communicate with her telepathically as her thrall.

"Well, relax, Araragi, it's not as if your life is in immediate danger. If your little sister looking a bit different is too hard on you, you're welcome to stay the night here," Miss Hachikuji offered considerately—while it wasn't exactly hard on me to see small Karen (amusing, more like), I didn't relish this turning into a drawn-out battle.

If I was getting accepted to college, I needed to go through the actual matriculation process... I had to return within the next few days at the latest.

"Oh, right... Yes, you did study hard. In that case, hmm, maybe forget about counting on Shinobu, and just wait stubbornly in the bathroom you came through, until the gate opens again?"

"..."

While the plan wasn't neat, it would certainly do—assuming that what happened once would happen again.

But there was no guarantee it would in the next few days—it might just take another thousand years was the issue here, and that issue was a dealbreaker. Little wonder Miss Hachikuji had discounted it at first.

Also, realistically speaking, I couldn't stand on guard forever in front of the sink. I mean, that space connected to the bath, which my parents and sisters used.

They'd chase me out of there every time they wanted to take a bath, like in the morning—I might somehow stand my ground against my little sisters, but I'd have to leave when it came to my parents. The gate could open during one of those intervals, which put that many holes in the plan.

Moreover, it'd be impossible to keep watch over my bathroom for twenty-four hours a day with dinner-plate eyes. Disconnected from Shinobu, I was nothing more than a regular human, and I needed to eat and sleep—how could I even live in a bathroom to begin with?

I'd be able to soak in the tub the moment I felt tired, of course, but really, what kind of benefit was—

"Oh!"

"Ahh!"

When I shouted as inspiration hit, Miss Hachikuji let out a super-cute scream of surprise—so cute I nearly lost my hold on the new idea (come to think of it, her scream during her young-girl days was "Graaah!"), but I just barely kept one pinky around its tail.

"Wh-What? Yelling like that all of a sudden."

"Kanbaru's home," I began to explain without preamble, but with a lot of gusto. "I think their cypress bathtub—"

007

In essence, you could call it a magic charm.

A trifling one that an elementary school girl might use—Kanbaru's home clearly has a lot of history to it, so it'd be odd for there not to be a tradition or two of the sort.

A year had already passed since I first heard of it, so I couldn't describe the specifics. I want to say it went something like this, though: the surface of the water in her home's cypress-wood bath reflected, on occasion, the image of the person you'd marry one day.

The legend is so cute even I hesitate to make any uncouth jokes or jabs about it, and I had to wonder if I should really be looking to it for help—but it was a different story when I considered that Toé Gaen, mother to Suruga Kanbaru, and older sister to Izuko Gaen, was tied to this legend.

It took on a very different complexion.

Though she'd passed away, her involvement in our storyline would utterly change the course of the tale—in fact, it's not an overstatement to say that she had something to do with the majority of the aberrations I'd experienced as a high school student.

Even if the legend came straight from the Kanbarus, to hear

that Kanbaru's father once saw a vision of Toé Gaen in that water's surface assured there was *something* about the wood bath.

Something.

It was worth a try, at least.

This was like *Nobita and the Steel Troops*, where he uses the bath in Shizuka's home to travel to another world. Hoping that it connected back to my world was expecting too much—but couldn't it work as a communication tool?

If I looked at the surface and saw someone other than me, wouldn't I be able to leave a message?

If you saw whoever you were going to marry in the future, I absolutely wanted it to be Hitagi there in the water, but if it just meant a lifelong partner, maybe I'd rather it be Shinobu—it'd be quicker that way.

I might not see anyone, of course.

I might just see my own stupid face reflected—but it did seem far more productive than staring into the bathroom mirror at my own home.

"Okay, then you go visit Suruga's—I'll go searching for other possibilities, just in case. I don't have any ideas left, but maybe other gods will have other ideas," Miss Hachikuji said, approving my plan. I had to admit, she might have matured, and we may have been in another world, but she was still such a good person, offering even to use her divine network.

Though…it did give me pause that Hachikuji simply called her "Suruga" in this mirrored land. Given their respective ages, it was appropriate—I really shouldn't be worrying myself over consistency.

In any case, I climbed down the mountain alone and began pedaling the BMX to Kanbaru's—and arrived in no time, as it wasn't far.

Once I knew that left and right were reversed, I had an easy enough time riding the bike. I'd also grown accustomed to seeing the flipped-around world. Humans can adapt to anything.

If I got too used to this world, though, it'd be a hassle once I returned—I'd end up only being able to write backwards, and soon my nickname would be Leonardo da Vinci.

People might start touting me as a universal genius.

I'd feel so self-conscious.

The Kanbaru residence—or rather, estate was so grand I almost felt like calling it the Kanbaru mansion. Some said it contained eleven TV sets.

I entered the "residence" about twice a month to clean up Kanbaru's room (and borrowed their cypress tub a number of times—the reason I was just barely able to recall it) but still shrink every time I stand in front of its gates.

Perhaps there were some things humans don't adapt to—and the gate had been flipped around as well, with even the doorphone on the opposite side.

Opposite.

The world fully mirrored.

It'd be hard to explain, but you can't just barge into someone else's bath (no matter how well you know the person). I needed to get Kanbaru's permission first…but was having trouble summoning the nerve to hit the call button.

I needed her permission, but come to think of it, in this mirrored world Kanbaru might be a completely different character from the junior I knew…

Going by the stats I'd compiled, cases like Tsukihi's, where someone hadn't changed, were in the minority. In the past I hadn't felt too reserved about relying on my close friend Kanbaru (what kind of a senior was I?), but nothing guaranteed she'd be the candid, gallant person who never failed to lend a helping hand.

I may respect you as a senior, Araragi-senpai, but letting you use my bath is out of the question, she might say, without any feeling even.

I'd never recover if I heard that from Kanbaru, in a different world or not. I'd carry the baggage for the rest of my life.

It kept my finger from hitting the button, but then...

"Pfft," I laughed—why was I worried?

Aside from Tsukihi, all the girls—whether it was Karen or Ononoki or Hachikuji—differed from the versions I knew but hadn't changed fundamentally as people.

Grownup Hachikuji was still helping me out. Ononoki's expressiveness exposed her nasty personality to the world, but you could say she was the same as ever.

Flipped around or reversed, they were still them—and Kanbaru would be too.

We had a relationship of trust, didn't we?

Why be so negative, anyway? In fact, the trait that always gave me pause might be turned around and canceled out.

A Kanbaru who isn't sex-obsessed.

A Kanbaru who isn't a masochist.

A Kanbaru who isn't shameless.

A Suruga Kanbaru who fancies just literature, always has her underwear on, and quietly walks along the sidewalk; considerate to the untalented, not prying when speaking to the timid, and ever-prudent—okay, she'd be unrecognizable at that point.

While I loved her boyish ways, I'd have no other chance of seeing her act gracefully. I felt excited when I thought about it that way.

Just what kind of Kanbaru would she be—yeah, why over-think this?

Maybe I'd find that I guessed exactly right. I'm not bad at reasoning.

After all the serious battles I'd recently faced, it didn't hurt to have the emotional wherewithal to enjoy laidback twists.

True, being transported to another world was unbelievably huge, but why not be a big man who welcomed such a crisis? The kind who quipped as bullets flew by.

I'd be like Space Pirate Cobra.

I made up my mind and used my Psychogun, or actually just my plain finger, to press the button—I think I pressed it.

But.

Something pressed back.

"...?!"

A fleeting moment.

I had no idea what had happened—of course not. Who, in modern-day Japan, ever pressed a button that pressed back? In any age or world, as a matter of fact, but I hadn't survived so many battles for nothing.

I'd been to hell and back, I played with fire without getting burned.

Even with what you might call zero fighting abilities, I could go toe-to-toe with anyone thanks to my first-rate danger avoidance—which is to say, skill at running away.

Well, I wasn't going toe-to-toe with anyone if I ran, but anyway, I had the presence of mind to spring back. I'd have sprained my right index finger otherwise.

If I were lucky, actually. My finger could've broken—into multiple pieces.

Because what pushed back wasn't strictly speaking the button, but rather the gatepost behind it—no, not even the gatepost. The doorphone and the gatepost were simply destroyed by the pressure applied to the other side.

And sure enough, what came sticking out of the pulverized post—was a fist.

"Ah..."

It flew too fast for the human eye to perceive it as such, and I must have recognized it only because I was familiar with it.

A fist—a paw. Because I knew about that Monkey's Paw...

"Aaaaaaaaaaaaaaaaaaaaaaaaaaaaaaaaaaaaaaaaaaaaaaaaaaaaaaaaaaaaaa aaaaaah!"

I'd like you to know that the scream wasn't mine.

Honestly, I was so dumbstruck I couldn't even scream—in other words, the cry belonged to the girl who appeared from the other side of the gate along with the Monkey's Paw.

A cry—be it a girl's, or a beast's.

"R..."

I finally began to speak.

It wasn't raining, or the least bit cloudy—but a figure in a hooded raincoat and rubber boots came crashing through where the gate once stood, and I spoke *her* name.

"Rainy Devil!"

No. Should I still have called *her* Suruga Kanbaru?

"A...aaaaaaaaaaaaaaaaaaaaaaaaaaaaaaaaaaaaaaaaaaaaaaaaaaaaaaaaa aah!" roared the Rainy Devil—or Suruga Kanbaru.

Before saying, just as before:

"I—I hate you I hate you—"

"...!"

Baths were the least of my worries.

If anything, I needed to avoid a bloodbath, but too stunned even to mumble that quip, I straddled the BMX—I couldn't believe it.

A lukewarm setup? Give me a break.

A highly hazardous aberration had shown up in the middle of the day—how much of a beatdown had I received at the hands of this demon monkey last May?

I also lost one of my favorite rides back then—I began to pedal, swearing I wouldn't lose the borrowed BMX and let history repeat itself to that degree.

Pedaling for dear life, dammit!

What kind of a world was this?!

Of all the things to happen, for the Rainy Devil to reappear because Kanbaru got mirrored…

"I—"

At my back, a voice that should've been distant…

"I hate you I hate you I hate you I hate you I hate you I hate you I hate you!"

Grew closer.

I knew I shouldn't look back. I needed to focus only on moving forward, but my fear got the better of me and I turned my head—I really shouldn't have.

Wall-running.

The Rainy Devil ran perpendicular to the wall surrounding the Kanbaru residence as she chased after me. Each step she took crushed and demolished the white surface, turning it into flour-like dust.

What a terrifying musclehead.

If there was any saving grace, she wore boots—and couldn't gather the kind of speed she could in running shoes.

Still, she seemed faster than the flipped BMX's top speed, and the distance between us continued to shrink—this was bad. Since my link to Shinobu had been cut and nothing about me was vampiric, I hadn't the durability to withstand a blow from the Monkey's Paw.

At this rate, I'd die in this nonsensical world before ever finding out if I'd gotten into college—come on, this inconsistency went too far! How could she have lived until now as the Rainy Devil? This was who Miss Hachikuji chummily called "Suruga"?!

I cursed and complained as I turned the handlebars—steering at this velocity was all but impossible, but I might earn myself some time if I veered away from the wall-running Kanbaru.

Fortunately, BMX bikes were made for acrobatic tricks, and I needed to resort to stunts if she beat me on speed.

But no, I soon learned how shortsighted my idea was.

A misconception.

I should've known that her legs' true power lay not in their speed, but in their jumping skills. The Rainy Devil kicked off the Kanbaru residence to leap parallel to the ground—thereby following my turn and still chasing straight after me.

Depending on how you looked at it, it was a vertical jump.

She caught up to me—passed me.

"I hate you I hate—!"

Her hatred only grew.

Packing it into her balled left fist, she descended in front of me and, still midair, swung it in my direction—wait, her left fist?

Huh? I forgot to hit the brakes, or even to take my hands off the handlebars to guard my vitals—*her left hand*?

No, that was how it went.

The paw Kanbaru once wished upon was a left hand. The original and authentic item had been a right hand, but the memento bequeathed to her by Toé Gaen, her mother, was a southpaw.

Kanbaru had kept her left arm wrapped up in bandages every day at all hours—because underneath was the furry limb of a beast, the price she'd paid for wishing upon an aberration.

As the Rainy Devil too—it was her left arm, as she wore a raincoat and tall rubber boots, that wrecked my body and my mountain bike.

The impression had been so strong that I hadn't noticed, but…it didn't make sense, did it? Even if you accepted that she'd become the Rainy Devil in this mirrored land—wouldn't her paw be her right hand?

Right hand, left hand.

Because mirrors—flip left and right.

If the original was a left hand.

Then it needed to be a right hand.

"—I! Hate! Youuuu! Ihateyouihateyouihateyouihateyouihate-youihateyou—!"

That was as far as my thoughts got.

As Kanbaru's howls gradually collapsed in on themselves, perhaps due to the Doppler effect, I rode right into the incomprehensible left hand—its destructive power had smashed a gate into dust and would surely reduce my body to putty.

"Heh…" I had to laugh.

I couldn't believe it. Despite Ogi's lectures, I was still hopeless—after all this time.

Suruga Kanbaru.

I don't want to die, but maybe it's not so bad if it's you, I found myself thinking—Koyomi Araragi is such a lost cause that it made me want to laugh, and to weep.

You were right, Ogi. But you know, even this late in the game, even in another world, my junior Kanbaru—is someone I just can't bring myself to hate.

"ihateyouihateyouihateyouihateyouihateyouihateyouihate-youihateyouihateyouihateyouihateyouihateyouihateyouihate-youihateyouihate—" "—myaaaahahahahahaha!"

Then.

The monkey's cry was joined by a cat's.

And I—was scooped up, bicycle and all.

008

Like a predator snatching prey in the savanna—is probably what it was. From my perspective as the prey, I'd been scooped away a split second before Kanbaru's left hand could sink into my heart. The predator, however, took me like it was nothing and might as well have been humming to herself.

The action centered around her—I should be treating her as the protagonist. Or maybe just as a cat.

In any case, once my eyes stopped spinning from the impact to my flank, I found myself completely elsewhere.

My self, completely elsewhere.

Kidnapped and taken someplace else—but also familiar. That is, if you accounted for the mirroring—this.

This was Shirohebi Park. Familiar to me even if I had only learned its true name the other day.

I was splayed out on the ground in its plaza.

Next to me was the BMX, its wheels klacking as they spun— thank goodness, it looked like Ogi's ride was fine for now.

The bike was one thing, but I'd have trouble saying I was. No, Kanbaru's fist hadn't grazed me or anything, I had no injuries— but this incredible fatigue coated every inch of my body.

I'd pedaled with all my strength to elude the Rainy Devil's pursuit, but that wasn't why. Even I'm not that feeble. No, I'd been sucked dry as I was abducted—yes, by the cat.

The special ability of the aberration known as the Afflicting Cat: energy drain.

"Myahahaha."

And then.

Opposite the bicycle, which was on either its left or right side, its right at least from my perspective—sat, on all fours with an amused look on her face...well, no need to put on airs now.

It was Black Hanekawa.

"..."

Though exhausted, I could at least move my eyes, so I looked her over—to find her with white snowy hair stretching to her back and large cat ears.

Also, she was in her underwear.

A polka-dot-patterned bra—something whose existence in the world is surprisingly difficult to confirm, a strapless one at that—along with black-and-white panties made out of a thick material and adorned with large frills on both the front and back. The clash between top and bottom gave off a different feeling from when they'd matched... No, this wasn't the time to be contemplating her underwear.

How should I describe this Black Hanekawa? Was this the initial design? Not Black Hanekawa from before the culture festival or after summer break, but during that nightmare of a Golden Week, when she was at her most feral and untouchable...

Then it was extremely dangerous for me to be splayed out in front of her like a fish on the chopping block—or maybe a mouse being toyed with by a cat. I may have escaped from the Rainy Devil, but my life was still under threat.

"And taking a catnap after being kidnapped by a cat. Lame, even as a pun..."

"Myaaahahahaha!"

But Black Hanekawa, with her low laughter threshold, cackled with glee as I muttered to myself. Please, could you not use Hanekawa's body to double over in hysterics in nothing but underwear?

"You really are an amewsing one, human—what a sharp wit you've got."

After cachinnating for a little while, she stood up to look down at me where I lay. Wasn't she aware that when she did that with breasts as large as Hanekawa's, I couldn't see her face?

"You nyoh, I haven't heard any thanks from you yet. Can't you at least try?"

"…"

I hesitated for a moment.

"Thank you," I then complied—it was true that she'd saved me, whatever her intentions had been and whatever she planned on doing to me next.

Of course, from my perspective, I was thanking her pair of breasts…

"Myahahaha. Nyo nyeed," Black Hanekawa said with delight after demanding my gratitude—the issue here wasn't her character, but her brains.

It seemed her intelligence level hadn't improved, and I was unsure of how to take the fact. Her idiocy was less a chink in her armor than a natural fort that made asking her for explanations pointless…

I didn't know how to approach her.

"Nyactually, how long are you planning on nyapping anyway, human? I myight've energy drained you when we touched, but it was only for a split second. It shouldn't have done too much damage."

"…"

Seriously, cat? You're far from the mark—I'm not staying

down to get you to lower your guard or anything, I literally can't move a finger…

Hanekawa liked to downplay herself as an innocent kitty and overestimate my abilities, and Black Hanekawa seemed to share that trait.

Despite my awful physical state, my mental state—my mind had started to clear. Perhaps thanks to having Tsubasa Hanekawa stand near me in her underwear even if it was in Black form.

Not an energy drain, but an energy injection—but now that my mind was clear, I found it full not of exclamation but question marks.

Not "Black Hanekawa! What are you doing here!"

But "Black Hanekawa? What are you doing here?"

?????

I mean, it didn't make sense, did it?

Black Hanekawa had been accepted into Tsubasa Hanekawa's heart back then, at the end of summer break, and should have disappeared forever.

Umm, hold on a second… That made it hard for me to stay calm for more reasons than one, but maybe the proper way to look at it was that Hanekawa's mirrored form is Black Hanekawa, just as Suruga Kanbaru's is the Rainy Devil?

Still. Hadn't Hanekawa gone on a trip overseas?

Was even that fact flipped around in this mirrored land? Yes, it was possible. A world where anything goes, where anything is conceivable, where contradictions are fine—

"Myaahaha. Looks like a lot's going through your head right nyow, human—but you're nyoverthinking it. You just nyeed to accept things as they are and as they appear, nyohkay?"

"As they appear…" Echoing her for no reason in particular, I looked up at her—or meant to, but as I should've known, all I saw was a massive amount of underboob. What good did it do me to accept its appearance?

I was going to have trouble taking any of this seriously unless she stood a little farther back, but that's when I noticed—and once I did, it almost felt strange that I hadn't until now.

Her bra and its unusual design were no excuse, I needed to feel ashamed as a Tsubasa Hanekawa devotee.

Well, given that this was how things should be, it was quite pointless to reflect too much on my error after the fact—but her chest.

It was her chest. Black Hanekawa, or Tsubasa Hanekawa's mammaries, taken not as a whole but divided into a left and right breast and observed thusly, revealed the right breast to be ever-so-slightly larger.

They say the left one is more likely to grow larger because of the heart's placement on that side of the body, but in Hanekawa's case, her right one is just a bit larger—probably because of all the use she gets out of her dominant hand while studying. The difference is minute, but my sharp eyes can't be deceived.

Putting aside the fact that she would put something sharp in said eyes if I told her—the difference was *the same* despite us being in a mirrored land.

Just like Kanbaru's "left hand."

It wasn't flipped around—hadn't been reversed.

"Wait, relax... Vision can only get me so far. I can't be sure and address this unease until I feel its root cause, those breasts, with my own hands."

"I'm nyot joking when I say you'd die if you touched my breasts in your condition. It'd be your chest nyeeding emyergency attention, nyot mine," quipped Black Hanekawa, taking a step back—allowing me to see her face at last.

"..."

I felt a little relieved.

Because her expression looked peaceful.

Although her design was the most ferocious and brutal one

from Golden Week, her mood seemed closest to Black Hanekawa at the end of summer break.

I guess that didn't match up, either... It felt inconsistent.

In that case, could I just think of this as a straightforward rescue?

"Hey, Black Hanekawa," I said, able to talk clearly at last. "Can I ask you just one question?"

"Sure. If it's something I can nyanswer."

"Yeah, literally true in your case... Anyway. I just wanted to check, we're in the land of mirrors now, right?"

To which Black Hanekawa responded, "Who nyohs," with a self-effacing smile. "It's nyot that I can't give you a nyanswer to that one—but as someone who lives in this world, I can't give you the one you want. Nyo matter what I say, it's nyot going to purrove anything."

"..."

"So I can't nyanswer your question, but I can give you a piece of advice. Don't go nyeer that monkey's home—I can imyagine why you'd visit it, but you're nyot going to get past that Monkey's Paw."

I didn't need to be told. But now that I had been, the number of question marks in my head only grew. She could "imyagine" why I'd visit Kanbaru's home? If anything, that's what I wanted to ask this world's Black Hanekawa...

"I'm going to reject that advice."

"Who knew advice is something you can reject?"

"I have to get in Kanbaru's bath, no matter what it takes."

"That'd be quite a puzzling line nyout of context."

"So let me change the question. *Who exactly asked you* to save me?"

"Wait a myanute, what makes you so certain that someone asked me to?"

"..."

74

Faced with this reply, I had no grounds to stand on and felt like I'd said something off the mark.

It was just that Black Hanekawa, this generation or any other, wouldn't go out of her way to help me—if she did, I assumed someone else's will had been involved.

"Nyahaha. I'll take a pass on that question too—and give you anyother piece of advice to replace the one you rejected. I nyoh you'll accept this one. If you have to go inside that home nyo myatter what, don't go alone. Go with a partnyer."

"A partner?"

"Hey, nyow, don't expect anything from me—as you've guessed, I hate you, Koyomi Araragi," Black Hanekawa said.

Using my name.

As far as I could recall, as an aberration she'd never spoken my, a human's, name—though maybe it was natural for her in this world.

"Cat—no, Hanekawa, tell me. What exactly…do you know?"

"I don't nyoh everything—I only nyoh what I nyoh."

Nyahahaha.

In the end, she'd answered none of my questions—nor did she wait for me to recover.

Because with that, Black Hanekawa left Shirohebi Park—slipping away like a stray cat whose eyes had met mine for just a brief moment.

009

I needed to rethink this all through.

To readjust my understanding.

Black Hanekawa might laugh again and tell me I was over-thinking things, but I wasn't capable of doing as little thinking as her—I needed to think. Bereft of my vampire skills, it was all I could do.

As shocked as I was when the great and holy Mayoi Hachikuji informed me that we were inside a mirror, I accepted it—but maybe it wasn't that simple.

Kanbaru's left hand. Hanekawa's right breast.

Nor was that all—the duo I encountered in quick succession had been flipped around in a way that seemed distinct from what I'd seen until then.

I mean, they'd turned into aberrations.

They'd aberrated. How did that make any sense?

A monkey and a cat. The Rainy Devil and Black Hanekawa—and you know, Tsukihi still bothered me too. Why had there been no change to her and her alone among everyone I'd met?

Dammit. It was times like these that made me regret how anti-social I was, or maybe just how few people I knew. There were passersby, but since I didn't know them to begin with, I didn't know how they'd changed, if they'd changed at all.

They say a friend in need is a friend indeed, and I was learning just how true that is by having so few... Pathetic.

As I thought this (and was finally able to move again), I settled on my next course of action—pride aside, taking Black Hanekawa's advice uncritically seemed risky, but sauntering back to Kanbaru's home unarmed went past reckless and straight into foolish territory.

I didn't know what she meant by finding a partner before heading to Kanbaru's. If I could call anyone that, it was Shinobu Oshino, but I needed to reach the Kanbarus' cypress bath precisely in order to contact my partner.

The reasoning already felt flimsy enough. Land of mirrors or not, it wasn't as if I could ignore moment-to-moment continuity.

So, the advice aside, I was going to head to the bookstore to grasp the situation, or maybe to reassess my strategic position. I decided on the location because, naturally, the sight of Black Hanekawa's body had ignited my passions, and I could use some dirty magazines—no, of course not.

While I had few real-world friends, I knew more than a little about historical figures from studying for my entrance exams. If I leafed through books that described them, I ought to be able to gauge how people had been flipped around in this world. A way to increase my sample size.

I wouldn't need to unfurl any massive historical tomes; reference books for grade schoolers should do. Descriptions of Nobunaga Oda and Ieyasu Tokugawa, of Napoleon and Lincoln, would show me how they'd changed from the figures I knew and aid me in understanding how this world worked.

When Miss Hachikuji and I had compared notes, we'd focused on nothing but scientific matters, so that'd been a blind spot. If personalities and bodies were flipped around, characters throughout the ages should've changed as well, even if history itself stayed the same. Maybe some people even differed the way Kanbaru and Hanekawa did... All right, I was probably expecting too much (though some historical figures turned into aberrations, didn't they?).

I might discover yet another pattern of transformations nonetheless. With that thought, I picked up the bicycle, made sure once more that it wasn't broken, and began pedaling toward the one large bookstore in town. Unsteadily—it'd taken a few hours for me to recover from Black Hanekawa's energy drain, so I did try to hurry to make up for lost time.

To cut to the chase, though, it was utterly fruitless, or rather, I ended up conducting a meaningless survey.

Well, the idea of looking into great historical figures wasn't meaningless in itself, but the failure came from looking to the written word for answers. I entered the store and immediately started deliberating on what book to buy only to find that I couldn't read all the flipped-around characters.

They were only mirrored, of course, so it wasn't too hard to decipher each character on its own, but when it came to the meaning of the passages, none of it stuck in my mind.

As if reading a book drained my energy—it was extremely wearying. I soon gave up on the approach. Not that I had any other plans if I gave up...

Return to Kita-Shirahebi Shrine? No, Miss Hachikuji probably wouldn't be back yet. In which case, I wanted to try something before meeting up with her.

Well... I was reluctant, or it was pretty much the last thing I wanted, but the only option seemed to be to go home and pay my respects to the tween doll plopped brazenly down in my little sisters' room. What I should've done at the very start...

Her dashing look and tone pissing me off had blotted out everything else, and asking someone who was experiencing these abnormalities hadn't seemed like a good idea. But why use that criterion to pick who to talk to if almost everyone in the world had been flipped around?

Whatever. If her dashing look pissed me off, I should just avert my gaze—come to think of it, her nasty personality wasn't new by any stretch.

I'd try to see her as conceited, not malicious. I steered toward my home—my sisters, Karen and Tsukihi, must have gone shopping, so now was a better opportunity than this morning to have an open conversation with Ononoki. Even if things took a turn for the worse and we ended up brawling, I could keep the damage to a minimum, or so I thought, but my plans always having a hitch in them held just as true in this mirrored land as it did in my original world. Maybe I should just call it nothing ever going the way I wanted.

No, even then, what happened next was too inconsistent a twist, or not to mince words, in bad taste—when I got home, parked the BMX, and entered from the front entrance, there in the house that should've been empty except for a doll, now that my sisters had left...

Stood a girl I didn't know—coming down from the second floor at the sound of the front door opening. I really had no idea who she was.

Shorts and a camisole with no bra.

A girl with shaggy short hair—not exactly in her underwear, but in an outfit that came close in terms of exposure.

Her attire seemed far too at-home for any guest my sisters might've invited over. Not even homewear but roomwear, like an open statement that she lived here. What, did I have a third little sister in this world? A bigger little sister, a littler little sister, and a middlish little sister? Things were already complicated enough now that my bigger little sister was littler than my littler little sister, so for a third little sister to appear—but wait, wasn't she coming across like the oldest of the three?

As I blinked in the grip of confusion, the girl looked at me and expressed her relief.

"Oh, it's just you, Koyomi. You scared me there."

For a moment I couldn't fathom why she'd feel relieved, but since my little sisters' shoes weren't by the front door (a pair of sandals I was seeing for the first time, not having noticed them in the morning, sat in their place—were they hers?), I realized she was afraid a burglar had come in while she was home alone. But hold on, home alone?

That really made her a third little sister... Her dismissive tone, though? Was she my big sister? Miss Hachikuji did theorize about Karen flipping around and turning into my older sister...

No, wait a sec. I'd thought I'd never seen this girl, but her voice sounded familiar...

While I wasn't the best at distinguishing between girls' voices, I'd heard this one before, only the tone was different—it used to berate me.

"Hm? What's the matter, Koyomi? Why're you just standing there?" asked the girl in the shorts, puzzled, as she descended the stairs rhythmically and closed the distance between us. She grabbed my hand and pulled me into my home.

I'd considered leaving, timidly enough, but instead hurried up and took off my shoes, forced to by her assertive attitude—I say forced, but she hadn't tugged my arm with all that much force, I'm just easily persuaded.

This overbearingness... I'd experienced it before...

"Hmmm? Huh? I thought you might've gone out, Koyomi, was it to the bookstore?" interrogated the girl in the shorts, keenly spotting the plastic bag in my other hand. She grinned. "You bought another dirty book? Ah, you're hopeless."

How did she know?! I omitted that whole bit—how did she know I'd purchased a photo collection where the mirrored characters didn't matter, and brought home *Cat-Eared Class Presidents of the World*?!

Only a little sister had that kind of intuition!

"Talk about rude. After living under the same roof with this cute a girl for almost a decade, you prefer books? Come on! But I guess we're like family at this point. Maybe I can't blame you."

"...Like family?"

In other words, not family?

Huh? Then seriously, who was she? Another freeloader, like Ononoki? But this girl was clearly human, not an aberration or a doll...right?

Almost a decade, though?

"C'mon, Koyomi. I know you want to enjoy that dirty book, but at least join me for a cup of tea. I was so bored holding the fort, I didn't know what to do! Listen, I have some sweets for the tea, and the perfect math puzzles," the girl in the shorts said, hauling me along into the living room.

Dammit, why couldn't I resist her?

I couldn't, at all. Partly because I was recovering from that energy drain, but I also couldn't disobey her on some instinctual level, her familiar voice enfeebling me—math puzzles?

...

......

....

"Wait, you're Sodachi Oikura?!"

"Whoa! Geez, don't scare me like that!" the girl in the shorts exclaimed in a familiar voice—that once showered me with abuse.

She sounded even more surprised than me.

"You're saying that now, Koyomi?! I've been living with you ever since elementary!"

010

Her impression was so different that I had no clue—but once I realized the truth, it seemed obvious. Of course she was *that* Oikura.

Sodachi Oikura.

Her hairstyle was different, and the Oikura I knew never exposed her limbs this much—most of all, the look in her eyes was just so different.

Once, they were so clouded that you worried she was afflicted with some kind of curse and was casting it on you with her gaze. Now, she was nothing but jovial.

"Hey! Hey! Isn't this puzzle amazing? This puzzle is amazing, and I'm amazing for figuring it out, don't you think?! It seems really hard, but look, the answer's obvious once you diagram it out! Don't you love this feeling? It's like a haze of mystery over the whole thing clearing up all at once!"

Oikura, who used to never come within three feet of me, as if she were dealing with some sort of waste product, now sat by my side on the sofa, her shoulder jostling against mine, not just dealing with me but sounding giddy. How was I supposed to recognize her?

She was a different individual, plain and simple.

This different, shorts-wearing Oikura, as far as I could tell from the fragments of information I gleaned from her words, had been in the Araragis' custody for eight years now—and we'd grown up on friendly terms, like brother and sister, though I'm not sure who was the older sibling in this case.

"Y-Yeah, sure, Sodachi…" Although nothing about it felt right, I called her by her first name. It was unnatural to use her family name if we weren't just childhood friends but living under the same roof—though it was going to be awkward whatever I called her given how weird the situation was. "You never fail to impress me. I've got to take my hat off to you for solving such a difficult problem."

The trauma carved into me during my first year of high school was so deep that I was trying to stay on her good side and pacify her with words even though her personality had been flipped. Of course, the Oikura I knew would have snapped at my obvious fawning, but this version was different.

"Hahaa! Koyomi praised me! Hooray!" she rejoiced like a good girl.

If the Oikura I knew, the difficult girl who wanted to be called Euler, saw herself acting this bright, cheerful, and merry, she might go on a rampage…

In fact, to be honest, I almost felt like running around and breaking things myself—it didn't make sense for me to be embarrassed, but I'd never imagined I'd be able to communicate with her like this. It felt like an impossible delusion, which made me blush.

"Hm? What's the matter, Koyomi? Your face is red. Could you be sick or something?"

Plop.

Oikura touched her forehead, already so close, to mine—like it was the most natural thing in the world. Stop! I wasn't the least bit happy, but she was going to make me start grinning!

"Hmm. Less hot than I thought," she said, her hand already working to solve the puzzle. She was writing down numbers with her left hand, but this didn't help me since I couldn't recall her dominant hand.

Then I had an idea.

"Hey, Sodachi... I forget, who's that mathematician you worship again? Euler?"

"Huh? What're you talking about? Euler is great, of course, but the mathematician I respect the most is Gauss. You know that!"

"..."

The difference was so minor that I didn't know what it signified. Did that count as being flipped around? Or rather, she was so fundamentally different that it was like being introduced to someone for the first time. Seriously, it made zero sense.

What was with this world? How did you flip that Oikura around to get this character?

Enjoying a placid, familial relationship with someone who was once on bad terms with me, or who hated me unilaterally with a vengeance, I should say, was yet another lukewarm, laid-back twist. Even so, I was too unaccustomed to all of this to know how to react.

I just couldn't accept the lack of tension.

I'd never met a female lead like this one.

"Okay, Koyomi, let's solve this problem together. I've gotten pretty far on it myself, or actually I do have an answer, but it feels like such a brute-force solution. There's nothing beautiful about trying every possibility, you know? There must be a cleaner way to solve it."

"Y-Yeah, sure, Sodachi..."

Even the numbers she wrote were mirrored, making the problem pointlessly hard, but I couldn't ignore her if I was her friendly older (younger?) brother—my plan of going to the second floor and asking Ononoki for help had been thwarted.

In fact, I was painting the perfect target on my back if the *shikigami* saw me like this—with that dashing look you couldn't even draw. But no, maybe not if this was the norm in this world? If this was Koyomi Araragi's usual behavior…

"Hm?"

Huh? Something gave me pause there.

It felt odd for a moment…like the closest I'd gotten to putting my finger on a hint for a clean solution—

"Lemme have some of your tea, Koyomi."

Oikura, who seemed to have finished off hers, took the teacup in front of me and elegantly sipped its contents. Not a problem on its own…

"Heheh! Second-hand kiss with Koyomi!"

When she didn't think twice about saying stuff like that, though, I didn't have any idea how to respond. This intimate, jokey Oikura sent my mind into the clouds, and I couldn't gather my thoughts.

I guess I was a noob at flirting because every relationship I'd managed to build involved arguing.

And so, I lost my train of thought.

"Phew," I sighed—well, maybe it was fine.

Why not just one Oikura like this, even if this wasn't an all-out parallel world but an inconsistent world full of contradictions—it might not lend a helping hand to the Oikura I knew, but family time with a girl who wasn't blessed in that department wasn't so terrible.

It resembled resignation, but I did at last reach such a state—could feel that way about a childhood friend who was still striving to find happiness.

"Hey…Sodachi. I have a question about Tsukihi."

That notion must have provided me with solid ground because

I put my concerns behind and launched into the matter at hand. Well, I ought to have been bringing it to Ononoki, but if this girl was saying we'd lived together for nearly a decade, she'd have to know my littler little sister better than the shikigami, who when it came down to it had started living with us only recently.

"Hmm? Tsukihi? She went shopping with Karen. They invited me too, but I wanted to tell you about this puzzle asap."

The point of my question didn't get across to her, and I should've known. She simply informed me of Tsukihi's current location—so I continued, "Has anything about her changed lately?"

No, that wouldn't work, either. Even if there'd been a change—some kind of reversal that I didn't notice, it'd be her natural state in this mirrored land.

"What kind of person was she, again?" I rephrased my question.

"Kind of person? What a weird thing to ask, Koyomi. Well, I see why you're worried about her. I am too. How's she going to make it in the world with that personality of hers?"

Forcing a smile, Oikura began conveying her impressions of Tsukihi Araragi as she understood her. As a girl talking about another girl, she went easier on her in some ways and harder in others, but on the whole none of it gainsaid my own impression of Tsukihi.

In which case, she really hadn't changed... Did some people change but not others, or was Tsukihi the sole exception?

If she was, I supposed I understood... If the formidable Oikura was this much of a mess (sorry), I ought to assume that most people were reversed in some way.

The existence of one such Oikura did no harm, but on the flip side, I couldn't deny also feeling that I didn't want to see her like this.

"..."

The flip side.

Right?

"Wow. Amazing, Koyomi, you figured it out. I know I get better grades than you, but I'm no match for you when it comes to this sort of thing. I don't mind, though, somehow it doesn't annoy me... Phew."

And then.

Once I finished solving the math puzzles she'd prepared, she plopped her head down on my shoulder—and something about it felt like a slight departure from the sisterly, familial vibe she'd been setting off.

"Hey, Sodachi—"

"I wonder what it is. It's strange," she interrupted me before I could chide her, not moving. "It's been like this since forever, right? But I find myself wanting it to be. Isn't that weird?"

"..."

"Is something wrong with me? You're here, Karen's here, Tsukihi's here... Uncle and Auntie are here, and you're all so nice to me, and we get along so well, like a real family, and I'm so happy, but—"

Suddenly, Sodachi Oikura...

Spoke like Sodachi Oikura: *I wonder why*—

"This all seems like a lie."

011

I ended up going back to Kita-Shirahebi Shrine without speaking to Ononoki—no, it's not like Oikura refused to free me from the living room even after I solved all her puzzles.

If anything, I had an opening.

She'd headed to the bathroom, saying she'd take a shower to freshen up and shake off her strange mood—and I used it as my cue to visit my little sisters' room.

Incidentally, she'd also issued a joking invitation: *You don't seem too well either, wanna join me?*

I firmly declined. There are some lines that even I won't cross. Too scary.

This entire emergency owed to washing my face to freshen up in the first place—I did take a casual glance at the bathroom mirror during our exchange, but it was nothing more than a mirror, as you might expect.

So then, to my little sisters' room.

Where Yotsugi Ononoki—wasn't present.

There were plenty of explanations for this—a variety of interpretations, but the most standard hypothesis was that she'd gone outside on her own for a walk.

But I didn't adopt the hypothesis.

Out of the variety of interpretations, I didn't choose it.

Even if her dashing look pissed me off, even if she spoke in a haughty tone, Ononoki was still Ononoki, an expert, regardless of her flaws.

An expert disappearing in this situation seemed like cause for alarm—I'd never admit it to her, even with a gun to my head, but I admired her brisk work and sense of responsibility.

Which meant there had been *something*, that *something* had occurred and urged her to take action—dammit.

If I'd known, I'd have put a lid on my irritation and heard her out in the morning, no matter what it took—I thought as I left home.

"I'm going out for a bit, Sodachi," I returned to the bathroom and told her from the other side of the frosted glass as she (judging by her silhouette) washed her hair, before taking off to Kita-Shi-rahebi on the BMX.

Miss Hachikuji should have returned by now; I needed to update my understanding of the situation and rethink my strategy.

A sudden plunge.

I'd been wrong to call this a lukewarm setup—I still didn't get what was going on, but I was possibly in a worse fix than ever before.

This reality was unsettling and improper.

Maybe it entailed actual risk.

Right, this wasn't some benign mirror country.

I'd asked if it was science fiction or fantasy, but come to think of it, weren't there also lots of ghost stories that involved mirrors?

Urban legends.

Street gossip.

Tall tales.

For instance—hadn't the mirror turned purple?

Agh, with my twentieth birthday not far away, I'd remembered the words: purple mirror.

How did the urban legend go again, were they cursed words that killed you if you still remembered them when you were twenty? I wanted to say there was another phrase to undo the curse, but I'd forgotten it.

Was it saying "Bloody Mary" three times?

No, that was a different mirror-related curse.

Not that any of this seemed relevant—it's just that there's no shortage of mirror-related aberrations. Even an ignorant fool like me could easily start listing them off.

In which case this world might be no land of mirrors, simply irrational and incoherent, but rather an aberrational phenomenon with a proper reason to it.

I returned to the foot of the mountain crowned by Kita-Shirahebi Shrine with the sense that I'd been sent back to the starting tile in a board game—not a good outcome in a game, but honestly? I wished I could start all over.

I all but dashed up the mountain as soon as I chained up the bike, a regular trail run. Sprinting up and down the stairs in such a short period of time reminded me of just the other day—not that those were the best memories.

Why would they be? Back then, the god enshrined at the shrine wasn't Hachikuji—and so.

I walked through the shrine's gate, indeed feeling like I'd returned to the very start—okay, that's an exaggeration, but like I'd been sent back about five squares.

"Heya, Araragi! It's Missy Mayoi! Looks to me like things haven't been going so good for you, huh? But don't worry! I thought that might happen, so just for you, just for you, just for you, Araragi! Your friend here used all her connections to bring over a super reliable helper!"

The great god Hachikuji pushily, and I really mean pushily, said this from her position in front of the shrine, to introduce a "god"—of all the people.

A girl I thought I'd never meet again, of all the people.

Someone I'd personally wounded, of all the people.

Of all the people, Nadeko Sengok—

"Hsshh hsshh hsshh! What's up, Big Brother Koyomi? That's right, it's me! Been a while, huh? So? You been doing good all this time? Hmmmm?!"

"..."

Nadeko Sengok-who?

012

I know, a character intro this late in the story is silly, but just in case, Nadeko Sengoku—whom Miss Hachikuji brought over after making use of all her connections—had been friends with Tsukihi Araragi, my little sister, since elementary school.

They did fall out of touch at one point but recently started seeing each other again—a resumption that began with my reunion with her, but thanks to a certain conman's schemes, I'd fallen out of touch with her myself, ironically.

Because around last New Year's she, an average middle school girl, became the shrine's god—a snake god.

Well, to get to the real root of the problem, it was probably karmic retribution for my actions, but let me omit that part if I may—none of that could be undone at this point.

I can think about what I've done on my own.

But Sengoku, with whom I'd cut ties, now stood before me— we weren't supposed to ever be in such close proximity. Do you have any idea what you've done, Big Sis?

Making a fool out of me even in another world, Hachikuji— I wanted to say, but I swallowed the words at the last second because this really was a different world.

Whoever this Sengok-who was, with her gaping maw and mocking "Hsshh hsshh hsshh!" (what was so funny?), a snake in more ways than one, it wasn't the Nadeko Sengoku that I knew. Nope, I didn't know of a Nadeko Sengoku like this.

There were, at absolute most, two types of Sengokus—an easy set to complete if she were made into trading cards.

First off was what I guess you'd call her basic form? The girl I crossed paths with on the stairs to this shrine—the introverted middle school version with a face covered in bangs and a tendency to look at the ground as she muttered. There were some changes in her hairstyle and clothing, but that was normal for anyone living a normal life.

The other type was the aforementioned snake god version— who took on a dreadful form, each of her hundred-thousand-plus strands of hair a white snake, like some kind of Medusa, her expressions so unleashed you could never imagine them coming from her basic self. The Sengoku that tried to kill me countless times, and in fact did, but let me omit that part as well.

It'd be long, and I don't want to talk about it.

Meanwhile, the audacious Sengoku standing next to Miss Hachikuji seemed like neither—sure, she was wearing Middle School #701's trademark dress uniform, but her hair was cropped short and entirely white, yet not made out of snakes. Her fearless, carefree, and savage expression did seem poised, at the same time, to bear down on me from on high and gobble me up.

How do I explain it? It felt like she'd placed herself in some kind of middle, that she was immature, even incomplete—in the middle of trying to change something about herself. Right, like an organism stirring to life from within an egg...

"I think you know who she is, Araragi, but let me introduce her in case you don't, having come from another world. This is my senior—or rather, my predecessor as a god. This is Miss Serpent."

"...I see."

Miss Serpent.

I nodded in understanding at Miss Hachikuji's words, but they weren't entering my brain—yes, partly because I was baffled by this sudden encounter with a girl that I thought I'd cut ties with.

But since we were in this land of mirrors, you could also say that it didn't count, even if it wasn't a good thing by any means. What baffled me the most was that I seemed to be wrong.

Given my experiences after climbing down the mountain, I'd started to suspect that this world consisted of my delusions.

Delusions might be too harsh.

To put it differently, I thought I might be dreaming—I may not have pinched my own cheek, but I'd considered the line of reasoning as I returned to the mountain.

A dubious dream—if Oikura found out about her utterly different iteration, which was in such bad taste, she'd kill me—but wasn't I still snoring away under the covers, despite thinking that I was awake, because my little sisters never came to wake me up?

It'd explain the lack of consistency and coherence—and make sense of nothing making sense.

A dream.

In other words, one of those it-was-all-just-a-dream stories.

A bit of a foul as a narrative technique, but using it just once didn't seem so bad? They do say that rules are made to be broken. In any case, by any reckoning, ...*and that was my dream* was more convincing than ...*and that was the land of mirrors I visited.*

Story quality aside.

Kanbaru being the Rainy Devil... Hanekawa, who should have been overseas, being Black Hanekawa, who should have vanished... I'd observed multiple examples of things that couldn't be explained as a simple reversal in some kind of mirrored land—yet my hypothesis of this all being a dream was its own convenient delusion.

Almost a piece of wishful thinking.

I mean, I at least knew about the Rainy Devil and Black Hanekawa...and if you insisted that I wanted Oikura to act that way, I'd have trouble arguing with you.

But—I didn't know. Did not know.

This Nadeko Sengoku, I did not know—neither god nor human, something in between, but also looking ahead to what was to be. I didn't know her, didn't even have the right to.

In other words.

If dreams are made of the thoughts and memories stored in your mind, I'd never dream of this Sengoku.

Nadeko Sengoku with her hair cropped short? Unthinkable, which meant this being a dream was unthinkable too.

"..."

Then what the hell was this world?

I was already at peak confusion, but now they were trying to set a new record? Miss Serpent? Didn't that name ring a bell, at least?

"Hsshh hsshh! I see."

Amused, Nadeko Sengok-who laughed—the timbre of her voice was Sengoku's, but the tone seemed rough or maybe vulgar, all wrong, making her feel so different I thought she had to be a twin sister.

Though I've yet to meet any real-life twins...

"Listen, you're overthinking things—just like the cat said."

"Huh?"

The cat? As in...Black Hanekawa? She did say I was overthinking things...but as far as I knew, Sengoku and Black Hanekawa never interacted?

I glanced over at Miss Hachikuji.

Who returned a wink.

That's not what I wanted from you... Also, you're awful at winking.

I gave up on her and faced Nadeko Sengok-who again—though communicating with her seemed challenging in its own way.

"Hmmmm? What is it, Big Brother Koyomi? You saying you don't understand? My point's not getting across? Well, I'd imagine as much. Hsshh hsshh!"

"…"

"Don't glare at me like that. It's not like I'm messing with you, okay? Listen here, I may not look it, but I was once the god of this shrine. I'm going to be more cooperative than the cat, at least."

Come here, Nadeko Sengok-who—Miss Serpent—beckoned me over.

There was something serpentine about both her gesture and her tongue, so I hesitated, but being scared wouldn't do me any good. I began approaching Miss Serpent and Miss Hachikuji, cautiously, step by step—

"Hup!"

Once I was within several feet of the young ladies, the more big-sisterly of the two leapt at me—and pushed me to the ground for no reason.

How many times was she planning on shoving me over in a shrine?

Or maybe a poisonous spider was about to attack me—I began to look around in shock, only for Miss Hachikuji to smile and speak.

"C'mon. What're you being all serious for? Isn't that exactly why everyone's saying you're overthinking things? It's not every day you get to come to a mirrored land, so you ought to relax and even try to enjoy it, kid."

"All right."

What a selfish lady, telling me to be serious when I was being silly, then telling me to lighten up once I turned cautious—but actually, she was right.

Imposing my image of Sengoku, from my original world, onto this one was unnecessary, and while caution usually paid off, I mustn't overdo it—*relax. Even try to enjoy it.*

True.

Getting straddled by a twenty-one-year-old Hachikuji would surely be a great story once I returned—and so I turned to Miss Serpent while still in that position.

"I appreciate your help," I thanked her belatedly.

"Hmmm? Eh, sure, if it's help you're seeking, that's what you'll get. I'm a god, after all—but that's not what I meant when I said you're overthinking this."

Continuing to pin me to the ground (why wouldn't she move?), and unfazed by Miss Serpent's denial, Miss Hachikuji said, "Oh, I see. Still, Araragi, lean on Miss Serpent here. Of all the gods and buddhas out there, she's the one you ought to count on the most!"

"Of all the gods... How?"

It sounded like hyperbole, but Miss Hachikuji didn't retract her overblown promotional statement. "Well, snakes are experts when it comes to mirrors," she said.

"Huh? Snakes are experts when it comes to mirrors?" I echoed, looking at Miss Serpent—and catching a glimpse under her dress from my position on the ground.

"Hm? Yeah, sure. What, you couldn't figure it out the moment you saw me? Why else would Big Sis Mayoi call me out here, Big Brother Koyomi?"

"Why?"

Wasn't it because she didn't know too many gods, having just become one herself? She'd gone to her senior—her predecessor—for help with this quandary...or was it something more?

"Listen, Araragi," Miss Hachikuji told me.

Proud of what she was about to say.

"The Japanese word for mirror originally comes from 'snake eyes'—*kaga-mi*. You didn't know?"

013

Of course I didn't.

Snakes being called *kaka* in old Japanese hadn't been required knowledge for my entrance exams—as much as the idea resisted being put to rest, this too was proof that I wasn't experiencing a dream.

Maybe the fact that Shinobu Oshino, someone previously compared to a sea serpent, laughed with a distinctive "Kakak!" sat deep in my mind, and theoretically you could connect the dots to arrive at a dream, but that was far too forced a payoff as far as foreshadowing goes—in any case, I hadn't even considered hoping for an expert on mirrors, but her appearance now, whether goddess or middle school student, was appreciated.

"Aren't you hungry, Araragi? It sounds like you haven't eaten anything all day. Let's eat and talk. C'mon, Miss Serpent, you too."

Now that she mentioned it, the tea Oikura made me was just about the only thing I'd consumed—I hadn't really noticed because the sight of her had filled me up on its own. Having lost all of my vampiric qualities, however, I needed proper nutrition if I didn't want to collapse.

And so, I was invited inside Kita-Shirahebi's main shrine for the first time and sat down to eat a meal prepared by Miss Hachikuji.

"Hold on, aren't these offerings?"

"That's right, they are."

"…"

I should've been the only person paying visits, so maybe they were Miss Serpent's offerings? And wait, was it okay to eat them?

As I sat there hesitating, Miss Hachikuji and Miss Serpent dug straight in. To avoid any awkwardness, I humbly joined them.

I doubt this bears repeating, but what a situation—I was sitting in a circle with two gods and having a meal.

Who exactly was I?

In the world I'd been living in until that morning, Mayoi Hachikuji was a god as a result of Nadeko Sengoku no longer being one—in other words, the two never reigned concurrently, but this was another point of incoherence, or maybe inconsistency in this world.

"Gulg glug glug glug." "Glug glug glug glug."

The two gods drank straight from sake bottles that also seemed to be offerings—Miss Mayoi, twenty-one years old, was one thing, but Miss Serpent, outwardly a middle school girl, was a sight to behold.

"Big Brother Koyomi—could you be thinking that mirrors show the world with left and right reversed?"

Miss Serpent got to no warning with the matter at hand—sorry, Miss Serpent got to the matter at hand with no warning.

So suddenly that I stumbled over my narration… How embarrassing for my tongue to slip in Hachikuji's presence, though hers didn't anymore.

"Ah, um, what? Could you repeat that?"

"Could you be thinking that mirrors show the world with left and right reversed—I'm asking you a question, hmmm?"

She spoke like she was trying to pick a fight with me. Was this some kind of stress interview? That wasn't why, but I couldn't make out her question's meaning even if I understood it.

Mirrors show the world with left and right reversed—yes, that's what I thought. The kind of common knowledge possessed even by an elementary schooler.

Why do you think mirrors show the world with left and right reversed? would have some kind of philosophical edge to it, so I wouldn't have minded it. Her question, though, seemed less philosophy and more Zen koan—was she going to tell me that it's in fact us who are reversed, that our mirrored forms are the truth?

No, wait.

Elementary schoolers probably didn't know about this property of mirrors, but honors-roll students like Hitagi and Oikura would point out that it's not left and right that are reversed, but front and back, strictly speaking... Is that what she meant? That was just semantics, though. The way we see it—the "mirror image"—remains the same.

"I've heard that if you take multiple mirrors, like on a vanity mirror," I offered, "and put them at a right angle and look at where they meet, left and right are where they should be... Is that what you want to say?"

Wasn't there some mirror that shows left and right correctly even as a flat surface, by making good use of reflections? I didn't know about this world's Rainy Devil, but Kanbaru did love new and unusual things, and I remembered seeing one as I cleaned her room.

"No, no—hsshh hsshh. That's not what I mean, I'm asking if, just looking into a mirror, *you think left and right are reversed.*"

"Well...yeah, I do. When I raise my right hand, my reflection raises its left, and if I raise my left leg, my reflection raises its right, doesn't it?"

"Huh. You do ballet stretches in front of the mirror? What a weirdo."

"It's just an example. Why would I?"

It's Karen who does them, not me. Did she in this world too?

"In any case, my reflection moves in the opposite way as me."

"Do you really think that?"

Relentlessly.

Miss Serpent closed in on me—my image of snakes was that they were persistent, and that's exactly how this situation was playing out.

"Don't you just think that because it's what everyone says?"

"D-Don't be ridiculous. Do I look like the type to be bound by common sense?"

True, mirrors reversing left and right—or front and back—was a piece of common knowledge, which is to say a preconception. If I were asked to explain a mirror as an object, that'd be how. I don't remember who, but someone must've explained a mirror to me that way, and I must've understood it that way: *Oh, so it's a board that shows reality, but with left and right flipped around.*

"Miss Serpent, are you saying that's not the case? What do you think, Miss Hachikuji?"

"I'll chime in with my opinion at the end. Keep going for now," the young lady replied.

With dignity. She sounded so authoritative.

Since I knew her back when she was ten, it was hard to tell if she was being serious, silly, or just glossing over the fact that she didn't have an opinion.

"You know the mirror test, don't you? To see if an animal— for example, a snake—recognizes itself in a mirror," Miss Serpent said. "But doesn't the animal recognize the reflection as itself precisely because left and right are flipped, and the image is its *counterpart*? If left and right moved exactly the same in the mirror, the animal would think it's moving in a different way, that it's a different creature—maybe. Hsshh hsshh."

"Well, the reflections do move with left and right reversed, so…"

"In any case, snakes don't have limbs, so your phrasing isn't convincing me—and anyway, mirrors don't give off any light. They just reflect the light that enters them, and the viewer just assumes that it's 'showing' an image. When you think of it that way, that's not the function of a mirror at all, is it?"

"Miss Serpent…" It felt like I was being toyed with—or straight-up being teased, so I replied in a somewhat stern tone, even though I was speaking to a god. "If a mirror doesn't show you the world with left and right reversed, then what exactly does it show?"

"The truth," Miss Serpent declared. "And no, Big Brother Koyomi, I'm not saying that there's a 'true' left and right. It's how mirrors were treated in ancient times—they were holy items."

"Oh… Yeah, magical mirrors and the like crop up all the time."

"Like Cinderella's mother's," Miss Hachikuji chimed in knowingly, when she'd confused Cinderella for Snow White. Still, it was a good example.

We have an unromantic explanation nowadays, but images in mirrors seemed quite wondrous in the past, so people naturally granted them some sort of meaning—hence all the aberrations revolving around mirrors.

They show the truth, huh?

"Shown the truth, Medusa turned to stone—but who wouldn't be petrified by someone with snakes for hair? Hsshh hsshh!" laughed Miss Serpent. Maybe I didn't get snake humor, but having witnessed a serpent-god Sengoku looking just that way, I didn't find it funny at all… Did that version of her never exist in this world?

"They show the truth? Okay, I admit that's suggestive, but so what? What kind of lesson am I supposed to take home here?"

Going on about lessons made me sound like that conman, but my only impression so far was that looking back on history could sure be edifying.

You call it the truth, but it's still facing the wrong way around, I almost wanted to say in a salty mood. While I'd made a four-yen offering to Miss Hachikuji, I couldn't take that attitude with Miss Serpent, who'd made a cameo appearance free of charge.

In hindsight, my donation to Miss Hachikuji was so meager I'd be better off not having paid anything. I suddenly felt like apologizing—sorry for my callous quips, even if I kept them to myself.

"Do you still not get it, Big Brother Koyomi? Listen here, I'm just trying to tell you that the same goes for this world. Viewed head-on, it might seem like left and right are flipped, but that doesn't mean it's reversed—it's not about deciding which one is correct, both of them are, okay?"

"What?" Both—were correct? The truth?

"This world might look like an inconsistent mess from where you stand, but just like your world, that all depends on if you lewd in the right way."

"Lewd in the right way..." I took her seriously, but wait, my world wasn't that lewd.

"Pardon me, view it in the right way."

"How do you make a mistake like that? How do you confuse those two phrases? They're practically opposites."

"Opposites, eh—hsshh hsshh."

Miss Serpent echoed my vacuous quip as if it were profound—hm?

"All right, fine, let me recap," she continued. "All the nice people you know who you've met in this world, whether your sisters or your friends or your juniors or your childhood acquaintances—along with me and Miss Mayoi. It's not like our left and right have been flipped around. You've started to figure that out by now, haven't you?"

" … "

"Yes. It's not that we're flipped around—we're out here as our honest selves, in our own way. We might be reflections, but we're not illusions—hsshh hsshh! Judging by the way you've been looking at me, I'm nothing like the me you know, to the point where you can't believe that we're the same people—but I'm sorry to say, this is also who I am."

I'm Nadeko Sengoku, Miss Serpent said.

Nadeko Sengoku said, in other words.

Even my dull self was beginning to see her point—but something about it wasn't sinking in. Was it some visceral reaction?

The logic that the reflection in the mirror is identical, is the same person, made sense for Tsubasa Hanekawa and Black Hanekawa, but I couldn't bring myself to accept it for anyone else.

Take the first person I met. If Karen got shorter, didn't her entire identity crumble away?

"People who're tall don't always wish it was that way—just as some people develop a complex over being short, others can about being tall. Your cute little sister only just graduated middle school, right? Do you think she's grown up enough on the inside—to catch up to her height?"

"On the inside…"

Well, when you put it that way, yes, her body had done all the growing but the person inside of it had yet to fill it out. She was still a child—it seemed to me, at least.

" … "

And?

If you adopted that approach with Tsukihi—Ononoki—Hachikuji—Kanbaru—Hanekawa—Oikura—Sengoku—the jumbled way they'd been flipped around finally started to line up along a common theme. But what did it mean?

"Hsshh hsshh. It's starting to come together now, so why don't we jump back a bit. You said that mirrors flip around left and right because when you raise your right arm, your left arm moves—but that example doesn't apply to a snake with no limbs. What would you say is flipped around in the case of a snake? How would you—how do you explain left and right being 'flipped around' to me?"

"I'd, um, use the shape of your scales, or the way they're lined up…"

"Don't picture literally explaining it to a snake. What are you, stupid? I'm asking how you'd explain left and right being flipped around to someone who lacks those concepts."

"Well…"

It was like a variation on the Ozma Problem. It might seem easy, but it's harder than you think. For example, moving your body to the right would make your counterpart move left—but the key is to explain left and right being reversed without using the words.

"The Ozma Problem reminds me of the Wizard of Oz," Miss Hachikuji chimed in with a comment that I could safely ignore (not quipping even silently at her expense now just made me seem cold). But as I continued to agonize over the question, I arrived at a very simple answer.

"That's it. You could just show them reflected letters."

"Hsshh hsshh. Letters?"

"Yeah. Well, there are a lot of symmetrical letters depending on the way you write them, so maybe use full words? Put that in a mirror and it'll be reflected with left and right switched around, which should let you explain a mirror's properties, right?"

Koyomi Araragi would be reflected as Ʞoγomi ȺⱤɐⱤɐϱi. Miss Serpent would be reflected as Miƨƨ Ƨɘɿqɘnƚ—the "mirrored letters" that made me give up at the bookstore.

Seeing them, it was immediately obvious that you weren't looking at a simple piece of glass, and that reality isn't being shown to you as it is.

"Yes."

That's it, Miss Serpent said.

Her facial expression was less of a *Right! You're smarter than I thought, Big Brother Koyomi!* and more of a *So you finally managed to put together the answer I wanted—look at all the work you made me do.* Well, then maybe you should've just given it to me up front in an itemized list.

Maybe gods had some kind of rule where they couldn't deliver messages too directly from on high, but I'd heard enough about mirrors; I was even reminded of that abandoned cram school and Oshino force-feeding me his extensive knowledge on aberrations. For her to look disappointed on top of it all was too much to handle.

Speaking of which, what became of that cram school in this world? It didn't exist in mine anymore. The designs of buildings and other sights around town were flipped around, but that was all I'd noticed...

"Okay, Big Brother Koyomi. Time for the next step."

"You weren't done yet?"

"Don't you worry, this is the last of it—we'll ask Miss Mayoi for her opinion after this."

"Huh?" Mayoi Hachikuji seemed honestly surprised to hear Miss Serpent mention her—she must've forgotten her own earlier statement.

I was right, it was just an excuse and she didn't have an opinion...

"If, out of the blue, someone showed you the words Ʞoγomi Ⱥⱥⱥⱥᴁi, not in a mirror but on a piece of paper—what would you do?" asked Miss Serpent.

"...So I'm playing the snake now? Do I also need to pretend that I have the brain of a reptile?"

"No, even yours should be up to it."

What a mean thing to say—well, of course Miss Serpent

would be partial to reptiles, she was a snake god.

Umm.

"Well, I'd probably just think of them as mirrored letters."

"But you don't know what a mirror is. Nor do you know what mirrored letters are."

"Okay, then I wouldn't think of them as mirrored letters, but that just means I don't know how to read. I'd still think of them as flipped—"

Hm? No, that wasn't it. I'd normally only think of mirrored letters as "flipped around" if I were in front of a mirror. Try to remember, what did I do when I struggled to read those history books?

Right.

I tried to read the pages from the opposite side, through the paper—an attempt that failed, but that meant if I saw mirrored letters on a piece of paper...

I'd probably turn the page to look at it from the inside out.

Yes. Mirrors didn't turn left and right around—

"They turn people—*inside out.*"

Now I understood.

For the first time since coming to this world, I finally got it—this was no mirrored land. Well, it was a totally correct understanding, but—the girls I'd seen hadn't been flipped around.

They were turned—inside out.

What was hidden inside of them was now on the outside.

Ah... That's why Tsukihi was the only one who hadn't changed, aside from her clothes—actually, even the clothes were a regular mistake by her standards, but in any case, that's the kind of person she is.

Someone with only one face—Tsukihi Araragi had no inner self that could appear, even in a mirror.

Yes.

Here, on the other side of that mirror, was an inner world.

108

014

To start with a discussion of terminology, the world you're placed in after completing a videogame used to be called a *secret world*—this might not be common knowledge since games these days tend not to have endings at all, but think of it as an especially hard stage, or maybe a bonus stage.

In my case, it meant the world on the other side of the surface, like the opposite side of a coin—you could also take it to mean an inside-out world.

I'd spent almost an entire day up to this point getting it all wrong. Of course, *a world where left and right are flipped around* and *an inside-out world* might not seem that different, and you might be thinking that they're the same thing at the end of the day. While that's true of the world as I saw it, it wasn't of the personalities that it contained.

I suppose Hanekawa's example is the easiest to understand. Black Hanekawa might not be Tsubasa Hanekawa, but it's not true either that they're two different people—nor is Black Hanekawa a fabrication who doesn't exist in the real world.

The aberration that appeared during Golden Week was both the *yokai* known as the Afflicting Cat and Tsubasa Hanekawa herself.

Something that saintly woman had repressed.

Her self and her long-suppressed pain.

That—was Tsubasa Hanekawa's inner self.

Oshino may have named it Black Hanekawa, but in truth, you could call the cat "Tsubasa Hanekawa" and Hanekawa "White Hanekawa"—and if we looked at this world from an inside-out perspective, the same applied to the others.

Seeing small Karen was so unconventional and novel that I felt a shock on the level of the discovery of a new continent—but as Miss Serpent said, Karen really was concerned about her height. The gap between her lack of growth as a person and her growing body existed in her mind.

It must've been there. If that inner part of her came to the surface—it'd take that form.

The way she looked wasn't at all new. It was a manifestation of her poor balance as a person.

In Ononoki's case, being a shikigami meant taking the form of an inexpressive, affectless doll lacking any intonation in her voice, but she'd told me in the past that she simply wasn't able to surface those qualities—couldn't display them on the outside, and that she wasn't inexpressive or affectless at all.

Taking into account Tadatsuru Teori's testimony, we might say that her interior in contrast to her exterior, who she was on the inside in contrast to on the outside, had been made visible.

In fact, my impression of Ononoki wasn't that her personality had changed but that her nasty personality had been exposed—and Mayoi Hachikuji's case was even easier.

Hachikuji, who previously appeared before me as a ten-year-old girl, was in fact a ghost who'd died ten-plus years ago. She'd be twenty-one if she'd aged normally.

She looked like a young girl on the outside but had the temperament of an adult woman on the inside. On the one hand, ghosts don't mature, time doesn't accumulate for aberrations, and you can't just tally up her mental age; on the other hand, even being sent to hell and becoming a god didn't annul her history of wandering the streets for eleven straight years.

I didn't understand it too well myself, but she had an inner side that was invisible to people like Kanbaru, who praised her to the skies and went on about cute young girls—and what I saw was what you got if you turned that inside out.

Speaking of Kanbaru, Suruga Kanbaru, her case was a little complicated—it was intertwined with her mother, Toé Kanbaru, and her aunt, Izuko Gaen. But if you looked at her on her own and spoke of her just in terms of inside and outside, her left hand—the Monkey's Paw—read the inner wishes of its owner from the start and granted them. Its very existence as an aberration was like a cheat code.

She wore a raincoat and tall rubber boots.

Her form as the Rainy Devil was the hidden, interior Suruga Kanbaru—while her attachment to me as her senior was genuine, she couldn't ever fully rid herself of the hatred she bore me.

It's not like something that never existed appeared.

It always existed there, always was there.

The distinctions make it sound like I was dealing with mathematical definitions, but you can simplify the problem by saying that the Rainy Devil was none other than Suruga Kanbaru—and speaking of math, there was Sodachi Oikura and her unwatchable version.

Honestly, I had yet to process what I'd witnessed. That open and free personality she'd never given a glimpse of, and the way she acted like one of the Araragis, might be something I'd daydreamed, but it was more for her sake, more than she'd ever ask for—so I'd like to think.

That happiness, too good to be true.

I wanted to believe from the bottom of my heart that Sodachi

Oikura hoped for that kind of thing—a girl like that on the other side of her prickly personality and hostile behavior did feel like some sort of saving grace.

Maybe I'm being too self-serving, but it's impossible for me to speak about her, a childhood friend, logically.

Compared to that, my evidence for Nadeko Sengoku's case might be slightly more convincing—because the god known as Miss Serpent, the indigenous god worshipped at Kita-Shirahebi Shrine, was something she'd hatched within her.

Maybe not quite a case of split personalities, but Shinobu and I had seen Sengoku speak with this serpent god once—a snake that had nested inside her, invisible to both of us.

That rough way of speaking, that rude, carefree behavior.

That too was Nadeko Sengoku—one and the same, as she said herself.

As hard as it was for me to accept, having only ever seen her as my little sister's friend, there was no Nadeko Sengoku who was simply reserved, introverted, and cute—something I had no choice but to accept with remorse.

Beneath the reserve was a childishness.

Beneath the introversion was aggression.

Beneath the cuteness was audacity, all there.

A Nadeko Sengoku who could explode, who could burst at any moment resided in Nadeko Sengoku—that's how it was.

I went back over my adventures through this world I saw as strange to find that it wasn't so at all. I'd simply been seeing these girls turned inside out.

This world allowed inconsistency and contradiction—not because it was a land of mirrors, but because the girls appeared as the characters they were in their own hearts and minds.

Freedom of thought.

Is that what you'd call it? It did center this world, which had felt so unstable and uncertain to me. It even changed the way I saw the sights, which simply seemed mirrored until then.

By the by, regarding what Miss Hachikuji told me about the etymology of "mirror" in Japanese, *kagami*, and how it's derived from "snake eyes," *kaga-mi*—there are of course many competing theories, one apparently being that it comes from "seeing shadows," or *kage-mi*. A device to see people's shadows.

Wherever there is light, there are shadows.

Whenever you see a surface, something exists underneath—everyone has another side to them.

Miss Serpent explained it to me in manga terms—out of nowhere, but I assumed it was for my own ease of understanding.

"I've heard you pick up certain bad habits when you're drawing faces looking left or right, depending on which hand you draw with—so when you draw a face looking in your weak direction, you check it later in a mirror, or even draw a face looking the other way on the back side and trace it over on the front. Yes, obverse and reverse are also about strengths and weaknesses—the same essence expressed in completely different manners."

The manga metaphor was easy for me to understand, but it was from an artist's perspective for some reason…

Hm. Okay, there were many types of reversals, and lazily, I'd harbored a major misunderstanding until now. Miss Serpent had been worth my time, and she'd just worked a miracle—still, hearing her interpretation made me wonder, *So what?*

Being in another world, in a place I saw as a foreign land, and not having the first clue as to how to return plagued me just the same as before.

This expert on mirrors had enlightened me with the knowledge that mirrors pierce a person's truth from the inside out, but there was no *Which is why you need to do this!* along with it.

Even if they weren't the girls I knew, they were still one side of them, so I'd resolved not to treat them with disdain—but I'd gained no answer or solution to the question of how to get back to my original world and why this had happened.

No, strictly speaking, she made a fairly sharp point about the why, even if it wasn't a full hypothesis—*she* in this case being not Miss Serpent, but Miss Hachikuji.

Lo and behold, she hadn't been bluffing about giving her opinion at the end—she did have one doubt, unrelated to Miss Serpent's take. A question she'd found herself with after we'd parted ways earlier that day.

"Well, putting aside this place being inside a mirror, or a mirrored land, or another world, or another dimension, whatever—there are people you know here, right? Like your family and friends, your juniors and childhood acquaintances?"

"Yup… In that sense, I haven't been tossed into a completely unfamiliar realm, but your point?"

"What about you? Where are you, Araragi?"

Me?

"You haven't met you, Araragi—isn't that strange? Everyone knows you, me and Miss Serpent included—we each have a relationship with you. Some of us, like Suruga, might try to attack you, but that's still a kind of relationship. But doesn't that mean you've existed in this world long before you ever came here?"

"…"

"In that case, where did that Araragi go? Your personality and behavior seem familiar to us…but you're not this world's Koyomi Araragi, are you? Shouldn't another Araragi aside from you—shouldn't your inner self be in this world?"

There we go. The idea, or maybe clue that slipped away from me when I was talking to Oikura…

The normal Koyomi Araragi.

Traveling through time with Shinobu, we'd talked about there being two patterns: "you" existing in the time traveled to, and "you" being absent. In this case, though, there was only one possibility.

If the girls here knew me, it didn't make sense for me not to exist—even if I wasn't here now, I had to be before now.

When I looked in the mirror this morning.

That mirror image that didn't line up with my movements.

Those eyes that seemed to glare at me—

"Could Araragi have gone to the other world, switching places with you, Araragi? And now he's confused by 'a nonsensical world where everything is consistent'... Heh, I think they'd be having a tougher time over there than we're having here."

"...That still makes things tough for us, too. We'd have to sync up perfectly with the other side when both of us return to our original worlds."

Oh—actually, if the me who wasn't me was in a world with Shinobu, things could get settled faster. We might be able to communicate with that world without using the Kanbarus' wooden bath.

No.

Even if that were true—even if the me from this world had gotten sucked into the other world to take my place, it still wouldn't go that well.

How would we pull off a perfectly synchronized two-man play? There was no guarantee that we thought the same way just because we were two sides of the same coin, the same person.

Twins can share the same genes but have different fingerprints. Why would the timing of our actions line up—this was the bigger issue.

Because.

Because thinking this through—judging by the examples of Black Hanekawa and the Rainy Devil, even if Koyomi Araragi existed in this world.

The flip side of Koyomi Araragi—was my nemesis.

It would have to be Ogi Oshino.

015

I wanted to complain if all of this was Ogi's plot. This is way too fast for you to be coming for revenge, how obsessed with retaliation are you, I know it's not on the heels of yesterday but this is still on the heels of the day before yesterday, I'd say, but what good would it do to make speculative comments to a person who wasn't even present—though the fact that the girl known for appearing at the most unexpected of times had yet to show herself for once did make me feel very uneasy. If this world's Ogi had been sent to the other world to take my place, that meant there were two Ogis over there, and well, just the thought was scary. The world I needed to return to would be enveloped in darkness. Two Ogis... I couldn't think of any way to deal with that. I nearly felt glad I wasn't present for it.

"True, Araragi, it doesn't change what we have to do—somehow sneak over to the bath in Suruga's place and communicate with the other world. I don't imagine avoiding the Rainy Devil's watchful eye would be easy, though."

"Yeah...I guess," I sighed.

"I know I'm repeating myself, but there's no point in panicking... Go to bed for today. You only have a regular human's stamina now, so resting is an important step in achieving your goals. What do you want to do? Wanna stay here at this shrine?"

"I appreciate the offer, but no, I think I'll go home… There's something I want to check there, anyway."

"Oh. Well, Miss Serpent and I will keep on going, so come by again tomorrow, maybe in the evening. If you do get the chance to go back to the other side, though, you of course shouldn't let it get away. Leave a letter behind or something if that happens."

"Okay… I'm sorry for causing you all this trouble."

"You haven't caused any trouble at all—and it's my job now to keep this town under control," Miss Hachikuji said, with dignity. She only recently became a god in this world too, but seeing her so in her element was somehow very reassuring.

So this was what divine favor felt like—even if Miss Serpent added, "Well, you're causing trouble for me, pulling me back in like this when I've retired." Although she spat this venom at me (in keeping with her nature as a poisonous snake), she also said, "Eh. I'm curious about what that cat is up to," hinting at something before going quiet.

Come to think of it, we'd never gotten to Miss Serpent and Black Hanekawa's relationship, and the snake god started heading back before I could ask… Maybe she'd never meant to tell me—not that it seemed important. Logic suggested that a third party had gotten involved if I'd been saved by Black Hanekawa, who hated me, but logic had no meaning in this world.

"This might be turning into a drawn-out campaign, but I can't stay here for too long," I griped. "There's paperwork I'll need to do to enroll if I passed my entrance exams."

"In the worst case, just have Shinobu take you back to the past once you've returned."

"That's the kind of obviously flawed solution from an episode of *Doraemon*…"

"By the way. In *Doraemon*, Nobita ends up getting married to

Shizuka because he changed his own future. But that means Shizuka has to get married to someone she used to look down on, when she should've married Dekisugi, a way better guy who's almost too good to be true. How are we supposed to feel about that?"

"…"

A view befitting a young woman. As a boy, I didn't know what to say.

In any case, I walked down the mountain, got on the BMX, and headed back home—where was the owner of the bike?

The BMX existing in this world implied that Ogi existed in it until at least the day before yesterday, but I couldn't say for sure… It was hard to live in a world that allowed for inconsistency.

It defanged all of my theories and reasoning.

I'm not clever by any stretch, but in my own way, I'd used my wits to get myself out of every situation thus far—so it felt like I'd lost a weapon here in a world with no use for wisdom. Even if that wisdom wasn't much to speak of.

Even my line of thought that a Nadeko Sengoku unlike any Nadeko I knew proved this wasn't a dream might be an instance of overthinking things—there was no rule saying that knowledge you didn't possess couldn't appear in a dream.

And even if this wasn't my dream, it might be someone else's—though that gave this story an SF tinge all over again.

…I suddenly wondered what Hitagi Senjogahara was like in this world. Oikura showed that you could be the complete opposite, and while I didn't have the bad taste to desire it, what was Hitagi Senjogahara like in a world where your inner self came to the surface?

I'd be lying if I said I wasn't curious.

Still, I had to admit it'd be in bad taste—even if it provided me with a hint on how to escape this world, it was only a pretext for sneaking a look at my girlfriend's heart.

Anything that'd make me unable to look her in the eyes after

I got back home was off limits—and as I swore this to myself, I arrived at the Araragi residence.

Half as a joke, I tried imagining how things might be for her. No harm in that, right? Maybe it was fine if a Hitagi still lived in the palatial estate that once stood, supposedly, near Shirohebi Park, where Black Hanekawa had taken me after kidnapping me.

The Valhalla Duo might be going strong, too, with no rupture between their time together in middle school and high school—it didn't link up with the Rainy Devil's existence, but consistency wasn't a thing in this mirrored land.

While this world was nothing but trouble for me, that made me wonder if it wasn't so bad after all—this place could even allow for a future where everyone's happy, that idea mocked by Oshino.

Well, it was nothing more than wishful thinking, and things naturally didn't turn out as I wanted—the detail I wanted to check at home ended up being a swing and a miss. I thought meeting my parents once they came back from their jobs might strengthen Miss Serpent's divine hypothesis (hy-apotheosis?) about this being an inside-out world, but their work was going late, and neither would be returning tonight.

Talk about bad timing... I did get what info I could from my little sisters and Oikura, but my parents, like Tsukihi, weren't too different from the people I knew.

I couldn't say for certain until I saw them, but then again, even if it wasn't at Tsukihi's level, neither was the type to have a hidden side... Of course, I'm sure part of it was the fact they were adults, and my parents.

You could turn their personalities inside out, but if you covered it all up with "adulthood," they wouldn't seem any different... I had to admit, I was a bit relieved. The feeling wasn't as strong as with Hitagi, but I didn't particularly want to see who my parents were on the inside.

I began to regret not taking Miss Hachikuji up on her kind offer if this was the outcome. In addition to not wanting to impose too much, I'd refused because my good sense told me that while a ten-year-young girl was one thing, staying the night with a twenty-one-year-old Hachikuji was out of the question.

The wall between minor and adult wasn't nothing, but if you just looked at the numbers, only three years separated us—seeing Mayoi Hachikuji as a woman didn't come easily at this point, but I still needed to draw a line.

Yes, I knew how to behave myself.

Or so I thought, but after I got out of the bath and saw there indeed wasn't anything strange about my bathroom mirror and felt dejected; after I put on an optimistic mask and decided to go to bed because everything might be back to normal when I woke up in the morning; once I entered my flipped-around room—

"Koyomi! Oh, you. You're gonna catch a cold if you don't dry off your hair. Not that it'd make you any less hot! Haha," Oikura said from her top bunk. She was wearing heart-patterned pajamas and reading a book of sample math questions.

…Come to think of it, I hadn't entered my room in this world, but I should've seen it coming.

Since Oikura lived with us and we only had a limited number of rooms, the kids—me, Karen, Tsukihi, and Oikura—had to form two pairs. Apparently, I was with Oikura.

Not spending the night with the older Miss Hachikuji was making me use the same bunk bed as Oikura, who was my age… I began putting together a sneaky escape to the sofa on the first floor, but it ended in failure.

"Whaaat? Why, why, why? Did I do something wrong?! Are you mad, Koyomi? Stop it, don't act so distant! What, are you seeing me as a girl now?!" asked Oikura, or someone else I didn't recognize, squashing my plan. As much as I dreaded an extended war, I didn't have a solid idea of when I'd be returning to my world, so I had to be careful not to act too suspicious.

Witnessing Oikura in such high spirits was probably insulting to her, but this Oikura didn't totally satisfy the theory that I was in an inside-out world where the internal was made external. There was the very practical matter of having to observe her... Talking to her made it clear that we did indeed live in the same room, but we at least respected each other's privacy when changing and the like, so I gave up resisting and got into the lower bunk bed.

As sad as it is to admit, I felt a little excited about getting in a bunk bed for the first time in so long... Back when I was little and sharing a room with my sisters, I'd insist on the top bunk (Karen, Tsukihi, and I rotated each night between a bunk bed and a single bed), but the bottom bunk was interesting in its own way. Knowing that someone was sleeping right above me felt odd—even apart from the said person being Oikura.

"Hey, Oiku—Sodachi. Do you know anything about mirrors?" I asked upwards after turning off the lights. I wouldn't say I was going all-in, but I should make effective use of anyone as smart as her.

With so much I couldn't say, my question had become pretty straightforward. Despite the complete change in her, Oikura's answer wasn't perfunctory and went beyond flipping things around.

"I guess I remember hearing that they never reflect an image accurately," she replied sleepily. "Because while mirrors reflect the light that hits them, it's impossible to reflect all the light. How did it go again? Normal mirrors are only about eighty percent reflective? They always end up absorbing some amount of light. So—mirrored images look blurrier than the real thing."

"..."

"We might look at ourselves in the mirror, but we only ever see a blurred image...can only know a blurry version of ourselves. Inaccurately, with a dim outline..."

I was intrigued and wanted to hear more, but it seemed Oikura had fallen asleep.

Mirrors aren't precise with their reflections.

Info that could turn into the first step of a solution, or maybe not—perhaps it was a careless question if my goal was to keep up appearances.

It also felt like I was hitting some kind of limit… Relying too much on gods like Miss Hachikuji and Miss Serpent didn't seem right, maybe I should take this opportunity to visit Kanbaru's home tomorrow with Oikura? No, probably not.

Find a partner.

That's what Black Hanekawa said—but that partner didn't exist in this world.

Someone I could rely on in a situation like this, without forethought…not even about the trouble I might cause. She really was the only one for me in the end, I thought, and before long I fell asleep too.

As I did, a dreamy notion went through my mind: I'd forgotten and couldn't remember, but maybe, back when I was a grade schooler and the Araragis had taken her in for a time, I'd drifted off to sleep with Oikura like this.

016

Someone woke me up right away.

Like they were waiting for me to fall asleep.

For a moment, I was in that state where I didn't know if I was asleep or awake, in a dream or in a daze, but even after that moment passed and I woke up, I didn't know what was going on.

"Shh."

There, standing by the bed with her index finger up against her mouth, the lights still off, was none other than the shikigami tween of unknown whereabouts, Yotsugi Ononoki.

It was Ononoki.

No, that wouldn't have been so confusing on its own—it was the usual level of eccentric (and harassing) behavior for her. Normally I'd have the mental composure to feel nice and relieved that she'd made it back home safe—but.

There was a reason that didn't happen.

"Kind monster sir, you need to get up without making a sound. Without waking up Big Sis Sodachi. Put on clothes so that you can go outside," Ononoki said, her tone uninflected, unfeeling, and flat—spoken with such little expression on her face that I knew exactly how she looked even in the dark, unlit room. That was why.

No expression, no emotion, just words, just standing there.

She did have that outfit on with the pants, but I was certain that she was the Yotsugi Ononoki I knew.

"...?"

What was going on? Why?

Why did yet another exception have to pop up just as I'd gotten used to this world and started doing my best to analyze it—where was the emotive Ononoki?

Then, this Ononoki said something to exacerbate my confusion.

In, of course, a flat tone.

There was no feeling behind her words, but they were as shocking as could be.

"Stay quiet and just follow me, monstieur. If you do, I'll take you to Shinobu—to the Kissshot Acerolaorion Heartunderblade who exists in this world."

017

"I should let you know in advance…not to get your hopes up too high. I've barely figured any of this out myself, and I'm far from being able to say I understand it all," Ononoki warned as we plodded along the streets at night. Wherever it was we were heading, the Unlimited Rulebook could have gotten us there in no time with a single hop, but I wasn't up to it in my current form.

A method of transportation that violent would kill any flesh-and-blood human.

So I was on foot, and not on the BMX, either—Ononoki could probably keep up with me even if I biked at full speed, but I didn't feel like trying. Though not as bad as the Unlimited Rulebook, riding that altered bike in the middle of the night was far too dangerous.

"Ononoki."

"What is it, monstieur?"

"Er, well…"

She'd replied in a flat tone, at her own leisure, not so much as looking in my direction—indeed the Ononoki I knew.

After assaulting me in my sleep…or just rousing me from it, she'd led me out of my home, careful not to wake Oikura or my sisters, and made me walk for quite some distance now. Yet I hadn't gotten used to her.

Okay, in terms of what I am and am not used to, this was the Ononoki I was used to and felt comfortable around—but why had she "flipped around" to being this way all of a sudden?

I had no idea what had caused the inside-out her to turn inside out again—not explaining a thing was also very much like her. I hesitated to ask her any direct questions and was tamely following her through town.

That makes me sound so passive, but I just couldn't ignore the name she'd spoken—Kissshot Acerolaorion Heartunderblade.

A vampire, who shouldn't exist in this mirrored land—no, wait. If this was more than a world "inside a mirror," then maybe it wasn't too strange for a vampire to exist here?

That seemed like a stretch—but if Ononoki really was going to take me to Shinobu (excuse the cautious wording, but the Ononoki I knew wouldn't think twice about telling that malicious of a lie), we'd move toward a solution in no time at all, wouldn't we? It'd save us the trouble of having to contact Shinobu on the other side.

If this side's Shinobu opened up a gate on this side, I'd be able to return to my original world—an immediate simplification of the plan.

The thought was exciting enough that being roused in the middle of the night felt fair. Sadly, I also realized that at no time in my whole career had a twist been so convenient.

My natural reaction was to brace myself.

It was like watching a movie and knowing, given how long it'd gone so far, that a certain twist could only be the middle act and not the climax—not that I should let my guard down, since my story could get lopped off, cut short before its finale.

In any case, I couldn't stay silent forever. The change in Ononoki intimidated me, and I was losing my motivation after all these dizzying twists and turns, but better to be the boy who cried wolf than the one who jumped at his own shadow.

I made my move.

"That outfit looks good on you."

Made my move, starting from a distance.

Hey, even the most talented boxer starts off with a few jabs.

"Thank you," Ononoki said, surprising me by taking the compliment—she wasn't the type, so her words, even if they were flat, stunned me. "Though this does feel wrong in its own way—I feel like I was wearing cuter clothes. Not that there's any point in complaining about such a trivial matter... In any case, they're not to my taste. No, maybe this is my taste... My taste, as well as my bad taste."

"..."

"Oh, you want me to explain, don't you? All right, I get it. I know what you're like, kind monster sir, from the way you like little girls to the way you like tween girls."

"Know me less narrowly, please. And that's not what I'm like, that's what I like... Not that those are my likes!"

"I am a professional, you know," Ononoki objected. "When you saw me and spoke to me this morning, you seemed sure that there was something off about this world... And the way you were acting, I started to feel like something was off too."

When you gaze into the abyss, the abyss gazes into you, Ononoki pulled out an awfully pretentious quote.

Put simply, she'd been surprised to see me surprised. I'd thought I'd managed to get out of that situation, even if I hadn't kept a cool head through it all. Her keen professional eyes drove home that I was just an amateur.

"What? Monstieur leaving without even trying to pull down my pants? Impossible, I thought. That doubt is where it all started."

"Please don't use that as a starting point. And when you say that, do you mean just take off your pants, or your underwear too?"

"Well, peer into your own bosom for the answer... Speaking of chests, it was also suspicious that the man who always used my chest, didn't."

"What do you even mean by that? How am I a man who's always using your chest?"

"It's my curse to be unable to let any grounds for concern go, you see. Once you left, I performed a self-check—what about my condition surprised you? I wondered what had us make out."

"Make out? I'm pretty sure we didn't."

"Sorry. I meant to say, *what had you creeped out.*"

"Those are nothing like each other. How do you make a mistake like that?"

Of course, anyone would feel creeped out if we really did make out...

"My maintenance couldn't pinpoint why you felt creeped out, but at least I realized that I was not currently in a state to perform at full capacity. I was defective as a monster, as a shikigami who serves Big Sis—and so."

I rebuilt my personality, she said—Yotsugi Ononoki did.

If ever she'd spoken in a monotone, it was as she said this line. The casual way she passed it off made it easier for me to digest. Oh, of course, yes, no, hold on, what did she just say? She rebuilt her personality?

"In other words, I *scrubbed* my character—polished it up. I'm not sure if I did a good job of it, but it seems to have gone well for the most part, judging by your reaction."

"..."

This was a bombshell...but she was right.

Now that she mentioned it, she was right.

As an artificial aberration, Yotsugi Ononoki didn't have a consistent character. She was always influenced by her surroundings, ever *shifting*—indeed like a mirror, always influenced by those

130

around her, always reflecting them.

It seemed more like a flaw than a characteristic, but to think it'd end up working this way...

While her ever-changing, kaleidoscopic personality had thrown me for multiple, painful loops, putting up with it had paid off. A smug expression and tone did hamper Ononoki's ability to do her job, so it made sense for her self-check to catch them.

It did...but having experienced for myself just how big of an ask it was for something to "make sense" in this world, I couldn't help but be impressed by Ononoki, who'd done it all on her own.

"Oh, it's hardly commendable. I couldn't have done it without your help. That's why I thanked you. Thank you, monstieur, for not taking off my pants."

"C'mon, it was nothing. I just didn't do what comes naturally to me."

Nope—just don't.

Let *that* come naturally.

But thinking too hard about it brought up a new set of questions—because if the Koyomi Araragi who existed in this world was Ogi Oshino, I couldn't see her ever doing such a thing.

I wouldn't, but she was even less likely to—Ogi stripping a doll naked and playing with it every morning betrayed who she was as a character more than anything I'd seen.

Too painful a sight.

All of this hinted at unexplained mysteries...but in any case, I felt encouraged that Ononoki had returned to being the character I knew.

"Of course, only someone like you who changes personalities like a dress-up doll changes clothes could do that."

She was the polar opposite of Tsukihi, who was herself because she only had one side to her. Ononoki's duality was so excessive that she could change even her inside-out self.

To use Oikura's mirror reflectivity analogy, her outlines were fuzzy from the beginning, so her image never got set in place.

"Like I said, it's not like I understand what's going on either—in fact, I'm really pushing it here. Changing who I am as a character to this degree is deviating pretty far from what's allowed of an aberration… I wouldn't be surprised if the Darkness showed up."

"!?"

The word sent a shiver down my spine—a visceral reaction.

Oh. So that concept existed in this world too.

The very embodiment of darkness seemed even less tenable than vampires in a mirrored land consisting of reflections of light, but I guess it didn't matter because it was non-existent from the outset.

It traumatized me even more than that snake god, but Ononoki remained serene—because she'd remade her personality to be that way, but still…

"And so, monstieur, there's only so much I can do. It'll threaten my existence if I go too wild," she said. "I can't vanish before fulfilling my promise to you, that we'd go and see the ocean together one day."

"…"

I'd made that cool-sounding of a promise?

While also pulling down her pants every morning?

Whatever the case, I now understood why Ononoki had turned back into the character I knew. It was news to me that she was best able to perform, in peak condition, when she was stone-faced and flat-toned, but maybe it was called being unaffected.

Even in martial arts, they do say that the ultimate stance is having no stance at all—being a doll with no personality meant she could play any role she wanted.

I'd learned once again that in spite of her freewheeling ways, Ononoki was surprisingly professional at all times.

"So, what did you do after that?" I asked her. "Are you saying that you went off to investigate this strange state of affairs, just like I went to Kita-Shirahebi Shrine to ask for help?"

"You went to Kita-Shirahebi Shrine... Huh. Tell me about that later, will you?"

"Oh, so you don't know what I've been doing." The offhanded way she'd brought up Shinobu's name made it feel like she knew every last thing I'd done today.

"Hey, don't be holding such high hopes for me. My head's pretty messed up right now because I put too much into reforming my personality—I assumed you were off doing something, monsieur, but it was just about as likely that you were off buying a present for Sodachi."

"How likely is that? Zero percent?"

"Well, she kept asking you. 'Koyomiii, you have to buy me one, buy it for me! Please! I'm not letting you go until you say yes!'"

"I've really been spoiling her, huh..."

What had she begged me for?

And just what kind of person was I in this world, trying to take off Ononoki's pants and indulging Oikura when it wasn't even her birthday (I felt pretty certain it wasn't)?

"Ah. Sodachi's going to feel so let down."

"Stop, don't pressure me like that," I said. "Any idea of letting her down is painful to me. Don't pile more tasks on top of what I already have on my plate... So, after surveying the town...you decided to have me and Shinobu meet?"

"Right. Of course, the former Heartunderblade is different from the former Heartunderblade you know. I'm not giving you the details yet, I want to enjoy seeing your reaction when you meet in person... Just be ready for it."

"Yeah, okay... Wait, you just want to see my reaction? That's your reason?"

"Yup. What're you gonna do about it?"

"Why are you even doubling down?"

Hmph.

While we didn't have a particularly good relationship back in my original world—let's just call it a long and bumpy ride—going back and forth with Ononoki "like usual" did help soothe my nerves.

Only, I had to think about Shinobu being different, as Ononoki put it. Maybe I needed to be not just ready, but on alert—because I couldn't begin to imagine what the other side of Shinobu was like, who her inner self was.

If she existed in this world, we could solve everything just by getting her to open a gate from this side—my line of thought went, but it was an optimistic one that ignored such issues.

Though it wasn't in this mirrored land, I'd met another iteration of Shinobu in another timeline—I'd encountered the aberration known as Kissshot Acerolaorion Heartunderblade.

She resented and abhorred me.

Enough to destroy the world.

That probably wasn't the exact form of Shinobu's other side, but no one could deny the possibility existed in her.

She'd lived for around six hundred years. There had to be many "other sides" to her—and to be frank, I wasn't confident I could accept them all.

This was no time for pathetic whining, though... So long as that monkey demon protected the Kanbarus' wood bath, we needed to try a different approach, if any existed.

"I know nothing," Ononoki said, "about the circumstances on your side... Do I get along with Big Sis *over there?*"

"Hm? Er, well," I stammered. I didn't really know the answer to that one. When I'd asked Miss Kagenui about their relationship—for whatever reason, she'd deflected the question.

"Hm. Well, I'd imagine as much."

Ononoki shrugged, taking my silence for an answer—her face showed no expression, so I couldn't tell if she felt any way about that.

It wouldn't have been Ononoki any other way, of course.

I felt a little bad—when I thought about it, I'd taken this world's Ononoki, who'd been living a peaceful, expressive life as a doll, and turned her into a flat, emotionless, doll-like doll. Maybe I needed to reflect on what I'd done.

It may have been her professionalism, but she didn't need to act just because she noticed this land of mirrors wasn't logically consistent.

"So, monstieur. Where did you go today, and whose pants did you take off?"

"Can't I get at least a little sentimental over you? If you want to know, ask me like a normal person."

"What was it? You went to Kita-Shirahebi first thing to take off Miss Mayoi's pants?"

"Imagine the kind of divine punishment that'd get me. Instant karma."

Bantering like this, I gave Ononoki a rough outline of my day. I was afraid it'd take a while—we might arrive at our destination before I was done (she still wouldn't tell me where we were going. Did she want to see my reaction to that, too?), but my fears proved groundless.

Then again, only two things had happened: I'd failed to enter the Kanbaru estate, and Black Hanekawa had saved me. My surprise over the personality differences I witnessed today was a subjective matter.

"Hm. So you met Miss Mayoi, Big Sis Monkey, Big Sis Cat, Big Sis Snake, and Big Sis Sodachi today, and took off their pants."

"At this point, you obviously mean their underwear too?"

"Oops. I forgot to include the Fire Sisters."

"No need for that."

"Wow, monstieur, impressive. Your little sisters' pants don't even count."

"Am I not impressing you in any other way? If that's what you took from everything I just said, even I'm gonna be depressed."

"Well, to me it just sounds like the regulars I know in the regular way I know them—but I do agree with you about one thing."

"Huh, what's that?"

"Looks like we're on the same page for once…"

"We're not in some kind of buddy-cop movie. We've agreed plenty of times before. What is it?" I asked again.

"Black Hanekawa saving you—is almost impossible if we went by my understanding of her."

Oh… I'd wondered if an "inside-out" Black Hanekawa also felt differently about me, but if that was the professional opinion of this world's Ononoki…

Then was my initial guess correct? She'd saved me on someone's request? I'd suspected it was Ononoki, but that seemed unlikely after this exchange.

"Who could it be, though? Who'd ask Black Hanekawa to save me?"

"Indeed. Who would ever want to save you? Certainly not me."

"That's not what I meant—the kind of person who'd go to Black Hanekawa with that request. Certainly not you? How about you stop being so hurtful? You're helping me right now, aren't you?"

"I want you to think that, just so I can abandon you at the last possible moment and enjoy the look on your face."

"How unbelievably nasty are you? Start over and remake your character again."

In any case, I'd hoped to glean some kind of clue from Ononoki, but she didn't seem to have any idea either. The mystery persisted.

Not that it had deepened—I was now able to talk to Ononoki like this, and it was by pushing forward that we'd make progress.

"Does Shinobu know I'm coming? I won't pepper you with questions if you don't want me to, but I'm just curious. Did you, uh, make an appointment?"

"I did. Don't worry, I'm not sure how it is in your world, but that woman and I are friends in this one."

"That absolutely can't be true. Even the phrase *that woman and I* sounds hostile... Hm?"

And then.

After coming this far, I knew where we were headed. Normally I'd realize sooner, but between it being nighttime and the streets being flipped around, it took me a little longer. I'd visited the location countless times over the past year.

The ruins that the vagrant expert known as Mèmè Oshino once treated as his castle and keep—the building beyond us was that former cram school.

In the world I knew, it had caught fire last summer and burned to the ground, but it still had to be fine here if that's where Ononoki was taking me.

Maybe in this world, instead of dwelling in my shadow, Shinobu continued to live in that classroom ever since she was there together with Oshino?

In that case, she might not be too amicable towards me...or rather, *Koyomi Araragi*.

I didn't think my life was in danger, especially with Ononoki around, but maybe I needed to get my guard up a little higher.

"What's wrong, monstieur? You suddenly went quiet. Did you die?"

"No, why'd I die? I was just thinking. Maybe I shouldn't be, since everyone keeps telling me I'm overthinking things, but I just can't help it."

"Teal, don't mink, as they like to say."

"You mean feel, don't think."

"It's the same thing—reach for the skies and don't stay too grounded. Your thoughts need to be free. As an outsider, you might find the right balance that I can't as someone who's always

137

lived in this world…or you might feel sorry that you got me involved in this and get on all fours to lick my boot."

"I do feel bad, but not that bad."

"Works for me. I don't want you licking my boot."

"Now it sounds like something else."

"Don't mind. I knew this day would come."

"…"

Huh? Another one of those cool lines you'd expect from an unlikely duo of crime-fighters? As in, it was clear we'd fight side by side eventually—but when I tried to ask her what she meant, it was a bit late for such questions.

We'd arrived at our destination.

My prediction turned out to be half right, half wrong—no, I'm grading myself too easily.

Objectively speaking, I was ninety percent wrong. I'd only gotten the location right.

Of course, it was sort of impressive that I'd gotten the location right at least: where the abandoned cram school Mèmè Oshino once treated as his castle and keep *used to stand*.

That much was right.

In my world, it'd caught fire and turned into a burnt-out field, leaving no traces behind. The same wasn't true in this world.

In fact—a completely *different building* stood there.

"Daze…"

I was so dazed that I actually said the word. I mean, I wouldn't be this surprised if I'd seen an office complex, a house, a store—simply another building.

Actually, it didn't matter where. I'd be just as surprised if *this* stood anywhere in town, former cram-school site or not.

"…"

There, on the real estate Mèmè Oshino once treated as his castle and keep, was an actual castle for goodness' sake.

018

I call it a castle, but it wasn't the domestic kind found in Nagoya or Kumamoto. Western style—a massive edifice atop plenty of square footage towering over all.

It shot into the sky.

Grand enough to qualify as a certified cultural asset, in my amateur opinion—soaring high in a Japanese suburb in the middle of nowhere, it seemed too surreal to be true.

Like a poorly faked photo.

It was hard to accept, easier to buy as some sort of 3D graphics—its style and its ancient, austere mood suggested that it hadn't been built on the site of that abandoned building but had stood there for many centuries—for six hundred years, so to speak.

"…"

This was a new one.

Over the course of the day I'd seen many humans, as well as aberrations, existing in a different way, but this was the first time any building or piece of scenery had transformed beyond being flipped around.

Did I need to gather something from this? It did tell me that my journey was entering the next stage.

"Shinobu…is here, right? She lives in this castle, doesn't she, Ononoki?"

"Yes, kind monster sir. She's here—she lives here. Heartunderblade, the former Kissshot Acerolaorion Heartunderblade. Now they call her Keepshot Castleorion Fortunderblade."

"Liar…what a blatant lie. You're not pulling that one on me."

"Well, you'd have found a castle this fantastic even if I didn't bring you here, but I thought I'd mediate between you two… Now, shall we?"

"G-Go in? This isn't the sort of place you just stroll into."

"A castle's not going to have an intercom, okay?"

True, it'd be such a letdown—the solemn structure felt like it might have sentries on guard, but they didn't seem to be around either.

It really was like a cultural asset in that sense, not a domicile. Then again, that seemed to suit a vampire.

I knew surprisingly little about vampires despite having turned into one and wasn't too familiar with their types of castles. Still, I'd believe it if you told me a legendary vampire lived here.

Its presence in our Podunk town felt as wrong as could be—but I followed after Ononoki.

The castle's halls and stairs were dark, and an eeriness overwhelmed any sense of majesty—did it not have electricity? To make it seem like the Middle Ages? This was more like actually from them…

"Speaking of which, Ononoki."

"What is it, kind monster sir?"

"About my adventures that I just told you about… I'd been convinced that Shinobu didn't exist in this world. Since vampires don't appear in mirrors, there wouldn't be any inside one, either. Miss Hachikuji thought so, too… Well, she didn't out and say it, but seemed to imply it. So why is Shinobu here? Why's she living in a castle she built?"

"There seems to be a bit of a misunderstanding…on your part, and on Miss Mayoi's. She only became a god recently and isn't perfect. Of course, as immature as she is, and despite how it may look, she's doing her absolute best."

"How condescending… How high of a pedestal are you putting yourself on to look down on her that hard?"

"Hey, that's part of what's inconsistent about this world. Kind monster sir, I call you kind monster sir, don't I?"

"Yep. That's been your name for me for some time."

"Do you know why I call you that?"

"Why? Well, yeah, I guess I do?"

"Oh. *Because I don't*," Ononoki said, making no sense at all.

"What's that supposed to—"

"A mirror world, or the flip side… It falls into place when you explain it that way. From my perspective, of course, your world seems narrow and constricted. The reverse reversed is the obverse—you might say, but really, it's still reversed," Ononoki intoned. Our dark surroundings didn't seem to affect an aberration like her, and she walked just as steadily as when we were outside. "Every coin has two sides…but you can also have a record with two A-sides. Don't you feel this world is a lot fairer and squarer than a world where you have to put on a happy face to hide what's underneath?"

"That's, er, um."

Don't be ridiculous. Like I'd ever feel that way.

Or so I began to say, but my judgment kicked in and I thought better of dissing the ways of this world too harshly. I was talking to one of its inhabitants—but this itself was an example of the "happy face" she mentioned, a surface at odds with my inner self.

A surface, and what lurks below.

Discussing them as opposites tends to give off the impression that the surface is good, while what lurks below is bad, but that's not always the case—smoothing over a mistake isn't fixing it, and

141

we shouldn't judge a book by its cover.

But going on to argue that authenticity lies beneath the surface, or that surface appearances are always false, doesn't seem right either—take Miss Serpent's gruff, disheveled attitude. That might be Sengoku's inner self, the real her, but the Sengoku I knew, who always had her eyes to the ground, was the real her too.

Inside, outside, both sides are you.

The quickest way to lose sight of yourself is actually to start going on about *your true self*—there's nothing wrong with going on a journey of self-discovery, but how do you even take the first step if you lack a self to begin with?

I did wonder about Shinobu. I'd been focusing on her relationship with me, but I was curious about the "inner side" of her other facets…

"This way. The former Heartunderblade is waiting for you in her bedchamber—not that that's what you should call her. She might not be Keepshot Castleorion Fortunderblade, but I don't know about Shinobu Oshino either."

"What do you mean? There's nothing *former* about her?"

"You're a sharp one. What a shame—one less thing for me to enjoy seeing."

Stop trying to enjoy this. Keep your enjoyment quota at zero.

But hold on, it meant that right now—that in this world, Shinobu hadn't lost what made her special as a vampire and was at the height of her powers.

Not the former Kissshot Acerolaorion Heartunderblade, not Shinobu Oshino, but the genuine Kissshot Acerolaorion Heartunderblade?

I suspected she wouldn't be in her little-girl form, but still… it forced me think of the Shinobu who destroyed the world in a different timeline. I needed to be even more on my toes than I was already.

Or so I thought, but when Ononoki finally led me to the bedchamber—a word that doesn't do justice to how big it was—and I saw her there, waiting for me on her luxurious and magnificent bed, I realized that my resolve fell short.

This world wasn't going to abide by my expectations—that said, while I didn't expect this, it wasn't an unbelievable, unfathomable twist either.

Seeing it, I could believe it.

Technically, I saw nothing. The bed was enveloped by a thin curtain, and I only saw dimly through it, but the silhouette was all I needed to figure out the rest.

I figured it all out.

"Thank you for venturing all this way, Sir Araragi, and well met. It is a pleasure to meet you—I suppose I should say. I am Kissshot Acerolaorion Heartunderblade."

Her cordial greeting sounded like something from another time.

But this elegant lady was no vampire.

She was human.

019

Ah, well—in that case, sure.

In that case.

Vampires aren't reflected in mirrors and therefore can't enter them—that was my logic for why Shinobu wasn't in my shadow. I'd accepted that my partner didn't exist in this world, but there was a hole in that logic.

A hole, or rather, an opening. The fact that I, my vampiric nature deleted, existed here was already the answer. If the same phenomenon had visited Shinobu, she too could exist.

No, putting it that way was misleading. The Shinobu Oshino I knew, or the former Heartunderblade as Ononoki called her, had indeed been left behind in the other world—but that didn't mean she didn't exist in this one.

Just as there was no big Karen in this world, while a small Karen existed, *it had its own Shinobu Oshino.*

Now I understood Ononoki's puzzling line—about why she called me kind monster sir, monstieur, and so on.

The reason was clear in the other world. Though it wasn't exactly polite, calling a one-time vampire thrall a monster made sense.

Miss Hachikuji and Miss Serpent saw me in the same way, but if vampires couldn't exist in this world, a vampire thrall shouldn't either. There was an inconsistency—they knew I'd fallen victim to a vampire but also weren't aware of any vampires, a contradiction.

Vampires indeed didn't exist in this world, so there was no need to call me a monster, but no vampires didn't mean no Shinobu Oshino. I'd forgotten until just now, but according to what I'd heard over spring break a year ago, the iron-blooded, hot-blooded, yet cold-blooded vampire, the Aberration Slayer Kissshot Acerola-orion Heartunderblade, was once human.

Six hundred years ago, she was human.

Of the highest stock—yes, the kind of princess who might live in a castle, who'd see her castle as her extension. That—was her other side.

The flip side of Shinobu Oshino.

"Please, there's no cause to feel so tense. Lift your head, Sir Araragi."

Lift my head.

I finally noticed that I'd been having these thoughts on bent knee—I couldn't believe it. I'd genuflected reflexively, not to the vampiric but human aura of nobility emanating from beyond the curtain.

I was no master of etiquette, but the pressure had prevented me from even standing up... No, pressure was too coarse a word. Frighteningly, it was something kinder—she'd soothed me to my knee from across the curtain.

Was this charisma? Magnetism?

I could raise my head after hearing her words, but awe filled my chest.

Meanwhile, Ononoki stood straight as a ruler next to me, which didn't surprise me. Still, some sort of barrier seemed to prevent her from drawing any closer to the bed.

This was no aberration but a human. A human being.

This was Kissshot Acerolaorion Heartunderblade, the human being, on the other side of the curtain—forget her golden age as a vampire, in terms of sheer power she was possibly weaker now than in her little-girl form. And yet.

As a human, she was nobler, more unapproachable than I'd ever experienced her. You couldn't help but pay your respects, almost by fiat, as if a spell had been cast.

"Allow me to remain beyond these curtains like so. Forgive my rudeness, conversing thus without showing my face," she said. If anything, though, it must've been out of consideration for me—of course it was. If I was feeling this way with a curtain between us, speaking face to face was too much for me. Unable to endure my own worthlessness, we couldn't carry on any conversation—even on one knee, I was managing to be myself only because I knew Shinobu Oshino, knew Kissshot Acerolaorion Heartunderblade as a vampire.

Who knew what I might be doing in the moment otherwise? Obviously, as a human, she didn't live in my shadow, but I saw why she lived alone on the outskirts of town. Exuding this kind of nobility just anywhere simply wouldn't do. No wonder she resided in quiet seclusion in this world, even if this grand castle belied that expression.

This explained why Miss Hachikuji and Miss Serpent weren't familiar with her... Did Ononoki know simply because she was an expert? No, maybe her investigation turned it up—I'd ask her about that later. I bet she was already plenty satisfied seeing me kneel the moment we met; she'd probably let me know.

For now, I needed to talk to Shinobu. As intimidating as the prospect was—

"It seems as though you have come from another world. Sir Araragi, from another world... To wit, you are the same, yet different from the personage I've come to know. Is that correct?"

"Y-Yes."

It took everything I had just to nod. There wasn't even a mirror around, but my stomach was turning inside out.

She'd called this world's Koyomi Araragi a personage... Between this, trying to take off Ononoki's pants, and heeding Oikura's pleas, I couldn't get any read on what he was like.

That's who I was inside? Not Ogi?

"Fate has brought us together, and I interact with another world. I would love for us to speak at length over tea but fear that there is no time—Sir Araragi. Pray describe your predicament in a fashion that even I may understand. Though you see me as an untrusted stranger, met for but the first time, put your faith in me. I offer no guarantee but would yet be of use."

"O-Okay," I nodded without a second thought.

I'd obliged a dying vampire last spring break, but felt even more coerced now—no, that's not the right word.

I wanted to serve her of my own free will.

How unbelievably dangerous.

This actually seemed to surpass being flipped or turned inside out, she felt like an altogether different person... That little girl carried this inside of her?

Her self-image was way too exalted.

This was no time for jabs, though, and the woman before me wasn't to blame. I did as she requested and described the chain of events since the morning, in even more precise detail than I'd just done for Ononoki. I also took the opportunity to sketch out the other world—I fought off the urge to convey everything about it to her noble presence, and instead kept it to a sketch, but that wasn't thanks to any feat of self-restraint. I simply didn't dare tell her that in this other world, she was a little girl who seemed happy spending her life eating donuts and lazing around all day.

Her being a vampire in that other world, though. I couldn't hide that one.

But even as I talked, a cooler part of my head determined that this Shinobu Oshino—milady Kissshot Acerolaorion Heartunderblade could never aid my lowly self. Noble or grand, a human is still a human. She was hardly a "fellow" human, but human all the same.

Shinobu could open a gate to another dimension even as a little girl because she was a vampire—the person before me, a human, wouldn't have that skill.

When Ononoki offered to take me to Shinobu, I didn't assume it meant an immediate solution, and my prediction seemed to have hit the mark... I could converse like this and seek her advice, but how could she, nothing but a human, succeed where not one but two gods had failed?

Well... That was no reason to cast aside someone's good favor, and simply speaking to her might make me feel better.

Though I wondered—princess had slipped something in about there being no time. What could that mean? I'd prepared myself for a long and drawn-out struggle... Was it just that she had plans after this?

Wondering, and kneeling the whole time, I finished my story.

"Thank you kindly. You have come from a very interesting world," princess shared her thoughts. She really did seem pleased, and perhaps wasn't just being polite.

I felt like some kind of adventurer returning from a long journey to report his experiences to a noblewoman—maybe I'd be sent back with a few gold pieces as a reward.

Still. An interesting world, huh?

Miss Hachikuji and Miss Serpent had what you might call the composure that came with being a god and showed close to no interest in my world, but yes, it was "another world" for this one's inhabitants. Endlessly interesting to a human, especially if you lived all alone in a castle.

"Our world must seem counterfeit to one such as you—still, to hear that I am a vampire. Truly, how interesting it would be, to be a demon."

"…"

It felt rude not to respond, but what was I to say? I couldn't reply with a casual *Yup, it's nice being a vampire.*

"Yet, to me, that is the counterfeit—each of us must be a fake to the other," princess echoed Ononoki's sentiment on the way here. Or maybe this was deeper, weightier.

If you told me what's on the surface, not underneath, is the counterfeit, an illusion that doesn't really exist, I'd concede the point—while always being your natural self isn't necessarily good, we live our lives falsifying so much about ourselves.

"Like the moon reflected on water," princess remarked poetically.

Our Shinobu would never say such a thing. But a reflection on water was an apt comparison—it was what I was after when I tried to sneak into Kanbaru's place.

Of course, I couldn't say for sure that it was the ticket back to my world…but it was the only guide I had.

"Alas, with but a human body, unlike myself in your world, this feat of opening a portal to another world is not for me to perform," princess lamented with what sounded like genuine regret. Please, I was not worthy—making such a princess feel bad was making me regretful. Should I take responsibility and crush my own throat?

…What the hell? Why was I even thinking about crushing my own throat?

"But I do believe I can provide some insight, if you would kindly lend your ear to the nonsense of one as naïve to the world as myself."

"Y-Yes. I would be most grateful."

Most grateful—that was part of my vocabulary?

"Heartunderblade," Ononoki jumped in. "He's holding on better than I thought, but can you hurry it up? Monstieur is gonna be in pretty bad shape soon. Your influence is growing in proportion to his resistance."

What did that even mean? A terribly impudent tone to take with milady, but unusually for Ononoki, she was concerned about my health.

"Sure, Ononoki," princess replied, using a more casual register with the shikigami—and just her name.

The versions I knew got along horribly, ignoring each other when they crossed paths at home, but surprisingly, that wasn't the case here... So Ononoki wasn't lying earlier—in which case, maybe there was mutual recognition in their heart of hearts. While that seemed like a good thing, I wished I'd found out some other way...

"Sir Araragi. It would seem wise for you to return to your own world as soon as possible—I understand Miss Hachikuji suggested you take a relaxed attitude, but she spoke from the perspective of a god. It would not be in line with human nature," princess confirmed what I'd thought after her earlier aside that there was no time. What an honor that my thoughts were in line with milady's—or no, daring to read them was so lacking in decency that I deserved death, many times over.

...Yikes, what was with my mindset here? I wasn't part of her retinue or anything. I wasn't so servile even as Shinobu's vampire thrall.

"To wit, your existence in this world is exerting a massive influence. An influence...perhaps I ought to say, a negative influence. If you would excuse my rude choice of words, Sir Araragi, you are a calamity inflicted upon this weak world."

Negative influence? Calamity? Inflicted?

Unconsidered, abusive words, ill-befitting milady's pretty and polite language, but somehow, they didn't shock me—and just seemed strange.

I mean, I felt like the victim, wrapped up here in some kind of massive calamity—but I was suddenly reminded of Mèmè Oshino.

—*I can't stand you playing the victim.*

A line he uttered often.

That expert hated people going around blaming aberrations as soon as anything happened and shunting responsibility—it isn't what I meant to do, but had I started to think that way at some point this time?

Was milady nudging me towards such an understanding?

What a blessing!

"This world may be counterfeit in your eyes, a place filled with contradictions that does not follow reason, but it exists by way of its own balance. You are threatening that balance. In truth… Ononoki may look to you as though she has returned to normal, but to me, she has transformed into something unusual."

"!"

I reflexively looked over at Ononoki—who flashed a sideway peace sign.

Why?

But princess was right—even if the shikigami *knew this day would come.* And from the way milady was speaking, was I going to make not just Ononoki but others *transform*?

"I shan't go so far, but it will inevitably cause strain. Sir Araragi, you are and are not Sir Araragi—yet we accept and understand you as him. For you and he are the same. The pending strain could very well undo our world entire."

"…"

The world? The scale was starting to get pretty huge. Well, I guess we were talking about worlds from the start. I needed to be more aware of that.

I'd interacted with Karen, Tsukihi, and Oikura in a way that wouldn't give away that I was from another world, but I couldn't have lined up exactly with their image of Koyomi Araragi (I doubt

I'm one-faced like Tsukihi)—they had to be finding me odd, just as Ononoki thought something was off.

In fact, Oikura had said as much. It could be responsible for that line of hers, *This all seems like a lie.*

Yet the girls recognized me as Koyomi Araragi regardless—because I was none other than Koyomi Araragi. Just like the person in front of me was Shinobu Oshino, however far removed her appearance...

"You must return to your world before this world suffers from *cognitive dissonance*—we would not survive that unharmed, nor would you, of course. Surely, it would be an alarming state of events. In fact, I have already started to be affected—my understanding of who Koyomi Araragi is *already grows dim.*"

"I..."

I want to know what kind of person I was in this world, I asked milady a question for the first time—more because it seemed like bad news if I didn't than out of curiosity.

I felt so guilty I might off with my own head if I didn't stay strong—but why? Yes, I was causing harm to this world, but that harm could still be rectified. Why was I turning so soon to the idea of atoning with my life?

Did I think it was that much of a sin to destroy her image of Koyomi Araragi?

"That—is something I will not tell you," she answered.

"I-Is it because...you've forgotten so much already that you can't?"

"No, it is not yet to that stage—though I fear it may come to that at this rate. I will not tell you because the knowledge may, perchance, have a negative influence on you. Ononoki, be sure not to say anything uncalled for yourself."

"Of course. I haven't said a word," the shikigami blatantly lied.

She told me all that stuff about pantsing girls...or was she kidding? What a malicious joke. Of course, it'd be more malicious if it wasn't a lie.

"B-But...I too wish to return as soon as I may."

What was with my language? Had I come to beg for forgiveness for not making my yearly tribute?

"As I intimated, we lack a means," princess noted. "We might near our lone prospect, the bathing tub at the Kanbaru manse, yet fail to contact the other side."

True. We were clinging onto the legend about their cypress bath as our one hope when it was nothing more than a silly magic charm. It involved Toé Kanbaru, but the legend itself originated with the Kanbarus, not the Gaens. Seriously, should we be relying on it?

How dare I bother milady with such a tale, I promptly ought to end my life right—wait, why did I want to die so much?!

"No good. He's at his limit, Shinobu."

Ononoki grabbed me by the scruff of my neck from beside and forced me to stand.

Huh? What?

"Time's up. I'm bringing him back with me. Wrap whatever you need to say up."

What an unreasonable request to make of milady!

By my own death, this impudence ought—no, the sin was truly my lowly self's for standing without princess' permission, I would die, I would die, I needed to die—

"All right. Sorry for the trouble, Ononoki."

"I don't mind. Same old, same old."

Ononoki sounded kind of cool. Her role here seemed downright unfair.

"Sir Araragi. You are not mistaken in proceeding down your path. But that will not suffice. Do not endeavor to carry this out alone, rather seek support. Be another's light in this world, just as you became mine—"

"Unlimited Rulebook," Ononoki said.

Before jumping—teal, don't mink.

154

020

"It seems that Shinobu is different in your world, kind monster sir...but it's dangerous to talk for too long to the noble you just met. To put it simply, being exposed to her grandeur *makes you want to die.* She told you at the beginning that you don't have much time, right? That there was no time to sit around and chat."

She did.

I assumed she was urging me to return to my world soon, but that's what she meant when she cautioned me.

Putting that aside, Ononoki's Unlimited Rulebook was just as potent in this world—well, honestly, she seemed far more effective with it here.

Exiting Shinobu's castle by smashing through multiple roofs, she landed on a nearby road, all while holding onto the scruff of my neck. Despite the decisive launch and landing, my brain wasn't as badly shaken as you might think.

Accompanying her Unlimited Rulebook as a "regular human" had been awful in the past. I'd gotten altitude sickness, and blacked out, and more—but it seemed she could control its speed in this world. She hadn't used it for our trip here just to milk me for info as we traveled.

Don't get me wrong, maybe she could in the other world too, but I doubt she had that kind of precision—though the real issue here might have been personality.

The Ononoki in this world had modified it to attain peak performance, but that was ultimately a quick fix. She couldn't be a carbon copy... In fact, maybe this Ononoki couldn't wield her strength with the same kind of reckless abandon.

Everything has its advantages and disadvantages.

And that's what saved me here.

"Being exposed to her grandeur makes you want to die? Well, okay, I admit I knelt automatically, but if it's that bad then it's no laughing matter. Is that why she also stayed behind a curtain?"

"Yup. If your eyes beheld her full beauty, you'd claw out your entrails on the spot."

"Why choose that gruesome a suicide method? Let me die easy."

I feel bad saying this, but getting away from that bedchamber brought me a profound sense of relief, which was why I could riff off of Ononoki. Given what I'd heard, though, I shouldn't even be engaging in banter.

I was destroying the balance of the world. Ononoki would cease to be Ononoki, and a chain reaction would ripple out, flipping everything around like a Reversi piece placed in just the right square.

"For a better understanding of the details," advised Ononoki, "you might want to read the fairy tale called 'Beautiful Princess' in the anime adaptation's fan book."

"I might, but don't say that when I'm trying to be serious. I don't want to play the straight man with you anymore, so could you not bait me?"

"I told you, don't mind. When you act self-conscious, it makes things harder for me. Stop reacting like a boy who just realized that a girl he's known since elementary school has started wearing a bra."

"What kind of example is that?"

"I'm just doing my job. In my case, if I try hard enough, I can even fix my changed personality—since it lacked a set form in the first place, once I send you back to the other side, I can take my sweet time."

"Fine, then."

"Getting back on track. If you can't find the fan book, go to your nearest bookstore and have them order it for you."

"Enough with the promo, what kind of track are you getting us back on? I couldn't read it anyway because all the characters would be flipped around... So that's what Shinobu was like when she was a human. A real princess." Sure, she'd told me, but frankly I'd had my doubts.

"Not necessarily. According to your hypothesis, that's just her *inner self*, not a reflection of the truth. The moon reflected on water, as she put it."

" ... "

"But yeah, in this world, she has too strong an effect on people, so she's chosen to live the solitary life of seclusion you just saw. Nobility so great it kills anyone who's granted an audience might spark a revolution—though she's human, she doesn't fit into that category."

So just as the noble vampire Kissshot Acerolaorion Heartunderblade exceeded vampiredom, as a human she exceeded humanity. I realized once again just how preposterous she was.

Someone I genuinely was no match for—I'd nearly killed myself in another world. Well, maybe my fate was to die for Shinobu no matter where I was.

Putting that aside.

I'd gotten out of a tight spot thanks to Ononoki (I might have made better use of our limited time together if she'd given me a proper explanation in advance, but what can we say, she wanted to see me react to our meeting by kneeling—I needed to be glad it wasn't watching me kill myself), but the counsel bestowed upon me by milady (I was still feeling the effect) had been truncated as a result. Um, what had she told me again?

"My path isn't mistaken...so I'm not wrong to think that the Kanbarus' wood bath offers an opening?"

"That must be what she meant. But she also said to seek support, remember? You wouldn't be able to do anything on your own."

Hm, the opposite of what Oshino used to say.

To be sure, it did line up with Black Hanekawa's advice about finding a partner...but hearing it from Shinobu, my foremost partner, actually made it harder for me to take action.

"Like if the girl you're after told you, 'Hurry up and find a girlfriend, I'm sure there's someone you like'?"

"Um, why do you keep on going back to grade school romances for your examples?"

"Given the way Miss Mayoi and Shinobu are this time, we're kind of low on the child factor."

"Stop being weirdly considerate, and just carry that weight as you are."

If Black Hanekawa meant Shinobu, there was no way I could work alongside that noblewoman—those suicidal impulses posed a greater danger than your average aberration.

She'd called me a calamity and negative influence, but maybe it owed to the way she thought about herself. She did have the power to destroy the world all by herself.

She knew how fragile it all was.

"Still," I said, "it's not like we can go back to the castle and ask her what she meant."

"Right. You're already at your limit of suicide points. You shouldn't see her until things have settled down—not that you can wait until they have."

"Excuse me, suicide points? The everyday phrasing isn't making me feel any better... But yeah, this isn't a situation where I can wait for things to cool off."

Support, huh?

True, it'd be great if someone could distract Kanbaru as I tried to sneak into her home. If she—the Rainy Devil—got drawn away for even five minutes, I could use the time to check out that wood bath and see if it served as a route to the outside world.

This, it goes without saying, was a challenge.

Finding such a collaborator in this foreign land... Even if I succeeded, the Rainy Devil's brutality was nearly unmatched among the aberrations I knew. Forget five minutes, no ordinary human could keep that aberration engaged for one—I'd only escaped to safety thanks to Black Hanekawa's help.

I couldn't tell how much of milady's advice to take at face value...but were I to look for support, who would it even be?

Asking Miss Hachikuji and Miss Serpent was out of the question. I couldn't call upon gods to fight for me.

"What do you think, Ononoki? Any ideas as far as what kind of character could distract the Rainy Devil?"

"Well, hmm," she folded her arms. "Let's see. As destructive and capable in battle as the Rainy Devil, also knows the details about your situation, understands and supports your position, recognizes the danger at hand and hence is motivated to work toward a solution, naturally possesses at least some expert knowledge, must have a method of fleeing if it comes down to it... I don't know if anyone like that exists."

"It's you!"

It was Ononoki.

021

After that, I went home (just one leap with the Unlimited Rulebook, easy as pie) and snuck under the sheets of the bottom bunk so Oikura wouldn't notice, while Ononoki slipped back into my sisters' room.

I treated it like a joke without meaning to, but leaning on Ononoki to revisit Kanbaru's home probably wasn't what Black Hanekawa and Shinobu were recommending at all.

We'd formed a common front a number of times in the other world, and she'd saved me a few times too, but *partner* didn't describe Ononoki's relationship to me—she has a master she serves as a shikigami.

A more partnerly partner—a violent onmyoji fighting polar bears at my world's North Pole right about now. I had no idea what she was doing in this one (maybe she fought penguins at the South Pole, I hear they're pretty tough), but it didn't seem right to ignore her and make Ononoki my partner.

Ononoki and I were already allied to some degree during my audience with Shinobu—if milady was suggesting that I turn to the shikigami, why advise me to *seek support* in that scene?

Who the heck were they talking about? I pondered the question but got nowhere because this time, I managed to go to sleep. I had the faint hope that this was one of those stories where you woke up to learn it was all just a dream, but my expectations were for naught.

"Koyomiiii! It's morning, it's morning! Wake up, you big old sleepyhead!"

I had to wonder if it was a dream after all, a convenient and far-too-embarrassing delusion, when Oikura woke me up with a cheerful flying splash.

Ah, so Oikura, not Karen and Tsukihi, roused Araragi awake every morning in this world... My earnest wish had come true of having a childhood friend who would do just that.

Moreover, the custom persisted even after I graduated, a fact that didn't apply to my cruel little sisters.

"C'mon, get out, I need to change! Or do you want to see me changing? Oooh, such a dirty mind, but I wouldn't mind if it's you. Look!"

"S-Stop it, you idiot. You're gonna make me sick," I said, leaving the room in a flurry—*make me sick* might come off as overly harsh, even with family, but I seriously didn't need that from Oikura, who'd drawn the shortest straw of all in this otherwise lukewarm setup.

Really? This was another side of her?

But when I turned around for an instant to close the door, Oikura had her back to me and both hands on her head.

As if her actions were making her wonder: *Is this really who I am?*

A negative influence brought on by me, as Shinobu put it—as someone who lived under the same roof, in the same room, Oikura would have spent the greatest amount of time with me. Perhaps that influence was felt most strongly by her.

Yikes, I needed to hurry if that was the case. As cringeworthy as she was, I didn't want to ruin her bright, cheery life as part of a happy family. Ruining her life three times was enough already.

"Oh, Koyomi! Good morning!"

I crossed paths with Karen on the stairs.

Seeing my already-short sister down them made her look even littler.

She seemed to have gotten out of the bath but wore outdoor clothes—was she planning to go out so early?

"Yep. I'm gonna have fun with Sodachi today!"

"Oh... Well, show her a good time, will you?"

"Excuse me? And who exactly are you to her?" Karen gave a sarcastic chuckle, but seeing her now, I almost wanted to do the same—no, that'd be rude.

She'd always worn a tracksuit when not in her school uniform, but sure, she was free to wear a skirt—wait, was this yet another aspect of her inner self?

A rough girl like her wishing she could look cute was like something out of a manga... I swore to myself that once I made it back to my world safe and sound, I'd be a tad kinder to her.

"See ya," I said, then walked down the stairs and passed her. Well, even if her appearance and fashion choices had changed, her core personality had stayed more or less the same. In that sense, she seemed to be in better shape than Oikura.

It made me wonder just how much of her emotions my childhood friend had been suppressing, just how much of everything she was keeping bottled up inside.

Where was she now, and what was she up to? All of a sudden, I was worrying if she was okay—and realized that I seriously needed to ask myself why Oikura, who'd left for another town, and Hanekawa, who'd gone overseas, were still here.

My vague, initial thought was that if this world was flipped around, then the girls who'd left were flipped around into still being here. That interpretation fell short if we took Miss Serpent's inside-out theory, though.

What exactly did you need to turn inside out for Black Hanekawa and my housemate, Sodachi, to stay in town? Thinking, I entered the bathroom.

It was to wash my face, and of course to check the bathroom mirror, but there stood Tsukihi, naked.

Was someone always naked in our house? What kind of home did I live in?

Sadly, it was a question I needed to ask not just in this world but in my original one too... Tsukihi seemed about to take a morning bath after Karen.

"Oh my. Good day to you, my brother," she greeted, and for a moment I suspected she'd undergone a change as well. But this little sister of mine could never be so refined on the inside. I figured she was only messing around as usual.

"Don't you good-day me."

"What, need to brush your teeth?"

"No, I'm washing my face..."

I checked the mirror as I spoke. Standing at an angle meant seeing Tsukihi reflected in it in nothing but her panties, so it felt like a joke, but in any case, it was just a regular old mirror.

I remembered what Oikura said about reflectivity—and indeed I could tell the nude Tsukihi in the mirror and the actual nude Tsukihi weren't identical.

They say that the ink stands out more in manga e-books, clearer than in print, but was it that kind of a difference?

Reflectivity... I got oddly hung up on the word—but maybe I only felt partial and lingered on it because it came from Oikura's lips.

It was just simple trivia about mirrors, right? She said standard mirrors are about eighty percent reflective, but what about non-standard ones? Were there hundred-percent-reflective mirrors too?

Would this world be different if I'd passed through one of

those? Maybe I only thought this thanks to how inconsistent and sloppy around the edges, how eighty-percent-finished this world seemed…

"What's wrong, Koyomi? Aren't you gonna wash your face? I can't take my bath until you do."

"Why not? You can, either way. Actually, it'd be easier for me to wash my face if you went in."

"Fine, I get it. Say no more. You want your adorable little sister to wash your face, don't you? Okay, then get ready."

"For what? I'm washing my own face, obviously." I pushed her aside to stand in front of the sink—only for her to reach over my shoulders from behind me like in some skit.

"I'm not good enough for you, huh?" she said.

"Why are you turning this into a shojo manga? With me as the heroine, too."

"Bellyflop!"

Gluing herself to my back like a baby koala, she hooked both of my arms as if she'd be attempting a backbreaker next. She wasn't Karen, though, and didn't know the first thing about martial arts. All she did was work the faucet.

With such force that a good amount of water came rushing out… She sure lived in this world the way she turned the correct handle, unlike me.

"Now let's get you all nice and clean!" she said, scooping warm water into both hands and washing my face—doing a surprisingly proper job of it despite her comedic posture.

A very versatile young lady.

It felt strange to have hands, or rather fingers that weren't my own touching my face. She repeatedly squished and squashed the meat and flesh that clung to my skull—hmm.

"Your hair's really in the way. Why don't you cut it?" she asked.

"Like you're one to talk. I bet we look like a yokai from behind."

Or from any angle.

"Gah, big brother, get outta my way. I can't see the soap. Could you use your mouth to take it from the dish and drop it into my hands?"

"Why should I after being treated like an obstacle? And with my mouth?"

In spite of my retort, I, the ever-kind older brother, grabbed the soap with my mouth. Tsukihi made a lather with it in her hands, then returned it to my mouth.

Don't use my mouth as a soap dish.

When I spat it out, it fell into the sink, so the pooled water naturally turned soapy even as it swirled towards the drain.

"Close your eyes, okay? You could go blind."

"Maybe if you got bleach in them, but that kind of warning is unwarranted over face soap."

"No, it's because this is my first time washing someone's face. I might poke your eyeballs with my fingernails."

"It's a little late for that warning."

"Eat lather!" yelled Tsukihi, covering my face in soapy bubbles—as powerful as her scream was, her hands were gentler than before. She seemed pretty good at this for her first time, but apparently wasn't satisfied. "Hmm, I don't know... Maybe I'll go ahead and borrow Sodachi's foam cleanser."

"No, you shouldn't—glurp! Glorp!"

She really made me eat lather.

You mustn't try to talk when your little sister is washing your face, but it was my first time too, you see.

"Well, I guess I'll let you off with this for today. I wash your face of you!" she said, starting to wash the soap off my face. The water had been running this entire time, and when I opened my eyes a crack, the sink was full and on the verge of overflowing.

I'd have shut it off with my hand if I could, but Tsukihi had tied up my arms with her own—fine, I just had to use my mouth again.

As I did...

"Grrf?!"

The foam was mostly gone from my face, but I still made that noise—actually having eaten lather.

I opened my eyes.

Right below—was a pool of water.

Closing the faucet calmed its surface, but it was soapy thanks to the bar I'd dropped, and opaque—increasing its reflectivity.

In other words, I saw my own face reflected there, albeit imperfectly, as my little sister washed it. And that face looked at me.

With a smirk.

022

What's happening, what's going on here, why on water and not a mirror—I thought as I opened my eyes wide, only to have Tsukihi actually stick her fingernails in them.

No surprise there, but she really knew how to mess up a clutch moment.

"You can't put it on me, I did warn you. Why can't you ever do as you're told, big brother?"

Ditching the final steps of washing my face, Tsukihi scurried away into the bath.

I wished I could be like her. Seriously, I felt jealous.

When I looked back down into the sink, all the soapy water had been sucked down the drain. I felt like I'd lost my chance to seize a hint that had appeared out of the blue, but maybe, against my own will, my face had been beaming thanks to the heavenly experience that was having someone wash it. I shouldn't feel too dejected...

I wanted to curse Tsukihi for interfering, but I wouldn't have seen anything at all if she hadn't had the bright idea to wash my face—so par for the course. After waiting for her, Karen, and Oikura to leave, I brought Ononoki out from my sisters' room and headed to Kanbaru's.

We traveled by BMX, not the Unlimited Rulebook, because there were people around during the day to see us—yes, riding two to a bike was against the rules, but strictly speaking, Ononoki is a doll. Legally, if we interpreted it as riding around with a doll on my shoulders, it was just fine.

"I gotta say, it's still pretty abnormal to be riding around with a doll on your shoulders," the shikigami took her turn to quip at me—Ogi hadn't lent me her bike's foot-rest accessory, so there was nothing I could do. "Monstieur, you give all kinds of characters shoulder rides. Who's left?"

"You're making it sound like I've given them to a majority of the cast. Going down the list, it's only about four people long, counting you."

"Me, Shinobu, the bigger little sister, and who else?"

I exercised my right to silence.

Since Ononoki wore pants in this world, nothing too wonderful happened during the ride. Thanks to her experience supporting Miss Kagenui with one finger (?), she did have an excellent sense of balance, and operating the bicycle wasn't the slightest bit harder—in fact, I felt like I was the one being steered because she held onto my hair like a pair of handlebars (making me look like I had pigtails).

We'd discussed what we would do at Kanbaru's the previous night, and I didn't imagine there'd be any changes to our plan, but I still saw fit to report the little incident.

"Huh, is that so," Ononoki said. "Well, it's not your fault that the water went down the drain. It doesn't seem too relevant, so don't worry about it—wait a sec," she pulled off a double-take from her double-decker perch. "Isn't that really important? Could the gate to the other world be in our bathroom after all, and not in the monkey girl's home?"

"*Our* bathroom, my ass."

"I'll be sure to tell Big Sis Sodachi the same."

"No, she's suffered enough! Anyway, it was only for a moment, and maybe I was just seeing things—I couldn't make it happen again, either. I'm not even sure what caused it."

"Right. A mirror the first time, and a reflection in the sink the second time... The location was the same, but the meaning seems different. I guess the constant is that you were washing your face? The necessary condition for reflective surfaces opening to another world: washing your face."

"What kinda condition is that? If that's all, I washed my face in the bath too... Either way, my reflection laughing, or not moving the way I do, isn't that important—if going back home is my goal, I need to see Shinobu, or someone who can contact Shinobu, in the reflection."

"Hm, true. Which makes today's mission quite important."

"Yeah, if possible, I'd like to end this today—I didn't want this to take more than a day. Like I was saying, Oikura, for example, is starting to feel my negative influence."

"..."

Huh? Why stay silent there? Ononoki suddenly going quiet worried me—was she angry? I suppose missing my opportunity earlier in the bathroom deserved a scolding.

"Monsieur. Have you noticed there's a simple solution to this disturbance?"

"A simple solution."

"Yes. A super-simple super-solution."

"I'm fine with super-simple, but a super-solution sounds a little scary." The wording suggested something along the lines of *die and you'll never worry again*—but if she was saying a solution existed, I had to hear her out. Coolly, trying to come across as not one bit afraid or anything about this proposal of hers, I prodded, "What is it?"

"It's a sort of Copenhagen interpretation."

"Copenhagen interpretation? That's some complicated stuff... Quantum mechanics, was it?" Since we can't fully grasp the present, predicting the future with perfect accuracy is impossible— but how did my current situation relate to that line of thinking?

"Aren't you supposed to be the straight man? I obviously meant Copernican revolution."

"How should I know?! They're practically the same thing!"

"Uh, the Copenhagen interpretation and Copernican revolutions aren't that similar," Ononoki criticized me for her own misstatement—but that aside, she restated, "It's a sort of Copernican revolution. Simply give up on returning to your original world and resign yourself to settling down in this one."

"Oh! I guess I could! You're a sharp one, Ononoki, now there's no need to sneak into Kanbaru's bath. Why don't we head straight to the Häagen-Dazs shop, I'll treat you to whatever you—hold on," I attempted a clumsy double-take, as the other half of the double-decker arrangement.

Ononoki just said, "Häagen-Dazs stores don't exist in Japan anymore."

Right. Seriously, though? It wasn't just this world...but we digress.

"How is that a solution? Even if it's some super-solution, it doesn't solve anything. If I continue to exist in this world—"

"That's only because you're trying to go back to yours and refusing to grow accustomed to this one. You're like a transfer student who just won't stop bragging about his hometown and speaking in his local dialect, souring the mood for the whole class."

"What's with the mean example?"

"If I may, I'm the kind protagonist who reaches out to the kid who's sticking out like a sore thumb."

"Oh, so this was another one of your grade-school rom-com metaphors..."

"Surrender and open your heart to this world, be influenced

and pressured by it instead, and you might go back to normal—from our point of view. Actually, it might never be more than a compromise...but I don't think you'd overpower our influence when we hold the majority."

"..."

This seemed to be an honest proposal, not some kind of joke—and looking at it objectively, Ononoki could be right.

If I gave up.

If I abandoned my world and decided to live here—I guess, in the vein of Ononoki's analogy, it'd be like getting lost at sea, drifting off to a distant land, and hunkering down there?

"I don't think it's a bad suggestion, monsieur. Not just because it'd maintain this world's balance, but for you too. I mean, you might not have realized this yet, but you aren't in any danger as long as you don't try to go back, you know?" Thanks to her usual monotone, Ononoki didn't sound like she was trying particularly hard to convince me, but she certainly was nudging me in a certain direction. "So long as you don't try to get near Kanbaru's home, the monkey shouldn't decide to attack you on her part. All it takes is a resolution to start living the hanky-panky life with Big Sis Sodachi from tomorrow."

"Like that's my goal here. As if I'm going to stay just so I can be all lovey-dovey with Oikura... Phew."

Perhaps the proposal was worth considering? It might end up being my only option—but I still only considered it through an objective lens. It wasn't yet worth so much as a moment's thought.

I felt bad toward Ononoki, who'd gone out of her way to come up with it, but settling down in this world meant leaving far too much behind in mine. As long as there was hope, I'd pursue it, even if it put my life in danger.

"You know you're putting my life in danger too, right?"

"W-Well, I..."

"It's fine, I'm already dead. I just had to ask—just wanted to ask. And it's not as if this plan is airtight," Ononoki said. "Even if you settled right in to your current position, there's no guarantee the real Koyomi Araragi isn't coming back."

"The real? Well, the real one to you guys, but don't make me sound like a fake."

"A double of the same person, the doppelganger phenomenon, is probably enough to destabilize the world on its own... I wonder, where did Koyomi Araragi go? Maybe you two did switch places, and he went to that other world."

"..."

Then my fear that there were now two Ogi Oshinos in that world might not be idle—assuming the Koyomi Araragi in this world took her form. But it'd explain why Oikura and I lived in the same room. No matter how close, a high school-aged boy and girl sharing a room was irregular.

Couldn't that be why she was second only to Ononoki, a professional and expert, in sensing that something was wrong? Koyomi Araragi's gender was different from Koyomi Araragi's... For my part, our closeness seemed wrong when I already had a girlfriend.

"Hmm..."

I just hoped things in the other world weren't hopeless, like Ogi and Ogi trying to kill each other—she embodied my feelings of self-negation, after all.

I guess I also needed to figure out what kind of relationship I had with Hitagi Senjogahara in this world, but that concern could wait until our mission today ended in failure. For now, I would focus on evading the Rainy Devil—a fainthearted approach, as opposed to eliminating her, but putting aside the Monkey's Paw, it wasn't as if I could eliminate Kanbaru herself.

I told myself that my sights were set just right—and just as I did.

"We're here," Ononoki said, pointing ahead in the direction

of a wall smashed into dust.

The result of Kanbaru running along it a day ago—even if consistency didn't matter in this world, destroyed objects didn't seem to repair themselves, and the gate to the Kanbaru estate past it was a shambles as well.

"All right, monstieur, let's follow the plan. I'll do what I can to buy you time, so don't rush your investigation. Feel free to take a dip in the tub while you're there."

"As if I'm in such a state of mind."

"Maybe not, but you do have plenty of time. Forget five minutes, I could buy you five hours."

I'd feel woozy if I took a bath for that long.

I wondered how I might reply, but couldn't at all—having spotted beyond the pulverized wall, on the grounds of the Kanbaru estate, a raincoat kicking up a cloud of rubble as it dashed straight toward us.

So far away just a second ago, it was now *this* close—the day before, I'd found it strange that she'd run along the wall for no apparent reason, but I understood as she sped through the grand, or formerly grand, Japanese garden.

She ran *splitting the ground with each step*—wrecking a wall sure beat destroying our planet. It implied that she had some degree of judgment and reason, but I wasn't in a place to be giving it any more thought.

"Just go, kind monster sir. Unlimited Rulebook—"

Ononoki leapt off of my shoulders, and the finger she'd used to indicate the demolished wall grew massive and destructive. It now pointed at Suruga Kanbaru, who was coming at us head-on, ready to collide.

A finger of havoc pointed at legs of havoc—Ononoki had been riding on my shoulder in part so her hands would be free. And so, the battle between the monkey and the corpse began.

023

I stepped aside and snuck away once this battle to the death commenced, successfully completing the first stage of my mission to infiltrate Kanbaru's home. The Rainy Devil tried to chase after me, of course, but Ononoki did a beautiful job getting in her way.

I should be fine, given the state the two were in as I left—five hours had to be an exaggeration, but if Ononoki focused on defense, she'd never succumb to the Rainy Devil.

If anything, she might accidentally beat the Rainy Devil, in other words eliminate her without meaning to, but the shikigami seemed to understand the meaning of moderation in this world, perhaps in contrast to her counterpart in my world. Unless the situation took an extreme turn, I didn't think it'd happen.

Which is to say it could, if the situation took an extreme turn—I was in no position to order Ononoki to risk her own demise and avoid delivering a fatal blow to Rainy Devil. This was no time to be relaxing, I needed to hurry up and investigate that bath.

In spite of my resolve, I immediately got lost. Kanbaru's place is just too big—not to mention, I'd forgotten that left and right were switched around. What sounded like an extensive construction project on the lawn as my background music, I ran this way and that (that way and this?) until I discovered the bath at last.

"Phew…" I caught my breath for a moment.

Ten hours after I first got the idea of coming here on Kita-Shirahebi's grounds, I'd pulled it off… It felt like some kind of accomplishment, but I still hadn't done anything. Everything so far was like getting tips from all around on how to run a marathon, and only now was I hearing the starter gun's bang.

By the way, where were Kanbaru's grandparents, who lived here with her? We did come when they might be out—was that paying off? Not that it mattered who I met so long as it wasn't the Rainy Devil, but it was better if our paths didn't cross.

I traversed the dressing room, which was larger than my bedroom, and opened the sliding wood door to the space that contained the bath—fortunately, it was already filled. A stroke of luck, since it'd take more than just fifteen or thirty minutes to fill one of this scale from zero. Could the Rainy Devil have taken a morning bath like Karen and Tsukihi?

Staring at the bathwater of one of my juniors felt a little immoral…but I moved straight to studying the surface—at a slant, to see as much reflected light as possible.

"…"

I don't know, I felt incredibly stupid accomplishing my goal here… What the hell I was up to, going so far as to involve a corpse doll? Nor was anything showing up on the surface, which almost felt like a forgone conclusion. Sure, the water did reflect the ceiling, but that was all—what was I gonna say to Ononoki?

No, I hadn't expected this to work, and yes, I was grasping at straws, but faced with this outcome, I had to wonder why I'd bothered grasping at them at all. Did I think I was some sort of alchemist who turned straw into gold?

I splashed around with my hand to make a few waves but only created ripples. I was already searching for deft explanations

I might give to keep Ononoki from making fun of me, but as I played around...

"Ah!" I remembered—the precise wording of the story I'd heard from Kanbaru. Right, the image of your future spouse appeared on the surface as you bathed. It was only a slight difference, but maybe standing outside the bath and looking at it, while clothed, diverged from the legend—hmm.

If this was a case of in for a penny, in for a pound, I was already in for that pound, but did I need to put up my whole wallet, or even my bank account? I couldn't return empty-handed after coming this far... Well, I might have to, but that was no reason not to try everything.

Ononoki was battling the Rainy Devil, that brutal aberration, for my sake. Not only was there risk, she'd see very little return. This was for her, too—I had to strip nude! And take a nice little bath!

Fortunately, having tested it with my hand, the water was still warm. The culprit couldn't have gone far—sorry, no, there was no need to reheat the bath.

I went back to the dressing room, threw off my clothes, and returned. Being naked in someone else's home never felt quite right, but even if I needed to hurry, I couldn't forget my manners. You don't enter a bath without washing yourself down first—though if we're talking about manners, using another family's bath without permission was a massive breach of them.

When I listened closely, unmistakable destruction pierced the air every now and then—the battle seemed to rage on. I couldn't give up when Ononoki was still fighting, I thought, and fought my own battle, lathering my body and showering it down... Preparations complete.

I entered the cypress tub. To take a bath.

Ooh, feels nice.

No, I needed to hurry.

To cut to the chase, after stripping, dipping in, and examining the water from an angle, nothing in particular happened—and honestly, I wasn't expecting anything to.

Yeah. Things never go that well.

Why did I ever think this was a brilliant plan? How embarrassing... There was something wrong with me, that was the only explanation.

Fine, time for a new plan—maybe I should start by looking for the other Koyomi Araragi who lived in this world? Probably Ogi, but if it wasn't Ogi...and then.

This was the quickest of dips, let alone counting to a hundred, but I stood up. That was when.

Rattle.

The wooden door to the bath slid open—what, how? Was the Rainy Devil here after defeating Ononoki? Impossible.

I was pretty sure the shikigami wouldn't lose so easily, but more to the point, Suruga Kanbaru as the Rainy Devil didn't open doors like a reasonable person. As she'd proved with the gate out front, she saw them as something to destroy, not use.

And indeed, it wasn't Suruga Kanbaru, the Rainy Devil, standing on the other side of the door—but nor was it Ononoki after accidentally defeating her opponent.

Nor either of Kanbaru's grandparents who'd been home the entire time. As roundabout as my description is, I have no surprise punch line.

Because I didn't know this person.

Someone I was meeting for the first time—stood there completely naked.

Someone I'd never seen, nude like I'd never seen.

"Huh? Who the hell are you?" the stranger asked, making no effort whatsoever to cover up. Grasping in one hand a towel that stayed slung against her shoulder—unfazed.

The nude stranger was demanding to know who my nude self

was.

"Hah, if you want to know someone's name, you ought to introduce yourself first," I summoned up everything I had to put up this front—as fazed as could be, desperate to hide my body, goading my stark naked and desperate self.

In any case, I couldn't run away, couldn't exit the bath without shoving aside this stranger who stood in the doorway. Since I didn't dare to identify myself, my only real option was to turn the question around.

"I'm Toé Gaen."

But she answered it, just like that.

"And now, who the hell are you? Better answer me this time, or else you're not long for this world."

024

Toé Gaen.

A name that has come up many times—but not someone I ever imagined popping up, which is why I hadn't introduced her properly.

Suruga Kanbaru's mother.

Izuko Gaen's older sister.

The individual who left Kanbaru the Monkey's Paw, the only person in this world for whom Izuko Gaen, the woman who knows everything, feels any awe and fear.

And—she's deceased.

Deceased... Right, she ought to have died in a traffic accident along with her husband, Kanbaru's grandparents' eldest son... So why was she here?

Why was she here now, bathing with me?

"Ah, sorry about that, sorry about threatening you. I never thought you'd be Suruga's senior, is all. You should've just told me in that case," Ms. Toé said in a laidback tone, with a hearty laugh—was *laidback* even the right word? She still wasn't making any attempt to hide her body...

She knew her breasts were hanging out in the open, didn't she?

Unable to leave due to this turn of events, I sat back down in the bath—sinking down to my shoulders, hiding as much of my body as I could, in contrast to Ms. Toé.

Call it unmanly, but I can't say I'm positive about my body.

"Araragi, was it? So, how's Suruga at school? I bet that idiot's getting into nothing but a bunch of stupid trouble."

"U-Um..."

Forget school, she was fighting an idiotically savage battle out on the front lawn—did Ms. Toé not know?

Maybe I shouldn't be surprised that people in this world acted in inconsistent ways, but then I was a confused mess—not having prepared myself emotionally for a hot-tub experience with my junior's mom.

And wait, wasn't she way too young?

I couldn't be sure because she lacked the surprisingly important factor in determining someone's age, namely, clothes...but how old was she, again? Was I told at some point that she was several years older than Miss Gaen?

Hard to say when she was fully au naturel, both in attire and makeup, but Miss Gaen had such a babyface she didn't look above thirty, and maybe the same went for her older sister? Either way, I suck at guessing women's ages even when they aren't naked. Or perhaps—

Perhaps I was seeing her as she was when she passed away in the accident. Like with Hachikuji in my world... Possible if this lady was a ghost.

Damn, I couldn't think straight.

My thoughts were all jumbled up—you couldn't blame me, with a naked lady right in front of me, but I needed to get ahold of myself.

"..."

I decided to approach the situation like a test and begin with the questions I did know the answers to. With the easiest bits—

first off, was this person really Toé Gaen, Kanbaru's mother?

Given the illogic and inconsistency of this world, trusting her self-reported info seemed to be my only choice, really.

But well, if you asked...I guess she looked similar?

To Miss Gaen, and to Kanbaru.

Personality-wise, she was definitively bolder, or less sensitive, but her build was similar: short and slim. She looked closer to Miss Gaen, if I had to pick one—didn't that make genetic sense for sisters? At the same time, Kanbaru had inherited her intense, driven eyes, her eyebrows, and more...

"Wow. You've got some nerve, ogling me like that. Just how thirsty are you?"

"Huh? N-No, I wasn't. Your face..." She'd misinterpreted my gaze (really, it was a misinterpretation), but her understandable reaction made me stammer. "I was looking at your face. I-I was just thinking how much you and Kanbaru look alike."

"Oh, she looks like me? Keheheh. I see, so her breasts have gotten this big."

"Er, no, like I said, your face..."

Come on, I've never seen Kanbaru's boobs. Just barely, but I haven't.

Hm? Hold on, something was off about this last exchange—she didn't know about Kanbaru's breasts getting bigger?

"..."

"Mm. Ha. Does it really matter if I didn't know?" Ms. Toé seemed to intuit my doubts. I suppose she and her little sister, Miss Gaen, had different values.

Well, maybe *values* overstated her lackadaisical attitude, but the big sis of a little sis who knew everything laughing that what you knew didn't really matter was...unfortunate.

Actually, I was remembering some stuff now, and this lady seemed pretty different from the image Miss Gaen had given me of her older sister...an extremely self-critical, austere person if I recalled correctly. I didn't see a hint of that.

She was an approachable mom—well, okay, even an approachable mom didn't normally bathe with her daughter's senior from school. Of course, I couldn't fault her or say there was anything wrong with her since I was a trespasser who could easily be handed over to the cops otherwise.

Family members don't always see one another as others do—and come to think of it, Miss Gaen's characterization of me was off the mark too. She thought I was stoic and no different from her big sister.

Maybe knowing everything didn't necessarily make you a good judge of character.

"Oh, no, I only calmed down after I got married—after I found myself a man, in other words," Ms. Toé answered before I could speak, seeming to anticipate my queries again.

No, hold on. Wasn't she a little too good at it? I wasn't planning on asking her anything that personal... If she'd seen it in my expression, then my face was far too eloquent.

"While I say I calmed down, I never got as lukewarm as this setup, so give a girl a pass—things happen once you become an adult, okay? Being told that I haven't changed one bit since the old days might make me happy, but it isn't true."

"Okay... Hm?"

A lukewarm setup—a silly line I'd used with Miss Hachikuji. Why would Ms. Toé know it? Hello...

It felt like she was seeing straight into my mind.

Yes, we were quite literally baring all, but did it really include my thoughts and feelings? I mean, I couldn't begin to read her intentions, for my part.

What was she, the mind-reading yokai *satori*?

"Wh-What—do you know?"

"Like. I. Said. Knowing, not knowing, none of it matters. What's important is understanding. You can know something, but it'll only go to waste if you can't use that knowledge, and half-assed knowledge can keep you from understanding by way of intuition." Ms. Toé smirked, running her fingers through her wet hair. "I'm telling you, even if you don't know something, you begin to get it just from seeing it."

"…"

The brilliant type.

I'd thought she might be like Oshino, or maybe her sister Miss Gaen, but these remarks made her seem completely different… In other words, did she not know anything when she stepped into the bath but manage to put together a rough guess as to my predicament? Just from my demeanor, speech, and behavior, even though I hadn't told her anything in particular?

Hard to say.

Maybe I was overestimating her. Maybe she'd only meant to describe our bathing together as a lukewarm setup. As far as hot-spring travelogues went, this was pretty tepid, after all…

"Of course, back in my day, suspense dramas always had a steamy little bath scene right in the middle. Keheheh. Are there restrictions on that kind of thing nowadays? You don't see too many tops on television lately."

"Tops? Er, no, um…"

Our conversation risked getting dangerously off-track, so I did my best to correct its course—or rather, the question here was how to get myself out of this.

I needed to escape this suspense drama.

No, hold on a second.

As Miss Gaen's sister, and having bequeathed the Monkey's Paw to Kanbaru, she was, if not an expert on aberrations, at least a pro…or I guess a wild card.

I didn't know if it applied in this one, but in my original world, I often came across her influence—the responsibility for Ogi's birth lay squarely on my shoulders, but it was also a fact that this lady was involved.

In which case... I had no idea why she was here now, but Kanbaru's mom or not, she was on bad terms with the Kanbarus and shouldn't be allowed on these premises—didn't I need to welcome this encounter? My idea of trying to communicate via the water's surface had been a bust, but if that failure meant getting to meet Ms. Toé, it turned my moonshot into an *all's well that ends well* scenario...

"Hm? You're staring at me again," she reacted sharply to my gaze for the second time—my assessing gaze. Ms. Toé then put both her hands behind her head, as if in resignation, and said, "Okay, I get it. We'll do it later, so just come to my room. You'd better keep this a secret from Suruga, though."

"No, that's not it!"

There was nothing okay about it!

Seeing it didn't always mean getting it, even for her—well, I suppose she was just kidding, but it was in pretty bad taste.

What kind of person was she?

Even if the lady didn't necessarily equal my mental image of Toé Gaen, this did seem to banish the notion that the land of mirrors was all my delusion or a dream. If you told me that somewhere inside of me, I wanted to see an energetic Sengoku or a playful Oikura, I couldn't argue with you, but even I didn't yearn to take a bath with the mom of one of my juniors.

What kind of unconscious was that?

"Ha... Seems like this has been an interesting development, I'm glad for you. A lot happens once you become an adult, but also when you're a kid, I guess? Hang in there, young man."

"And what am I to do with such easy advice?"

"Oh, you wanted advice? Well, I suppose you might—but you see, Araragi. I'm not anyone's idea of a life coach."

"..."

"I mean that in all sorts of ways. Considering your situation and given what you've done for Suruga, I want to help you, but I don't know about butting into this story when no one's asked me to."

She was being awfully mystifying for someone so laidback. How was I to interpret that? What I'd done for Kanbaru…in this world, or in the other world? I had no idea, and couldn't even tell if I should. As much as I wanted to bombard her with questions, I needed to be careful, as a potential negative influence on this world.

In her case, though, she proactively—or rather, spontaneously figured out the situation just by looking at me. If I didn't want to influence this world, my best course of action was to hurry up and get out of the bath and retreat to Ononoki's position.

Yet escaping from this place meant running away naked. Without so much as a towel, I'd be baring my ass to Ms. Toé.

How embarrassing!

Putting aside my own shame, turning and showing my butt to the mom of a junior I felt indebted to was beyond rude.

I hoped that she might get out first, but Ms. Toé, her scrub towel folded atop her head, looked poised for a long soak. If only I could act so unconcerned.

"…"

"About what I was saying about knowing and not knowing—things aren't that simple here, Araragi."

"E-Excuse me?"

I'd gone silent, only for her to start speaking. I wasn't asking her any questions, but the result was the same if she was going to talk to me—and still short of a course of action, I was barely able to react. My hesitation must've been one of those things that didn't matter to Ms. Toé, who continued, "Knowing and not knowing aren't dualistic. My little sister has pursued knowing by removing any traces of not knowing, and your friend Miss Hanekawa has kept both knowing and not knowing as close parts of herself, but both of them are overlooking a crucial fact. Which is that a lot of knowledge is wrongly known—you think you know but have gotten it wrong. That's why understanding is so important in matters."

"…You know Hanekawa?"

Did she mean this world's Black Hanekawa, or the Tsubasa Hanekawa I knew who'd left the country? Also, she didn't mention Ogi, who professed not to know anything, but was that because Ms. Toé didn't know her or—dammit, the more I tried to think, the more I was spinning my wheels.

I was getting too heated and about to blow my top, and not because I was sitting in a bath.

"Can't say I know her. I understand her a little, that's all—how about you, Araragi? How well do you understand your friend? Maybe you don't get a thing about the thinking of your friend who decided to go overseas."

"…"

That word *overseas* meant she was talking about the Hanekawa I knew. Okay, so now this lady who shouldn't have known anything about me when she'd entered the bath grasped my situation perfectly. At what point had she started asking leading questions and gauging my reactions? She was on an altogether different level.

It was counterproductive to act awkward and reserved around her, and I found myself in a state of resignation, which is to say, I decided to stop trying to hide things—my inner thoughts, I mean, not the details of my anatomy. Nor would she be particularly surprised whatever I confessed now.

I shared why I now sat in this bath, what had compelled me to do so. I hadn't forgotten about the influence I might have—it had forced Ononoki to "change"—but felt like it didn't really apply to her.

This was only instinct, but she didn't seem the type to be

influenced by me. She wouldn't come under anyone's influence, was above influence. She just digested it all.

"Hmm…so you came here believing in this magic charm? What a pure-hearted maiden you are," Ms. Toé said with a be-mused nod after hearing me out. "Reminds me of a student of mine. Liked magic charms, or maybe I should say curses… But you might as well give up on that approach. This bath—"

Splash, she slapped the water's surface.

"—is nothing but a bath. If anyone ever saw something on its surface, it's on the person who saw it."

"Is that so."

Yeah. I mean, I knew that. Still, I'd been hopeful because I'd heard the story as an episode involving Toé Gaen. Having it de-nied in person made it sound all the more ridiculous.

"Oh, no, don't be embarrassed. I feel kind of bad that I was the reason you got your hopes up," she consoled me, but when I thought about how excited I'd gotten, how Ononoki was locked in battle, my shame wasn't so easily wiped away.

Also, I was naked. How could I not be embarrassed?

"It sounds like my little sister and Oshino have gone around saying all kinds of things about me, but this is what happens when you meet a legend for yourself. It's like reading about a great his-torical figure only to find a slew of scandals or learning about someone else who was a lot greater. Sorry for being such a plain old lady," Ms. Toé said all too candidly—but the very fact that she could hinted that she wasn't just anybody.

I had to wonder. She'd declared her lack of interest in butting into this story, so I wasn't coming clean to get her advice—but having told her everything, I felt like that process had been nec-essary here. Until now, I'd been explaining stuff so others would understand, but this time it seemed to be for my own sake: a way of straightening out my own thoughts.

"Well, there's not much I have to say," Ms. Toé cushioned our conversation. "After having you tell me all that, I'd be terribly cold to do nothing in return, though. All right, Araragi, let me wash your back."

She stood.

With a sploosh.

Even as I was feeling embarrassed every which way, Ms. Toé continued to show no modesty whatsoever—and walked right over to the shower area.

"C'mon, hurry up. It's not every day that you get to have your back washed by a Gaen."

It's not every day that you get to have your back washed by anyone, a Gaen or not. Still, and even though Ms. Toé was losing no time working up a lather with her towel, I answered, "N-No, I'm fine. I've already washed myself down."

"Hey, it's fine," she said, not taking no for an answer. "You can't do a proper job of washing your own back. Not that you can count on me to do any better. I've never even washed my husband's back."

"Ma'am, maybe don't share anything that heavy when we're meeting for the first time?"

"But we're not meeting for the first time," she casually informed me. "My left hand—has met you, hasn't it?"

"..."

"You haven't heard about that yet, have you, Araragi—aren't you curious? About why I gave that wish-granting Monkey's Paw to my daughter...to Suruga."

025

Right.

Mirrors reversed right and left, flipped front and back, turned everything inside out—it was probably the same no matter how you described it, but from my point of view, it was all very *through a glass, darkly.*

I thought this facing the mirror right in front of where I sat outside the tub as Ms. Toé washed my back—yeah, I had that realization because staring into the mirror was all I could do. A practical stranger was washing my back, even if I'd heard her name before, and I was nervous.

You see, I could place my palm against the mirror to high-five my reflected self, but upon closer inspection, there was a looking glass-deep gap between our hands.

We could never come into contact. The reflected me, on the mirror's surface or not, existed on the other side of that glass—you might even say the mirror image was reflected on its reverse face.

Was the true essence of a mirror just its silver coating and the rest nothing more than a transparent sheet of glass? Was I looking at a mirror, a piece of glass, or myself? What is it that we see when we face a mirror?

Reflected light? Really?

Pondering these ideas wasn't going to let me escape my predicament, but at least it helped me escape reality, which is to say ignore it, for the time being.

"You've got a nice, muscular back. That's a young man for you."

"Um, I have no idea what kind of back I have... Plus, the one simple trick behind my physique is that I was a vampire..."

"A vampire? Oh, okay, you did tell me about that just now. What a convenient fitness regimen. You wouldn't believe how much work I put in to maintain this figure," Ms. Toé said, scrubbing my back with her towel—it felt more like she was shaving my back than washing it.

Was she really using a towel? Wasn't it a rough sponge?

What a world I'd gotten myself into—my little sister washing my face in the morning, my junior's mom washing my back in the afternoon... Who was going to wash what part of me tonight? My instincts told me to be on the lookout for Oikura...

I needed to solve this before night fell.

To protect Sodachi Oikura!

From myself...

"Washing your back almost makes me feel like you're my grandpa, but I guess the paw you wanted to talk about was a monkey's."

"U-Uh huh."

Of course. That's why I was submitting myself to this bizarre exercise—but in that case, there was another thing I wanted to ask: yes, I was letting her wash my back so I could hear more about the Monkey's Paw, a vital item to us, but why was she so eager to wash it that it was what she got out of the bargain? If I were to believe her, it wasn't because she enjoyed washing young men's backs... I admit I've had my fun playing with the young, little, and tween girls that were Hachikuji, Shinobu, and Onono-

194

ki, but it was dawning on me that I too, legally speaking, would be classified as a minor.

"Right, I don't want to sound out of line," I said, "but from my perspective...speaking only based on my own values and about the world I came from, I'm not sure leaving Kanbaru the Monkey's Paw was the best thing for her."

In fact, that wasn't limited to my world. Whatever happened—or didn't happen—beforehand, the ill effects of the Monkey's Paw had to be responsible for Kanbaru becoming the Rainy Devil here as well...

"Oh, it's not like I had any clear intention in mind when I gifted it to her. I wasn't trying to help her, nor was I trying to spite her—I think? The other me, too."

"..."

A subtle reply. It was unclear whether the Ms. Toé with me now was alive or dead—but one thing was certain.

The mirror embedded in the Kanbarus' bath wall, the mirror that had occasioned me to ponder its *thickness*, reflected me and only me.

Ms. Toé—wasn't behind me.

It didn't reflect her nude body. How to interpret the unexpected but clear fact facing me now.

Once, when I took a bath with my little sister, I was the one who didn't appear in the mirror as we washed each other's hair. That's how I learned that my transformation into a vampire was progressing past a certain threshold... If Ms. Toé had no reflection either, did it mean she was a vampire?

No, I could rule that out. Vampires didn't exist in this world—"here" was inside a mirror, and I needed to flip around my interpretation.

This was probably how her absence in what I saw as my original world, what this side saw as the other world, manifested itself—so then, was Toé Gaen dead in the other world but alive in this one?

Maybe she was a ghost who only existed in a mirror. I could imagine that sort of scary story, and if anything, the idea helped calm me down. It was a lot less stressful than my junior's mom being here in the flesh, alive, and washing my back.

"The Monkey's Paw, or rather its source the Rainy Devil, is actually my avatar, as you already know—it was my flip side, a flip side attacking myself. That's the kind of family we Gaens have been for generations...experts at *creating monsters*."

"Creating—monsters."

"You know that my sorry excuse for a sister worked with some of her friends to create a corpse aberration, right? It was a variation on this theme—she'd deny it, but in the end, she's the true inheritor of the gifts of our lineage. Even if the path she chose, for whatever reason, is to rid the world of monsters."

On your side too, Ms. Toé added.

Too—so Miss Gaen was an expert yokai exterminator, the big boss of them all, on this side as well?

That was sort of comforting...being one of the few things this world and the other had in common—though it was hardly a feel-good moment when you analyzed Miss Gaen's reasons for choosing such a path.

"It's a question of how you face your other side," Ms. Toé went on. "It might be your flip side, but you shouldn't stand back to back with it—that's what I think. How you see your own back."

She began scrubbing my back even harder, with her bare hands. I didn't know when, but at some point, she'd stopped using her towel.

A far cry from Tsukihi's gentle touch, this was more like being scratched—hard. At this rate, I was going to end up as a scratch-board.

"Your own back? Unless you've got a real long neck, you'll need a mirror," I said.

"Right. Mirrors make you face yourself from various angles—that's its function as a device, after all, and the Rainy Devil was my mirror."

"But didn't you get rid of it by giving it that name? You didn't just face it, you defeated it…"

"While the Kanbarus took Suruga in, there's no question that she has Gaen blood in her. She'll end up facing herself just like my sister and I—maybe I did hope the paw would help. That left hand is just one part of the Rainy Devil, and it'll simply vanish if there's no use for it."

"Now that you mention it, I forget when, but Oshino—Mèmè Oshino was wondering where the rest of the Rainy Devil was. Um, at least in my world, Kanbaru only inherited that left hand…"

"I scattered them all around. They're safe as long as they're not together, but it might be dangerous if someone collects them. It's my avatar, you see."

"What a casually scary remark."

"Oh, no. I say that, but they're mummified. It's the corpse of an aberration, really—neither poison nor medicine, just a corpse. Don't be too worried, but if you happen across them, could you dispose of them for me? The sins of the mother are visited upon the daughter, but they also say that kids grow with or without parents… Tell Suruga for me when the time seems right, will you? Tell her there's no need to cherish it for life, that I really only wanted to tell her one thing—don't turn out like me."

"I could never. Not that. As a mother's words to her daughter?"

"Listen to yourself, an eighteen-year-old boy preaching about motherhood? What exactly do you think you know about being a mother?" Ms. Toé teased me, and I had no reply—I'd never been a mother, I'd never be a mother, I even had a strained relationship with my mother.

"…"

"Keheheh, sorry. You're right, it's a heavy message to ask some-one else to deliver. I take it back…but if Suruga ends up facing herself and seems stuck, do lend her a hand, will you?"

At this point, Ms. Toé was speaking purely about the other side—what a mysterious person. I was beginning to see why even someone like Miss Gaen chose her words carefully when (and only when) it came to her big sister.

Reaching past my head to grab the showerhead, Ms. Toé be-gan rinsing my back—torture time must've come to an end.

My back had been going numb, but now it burned—the hot water stung. Was I bleeding?

"If you can't be medicine, be poison. Otherwise you're noth-ing but water," Ms. Toé said over the noise the water was making. "That's what I told her, raising her—I wonder how much of my point got through? Maybe I just thought I was speaking to her, but was actually trying to get through to myself. She saw me as her parent, and my sister saw me as her big sister, but looking back—I was just a crybaby and a devil."

A weakling, she said. She sounded her usual self, so maybe it was just my impression, but was she whining?

"The best I could manage was to defeat that devil, while you, Araragi—protected your double. In which case, stick to your path. Darkness or light, that's your partner for sure."

"Partner?"

I looked behind me at that word.

Partner.

Find one, Black Hanekawa had told me—maybe it was sheer coincidence, but if Ms. Toé was using that word now, I had to ask what she meant.

I had to but didn't get the chance.

Because when I looked, I found no one there. Just as the mir-ror had shown, I was alone in this room with a cypress bath.

Since when? Or was it from the beginning?

Toé Gaen was gone, leaving behind just her towel—the showerhead lying on the floor.

"..."

I quietly placed it back on its hook, shut off the running water, and picked up the towel.

Well, at least the towel proved that our conversation wasn't just a fantasy I concocted once it became clear that Koyomi Araragi wasn't going to establish comms via any cypress bath—an excuse to give to Ononoki, but hey, while we're at it, I guess my smarting back was also proof?

It tingled and throbbed to the point that I honestly wondered if I was bleeding... Not to underscore my dialogue with Ms. Toé and needing a mirror to face my back, but I stood up to do just that. Then—

I gasped.

In the reflection I'd twisted my neck to see, my back wasn't bleeding, but there were welts all across it as if I'd been sentenced to a lashing—and they formed words.

In proper, mirrored characters.

There in the looking glass, they were easy to make out.

"NAOETSUHIGH"

It seemed I had my next destination.

026

"You think it's funny, shit-for-brains? I ought to kill you."

When I recounted the whole business to Ononoki, she abused me with some filthy language—she'd never gone on such a tirade against me, in this world or the other.

She did maintain her expressionless face and affectless tone, but had she been this world's original Ononoki, I imagine her look would have been anything but dashing.

"Who actually agrees to take a bath in that situation? With a married woman, at that. Who's yet to follow her husband in death."

"Um, I don't know about that last part…"

If she was a ghost, she already was dead along with her husband. Ononoki also needed to be careful about her sexist assumptions—though among men, the same concept was called a pledge of eternal friendship, say, or the Oath of the Peach Garden.

We'd left the Kanbaru estate by now and moved to Shirohebi Park—not that we needed to be there, but I'd evaded the Rainy Devil the day before by coming here, so we rehashed the same pattern.

After getting out of the bath, I'd exited out to the yard, gotten on my bike, and jumped into Kanbaru and Ononoki's battle, and the shikigami had taken that as her cue.

"Unlimited Rulebook—"

We'd shot into the sky.

As far as I could tell, the Rainy Devil hadn't taken any significant damage, with just a few scraps missing from her raincoat.

Ononoki had managed to accomplish her mission, fighting to buy me time but holding back and not injuring her opponent—what a professional.

I wanted her to know that I, an amateur, had also done good work, so once we arrived at the park's plaza, I related the ghost story I'd experienced in the wood bath—only to trigger the above verbal abuse.

"Sheesh... I feel like a kitty who caught a mouse and brought it to his master to be praised but who got yelled at instead."

"What you did wasn't so good."

"The simile is, though." I thought comparing myself to a feline when I didn't care for cats expressed the depth of my shock.

"Also, casting me as your master? It violates good-faith principles. You'd be Big Sis' sub-shikigami."

"A sub-shikigami? Is that a real concept? Wouldn't want to be under Miss Kagenui's umbrella..."

I looked around the park as I said this—fortunately, there were no witnesses, or rather no one had overheard my exchange with Ononoki.

Anyway, I'd ended up taking a rather long bath, and it was already past noon. My plan was to visit Kita-Shirahebi Shrine again at night, and we still had the time for one other action.

"So, Ononoki. I was thinking of going to NAOETSUHIGH... er, Naoetsu High, but what do you say?"

"Hmm... Well, I guess that's our only option if we don't have any other leads. Meanwhile, if you want to know how I feel, I'm not terribly excited about following Miss Gaen's sister's advice."

Feel, excited—words that didn't quite suit Ononoki.

"Advice, it probably isn't," I said. "She told me she wouldn't give me any—I think it's a suggestion, or maybe a screening process...something like a hint that we're free to discard."

That just might be where she drew the line, I thought—just as Oshino had one when it came to saving others, she might be limiting her assistance on account of her cheat-grade skills, intentionally or not.

That was my impression.

"You keep on talking about these stigmata, monstieur, but you still haven't shown them to me."

"What? You wanna look? You're telling me to strip here? I'm feeling a little shy..."

"You're acting legitimately self-conscious when your story's so phony that I can't believe it without some kind of proof. Aren't you just making stuff up to cover for the fact that you found nothing?"

"D-Don't be ridiculous. I'd never cover up a blunder."

I'd tried to come up with something, yes, but my dithering had led to getting my back washed by a married woman.

"Okay, turn around," Ononoki said like a doctor—how funny, a doll was playing doctor with a guy.

I pulled up my shirt.

"Are you kidding me?"

"Huh? What? Why that tone? And why those words?"

"There's not a thing there. Just a well-toned back."

"I'm not sure how to respond to that compliment...but seriously?"

"Seriously."

"No..."

I twisted my neck but naturally couldn't see my own back. Still, how could Ononoki not see those impressive welts?

Yet now that she said so, the pain had vanished at some

point... In the bath mirror, those nail marks had made me wonder if they'd ever disappear, but I suppose Ms. Toé had shown me some consideration. In that case, however, they'd gone away a little too soon...

"N-No, they were there until just now. NAOETSUHIGH, it said right on my back, in mirrored characters."

"Wow. Desperate, aren't you? A boy who gets trapped in his own lies about having a cute pen pal level of desperate."

"No elementary school rom-com metaphors please, this isn't a joke. I'm serious, Ononoki, look at my eyes! Are these the eyes of a liar?!"

"It's the first time anyone tried that line on me. This isn't a manga, looking at your eyes won't tell me anything. That's just called a staring contest. Want me to make a funny face while we're at it?"

"Look at my pupils!"

"Are they dilated or something? A whole other kind of suspicious. Anyway, I'm not an ophthalmologist. But I wish the lady had gone for a nice, full sentence."

"You're traumatizing me!"

Like I'd let her scar me in essay form!

Capital letters were bad enough!

"...Um, Ononoki, are you saying you believe it now? My tale of adventure that unfolded as you were busy fighting the Rainy Devil?"

"Not sure if you should be calling it that, but...if you're going to lie, try and tell a more believable lie."

"Wait, are you criticizing me now?"

"Sorry. I meant to say that if you were lying, you'd try and tell a more believable lie... I'm afraid I blurted out my creed."

"Your rephrasing was empty cant, then."

"Whatever the case, it's not like we have any other course of action. Right now I'm hung up on the fact that it was Miss Gaen's big sister who gave you that advice…or hint, as you put it."

Just like in my world, the name Toé Gaen carried *that kind* of connotation. Having met her, I could see why… Even apart from that, I didn't particularly want to visit Naoetsu High.

I preferred not to, in fact. A place I thought I was done with—what sort of face was I going to wear walking into my alma mater when I'd gotten down on all fours and apologized in the teachers' room on graduation day?

But at this hour, maybe school was out…and there weren't too many people. Sure, a good opportunity to sneak in, but alumnus or not, I was an outsider now, and they might get really mad at me (I'd be lucky if it ended there).

"Let's see… I'm one thing, but you'd stand out, Ononoki…"

"True, my cuteness attracts a lot of attention, wherever I go."

"…"

No, I was saying that a tween girl couldn't avoid standing out at a high school… If she was joking, it wasn't really her brand of humor—there was somewhat of a deviation between this Ononoki and the one I knew after all.

Berating me earlier felt like another variant of that, but just as I was thinking about what to do—

"That's it. Why don't we split up?" she proposed. "If there's no risk of the Rainy Devil coming into the picture, which is to say, of a battle erupting, I don't need to be with you. I'll try a different route while you head to Naoetsu High."

"A different route? Like?"

"Well, I only thought of it just now… Searching for a good excuse not to go there, because I really don't want to do as Miss Gaen's sister says, I had an idea."

"Are you being cautious, or do you just hate her? How unwilling can you be to visit Naoetsu High?"

"Let me try checking with Black Hanekawa—checking with her, or maybe finding her… Why she decided to save you is still a big question for me. I'm going to clear that up."

"Any idea where she might be?"

"No, but it'd be negligence if I used that as an excuse and didn't even try. Nothing wrong with looking for a lost cat now and then. I feel like a P.I."

"Well…"

It did seem like a good enough reason to reject Ms. Toé's hint—while I didn't know what I might find at Naoetsu High, contacting Black Hanekawa would undoubtedly represent significant progress.

Even if Ononoki located her, it'd be no walk in the park getting anything out of Black Hanekawa. Still, I wanted to know who had asked her to save me.

"Also," said Ononoki, "I probably won't get anywhere with it, but I'd like to see Shinobu again first."

"What? That's kind of worrisome… Will you be okay?"

"Heh. Never thought you'd worry yourself over the likes of me."

"There you go again, like we're in some buddy-cop movie… It's either that or a grade school romance, huh? Your repertoire's way too narrow."

"Don't worry, you saw for yourself how Shinobu's aura doesn't really work on me. I'm not saying it doesn't affect me at all, but it's still better than you going. I might get to hear the final bit of a conversation that got cut short… Of course, that selfish princess is more stubborn than you'd expect, and she might not talk unless it's directly to you, which is why I woke you up in the middle of the night, but I'll figure something out. I'll try reverse-prostrating myself and asking her."

"Okay. Thanks for begging on my behalf—hold on, reverse-prostrating?"

"The esoteric technique known as a back bridge. Primarily, bending your body backwards."

"Who do you think you are to assume such a cocky pose before milady... But how well do you think that'll all go? You said you have no idea where Black Hanekawa is, and you might not get anywhere with Shinobu, but if it's more promising than going to Naoetsu High, I could also—"

"Keep in mind that I only came up with these ideas because I don't want to go to Naoetsu High... If you came with me, I'd have to accompany you to Naoetsu High as a show of thanks."

She was telling me this to my face—did she hate Ms. Toé that much?

"Hence a plan you'd specifically have trouble coming along on. Your lack of mobility would only get in the way of chasing after Black Hanekawa, and you'd shrivel up and wither if you visited Shinobu—so. Give up yet?"

"I give up."

Well argued on her part.

It was educational, the way she weaved logical reasons for not doing something she didn't want to do. I hadn't been making excuses, but in contrast, how nonsensical my account of seeing nothing on the bathwater surface, meeting Kanbaru's mom instead, taking a soak with her, and receiving a message on my back must have sounded to Ononoki.

"In that case," she said, "let's meet back here in about three hours and then head to Kita-Shirahebi Shrine. We'll squeeze the most out of our time if we join up at the last second and jump over with my Unlimited Rulebook, instead of meeting up there. You go gather firewood at Naoetsu High, and I'll wash our laundry with Black Hanekawa and Shinobu."

"Did you just try to broaden your analogy repertoire and fail miserably? Your folktale reference even managed to muddy your point... Well, I don't think I'll be in any danger, but you be careful. Shinobu's one thing, but Black Hanekawa seems plenty dangerous in this world, too. I mean, she can drain your energy."

"Her energy drain doesn't mean much to me. I'm a corpse, okay?"

"Oh yeah? I didn't know."

"If we're talking about danger, I think you'll be in more of it, monstieur. You may not get in any battles, but doing exactly as Miss Gaen's sister says? It's bound to be costly—I think something is going to happen."

"..."

To be honest, I wasn't sensing any danger. What about Ms. Toé was making Ononoki this wary?

Of course, depending on how you looked at it, her intense caution was an expression of high esteem—if there wouldn't be any battles, it seemed worth going there just on my own.

"Should I drop by my house first and change into my school uniform, in that case?" I asked Ononoki. "Would it be better if I pretended to be a high schooler?"

I hadn't thought I'd ever wear my uniform again, but it looked like I had to one last time... Oikura should be out with my little sisters, so there was no risk of running into her even if I went back to my room.

"I think so. I'll escort you. I feel bad about abandoning you, it's the least I can do."

"Maybe don't abandon me and don't feel bad in the first place?"

That said, her relationship with Miss Gaen was probably at play here. To begin with, Ononoki didn't need to be helping me at all.

"Fine, please just take me home then. But you be careful too and don't try anything reckless," I warned her, knowing just how terrifying Black Hanekawa could be, and concluded our briefing...giving the matter no further thought.

But I ought to have given far more weight to Ononoki's misgivings—I'd yet to see just how terrifying Toé Gaen could be.

At her guidance, I was heading to Naoetsu High—and while I'd lived to tell numerous tales of aberrations, just barely making it through, I'd be coming face to face with a hair-raising, supreme terror like none other.

027

Or so I say, but it wasn't the destination Ms. Toé gave me, Naoe-tsu High, where I faced this terror.

It happened at an earlier stage.

After Ononoki transported me back to the Araragi residence so I could drop in, I bumped into this dreadful situation in my, or rather, Koyomi and Sodachi's room.

It felt like trying to pick the right gear and stocking back up on recovery items before a big boss fight but instead getting attacked by the arms shop owner and getting a game over. Now, let me tell you this in advance: If you're one of those Oikura fans who loves to see terrible things happen to her, sorry but she wasn't there.

Fortunately, she was out shopping with Karen and Tsukihi—the Araragi residence was empty, and it was going well at first.

Smooth sailing.

The problem occurred when I opened my room closet to change into the outfit that my stealth mission at Naoetsu High demanded—my second in a row after infiltrating the Kanbaru estate. In other words, when I tried to get my school uniform.

It wasn't there.

Hm, had it already been thrown out? That seemed impossible…

Maybe it was in Oikura's closet? We were family living in the same room, but I couldn't open it without even asking…so I checked every piece of clothing hanging in my own, one at a time, until at last—I found it.

No, not my school uniform.

Well—when I use that term, I picture the outfit I wore for three years, that tight-collared jacket and trousers, and maybe I just wasn't accustomed to describing it as such, but it was one in its own way. At least, it was a uniform you wore to school, and calling it a school uniform was totally proper.

A sailor-style blouse. A skirt.

What a girl calls a school uniform—the hard problem that arose here wasn't one of nomenclature.

"Oh. Oh. Oh."

I see.

You see?

If this world was inside out rather than flipped around sideways—if Koyomi Araragi lived here as Ogi Oshino, just as Tsubasa Hanekawa had become Black Hanekawa, this made sense. My school uniform would be a girl's rather than a boy's.

I've heard about new major leaguers finding cosplay outfits in their lockers as a form of hazing, and I guess this was the land of mirrors doing the same to me, an outsider. I hadn't noticed because I'd been wearing jeans, a t-shirt, and a hoodie, which is to say my usual outfit, but now it seemed certain that in this world Koyomi Araragi was Ogi Oshino.

Perhaps sharing a room with Oikura, and Ms. Toé not hesitating to bathe with me, were manifestations of the same inconsistency, or maybe incoherency… Okay, in Ms. Toé's case, I guess it was just a matter of personality, but Oikura's overfriendly openness made a little more sense if she'd been interacting with another girl.

She did chase me out of the room to get changed, but also jokingly invited me to take a bath with her on the first day.

"Nkk..."

I gritted my teeth.

Did I have no choice? The one thing I'd managed to avoid the entire series...the red line that I drew. There might've been little girls and mature ladies and the brushing of teeth, all sorts of stuff, but had I gotten carried away? I wasn't the type, it just wasn't me, and I'd thought I was all talk. That I was different from those other protagonists, the nonsense-users, the sister-obsessed middle schoolers, the swordless swordsmen, and the legendary heroes...

But I, too, was on team comic relief.

Okay, then, best not to brood over this.

Let's hurry up and get this on. Let's hurry up and get this going. We're already eating pretty far into our page count. At times like these, the greatest form of resistance is not resisting at all.

I began putting on the Naoetsu High girl's uniform—I really didn't get how consistency worked in this instance because Ogi and I should've worn completely different sizes, even if I'm on the small side. Yet the uniform fit so well it seemed tailor-made for me.

Maybe it had been.

Having come into contact with girls' clothes more than once during my adventures, fortuitously, I wasn't clueless about how you put them on. Since dressing someone else was indeed flipped left-right compared to wearing them yourself, after some effort it came together.

I was lucky that Ogi preferred to wear stockings—I lacked the fashion sense to care too much, but going out with bare legs was one of my few hang-ups. Nothing more undignified in a man.

All right, changed and ready to go. My plan had been to hop into my uniform and turn right back, but I'd ended up spending more time than I expected—I skipped down the steps two at a time and exited our house.

I hadn't looked in the mirror. Why would I?

Thanks to having let my hair grow out, I'd seem way too earnest about this.

Once outside, I realized just how anxious girls' clothes made me feel—and not just because this was my first time. I was left speechless by how defenseless a skirt left you.

A mere breeze could deal some damage to me. I had to respect girls if they went through high school in this kind of armor—and felt like apologizing to Hanekawa in particular.

But this was no time to be understanding Scottish culture. I straddled the BMX (and learned just how risky even getting on a bike seat was. I'd have never known otherwise—Ms. Toé was right about how knowing or not knowing wasn't what mattered, the point was to understand), then started pedaling toward Naoetsu High.

I thought I wouldn't ever, not anymore—would be an overstatement, but I didn't think I'd be rushing my way to school like this anytime soon, certainly not after just one day. In a girl's uniform was even more unexpected, but actually, this was no longer even my way to school.

That thought did make me a little melancholic. Whether I wore a boy's uniform or a girl's, whether I biked or walked—in any case, I was no longer a high school student.

I had no title. You might say I was therefore in another world, wherever I was, but getting lost in thought like this while I was biking wasn't safe, so I focused on focusing.

Once I did, it felt a little strange—yes, strange. Not a little, quite strange.

It was odd. I'd accepted my uniform being a girl's without much unease because if Koyomi Araragi existed in this world, he'd be Ogi. According to that logic, though, all of my clothes should've been feminine. Jeans, t-shirts, hoodies, pajamas, and the like are unisex—that had been my earlier rationalization, but I'd been overlooking the issue of underwear.

If all of my clothes really had changed, I should've noticed last night when I got out of the bath. As I put on Ogi's panties, or when I wore a bra—how do you explain that?

Of course, you couldn't expect too much logic out of this world. Why try to make honest sense out of it when I couldn't be taking Ogi's place to begin with? Still, this was intriguing.

Because—it was the other way around. Backwards.

The true nature of my odd feeling became clear when I considered the examples of Ononoki, Oikura, and Shinobu.

Ononoki thought something was off when I appeared before her from another world, and she modified herself to cope with it—yeah, the tween was just preposterous, but in any case, by doing so, she grew closer to the Ononoki I knew.

Oikura didn't know I was a visitor from another world and treated me the same. The issues it caused seemed to torment her, and she could be inching toward the truth given her smarts.

Shinobu, too, said her memories of this world's Koyomi Araragi were growing dim—her common sense was being replaced by mine.

That was the negative influence I had here, my effect on this world as an alien element—but wasn't it strange, then, that a closet full of my clothes yesterday contained Ogi's today?

Wasn't the vector pointing the other way around? The direction of the change made sense if I'd worn Ogi's underwear yesterday and my school jacket today, but when a jacket turned into a skirt—

"…"

It was too strange to overlook. Or so it seemed, but I also felt like contradictions on that level didn't matter anymore.

Didn't one way or the other.

I admit, a guy taking a bath with his junior's mom and then fussing over these details has hardly any authority—I'd been failing to behave in a reasonable manner for some time now.

Yes, that.

In other words—at the same time as I was influencing this world, was it influencing me? Was I *becoming* Ogi?

Beyond just my clothes, was I, myself, turning into a... mean-spirited, or let's say awful to deal with girl like her? It seemed ridiculous, but also completely possible—even the far more legitimate outcome.

Heat moves from hot to cold. Even if I had a strong influence on this world, just how much could a single drop of hot water affect an entire pool?

It'd get leveled out in no time. I'd turn into just another scoop of cold water.

Nothing but water.

I needed to do as Shinobu said and return to my world as soon as possible, literally asap.

Otherwise—I'd be lost.

I'd vanish.

Losing the part of me that should stay me no matter what.

I would go away.

Just as I lost my title when I graduated.

Koyomi Araragi would be erased.

And that—was the supreme, hair-raising terror.

028

Around this time, Yotsugi Ononoki, who was now acting independently, had gone to Shinobu Oshino—or Keepshot Castleorion Fortunderblade, that's to say Kissshot Acerolaorion Heartunderblade in her peak form, but in her peak form as a human—and finished her audience and exited the palace. An impressive show of initiative when my own drama had been to wear or not to wear, her actions conformed to our expectations of an expert.

More than enough talent to make up for a nasty personality—and yet, she would regret to report that she'd gained nothing from the audience.

According to her subsequent explanation: "Well, she might make herself out to be important, but she's no monster. The only unique thing about her is her charisma—it's not as if she's omniscient or omnipotent."

Being a corpse made it harder for Kissshot Acerolaorion Heartunderblade's grandeur to affect her, but it still did to some extent. Perhaps having no choice but to keep their conversation brief, she'd left empty-handed—unfortunate, but then her solo quest's main purpose was not having to heed Miss Gaen's sister's instructions, so perhaps it was all the same to Ononoki.

As much as that pissed me off, nothing would be more futile than to comment on it. She hadn't exactly strayed from her path and slacked off, and had done her job properly. Far be it from me to complain—in fact, it wasn't her job in the first place.

All right, Yotsugi Ononoki said, wiping her memory of her fruitless audience and moving on to her next item—in other words, finding Black Hanekawa.

Who knew *something*. Maybe just what she knew—but she did know.

In which case, we needed to ask her. Lacking a single clue as to her location, the only option was to comb through our town—well, no, I wouldn't say we didn't have any idea.

Like we said, Miss Serpent—this world's Nadeko Sengoku spoke as though she knew Black Hanekawa, and that might be considered a clue. Miss Serpent wasn't interested in discussing the matter, and since I couldn't bring myself to be assertive with Nadeko Sengoku, I'd had trouble digging into the topic. Yotsugi Ononoki, on the other hand, had no such qualms.

She could dive head-first if she wanted.

While we weren't sure that Miss Serpent would answer—not to mention the obscurity of her own whereabouts—we couldn't be any more certain about the location of her "friend"…or should we say successor.

A place Ononoki knew quite well herself, one she'd visited a number of times—Kita-Shirahebi Shrine. No need even to set any coordinates.

Unlimited Rulebook, was all it took. Uttering the words with no emotion, no expression—she flew.

Soaring at top speed now that she had no cargo, namely me getting in the way and weighing her down, she arrived at Kita-Shirahebi a dozen or so seconds later. Her body, her dead body, absorbed the impact so as not to destroy her destination—an impressive, environmentally-friendly landing that surprised no one, coming from her. But then…

Hm?

Yotsugi Ononoki's expressionless face wavered.

She didn't smile, nor did she put on a dashing look, but the expressionless one she'd settled on, so seemingly fixed, now cracked the tiniest bit.

Her current personality may have been a rush job, but what really surprised her was feeling perturbed at all while in full work mode. Well, chalk that up to this being another world and remaking herself to belong to *the other side*—she looked at what lay before her again.

In her defense, the sight would've surprised anyone, not just Ononoki.

The great god Mayoi Hachikuji and Miss Serpent—just the fact that those two people, or gods, were there was providential, as it meant skipping the preliminary step of talking to Miss Hachikuji to find Miss Serpent. Wary as Ononoki might be of such a convenient development, she'd take it.

But there, drinking hard with the duo, was a third individual—or rather, a little girl.

Who wouldn't be stunned to see an elementary schooler with braided hair and glasses—scratch that, an elementary schooler joining in on a drunken revel?

Unbelievable, I thought the little-girl factor rested entirely on me this time, Ononoki muttered in a solemn (rather than flat) tone, appraising the little girl—whose cheeks were flushed but not out of bashfulness.

"Hnm? Mrowww?" the little girl slurred with a sloppy smile on her face. "Tsubasa Hanyekawa here. Myahaha."

"…"

This actually allowed Ononoki to regain her composure.

It goes without saying that she didn't know Hanekawa at six years old. In fact, the shikigami barely knew Tsubasa Hanekawa, and even her familiarity with Black Hanekawa was limited to what I'd told her.

But if anything, this scene was easier to accept if the drunken little girl claimed to be Tsubasa Hanekawa—it was at least less scandalous than a regular little girl getting drunk.

"Miss Hachikuji. What's going on here?" the shikigami asked the lone individual present old enough to legally consume alcohol, who seemed to have a nice buzz going on too.

"Hm? Oh," she replied, sounding surprisingly sober. She was sitting there cross-legged on the ground, but perhaps gods were best when they weren't too uptight. "What's going on here is that Tsubasa Hanekawa's got more than one other side to her, though you still have her beat. Her early childhood is certainly one of her inner selves, while on the outside—well, since we haven't seen that little tiger of ours yet, maybe it all got settled."

"…"

Ononoki tilted her head in confusion at what purported to be an explanation. An outsider to the incidents involving Hanekawa, it didn't mean a thing to her.

She didn't know what was being said.

But ignoring what she didn't understand was Ononoki's specialty—her special move, even. She didn't expect any correct information from a drunk, anyway, and decided to just go over the important points one more time.

"So Black Hanekawa—is another pattern of Tsubasa Hane-kawa, yes? Of course, thanks to kind monster sir breaking me in, I can't grasp this world properly anymore…"

Breaking in sounded a little too violent, but this was a real issue for her—she could no longer accept what was "obvious" in this world as such.

She'd modified her own personality into one that stressed logic and reason.

"Yep, you got it—hsshh hsshh!"

220

This of course was Miss Serpent, wasted too, nodding in reply. Ononoki enjoyed no real familiarity with Nadeko Sengoku either, but their ties were far from shallow. At least, in the world I knew—but those memories both existed and didn't. How did that work in this case?

"Because Tsubasa Hanekawa's an honest-to-god case of multiple personalities, unlike me. Hsshh hsshh hsshh."

"I see..."

Though Ononoki nodded, she calmly determined that this trip was fruitless in its own way—Miss Serpent aside, leaping straight to discovering Hanekawa, the very person she was looking for, went beyond convenient and into too-good-to-be-true territory. Finding them all drunk here almost made it feel like her trail had been cut short.

She might have managed to extract info from the six-year-old Hanekawa, something like a double of Black Hanekawa, a double herself, if she weren't inebriated—or maybe not. Talking to a six-year-old girl, whether or not she was drunk, wasn't much better, she thought.

Ononoki was being a little naive, or as someone who didn't know Hanekawa, committing an unavoidable error. (Six or not, drunk or not, Hanekawa was still Hanekawa. Asking her a question would still get you a response). Unwilling to return empty-handed, however, she chose to join the three-person ring and sat herself down. Not to take part in the booze-soaked revelry, of course—alcohol was nothing more than a preservative to a corpse like her.

A third party objectively examining this scene and hypothesizing the appropriate course of action would, we imagine, have her conclude her solo quest and meet with me at Naoetsu High, where I now headed—but Ononoki, who'd rather be drawn and quartered, pretended not to notice this option.

Or really didn't notice. She just didn't want to that much.

"Well, aren't you all carefree, drinking like this when kind monster sir is in so much trouble," Ononoki scolded the three females, two of whom were gods. Humans have a tendency to attack others when they feel guilty, and the same seemed to go for corpses.

Perhaps, in terms of social standing, this didn't count as being disrespectful because as a shikigami, she was technically a god too.

"Oh, that stuff will be fine," Miss Hachikuji answered—now that she was drunk, her already reversed voice sounded even more falsetto, but her words had a strange sense of certainty at their core. "I just heard from little Tsubasa here... That's why we're drinking to celebrate."

"Celebration. Myahaha," the girl laughed, though Ononoki didn't know what was so funny.

"Hsshh hsshh hsshh hsshh," Miss Serpent joined in.

Ononoki, unable to blend into the already established mood, felt left out and uncomfortable (she actually did), but it wasn't enough for her to take a cue and leave.

Doing so meant going to Naoetsu High, which was out of the question.

"There've been various misconceptions, on my part, on everyone else's—Koyomi Araragi included, of course," Miss Hachikuji continued. "Maybe on your part too. No, that's not it—you could say this entire world is the product of a massive misconception."

"I'm not sure I get you..." Though wary about heeding the opinion of a drunk, Ononoki translated the remark and interpreted it as best she could. "Should I look at it like this? Judging by your calm...or loose demeanor, this situation, this case, has been settled."

"To be precise, it's heading toward a solution, mrow," responded the six-year-old Hanekawa, her tone anything but settled. "It's Araragi himself who's nyow heading toward it—mew could say it's always been that simple from the start. This is a tail of him coming to an understanding, and all we nyeeded to do was wait fur him to nyotice."

"Notice?"

"*Nyotice the existence of his partnyer*—though that partnyer *getting caged in* due to a mistake made things a little complicated... It would've all ended on the first day, nyotherwise. This is like a continyuation of the end. That's why I've had to run around everywhere, pouncing and pawing... Rolly-rolly."

"..."

If she was saying anything important, Ononoki couldn't quite figure it out. Still, she did get the vague nyoutline.

Or rather, outline—her job was over. It was an intuition that also sank into her. She could just stay here for the rest of this episode.

She understood—that she only had to wait with these three drunks for Koyomi Araragi to return via Naoetsu High.

This was far from the sense of accomplishment you felt after a job well done—in fact, the realization came with a sense of loss, like something had slipped out of her hands.

But never mind. She knew this day would come.

029

I arrived at Naoetsu High, parked the BMX in the bike lot, and entered its grounds. The air about this place felt completely different.

Not just because everything had been flipped around—there was a gentle sense of rejection, as though I were never meant to come here.

Maybe it had to do with my own mindset?

I started getting the sense that maybe this was what it meant to graduate. I'd felt refreshed in a way after graduating, but coming back here, it was almost like I'd been shoved through the place and extruded out the other end.

I'd had similar thoughts visiting my middle school with Ogi, but all it took was a day's time to feel this way. It wasn't sorrow, nor emptiness, but I think it did come down to my emotions.

Ruminating, I entered the school's halls—Ms. Toé had only written "NAOETSUHIGH" on my back.

Those coordinates were fairly specific, but the Naoetsu High campus was by no means small, so it was hard to decide where to go next—or so I say, but I knew I needed to head to my last classroom first. The one where I spent my days with Hitagi

Senjogahara and Tsubasa Hanekawa.

I didn't know what, or who, would be there, but I climbed the stairs until I arrived at the top floor.

Fortunately, I didn't run into anyone. Classes were done for the day, and the students had filed out. As for the Rainy Devil, or Suruga Kanbaru, she probably hadn't even been here—was she okay in this world? Did she ever come to school? Then again, according to Ms. Toé, those loose ends didn't necessarily have to meet.

This all ran through my mind as I opened the door to a classroom that was so fresh in my memory it didn't even feel nostalgic—and to cut to the chase, I found nothing. The tidied classroom's air just made me feel even more out of place, and naturally, no one else was there, either.

"…"

A swing and a miss? No, Ms. Toé had pointed this way, and it didn't make sense for there to be nothing—did I need to go somewhere else? To another classroom I'd used? How about the gym, or the teachers' room where I'd gotten on my hands and knees? Maybe the athletic field that had hosted more than one battle with an aberration... I could think of a number of places, but none of them stood out.

None of them fit. Ms. Toé never said it'd be a spot I knew well, of course, but given what she must've meant by finding my partner, she did seem to hint at some place connected to Koyomi Araragi... That said, the classrooms I'd used during my first and second years didn't seem likely—I had even less of a connection to them, a year or two having passed since I'd stopped using them to hand them down to my juniors. If this classroom wasn't it, it couldn't be those either...

Could it be the athletic field, after all? It was linked to aberrations.

Or maybe the P.E. shed. That was more linked to Hanekawa

than to aberrations, though…and I felt vaguely awkward about searching it so soon.

And then—I struck upon a different possibility altogether.

If we were talking about my connections to a place, there was a classroom with a deeper tie to me than the one where I spent my senior year. The cause of my time as a high schooler being not all too spectacular, a place where time stopped.

If that was it, I knew for certain who would be there—it felt like I'd just been slapped in the face with the answer.

That happened often with the math puzzles Oikura loved so much. They looked difficult, even impossible, but you figured them out the moment you realized the questioner's intent. That kind of feeling.

Of course.

That's all I could say.

I left the classroom—that was no longer mine.

030

I couldn't believe how casually she sat there.

"Hey, you're late—I've been waiting for ages, my dear senior," I was greeted by a line her uncle might use.

Ogi Oshino.

Ogi. My junior, a first-year at Naoetsu High.

Her impression of her uncle, Mèmè Oshino, may have been her way of getting back at me for the other day. She'd done a pretty good job of it, too.

Yeah, you could tell they were related.

"But wait, what's with that getup? Are you seriously cosplaying me?"

"You say that, but aren't you cosplaying me right back?" I asked in return. Ogi wore a Naoetsu High uniform, which is to say a high-collared jacket, there where she sat on one of the classroom's desks.

A Year 1, Class 3 desk.

But not the *current* Year 1, Class 3, nor an *extant* Year 1, Class 3. It wasn't the classroom once used by me, or later by any of my juniors—no.

The ghost of a classroom that never should have existed, that

Ogi and I wandered into and *got trapped in* not long after she transferred to my school, a room that shouldn't exist at Naoetsu High going by its blueprint—the apparitional Year 1, Class 3.

The place where it all began for Koyomi Araragi and Ogi Oshino, as it were.

"Well, *this* is just a joke. Though *that* was just a joke, too," Ogi said, bemused, her cheeks puffed out like she was trying not to laugh—I guess I looked that funny cosplaying her. "No one told you? Or was everyone just playing along? You absolutely didn't need to wear my uniform just because yours had been swapped out for it."

"Oh."

"Is that all you have to say? 'Oh'? You really are such a fool—but I suppose that's also one of your virtues. Don't worry, nothing too terrible is happening here."

Was that meant to be reassuring?

I had to wonder as I took my seat, finding the chair I'd used at the time. I looked at the clock, and while it was flipped around, its hands were moving, unlike before. After time had started to move back then, it hadn't stopped.

I was all alone with Ogi like before, though—or no, maybe I should say I was by myself?

She was my double, after all. My shadow, my copy, myself as reflected in a mirror.

Ogi Oshino, therefore—*was none other than my partner.*

"Wait, hm? Isn't that weird?"

"Huh? What is it, Araragi-senpai? There's nothing weird going on here." Ogi tilted her head—the way she always did to play dumb.

"Well...aren't you this world's Koyomi Araragi? Since you weren't in it, I was going to turn into you from the pressure this world exerted on me... But if you're here, why was my uniform replaced by a girl's?"

I had the vague notion that this world's Ogi—or this world's Araragi—had gone over to my original world and switched places with me, but if she was here, then maybe not?

Well, as rude as it might sound, she was even more anything-goes than this world, so maybe it was fine for there to be two, or even three of her... Did one go to my world, while another didn't?

"You've thought of all kinds of things, haven't you—you think too much. I'm pretty sure I told Black Hanekawa."

"Huh? You told her? Black Hanekawa? What do you mean..."

But there was only one thing it could mean.

Ogi had been the one to ask that cat to rescue me—she was me, after all, so it made perfect sense once I had the thought. I'd never considered it because Hanekawa and Ogi were on worse than bad terms, but maybe a partnership between them was possible in an inside-out world.

"Thinking too much... Maybe you're right. But I can't be thoughtless here, can I? Without an adequate amount of thinking, and adequate understanding—"

"Is that Ms. Toé's view of things? In the end, though, reason can only get you so far. As strange as that is for me to say." Ogi smirked—a bottomless smile. "No, don't worry, Araragi-senpai. You've reached your goal. You have no further destination after this. You know something?"

"What now?" I replied warily.

If she wanted to start comparing answers with me, how could I not be wary—how, when finding my partner, as everyone had urged me to do, actually meant finding the culprit?

I wasn't ruling out the chance that this was Ogi's all-too-speedy revenge. What she was about to deliver might not be her solution to the puzzle, but a confession.

"Did it never occur to you that this might all be a dream?" she asked me.

231

"Huh? Oh, uh..." The changeup of a question caught me off guard and took the wind out of my sails—what, was she going to hold out here? "I did think about that. More than once... I mean, who wouldn't in this situation? An illogical world full of contradictions where causes don't cause... A lucid dream, is that what you call it? I still think that this might be nothing more than a dream."

"Yes, you're right. It really is like a perfect dream, whether you're getting in a bath with Kanbaru's mom or putting on my school uniform."

"Um, could you not phrase it like I wanted to do those things?"

"Oikura, that hell-sent girl, is here leading such a joyful life. Didn't you want to see that, at least?"

"Oikura? Hell-sent..." I'd never met someone who used that phrase before. Well, I guess it was technically me using it, but it suited that girl to a t. "How do I put it, though. It wouldn't quite make sense if this was a dream. Things that I don't wish for happen here, and the place is teeming with things I don't know."

"Heheheh, I wonder. This idea that what you don't know can't appear in a dream is actually baseless. And nightmares are a thing, aren't they?"

"I considered that, but...are you saying this world is something that I dreamed up? Am I sleeping at home in my bed, still unable to wake up? Do I have this much trouble waking up if my sisters don't do it for me?"

"That, or you got in a traffic accident like Hachikuji or Ms. Toé as you headed back from graduation, riding happily along on my BMX, and you're in a hospital, wandering the border between life and death—it's a vision you're having on the brink of death."

"..."

"No, Shinobu would surely save you in that situation. That's what I'd call overthinking."

It's an illustration, Ogi said. She was as mysterious as ever,

232

with her clear words and murky intent—hard to accept in a partner and double.

"Then what about this?" she went on. "I personally would call it a pretty convincing hypothesis."

"What is it this time? Give it to me, at this point I'm ready to hear whatever you've got."

"Relax, this is my last hypothesis—no need to brace yourself. Everything broke down between you and Sodachi Oikura two years ago in this classroom, right?"

"...Yeah." Sure, things had broken down between me and my former childhood friend long before then—but that day, that time, was decisive.

"Right, right. And you met Kissshot Acerolaorion Heartunderblade during spring break a year ago—so much has happened since then. You got to know Tsubasa Hanekawa, you fell in love with Hitagi Senjogahara, you became pals with Mayoi Hachikuji, you played around with Suruga Kanbaru, you were reacquainted with Nadeko Sengoku—you came across many names in many places, whether it was my uncle, Yozuru Kagenui, Deishu Kaiki, Yotsugi Ononoki, Tadatsuru Teori, or Seishiro Shishirui."

"So? A recap, like now? Are you trying to get your yearbook signed when graduation is already over?"

"Say," Ogi ignored my awkward attempt at a dismissal to continue—to present me with her final hypothesis. "*Say it was all a dream—then what?*"

Not just this tale.

Every tale until now—what if it was all just a dream.

031

Battling on the precipice of death against Kissshot Acerolaorion
Heartunderblade.
Being saved by Mèmè Oshino.
Facing Tsubasa Hanekawa—Black Hanekawa.
Catching Hitagi Senjogahara at the bottom of the stairs.
Walking Mayoi Hachikuji home.
Competing for a girl's heart with Suruga Kanbaru.
Freeing Nadeko Sengoku from a charm.
Facing Black Hanekawa again.
Reconciling with Shinobu Oshino.
Banishing Deishu Kaiki.
Fighting Yotsugi Ononoki.
Getting spared by Yozuru Kagenui.
Having Tsubasa Hanekawa confess to me.
Failing to save Mayoi Hachikuji and parting ways.
Confronting Seishiro Shishirui.
Getting reintroduced to Sodachi Oikura.
Failing to save Nadeko Sengoku after all.
Sitting in Tadatsuru Teori's sights.
And settling it all with Ogi Oshino.

An entire year—our year-long tale, all just a dream? I hadn't wandered into another world—but only woken up?

Just as many people do every morning.

I simply woke up? All that sorrow, joy, loneliness, frustration, pain, and fun, all the smiles, tears, words, and strength, all the life and death—was all just something I dreamed? This inconsistent, contradictory world was in fact real, was the original world that I always existed in?

Both sides see the other as the counterfeit—Shinobu had told me, but only my world was the counterfeit?

Only I was the counterfeit. The world had always been universal.

Next morning—I'd wake up as always.

"If you're saying all of it is a dream…" I—Koyomi Araragi, answered. "I'd say I had a wonderful dream, stretch my arms—and know with a smile on my face that an incredible day awaits me."

"An answer you could only dream of."

In that case, let me retract my hypothesis, Ogi said with a shrug—excuse me, what?

"I said I take back my hypothetical. It can't be true. So, why don't we cut out the small talk and get to the topic at hand?"

"Small talk?!"

Hold on, hold on, hold on! It all seemed pretty serious to me! We neatly summed up all the previous installments and drummed up a crisis that threatened to turn everything on its head, ruining it all!

"Ha haa. Even I don't have the courage."

"I'd say faking me out with something that malicious is pretty brave… Wait, so it's not true? The entire series of tales so far wasn't just a dream?"

"I guarantee it. I mean, just how long would you have to be dreaming for that to be true? Speaking of which, did we discuss it the other day—the butterfly dream? Where you can't tell if you're a human being dreaming of having become a butterfly, or a butterfly dreaming of having become a human being—which would be just a dream when you wake up?"

"Oh...if you put it that way, I guess the idea of experiences all being a dream is thought-provoking."

"But, Araragi-senpai. However thought-provoking, don't you think there's an innegligible hole in it?"

"A hole?" Was she claiming to have found one in a famous anecdote that people have been telling for thousands of years? Now, this was big.

"Challenging historical fact is a part of period mysteries. Just because something is written down in an ancient text doesn't make it indisputable—for example, did the Honnoji Incident really happen?"

"You're saying the butterfly dream isn't real? Is that it?"

"My conclusion is that it never happened—it was just a type of thought experiment by an ancient philosopher. That it, if anything, is a hypothesis. A metaphor. In other words, it's saying, 'I was dreaming. In my dream, I was a butterfly, floating from flower to flower—and then I woke up. I was a human. But then the thought struck me, could I simply be a butterfly dreaming that I'd become human...'"

"I don't see that as contradictory. At least, you can't disprove it in theory."

"But for an entirely emotional argument against it, I'd say, *Who the hell dreams of becoming a butterfly?!*"

There's my double for you. She delivered the quip exactly as I would, in an identical tone—then, a beat later...

"No matter how fantastical a dream, *you're never going to not be you.* Or—has that ever happened to you? Have you ever dreamed of being a butterfly? It doesn't have to be a butterfly. A dream where you're a dog, say, or a bird."

No, I couldn't say I had.

I was pretty sure, too... I'd had a lot of dreams in my life, but they were always from my own point of view—I'd never been anyone other than myself. Even if I budged and pretended that I'd dreamed of being a butterfly, that'd still be a dream about nothing more than *me as a butterfly*. Plus, I didn't imagine a butterfly had the mental capacity in the first place to dream of becoming human.

"Indeed. Dreams are always had from the dreamer's perspective. Butterflies must not be able to recognize themselves in mirrors—but anyway, that's why it's a kind of metaphor. He used the example of a butterfly for ease of understanding. In other words, nothing but-a-flight of fancy," Ogi punned. "*It was all just a dream* endings are considered off-limits not because they're cowardly and unfair, but because they aren't realistic. They aren't convincing— you couldn't possibly accept everything so far being a dream, could you?"

"True, but..."

As her senior, and as her partner, I wanted to respond to her big lie, which had felt a little too true-to-life—but I wasn't going to let Ogi's mean tricks get to me at this point. Sheesh, what was it that this girl wanted to do? Don't confuse me as a prank.

"In that case, what *is* happening to me? You're saying that this isn't a dream either, right? This world, that world. Inside a mirror, the land of mirrors—left and right being flipped around, everything being inside out, it's all so incoherent that my brain can barely handle it. If there's something you know, tell me, I'd really appreciate it. Ogi, what exactly do you know?"

"I don't know anything—you're the one who knows. And the work of understanding falls on you too," she said. "It's because you're so slow to understand that you end up having to cosplay me in an unsightly display."

"Oh...right." Calling me unsightly was going too far, but having nothing to say in return, I asked a question to shift the topic, to hide my embarrassment so to speak. "Whatever this world is, if you exist in it, I don't see any reason for the school uniform in my closet to change into a girl's uniform—could you start by explaining that?"

"I don't think that's where I should begin...and didn't I explain that already?"

"What? No, I don't remember ever getting an explanation?"

"I told you *that* was just a joke too, right at the outset."

"..."

Had she? Ah, yes, but I hadn't taken her meaning. Though I certainly remembered thinking that me cosplaying her as she cosplayed me was some sort of sick joke...

"It should go without saying," averred Ogi, "but let me play the boor and give you the details. You were taking too long sitting back and enjoying your time here flirting with Miss Oikura, so I got annoyed and thought to tease you by swapping my uniform with yours."

"How does that go without saying?!"

Like I'd ever figure out from a single line that she'd been so proactive!

What was the point of this costume change, then?!

"Please don't get so upset. Listen, I wasn't expecting this either. I thought maybe you'd get a little flustered if you saw that your uniform had changed. But you went so far past flustered that you even put on a pair of stockings... I don't think that's normal."

In fact, I ended up being the flustered one, Ogi noted. *I panicked and put a barrier around the whole school.*

So not encountering anyone or being spotted on campus wasn't just dumb luck...

In the end, the change in my school uniform—the idea of changes coming from the opposite vector—was only a prank on Ogi's part.

"Also, while I'm confessing here," she said, "the smirking face you saw in the bathroom mirror when Tsukihi washed your face was also me."

"Not the kind of thing you just tack on to a confession... Seriously? You can do that?"

"Yes. It's hardly impressive, you and I are the same person. Or rather, that was about all I could do, trapped here in this classroom. To fan your sense of crisis, of course."

"..."

Oh. While I was furious, this gave me some respite. For the time being, the idea of me no longer being me, the loss of Koyomi Araragi, was ruled out. But it only meant that the world exerted no pressure on me, and didn't do away with the pressure I put on the world.

Ogi trying to make me fret implied that I needed to hurry up and go home. It was a sort of request on her part, in which case I shouldn't be mad at her—nor would I be awarded any injury time at the end here.

"But even if you're telling me to go home, I don't know how," I grumbled. "Unless you're able to create a gate to the other world like Shinobu? Actually, which are you anyway? The Ogi who's my double, or Ogi, this world's Koyomi Araragi? You could even be both..."

"I'm your double," she answered with unexpected candor— Ogi never answered a simple question with a simple answer, so I was a bit stunned.

Was she being so forthcoming because of how much laid ahead of us? She'd said no more small talk, but were we already on the main topic? Or were we still on the runup—I did hope this was at least the prologue.

"I'm your Ogi Oshino."

"Could you not phrase it that way? Our distance is already awkward enough now that I've learned your true identity."

"How cold—you might be surprised to hear this, but I'm grateful to you in my own way, okay? You risked your life to save me from the Darkness' judgment, and I'd like to pay you back for what you did."

Her tone was far too hollow for me to believe her, but I couldn't ignore her if she put it that way. I was surprised though, I'll admit.

"My double... Does that mean you came into this land of mirrors along with me? I guess you could come to this side as yourself, unlike Shinobu, a vampire... But that does bring back another problem that I thought was solved. In that case, where did the inside-out Koyomi Araragi that should exist in this world go?"

"..."

Oh? Even if it was standard operating procedure for Ogi not to give a straight answer, going silent was unusual—she loved running her mouth just as much as her uncle, or maybe even more than him.

"Ogi?"

"Has anyone talked to you yet...about the reflectivity of mirrors?" she asked, fixing her eyes on me after I called her name—with those black orbs that sucked you in.

"Has anyone... As my double, aren't you aware of my every deed? Oikura told me."

"You're misunderstanding something. It's not as if I grasped everything about you—there'd be no point in my existence. Overlapping and failing to at the same time is what allows me to be my own critic."

Miss Oikura, you say? Just the kind of role she'd play, Ogi laughed. "Yes, the reflectivity of the average mirror is about eighty percent—you could say the rest is blurred, but also that the twenty-or-so percent is whittled away in reflection, and sentenced to death."

"Sentenced to death..."

Right.

We always tend to focus on the larger proportion, on the eighty percent, but if we looked to the remaining twenty percent—well, no, we can't see it.

Because there's no light there. It's absorbed, never reflected back.

"So…Koyomi Araragi never existed in this world to begin with?"

I belonged to the twenty percent that didn't exist? No wonder I couldn't find him no matter how hard I looked. Searching for something that exists is simple compared to searching for something that doesn't—you can seek something that is, but how do you find something that isn't? I was part of the light absorbed by a mirror and not reflected—no, wait.

That couldn't be it—I'd seen myself in the mirror before being sucked into it yesterday, and that's where this whole story began. When I was more vampiric and mirrors didn't reflect me, you might've said that, but not anymore. Even if you ignored that line of reasoning and accepted that I was part of the twenty percent that was left un-reflected, you could still ask, *So what?*

It wasn't as if I'd been sucked into the mirror because I was the light it didn't absorb—because then a lot more than just me would have been sucked in.

"…Is this another hypothesis of yours, Ogi?"

"No, no, you're jumping to the wrong conclusion. I'm not trying to dredge up hypotheses, nor your emotions for that matter… Well, how should I put it. You've jumped to the wrong conclusion, that really is the best way to phrase it."

Hearing this was vexing—jumping to conclusions. Yes, doing so one too many times might be to blame for my predicament. Hadn't I jumped from one conclusion to the next throughout high school?

"But it's not as if I dislike that impatience of yours," Ogi said. "And your kindness, I suppose, how you sympathize with the

242

excised twenty percent."

"…"

She then beckoned me over—what a presumptuous girl, summoning her senior, but I couldn't complain when I was used to Kanbaru doing just that. I stood up and moved over—only now noticing that the seat my double had taken was Oikura's.

God, she really did like staging every last detail.

"Heyyy!" she called out as I approached, motioning for a high five—what the heck?

"Heyyy," I complied.

A nice *smack* filled the room.

"So, what's this about?"

"Well, you know," Ogi said. "You and I are mirror images of the same person—flip sides of each other, yes, but we can't put our hands together like this with a mirror between us, right?"

"…"

I'd had that thought before. When and where?

Strictly speaking, when we talk about a mirror's face, we're referring to the silver coating applied to its backside, so there's always going to be a gap equal to the depth of the glass between your hand and your reflection's, even if you try to make them touch—

"It was when Ms. Toé washed your back. Could you not pretend something that shocking never happened?"

"Oh, was it? It totally slipped my mind since it was nothing to me… Anyway, is that important?"

"We're talking about a mirror's thickness, stop playing thick yourself. What I'm saying is that if you want to enter a mirror—if you want to travel to the land of mirrors—you first need to *physically pass through the glass.*"

You first need a portable portal like a pass loop, Ogi used one of Doraemon's secret tools as an example.

I wasn't so sure about minding physical phenomena in the

context of a feat as fantasyish as entering a mirror, though...

"Fine," I said, "it'd be one thing if I was reflected on water or on polished iron, but with a mirror, the glass acts as a gate I need to pass through first. I get what you're saying, but...so what?"

"So what? So that's the answer—don't you remember what I told you when we were stuck here before?"

"Hm? You told me a whole lot of things. To be specific?"

"Vampires."

Vampires can't enter a room without permission.

Right, she'd said that—which is why we'd been trapped, or why we couldn't get out. And the characteristic meant that as someone with a vampiric aspect, passing through the glass in the first place was much harder than entering a mirror... Even if I could leave my vampiric aspect on the other side in order to do so, it's not like humans can pass through glass. Then again, that rendered everything moot.

In which case, what was this girl trying to say? It felt like she was still toying around with hypotheses...or were we in fact closing in on the solution?

"It's not good to overthink things, but you shouldn't be thoughtless, either—you're right about that, Araragi-senpai. Also, you're thinking about this the wrong way around."

"Hm?"

"You may not be able to pass to the other side of a sheet of glass, but even a vampire can be *pulled into it* from this side."

"Hm?"

"You know how we just discussed all of it being a dream? Well—that's not the case, but what about this? I don't think you can disprove the idea that *this* isn't the real world yet."

I didn't follow. Was she switching topics again without me noticing, maybe going back to an old one? "No, Ogi... If this were the real world, the other side would be the counterfeit. Whether I'm in a dream or in a mirror."

"Don't think of that side as inside a mirror, think of this one as outside it—now do you understand?"

"I don't. You're only making this more confusing—inside, outside, isn't it all the same?"

If we were *outside a mirror*, didn't that place my previous world *inside a mirror*, after all? Actually, no—there was one last possibility I had to consider.

It would never come from me, but had been prompted by Ogi—*the opposite of it all being a dream.*

If I'd always lived in this land of mirrors but been expelled from it—but no, wasn't that only a matter of perspective? It wouldn't change the fact of me being me and barely functioned as an answer to Ogi's question.

So long as I couldn't pass through a sheet of glass, I couldn't enter or exit any land of mirrors—pulled into it? Like *pulling up* a drowning man grasping at straws?

Sure, I couldn't swim, but splashing around in bathwater and checking its temperature wasn't beyond me—no.

Even if you could pull something in through its surface, or that of a mirror across a pane of glass, from the other side—what exactly had I offered a hand to?

"The twenty percent, that's what," Ogi said. "The light that should've been absorbed *and never reflected*—you scooped it up and rescued it. *You opened the gate* and brought it to this side for safety. You ended up *making* this world into the land of mirrors. You haven't come to it—*you pulled it in*. Almost like they say the ancient gods pulled all of Japan together as one."

032

That, of course, was another joke.

I expected Ogi to follow up with a line like that, but she didn't. *Honestly, one wrong step there and it would've been a disaster*, she said instead, as if to frighten me.

She seemed to be having fun.

"You didn't get caught up in this land of mirrors, Araragi-senpai, you got it caught up with you."

"…"

"Of course, this town is the only thing being affected, in spite of all the talk of worlds and lands—but please do be careful going forward. I'm not sure how much you realize this, but you've subdued a legendary vampire, built amicable relationships with gods, and are one and the same as me, someone with all kinds of elements from all kinds of aberrations. You suggested earlier that anything goes with me, but I'd say you're pretty anything-goes yourself."

Then the culprit wasn't Ogi.

It was me—okay, it was Koyomi Araragi either way. But it didn't change the fact that I was playing solitaire. It didn't, but...

"Isn't this already a disaster? You could put me on the same level as Shinobu when she destroyed the world in another time-line. Messing up an entire town—"

"Oh, no. This is still just a counterfeit. I said you pulled this land together, but it's not like you did that physically. It's only a question of how you feel about it. If that side is a counterfeit, then so is this one—just like Miss Shinobu said. All you did was bring a sense of *maybe it's all my imagination* to the entire town. It's not as if anything you did stopped being history, right? You only modestly rescued the light that was lost, the light that had gone out of sight—you only gave everyone a tiny little reminder of the forgotten ones, those feelings that had been left behind."

Though you did put us in a dangerous spot, she said consolingly—well, no, I was sure it was just mean-spirited nagging.

"It won't be a problem if you act appropriately from here. Yes, to put it as you might, it'll just seem like you had a wonderful little dream."

"Appropriately..." I sat down, all the strength instantly draining from my body. "It seems to me like there's a lot you're going to have to tell me if I want to do that."

"Yes, and that's why I'm here—we couldn't bother any experts over something like this. I was impressed by Yotsugi Ononoki's emergency response, but this story of aberrations is compact enough that we can handle it between you and me... Do be careful going forward, though. Don't forget that we're marked by those experts for observation."

"..."

True. A chilling thought.

If Miss Gaen got word of this—fine, she knew everything, so maybe she already did. I could imagine how pissed she was at me for stirring up trouble all over again, after we'd pacified the town by settling that whole series of incidents... In fact, she might more than just scold me.

"No," disagreed Ogi, "while she might know about this affair,

248

she hasn't the right to blow her top. She was the one who *left behind* Toé Gaen's existence, after all, here in this town—and while it turned out for the best, I doubt it had been on purpose. It sure would've taken you longer to arrive at this classroom, though, without Ms. Toé."

"I don't get it... If you want to hurry me up so badly, why not come meet me at my house instead of sitting cooped up in this classroom?"

"Like I said, I was locked in—because this classroom was established as where I belong. *This* is my own lingering regret—or mistake, or stroke of bad luck... I failed to secure a good place for myself. That's why messing with you in a roundabout way was the best I could do—anything may go when it comes to me, but I'm not omnipotent."

"..."

"Miss Gaen must have left Ms. Toé behind due to some bitter memories, but I bet it was a simple case of lingering regret for Miss Hanekawa. Saying goodbye to everyone must've been very difficult. Almost like a six-year-old child, don't you think? Then again, that might be why we could work in tandem..."

And yet she left with a big smile on her face. That big-breasted girl is as foolish as they come, Ogi laughed—apparently disliking Hanekawa as always.

Still, she'd allied herself with the class president among class presidents when this wasn't even the land of mirrors. Did that mean there'd been a change in her nevertheless?

Just as I'd changed—perhaps Ogi could, too?

"Hanekawa...felt that way when she left? She's my friend, but I didn't do anything to show her I understood that at all."

"That large-chested senior of mine would only hate it if someone saw straight through her, friend or not. She's the kind of person who hides many things and has lots of secrets—you don't believe Miss Oikura wanted you to know that she hoped to be better friends with you when she left this town, do you?"

"…"

"Then there's Kissshot Acerolaorion Heartunderblade when she was a human, and those vestiges of the living Yotsugi Ononoki—and Karen Araragi's complex about not being girly. Mayoi Hachikuji, who could never become an adult—and the savagery lurking in Nadeko Sengoku and Suruga Kanbaru. These were all forgotten, or were things they wish they could forget. You took *all those things* that were left behind and brought them to this side. That's how you created—the so-called land of mirrors."

It's like some sort of light-based magic trick, Ogi quipped—and also that if she used black magic, I must use white magic.

That made sense. If she belonged to the element of darkness, my element was light, in contrast to her—though it sounds like bragging to assign yourself light as an element. I was buying myself shoes I could never fill.

"The mirror was nothing more than a catalyst—or maybe a detonator, but in any case, it only provided the chance. Of course, a mirror being the cue for all this did cause everything in the world to be flipped around."

"If I didn't get caught up in the land of mirrors but got it caught up with me—then I guess this was far from a lukewarm setup. Hm? In that case, did Ononoki and Oikura feel that something about the world was off not because of the negative effects that I had on it as an outsider, but rather because of its shortcomings?"

"I'd call them excesses, not shortcomings. You dragged another twenty percent from the land of mirrors, giving this place a hundred and twenty percent—it's going to run over, beyond capacity like that. Either way, it doesn't have much to do with them interacting with you. So if you feel like it, you're welcome to fool around with Miss Oikura."

Just as with Ms. Toé and Black Hanekawa, she's not the real thing, though—Ogi said. That was a relief, or rather, I needed to straighten out the situation before the real Oikura came back to this town by some mistake.

"I need to figure something out...or wait...can we return things back to the way they were? Can we make this inconsistent world into a consistent one again?"

"I wouldn't call it going back to the way things were. It might be more like moving forward—with an extra twenty percent in tow. Everyone regained what they'd lost, if only temporarily, so there will of course be some effect. That would be the influence you exert, if anything—for example, I imagine Miss Kanbaru is going to dream about Ms. Toé for a little while. Nothing more serious than that."

"Can I really think of this as not having done anything serious?"

I couldn't tell if Ogi was trying to be considerate, or if she was trying to bully me... Still, it was a load off my chest to know that despite inconveniencing everyone, I hadn't done them any harm.

How would I ever forgive myself if Shinobu, who'd even taken the form of a little girl, could no longer be certified as harmless?

"Ha haa. You know, I think this turned out to be a good test case."

"A test case? Of what?"

"You foolishly saved me when I should've been sucked up by the Darkness. My uncle may have supported your intentions there, but it's not as if all those experts wholeheartedly approve of what you did. I think it's clear as day that no small number of ungenerous characters would have rather seen a dangerous element like myself disappear."

I count myself among them by the way, said a self-flagellating Ogi—while she often said these kinds of things to feign humility, I could tell she really meant it now.

"Yet this time, I acted as your safety valve—letting me live had some meaning. Forget being certified as harmless, I think this confirms it as fact. The surveillance level on you could rise a bit, though."

"…"

The surveillance level? I didn't need any more freeloaders. Ononoki was plenty on her own.

"Of course, walking away from this situation as it stands will have them swooping in and crushing it with all their might. Miss Gaen will get ready to face off against her sister, I'm sure—would you like that? I do think it's a valid option. We could live in this inconsistent world forever."

"Don't make me weird offers. Why would I ever want that? I just want to hurry up and go home…or I guess that's not how I should put it. I'm already home. Um…"

How should I word it?

Release the twenty percent of light I pulled into this world back through the mirror? How would I go about doing that? I didn't even know how I pulled it here in the first place…

"I do want—to hurry up and proceed."

"Ha haa. And again, that's why I'm here—I take care of your mess-ups. Just as you take care of mine."

"Kind of feels like an unfair peace treaty to me…"

No, I couldn't say that as a fact. This could have turned into a genuine calamity—both Ogi and Shinobu called it a counterfeit, but when a screen is exposed to light for too long, that light can burn itself in. If I'd accepted Ogi's offer just now—this world would be permanent.

She'd put a stop to it at the last second, and I sincerely owed her. I'd thought this might be her all-too-speedy revenge, but in fact it had been her payback that was speedy.

Her payback in a backwards world.

Though I wish I could come up with a better line than that.

"Um, could you please wait a second? I'm going to bring something out," Ogi said, sticking her hand in her school jacket and fishing around before pulling out a bare Blu-ray—why stick it uncased in your uniform, I wondered, what if you scratched the disc, but no, it was no Blu-ray.

Because it was pure black.

Black like darkness.

A Blu-ray was a reflective silver on at least one side—while on both sides of the palm-sized, disc-shaped object Ogi held by the edges, as if to keep any fingerprints from getting on it, was a shade of black that felt like it could suck you in.

"Um...was that how PlayStation 1 games were?"

"Bingo. But this isn't a PlayStation 1 game—I do have a PSX at home and would be happy to play with you, just not this. Because..."

Ogi threw it at me side-armed, like a frisbee—why make it so hard to catch when we were so close, I wasn't a dog, I thought, but I somehow grabbed it, using my torso as a net.

"Look," she urged.

And all I needed to do was look—because you couldn't play this on a console when it had no donut hole.

A perfectly disc-shaped object, the kind you might expect to see in a math textbook—even a jet-black game disk might reflect something, but this one didn't.

It reflected nothing to an excessive degree.

A flat, total black, like it had been painted.

Almost seeming to absorb any and all light that hit it—darkness.

"..."

I returned the black object to Ogi with trepidation, as if I were handling a bomb. "Don't act so scared," she said, taking it and raising it overhead before continuing, "Zero percent reflectivity—a mirror that's a hundred percent absorbent."

A mirror...that black?

Well, like she said—it was zero percent reflective.

"I was bored, stuck here in this classroom. Crafting something like this was about all I could do—using the blackboard."

"The blackboard?"

I glanced over...and looking closely, found a chip missing from the corner. I had no idea what kind of tools and technology she'd used to create a disc out of it, though... That was some impressive DIY work.

I never imagined a piece of Year 1, Class 3 classroom's ghost, which I'd fixed in place, could take such a form... Was it like plucking a four-leaf clover to keep with you?

"I guess," affirmed Ogi. "It carries just as much supernatural power, if not more. You're planning on visiting Kita-Shirahebi after this, right? In that case, I want you to offer it to the shrine there—it's what you might call a votive object."

"A votive object..."

This reminded me—as items that reflected the truth, mirrors were seen as holy since ancient times. Forget votive objects, they could even be treated like dwellings for the divine. Could Ogi's handmade mirror, this black mirror, be one?

"Call it a gift to congratulate Hachikuji on her new post as god—it seems like she wasn't able to fully deal with this situation, which is no surprise given that she only became a deity thanks to a sophistic technicality, but in reality, as the god meant to protect this town, she's the one who needs to settle this all peacefully, not me. I suppose I'll let her take the credit."

"That shrine is the heart of this town. What's going to happen when I place it there? If it has zero reflectivity, it doesn't just show you nothing...it can even suck light into itself, right?"

"Well, it's going to suck up that twenty percent of light that would have been lost if you hadn't guided it here—lingering regrets and remnants that ought to have faded into obscurity. Part of a shrine's job to accept those, right? Kita-Shirahebi is also an air pocket that attracts the stuff that aberrations are made of, and now that Mister Shishirui is no longer with us, it requires a tool to help it absorb wayward thoughts."

True. It was asking too much of Hachikuji, who only happened to become a god due to the way everything progressed, to keep the town tranquil and pacified all on her own. We might have tied up those loose ends, all too neatly, but if there were any remaining openings, or maybe concerns, it was this.

Miss Gaen would surely continue to follow up on the situation, but it wasn't as if she could spend all her time worrying about one town... I didn't see the harm in bringing over one of these votive objects, or a cheat item.

"Okay. I'll offer it to the shrine."

"I appreciate it. By the way, you'll know it's time to swap it out once it's turned completely white."

"So it's like a filter? How long does it last?"

"A few centuries, under normal circumstances...but then we're talking about this town. A town once attacked by a legendary vampire, a town that you now grace with your presence—who knows, it might only last a few months."

"You really know how to scare me."

This time, Ogi offered the black mirror to me with care, and I took it with reverence—if what she said was true, offering it to the shrine wouldn't fix everything. I needed to keep on frequenting Kita-Shirahebi, I thought—hm?

"What's the matter, Araragi-senpai?"

Just as Ogi handed me the mirror and we both held it, together.

Just as Ogi and I faced each other, with what was still a mirror between us, even if it was zero percent reflective—a black mirror between us, its front side indistinguishable from its back, I thought, *Hold on.*

My doubts were reignited.

Ogi's flowing delivery made me think that all the mysteries

had been solved, that we even had countermeasures—but one vital point remained vague.

I got that I'd scooped up this lost twenty percent from the other side of the mirror at that moment—but still didn't know why.

Rescuing these poor little regrets left lingering behind to fade away and giving them form sounded nice, but I hadn't meant to do anything so noble.

In fact, I hadn't known anything about reflectivity and the like until Oikura ('s residual thoughts?) bothered to school me.

Yes, I'd reached out to the mirror yesterday morning because something seemed wrong with the me I saw in it—my reflected self in the mirror. It had stopped.

"Unlike the reflection I saw in the sink, that wasn't you, right? Then what exactly—"

"Come up with the answer to that one on your own, at least. Think about it, reflect on it."

"You mean it requires self-reflection?"

"Yes, I suppose. Really, consider what you've done...or so I say, but we'd be back at square one if you started overthinking things again. I'll borrow a page from my predecessors and just give you a hint."

Ogi let go of the black mirror.

And said: "Who exactly are you?"

What, she wanted me to say it? My expression turned sober and austere, but I couldn't reply to her question any other way. Even a lukewarm setup needed a reasonably serious conclusion.

So I answered her, looking into the dark black mirror.

"Koyomi Araragi here. Just the man you see."

And then I understood.

Of course.

My own lingering regrets.

033

The epilogue, or maybe just a log in this case?

Either way, I was the one to rouse myself the next day, not my little sisters Karen and Tsukihi—I did have some help from an alarm clock if we're splitting hairs, but I think it still counts.

I was alone in my room, of course, with no childhood friend sharing it with me. Getting ready to leave the house, I saw my tall little sister, and my other little sister who was the exact same; I flipped the skirt of an expressionless doll, then headed to the bathroom mirror to straighten out my hair, when the doorbell rang.

It was Hitagi Senjogahara.

Not a second off our agreed-upon time. Did she wear a stopwatch for a wristwatch, or what? Either way, I stepped outside with a *see ya later*—

"Good morning, Koyomi," she waved at me from the other side of the gate, her hair in pigtails.

I nearly lost my balance.

To go into more detail before I regain my balance, Hitagi Senjogahara had on pigtails, a miniskirt, a smaller t-shirt that emphasized her figure ever so slightly, and a shawl draped over her.

She looked like a nymph who'd fallen from heaven.

Oh no. I froze, afraid this entire dimension had been twisted in some way again, but…

"Just trying to imitate Miss Hanekawa is only going to leave me depressed. I thought I'd go big and went for a makeover. What do you think? Am I on point?" she explained.

If I had to pick one or the other, she was off point. I couldn't figure out why her style was regressing the moment she graduated, but when I asked her, she replied:

"*Mature* isn't such a compliment now that I'm not a high school student anymore, so I thought I'd go for a youthful look."

It seemed Hitagi had her own thoughts about graduating from high school. What in the world was she thinking, though? Maybe it was a serious problem for a girl.

"Still, Hitagi. Isn't your skirt too short? Your legs are extra-long to begin with, so it's a pretty overboard look. You're going to make your boyfriend worry."

"Overboard? How rude. It's fine, it might look like a skirt, but these are actually shorts where the fabric around the outside is designed to look like a skirt. It's a marvelous garment that fulfills a lady's desire to wear a cute skirt without showing off her underwear."

"They make clothes like that?" The world was full of things I didn't know—I shouldn't have been satisfied simply wearing Ogi's skirt… "Is it like a running skirt? Anyway, this is a big makeover for you."

"Heh. Well, I wouldn't have minded showing off even more skin when I consider the peaks of excitement I'll be feeling when we find out you got into college."

"Doesn't that mean it'll be hell on earth if I got rejected?"

Anyway, warming up to each other from having this conversation right off the bat, we left—to visit none other than my first-choice school, which had already accepted Hitagi Senjogahara.

Actually, that description is the other way around. The college was Hitagi Senjogahara's first-choice school, and I'd done my best to get in so I could attend the same school as my girlfriend… But it's easy for the order of things to get flipped around, and if I found myself on the wrong side of the school's gates, I'd be the one turned inside out.

"So," Hitagi fished for info as we walked to the bus stop, "how did it go this time around? I'd be happy to hear all about it, if you want to tell me. I think you might feel better if you did."

"…I wouldn't say an envious position, but you've certainly settled into a delicious one."

In terms of resourcefulness, she was on a different level from the likes of Oikura. I wished I could be like Hitagi someday and just get to listen to stories of other people's adventures from a safe distance.

"Well, you know," she said. "If this were *Columbo*, my goal is to be the missus."

"That's as delicious as it gets." A hall-of-fame role as far as never being in danger—though even Mrs. Columbo was once targeted by a killer.

"In other words, I may have allowed Hachikuji to be this town's lord, but there's no way I'd let anyone else be your lady."

"I'm happy to hear that, but are you really telling me there was a time you were angling to become a god?"

No fact could raise more hairs.

In any case, I gave Hitagi an outline of the last couple of days—naturally, she'd experienced them as well, but when I'd surveyed Karen, Tsukihi, and Ononoki about the topic, their recollection of what had happened seemed vague.

Light had flooded the entire town, creating enough confusion to make you think you were in another world, and yet no one found it strange. They just went along with their lives, facing today as another day—looking to the future just a little bit more than yesterday.

I guess I shouldn't expect anything else from a logical world?

Consistency worked itself out when it came to this kind of thing, it seemed—maybe Ogi was right and it was all just an issue of mindset, but at the same time, I couldn't shake the feeling that it was all very slipshod.

This left me with some thoughts I hadn't sorted through as a first party in the matter, but Hitagi turned out to be right. I did feel a little better telling her about it all.

"You did a good job," she said with a smile, applauding after she'd finished hearing me out—well, she clapped twice above her head and a little to the left, so it seemed more like a flamenco move than applause.

Or maybe she'd summoned ninjas?

"That was quite the satisfying story. I would say its message comes off a little too strong, though. Were you too fired up over your first case since graduating high school?"

"There's no message. I'd be happy if it earned the label of a slapstick comedy now that it's over."

"You know, Koyomi, I actually kind of like the way you're so aggressive about toeing the line between cheating on me and not. Keep on keeping me on pins and needles, okay?"

"What kind of woman are you? Hearing you say that puts me on pins and needles, if anything. And that wasn't the point... Were you even listening?"

"Of course. I'd never fail to, Koyomi. You really have grown over the last year. You might require support, and from so many women too, but it's as if you solved everything on your own."

"On my own, no..."

I wasn't sure how to count Ogi. She was a partner, but she was me.

Either way, though, I had everyone to thank.

"Oh, you're always so modest. Look at how you've matured. Can I start calling you Daddy?"

"That's not even funny. Who matures that much in a couple of days?"

"You know how people wonder why mirrors reverse left and right, but not up and down?"

If we were talking about lines, she shifted lines of conversation as smoothly as ever. "Oh, yeah... That's like a trick question, right? Where if you put a mirror on the floor and stand on top of it, it does reverse up and down."

"Yes. In other words, up, down, left, and right are all about perspective—but aren't there facets of it that you're still missing? I doubt you've forgotten everything you learned about science already—so you know how when we see things through our eyes, the eyeball acts as a lens that reflects the image it receives from light on the retina, reversing it?"

"Oh, yeah..." That was something I learned in human anatomy class during elementary or middle school, not while studying for college entrance exams, but I did recall—that while mirrors were mirrors, there was also the question of the lens. "And?"

"Well, it was just such a mystery to me as a child. Why don't we see the world in reverse, even though it looks that way on the retina?"

"Oh, umm."

Umm, what was the answer to that?

I felt like I'd read about it in a trivia book, not any textbook... That because up and down are relative just like left and right, our brains adjust what we see even if it's upside down—or something?

"It's a matter of practice, in other words," Hitagi said. "Just like how you were so in love with the idea of being left-handed that you wore your watch on your right wrist and practiced writing with your left hand."

"You aren't going to let that one go, are you..."

Personally, I wished that my actions then belonged to the twenty percent—though I did continue to wear my watch on my right wrist.

It was a habit by now.

But she'd said practice, not habit.

"How did it all start in the first place?" she asked me. "It was a little abstract and hard to understand, but why did your mirror image stop in the mirror, again?"

"Like I said—it was regret that lingered there. A symbol of it all. Now that I've graduated, lost my title as student, and am trying to move on, it was the part of Koyomi Araragi that I'm trying to leave behind."

"…"

"In other words, those were the regrets I tried to put behind me yesterday, and leave there—but I missed it all so much that I ended up reaching out for them. The stuff about me rescuing the lost twenty percent was a consequence of that—nothing but a byproduct. All I tried to do when I saw myself in the mirror for the first time in so long was to remember something I was close to forgetting."

Everything else had only gotten wrapped up in it.

Entangled in an act I performed for my own sake.

Ogi was right, I needed to think about what I'd done.

I'd forced the entire town to partake in my own sentimentality, in my meddling with a mirrored world…

"True, but it must've been fun for everyone, no? It's not as if you put anyone's life in danger," Hitagi said offhandedly.

She hardly understood the gravity of it—that's an irresponsible spectator for you.

"People influence the world around them just by passing someone on the street. You shouldn't worry about it too much. I've caused a lot of folks trouble over the course of my life, but I believe they grew as people by overcoming those troubles."

"That's the most selfish excuse I've ever heard."

"Someday, they'll say they're the individuals they are now

thanks to the trouble I caused them."

"They wouldn't be complimenting you…"

"People are tougher than you'd expect. A world where every-thing is inside out—I have to admit, I'd be interested to know how I was in that world," Hitagi brought up a topic that interested me very much as well, to be honest.

"Hmm, well, I never got a chance to meet you. I think it's one of those things better left to the imagination."

"Why? You should've gone and met me. I appreciate your con-sideration, but I wish you'd be a little rougher with me. But maybe that's only the kind of thing a spoiled girl asks for. Still, what were they, anyway? These lingering regrets of yours, Koyomi—were you able to address them?"

"It was because I did, according to Ogi, that we managed to regain control. And that's why she could create the black mirror, or something. I actually don't know what they are myself."

"What? Really?"

"Yeah…but that's what makes it something I've forgotten and left behind. Of all my experiences in the virtual land of mirrors, I don't know which was my own regret—maybe there was more than one."

While they were the lingering regrets of all the girls—they were mine as well, according to Ogi. Their twenty percent, and my twenty percent too.

Feelings forgotten and left behind.

Maybe I wanted to apologize about the time I saw Karen in a skirt and laughed. Maybe Ononoki being a doll didn't allay my remorse for making her attack Tadatsuru Teori. I couldn't save Hachikuji and had her deified. I could never do anything about Kanbaru's left arm as a student. I couldn't come to Oikura's aid sooner. As far as Sengoku, that one goes without saying—and I continued to bind Shinobu to my shadow.

Year 1, Class 3—and so much more.

I had a mountain of regrets.

I couldn't claim that I'd graduated with a clear conscience—even if I did, I could never say for certain.

I merely remembered it and faced it.

That was probably enough.

I wouldn't be able to shoulder it all, nor could I carry it with me.

I wasn't Hanekawa or Oikura, but I still needed to pack as light as possible for my journey—I only had so much space in my suitcase.

Still, there was nothing wrong with thinking back on it every now and then, yes?

"Yes...you're right. I suppose your regrets linger because you leave them behind. Leaving little bits of your heart along the path, à la Hansel and Gretel, might be kind of convenient—for fondly looking back on it."

"I'm not sure that's how it works, but yeah, that'd be neat."

"If you don't know, though, that makes me wonder. Which of those regrets were yours? I feel like everyone's slightly skewed image of you might be a hint. The ideal Koyomi Araragi—and the mirrored Koyomi Araragi. I'm just being silly... I wouldn't keep wearing my hair in these childish pigtails if your regret was not getting to bathe with Kanbaru's mom, though."

"Don't worry, I'm pretty sure that wasn't it... Also, there's one thing I can say for certain."

Then—putting my arm around Hitagi's shoulder as she walked beside me, I tugged her close.

"I didn't have any regrets when it comes to you. Because we're always going to be together from now on."

"Let's wait until we see your exam results. We're going to be far apart if you don't get in."

Her words were more ruthless than realistic, but she didn't try to brush off my arm—a relief, given all the courage it took to put it there.

We'd managed to walk quite a distance while we chatted. One more pedestrian crossing and we'd be at our bus stop—not our final destination, of course, just a checkpoint. We needed to get on a train, keep on walking, climb some stairs, cross a pedestrian bridge, get on an elevator, get on an escalator, and walk some more.

"By the way," Hitagi said as we stood side by side at a red light. "Remember what we said about *sansukumi*, the original form of rock-paper-scissors—one of the reasons Hachikuji became a god? I heard that the slug in that game used to be a centipede."

"A centipede? Really?"

"Yes, I don't remember why, but what started out as a game of frog, snake, and centipede turned into frog-snake-slug over the years... I guess if you think of which one a snake would hate more, the hundred-legged centipede makes more sense."

Hm, no legs at all versus a hundred. That did make sense.

"Of course, I'd flinch if I saw any of them. Frog, snake, slug, or centipede."

"Seriously? My impression was that you didn't mind that sort of thing."

"I'm a girl, okay," teased Hitagi, grabbing both of her pigtails and flapping them around.

What? So cute...

Speaking of flinching, though. And centipedes.

"It only happens every once in a while," I said, "but I've always had this problem. Waiting for a pedestrian light to change, I suddenly can't figure out which foot I should start with when it turns green. Do I take the first step with my right foot, or with my left? I should probably just make a rule about it, like some kind of superstition."

Thinking leads to hesitation.

Yes, you could call it overthinking and yell at me to hurry up and take that step, but if it were that easy, it wouldn't be a problem in the first place. No conceptual leaps come from overthinking things, I've been told time and again, but it's not as if humans can stop thinking.

My mind might know that I need to move forward, but my legs just won't.

Like my body is flinching.

As if my feet are choking—I sit there, unable to take a single step, like the centipede who forgets how to walk.

Even if I know it's nothing major that could define my fate, it leaves me not knowing which way to go.

My body, rather than my thoughts, gets left behind.

"That's your problem?" asked Hitagi, guffawing. She never used to laugh with such hearty cheer—but she was a lively young woman now. "If you don't know which foot to start with, you just have to do this."

She made sure the light had turned green. Checking both ways to make sure it was safe—she crouched.

Hitagi Senjogahara lowered her center of gravity, and then…

"Hup!"

Jumped forward with both legs.

Teal, don't mink.

With my arm still wrapped around the former track runner's shoulder, her resilient legs pulled me along. I rushed to trail after her, not wanting to be left behind, moving forward—leaping towards the light, with an extra twenty percent.

Ending the tale that continued for so long.

Recalling my remembrances, leaving behind what lingered.

The margins open for notes, a note in the air.

We flew to our next tale.

Afterword

Taking my life until now and thinking about the proportion of *things I've done* and *things I haven't done*, the latter is overwhelmingly larger, which makes total sense, because when you're *doing something*, you're ultimately *not doing everything else.* Furthermore, *working at something* means *slacking off on everything else.* When I read about great historical figures, the absurd amount of effort geniuses spend for their goals often leaves me speechless, but on second thought, weren't they neglecting quite a large portion of the rest of their lives? Could it be that we can't do everything in the end, that we always have to give up on something? Choosing one form of happiness means sacrificing other forms—and the antonym of fortune is not misfortune, but other fortunes? Not infrequently, when you think "I did it!" you've lost much of whatever else is important to you, and as you keep on doing that, things proceed to a point where there's no turning back, or something like that. Still, it's unrealistic to do just a little bit of lots of things, or at least it wouldn't be very fruitful. Of course, they also say that mastery in one thing leads to all things, and what you learn by plumbing the depths of one field can in fact apply to others, so doing something is certainly better than doing nothing at all. But in that case, since the difference between *doing* and *being able to* is quite salient, it'd be pretty rough if *what you did* equaled *what you couldn't.* Just accumulating more regret and remorse the more you do something is depressing, but I also feel that thinking "if only I'd done it *so*" actually leads to more than you'd expect.

And so, here's a bonus installment of the *MONOGATARI* series. One last stubborn book. The actual final volume was the one before this, *End Tale Part 03*, so I wanted to go back to the roots of what it means to read a novel, which is to say I aimed for a book that you can read or just as well not. In that spirit, it's filled to the brim with unignorable contradictions. A worldview that doesn't require thinking about how to pay off foreshadowing is nice in its own way. It'd be a problem if I always did that, though. Anyway, this has been *End Tale (Cont.)*, "Final Chapter: Koyomi Reverse," or not knowing when to quit. Oh, speaking of which, it's a little late, but I changed the subtitle from "Koyomi Book" because that obviously deserved to be a *Calendar Tale* subtitle instead.

We see a happy Miss Sodachi Oikura on the cover here. So cute! I was asking for a lot when I pushed for the choice, but VOFAN did an incredible job. Thank you. I'd also like to give my deepest thanks to all of you who've read all of the installments of the *MONOGATARI* series. Even this one, which you could just as well not—I couldn't be happier.

Great work, everyone!

NISIOISIN

NISIOISIN

Art by
Kinako

The Dark St★r that Shines for You Alone

1 Pretty Boy Detective Club

JOIN THE CLUB

Ten years ago, Mayumi Dojima saw a star...and she's been searching for it ever since. The mysterious organization that solves (and causes?) all the problems at Yubiwa Academy—the *Pretty Boy Detective Club* is on the case! Five beautiful youths, each more eccentric than the last, united only by their devotion to the aesthetics of mystery-solving. Together they find much, much more than they bargained for.

AVAILABLE NOW!

OWARIMONOGATARI

END TALE

PART 01

NISIOISIN

VERTICAL.

OWARIMONOGATARI
End Tale
Part 01

NISIOISIN

Art by VOFAN

Translated by Ko Ransom

VERTICAL.

CHAPTER ONE OGI FORMULA

CHAPTER TWO SODACHI RIDDLE

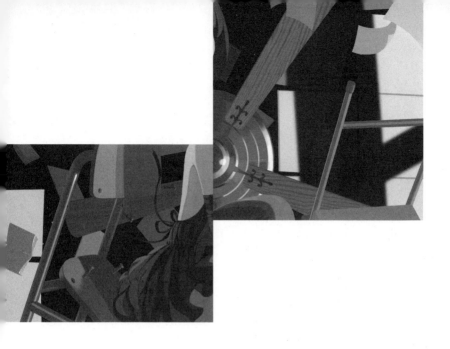

CHAPTER THREE   SODACHI LOST

OWARIMONOGATARI, PART 01

© 2013 NISIOISIN
All rights reserved.

First published in Japan in 2013 by
Kodansha Ltd., Tokyo.
Publication rights for this English edition
arranged through Kodansha Ltd., Tokyo.

Published by Vertical, an imprint of
Kodansha USA Publishing, LLC, 2019

ISBN 978-1-947194-90-8

Manufactured in the United States
of America

First Edition

Second Printing

Kodansha USA Publishing, LLC
451 Park Avenue South
7th Floor
New York, NY 10016

www.readvertical.com

CHAPTER ONE
OGI FORMULA

$$f(x) = \lim_{\to 0} \frac{f(x+\Delta)}{\Delta x}$$

$$\frac{\sqrt{\sum_{i=1}^{n}(x_i - \bar{x})^2}}{n-1} \quad S_\Delta = \sqrt{P(p-a}$$

$$\sum_{i=1}^{n} x_i \qquad \mu = \frac{\sum_{i=1}^{N} x_i}{N}$$

$$\frac{1}{n} \qquad \frac{1}{n^2} =$$

$$\left(\frac{1}{\sqrt{2}} + \frac{1}{2^2} + \frac{1}{2}\right)$$

$$x H(-x^2)$$

$$\gamma = \lim_{n\to\infty}\left(1 + \frac{1}{2} + \frac{1}{3} + \frac{1}{4}\right)$$

$$e^x = \sum_{n=0}^{\infty} \frac{x^n}{n!} = \lim_{n\to}$$

$$P^p > \sum_{j=0,\, j\neq p}^{n} A_p$$

$$p = 2\vartheta \qquad e^{i\varphi} = c$$

$$f'(x) = \lim_{x\to 0} \frac{f(x+\Delta x)}{\Delta x}$$

001

Ogi Oshino is Ogi Oshino. That is the entirety of what can be said as far as that transfer student is concerned. Once you state her name, there's nothing left to say on the subject. You could of course make the point that everyone is someone and absolutely no one else—ultimately, that is all that should be said about any person. Tsubasa Hanekawa is Tsubasa Hanekawa, and Hitagi Senjogahara is Hitagi Senjogahara—yes, just as Koyomi Araragi is Koyomi Araragi. But even then, Ogi Oshino was just so Ogi Oshino. She was so singularly Ogi Oshino that she was nothing else. Ogi Oshino is Ogi Oshino in the same way you don't like things you don't like, how no means no. Any further discussion would be fruitless, utterly so. In the sense that she's so firmly defined, so wholly decided and determined, so completely unshakable, she is extremely mathematical—yes, second only to how much she is Ogi Oshino.

Speaking of math, are you familiar with what they call the most beautiful formula in the history of mathematics? Wait, don't even answer that, you'll recall it once you hear it. If you ask me, forget math, I want to say it's the most beautiful formula in human history: $e^{i\pi} + 1 = 0$. Also known as Euler's Formula. It uses e, the base of the natural logarithm, π, the ratio of a circle's circumference to its diameter, i, the unit imaginary number, then 1 and 0 all in the same graceful formula, as if it had come together by such designed necessity that if there is a God, it'd be the most convincing evidence for His existence.

What's interesting—rather, what's beautiful is how this formula had to exist. There's your answer if you ever get asked that on a test. In other words, Euler's Formula is not a product of human expression but of human excavation. Even if mankind had never existed in this world, even if there wasn't a single brain to think about the base of the natural logarithm, the ratio of a circle's circumference to its diameter, imaginary numbers, 1, or 0, the base of the natural logarithm raised to the power of the ratio of a circle's circumference to its diameter multiplied by the unit imaginary number added to one *would have still been* 0.

It's beautiful—but when you think about it in that way, it's also scary.

It seems that in society these days, what we call the world is a vague and hazy thing mutable and subject to being turned on its head with the greatest of ease, yesterday's common sense becoming today's senselessness, the rules in the morning breaking the rules at night, not one value set in stone, all of us aimless and adrift, which is why the future as a blank slate is the only thing that can give us hope—or so it seems, but really, isn't the future, which is to say the unknown, already determined, and we just don't know? Instead of it being the unknown, maybe we're just uninformed?

If someone who doesn't know the ratio of a circle's circumference to its diameter calculated it, the result would be pi. The theory of relativity was always there, even if Einstein never used the full powers of his brilliance. You don't have to know who Beethoven is in order to produce the sounds of *Symphony No. 5*, you just have to play the notes from its score—what, you wouldn't be as moved? In that case, just play it *the same way as the version that does move you*. As hard as it is to believe, likewise you don't have to be the genius among geniuses Vincent van Gogh to come up with *Sunflowers*, even the rankest of novices could, simply by using the same strokes, pressure, and materials in the same environment from the same perspective to paint the same flowers. Let monkeys bash typewriters for long enough and they'll eventually produce Shakespeare, right?

Answers don't change—laws don't change.

When people feel that something has "changed" or "become new," it's nothing more than a cute little illusion arising from *the fact that a different, pre-existing program has been executed.*

In that sense, there's nothing in the world or its future that even resembles a "playful ambiguity" or "vague margin." What exists are only hard laws that state, "Do X and Y will happen." Just as how you don't like things you don't like, how no means no—not only is what's set in stone set in stone, there is no room there to impose your will, no opening for your heart. Therefore, all expression is only excavation, all that's devised is only discovered. No, even these discoveries may only be rediscoveries—even the impossible task that continues to torment me as I desperately seek its solution might have a ready-made model answer, all of my trial and error nothing more than a detour on the way to arriving at it—from the perspective of someone in the know.

Someone in the know.

A monster, perhaps.

Still, Ogi Oshino, that transfer student, might offer some frank advice regarding even the beauty of Euler's Formula.

Something like this.

"Yes, it's beautiful—so beautiful and gorgeous that I could faint. The most beautiful part of all is the way the answer is zero. That said, I feel like there isn't really any reason to calculate all that out if the answer is just going to be zero."

Upon hearing this, I would think: Ogi Oshino is Ogi Oshino, and that's all there is to say about it. Everything is zero before her, and no matter how unlike herself she may act, that act becomes so much like her—and so this is a tale about math.

Let's do some studying.

I know some of you might put your guard up when you hear the word *math*, so we could break that down and say this is a story about arithmetic—or to be even more straightforward, a story about numbers. After all, this is a story whose solution is decided by the larger number— which is to say, it's a story about majority rule.

Majority rule.

The one way to turn even something wrong into the truth.

A building-block system that seeks collusion, not happiness.

Our inequality formula, for formulating iniquity.

You could say it's the one true human invention—as well as the ugliest formula in human history.

002

If any of you've experienced being locked in an enigmatic classroom alone with an underclassman you're meeting for the first time and an hour has already passed, I would've loved to ask you for advice—of course, my phone seemed to be out of service, and the room appeared to block any wi-fi signal as well. Even seeking outside advice appeared to be beyond me.

"No good, Araragi-senpai—" she said.

Ogi trotted over to me with tiny steps as I frantically used the full strength of my hands and feet to try and open the classroom's front door.

"Oh, um, I don't mean that you're no good. I tried a lot of different things, but neither large window nor high window budged an inch, is what I'm trying to say."

"...How'd I ever misinterpret it as 'no-good Araragi-senpai' in this situation?"

What kind of an aside was that?

"No good, either," I said, slightly upset.

"No good, huh? That's what I thought."

"You're doing it on purpose, aren't you? Trying to make *me* sound no good."

Oh, not even a smidge—Ogi denied with the smile of someone playing dumb. Then again, despite her full, bright smile, she didn't seem to

13

me like someone who liked jokes too much. I decided to believe her for the time being.

From the moment we learned that we were apparently locked in there, Ogi and I had divided up the labor and attempted every escape method possible—me trying the regular entrances and exits, which is to say the doors at the front and back, while she investigated the windows.

"It isn't like they're locked… It's like they've been fixed in place with glue or something," I gave my thoughts on the matter, stretching my numbed arms around and around, after close to an hour in combat with the doors. As a senior, it was a little embarrassing to have spent a full hour to come to an "or something" conclusion, but facts were facts.

Meanwhile, Ogi—a Naoetsu High novice, a freshman and transfer student—shared her own better-informed findings with a soft smile.

"Right, as stated above, the windows are not budging one inch. Regarding any locks, the crescent ones installed on the windows are mobile. You can engage and disengage them freely—they can even be locked once engaged. The all-important window frame is immobile, though. When the crescent locks are engaged, of course, but also when they aren't—as if they've been fixed in place with glue 'or something,' as you put it."

"…"

By imitating my childish expression at the end, was she deferring to me, as her senior, or trying to insult me? Debatable.

"Every window, without exception?"

"Yes. Of course I gave each one a try. I'd never use a sample survey to cut corners—the large windows, the high windows, the hallway windows, the gym-side windows."

They don't move, she reported.

"The gym-side windows…" I muttered, turning to look in *that direction.* To be honest, it wasn't the fact we were locked in, but that side, *that direction,* that was the real problem.

True, there was nothing visibly off about it—there was no world of demons on the other side of the window, no pack of dinosaurs or sea of flames. All I saw was a plain gym—Naoetsu High's regular old gym. The basketball team that Kanbaru retired from was probably busy at work inside—well, I couldn't hear any sounds coming from it, but maybe any external noise had been shut out from the classroom?

The ban on entering and exiting was comprehensive if it included sound, but even that didn't seem to be a problem—*not compared to what I saw on the other side of the window.* No, like I said, the gym was just a plain gym.

Nothing unusual about the sight—except, *we shouldn't have been able to see the gym given the angle of the school building we were in.*

"Normally, we should be seeing the school field from here."

Yes, this building that Ogi and I had walked to stood parallel to the athletic field—we should've been able to espy the baseball team or the track team from where we were, not the indoor basketball team.

"..."

I felt like sticking my body out of the window, turning my head to look about, and getting a better understanding of what I was seeing outside, but even that was out of the question since the windows didn't so much as open. All I could do was get an unnatural, uncanny feeling from our regular old gym.

Or maybe I was confused? Could I have come to a building facing the gym by accident, instead of the building facing the athletic grounds? No, I'd never make such an awful mistake, not when I was trying to show off to an underclassman I was meeting for the first time.

To begin with, the *way* we could see the gym from the window was unnatural. We were supposed to be on the third floor. Unless we were on the fifth floor, or at least the fourth, the roof shouldn't have been visible—if I'd brought us to the wrong building, though, it was certainly possible we were on the wrong floor...

But even if seeing something that shouldn't have been there was due to some mishap, it didn't change the fact that Ogi and I were currently shut in a room.

Still, apart from sticking my body out of a window, was there no way of figuring out what floor we were on? Just as I was spinning my wheels—

"Then maybe it's about time," Ogi said.

"About time? For what?"

"To take to—more extreme measures. I mean, both you and I are going to starve if we don't do something. We'll starve and wither and die."

"Yeah, I guess…"

Starving to death sounded a bit exaggerated at this point in time, but it was an inevitability if we continued to be stuck there. I mean, I felt confident that I could endure a little hunger, but the same couldn't be said about Ogi, who was still in the middle of her growth spurt.

"But more extreme measures?"

When I turned to ask her what she meant, I saw there was no reason to—it was clear as day. Ogi was holding up, with both arms, one of the many desks that lined the classroom. As if it was cleaning time and they needed to be moved, so that the floor could be wiped down—but she wanted to do the complete opposite, to make a mess.

"One, two…"

On her own count, Ogi tossed the desk at the window. Not the hallway window, but the gym-side one (which should have been facing the athletic grounds). *The hallway window was too dangerous, in case someone was walking on the other side,* she told me later, but I don't see much of a difference in risk between that and hurling it out of the building. In fact, the added potential energy (whether we were on the third floor or the fifth) could make both the broken glass and the flying desk that much more dangerous—but such fears turned out to be groundless.

The desk that Ogi threw at the window, which is to say at the glass, oh-so-naturally bounced off it like a Super Ball off a hard wall, expelling the contents—textbooks, notebooks, pencil case—onto the classroom floor. It seemed the owner wasn't much for taking homework home, and the jumble could only be described as a pitiful sight. As for the desk, it came to a rest upside down, but not before a number of bounces.

There wasn't a single scratch on the glass.

On that same note, the desk that came bouncing back, as well as its scattered contents, wasn't destroyed or cracked. The "extreme measure" Ogi had taken—resulted in no results whatsoever.

"Maybe you could've thrown a desk that didn't have anything in it? Considering the aftermath," I nitpicked—but really, if we were going to go there, did she have to force herself to toss a desk? Wasn't, uh, a chair easier to hold? This was glass she was trying to break, so even if using her bare hands was out of the question, why would a slender-armed girl like her, by no means well-built, choose a desk—but my doubts were soon addressed.

Which is to say, Ogi picked up a ballpoint pen (which was once inside a pencil case) from among the stuff scattered on the floor. With it in hand, she walked toward the blackboard. As if tossing not a chair but a packed desk at the window had killed two birds with one stone, and she'd saved herself the trouble of extracting the pen. Call it rational, or lazy—but as my doubt was addressed, a new one popped up. What exactly was she going to do with the pen? A click drew my attention, and it seemed she'd extended its tip, but you wrote on blackboards with chalk, not with—

"!"

I didn't even have time to stop her. She scraped the blackboard with the ballpoint pen. Across the classroom, more sealed than usual, that awful screeching noise that torments the nerves worse than any other—didn't spread.

There was no sound.

It didn't seem like she'd held back, she'd slashed as if she were wielding a katana, yet no marks were left behind on the blackboard, not even the pen's ink. I almost began to think that my eyes had been tricked into thinking she'd scratched it while she'd whiffed somehow.

"...No good. Hmm."

"Wh-What were you trying to do there, Ogi?"

"Well, since I couldn't destroy the window with a strike, I thought I'd try to shatter it using acoustic resonance," she casually informed me. So this girl nonchalantly attempted something as advanced as destroy a window through sonic force—but she'd failed. And as if she'd accounted for this from the start, her expression stayed nonchalant as she tossed the pen to the floor.

Throwing a desk to try to break a window and to procure a ballpoint pen at the same time might be rational, but leaving such a mess in the process is surely irrational, I thought, tidying up the area to return the classroom to its original state. Ah, but then, wasn't it rational in its own way to make such a big mess that I'd want to clean up, just as I was doing?

"Hm?"

As I gathered the textbooks and placed them inside the desk that I'd flipped back up, I caught a glimpse of the name written on them in sharpie: *Fukado, Class 1-3*.

So this was a first-year classroom? It had to be since that's what it said… I hadn't looked closely at the sign upon entering; in fact, I didn't even recall if there was a sign to begin with. But wait—Fukado? Fukado… Well, I guess it was a common enough name?

"I'm sorry to interrupt you when you're busy at work, but could you please come over this way?"

Ogi's voice derailed my train of thought. I wanted to tell her I was busy tidying up the mess she'd made, but I stopped picking up for a moment anyway and began walking toward the front door—which I'd been battling until moments earlier, and where Ogi had moved without me noticing.

"Oh, no, no—back up a step, please. A little to the right, no, too much, to the left. Hmm, back half a step. Okay, now puff out your chest a little."

…Her instructions were so detailed. I didn't have a clue as to what she was trying to do, or why she was trying to do it—because I was assuming she'd decided to give her violent approaches toward the classroom a rest after throwing a desk at a window and scraping the blackboard. But no, she had another trick to try. And it was one hell of a violent one.

Just as I thought she was bending her knees low, Ogi unleashed a powerful elbow thrust into my solar plexus—ripping straight through me before my reflexes could spring into action.

"Ghaak!"

With my chest puffed out just as instructed, my body acted like a spring, bending at a right angle before falling head over heels and collapsing on the spot. My head nearly hit the door, thanks to the sheer force—but only grazed it, and I lay cowering on the floor.

18

"Kha…k. Wh-What… Ogi, you…"

"Hm. No good after all," she deadpanned, looking at me with scorn as I struggled to so much as breathe. She showed zero signs of guilt. "Well, I just thought I might be able to erode the door with stomach acid. You know, even if strikes and resonance don't work, we might still be able to melt it away. Looks like that approach doesn't get it done either, though. All we did was make the door filthy. Not that a couple of drops of your stomach acid would dissolve the entire thing, anyway—wipe it down for me later, okay?"

"…"

She'd aimed not for my solar plexus but my stomach—her goal had been to make me spew bile. The girl did some crazy things with that gentle expression of hers. Why did I have to get sucker-punched by a girl I was meeting for the first time? What had I done to deserve this?

"Oh, sorry. Did that hurt?" she asked so shamelessly that I couldn't even be mad. In fact, it was almost refreshing—and to tell the truth, I was fortunate enough to be used to this level of violence, given my home environment.

What kind of domestic abusers did I live with to be used to getting punched in the stomach?

Forget this life, I must be dealing with karma from a previous one.

"Not really. It's no big deal," I tried to keep up appearances as I got up. Then again, while acting calm was one thing, if this was what I got for trying to impress an underclassman, it was probably about time I reconsidered my stance.

"Ah, I knew I could count on you. I wouldn't have minded spewing my own stomach acid, but I thought it might be a little too extreme of a visual. You're the type who'd rather hock up his own digestive juices than make a girl puke hers, so I saw fit to defer to you."

"How very considerate… And yes, I'm the type who'd rather spit up his own stomach acid than cause a girl to do the same."

This was far too specific as far as personality traits go, not to mention the bizarre underlying assumption that someone had to vomit, but I went along with Ogi's conversation as she stood there, smiling. Whether it was the smile of someone relying on an upperclassman's kindness, or of

19

someone making a total fool of him, was once again hard to tell.

So unfathomable.

It really did make sense that she was *his* niece—despite looking nothing at all like him.

"In any case," I said, "this means the windows and the doors can't be destroyed. We of course don't have any professional tools at our disposal, so I doubt we'd be able to plow through a wall, either."

"If only we had some plastic explosives," Ogi remarked—troublingly, since I could see her using a bomb without a second thought if she had access to one, considering how quick she'd been to elbow me. Of course, whether or not that would work was a different question—we might not come out of it unscathed, for one thing.

"Yikes. Looks like we're in this for the long haul. The real threat here is driving ourselves crazy by struggling and failing to get out. Let's just wait for someone on the outside to help us, Ogi—luckily, Kanbaru knows we're here," I said magisterially, in as bright and cheerful of a tone as I could manage.

I wasn't as relaxed as that, to be honest, but I wanted to make this junior of mine feel safe and show her just how mature I was. From her perspective, just being locked in the same space as a boy she was meeting for the first time must have been worrying enough... In that light, her earlier elbow strike could be interpreted as a kind of threat, an expression of her apprehension.

Whatever the case, it felt like I was being tested as a man through my actions. Or that the wrong choice could lead to my downfall.

"I wonder." Ogi sounded calm, not concerned at all—but might have been putting on a brave face just like me. "As a big fan of hers, I'd love it too if Kanbaru-senpai saved us—but I'm afraid our chances of anyone on the outside rescuing us are slim."

"Hm? Why's that? Two students suddenly disappearing after school—someone would have to notice that, even if it wasn't Kanbaru. There'd be an uproar, among your classmates, and mine."

Uproar might have been an exaggeration—my own classmates, at least, would treat my disappearance as nothing out of the ordinary. Including Senjogahara and Hanekawa. But in Ogi's case, a fresh transfer going missing would get people talking.

"Plus," I went on, "they'd know we never left school since we didn't take our bags. Soon enough, someone would find us here—"

"You really do like depending on other people, don't you? Even though—people just go and get saved on their own."

"!?"

"I'm sorry. That's *my uncle's creed*—not anything to do with you or me. That said, while counting on others isn't such a bad thing, we mustn't give up on trying to escape on our own just yet. I say that because..."

Ogi pointed—at the clock hanging above the blackboard. And I froze the moment I saw it.

The clock's hands.

From the moment we'd entered the classroom—the hands of the clock hadn't budged *a single second or minute*. We should have been locked in for over an hour by now—but not a second had passed inside the classroom.

"Do you think it's out of batteries? Because I certainly don't," Ogi said, smirking.

003

It all started on a late October day, exactly half a year after I was attacked by a golden-haired, golden-eyed vampire during spring break. Just as I was about to have lunch at my homeroom desk, my lovable junior Suruga Kanbaru came to visit.

"Hey there, Araragi-senpai! It's me, Suruga Kanbaru!"

She was as energetic as ever.

"So you're alone! All alone, huh?!"

She was also as rude as ever.

"I don't know if I'd say alone," I struggled to come up with an excuse. Well, part of me was simply overwhelmed and shrank in the face of all her positive energy. "Senjogahara and Hanekawa have gotten really chummy ever since second term started... Now they won't eat with me."

They were on a lunch date, no doubt. It was a rare case of female friendship overcoming romance.

"Huh. Then why not eat with some of your other friends? There's nothing sadder than lunching alone," pressed Kanbaru, with no consideration whatsoever. I didn't dispute her point, but it's also true that humans need to eat to survive—even if they don't have any friends. Sadness, desolation, they're a part of life, aren't they?

Still, I couldn't believe her. She'd walked into a third-year classroom undaunted—as if she might even grab an open seat without asking.

Retired or not, it was indeed the kind of move you'd expect from a former star the entire school over.

"But I'm here with some good news for my sad little senior."

"Good news? Interesting, tell me more. I love good news."

I wasn't that interested, but any topic was preferable to how sad I was eating lunch on my own—whether it was international relations, talk about the IT industry, good news, or bad news.

"Okay. There's actually a girl I want to introduce you to," Kanbaru said, pointing her left hand, wrapped again and again in a bandage, toward the entrance—where a petite girl stood in the hallway, half her body peeking inside.

"…"

Kanbaru wanted to introduce me to…that girl? Who could it be, I'd never seen her before—no, of course I hadn't if she wanted to introduce us. A junior from her time on the basketball team? But why would Kanbaru want to introduce me to the girl, a stranger? Looking at her, I got the feeling she was a first-year… She was too far for me to see her class pin, though.

"Cute, right?" Kanbaru said, as if that dispelled any and all doubts—but sure, that's actually kind of how the world works.

"I know it's pretty risky to introduce you to a cute girl, but what was I supposed to do? She asked me to introduce you herself. It was a bitter decision! Phew, good thing Senjogahara-senpai and Hanekawa-senpai happen to be out."

"How exactly do you see me?"

"As being closer to human than beast."

"Correct, but…"

It almost seemed like she'd timed her visit. Senjogahara and Hanekawa weren't around, just so happening to be somewhere else today, but they had lunch in our classroom more often than not (in which case I was still excluded). Kanbaru couldn't have been waiting for this moment, though—could she?

In any case, introduce me to a girl?

As you know, I don't have the most social of personalities and am not a big fan of meeting new people, whatever their age or gender, but I didn't expect the hyper-social Kanbaru, who loved meeting people she didn't know, to understand the subtleties at play here.

If I told her, *Sorry, I'm not great at meeting people for the first time,* I'd simply be met with, *Ah! Then let's work on getting better at it!*

Of course, I had "introduced" Kanbaru to someone two months earlier. I was more of an intermediary than an introducer, but I still felt guilty about bringing a rather dangerous individual into her life, even if I'd had no choice. And in fact, I'd also introduced her to my violent little sister Karen before that. So if Kanbaru wanted to introduce me to someone, I had to oblige her, whoever it might be. Seriously, her network of friends was so vast that it could be anyone.

Not that the girl waiting for Kanbaru's cue outside the classroom looked shady, but there was something…indescribable about her.

"Don't worry, my senior. Everything is going to be okay." Kanbaru grinned as if she'd detected my unease. "I made sure she took off her underwear."

"Go back to wherever it is you came from, and stay there!"

"Please, relax. I know I said I made her take off her underwear, but I'm just talking about her panties. She still has her bra on. You're the type who likes to take a girl's bra off himself, yes?"

"You come into our third-year classroom to say this?! I don't belong to any type or team!"

Given Kanbaru's fame at our school, the other students were already paying attention to our conversation—finding it odd that we were having one. Fortunately, no one around us seemed to have heard any of her perverted words—only my verbal abuse aimed at her. All I had to suffer through were the pointed looks of criticism for daring to act like her senior. In other words, it wasn't at all fortunate for me, but it was at least more fortunate than the world discovering how much of a freak Kanbaru is.

"Huh? So you even want to take her panties off yourself? What a man. When it comes to girls, you really want to take the situation by the collar. Oh, but I don't mean that in a BDSM way."

"Yeah, I wish I could put a collar on you, and I don't mean that in a BDSM way either."

What I really wanted to put on her was a bell. But this was just Kanbaru's idea of a joke, her way of saying hello. I'd gotten used to it by now.

"And, what's with the girl? What's her true identity? You want to introduce her to me? I'm not someone worth being introduced to. Do you know what Koyomi Araragi's catchphrase is? The man who always has to introduce himself."

"What a sad catchphrase. It's not even catchy. Listen, she says she wants advice—from you. That's why I want you to meet her."

"Advice, from me? Hold on, now it's really getting ridiculous. Do you know how often people give the advice, 'No matter who you ask for advice, just don't ask Araragi'?"

"Really? People around here are giving that kind of advice? I'll beat them up if they are."

"Stop, stop, stop! I'm kidding, I'm kidding!" I found myself having to talk down Kanbaru, who was glaring at my classmates with an un-civil air about her. From their perspective, it must have looked like I was refusing to let the star athlete cut our conversation short and leave (further plummeting my favorability rating), but listen—I saved all of you. It was all the more urgent since she'd proved a couple of months ago that her left hand still had the power to beat anyone up.

"So, u-um, what's this about advice? I-I mean, I'm the Fire Sisters' big brother after all, I've been known to give advice. I don't mind one bit, she does have an introduction from you."

"I haven't heard the details myself, but it seems like it has something to do with aberrations."

"Wha…"

With aberrations?

Kanbaru saw my uneasy expression and said, "Yeah, it seems like she knows about them. She knew about my left hand, too, and about your blood. She said—her uncle told her."

"Her uncle…"

"She's a first-year who just transferred into this school. I was shocked to hear it, but apparently she's Mister Oshino's niece. Her name's Ogi Oshino."

I turned my still-uneasy face to her for another look—to look at half of Ogi Oshino. That's when our eyes met for the first time.

Her eyes were black—like they could suck you in.

004

"It's funny, you see."

"Funny."

"It's strange."

"Strange."

"In other words—it's abnormal."

"Abnormal. And—"

Errant.

Ogi Oshino pointed to a sketch in the notebook sitting open on top of my desk—and spoke in an unconcerned tone. I recalled facing Miss Gaen and doing something similar in August, but we used a tablet in that meeting, not a notebook. It's not unusual for high schoolers to be using tablets these days, but maybe analog technology suited her better, as you might expect from Oshino's niece.

There in the notebook was a structural layout of Naoetsu High. I could see why she'd show it to someone she'd only met for the first time; it was impressive, so good it made me wonder if she'd used professional tools to draw it. You could take it and post it by the entrance of the building if you wanted.

"It's funny, you see," Ogi repeated, still pointing to a specific part of the layout.

"…"

As we spoke, I split my time about evenly between looking at the diagram and at her—at her eyes. Those eyes that seemed like they could suck me in.

It reminded me of how Miss Gaen once called herself "Mèmè Oshino's little sister." While at the time I wondered why it was little and not big sister—and thought that she said the most arbitrary things—I suppose there was at least someone real she was hinting at with that title. Come to think of it, of course Miss Gaen wouldn't say anything arbitrary.

Still, why was that expert's niece transferring into my school after he left our town in June? Kanbaru probably dismissed it with nothing more than a *fate brings people together in the strangest ways*, but as someone who'd experienced what happened with Hachikuji…

"Uh, are you listening to me?"

"Er, um…" I quickly gathered myself when she noticed how distracted I was. "Wh-Why don't you sit down, Ogi-chan? I was just thinking it must be hard for you to explain all this when you're standing. The chairs around there belong to kids who're on the athletic grounds, and they probably won't be coming back until the bell."

I tried this excuse because I did feel guilty about sitting there and forcing an underclassman I was meeting for the first time to stand, but Ogi declined. Kanbaru never ended up sitting either, but the way Ogi declined was what amazed me.

"Sorry, but I'm afraid I'm a germophobe. I don't want to sit in a chair when I don't know who's been using it."

"…Is that so."

A germophobe. Well, I thought, guess she'd never be able to live in that abandoned, no longer existent cram school the way her uncle had.

"I wouldn't mind sitting on your lap, though."

"Stop it."

"Ooh, I bet you were thinking something naughty just now!"

Ogi clapped with glee. She was just goofing off like any high school freshman, but that wasn't enough to do away with the unfathomable impression she gave off.

"You're the one who said something naughty. You can stand there as punishment."

"Man, you're so strict."

"And, what were we talking about? What's funny again?"

"The bone on your arm that makes it numb if you hit it—nah, I don't mean funny in a humerus way... Well, okay, I'm a transfer student, right? I've had to transfer schools a lot thanks to what you'd call family issues, or maybe personal issues. So often that I don't even remember how many schools I've transferred into."

"Huh... That must be tough. Now that I think about it, I guess Kanbaru transferred schools when she was in elementary, too..."

Kanbaru was now gone, by the way. She'd run off somewhere just as soon as she'd introduced me to Ogi. A busy young lady—or maybe she didn't think she should listen to the details of this conversation?

"Yeah, transferring really must be tough. The entire environment around you changes."

"True. But I've grown used to it. Anyway, every time I transfer into a new school, there's something I do right away. What do you think that is?"

"What do I think... Say hello to the teachers?"

"I don't always."

"Wait, you don't?"

"Well—I make diagrams like these."

Ogi flipped through the pages of the notebook. I could tell it was new, but a lot of its pages had been filled with diagrams of the school's buildings. She'd depicted Naoetsu High in a fairly detailed way. There weren't just flat layouts, but three-dimensional ones, too—how had she drawn a bird's-eye view of the whole school? It almost looked like aerial photography.

"You could call it a habit of mine. I want to get a grasp on the school that's going to host me—do you think that's strange?"

"No, not really..."

To be honest, I did think it was pretty eccentric, but I actually knew two or so people who'd done something similar when they were starting at Naoetsu. I couldn't call it outright strange. What shocked me more was that those two or so people weren't the only ones.

31

I was just meeting Ogi for the first time, and she was the niece of that tricky dude Oshino. I'd been cautious, approaching her from a distance, so to speak, but I found this bit of odd behavior endearing.

"I like mysteries that take place in mansions," she said. "Just seeing a blueprint at the beginning of a book gets me interested. That's why every time I start life at a new school, I draw layouts like these—not that I'm expecting anyone to get murdered." She laughed, but it was hard to take it entirely as a quip because she somehow seemed so mysterious. If she'd told me that she was drawing a map for when a case did occur, I might have believed her.

"Huh... Let me take a look."

"Hm? At my panties?"

"No, at your notebook..."

It was just the kind of thing that Kanbaru's protégée would say. The former star's perverted ways were a bit of a secret thanks to the efforts of those who knew her best, so her influence on Ogi made me think that the two must be close (though given what she just said, Kanbaru instructing her to take off her underwear was just talk). But then, how had Ogi gotten close to Kanbaru in the short time since she'd transferred to our school? Kanbaru did have a habit of making friends with everyone, though—and so I flipped through the notebook from cover to cover. Looking at the school that way, I realized how many of its facilities I knew nothing about despite being a student here for nearly three years. It was like I'd been shown just how halfhearted my time at Naoetsu High had been.

"...By the way, you're really good at drawing, Ogi. I'm not that good at reading maps, so I'm normally confused by this kind of thing, but your notebook makes me feel like I'm right there walking through the school."

"I am most humbly honored by your praise. In that case, I'm sure you understand—why I think something's funny."

"Hm? Like..." I didn't understand. I hadn't meant to flatter her, but now my compliment sounded phony. I forced myself to come up with something like an opinion. "The fact that there's too many buildings? Given the size of the student body, we could probably do away with one or—"

"That's not it. What are you, a fool?"

Harsh words, delivered in a polite tone. For a second I thought I'd angered her, but apparently not, as her expression was as beaming as ever—did her unique speech owe to transferring from one school to the next? There are cases where a horrible name to call someone in one place is a regular way to address them in others.

"That's just because of Japan's declining population. They must have needed this many in the past. We can infer that the large number of empty classrooms is simply the result of the number of current students being lower compared to when the school came into being. That's not what I'm talking about—this right here is."

"Where?"

"Here."

Ogi took her notebook back, opened it to a different page, and pointed—at the same place she was pointing a few moments earlier. But nothing there struck me as particularly funny.

"The layout here is strange." Fed up with waiting for an answer from a fool, which is to say from me, Ogi began explaining.

"Strange, or maybe unnatural—just look at the floors right above and below it," she said, flipping between the adjacent pages. "They have rooms here like they should, right? It's funny that this one room is missing in between them."

"Funny..." I looked at the layout once again, this time with these preconceptions and prejudices in mind, but still didn't see it. "But the third floor does have this room. The AV room..."

"*That's because the layout is wrong.* Wrong, or well, I did draw these to reflect reality, but the actual AV room isn't this long. You must have noticed that it's drawn about one-and-a-half times longer compared to the surrounding rooms."

"Hmmm."

True, maybe it did look that way compared to the classrooms around it—the AV room I'd used a number of times during my time as a student wasn't this large. It still didn't seem like an impermissibly large error, though... And it wasn't as if Ogi had drawn her plans with the kind of serious measuring tools they used on a construction site. She'd probably overlooked a classroom on one of the floors, or got her units wrong, or made some other kind of error that manifested in the AV room getting a little longer.

"What's that? You're not doubting me, are you? Oh, that really hurts."

"I know you don't like me enough to be wounded by me doubting you."

"No, I'm quite enamored with you—I have a thing for easily tricked fools."

Casually calling me a fool again... It'd be one thing if she was contemptuous, the way Senjogahara once was, but given Ogi's smile, I couldn't tell if she was being guileless or malicious. It was causing cognitive dissonance.

"I don't make mistakes. If this is a mistake, I'll strip down and use my wide-open arms in place of a ruler to remeasure the entire school."

"Are you always so careless about making promises?"

Me, I'd never promise such a thing, no matter how confident I was.

"It isn't a mistake..." Ogi paused and chuckled. "If this were a mystery novel, a floor plan not lining up with reality would, in most cases, mean there's a hidden room. Now, what should we do? What if there was enough space here for an entire room stuffed full of treasure?"

"Hidden treasure at a school? And I doubt it'd become ours just because we found it."

"You need to dream a little—kids studying for exams turn into such realists."

"Even if it wasn't a mistake on your part when you were drawing these, wouldn't it make sense to assume it's a mistake on the builders' part? In other words, it's dead space just buried in concrete—"

I didn't recall there being any concrete wall next to the AV room—but if you asked me what it did look like, I couldn't tell you. All you really need to know as a student is the location of your homeroom.

"Maybe. Of course, that would be best. No, it'd be best if it were stuffed full of treasure, but I'd be fine if it were stuffed full of concrete. But if..." Saying something improper, or imprudent, seemed to excite

Ogi so much that she could barely hold herself back. *"If this is some kind of aberrational phenomenon*—we ought to look into it before anyone gets hurt."

"..."

My honest impression—was that she was jumping to conclusions. Yes, it was strange that the layout didn't line up with reality, but you couldn't go straight from that to an aberrational phenomenon. Even her hidden-room theory was more believable—though maybe you could find an aberration like that if you dug through the literature.

And anyway, Shinobu would notice if there was something like that at our school—in fact, how could Oshino not have caught on as early as spring break? Yeah, he'd definitely say, *I don't like it when people blame everything on aberrations as soon as something strange happens.*

I couldn't dismiss her opinion out of hand, though, precisely because she was Oshino's niece—and because the two or so people who'd surveyed every inch of Naoetsu High when they entered, namely Tsubasa Hanekawa and Hitagi Senjogahara, hadn't said a thing about this dead space.

If it really existed—whether it had anything to do with aberrations or not—Ogi had spotted something unusual immediately after transferring in like it was obvious, when not only Tsubasa Hanekawa, who knew everything, and Hitagi Senjogahara, at the height of her desperate self-preservation, hadn't.

This fact—no, it was only a possibility at this point, but I wasn't so dry that my curiosity wasn't piqued by the possibility.

"Even if it's an aberration, we don't know that it's harmful...but I suppose I do agree, we should look into it just in case," I said, prudently and a little too turgidly. I didn't want her to think that I was hopping straight onto an underclassman's proposal; I wanted to keep up the appearances I no longer cared to with Kanbaru.

"Aw, that's great. I knew I could count on Araragi-senpai. Please come and meet me today after school, then. Visiting a third-year classroom makes me nervous, you know?"

How cute of her, and unlike Kanbaru. She was effectively telling a senior she'd only just met to come to her, which was rude, but I didn't even notice.

"Okay, I just need to come to your classroom? But this can't go too late, okay? I might get assassinated if someone mistakenly thinks that I'm off having fun after school with one of my juniors."

"I won't keep you long, of course. Maybe fifteen minutes? That should be more than enough time to realize it's nothing. It'll only take a minute."

Or fifteen, Ogi said, looking cheery. Seeing her act this way made me think that all the talk about floor plans and aberrations was nothing more than an excuse. Maybe this girl, at a brand-new school where she didn't know people, just wanted to get along with an indirect acquaintance like me, I thought conceitedly—of course, the truth was something else.

Fifteen minutes wasn't anywhere near enough for our investigation—and I still didn't know how long it would take.

005

I went to visit Ogi after school like I'd said, and from there we briskly walked over to the building where the AV room was located. Ogi took the lead. This made me feel like I was the transfer student and she was showing me around school. She talked to me about all kinds of things on our way there—so I wouldn't get bored, I assumed. Things like "the law in serialized manga where editors write really long copy for titles they're not confident about (on the other hand, copy for popular manga is short)" or "the law where the more expensive something gets, the slower it goes (the speed at which food is served at a restaurant, paying the bill, the delivery of goods, wrapping a present)," stuff she came up with herself. It seemed that she was a fan of laws. Seeing her talk on and on made me think there was indeed something about her that took after Mèmè Oshino. There was also something about it that made her feel like a fresh high school girl. I savored both the nostalgia and the freshness of it as we arrived at our destination. And at our destination, the third floor of the school building in question, next to the AV room, sure enough.

There it was.

A classroom.

"See, Ogi? Take a look at that. There's a regular classroom right here. You overlooked it, that's all. In other words, you added the space taken up by this classroom to your drawing of the AV room. Now it's clear that you made a mistake. So I think it's time for you to strip down and use your wide-open arms in place of a ruler to remeasure the entire school. Maybe I'll have you measure my body while you're at it. I feel like I've grown lately," I didn't actually say.

After all, *it was far stranger for there to be a classroom here than not*— in a building full of special classrooms, why was there a regular one, like it had sprouted up out of nowhere? It was so out of place that it left an impression, and I absolutely would've remembered it. Even if I didn't remember it looking at a floor plan, I definitely would after seeing it in person.

"Hmm? What could this classroom be? It wasn't here when I visited the area to draw my layout. What a big, old mystery," Ogi said, flatly for some reason—grinning as always. It almost looked like she was enjoying this.

"Anyway...let's go inside."

It was the wrong decision. It seems obvious that I should have stepped back, come up with a plan, and returned. I should have drawn on Hanekawa's wisdom and consulted Shinobu, who was sleeping in my shadow—but I wanted to show my underclassman that I was reliable, so I recklessly opened the door and walked inside.

Like a fool.

From the outside, it seemed like no one was there, but the door was unlocked, making it easy to enter—no one, indeed.

Just rows of desks and chairs, as well as a teacher's desk and a locker for cleaning supplies.

An empty classroom—nothing odd about that. The fact is, the unticking clock and the gym being visible from the windows already stood out, but I had yet to notice. It certainly wasn't stuffed full of treasure, and as far as I could see, it was a plain classroom. Assuming I'd just remembered wrong and that it'd always been right here, I felt relieved, not noticing—not noticing a single thing I should have.

Ogi entered the classroom as well.

Then closed the door.

"And that brings us to now..."

I looked at the clock above the blackboard, then compared it to my wristwatch—noting the disparity between the time my watch displayed and the (stopped) time on the hanging clock.

My watch was operating like nothing had happened, so it was possible that the clock on the wall was out of batteries, but Ogi hadn't dismissed that possibility out of hand. If time was stopped inside the classroom, to some degree that explained why the doors wouldn't budge and the windows wouldn't break. A class where time had stopped—or no, maybe I ought to call it a class where time didn't pass?

"I guess the question is how fixed in time it really is," Ogi said, facing the blackboard again. It wasn't a ballpoint pen in her hands now, but a regular implement for writing on a blackboard, which is to say chalk. "That's right, blackboard chalk. But I'm old-fashioned, so I prefer to call it slate."

With that, she drew a line across the blackboard.

While the ballpoint pen had failed to leave a mark on it, this time she managed to draw a clear white line on the board.

"Wh... Whoa," I exclaimed, not so much at the experiment result showing that you could draw on the blackboard with chalk, but at the level of activity with which Ogi performed test after test. Weren't people normally more cautious in a sealed environment like ours?

"Hahaha. Looks like chalk works. I wonder what the logic is here. What about this?" Ogi then held the chalk sideways to draw a thick line. It was a forbidden way of using chalk that consumed a piece in the blink of an eye. Still, she could draw that way. Her thick line bent back and forth as she drew a love umbrella.

From there, she held the chalk vertically again and wrote "Koyomi" and "Ogi" under each side of the umbrella.

"Hahaha! Just messing around!"

"This really isn't the time for that, Ogi..."

Oops. If anything, this wasn't the time for me to be getting ticked off by an underclassman's silly joke—I should've been coming up with my own experiments, my own trials and errors to figure out how to escape from the locked room.

"Will the lights turn on?" We hadn't tried the switches yet since there was more than enough light coming through the window—but I tried flicking them all on. All of them at the same time, in our situation, showed how slovenly I am, but the fluorescent tubes on the ceiling lit up anyway. "So there's electricity... I guess this place functions as a class-room, at least?"

I wasn't sure... Still, if it was getting electricity, then as a last-ditch escape method we could use an outlet to light a spark and cause a fire. Tsukihi had done something similar in the past to help Karen (quite lit-erally the Fire Sisters), but while it was probably safer than an explosion, we ran the risk of suffocating if we started a fire in an enclosed space, making it an honest-to-goodness last-ditch method.

"Is there a danger," I muttered, "of us suffocating even if we didn't? I wonder how fast a human being consumes oxygen. We'd run out even-tually if this goes on for too long..."

"I don't know about that one. This is a classroom, after all—it might be a locked room, but I doubt we're sealed off from even the atmosphere. Maybe if someone used tape to trap us in here, but enough air should be seeping through the window frames and all to keep two humans alive."

"Oh... That's a relief."

Though I said I was relieved, I noticed that Ogi had used the words *locked room*. She probably just happened to choose them, of course, but maybe she was right.

Locked room might be a more fitting term for our situation than *enclosed space* if we weren't in an airtight environment.

Sheesh.

Guided by a blueprint to a hidden room like something out of a mystery novel—we now found ourselves in a locked room. Not a bad setup, but it had a lamentable lack of a detective.

"What do you think, Araragi-senpai?"

"What do I think? Well...what am I supposed to?"

I had to admit—that a floor plan that didn't seem quite right and my inability to recall the classroom could be put down to some misunder-standing, but there was no logical explanation for ending up in a locked room. My only choice was to explain it illogically, as an absurdity.

"But Ogi. If an aberration is doing this—what kind of aberration is it? Is there some aberration that locks people in a classroom?"

"Hard to say. Unlike my uncle, I'm not versed in that old-timey lore. I only know major aberrations, the kinds that show up in manga and movies," she either played dumb or acted modest—with such unfathomable snickering that it made me think she actually did know. It was the same when I talked to Oshino—I couldn't help but distrust him. Seeing my suspicious eyes on her, Ogi continued.

"But I'm sure there has to be some kind of aberration that keeps you from leaving a locked room. The type you hear about most doesn't let you leave until the next visitor shows up and you trick them into walking in so that you can leave. That sort of thing."

Yes, I'd heard that kind of ghost story—so were we stuck in this classroom until someone else showed up? No, that couldn't be right, it wasn't as if anyone trapped inside had left when we walked in. Even if this was an aberration, it was a different type of phenomenon.

"Ah, I was so afraid a fool like you might go along with that hypothesis." Ogi smiled gently—she was cutest whenever she called me a fool, but what was it? I kept missing my chance to scold her. "I can say this much, though. *For every aberration, there is a reason*—you see."

"..."

Wasn't that another one of Oshino's lines? In which case, the inference was that figuring this reason out would help us escape...

"Still, why'd we be unable to leave a classroom? And why should a clock stop the way—"

"Maybe the time its hands stopped on is the key? I mean—doesn't the ridiculous time they've stopped on feel odd?"

The clock hanging on the wall read a little before six—5:58, to be exact. As for my wristwatch, it said 4:45. Ogi and I must have started our investigation at around 3:30—so an hour and fifteen minutes had already passed since the onset of our abnormal situation.

"Even if that clock stopping a little before six is the key, is that supposed to be a.m. or p.m.? You can't tell with an analog clock."

"I think it's p.m.—judging from the view outside."

"Hm? Wait, really? If anything..."

Referencing the scene beyond the windows hadn't occurred to me. While I was quietly impressed by Ogi, I didn't want to betray my lack of insight to an underclassman, forcing me to find faults in her argument. I keenly hated how small of a person I was.

"Wouldn't it be darker out if it was six in the evening? At this time of the year—you might not know this because you're a transfer student, Ogi, but the sun around here sets pretty early once it's October."

"It does? Huh, I learn so much from talking to you. I still think it's 6 p.m., though—look at the direction of the shadow cast by the gym. The sun would have to be in the west for it to look that way."

"Mmm...okay. But we're facing—wait, no. We shouldn't base our direction off of this building's position since we're seeing the wrong thing from the window. We ought to use the gym's position instead. And it faces east-west," I muttered, recalling Ogi's gym page—fine. In that case, yes, the clock was showing 5:58 p.m.

"Six in the evening is when school closes for the day, right? Heh, so we'll be able to leave in time—oh, or maybe it's still 3:30 outside if the clock is stopped?"

"That would mean my wristwatch is malfunctioning here. This is getting annoying..."

"What're you talking about, time travel is a walk in the park for you," Ogi said—hm?

Hold on, she shouldn't know anything about the time travel stuff, it happened after Oshino left town—

"Details aside, we sure are in a bind, aren't we? If time isn't moving forward, that means night is never going to come. In other words, you won't be able to rely on that nightwalker...er, Miss Shinobu."

"Mm. Oh, I guess not."

Shinobu Oshino, the vampire who lives in my shadow, formerly known as the Aberration Slayer, is like a natural predator to any and all aberrational phenomena—an aberration who eats other aberrations. If she could make an appearance, she'd surely consume whatever we were facing, maybe even the whole classroom. But it was quite a lot of work luring out someone nocturnal like her at the awkward hour of "just before six in the evening." It wasn't impossible...but there was no telling how many donuts she'd demand in return.

"I don't know," I said. "Even if time isn't flowing in this classroom, it's moving for me—so maybe it is inside my shadow for Shinobu, too?"

"We don't know for sure if time is flowing for you. It could be that only your will is active, while time has stopped for your body. I mean, I hope that our physiologies aren't moving through time."

"Why not?"

"What're we going to do if we want to pee?"

"..."

A serious problem, indeed. I was doing my best not to think about it, but more than hunger or thirst, that was the most pressing issue—if anything, though, Ogi kept calm as she said this.

"I've heard all about your heroics, but even if you're known as our era's Junichiro Tanizaki, you couldn't possibly be into watching a girl pee and vice versa."

"Who are you calling our era's Tanizaki?"

"If time really has stopped in this classroom right before six—why would that be?" asked Ogi, putting us back on track.

"What do you mean, why..."

"Let me rephrase that. Six in the evening, time to leave school. What meaning does this phenomenon hold, where two students are trapped in a classroom at the exact time when they ought to be leaving?"

"Not going home, even when it's time to..."

She was right. It did seem odd—in fact, as far as school-related aberrations go, the type meant to teach some sort of lesson was the most common—like attacking students who loiter on the premises.

"Is this what you'd call detention?" said Ogi.

"Detention..."

Hm. Why was I getting hung up on that word? The reason wasn't coming to me, but I got the vague sense that it meant something.

It felt like it stirred my memories—detention?

"Have you ever had to stay after school for some remedial session, Araragi-senpai? Hahaha. I can't say I have. You might be surprised to know, but I'm on the smarter side."

"Can't say I have, either..."

"Oh, wow."

Though Ogi acted impressed, it wasn't smarts that kept me from doing detention or remedial work; I'd just skip any. Not that I could now, since I was hoping to take college entrance exams...but yes, last year or the year before that...especially when I was a first-year—a first-year?

"What's the matter? Your fate doesn't look well—I mean, your face."

"Hm? Really? Sorry, I was just...feeling dizzy."

"No need to apologize. No need at all. Being burdened with a helpless underclassman must be taxing. Would you like to sit down on one of those chairs? I'm sure you're not a germophobe like me—but if you insist, I can lend you my lap."

"Where exactly on your lent lap would I sit? If I borrowed it when you're not sitting, that would be a gymnastic formation. Seriously..."

I was starting to get used to Ogi's teasing. As her senior, I should've been putting her in her place (right, before it was too late as with Kanbaru), but I honestly did feel dizzy with a slight headache. I took Ogi's suggestion and decided to sit down for a moment—not on her lap, of course, but in one of the classroom's many chairs. I could see this going for a long time, so there was no point in overexerting myself now. I moved, pulled out a chair, and sat in it.

"Why did you sit there?" she asked as soon as I did, or maybe even a little before I did.

Huh, what? Why? She was the one who'd suggested it.

"No, that's not what I mean—this classroom is full of chairs, so I wanted to know why you picked that one."

"..."

Why'd there be a reason? I just felt like it—I thought of saying, but now that she'd asked, I couldn't figure out the answer. If I was sitting down because I was tired, it made the most sense to pick the closest chair—so why get moving, wind my way through the desks, pass up a number of other chairs, and finally sit in the fourth seat from the front, third from the right?

I just felt like it was of course the only answer I could give...

"Felt like it," Ogi said. "You just felt like—that was the easiest chair to sit in? It looked the most comfortable?"

"I don't think there's much difference in how comfortable any of these chairs are... It's just—"

"Just what?"

"Like I felt *used to sitting here*."

I myself thought that was an odd thing to say. Stumped as I was for an answer, *used to*—in a room I was visiting for the first time? Sure, if I need to rest in our classroom, even though all of the chairs are basically the same—I might unconsciously pick the most familiar seat, my own, to sit in…but this wasn't even close to being our classroom.

"Is that really true?"

"Huh? What? What'd you just say, Ogi?"

"Oh, I'm just throwing every possibility at the wall—and I just realized that maybe this isn't the first time you've come here. When you needed to take a seat, could you have gone straight to a specific chair because you've sat in it before?"

"…Sorry, that one's too out there for me," I replied with a half-smile—yeah, that didn't seem like a hypothesis worth serious consideration. Ogi was playing around and teasing me again. "I didn't even know there was a classroom here until now—"

"It wasn't here when I did my first survey, either. But it appeared when I came with you—so it strikes me as completely natural that it has something to do with you."

"Hm… Is that what it means."

To be honest, I wondered if Ogi wasn't the cause since she had discovered the aberrational phenomenon—but from her perspective, I was the suspicious one.

"You even said it yourself, Araragi-senpai. The view out of the window seemed familiar to you."

"Huh? Did I?"

"You did. Right when we entered, before we noticed we were trapped."

I didn't remember this—but I must have if she was so certain. I must've forgotten once I realized I was in a locked room.

Still seated, I took another look out the window—where I could see the gym. At our angle, from this floor of this building, we shouldn't have been able to—and the view from my seat was a little different from the one by the window. I couldn't see the roof anymore, and instead mountains loomed off in the distance, and it did seem…

My memories.

They were being stirred.

"Hm… I remember seeing this. But…"

"But?" echoed Ogi, more cross-examining than following up—she'd gotten close to my seat without my noticing. She hadn't made a sound, and she was so close that I found myself a little flustered. I started to talk, as if to gloss over the situation.

"Well… I wouldn't say I feel particularly nostalgic. Actually, it's kind of unpleasant…"

"Unpleasant? Really? I think it's a nice view—this location, this situation. We were saying that despite being on the third floor, it felt more like the fourth or fifth floor, but it's definitely the fifth at this height."

"Fifth floor…"

Fifth floor—in which case.

Right… I needed to rethink this. The view was an impossibility from this floor of this building. What if this was the fifth floor, and I was in a classroom in a building that faced the gym—what if I was where I could see this?

I was familiar—with such a classroom.

Fukado.

"…!"

"Uh oh. What's the matter—it's not like something came to you? Sorry if I was insensitive," Ogi said like she was apologizing. No, she wasn't apologizing, she was savoring this. She'd changed positions again at some point and now stood directly behind me. "Did you just recall—something you didn't want to recall?"

"No, that's…not it. I haven't recalled anything."

Indeed, I hadn't. Because *I'd never forgotten it to begin with*—how could I ever forget what happened? I bit my lips, went silent, and stuck my hand inside the desk—to search inside the seat I chose, claiming it was comfortable. The owner had to be pretty averse to studying at home; it was crammed with textbooks. I pulled one out and examined its back cover. There it said: *Year 1, Class 3—Araragi*.

"Guh…"

I covered my mouth and instantly moved to hide the name—but was too late. Ogi spotted it from over my shoulder.

"Wait a sec. Did that textbook just now say 'Araragi' on it? That's funny, that's strange, why could that be—why would your textbook be here in this classroom? Did you slip it in while I wasn't looking? Please, don't you know outside items aren't allowed in this classroom?"

Just kidding, it's not like this is a test, there's no such rule, Ogi added slimily—somehow without ditching her easy tone. A test. That's right, a test. Each word she uttered stirred my memories and stung them—not like a rose's thorns, but like a porcupine's quills.

Now desperate, I asked her: "Ogi… What do you know?"

"Nothing. *You're the one who knows.* For example—"

Ogi reached for the seat next to mine. From the desk, she extracted a random textbook—then flipped it over and read the name on it. *Year 1, Class 3. Toishima.*

"You must know this Toishima person, too?"

"Yeah… I…"

I did.

Suisen Toishima. Everyone called her Sui for short—was she in the flower arrangement club? She was always laughing and smiling, no matter what you asked her or said to her. Didn't her friends always caution her that laughing with her mouth wide open wasn't ladylike? If anything, though, the boys liked her for her hearty laughter. The teachers did too. Hadn't she been like a savior, in fact, for teachers who liked to joke during class? Right, and she was so serious about seat reassignments… and seemed pretty unhappy in this one, fourth from the front, second from the right, a half-assed position. Sitting right next to someone who looked so dissatisfied was bewildering at first, but then I came to realize it was a special front-row seat for hearing her laughter.

"She wore her hair in French braids… I knew just how long it took to do that because my little sister is like a walking hair catalog, and I always thought about the amount of work it must take her every morning. I never brought it up, though…"

"You sure do know a lot about this Miss Toishima."

"No… Any classmate would know that much. I—"

I hadn't known anything—after all.

This was back when I hadn't—there were a lot of things I hadn't known.

"Then what about Fukado? What kind of person sat at the desk I flipped over?"

It seemed that Ogi, too, had seen the name on that textbook. So she had, but not brought it up until now—well, that wasn't odd. It's not as if the name had anything to do with her.

"Shimono Fukado. Now her, I was scared of... Not because she did anything in particular. I think she was harmless. I guess she was just ridiculously good at putting forth a personality? To be blunt, she acted cute. She came to school wearing the kinds of fancy hair accessories you only ever see in anime, she'd get told not to all the time, and she'd get this look on her face like, 'I don't understand why you're so mad at me.' It was obvious that she knew... Maybe because she thought that being smart or a good student wasn't cute, she'd do badly on tests on purpose—I won't say she played dumb, but it was kind of like that. I think her goal for the future was 'becoming a mom'—even an oaf like me could easily tell that 'becoming a bride' was the more girlish answer, so maybe she meant it. But when she smiled, her eyes never did, as far as I know."

Damn. I was talking too much. I couldn't stop once I'd started, though. It was like the floodgates had opened and the words were spilling forth—hadn't I decided not to think about it anymore, even if I couldn't forget it?

I'd thought I'd decided.

Why? Why was Year 1, Class 3—my classroom from two years earlier, here now? Just before six. 5:58 p.m. Right before it was time to go home. We needed to go home—but couldn't.

This classroom—that no one could leave.

"Ogi? Is there anything around that might tell us the date?"

"The date?"

"Yeah. Like what today—or no, what month and day it is in this classroom. I need to know."

"Well, it's right there on the blackboard. Just take a look."

Ogi was directly behind me now for the third time. Drawing her face close to mine, she put her arm around my shoulder and pointed at the blackboard. At its right-hand corner. Why hadn't I noticed until now? "Today's" date in this classroom was right there—along with the names of those who were on day duty.

July 15. Thursday. Koma / Marizumi.

"...!"

"Oh, so today's July fifteenth—now it makes sense for it to be so bright outside. Hmm, so then, did something happen in this classroom— Year 1, Class 3, I suppose—at around six on Thursday, July fifteenth? Something regretful, I'm sure. And that regret must've borne fruit as this aberration," remarked Ogi, broadly, as if none of it really mattered—I almost found myself protesting and saying it was more serious than that, but I couldn't. The biggest reason being that I didn't want to yell at a girl who was my underclassman—but also, she was completely on the mark when I thought about it.

What happened in this classroom on that day—really didn't matter, which is exactly why it was so unbearable. Who knew what the space was being used for now. An afterschool class council meeting held on July fifteenth in the Year 1, Class 3 room, located in the center of the fifth floor of that building facing the gym. A gathering of the class council that might be termed a trial. There we condemned one another over a certain incident—asserting our own innocence and imputing guilt to others. There were objections, and there was the right to remain silent. There were testimonies, and there was perjury. And I—Koyomi Araragi of Year 1, Class 3, sat at the center of this tumultuous trial.

Right.

Wasn't that when it started?

When I first started to say it?

"I don't make friends—making friends would lower my intensity as a human," Ogi preempted me. Preempted, as if to block my escape route. To chase me down a dead end.

Her face, still to the side of mine, drew even closer. Our cheeks almost touched now. She wasn't just close, her dainty chin was resting on top of my shoulder.

"That was your favorite line—though it seems you've stopped saying it ever since Tsubasa Hanekawa came into your life. Ah, we really do change through meeting people, don't we—so let me ask this, out of curiosity. How did you change when you were in this class? How did Fukado, how did Toishima, how did Koma, how did Marizumi— change you?"

"Change…m—"

"I've heard your personality changed quite a bit between middle school and high school. Could the reason for that possibly be found in this classroom?"

Who told her that? Well, some people did know, of course—but this was the past, and the only ones who'd bother digging it up now were the Fire Sisters.

"What happened, Araragi-senpai? Here in this classroom. That day. That time," Ogi whispered the words like she was cornering me.

One of her arms was around my neck, and I felt like I was being throttled—and understood what people meant when they spoke of being hanged with a silk noose.

"Let's talk about it—Koyomi Araragi," she muttered, murmured. "You'll feel better once you do. No matter how awful a memory might be, talk about it and it'll turn into nothing more than a tale."

"A tale…"

"Don't worry, I'll listen. I might not look it, but I'm someone you can really *talk to*."

"…"

I did everything to maintain my composure, even then—even under those circumstances, I didn't want to embarrass myself in front of my junior. How vain am I?

"We can't leave," I said.

"Excuse me?"

"We can't leave—we aren't allowed to exit this classroom until we figure out the culprit. That's what we did—*that's what we forced upon ourselves* in that class council. And as unbelievable as this sounds…I was the chairman."

006

If you were to ask me what kind of person Koyomi Araragi was during his first year of high school, I guess a self-evaluation finds someone less difficult than I am now, while a self-examination finds someone more honest and straightforward than I am now. I also hadn't been attacked by a vampire, of course, so I could state with confidence that I was a human day and night.

Now, then. Naoetsu Private High School, which I attend and which Ogi transferred into, is quite the prep school—we even have classes on Saturdays, and it'd be hard to call it an average high school in that sense. The exam to get in is fairly hard, too. Maybe it was a miracle that I overcame this barrier—no, "miracle" might be going too far. It'd be more accurate to say that I passed thanks to some sort of mistake. I mean, I had to pay a pretty high price to compensate for the mistake of doing whatever it took to get in—it wasn't long before I couldn't keep up with Naoetsu High's over-the-top curriculum. From the time you're a freshman, you're in classes that are preparing you for college entrance exams. No fun allowed, and that was a pretty big culture shock for me. Still, I'd gotten in (due to some sort of mistake or not), and in those days I thought I should accept my fate and stick it out. Yes, until the end of our first term, right before summer break. Until just after finals, I guess I should say? Well, whatever the case, until what happened after school on July fifteenth.

July fifteenth. The day I gave up on being serious, on being an honest and straightforward student—and decided to sink to being what Tsubasa Hanekawa would call a delinquent. The truth is, I just became your standard washout. Even if that day and its events never happened, I'd have fallen behind before long.

In any case, on July fifteenth two years ago, I finished ignoring my incomprehensible classes (I wasn't even trying to keep up. I mean, I was leaving my textbooks at school) and, mentally exhausted, was getting ready to make my way home. It's almost summer break, it's almost summer break, it's almost summer break, I chanted in my mind like a spell—not that summer break boded well, considering how much homework we'd be getting.

I'd somehow survived our first term, but couldn't stand the thought of going on that way until graduation. In fact, I hadn't made it through first term yet—and in the end, wouldn't.

Shadows. Three of them—blocked my path as I walked down the hallway. Feeling drained, barely noticing them in time, I almost collided with them.

"Araragi," a voice called.

When I finally lifted my downturned eyes, I saw three of my classmates.

"Got a second?"

It was Arikure who said this as I stood there—Biwa Arikure. A mean girl who seemed to find a way to complain about everything. To be honest, a type I don't really like—and I doubt any boys had a favorable view of her. She always had her hands in her skirt pockets, and it wasn't some blatant attempt to act bad. It was to protect her hands—when she did take them out, they were gloved, still fully protected. Something about her wanting to become a pianist—*good thing you can't hear her personality*, you might badmouth her, but apparently, she was reasonably accomplished. Not that I'd ever heard her play, but rumors aren't always just rumors.

In any case, getting stopped by a girl I didn't like when I felt so drained was pretty rough.

"Sorry, there's something important I have to do now, called going home…"

"What, you think you're better than me?" she said as if to pick a fight—I didn't think I was, but she must've thought I was messing with her. That's one part of me that continues to stay the same.

Two girls stood behind Arikure—whose nickname, I believe, was Arikui, or anteater—and one of them, Kijikiri, was silent. In fact, spaced out somehow, she wouldn't even look at me. That's the kind of person she was, proceeding at her own pace, or maybe laidback. Sometimes she'd stay behind for no reason, and come to think of it, even be absent without telling anyone. Hoka Kijikiri was a capricious girl with a strange way of life—people even said she lived in a different world. That's why I was surprised. Why would she team up with Arikure to block my path? Not that she'd strayed from her indifferent stance, just standing there and looking away.

"No, I really do have to get home. I have an obligation to. Going home is one of my three great obligations. I haven't told anyone else, but my little sister in sixth grade got herself mixed up in a huge fight—or actually, stirred up a huge fight, and I can't afford to take my eyes off of her."

"Huh? Stop with the jokes already. I hate that kind of stuff more than anything," Arikure complained like I'd truly offended her—it wasn't a joke, but to be fair, my beloved little sisters had yet to be known as the Fire Sisters of Tsuganoki Second Middle School. My words must've come off as nothing more than a lie.

"Now, now. Calm down," said the last girl, Tone, to soothe her, as if she were a wild mare. "We're sorry to bother you when you're busy, but please come back to the classroom with us. We won't take that much of your time. You'd be a great help."

Won't take that much of your time. Those words ended up being a lie, but I'm sure she didn't mean to deceive me.

Jiku Tone. Her nickname was Icing—not the frozen kind, but after the character for "sugar" in her name (stay with me, but Year 1 Class 3 also had a boy, Higuma, with the character for "ice"). She always looked happy, infectiously so. The healing type, to use a once-fashionable term.

53

Her name and nickname suggested that she liked sweets, but she was an all-round glutton. While she never seemed unhappy, according to herself she was happiest when she was eating. A regular customer at all-you-can-eat buffets.

"…"

I knew the basics about each girl, having studied hard alongside them for an entire term, but wasn't aware that they operated as a group. Actually, I think this was the first time I'd seen them together.

As I wondered what could have brought them together, Arikure ran out of patience. "You're being so irritating, Araragi," she accused angrily. "Are you coming or not? Decide already. It's fine with me if you don't."

"I will. That's all you want, right?"

If I were a little wiser, I probably wouldn't have agreed—I did sense the menacing mood. I had yet to give up on my life as a high school student, though. *Why these three?* I wondered, but looking back on it, what a good team they made. The unpleasant, pardon me, the aggressive Arikure in front; Kijikiri behind her, untouchable, or simply hard to communicate with; the healing Tone. A lineup you'd rather not face in a fight, handling them the wrong way could hobble the rest of my high school days. I ended up crippling most of my future as a high schooler anyway, but my only option at the time was to go with them.

We returned to the classroom, Year 1 Class 3's, on the fifth floor of the school building facing the gym. Two students stood by the door, waiting for us, and that's when it all made sense. One boy and one girl, and the boy wasn't the problem here. The issue was the girl glaring at me with open hostility—a sharp stare as if her parents' murderer stood behind me.

Her name was Sodachi Oikura. While she wanted people to call her Euler, they actually called her How Much. This was of course because her name, Oikura, could also be read as "how much"—which was quite fitting for someone who looked at you so appraisingly. Not that we were on good enough terms to call each other by any nicknames—if anything, I was her enemy.

She was the class president. These days, that could only refer to Tsubasa Hanekawa, globally speaking (at least for me), but her reputation had yet to spread so far. Hence...

"Class President Oikura," I said, judging that the situation called for her title. "What're you doing here? Are you the one who asked for me?"

"Hurry up and go inside. Everyone's waiting for you," she replied coldly and entered the classroom. The boy with her followed behind—if you're curious, this was Tsuma Shui, our class vice president. If you took dead seriousness and molded it into a high school freshman, the model Naoetsu High pupil, you'd get him. I touched on how Oikura was with me, but she was harsh overall, and I personally saw him as more of a class president than her. According to him, though, he was more of "the bureaucratic type" who preferred to play "a supporting role." What kind of high schooler is the bureaucratic type, I thought and didn't believe him at first, but he stayed in Oikura's shadow during that entire first term, helping her lead the class—so I guess that sort of talent exists. I did see him just once at an arcade, where he moved with incredible precision for a dancing game. I felt like I'd seen a side of him I shouldn't have, but ever since I couldn't hate him even if he wasn't the type I got along with. I carefully avoided any conflict with Oikura partly for his sake, but I bet he barely noticed me...

"You heard her, Araragi. She said to come in. Go," Arikure prompted me. I shrugged and entered the classroom as I was told. Oikura never answered the question, but she must've asked the trio to fetch me—instead of doing so herself. Why? Because we would've gotten in a fight, and she wanted to maintain her dignity? In any case, it made perfect sense if she was the mind behind the well-selected team. What gave me pause, though, were her words—*everyone's waiting for you*. What did that mean? Was I the kind of hero who could make everyone eagerly await me? Who was "everyone" in the first place?

I went in and learned that "everyone" was quite literal—every last member of Year 1, Class 3 was assembled there.

007

"Huh. Everyone—so the full class," Ogi said. "It's abandoned now, but every seat was filled back then. I see, I see. Time waits for no man, a decade can pass in the blink of an eye."

"Yeah... Wait, it's only been two years, not ten, and technically, the seats belonging to the trio who'd come for me were empty. Also, the class vice president Shui was sitting, but Oikura was standing at the teacher's desk."

"On top of it?"

"She wasn't that eccentric a class president, okay? Anyway, standing at the desk, she declared, 'Now that we've secured our deserter, I'd like to begin this special session of our class council.'"

"Deserter? How harsh—Miss Oikura must've been pretty scary. I'd never poke fun at her. She's still here as a third-year, right?"

"Yeah. I guess..."

I tried to keep it vague because I really didn't want to discuss it. I put us right back on track—taking us back to the past.

"A special session of the class council isn't normally something you'd do after school, but Oikura was charismatic enough to make it happen."

"Huh... Still, it's weird. You didn't know about this meeting until just before it happened? That must be why they sent someone to get you, and why they called you a deserter. Why didn't you know about it?"

"A simple lapse in communication…apparently. The message reached the rest of the class, whether by folded notes or text message or whatever, but it never made it to me."

"What? Sounds like…" For the first time, the smile receded from Ogi's ever-snickering face, to give way to a look of shock and disgust. When people as fair-skinned as her turn pale, they seriously look light blue, like some color sample. "…you were what we might call—an outcast?"

"Excuse me? Could you not be so quick to call people wannabe radio shows?"

"Don't mishear people in ways that expose your dated ideas about tech. Anyway, you didn't have any friends even before you started saying stupid things like 'making friends would lower my intensity as a human'!"

"You're somewhat mistaken." Though not completely mistaken… "This is a tale about how someone who had no friends came to need no friends."

"Exactly what an outcast'd say," commented Ogi, still straight-faced. The pale one showed no interest in sympathizing. If anything, she disdained me—the reverence I was owed as her senior gone. "It's a sad thing to have no friends…"

"I don't need you to preach at me."

"Then stop acting so pious… All right, now sit up straight and tell me what happened. This so-called special session of the class council. What was its business—for today?"

008

"We're gathered here today to find the culprit," Oikura began before I could even take a seat, while the three girls who'd found me had followed Shui's lead and done so. Completely ignoring that I was just standing there, dumbfounded by the bizarreness of everyone being in class despite school having ended, the class president continued, "Understand that no one will be allowed out of this classroom until we find the culprit, or the culprit comes forward."

Her tone was harsh—even I'd rarely heard her speak that way, and she considered me an enemy. Her voice told you she'd accept no counterargument. She had no intention of coming to a compromise, and to be frank, this soured the mood inside the classroom. The air was the very picture of hostility—though I guess you can't illustrate air.

"This is a secret meeting of the class council, no outsiders allowed. Please turn off your cell phones and participate once you have cut off all external communication—Araragi. What are you doing?" said Oikura, finally turning to me. "Close the door. Can you not even close a door?"

I thought she was going to suggest that I sit, but was scolded instead for leaving the door open. I felt like bitching—it wasn't as if leaving the door open would cause any problems, but maybe she was expressing her determination not to let anyone out.

Then I noticed that all the windows were shut too. This was summer, and locking down a classroom with no air conditioning was a pretty rough thing to do to yourself... Was she trying to create the most inhospitable environment possible? Did she think that she might get lucky and induce the culprit to come forward? And wait, what was this stuff about a culprit? Could she be talking about a mystery novel? No—that wasn't something you'd gather everyone to discuss after school, was it?

I took a look at the seat farthest to the back on the gym side—six rows behind Fukado's, it belonged to Hitagi Senjogahara. The fragile-looking, most beautiful girl in class, whom I'd been too frightened to speak to, who seemed somehow noble and extremely sickly, like the heroine in a piece of sanatorium literature, who in fact skipped school all the time—it felt like she'd been absent for more than half of first term. If she was in attendance, it had to be pretty serious.

Someone could suffer heat stroke in a classroom as hot as ours, especially the sickly Senjogahara...

"President Oikura. What do you mean, 'find the culprit'?"

"Shut up. Please, just don't talk. I'm about to explain. I'm following a plan."

Scolded. Sternly, too. Even if you asked her weight, no normal girl would answer in such a tone. I fell silent—what else was I going to do in response to her request—but let me tell you, I didn't recall doing anything to her that merited such hatred. Most of the hostility she directed at me was unearned.

While I fell silent, hoping not to trouble the vice president by daring to ask another question—

"Come on, Oikura. What're you talking about? Why do you get to run this?" a voice seemed to taunt the teacher's desk from right in front of it. It was Okitada Koma. His legs crossed and looking as annoyed as could be, he objected, "You're one of the suspects, too—in fact, aren't you the prime suspect? Everyone's just too scared to say it."

The air grew even more tense. Normally, Koma's voice was too gorgeous to have this effect on anyone, no matter how harsh the words—but even his angel's voice couldn't gloss over or cover up the nerve-wracking content here. I didn't understand what was going on, but I guess he decided to say what everyone was thinking and hit a sore spot? Few others in our class could do this. Certainly not me, especially when I didn't understand the situation—though it seemed I was the only one in the dark. Had it been explained to everyone while I was on my way? That would suck... Did they lasso me in here and leave me out of the loop at the same time?

"Yes, Koma, I understand that," Oikura agreed. "Thank you for fulfilling your role as a student on day duty and voicing your honest opinion."

Compared to the way she spoke to me, she was polite with him for some reason—in fact, I was the only boy she was rude to as far as I knew. Why the special treatment? I wished I could tell her to stop, but of course I didn't.

"I'm only here in this position provisionally as we begin this session. I'll be handing it over and stepping down once I do—however, as a concerned party, and especially, as you point out, as the most likely suspect, I thought it'd be appropriate for me to give an overview of the situation. I know you're eager to get to cram school, but please, would you zip your mouth up for just a little longer?"

"Kch," Koma muttered in lieu of a response, but went quiet—seemingly annoyed that she'd brought up his cram-school attendance. He was an unusual case, a student who'd applied to Naoetsu High as a backup. Since he was here, he'd failed to get into his first choice—making it a bit hard for him to blend into our class. In fact, his conceited attitude reflected this and also helped him speak out against Oikura without fear. But even he couldn't make the class president back down. There's nothing wrong with a first-year attending cram school (at Naoetsu High, it's deemed praiseworthy), but then again, everyone has his own complexes.

"We got off track thanks to Araragi and Koma—but allow me to explain once more since not everyone seems to understand the situation," Oikura oh-so-subtly shifted the blame before beginning.

Still, I had to give credit where credit was due because she laid it out in simple terms.

"The incident occurred last Wednesday. All of you recall the open signups for the study sessions to be held in this classroom, correct?"

I didn't. In fact, I knew nothing about it. When were there signups?

They were doing something without telling me? A study session? Last Wednesday, meaning right before finals—to prepare for our tests, then.

"Raise your hand if you took part in the study session," requested Oikura, and half the class did. Their hands came down too fast for me to count, but there'd been more than fifteen—a session of a decent size.

Of course, that also meant that about half of the class, myself included, had skipped it—Koma, who'd just spoken up, hadn't raised his hand, for example.

Oikura hadn't either but said, "Yes. And of course, I did too."

I didn't see why this was supposed to be obvious. Because she would have organized the event, as a matter of course? Because raising your hand was an unladylike pose? Whatever the reason, I found it unpleasant. She was implicitly blaming anyone who hadn't participated—you uncooperative, selfish bunch, she seemed to be saying. True, I, at least, was guilty as charged...

"For anyone who was absent, the session was primarily for the purpose of studying mathematics."

Putting aside the fact that not participating in a voluntary session had suddenly turned into an absence—yes, we had two tests the next day, Thursday: math, as well as health and physical education. Health and P.E. first period, then math second period. Thus, the study session had been limited to math—no one would group up to study health and physical education.

"It was a truly wonderful session, where we learned from one another concepts we didn't understand, teaching and furthering each other—I'm very proud to have been able to hold such an event," Oikura stated as if she deserved all the credit. Well, she probably did. Though she wasn't exactly popular, there was a reason an unpopular person had been voted class president in a fair election.

"However, something occurred that cast a shadow on this auspicious event—which is why I've gathered you all here today. I believe it's our duty as Naoetsu High students to gather at such times, to deal with such situations."

"Um," a voice asked to speak as a timid hand rose. It belonged to Hayamachi, a girl who sat next to Koma right in front of the teacher's desk. "Maybe I'm too stupid to understand, Oikura... But if this is a problem that occurred at the study session, shouldn't the students at the study session work it out themselves? I didn't even know there was a study session..."

I had an ally. Not that Hayamachi—Seiko Hayamachi—saw me as anything close to an ally.

"Miss Hayamachi. First of all, please retract your statement, 'I'm too stupid to understand.' It's offensive to the rest of the class," Oikura said. Offensive because Hayamachi was something of a genius, despite her appearance—not the politest thing to say, but that's how students at Naoetsu High see any classmate who comes to school with painted nails, more-than-light makeup, and hair dyed brown. Actually, she was more of the hardworking type than a genius...but in terms of how unpleasant Oikura found her, she must've been right next to Koma (in addition to their physical positions, in other words).

That said, Oikura didn't seem to hate her as much as me—the class president didn't just find me unpleasant, but offensive.

"Well, I only said I was stupid because I am stupid," replied Hayamachi, not retracting her statement at all as she twirled her hair.

"The problem is what happened after our math tests were returned," Oikura said, ignoring her unrepentant classmate. "Every one of you conscientious students who participated in the study session got a good score—a wonderful thing. But that's where a problem arose. No, let's call it a suspicion, not a problem. A suspicion arose."

"Suspicion?" I reacted to the word.

Oikura glared at me. Unconscientious students weren't even allowed to mutter a word in reaction, it seemed. I noticed Tetsujo looking at me with sympathy in her eyes. Komichi Tetsujo. Member of the softball team. If Oikura was the leader of our class, she was the mediator. Given her personality, she was concerned about the friction between me and Oikura, but at the moment, meeker than usual, she wasn't speaking up. Was a sympathetic look the most she could do for me here? Sorry, but it meant nothing. Though maybe it beat jumping in and starting a heated argument with the class president—not that there could ever be one between the sharp-tongued Oikura and the above-the-fray Tetsujo.

"To put it plainly, this suspicion is a suspicion of cheating. Compared to those who were absent from the study session, the test scores of the students who did participate were *too high*," Oikura said. "There is a gap of about twenty points on average between students who participated and those who were absent. A ten-or-so point difference could be credited to a study session, but a twenty-point difference is too significant to ignore. Some form of foul play must have occurred."

"…"

Foul play—cheating.

So "finding the culprit" was about figuring out who cheated—wait, but in this case…

"Hold on, izzat what'cha call cheating? I thought cheating was like, taking a peek at someone's answers during a test," piped up Mebe, who sat behind Tetsujo—Miawa Mebe. A student from the west side of Japan nicknamed Whip. Nothing in her name referred to whip(ped cream), but she'd gotten a dessert-related nickname thanks to her friendship with Tone. Her approachable personality meant a reasonably friendly relationship with even Oikura (a miracle in my eyes—I wanted to beg her to teach me but had never spoken to the girl, who was approachable) and being able to make her point frankly.

"You're right."

Sure enough, Oikura stayed calm. Wait, had Mebe attended the study session? I hadn't paid too much attention when everyone raised their hands, so I couldn't be sure…

"My suspicion is that the foul play took the following form. *A certain someone*," Oikura worded it in a way that exuded intense animosity— on par with what she felt for me, "acquired the test questions from the teachers' room, then quietly introduced their contents into the study session. As a result, all of the students who participated got higher scores."

"Huh? But why'd you wanna do that?" Mebe tilted her head. "Test questions? If you got 'em unfairly, why not keep 'em to yerself? Teaching everyone in the session would be like—"

"I can think of a number of reasons why someone would do that and cannot pick just one. Camouflage, perhaps, or it might've been for the thrill of it," answered Oikura, only giving two possible reasons. I guess listing every reason she could think of was too laborious, and her plan was to consider motive later. "In any case, it'd be unforgivable if someone did indeed sully our sacred study session along with our inviolable final exam—and I don't want any of you who were absent to assume this has nothing to do with you, either. This is a problem for all of Year 1 Class 3. To repeat myself…"

She banged on the table. For some reason, Sodachi Oikura glared at me as she continued—like it was a declaration of war.

"Understand that no one will be allowed out of this classroom until we find the culprit, or the culprit comes forward."

009

"Haha. We started off looking for a hidden room from a blueprint, got ourselves into a locked room, and now we're trying to identify the perp? It's really getting to seem like we're in a mystery novel. What an interesting story. Both exciting and eccentric."

"There's nothing interesting about it... I'm sure you can guess how things turned out when a bunch of amateurs got together to finger a culprit." I shook my head at Ogi's optimism. I'd barely started telling the story, and I already felt pretty depressed—why I was sharing all this with a girl I'd met for the first time?

I hadn't even told Shinobu.

"Heh. Still, she sounds quite stern, this old Ikura—sorry, Oikura."

"Old Ikura? Ha, funny mistake to make... Should've said that one to her face."

Not that I had anything close to the courage to do so—back then, I'd been afraid of her for real. There's something extra frightening about people who're incomprehensibly hostile to you.

"Of course, I'd yet to learn that her brand of sternness was cute compared to Senjogahara—who had malice in her heart, not hostility."

"Ah. I didn't want to interrupt you, but you just reminded me. You referred to a Senjogahara in your story, but am I right to assume that's the same Senjogahara who's now your girlfriend? The witch with a poison tongue, the *tsundere* queen Senjogahara?"

"What kinds of stories have you heard about her? But yeah, you're right."

She'd had a change of heart and was reformed—but the fact that the girl then known as a flower in a bell jar (really a rose that was all thorns), the heroine in a piece of sanatorium literature (really the monster in a horror novel), and a cloistered princess (really an animal that needed to be caged) is my girlfriend two years later just goes to show that relationships work in the strangest ways.

That said…no other classmate from back then is still on good terms with me.

"I didn't know her true identity at the time, so let's just say she used to be the sickly, cloistered princess."

"Well, then sure, let's both say it," Ogi egged me on happily—I guess she was a good listener, or at least she genuinely seemed to be relishing my story. There was nothing pleasant about telling it, but I couldn't stop while she acted this way. It's weird, but it felt like my mouth had a mind of its own—and spoke independent of me.

"Umm. Where was I again?"

"The part where Oikura declared no one would be leaving the classroom until the culprit was exposed. Hm? Was it to you that she ceded the position of chair? You said you presided over a class council meeting."

"Oh, right—that's where I took over."

"I see. So basically she was the *kari-oya*, and you became the actual dealer once she rolled the dice."

"A mahjong metaphor only makes things harder to understand…" Ogi apparently had some very mature hobbies. Maybe she knew how to play *hanafuda*, too?

"Fine, no one literally rolled dice. She decided of her own will to name you chair, didn't she? And that's why she left you standing instead of letting you sit."

"Yup—that's it." Even if I didn't see the need to keep me standing the whole time.

"I don't get it in that case. Why pick you? Didn't anyone protest?"

"It's not like everyone was in favor of it, of course—like this one

boy, Shinaniwa. Ayazute Shinaniwa, who was like elitism personified…
He had a habit of looking down on people, and guys like me were as far
down as he could look. He was pretty adamantly against it."

"All kinds of people hate you, huh? An elitist… It does seem like
there are a lot of those in this school. Maybe that's where Oikura's harshness was coming from? But don't worry, Araragi-senpai, being hated is
a virtue."

"Put a little more thought into it when you praise people… I almost
agreed with you for a second, but no, of course being hated isn't a virtue.
And it wasn't like Shinaniwa hated me or anything, he just looked down
on me."

"Is there really a difference? Anyway, did this Shinaniwa take part in
the study session, too?"

"No—he was the type to study alone. He wasn't as exclusionary as
Koma, though. The kid looked down on people he thought were beneath
him and even cut them off at times, but he was really friendly with anyone he saw to be on his level or above."

"Sounds like he's the worst."

"He wasn't a bad guy."

Wasn't a bad guy—another line I could utter only because we weren't
close. What did I know about Ayazute Shinaniwa or Sodachi Oikura?
Familiarity with a guy's profile doesn't make you his friend.

"But everyone in class, including this current third-year, Shinaniwa,
accepted you as chair in the end," Ogi said. "Why was that?"

"Well, someone from the study session running the meeting would
be bad, right? Just like how Koma pointed out that Oikura was the most
likely suspect. About half of the class lost any right to be chair—but that
didn't mean anyone from the remaining half would do. We were there
because of a math test, after all. We'd be examining the questions asked
on it, so you couldn't leave it to someone with only so-so math grades."

"Huh, well, I suppose." Since we weren't going through and veri-
fying the answers, being poor at math wouldn't have been an issue—
Ogi seemed to want to say, but she simply nodded for the time being. "Still, the average score of the students who were absent—or who
didn't participate in the study session was twenty points lower than the

average of the students who did. Did anyone in the non-participating group score high enough to rival the study-session students?"

"Sure—I mean, I want to say Hayamachi got a 92. The participants weren't the only people who did well on the final, which did make things a little complicated. Only one student, though, got a higher score than everyone from the study session. Yours truly."

"What…"

"Which is why—I was chosen to chair the meeting."

010

100 points.

100 points out of 100—was my score on the math final. Sodachi Oikura had the next highest, a 99 (the highest score out of anyone from the study session).

I was all but unable to keep up with Naoetsu High's curriculum, math being the one exception—it sounds like I'm bragging to say it was my best subject, but math was easier for me because you didn't have to think. Still, a perfect score was a little too good—which is why I felt more anxiety than joy when I got my test back. Wouldn't there be some sort of blowback, I wondered, and my prediction had been spot-on.

I couldn't believe it—had I picked that short of a straw? I stood at the teacher's desk, but actually wanted to hide underneath it. So that was how my teachers (or Oikura) saw the classroom—I couldn't bear all the eyes on me. I was grateful for students like Kijikiri and Senjogahara who were looking away, uninterested.

"All right, Araragi. Think you could start speeding us along? Prove our innocence for us," urged Oikura, her words full of hostility and sarcasm—her seat may have been in the back, but the five chairs' worth of distance between us did nothing to damper the pressure coming from her.

I assume you've figured this out already, but her pathological hatred for me stemmed from my being good at math. She was convinced it was thanks to me and my higher math scores that no one called her Euler. Her resentment went beyond unjustified, it was indiscriminate. Naturally, I couldn't accept this and even tried (recklessly) arguing with her— *come on, your scores are so much higher than mine in every subject that we're not even in competition*—but that was in fact the very reason for her fury, according to her. She said it was like monkeys typing out Shakespeare in front of someone who wanted to become a novelist. What an awful thing to say…

I wasn't going to go out of my way to do poorly in math, my island of hope in the sea of Naoetsu High's curriculum… I wished she'd work to surpass me of her own accord, but that chance vanished once I got a perfect score.

"Of course, since you were the only one to get a perfect score, Araragi, we can't count out the possibility that you stole the answers," Oikura said combatively. What? Hadn't she appointed me? Was it my duty as chair to counter this spiteful jab of an opinion?

"That seems like kind of a stretch," a voice said in my place. Well, maybe not in my place, but the words were spoken to Oikura by a student sitting directly in front of her, Keiri Ashine—Year 1 Class 3's student no. 1. He was student no. 1, and I was no. 2—our consecutive roll-call numbers meant we were somewhat friendly. Okay, maybe not friendly, but we'd at least spoken before, and that trivial little link might have moved him to defend me. Like Mebe, he was one of the few students on good terms with Oikura—but in his case, he had some degree of influence over nearly every girl in class, not just her. His nickname was straight-up Handsome, after all. He wasn't the kind of guy you could describe in superficial, flashy terms like "hunky"—plus, he was good-natured if he had no reservations about interacting with someone as bothersome as me. Handsome and a good guy. No faults to find with him, and he continued his faultless argument.

"Since Araragi didn't even know that the study session existed, he wasn't in touch with anyone in it. How could he have had an impact on their average score? And didn't you pick him as chair partly because he has no conflicts of interest with anyone in class?"

"W-Well, true…"

Oikura faltered in a rare display for her—so even our class appraiser had a weakness for handsome boys. How disappointing, but even more disappointing was his remark that I had *no conflicts of interest with anyone in class*. He'd stood up for me just to cut me down where I stood.

It was true, though… At any kind of class council event, whether it involved being in groups of two or three or four, I, Koyomi Araragi, was always the one student left over at the end—and perhaps my lack of connections actually qualified me for the independent position of chair.

As depressing a job as it was…

"Okay, then," I said, "let's start by having everyone in the study session raise their hands, please."

I considered wording it as more of an arrogant command but didn't want to make any unnecessary waves. I'd act humble and proceed in a businesslike manner. To be honest, I didn't see how any amount of talk could reveal the culprit…but either way, I had to take care of this. The students whose arms had shot up for Oikura raised them slowly this time as if they were eyeing one another.

"I want you to keep your hands raised. I'm going to write your names on the blackboard."

"Oh, I can do that," Gekizaka volunteered, standing up. She was assuming the position of court clerk, an assertive move that was very much like her. Well, she had her hand raised until just a moment ago, which made her one of the suspects… But no, what was the harm in letting her be a simple clerk, even if she'd been in the study session? Gekizaka threaded her way through the seats to the front before I could accept her offer, and started by writing her own name on the blackboard. Some students looked at her as they would a traitor—they had their hands raised, naturally.

Or maybe they just found her pushiness suspicious—and Nageki Gekizaka's candid personality always made the girl an easy target for doubt. She never seemed to pay enough attention to the wall or fence between boys and girls and casually touched students of the opposite sex, which often resulted in trouble… You know, the kind of girl who made guys wonder, *Is she actually into me?* On that occasion too, I couldn't deny harboring some level of groundless suspicion simply because she'd volunteered. Maybe boys are just stupid, but in any case, her name wasn't solely responsible for her nickname Nagekiss. She returned to her seat—two rows in front of Senjogahara—after writing the names of every student with a raised hand, in addition to her own, on the blackboard.

Now I knew the names of the nineteen students who'd participated in the study session. Gekizaka had written only their last names, in whatever haphazard order she noticed them, but let me give their full names here, ordered by the Japanese syllabary:

1: Keiri Ashine 2: Michisada Igami 3: Sodachi Oikura 4: Enji Kikigoe 5: Hoka Kijikiri 6: Aizu Kube 7: Nageki Gekizaka 8: So-sho Kodo 9: Tsuma Shui 10: Judo Shuzawa 11: Kokushi Su'uchi 12: Ki'ichigo Daino 13: Choka Nagagutsu 14: Roka Haga 15: Sekiro Higuma 16: Joro Hishigata 17: Shijima Fudo 18: Kabe Madomura 19: Shokei Yoki

011

"Huh! So you narrowed it down to nineteen suspects—this is getting exciting. Or maybe that's inappropriate. Am I in trouble? Heheh," Ogi said, showing self-restraint but laughing openly. It made me want to throw some water on her enjoyment.

"It's not that simple. Yes, everyone in the study session was suspicious, but that didn't clear everyone who hadn't participated of all doubt," I noted. I wasn't just throwing some water, I was trying to drown her enjoyment. "To give an extreme example, someone might have stolen the answers and put them in the head of someone in the study session, indirectly influencing how they answered the test questions."

"Indirectly, you say. Hmm, possible, I guess," Ogi said, amused.

Any wet blanket I could throw was going to land on red-hot rocks, and the only thing that was flailing its arms was my dignity. "If the plan was to have fun by raising the class's average score, that'd be the best way…"

"Would that really be so fun?"

"Who knows, I wasn't the one—but think about it. It'd be fun if you didn't care about the consequences. It'd make you feel like a god."

"Playing god… I don't think I approve."

Hm? It felt odd that her reaction had gotten a little more negative. Maybe as Oshino's niece, she was sensitive to talk of the divine? I told myself this before putting us back on track.

"In any case, you could supply the info to the study session without being a part of it."

"If that's what happened—the culprit would be a student who didn't participate in the study session who got a good score on the test," conjectured Ogi. "In other words, someone who got a grade on the same level as the students in the study session despite not being a part of it—other than you, of course."

"Hah. Sure, sure, I had no conflicts of interest with anyone in class…" Oikura might have glared at me, but there was only conflict between us, not any kind of interest.

"Oh, don't pout like that. Here, I'll be kind to you."

With that, Ogi put both of her arms around my neck. In an instant, they were wrapped around my throat—like she was a scarf or something.

"I think you're a little close," I finally cautioned my underclassman, as a guy with a girlfriend.

"Excuse me. This level of distance is normal where I grew up. Just think of it as the kind of friendly physical contact that Gekizaka gave everyone," Ogi retorted, unembarrassed.

Gekizaka was never that handsy with anyone, I'm pretty sure…

"Anyway, please continue—which one of the nineteen was the culprit?"

"Didn't I just say it wasn't necessarily one of them? And even if it was a student who skipped the session, he or she might not have done well on the test. You might get a bad score on purpose to avoid suspicion, in fact. So everyone's back to being a suspect."

"Intentionally? Who'd go that far on an all-important test?"

"You might, or you might not—I'm trying to convey that we didn't know anything. I'm going to go ahead and spoil it here, Ogi. We failed to identify the culprit at that meeting."

"What?"

"In that sense, there's no neat conclusion to this story, just confusion. The class council's investigation turned into a class-wide castigation. Things got as ugly as they could, and it seemed pointless to everyone by the end, whether you were Oikura or Shui or Tetsujo. Basically, it fell apart, and we weren't able to learn anything at all. And then—"

"Oh, okay!"

Ogi smacked both of my shoulders, going beyond physical contact to plain assault. The longer I talked about this, the more depressed I felt—jumping to the end was my idea of cutting the whole thing short, but it had given her an idea.

"Now I know how we can escape from here. We just have to solve the unsolved case from two years ago and then we can leave."

"What...do you mean?"

"Oikura declared that no one would be allowed out of this classroom until the culprit was revealed. Which means *identifying the perpetrator of that case*—is how we escape this room. Am I right?"

"..."

Was she right? Well, if the classroom was a faithful recreation of what took place that day after school in Year 1 Class 3, then...she was.

We'd learned nothing through the fierce debate (a nice way to put it, "pandemonium" would be more accurate) that lasted until it was time to leave the premises. *That's* how the class council ended—yet the clock in the room was stopped *right before* closing time.

The windows were locked, the doors were shut tight—we couldn't get out.

"The regret left behind in Year 1 Class 3's hearts that day must have taken form as this structural gap," Ogi insisted. "Call it the ghost of the class council meeting."

"A ghost, of a meeting? Are you claiming we've been trapped by something that nonsensical? And why me..."

"Hard to say. Maybe because *you're the one it still bothers most*—you never know, your life did change that day."

"It changed?"

"Since that day, you've avoided thinking about what happened. You've been dodging it—you've never forgotten about it but never thought about it either. But it's come at last—the day when you have to face your past. Time to unravel this mystery."

I didn't know how Ogi could be so sure... There could be plenty of other reasons for this aberration.

She grinned—invitingly.

"I'd be happy to help you reason through it, if I can manage to be of any use. Go down the list, and tell me what happened. Let's start with those nineteen suspects' profiles. At the end of the day, they're the most suspicious, right?"

"Okay...I'll go down the list. I'm skipping the ones I already talked about, though—"

012

1: Keiri Ashine—already introduced.

2: Michisada Igami—apparently called Doctor because of the character for "medicine" in his name, it wasn't as if his parents were doctors. Still, they seemed to be reasonably wealthy, and he was well known for his generous nature. He never went as far as to modify his school uniform, but I heard rumors that his street clothes were pretty flashy. They said he'd brought snacks for everyone to the study session. However, he strongly insisted that he couldn't be the culprit—the reason being that he'd only gotten a 68.

"Who would raise everyone's scores, come to the study session, and still get a 68 on his own test?"

While his argument made sense, it didn't clear him of all suspicion for reasons stated earlier. There was a high material chance that you committed the crime if you participated in the study session. By the way, he was the only participant who scored in the 60s. There weren't even students who scored in the 70s; everyone else received an 80 or above. A single student getting an unusually bad score might be termed suspicious.

3: Sodachi Oikura—already introduced.

4: Enji Kikigoe—you could say he was more suspect than Ashine, specifically because he was known to be a prankster. Once, he planted a paper-cutter blade inside a blackboard eraser so it'd screech the next time someone went to erase some chalk—fortunately, this was discovered in time. Otherwise, we'd have been lucky if only a window or two shattered. "I don't do any pranks that inconvenience anyone," the kid said, convincing nobody.

What's funny was that his first name, which included the character for "smoke," earned him the nickname Spy, making him seem that much more suspicious—though I'm sure he only found it galling, not funny, that his parents' sensibility was cause for suspicion.

5: Hoka Kijikiri—already introduced. As a special note, it'd be closer to the truth to say that she'd absentmindedly been sitting in the classroom when the study session took place around her. She did get a good score, however, and since she was at the scene, she couldn't have heard nothing...

6: Aizu Kube—known as the library assistant, even though Naoetsu High had no such position. It was the school's ethos not to let us do anything but pursue our studies—she only got the title because she loved to read. She read on the way to school, of course, and during breaks, and sometimes even during class—a true warrior that read *Rilla of Ingleside* as a high school freshman. There was one other student in our class addicted to the printed word, Hitagi Senjogahara, but while she was an indiscriminate reader, Kube had a special love for classic foreign novels. Hadn't gone so far as to read during the study session, apparently.

7: Nageki Gekizaka—already introduced.

8: Sosho Kodo—a tall student on the girls' volleyball team. For some strange reason, she had a tan despite playing an indoor sport. I suppose the running and muscle-building parts happened outdoors. In any case, the rare example of a student who devoted herself to extracurriculars in a class that mostly went straight home after school. She had a contradictory personality, coarse yet high-strung—might be overstating the case in a mere introduction, but to put it simply, she hated it when anyone used her things but was always using other people's things. She'd borrow pens, notebooks, and textbooks without asking, even destroying, ripping, and losing them, but never let anyone borrow anything of hers. She got livid, too, if you went ahead without asking first... According to

Fuyunami, an old friend of hers, Kodo was "mentally immature." Clubs and teams went on hiatus before testing periods, so she had no problem taking part in the study session.

9: Tsuma Shui—already introduced. While Oikura ran the study session, naturally the vice president supported her. "If Oikura is the most likely suspect, I'm just as likely of a suspect," he said calmly—no doubt an attempt to shoulder some of the suspicion placed on Oikura, to which she replied, "It doesn't make sense for there to be two most likely suspects. I'm the most likely." She had to be number one at everything, even when it came to suspicion.

10: Judo Shuzawa—even if he hadn't raised his hand, everyone would have assumed he'd taken part in the study session. Shuzawa didn't seem to realize it himself, but he was the kind of boy who loved these kinds of events. I guess he liked study sessions, or maybe just teaching people things? He always wanted to teach. He "taught" me a lot of things for our midterms, but I was more bothered by his pushiness than grateful for his help. I say that because he didn't care one bit whether I understood him—still, his eager-to-teach personality matched the assumed profile of our culprit. This probably has nothing to do with any of the above, but he also wore a watch on each wrist. "It keeps me from being unbalanced"—mental balance might be what he really lacked.

11: Kokushi Su'uchi—an understated student. By which I mean he had no notable qualities and tried to hide among the rest of us. As a fellow student on the less popular side, I'd interacted with him before, but without getting any kind of read on him. It was unclear what Su'uchi liked and what he disliked. Of course, he wasn't going to open up to someone like me. He didn't seem like the type to participate in a study session, but if he had without incident, I guess he wasn't particularly antisocial. In other words, I was the only one of us who thought we were alike.

12: Ki'ichigo Daino—while I thought the girl's first name, "raspberry," was the more distinctive of the two, for whatever reason both the boys and the girls in class took the beginning of her last name and called her Daa. She was eloquent, a born talker, and built a logical case for just how not suspicious she was—convincing me that whoever the culprit was, it couldn't have been her. When I thought about it afterwards, she wasn't convincing at all. She seemed to be in a real rush to leave, maybe she had somewhere to be—we all wanted to go home, though. Even I wanted to go home already.

13: Choka Nagagutsu—simply put, the class clown. He was the one who set the mood in Year 1 Class 3. But a lot of the girls hated him. Like, actually hated him. He had a tendency to go overboard and make them cry—okay, not often enough to call it a tendency, but in high school you don't forget when someone makes a girl cry. The impression was burned into our minds. Maybe the problem was that the kid didn't seem sorry at all. Oikura had half given up on him—why wasn't she bothering to give up on me too? He showed up for the study session but didn't take it very seriously, treating the whole thing as a joke, depending on who you asked. Did his presence actually drag down their average?

14: Roka Haga—an athletic girl on the track team, but also a gamer. A problem child who brought portable gaming systems to school and had them confiscated. She even played during class with the sound off—Kube read novels during class, but this was verboten on a whole other level. Yet she took part in the study session because her midterm results had been awful thanks to her track and videogame commitments. She needed to recover from that—and her efforts paid off, earning her a 96. Thus, like Oikura, she was disappointed that her achievement had been called into question. It made me a little curious to know how she did in her other classes.

15: Sekiro Higuma—a student council president during middle school, he ran against Oikura in our election at the beginning of the term. Losing only by a slight margin, he was nominated for vice president, but apparently not interested, he withdrew himself (it didn't sound like he'd become class president during middle school out of personal ambition, either—more like, the teacher forced him to). This stance of his struck people as modest and virtuous and made him popular with the girls—he was second only to the "handsome" Ashikura. Initially known as Ice thanks to the character "hi" in his surname. This was too similar to Tone's nickname of Icing, and he started getting called Kilo for the "kiro" in his given name.

16: Joro Hishigata—a member of the softball team and our dependable big sis type. Unmistakably one of the core pieces of our class, alongside Oikura's charisma-through-fear and Tetsujo's oddly unreliable mediation. As a girl she did make a habit of siding with the girls—but boys respected her too, cowed by how she never took so much as a half step back in the face of anyone, even a boy. She certainly could've worked on her temper, though.

17: Shijima Fudo—a girl on the swimming team. She lied and said her father was a professional baseball player, a mysterious fabrication she couldn't easily take back. She had brown hair, but unlike Hayamachi claimed it was due to all the chlorine in the pool—this too may have been a lie. She was at the study session, which we knew for sure thanks to witnesses.

18: Kabe Madomura—another one of the few students involved in extracurriculars. The light music club, too. To think that Naoetsu High had any activity that fun-focused. His often-standing hair wasn't an expression of his rock-and-roll spirit though, just bedhead. Kind of a letdown. Good English thanks to all the Western music he grew up on, while math, he admitted, wasn't his forte, hence his presence at the study session—did he really need to lead in with that stuff about being good at English?

19: Shokei Yoki—an old-fashioned kid. An anachronism, even. He was given to asking *what it means to be a man*, annoying us boys, let alone the girls, with his sweaty talk. He just kept going on about masculinity, oblivious to our reaction... If you put up with it, though, he sometimes said surprisingly substantial stuff—*what it means to be a man* was actually about being a gentleman, not that it made him any less of an anachronism. Still, he had a bad habit of being blustery and was the first one to suggest that Kikigoe, the prankster Spy, was suspicious.

In total—nineteen individuals.

These nineteen had taken part in the study session held the day before the final. The culprit may have been among them, or perhaps not.

013

"So most of Year 1 Class 3 weren't in any extracurriculars... Do you mind me asking about that, Araragi-senpai? How many others were in clubs or on teams?"

"Huh? Why do you wanna know?"

"When you're laying the truth bare, you never know what might turn out to be a hint. After saying there weren't many club members, you described three in a row who were toward the end. It made me wonder. I'd like to look into whatever sets I can."

Laying the truth bare sounded a little extreme, but I answered her anyway. The study-session people who were in clubs were Kodo, on the volleyball team; Haga, on the track team; Hishigata, on the softball team; Fudo, on the swimming team; and Madomura, in the light music club. Those five—and Ogi was right, there did happen to be three in a row based on how I organized the list, but five out of nineteen still seemed on the low side.

"Yes. Which is why I want to know about the non-participants who were in clubs and on teams—didn't you say at the beginning that Suisen Toishima was in the flower arrangement club? And that Tetsujo, the class mediator who led you guys alongside Sodachi Oikura, was a member of the softball team?"

"Oh...yeah, with Hishigata."

"I see. The softball team—who else in your class was on it?"

"No one. Whatever you're hoping to get from this…like every other extracurricular at our school, the softball team was plagued every year by a lack of members. I want to say that Tetsujo invited Hishigata to join? As far as other kids who skipped the session, Shinaniwa was on the track team, like Haga. And Fuyunami played volleyball."

"Fuyunami. You mentioned him once before—right, childhood friends with Kodo. Huh. Childhood friends playing the same sport. Kind of romantic."

"I'm pretty sure the boys' team and the girls' team are basically different clubs…"

Well, it was just a prediction, or preconception—as if I, who'd been going straight home ever since middle school, knew anything about how clubs operated.

"Fuyunami—Saka'atsu Fuyunami joined the volleyball team to get taller. Seriously, boys like him exist. They buy the urban legend that if you compete in sports where height matters, like volleyball or basketball, your body meets that demand and grows… I think it's BS, though."

"A-ha. Which is why you don't bother with any extracurriculars."

"Let's not go into that. But yeah, Fuyunami is about my height… I don't know if he thought we were buddies or what, but he approached me at the start of the school year—that's when he told me Kodo was mentally immature. Maybe hanging around with other short boys gave him no comfort because he distanced himself from me pretty quickly. After that, he made friends with guys with more solid builds, like Higuma."

"Ah. How do I put it… Seems like his childhood friend wasn't the only mentally immature one—not terribly romantic."

"Then there's Mizaki, a member of the art club… Oh, right. I almost forgot, Yuba was on the baseball team."

"Mizaki. Yuba. Both names I'm hearing for the first time."

"Yeah—Mizaki's full name is Meibi Mizaki. Everyone called him P'raps because of his first name."

"P'raps… Year 1 Class 3 had a unique sensibility when it came to nicknames, I see. By the way, what was yours?"

"I didn't have one."

"Sorry that I asked," Ogi muttered apologetically—I much preferred her smirking and calling me a fool to the look now on her face.

"Mizaki was a real artist and free spirit. He didn't quite fit in. Maybe he, rather than Su'uchi, was the student whose position resembled mine. He didn't take part in the study session, either."

"But did have a nickname."

"I guess. The girls would ask him to draw them during break, so they didn't hate him, at least..."

Which reminded me—Oikura had modeled for him too. I realized, belatedly, that his artistic temperament was actually his way of socializing.

"And Yuba? You seem to have nearly forgotten some of these people—were they that non-notable?"

"Oh, the opposite. Yuba was extra-notable—it's just that he was only on the baseball team on paper. A total ghost member, which is why his name slipped my mind—Shokunori Yuba."

"A ghost member. He must have something to do with this ghostly classroom."

"Um, I don't think so?"

While we ought to be thinking of every possibility, tying an ever-absent sports team member to a supernatural phenomenon was a bit much.

"But he was very notable?"

"Have Kanbaru or Oshino or anyone told you that I tend to skip school a lot?"

"Oh, well, to an extent," Ogi decided to play dumb for whatever reason. So she wasn't always trying to be a know-it-all.

"Yuba was already skipping school more than me during the first term of our freshman year. He'd show up late, leave early, and not even attend classes he didn't like. Kijikiri was absent a lot too, but it was a little different with her... Yeah, the only one who came to school less than Yuba was Senjogahara, who was in and out of the hospital."

"So a true delinquent, unlike your delinquency-lite?"

"I wouldn't say that... But there was something menacing about him. It made you think twice about bringing up his conduct with him..."

He had piercing eyes and a shaved head—"

Well, maybe his head was shaved because he was on the baseball team—ghost member or not.

"How scary. I'd better avoid him during my time here."

"No need to worry. He already quit."

"Oh my. Is that so?"

"Right after that class council meeting—maybe he lost hope, like me. Friends, classmates, unity—maybe he got bored of it all."

What was he up to these days?

I wouldn't have known how to ask him back then, but I felt like I did now.

"By the way, Yuba scored a zero on that final."

"A zero? No, you don't actually mean zero—it's actually a feat to get a zero."

"He turned in a blank test—I think he was trying to make a point. Maybe his act of rebellion makes him suspicious. Leaking the answers then getting a zero yourself would be one way to turn the entire idea of testing into a joke."

"I doubt it—still, people believe in all sorts of things. Did someone who look so threatening have a route for leaking the answers, though?"

"Yeah. We were afraid of him, but somehow, he wasn't isolated—by the way, everyone called him Chin Prop. Because even when he did show up to class, he'd take this defiant pose, propping up his chin—same goes for during the class council meeting."

"So even he had a nickname, but not you. A powerful anecdote."

"…That's everyone in a club or team. All the others went straight home. Not that many, right? Oh, I should mention—a girl named Waritori. She wasn't in any extracurricular but went to a serious-sounding dojo after school. Practical kendo, or something…"

Not that I knew what *practical* meant in that context, but it must've been like the karate school that my little sister Karen attends.

"Shitsue Waritori—at first I thought she was in the kendo club because she sometimes wore her *gi* to class. She was one of the harder girls to approach. Not like she swung a bamboo sword around, but she'd start beating on you with a broom if there was a problem. You could say she was violent, or maybe quick to put her hands on you—or her rod. Only Hishigata got into fights quicker than her."

"Sounds like she lacked mental discipline. An awful lot of mentally immature students in that class."

"Maybe, being practical, her dojo wasn't into the whole discipline thing? Anyway, this was two years ago—during our first year of high school. Of course we were all immature—boys, girls, and not just Kodo, Fuyunami, or Waritori."

Oikura, and me too.

Immature, inexperienced—not fully formed.

If only we'd been aware of that back then—things'd be different two years later.

"Then again," Ogi reminded me, "thanks to that experience you met Miss Shinobu and Miss Hanekawa and are dating Miss Senjogahara. The night is always darkest just before dawn."

"Well, I guess..." She'd wrapped my life up in a neat little package.

"In any case, that was very helpful. Thank you so much. Sorry for interrupting you, but I've closed in on the truth about most everything here. Please, continue. After you had the names of the nineteen most likely suspects written out on the blackboard, what happened?" prodded Ogi, so naturally that I didn't notice—just how casually she'd said *closed in on the truth*.

"As soon as we wrote down the nineteen names, Arikure began to complain—about something we've brought up. The culprit wasn't necessarily one of the nineteen..."

014

"Hold on. It seems like you've already made up your minds that it's one of these students—but that's not necessarily true, is it? Even if Haya-machi wants to go home because she thinks her absence at the meeting proves her innocence."

I didn't think Hayamachi had gone that far, but she didn't bother to defend herself, probably not interested in dealing with Arikure. Still, that'd cast suspicion on everyone who skipped the study session too, including Arikure. Did she love complaining so much that the cost didn't matter?

That wasn't the case, of course... "Anyone who got a high score is suspect, even if they didn't attend the study session," she argued—having gotten a 65, this put her in the clear (but not Hayamachi, with her 92). On the other hand, since the culprit might've done badly on purpose to avoid detection (in the extreme case, submitting a blank sheet and scoring a zero as Yuba did), it was a weak argument.

"Okay, then let's add to the list students who didn't participate but got...say a 90 or above," I proposed grudgingly—a compromise if there ever was one. If anyone insisted that students with low scores were also suspicious, everyone in class would be on the blackboard—what was this, roll call?

The non-participants with scores of 90 or above were as follows, in the same order as before—since there were so few, I wrote them myself rather than bother Gekizaka.

1: Koyomi Araragi (100) 2: Okitada Koma (97) 3: Hitagi Senjogahara (98) 4: Seiko Hayamachi (92) 5: Miawa Mebe (95)

…The list made me realize it included a lot of suspicious characters, like me. Mebe, however, was the most conspicuous. She wasn't seen as someone who got good grades. Meanwhile, my math skills were well known (and even called puzzling), Koma went to cram school, while Senjogahara and Hayamachi were famous for their excellent grades. There stood Mebe in contrast—not that her academics were always sitting below average. Couldn't she have her good days?

Test results were posted for all to see, so everyone knew everyone else's scores. But when we applied specific conditions to narrow it down to just this group, her score did seem somehow unnatural—and Arikure, who'd been the catalyst for this, looked perplexed too. She must not have intended to attack anyone in particular.

As for Mebe, she was at a loss. "Huh? Hold on, naw…"

This seemed like a normal reaction to being questioned, if not suspected, by her classmates. It also looked like she was acting guilty, but that was probably biased.

"No way, I dunno. I've got nothing to do with it."

"Could you not finger a culprit based on nothing, Araragi?" said Oikura, like it was my fault—she was shielding one of her few friends. No one objected because she was, in fact, right: Mebe's 95 didn't prove she'd done anything wrong.

"Wait, hold on," another student raised her hand. It belonged to Ukitobi, who sat behind Hayamachi. "Um…so I probably got the lowest score out of all the girls? Which is why this might sound like an excuse? But I think this math test was pretty hard—could you solve the questions if you knew the answers?"

"…?"

It took me a moment to take her meaning. Maybe she didn't really get what she was saying, either.

Arikure spoke again. "What are you talking about? Of course you could if you knew the answers. You'd just have to memorize them…"

But it seemed she, too, understood Ukitobi's inarticulate remark.

Right, putting aside motive, a method as blatant as getting everyone to memorize the answers didn't work if the culprit was introducing the test's contents to a whole study session. Maybe if it was just two or three people, but with a group of nineteen, someone was bound to report it—in common parlance, you'd have a snitch. This crime couldn't have that many partners; the contents needed to be imprinted unconsciously in the minds of the majority of the participants.

Still, their average was just too high... I mean, everyone other than Igami getting an 80 or higher? Sharing the info in a subtle manner wouldn't lead to such a result.

"But if we started asking that, there'd be no end to it," Ukitobi admitted, as if to dispel the silence her comment had brought on—Kyusu Ukitobi. I want to say she got a 57—the lowest score out of all the girls, or rather, aside from Yuba. Yet she'd made the lone brilliant point in our meeting. I didn't have any sort of impression of her until then—must've been one of those kids who was smart, just bad at studying. The type shows up all the time in manga, but I'd never met one in real life. I couldn't help but stare.

"S-Sorry, Araragi. That wasn't my intention," she apologized. I was admiring, not accusing, her—a sad misunderstanding, but not one I could clear up.

"Actually, why are we assuming there was foul play in the first place?"

This was Daino. It was as if she'd been waiting for everyone to settle down so she could launch into one of her eloquent speeches.

"As someone who worked very hard for this test, I'm finding this very unpleasant, to be frank. The average score of students who participated in a study session exceeding the rest by twenty points is eminently possible. Not to mention, the latter's average was dragged down by a certain somebody." She was referring of course to Yuba—the air grew even chillier when she jerked his chain, but the class menace didn't seem to mind at all. His chin propped in his hand like always, he only glanced at Daino.

"You had Araragi to make up for all the points Yuba lost," Oikura said, her voice dripping with sarcasm—*why*, I wanted to ask. Me, just an innocent bystander! "Still, Miss Daino, you are right. It certainly is unpleasant to be suspected of something you have absolutely no recollection of. That's why we need to clear ourselves of such suspicion."

It was a non-answer—she'd agreed without amending her own view. When you did that, the individual in the weaker position could only back down, and indeed Daino shut up. Reluctantly.

…I'd later come to learn that the meeting hadn't been summoned at the school's behest. It was Oikura's idea from start to finish. She saw the posted test results, felt like something was wrong, calculated the averages herself, compared them, analyzed them, deepened her suspicion—and decided to clear herself of any doubt before any could surface.

As if she couldn't allow even the possibility of suspicion in her life— hence she was dragging all of her classmates into it. How unreasonable, and two years later, I still didn't support her, but I had to acknowledge her sense of pride. Otherwise, she'd come up empty—*given the sorry outcome of all her pride*, maybe she did anyway.

"'If we started asking that, there'd be no end to it'? Well, then I find it hard to believe that any study session took place to begin with."

The outrageous words came from the mouth of Marizumi, one of the students on day duty. A girl who wore a baggy uniform allegedly handed down from an older sister who was on the large side—she didn't seem to care much about fashion, and her hair was as disheveled as if someone had taken random snips at it with a pair of scissors. Normally treated as a weirdo and kept at a distance. Her statement hushed us for a different reason than Ukitobi's.

"There isn't a single thing in this world that we can know for certain. Maybe there wasn't actually any study session at all. How can we be sure those nineteen people aren't colluding to tell the same lie?"

"Don't be ridiculous, Marizumi."

"I'm not being ridiculous. I'm totally serious."

Not even Oikura's glare could move her—while Hyoi Marizumi could interact with our class president and not flinch, the rest of us did. We knew there'd be collateral damage.

"Say something, Araragi… Aren't you the chair?!"

What'd I tell you.

"Um...while I do agree that we should consider all possibilities, the idea that the study session never occurred does seem a little too fantastical..."

"It's the logically improbable truth."

"What?"

I was flummoxed for a moment, unsure of what Marizumi had just said—she was trying to shorten one of Sherlock Holmes's famous lines, but abbreviating it to that degree altered its sense.

"Come on," intervened Oikura, irritated at me. "You're both weirdos, you can communicate."

How Much was going too far with that.

But Marizumi kept a straight face as she responded to the transgression.

"Please don't lump me together with Araragi."

It was a lot to take in.

This was becoming a meeting where we took a close look at just how isolated, or even segregated I was from the rest of the class—when a student quietly raised a hand. I assumed she'd speak next, but she remained silent, her hand up. I realized she was waiting to be called on, so that's what I did as chair.

"Sunahama, do you have something to add?"

"I know it's an aggravating theory to have to refute, but I thought I'd give testimony that the meeting did take place."

Sunahama—Ruise Sunahama sounded absolutely fed up. Like she should never have had to carry out the task. As someone who'd been appointed chair against his own wishes, I wanted to express my sympathy. I kept the feeling to myself because she'd probably reject my overture. "What is it?" I instead encouraged her to continue.

"Well, I was on day duty the day of the math final...so I had to get to school early and get the classroom ready. I remember very well how all of you in the study session," she said, throwing an annoyed glance at Oikura, "had left without cleaning up your mess. I was burdened with putting everything away. Nagagutsu, the boy on day duty, was nowhere in sight, so I ended up getting help from Whip, and Joe, and Hooky, who were also there early. We lined everyone's desks back up, wiped the blackboard clean, took out the trash, and more. Seriously, can't you at least clean up your snacks before going home?!"

This was enough to silence even Oikura—up against the school's closing time, they must've just grabbed their things and headed out...

Sunahama, generally the lazy type, couldn't let the mess stand when it came down to it—the girl was a clean freak, though probably not a germophobe. The study session was inconsiderate to leave the classroom in such a mess the day before a girl like her was on cleaning duty...

Sunahama could be lying had she been all alone, and Marizumi would have cross-examined her, but even the die-hard skeptic would shelve her excessive suspicion if Mebe and Tetsujo ("Joe") and Fukuishi ("Hooky") all gave the same testimony. Testimony from Tetsujo, the class mediator, would be especially credible.

Yet none of the three, namely Miawa Mebe, Komichi Tetsujo, and Tenko Fukuishi, backed up Sunahama with any vigor—they didn't deny her claim, but that was all. Though a little leery of their muted reaction, Sunahama seemed to chalk it up to their fear of Oikura, the leader of the study session. While that made sense for Tetsujo and Fukuishi, what about the sociable, friendly, precious girl on good terms with the class president? Mebe shouldn't have been afraid of Oikura.

"Is that correct, Fukuishi?" I tried to verify just in case. Asking Mebe directly would have been too obvious—as I expected, Fukuishi nodded meekly. She tended to keep to herself and was never assertive, so you could say a simple nod from her signaled strenuous agreement. This was someone so introverted that it took her more than two months into the school year to correct either her teachers or her classmates on the pronunciation of her name, which had mistakenly been entered as *Fukuseki*.

Should I seek Tetsujo's verbal confirmation as well? Or should I go straight to Mebe? She might not go into much detail thanks to the awkwardness just moments ago. In which case, she could remain silent even if I asked her.

As I sat there, lost on what to do, a voice cut in: "Let's say there really was a study session—well, I know it did, since I took part in it."

Higuma hadn't even raised his hand. Was he finally making good on his middle-school stint as student council president? Maybe he couldn't bear to watch my hopeless attempt to lead us forward. I was all for it. In fact, he could take my place if he wanted.

"Let's say someone—directly or indirectly—leaked the answers to the study session. The practical issue with that scenario is that we'd notice. It would feel blatant."

"Not necessarily," Waritori disagreed. Having gone to the same middle school, the grumpy girl was relatively mellow towards him (or at least spared him the rod). "Maybe they did it in a natural way so no one would catch on."

"That'd be possible in a group of two or three, but we're talking more than a dozen people. Someone's going to think it's strange. Getting everyone to memorize the answers outright is clearly out of the question, but slyly imprinting the answers on our unconscious also sounds like a tall order. You can't fool so many people at once."

Higuma, who once dealt with the hoi polloi, which is to say an entire student body when he was student council president, would think so—but in that case, we were left emptyhanded. It'd be like the crime never happened.

But maybe that was fine—and the reason why Higuma was speaking up. Maybe he wanted to settle our meeting that way.

Yet Oikura wasn't having it. She was dead set on continuing the search for the culprit.

"Then let's go over the actual contents of the test. We'll use testimony from everyone who participated in the study session to see how much of what we discussed there appeared on the final."

In order to identify the culprit.

No one leaving the classroom until we did.

015

"So, were you able to figure it out? Sorry, not the culprit, but—the stuff about the overlapping questions."

"No. It'd been a week. It was easy to say, but pinning anything down was impossible because everyone's memories had gotten fuzzy."

A particularly unproductive segment of our already unproductive meeting, it was especially vexing for those of us who skipped the session.

"I bet," Ogi nodded. "That said, the session had an impact on the participants' grades, right? Out of all the stuff they studied…some of it hit the mark, so to speak?"

"Well, yeah. Specifically, when it came to the bigger questions— there were around three that were particularly difficult. We established that most of the participants got them right, while the non-participants tended to get them wrong. I want to say the problems involved limits, indefinite integrals, and probability distributions."

"Is that the kind of stuff you cover during your first year? I thought those don't show up until Math III or Math C."

"It might not make sense to you since you just transferred, but that's what's so ridiculous about Naoetsu High's curriculum. The tests are meant to prepare you for entrance exams from your first year, that's their policy—in fact, college-level higher-math problems crop up on our mid-terms. We do cover the subjects in class, so some people can solve them."

"You, for instance?"

"Well."

Now it sounded like I was bragging. I didn't mean to boast that I could do math…but given how little effort I put into it, I couldn't be modest either. I almost felt guilty, like I wasn't playing by the rules, when she mentioned me.

"As far as those three," I said, "it turned out they did work on similar problems during the study session… We couldn't pin down who brought them up, though."

To be precise, there were a number of suspects, but no evidence. If the person in question denied it, that was that. Denial. Or silence. Naturally, no one wanted to say anything that would cast doubt on themselves—that's where the meeting really started to break down, and there was nothing its incompetent chair could do to stop it.

"At the study session, the nineteen participants taught each other things they didn't understand, working on the kinds of problems that might appear on the test. It wasn't like there were specific 'teachers' and 'students'—but if you had to pick out the leaders, they said there were six."

"Six of them?"

"Right. Oikura, who had the idea for the session. Shui, the class vice president who supported her. The assertive Gekizaka. Shuzawa, who was always eager to teach. Hishigata, the big-sis character. And Higuma, the former student council president. Those six were on the teaching side for the most part. They were the ones who'd have done well on the test anyway—which some people thought made them suspicious."

The thing about those six was that they weren't just smart but help-ful—Oikura may have been domineering, but someone who felt only disdain for others would never organize a study session. Sure, some part of her wanted to show off, and the other five's generosity may have come with its own strings attached, but goodwill fomenting suspicion sounded like a raw deal.

"We also started getting testimony that were clearly lies meant to cover for one another—and it was the chair's job to shut this down and keep the meeting going. I can't say it felt great since their intent wasn't malicious."

"Well-meant lies are trickier than ill-meant truths, huh?"

"More or less. But a lot of problems they tackled in the study session never showed up on the final... If anything, some simpler ones never came up during the session—which does make it seem like it was all just a coincidence."

"A coincidence... Well, yes. That's one possible solution—but not the one you picked."

Ogi was still whispering in my ear and grinning. It was hard to tell whether I was telling the story to her or the other way around given her posture. Did I only think I was narrating to her when in reality, I was listening? How confusing.

But no, this was my tale—and classroom. Wherein I was confined after school that day, wherein various thoughts and feelings were sealed away, and trapped.

"I see, I see. That's what it was—forced to stand in the middle of ugly exchanges, incoherent arguments, and barren squabbles, you developed a real distaste for the creatures called human beings. The well-meant covering-up, buck-passing, and finger-pointing made you despair—and lose sight of justice and generosity and all that. You reached a conclusion: *I don't need friends.* So many classmates lowering their intensity as humans through friendship was traumatizing—right?"

"Wrong."

"Oh?" Ogi sounded surprised by my denial. Puzzled, even. But then, I wasn't sure how certain she'd been about her reasoning. She was, after all, the niece of that man who spoke like he saw through everything.

"If anything, that's how it should have been. That whole discussion should have made me despair—but some part of me still believed in things like justice and truth. Probably because I was young then."

Young then. Not words an eighteen-year-old ought to utter about his sixteen-year-old self—would *childish* have been better?

"In fact, I was vaguely happy."

"Happy?"

"Covering for each other, trying to end the ridiculous meeting asap, eventually even suggesting you might've been to blame—or holding a meeting in the first place to wipe away any doubts, as Oikura had done, wasn't evil to say the least. Maybe you won't understand, it might sound like I'm trying to put on a brave face..."

I paused—hesitated somewhat to say the words. Still, I had to. It was deceitful not to.

"I felt like it was the *right* sort of discussion. We all did, I believe. Even Marizumi, and Yuba, and Kijikiri."

Senjogahara might've been the only exception. I haven't spoken to her about that time—how did she feel about it? No idea.

"That's why, Ogi. It wasn't the discussion that made me despair, but the conclusion. No one saw it coming—we were pursuing what was right, but then made a fatal mistake. That's when I lost sight of my idea of justice."

Lost sight of it—I should have refused from the start, and never let Oikura force the role of chair onto me—shaken Arikure off and gone home, who cares what people might think.

"The conclusion," said Ogi. "But the conclusion was that you couldn't figure out who the culprit was—sure, a disappointing way for your discussion to end, but falling into despair?"

"Yeah. That's the thing. We couldn't figure out who the culprit was—*but that's not to say we didn't decide on one.*"

"Huh?"

"*That was the reason for my despair.* The reality that people will make decisions about everything, even about things they don't know—that's what made me lose hope."

I lost hope.

To the point where I'd say—I don't need friends.

I cut ties.

"I see—I see, I see... In that case," Ogi murmured like she was caressing—or choking me gently, "how about you tell me what happened next? Isn't it about time to leave school? You've been arguing in a locked room for over two hours, everyone must be near their breaking point. And there at that point...what kind of conclusion did you reach? Where did you end up?"

"..."

"Ahhh, I wanna knowww. What could've happened? I hope after all the twists and turns you managed to blunder your way past your plentiful troubles and paltry turmoil and every last one of you were left as happy as could beeeee…"

"…"

I knew it didn't leave us happy—but in that case, how did it leave us?

016

A major reason that actual debates and negotiations don't proceed in the smooth, logical way they do in plays is that *people don't listen to each other*—accepting neither their opponents' statements nor their right to make them, interrupting before any points can be made, cutting others off with their own, yelling over everything from start to finish. Moving down a terrible path that's the precise opposite of smooth logic, it all brings only fatigue. If you forced me nonetheless to produce minutes for the meeting after that, it would look as follows.

"Whatever, this is pointless. Let's just say I'm the culprit and be done with this discussion." "How is that supposed to settle anything? Are you covering for someone? I bet you know who did it, don't you?" "Is there really a culprit here to begin with?" "We said we'd assume there was while we talked about this. Don't try to make us go back on it." "I mean, realistically speaking, could anyone really steal test questions out of the teachers' room?" "You're asking if it's physically possible, not ethically?" "No, I'm talking about guts here." "Don't be ridiculous. What does that have to do with our discussion? Everyone's lying here, that's all." "I'm sorry, can we please all raise our hands before speaking from now on?" "I can't stand listening to any more of this." "Teachers make test questions on computers these days. You could get them without sneaking into the teachers' room if you hacked them." "You watch too many TV shows."

"To repeat myself, I think it was Oikura who taught us the last question on the test during the study session. I'm not certain, though." "If you're not certain, then don't speak up. How would you take responsibility for ruining someone's life? You've always been like that, you know." "Please raise your hand." "Listen, I just want to go home. Can you do this somewhere without me?" "We're not letting you leave." "They might say you did it if you leave." "Fine with me—I just have to be the bad guy, right?" "Gross, stop trying to act cool. What're you trying to pull here? The other day—" "Higuma would never." "You were invited to the study session, but didn't show up. May I ask why?" "Are you really going to suspect me?" "I thought you weren't that kind of person." "Excuse me. Everyone. Please settle down. Let's stay calm." "How are we supposed to be calm?!" "Haven't we had enough? If something's suspicious, why not let sensei handle it?" "I think there's meaning in trying to correct our own mistakes. We ought to handle our own business." "I said I don't have anything to do with this!" "Raise your hand before you speak—" "And anyway, if Araragi got a perfect score, it was possible to solve every problem on the test. Claiming that there had to be cheating or foul play makes no sense." "Ugh. I'm starting to get annoyed. I want to leave already." "Leave if you want. Become the culprit." "What right do you have to talk? You didn't even get the trig problems right." "What about you? Who gets the geometry questions wrong?! You could tell the figures were similar just by looking at them!" "Why don't we do it this way? We put up the names of everyone who got the three big problems right but not the smaller ones, and—" "What'd be the point?" "Why're you acting like that? Stop being so emotional. Let's think about this logically, everyone." "Don't think. Feel." "This isn't the time for jokes, Nagagutsu!" "Senjogahara, you've been quiet this whole time. What do you think?" "I don't know." "Hey, everyone. There's something I want to say." "Say it later!" "Keep your voice down. It's pathetic." "Pathetic!" "What are you scared of? Feeling guilty much?" "The one thing we've established is that I didn't do it!" "You're the only one dumb enough to believe that." "Excuse me? I'd like you to take that back." "Araragi, you need to lead us." "Easy for you to say—" "Couldn't it have been plain cheating? Like a whole group of students cheating." "That'd still implicate someone from the study session." "And the other subjects? There weren't polarized scores for them, were there?" "It's not like we had study sessions for them. With a little thought you'd realize that yourself." "Why should I know?" "So, the culprit didn't steal any other tests? Why not steal tests for other subjects while you're there?" "Stop acting like you're an expert. What do you think you are, a detective?" "Then anyone with high scores in other subjects is suspicious?" "Why did we only have a study session for math to begin with? I would've attended a history one." "Obviously because it'd look bad if the math average was low for a class whose homeroom teacher taught math. In other words, it's about appearances. Our dear class president wanted to score points with sensei." "That's not why. It's because mathematics is the most beautiful of all the disciplines." "You're literally the only one who thinks that. What does that even mean? Beautiful? So, you just felt like it." "It always has to be about you, huh?" "I hate math, personally." "You don't understand the beauty of math?" "Schoolwork isn't about love or hate. Why are you even at Naoetsu High?" "What, jealous?" "What'd you just say?!" "Please don't fight." "We're not fighting, it's because a certain someone is spouting nonsense that it's weird for me to be at this school—" "I didn't go that far!" "I don't care about math, I'm a humanities person. I'm planning on applying to a school that doesn't have a math exam." "Oh, me too." "Stop trying to piggyback on other people's comments, will you?" "Why are you lashing out at me?" "All of you have gotten so quiet all of a sudden. What gives?" "I'm just staying silent because there's nothing for me to say." "I have an alibi!" "An alibi, when we don't even know when the crime took place?" "I have someone to testify. On my behalf. Someone who'd guarantee I'd never do such a thing." "What about motive? Would someone do this just for kicks?" "Generally speaking, the culprit wouldn't stand to benefit if the class's average score rose. Wouldn't you normally be happier if the overall score went down?" "Then this isn't a general or normal case." "Are you trying to say something here? Out with it." "I'm saying there isn't, and there's nothing I want to say." "These are leading questions." "Are you all done yet? I'm sick and tired of this. I had plans to go on a date today." "Wait, you two are still going out?" "It's my call, isn't it?" "Can I take a nap?" "Come on, let's go through and think about what happened in order. It started with news about a study session getting passed around in class, and—" "Why didn't that note make it to me? I'd have never found out if Hishigata hadn't told me. Were you trying to avoid me? Are you bullying me? Do you not like me?" "No, of course it wasn't intentional… It's just that you weren't there…" "Let's all get along, okay?" "It's too late for that. I mean, people think I did it! I haven't done anything wrong!" "There's no smoke without fire." "You know, that's the thing with you." "Oh?! That's my line!" "Yeah, why ever have a study session! Studying is something you do alone!"

…No one was raising a hand at this point. It'd become an assembly where everyone just said what they felt like saying. The template of a fruitless discussion, a space where every line sounded typical and devoid of any creativity. I mentioned plays earlier, and at this point it was like a bunch of hammy actors rehearsing their flat delivery.

We were managing to hurt one another, but without speaking our minds. A true wasteland. A true hellhole.

I remained on top of things as long as it was still one discussion, but once smaller squabbles started popping up, it got impossible to control. I don't mean to justify myself, but regardless of who was chair, it was probably the fated outcome—and in the chaos, I weaved my way through the rows to where Oikura sat glumly.

"This isn't going any further. There's no way to get it back under control." It was 5:58, and I gave her my notice—or rather, declaration of surrender. What I'd been defeated at, I didn't know, but I certainly couldn't fulfill the role assigned to me, out of spite or not, by the class president. "Give me a break. We should end this before it gets any worse."

"What are you whining for? You got a better score than me and you want to give up?"

Oikura glared at me—but her glare lacked the intensity it had at the beginning. She was exhausted, too. While my surrender was nothing more than me throwing in the towel, I also told myself that I was rescuing her.

"That's right. I'm giving up. It's hopeless."

"I'm not letting anyone leave…until we find the culprit."

"There's no way. Everyone's going home once the closing bell rings.

You must know that yourself," I leveled with her—maybe I shouldn't have. Someone had to say it, but even if I didn't, Tetsujo or Shui could. That it was me of all people, though, incited her.

I'd forgotten.

Just how much Oikura hated me.

I should have passively, irresponsibly ceded the awful task to someone else. Was I really dispensing advice to her out of some sense of duty? Or was I hoping for something? She simply saw me as a rival, and down deep, didn't really hate me? Was I so conceited that I thought we'd be on good terms one day—since she was just playing hard to get?

The truth was different.

With heartfelt contempt, which surpassed her exhaustion, she spat, "I hate you."

She stood—and made a beeline to the teacher's desk, leaving me behind. She slammed her hands on it to get everyone's attention. She did, yet the commotion didn't abate—which is why she shouted:

"Everyone!"

With this, the room finally fell silent, but everyone looked gloomy and disgusted, and wasn't hiding it—they must have thought that a new chair at this point would do nothing to tighten all the screws that had come loose. I myself felt like reorganizing the meeting would only bring us back to square one—any change in chairs should have come earlier. Just as I expected, Koma, the first student to have complained, was about to lodge another complaint—but Oikura held even that at bay.

"Everyone!" she repeated. "I think we've discussed the matter sufficiently."

Oh, I thought, forgetting her parting show of contempt and breathing a sigh of relief. So Oikura, too, had given up and wanted to wrap this meeting. As the one who'd convened the class council—or perhaps who'd arranged the study session—she was going to draw the line and bring this to a close. We hadn't come to a conclusion, nor had we found the culprit, nor had the culprit come forward, but we all did our best, came together—she'd spout such lines, maybe make us give ourselves a round of applause, and let everyone go. Yes, the mood would be awkward and unpleasant in our class for a while, but she was going to choose the best way to settle this...

Nope, no such luck. She would search for this culprit until the bitter end. A smart girl like her didn't need me to tell her that we had to bring things to an end—but dead set on coming to a conclusion no matter what, if adjourn we must—she said, "So I'm going to take a vote."

Foolish—and irredeemable.

The worst option.

This proclamation.

"We'll decide who the culprit is by majority vote."

017

I still wonder—just what kind of result was Oikura hoping for, anyway? What kind of conclusion did she think her proposal would bring us to? Was a conclusion all that mattered to her, even if it wasn't the truth?

You can decide even if you don't know.

Finger, even if things are unclear.

Then again, she said it from the start. The meeting would continue until we found the culprit, or the culprit came forward—she never said it'd go on "until we know who the culprit is."

"...I always tended to be the class loner. One time in middle school, we even had a council meeting about it. Like, to acculturate me, which does sound absurd in retrospect, and as the discussion unfolded, it started to make less and less sense. At some point it devolved into a session where everyone criticized me and my uncooperativeness. I guess meetings easily lose direction that way. I didn't think much of it because by preferring to be alone, I was partly to blame. I had no complaints about the conclusion, either: *Araragi should work to get along with everyone.* But choosing a culprit based on a majority vote?"

"I see what you mean—but can't wholly dismiss the idea. Jury systems are common in the West, and a lay judge system is taking root even in Japan. Of course, juries require a unanimous decision, and even lay decisions aren't made by simple majority... But if you did discuss everything, maybe Oikura made the right decision," Ogi whispered by my ear, as if to console me. If I wasn't careful, I might let her—but no. That's not how it was. She was just going over the theory—what happened was that we made the wrong decision. I ought to have stopped Oikura, even if it meant slugging her.

Yet the majority vote proceeded.

Not even with a secret ballot, but with a show of hands. Year 1 Class 3 was asked to raise our hand for one of the names she called out in order of roll-call number.

Who thinks no. 2, Koyomi Araragi, is the culprit.

Please raise your hand.

"Huh, really, is that what happened... And the majority spoke and framed you as the culprit—now I see why it wasn't the discussion but the conclusion that made you despair. Yes, it makes sense for someone to lose faith in humanity in that case. Please accept my sincerest sympathies."

"No. Oikura was the only one who voted for me."

"Wha?"

"The majority raised their hand when she called no. 6—Sodachi Oikura."

It brought everything to an end.

No need to call out the remaining students' names and ask for a show of hands—even if she'd tried, I doubt Oikura could even speak.

I'll never forget the look of despair on her face. That despair—must have snagged me as well.

No one ever saw Oikura at Naoetsu High again. Not because she dropped out like Yuba—she was still registered. But she stopped coming to school entirely, for classes or for tests. Despite her absence, she received some sort of special treatment thanks to her smarts and wasn't held back, and apparently was matriculated in one of the third-year classes—though no one knew which one.

Some said she reaped what she sowed, while others more bluntly called it digging her own grave—and yes, in hindsight, what else did she expect from a majority vote? She'd confined everyone after school, trapping them in a space high on the discomfort index, and grilled us mercilessly. Something was very wrong with you if you thought it wouldn't result in malice—but realizing that people hate you isn't easy. Just as I hadn't grasped, in any true sense, her violent contempt for me.

I could only watch as she walked into the jaws of death—I couldn't save her. I doubt she wanted me to, but still—shouldn't I have known? How else could it have turned out? Was I hoping to witness the fall of a girl who'd been hostile to me forever? Wasn't I just wishing for that look of despair on her face, which'd be so vindicating for me? No—I was fully convinced I'd be the culprit in a majority vote, and that might have been Oikura's plan. It didn't seem too terrible, actually. Someone who obviously wasn't the culprit being named as the culprit offered a clean conclusion that left the least behind to fester—so much the better since the heinous election would end at no. 2…

My naive read on the situation made me turn a blind eye. In that sense, no. 1 being Ashine also led me astray—no way they'd treat a polite, handsome guy, the peacemaker from start to finish, as a criminal.

But more importantly—the responsibility for her ruin did lie with me if I was the reason why she grew intransigent and ran amok.

I don't mean to say that was why.

I don't—but I started taking even more days off, played hooky more often. Because not seeing Oikura at school left me with this viscous sensation that was a little like guilt.

Also, since that day.

I never once got a perfect score in math.

"Do you really need to feel so responsible? You said from the beginning—Oikura was a prime suspect. Maybe all those votes for her were fair and impartial."

"I'm sure some hands went up for that reason… It was an excellent excuse, but at least a few must've believed it for real—I tried telling myself that, but remember what I said? She decided on her own to hold the meeting, not because anyone asked her. It was meant to clear her of suspicion *because* she was a prime suspect… Ironically, it ratified those doubts, but why call for a meeting if she was the culprit? That one fact is enough for me to declare that it wasn't her."

"Heh. I see. Declare, huh?"

"…Anyway, the class council ended up giving birth to a false charge—which, at the end of the day, was karmic retribution. Still—"

"It's more like being hoist by your own petard. Blowing yourself up with a bomb that you set. Hah, what a clown, when I put it that way."

Ogi laughed. It was laughable—Oikura, along with the rest of us, had been in a farce.

Even so, I said.

"Seeing a false truth get forged—witnessing such a stupid decision made everything feel so messed up. It messed *me* up. The majority, most of the students, raised their hands as one, without any prior arrangement or agreement, not even through glances. That moment when they decided on the truth, and justice was settled—is the scariest thing I ever saw. Speaking of losing sight, that was when."

Losing sight?

No, I lost so much more.

"Until then, I believed in something like the idea of rightness—that there are things in the world that are right, and that it's a question of if you can do them or not. But that's when I learned that no matter how wrong or cruel or stupid, as long as enough people agree, it *becomes right.*"

If a million people approve, even an obvious mistake, a foolish failure, becomes right—the heavens revolved around the Earth so long as everyone in the world believed it.

Majority vote, the ugliest formula ever invented by humanity. The most unjust, unequal formula.

But that was justice.

Everyone said it was right—so it was right.

"Ahaha. What an extreme argument—madly rushing from one extreme to the other. That's no different from saying everything that sells well is trash."

"Maybe. Maybe I'm being dumb. But if a million people showed up to agree, even my dumb opinion becomes right. I learned that you can mass-produce all the justice you could ever want—that justice arises from numbers. It's about establishing a majority. That's why I chose solitude over establishment."

I don't need friends—they'll only lower my intensity as a human.

That's—what I ended up saying.

"It was the only way I could protect my own sense of things. My only choice was not belonging to any faction or gang. Of course, it all came tumbling down during spring break two years later... I know it ended up going long, but this has been the tale of Koyomi Araragi. Thank you for listening, Ogi. You know, you said it. It was nothing, now that I've talked about it. I feel all better now."

"Well that's no good."

"Hm?"

"I'm saying you shouldn't be feeling all better quite yet."

Stepping away from my neck area at last, she quietly appeared in front of me. It'd been a while since I last got a head-on view of her smile—so cute, it was almost uncanny.

"We can't leave if the tale ends with Oikura not being the culprit—have you forgotten? We need to identify the culprit to exit this classroom. The culprit you couldn't identify that day—through majority vote."

We'll have to decide instead.

Or so said Ogi.

Now that she mentioned it, yes. Wait, no, that was only her hypothesis... "You mean Oikura's deep-seated grudge from that day created this classroom? That does make me getting trapped in here seem like fate."

Oikura.

Had she still not forgiven me?

Was she the same as that day?

Did she hate me as much as ever?

I hate you.

"Nah, she's probably forgotten about you. That's how things go."

"Then what about this classroom?"

"Didn't I tell you? I think your mind gave birth to it. That's my definition—a classroom created by your mind, by your regret. If you'd pinned down the culprit that day, Sodachi Oikura wouldn't have met her downfall. And—"

You wouldn't have lost your sense of justice.

It's your regret that created this classroom.

If the school's closing time had never come that day—5:58.

That's where the clock was stopped. Stopped time—suspended.

Time continued to stagnate, for over two years.

"You've been after that sense of justice ever since you lost it that day—and created this classroom to retrieve it."

"I did?"

Was that possible? It's not as if I had Shinobu's power to generate matter, so for me to create a room would be—but then again, every aberration has its reasons. In that case, me being the reason—was enough.

"Okay, but justice?"

We were talking about two years ago. How could we figure out the culprit now, when our whole discussion came up empty back then? Were Ogi and I going to be trapped here forever, unable to leave school for eternity?

No, forget about me, but Ogi didn't deserve this. Even if our misadventure started with her, it was too much for me to bear. In that case, there was only one course of action. No matter how impossible, we had to do what had to be done.

"Okay, we'll redo that meeting," I said. "This time we can't just find someone guilty, we have to find the true culprit—"

"Er, no? If it's the true culprit you want, I already know."

Ogi blithely thwarted—my determination.

"*And I think you know, too*—who really should have been condemned at the class council. The one who ruined your, as Oikura might put it, sacred math final. That much was clear—from hearing you speak. You feel awful about what happened to Oikura because unconsciously, you know who the culprit is. Otherwise you wouldn't have *told it that way.*"

"Told it—what way?"

"You deliberately hid one piece of info in your account *to avoid casting doubt on a certain individual.* In that sense, you're covering for the true culprit, whether you mean to or not. You're covering up the truth. That's why you feel so guilty about Oikura, who had to take the blame."

"...?"

Deliberately? Covering up? Don't be ridiculous, what was I hiding? I'll never forget what happened in that meeting. Whatever I might try to hide, I couldn't.

"Right, you couldn't. It tells me your unconscious knew the identity of the culprit—you've been averting your gaze from it the whole time. Just like Tsubasa Hanekawa used to."

"…"

I didn't get it.

What was this girl saying?

What did this girl know?

"I don't know anything—you're the one who does, my dear senior. Koyomi Araragi."

"I—"

"And with a clearing of the throat, the great detective gathered them all and began—but there's no great detective here, so I guess I'll do it instead. Ahem! Why don't we begin the solemn business of figuring out whodunnit, in part to mourn the idiot, dunce, and fool brought to ruin by the weight of her own sins, Sodachi Oikura, as it is what she too wanted. Oh, I nearly forgot, something does need to be said if this is a whodunnit. Convention is important, you see, whether you're banishing aberrations or solving mysteries."

Ogi snickered at my puzzled look.

Ogi Oshino, Mèmè Oshino's niece and transfer student, turned around—then struck a pose like a kabuki actor, facing no one but the blackboard. I couldn't catch her expression because of the angle, but I could almost see it.

"I challenge the reader."

018

"Komichi Tetsujo is the culprit."

No preface, no pause, no build-up.

The words casually slipped out of Ogi Oshino.

In response—to hearing that the culprit was someone so "unexpect-ed"—I was surprisingly unsurprised. It did nothing to move me, my heart was unshaken. Why? *It should have been news to me.*

Could some part of me have known, like Ogi said? That the crime was *hers*? And that Sodachi Oikura was a victim, the patsy?

"Shall I continue?" asked Ogi.

"...Yeah," I managed.

She didn't need to say more, having spoken the name—but I had a duty to listen. A duty, as the tale's narrator, to hear the truth of the mat-ter—to listen rather than tell.

"What made you suspicious of Tetsujo? She was basically in the same position as the rest of us. Sure, her name came up a few more times than average, but couldn't you also say—the less they're mentioned, the more suspicious? If I was being arbitrary."

"It wasn't the frequency—my initial doubt involved how many of you there were."

"How many of us?"

"Thirty-eight. The number of characters who appeared in your tale—I counted them. Then I counted them again, so I'm pretty certain. But it doesn't make sense."

"It doesn't? Why not? It seems like a normal number of students."

"It's not that."

Ogi took a look around the Year 1 Class 3 classroom. As if to inspect every empty seat—as if to observe them.

"I believe you said the following, when you spoke of just how isolated you were: whether it was groups of two, three, or four, you were always the one left over. That doesn't make sense. If there were thirty-eight students in your class, that number is divisible by two, and two students would be left over for groups of three and four. There are no situations in which just one student is."

Agh—I couldn't even manage a response.

She was right—and it wasn't even math, it was simple arithmetic.

"Mathematics isn't my strong suit. Math III or Math C are far beyond me. Still, I can do division. Well, let's look for a number that leaves a remainder of one, whether we divide it by two, three, or four. Does that just barely count as mathematics? We simply have to find a common multiple of the three numbers, then add one."

"..."

"The least common multiple of 2, 3, and 4 is 12. 12 plus 1 is 13. An odd coincidence, given that you were in Class 1-3, but nowhere near enough students. Let's go to the next common multiple—which we can find by multiplying by 2. 24. 24 plus 1 is 25. A fair number of classes around Japan are that size, but you described the study session as comprising about half of the class. You couldn't call 19 of 25 'about half.' So let's give it one more try. Multiply the least common multiple by 3 to get 36—plus one. 37. Thirty-seven. Isn't that the correct number of students in Year 1 Class 3?"

"There was one outsider in there with us? But think about Oikura's decree. She specifically said no outsiders allowed, so how—"

"True. There shouldn't be. But her rule could be taken to mean that it's fine *if you're a part of Year 1 Class 3*. For instance..."

Its homeroom teacher.

Ogi spoke the words with a nasty smile.

"As you noted at the very beginning—you found every last member of Year 1 Class 3 assembled there. Yes, and you used the word *member*. Not every *student* of Year 1 Class 3. Of course. You could call your homeroom teacher a member of Year 1 Class 3. It wouldn't be odd for a teacher to attend a class council."

"…"

"From there, going back over your introductions of the thirty-eight, you used words like 'student,' 'kid,' 'boy,' 'girl,' 'uniform,' 'classmate,' 'first-year,' 'high schooler,' 'club member,' and so on to describe all of them *except for one*—that being Komichi Tetsujo. And so, through a fundamental element of both mystery novels and mathematics, the process of elimination—and of non-contradiction—I could identify Tetsujo as the culprit. Oops, should I be using her title? Should I say Tetsujo-sensei? Then again, it sounds like she went by Joe, and you yourself didn't bother, either. She seems pretty laidback, so I guess it's fine?"

Ogi grinned, then continued.

"When you said she was on the softball team, you probably meant as its adviser—now really, you talk in such misleading ways. Oh, but you did call her above-the-fray. Was that meant to be allusive, now that I think about it?"

"Nah, I wasn't trying to be."

"Haha, is that so."

"…"

"Furthermore, when the three girls brought you to the classroom, I said that all of the seats must have been filled, to which you said that technically, Arikure, Kijikiri, Tone, and Oikura's were open—but that doesn't seem right, does it? *It'd be strange unless your seat was open, too—* or could anyone have taken in it? Like, say, your homeroom teacher?"

It's not that Oikura wouldn't let you sit, you couldn't to begin with— remarked Ogi.

"Just corroborating evidence, of course. A small detail. So, tell me. Is my deduction, that Komichi Tetsujo was not a student but a teacher, completely off the mark? Am I just nitpicking?"

"You got it. You're right—there were thirty-seven students in Year 1 Class 3. There were thirty-eight people at the class council, including

Tetsujo, our homeroom teacher. But," I said, as if I needed to give a forceful rebuttal—as if I'd been fingered as the culprit. "Just because Tetsujo was our teacher doesn't mean she's automatically the culprit. All it means is that we had a friendly teacher who'd sit in a student's seat during a class council meeting—"

"The mediator! What a clever way to refer to a homeroom teacher..."

Ogi laughed, almost ignoring me.

Her attitude made me lean forward in my chair. "Hey—"

"Of course, I would have suspected your homeroom teacher even if Tetsujo wasn't there, even if her name never came up at all. Someone said it as the meeting began to break down, right? Could anyone really find out the questions on a test before it's given?"

Ogi stepped toward my leaning body—our faces were far too close, and I shrank back. Weak...

"It'd be so hard. Sneak into the teachers' room? Hack the computer system? What kind of culprit would do something like that just for kicks?"

"Teachers are free to go in and out of the teachers' room, but that's not enough of a reason to doubt—"

"Please don't play dumb, not after how far we've come—this, too, was brought up as the meeting broke down, if I'm not mistaken. Year 1 Class 3's homeroom teacher was a math teacher. Komichi Tetsujo taught math. Given that position, it's not an issue of prior knowledge. *She was making the questions.* There was zero risk."

Ogi really had listened carefully, to even the smallest details.

An honest-to-God good listener.

"*Even if that was true,*" I said, "how could she get the questions she made to the study session? Tetsujo didn't take part in it. Not that a teacher ever would...unlike with class council meetings. So how did she leak the info? Through whom?"

"She didn't have to go through anyone, and neither did the information. Who was it again, Higuma? They'd have found it unnatural if someone tried to leak the test questions. It was only his impression, so I'm not sure if I should buy it, but his testimony is worth considering. One more thing, an important point—why not leak all of the questions if you're going to leak? I don't see a reason to leak just part of the test."

"If you're going to say that, why leak them in the first place?"

"*That will be made clear later.* The logical answer would be that Tetsujo didn't disseminate the information to the study session—it was nothing but a wholesome place of mutual learning and betterment. Just as Oikura wanted."

"Then why did the nineteen students in the session—"

"Simple. Tetsujo was in a position to create the test questions. In that case, *she just needed to have them match up with what the study session covered.*"

"!"

An exclamation mark, on cue—but I still wasn't shocked. The very picture of composure, my mind accepted Ogi's "surprising truth."

"Sunahama, on day duty, complained about having to clean up after the study session early in the morning, right? She had Tetsujo and Mebe and Fukuishi help her. What kind of cleaning up did they do? Come on, won't you tell me? How did they clean up after them?"

"They threw out bags of snacks and straightened the desks."

"The other thing!"

"And erased the blackboard, I guess."

I'd hesitated to reply—the blackboard.

Yes, in heavy use during the class council meeting—but any study session had to involve examples on a blackboard too. In other words, the participants had left traces of their session on the blackboard for all to see.

The surface of a blackboard is only so large, of course, so they must have written and erased and written again. Not everything they put there would have been legible, but—

"You'd be able to read a *portion* of it," I admitted.

"Yes indeed. And if you knew what they went over at the study session, you could create matching test questions. It was the day of the final, of course. Even if you could change the questions, I'm sure you could only change a *portion* of them anyway."

So only a portion of the questions lined up with the study session because she couldn't get a full picture of it from the blackboard—and because there wasn't enough time.

"We had math during second period, so she'd have reworked the questions during our P.E. test... Could we chalk Mebe's high score up to the fact that like Tetsujo, she saw the questions while she was cleaning up before class—and they were imprinted on her mind?"

"Right," Ogi concurred. "She must have realized during the meeting, which explains her discomfort. She must not have wanted to slip up and say anything that'd lump her in with the participants. Of course, there were also some students like Sunahama and Fukuishi who looked at the blackboard and didn't learn a thing. I think we should call that a show of talent from Mebe."

True—not every student can get math questions right just by knowing them ahead of time.

"And Tetsujo must have thought so too—I bet she was surprised when the average score went up by so much. Only Igami participated in the session and got a bad score, while everyone else got an 80 or higher? Really? What really blindsided her, though, was Oikura holding this whodunnit meeting. I'm sure Tetsujo's heart was pounding the whole time—she thought her crime might come to light."

"...To the point that she couldn't mediate between me and Oikura."

I pulled back—Ogi creeped toward me. She continued, a desk in between us, but close enough for me to feel her breath.

"We might also surmise that she took part in the meeting out of fear. In order to lead the discussion if it came down to it, you see. Not that she should've been worried. No one is going to think that the teacher, of all people, is the perp—it'd be like the detective or the police being the culprit of a mystery novel, a real blind spot for people. Then again, stories where the detective or the police are the culprit have been done to death. Seriously, did no one suspect the teacher?"

"No one."

"Other than you."

"Well, if you're going to say I did, I'm sure everyone else did too. But we were trying to convince ourselves there was no way."

Were we relieved, then? That the majority vote came to an end at suspect no. 6? No, it didn't matter how far down the roll we went, our homeroom teacher wasn't on it. Her name would never have been called.

"What's left—um, the motive?" said Ogi. "The motivation behind the crime. Not leaking the questions, exactly, but whatever it is she did."

"Oh… You promised you'd make that clear later, does that mean you have that figured out, too?"

"It'd be a nonsensical crime for a student. Even for thrills, it's hard to figure out a motive. Raising the average score would have the relative effect of worsening the grade deviation among the students, one of the most important methods of ranking them. If I had to come up with something, maybe boosting the reputation of whoever—Oikura, in this case? But then, why convene the class council? As you said, it'd be something she absolutely shouldn't do. But there's one person whose reputation rose if the class average rose—that being math teacher Tetsujo, also Year 1 Class 3's homeroom teacher. It would reflect well on her skills of instruction and guidance—and that was her motive."

"But in that case…"

In that case, she could just tell us during class, "This will appear on the final." Why go to the trouble of lining the test up with her students' predictions—

"No, no. She'd be found out, if she did it in class. It had to be subtle—though she went a little too far. Three questions is too much. She should've kept it to one or two swapped in at the last second—seems she underestimated the academic abilities of her students."

Yeah. It also meant she made light of her own abilities as an instructor—her own class had managed to come up with the problems.

And as a result—

She lost one of her best students.

"Anything else, Araragi-senpai?"

"Why would there be…"

"Ah. Then why don't we get going."

With that—beaming back at me and my curt answer, Ogi hopped away and made her way to the door, with light footsteps, insouciant.

"You can leave now," she put her hand on the door and said.

"Yeah…"

I followed Ogi's footsteps with plodding ones. Looking down at my wristwatch, I saw that it was 5:58, the exact same time as the classroom clock. The angle of the hands agreed at last, like the stars aligning. Even a broken clock is right two times a day—no.

The clock hanging in the classroom—must have started ticking again.

Like the gig was up.

Because Ogi—because I had come out with the answer.

Because I went and identified the culprit—time resumed.

The bell announcing the end of the day would be ringing soon.

"What do you mean, I can leave?"

"Excuse me?"

"Well, it was an odd way to put it... What did you mean by that?"

"Oh. Do you not know? Vampires need permission from someone inside a building or a room in order to enter it."

"Right... I've never experienced that myself, though."

"Well, Shinobu is a special model. But since you couldn't exit here rather than enter, I thought I'd try telling you that you could. A little incantation meant to put you at ease."

"You're almost making it sound like you were the one who locked me in."

"Don't be silly. I'd never lock you in a room. Why would I ever," Ogi defended herself with a chuckle. "You were trapped by your own past. This whole time, for two years. Isn't that right?"

"..."

"Just a guess, of course. But think of what it must feel like for a teacher, someone meant to symbolize fairness to a student, to do something dishonest—and a friendly, trusted teacher who acted as the class mediator, at that. Who could blame you for closing off your heart, out of a sense of betrayal? It destroyed one student, after all—she's been promoted despite her attendance partly because of her excellent marks, but isn't it also atonement on Tetsujo's part?"

"Atonement? No, it's an excuse. She just wants to believe that she's a decent human being," I muttered, in a harsher tone than I expected. As if to distract from this, I put a hand on the classroom door to open it—but Ogi gently laid her hand on top of mine a moment before I could.

What happened next.

You need to tell me.

Until you do—I won't let you leave.

She seemed to be saying this.

"What made me give up…"

So I did. Digging up memories I'd locked away, unable to ever forget, of the meeting that had taken place in this classroom two years ago, on July fifteenth—

Recalling—that majority vote.

The true reason I gave up on justice.

I didn't despair because of the meeting itself—because of the vote itself.

It wasn't the aspect of truth itself.

All right, next.

No. 6.

Who thinks the culprit is me—Sodachi Oikura.

Please raise your hand.

"I gave up on justice because…"

I gave up on justice because.

"There, among all my classmates designating Oikura as the culprit…was Tetsujo, our teacher, her hand raised straight. That's why."

The bell rang.

The door opened.

Now let's go home—the meeting is over.

You can't stay at school forever.

019

The epilogue, or maybe, the punch line of this story.

The next day, I was roused from bed by my little sisters Karen and Tsukihi, who, unlike me, still believe that such a thing as immutable justice exists in the world, and I headed to school—on foot, as I still couldn't buy a new bicycle. I guess it was good for my health. On a whim, I stopped by the AV room before heading to my classroom. More precisely, next to the AV room.

And, as if it was the most natural thing.

There was no empty classroom—not even the dead space from Ogi's notebook. Just the AV room, a plain corner room, not even longer than average by the length of one classroom.

Ah, another supernatural phenomenon, I thought, but no, that couldn't be it. Ogi had just measured wrong, that's all. She'd created a nonexistent space in the process of mapping out the school's buildings.

There was nothing here.

Nothing happened here.

No hidden or locked room, no whodunnit.

No surprising truth—no class council and no majority vote.

All of it was in the past, over and done.

Still, I thought, I ought to let Ogi know—I'd have Kanbaru connect us next time we met since I didn't have her contact info. Musing, I moved buildings and headed to my classroom.

I passed by the teachers' room on the way... Komichi Tetsujo wouldn't be there. No, she didn't quit out of a guilty conscience or get dismissed after her wrongdoing was uncovered. It was for an auspicious reason, she was pregnant and on maternity leave—loved by her students, she received congratulations from all as she left. She wouldn't be coming back to school before I graduated, even if you didn't take into account the time she'd take off to care for her baby. I doubt Tetsujo and I would ever, in our lives, meet again.

I had no feelings about that.

After I saw her raise her hand from the back that day two years ago, she'd stopped being a teacher or a grownup to me—to be honest, I'm unsure how much of the truth of this case I'd known, whether in my conscious or subconscious mind, but *if there was a reason I never spoke about her like she was a teacher* throughout my tale, that would be it. Under no circumstances was I trying to cover for her, as Ogi put it. I bet it'd only net me an insincere reply if I told her, though. *Ohhh, is that so? Verrry educational.*

I walked past the teachers' room with no change in my stride. I arrived at my current, third-year classroom—but as I tried to enter, I nearly bumped into Hanekawa, who'd just exited.

"Ah. 'Morning, Araragi."

"Oh. Good morning, Hanekawa."

"Bad timing."

"Excuse me?"

"It might be better if you don't go in there."

"What?"

"Hup!" Hanekawa separated me from the classroom by pushing me away from it with both palms—the cutest palm strikes ever. Once we'd moved back several feet, she whispered into my ear, "Did you ever notice the one empty seat in our class, Araragi?"

"Hm? Mm. Yeah. I guess... I thought it was a back-up chair, what about it?" I replied, still clueless—an empty seat? "Why, did you come to class today to find a ghost sitting in it? You'll need more than a ghost to scare me off at this point."

"Not a ghost—a person was sitting in it. A classmate who hasn't come to school in ages suddenly decided to show up today."

"Huh…really? So then the seat belonged to this person. That's a surprise, we had one more classmate than I thought. But why does that mean I shouldn't go inside?"

"Because it's Miss Oikura," Tsubasa Hanekawa said. Solemnly, with a concerned look that seemed to presage a tragedy that was about to befall me. "Sodachi Oikura—seems to have been studying at home for two years, and as if in exchange for Miss Tetsujo, she's back at school. You two are on bad terms, right?"

CHAPTER TWO
SODACHI RIDDLE

S ODACHI OI KURA

001

Sodachi Oikura hated me. With the kind of deep hatred you might feel for a homewrecker—in fact, I couldn't help but wonder what you had to do to become so hated, or to hate so much. Think about her position. Hating a specific person to that degree had to be pretty stressful. Granted, I'm not the most likable person, neither too amiable nor attractive—but even then, I couldn't recall doing anything that deserved being glared at with eyes like hers. Well, I suppose there's one reason I'm aware of, which is that I was better than her at math—but it's not as if that actually harmed her. And in retrospect, it feels like her glare was set on me from the first time I met her in Year 1 Class 3's classroom, soon after we entered Naoetsu High—does that sound paranoid? It's not as if she had access to my entrance exam results, I don't even know myself what I got. And anyway, in terms of the final linked to that fateful meeting, I only happened to get a perfect score that time around. It wasn't consistent—she must've had good days during first term and outscored me on quizzes, and math is a broad, catch-all term to begin with. Surely she understood some things better than me.

   She couldn't have honestly believed I was to blame for no one calling her Euler. Come to think of it, did a high school girl really want such a nickname? Wasn't it just a pretext? No one can dispute Euler's greatness as a mathematician, but what you go by is something else entirely. I respect Tsubasa Hanekawa, for example, but have no desire to be called Tsubasa or Hanekawa.

Oikura must have misunderstood me.

Just as I misunderstood her.

Misunderstandings tend to multiply.

That's what I think—but there's this other striking thought I have, something else that I think is strange, which is that while Sodachi Oikura hated me, I in no way hated Sodachi Oikura. I think that's very unusual. In general, it's really hard not to hate someone who hates you. Not that I liked her, of course—I'm not twisted enough to adore someone who glares at me all the time and subjects me to prickling acts of spite that might not be outright attacks. Such high-level twistedness isn't for me. Still, while I found her attitude dislikable, I couldn't say I hated it.

I couldn't.

Why not?

A far more serious question, in a way, than why she hated me so: why couldn't I hate her? In fact, temperamentally and philosophically "incompatible" with the Naoetsu High student body, I might've even held her in relatively high regard, though I'd never go so far as to say I had a good impression of her.

Thinking well of people just because they're great at math, or love math—I'm not so good-natured, or simple. Maybe it was part of why I found it hard to repudiate her. But if I kept her in mind, if my memories never let go of her even after she stopped coming to school, after she couldn't due to her own highly unsympathetic act of self-destruction, it involved something other than academics.

Or so I thought.

Vague, half-formed thoughts—about a girl I believed I'd never meet again. Yet running into her at school two years later forced me to face that old question.

Not just face.

I was pressed for an answer—for a solution. I'd come to know why she hated me, why I couldn't hate her, what she was to me, what I was to her, what we weren't to each other. Truths revealed after two years, as well as truths revealed after five.

Revealed.

And exposed.

Actually, we can cut out the hyperbole and suspense.

I can even divulge the solution right now. Turns out math was entrenched in our conflict, and I was, in fact, a sort of homewrecker to her—or worse. Also: some things, you never forget, and some things, you do forget.

When you can't recall why someone hates you—it could be that you just forgot why.

Mathematically, then.

Or perhaps dramatically, in the manner of a mystery novel, I set forth this problem—prove the following:

Why, when Sodachi Oikura hates Koyomi Araragi, can Koyomi Araragi not hate Sodachi Oikura?

Ignore Ogi Oshino when answering this problem.

002

It can be embarrassing to visit your alma mater—and I confess I'd never once returned to Public Middle School #701 since graduating. Despite it being in walking distance, I didn't bring myself there for nearly three years—then again, it's not like I had any particular reason to head back there after receiving my diploma. Only natural. I hadn't belonged to any sort of club I could go back and visit as an alumnus, either.

In fact, you could say I'd started to forget that I was ever a middle schooler—but after taking one step through its nostalgic gates, a torrent of memories came rushing back to me. I remembered so many things all of a sudden—good things, bad things, things that didn't matter, even awkward things.

I remembered.

What the disconnected memories had in common was probably embarrassment—but to my chagrin, none of the roused remembrances were of what Oikura hinted at.

I couldn't conjure or come up with anything.

"Heheh. This is where you went to middle school? No wonder it feels so stately," Ogi said, grinning next to me. Her attitude made it hard to tell how serious she was being, and I wondered whether she got it from her uncle.

There was nothing stately about it. MS 701 was as bland as could be.

It was a plain, ordinary middle school in a provincial city, unworthy of special attention.

Then again, I did think it was special just because I'd gone there.

Is that what Ogi was getting at?

"It feels a little strange, though," I said. "Even after I graduated from it, this middle school is still right here, doing its middle-school thing."

"Of course it is. What kind of place exists for no one's sake but your own? Just because a place is important to you, that doesn't mean you're important to it—you're such a fool."

A true fool, laughed Ogi.

Fine, maybe it was laughable—better than leaving her at a loss for words. It was about four in the afternoon, and the students, done with classes for the day, stared at us with suspicion as we stood by its gates. They left school like it was the most natural thing to do, the way I had—and tomorrow, they'd return like it was the most natural thing to do. Believing the cycle would last forever, not yet knowing that it'd come to a sudden end as soon as they graduated—

"Um. Remind me, do your two honorable younger sisters deign to grace this place with their presence?"

"Why so excessively polite when you're talking about my sisters? No, they don't—they're at a private school."

"Ah, right. Tsuganoki Second Middle's Fire Sisters, was it? By the way, what is Tsuganoki Second Middle short for?"

"Tsuganoki Middle School #2… Anyway, my friend here at MS 701 is called Nadeko Sengoku, and…uh oh. Should've contacted her ahead of time so she could accompany us."

Graduate or not, I felt a little awkward walking into the school. Any way you cut it, it's such a crazy world out there. I probably wouldn't be treated as some kind of suspicious individual, but some teacher might say something if we wandered about too much.

"We're fine. Stand tall, there's no need to be afraid. *Just pretend it's three years ago,*" encouraged Ogi. Reservations about high schoolers stepping foot into a middle school weren't for her—unlike me, she'd been a middle school student until the previous year. Maybe it wasn't very worrying for her.

Still, and also unlike me, MS 701 was in no way her territory. She was totally ignorant of the place, never having seen, heard, or been to it before, so it made sense for her to be a little anxious, and yet—

"Haha! When you put it that way, I'm ignorant of most places. I don't know anything," Ogi said and resumed walking, with her small stride. "Let's go. It's far more suspicious for us to vacantly linger by the gates—you don't want them calling a policeman on us, do you? We'll be swift. In, and out. What you might call a touch-and-go. The shoe cupboards, was it?"

"Oh, yeah. The shoe cupboards."

Ogi was on her way, and I followed behind, flustered. Like the day before, when I was locked in a room with her, the decisiveness and speed with which she acted was amazing. As someone liable to get lost in his own thoughts and entangled in speculation, her recklessness had me wrapped around her little finger. You could say she had me off balance— feeling the need to reclaim my status as her senior, I overtook her with long, fast strides.

"The shoe cupboards—that's what Oikura said. Not that I'm positive she was telling the truth. This is Oikura we're dealing with, she might've told some sort of irresponsible lie to torment me."

"An irresponsible lie—that does seem possible. Yes, it does indeed. There are just so many liars out there in the world." Ogi seemed to be enjoying herself. I won't say she was acting like this was a picnic—it wasn't her problem at the end of the day. "This shoe cupboard, then, will be nothing but a bunch of wasted leg work. Still a worthwhile afterschool activity, to have gotten the opportunity to accompany my dear senior Araragi."

"Stop sounding like Kanbaru with that 'dear senior' and 'opportunity to accompany'—why'd you ever respect me?"

"Please, be a little more self-aware. The stories I've heard of you facing aberrations here in this town for the past half-year make you worthy of quite a lot of respect. Are you trying to get me to go down the list, one by one? You must remember it all, it's in your bones."

"In my bones."

"Yes. I'm talking about your memories."

"…"

True, I couldn't claim the memories weren't a part of me—I'd just have to overlook how unmistakably influenced by Kanbaru she sounded.

Overlook, or maybe put up with, or maybe ignore.

It was an issue I'd have to deal with someday, but the one I needed to address at the moment was Sodachi Oikura.

A serious issue I couldn't simply put up with—an issue thrust before me with all the weight of her sudden appearance at school after two straight years of absence.

I couldn't approach this with my guard down.

Sure, Oikura coming back to school before graduation and for the first time since that meeting was something to be celebrated, but—

"Heheh, what a strange coincidence. I suppose these things really do happen. You told me about her, and you were reunited the next day—a twist of fate indeed."

"I admit I was surprised… I didn't even know we were in the same class."

That I didn't was a shock in itself, of course, no matter how uninterested in my surroundings and disconnected from my class I might be. When I went and checked, though, her name really was on the roll. As this year's class vice president at least in name, you could call my oversight a blameworthy case of negligence. Did I deliberately ignore it? Had I not noticed because—doing so would remind me of that day and the class council?

Of those memories?

"Heheh. Heheh. Heheheheh. Oh, life is just one surprise after the next. You never know what might happen—which is why it's so much fun."

"I'd call it the opposite of fun."

Ogi seemed to be enjoying herself, but my heart was actually quite heavy—if what happened today was continuing on into tomorrow and beyond, this was no time to be worried about entrance exams. Right, what if today was just a warm-up—I had to deal with this asap, before the main event began.

"And thus—the *getabako*."

144

"Yeah. The shoe cupboards."

They weren't "geta boxes" anymore—no middle schooler was going to wear wooden sandals to school in this day and age (I doubt the regulations even permitted it).

Ogi and I entered the building—and arrived in front of the shoe cupboard in question. Well, Oikura hadn't directed me to the cupboard itself—but its contents.

Inside the cupboard...

"So, which one is it? Which did you use when you were a first-year?" asked Ogi.

"Oh... If we're looking for the first-years' corner..." I replied, guiding her.

Maybe *corner* wasn't accurate ("area" would be more like it), but what could I do? The word came to my mouth and slipped out in the moment. It wasn't worth correcting—so I led Ogi. Yes, around here, if nothing changed since my days...

"It's actually surprising how well I remember—it's like my body does, rather than my mind." The school's very existence had been hazy to me until just moments ago, but now that I'd gone and stepped foot inside, it was as if my feet knew the way—they moved of their own accord.

"Heheh. Is that so? Well, I understand the feeling, as someone who's transferred all around—a memory that seemed to be nowhere in your conscious mind getting dug up all of a sudden. It really is such a flimsy thing... You think you remembered, or recalled, something, but that could be far from the truth," Ogi said. Her strange and bothersome remark made me all the more anxious, but I identified the space I undoubtedly used at the time.

I identified it.

This seems obvious, but it was another student's now, so it wasn't as if the label read "Araragi" like five years ago. Still...

"This is it, huh? The spot where the new middle schooler Koyomi Araragi swapped his outdoor shoes for indoor slippers each and every day—how moving."

"Moving? Me swapping one pair of footwear for another?"

"What kind of young gentleman were you?"

"Young gentleman…"

I was a middle schooler.

Come on.

That said, a high schooler can't help thinking of a first-year middle schooler as young. And in fact, I was such a child then that I acted painfully childish—take the way I saw truth.

Or justice. I never doubted their existence.

I'd resolved to always do the right thing. Yes, just like my younger siblings, the Fire Sisters.

A bloated self-consciousness—what's more childish than that?

"Oops. You've gone quiet all of a sudden. Is something the matter? Oh, you. Staying silent like that, you seem all the more manly. You're going to make me fall in love with you at this rate."

"Um, no…"

"You realize you're in for a rough time if I do fall in love with you."

"Yeah, I can definitely see that one." I don't know, but somehow hearing her praise me wasn't embarrassing, unlike with Kanbaru. Part of it is that Ogi was clearly teasing me (or being malicious)—in that sense, I guess Kanbaru's bombastic accolades were convincing (sincere?) to some extent… "I'm just wondering what to do—we've come here, just like Oikura said, but what's next?"

The shoe cupboard. Inside—the one I used as a first-year middle schooler. I felt compelled to come and see, but now that I was here, all I remembered was its exact location.

This was our terminus—a dead end.

Why did Oikura want me to come here? Well, not that literally checking out my middle-school shoe cupboard was the point… But then, what was she trying to tell me?

"What next? There's only one thing to do next. Look inside." Before I could stop her, unhalting, untroubled, and unstraying, Ogi—put a hand on the space I used during my first year of middle school.

She popped it open.

Even as I turned pale, taken aback—yes, according to Oikura, the contents were the issue, so we'd have had to at some point. But it belonged to someone else now—an adorable (or maybe not) first-year middle schooler, a stranger. Entering the grounds without permission was a problem to begin with, but we were dealing with a student's shoe locker here. You didn't have to be particularly considerate of privacy issues to know it shouldn't be tossed open, thus my cold feet. I'd felt like our investigation had hit a brick wall, but Ogi had gone up to this wall, to this terminus and dead end, and hopped over it with ease like a hurdle in an obstacle race.

Fearsome, the Oshino bloodline.

They didn't think twice about jettisoning a little bit of their ethics for the sake of an investigation—I had a similar thought the day before, but she really was born to be inquisitive.

Prompt in assessment and decision.

Her capability for resolute action seemed to engulf all else. Couldn't she at least warn me first, though?

"Haha. You say that, but don't tell me you were going to wait for the student whose shoe box this is to show up, so you could explain the situation and ask for permission to look inside."

"Um, that seems like a sensible plan to me?"

"You're so patient—one of your virtues, but no matter how patient you are, time waits for no man. If we lay in wait for a middle schooler, we'd be full-fledged suspicious individuals at that point. Think about your bright future, which you'd be throwing down the drain."

"Okay, but isn't it an even bigger problem to open a middle schooler's shoe locker without permission?"

"It's okay, I'll lie if they find us and say I wanted to drop a love letter into the kid's box. There's no law out there that says I can't lie, not when the world is so full of liars. You can be my trusty senior who agreed to tag along with my timid self."

"Oh, okay. Yeah, a good setup. I like my role, too. But you know, Ogi, it might be a girl using that box now, given the penmanship."

"Then you were the one planning to drop off the love letter. I'll be your junior who's tagging along."

"A high school senior bringing along one of his juniors to drop off a love letter to a first-year middle schooler? Feels like you've flipped a great setup into an awful one... Come on, that's too fatal a drop for me and

147

my role."

"Ah, what's this? There are indoor slippers in here, which means its current user has already left. It'd have been impossible to get permission in advance. Why care when you get results. Hm? What do we have here?"

Having noticed something, she stuck her hand inside. My request flew into the ether as Ogi, for whom "not caring if you get results" was a commendable attitude, moved once more to promptly assessed and decided action, but what could it be? Something suspicious about the slippers?

What she extracted from the cupboard, however, wasn't footwear.

Three.

There were three—envelopes.

"En...velopes?"

Huh?

We'd been kidding, but love letters, in this day and age? *Billets-doux?* And three of them? What, was the user of this box, mister first-year middle schooler who'd already gone home, popular with the ladies?

Kids these days...

Was he the protagonist of a light novel?

Was that kind of story unfolding at my old middle school?

"Mmm, no. Sorry to interrupt you when you're feeling so giggly, but these don't seem to be love letters—and they're all from the same person, anyway."

"All three? Well, if that's what you say... And also, I'm not feeling giggly, but whatever, you shouldn't be grabbing someone's private correspondence. You need to put them back right now."

I had to scold her. We hadn't come to my alma mater to infringe on the privacy of middle schoolers.

Yet she was utterly nonchalant. "I dunno. Take a look at these envelopes—they're labeled *a, b,* and *c* in big letters on the front. By hand, too. The handwriting seems to belong to one person, but who'd use this kind of lettering on a love letter?"

What kind of love-lettering would that be, Ogi mumbled.

Yes, it did seem off, or rather, odd—all the more so since each letter was written exactly as you'd see it in math class if it were a variable. Now, first year of middle school, that's right around the time you go from arithmetic to mathematics, which meant it was about when you'd start using that kind of notation—still, hold on.

"Still, you shouldn't look at someone's private letters without permission. Listen to me, I don't care if it's for the sake of fieldwork—"

"But...these letters are addressed to you."

Ogi turned the envelopes around.

And yes, it said: *To Koyomi Araragi, 1-3.*

All three of them.

"What..."

"Hmmmmm. What could we possibly have here? My, myyyy, how straaaange. Ohhh, it just doesn't make sense," Ogi cried out with an unsettling smirk—and that's when I remembered, like I'd been hit by a bolt of lightning.

What Oikura was trying to say.

I remembered.

Almost to the point of forgetting everything else.

How true.

It really is such a flimsy thing—human memory, as dodgy as my life itself.

003

The memory I'd recalled was still a chaotic mess—so let me first explain the situation to you. It had led me to visit my alma mater, with all the embarrassment and nostalgia that it entailed.

The morning after I escaped from a classroom after being locked in with transfer student Ogi Oshino, I walked through the halls on my way to class when Hanekawa stopped me. Because Sodachi Oikura was inside, Hanekawa said—because she had come back to school for the first time in two years.

"You two are on bad terms, right? I just thought it might be better to mentally prepare yourself first."

I could expect no less from a class president among class presidents.

Tsubasa Hanekawa, the class president of all under heaven.

Her thoughtfulness about such matters was impeccable—I'm sure that class council wouldn't have ended the way it did if she'd been the president of Year 1 Class 3. Surely we would have avoided that tragedy. Of course, if she'd been in our class, the true culprit might have been identified on the spot... How might things have gone then? I wouldn't call it the better outcome without any reservations.

Every student from that meeting, myself and Senjogahara included, kept our mouths shut about what happened. Hanekawa couldn't have known—but it seemed that my differences with Oikura were well known to begin with. Some people at that meeting even theorized that I brought about her downfall—however much it upset me to hear.

Hanekawa didn't take the opportunity to ask me, "Araragi, what happened between you and Miss Oikura?" Maybe she thought it wasn't a topic she ought to dig into—even so, it was a pressing matter.

If Oikura and I caused some sort of issue in class that was too big to overlook, Hanekawa would interrogate me and Senjogahara, aggressively too.

That'd be no good.

I didn't want people knowing about that meeting.

I didn't want Hanekawa knowing I, of all people, had been the chair. Hanekawa being Hanekawa, she wouldn't castigate me—if anything, she'd gently admonish me, but I still didn't want to tell her. I didn't want to talk about this lightheartedly, nor, for that matter, with a heavy heart.

In fact, I was needling myself over the way I'd blabbed on to Ogi the day before, when I hadn't even told Shinobu about what happened two years ago—regardless of how necessary it may have been to escape from that locked room.

I had to maintain the most peaceful relationship possible with Oikura now that she was here—Hanekawa wouldn't launch an investigation if I led a regular, trouble-free life. Did I also need to make sure Senjogahara kept her mouth shut? Not that I knew how she felt about that incident...

She thought about things in a different way than she did back then, anyway.

"Ha ha ha!"

I let out a strained laugh.

Hanekawa, you're worrying too much, it was meant to say—but fell flat. She stood there looking at me like I was this bizarre thing. The kind of look you'd give a friend who started acting crazy—just how forced was my laugh?

I continued, "It's nothing worth worrying about." I considered clearing my throat, but didn't. "Bad terms, maybe, but that's two years ago, the distant past. I don't have any concerns. None at all. I appreciate the consideration, but I could've walked straight into that classroom and

152

nothing would've happened."

"Hm. Hmm. Really?"

"Uh huh, really. And I'm sure she's forgotten about me, too," I guaranteed as Hanekawa seemed to ponder the situation.

This too fell flat, only making her needlessly suspicious. I venture to say this because of her reply.

"Well, Miss Oikura asked me. About how you're doing now, what you're doing now, what you're like now."

She super remembered me. And she was super obsessed—scarily enough. Suddenly, I didn't want to walk into my classroom anymore. I'd have done a U-turn and headed straight back home if I didn't have to worry about my attendance.

"She wanted to know if you'd gotten taller, what you have for lunch, and around what time you get to school."

"That's a lot of questions…"

"I did answer her, of course, as long as they were harmless. I thought it'd be strange if I didn't."

"Wh-What do you mean, harmless?"

"Stuff everyone knows. Like how you're the vice president, or how you've gotten your act straight lately… That much."

I didn't tell her about Shinobu, or about aberrations, of course—Hanekawa assured. Right, that wouldn't be harmless. Afflicting, more like.

"Also, I didn't tell her about Miss Senjogahara because the situation seemed somewhat fraught—after all, she hasn't come to school yet. I do think you ought to set a goal for before she does arrive, though."

"A goal?"

"I'm suggesting that you talk to her. You're classmates. You can't spend the remaining months together without ever coming in contact. Yes?"

"Hmm…" Wow, she saw through my plan of trying to ignore Oikura for the rest of the year? Surely our classroom offered some sort of dead angle—

"I can't have you ruining the mood of the class, either. Even if Miss Oikura holds some sort of a grudge, if you're as unconcerned about her as you say, you should be able to meet her halfway."

How could this be happening. She'd used my own words against me.

Halfway? If her attitude towards me was the same as two years ago, it was all scorched earth... Who knew what kind of minefield I'd be walking into.

I've heard some landmines are designed not to deliver lethal wounds and just blow away your legs and make you suffer as much as possible...

Hanekawa wanted me to step on it?

"But Araragi, wait just a sec, okay? I need to talk to our homeroom teacher about the reinstatement process for Miss Oikura—at the teachers' room. Would you like to come with me? You're the vice president, after all."

"Mm..."

Oikura hadn't withdrawn from school, so "reinstatement" was just a way of speaking. Still, Hanekawa stepping away for a moment provided me with an excellent opportunity, especially if Senjogahara hadn't arrived yet—if I went in now, I wouldn't have to mind anyone else.

A perfect chance.

Once in a lifetime.

Having to mind only two pairs of eyes said something about my life, but didn't make it any less of a rare chance—so I cordially declined Hanekawa's invitation (though, cordially or not, I was in a sense neglecting my duties).

"I'll resolve everything with Oikura by the time you get back," I said. "There's only half a year left until we graduate. I'd like to enjoy my youth, you know?"

"Hm... You've really grown, Araragi."

Hanekawa sounded impressed, but it was a stopgap measure at best—and I had no way of making good on my promise that I'd resolve everything before she returned.

004

I entered the classroom—the "empty seat" kept open for Oikura all this time was pretty far from mine, giving me some degree of comfort.

Given what Hanekawa had just told me—and even if that wasn't the case—I couldn't ignore Oikura. Still, I assumed I could at least place my bag down at my seat, sit down, and breathe for a moment. The plan was to inspect Oikura while doing this, then come up with a plan based on her attitude and mood. I'd be jumping the gun in a sense, kind of like how people who're quick at doing calculations start thinking about how to solve a problem before they're even done hearing it. Unfortunately, someone called me on my foul. No, that's not accurate—because I didn't even get a chance to execute my so-called plan.

Oikura had taken my seat.

It didn't matter if Hanekawa told her or not, because really, she could ask anyone where I sat and they'd tell her—it wasn't as if no other former Year 1 Class 3 students were in our class. Well, actually, even if she did ask someone, I doubted she'd ask someone from 1-3. She'd probably avoid them.

Oikura would.

In any case, I tried to pull off a feint, but she'd gotten the jump on me—or rather, it felt like she'd jumped me, and I had to admit, it did feel strange. Yes, Oikura hated me since long ago, but was it to the point that she'd try to pick a fight with me this openly? You could almost call it an attack. How was it any different from physical violence? She seemed to be challenging me to battle—I considered answering this declaration of war by going over to her seat (the one that had always been empty) and sitting in it, but allowing myself to be provoked would only drag me into a quagmire. On second thought, it was times like these that called on me to be a cool and collected gentleman. I calmly walked with the most graceful of steps toward my seat and Oikura like a movie star on the red carpet, or perhaps a bride down the wedding aisle.

You can tell by my nonsense metaphors that I was in fact quite shaken, but in any case—

"Hey, you know that's my seat," I said.

Calmly.

As calmly as possible.

"Hm? Hold on. Aren't you Oikura? That's right, you're Oikura! Whoa, what a surprise! Oikura, my old classmate from when I was a first-year, two whole years in the past! I wonder if you remember me. You've probably forgotten me, but you know, number two, Araragi! Number two!"

My entire profile consisted of my roll-call number.

And, while I meant for this self-introduction to cleverly imply that yes, How Much, I know that's how little I'm worth to you, she only replied, in a low voice:

"...I remember. Of course I do."

Not just a low voice, the lowest.

The kind of voice that might arise from the lowest depths of hell—over the past six months, I'd faced countless crises, squared off against no shortage of dangerous characters, and could say without exaggeration that I'd been pushed to the brink of death again and again, but this voice made me want to flinch.

All my experience meant nothing—what exactly had she gone through?

"How could I ever forget you—Araragi."

Oikura let out my name with so much hatred that I bet she'd speak the devil's name with more cheer in comparison. She more spit it out than let it out, leaving no room whatsoever for compromise. This wasn't scorched earth, this was like a barrier.

Or maybe just—a deep ravine?

"I'm glad you remember me... Yes. That makes me, Araragi, roll-call number two, happy," I said as I observed Oikura, whom I was seeing for the first time in two years. She seemed to have grown, though that seems obvious enough—she'd gone from being a first-year high school student to a third-year high school student. Her details were a little more childish in my memories, but that seemed to have disappeared entirely. As far as changes, though, the most prominent of all was her gaze—the gaze she summoned to glare at me.

Her gaze.

Now even sharper than two years ago—it seemed to have a keener edge to it. Unless her eyesight had gotten worse from spending the past two years playing too many video games, her hatred and revulsion for me must have grown the entire time—negative growth, as they say.

More than her body had grown—which was fine, but why would her hatred toward me grow?

It's not like we'd been meeting or anything.

"So. You're sitting in my seat," I repeated patiently.

Don't ever get impatient when you're dealing with wild beasts—fall into agitation or panic and you doom yourself to be eaten. Most important of all, remain unshaken and unperturbed before a predator.

"You seem to be doing well, unlike me," the predator said, ignoring my words.

She offered a meager smile—kindly teaching me that smiling isn't always a sign of good intentions.

"Of course, my life is a total mess thanks to you."

"Thanks to me?"

I didn't know what she meant—was she talking about the class council meeting? No, how did that make sense? Sure, Oikura stopped coming to school, and that might have made a total mess of her life, but the unanimous opinion was that she'd caused her own downfall. She'd reaped what she sowed, and shouldn't be holding a grudge against anyone. Don't tell me she believed the theory that I'd intentionally brought

157

her low? Did she even think that I was the true culprit?

How ridiculous—I thought, but it belonged to the realm of possibility. This was, after all, about what someone believed, and anyone is free to believe anything.

A solo majority vote always ends in a unanimous decision.

If Oikura thought I was the culprit, I was the culprit.

If Oikura thought I caused her downfall, I had to accept that fact—

"Looks like you're leading a happy life," she continued.

I noticed there was something unnatural about the way she spoke—a weak vibrato, like she wasn't too used to talking, as if she didn't have full control over the volume of her voice.

She hadn't come to school for two years, and perhaps hadn't talked to anyone in a while. In that case, saying anything too stimulating was unwise—though it was hard to say at this point what would constitute a wise move.

I guess neither wisdom nor moves had been a big part of her life for some time…

I began to regret not going to the teachers' room with Hanekawa, but as it always is with regret, I was too late.

"I'm so jealous. You were studying, trying to get into college, and finding a girlfriend while I shut myself in at home. It's all been smooth sailing for you, hasn't it?"

"Yeah. Thanks," I said, the most I could muster in reply.

It seemed she'd asked more than just Hanekawa about me—studying was one thing, but Hanekawa wouldn't babble about me wanting to go to college and other private stuff. She told me she'd left out Senjogahara, but it wasn't as if our relationship was a secret. Someone else must have brought it up. It didn't take a masterful investigation.

But there was something unhealthy about Oikura.

Something extremely sick.

She'd come back to school after two years, and the first thing she did was ask everyone about me—didn't she worry about the kind of impression it gave? Going around and asking about Koyomi Araragi? In fact, her eccentric behavior bothered Hanekawa to the point that she decided to caution me in advance. Not that I didn't seem to be making an active mockery of her advice.

Oikura was a pretty harsh person two years ago, not easy to get along with, but I didn't recall her being this poor of a communicator, this incapable of managing her relationships with others.

Had that incident changed her, after all?

Or perhaps set her down a rather distorted path—twisted and turning.

"Thanks? *Thanks*? Hah... What did I do for you? It's not like I was here at school."

"No, I meant..."

Now she wanted to nitpick my empty platitudes?

Not to mention, it felt more like her nails digging into me than her picking nits.

"Hmph," she snorted. "I'm sure you could get into any college you want, if you felt like it."

"I-I wouldn't say that, I'm in a real rough spot," I shrugged and replied jokingly to her words soaked in—no, dripping with sarcasm. The real rough spot I found myself in was keeping the mood from growing dark, not that my efforts were paying off.

It went beyond me. The air in the entire room felt suffocating—I almost wondered if the oxygen around us had been replaced with precious metals. Not one student in class chatted away. They all seemed to be focused on us.

My reputation was going to take yet another hit.

I was doing all the right things, and yet my reputation was going down the drain? How unfair.

"No need to be modest. You're still good at math, aren't you?"

Oikura said this sneeringly. The snide remark seemed to be no motive and all malice.

"You must think 'Euler' suits you better than it does me."

"..."

There was something laughable about the way she fixated on this point, and it seemed even dumber when that piercing glare accompanied it—if you want to know what the object of that piercing glare thought.

"Well, I guess you could say I'm good at math, or more that it's my one lifeline."

"Still getting perfect score after perfect score?"

"No, as far as my scores—"

I couldn't say it. That of all subjects, I'd never gotten a perfect score in math since that day—I had the experience lately in other subjects, math was the only one where I couldn't make it happen.

Or shouldn't.

A compulsion coming from somewhere.

From somewhere? No, I knew where.

It came from *right here.*

"And you have a girlfriend now? That must be thanks to math, too."

"No, that's a bit…"

Of a stretch.

At the same time, I realized that while Oikura's questioning may have turned up the fact that I had a girlfriend, she didn't seem to have learned it was Senjogahara.

Because Oikura wouldn't have let that go if she'd known—how could she ignore the news that Koyomi Araragi had captured the heart of Hitagi Senjogahara, the cloistered princess, the flower in a bell jar?

What a stroke of luck. Perhaps whoever told Oikura that I had a girlfriend sensed something disquieting, either from the start or as they spoke—disquieting, or some sort of unusual vibe.

In that case, I resolved anew, I at least needed to get her out of my seat before Senjogahara got to school—but ultimately, it's not as if my mere resolve meant anything.

"It's all thanks to math," Oikura repeated nonsensically. "Punks like you really grind my gears—I could have all the resentment in the world and it still wouldn't be enough. My hatred for you just keeps on bubbling up whether I want it to or not. A bottomless spring of disgust."

"Punks like me… Gosh, that's a little extreme," I attempted to mollify the now openly hostile Oikura. To keep us on a peaceful, or at least conciliatory path—yet she only kept her sights trained on me. In fact, her expression grew even harsher.

"I hate you," she stated.

The same words I'd heard in that classroom two years ago.

"I hate that attitude of yours—wrapping everything up in a nice, noncommittal way. You try to compromise, to smooth everything over, just like back then, when—" she said before gulping her words.

No, it seemed more like she'd lost them when they got stuck in her throat. This girl who hadn't done much speaking in a while had apparently messed her throat up by suddenly taking a furious tone.

In fact, she had a mild coughing fit.

I approached her, concerned, but—

"Don't touch me," she rejected me.

This is what it meant for someone to be *brusque*.

"I don't want someone like you worrying about me—what good could possibly come out of that?"

"Is that so."

I stepped away. As requested.

I got to thinking.

Just like back then, when—Oikura had said. *Back then* naturally meant when I was a first-year. Did she mean the way I tried to bring the meeting to an inconclusive end?

Speaking of, she reached the decision to take a majority vote after learning of my stance. A decision, or maybe a boiling point—maybe she felt some kind of unjustified resentment over it? Unjustified from my point of view, of course, while she surely saw it as a legitimate grudge. Spending two whole years keenly aware of her grudge would explain the way she glared at me now.

It was unreasonable—but not unjustified.

"I-I hate you. I hate you. I hate you, okay?" she went on, like some firebrand trying to win over a crowd—like a dam had burst, spilling out words.

Her own words lit a flame in her, drove her into a frenzy.

"I don't even want to see your face. The fact that you exist in this world at all is disgusting."

"That bad…"

You have no choice but to go on the defensive when someone attacks you to that degree—I felt my emotions cooling off. Faced with a wild beast, I effortlessly fell into a state of calm serenity. Settled into, more

161

like. Her rant was appalling and left me cold—but it was also fear, a cold sensation in my guts over not knowing what to do, or what she might do.

She was comical in a way, hating me to this extent, so it was possible to see her as foolish, but I couldn't laugh at her so easily. Even if I did, it'd surely be forced.

Just like Oikura's agitation.

My laugh would be peculiar.

"Seems like you really hate happy people."

I wanted to ask her why she bothered coming to school if she didn't want to see my face, but that was like telling her to go home after she'd finally decided otherwise after her long absence. Instead, I tried to evade her attacks by generalizing.

But no, she shook her head as if I said the stupidest things.

"I like happy people."

Right, she'd refute anything I said at this point. She'd say left if I said right, down if I said up—but she seemed to mean it.

"Seeing them makes me happy—what I hate are people who don't know why they're happy. People who don't even try to consider why they're happy."

" ... "

"I hate water that thinks it made itself boil. I hate seasons that think they came about naturally. I hate the Sun for thinking it rises all on its own—I hate it, I hate it, I ha-ha-hate it—I hate it. I hate you."

Oikura's eyes glowed.

Like they were aflame—like they were inflamed.

I had no idea anything could glow in such a disgusting way.

"I hate it hate it hate it hate it hate it. I ha-ha—hate it. I hate everything. I hate it, no exceptions. I hate it, no takebacks. I hate it, I hate it—I hate the hate of hate that hates hate because hating hate hates hate."

"Oikura..."

Oh crap—I thought. I was wrong, totally wrong.

It was the kind of mistake you make when you're being attacked—you're the underdog being viciously harassed by someone with an advantage over you. If you don't strike back, if you don't stand strong, you're going to let yourself be mauled—no, maybe *mistake* is an overstatement.

162

I'd be beaten into submission if I didn't strike back and stand strong.

Oikura was certainly being hostile toward me.

Her attitude was threatening and aggressive—but even if it meant getting beaten into submission, it should've been unthinkable for me to strike back at her.

It'd be a different story if this was the Oikura from two years ago.

But I couldn't now.

I mean, now she was—fragile.

Almost like a piece of glass. If I tried to strike back and defend myself in the wrong way, the slightest nudge from my hand could shatter her into a thousand pieces. Who knows what would have happened if I dared tell her to go home? What could I do or say to someone coming after me in such a perilous emotional state?

Even the way she took my seat for starters—might have been more defensive than offensive, a way to protect herself and her mind.

She lacked any and all equilibrium.

I felt, well, awful.

She'd been so cool and commanding, but now appeared this weak and frail—I'd have preferred the return of a more aggressive Oikura.

A former foe returns, but weakened—who wants to watch a drama like that?

She was no wild beast.

She was like a scared little animal.

If anything, it was Oikura who saw me as a ferocious, wild beast.

The predator.

Touching her would leave me hurt, but shatter her.

This difference in power *forced* me to go easy on her.

"Why aren't you talking? Don't tell me you're feeling sympathetic, Araragi. You, feel sympathy for me? Your suh-sympathy isn't worth a cent to—"

"Hold on, Oikura. Ho-o-o-ld on. Calm down. I'll leave for a bit, okay? Cool your head while I'm gone. You can keep on sitting in that seat…"

My attitude only seemed to irritate Oikura—she stood up indignantly. The way she stood the moment I said it was okay to sit was, in a sense, consistent, but this was no time to be impressed.

"Araragi. You-you, don't know anything—you act like you do as you live your comfortable little life, not even considering why you're happy. You don't know—you've forgotten. College exams? Girlfriends? Duh-d-d-d-don't give me that crap."

"A-Again—Oikura."

I didn't think I was giving her crap, but nothing would come out of arguing here. Perhaps the biggest load of crap to her was when I tried to act serious. Not to mention, it's a terrible idea to contradict someone who's emotionally off-balance—I had to affirm everything coming out of her mouth, just as she denied everything coming from mine.

Or so I thought, but she wasn't even letting me affirm her. Or speak in the first place. She interrupted me as I tried, endlessly unfurling her pet theories and personal opinions before I could so much as nod.

"It's because people like you are in power—that I'm never going to be saved. I hate people who think they're the only ones responsible for the way they live—who think they can live all on their own. I hate people who flatter themselves by thinking they can make it on their own if it really came down to it—people with the nerve to say they don't need anyone's help."

"..."

"*You can never be happy unless someone saves you*—I hate idiots who don't even realize that, I hate them so much it's killing me."

What had driven her to this point?

That class council meeting?

The two years of depression that followed?

Or something else I wasn't aware of…

"I-I agree, it's important for people to help each other out. Yeah, Oikura, you're right, people never go and get saved on their own, definitely not. I'm always thinking the same thing, those ungrateful people who think they're on their own are unforgivable—"

I'm probably not cut out for flattery. To think that going along with someone's opinion could be this hard… But permit me to make the bare minimum of an excuse—no one could stay on the same page as Oikura here.

"You're the unforgivable one, Araragi. No one is more ungrateful than you. You're complacent—I mean, what about your idea of justice?"

"Justice?"

"*Or are you telling me you don't remember?* What was inside that shoe cupboard during our first year of middle school?"

What was inside the shoe cupboard.

The words came from nowhere.

It felt like the flow of our conversation had been interrupted—*what was inside that shoe cupboard during our first year of middle school?* What was that supposed to mean? I couldn't figure out what the words meant beyond a literal level—at all. Oikura looked almost triumphant when she noticed my bewilderment.

"See? I knew it. You don't remember a thing. You don't know what you're made up of."

What I'm made up of.

I didn't know.

Why did the words strike so hard—pierce my heart, even. And come out the other side.

"Oikura, what do you mean by—"

"Nothing. Because I hate meaning. I hate everything. I hate hate and hate and I hate the hate of hate of hate at the hate in hate—I hate hate hate hate hate hate hate hate hate hate hate hate hate hate hate hate hate hate hate hate hate hate hate!"

Now this was going too far.

Though I'd unfortunately seen people in her state multiple times—and while I knew it was better to just let it all come out, we were in a classroom with all these pairs of eyes surrounding us.

I could end a little quarrel or argument by saying I was in the wrong, no matter how it unfolded—my reputation be damned.

But this kind of fierce, almost panicked paroxysm would ruin Oikura's reputation. How could it not? Our class already had preconceived notions of her, the way she'd come to school out of nowhere after being absent for all this time.

Sodachi Oikura.

I needed to find some way to calm her down.

The thought drove me to hold her shoulders as if I were supporting her. I tried to shake her and speak to her with whatever words came to mind. But before I could say anything—not that I knew what to say, and the only correct course of action might have been to sprint away at full speed—Oikura screamed.

"I told you—don't touch me!"

She sounded like a child.

And acted in the thoughtless manner of a child—atop the desk Oikura occupied, my desk, sat a ballpoint pen. An extra-fine ballpoint pen—I didn't know why it was there. The only explanation seemed to be that someone *just so happened* to place it there, and true, it was the kind of ballpoint pen you might find sitting around anywhere in a school. Oikura grabbed it and swung it at my hand, which was on her shoulder.

"Mgh!"

Well.

I wasn't trying to act tough or anything (why do that in front of Oikura now?), but if I'm being honest, I think I could have dodged it.

It was a ballpoint pen swung by a high school girl, and a diminished one at that, after the fierce battles I'd experienced over the past six months—and yet, its tip pierced the back of my hand.

It didn't make it out the other side, stopping when it hit the knuckle of my middle finger—which gave me some comfort. Had the tip fully penetrated my hand and stabbed into Oikura's shoulder, there'd have been no point in choosing not to avoid it.

I can say this with confidence.

Had I let go of Oikura's shoulder and evaded the pen, she'd have stabbed her own shoulder with it—so thoughtless, spontaneous, and reflexive was her act.

It actually helped her regain some degree of her senses.

"Oh..." she said, betraying a glimpse of regret.

Still, I wasn't in a place where I could attend to her. I had to hide the wound as soon as possible for two reasons.

The first, of course, concerned Oikura's future—she'd performed the brutal act out in the open, but our classmates had been watching our argument from a distance. They should buy that she never stabbed me, that she stopped just short if I hid the wound... Well, could buy it. The other reason was extremely self-serving—the wound would heal in no time at all due to the vampiric aftereffects lingering in my body.

It'd be a problem if they saw it healing.

I never imagined I'd sustain this kind of damage in a place of learning, but whatever the case, I really needed to get away from here, now, while Oikura sat dumbstruck. Then—

Hiding the back of my hand, I spun, but had to stop my feet from moving. I had to stop them, or they just stopped. Not just my legs, every one of my actions.

My escape and thought processes.

Because her form came into sight—the form of Hitagi Senjogahara as she opened the door and entered the classroom.

From there.

With the flat affect she once carried herself with—with a flatter affect than ever before, Senjogahara looked at my hand, pierced by the pen, as well as Oikura.

"..."

What now?

005

Upon further inspection, a body resembling Hanekawa's clung to Senjogahara around her hips. And looked exhausted. A fairly rare state to see the class president in, but the sight of her gave me more or less of an idea of what had happened. In other words, what took place somewhere else before Hitagi Senjogahara and Tsubasa Hanekawa's arrival.

After we parted ways, Hanekawa must've conducted whatever procedures were needed to reinstate (?) Oikura in the teachers' room, and while I have no way of being sure whether it happened before or after she finished her business there, she had a chance encounter with Senjogahara, who arrived at school. More of an ill-fated encounter, considering Hanekawa's current state—but in any case, she must've told Senjoghara about Oikura coming to school. Naturally, Hanekawa at least knew that Oikura and Senjogahara were once classmates—and maybe the conversation even led to her stating that Oikura and I were meeting now.

Hanekawa wouldn't have said this with any sort of urgency, but from the point of view of Senjogahara, who knew of the "differences" between me and Oikura on a deeper, closer level than her, it'd have sounded like a notice of quite the storm brewing.

And she'd sped to the classroom like the wind—dragging Hanekawa along. It seemed her legs were every bit as powerful as when she was the star of the track team—or maybe she'd built them back up to that level? In any case, Senjogahara (and Hanekawa) appeared in the classroom at the worst possible moment.

"You're fucking dead," Senjogahara said.

I'd like you to note that the words came from her after she seemed to have turned a new leaf. It threatened to undo all her work until now, but she was just that full of quiet fury.

"Only I'm allowed to stab Araragi with stationery—no matter how much of that character I've abandoned, I won't stand for any reuse of it."

That's what you're mad about?

Be mad that your boyfriend got stabbed.

"M-Miss Senjogahara, please wai—"

In spite of her ragged state, Hanekawa did a laudable job trying to fulfill her duty as both class president and friend, but regrettably, she lacked the physical strength.

Senjogahara walked straight toward us.

Ready to throw herself straight into a sea of mines.

"Miss Senjogahara."

And then.

Oikura noticed—her former classmate.

As president and leader of Year 1 Class 3, Oikura had to remember a classmate as distinctive as Hitagi Senjogahara, the weakly honors student.

I had no idea what kind of relationship Senjogahara, once considered untouchable, used to have with Oikura—but whatever friendly relations they may have once had, even if they'd been the closest and best of friends, weren't about to resume now.

The air was just that tense.

On Senjogahara's side, of course—and on Oikura's as well.

"Oh. So that's how it is. I get it now," Oikura said. A contemptuous smile crept onto her face. "You're going out with Araragi—how far you've fallen."

"..."

This actually had the effect of bringing Senjogahara back to her senses. As someone with crisis-management abilities and observational skills far superior to mine, she must have instantly recognized Sodachi

Oikura's mental and emotional state.

She recognized the danger—the fragility there.

An aggression built upon weakness that permitted no counterattack.

The old Senjogahara would have surely gone right ahead and opposed Oikura, but—

"Miss Hanekawa. It's fine. You can let go of me," the "fallen" Senjogahara said. "I'm sorry. It was nothing."

"Are you sure?" asked Hanekawa, having been dragged all this way, as she moved away from her hips. The most right-minded, good-hearted person here, she had drawn the short straw.

"It's fine. Thank you. I'm always grateful for your self-sacrificing friendship."

"You're very welcome…"

"As a show of gratitude, I'll be your hug pillow one of these days."

"I don't know about saying that at school, Miss Senjogahara…"

I promptly hid my stabbed hand behind my back.

Hanekawa gave me a questioning look, but even in her exhausted state she wisely decided that now was not the time and returned her gaze to Senjogahara, Oikura, and the tense situation between them.

It almost seemed like a face-off between the two stationery girls, new and old—but Senjogahara was already somewhat relaxed. This, however, seemed only to goad Oikura.

Of course—she hated everything now. Was there anything that wouldn't goad her on?

"What do you mean, it's nothing? Are you saying that I'm nothing? Just look at how great you're doing now. You used to be a useless sick girl who couldn't do a thing unless I took care of you."

"You seem terribly busy holding me up and bringing me down—Miss Oikura. But yes, it's true that you did a lot for me. You never punched down," Senjogahara said flatly.

It brought me back—but her affect, or lack thereof, seemed somewhat strained. She was puffing herself up in a way, when she didn't need to, and it was to maintain some kind of balance with Oikura.

"Not that you have the capacity for kindness towards anyone now, sick or not."

"So are you better, Miss Senjogahara?"

"Yes. Thank you."

This thank-you seemed to irritate Oikura once again—I'd given her my own empty thanks, but apparently she hated hearing the words.

"Did Araragi decide to apply for college because you've been looking after him? If that's the case—you ought to stop, it's pointless. He's never going to appreciate it no matter what you do for him. He thinks he lives his life all on his own. No matter how much you do, he's going to keep on thinking that he did it all thanks to himself."

"Well, you might be right."

Hey now.

Don't just accept it, I thought—but like me, Senjogahara must have felt that contradicting Oikura now was a bad idea. Maybe what looked to be a solid discussion had already collapsed, and the issue at hand was how to bring this situation to an end.

A way to lower the curtain.

Ultimately, the only way was to tear the curtain to shreds—notwithstanding Hanekawa's presence. I shuddered with fear when I thought about all that implied.

"But really, it doesn't matter—it's not like I'm seeking a reward. What I want is for Araragi to attend college with me, so I'm not going to hope for anything beyond that."

The ironclad assumption was that she would get in (she could talk this way because she was all but guaranteed recommendation-based admission)—and something or other, possibly the part about not "seeking a reward," ticked off Oikura. She flew off the handle yet again—and sent her palm flying toward Senjogahara.

A slap.

Fortunately, there was no stationery nearby—fortunately for Oikura, I mean. Because Senjogahara's counterattack would have surely involved that piece of stationery.

Devastating, in her hands—even an eraser dealt more damage than the strike she did deliver in return, with her fist.

"Mgh!"

The entire class fell silent.

I, who was too late to stop them, and Hanekawa, who foolishly believed Senjogahara and let go of her, and our classmates, who watched at a distance, and of course the clobbered Oikura.

She crumpled to the floor and didn't get up.

While you might call this the rare example of rock earning a win over paper, Senjogahara, the winner—despite being as expressionless as she had been in her old days—looked like she knew she'd done something wrong.

Well, yeah. You can't rock someone with a punch like that...

"Araragi," Senjogahara said in a quiet voice only I could hear. "I'm going to pass out too, so please take care of the rest."

What?

Before I could finish reacting, she fainted on the spot like an anemic student passing out during morning assembly as the principal gave one of his long sermons.

With an even more dramatic noise than when Oikura collapsed.

And she'd fallen completely unconscious, not so much as breaking her fall.

It was such an impressive display of playing dead that even I had trouble telling if it was real. Was she a ladybug or something?

And with this, the early-morning commotion came to a shocking end, with two girls pitifully splayed on the floor.

In other words, Hanekawa, the class president, and I, the vice president, had been left to handle the aftermath—but I'll skip over what happened next. As a true devotee of Tsubasa Hanekawa, I don't want to have to depict her swamped and exhausted.

006

With the flashback over, we'll move back into the present. In other words, after school, visiting the shoe cupboards of my dear old alma mater, Public Middle School #701, in order to learn the truth about Oikura's weird remark.

"Wait, what? That's strange, how does that flashback explain why you're here at this middle school with me, Ogi?"

"Oh, you. What are you talking about? You know, you always say the funniest things. I, your laudable junior, came to thank you for what happened yesterday, and that's when you told me about this, remember? And then, my humble self presumptuously proposed that you try visiting your former middle school. I couldn't simply ignore what came from a proposal I made, which is why I'm accompanying you, however pushy I realize that may be."

Who knows, maybe I might be able to help you in some way by being here—Ogi said.

That's what happened? Really?

But, well, I couldn't think of a particular reason for her to lie, so it was probably true. How careless of me, I'd rushed to tell someone about my battle with Oikura? Maybe I'd started to open my heart up to Ogi after being trapped alongside her the day before. If so, Koyomi Araragi was being quite sociable toward a transfer student he'd only met a day ago.

Not that it was a change for the worse.

With my doubts fully dispelled, I turned my attention to the three envelopes addressed to me that had been in my former shoe cupboard.

Three letters to me in a middle-school shoe box I hadn't used for nearly three years since graduating—the situation was already out of the ordinary at that point, but there were also the letters on each envelope.

The letters *a*, *b*, and *c*—written by hand, had shaken my psyche to the core.

Sodachi Oikura.

They reminded me of her rant—the three alphabetic marks made me recall something I'd forgotten.

"What could this mean? Oh, I just can't figure it out. I'm sure these letters are to you, but why send three letters at once to the same person? Ah, what a mystery—there is that classic masterpiece of detective fiction that gets brought up all the time, 'The Purloined Letter,' but this is more like 'The Conjoined Letters.' It would be interesting if they were advance notices of a crime, though."

"You don't have to stretch the situation to make it sound like a mystery. Or to bring up what you call an over-referenced story yet again."

Yes, I remembered now—I remembered *that much*. How I acted next, faced with another set of three letters five years ago.

"Ogi—it's not complicated. We just have to open the envelopes to solve this mystery."

"Really? Then let's take a look," Ogi said, unsealing one of them.

She was as unhesitant as ever, but when I say she unsealed one, I don't mean she ripped it open. It was kind of girlish, the way she carefully peeled it open. I won't say that I did rip them open five years ago, but I must've been a little rougher... Anyway, she opened the *a* envelope.

"Hm?" Ogi tilted her head as she looked at the piece of paper inside. She didn't need to show me. It must have read:

"The *b* envelope is the wrong one. Will you switch your choice to the *c* envelope?"

Yes, how could I forget.

Down to the details of the phrasing—every last part of speech.

If anything, I couldn't figure out how I'd forgotten it all until now…

"What does this mean? I don't have a clue, it doesn't make any sense—is this some kind of code?"

"It's more of a quiz than a code."

"Why would you say that when you haven't even looked at it?"

Ogi handed me the note—it read exactly as I thought it would, and the childish handwriting was also just as I imagined. If someone told me it was the actual letter I'd received five years ago, I'd almost believe it—but that couldn't be. How could a letter from five years ago be here?

…But then, where had I put the letter?

The letter that changed my life when I received it.

Where had it—disappeared to?

Why had I—lost it?

"Your expression says that you expected this, but what about it is a quiz? It talks about switching to the *c* envelope, but I don't know what it means for *b* to be the wrong one to begin with."

"This is a famous puzzle known as the Monty Hall problem. A game of probability that any math enthusiast has come across," I explained.

Giving Ogi the same explanation I once received.

"The Monty Hole problem? Huh? Something to do with astronomy? Like black holes and white holes—"

"No, Monty *Hall*. It's the name of a television program and doesn't have anything to do with the actual question. It's one of many probability problems with an answer at odds with your intuition."

"At odds with your intuition? Like a paradox?"

"I guess you could say that…but it's not technically a paradox. Nothing about the answer contradicts reality."

The Monty Hall problem.

There are three doors, A, B, and C, and a fabulous prize is hidden behind one—the player first chooses one door out of the three.

After the door is chosen, the host of the program opens one of the other two doors. It's the wrong door, and the player learns this fact. Given this information, the player is allowed the opportunity to choose a second time—stay with the door you picked, or switch and pick the remaining door.

That is the puzzle, in a nutshell.

"Huh," Ogi nodded.

As a good listener and someone with good comprehension, she now had a rough understanding of the game, I assumed. At the same time, there was also a slight sense of "So what?" about her. Perhaps she wondered what about this game was so exciting.

So, to encourage her.

"What do you think?" I asked.

Just as I once was.

"Um, what do I think? Well, I understand that the letter inside envelope *a* is imitating this puzzle."

"What would you do, Ogi? You picked envelope *a* and now you've been told that envelope *b* is wrong. Will you switch your choice to *c*?"

"Ummm."

Ogi looked back and forth between the empty *a* envelope and envelope *c*. She thought for about five seconds before saying, "Isn't the probability the same either way?"

Yes, the answer that puts her right in the asker's trap—but also the answer that anyone, including myself five years ago, would give at first, without a significant background in mathematics.

"If you don't find out the answer until later, and only one of A, B, and C is the right choice, then each one has a one-third chance of being right," Ogi said. "It'd be a different story if you found out that B was wrong before you made your first choice, of course."

"Yes. But changing your answer here is the right choice—switching from A to C."

"Is that really true?" asked Ogi, politely. Her curiosity didn't seem particularly piqued. And, well, the concept behind the question gets a little confusing when you start talking about shifting probabilities, boring anyone who was never interested.

It greatly piqued my curiosity five years ago—but it was a bit unfair to expect the same kind of excitement from Ogi.

"Why does that happen? I sure would like to know. Won't you tell me?" she said, sounding like she didn't really care.

Her consideration made me happy, but I wished she'd be a little more considerate with her consideration.

While it hurt to be acting like a math nerd giving a fiery lecture to a bored audience, I had to if I were to connect the topic to the three envelopes. I pretended not to notice Ogi's listlessness.

Acting like I wasn't sensitive required some sensitivity.

"The most popular explanation is to ask you to imagine this problem with a hundred doors, not three. Choose one door out of those hundred that you think the fabulous prize sits behind."

"Okay, chosen. Now what?"

"Of the remaining ninety-nine doors, ninety-eight are opened and shown to be wrong—you don't know if the one remaining door is right or not, but what would you do if you were allowed to change your selection?"

"In that case," Ogi said pensively, looking at the shoe cupboard. Perhaps she was overlaying a mental illustration of the Monty Hall problem on top of the long row of boxes—something I didn't have the quick wit to do in the past. Whether or not she had an interest in math, Ogi did seem to have a nimble mind in general.

If only one of the boxes is the right answer—and you chose one—and then you were left with only one other option, shown that all the rest were wrong—

"Well, I guess I'd change my pick in that case."

"Right?"

"But you've changed the problem," she made her dissatisfaction clear. She wasn't buying my explanation—of course, I did expect this to some extent. "Picking one door out of three and having one of the other doors disappear doesn't seem like the same problem as picking one door out of a hundred and having ninety-eight of the others disappear."

"Well, yeah…"

It's obvious in this case that the one final option, the survivor of 1/99 odds, seems more correct than the 1/100 choice you first made. But it's hard to go from that and successfully appeal to someone's impression that the same goes with three doors for the same reason—naturally, because the problem has to do with math, not impressions.

"Then let's go with the solution that I heard."

I decided to back down and try another approach—sometimes a detour can prove to be a shortcut.

It seemed to be the quickest way. The shortest path isn't always the most expedient one.

"First, let's think about if A is the right answer. In this case, switch choices and you'll always be wrong. It doesn't matter whether the game show host opens door B or C, the player is guaranteed to lose by changing doors. Therefore, not switching is the right move—therefore, it's better not to switch if A is the correct answer. Right?"

"Yes. I get that."

"Then let's think about it when B is the right answer. The host has no choice but to open door C if the player has chosen A, one of the two incorrect doors. In other words, the player only has two choices, A or B. Switch and you're right, don't switch and you're wrong—so it's better to switch if the answer is B."

"I see. Well, I get that too."

"Finally, when C is the right answer—this follows the same pattern as when the answer is B. Given that the player has chosen A and the right answer is C, the host can only open door B. This gives you the two options of A or C, where not switching is wrong and switching is right, making it better for you to switch."

"It—does?"

"Imagine the paths toward getting the answer right for all three cases, A, B, and C. There are two cases where switching is better, and one where switching leaves you worse off. In other words, not switching gives you a one-third chance of getting it right, while there's a two-thirds chance that switching is beneficial."

And of course, the calculations are the same if the player picks door B or door C—which is why the optimal action for the player to take in the Monty Hall problem is to change their selection.

This proof left my first-year middle schooler self in shock—but while I wouldn't call Ogi's reaction apathetic, it was still on the level of, *Ah. Okay, I understand.*

So it didn't leave a high schooler stunned… Yes, maybe these kinds of math problems hit hardest when you're in late elementary to middle school. In that case, I'd encountered it at the right time.

Well, maybe not encountered.

I was introduced to it—taught it.

By the individual who had left three envelopes in my shoe box.

"This is kind of an aside," said Ogi, "but did this TV show know this when they ran the game? Was it a program meant to amuse viewers by letting them watch players be fooled by their human instincts into being unable to pick the optimal solution?"

"No, apparently not—it seems like no one thought a player could double their chances until it was pointed out in a magazine, not the staff working on the show or its viewers. I guess you could say that's weird…"

It really was weird.

Why else would someone come up with a game involving such odd mechanics—if they thought that your chances stayed the same, how would the game be any different from just choosing one door out of the three? Even if it was meant as a kind of countdown, it seemed so meaningless.

It had become a famous question, the Monty Hall problem, precisely because someone had shown its solution to be so counterintuitive—but the problem existing in the first place felt like some sort of nauseating inversion of ends and means, almost like if aberrations existed prior to aberrational phenomena.

As if children existed before their parents, and that's what was truly weird about it—how had the creator of the problem come up with the game?

"Heh. I see—well, I guess it's suggestive."

"Hm? What's suggestive of what?"

"Oh, nothing. I'm just talking to myself—for now. No need to worry, we're not going to get to that for a while. So, to summarize and apply this to the envelopes, you're saying that it's the right answer to change our selection from *a*, the first envelope I opened, to *c*."

But I already did open the a *envelope, didn't I,* Ogi pointed out mercilessly. I wished she'd overlook the fact. These three envelopes weren't some kind of project put together by a TV show—that wasn't who sent them.

The person who did, through my shoe locker, was a first-year middle schooler at the time, like me.

"In that case, let's open the *c* envelope—let's play right into expectations. And what's this? A map? There seems to be some kind of marking on the map, too," Ogi said in an overly explanatory style. She didn't delay opening the *c* envelope for a single moment once she knew it was the right answer. Though I wasn't fully on board with it, I could learn something from her drive.

Had I possessed half of her drive during that morning's commotion, it never would have ended in that awful way. I'd have been able to stop Oikura, or if not her, then Senjogahara—

"In other words, we should go to the place shown on the map? Huh... It doesn't seem awfully far. This isn't—a treasure map, is it? And by the way, what was in the *b* envelope? Let's take a look."

Ogi briskly opened the *b* envelope as well.

What drive...

She had no intention of playing by the rules—or rather, she was playing by an entirely different set of them. Firm rules, rules that made any others just about meaningless.

"Oh? This envelope was empty from the start. Does that mean it's the wrong choice? Hm—the Monty Hall problem. But this entire chain of events only worked out because we opened the *a* envelope first. Wouldn't it not make any sense if I'd started by opening the *b* or *c* envelope?"

"Well, yeah—but it was unlikely that you would. If you have three envelopes marked *a*, *b*, and *c*, most people are going to start by opening *a*."

"Ah, is that so. Yes, yes, I see. Hmm—what a clever grasp of human psychology. And look at me, I went and sided right with the majority. It seems that whoever placed these letters in your shoe box had a lot of confidence in their own intellect. Though I don't see the sender's name on either side of the envelopes."

So, naturally, Ogi continued.

"We're going to the place shown on the map next—a journey tracing your memories. We're on a tour, tracking a young Araragi's footsteps."

"Yeah... That's right," I said, reminiscing.

Actually, we could just cancel the tour then and there, now that I remembered most of everything that had happened. In other words, I could tell Ogi that our journey had come to an end, and perhaps that would have been the right thing to do as her senior—I'd made her tag along for my sake. But I couldn't stand not going, not after coming this far.

Going there—going to the place that a young Araragi frequented every single day one summer.

I had to go.

"Let's, Ogi. To the coordinates shown on that map—wait, what?" I found myself saying again. Because at some point, she'd disappeared from in front of the shoe cupboard—no doubt acting before waiting to hear my reply.

Come on, give me a break.

Cutting short my attempt to look cool...

Just how aggressive could one person be? And why bother checking with me if she was just going ahead with it? What was she doing ditching her travel companion, even if we were at my alma mater? All this ran through my mind as I chased after Ogi. She might already be past the school gates with that drive of hers, I thought. But I didn't have to exhaust myself going after her, she'd stopped only a little ahead of me.

Had she decided to wait on me and my slow decision-making abilities?

She stood at the shoe-cupboard corner for the second-years.

Vacantly staring at one of the labels.

"Sorry to make you wait," I apologized. She'd been the one to go ahead without asking, but I wasn't about to criticize her for that.

"Oh, no, it's fine, you fool. Don't you worry," answered Ogi, before starting to walk again. I'd gotten pretty used to the way she called me a fool, but it did surprise me when it came out of nowhere.

"Hm..."

I passed my eyes over the nearby boxes and found Sengoku's name on one. Well, of course, she'd have one since she was a student here but—hmmm? It kind of seemed like Ogi had been staring at this particular one—was I imagining things?

007

Ogi and I followed the map contained inside envelope *c* to arrive at what might be called a flag lot in a new housing development not far from Public Middle School #701. Standing there, surrounded on all four sides by homes, was a dilapidated house. So perhaps it would be more accurate to say it was crumbling there, not standing there—in botanical terms, it seemed withered. Yet this derelict building was the exact place frequented by first-year middle schooler Koyomi Araragi.

"Hm. Could this be like the abandoned former cram school that I hear my uncle used as his bedroom while he stayed in this town?"

"Ah...yeah, I guess so."

True, this secluded, rundown home did bring to mind that no-longer-standing building. You could even say the two places were just about as deeply memorable to me.

But. That said. I went to that abandoned building so many times to visit Oshino, to give blood to Shinobu—so why hadn't I ever thought about this place? It seemed completely reasonable to make the association at least once.

I couldn't help but be puzzled.

Now Oikura's words made sense.

She hated water that thinks it made itself boil.

She hated people who don't know why they're happy.

Ungrateful people who lived their happy little lives—now I understood.

She was exactly right—neither more nor less. It wasn't any exaggeration to say that by completely forgetting about this dilapidated place, I'd forgotten why I was me.

It was like carrying on with my life having forgotten the name of my parents.

How embarrassing—no.

How shameful.

Was this what Ogi meant moments ago by "suggestive"? Aberrations existing before aberrational phenomena—but as far as she was concerned...

"It's so rundown it's dangerous. It's at the mercy of the elements and not even being maintained. I'm a germophobe, unlike my uncle, so I could never live in a place like this. You've got to be kidding me."

She didn't hesitate to slander wholesale a place that held a treasured spot in my memories—I'd be lying to say it didn't offend me, but how convincing would a scolding be from someone who'd forgotten about it until just moments ago?

It'd be brazen—transparent and shameless.

Not to mention, unlike her uncle, Ogi was young and innocent. Only natural for her to dislike a place like this.

I spoke.

Recalling the figure of a girl—of that girl.

"I used to meet a girl in this deserted place..."

"Hm. Why would you do that?"

While my words brimmed with emotion, Ogi's were rather sharp. Her tone lacked any trace of sentiment. She seemed to find this crumbling home extremely displeasing—but not enough for that spirit of investigation at her core to shrivel. She took a look at the nameplate at the gate as soon as she detected a break in the conversation.

She took a look, but there wasn't any plate where one ought to go, only an old piece of rubber tape, rudely stuck there. We didn't even need to try the intercom next to it to tell that it was broken.

"Since there's a trace of a nameplate, this place must have been a regular home, right? I mean, there are nothing but homes all around it."

"Who knows," I answered. "I'm not that familiar with this area. I never was. I was never aware of any nameplate as a middle schooler." Ogi really was sharp. Even if we couldn't press the button on the intercom, she knew which buttons to press when it came to fieldwork. "But it was to do homework, rather than fieldwork, that I frequented this place. A home, huh…"

I looked at the crumbling house again. Despite having slept over in that abandoned cram school like Oshino, I hesitated to walk inside. More because it seemed in danger of collapsing than for any sanitary reasons—but I hadn't come all this way just to look at it from the outside and turn tail.

There was no getting off this ride—or rather.

What goes up—must come down.

No, maybe I was only digging myself in deeper here…

"You know, I called it a haunted house back then."

"Heh. A haunted house—that you visited every day for a whole summer? How spooky. Our tale's suddenly turned into a ghost story."

"Well, yes… An old-fashioned one."

I opened the gate and walked inside. Maybe it was trespassing since someone surely owned the land, but unless I stepped in, the story couldn't unfold. Entering the premises felt a bit like treading into my own mind without taking off my shoes, but that was just another feeling I had to ignore.

I had to if I were to face it.

If I were to face my past—

"Heh," chuckled Ogi. "People must live facing the future, but every now and then, the past catches up to you—I guess? At least in this case. Humans live their lives having forgotten pretty big things. That goes for me too—but when something suddenly triggers our memories, we act surprised. Let's hope all that comes out of this ghost story is a jump scare. Heheheh…"

Ogi briskly skipped along the stepping-stones behind me, and we arrived at the entrance. A rusted sign, which hadn't been visible from the front gate, hung on its handle.

For Sale.

Underneath were the name and contact info for a management agency, but the rust made it illegible—I couldn't even be sure the company still existed.

"This sign wasn't here when I was visiting this place. It must be under new management compared to five years ago—"

It might even have changed hands more than once. That's just how long a period five years is—and while the place looked like the same haunted house to my memory-tinted eyes, I had to admit it was a building, not some sort of immortal vampire. It had to change.

It was only a "haunted house" because that's what I felt like calling it.

In fact, it was just a derelict house.

"Heh. Yes, you're right. Still, I wouldn't want to come by here at night. Let's go home before it gets dark."

"Yeah, I know—I'm not going to make you hang around with me for that long."

I looked at my watch. It was before five in the afternoon.

At this time of the year, evening turned to night before you knew it. If we really were to go home before it got dark, I basically had no time to waste.

I put my hand on the handle. Surprisingly—or maybe naturally, the door was locked. It resisted me.

The place did have a new proprietor, then—no one ever locked the front door back when I used to visit.

The door would just open for me.

Welcomingly.

"Well, we could force it open…but why don't we try one of the windows? I'm sure we can find one to enter through, they've been sitting here for the breaking all this time."

As I made this lukewarm proposal, Ogi was already getting to it, but she must have only heard the first half. The entrance was weather-beaten, but it still was an entrance, and it was against it that my junior slammed her body.

Seriously?

Dealing with a stubborn door by charging into it (with a shoulder tackle?) was something I'd only ever seen in crime dramas—just how obsessed with mysteries was this girl?

In any case, whether you've been locked in a room or are going after a holed-up criminal, trying to force a closed door by slamming into it is inefficient. The area of impact is too large, and the momentum spreads out. It's more logical to focus on a specific point, kicking down the door at the area around its lock—when the riot police charges into a closed space, they use a ram as if they're going to sound a temple bell, to smash their way in. We needed none of this reasoning, though. The entrance had exceeded its lifespan, and a solid slam from the slender body of a high school freshman brought it down easily.

"Okay," Ogi said, "let's hurry up and go inside. The neighbors might call the police after hearing that noise."

She hastily entered the building, her already-swift actions accelerating further, and I could barely keep up. This should've been a journey through my memories, but all of a sudden it felt like she'd taken the reins—or had she held them from the beginning?

"If the police show up, I'll say that we got lost, so make sure our stories are straight," she advised.

"Why do you seem so used to doing this?" I asked with some disbelief, but maybe she actually was. I didn't imagine she was some sort of abandoned-building aficionado, given her earlier antipathy, but she must regularly perform various kinds of fieldwork just like her uncle. I suppose she gets questioned by the police or reported to the authorities by neighbors? When we were entering Public Middle School #701, she was on high alert, too.

Being concerned about the police made her a very delinquent young woman despite her spick-and-span image, but I wasn't too different. We were both on the watch for the authorities as we went about our lives, so I couldn't scold her as her senior. How many faces would I need to do that? Two wouldn't cut it.

"Don't worry, I'll give them the same story. Getting lost is embarrassing as a high schooler, but better than getting my whole life derailed."

"Getting your life derailed? What's that supposed to mean?" my partner found fault with my words. "Sure, they might get mad at you, but it's not like your whole life is going to get derailed just because you were questioned by the police. For the most part, those kinds of people are on the side of us upstanding citizens. Just how much of a coward are you?"

"Well, you know. In my case, both of my parents are police officers, so—"

"Your parents are police officers!" Ogi reacted dramatically.

Hm?

Why did I say that?

Both parents in the Araragi household, both father and mother, being police officers was one of my most private facts, and I told as few people as possible—some of my most highly classified pieces of information, withheld from Hanekawa and even Senjogahara. Why leak it to a transfer student I met for the first time just yesterday?

It was hard to believe. I could only chalk it up to letting my guard down.

Yes, my guard had come down visiting this nostalgic spot, what else could it be—but no amount of regret could take back the words that had come out of my mouth. *Both of my parents are police officers* was powerful bait to a mystery buff like Ogi, and she was acting like a fish on a line I never meant to cast.

"Why didn't you tell me? How awful, how could you keep something like that from me, how amazing!"

"Well, it's not something you'd come out and tell someone you've just met—"

"What greater tradition is there in mysteries than having a police officer as a close relative? My goodness, I always knew you were a senior deserving of respect, but I never thought you were royalty!"

"...I guess there are a lot of mysteries like that."

It did seem more like a TV or film setup to me than a mystery novel motif—but now that she mentioned it, a Japanese detective fiction lion, Mitsuhiko Asami, fit the bill.

"In that case, no need to worry. If someone did report us and the police biked over here, your parents could just bail us out. Can't you hear the officer interrogating us saying it already? 'Oh! I never imagined that you were Commissioner Araragi's son!'"

"Neither of my parents are that high up. And anyway, they aren't the type to bail out their son if he got himself in a fix," I retorted in a pained voice.

No, more in pain generally.

As much as I didn't want to discuss my parents, it was going to be difficult to change the subject and cut this short without any sort of explanation, given how deeply Ogi had her teeth in it.

She really was good at drawing things out of you. I didn't think I was particularly loose-lipped…

"If anything, they're the kind of strict parents who'd never forgive their kids for breaking rules. They disciplined me as a kid by taking me to the nearest police box any time I did something bad."

"A police box? Now that's scary—I could even see that traumatizing you."

Well.

It probably did.

Quite the trauma.

But it, too, was part of the past that created the present-day me—I consist of many things. I'm built of many things. The issue is the degree to which I'm aware of it—whether I remember it or not.

I hate people who don't know what they're made up of—Oikura had told me. Now that I remembered this dilapidated house, I had to admit, I saw what she was trying to say.

This place.

That girl. That I lived having forgotten them—did mean I didn't know what I'm made up of.

I hadn't remembered, after all.

"They haven't done it to me in a while, but I can't even imagine what kind of discipline would be awaiting me at home if I got taken into custody. All that time off would only make it worse."

Maybe I wouldn't have had to worry about it six months earlier, when my parents had half-abandoned my high-school-washout self, but now I was starting to see signs of reconciliation as far as that part of our relationship. I wouldn't want to let it go to waste, even if I was still waist-deep in teen rebellion.

"So, Ogi. I'm going to be as scared of the police as I can. If the worst does happen, I'm sorry, but I want you to play the role of a delicate little high school girl."

"Haha. Well, it's not like I have to play a role, I really am a delicate little high school girl. Don't worry, I won't testify, even by mistake, that you forced me to come into this abandoned home."

"How would you even make that big of a mistake?"

Forget about custody, they'd arrest me for that.

I'd have committed a huge mistake.

Anyway, we went straight into the derelict house via the broken (by us) front door—I think this goes without saying, but we kept our shoes on. While manners would have us taking them off, it's not as though an abandoned home had slippers for visitors.

The floor was of course not in a state where Ogi, the germophobe, could walk on it, and stepping on any of the scattered glass or odd scraps of wood and metal could cause injury or worse. Tetanus isn't as far-removed a disease from our lives as you might think.

"Speaking of tetanus," Ogi began to ask, walking at a rather leisurely pace down the hall compared to her entry.

Her slower speed was due to the lack of electricity (even if the building did have it, every one of its light bulbs was broken) and the dark interior, as well as our fieldworker inspecting the area around her as she walked. For my part, nostalgia had me looking around, so I didn't feel that she was going particularly slow.

"Is the back of your hand that Miss Oikura stabbed okay?"

"Hm? What, are you worried about me?"

"Of course I am. How could I, Ogi Oshino, your faithful junior, not be worried about her esteemed senior Araragi? Please be careful, that body doesn't belong to you alone," she said, not making any sense.

Yet another form of teasing—Oshino's jokes were similar, now that I thought about it. I didn't get their brand of humor. Just how disconnected were they from the rest of the world?

"No worries, as you know, I have a vampire's constitution. It's already healed up without a scar. Fortunately, in the ensuing commotion..."

The commotion that was two girls passing out.

"I was able to fudge whether or not I'd really gotten stabbed with a pen. Senjogahara's arrival was a blessing, if you look at it that way."

"Or you're that weak of a presence in class—weak to the point that you can vanish without anyone figuring anything out. I guess you're not that different from two years ago in that sense?"

Ogi snickered. Maybe she really was making fun of me.

Pondering this, I continued.

"Oikura ended up spending the whole day in the nurse's room. Too bad—just when she'd finally made it to school."

As for Senjogahara, she left early. She would have been taken to the nurse's room as well, but when the teacher wasn't looking, she made herself scarce—what was she, a master thief or something?

"Haha. I see, I see. I can only imagine how hard that must have been on Miss Hanekawa."

"You said it—and I went off on this journey through my memories to try to lessen any part of that load, but...well, at least it seems like it won't be in vain. Not that this will leave me feeling great..."

"I wonder. If there's one thing I could say—" Ogi turned to face me. "The theory that Miss Oikura holds a grudge against you because of what happened at the class council two years ago—probably doesn't hold up."

"Hm?"

"The chances that she mistakenly believes that you brought about her downfall, or are the culprit who leaked the test answers, are strikingly low. Why, you ask?" said Ogi, amused.

Well, I didn't ask.

While she hadn't enjoyed the Monty Hall problem all too much, she must have a fundamental love for mysteries and solving them, whether it was this or our earlier time in the classroom. Maybe even her germophobia was the inverse of a personality that loved to take messy situations and give them order. Though you could just call her a mystery nerd... Anyway, her assertion made me want to hear why the chances were low—whether or not I was asking.

"It's simple. Because she came to school."

"What do you mean by that?"

It was odd, now that she mentioned it.

A mystery.

Oikura had refused to come to school for two years after the majority vote, so why appear out of nowhere today—with zero warning signs. It was almost as if Ogi and I picking up where that meeting left off and pinning down the culprit, locked in that classroom, had triggered it. But it was a pretty big stretch to claim the two were related. Things happening in a specific order didn't imply causation—it made even less sense than a butterfly flapping its wings and causing a tornado.

"What I mean by that—well, Miss Hanekawa said it from the start. Tetsujo-sensei went on maternity leave, and Miss Oikura came to school as if to replace her—"

"…"

Hanekawa did say that.

Right.

I'd completely forgotten thanks to the commotion that followed…

"In other words," explained Ogi, "Miss Oikura could come to school because Tetsujo-sensei is *no longer at* Naoetsu High."

"…Which means, she knows who the culprit was."

She knew—or rather, figured it out.

During the majority vote.

When Tetsujo raised her hand after the class was asked who thought Oikura had done it—or maybe she only realized during the two years she spent "shut in at home," as she put it. I didn't know, but essentially, she figured out that her homeroom teacher had framed her.

"…"

Not as if it improved Oikura's situation—if anything, it must have been the reason why she couldn't come to school. If it was me, I doubt I could ever return even if Tetsujo was gone.

In that sense, she was tough mentally.

"Tough? I don't know, it looks to me like she's bullying herself and enjoying it."

"Bullying herself…"

"She's so weak. A heavyweight weakling, even. She tries to put herself in bad situations, intentionally driving herself into corners—and isn't there only one thing she could want from that? You might even call it a roundabout suicide. No matter how awful things get, maybe they aren't ruinous enough for her," Ogi said nastily.

I guess she could be this biting about Oikura because they'd never met, but then again, this was Ogi. She might say the exact same thing to Oikura's face.

Even in the face of someone so weak, who'd crumble at a touch, she might refuse to ease up.

Saying, *Fool.*

"In any case, what we do know is that Miss Oikura has never given voice to her grudges or hatred for you in relation to the class council."

"Never given voice to her hatred…"

What was she doing making it sound so romantic?

But true—even if the class council transformed her personality and temperament, it wasn't her immediate reason for hating me.

That's what Ogi meant.

Because as far as that went, Oikura hated me from the day we met in Year 1 Class 3.

She hated me—like you'd hate a homewrecker.

"She hates water that thinks it made itself boil, was it? She says the most interesting things. In other words, Miss Oikura simply couldn't stand the way you live not knowing, even forgetting your roots. But when you really dig into it, that seems odd too. Plenty of people forget about the past. Like I was saying—I've lost most of my elementary-school self to oblivion, to the point that I wonder if I was born just recently and don't have any past at all."

"Born just recently… What, like the five-minute hypothesis?"

"So then why does Miss Oikura hate only you like you're some sort of homewrecker? How strange, how unusual, how suspicious—how frightening."

"Frightening?"

"Yes—due to the difference," Ogi said, enjoying every moment of this. She couldn't actually be frightened, but indeed, people who hate you and attack you for no good reason are the scariest thing in the world.

If you don't understand their goal, you can't deal with them—in order to fight, you must first know what your opponent considers just. What Sodachi Oikura thought was right, what she believed was right—this trip was in part to figure that out.

"Hahaha. I see, well said, Araragi-senpai. But be careful. While you can't fight without understanding what your opponent considers just, you'll be unable to fight if you start believing that justice is on their side. If you think they're no less right, or righter than you, it's too late—how do you fight then?"

"…"

"Speechless? Are you thinking you'd be fine even if that happened? Or have you already understood what Miss Oikura considers just—and lost the will to fight?"

I wouldn't say that.

I understood something—a mistake that Koyomi Araragi made that might be the flip side of Oikura's righteousness.

My own mistake.

I couldn't be certain yet—couldn't claim to have remembered it all, or to have a perfect understanding of what she was trying to say. I'd have to reach the deepest part of this derelict house to grasp that.

That's where it was—my truth.

It had to be.

The prologue and epilogue that needed to be told, of my tale.

Certainly not a monologue, but a dialogue—with *her*.

"We should've brought a flashlight," Ogi griped in response to my silence as she began walking again. "I'd have brought my set of fieldwork tools if I had the time. Since we came straight from school, all I have are my cosmetics."

"Isn't it against the rules to have cosmetics with you?"

"Well, I've only just transferred. I don't know the rules yet, you see."

Ogi's plan, as she spouted her convenient logic, must have been to keep on searching, but there was no need. Climbing the stairs and looking at a certain room on the second floor would suffice.

When I made my way up the perilous stairs, which threatened to collapse underfoot, and entered the room—

I was already certain.

"Yikes, this one looks just as terrible on the inside. I know you called this building a haunted house, but that's literally what this place is," Ogi dispraised, holding a handkerchief to her mouth. Maybe it was too dusty—she seemed truly revolted. "But dilapidated as it is, you can see signs of repair: rubber tape on the broken windows, putty on the cracks in the wall. The management's earning their keep—or maybe there was a time when they did?"

"Beats me. Even if someone did some work on this place, it was management that existed before I started showing up here—the windows already looked like this by the time I came by."

"Is that so?"

"Yeah. In that sense, this place is exactly like it was five years ago. Unchanged. As if time—has stopped."

Like the classroom we'd wandered into the day before.

Actually, no. The dust and stagnant air that Ogi hated so much spoke to the passage of time. It wasn't as if time had really stopped like with that supernatural phenomenon.

But coming here—instantly transported my heart and mind back by five years.

It felt more like traveling through time than actual time travel did.

"See the low, small table over there? We used it."

"You used it? How? As a chair?"

"No…"

"I don't really get this to begin with."

Even if the low table was a chair, Ogi didn't want to use any that who-knows-who had sat in. She'd never perch on a table covered in splinters and a thin layer of grime. If she moved stuff around with her feet, she could make a place on the floor to sit like I used to, but even I thought it might be unsanitary with so much dust.

Would it not have bothered me five years ago?

Kids can be fearless that way.

"Why keep coming back to these ruins every day for an entire summer? Your behavior just doesn't make sense—were you an adventure-loving grade schooler, or what?"

"Says the fieldwork-loving high schooler. Of course it doesn't make sense, kids never do. I don't know why. My mindset then was nothing like it is now."

That might go for everyone. This wasn't just a difference between children and adults, but between the past and the future.

When I look back on this a dozen years later, eighteen-year-old Koyomi Araragi's behavior would surely seem mysterious—I'd tilt my head and wonder, why talk about myself in a derelict building to a transfer student I'd only just met?

Okay, I was already wondering.

A real-time mystery.

Seriously, why did my tongue get so loose around her? When she asked, I even answered questions I could cover up with a throwaway lie.

By the time I noticed, I'd given my answer.

Ogi was a good listener, but maybe she was a good interviewer too? Oshino had been an expert talker despite how frivolous he seemed—and I guess his niece took after him. Interviews and hearings must be an important part of fieldwork, after all.

In any case, I began to tell her.

About what happened five years ago.

About who I met—and what we did together.

About the stuff that Koyomi Araragi—was made up of.

I told her.

I told my tale.

008

Five years ago.

In other words, the kind of person Koyomi Araragi was in his first year of middle school—to be honest, I'm not certain, but I doubt he was as twisted as I am now. A straightforward, pure, earnest, so-called regular kid.

The kind of regular kid you can find anywhere.

Liar, you might be saying, but really, that's how most children are before they hit their rebellious phase, before their voice changes—and I was no exception. I did of course think I was special, because who doesn't think that about themselves, but in hindsight, yes—I was a plain kid, the kind you can find anywhere. The common child, distributed far and wide across Japan.

Although young, banal Araragi never imagined he'd be attacked by a vampire and gain immortality, if he were to pick out something special about himself, both of his parents were police officers—who made peace, justice, and safety their principles. And it was under their influence that his personality developed.

That he was reared.

Inevitably—or because his parents' methods were successful up to that point—young Araragi had a relatively strong sense of right and wrong.

Yes.

As much as I hate to admit it, I was a righteous middle schooler on par with my lovable little sisters who profess to be defenders of justice—though I never had their kind of perilous drive, nor a violent streak (Karen) or a strategic mind (Tsukihi). Furthermore, while they operate as a unit, I acted on my own. To compare us to superheroes, they were a team of transforming rangers, while I was like Kamen Rider.

I'd love the Fire Sisters a little more if they were at least Pretty Cures—love them more than I should, but in any case, my dispute with the Fire Sisters' activities in the name of justice, the reason I can't help but take a negative view, has at least a little to do with the fact that they remind me of my old self.

A case of like repelling like—of blood making you sicker than water.

A stew of love and hate.

No, maybe it's simple jealousy—that they still believe in the kind of righteousness and justice that vanished in me as a high school freshman.

Those two are able to believe that there are things in this world that are right, and just, regardless of perspective, no matter how many people try to say otherwise—still straightforward, pure, and earnest.

Unlike me.

Very unlike me.

I'm sure they'll run into the same wall someday, and when they do, I need to absorb as much of the shock as possible, as their older brother, as their forebear and forerunner, but that was yet to be—I need to be talking about the past now.

About five years ago.

Back when his parents were still raising their son successfully, young Koyomi Araragi became a middle school student without incident, diligently applying himself to academic pursuits. Yet one day, around the time that first term was coming to an end, he found himself a little fretful. Maybe not a little, but quite fretful—the final exam he'd just gotten back indicated less than satisfactory results.

They weren't downright tragic, but he could see what it foreshadowed—understood better than anyone else.

He was in trouble if this continued.

He was in the danger zone.

In other words, as he rose from elementary to middle school, so did the level of his courses, and he was starting to have trouble keeping up. Still, midterms had been like an extension of his elementary classes.

Once finals rolled around, however, it was as if his courses had finished warming up and started to get serious—especially math.

As the name changed from "Arithmetic" to "Mathematics," the difficulty spiked an incredible degree, and it now stood in young Araragi's way.

Today, after having tasted much more of what life has to offer, both the sweet and the bitter, I might brush it off, switch gears, and decide to work harder next term and not take it as some dire omen. But this was five years ago, before my personality was twisted—you could say we're talking about a Koyomi Araragi back when he lacked flexibility.

He was in trouble if this continued, he thought—*he wouldn't be able to stick to what's right*. While not so cornered as to use those precise words, the idea that he wouldn't be able to accomplish the righteous act that is learning was more embarrassing to him than any score.

I know I just used the phrase *back when his parents were still raising their son successfully*, but you could say their methods had failed at this point—doggedly emphasizing what's right might produce a child that does no wrong, but he also can't excuse failure. When he fails, he blames himself more than necessary and has trouble getting back up—that's the kind of child you end up with. And in fact, that's what happened to me during my first year of high school, and here we are.

Not that I resent my parents, how could I? Yes, there are still some negative feelings between us, and they're still very worried, but at least they support me now that I've gotten back on my feet thanks to Hanekawa and Senjogahara. As far as how they chose to raise their children, they seem to have learned from their mistakes and made course corrections for my two little sisters, so why say anything now?

But—how did my righteousness-revering heart not break until July fifteenth of my first year in high school? How did my poor score not shatter it to pieces during my first year of middle school? It was because my shoe locker contained three envelopes as I left school.

a, b, c.

Like that.

Three envelopes marked with handwritten alphabetic letters.

Please don't condemn him for this, but young Araragi thought they were love letters at first. He thought his box contained three love letters. Look at that, he thought, the girls love me—such is the mind of a first-year middle schooler.

Despite the presence of the first three letters of the alphabet, it was enough to make him forget about his poor score for a moment. But then he noticed that the three markings and the "To Araragi" had the same handwriting, belonging to one person. He tilted his head.

Why would anyone leave three letters in his shoebox? There was no logical reason, which is to say, this situation was far from right, and he was confused.

His confusion only lasted until he opened envelope *a*—after reading the note found therein, he saw that it was some sort of quiz.

I didn't know about the Monty Hall problem then, but when it was thrust upon me, it piqued my interest. My interest, or maybe my curiosity—after thinking it over a bit, I opened envelope *c*.

I hadn't changed my selection from *a* to *c* after calculating the probabilities and determining that it was the optimal choice—young Araragi was no genius. I just had the vague notion that if someone gave me this problem, changing my answer seemed like the right thing to do. I opened envelope *c* as if I were following the questioner's intent.

The quiz could betray that authorial intent, as the real Monty Hall problem did—and my reasoning may not have been praiseworthy, but ultimately, I made the right choice. You could also say it didn't matter either way. Unable to keep myself from opening both envelopes in the end, I'd have headed to the location indicated on the map in envelope *c* no matter what.

Why obey the instructions in a letter from an unknown sender and take a detour on my way home from school? I have no logical explanation for my unsafe decision—thinking about it now, I probably should have ignored such a bizarre piece of correspondence.

But I.

Koyomi Araragi wanted to know.

It was curiosity.

He was curious about the curious.

He had a love for it.

It's not as if he knew the intent behind the quiz or what the missive meant, yet—that was the exact reason he wanted to know.

The intent, the meaning.

His youthful intellectual curiosity led him to an abandoned home in a residential development—a new area for him, so young Araragi had no idea such ruins were hidden within.

Its appearance frightened him, of course.

He wanted to leave at once—the ruins were irrationally scary. No sign reading "No Trespassing" hung there, but he still thought it was a place he shouldn't enter. An abandoned building wouldn't scare me these days, now that I've gotten used to that former cram school, but this was a first-year middle schooler—young Araragi didn't have the mental fortitude to endure such a solo test of courage.

As a boy who revered righteousness and believed in justice, he hated evil and wouldn't hesitate to battle it (I now blush to recall). At the same time, he didn't have the strength of heart to face his fear or this darkness.

The boy who claimed that right was unconditionally right also found the scary to be unconditionally scary.

The story would end there had he gone home, but that's not what happened—very fortunately for me.

"You came, Araragi."

And.

A lone girl appeared from the ruins.

She appeared.

"If you're here, does that mean you solved the quiz?"

"…"

He was silent because he was stunned. For a sweet young girl to emerge from a crumbling, abandoned building was such a fantastic, even perverted sight that it felt unreal to him—leaving him speechless.

Had he wandered into another dimension, he even wondered.

The girl seemed fragile to the point of transparency—like a ghost.

And that's why.

Koyomi Araragi decided to call the abandoned home—a haunted house.

"The question. I..."

Sure enough.

Forgetting even to keep up any childish appearances, I gave this girl, who seemed to be the letters' sender, an honest answer.

"I didn't solve it. I changed my answer, but I don't know why c was right..."

"I see."

The girl didn't seem disappointed to hear that I'd answered based on a hunch. She only smiled.

She looked so happy as she smiled.

"Then we can start by analyzing the problem. Come in, Araragi."

"What?"

"Let's study. Why don't we get smarter together?"

009

"Hah—ahaha," Ogi laughed, having heard this much. "Comical, in a way. What a silly memory, I'd declare it to be nothing but the product of your delusions if you weren't the lord and master of Miss Kanbaru, who I'm a big fan of."

"Listen, call my memories silly if you want. But in exchange, retract the product of Kanbaru's delusions that you just repeated about me being her lord and master," I interrupted my story to respond to Ogi. "She and I have a healthy, wholesome junior-senior relationship."

"Heh, is that so—I'd like my relationship with you to be that way too. Um, what were we talking about again? To summarize, a ghost girl who came creeping and crawling out of this derelict house sent you the letters?"

"No, no, that's not it at all," I said, flustered. "I didn't have anything to do with aberrations until spring break between my second and third years of high school, when I was attacked by a vampire. This was a living, breathing human being, not a ghost—she hadn't materialized on the spot, she just showed up before me and decided to wait inside." A failure as a narrator, I'd spoken in a misleading way. "I would've figured it out with a closer look. Wait, no, I think I knew on first glance. I mean, she wore MS 701's uniform, the school we just came from."

"A school uniform? Oh, but now that you mention it, you did say that a first-year middle schooler sent the letters. Which would mean... that you and this girl were classmates?"

"Yes, it would."

Yes.

That's what it should mean—probably.

"You're saying you made a girl wait for you here in this derelict house? You were one bad boy, even back then. What a ladykiller," Ogi teased me off-hand. I wished she'd put a little more effort into it if she was going to. "Were those envelopes love letters, after all? Was it a sly strategy by this girl to lure you to a remote location and deliver you a glorious confession?"

"Glorious..."

What a bizarre way to put it. I couldn't even tell if she was being facetious.

"It wasn't a love letter. And of course, it wasn't a sly strategy, either. Classmate or not, I was only meeting her for the first time. It's not like we had any kind of interaction before that."

"Hm. There's no law against sending a love letter to someone you haven't interacted with—if anything, they tend to get sent to people you don't know all that well. But I suppose it'd be an odd love letter—using some sort of math problem to attract someone's interest."

"Yeah. And that wasn't it at all. According to her, she sent letters to multiple other people. I was the only one to show up at the meeting spot."

"The only one brazen enough."

"Brazen? Well, I guess so."

Aloof might've been the better word.

You could say I totally lacked the ability to sense danger.

Not only had I come to a derelict home because a letter had sent me there, I entered it because a strange girl invited me in. It was too risky an act for a child. Unsafe and imprudent, and that's being generous. But it's due to these dangerous acts—that I am who I am today.

"At the very least, I'd have started to dislike math if not for that summer—I'd have come to hate it. I doubt I would've been able to enter Naoetsu High."

Which meant never meeting Hanekawa or Senjogahara—there's no way to know for sure, but I'd probably be a very different person today.

That's not something I'd want.

"I see, I think I'm starting to get a vague idea. Of what exactly Miss Oikura wanted to say—but I don't get the full connection yet. I don't want to jump to conclusions. Let me listen to my foolish senior's story to the end."

"Yeah...you should. The real heart of the story comes next."

"Well, why don't you just come out and say it? I promise not to think any less of you for it. Even if it was pure intellectual curiosity that got you to waltz up to this derelict house, you entered faithfully because this ghost girl was cute, didn't you?"

"Could you not vulgarize my precious memories?!"

"Well..." Though I raised my voice, Ogi remained undaunted. She was so above it all. "That's just how first-year middle school boys are. All you cared about was that this girl was cute. I'm not conceding this point to you. Young Araragi would have shown a little more caution otherwise. If it was a brawny bandit of a man who'd come out, would you have followed him in?"

"A brawny bandit? I'd run away like mad whatever the context is."

"So, was this ghost girl cute?" pressed Ogi, as if her investigation hinged on this point. How crass... "Most boys wouldn't stand a chance against a cute girl telling them let's study and get smarter together—and that's what happened, right? I can tell you're trying to make it sound like either a heartwarming or a scary story, but in any case, this girl was sweet. End of story, yes?"

"Fine, I'll admit that wasn't completely out of the picture, so please leave it at that," I surrendered. It felt like my memories had been sullied—but then again, it's not like she could really sully or do much else to a memory I'd forgotten until a few moments ago. "But allow me to insist for the sake of my former self's honor: I was also drawn to what she said about analyzing the problem. The letter was perfectly in tune with my tastes that way. To the point that I could hardly believe that anyone could ignore it."

"Hardly believe, huh? I probably would have ignored it," Ogi said dismissively. "Whatever the case, let's hear the rest of your story. About your fateful summer escapade. About the rest—of your secret rendez-vous with this mysterious girl."

"..."

Her word choice, *escapade*, gave me pause, and *secret rendezvous* bothered me even more. Yes, maybe they described what happened, but I never thought of it in such furtive terms, nor felt ashamed or guilty about any of it.

And that's why.

The right term for my meetings with the girl, which began that day—would be *study session*.

010

"And so, your chances of getting it right are higher if you switch from envelope *a* to envelope *c*. Twice as high. They call this the Monty Hall problem," the girl finished explaining, and now it finally made sense. I felt like shouting out loud.

This is fun!

That was my reaction—the first time since elementary school that I felt like studying could be fun. Even if getting good grades was the right thing to do, I wasn't having any fun. Sure, getting a 90 made me happier than getting an 80, but it just wasn't the same.

Listening to her explanation, I discovered that *studying* could be *fun*—and that seemed far more valuable than anything else I'd been learning. This of course had to be in part because of how skilled the girl was at teaching.

Conveying a problem whose solution is at odds with our intuition, like the Monty Hall puzzle, is difficult—take how I tried and failed with Ogi, for instance.

"This is fun!" I had exclaimed. Out loud.

Yes, this was before I grew bitter, before I gave up, before I washed out, back when I was straightforward. I was more affable than I am now, but not the type to be so honest about his feelings with a stranger.

I must have found it just that fun.

It was shocking.

It's okay for studying to be fun—the idea had never occurred to me. I would have found it immoral, somehow criminal.

If you asked police officers devoted to justice—one of my parents, or someone else, it doesn't matter—why they carried out their duties, they'd get bashed for replying, *Because it's fun*. If a politician whose actions affect a nation said *politics is fun*, the remark could even be used to force a resignation.

Likewise.

You should never say that studying is fun—I thought it was forbidden.

But in fact.

The girl's explanation was fun—so much so that I wanted to scream.

It was like the first time I ever read a novel. I'd vaguely seen comics as fun and novels as serious, and having my ignorance shattered was refreshing.

Of course, the Monty Hall problem wouldn't show up in a middle-school math class, so it wasn't directly connected to my coursework. That didn't matter, though.

Before I knew it, I was asking her, "Are there any more problems like that?!"

"Yup. Lots of them," she replied with a smile. "I can teach you as many as you want. As long as you promise to love math even more. As long as you keep loving math."

I was happy.

Her words made me happy—to be clear, young Araragi was close to hating math after receiving those miserable results on his final exam. He nearly hated this new subject, nothing like the arithmetic he so excelled at in elementary school—but that was all wiped clean from his mind. He even felt as though he'd loved math since he was born, ceaselessly.

It was a bit extreme, even for a child's thoughts.

I'll admit that myself.

I might have chewed out any guy who flip-flopped like that, whether or not he tried to hide it. Meanwhile, the girl didn't look bothered in the least when I swore to unconditionally love math.

"Okay, then," she said. "Starting tomorrow, let's keep on studying here together."

I could keep on loving math.

To jump to the end of this story, I upheld my vow. Even after my grades plunged to a washout's at Naoetsu High, I maintained at least a certain standard in math.

But I'd forgotten my all-important vow until just now.

I'd forgotten the cause, producing only effect.

What to make of that?

"It's getting late, Araragi, so I'll just give you some homework. Think about it on your own, come up with an answer, and return here on your way home from school tomorrow."

"Huh? Oh, okay."

My faint disappointment that today was coming to an end was over-shadowed by excitement: there was not only a tomorrow, there would be many tomorrows.

"It's a promise. Promise you'll come. That you won't get bored of math."

"Yeah. I get it."

"Then here's your question," the girl said, pulling five cards out of her pocket. It seemed she had prepared this "homework" for young Araragi in advance.

There seemed to be numbers, symbols, letters, and kanji characters on both sides of the cards. Without showing them to young Araragi, the girl lined them up on the floor of the derelict house.

"There are five cards here. What is the minimum number of cards you have to flip in order to prove that a number is always on the opposite side of a card showing a character?"

011

"Ah...I've heard that question before. But what was the answer, I've forgotten." Ogi tilted her head. "I want to say that what's important here is that a character doesn't always have to be on the flip side of a card showing a number? It didn't interest me too much, but did the question shatter your heart into pieces yet again? Did it send a second arrow through your first-year middle-schooler heart?"

"Do you have to put it that way?"

Well, she was right.

If she wanted to call it a second arrow, that's exactly what it was.

Now that I had my homework, I went home and thought about the problem as promised. The joy I felt when I came up with the answer drove me even further into joyful obsession.

To put it simply.

I'd become a slave to math.

"A slave—hmm. I was expecting a story of a gentle romance from your early days, but I see the ground has shifted. This is starting to sound like a manga ad for a massive test-prep company."

"If you want to be objective about it, I was basically going to cram school. I kept on coming to these ruins from the end of first term all throughout summer break. I kept on studying with the mysterious girl."

To be precise, it was more one-way than me studying with her. She taught me—taught me fun math that didn't have much to do with my coursework.

She was also the one to teach me about the most beautiful formula in human history, Euler's—and I can still rattle off all of this "math" that, if we're being honest, is useless at school.

I hadn't forgotten anything I learned there.

I'd forgotten just one thing.

The girl who'd taught it to me.

"It didn't feel like studying to me at all. More like coming to play every day... Honestly, this place was our secret base. Or maybe a secret cram school?"

"Cram school... Which reminds me, wasn't the abandoned building where my uncle lived for a while a former cram school?"

"Yeah. It managed to stay afloat until a few years ago, but sounds like pressure from a corporate chain that moved into town gave it financial troubles until it closed down."

"Financial troubles. Then after it went down in flames, the building went up in flames. Tragic."

"..."

Um.

It seemed to me like she'd gone out of her way to play up the tragic aspect...

"The same might befall this place someday if it stays abandoned," noted Ogi. "You do hear about abandoned buildings getting burned down by suspicious fires all the time. Of course, by the looks of it, it might collapse before it goes up in flames. I can't believe you were holding study sessions here almost every day."

"Well, yeah. It does seem strange when I look back on it now... We could've used the public library, or the school library, lots of other options. But she was fixated on this place. She said she'd only study here."

The next day.

Having solved my homework (in my own unique way, though I ended up being right when we compared answers), we met in our room in the derelict house, where she set out that rule. While she was usually

214

kind, if also a bit precarious, that was the one time she made me promise sternly—there were conditions in order for these study sessions to continue.

Three conditions.

One of them being that they'd take place here—in the farthest room of the second floor of this derelict house.

"Three conditions… Hey, now, that wasn't the deal. I mean, didn't she offer just the day before to teach young Araragi to his heart's content if he'd keep on loving math? How unfair. And contradictory. There's no consistency here. The whole narrative's falling apart."

"You really are a nitpicker, aren't you… Sure, looking back on it now, you're right. Not one of the points in your little lecture is wrong. But isn't it a very human thing to add on conditions?"

To repeat, she was a middle school first-year, *someone* in the same class as me—not any kind of officially licensed cram school instructor, so tacking on extra conditions didn't put her in violation of any code of ethics.

"Is that so. Well, and the other two? That you'd pay her a fee? The way you're paying Miss Senjogahara and Miss Hanekawa every month?"

"Don't spread fake rumors. I'm not paying a monthly fee to Senjogahara or Hanekawa."

"Ah, right—I guess Miss Senjogahara's stance is that she won't seek anything in return. I'm sure Miss Hanekawa is the same way."

"…"

Actually, why did she know this about Senjogahara and Hanekawa when she'd never met them—even supposing she'd heard about them from Oshino or Kanbaru?

"Funny how you're so insistent that you don't pay them. It'd be even funnier if you said, *I pay them in gratitude.*"

"…So the second condition is that we'd keep our study sessions here a secret between us. That we wouldn't tell anyone. As for the third condition—"

Don't ask my name.

Don't try to find out who I am.

Don't ask me anything—except about math.

"That was it."

"What was she, the math fairy?" Ogi blurted out her uncensored impression.

Well, I couldn't blame her—not only had I been captivated by her aura, I'd been enchanted by math and how fun it was. I didn't see it quite in the same way as Ogi, but when you boiled it down, it did sound like a fairytale.

The girl spoke and acted like someone from a dream world disconnected from ours.

"Did you ask why she was giving you these conditions? Why your secret meetings had to take place in this dilapidated house, or why you couldn't tell anyone else about your study sessions, or why you shouldn't look into her true identity? You must have asked?"

To listen to Ogi, no investigator worth her salt would be so amiss, but my unfortunate self, Koyomi Araragi, was no investigator.

"That went against condition three." *Don't ask me anything.* "That's why I didn't ask—I accepted the conditions, no ifs, ands, or buts."

"Studying math and logic puzzles without those? You're the type who walks straight into scams, I bet."

"But I can also say that the girl never demanded anything else. Really, not a thing. Just the three conditions, along with what she said at the beginning. She never wanted anything like a private-tutoring fee or a monthly payment or tuition. I felt bad about her just teaching me and never doing anything in return, so I brought her some snacks one day, but she wouldn't even allow me to offer them to her. 'I'm not doing this—'"

I'm not doing this because I want to be rewarded.

You see.

All I want is for you to love math, Araragi.

There's nothing I want but that.

I'm glad I'm getting to teach you math.

So please.

Don't stop loving math.

"That's what she said."

"You're only making her sound more like the math fairy...or maybe less of a test-prep ad and more of a manga guide to learning math. Oh, or could it be a science-minded mystery full of math-based tricks?"

"This story doesn't pass muster as a science-minded mystery, does it? It's too illogical. The study sessions end up coming to a sudden end one day, too—leaving behind unsolved mysteries."

"They never got solved?"

"If anything, I was only left with more questions. But anyway, I agreed to all the conditions and started coming to these ruins every day."

"Every single day? Literally?"

"Every single day. Literally."

"Huh—how singleminded of you."

Ogi sounded impressed, and in fact, I was surprised by my own actions, describing them out loud like this. While I'm devoted to studying for my entrance exams, I'm still not as fervent about my studies as I was then.

Strictly speaking, of course, our sessions weren't my studies. It was more the kind of trivia a middle schooler loves than it was math—making me a bit like a game-obsessed kid.

Karen and Tsukihi, the Fire Sisters—though they weren't called that at the time, both being in elementary school—even complained that I stopped being as friendly once I started middle school and didn't play with them anymore.

That aspect of our poor sibling relationship was improving lately— but while I'd chalked up its deterioration to a typical shift in attitude between elementary and middle school, now that I considered it, the sudden "unfriendliness" might have been due to the fact that I'd silently gone off somewhere every day that summer.

It seemed likely—which meant that at the time, I was so engrossed in math that I couldn't be bothered with anything else, even my own family.

"Your story starts to take on a new light if you weren't considerate of your own surroundings—if it got so bad that it had a negative effect on your regular life. At the very least, it'd be more of a ghost story than a heartwarming tale. Were you okay?" asked Ogi, a note of concern in her voice.

In other words, the situation, looked at objectively, worried even a girl who tended to find everything amusing.

"Well, of course you were okay. Otherwise you wouldn't be here talking to me now."

"If it kept on going, then who knows—but like I said earlier, these study sessions came to a sudden end one day."

"An end."

"Yes. An abrupt end. On the last day of summer break. I visited this place like always, but—"

012

Young Araragi visited the derelict house like always, but that day, the girl who never failed to arrive before him—so she could finish preparing for their session—wasn't there.

That day—for the first time.

Young Araragi found this a little odd, of course, but interpreted the situation in an idyllic manner. Well, he thought, given enough meetings, this was bound to happen sooner or later. He sat and waited for the girl.

No doubt, he optimistically believed, the "math" she was teaching him today took a long time to prepare, hence her tardiness. He even grew excited—but no matter how much time passed, no matter how long he waited, she wouldn't come.

Only after the sun had set did young Araragi belatedly begin searching the home—but she was nowhere to be found. She wasn't hiding somewhere to scare him.

He ended up returning to the room—the farthest one on the second floor, and spent the final night of his summer break there. Raised by his parents to accept correctness as one of his principles, he was staying the night away from home without permission for the first time—sadly to no avail.

His unauthorized sleepover left him empty-handed.

Morning came, but she did not come.

Young Araragi needed to go to school, so he had no choice but to leave the derelict house behind—of course, once the start-of-term ceremony ended, he'd stop by his home then return to the ruins, before the day was out. That was his plan, but he had the vague feeling that it would be futile.

Because during his night there, he found an envelope beneath the low table. An envelope, sloppily Scotch-taped to the back side of the low table where young Araragi and the mysterious girl studied. An envelope that resembled the ones that had been deposited in his shoe locker.

No letters were written on the front, nor was it addressed or signed. The same envelope, but blank—and it was empty too.

Just like the *b* envelope from before.

It was empty—a wrong answer.

He wasn't so wise a boy as to take its meaning, or perhaps it had no meaning at all—but Koyomi Araragi, first-year middle schooler, had a thought.

It's over.

I won't be learning any more math from her here.

Such was his suspicion—and indeed, I was right.

Not only did I revisit the empty home that day, I continued to do so on days after that, just as I'd promised and at the time I'd promised, but she never came to teach me about how fun math could be.

I kept up my visits.

Stubbornly. Persistently.

But at some point, I ceased to.

If any one thing made me stop, it might have been the realization that the girl *didn't seem to be* one of my classmates.

Based on the third condition, I didn't look into her identity for quite a while after she vanished, but I came to the end of my rope at last and began investigating the other classes.

As someone without any sort of a network, of course, it was a passive investigation that involved sneaking peeks into other classes—but the girl I'd met for so many hours one summer was neither a classmate nor even an upperclassman.

She wore a MS 701 uniform, she had on a first-year's pin, and those letters had been placed in my shoe locker, so I'd assumed that she was a classmate—but given the fact she wasn't there at school, perhaps she'd been an outsider.

Not just from outside my school.

For all I knew, she'd come from outside this world.

A ghost in a haunted house—I didn't really think that, but it was as if her entire existence had vanished, and young Araragi—yes, it made him quiver.

He was scared.

That, probably, was when she began to scare him.

Thus—he stopped going near the abandoned home.

Thus—he forgot about her.

But—the one thing he didn't forget was the math he learned from her there, and young Araragi's grades began to rally after second term, supported most of all by his math scores.

In other words, his life had reverted to the state it was in before he started visiting the rundown home—nothing had changed in the long run, but one thing was different for certain.

For the most part, young Araragi kept up his steadfast pursuit of the right and just—at times going overboard and facing terrible repercussions for it—but when it came to math and math alone, he pursued fun.

If not for that foundation.

Once that class council meeting shattered his sense of justice—most likely there'd have been nothing left of his heart.

Math could be fun.

Life could be fun.

The world could be fun. It's because she taught him this—that I am who I am today.

I was made up of that summer.

013

"Huh? Wait, but to cut to the chase, that mysterious girl is Miss Oikura, right?"

Ogi's casual comment summarized so much that she had all but ruined my story. She checked her watch as she spoke—as a girl she might have a curfew, but as a proud mystery fan, you'd think she'd be a little more proper in presenting the solution.

"Hold on, you can't call it the solution," she objected. "If anything, I'd call it excessive misdirection if the girl is anyone but Miss Oikura. It'd be labelled unfair. Though it'd be fun in its own way if it turned out to be me. *I said not to tell anyone, you broke our promise to keep those study sessions a secret*—you know, like the Snow Woman."

Not that I had any reason to keep upholding the conditions, now that the study sessions had come to a unilateral end, but it did feel a little weird that I'd told her all of this—which meant her remark didn't sound all that funny to me.

Of course, it goes without saying that the girl wasn't Ogi.

Her smile looked nothing like the girl's.

"Well, you wouldn't tell me when I asked about her looks, so I did think she had to be an established character. You'd be giving it away if you described her outward appearance."

"I see." She got to engage in something resembling deduction—still, you'd be hard-pressed to call it mystery-solving.

"Though it'd be so interesting if the girl was Miss Senjogahara."

"Nope, it wouldn't be."

Unfortunately, Senjogahara was busy being a track athlete back then and didn't have the spare time to teach me, a student at another school. All she could say about that summer was how much she ran.

"In that case, Ogi. How do you explain the girl—young Oikura *not being* at Public Middle School #701 after summer break? How do you prove she wasn't the math fairy?"

"While it'd be pretty tough work proving the nonexistence of fairies, you don't have to use a theory as fantastic as that to explain why she was nowhere to be found at your middle school once second term started. She transferred," Ogi replied briskly.

As a transfer student herself, she didn't find it special or rare.

"And it's because she transferred that no matter how hard you searched, peeking even into the classrooms of your upperclassmen, you couldn't find her. It also explains why she never showed up again for your study sessions. It's far more likely than the possibility that a student from another school had been wearing your school's uniform—though that'd be the case with the Senjogahara theory—or a student from another school sneaking in and dropping letters into random shoe cupboards. But there's one hole in this line of inference, isn't there?"

Ogi put the point on the table herself before I could point it out.

"Miss Oikura and you had *already been classmates*—the way you've described things until now, you only met her for the first time after entering Naoetsu High."

" … "

"You said she hated you from the day you first met in Year 1 Class 3. Was that some kind of narrative trick, where you meant the first time you met in that classroom, but not the first time in general?" asked Ogi with a grin—but she was still showing quite a lot of consideration to her senior by interpreting it that way.

The truth was different.

Simpler by much, and easy to understand.

You couldn't even begin to call it a trick.

"*I only thought it was our first meeting*—in other words, I had totally forgotten about young Oikura. Forgotten who I had to thank for being good at math, forgotten how indebted I was to her. And I treated her as a regular classmate."

So of course—she hated me.

Calling me ungrateful here would be generous.

She had to have remembered me—and then my ungrateful self went and snatched a perfect score from under her, making her hate me all the more.

I hate water that thinks it made itself boil.

Yes, indeed.

I was water—terrible, conceited water.

I thought I was *somehow* good at math—when I wouldn't be the person I am now if I never spent that summer with Oikura.

"She was saying that everything I am today is thanks to math—even the fact I'm dating Senjogahara. But maybe she wanted to say it's thanks to her—"

Thanks. To her.

The empty compliment I'd given her.

I really did have her to thank.

"She likes happy people," Ogi said, "but she hates people who don't know why they're happy—was that it? Oh, and what else, she hates people who don't know what they're made up of? Heh, what profound words now that you've remembered all these things."

"In any case…"

I had a lot to think about, and a lot to reflect on—I felt a lot of regret, but at the same time, part of me felt like it was all in the past.

And it was.

More than two years ago—add three more years.

Memories are nothing but that, memories. Remembering them now wasn't going to change the present—however.

However.

"I need to apologize to Oikura tomorrow. I'm sure that won't make her stop hating and start liking me, and it probably won't make her feel better—but I need to apologize, so I will."

"Oh? You seem a little reluctant."

"Sure," I nodded, "it's not like I don't have some complaints of my own. Even if she had to transfer schools or whatever, she could have at least said something before she left."

How could she not even say goodbye?

It's not like she was Mèmè Oshino.

"How am I supposed to figure anything out from an empty envelope? And if she'd said something when we met again in Year 1 Class 3, I'd have remembered everything on the spot. Telling me now, after all this time..."

Too late.

I couldn't help but feel that way.

While I knew it was cruel to attack Oikura, I found it hard to overlook all of my festering discontent—not when I thought about the high school life we could have enjoyed.

We'd lost out, I couldn't help but feel.

Had I known, I couldn't stop myself from thinking, even that class council meeting might not have ended the way it did.

"Heh. When you met again?" Ogi said with a mischievous grin. "I was the girl from back then, Araragi, it's so nice to see you, oh, did you really forget about me, come on, you're the worst, oh you, talk about coldhearted! But that's just what I l-o-v-e☆ about you! If she said something like that?"

"I've never met any character on that sublime a level in the world of this story..."

"Well, in that case."

And then.

Ogi's expression suddenly turned from cheeky to solemn.

"Maybe you should think about why she didn't say that."

"Huh?"

"And *why she left without saying a thing*—you need to think about that, too. If you don't and you apologize tomorrow, you might only make the situation worse."

Ogi's tone seemed oddly certain despite her use of the word *might*.

"If you can't figure it out, then you need to keep thinking. You need to think until you figure out the reason. You need to solve anything that seems ambiguous. Nothing angers a victim more than an empty apology, after all."

"Victim? Come on, Ogi. Give me a break—don't you think that's going a little far? Sure, I committed an unthinkable social faux pas in forgetting about someone who did a lot for me, but I wouldn't say I victimized her—"

"You're right. You didn't do anything wrong, you're just a fool. A hopelessly hopeless fool."

"…?"

Ogi sneered at my confusion.

If that was the sort of smile you bestowed on a fool—perhaps it was far too kind.

"Ogi, what exactly—are you saying you know?"

"I don't know anything. You're the one who knows—Araragi-senpai."

"Me…"

Something I knew?

Something—I was forgetting.

"I think we ought to borrow a page from Miss Oikura's younger days and treat ourselves to a quiz. Here's your problem."

Ogi put up a finger like she was some kind of TV host. No—maybe like she was some famous detective? As a proud mystery fan, she did have that much down.

"Sodachi Oikura hates Koyomi Araragi as if he was a homewrecker. This is because Koyomi Araragi failed to meet Sodachi Oikura's expectations—and so she transferred schools without saying a word to him. Now, *what exactly did Sodachi Oikura hope to get from Koyomi Araragi?*"

"What did she—hope to get from me?"

"A hint. It involves your parents' profession—you have 120 seconds."

Two minutes, in other words.

Way too short a time.

Then again, I could be given two years, the same amount of time Oikura spent depressed, and still not come up with an answer.

014

"Basically, Miss Oikura wanted something in return for—how would you put it, teaching you how fun or whatever math could be."

Two minutes later.

Ogi divulged the solution without giving me a single second of extra time—just how antsy was she to go home?

"In return?"

"Yes—of all the things Miss Senjogahara did or said, that bothered Miss Oikura the most, didn't it? She's teaching you without seeking anything in return—this irritated the girl who once conducted study sessions with you."

Enough to make her get physical.

"Don't tell me you actually believed her. That she'd be happy so long as you loved math and kept loving it forever? It's something a fairy would say."

"…"

"What was it, she turned down the snacks you brought her to show your gratitude? But if you read into that, perhaps she wouldn't accept them because she needed more from you in return than some snacks? Seems like you couldn't look at yourself objectively once your eyes were opened to how much fun math could be, but from an outside perspective, those envelopes at the beginning were suspicious. They smell like a trap."

A trap.

Or I guess a baited hook—Ogi continued.

"Sending letters to other students but you being the only one to show up was a lie. A total fib. Actually, she wanted to reel you in and no one else. Doesn't it seem hard to believe that you were the only one to bite if she sent letters to multiple people?"

"Hard to believe? Okay, maybe it's conceited to think that I'm special, but it seems possible. In terms of probability."

"In terms of probability, you are special. Without a doubt."

"…"

"We'll talk about how you're special later, but she targeted you alone precisely because you're special—if young Oikura wanted to invite more people to her study sessions, she would have kept casting her lines, don't you think? There should have been ways for her to promote them even after summer break began. Yet no one but you showed up all summer. What does that mean? What does it mean if you two were alone the entire time?"

So that was her line of reasoning.

Refuting it was difficult, I couldn't deny it—she was probably right. Had Oikura picked her targets and planted letters for all of them, it'd be strange for her plan to have worked only on me. To begin with, it was hard to imagine a large study session getting together at this abandoned home, in this room.

From the very start.

I was to be the only participant.

That's what she ran.

That's what the young girl—planned.

"Miss Oikura knew your math grades were falling, so she must've played to that and planted letters that would interest you in your shoe box. A math problem for a boy thinking about how he needed to do something about his math score—I'd say that's a good lure."

"In that case, what does that say about me for waltzing in here…"

Oikura met me with a smile, but she might have been trying to stifle a laugh—it had all worked on me so perfectly.

"No, no. It didn't work on you perfectly—turns out making other people act exactly according to plan is hard. Personally, I'd say that while you're a fool, Miss Oikura is quite the fool herself."

In short, the real world doesn't work as neatly as math does, Ogi said. The kind of line a math-hater relishes—I wanted to argue the point as a math-lover, but I had to keep quiet here.

Indeed, I didn't know.

What Oikura wanted from me in return back then—I didn't have the first idea what she'd tried to make me do.

Ogi looked at me, satisfied.

Then spoke again.

"But if I had to say which of you was the bigger fool, it would have to be you—because if not for your misunderstanding, I doubt any of this would be happening."

"My misunderstanding?"

"That said, your future might have turned out differently if not for your misunderstanding. You might not be getting along with Miss Hanekawa and Miss Senjogahara the way you are now—so maybe it was a good outcome for you. In that sense, you had great foresight, so don't feel down," Ogi comforted me.

Not that I could tell if she was comforting me or insulting me.

All I knew was that I didn't have any foresight at all.

"Ogi, there's no need to console me, just say it. What kind of misunderstanding was there on my part five years ago?"

"Tell me," she said, as if to deflect my demand—but she wasn't going to drag this out more than necessary if she really wanted to go home.

In fact, she gave it to me straight.

Mercilessly, in a way.

"You're quite familiar with the ruins of the cram school in this town where my uncle, Mèmè Oshino, once lived."

"Hm? Yeah, of course. I told you I even stayed the night there."

"You also said something else. This abandoned home is just about as rundown as those ruins—right?"

"Yeah, and?"

"Don't you find that strange? Why would a cram school, freshly abandoned as of just a few years ago, look *just as rundown* as a home that had already fallen into disuse five years ago?"

"Huh?"

Hm?

Well, that's... Hm?

Was that—strange?

Yes—it was.

The abandoned school and abandoned home shared something in common, which was that they were deteriorating, unoccupied buildings—but it seemed strange that they'd age in such different ways, at such different speeds.

This house had already been abandoned five years ago. It should have deteriorated far worse over the last five years—but it was in a *similar state* as a building that had been in operation until just a few years ago, *which was impossible.* A few years, so two or three...at the most, five years, meaning...

The notion that time had stopped here was mere sentiment.

In reality, five years had passed.

Right—the logical conclusion would be...that until a few years ago, the building we found ourselves in *wasn't an abandoned home*—but what did that mean?

"..."

I put my hand over my mouth. So that I wouldn't make any weird noises.

So that I wouldn't scream in the face of the truth confronting me.

Let's just say.

If, when I visited this place during my first year of middle school, *it hadn't been an abandoned home...*

"This isn't the place I was visiting five years ago? The abandoned home where I met with Oikura that summer is in a totally different place—"

"No, that's not it. We followed a map to come here, remember? The same map as five years ago."

Then we'd read the map wrong.

And there was no guarantee that the map from five years ago was identical to today's—it seemed a little late to say this, but it was also weird that the letters I received five years ago were there today.

This excuse came to mind, but I didn't give voice to it—because I was the expert witness here. I knew for certain that this was the same house I'd visited five years ago—which meant.

Which meant only one thing.

This wasn't an abandoned home five years ago—and so.

And so.

"That's right," Ogi said.

With less mercy than ever. And with less ado.

"Five years ago—*this wasn't an abandoned home.* That's what you misunderstood—this was *Sodachi Oikura's home.*"

015

What I understood the least—as I had wondered time and time again—was how I'd forgotten about coming here every day for a whole summer five years ago. Childhood memories or not, could I really forget a summer that acted as such a major turning point in my life, a piece of it that important?

How?

I could understand forgetting it as a way to protect my psyche if it was some sort of awful, traumatic memory—but it led to me loving math. If anything, it was a positive memory.

A positive experience.

How had I forgotten it until now? Until this very moment?

Because of that, I hadn't noticed that Oikura and I knew each other. I could only see our reunion as a first meeting.

If there was any one *clear reason* for this memory lapse that made sense to me—

If there was a reason, paradoxically.

It was that the memory *hadn't been positive at all*—that if I really thought about it, it might in fact become traumatic…

A truth I wanted to forget.

A reality to be shunned.

If that's what existed here…

"The home—Oikura lived in?"

"It used to have a nameplate, right? Not now, but I think you used to be able to find the characters 'Oikura' there. On what grounds? Well, you found it curious, too. *Why hold a study session in an abandoned home*—the answer is that *this wasn't an abandoned home*."

"No, that's not what I mean—even if this place hadn't been abandoned five years ago, there's no guarantee it was Oikura's home."

"Then why did she always get here before you? Don't you find it strange that she never failed to arrive at your meeting place before you, not even once?"

"…"

Was it—strange?

It was, to the point where I wondered why I hadn't noticed. To the point where you could say that I really had noticed and only pretended I hadn't—in which case, I'd have nothing to say for myself.

"Miss Oikura was always waiting here *because it was her home*—of course, you might have been the first to leave school because of how long each of you loitered around your homeroom, but then, most of your study sessions took place during summer break. She came out of this home on the first day because she lived here. And anyway, once we realize this place wasn't abandoned five years ago, it only makes sense for it to be her home or yours, if you held your study sessions here. This isn't your address, so we can determine it to be Miss Oikura's home by process of elimination."

"The process of elimination again…"

And not the process of eliminating one option out of three—eliminating the one wrong option of two. There was no debating this solution.

It was overwhelmingly—right.

"So Oikura invited me to her house… I guess that does feel more like a study session than if we met in an abandoned home—but still."

It surprised me to learn that I'd managed to enter a girl's room as a mere first-year middle-school boy—but no bittersweet sensation filled me.

After all, back then.

I didn't think this home—was a home.

Right. I called it a haunted house, and—

"Okay then. I'm sorry to crack the whip just as you're busy being shocked, but we're getting to the most important part of my line of reasoning. Five years ago, *did you think her home was abandoned?* Did you think it was a haunted house?"

"Are you saying I'm misremembering?"

"No, misunderstanding. I'm pretty sure your memories are correct. You've given specific testimony, saying that the windows in this room were already as broken as they are now—so you're not misremembering, you're misunderstanding."

"..."

The tape-reinforced windows.

The cracked, putty-filled walls.

The messy rooms and messy hallways.

It wasn't an abandoned home—but it was wrecked to the point that you'd mistake it for one.

If this led to a conclusion—if there was a conclusion here you'd want to shun.

If it was a home that people lived in at the time.

And it was still that wrecked.

"...There was violence in the family."

Violence in the family.

Domestic abuse.

I tried to say it plainly, without any emotion.

Like a TV reporter reading off a script.

But I couldn't hold back the visceral revulsion—I now stood in that kind of a home, and it disgusted me.

And five years ago.

I had been hard at work studying here, at the site of a crime, and nothing could stop me from hating myself for it.

"That's right."

Meanwhile, Ogi was impressively unemotional. She grinned, then twirled around to take a look at the ruined room, as if the truth she'd arrived at made her feel nothing at all.

"You'd have to intentionally destroy a residence for it to be in such a disastrous state that you'd mistake it for an abandoned home—shatter the windows, beat the walls, demolish the furniture. Is the broken intercom broken for the same reason?"

A crumbling home.

A wrecked home—a broken home.

Wounded.

A home that could fall apart at any moment.

Now I understood. It wasn't an abandoned home—but.

A right and proper first-year middle schooler, who was ignorant about the world and could only think of a home as a peaceful, warm, and comforting place, foolishly misunderstood it to be abandoned.

Haunted by ghosts?

What was I talking about? How ridiculous.

This place was as human as it got.

"Oikura…couldn't have been the one."

She wouldn't have invited me to her home if she were perpetrating the violence.

"So her father? Or her mother…"

"Haha. Even my gray matter can't figure out which of the two it was. But one or the other, no doubt. It takes a whole lot of work to destroy an entire home to this degree all alone, though. It just might have been both of them," Ogi blithely offered a terrible thought.

The worst part about it was that it sounded completely plausible.

"It seems Miss Oikura was brought up in quite the tragic household environment. I guess we can't blame you, snugly raised in your peaceful household, for shoving your memories of an entire summer spent here to the furthest corners and darkest depths of your psyche. If there's any saving grace, it's that the violence was never aimed at Miss Oikura's body—or at least any exposed parts of her skin."

"…"

At least, huh?

That was far too miniscule a saving grace.

"Transferring once second term started also makes sense in that case—her family, on the verge of crumbling, finally did. This is of course groundless speculation, but couldn't Miss Oikura have changed her name then as well? That'd make the name once found on this home's front plate uncertain, but…either way, is that why you thought you were meeting her for the first time when you were reunited in Year 1 Class 3 at Naoetsu High? If you'd been in the same middle school, you should have at least heard her name, interaction or no."

You still ought to have recognized her face, though, Ogi said, spreading his arms—this seemed to be her idea of a joke.

I wished she wouldn't weave jokes into her deduction.

Especially in situations like this.

"In any case, we can be sure that the Oikura family would have been at its limits back then—and she wanted to do something about it."

"Something? Like what?"

"Something. Anything. *That's* why she called you here. In other words, that's what she wanted from you in exchange. Even if I'm wrong, it wasn't snacks she was after. Creating a new fan of mathematics was her method, not her goal."

"No, hold on a second. Fixing a family crumbling as a result of violence? That's asking too much. What did she expect from a middle-school kid? I might've been acting in some Fire Sisterish ways back then, but at the end of the day, it was basically just child's play—"

"You've got the order reversed. The Fire Sisters are acting in Koyomish ways—"

"W-Well, fine, that's true."

"She never expected that much out of you, of course. If she did, she'd probably just ask you for help instead of going such an indirect route—which is where your parents come in."

"My parents…"

"They're police officers, aren't they?"

Your honorable parents, who showed you what was right. She expected you to report back to them about the state of the Oikuras.

"If you did—the police would intervene in her domestic situation. To be honest, I don't see that solving anything, but it would be a last-ditch plan to save a family on the verge of collapse."

"…"

Why be so roundabout, just report the situation yourself—an

outsider might say. If only things were so easy—domestic violence is abuse that stays within a family, so those on the outside have to make moves from their outside position.

Still…

"Still, I'd been sworn to secrecy…by Oikura herself. She said I couldn't tell anyone about our meetings here."

My sisters and I even stopped getting along as a result.

Why would she say that?

"Yes—just like Snow Woman. I think Miss Oikura didn't want to be the one to accuse her family, no matter what. She would feel guilty about exposing them, or perhaps she feared retribution—maybe it was another case of both?"

"So, she wanted me to tell my parents about the state of her family, but *of my own accord*? That's what you're saying her plan was?"

And it was with this plan that she taught me math—not that the idea even made me angry. I didn't have any right to be mad in the first place. Honest to a fault—to the point I ruined my relationship with my little sisters—I never told anyone about my trips to this abandoned, or rather, Oikura's home, just as promised.

I didn't even think it was her home to begin with.

I simply learned math from her, without a care in the world.

I paid her nothing in return—and just exploited her.

I took from her.

When she said that no good could possibly come out of someone like me worrying about her, she wasn't acting tough or exaggerating. She meant exactly what she said.

My life is a total mess thanks to you.

She'd said that as well.

It too was exactly right.

Her life was a total mess—and I'd walked away.

I'd—neglected her.

"That means they must've been somewhere in this house," I said. "Right? They never showed themselves—but Oikura's parents were here."

"Well, yes. They probably were. Although they never came out to offer their guest tea and snacks, I guess they weren't so deviant as to be violent toward another family's child."

"…"

But that also meant that I protected Oikura by coming to this home—because I was nothing more than a "guest" who'd leave after a few hours. Back to his own home. I didn't want to think about the kind of storm that must have blown through this place after I did.

I didn't want to think about it.

What she must have looked like under her school uniform.

"So I did nothing that Oikura wanted me to do—and yet I took just the knowledge that she'd given me and sucked it all up."

Of course she'd hate me for that.

Who wouldn't—hold a grudge.

Forget ungrateful, I was a thief.

No wonder she never bothered saying goodbye—how did she feel as she kept teaching me math every day?

Ogi called it indirect, but the route Oikura hit upon after summoning all of her knowledge and bravery turned out to be fruitless. How had she felt about that?

I may have only been the intermediary, but maybe she thought she was the fool for ever relying on me—Ogi was right, though. Compared to her, I was the far bigger fool.

The empty envelope Oikura stuck under the low table was a perfect expression of the kind of guy I was.

Empty. The wrong choice.

An unreliable guy.

"Heheh. Well, I guess that's about it." Ogi checked her watch once more—as if she'd been timing herself to see how fast she could solve this mystery. What kind of person speed-ran this? "If my memory serves me correctly, you began this investigation to look into the reason Miss Oikura hated you like you were some kind of homewrecker—and I feel we've more or less accomplished that goal now. As such, I do think it's about time to pack up and go, but if you have any final remarks, please, go ahead."

Some kind of homewrecker.

In reality, though, that wasn't it. Oikura *wanted* me to be a homewrecker—did it get any more ironic than that?

I thought about mentioning this, but final remarks needed to be more comprehensive than that.

"I've been feeling very fortunate—I can't deny that it's been smooth sailing for me, and I'm happy. I have friends, I have a girlfriend, I have juniors—I'm very, very happy. But," I said.

"I've started to hate my happy self just a little bit."

Ogi grinned in reply. "Then I'll love you enough to make up for that. And depending on how you look at it, it's a good thing you haven't gone so far as to start hating math."

"You're right about that."

True.

No matter what I might start to hate, even if I've lost sight of justice, math is the one thing I'll always love. You could even call it a kind of curse.

016

The epilogue, or maybe, the punch line of this story.

The next day, I was roused from bed as usual by my little sisters Karen and Tsukihi before trudging my way to school with heavy footsteps. The truth was clear now. The reality of the situation had been exposed. My forgotten memories had been dredged up and I'd learned what they meant, but what I needed to do stayed the same—improve my relationship with Sodachi Oikura.

Our feud two years earlier.

Our missed connection five years ago.

Both misdeeds and mistakes far too late to take back, I couldn't redo any of it—which was exactly why I couldn't fail now. At the very least, I had to be careful to make sure we never had another commotion like yesterday's.

As I passed through the gates of Naoetsu High while thinking this, I saw Tsubasa Hanekawa trudging along with even heavier footsteps as if she alone shouldered all the troubles of this world.

She normally walked with excellent posture, so seeing her hunched over… Well, she was second only to me as far as being concerned about the hostility between Senjogahara and Oikura. We needed to work together as class president and vice president to tackle the situation, I thought, and called out to her from behind.

I then spoke openly to her about what I'd learned over the last couple of days about my relationship with Oikura—confessing all my thickheaded foolishness, which didn't feel great, but I couldn't keep it a secret from Hanekawa now. Not when we found ourselves in this spot.

It did seem wise to wait and see a little longer before telling Senjogahara about this one...

Either way, I braced myself for the unsparing reaction I deserved, but to my surprise Hanekawa said:

"Ogi Oshino?"

She'd reacted to Ogi's name.

"Mister Oshino's—niece?"

"Um...yeah. I figured a lot out thanks to her. I guess you could say it runs in the Oshino family, she was quite the detective. I doubt I could have solved yesterday's mystery or the day before's without her."

"..."

Hanekawa seemed to ponder this—silently.

More sternly than you'd expect.

"Are you sure that's who she is?"

"Huh? Yeah. I'm certain, Kanbaru introduced us," I said, realizing that Kanbaru's introduction was no guarantee at all of her identity being authentic. Something about her felt unfathomable—but now I realized I hadn't fathomed a thing about her.

I don't know anything.

You're the one who knows.

But it seemed like I didn't know anything, either.

What else—did I know?

"Araragi. It pains me to have to say something that would only keep picking at this wound..."

Hanekawa faced me. It was very much like her not to comfort me in a half-hearted manner—but even she seemed to balk at the thought of piling on me.

Don't worry about me, I urged her, say it.

If anything, I didn't want more causes for regret after coming this far. If Hanekawa noticed something from her point of view, I wanted her to come out and say it.

We entered the school building and began climbing the stairs to our class as we continued our conversation side by side.

"It wouldn't be strange for her to learn, somehow, that you'd hit a wall with math during your first-year, first-term finals in middle school. And I could see her putting the Monty Hall problem in your shoe locker and playing upon that. But—how did Miss Oikura learn the most vital fact in her plan, that your parents are police officers?"

"Huh..."

"Weren't you doing your best to hide it?"

Right.

Even Hanekawa didn't know what my parents did until my little sisters told her just the other day. I had a habit of not telling anyone, even when asked, to avoid any extraneous or unnecessary trouble—so why?

Why did Oikura know?

How?

"Well, maybe she just happened to find out some way or another," Hanekawa said, qualifying her query, "but couldn't there still be something? I don't know what, but something. Some kind of memory—involving you and Miss Oikura that you have to go further back to remember. A door you have to open."

As far as memories—and families were concerned, Tsubasa Hanekawa had more to say than the average person. The words carried a lot of weight when they came from this girl with mismatched wings.

A memory I needed to go further back to remember.

A door I needed to open.

If they existed, they'd be from a time before I was even a middle schooler—around the time Oikura and I were in grade school... What could have possibly happened then?

Could there really be something I was still forgetting—on top of all that?

If there was.

Just how big of a fool was Koyomi Araragi?

Was there no end to my foolishness?

—How could I ever forget you.

Oikura said that to me. Which meant she must remember. About this fool, two years ago, five years ago, and even before that.

I arrived in front of the classroom—whether or not Sodachi Oikura was there on the other side was an impossible proof.

CHAPTER THREE
SODACHI LOST

TSUBASA HANEKA

001

So let us now return to the topic of Ogi Oshino—or so I say, but ultimately, she is her and nothing else. Whether we start, repeat, or return to
this basic topic, that is the entirety of what can be said about her. Were
you to depict the being that is Ogi Oshino in a novel, it would end after
a single line. And you know, as someone who tends to ramble on, I have
to say I'm very grateful to have a heroine like her.

Ogi Oshino was Ogi Oshino—and they all lived happily ever after.
One line.

And if you were to stretch that idea to an extreme, to as far as it
could possibly go, you could summarize anyone in this way—though
Ryunosuke Akutagawa is known for saying that life is not worth a single
line of Baudelaire, you could sum up any life, whether Baudelaire's or
Ryunosuke Akutagawa's, in a single line if you wanted. It's what would
end up happening. Were you to fit any life into lines, whether a great
man's or an average one's, it'd be a single line long. Saying these kinds of
things may get me criticized for being pessimistic or abject—you might
say that humans, any human, isn't something so flimsy and frivolous
that you could speak about their life using only a single line. Yes, I'd of
course like to think that myself—I'd hate for my life to be spoken of in
just one line. Were you to speak it, were you to tell it, I'd like it to be at
least a book long. An ebook? No good, I need a cover—not just paper,

but some kind of front cover. And I'd want a spine that's even stronger. I'd want my spine to tell of me when I'm lined up on a bookshelf. I want to be a book whose spine tells an entire story. So I'd like it if the idea that you can say everything about a person in a single line wasn't true—and that's all I can think about faced with living proof that you can, Ogi Oshino.

Were I to say that—

"No, no, your romantic ideas are absolutely right. Anyone has enough substance to be turned into a full volume," our perp would likely answer with a grin—her jet-black eyes fixed on me as she pierced me with her words. "Of course, whether anyone would bother reading that book is a different question."

Are you trying to say that a book that goes unread is worthless?

"What I'm saying—is that you can't put a price on a book that goes unread. Price and value are two different things. Asking about value is nearly a completely different question from asking about price."

Hearing this would remind me of the girl who'd been nicknamed How Much—which of the two was she asking about? Price? Or value? Price, something determined by the balance of supply and demand—or value, something fixed. Was it weight, or was it mass? Of course, that might be too cruel of a question to ask her after she learned that value was something determined by majority vote.

"It's presumptuous to think that someone will read an entire book in today's society—you've got to think of it as its existence being more than enough. While I might be a humanities person who loves to read, unless you can find satisfaction in seeing that your shelves are filled with unread books, you can't ever be a bookworm."

But, she said. *If you still wanted someone to read you.*

"You ought to come up with a one-second summary—you ought to say it in a phrase, you ought to convey any knowledge or tales in a second. If you can't, who's going to bother listening to a story like yours?"

No one's going to read you.

Now it made sense.

All of those novels popping up lately with full sentences for titles and striking sales copy might in fact be based on that reasoning—one line. One phrase. No, it's ultimately the tale that conveys its meaning in a single word that's most desired these days—and so.

While we've been studying math for a bit now, let's end with a language arts class—here is your question. There's no need to prepare for it, of course—it's the type of question we all know.

Give a response on something or other in so many words.

While my childish mind didn't understand the reason behind limiting the number of words for these questions you encounter in elementary school, I know why quite well when I think about it now—the ability to briefly summarize is essential when discussing language. If you think about it, the purpose of words, their role, is to *convey*—and nothing else.

There are of course things that aren't conveyed.

Things that don't get conveyed even after you've run out of words—even if they are, you might still forget them.

As I've already said about Ogi Oshino—were we to center the question around her, it would be, "Discuss Ogi Oshino in three words or fewer," and the answer would be "Ogi Oshino." So here is my final question for you—"How much of a fool is Koyomi Araragi?"

Answer in twenty words or fewer.

However, the words "Ogi Oshino" must appear in your answer.

002

Come to think of it, this may have been my first time since August doing anything with Hanekawa—which of course isn't to say that we'd done nothing at all together for the previous two months or so, we were class president and vice president, but it really had been quite a while since we last did something big together as a two-man cell.

An event.

An incident, you could even say.

Still, it wasn't all fun and games—unfortunately, I wasn't in a state of mind to let me get flustered over working alongside Tsubasa Hanekawa, class president among class presidents, a grand figure whose name will surely be remembered throughout history.

This was because my gait was so extremely heavy that it now seemed fettered by something resembling Saturn's gravity—for you see, our two-man cell's goal, the "something big" we needed to come upon…

My pace as I walked toward it was just as heavy, just as weighty as my mood.

"So—did you figure it out, Araragi?" asked Hanekawa.

Like she'd finally asked a question she'd been waiting for the perfect time to spring.

Classes had finished for the day, we had left Naoetsu High, and we were on our way together—but not on the road back to my home or

Hanekawa's.

"Why did Miss Oikura know your parents' profession?"

"Mmh... Uh," I muttered with a vague nod.

Most people would probably see this as trying to gloss over something you didn't know—in fact, it was the complete opposite. There are also things that people try to gloss over *because they do know*, because they understand—but while it had only been an unconscious reaction, what could be more meaningless than lying or glossing over something in the face of Tsubasa Hanekawa?

"I figured it out," I drooped my head and said. "I checked with Sengoku, so I'm sure of it."

"Um, why are you hanging your head when you did?"

"My head's like a fruit, the riper it is, the more it sags."

"I see... You kind of seem out of it today. You look like someone who visits a friend at a hospital only to show up looking sicker than them. What's the matter with you?"

"..."

A hospital visit, huh.

Then again, that was the kind of gentle, roundabout rephrasing of reality that I knew Hanekawa for. Were you to give a cold and precise account of the truth, this was more like a home visit—by a class president and vice president. Though we'd never conducted one of these in our half-year since taking office, we had no choice.

I say that because I wasn't blameless regarding this situation—or rather, the trained eye would have no option but to place the responsibility for it entirely on me. The *girl being visited* had to place all the blame on me, in particular—and knowing this made my steps heavy.

Like I was on Saturn.

In fact, I'd been feeling so uncomfortably out of place for the last few days that it really felt like I'd been taken to another planet—and told that it was in fact my birthplace, awkwardly enough.

"It'd make anyone want to hang their head. I wasn't able to remember no matter how hard I tried, but then it came right back to me once I did what you suggested. You really do know everything, Hanekawa."

"I don't know everything. I only know what I know," she answered casually. This much was business as usual, but then she added, "I can't say I know everything when I don't know what Ogi knows."

" … "

Ogi.

Ogi Oshino.

"Are we okay?" asked Hanekawa. "She's not tailing us, is she?"

"Tailing us… What, do you think she's an assassin or something?" I replied, half-dumbfounded, but Hanekawa wasn't kidding, and she stopped to look behind her. She'd waited until we stood at a point with few blind spots—she did live here, but still, this class president had no need for a map app.

"An assassin? Do you mean a detective?"

Had Ogi, a transfer student with little knowledge of the area, been tailing us, it should have been easy to find her by turning around here and straining our eyes—but even Hanekawa couldn't spot our unseen tail, our unseen detective.

She wasn't satisfied, though. "Hmm, I would have preferred it if she'd come along with us—in this case, at least. I could've given her the slip."

"Aren't you acting a little paranoid?"

"No, but think about it. Even if she isn't tailing us, she might have gone ahead of us. It's clear where we're headed, so taking the time to look up the location would be the less risky move—making it the more annoying and harder-to-defend-against scenario. It's not easy to look up another student's address these days, but not impossible… I don't think I'm being paranoid."

"If you're not being paranoid, then you're overestimating Ogi. Yes, she's Oshino's niece, so she does seem *reasonably* smart, but she's still a child, or you know, a freshman. Charmingly innocent. It's my duty as her senior to keep her from becoming like Oshino, as well as my way of repaying him."

"Your way of repaying him… Well, that is a wonderful mindset."

Hanekawa began walking again.

Her tone had been relatively harsh, considering she'd complimented me.

"How admirable," she continued. "And here I was thinking that you'd gotten obsessed with yet another cute little underclassman who'd appeared on the scene."

"What do you mean, yet another…"

"Weren't you acting in a similar way with Miss Kanbaru? If that really is your mindset, I'd like you to stop giving off the impression that you're preoccupied with an underclassman just as our class is going through all these problems."

"I'll take that to heart."

"Good."

I don't know if you'd call it being serious or being stuffy.

But this part about her never changed.

No, maybe it had.

Either way, Tsubasa Hanekawa was clearly no big fan of Ogi's—but it was true that our transfer student didn't have the most approachable personality.

And she was awfully enigmatic.

Even if you conceded all of that, though, you had to admit that she was far more approachable than Oikura was now—

"Just to make sure," Hanekawa said. "You'd forgotten about your time in middle school with Miss Oikura until you accompanied Ogi on her fieldwork, correct?"

"Hm? Actually, no, it's the other way around, she accompanied me on my fieldwork. She came along with me for the most part—she just helped me remember Oikura. Yeah, I guess I feel bad about troubling Ogi when I think of it that way. I shouldn't carelessly get my juniors involved in my personal business. I'll have to make it up to her later."

"Hm. Hmmm. You're not understanding me for some reason. Maybe I'm not putting it the right way?" Hanekawa tilted her head. "From my perspective, she's as dangerous as they get."

"Dangerous? Are you talking about Oikura?"

"See? We're talking past each other. It's almost like you're intentionally avoiding my point—but whatever. It probably just means we can't talk about it yet."

"What do you mean?"

"I'm saying there are limits to what a person can do—but that's exactly why we need to do everything we can. It's easier to walk along the edges of your limits when you can see them."

It was a superhuman thing to say—and extremely human at the same time. I say this because the old Hanekawa wouldn't have thought twice about stepping over those lines.

I think it goes without saying, of course, that her way of trying to get as close as possible to the kinds of lines that most people avoid showed her mental fortitude. Then again, you're not going to set a goal of taking a post-graduation trip around the world without that kind of inner toughness.

I sincerely respected her.

That made it all the more disappointing to see her in the grips of a line of reasoning so far off the mark.

I might need to talk to her about it before we arrived at our destination. I needed to put aside any personal feelings born out of my adoration of Hanekawa, because I didn't want the situation to get any more complicated.

"Hanekawa. If you think that Ogi feels hostility toward Oikura, you're wrong. The two haven't even met. Though, hearing my story, her eccentricity might've aroused interest—"

"That's not what I'm worried about. No part of me whatsoever is concerned about whether or not Ogi has Miss Oikura in her sights. What I am worried about is—"

"Is?"

"You—Araragi."

Something you don't understand well might have you in its sights— Hanekawa warned.

"Something I don't understand?"

"Or maybe—*something unwelcome.*"

True, you couldn't deny that Ogi was unfathomable—and she certainly had me in her sights.

But what was Hanekawa saying?

What was she saying—and what did she want to say?

What couldn't she say?

"To be honest, I don't know if you can defend against it all."

"Defend against…"

"You call what happened during spring break hell—but your ordeals might have only begun."

My ordeals.

No, no way, Hanekawa was going through far more of an ordeal. Our ill-fated class president, not me, I thought, when—

We'd been busy rambling back and forth, but class president Tsubasa Hanekawa and vice president Koyomi Araragi reached their destination: Sodachi Oikura's current address.

003

After two years of absence stemming from the Year 1 Class 3 meeting held on July fifteenth, former class president Sodachi Oikura had at last, whether because the time was right or in spite of it all, returned to school, only to stop coming again the next day. She didn't come the next day, or the day after that—which is to say she'd gone back to being absent from school. No, she hadn't even been present for classes on that first day, so the records would only show an uninterrupted streak of absence. If you witnessed the incident that occurred early that fateful morning, her resumed absence was the result of her delirious behavior—this in no way precludes casting doubt on the view that it was my fault, but unfortunately, there were also witnesses to the violence wrought by Senjogahara's fist. The quick thinking that led to her collapsing on the spot somehow managed to keep her out of trouble, but it was only a stopgap measure—though of course, Oikura had been the one to strike first.

Just as I'd hoped, no one was sure if she'd stabbed the back of my hand with a ballpoint pen. But if a girl resuming her absence after finally returning to school ever got connected to a grand brawl, it was sure to become an issue.

While free-spirited and uncontrollable students like Kanbaru obscure the fact, Naoetsu High is in general a full-fledged prep school, meaning it is exceptionally strict when it comes to scandals.

In other words, Sodachi Oikura taking off from school again also endangered Hitagi Senjogahara's position to some degree, since the situation now involved her—though of course, we're talking about a clever girl here.

Keenly aware of the disquieting mood at school, she hadn't returned since that day either. Senjogahara took a leave of absence (?) in synch with Oikura. The stated reason was probably anemia, or perhaps minor fracturing (from hitting Oikura with her fist), but as far as people like Hanekawa and I, with our deep understanding of Senjogahara, were concerned, she was one hundred percent faking it.

She'd lived thinking only about her own self-protection once upon a time—though the old Senjogahara would never confront Oikura and precipitate such a commotion, not even by accident.

Whatever the case, it looked like one of those situations where no one involved in a fight is truly innocent. Senjogahara succeeded in making it hard for outside parties to comment, for which I commend her— but you could also call it reaping what you sow.

Anyway, Oikura had stopped coming to school, and so had Senjogahara. On the second day, class president Tsubasa Hanekawa decided to act.

"Miss Senjogahara could lose her recommendation at this rate," she cautioned me.

"Wait... Why? You mean her college recommendation, right? Due to a violent scandal?"

"Nope, that's not why. She managed to make both sides look guilty—but simply as a matter of attendance. She might not be as bad as you, but she's taking a lot of days off."

"Oh, I guess so..."

Come to think of it, her attendance rate during her first and second years could hardly be worse. It was of course because of her so-called illness, so while she'd returned to living like a regular high school student since May—

"She was sick with the flu or something in August when you weren't around. I'm sure she'd have no trouble at all getting in by way of exams even if her recommendation got rescinded, but a canceled recommendation is a fairly big deal that could have repercussions for our juniors—we need to solve this problem."

We.

That included me.

Already.

"Okay, but how? Do we go to Senjogahara's, tell her she has to stop pretending to be sick, and drag her out of bed?"

Not that she'd be cooped up, since it was a feigned illness. Judging from the less-than-perfect lies she always told, she could be out shopping.

She really did worry me in so many ways.

"It's not just Miss Senjogahara—we need to be worried about Miss Oikura, too."

"Oikura?"

"Yes. Miss Oikura, too—aren't you worried about her?"

"…"

Hearing a statement that certain made it hard to contradict…but to be honest, I didn't know if *worried* summed up everything I felt about Oikura.

Not to say it didn't affect me to know that she'd gone back to being a "shut-in"—but I didn't know how to approach her when I thought about the relationship between us that I'd uncovered the other day.

It felt too late to thank her or apologize to her—okay, that was nothing more than a convenient excuse. If I'm being honest, it felt awkward and shameful, and that was the real reason I didn't want to have to face her.

You often hear people say you ought to live your life looking to the future, not the past.

You can't change the past, but you can alter the future.

That kind of thing.

Absolutely, yes, it's exactly as they say—but facing the future in order to turn away from the past didn't feel like looking ahead, it felt backwards.

A negative way to be forward-looking.

We ought to live looking both to the future and the past—and I was a man as far removed from that as you could get.

Whether I faced the past or the future, my eyes were shut as I tried to maintain the status quo.

That's who I was.

"Yeah, I guess I'm worried," I ended up saying.

The words must have sounded reluctant.

Or rather, objectionable and offensive.

"But it's like I told you yesterday—I'm at a point where I even think it might be better if I don't bother her right now. It does concern me that she's stopped coming to school again, but I have to admit, some part of me feels relieved."

"Coming out and saying that is fine, you know," Hanekawa approved with forced cheer.

Since both parties involved in the incident weren't coming to school, some of the fallout was starting to come the class president's way—which did make her look exhausted, but here she was, as plucky as ever.

"It's okay to say that. No one's going to hear that and think you're trying to gloss over the situation—and it's not as if keeping up appearances is the only thing that matters."

"I'm glad you think so."

I wasn't thanking her so much as I was being honest with her— Tsubasa Hanekawa was always there to mend my heart whenever it neared its breaking point. In fact, that's how it's been since spring break.

This whole time.

"Hanekawa, if you have some kind of idea, I'll help out, of course. Whatever it is you have planned, it did come from your brain. Are you basically plotting to get them to make up?"

"Mmh. Mmmm—making up might be a little too much to ask. Especially out of the blue... They did have a fistfight. The old Miss Senjogahara might have been fine with it, but I don't know about now."

"Yeah...not now," I agreed.

In fact, I started to feel embarrassed about asking a stupid question—this was actually an instance where Senjogahara's reformation acted as a negative. You might not expect it, but the number of instances was a lot higher than one.

It was at times like these when I felt that the old Hitagi Senjogahara, tense and thinking only of her own self-protection, was really gone. You could say she'd left it up to me to figure out a plan and clean up after her mess, but she was also just staying away from school because something happened there that bothered her.

It wasn't stubbornness or strategy.

Really, she was being a regular girl.

A high school girl.

But if you were defining her that way, you needed to see Oikura in the same light.

It wouldn't be fair otherwise.

Given our history, I couldn't help but be biased and prejudiced and see Oikura's actions as being exceptional and out of the ordinary. I couldn't prevent myself from finding some kind of deeper meaning in what she did, but I also needed to step away from our connection—however impossible it was to forget—and look at her as a fellow classmate.

Which meant I couldn't just neglect her.

"So, Araragi. My plan is to go for a home visit after school today—to visit both Miss Senjogahara and Miss Oikura."

"Hm?" I replied, caught unawares.

It seemed like a natural guess as to where the conversation would go next, or a natural turn even if I didn't guess it. I was more surprised than I needed to be.

I shouldn't have been hm-ing this late in the day.

"If it's Miss Oikura's address you're wondering about, I got it from our homeroom teacher—but this is where we get to what I wanted to discuss," Hanekawa said, intimating that the class president and vice president visiting the two at home to resolve this situation was a predetermined procedure and path open to no discussion whatsoever. "We're so short on time that I thought we could split the work—who would you rather visit? Miss Senjogahara or Miss Oikura?"

"…"

"I'll leave it up to you."

The question was like some kind of psychological game.

But it was no game at all and didn't involve logic—only my psyche.

004

Pay a visit to my girlfriend's home, or pay a visit to my mortal enemy's home.

Quite the extreme choice, but I ended up picking the latter—you might say that I was making a masochistic, self-flagellating decision to corner myself, just like Oikura. And you'd be right, I did let my self-flagellating impulses take over.

Someone like Koyomi Araragi would never face Sodachi Oikura otherwise—and whatever she thought of me, I wouldn't be able to think about myself in any way at all unless I made a change.

I gave myself over to that feeling—Oikura would only find it annoying, and she probably hated that part of me, but regardless of how much hate I attracted, it wasn't as if I could suddenly stop being me.

I am me.

Koyomi Araragi is Koyomi Araragi.

But there was another, no, two other elements here—one being my exact relation to Oikura. As Hanekawa pointed out the day before, why did Oikura know what my parents did? And indeed, following her advice led me to the answer, miraculously solving the mystery. Miraculously, or promptly. And no, I'd only found an answer, I didn't know for sure if I could call it a solution—but in any case, my relation to her during our first year of high school, during our first year of middle school, and now, during elementary school, all sat there in my mind.

I wanted to use that as a base.

And I wanted to talk to her again.

...To be honest, I didn't, and I knew we wouldn't have a proper conversation in more ways than one, but there are times when you just have to leap into a bottomless swamp even if it's illogical or straight-up suicidal.

It had to happen.

The second element, though, was extremely practical, or perhaps pragmatic, which is that if I went to visit Senjogahara, I would without a doubt treat her with kindness—which wouldn't help her. To be fair, she'd helped me, or even taken my place by confronting Oikura for me, so I had no right at all to act stern even if you disregard the fact that we're going out. No, sorry, don't disregard that. Anyway, I had a better relationship with Senjogahara than I did with myself—an ironclad case for letting Hanekawa, who could be open and unsparing with her, handle that situation.

"Yes, you're right, I agree. I thought you'd choose Miss Senjogahara despite all of that—but I guess this is part of who you are," Hanekawa said. "Then let me handle Miss Senjogahara, and you do whatever you can to drag Miss Oikura back to school. It might be impossible to make them friends, or to get them to reconcile...but leaving things as they stand is just going to bring both of them unhappiness."

We needed to get Senjogahara to stop playing hooky so that her college recommendation wouldn't be rescinded—and we couldn't allow Oikura to keep doing this either, not after she'd returned to school, however halfheartedly. The two might come to blows if they met in class again—but taking care to make sure that didn't happen was part of the class president and vice president's job.

Even if we weren't up to it, we had to do all we could.

That might sound snide, considering that Oikura once abandoned her own job as class president—but whatever, the decision was made for me, class vice president, to wait until after school to visit her current place of residence.

Hm?

You want to know why I met up with Hanekawa again, when we were going to act separately? Well, this is how that happened—and I personally see this as one of her ordeals, or rather an illustration of her fretfulness. After the final bell, I got Oikura's address from Hanekawa, who still had some business at school, and started off on my own—but just as I neared the school gates.

"Hmmm? Well, if it isn't Araragi-senpai!"

Ogi Oshino called out to me.

"Oh… Ogi."

I.

I kind of felt like the air had been let out of my balloon just as I was getting ready to take off—nothing in particular had happened, but it was as if I'd finally prepared myself to go off and tackle a very important matter only to have someone offer me a cup of tea and a seat. I doubt you understand what I'm trying to say here, and I don't either. But if someone offers you some tea, you can't leave as soon as you take it.

"Ogi…are you heading home?"

"Home? Um…no?" She clapped her hands. With a smile. "What are you talking about? We agreed to meet here, remember? Our promise was to meet by the school gates at 3:42 p.m. And look at you, right on the dot, you're so punctual. You're so serious when it comes to this kind of thing—you fool."

"Hm??"

I tilted my head.

I couldn't recall making the promise—it was nowhere to be found in my memories. But, well, it had to be true, if Ogi said so. Though the way she called out to me just now didn't make much sense in that case. Not to mention, 3:42 p.m. seemed like too exact of a meeting time.

Uh oh, had I forgotten a promise I'd made to a junior? What an awful example I was setting. How was I supposed to put on airs now?

"Yaaay, hooray! My senior Araragi is taking me to a sushi restaurant, and not one of those cheap revolving ones either."

"Did I really promise you that?! Me?!"

"Of course you did. You said it was to celebrate my transferring into this school."

"A nice sushi meal to celebrate transferring schools… What in the world has transferred here into my school?" I said jokingly, but it was also a very sincere question—what exactly had transferred here into my school?

"And you promised you'd take me out to a bar afterwards."

"A bar? Like a salad bar?"

One expensive junior had transferred into my school. Even if she meant a salad bar.

But whether or not I'd made such a promise, today was the one day I couldn't go to a sushi restaurant or a bar—feeling bad, I gave her a sincere apology.

"I'm sorry to say, Ogi, I won't be able to make good on my promise."

"Huh, that's a pretty cool-sounding line. Wow, a cool line as you're breaking a promise. What, no money?"

"Don't be ridiculous. I'm a multimillionaire."

If I was going to break a promise, I might as well lie while I was at it.

As if I was barely sorry—well, maybe I was being a different kind of sorry.

"I have to drop by Oikura's place."

"Ohh? Back to that abandoned home, then?"

"No, not the abandoned one. Her current one…"

Mmf.

I was running my mouth again with her—I needed to reel this in, lest I get a reputation as someone with loose lips.

I shut them tight.

Then—Ogi touched my lips with her index finger. She brushed it across them, like she was putting lip gloss on me.

"What're you doing?!"

I couldn't keep from reacting to this fetishistic move, but it seemed there was no sexual meaning behind it.

"No, I was just seeing if I could unzip your lips," she said brazenly, breezily. "Though I'm sure it's more like velcro—please, tell me more. What happened? Just look at how fast you've unlocked her heart, you're on good enough terms to get yourself invited to Miss Oikura's home after what happened yesterday—or the day before that, I guess. What leaps and bounds you've made, you need to report on how this has all come to be, you fool," she ended with an order.

Something about the way she spoke was just so unnatural.

"No, we're not on good terms, and I didn't unlock her heart or anything. I haven't been invited, I'm basically forcing my way in. She stopped coming to school again yesterday—though she'd barely showed up the day before that," I said, having no choice but to explain.

I did have some degree of accountability here, given that I'd broken my promise to celebrate her transfer.

I reported the current dilemma: Tsubasa Hanekawa had decided to act because both Senjogahara's position and Oikura's future were in a bad place unless we did something—wait, reported? That makes it sound like she was my superior…but it feels like the right word to use, so I'll leave it be.

"—And that's what happened."

"So that's what happened? Hm… You know, it's going to turn into a fight if you head there by yourself," Ogi said with a thoughtful look after hearing me out. "You're just going to resume the argument you had in the classroom, only in Miss Oikura's home—don't you think?"

"Yeah, part of me does… That is a worry."

"You should've handled Miss Senjogahara, while Miss Hanekawa handled Miss Oikura—you've been assigned to the wrong post."

"Hmm, well, you might be right."

Her remark did seem on point if the idea was to settle this peaceful-ly—but peace in this situation looked awfully like closing our eyes, and I didn't think we could arrive at a solution with our eyes shut.

Hanekawa had the kind of personality that hated work for the sake of work, work in order to create an alibi—and in this case, even I, her vice president famous for his slipshod work, felt the same way.

"Hmm—but what about her family environment?" asked Ogi. "It seemed pretty dire, didn't it? Charging into that seems more than dan-gerous, it seems foolish. I can't recommend it."

"Oh, we don't have to worry about that… I haven't heard the details, but it looks like she's living away from her parents."

"Away from her parents? A-ha. So she's been placed under the care of her relatives?"

"No. Living alone, apparently."

"Huh—well, how interesting."

Her heart may have been sent racing by a "backstory" you only saw in manga—a high schooler living by herself.

"Her parents must have gotten divorced or something five years ago, just like you said—or I guess you could say her family fell apart. Then she returned here two years ago. I'm sure that technically—or legally speaking—she has guardians..."

"I see. So the blind guess was the right one. Though that does create its own problem, my foolish senior. In essence, you are about to visit the home of a girl who, for all intents and purposes, is living alone. That's no good."

"It isn't?"

"It isn't, at all. No gentleman should ever do that. Miss Hanekawa may trust you, but I'm sorry to say that in general, a boy going on his own to visit a girl living by herself will raise doubts. It's not something he should do if he already has a partner."

"Hmm."

Hearing her put it that way...made me think she might be right.

While I didn't think I needed to be so concerned about how every little social grace and matter of manners between the sexes reflected upon me when I was only in high school, I did want to avoid any unnecessary misunderstanding. It'd be one thing if it was just me, but if those kinds of rumors got started about Oikura, someone who hated me, she might seriously end up committing suicide.

Suicide...

The inauspicious word happened to come to me, and I shivered when I realized just how realistic it sounded—right.

Whether or not Hanekawa was the more appropriate choice for the visit, regardless of how Oikura now lived, no matter what misunderstandings might be created—I needed to approach her in a way that didn't put her in any worse of a situation.

Not as atonement for failing to give her the help she sought five years ago, and it certainly wouldn't be enough to make amends for it—but

I was faced with a very real question.

"I see you're having trouble coming to a decision."

Ogi shrugged as if to sigh. She seemed quite serious about stopping me from going to Oikura's home, and I could tell that her advice came from a place of kindness. I felt like I had no choice but to accept it, and she seemed to realize this.

"I was so looking forward to that unrevolving sushi…"

Or maybe it came from a place of hunger, not kindness? Either way, as bad as I felt about having to cancel our plans, my feelings of relief trumped all.

I couldn't stand around and talk for too long, in any case. I began to wrap things up.

"Anyway, Ogi."

"Oh, right! I just might have an idea," she cut off my wrap-up.

Because she just might have an idea.

"Why don't you bring my humble self with you to the home visit?"

"Wait. You, Ogi? I appreciate the offer, but…"

Hm? Did I appreciate it?

What about her accompanying me made me feel appreciative? Oh, but Ogi's earlier reasons for me not visiting Oikura's home only applied if I went alone.

"In other words, you're fine just as long as you're not alone. Especially because, you know, I'm a girl. I'm sure Miss Oikura's heart will be a bit soothed if I'm with you."

"She's not really the type to be soothed because she's dealing with a girl…"

Maybe if she was dealing with a junior?

No, she'd unleashed a slap on Senjogahara who, better or not, Oikura saw as a weakly girl… I couldn't see someone who wasn't kind to the sick being kind to her juniors.

Still, it did beat the two of us being alone—yes, it was a good idea. It even made me wonder why I hadn't come up with it myself.

"I'm a good listener, as you know—Miss Oikura might tell us all kinds of things if I'm there."

"All kinds of things."

"At the end of the day, socializing is information warfare. There's no downside to knowing about your opponent. You've been able to recall who she was after remembering what happened at the class council and during summer break when you were a first-year middle schooler, but you haven't had any sort of proper conversation with the present Miss Oikura. I'll insert myself so that the situation between you two doesn't escalate into an argument. It's too late to get off this ride, just let me handle the burden," Ogi said with a smile, as if her proposal came from a place of pure benevolence.

There seemed to be no reason for me to reject her offer. If I had to come up with one, it would be my hesitance to take a junior to an utter war zone instead of the stationary sushi meal I'd promised... Then again, Ogi also seemed the type to enjoy raw fights over raw fish.

She loved fieldwork, probes, investigations, inquiries—though in reality, she was also nothing more than a rubbernecker.

How could I turn down this wildly curious girl's offer? As long as I was prepared, how could I possibly fail to protect one underclassman even if Oikura ended up going berserk again?

"Okay then, Ogi. Come along with me."

"All right, thanks for asking."

"Don't ask her!"

Hm?

Whose line was that last one? There's no speaker tag attached to it, I thought as I turned—to find Hanekawa, apparently finished with whatever business she had, catching up to me as I wasted time standing and talking by the school gates.

005

"You mustn't ask her, Araragi," Hanekawa panted. She must have run to the gates from our school building. Had she left like usual, ready to head toward Senjogahara's home, only to find me and Ogi speaking by the gates and dashed over to us in a panic?

Ogi smiled.

She smiled as she looked at Hanekawa.

"Hanekawa…"

I didn't understand what was happening, so I tried saying her name for now. Sort of like the way you invoke God's name when you're in a bad spot, but true to form, Hanekawa calmed her breathing, looked up, and answered me.

"You know you shouldn't—you can't get an underclassman involved with an in-class dispute."

"Mm?"

Oh.

That's what she meant? That's what it was?

I'd wondered what it could be, the way she yelled my name in the kind of desperate tone you'd use to stop a friend from starting down a path of sin, but it turned out that she only wanted to give me some very common sense.

She was absolutely right, too.

Yes, you shouldn't get an outsider involved with internal affairs—even if Ogi offered to do so.

Upon reconsideration, it wasn't even worth considering.

"Ogi—"

"No, no, no, no. There's no need to be so strangely considerate—it'd only hurt more," Ogi interrupted me. While her tone sounded humble, her stance was firm, unwilling to cede a single step. "Please, you have to let me come along with you—I won't get in your way or anything. I just want to help you in any small way I can. Think of how mean you'd be to agree only to turn me down later."

"Urk."

She'd put me in a tight spot.

Even I could tell that she wasn't saying this because she wanted to help me out—I assumed it was a manifestation of her leering curiosity, but true, it'd be mean to turn her down after saying yes.

"If it's me you're worried about, don't be—I don't mind one bit," she said. "If anything, I'm shocked that you'd be so standoffish after all we've gone through together. Floored, I tell you. I thought we had a relationship."

"What kind of relationship do you and Araragi have, exactly?"

Just as Ogi nearly bowled me over with her pushiness (an Oshino trademark?), or rather, her momentum, Hanekawa jumped in.

I was surprised to see her, of all people, do this. I never saw Hanekawa as the type to insert herself in a situation between two people—but then again, she'd sprinted over here.

When I thought about it that way, of course she was going to butt in.

"You and Araragi met for the first time just three days ago, right?" she asked—still smiling, of course. Going by her smile alone, she was gently scolding a selfish underclassman.

"That's right," Ogi agreed for the moment. "But relationships aren't always about time—in fact, he and I became kindred spirits in no time at all. We've been locked in a strange classroom together, gone on an adventure in an abandoned home together. The two of us have shared experiences that would normally seem impossible—isn't that right, Araragi-senpai?"

"Hm? Oh, well, yeah."

I mean, I'd been willing to take her out to a sushi-doesn't-go-round when I'm just a high school student. I wouldn't do that unless we were real kindred spirits, huh?

"Oh, I heard," Hanekawa said. "It seems like you've done quite a lot for Araragi—for a very important friend of mine, and so I'd been wanting to thank you." She was now physically getting between me and Ogi in addition to doing so conversationally. And then, for all to hear—

"*But of course, I'd have done a better job.*"

"..."

Ogi went quiet. She froze, with a smile—with something resembling a smile still on her face.

Hold on, what was going on here?

This may have been my first time seeing Hanekawa act this aggressive. Even if it wasn't, it'd been a really long time. Like—spring break, maybe? Spring break—when Tsubasa Hanekawa got between me and a legendary vampire?

"Hmm..."

After a long and heavy silence.

Ogi finally opened her mouth.

"Is that so—yes, I suppose. I'm sure you'd have done a better job, Miss Hanekawa—you're a genius, after all. Yes, I've heard all about that from my uncle."

"When you say your uncle, do you mean Mister Oshino?"

"Yes. I'm his niece, you know."

This elicited a slight reaction from Hanekawa, who paid a lot of respect to Oshino. You could even say she'd been infatuated with the way he lived. It made sense for her to react to his name—but in that case, you'd think she'd pay his niece some respect too... Her attitude toward Ogi was the opposite of what you'd call respectful.

"Then again—all that genius is meaningless unless you can make use of it. In the end, I was the one to be by his side at those times."

Ogi slipped away from her position in front of Hanekawa—as if her gaze meant nothing. I doubt I'd be able to move if Hanekawa decided to stare me down head-on—I'd be petrified in more ways than one, but

Ogi didn't seem the least bit daunted.

What mental toughness.

That's Oshino's niece for you.

Unbelievably enough, Ogi then tried striking back.

"Your genius is such that even my uncle was frightened of it, I hear—yes, but when I consider that, you're not quite as impressive as I was led to believe. The Tsubasa Hanekawa I'd heard about—would never be absent when Koyomi Araragi was in danger."

"…"

"So I'll graciously accept your thanks. What an honor it is. You may have been able to do a better job, but in the end, you didn't do anything. And when you say a better job," provoked Ogi, "don't you mean back when you were in your prime?"

I could describe her attitude and tone as the same as what she used with me. Ogi treated everyone in the same, consistent way—but while she could say that stuff to me, I wasn't going to turn a blind eye to her treating Hanekawa this way.

I scolded her. Sternly.

"Hold on, Ogi—what a thing to say. Some lines shouldn't be crossed. What do you know about Hanekawa, anyway?"

"I don't know anything," Ogi replied. Gently. "You're the one who knows. About Miss Hanekawa's past and present, and about her future—yes, that, at least, isn't the kind of thing I should be talking about."

That, at least.

She spoke as if the existence of other things she should comment on was a given—her tone so certain that it seemed to preclude any further questioning.

"Well, Miss Hanekawa. I'm not foolish enough to try and compete with you. I wouldn't want to do anything rude and earn the hatred of my beloved senior Araragi—so why don't we agree to coexist. Now if you'll excuse me."

Ogi suddenly orbited around to behind where I stood, as if to circumvent Hanekawa—the girl was always at my back before I knew it. And look, now I found myself in between Hanekawa and Ogi. Please, it was the last place I wanted to be.

"Now go ahead, you're going to visit Miss Senjogahara's home, aren't you? Her home seems to be the farther one, so shouldn't you hurry along?"

"The farther one?" Hanekawa seemed to twitch.

She must have thought that even if Ogi had learned Oikura's address from me, it was odd for her to know Senjogahara's—and in that sense, I should have reacted even more myself. After all, I hadn't given her Oikura's current address, let alone Senjogahara's.

But this feeling I got from Ogi.

The feeling that *she knew what wasn't known*—I'd gotten pretty accustomed to it.

However menacing and outlandish it may have seemed to Hanekawa.

"No need to worry. If you don't want your precious friend asking something of an underclassman, that doesn't have to happen. I was the one to propose it, after all—this can be me deciding on my own to accompany him. Like a guardian spirit."

A guardian spirit.

It sounded oddly realistic when it came from behind me—though it's odd to call any statement having to do with spirits *realistic*.

"You wouldn't mind that, would you? You know, like the kind of uninvited assistant you see all the time in mystery novels."

More talk of mystery novels, and at a time like this. I was starting to feel a bit fed up with just how obsessed with them she was. Not that uninvited assistants could be called much of an officially recognized element of mystery fiction—and really, her role was more a detective's two and three days ago, not an assistant's.

An uninvited assistant?

This was really starting to sound like fan stuff now.

"I'm sure I'd be of help to him, and knowing that, I couldn't possibly not be by his side. I can't just leave him alone when something is troubling him—I'd like to be able to save him."

"I thought people just go and get saved on their own?" countered Hanekawa.

"That's my uncle's stance. Mine is closer to the folktale about the crane who returns a favor."

"A crane?" Hanekawa sounded confused. She must not have understood what Ogi meant—neither had I. There didn't seem to be anything crane-like at all about Ogi's actions.

"Or the story of the old man who offered his umbrellas to Buddhist statues. What I'm trying to say is that my rule is to pay back any favors with interest. I want people to say, 'Hey, your gratitude tab wasn't this big!' Araragi-senpai has been so kind to me, a fresh transfer to this school—I'd like to repay that favor even if it means putting myself on the line."

I'd been that kind to her after she transferred? Really? Oh, maybe she meant helping her with her map of the school? True, while I might have been the one to learn the truth behind the class council meeting, I was originally there to help her with her fieldwork. She did tag along with me for my own fieldwork the next day, though... But that was probably what she meant by paying me back with interest.

Not that I knew how serious she was being.

"Araragi."

Dealing with Ogi would get her nowhere—Hanekawa's attitude probably wasn't that extreme, but she called my name. I felt nervous, wondering if she was going to attack me now, but no.

She said this instead.

"Change of plans. I'm going to Miss Oikura's home too. With you, Araragi."

This one surprised me.

She almost never changed plans once she'd decided on them—she couldn't stand fickle policies.

"No complaints then. Right, Ogi? Your problem—is that you don't want Araragi, a lone boy, going to Miss Oikura's home. If I go with him, it's no longer an issue. You have no more pretext."

"..."

Ogi went silent as she stood at my back. I couldn't see her at all, and wondered what kind of expression she had on... Could she actually be smiling like always?

Was she keeping it up even after Hanekawa had gotten Ogi's

pretext right through sheer conjecture?

A moment passed, and then—

"Whether there's a problem or not, don't you have to go visit Miss Senjogahara's home?" said Ogi. "What kind of person puts their good friend last like that?"

"My conversation with her will be a long one, so I'll ask her to let me stay the night. It's been a while, but I think we'll have a pajama party."

A pajama party?

What an enticing event… Was I invited too? I didn't have a ticket, but maybe there were plus-ones?

"Good enough for you? After all—I can do a better job than you."

"Not everything is about how good of a job you can do—a job done too well lacks balance. There's no happy medium there. Though I do think you know that quite well. But good and bad aside," Ogi said, "I don't get to decide. It's up to Araragi-senpai."

"Huh?"

"Will you go with me? Or will you go with Miss Hanekawa? I'd like you to decide. We defer to your decision. Both Miss Hanekawa and I will do as you say. Yes?"

Ogi was issuing another challenge to Hanekawa—who wasn't necessarily accepting it but must've thought that her only choice was to go along with it.

"You're right," she nodded. "You choose, Araragi. This isn't something I can force you to do."

"…"

I'd been given a pretty big choice.

No, like Ogi said—it wasn't a choice, but a decision.

While the three of us going together seemed like the most peaceful option, now that Hanekawa and Ogi were fairly at odds with each other, it could be dangerous in its own way. We were talking about Oikura, with whom I was at odds myself, and I didn't want to take on any further risk. That said, knowing that a dispute awaited me didn't mean I should choose neither of them—it wasn't going to be that rough.

So I had to make a decision.

Do I visit Oikura with Ogi, or do I visit her with Hanekawa?

Two choices. Pick one.

You could also see this as me having to reject one of two offers, both of which I was happy to have received—so I needed to give this consideration.

Ogi did seem like the better choice.

Yeah.

It's not like fieldwork is a first-come, first-served affair, but she was the first to say she'd go with me. Not to mention, I'd already broken my earlier promise to her (the sushi), and she seemed to be the clear pick as far as anything having to do with Oikura. This all started with our investigation of a school building—it's not as if she bore some sort of responsibility regarding Oikura, but it made sense for her to see this through to the end.

Well, for *us* to see this through to the end, I guess?

Moreover, as was the case two days ago, I really didn't want Hanekawa to see the acrimony between me and Oikura—while Hanekawa might be able to mediate between us, I just didn't feel good about arguing with Oikura in her presence. Ogi apparently looked untrustworthy to Hanekawa—which is why she was worried for me, but that was my fault for misrepresenting her.

I'd take responsibility for the rift between the two by creating an opportunity to mend it at a later date, but for now, it seemed best if I visited Oikura with Ogi while Hanekawa just went to Senjogahara's place as originally planned.

Just as I was about to reach this conclusion, Ogi spoke as if to help me along.

"Hey, senpai. You don't want to trouble someone you're already indebted to over a personal issue. If it's an internal affair, she's just as external to it as I am. You'd never put Miss Hanekawa in a bad spot, right?"

Why yes, Ogi was exactly right. The girl always said the rightest things.

"I promise—if you go with me, then no matter what mystery we find there, I'll present you with yet another solution."

"..."

Well, if she was willing to go that far—my conclusion was on the verge of making its way out of my throat, but that was when it happened. Hanekawa followed suit with an expression that was more serious than anything I'd ever seen on her face.

"I promise too, Araragi. If you go with me," she said, "I'll let you touch my boobs."

006

And so, Hanekawa and I now arrived at Oikura's home.

Given how many times she'd moved, I was a bit worried, but as if to allay my fears, what stood before us was at least an apartment building that didn't seem very old—and not a derelict house.

"Room 444? The number for death three times in a row, I guess the management here isn't too spiritual."

"This might actually be public housing, not a commercial apartment building."

We climbed the stairs as we talked. The place had no elevator—while it wasn't old, it was hardly modern. It somehow lacked the kind of glamor we youngsters associate with *living on one's own*. If anything, it looked like a place for families…

That she would be living alone in a place for families seemed off in its own way—here was Hanekawa's view on that.

"She—Miss Oikura—must be getting some sort of subsidy."

"A subsidy?"

"Yes. From the government—and it feels like they might have introduced her to this complex as a part of that."

"…"

If Hanekawa's conjecture was right and Oikura did receive a subsidy from the state or local government—it wasn't hard to see why. She'd been living in a house that could be mistaken for an abandoned home—and when I considered her circumstances at the beginning of our relationship, during our time in elementary school…

But why had I forgotten something that even Sengoku remembered? No, it wasn't just me—what about my sisters?

I still hadn't gotten an opportunity to ask them, but…I wondered, did Karen and Tsukihi remember Sodachi Oikura?

"Now that I think of it, maybe I'm a cold guy—I'd forgotten about Sengoku too, after all. I didn't recognize her at first."

"I don't think you can be blamed for that. You didn't have a particularly memorable relationship with Sengoku or Miss Oikura at the time, right?"

Well, sure.

Still, it was one thing to forget Sengoku, whom Tsukihi had brought over as a friend—I should've established the kind of relationship with Oikura that persisted in my mind. Had I done so, I probably wouldn't have overlooked her SOS during our first year of middle school. Even the class council meeting during our first year of high school—might never have taken place.

"Don't blame your past self too much. That's not reflection, you know," Hanekawa said upon seeing my expression. "Making your past self the villain and protecting your present self will make you repeat the same mistakes forever—just imagine. Living the kind of life where you're always being blamed by your future self? Does that seem like fun to you?"

"There's nothing fun about it."

Not fun.

The words felt different when they came from a girl who didn't blame or attack the past but faced it head-on. They carried weight.

That's right.

This was about the here and now, not the past.

How I acted here—how I faced Oikura. Not the old Oikura, but Oikura now. It was about what I was going to do, not what I did back then—however trite that may sound.

We arrived on the fourth floor, where Oikura lived. As a mockery of a vampire, my breathing was of course unbothered by the trip, but Hanekawa's was calm too. She really was an all-powerful class president. Even her base stamina was impressive.

"Okay, Araragi. Just wait a second."

"Hm? Here in the stairwell? Why?"

"Miss Oikura lives alone, right? It might be embarrassing if we rang the doorbell and she came out still in pajamas or loungewear."

"..."

I couldn't believe she had such an unlikely scenario in mind... With defenses like that, no wonder I never had the chance to see Hanekawa in street clothes.

I just did as I was told.

The stuff about pajamas aside, it was probably a good idea to have Oikura speak to Hanekawa alone at first—though of course I'd leap out if I detected even the slightest attempt to harm Hanekawa coming from Oikura.

And so, Hanekawa went up to Oikura's door alone and rang the intercom. Judging by the sound, it wasn't a modern one with a camera or the feature to talk through it—more of a doorbell. You could either talk to someone from the other side of the door or open it and come outside—only increasing the chances of an embarrassing moment.

The class president was amazing.

She'd managed to avoid an entire scene.

But while I was busy admiring her judgment, what happened surpassed her judgment—or undercut it.

The door did open.

It seemed to have a chain attached to it, so I could hear a clang as it ran its length.

I then heard Oikura's voice.

"Who's there."

While I thought her careless for simply opening her door for an unidentified visitor, chain or not, maybe she'd seen someone wearing her school's uniform through a fisheye lens. Even if she couldn't identify Hanekawa, a girl she'd barely crossed paths with a few days earlier, she'd at least open the door for someone from school, a student and a girl—

making me think that she may not have opened it had I been standing there.

Good thing I hadn't come on my own, I thought as Hanekawa and Oikura began going back and forth. I call it a back and forth, but it didn't seem like much of a conversation—Hanekawa was doggedly trying to persuade Oikura.

Even she couldn't make it happen, though...

I heard them both talk for a bit, in the dark about what they were discussing—was Hanekawa asking for Oikura to let her in, or to come back to school? No, it seemed like something else. What could they be arguing about?

While I say *arguing*, it was nothing like what happened earlier by the school gates with Ogi. I decided I didn't need to leap out of the shadows.

What was that ghastly showdown, anyway?

Many of you might have gotten the wrong idea, but I didn't choose Hanekawa to be my partner over Ogi because I was ensorcelled by her chest—I chose her because I sensed something far out of the ordinary if the situation was pushing her to say what she did.

Perhaps, as Ogi said, Hanekawa was past her prime, and I should have come here with Ogi given the flow of things. Perhaps Hanekawa was all wrong about Ogi, and I was putting my friend in harm's way for no good reason.

But I didn't want to become someone who couldn't choose Hanekawa after she went that far—after she said that for me. Even if Hanekawa was wrong, even if I was wrong, Tsubasa Hanekawa had to be the right answer to that question.

I did feel bad for Ogi, though...

I'd make sure to follow up. Yes, I'd become the kind of person capable of that, too.

That's right, I don't know about stationary sushi, but I could at least take her to a revolving place...

As I was thinking about all this, Hanekawa returned to where I stood—she seemed somehow exhausted. Maybe she'd been turned away unceremoniously? No, she wouldn't just give up. What was it, then? What happened?

"It's okay, Araragi. Come out," she said listlessly.

Her eyes were dead... Just how unproductive of a conversation was it?

"I can come out? But—"

"You can go in. Into her apartment. But to spoil it for you, she's still in her pajamas."

"Hm? Wait, but isn't that exactly what you were trying to prevent?"

"She said you aren't worth the effort of changing clothes... I tried my best to convince her otherwise, but the more I argued, the more stubborn she got. Eventually she said she wouldn't change under any circumstances, and that if I kept arguing she'd come out here naked."

So I bent, Hanekawa said.

Oikura had been menacing—though on a matter that was as stupid as could be.

"Don't worry. Even I'm not so shallow enough to get excited over a girl wearing pajamas in this kind of situation."

"I don't know," Hanekawa said, wounding me with a doubtful look. "Coming from someone who's just after my boobs..."

"..."

She understood less about the way I felt than anyone.

Sad, but then, who could blame her—let bygones be bygones (though we're talking about my own past behavior), and face the present instead.

Hanekawa was one thing, but why wasn't Oikura shooing me away—probably because it'd spell defeat. She'd refused to change clothes for the same reason. Now that the gates were open, though, I had to step through them. Even if she'd raised the portcullis just to declare war, my only choice was to accept.

Because that—was probably my role as Sodachi Oikura's childhood friend.

007

Childhood friends.

I'd never even considered that I always had one, but it seemed that my relationship with Oikura was something infinitesimally close to that fantasy. She was a childhood friend, or maybe a friend from long ago—in any case, I, Koyomi Araragi, and she, Sodachi Oikura, had been well acquainted.

The circumstances were slightly unusual, though. She didn't live nearby the way Sengoku did, nor did we go to the same elementary school—so allow me to give a brief explanation of these *slightly unusual* circumstances before I face Oikura. I'm very sorry to all of you who were looking forward to Oikura in her pajamas, but stay with me for a moment as I talk about the past.

Both of my parents work as police officers, and I've done my best not to tell anyone ever since I was little. From before I can remember. A question on my homework might say, "What do your mom and dad do," and I still wouldn't reveal their profession. Why did I so assiduously conceal my parents' job? Looking back on it, the answer is that I did as my parents said, at least as a child. In other words, they'd taught me not to discuss their work if at all possible—it's not a memory that comes up unless I try to recall it, but this seems to be the reason.

As a too-obedient youth, I did as they said without asking why. And

I've swallowed it whole from then to the present day—but now that I think about it, the admonition had dual meanings. One was ethical: I shouldn't be frivolous and recklessly publicize to strangers that my parents are police, a profession with some social significance. My parents sought what was right and wanted to instill a lesson with their gag order—from a reasoning standpoint. As for the other meaning, you could say it was their emotions speaking, not any sort of reasoning. In other words, publicizing that my parents were police officers could expose me to danger—it was a management issue.

Risk management, so to speak—my parents were worried that their jobs could result in harm coming to their kids. While it was overprotective in a way, I don't think you could call it overblown. At least, I understand their concerns now that I'm eighteen. I'd lived my life simply proud of the fact that my parents were both police officers and wanted to brag about it—so while at first I might have questioned or even felt scared about not being able to tell anyone, I was won over by my parents' warning that *heroes ought to hide their true identities.*

Of course, now you have Karen, too stupid to hide her parents' profession well, and Tsukihi, who makes full and skillful use of the fact that her parents are police officers—the existence of Tsuganoki Second Middle School's Fire Sisters have made it almost pointless to keep hiding my parents' occupation—but as they say, old habits die hard. Just as it's hard to parse the actual meaning of that phrase off the cuff—do old habits suffer intense deaths?—once an act is etched into your mind, it's hard to correct even if you lose sight of the original goal or your memory of it altogether. So I've continued to hide what my parents do, and you could call it meaningless if you want…but there was at least a reason behind my actions or lack thereof back during my first year of middle school. Back when I spent an entire summer with a younger Oikura.

The summer I spent in a derelict house.

The summer I spent growing to love math.

I already knew, thanks to Ogi, what that summer hid—I'd ignored the SOS Oikura sent me, but then, she shouldn't have known the premise for that SOS, namely my parents' job.

Even my few friends didn't know what they did, so how could

Oikura have found out? The precise question Hanekawa tossed my way early yesterday morning.

I didn't have an answer.

I didn't have any idea—I felt at the time that it hinted at some special relationship with Oikura, but without any basis in fact. What exactly did she know about me? How much did she know? It felt nothing short of uncanny, but if there was something else between me and her, it had to be from back in elementary school…

Yet my memories of our first year in middle school were fuzzy enough. How was I supposed to recall even-more distant memories of my time in elementary?

As I worried myself, Hanekawa, who'd presented the doubt to me in the first place, advised, "If you just can't remember, why not try asking your parents? Your parents watch you, you know—well, how convincing, coming from me, but as far as I know, your father and mother kept a proper eye on you."

They did seem proper, she said.

Hmm—I didn't expect her to understand all the current strife between me and my parents, but the words came from someone who'd come in contact with them. For certain reasons, she'd stayed at the Araragi residence during my own absence.

I could allow it—not that I was in a position to sound so high and mighty. I decided to take her advice without a second thought—these were Hanekawa's words at the end of the day. She could tell me to eat a shoe and I just might.

Sure enough, the answer became clear.

Oikura and I had met during elementary school—

In other words, we were childhood friends.

To be precise, it happened around the time I was a sixth grader—around the time I played with Sengoku and other friends Tsukihi would bring over.

That's when I met Sodachi Oikura.

It's not like we played together, though, and we didn't attend the same school, either. I'm sure she would have been more memorable if she did—my memory of her might have been different, too. At least, I'd have talked to her and retained memories of her, just like how I spoke to Sengoku and retained memories of her—even if Oikura had a different name back then.

It impressed me that Sengoku did remember her, but according to Sengoku, "Nadeko doesn't have many memories of her time in elementary, so she really remembers playing with Tsukihi—we called her Rara then. And of course, Nadeko's time playing with you too, Big Brother Koyomi."

She says the cutest things—but whatever the case, I never played with Oikura.

We didn't go to the same school, we didn't play together, and she wasn't even a neighbor. I could see how you might want to ask if we could really be called childhood friends—but however temporary a period in your life.

If you *live with someone*, whether you play with them or not, regardless of how short the time, can't you call that person a childhood friend?

I think you can, at least.

I might have worded this all in a slightly confusing way, but in essence—something happened one day.

One day.

I say that like I'm recalling all of this, but unlike the class council meeting I never forgot or the summer at the derelict house I did recollect, I honestly and truly don't remember. It's nowhere to be found in my memories. I asked my parents, and it's what they told me—and Sengoku remembered it, so I've verified it. For my part, I've lost any and all memories of it. I doubt I'll ever recover them—but anyway, one day.

My parents brought a girl home with them.

This girl, of course, was Sodachi Oikura, as she's called now. Apparently, they told me and my two sisters that she'd be staying with us for a while, so we should be nice to her—without any real explanation.

At the time, I was a child who saw no one and nothing as more important than my parents. Karen and Tsukihi were still young, in third and second grade, respectively—so we didn't particularly object to this sudden and unexplained notification, but I now know why, and I also know why they couldn't tell their elementary-aged children why.

In other words, my parents had taken the juvenile Oikura to their own home as a way to protect her from her "household"—the "household" where violence must have been running rampant.

This is only a guess, since I don't know for sure how society worked at the time, but I assume it was even harder than it is now for a public agency to enter into a private household. My parents' actions—temporarily taking Oikura into their own home—were probably what you'd call borderline, or at least not something to be officially recognized. What you might call extralegal measures—my parents didn't go into details here. What's important is that Oikura lived in my home, and that she met me then, and—however obvious this might be, she knew what my parents did.

So it was simple.

Oikura had met my parents, police officers—it wasn't about having any info.

In that case, Ogi's reasoning required a bit of correction, or maybe a few small adjustments—the outline might not change, but it did also answer Hanekawa's question. I'll start getting into that later—but as far as how the juvenile Oikura whom I didn't remember at all acted, according to my parents, and according to Sengoku, she was *a girl who didn't talk at all*. It must have been extreme if an introvert like Sengoku described her that way—at the same time, I've met another girl who wouldn't talk, making it easier for me to imagine. I mean, of course, Shinobu Oshino back when she lived in the abandoned cram school and not in my shadow—Shinobu back when all she did was glare at me without a single sound making it out of her mouth.

"It seemed like you had someone kind of strange with you. She didn't want to play with us, but she didn't try to leave the room, either—and she wouldn't talk."

Sengoku's words.

The more I heard about this girl, the more she sounded like the former Shinobu, but the former Shinobu had a good reason not to talk or budge—in other words, we should assume that juvenile Oikura had one as well.

Her household environment, most likely—juvenile Oikura wouldn't open her heart even after being taken into protection, which is to say at our home. No, it's hard to tell if she even understood what a household was—my mother said.

It also seemed like she didn't understand why she was with us, causing her to stiffen up—my mother continued.

She might have actually seen it at the time as being abducted and taken to an unknown home. Even if she didn't, she might not have known what it meant to be taken into protection—according to my mother again.

God.

Not something you could tell a child.

In any case, what I heard about Oikura's personality back then was different from her personality at any of the times I'd known her. It seemed inconsistent. Weren't we talking about a totally different person who happened to be around the same age? But as far as I could tell from descriptions of her appearance, it was indeed Oikura.

Sodachi Oikura.

I couldn't help but wonder which was the true Sodachi Oikura, but I suppose the answer would be: *They're all Sodachi Oikura*. She wouldn't want me talking about her "true self" like I knew anything about her, at the very least—so.

I was totally unable to recall the fact that juvenile Oikura had temporarily stayed at my home, that we once lived together—I felt a little bewildered at this truth delivered by my parents and Sengoku (I'd be lying if I said that no part of me wondered if they might be conspiring to trick me, but how would my parents and Sengoku get their stories straight?). However, it did bring one clear fact back to mind. Not about Oikura, or about when she was around, but...

I remembered how the juvenile Oikura disappeared.

The feeling that someone had left our home—that I'd lost something.

I could liken it to the feeling of losing sight of what is just and right during that class council meeting—or of losing a kindred spirit at that abandoned home.

That feeling of loss.

She'd been the first one to plant it in me.

I didn't know what it was, but I'd experienced losing something, or having lost something—and I now recalled it clearly.

That feeling of loss.

I remembered.

However it happened, she suddenly disappeared—though it seems that juvenile Oikura had decided on her own to return to her home.

On her own...

Her parents hadn't come to get her back, nor had mine decided they couldn't keep her under their protection anymore for whatever reason—juvenile Oikura decided on her own to leave *my home* to return to *her home*.

I guess that at the end of the day, children's parents are their parents, and their only home is their home—however wretched those parents and miserable that home may be.

That's how my dad put it—and maybe he was right. At least, juvenile Oikura must have thought so and found her actions to be correct when she disappeared.

My parents didn't go into detail about that, either, but I'm sure there were more troubles after she returned home—when I think of the future that awaited her, Oikura's case must not have been resolved in any way my parents had hoped for.

It's hard for a DV situation to be resolved unless someone on the inside sends out an SOS—if no one thinks the problem is a problem, no one is going to go solve it.

That's how my parents wrapped things up.

They must have jumped to the conclusion that I'd suddenly recalled something from when I was a child—that I'd remembered the juvenile who once lived with us. I'd come to ask them about her—but in fact, I hadn't remembered anything at all and only knew about the episodes that followed.

About what was in store for Sodachi Oikura.

Her tragic life.

She'd tried to send out an SOS to my parents through me about a year later—and her SOS had stopped at me.

I didn't remember Oikura when we found ourselves at the same middle school—I never had the chance to see her there because we were in different classes, but I still had no clue who she was even when we met in the derelict house. Of course, her personality had changed completely, and of course, she gave off a very different vibe, but—

Given the fact that she left our home without any notice, without a word, I can't help but think that the reason I didn't was that I'd lost her in more ways than one.

She vanished.

And I was a cold person.

008

She looked even more pajamaed than I expected.

I'd prepared myself emotionally for this, and as a man who'd made it through countless battlefields, I felt ready for any strange twist or turn, but there in the public-housing unit stood the very image of a girl in pajamas that a high school boy would conjure, a fastball straight down the middle.

Hanekawa whispered in my ear.

"I think her sense of fashion ended up getting refined in this direction because of how long she's spent in her room…"

A-ha.

Just as Hanekawa's household environment caused her own sense of fashion to head in an "underwear" direction? But more pressing than that was the danger posed by Hanekawa whispering in my ear and making me feel like nothing else really mattered. Unlike the sensation of Ogi whispering in my ear—not that the two could be compared.

Oikura undid the door chain and greeted us with an imposing stance, her arms folded. With what seemed like swagger, she said, "I'm impressed you came. I have to admit, I admire your guts, AraraG…"

AraraG?

Huh? I wondered what kind of mean-spirited abuse this could be, but she'd simply misspoken.

"Agh…" She scowled openly. "Why's your name have to be so im-popossible to renounce…" she misspoke yet again (I assume she was trying to say "impossible to pronounce"). It might have been cute if she'd followed up with *Sorry, a slip of the tongue*, but she only turned her back to me and walked down the hall.

Stomp, stomp.

Hanekawa closed the door behind us and locked it. If I'm being honest, part of me wanted her to leave it unlocked so it'd be easier to escape, but I didn't see that happening—yes, I needed to emulate Hanekawa's mental toughness at times like these.

Especially if I was about to face Oikura.

Hanekawa took off her shoes and passed by me.

With these hushed words: "This is a family rental, two bedrooms with a living room, dining room, and kitchen. But there are only two pairs of women's shoes here, and they're the same size. We now know for a fact she lives alone. She might be acting that way, but from the smell in the air, I think she made some tea while I went to get you, so be ready to thank her."

My brain couldn't process so much sudden info—though it was also incredible that she'd grasped the layout of the entire home just by entering it.

It hadn't even crossed my mind that we might have bad info, that Oikura might not be living alone—was Tsubasa Hanekawa still in her prime, or what? If anything, she might have grown by facing her past and her self—and she was in fact right, tea sat ready there in the dining room.

She wasn't entirely right, though. There were only two cups of tea—one in front of Oikura, seated at the table, and another. In short, no tea for me.

I guess even Hanekawa couldn't fully comprehend just how much Oikura hated me? Not that it bothered me now.

The spartan room actually attracted more of my attention. No, it went beyond attention. The room felt horribly off, like some sort of spot-the-mistake puzzle.

There was a table. But only one chair, which Oikura sat in—even if she'd put them away out of spite for me, she'd have left one for Hanekawa, so there must have only been one from the start.

No curtains. Well, lace curtains. But that was all. Looking up at the ceiling, I found only one fluorescent bulb.

I thought back and remembered the welcome mat at the entrance, but the rooms contained no rugs or carpets. The tea seemed to come with everything you'd want—sugar, milk, spoons—but the cups weren't on saucers.

There were lots of other things. It felt like just a little was always missing from these rooms—revealing not so much their tenant's disposition, but the fact that something was off, even uncanny.

If I were to be less delicate, I'd say it went beyond uncanny and made it all the way to unsightly—Hanekawa must have had an even stronger sense of this bizarre feeling but betrayed no signs of it.

"Um," she began.

With no chair, she of course couldn't sit, but she faced Oikura from across the table.

"You seem to be doing well, Miss Oikura. I'm glad."

"Yeah? Does it really seem that way?" retorted Oikura, pointing at her cheek. It didn't look too bad, but it was red and swollen—you could say that was to be expected, since she'd been punched there. Senjogahara's slapped cheek was surely still swollen as well, though. "I can't believe it... Just how big of an act was that girl putting on? I knew she was more than a sickly, mild-mannered girl, but still..."

Then Oikura looked—or glared at me.

"You know, maybe I should sue her for assault. I'll go to a doctor before this swelling subsides and get a medical certificate. Shouldn't that be enough to get her recommendation or whatever taken away?"

"You two are even. You did hit her first. It'd be considered self-defense if it came down to it."

"I wonder about that," Oikura threw out. True, it might be hard to claim self-defense in that situation. Not so much even, they were both losers here.

I sighed and glanced at Hanekawa. I tried to make eye contact with her. Would my point get across to her—I wondered, but forget about reciprocating, Hanekawa was already on the move.

How sharp was she?

I'd tried to make eye contact with air—what could feel emptier than that? Anyway, with a natural motion, Hanekawa reached for the cup of tea.

It's human reflex to notice motion in your field of vision—and the glaring Oikura was no exception as her eyes followed Hanekawa.

I quickly went around the table as if to leap on this moment and touched Oikura's cheek, which is to say her injury, with my index finger.

"Hey... What're you..."

Oikura's chair swung back and thunked against the floor, but it was too late. I'd returned to my original position like some kind of touch-and-go—not that I particularly needed to rush back once I'd accomplished my goal, but I might get slapped if I stayed around for too long...

"Wh-What're you... Poking my cheek? Again and again?! You think we're so close it's okay to mess around with me like that? Are you trying to get yourself sued?!"

Putting aside whether or not poking someone's cheek is a crime (and I didn't do it again and again)—I pointed at Oikura with the opposite hand as the one I poked her with. The index finger of the hand I used to poke her cheek was still bleeding from a safety-pin prick—though it would soon heal.

Just like her cheek.

"I don't think you'd be able to get a medical certificate if you went to a doctor with that cheek, Oikura."

"Huh? Hm? What?"

She seemed to marvel at the cheek I'd healed using my blood—which is to say, a vampire's—as if she didn't know what was going on. Well, of course she didn't, who would ever think that a poke would heal your cheek? She must have interpreted it as nothing more than a way to ascertain whether or not it had healed.

While part of it must have been her unwillingness to believe in a supernatural phenomenon, I also think she hated having any kind of favor bestowed on her by me. I doubt she was being serious when she said she'd sue Senjogahara, but it was also true that my girlfriend had gone a little too far in hitting Oikura with a closed fist. Sorting out the aftermath seemed like the right thing to do.

"Gah... That swelling healed after just two nights? I can't believe how fast my body recovers..."

She credited her own recuperative abilities for erasing her basis for harassing me, and seemed chagrined that her anger had lost its focal point.

Hanekawa didn't take the cup she'd reached for. Instead, she returned to her original position.

"It looks like you're healthy and fine," she said. "You'll be able to come back to school starting tomorrow, won't you, Miss Oikura?"

"So you're here as class president? Um...Miss Hanekawa, was it?"

Whether Oikura really didn't remember Hanekawa or was just playing dumb, I couldn't be sure. As someone who hadn't been to school since the first term of her first year, she wouldn't know just how much of a threat Hanekawa posed...which meant that Oikura faced a towering foe without even realizing it. The power imbalance between the two seemed comical from where I stood, but it also presented a problem.

Sodachi Oikura—the current Sodachi Oikura was just so weak, so notably fragile that a jab from us to test the waters could demolish her.

"That's right. Tsubasa Hanekawa," Hanekawa replied with a smile.

Well, she didn't have any sort of vested interest in Oikura the way Senjogahara and I did. The situation between the two couldn't turn that oppositional.

I was feeling glad that I'd come here with Hanekawa—but I couldn't allow myself to rely on that fact. She'd tried to send me here on my own at first because she thought that would be the better move. Either for my sake or Oikura's.

Ogi prevented that from happening—and the current situation wasn't what Hanekawa had hoped for.

"So I guess you came to get me because the teachers asked you? Um... Who was our homeroom teacher again?"

"Hoshina, a very good homeroom teacher."

"A good teacher? Are you trying to claim that good teachers exist?"

Oikura had a grin on her face. It might be a grimace, but it was probably the former—there was no need here to grin through any pain.

So she did know about Tetsujo.

Ogi's reasoning that said Oikura had come to school because Tetsujo was gone seemed to be right on the mark.

"I know because I used to be class president myself—aren't you just letting yourself be used however the teachers want, Miss Hanekawa?"

"Hm. Hmm. I never thought about it that way, but you're right, I suppose you could see it that way," Hanekawa deflected Oikura's spiteful words. This kind of reply, neither a denial nor an acceptance, was the most effective way to deal with Oikura as she was now. You could really see Tsubasa Hanekawa's skill from the fact that even her small talk had a point to it.

While she was out-argued as far as the pajamas, you could say she was conceding a point she could afford to lose, letting Oikura save face ahead of time.

Or perhaps—it was just making Hanekawa more serious.

As for Oikura, she wasn't even a shadow of her former self, but once upon a time she'd been the brave and widely known leader of our class. She seemed to realize through this brief exchange that Tsubasa Hanekawa was no mere class president, and stopped saying anything unnecessary that might come off as aggressive. She must not have wanted to find herself on the wrong side of a surprise attack.

Pride had something to do with her inviting us into her room, but it was her terrain, quite literally her home turf (and in fact, she did act more self-assured compared to the way she'd been in our classroom). But it appeared as though she noticed the situation before her wasn't exactly what she'd imagined. Not that the Oikura we now faced would ever consider retreating—unlike two years ago.

Her eyes, which is to say her crosshairs, were back on me.

She focused her gaze and took aim.

"So," she said. "I can see why Miss Hanekawa is here, but why you? A—A, ra, ra, gi."

She said my name slowly this time so as not to stumble over it.

"I don't want to have to see your face, and I'm sure you don't want to have to see mine either. As far as I remember, the two of us are on horrible terms. Or perhaps I am mistaken?"

I could hear her forcing herself to sound polite—like some sort of elementary school student.

But I saw this as an opportunity—it'd be pointless to wait for the perfect moment. There was no such thing as a best or right moment when it came to me and Oikura. Even if one did exist, it was two years, five years, maybe even six years ago. It had long passed. For now, I'd just think about avoiding the worst possible moment.

I'd just think about Oikura.

For now, I'd exist for her.

"You're not mistaken. But I think there's more to it than that—isn't that what you taught me the day before yesterday?"

"!"

She looked shocked.

Was my recollection of the derelict house that unforeseen? Or maybe—she just found it unfortunate.

But if it was, I doubled down.

"There's even what happened in elementary school."

"Ah... Mh—"

Oikura then did something unexpected. She snatched her teacup and threw it at me!

This left a bitter taste in my mouth. No, not the tea, the situation.

A ballpoint pen was one thing (though she did get me with one of those as well), but how could I dodge an airborne splash of liquid? I wasn't capable of the kind of teleportation that would require. I'd be covered in freshly brewed tea—the burns would be one thing, but what really worried me was that Oikura would see them healing. She might even connect the dots and figure out that I'd healed her cheek.

My mind worked through all of this, but my body didn't react. Even if it did, this was the kind of crisis where I could only hunch over—but Hanekawa saved me yet again.

I don't know when, I really don't, but she'd taken a half-step in my direction and stopped the flying cup before it could hit me.

No.

She didn't stop it, she took it.

She didn't sacrifice herself to protect me, not at all. She simply reached out, grabbed the handle of the cup as it spun through the air, twirled it in her hand seemingly around the overflowing liquid to kill its momentum, and placed it right back on the table. A little spilled out when she put it there, but no more.

Oikura's eyes were wide open.

The girl who had her thin-eyed glare on me this entire time. Not that I could blame her, I knew just how amazing Hanekawa was, and I bet I was just as wide-eyed.

It really did seem like she'd leveled up after what happened on the heels of summer break... Or maybe, in the past, she wouldn't have spilled a single drop at the end there.

"Hm? Oh, you know. I was prepared, thinking it might be dangerous if Miss Oikura threw her tea... I learned my lesson after being unable to stop Miss Senjogahara the day before yesterday."

"..."

Lesson? She'd earned an entire degree.

You could never be too careful around this girl when she learned her lessons.

So far, the only issue she hadn't been able to neutralize was Oikura's pajamas... It was like I couldn't even get into trouble around her.

Even if she'd conceded or surrendered the point with the pajamas, it felt like she'd already earned it back—I began to think that I might go right back to my conversation with Oikura, but of course, life is never that simple.

Whatever inhuman danger-foiling skills Hanekawa boasted, in the end, it was Oikura that I had to face, not her.

Koyomi Araragi did.

"Oikura," I said.

With resolve.

"Let's talk—about the past. About you and me."

"..."

Oikura went quiet for a moment. And then—

"I hate you," she said.

Words I'd heard a number of times already.

Even so, they hurt me every time she said them.

009

"I want you to find my missing mother."

Many twists and turns later.

Oikura eventually said this.

"If you do, I wouldn't mind going to school for you—or even apologizing to Miss Senjogahara."

To explain how our discussion ended in such a bizarre, or even off-the-mark place, I need to go into Sodachi Oikura's history from her perspective. In other words, how she spent her days after leaving this town—and the kind of person she was, there out of my sight.

That kind of story.

A manhunt is of course a staple element of mysteries, whodun-nits, and detective stories, so it's not as if this twist turned us in a weird direction. If anything, it flowed naturally—but I still need to describe the channel that it took to this point.

"So you remembered... What's more, it looks like you've finally understood what I tried to do back then, after five whole years. Which means—you must really think I'm an idiot," Oikura began.

Bitterly.

Hanekawa taking the teacup must have been impossible for her to process because she was pretending that it never happened.

"The way I tried so hard to pander to you and get you to save me..."

"Pander to me?"

Is that how she saw it?

During the summer break I'd remembered—I had been the fool for not answering her call for help. It could even sound like a heartwarming episode in the hands of a skilled narrator, but Oikura describing her fey demeanor and joyful smile as "pandering" only trampled on my tattered memories.

I couldn't complain, though.

Yes, it was the same memory as mine, but seen through her eyes—however she wanted to tarnish it was her choice and hers alone.

Still, how could you describe it as anything but bankrupt when she criticized me for forgetting about it and cursed me for remembering it? Not that I wanted to put any failures of her current personality up for debate after everything we'd gone through...

"Wh-What an idiot," she said.

I fully assumed this to be more abuse hurled my way—her sneering at me for never noticing, when she'd kindly taught me math.

But I was wrong—this time I was wrong.

The "idiot" she talked about was herself this time.

"What an idiot, what an idiot, what an idiot... I am such an idiot! I-I'm so embarrassed that I ever pandered to someone like you hoping you'd save me! I-I threw away my pride to flatter and suck up to someone like you! I licked your boots clean! Emotionally!"

"..."

"I tried to fix one failure and failed in an even worse way... I'm so embarrassed, I'm so ashamed! I'm so embarrassed, I'm so ashamed—I want to die!"

I want to disappear!

She screamed and collapsed on the table.

I heard an awful whack.

It sounded so bad I thought she might have split her head open—but her face rose seconds later. She returned looking determined. A grinning, resolute, threatening look. What kind of switch had been flipped in her mind?

I want to disappear.

Literally speaking, she did "disappear"...

The failure she'd tried to fix must have meant her custody at the Araragi residence—where she said nothing and opened up to no one. She must have meant the way she failed by not pandering to anyone, if you wanted to put it that way, and going back to her desolate home alone.

If that had resulted in her roundabout cry for help, I did have to admit she'd made a distinctive, or rather, a very unusual choice—but it also underscored the reason why she couldn't go directly to my parents for that help. In short, she felt self-conscious about how she'd swatted away their outstretched hands in the past.

"But, Araragi. I think the same thing would have happened, even if it wasn't me. I don't think there's anything special about my misfortune. These kinds of things. They happen all the time. Don't you think? You couldn't possibly feel any sympathy for me."

"..."

"There are a lot of people in worse situations than me. All over Japan. All over the world. All over the papers. I don't have some incurable disease, I'm not starving, I'm not caught up in some war, I'm not getting beaten by some stranger for no good reason. I'm not misfortunate, I'm not misfortunate, I'm not misfortunate. Right? Don't you agree?"

"..."

Though she was asking me to agree with her, I couldn't say anything—if there was one thing I could say, her misfortune was so deep that pointing to people who were more misfortunate was the only way she could affirm herself.

There are a lot of people in worse situations than me—that's not something you say about yourself, is it?

"So don't take pity on me—it makes me want to die when someone I hate as much as you takes pity on me."

"I don't think there's anything I could say to you that would make a difference. Because I haven't paid you back in any way for what I received from you."

I was water that thought I'd made myself boil.

I had only been on the receiving end with Oikura—in other words,

309

I only ever took from her. There was nothing I could give her now, nothing that could be taken back.

"So if you say not to pity you, I won't. If you say you don't want me to atone, I of course won't."

"What, are you trying to act cool or something? Do you think you're being gallant with that attitude? You're a decent human being? Is that supposed to be manly? All you're doing is giving up."

"Yeah—but aren't I giving up in the same way you did?"

Oh no.

I argued back without thinking—I always let my guard down when it feels like I'm in a real conversation. In reality, only I felt that way. It was a one-way street—or two opposing lanes of traffic, right and left, cars zooming by one another, head-on collisions just one little steering error away.

I thought she might throw something at me again, but nothing sat in front of her, even her spoon or sugar bowl. On further inspection, Hanekawa had them all for some reason—when did she take the opportunity to confiscate them? I hadn't noticed...

Hanekawa wasn't inserting herself into our individual strokes, but she would at least create a situation that allowed us to rally. Her position was more a referee's than a partner's, but I was grateful to have someone who'd make fair calls.

"What was I supposed to do? It wasn't my fault. It's my parents' fault that I give up, that I run away whenever things are too much for me."

It's my parents' fault.

Oikura spoke begrudgingly. She threw words my way instead of objects—words that made flying objects seem like the more preferable of the two.

"It's my parents' responsibility that I'm like this now."

"What are those parents doing now?"

"Oh? What's this, you're worried about me! Little old me and my family situation! Why the change, you never once stopped to consider it back in middle school."

Words soaked in cutting sarcasm, but the kind of sarcasm that seemed to wound the speaker too. They could only have come from someone who'd been cut to the bone.

"They had themselves a happy divorce after you didn't save me. My mother took me and left this town... As for what my male parent is doing now, I don't have the first clue."

My male parent—that was how she put it.

It was quite clear how she felt about him. Which suggested that it was her father who'd wrought havoc on that house—he must've been responsible for the violence in that trashed household.

I wasn't expecting Oikura to have enough extra room in her mind at this point to figure out my line of thinking, but she said, "That's right. My male parent made that house the way it was. That piece of trash."

Her face was red, but with what seemed like shame, not anger— perhaps she felt embarrassed over being such a fool in elementary school that she made the decision to return to the custody of such a piece of trash.

Or perhaps she felt like there was no period in her life when she wasn't a fool—and it embarrassed her.

"My mother would hit me *now and then*, that's all. To take her mind off of him hitting her," she continued—then paused for a moment, as if to wait for my reaction. She had just told us about being the final link in a chain of violence—but didn't seek compassion. Not at all. So I had no idea at all how to respond, or what the right answer was.

Once, she'd wanted me to save her—what did she want now?

I didn't know.

The question seemed worse than illogical.

In the end, all I could do was ask a question.

"Did you decide then to go with your mother, since she was the better choice of the two?"

But Oikura only sneered back.

"Do you think I was in a position to make any kind of decision? Back then—adults just made all the decisions on their own. I guess you could say my mother was the better choice, but really, society must have seen her as a victim when I look back on it now—and I thought the same back then, too."

Just as she thought her male parent was her father back in elementary school, she thought her mother was a victim back in middle school?

It went beyond hopeless.

No, what right did I have to make comments about hope when I'd been responsible for keeping it from shining on her life—however, that's not where the hopelessness in Oikura's life ended.

Not by a long shot.

It would be a little more than two years until she entered high school. The period between her second term in middle school to the time she graduated—hopelessness descended upon her again while she'd been away from this town. Misfortune descended upon her.

A kind of misfortune not nearly as bad as incurable illness, starvation, or war: the disappearance of her mother, as she mentioned at the start. The girl deserved at least one decent thing happening in her life— but so far, nothing. It was always in shambles, just like the balance of the room's furnishings.

It was a mess, and—lacked so much.

"I don't know just how great of a person you are—well, I do know just how base of a person you are, but you'd have turned out the same way with parents like mine. I mean, I wish they were police officers."

"It's not like parents get to choose their children," I argued needlessly again. The words were in part self-reproach, but they seemed to strike her heart much harder than I expected. She looked astounded.

Then she nodded. "Yes. My mother said the exact same thing—to me."

To be honest, I had big expectations, she said. *That my life might reverse course. That it might be my big turning point.*

"I'd been off the mark in hoping that you'd do what I wanted you to do, but I still had expectations. I thought nothing worse could happen now that my family had fallen apart. I told myself I'd already seen rock bottom. Really, that household had always been broken, even when I was an elementary schooler—I knew what was coming. But I thought failing meant I'd be able to get back up and try again. That after all the tragedy, someone like me would get to lead a happy life. That's what I expected because it wouldn't make sense otherwise—but that's not what happened at all. My life kept on being tragic."

312

"You're saying the violence continued? From your…mother?"

"Wrong. Were you not listening to me? My mother hit me to take her mind off of my male parent hitting her. She wasn't going to hit me now that the piece of trash was gone."

"…"

I still had trouble accepting that premise, but if her logic held up, it did at least mean the chain of violence had been broken. In that case, though, what was so tragic?

"One of my grounds for blaming my parents, the reason I've shut myself in like this for over two years—"

My mother shut herself in too.

"As soon as we became a single-mother household, the divorce finally caught up to her. She shut herself in a room of our new home and stopped coming out."

"She stopped—"

"Can you even imagine what it's like for one of your parents to shut herself in? I had to take care of her as a first-year middle schooler—isn't that laughable?"

Go ahead, laugh, she hounded me, laughing herself—maybe because she'd remembered those times, or maybe because she found it funny that I'd been rendered speechless. I couldn't tell.

"There are lots of books and shows out there for parents whose kids are shut-ins—but nothing about how to handle a shut-in parent. So back then… Well, back then, I guess I swore I'd never shut myself in no matter what happened. I didn't think twice about breaking that vow a few years later, of course."

But my mother's case was a serious one, an extreme case of withdrawal. I look completely normal in comparison, Oikura said. She was saying she wasn't as broken as her mother.

"It really was awful. She shut herself in a room with a locking door and curled into a ball in the corner. I had to bring and take away all her meals. It wasn't long until she stopped eating altogether. Not only did my mother board up the windows, she kept the curtains shut all day long, making the room pitch black. Total darkness. She even unscrewed the bulbs so that no one could turn on the lights. And she kept on muttering to herself...muttering on and on about how parents don't get to choose their children. At some point she even started to ignore anything I said to her—like an adolescent or something. She was far more the adolescent than my middle-school self, much more the rebel. You sometimes hear about children giving birth to children—but I was a child taking care of a child."

Had the collapse of their household broken Oikura's mother's spirit? Had their household, violent or not, made her happy—supporting her heart and mind?

In any case, no, I couldn't imagine—what a daughter must feel when her mother falls into a state like that. Maybe Senjogahara could show some degree of understanding—no, even her case was different. She never had to take care of her mother.

"My grades at school plummeted. It felt so frustrating... All those kids dumber than me, passing me by. All because I was a good girl who cared for her mother... Well, the school did seem to consider my situation and offered me their egotistical sympathy by bumping my grades. Heh, I mean, how else would I have ever gotten into Naoetsu High with grades and a transcript like that..."

Perhaps that was why she seemed so unnecessarily proud to be a Naoetsu High student in my first-year eyes. Perhaps it was part of the reason for her math complex involving me as well.

Something she should have been able to do but couldn't. Unable to make use of her talents as opportunities were stolen from her—that feeling of being left behind. Given her pride, that multi-year stretch would have been an unimaginable struggle.

"But still, your mother is your mother—your mom is your mom. And your parent is your parent. I'd already lost one of them, so I thought I needed to be careful not to lose the other. That she'd decide to leave her room someday. That maybe she'd even apologize to me for saying things like *parents can't choose their children*—maybe she'd say she was glad to have had me. After all, you never know what's going to happen in this world, right? No one knows what the future holds. Or are you going to say that the future is predetermined and locked in place?"

Oikura coughed here—not to pause, but as if she'd choked on

something. She'd had trouble saying my name, too, so it did seem like she wasn't used to talking.

"Fortunately, Japan has relatively substantial social welfare programs. Even if my mother didn't earn money, even if my male parent never sent alimony or child support, get the right documents in order and a mother with one child can get enough to just barely put food on the table. So I never once thought life would be better if my mother disappeared—that I can be sure of."

Then it resumed. Her madness.

"I mean, I prayed every single night. Please, keep me from thinking life would be better if my mother disappeared. Please, keep me from thinking life would be better if my mother disappeared. Please, keep me from thinking life would be better if my mother disappeared. Please, keep me from thinking life would be better if my mother disappeared."

But.

My mother disappeared.

Against my wishes.

"She disappeared one day, without saying a word to me, without telling me anything—I came home from school and my mother was gone. She disappeared all of a sudden, without warning—just like me, wouldn't you say?"

They say girls take after their male parents, but I think I'm more like my mother—and.

Oikura laughed. I suppose she had her mother's laugh.

010

"That's right. I made dinner and took it to her room. When I unlocked the door and went in, it was deserted—with not even a letter left behind. I say she disappeared suddenly and without any notice, but could there have been some kind of sign? Maybe not a sign, but a feeling... I felt like my mother was going to leave me behind and go off somewhere. Just like the way my male parent went off somewhere."

My parents.

I don't know where either of them is now.

Oikura spoke the words—killing any emotions in her voice.

Just as she'd killed her self.

Just as she'd butchered her own heart.

"She seemed to reminisce about the old days, so at first I thought she went off to wherever he was... The thought made me not want to look for her, but that might be the case when I think about it now. She didn't want to try all over again, she was only grieving over her misfortune that was the divorce—in any case, it freed me from having to take care of my mother. I caught back up on my studies. I found a relative who could technically be my guardian and returned to this town thanks to assistance from the state. I didn't really want to come back since I didn't want to have to meet you...but this was the only open spot."

By open spot, she must have meant a place to live. Yet another correct read by Hanekawa—she needed to consider a career in fortune-telling or something.

Hanekawa, however, had a troubled expression on her face.

Hm? What was it? Was something in Oikura's story giving her pause? True, it was difficult to listen to, but her expression didn't exactly match the situation...

I didn't understand, but if Hanekawa was deep in thought, I needed to be on even higher alert.

"So why did you decide to live alone?" I asked. "A relative who's only technically your guardian is still a relative. And why bother moving when you could have kept on living in the home you shared with your mother? You said yourself you didn't want to come back to this town."

"Because it was a dump. Taking care of my mother kept me so busy that I didn't have the time to do anything like clean. It was too big for one person to manage, anyway... I thought it'd be better to ditch the whole house rather than get to work cleaning it."

Ditch the whole house.

Ditch.

Could she have hesitated? No, I doubted it. If she'd been pushed to that point, it must not have been something worth protecting or caring for.

With no home and no household—why keep protecting a plain house?

"I put the lessons I learned to use and decided to go light on the furniture here. Nice and tidy, isn't it?"

In an unusual move (maybe just a blunder from her perspective), she looked to me for agreement. I might have obliged her, but couldn't—not in this room.

Yes, it was nice and tidy, but not because it was light on the furniture. It was devoid of furniture—the room lacked balance because she was putting whatever lessons she'd learned to use.

Learned them?

If anything, those lessons were dead.

This wasn't what you called ordered or tidy.

Also, she'd ignored my first question, surely on purpose. Why

318

choose to live alone when she had a nominal guardian—was it such a stupid question that she couldn't bother to answer it? Well, maybe it was. It answered itself.

She'd spent two years straight caring for her caretaker—being placed under anyone's care must sound like an absurd joke to her. I didn't know how it all worked legally—but it seemed that Oikura had taken care of the problem now that she'd managed to receive public assistance and live alone here in public housing.

In any case, Sodachi Oikura returned to her hometown—the town where she spent her days as a young child.

I already knew what came after that.

She and I were reunited at Naoetsu High, but I'd forgotten about her in every conceivable way, and just as she thought she'd built a place for herself as the class leader, her homeroom teacher and classmates brought her low—or rather, she fell in a pit of her own digging. Then, she spent two years in this room.

Shutting herself in, just like her mother.

Regardless of any differences in the gravity of their circumstances, she'd spent just about the same amount of time shutting herself in a room as her mother—and then the day before yesterday, having learned somehow that Tetsujo had gone on maternity leave, she finally decided to return to school. Of course, this return, too, hit a snag…

"Do you understand? I'm not that misfortunate," Oikura concluded.

Rather proudly, in fact.

With a tense grin.

"Could happen to anyone, right? Happens all the time to people, to one extent or another… You could barely call it a story of struggle. Okay, I might've had a little harder time than the average person, but how can anyone survive in this world if you're going to say that? Sure, it's unusual that I had a shut-in for a parent, but I should be grateful for the precious and rare experience. I'm not the only misfortunate person in the world, so I need to keep working on things. I think I'm on the fortunate side, seeing as I'm alive."

"…"

I couldn't call this an argument she placed before me, given how

319

flimsy it was—she probably believed her own words less than anyone.

"So again, I don't need your sympathy… You don't need to apologize or atone, Araragi. Forget about any kind of penance. Just talking about this kind of feels like a load's been taken off my back, anyway…"

You'll feel better once you talk about it.

Those words—who had said them to me?

"And all of that is in the past—whatever old stories you're looking for are ancient history. They're all tales that have come to an end. I know I picked fights with you because you annoyed me…but I don't want you to do anything for me after all this time. If I had to make a request, then—"

Could you leave?

That's what she said.

She seemed to have grown smaller over the course of the hour—one or maybe two times over. It went without saying that her situation wasn't any better just because she finished talking about it all, but it did look like she'd been exorcised of something, all the pride she'd expended to face me dissipating—was that it?

Was Oikura picking fights with me ever since my first year in high school not because of anything that had to do with math, or because I hadn't given her the help she'd wanted—but because I'd forgotten everything about my two interactions with her? Was that the key? And now that it was all clear, now that she'd made me remember, now that she made me know and thrown it all in my face, did she no longer feel possessed?

I'm sure Ogi would laugh if I said that. Oh, how she'd laugh—Miss Oikura hates you because she resents you, isn't that obvious, she'd say.

"…"

This was her residence, so we had no choice or room to fight if she was telling us to leave. We'd have to—but we hadn't completed our goal of getting her to come to class. We might as well have not come at all if we were going to leave now—and so I thought I'd say something to Oikura for the time being, but just as I began calling her name, *O—* I was interrupted.

"Miss Oikura," Hanekawa finally spoke up—but with an odd

question, one that seemed out of place and off topic. "Did you say—you unlocked the door?"

"Huh? What?"

Oikura looked confused for a moment, as if she didn't understand the words—but she'd used them herself, and quickly realized that Hanekawa was referring to the time she discovered her mother was missing.

"Yes—that's right." Oikura nodded. "I unlocked the door and went inside, and my mother had disappeared…"

"But the windows were boarded up, right? And if the door was locked," Hanekawa repeated—"how did your mother leave?"

011

Hanekawa's point startled me—I'd completely failed to ask about this, but yes, it was strange. I never expected to encounter another "locked room" after all that had happened, and the circumstances around this case were different from that strange classroom I'd been trapped in with Ogi. A plain locked room with no relation to aberrations, and one that suggested foul play—this really was like a mystery novel.

A simple, uncomplicated locked room, making it impossible to know where to start—a room with boarded-up windows and a locked door? The structure was too simple for it to contain any kind of tricks. And Oikura was saying that a human being vanished from inside of it?

A disappearance from inside a locked room.

A universal theme, yes, but...

"How? Through the door, how else?"

But Oikura, a party to the case, didn't seem to get what Hanekawa was saying—and was wondering why she was so caught up in minor details.

"You just have to turn the lock from the inside to open the door. Then she can leave, right?"

"Was it an auto-locking door?"

"Just how modern do you think our place was? It was an old rental, so it had a normal lock. The key was sitting around somewhere or other, though, so she must have locked it again as she left."

Oh.

Well, that did serve as one logical explanation—but I felt I knew what Hanekawa was thinking. Would a person who was about to disappear go to the trouble of locking a door back up?

Wherever she was disappearing to, wouldn't she want to leave the scene as quickly as possible to pull off her disappearing act? At least, it was hard to imagine she had the presence of mind to search for a key that lay *somewhere or other*. Even if she did have the time.

In other words, the fact that Oikura *had to open* the lock when she discovered her mother's disappearance didn't make logical sense.

"Why do you care about such a minor detail—I could be misremembering, or maybe my mother locked it for no real reason. Thinking it was better."

"Well, okay, sure—" Hanekawa said.

It was as if she was only pretending to listen to Oikura's view—well, she did listen, but not as if she was taking it into consideration. Hanekawa's feeling that something was off must have come from Oikura's story as a whole, not just this point—the mother's disappearance was the part that broke it all apart. Not that I had any idea what had precipitated her doubts...

But yes, overwhelmed by Oikura's story, by her upbringing, I'd neglected to do much thinking at all—but that was just me.

Oikura's view did have some merit to it, of course. Faced with Sodachi Oikura, a girl who rationality stood no chance against, who in fact only ever acted counter to rationality, it didn't seem that strange for a person to go out of her way to scrupulously lock up as she disappeared.

Hm. But speaking of locking up...

"In that case, Oikura," I said. "Forget about the door to the room, what about your front door? Was it open? Or was it locked?"

"Huh? Why would you bother asking... I don't remember," she replied sourly. "If I don't remember, that means it didn't make an impression on me, so I guess it was locked? If it had been open, I'd have thought something was strange from that moment."

"..."

That would mean Oikura's mother not only made sure to lock up the door to her room before leaving, but the front door as well…

"I guess she wanted to make sure no burglars got in for the sake of the daughter she was leaving behind? I'm sure there was a spare key to the front door lying around somewhere…"

Probably not anywhere as obvious as under a potted plant, but surely you could find some kind of extra key to the front door with a little bit of searching, just like you could find a key to that room. At least, it wasn't physically impossible.

"So that burglars wouldn't come in, for my sake? My mother would never do something so admirable. She'd never act like some kind of guardian."

I'd been defending Oikura's view, if anything, but she shot me down… In the face of this irrationality, whether or not a door or two had been locked or unlocked seemed less significant.

Still, Hanekawa continued to think.

Almost as if she felt troubled—what exactly was she trying to focus on? At this rate, I couldn't possibly ask her about her promise to let me touch her chest, not that it was on my mind at all, of course.

Oikura seemed irritated.

"I don't get it… Does my mother's disappearance interest you that much? Why?" she said. "I don't understand most of what my mother did. I don't know why she suddenly disappeared—or why she let her spirit be broken over that man. I don't understand why she wanted to stick with someone like him when he kept hitting her. Did I say this already? Or did I not? It wasn't my mother, subjected to violence, who said she wanted a divorce, but my male parent—I really don't get it. What is with my family? Well, we're not a family anymore—we never were from the start. What's with me? Tell me, Araragi…do you have any idea how I felt when I was taken into protection at your home?"

"Huh?"

"I thought *you were putting on some kind of show*—because I thought my house, my household was the norm. I couldn't believe that a house with unbroken windows, unbroken walls, unbroken floors, a tidy little house like that—a household that peaceful could actually exist. That's why I just kept glaring at you all—glaring at you without saying a word. Do you remember that?"

"Yeah..."

I nodded, but this was a lie. I didn't remember anything about that time. But just as Sengoku remembered it clearly—Oikura had found it an intense experience as well.

It was all too bright, she said.

...I'm going to go ahead and say here that while my family might be unique in that both of my parents are police officers, we aren't particularly special—I think we're a very normal household.

When we didn't get along, we didn't get along, just like normal.

It was too bright for her.

The completely normal.

Even the ways we didn't get along.

"It was too bright for me—and so I ran away. It dazzled my eyes and I thought I'd go blind. I thought the warmth, the comfort there would destroy me. But it was no good. Too late. Once I saw that, I realized how miserable my own house was."

It would've been better if I didn't know.

It would've been better if you and I.

If we had never met—said Oikura.

"Once I realized that, it was hopeless—when I tried to act out and do something about it, I was called rebellious. It got me hit even more. I was beaten when people wouldn't see, in places people couldn't see. But while I'd run away once, I couldn't do it again. Not anymore. Which is why I even thought it was some kind of fate that we met again in middle school—I tried so hard to pander to you, remember?"

"..."

"Of course, as a result, I was a little too harsh with you when we were reunited for a second time in high school... Not that it mattered, since you'd forgotten about me anyway."

And now she was an emotionally unstable girl during this, our third time being reunited. As if all of her personalities had merged...

She'd walked a terrible road.

She had lost her way—to the point where I wondered how one person could stray so far.

"God... Things never go well for me, do they. Just as I thought I could finally start over now that Tetsujo is gone, I get put in the same class as you again. Unbelievable."

It really does feel like some kind of fate, Oikura continued.

"Some kind of cursed fate. You show up at every turning point in my life to spread disaster everywhere."

"It's my fault?"

"Yes. My life is a total mess thanks to you—no."

She shook her head.

Forcefully.

"I know. It's not your fault, I'm the one to blame—it's not even my parents' fault. My mother was right, she'd have had a more decent life if she'd given birth to anyone but me. I'm to blame. I'm to blame. I'm to blame."

I'm to hate.

I hate me.

"But you know, Araragi, I can't keep going unless I make it your fault. I'm sorry, but won't you play the villain for me? It's no good anymore, making my parents the villains just isn't enough."

"Oikura—"

"Why doesn't it ever go well? I'm doing everything I should be doing. I'm working hard, I'm giving it my all... Sure, I'm messed up in a lot of ways, whether it's my personality or my head, but...I haven't done anything so bad that I deserve this kind of punishment, have I? Tell me, Araragi. You're happy right now, aren't you? And if you think I've done anything at all to contribute to that, if you'll think that for my sake, then tell me. Why can't I be happy?"

"You can't be happy because..."

It was Hanekawa who answered—before I even got a chance to think.

"You're not trying to be happy. No one can make you happy when you're not even trying."

"Sounds like you know this from experience."

"I don't know everything. I only know what I know."

For some reason, Oikura's expression relaxed when she heard Hanekawa's harsh words. Then—

"You know, you're exactly right. Bingo," she said—as if this was some kind of quiz with a prize attached. "I mean, I'm so fragile that I'd be crushed like a bug if I ever was happy. Both my eyes and my body, destroyed. I can't bear the weight of happiness. I'd rather be soaked from head to toe in lukewarm unhappiness and make do with it than be happy after all this time. I want to live with drenched shoes. And that's what I've done... Yeah. I don't want to be happy after all this time. It's too late."

Too late.

In that case, when could I have made it in time?

Two years ago? Five years ago? Six years ago?

Or was it already too late before any of that—for my childhood friend.

Was it all in the past, something that couldn't be undone at this point, too late and irrecoverable? No.

It wasn't.

That wasn't it.

Hanekawa was right, attacking your old self isn't learning from the past, but a way to avoid responsibility—but that doesn't mean the right thing to do is to give up and cut the past loose. I don't know what the right thing to do is—I don't know what's right. It's something I've lost sight of, something I've lost.

But I did feel like I knew when something was wrong, and I wasn't wrong to think it was wrong to leave her like this and go home.

"There's no such thing," I said. "There's no such thing in this world as happiness so heavy it'd crush you. Happiness isn't bright or heavy. Stop overestimating happiness. Happiness in all its forms suits you fine."

It's perfect for you.

Tailor-made—it'd look just right on you.

"So don't hate happiness like that. Don't hate the world, don't hate everything around you—don't hate yourself. All of that hate in you, give it to me—I'll accept it, so please, you need to start loving yourself more."

Start loving Sodachi Oikura.

You can hate me as much as you want—so just love yourself.

At least as much as I used to love you.

"It's true, I'm happy now—which is why I can say this! This kind of thing is normal for anyone!"

Nudge.

I felt a light jab to my side—it was Hanekawa.

This brought me back to my senses.

What was I saying? What was I doing? Hanekawa was finally talking to Oikura and I'd interrupted her—I should have left the rest up to Hanekawa once she got started. But I had to butt in.

I gritted my teeth, ready to be scolded—but she just pulled her hand back and whispered so that only I could hear.

"Nice one."

It did relieve me to know that my reckless words hadn't displeased her—but the question remained.

Of how exactly Sodachi Oikura took them—my reckless, even ungrateful words aimed at this girl, who had undoubtedly been responsible in part for my happiness. And she took them by saying—

"Town Hall."

Town Hall?

She looked up—like she was tired.

"Someone from Town Hall is coming soon. I'm sorry to say this just as you're getting this passionate, but really, could you please go home? They're going to check if everything is fine with my living situation… If I'm being honest with you, they're just barely overlooking the fact that I'm not going to school. It'd be really bad if they saw me arguing with my classmates."

An excuse to drive us off?

But in that case, wouldn't she have used it earlier?

Which meant it wasn't a lie. At least, Hanekawa seemed to come to that conclusion.

"Oh. Then we'll leave for today," she nodded. "But we're coming back again tomorrow. And the day after, weekend or not. It might annoy you, but that's how we do things. We annoy the people we like."

Oh, oops, Hanekawa continued, tacking on another comment.

"I almost forgot. I ought to say this first. I actually kind of like you a lot now."

"…"

Those words.

Those words from Tsubasa Hanekawa made Sodachi Oikura look sincerely troubled—and she looked at the floor, resentfully it seemed.

"In that case," she said.

In that case, you two.

"I want you to find my missing mother. If you do, I wouldn't mind going to school for you—or even apologizing to Miss Senjogahara."

012

Hanekawa and I, class president and vice president, should have been happy to know the exact goal we needed to work toward—but when I thought about it, it could also be seen as Oikura brushing us off, a declaration that *she wasn't coming to school if we didn't find her mother.*

"I would be fine with that—the fact that we're seeing even the smallest signs of the misunderstanding between you and Miss Oikura starting to thaw is really as good as it can get."

"Signs of it thawing, huh? Well, if you're okay with it."

In reality, we must not have done much more than stir Oikura's emotions. They might settle back into stubbornness by tomorrow—and if not tomorrow, then the day after.

The sculpture that was her hatred for me had spent two, five, or maybe even six years hardening and settling into place. It wouldn't be that easy to melt it all down—we had to approach this with patience.

"But should you really say that's as good as it can get, President Hanekawa? Our mission is to get her to go to school."

"I don't plan on forcing her to do anything so long as she settles things with Miss Senjogahara, or at least cools them down—high school isn't worth attending begrudgingly, anyway."

So even Hanekawa, with her commitment to seriousness, was going to say that—but true, it did feel like I had no right to urge Oikura to go to school. She wouldn't have to go to school to graduate and head to college, she only needed to make sure she got good grades. There was no need for her to force herself to live a miserable school life—but.

"Yes, *but*, if she can have an enjoyable school life," said Hanekawa, "I want her to live it, even if it means forcing her—for the half-year she has left. Your adolescence is your adolescence, even if it's short. She's going to have to apologize to Miss Senjogahara."

"That seems like the toughest problem of all to me..."

"If you're going to be solving problems, isn't it more fun to start with the hard ones?"

We left Oikura's place, climbed down the stairs, exited the building, then moved to the plaza inside the apartment block—it seemed like the kind of plaza where residents would have their children play, but it was deserted, either as a result of the time of day or for some other reason.

The desolate sight was sad, but just right for thinking. We decided to consider things there—to consider the case of Oikura's mother's disappearance from the locked room.

Of course, it was only a disappearance from a locked room if you looked at it from a mystery-novel perspective. In fantasy fiction, it was called being "spirited away"—after all, an adult human being had vanished like smoke into thin air.

What I expected was that we'd each go back home and bring our findings to school the next day after a night of consideration, to discuss the matter and come to a conclusion—I assumed we'd be on that kind of schedule. But maybe that's the difference between genius and mediocrity because Hanekawa said, "Okay, let's at least figure out what direction to go in while Miss Oikura's dealing with Town Hall. If we can come up with a good enough conclusion here, we'll be able to report back to her after this person leaves."

True, this would let us make a deal before Oikura's emotions had settled back down, and it would be ideal if she and Senjogahara came back to school the very next day... I could have thought for a century and not come up with the idea.

Putting aside the question of how realistic it was for two high school students to search for a missing person, something a real-life detective would dedicate a huge amount of resources to—smart people are just so quick on their feet. These thoughts ran through my mind as I tried what seemed like a good starting point.

"I know what Oikura said—but I agree, something seems strange. I'm siding with you here. It doesn't make sense for her mother to lock up if she left on her own. The front door is one thing, but the lock to the room she'd shut herself in? That seems especially—"

"I think the front door is strange enough on its own—I think Miss Oikura is right about that...even if she was just reflexively disagreeing with us. It really doesn't make sense for someone in that tight of a psychological spot to bother locking the door to a house she's not planning on returning to," Hanekawa took the baton from me—even for her this seemed more like a brainstorming session than careful consideration. It felt like she'd replied with whatever came to mind.

It was hard to tell if clearing up those doubts would help us at all... to solve the mystery of the locked room? No, I'll just say pinning down her mother's whereabouts. It even seemed unlikely, but it was the biggest clue we could see at the moment.

"What possibilities can you think of, in that case? If Oikura's mother wasn't the one to lock the door—was she abducted? Did a kidnapper grab her mother and return the locks to their original positions as a form of camouflage?"

"Well, yes. That's possible," Hanekawa said. "It would make more sense for a kidnapper to resort to camouflage than someone trying to go missing—that, or an accident."

"Like what?"

"As in she never had plans to disappear. She just felt like going out— so she locked her door to make sure no one came into the room while she was away. And she locked the front door as one does. Then she got into or encountered some kind of accident while she was out, making it impossible for her to return—or it's possible that she felt like disappearing while she was out."

"That does seem to be the best explanation we have right now."

It was pretty hard to imagine what wanting to vanish felt like, but this did seem like a far more likely kind of whim than Oikura's theory that her mother locked the room and the front door because she felt like it—but then Hanekawa continued, "I don't understand why she'd randomly go outside after shutting herself in for all that time." She shook her head. "Despite being a shut-in for two years, one day she randomly decides to go outside and randomly gets the idea to disappear? I could maybe accept one of those things happening, but both seems a little unreasonable."

"Well, no. It's only Oikura's impression that she hadn't left that room for two years. Who knows, she might have been sneaking out and doing some shopping while Oikura was at school."

"Why bother sneaking out? We're talking about an adult, it's not like anyone would get mad at her if they found out."

"But in their case, Oikura was taking care of her mother—and maybe she'd quit if she saw her mother strolling around town."

What kind of a mother was I talking about? It was of course just a hypothesis, an example that I was proposing. Our missing person being Oikura's mother, who had been under her own daughter's care, though, was neither a hypothesis nor an example.

"Okay, you've convinced me. Keep going."

"So, then…she left home, the way she always did. Though I'm sure it'd be hard to make sure not just Oikura but no one at all saw her… And then one day she came up with the idea of running off?"

The context didn't seem to make sense when I tried to connect the dots with the first half of my idea. While it seemed improbable that someone who'd isolated herself from society for two years not only went outside but suddenly had the idea of vanishing while doing so, it seemed even more improbable for a pseudo-shut-in who'd been going outside in good health nearly every day suddenly deciding to vanish. She would have been living a normal life, after all.

While I'm sure disappearances happen more often than locked-room mysteries and humans getting spirited away, it isn't the kind of thing you'd be thinking about if you're living a normal life—compared to that, it felt more realistic for a person who'd been a shut-in for two years to make a promise to herself to vanish.

Not that this was entirely about what felt realistic…

334

"Of all the ideas we've had until now, the only one involving some-one else is kidnapping—can you think of any reason someone would kidnap not a child, but an adult, an adult at her residence at that? For ransom?"

"No, their family was living on government assistance... It couldn't have been for money. If they were targeting her in her home, they'd done their research... And it's not like there was any demand for money in the first place, right?"

"So it was herself they were after? Who could have a motive to kid-nap Oikura's mother—her father? Oikura doesn't even know where he lives."

"Hm... I guess he would be one likely suspect."

At first, Oikura seemed to have suspected that her missing mother had gone to her father's, but in this case, it would have been the opposite, her father going to her mother. He'd been the one to file for divorce, but it did seem quite possible for an old flame to have reignited in him...

"That also raises the possibility that both of them felt like their relationship had been rekindled—in which case they eloped. I mean, she would have at least put up a little bit of a fight if it had been a forced abduction, right? And Oikura would have noticed whatever marks were left behind... No markings means that her mother could have been abducted after coming to some sort of agreement, even if it was a forced one."

"Hold on, Araragi. It's possible for a forceful abduction to leave no traces."

"Hm?"

"Well, Miss Oikura's home may be nice and tidy at the moment, but at one point, she didn't have the time to clean and it was full of trash, remember? If the place was a mess to begin with, she might not have noticed a scuffle."

"Oh. Yeah... I guess you could compare it to Kanbaru's room?"

A room on the level of Kanbaru's might actually end up tidier if you had a fight in it, but assuming it hadn't been quite that messy, Hanekawa was right.

"But of course, it's possible that she agreed to leave, that she decided to set off on a journey—maybe even with someone else, not necessarily Miss Oikura's father."

"Like who? Do you have anyone in mind?"

"No, no one—I just wonder if she'd really leave her daughter behind like she was eloping if it was her ex-husband."

"Elopement, huh—but in that case, getting a new start with her old husband seems like a possible explanation for leaving Oikura behind. They could try to make it work again if it was just the two of them—or something like that."

"You seem quite familiar with male psychology, Araragi."

"No, hold on, I don't mean it like that—"

"I'm joking. That is something we'll have to look into if we're going to figure out where Miss Oikura's mother went, though."

Hanekawa clapped her hands together as if to mark a take. Maybe she wanted to punctuate the conversation here. I think it goes without saying, but she wasn't applauding.

"I think we should consider at this point that locating her won't necessarily be desirable for Miss Oikura. Of course, it was unlikely from the start that we'd end up with any happy outcome…"

"Well, yeah… If the signs really do point to a conclusion like her parents eloping on their own and leaving Oikura behind, I'd have a tough time telling her. No matter how I think about it."

"It could be worse than just having a tough time. We might not be able to tell her at all."

"What do you mean?"

"We should think of this separately from the locked room—but we can't ignore the possibility that her missing mother is no longer with us. To take that a step further—her mother may have been killed by someone before this disappearance, or by the time she went missing."

"Killed…"

"I know people are split on whether it's easier to carry a corpse as compared to a live body…but the perp thought that a dead body would be easier to carry, since it wouldn't struggle."

"Hmm… You just as often hear that it's hard to carry a corpse because it's stiff and won't try to support itself. People do seem to be split on that…but I guess there's room to speculate which side of the argument the perp would be on. But," I said. "Now that we've come this far, I think we need to tell Oikura about whatever we find, no matter how painful—or maybe not 'we,' it's my duty. I'm sure she doesn't expect to see her mother again, either."

"That's the thing."

"Hm?"

"It comes down to *why* Miss Oikura gave us this important mission of finding her mother—isn't that hard to understand?"

"Well…"

It vaguely seemed like a reasonable assumption that a daughter would want to find her mother, so it'd be a request she might make, but…it wasn't as if she liked her mother. Her mother was only a bit better than her father, and the difference between the two may not have been that large. I didn't know how Oikura mentally classified her mother or processed their relationship—but I did know for sure that this wasn't about her finding her mother because she wanted to live with her again.

What was Oikura after when she sent us looking for her mother? She surely would have gone with something else if she was only looking for an excuse to shoo us away…

Oikura's goal.

What was it—that she wanted to know?

"I don't know," I said, "but…there's probably something that she just can't come to terms with, and it's been nagging at her all this time… Don't you think that's possible? In other words, despite everything she said to us, she thinks there's something strange about the circumstances of her mother's disappearance in her heart of hearts. Vanishing out of the blue like that… She mentioned that she takes after her mother, and who knows, maybe that's why she's scared. She's afraid that she might disappear all of a sudden herself, for no reason at all—that she might fade away like a puff of smoke."

Vanish.

Just like she did in elementary school.

Not funny… I wasn't letting her.

I wasn't letting Oikura vanish—not again.

Practically speaking, even if locating her mother proved to be impossible, we would certainly get another chance to speak to Oikura if we came up with some line of thinking that provided a hint—not that I wanted her thanks or anything.

You know what it was?

This is what I thought—

It might not be so bad if I lowered my intensity as a human yet another degree from where it was now.

"Okay."

Hanekawa again.

"Let's start again from the very beginning and summarize all our doubts about her mother's disappearance. We'll decide which to keep and which to throw out—I know we didn't come up with any decisive plans for a solution, but I really do think this is the most vital part. In other words, how did the room get locked? You don't know, do you?"

"Right. I don't know."

"Reaaally? You don't know?"

And then.

Darkness suddenly interrupted my time with Hanekawa—a blackout, like day had switched to night in an instant.

It was only an illusion, though. It was still before dusk—grown-out black hair had fallen across my face, that was all. It belonged to Ogi Oshino.

Ogi Oshino—Ogi.

Ogi was here.

"Huh, that's kind of disappointing. You can't figure out the mystery behind a locked room? I know that you're a fool, Araragi-senpai, but even you, Miss Hanekawa?"

"…"

Hanekawa looked up.

Why is Ogi here—is that what she thought? No, not at this point. Hanekawa herself said that while it had taken some time to look up Oikura's current address, it wasn't by any means impossible—the "annoying" scenario she'd brought up. Ogi going back to school and looking up the address.

She grinned at us.

But even her smile was pretty scary in that case.

"Oh, I was just so curious, so I decided to come and check in on you, even though I knew I was being invasive. I thought there might be a chance you couldn't be of any help, Miss Hanekawa...and I was right, sure enough. Heheh, I really do think you might be past your prime. Heheh, heheh. And to think that someone of your level snatched Araragi-senpai from me and walked off with him. It makes me want to laugh—my goodness."

Ogi forced herself between Hanekawa and me, squeezing her body to fit there like some kind of battle for seats in a crowded train.

Even Hanekawa had to give in.

Part of her seemed baffled—though she couldn't have been confused by the fact that Ogi was here, having predicted that she'd make it here before us. If Hanekawa found anything strange about this situation, it wasn't Ogi's presence, but why she was speaking to us now, at this exact point in time.

I didn't know either—a grudge over what happened at the school gate?

"Yes, all that work you did luring him with those lumps of flesh on your chest—and nothing to show for it? Hah hah hah."

A serious grudge...

I'd planned to follow up the next day, but it seemed I was too late. My leg work was only that of an average person, and I was going to have to pay for my torpor.

"Oh, how embarrassing. How embarrassing. I'd be so embarrassed that I couldn't keep going. Getting him to pick me by seducing him with my feminine charms, only to cause him more trouble than if he'd gone alone? Even I look pitiful here, when I think about it. He wouldn't have had to feel this way if only I'd been with him, but now it's turned out like this because I let your breasts steal him away."

Ogi turned to face me. She really seemed to be enjoying this. She was savoring the situation from the bottom of her heart. In other words, she enjoyed wedging herself in between me and Hanekawa.

"I'm sorry for making you feel so uneasy. Really, I am. If only you'd picked me back there. But I won't blame you! I won't blame you. That's right, I won't. Everyone makes mistakes, after all—isn't that right, Miss Hanekawa?" she said, twisting her head to look at Hanekawa next. "You'll forgive him too, won't you? For making the huge blunder of choosing you. You know, why don't you say it to him out loud? 'You aren't to blame for my foolishness, Araragi'—"

"…"

Hanekawa continued to say nothing to Ogi's show of utter disrespect—maybe she couldn't say anything? I had to, though. Ogi could act however she wanted towards me, but I wouldn't stand for her being this high-handed with Hanekawa.

"Hey, Ogi—"

"*Personally…*" Ogi swung back around to face me. It felt for a moment like only her neck had rotated 180 degrees to face me, but I must have been seeing things. "*Personally, I've already figured out that locked room.*"

"What?"

"And where her mother might have gone off to—well, for the most part."

To some degree.

Ogi chuckled faintly—as if to laugh at Hanekawa behind her. Though she faced me, her words were meant to attack Hanekawa.

"In fact, I can't believe there's someone who hasn't figured it out, especially that there's someone with big breasts who hasn't. You have to be pretty stupid to be unable to figure out this mystery. I bet even you've figured it out actually, haven't you, Araragi-senpai? You're only playing along for the sake of a certain someone whose name starts with an H. It's unthinkable for anyone not to have figured this out. At least, anyone who tried to plunder someone else's fieldwork partner."

"O-Ogi—hold on, it's not like you've heard much about this situation yourself. You only heard a few scraps of our conversation as you arrived here, right? I don't see how you could solve this mystery with that alone…"

"No, a few scraps are more than enough here. So long as you don't have big breasts."

"…"

Her hostility toward big breasts was relentless.

It seemed that what really got to Ogi wasn't the fact that her field-work partner had been taken away, but that he'd been taken away by big breasts—I felt like I was finally getting a glimpse of her younger age.

Leaving that aside—what did it mean? Ogi claimed the locked room was simple, even if she was exaggerating to annoy Hanekawa.

Ogi's main investigatory tool was listening. As far as I knew, she wasn't like one of those master detectives who solved a mystery immediately upon arriving at a scene—no, but at the same time, I couldn't imagine it all being an act when she'd so deftly dismantled what happened at the class council meeting and in the derelict house. If she said she'd solved it, she really must have—the mystery of Oikura's mother's disappearance.

Ogi even claimed to know where she'd gone—qualified with a *for the most part*, of course, but it'd still be impressive. It might be enough to satisfy Oikura—getting her to come back to school.

Even then, it was hard to believe.

Mèmè Oshino's niece or not, how much could she have understood after hearing so little info?

"Ogi. Ogi—Ogi Oshino. What exactly—do you know?"

"I don't know anything. It's you who knows—her in elementary school, her in middle school, her in high school. You know Sodachi Oikura—so it shouldn't be too difficult to pin down the truth about her mother."

So long as you don't have big breasts, she insisted.

"Speaking of, Miss Hanekawa. You used to have braids and glasses, right? It was a good choice to stop wearing those. You'd be committing fraud dressing up to look that smart when you can't even solve a problem like this one. You'd be arrested, nabbed. But while this might have been an extremely simple practice question for me, if you seriously can't figure it out, Miss Hanekawa, I suppose I could indulge you, since I want to be a good underclassman to you two. All you have to do is apologize for your big breasts."

Apologize for her big breasts?

The weirdest situation ever.

Ogi seemed to mean it, though. She stood up from her spot between us to stand directly in front of Hanekawa—facing her.

"'I let all of my nourishment go to my boobs. Ogi, my junior, I just can't solve this paltry question, so please, tell me the answer. I promise I'll never snatch Araragi away from you again.' Say that to me and I wouldn't mind giving you the model answer."

Clearly enjoying herself, Ogi stood there smirking—of course, none of this had anything to do with her since she'd never met Oikura, who was just an investigation topic. It made sense that Ogi was treating it as some kind of game.

For me and Hanekawa, though, this was no game at all—we could afford to be stubborn here if it was, but this involved Oikura's life.

Afraid that Hanekawa was going to fold, I stepped in.

"Ogi!" I yelled her name a little emphatically. "I'll ask you. I'll be the one to ask. That's good enough, isn't it? So if you know, please, tell us. What happened to the Oikuras three years ago?"

"Really? Now, what should I do? I'm legitimately mad at Miss Hanekawa, but I can't say no if you're asking. You just have that effect on me."

She seemed to be enjoying herself even more.

"What do you think, Miss Hanekawa? Shall I do as he asks? Shall I forgive his betrayal? Even you'd be able to figure it out then, so please, don't stay so silent and answer me, I'm going to the trouble of asking you so that you can save face."

Hanekawa didn't answer. She only looked at Ogi—even in this situation, she seemed to be analyzing the presence that was Ogi Oshino.

Her true form.

Trying to see into her.

Trying to see past her.

"It's so boring when you don't say anything. You really aren't as impressive as my uncle made you sound. You know, I bet you weren't even that much to speak of in your prime. Everyone around you just held you up higher than you deserved. Fine, then. In that case, Araragi-senpai."

Ogi let out a sigh, as if she was bored of poking fun at Hanekawa, and spoke to me.

"'I made a mistake in choosing someone as unimpressive as Hanekawa. You are my only partner, Ogi. I like you more than Hanekawa, Ogi.' Say that and I'll give you the answer. The truth and all."

"Wha…"

I hesitated.

She expected me to say that?

"I'm not compromising on this condition. I don't want you changing a single syllable, okay? Not even, 'Ogi, I like your just-right chest over Hanekawa's giant breasts.' What's the matter? There's no need to hesitate, is there? Miss Oikura is sure to be happy to learn the answer—isn't now the time for you to repay her for all she did? Or are you still going to prioritize Miss Hanekawa's chest?"

Mixing in all that chest talk made it confusing, but she was right.

If this was for Oikura's sake—for Oikura's sake.

There was only one decision I could make. I could never abnegate my beliefs with words like those, but if I were to refuse, she might force Hanekawa to make a request she should never have to make—she might be forced to admit defeat to Ogi. That'd be even worse. Even if Ogi reached the solution before Hanekawa here…I didn't want Hanekawa to admit defeat.

I didn't want to see Hanekawa like that.

It was a terrible prisoner's dilemma, but I was just going to have to fold before she did…

"You'd better not, Araragi."

Then.

Hanekawa spoke.

"Don't say it—even if it's a lie, even if it's for my sake, I still don't want you saying anything like that."

"B-But, Hanekawa—"

"I won't say it, either. I'm going to snatch you away as many times as I like."

Then she stood.

"Ogi. I want you to give me ten seconds to prove it—that Araragi was right to pick me."

"Ten."

Ogi began her countdown. No discussions, no negotiations. Right, the lightness of Ogi's footwork, the speed at which she made decisions was brilliant. Her rivalry with Tsubasa Hanekawa existed on more than a verbal level.

"Nine."

Hanekawa began to move swiftly. What was she doing, where was she going? She headed toward the water fountains in the corner of the plaza. The water fountains? She felt thirsty? At a time like this?

"Eight."

No.

Once she turned the spigot, she plunged her head into the stream below!

"Seven."

The valve was as open as it could go. What seemed like a waterfall drenched Hanekawa's head. She was like one of those ascetics. Was she trying to cool her head? That forcefully? Was she trying to cool down—because Ogi's provocations had gotten her worked up?

"Six."

Half of her time limit had passed. If this were a test, Hanekawa would already be checking her answers, but no, she was still busy bathing. She must have said *ten seconds* to keep Ogi at bay—I panicked. Shouldn't she have asked for at least thirty seconds, if not a minute? Then again, she must have thought that Ogi wouldn't accept the duel otherwise.

"Five."

She closed the spigot. Hanekawa quickly shook her head, like a cat who'd been in the rain—and something appeared different about her hair. Any dye in it had fallen off, showing about half a head's worth of white hair mixed in it. From afar, the black and white blended to make the whole look gray.

Gray matter, Ogi muttered before continuing—

"Four."

Hanekawa returned to us with quick, long strides—forget about her head, even her uniform was drenched. It looked like a storm had opened up on her and no one else. She returned, then sat again, grandly. Water flew from her speed and force, but her intensity kept me from trying to wipe it off.

"Three."

Hanekawa thought.

"Two."

Hanekawa thought.

"One."

Hanekawa thought.

"Z—"

"You don't need to count to zero."

Hanekawa finished thinking.

"I win."

013

"I win, but this is…"

Though Tsubasa Hanekawa declared victory, she seemed in no way haughty or proud—neither the victoriousness of victory, nor the winnerliness of a winner. I saw distress on her face if anything, like she'd savored the taste of defeat.

Ogi, meanwhile, was unchanged. Not a thing about her had changed. She was still grinning, even after Hanekawa's proclamation—no, Ogi even looked to be enjoying this.

I had no idea what to do while the two fought this battle of wits off in another dimension. Knowing nothing, about either the mystery or their thoughts, I could only sit there quietly.

"You…"

Hanekawa spoke at last.

As if she couldn't believe it.

"You really came up with this as your first theory? Minus any examination? You heard a fragment of our conversation…and came straight to this truth?"

"Yes," Ogi nodded. "That's where the thinking started—I took that hunch and, with some deduction, straightened out the story. Any other possibilities do seem very unlikely, after all."

"How exactly does your brain work? Thinking of this off the bat isn't the act of a sane person."

Not the act of a sane person—Hanekawa used words that were unusually strong for her, but her facial expression made it clear that even they weren't enough.

"You arrived at the same truth in the end, didn't you? In that case, what right do you have to say that? You're just as bad as me. It's just a matter of speed. There's no definitive difference between me and you. And—isn't Miss Oikura the one acting the least sane?"

"…"

"She is by far the least sane one here."

"…"

Hanekawa said nothing in response. Even though she'd been told that her classmate, Oikura, wasn't sane—what was going on here? What was this truth that Ogi, then Hanekawa, arrived upon?

"Araragi… We can't."

Hanekawa said this facing me—but not looking at me.

"We can't… There's no way we can tell Miss Oikura. I know you wanted to give her the truth, no matter what… I know you said it's your duty, but even you're going to change your mind once you hear this."

"Change my mind…"

"Awww, you can't do that, Miss Hanekawa. You can't indulge the foolish—you've got to make him think for himself a bit. He'll be a fool forever otherwise. No matter how much time passes," Ogi jumped in gleefully. "We need him to come up with it, too—the truth of the matter that's sickening even to come upon."

It seemed this was letting her get over everything with Hanekawa, even her large breasts. Ogi may have lost the battle, but making Hanekawa come up with this mad truth was enough to satisfy her.

But what could it be? A truth that's sickening even to come upon? A truth we can't tell Oikura? A truth we can never speak? Was there really anything we couldn't tell Oikura, after all she'd already gone through?

Something that surpassed, that undercut the status quo?

"So you want me to come up with this awful truth, but—"

"Hint 1. Miss Oikura's mother is already deceased," Ogi declared.

Okay, that was one of the possibilities I'd considered—but why did

Ogi, then Hanekawa, come to that conclusion?

"She's dead... Which means, okay... Oikura's dad killed her mom or something? And this led to her bizarre disappearance. The way she vanished as if she'd been spirited away—"

"Completely wrong." Ogi shook her head. She graded my answer harshly without even letting me finish. "You're so kind. That's the worst possible truth of the matter you can think of? All right, Miss Hanekawa. Please go ahead with hint 2."

"M-Me?"

"Yes. I opposed you over your chest, but we share a common interest in wanting to educate him, do we not? Let's work together to teach him. You're even acting as his home tutor, aren't you?"

"..."

A brief silence, and then—

"Hint 2."

Hanekawa must have decided that while keeping the truth from Oikura was one thing, she couldn't hide it from me as well. Still, it seemed like she'd been given a difficult role—like she'd sooner play the villain. I needed to arrive at the answer quickly to spare Hanekawa, but...

"Just as you mistook Miss Oikura's home for an abandoned one when you were in middle school, Miss Oikura misunderstood something herself—she misunderstood something about her mother. She still does."

"Oh, Miss Hanekawa. You're giving him too many hints. I did too, in the first chapter, but—how indulgent. You're oh-so-indulgent. You must be the one to blame for Araragi-senpai's sorry state."

"..."

Though she said Hanekawa had given me too many hints, I still didn't have any idea.

The worst possible truth. The worst possible truth. The worst possible truth.

A misunderstanding.

"Her mother was murdered...and the culprit is Oikura, and she doesn't realize it...or something?"

I tried saying the first thing that came to mind, praying it was wrong. There'd be so little hope in a truth like that—but if hopelessness was what backed up the right answer, was this it? Was this the worst possible truth?

"Bzzt."

Ogi shook her head. I breathed a sigh of relief. This was no time to feel relieved, though—because if that was wrong, an even worse truth lay in store for me.

"I'll concede the possibility that Miss Oikura's story is entirely fiction, that she made it up from A to Z, and that really she killed her mother under completely different circumstances—but we'd never get anywhere if we started with such doubts. Yes, narrators can be unreliable, but at a certain point we have to decide to believe what other people say. Believe one another—we need to, don't we? Don't we, Araragi-senpai?"

Her words rang so hollow.

But she was right.

So, if I were to believe Oikura's words—while also knowing that she'd misunderstood something.

If there was any kind of discrepancy there.

"Hint 3. Disappearing from a locked room does not necessarily mean escaping from that locked room."

As Ogi said this, she circled behind me again—she really did like taking my back.

Disappearance and escape were different?

True.

For example, there's the classic mystery novel trick that'd surprise no one these days—in fact, it'd be more of a surprise if an author innocently used it—where the culprit hides somewhere in the locked room together with the victim's body. The trick where it looks like he's escaped, when in reality he's still inside. In other words...

"In other words, when Oikura unlocked the door and walked inside, her mother was still there...and hid behind the door or something before sneaking behind Oikura to leave the house?"

"Bzzt. What would be the point?"

True.

It'd be pointless.

Why leave the room while Oikura was home, yet out of her sight, when the house was empty as she went to school?

It was a pointless risk.

The trick might be a possibility if her mother had been locked inside the room by someone else—but she'd shut herself in.

Though this was a locked-room case, it wasn't the kind of mystery that involved some sort of trick.

"Hint 4. So, Araragi, if her mother passed away, why couldn't she find the body? Why does Miss Oikura continue to treat her mother as missing?"

"…"

I'm sure it was by design, but it was as if Ogi had set up a situation where she and Hanekawa, two towering talents, took turns attacking me. I really wanted to come up with the answer, since I knew this was the last thing Hanekawa wanted to do—but if nothing was clicking in my brain, was it because my brain was refusing to click?

She couldn't find the body…

In other words, Ogi's roundabout way of saying she knew where Oikura's mother had gone off to *for the most part* must have meant she was dead and likely somewhere in the next life… Or did *for the most part* also include her still-missing corpse?

"Hint 5," Ogi continued, not pausing for an answer. "There are some things that even an excellent listener like me won't fully get from a tale told orally. While I may have only heard it secondhand this time around—I doubt I would have understood the exact details about *that* from Miss Oikura's story even if you'd picked me to be your partner. Thus, our investigatory fieldwork ought to go beyond interviews to include good, old-fashioned leg work in the form of an on-site survey—but what exactly could I be talking about?"

"Hint 6," Hanekawa took her turn. She wanted to end this as soon as possible. I felt irritated at myself for not being able to make it happen. "Miss Oikura had no time to clean up at her previous house. It was full of trash."

"Hint 7. Her mother suddenly disappeared one day. Suddenly one day, suddenly on that day. So what about the day before that?"

Ogi wasn't pausing either.

They were firing off hints at this fool.

"Hint 8. Miss Oikura's mother had been left with a terribly weak heart and mind when her family collapsed. To the point that she shut herself in. To the point where she lost the will to live."

"Hint 9. Miss Oikura looked after her mother, but it seems that at some point she stopped eating entirely. Have you interpreted this 'entirely' to mean 'she must have eaten at least a little bit'? Have you decided on your own to go with a mild interpretation?"

"Hint 10. Miss Oikura said that her mother stopped responding entirely to anything she said...didn't she?"

"Hint 11. And that she stopped moving from her corner of the room."

"Hint 12. She didn't eat, didn't listen, didn't speak, didn't talk. Would you call that living?"

"Hint 13. Really, could a middle schooler care for a parent who'd shut herself in over a span of not just months, but years? Caring for a corpse might be another story, of course."

"Hint 14. I wonder how long a human corpse retains its form."

"Hint 15. The answer to hint 5 is 'smell'—smell is just so hard to pick up on through an interview. You didn't get much of a sense of smell from Miss Oikura's story, did you? Taste is another very sensory thing, but we have a wide variety of ways of describing taste. Sweet, spicy, sour. For smells, we really just have good smells and bad smells. Aside from that, we're only left with direct comparisons. The smell of roses. The smell of rain. The smell of milk. The smell of rotten eggs—the smell of a rotting corpse."

"Hint 16. But a house packed with trash might envelop it all...even if there was a corpse there, and even if that corpse was in the process of rotting, the neighbors might not notice."

"Hint 17."

"Hint 18."

"Hint 19."

"Hint 20." "Hint 21." "Hint 22." "Hint 23." "Hint 24." "Hint 25." "Hint 26." "Hint 27." "Hint 28." "Hint 29." "Hint 30." "Hint 31." "Hint

32." "Hint 33." "Hint 34." "Hint 35." "Hint 36." "Hint 37." "Hint 38." "Hint 39." "Hint 40." "Hint 41." "Hint 42." "Hint 43." "Hint 44." "Hint 45." "Hint 46." "Hint 47." "Hint 48." "Hint 49." "Hint 50."

"I get it already!"

I shouted.

Or wailed.

I was nearly shrieking.

"You're saying that—for most of those two years! *Oikura was taking care of her mother's corpse!* Until it fully rotted! Until it was so fully rotten *that it disappeared*, and that she never noticed!"

Yes—that's right.

I'd overlooked the truth during the class council meeting two years ago.

And in that derelict house, five years ago.

I still couldn't remember my childhood friend from six years ago.

And so.

I couldn't run now. I couldn't avoid it now.

I had to face it. Sodachi Oikura's tragedy—Sodachi Oikura's madness.

That's what it means to move forward.

What it means to properly face Oikura.

"A brilliant answer. Look at that! All it took was some effort—arriving at the truth of the matter after a mere fifty hints. You might be a fool, but you show some promise."

Promise.

No, Ogi actually seemed impressed as she clapped with joy as if she were offering me her unqualified praise.

"Yes—yes, so in that sense, Miss Oikura's mother didn't disappear suddenly. She disappeared *gradually*. After refusing to eat, she gradually starved to death and gradually began to rot. And once she decomposed to the point that her body was unrecognizable—once it had fully *melted* into the room, Miss Oikura realized that her mother had *gone somewhere*."

Ogi continued as if she were making an aside.

353

"It's like water evaporating. She hates water that thinks it made itself boil—was it? Well, you can say that her mother did make herself boil."

"Water…"

"Have you ever kept bell crickets?" asked Ogi, gleefully bringing up an example. She was trying to explain the situation with an easy-to-understand analogy—so that the utterly tragic truth would be clear to anyone. "Well, I have… I like the sound they make. This is back when I was in elementary or so, though. Anyway, you feed them with cucumbers. Bell crickets just love cucumbers. I'd check in later to find that the cucumbers had vanished and think, wow, bugs have such incredible appetites! But apparently, it was something else. Cucumbers are mostly water, so they'd just evaporated and gone all thin."

Oh, and also, the bell crickets were wiped out because they ate those rotten cucumbers, Ogi said, tacking on an unnecessary and unpleasant bit of detail.

"Miss Oikura's mother also *evaporated*—humans do have a lot of water in them, after all. Disappearing into thin air, and evaporating. They end up meaning the same thing here, in an ironic twist—but that solves the case of the locked room, as well as the two locked doors. In that case, it's only natural that the front door and the room were locked. Her mother never left the room in the first place. She hadn't vanished like smoke—she vanished like water."

"But humans aren't made entirely of water. What about the *rest*?"

It was all I could do to pose that question—but Ogi simply answered, "Didn't I suggest something about that at around hint 29? The fact that there haven't been any real problems until now," she stated plainly, "must mean that they dealt with her alongside the garbage when they dealt with a house full of trash."

She spoke plainly about a human being disposed of alongside trash.

"It might even be the case—that an environment like that helped speed along the decomposition of a body."

"Then what," I asked.

Fearfully, bracing myself for an even more terrifying truth.

"It was…suicide by starvation?"

"I wonder. She may have lost her will to live, but I don't think you call that suicide. Losing the will to live and wanting to die are two different things in the human heart. But I'm sure people will be split on this. Shall we take a majority vote? What do you say, Miss Hanekawa? There's no way, right? A mother would never choose suicide and leave her daughter behind."

Hanekawa didn't answer.

Ogi must not have known. How could she?

She said she didn't know anything, so she must not have known—that Hanekawa's birth mother did just that, commit suicide and leave her daughter behind.

She could never have asked that if she'd known.

"All I think," Hanekawa said quietly.

Quietly, painfully.

"Is that Miss Oikura ought to live her life not knowing about this and never knowing about it."

"Yes. It would be better. But I bet a little part of her must think that something is strange here. Which is the reason she asked you two to investigate. Why did she ask you to find her mother? That's why. A feeling that something is off, that she's covered something up—a feeling that she's pretending not to notice something. She must have had those kinds of thoughts—for the last three years. And she will for the rest of her life, too."

"No. Until today," I said.

To Ogi—and to Hanekawa.

"I'm telling her. I'll be the one to tell her. I'm going back to Oikura's room right now to tell her everything."

"What?"

Hanekawa raised her voice in shock, and while Ogi didn't, she looked surprised as well. Personally, I didn't think I was saying anything surprising—I was just going to do what I needed to do.

"That person from Town Hall must have left by now—so I'll go by myself, you two can just wait here."

"A-Araragi... Are you serious?"

"I am. Didn't I just tell you? I've been ignoring Oikura for all this time—for over six years. I haven't been able to look her straight in the eye, just like she wasn't able to face her mother's death. That's why I can't neglect Oikura any more than I already have," I replied to Hanekawa.

"There's no telling what might happen, Araragi-senpai—Miss Oikura might end up hating you even more than she already does."

"Don't worry, she can't hate me any more than she does now. Even if she can, if she's able to love herself through hating me, I'd prefer that," I replied to Ogi.

Then I began walking—to Oikura's place.

Not to apologize, not to atone.

To speak, to tell.

Yes, I was going to teach her.

As her senior just a few steps further down the road to happiness, I would teach her how to get started on it—of course, my pupil was the highly gifted Oikura. Once she had the basics down, she'd surely overtake me. Even when it came to happiness... Not that it was a competition. If she overtook me, I could just start learning from her. We could learn from each other, each of us teaching and furthering the other.

We could hold study sessions.

We were as foolish as people could be, but—

Why don't we get smarter together?

Let's be as happy as we should be.

"Is that really how you're going to repay her kindness? With malice?"

I could hear Ogi's voice from afar—and it made me think. Even if it was malice, I was so glad I had something I could give back to Oikura.

014

The epilogue, or maybe, the punch line of this story.

The next day, I was roused from bed as usual by my little sisters Karen and Tsukihi and headed to school—as I did, I asked my sisters something. I was able to hide her name from them because it had changed in the interim, but I asked them if they remembered a girl who had stayed at our home back during elementary school. Neither of them remembered. Just as I thought that's how it goes, it turned out the circumstances were different. There were so many children like that during so many different periods that they didn't know who I was talking about—it seemed I had many other forgotten childhood friends. I was disgusted with myself. I felt embarrassed about ever saying I wanted a childhood friend who'd come to wake me up every morning when in reality I'd had so many childhood friends. There'd be no point in hating myself any more than I already did, though. Oikura would hate me plenty.

She ended up not coming to school—I went to school that day but didn't find her there. While this meant she'd scrapped our promise, I couldn't exactly blame her.

"Like I said earlier…they were just barely overlooking my situation. And they said no more," Oikura told me.

I'd returned to her single-occupancy room after all that.

"The person who came from Town Hall…told me that I can't keep living on my own. They said they're going to cut my assistance by about half, so I can't keep living here. Apparently, a family is going to live here next—but that's fine. It sounds like they found public housing that's a little smaller…so I'm going to move."

I'm going to transfer out of Naoetsu High—she said. She was shockingly calm—could her strength have left her after the conversation with Town Hall, with her life alone coming to an end, with this announcement that it was over? No, that's not it.

It was probably how Oikura was when it was just the two of us, the two of us talking—like over summer break during our first year of middle school. I understood now that her violent behavior in class was forced and a way to threaten people because she was in public—she was the type to get flustered in crowded places. In that sense, Hanekawa made the right decision when she tried to get me to visit her alone.

She also briskly accepted all of our speculation about her mother when I told her, and it was almost deflating.

"Oh—yeah, I should've known," she said.

It was how I'd reacted in the locked classroom when Ogi said the culprit was Komichi Tetsujo.

So she more or less knew? Unconsciously? No—probably not. She might have said the same thing no matter what.

She should've known.

Those were her thoughts on life.

"I knew I'd need to leave this town soon… But just as I found out, I went to school because I learned that Tetsujo would be taking time off. I thought that something might happen, that something might change. Then…"

Then.

Did something happen—did something change? Maybe nothing did, nothing changed. Maybe she only grew to hate me more. In the end—maybe she should've known. We spoke for a little longer, and I went home. I didn't stop anywhere on my way back.

So… To summarize, telling her, my childhood friend, the truth did nothing to improve our relationship, but it didn't do anything to make it worse, either. She would suddenly disappear, just like six years ago, just like five years ago—which is why I headed to school without any concerns about running into her in class... I walked over as always, but as I did, the rousing sound of a bike's wheels began to catch up to me.

It was Ogi.

So she gracefully biked her way to and from school?

It was a pretty nice bike, too.

"Hiii, Araragi-senpai."

"Hiii? Ogi, why'd you leave before I got back yesterday? I told you to wait."

"Miss Hanekawa said we ought to leave."

"Why would Hanekawa say that?"

"She meant it in a nice way. Like, we ought to give those two some space..."

"No, she wasn't being nice. I left her apartment pretty soon, you know... But you weren't anywhere to be found in that plaza. Do you have any idea how surprised I was?"

Whatever.

It wasn't serious enough to criticize her over.

I wonder what Ogi and Hanekawa had talked about. While I doubted they hit it off...I wished the two could at least come to some kind of understanding.

"I was the loser yesterday," Ogi said.

As she did, she gave a little bow—though she didn't get off her bike.

"I'm sorry. To be honest, I underestimated you. I was convinced you'd run off with your tail between your legs—you showed me some guts that I didn't know you had at the end there."

"...I don't really understand your standards when it comes to wins versus losses. You got me worked up, and Hanekawa too. What were you trying to do?"

A basic question.

"It kind of strikes me as strange. Just as soon as you transferred here, Tetsujo went on maternity leave, Oikura started coming to school, and then she went off and transferred just as suddenly. All these things that had come to a pause, these things we were pretending not to see, have suddenly started to move again, as if we suddenly remembered them…"

"Huh, Miss Oikura's going to transfer? I didn't know," Ogi said, ignoring my question. "I did think she made a good casting choice—in a way she was like the origin of all the heroines we've seen so far. I guess you could say she had the perfect character to get you all shaken up? Still, not everything went according to plan. That was a miscalculation—or rather, a missed expectation, which is to say, you deserve the credit here. I did expect Miss Oikura to add a little more chaos to the mix, though. I hope things go well for her at her new school. I'm sure she'll be able to succeed in a new world where nobody knows her. And that's thanks to you. It's all thanks to you."

"…What are you doing here, Ogi? Do you live nearby?"

Feeling that we were going nowhere fast, I changed the subject.

"Oh, you. Are you trying to figure out where I live? Remind me never to let my guard down around you.

"I was just looking for a lost child," she continued. "That's where it all started, after all."

"…"

Looking for a lost child? What a strange thing to say. Didn't she mean—she was lost, and looking for the right way? I could show her the way to school if she didn't know it, I thought—but she'd already begun to pedal again before I could say anything.

"I lost this time around, but if you'll allow me to be just a little bit of a sore loser, my first move was only exploratory. I managed to meet my goal of seeing how you'd act around a childhood friend, so you could even say that losing was the perfect thing for me to do if I wanted to maintain a balance. Do be careful. There's no guarantee things will go this well next time. Journeys at night aren't the only time in life when every new step is taken into darkness."

She pedaled off in the opposite direction from school… Was she okay? While I worried about her, it wasn't as if I could do anything. I decided to stop seeing her off and to head on to school.

On my way there, I ran into Hanekawa. Or rather, she was there waiting for me at the school gates—she must have been waiting for a while, I thought, but when I asked, she said she'd only been there for about a minute. As if she'd predicted when I would come to school—the minute she was off must have been the minute I spent talking to Ogi. Did this mean that an invisible battle between Hanekawa and Ogi was still playing out? Whatever the case, I told her about what happened with Oikura.

"I see... That's too bad. I thought we could become friends."

Hanekawa did sound disappointed, but at the same time, she looked somewhat relieved. The sort of relief you might feel when you've escaped some kind of nightmare scenario—but I probably didn't know the nature of the nightmare scenario Hanekawa had in mind.

"Well, I guess we should celebrate this new step in her life," she said.

"Yeah. Ogi said the same thing."

"Could you go ahead and go to class, Araragi? I need to submit a notice of absence."

"Yeah, sure... Wait, a notice of absence? Huh? What, are you leaving Naoetsu High too?"

"Nope. I said absence. You know how I'm planning on wandering around after graduation. I thought I'd go scout out some locations for that. Just a little trip around the world. I'm going to be leaving you on your own for about a month, so take care of things while I'm gone, okay?"

She was sure leaving a lot in my hands...

And a little trip around the world?

She made it sound like a lap around the athletic field.

Yes, I'd heard about her graduation trip, but...location scouting for it? Methodical people's brains really do work in a different way... She far surpassed my imagination, like an airplane flying overhead.

"I'll be sure to say hello if I come across Mister Oshino during my trip."

Oshino? I didn't see him going overseas too often... I had a hard time imagining him with a passport. Oh, but a trip around the world would include Japan, so it did at least seem like a possibility that they might meet.

In any case, I had no reason to stop Hanekawa. She may have brought it up far too suddenly, but I guess it was just another example of her quick footwork. I felt a little sad to know I wouldn't get to see her for a whole month, but I did everything I could to let that not show and send her off with cheer.

"Okay, then. If you do run into Oshino somewhere, let him know we met his niece."

"Yeah. Well, that's basically what I'm trying to do."

And so I arrived at my classroom, alone once again—and of course, I sat in my empty seat. The moment that I did, my cell phone rang. Uh oh, I'd forgotten to turn it off because I'd met Hanekawa by the school gates.

What a blunder.

Phew, that was dangerous—Hanekawa would have been shockingly mad if it had gone off around her.

New text message.

It was from Senjogahara.

"DEAR KOYOKOYO STOP MY FINGERS SERIOUSLY WERE FRACTURED SO I WILL BE GOING TO SCHOOL TODAY AFTER VISITING THE HOSPITAL STOP"

Why write it like a telegram…

The message might have started off cute, with that "Dear Koyokoyo," but it said she'd actually broken her fingers when she punched Oikura. Well, she probably did deserve that level of comeuppance… which explained why she was going to the hospital instead of relying on my blood. It did seem like she would attend school today, though she'd be late. Did the thought that she might see Oikura never cross her mind? I still hadn't told Senjogahara about what happened—I thought, as the next message arrived.

"DEAR YOKOYOKO STOP"

Yokoyoko? Had she developed dyslexia? No, she must have just typed "Koyokoyo" wrong. First the telegram-style message, then this. She amused herself in strange ways…

"MISS OIKURA CAME TO APOLOGIZE TO ME THIS MORNING STOP I FORGAVE HER STOP I AM OKAY NOW PARENTHETICALLY THOUGH MY FINGERS ARE FRACTURED STOP"

These messages were so annoying to read... Hm?

What? Oikura had gone to apologize? How did she know where Senjogahara lived? Senjogahara had entered a false address into the school's records, and as far as I knew, she hadn't corrected it... Oh, right. Oikura had gone to take care of Senjogahara back when she was sickly during our first year. Now that I thought about it, Oikura knew that Senjogahara would be going to college on a recommendation... If she knew that, did it mean she'd been concerned about Senjogahara even during her time as a shut-in?

Going to apologize, though...

Oikura had apparently kept her promise to make up with Senjogahara. And since the issue was resolved, Senjogahara could come back to school starting today—whatever the case, good. I needed to forward these messages to Hanekawa before she went off on her journey.

Then the third message arrived.

"SORRY FOR MAKING YOU WORRY KOYOKOYO STOP I WILL GIVE YOU LOTS OF SLOPPY KISSES DURING OUR NEXT DATE SO FORGIVE ME PLEASE OKAY STOP ☆☆☆ I AM A FREAK FOR YOUR FRENCH KISSES ☆☆☆☆☆☆ STOP"

How was I going to forward them to Hanekawa now?!

Just as I thought about putting my phone away, the fourth and final message arrived.

"A MESSAGE FROM MISS OIKURA STOP UNDER YOUR DESK SHE SAYS STOP BEST FISHES HI TIKI."

Best fishes hi tiki?

What kind of ending was that? Was she trying to say we should get fish at a Polynesian restaurant? And maybe "Yokoyoko" was part of that, some sort of South Pacific greeting? But no, it was probably just another typo, and she meant to say "Best wishes, Hitagi."

Great, now I began to wonder if she'd misspelled anything else. A message from Miss Oikura? Under your desk? What could it all mean, I wondered, but tried feeling around under my seat anyway—and.

I found something stuck there. Something like a piece of paper, held in place with masking tape—I peeled it off and took it in my hands.

It was an envelope. A thin, modern envelope with a design on it that I couldn't remember ever seeing before—but while I didn't remember seeing it, the envelope did feel familiar. Couldn't I have found a similar envelope under a low table in a derelict house five years ago, during summer break?

That envelope was empty.

Feel alone told me this one held a note—the envelope may not have listed a sender or recipient on either side, but someone had stuck it under my desk.

Sodachi Oikura.

She'd kept every one of her promises.

She must have come to school so early that even most of our teachers hadn't arrived yet—and she'd placed this envelope under my desk.

The kind of girl who suddenly disappeared, without any warning. That was the kind of girl Oikura—no longer seemed to be. A small change, but a change in her. It made me happy, but also a little sad. Like she'd gone ahead and left me behind.

In that case, I needed to prove that I'd grown, too. Instead of tearing the envelope apart like I had five years ago, I opened it as carefully as I could—and extracted multiple sheets of paper. Now then. Did they contain a math quiz, or was it an uncharacteristic letter of thanks— perhaps an insulting, abusive message? It could be all three—let's take a look.

"Heh."

I broke out smiling.

Hey.

What do you think it said?

Afterword

When I belatedly think about how unreliable human memory can be, I realize that forgetting something doesn't particularly mean that it's just gone for you. This isn't about how forgetting and losing are two different things, or how you might actually remember something you thought you'd forgotten. This is about cause and effect—in other words, even if you've forgotten all about learning how to ride a bicycle, it doesn't mean you're unable to ride one, and not remembering where you read something doesn't mean you're unable to make use of the knowledge. That kind of thing. Forgetting doesn't result in a chain reaction. Going into more detail would require discussing the difference between episodic and other types of memory, and conflating all that stuff when you talk about it really is a mistake to begin with, but when I close my eyes to that fact and think about it, I find it somehow encouraging that forgetting something doesn't mean it never happened. You could even say that it allows us to delude ourselves into believing that in this uncertain world of ours, some things are certain. Speaking of delusions, a bothersome type of case here is when you aren't forgetting something but remembering it incorrectly. In other words, you think you remember learning how to ride a bicycle, but the episode was entirely different, or you've mixed up a tome that dispensed valuable knowledge with another book—not impossible, and when it happens, what an uncertain place it makes our world. What is right, and what isn't right? What is true, and what isn't true? If my memory serves me correctly—or turning that phrase inside out, if my memory serves me incorrectly, having to check myself at every turn makes for a pretty miserable life. Maybe we should just chuck these doubts?

And so, this has been part seventeen of the *MONOGATARI* series. Volume number seventeen. I think it goes without saying that this is the longest NISIOISIN series in history by a bit, but what a mess it all becomes once you get this far along. Seventeen volumes? You can't casually recommend that long a series, can you? Reading seventeen books is quite a feat. As for the author, it gets daunting, and my pen threatens to flow less freely. That's why I decided to return to where I began and write this once more entirely, one hundred percent as a hobby. Now, of course, it led to such an outpouring that the work ended up getting split into separate volumes… But the hobby-esque latitude there is nice in its own way. Tasteful, even. And so, this has been *OWARIMONOGATARI Part 01*, "Chapter One: Ogi Formula," "Chapter Two: Sodachi Riddle," and "Chapter Three: Sodachi Lost."

Ogi Oshino, who spent Second Season shrouded in mystery, has finally started to take off the veil and even made it onto the cover. Thank you very much, VOFAN. The End Tale is moving on to its latter part, and I'll do what I can to keep there from being a middle part.

NISIOISIN

OWARIMONOGATARI

END TALE

PART 02

NISIOISIN

VERTICAL.

OWARIMONOGATARI
End Tale

Part 02

NISIOISIN

Art by VOFAN

Translated by Ko Ransom

VERTICAL.

OWARIMONOGATARI, PART 02

© 2014 NISIOISIN
All rights reserved.

First published in Japan in 2014 by
Kodansha Ltd., Tokyo.
Publication rights for this English edition
arranged through Kodansha Ltd., Tokyo.

Published by Vertical, an imprint of
Kodansha USA Publishing, LLC, 2020

ISBN 978-1-947194-92-2

Manufactured in the United States
of America

First Edition

Second Printing

Kodansha USA Publishing, LLC
451 Park Avenue South
7th Floor
New York, NY 10016

www.readvertical.com

CHAPTER FOUR SHINOBU MAIL

CHAPTER FOUR
SHINOBU MAIL

SHINOBU OSHINO

001

If only it wasn't for Ogi Oshino. I can't help but think that when I try to summarize the back half of my senior year—I mean, I seriously want to think so. There's no need to go on and on about how the antics of this girl, who transferred into Naoetsu High as a freshman during second term, ravaged and savaged my adolescence. All that needs to be said is—if only it wasn't for Ogi Oshino.

I do realize, fully, that this is a selfish, shameful, and lameful act of blame-shifting—I say it knowing that. If only it wasn't for Ogi Oshino? What a foolish and foolhardy argument, I ought to feel like killing my-self the moment I think of it, no need for you to point that out, I'm well aware. To begin with, even if she never existed, it's hard to imagine the back half of my senior year being all that different, though it couldn't have been identical. There was something untenable about my style from the start—clearly, one day, I would hit my limit. Experts of all kinds had pointed this out to me plenty of times, after all. My indecisive self was going to have to pay the painful, scathing price for riding the fence to the end, for pretending to overlook it all, for not seeing anything through or resolutely stepping out on my own. My karma being visited upon me was inevitable, not anything supernatural but rather the perfectly natural fact of the way of the world.

Ogi Oshino isn't to blame.

Koyomi Araragi is.

But then, if it wasn't for me, if only I didn't exist, would this, that, and everything have proceeded in a good, correct manner? I don't think you could say that at all either. Good and correct, what would that be in the first place? What does that even mean? If only it wasn't for Koyomi Araragi—if you were to ask me if anything would be different were the wish granted, I'd have to shake my head no. Even if I wasn't around, someone else would have saved Hitagi Senjogahara—and, no doubt, guided Mayoi Hachikuji—saved Suruga Kanbaru, Nadeko Sengoku, Tsubasa Hanekawa, all of them, and possibly in a far defter way than I ever did. Sure, I played a part in their fate, but nothing at all said it had to be me—we're talking about girls as strong, as tough, as determined as them. The truth is that their lives didn't require me.

When they happened to cross paths—it was with me, that's all.

Just like encountering a *yokai* on the street at night, or to be particular, the way I encountered, during spring break, a golden-haired, golden-eyed vampire with her limbs torn off as I was walking down a street. So it's nothing. Even before I became a vampire, I was already something of a cryptid.

When I think about it now, rather than me playing a part in their fate, it seems much more like I got them mixed up in my own irascible fate.

If only it wasn't for Koyomi Araragi.

In fact, maybe that's what those girls think—I think I've twisted so many people's fates that I couldn't blame them if they did.

No.

It wasn't their fates—but tales that I twisted.

And now I was having to deal with the repercussions—you could say like an eraser being flung away by a curved and bent ruler trying to *straighten itself out*. An eraser flying so far, who knows where it'll land— an eraser that flies out of the classroom window and falls into a flower bed, never to be found again as it crumbles away.

That must make Ogi Oshino the ruler.

Straight and precise.

An intransigent rule of a ruler.

10

I was wondering why she'd appeared before me, what for—but it must've been to draw a line, like a ruler.

She'd come to draw the line.

To give me a clear standard, that here and beyond was no good, that up to here was okay, not allowing a margin of error of even a fraction of an inch. Mayoi Hachikuji and Nadeko Sengoku were on the other side of the line, while Tsubasa Hanekawa and Sodachi Oikura were on this side of the line. As simple as that.

A borderline?

No, a goal line.

There was no room for straddling the line or judgment calls. That was like calling for war.

"Well, it wouldn't be logical—you know, as in l-Ogi-cal?"

And so.

Now that the presence of Ogi Oshino, who brazenly interrupts even my prologue, the only place where I can show off this time around, has been re-introduced… Sadly the tale that I'm presenting for the sake of the end of the end of the end doesn't begin on the grounds of Kita-Shi-rahebi Shrine, where I met Mayoi Hachikuji again. Before we can begin the endgame and be all at the end-all, there's just one more tale left that I must reveal to you. My dear readers, don't tell me you've forgotten.

I wish you had, frankly, and even more that I have—then I'd be able to close out my tale, furtively, meekly hiding that it ever happened.

"Way too tall of an order, Araragi-senpai—did you really think you could hide something from me? I wish you wouldn't be so reckless. I'm the nemesis of lies and deception. A predator who preys on procrastination and postponement. Even you must know what happened to Deishu Kaiki, that superlative con man, right? So please, start talking unless you want to end up like him. About what happened then—the story you've so obstinately covered up for all this time," Ogi Oshino says, pressing herself against me. Psychologically.

Judging by the looks of her, she already knows everything about what happened then, but if I were to ask her, she'd feign ignorance for sure.

"I don't know anything—you're the one who knows, Araragi-senpai."

She'd be right.

I do know—I know so very well.

Of course, that's why I wanted to hide it.

But that's why I have to tell it.

This is going to be a long one, I tell her.

"Fine with me. That's why, in between the first and last parts of this title, I crammed in—sorry, prepared a middle part for you," Ogi says nonsensically.

I won't ask her what that's supposed to mean—I could find the same question shot straight back at me.

After all, I'm about to talk about something that makes even less sense, an incident that happened more than two months before she transferred into my school.

Right after summer break ended and second term started.

The tale begins with Koyomi Araragi's experience of being almost fully "human" for the first time in half a year, after having his link to a vampire severed. Going neither to school nor his home and instead spending what seems like more time than he knows what to do with hiding out in a classroom of the ruined cram school where the expert Mèmè Oshino once made his roost—that's where the tale begins. Or that's from where it ends.

And *his* life.

His long-running life, too—comes at last to an end.

002

"What up, senpai! Long time no see!"

I feel I should clarify here that my junior Suruga Kanbaru is extremely well-mannered—at least, she's one of the few people younger than me who treats me, someone as unworthy as me, with respect. Perhaps I ought to say the only one—and while she never resorts to openly humble or formal language with me, she always maintains a certain level of politeness when we interact, even though I outrank her only in age. Maybe it's her straightforward personality, maybe it's her upbringing in a basically well-off family.

To put it in simpler terms, though she sometimes speaks to me as if we're in the same year, she isn't the type to make her appearance with an offhanded greeting like "What up!"

I'd like you to understand that it was an exception, and well, I could understand her excitement. It was completely natural for her to be so hyped up that day, or more specifically, that night—the night of August twenty-third, as she arrived in the second-floor classroom of the now-familiar abandoned cram school, which wasn't exactly a symbol, but at least a kind of landmark among us.

The reason being—it may not come off sounding great, but there weren't many situations where I'd ask Kanbaru to meet me. A girl who described herself as "someone who finds meaning in life simply by being of use to you, my honorable senior Araragi," "a part to be used by my honorable senior Araragi," and "a disposable tool to be used by my honorable senior Araragi," I could even understand why she leapt into the classroom after kicking down its door, giddy with joy—never mind, forget about it. Not when she refers to herself in those incomprehensible ways.

My life's to-do list never included having my girlfriend's junior get so attached to me…

That said, for the first thing coming out of her mouth to be that energetic and rather unsophisticated "Long time no see!" was, in the end, not wholly inappropriate.

If you were to ask me why, I'd give you the following answer: because a knee belonging to Kanbaru, confident in her ability to run, made contact with my cheek, located about five feet above the floor, since I was just standing and not sitting in a chair or anything.

It made contact.

By *made contact*, I mean that less in the "touched" sense and more in the "tackled" kind of way. In a soccer match, the flying knee, bearing all of her weight and speed, would have surely earned her an immediate red card. Since she's a basketball player, maybe I should compare it to a flagrant foul resulting in instant ejection—but you don't normally see many flying knees in basketball.

In any case, what I'm trying to say is that her greeting would've been appropriate if, instead of *long time no see*, it was *long time no knee*.

"Ghaah!"

Of course she injured my cheek, but that only covers the superficial issue of where she made contact, as the damage made its way to my cheekbone, inner cheek, oral cavity, cranium, and even my gray matter—it felt like the shockwave penetrating my head could even destroy the classroom wall behind me.

True, what actually cracked the classroom wall behind me was my own body, thrown into the air like a scrap of paper by the force of her flying knee.

"Ghuurk!"

I let out a second moan as my back hit the wall. I wish I could've let out something a little more stylish—sounding like a frog being run over by a car isn't a very cool act.

"Not that I could hope to look cool in any situation involving me getting kneed by my junior as soon as we meet."

"Wow, my dear senior. You really are at the top of your game. Setting up to get kneed during this time of need? You showed me up there."

Having made a beautiful landing, her mid-air balance undisturbed by her strike, Kanbaru nodded, looking at me as if I'd moved her to her core. A look of respect—it made me want to ask her what she saw in this crushed frog, and also, I hadn't set myself up to get kneed in a time of need.

What would that do for me?

"Well," Kanbaru said, "if I may speak for myself here, I'd prefer to describe it as you getting punked by my patella. The thought of my knees acting like handsome young ruffians brings me just a little bit of joy."

"Could you please not use words like 'joy' in this sort of context? And how are you sure these punks are handsome?"

"Actually, I see them more as impressionable little boys. Doesn't the world seem like a bit of a better place if little boys were living on our knees?"

"Don't describe anything as being a 'better place' in this context, either. There are no little boys living on my knees."

I stood.

As I did, I held a hand against my kicked cheek—my brain actually seemed fine, but dammit, the inside of my mouth had suffered cuts, making every retort difficult. I was tasting my blood like mad and it was like eating iron. But how could I not partake when Kanbaru was providing such a stand-up act?

"And wait," I objected, "if I should be going after you about anything, it's the fact that you kneed me, your senior, and haven't spoken an apologetic word about it."

"Apologize? Haha! What're you talking about? Am I, your faithful junior Suruga Kanbaru, not now like a part of your body?" Putting her hands in front of her chest, she continued, "You wouldn't apologize to yourself for kneeing your own cheek, would you?"

"What eloquently awful logic!"

"Come on, you don't need to keep acting so exasperated. Listen, I understand the way my senior feels better than anyone. You're just pretending like you're worried about the damage to your cheek when what you're really concerned about is whether or not I, an athlete, hurt my knee."

"Sounds like a great senior, but whoever that is, he sure ain't me!"

It was impossible to get an apology out of her...

Was it okay to have a junior like this one?

"Sorry to let you down, Kanbaru, but the only thing I'm worried about right now is my own body."

"So in other words, my body?"

"You're making it sound more and more like I'm the disposable tool here."

"If I'm being honest, part of me thinks that I don't have to apologize for a near-miss as minor as that given how good your body is at healing itself."

"I hope you don't think that honesty can get you out of any situation!"

A frightening girl.

Had I put myself in a fairly dangerous situation by being alone in these ruins, in the middle of the night, with someone this terrifying?

Still, she'd responded to my sudden request for her presence—and come running, giddy with joy. I should've been thanking her.

Especially when I considered what was to come.

What I was about to request of her.

"Yikes, you even chipped my teeth a little."

I'd felt something like pebbles inside my mouth and spat them out, only to find fragments of my own tooth.

"Even if I'm only a mockery of one, shattering a vampire's fang with a knee? What exactly is up with you?"

"It's only because you're not getting enough calcium in your daily diet."

Kanbaru was not going to apologize.

I needed some calcium asap. Not because of anything to do with my teeth, just to hold back my anger.

"You should learn from me. I've never once gotten a cavity, and I can open most bottles with my teeth."

"Don't open bottles with your teeth."

"But that shampoo I had to deal with the other day was a formidable foe."

"I don't even want to think about a situation that requires you to open a bottle of shampoo with your mouth."

Naked in the bath and chomping on a bottle of shampoo—what kind of a cavewoman did I have for a junior?

True, a chipped tooth wasn't an issue, it'd heal soon enough—but while I had a vampire's powers of regeneration, a mockery is only a mockery at the end of the day.

What's more.

As I was now—I'd been stripped of even that mockery of an ability. It did seem better to wait to introduce this fact to Kanbaru. I didn't want to worry her by bringing it up out of nowhere, and it was a somewhat complicated story...

I looked at her again.

She wore her grown-out hair in two tufts that reached her shoulders over her track jacket. She looked like she was in the middle of a jog, but there wasn't a drop of sweat on her, nor was her breathing belabored. She must've run all the way (with all the extra momentum leading to that knee strike), but that's a former star of the basketball team for you. It took more than a full sprint to make her tired, though you've got to wonder what it would take to tire out someone who doesn't get tired from a full sprint.

With her hair grown out, she looked a little less boyish than when I first met her, but the bandage wrapped around her left arm was still an odd note. As was the true nature of her hidden arm, ostensibly injured in an accident during practice—

"Hm? What's the matter, my dear senior? Why're you suddenly leering at my proportions?"

"I'm not."

"Huh? If you aren't, what of mine are you looking at? What do I

17

have worth a look other than my proportions?"

"I don't even know what that's supposed to mean, but stop being so modest. You're Naoetsu High's star athlete."

"I've retired."

"As someone whose life is threatened day and night by the members of your fan club, I find that hard to accept."

The posse included my own little sister (bigger one). Your own flesh and blood being after your life is a truly gloomy thing.

"Heheh. No need to leer at me. Don't you worry when it comes to me."

"? Worry? ? Who said I was worried about you?"

"Oh, stop playing stupid. Minding the details like always. But have a little more faith in your juniors," Kanbaru chided me. "It's okay, I made sure to take off my bra."

"Goddammit, I am worried about you!"

It really hurt to make this retort since my shattered tooth, sharp despite my temporarily broken link with Shinobu, cut up the inside of my mouth and made me spit blood.

The fact that she was wearing a track jacket, though, gave me quiet relief. At least she hadn't mistaken this for some kind of tryst…

"It might be hard to see because it's made of regrettably thick material, but I, Suruga Kanbaru, cannot lie to her senior. From my waist up, my bare skin is currently in contact with my jacket."

"What about your waist down? You're making me worry."

"In that case, I wouldn't mind unzipping right now. I, Suruga Kanbaru, have nothing to hide."

"You keep on saying 'I, Suruga Kanbaru' like you're so proud of yourself today, but personally, I think you ought to stay anonymous until you learn what it means to have discretion."

"I know what it means to have discretion. Who do you take me for?"

"I wonder if you even know what it means to have a sense of shame."

"What's the matter? You seem so dissatisfied. Oh, wait. Are you in the camp of people who like to undo a girl's bra themselves?"

"Camp? This isn't some kind of ideological war."

"Oh, so that's what it is. How ironic. By taking off my bra, I took myself off your list of potential romantic partners."

"I'd say you've taken yourself off the path of all that is right."

A line that might sound pretty cool on its own.

But I was just scolding my bra-less junior.

"What? But why else would you want to meet me at a place like this, at this hour?"

"'Why else'? What kind of why are you thinking about?"

"You finally feel ready to accept my chastity, right?"

"Right no!"

My calcium deficiency was starting to affect my ability to form sentences.

And that's why she got so excited that she kneed me in my cheek?

"I know this is your first appearance in a while, Kanbaru, but aren't you acting a little too excited?"

"Maybe I am. I never imagined I'd have to go this long without taking the stage. I was starting to worry that I'd done something wrong."

"Well, it'd be hard to say that you haven't…"

Not when her every word was so dangerous.

In a way, she was a far more dangerous character than Shinobu.

"The rules of basketball kept on changing while I was waiting my turn. Not just the rules, in fact, they changed the entire court. Even I was shocked by that one."

"And what about me? We've been wasting so much time that the entire college admissions process is gonna change before I graduate…"

Oops. A little too meta?

Let's get back on track.

"Anyway, I don't intend on taking your chastity."

"Aw, that sucks."

"Is that really going to be your reaction? Do you really have to put it that way?"

"Even so. You invited a young lady, which is to say a girl, here. An abandoned location. In the middle of the night. All on her own. With a suggestive text message. At that moment, I think, you forfeited the right to act surprised, about being taken that way."

"Agh…"

What could I possibly say to that?

All of those commas and short sentences?

Whether or not my message was suggestive, as someone with a girlfriend to whom I've promised my future, I guess I should've done everything I could to avoid such a misunderstanding. In fact, making biweekly visits to the garbage dump known as Kanbaru's to clean it up was also kind of an issue.

Even if this meeting was mandated by a promise—

"Also, I was going so fast just now that I ended up in a classroom on the third floor and not the second, and there was a bed up there made out of desks. Isn't that something that you put together?"

"What? I honestly don't know what you're talking about... A bed?"

What was going on?

Had someone decided to live here unbeknownst to me?

"Look at you, playing stupid yet again."

"'Yet again'? I'm not really the type to play stupid, you know..."

"I think you could say that we're common-law married at this point? It'd be fine for you to go ahead and take my chastity, right?"

"Right no... Sheesh."

Common-law married?

Nothing about this girl was common or lawful.

"But listen, Kanbaru. If I'm being serious, the bond that's our friendship goes beyond the walls of junior and senior, or of man and woman." Some people may laugh at the thought of a friendship between a man and a woman, but I did feel this way.

"Hm. I'm most honored and grateful to hear that. And, my senior, I completely agree with just about all of it."

"Just about?"

"I think what I'm feeling, for my part, is lust."

"Then we're talking about two entirely different things!"

"A lust that goes beyond the walls of man and woman. In other words, I'd be just as filled as lust for you even if I was a boy. There's not a day that goes by when I don't think that it's fate."

"Could you please chill out? For just one day out of the year?"

Good thing she's a girl, in that case.

Seriously.

"All right," Kanbaru said, "it's been a while since I've gotten all riled up with you. I'm starting to feel hot, would it be okay if I took off my jacket?"

"Sure, just hang it somewhere around th—wait, no, it's not! You're not wearing anything underneath that jacket, right?!"

"Tch. You figured it out."

"Did you just click your tongue at me? Your senior?!"

"No, but I did use it to lick my lips."

"That's even scarier."

"Or maybe I smacked my lips."

"Are you thinking about eating me or something? Anyway, keep your jacket on. Um…so let's get to the reason I asked you to come here," I got to the point at last.

It almost felt a little too late. I'd have loved to go on joking around with Kanbaru all night—but no, that wouldn't do.

"Hm. There's something you wanted to ask me?"

"Yup, there is."

"I'd convinced myself that it had to do with my chastity, but it seems I jumped to conclusions."

"That conclusion is so far removed from reality that even you couldn't get there with a jump. There's never going to be a day when I'd ask you that."

For the record, the message I sent Kanbaru that morning read as follows:

"come to second floor classroom tonight at 9 alone i need to ask you something"—I'd like to think of its somewhat poor composition as part of its charm.

You have to consider the situation I was in when I sent it, too.

"What I wanted to ask you…was basically to help me out with something, if you're willing," I said, switching to a more serious demeanor. "But if I'm being upfront with you, I'd like you to turn me down—"

"I'd never say no to you!" exclaimed Kanbaru.

I'd thought she might. Anyone could predict her reply.

"How could I, Suruga Kanbaru, ever refuse to meet the demands of my senior Araragi? You could ask me to move heaven and earth, and I'd do it!"

"Okay…" She was looking at me with a glare that could move heaven and earth all on its own, and I was flustered. "Well, it's not exactly my demand, I'm just an intermediary—what's more, I can't really give you many details about this thing I want you to help with…"

"You don't know the details?"

"Yeah. I don't know anything."

My ignorance was probably by design—if I knew more, I might veto it before the request traveled any further, but I didn't know and couldn't dismiss it out of hand on Kanbaru's behalf.

I had to leave it up to her.

I had to, given the nature of the request, too.

"So," I continued, "if you say no, that's all there is to it, which is why that's preferable—but if you insist on helping, I'll do everything I can to make sure no harm comes to you."

"Hah! Harm coming to me? There's no need for you to worry. If you just have to worry, then go ahead and focus on one part of my body, namely my chest area."

"I'm not going ahead."

The world doesn't need a guy who thinks only about the boobs of his juniors. And how would he, anyway? Like, *hmm, she's not wearing a bra today*…or something? Not that I knew if the no bra thing was a joke—we'd moved on to the matter at hand before I could ever find out.

Eight or nine out of ten, it was a joke, but Kanbaru just might do something like that, which is why I was so worried, and also why I couldn't take my eyes off of her.

No, I'm not saying that I couldn't take my eyes off her boobs.

"If anything, I, Suruga Kanbaru, would feel sad to see you worrying yourself over me. To be specific, about as sad as you'd feel when your favorite musician's best-of album doesn't include your favorite song of theirs."

"That really is specific."

"Where you end up thinking, 'Oh, so this artist doesn't consider that song as one of their best…'"

Kanbaru's shoulders slumped.

It sounded like a recent real-life occurrence, given her reaction.

But Suruga Kanbaru, with her brisk temperament, soon seemed to get over it. She looked back up and said, "Well, I guess I should just think of it as me noticing the greatness in them that they didn't notice themselves."

What a positive person. Positively reckless.

"And so, I'm happy that you're willing to rely on me, given how reserved you can be with me. Don't hold yourself back...sorry, don't hold anything back from me."

"You at least corrected yourself, but I dunno..."

That said, she just might have figured out what I was going to say.

Hanekawa and Senjogahara were one thing, but I wouldn't have asked Kanbaru like this unless it was serious. Even she knew that.

Right. Just like the time we visited that rundown shrine.

"If that's what you wanted to know, I think you already have the answer: I came running here in spite of everything."

"Yeah—well, I guess so."

"I just can't stop wanting to serve you. I came all the way here even though I had a book I wanted to read tonight."

"..."

Suddenly she was just trying to guilt-trip me.

For all her good manners, she really was rude.

A book she wanted to read?

That was my competition, as her senior? Some book?

"You say that, but books embody human knowledge. No matter how great you are, it's awfully presumptuous of you to think that you're a match for human history."

"No, Kanbaru, I'm not that presumptuous, but can't your book wait? You don't have to read it tonight, do you?"

"I could come running to you any time I want, too. Didn't have to be tonight."

You're playing by the same rules, she said.

For someone who wanted to serve me, she was coming off as awfully self-serving.

"And anyway, I bet this book you want to read is one of your boys' love novels, right?"

"What's this now? I don't get to see this every day. One of your predictions missing its mark? Of all the times for your read to be off, it was about a book?"

"Stop trying so hard to sound clever. So, you read other kinds of books?"

"Of course. A wide variety of them."

Really? Honestly, this surprised me. BL was all I ever dug up when I cleaned her room—but then, she did count Senjogahara as her senior and mentor. Maybe, having learned from that indiscriminate reader, it wasn't so surprising that Kanbaru read widely.

"That's how it is now that I've retired from the basketball team. I'm working hard every single day and night to broaden my horizons as a person."

"Wow, Kanbaru. I underestimated you."

"That's why I've been growing out my hair, too. Think of it as my effort to broaden my options for kinky stuff. Brings a tear to your eye, doesn't it?"

"It certainly does."

As her senior, it was enough to make me want to cry.

Still, I absolutely needed to know what kind of books she consumed. I decided to ask her more about her reading habits.

"In that case, Kanbaru. What exactly were you planning on reading tonight?"

"What else? A little something by the great Shugoro Yamamoto."

What else? I could have come up with a lot of things, but not that. A literary eminence from the last century? Even I, someone who doesn't read many books, knew the name. I had to admit, I'd underestimated Kanbaru. The likes of me couldn't hope to compete with the works of Shugoro Yamamoto.

But I didn't feel particularly frustrated or powerless. If anything, I was glad that she was reading regular and proper books. It looked like I could play the part of a pretty respectable senior.

"Out of curiosity, what by Shugoro Yamamoto? If you think something's worth reading, I'd like to check it out too."

"Huh? Well, I have plenty of BL novels I could recommend, in that case."

"Could we please start off with some Yamamoto?"

"I see. Then," Kanbaru told me the title of the book, "it's called *Beautiful Girls Take the Lead*."

"Liar!" I screamed. "The great Shugoro Yamamoto writing a book with a title like that?!"

"Hm? He really did, so what am I supposed to say… Though it's out of print and unavailable in stores lately."

"…"

Apparently, it wasn't a lie. My straight-man instincts had gotten the better of me…

Now that I thought about it, didn't Yamamoto turn down a prestigious prize for a book called *Lives of Great Japanese Women* or something? Was *Beautiful Girls* a variation on that?

"It's a collection of short stories that ran in *Shojo Club*. Y'hear me? *Shojo Club*."

"You're almost making it sound like an underground work that ran in an underground magazine, but I bet it's just YA? Something you'd call a light novel these days?"

"Well, light novels these days are a lot like erotica!"

"Please don't say erotica."

I didn't know what else by Yamamoto she'd read, but she must've chosen *Beautiful Girls Take the Lead* because of its title.

In fact, she must've bought it by accident.

"By the way, I only feel comfortable saying this now that it's established," prefaced Kanbaru, "but something about abbreviating light novels as *LN's* feels wrong to me. The same way people from San Francisco don't like it when you call it *San Fran*."

"Say something before it's established, not afterwards."

"I don't want to cause any kind of controversy."

"You don't? But yeah, I see what you mean… How should we abbreviate them, then? *Novels*? That'd be confusing…" Speaking of novels, it seems that some fans of literary fiction don't like having it called *lit-fic*—and of course, some people don't even like the term *light novel* to begin with.

"A certain nationally beloved anime series might not have become as popular if it had been called *San-Fran*!"

"Sakuragaoka High School isn't even in San Francisco, that'd be why. But going back to these girls who take the lead, is it in the sense of, say, leading an army into battle on horseback?"

"Probably. But according to Sigmund Freud, horses are a sexual motif."

"Most things are, according to Freud."

I retract my earlier statement.

Kanbaru needed to give me back that gladness I felt for her.

"Apologize. To Shugoro Yamamoto, for reading his work for impure reasons."

"I know I show you a lot of respect, but I don't want you bossing me around when it comes to how I read. A work belongs to its readers as soon as it's released. Shouldn't we respect individual readers' freedom to have whatever feelings and intentions they want toward a novel?"

"Oh, now you're going to take the moral high ground?"

"If anything, introducing the work in a fun and familiar way might encourage younger readers like you, who probably think of Shugoro Yamamoto as a hard-to-approach writer of dry novels, an author that a literary award has been named after, to try picking him up for a change. That's right, Shugoro Yamamoto's *Beautiful Girls Take the Lead*."

"You're not wrong, I suppose…"

As someone who's read none of the man's work, I'm far from qualified to tell you whether you ought to start with *Beautiful Girls Take the Lead*, but readers are free to make that choice as well. Some people must even find joy in starting a series with its final volume—though reading a detective novel from its solution first does strike me as a little too free.

"It might cause his sales to spike," Kanbaru argued. "It might result in a new appreciation for *Beautiful Girls Take the Lead*."

"Aren't little-known books little known for a reason? Isn't that why it's out of print and unavailable in stores?"

"Hah. Now that more books are being digitized, we're entering an era where 'out of print' won't mean much. We'll prize precisely those books that go out of print. That's right, I'm Naoetsu High's very own Biblia Antique Books."

"I imagine that minors wouldn't be allowed in." And any book that features her as the protagonist should have the blurb, *Unread by the greats! Never discussed in other works of fiction!*

"Hmph. If we're going down that path, I could come up with plenty of variations. Like, *Ignored by the Japan Bookstore Awards! A volume that even a bookseller could never recommend!*"

"Actually, I'd like to read that one…"

"How about *The gentle horror novel that never sent a single chill down a spine is here at last!* or *The bizarre work that no one ever discussed online!* or *The controversial tear-jerker that brought none of its readers to tears, now in paperback!*"

"There are a lot of ways to spin negatives…but people aren't going to overlook all your flaws just because you call yourself controversial. Why do a paperback of a controversial tear-jerker that brought none of its readers to tears? Where's the demand?"

"You know how it is. You want to hold on to the co-op deal you got for the New In Paperback table…"

"Stop carrying water for publishers."

"Still. Kanbaru Biblia Antique Books, or Cambrian Antique Books for short, has an impressive selection of products. It's full of titles that might run afoul of future laws."

"Then minors aren't allowed in, after all. The Book Burners are going to torch your place."

"You never know, I might get to be in a roundtable with Miss Shioriko and Miss Yomiko."

"A bookseller and a booklover with book puns as names. Why would you be alongside them?"

"For everything else. Who's going to take care of the remainders?"

"I think I get it now, but…please, don't say those kinds of things around me."

"Fine, then why don't you start your own bookstore? Koyomi Academy's very own Biblia Antique Books."

"Hey, I'm just as much of a Naoetsu High student as you! Why do I need to transfer schools to open a used bookstore?! I have to go that far to avoid any competition?!"

Wait, where was that from, though? Koyomi Academy? It felt like I'd heard it before.

"Oh, right. The school from *Happy Lesson*."

"Bullseye. I'm impressed you were so quick to remember. There's my dear senior."

"Don't test your seniors. Why am I taking an anime and manga pop quiz? What kind of Magic Academy have I found myself enrolled in? Also, we already made a reference to *Happy Lesson* once."

"We can talk about it as many times as we want. I lost my mother, right? No wonder I'm attracted to a story about five teachers barging into a student's home to become his moms."

"Kanbaru…" Catching a bittersweet expression on the face of my ever-bold junior, I felt a brief tug at my heartstrings—hold on, no. You can't bring up something as emotional as your mother's demise in the middle of inane banter.

"By the way, of his five moms, my favorite is Miss Uzuki Shitenno. What do you think, senpai?"

"You'd move this conversation forward? Miss Shitenno looks the least motherly of them all."

"Don't I get to have some input about what seems motherly to me?"

"As if you ever consider anyone else's."

"Hm? What's the matter, don't tell me you're a fan of Miss Fumi-tsuki Nanakorobi."

"She's not one of the mommy-teachers."

Setting traps, eh?

"Anyway, this is how you do it," my junior declared. "Keep up this kind of grassroots activism, and we'll get to see a Blu-ray box set go on sale one day. Heheheh, Kanbaru Biblia Antique Books is going to have that one right on its new video releases shelf."

"Just to make sure, you know we don't have that kind of influence?"

Uh, what were we discussing again? We'd been chatting about beautiful young fictional men and women for long enough…

Oh, right.

Kanbaru had refused to turn down my request, as I'd feared—fine, then. I'd just have to prepare myself for what was to come.

And anyway.

When I thought about it, I had no right to put a stop on this—and even less of an ability to do so. Were I to avoid Kanbaru, I knew what *she* would do.

She would undoubtedly contact my junior through some other route—in which case, I felt better about that contact happening in a place where I could see it.

What I might or might not be able to do was a different question altogether. Just because you can see something happening doesn't mean you can reach out and get involved in it...

"Okay, Kanbaru. So about this request—sorry to be this abrupt about it, but could you follow me?"

"Hm? Oh, there's nothing for us to do here?"

"Yeah, I only used it as a meeting place."

"Huh... Then why not just meet at one of our homes?"

Her vague doubt, now that she mentioned it, was on the mark. Wait, why did I choose this abandoned cram school as our meeting place again?

I wanted to say there was something...

"Well, it doesn't matter," Kanbaru said. "I won't sweat the details— I'll go anywhere. Don't worry, I composed my will and testament."

"That's a little scary?!"

Yikes, her grandparents might find what surely read like a suicide note!

"A will and testament written up by a minor?"

"It starts, *By the time you read this letter, I doubt I am still of this world.*"

"Very romantic, but..."

How uncool she'd look when they found out she was still of this world.

"Kanbaru, there's no need for you to act that way. We're just going to another meeting spot. A rendezvous, I guess—there's someone I want you to meet."

"Really, now. I can't believe you sometimes. So, how'd you talk me up to get her interested? My grades? My connections? How popular I am?"

"Rendezvous as in meet, not as in date. She said she wanted an introduction to you, so..."

"Hmm. Fine. If that's what you say, it's as good as gold."

"I wish you'd trust me only half as much as you do...but it'll be okay." I was trying to soothe her nerves with empty words. "At least, this isn't me playing matchmaker or middleman for some boy or girl who's interested in confessing to you."

"I wouldn't mind an introduction like that, though. I'd just turn them down."

"..."

She took after her esteemed senior Senjogahara when it came to how unconcerned she was about that sort of thing.

How she didn't treat everyone the way she treated me put me against the wall in its own way.

I'd have almost preferred to introduce Kanbaru to some boy or girl over having to introduce her to someone like *her*. I could use some empty words myself.

"Of course," Kanbaru said, "it'd be different if the punch line ends up being: *And the person I want to introduce you to...is me!*"

"Stop trying to sneak your way into a romantic relationship with me. Just how much of a man-eater are you?"

"Oh, I don't want a romantic relationship. Just a physical one. As a man-eater, I merely seek prey."

"You're sending a shiver down my spine."

"I don't believe in emotional connections."

"Who hurt you... Geez, what even goes through your mind as you live life?"

"I think you ought to go to a hospital to get yourself checked out if you think that anything goes through my mind," Kanbaru answered with a smile.

A stylish line, but little more. Doesn't work unless the right person says it...

"Let's get back on track," she urged.

I was glad she realized we'd gotten off of it.

"Okie dokie, my senior Araragi. I get what's going on now. So let's get going, it's time for me to meet this person I don't know in a location I don't know!"

"You really are incredible, you know that?"

Just so bold. So bold that maybe she could stand toe-to-toe with *her*, a person I was only ever overwhelmed by.

"And away we go!"

Then—

Right as Kanbaru used her bandaged left arm to pump her fist, it happened.

003

Bam.

Bam, bam.

Bam, bam, bam—I heard a knocking at the door.

A knocking at the door of the classroom we were using as a meeting spot—a, well, standard sliding double door that creaked the way you'd expect an abandoned building's door to when you opened or closed it.

It seemed that Kanbaru had conscientiously locked it behind her upon entering—giving you a glimpse into her good upbringing, but then, after so properly closing the classroom door, she'd proceeded to land a tooth-shattering flying knee on my face. But I could grill her, or rather rebuke her about this, later.

Bam.

Bam, bam.

Bam, bam, bam.

The sound of knocking at the door, but not a violent one. Polite, if anything—a quiet, regular knock. But hearing such propriety, I couldn't help but feel like something was wrong.

Of course I did. A gentleman can be as proper and dignified as he wants, but it only makes him seem creepier if you're meeting him deep in a dark forest—likewise the polite knock I now heard in an abandoned building in the middle of the night.

It was more than enough to make me nervous.

"Huh? What's this, a visitor? Come in," Kanbaru said.

…She wasn't nervous at all.

A heart of iron, despite only being a second-year high school student. You could tell she used to compete at the national level.

"Hm? My senior Araragi, isn't it this acquaintance of yours? You invited someone other than me here?"

"No, you're the only one—"

A visitor?

What, did *she* get impatient because Kanbaru and I were spending more time than I expected enjoying our pointless banter? Had *she* sent someone for us? Was that it?

The thought crossed my mind, but it seemed impossible.

It wasn't as if I'd spent that much time talking to Kanbaru, after all—yes, we'd rambled, but mostly in terms of topic, not length—and even if we'd rambled on for a long time, I couldn't imagine *her* ever getting impatient.

Her perception of the world involved spans of time different from mine—so then, who was it? Who now visited this classroom?

My foolish self got excited at the off-chance that maybe it was Shinobu. My link to her was down after having been severed, but maybe she'd used some other method to track me down?

That of course wasn't the case—but I'd later learn that while my notion missed the mark, it wasn't by far, *in more ways than one.*

In any case.

With Kanbaru's permission, the creaking door opened and into the classroom entered—toward us entered a suit of armor.

"…!"

Armor?

Nope, armor—undoubtedly armor.

Armor is the right word.

But was it right for this armor to have appeared?

What exactly was the context—what exactly transpired for an armored warrior to appear? Just moments ago, Kanbaru and I were enjoying a nice little conversation—so why?

My mind, according to its standard and proper routines, began to process this armored warrior who had suddenly appeared. *Is this some sort of anachronistic cosplay?* My thoughts started to lumber forward with optimistic, almost tortoise-like steps—but meanwhile those of the famously swift and agile Suruga Kanbaru were as quick as a hare's.

No.

To be more accurate, I doubt she thought at all—Suruga Kanbaru started to move the moment the door opened and the armored warrior came clanging in.

She held high her bandaged left arm.

And leapt toward the armor.

"K-Kanbaru!"

"Get down!" she yelled, even taking my safety into account—and slammed her left fist into the armor's torso, at the center of its trunk.

Though technically speaking, the left fist wasn't hers.

It was an aberration's.

And so while a normal bare fist would be liable to break if you used it to punch a suit of armor, it was the armor that broke in this case—one straight punch from Kanbaru was all it took to reduce it to pieces.

All in the blink of an eye.

It did seem a bit extreme to punch it, no questions asked, before we knew what the hell it was, but the sheer speed of Kanbaru's reaction to a suspicious figure was praiseworthy.

Lacking the courage to slug an armored warrior in any situation at all, I could only follow her request (order?) and reflexively lie down (my hands behind my head without a second thought, like some civilian surrendering to an army). It was then that I witnessed something even more shocking than her decision-making abilities.

The scattered armor.

I assumed the person wearing it would be exposed, their identity clear, no matter who they may be.

But—that didn't happen.

Inside the armor—was nothing.

"…"

This was enough to put even Kanbaru at a loss for words—she

silently stepped backwards until she reached me. You could say she ran backwards. Super-fast. Honestly, when it comes to her physical abilities, what deserves special note isn't so much the destructive power of her aberrational left fist but everything about her from the waist down that she tempered and trained through her own stubborn, steadfast will.

"Hold on a second," she objected. "Could you please not focus on everything about me from the waist down at a time like this? At least consider reading the room here."

"Well, then stop reading my mind. I specifically said everything you trained, meaning your legs. What else would I be talking about?"

I rose from my defensive state as I bickered with her—my eyes never leaving the scattered armor, of course.

A full set of armor.

Kanbaru's strike had sent it flying into pieces—but when I looked closely, none of the parts were damaged or broken. Like a set of toy blocks that had fallen over. The armor had gone flying a little too easily, no matter how powerful Kanbaru's strike, but it made perfect sense if the suit was empty.

"I'd say it was more like a shell," Kanbaru remarked. "It was strange how little of an impact I felt. I nearly thought I'd missed—what is that thing? Your friend?"

"I don't have any friends who are armor."

"I wonder, what kind of friends *do* you have?"

"…"

I couldn't answer her in a timely manner.

I just didn't have many friends she didn't know already.

In any case, I didn't know any walking sets of armor that were empty too—as a friend or otherwise.

I didn't know.

Even any aberration.

"So, at the very least, this armored warrior isn't the person you wanted to introduce to me."

"Wait…you punched it when you weren't sure?"

What was she planning on doing if it really was cosplay or someone's idea of a surprise?

"What was I planning? Well, I'd apologize. I simply did what I had to do at the moment to provide you the protection you deserve."

"..."

What a scary junior. She was never rattled.

Still, her powers of judgment and combat were equally reliable—I didn't know what *she* wanted from Kanbaru, but with my link to Shinobu severed, I certainly wasn't the more useful teen of us two.

In any case, whatever aberration or frightful apparition this was, Kanbaru had settled things before they could even get started—okay, scattered more than settled.

She really sucked at keeping a room tidy.

Was this related to *her* request? Did I need to let *her* know about this?

"Hm?" Kanbaru tilted her head. "Let's see…what do we have here."

"What's the matter?"

"Well, I thought it was a full set of armor, but upon closer inspection, it's missing something."

"It is?"

"Yeah. We've got a few suits of armor at my home—compared to them, this guy is short a vital piece."

"..."

A few suits of armor? What kind of a home was that?

Well, it was a grand Japanese-style estate… *A few* might be an exaggeration, but it wouldn't be surprising if she were familiar with at least one set.

"I didn't notice anything myself, Kanbaru—hmm, okay. If you know so much about suits of armor, could you put it back together?"

"What? Me?" She pointed at her own confused face.

Despite all the business about pledging her loyalty to me, Kanbaru wasn't used to being put to work for the most part. Not a useful teen at all in that sense, she was a diva.

I said, "It's not like I know how a suit of armor fits together."

"Then I'll give you instructions. Why don't you give it a shot?"

"You don't even think twice about putting your dear senior to work, do you? But fine. I'll show you I'm a man, capable of more than lying prone and taking cover when he's told to. I'm just as capable of being supine."

"If there's anything I don't want to see, it's a senior I respect demonstrating that ability in public... But why put this thing back together anyway?"

"Well, if we did, it just might start moving again..."

We needed to get ourselves over to our next meeting spot once we'd convened without incident. As things stood, though, our meet-up was hardly "without incident." To be frank, I didn't want any additional trouble and considered pretending that none of this stuff with the armor ever happened, and walking off—but I was fresh off a first-hand experience of what happens when you walk away from seeds of trouble and allow them to sprout.

I lacked any sort of knowledge or wisdom about our situation but still needed to do everything I could. It couldn't take that much time to build this suit of armor back up if Kanbaru knew how it fit together.

"No, I think it's gonna take a while... Don't you know how heavy a suit of armor is? This isn't like putting together a toy model or something."

"Ah... Not that I've ever assembled a toy model."

"Hm, really? I'm surprised to hear that from you, given your many interests."

"Don't laud my many interests just to keep on chatting. It's not like I never touched one, I just never completed one."

"Oh, I get you. I buy model kits all the time, but never take them out of the box."

"Okay, in that case, don't lump me in with your ilk."

And so on.

If anything was a waste of time, it was these kinds of conversations—but as a result, I was spared the onerous task of reassembling the scattered armor (in accordance with my junior's instructions). Not because she did it herself—our diva never labors.

It moved.

Without us laying a finger on it—in fact, without us even approaching it. Each of the scattered pieces began moving on its own nonetheless.

Like a video being played in reverse.

Moving on its own—*it put itself back together.*

As if the empty armor had been a lifeform—it creaked and clanged itself back into consciousness.

Forming itself back into life—like a lifeform.

The helmet, the chestplate, the robes, the gauntlets, the greaves, the mask, the shoulder guards, the socks, the straw sandals, and the riding shoes came together—*completing* the armored warrior we had seen.

In that abandoned building with no electricity, lit only by the moon and stars, I hadn't gotten a good look at the armored warrior earlier—but now that I had another chance.

Now that I saw it again, I realized just how loud and flashy it was.

Bright red armor.

What was this kind of armor called again—*akazonae?*

No, the color almost seemed to go beyond red, as if it was blood—I could only watch dumbfounded at something so unbelievable, but I did notice one new thing.

A new discovery, or rather, I understood Kanbaru's remark—that it was missing something. Now that I could view its full figure, the missing piece was clear.

What the armor *lacked*.

Putting aside that there was nothing inside it, of course, what the otherwise full set of equipment lacked was—

"…■■■■"

Huh?

It spoke?

The empty suit of armor—the shell—devoid of any contents?

No way, impossible. Some breeze must have passed through the hollow suit. It sounded far too muffled to be any kind of voice…at…

"Get back!"

all—once again Kanbaru moved faster than my synapses could fire. Nimbly. She brandished her left arm anew—then entered the armor's space without a moment's hesitation and smashed it square in the middle.

An empty set of armor not only moving but automatically putting itself back together was shocking to say the least, but Kanbaru reacted to the anomaly at a speed that sent a shiver down my spine. I did as she bade and got back.

It was a great mystery why she stayed so devoted to a senior like me (in my defense, I didn't back up because I was scared of the armor, my body just obeyed Kanbaru without any mental input—maybe that's even more pathetic?); whatever the reason, she had the kind of unhesitating personality that stepped on the gas in the face of danger.

But.

This time—the armor didn't come crashing apart.

Rather than scattering—it staggered back, unable to absorb the entire impact, but stood in place.

No.

It didn't just stand in place—it lurched back and used its left arm, its empty left arm, to try to grab Kanbaru.

Its movements sluggish.

It tried to grab Kanbaru's head from above—she's by no means a short girl, but the armored warrior was easily a foot and a half taller than her. Not having balked at their height difference in the first place, she of course didn't cower when that left arm reached out in reaction.

She avoided it by a hair's width—and slipped past to deal another blow, as if to counter, aiming not at its torso this time but at its chin. Not an uppercut—a laser-straight punch from below.

Naturally, it wasn't clear if aiming at what would normally be a weak spot meant anything up against an empty suit of armor—but Suruga Kanbaru's movements, far more familiar with brawling than mine, were enough to make me swear: *Crap, I need to make sure I never piss her off. She's got my unconditional obedience as her senior.*

Why was an athlete like her so comfortable in a brawl? Maybe you couldn't make it to the top in jock-land without being at least a little tough...

I'd fought her in this very classroom after she'd been poisoned by an aberration, and come to think of it, her movements then were pretty skillful too.

I doubted they were at the level of the Fire Sisters' designated brawn, but simply having full control over her body impressed my still-stunned self to no end.

This was no time to be impressed, though.

I think that goes without saying.

The armor's movements were dull, while Kanbaru's were swift, and not even relatively. While one blow might not have been enough to scatter the armor again, I wondered if it'd break after two or three.

The armor's *missing equipment* also encouraged this thought—but that isn't what happened.

Though Kanbaru dodged its grabbing arm, even a punch to the jaw did nothing but shake the warrior's helmet. She tried to hit it with a third shot—but suddenly fell to her knees.

She slumped over.

And collapsed.

"?! Kanbaru?!"

"S-Stay back!"

I could tell from her voice that she felt just as perplexed, but that's what she said. Pinning me in place with those words, she rose from her position on the floor, on one knee, before charging at the armored warrior's legs like a runner from a crouch start.

This wasn't a body-press, it was a tackle.

The armor wouldn't fall to punches, so now she tried to take it down by brute force—indeed, even if she couldn't send it flying into pieces, its own weight could scatter it if she smashed it against the floor. That must've been her goal, but even a rocket-propelled double-leg takedown, powered by Kanbaru's muscles, ended in failure.

"...!"

This time—it didn't waver one inch.

It didn't sway, nor even shake.

It didn't need to adjust its footing—the armored warrior withstood the tackle and merely stood at attention as if roots had grown from its feet.

What? It almost felt like...

The thing was getting tougher and tougher.

One strike broke it apart at first—then it only staggered—then it was only shaken—and then it didn't budge an inch? The progression was far too quick to be explained away as the armored warrior acclimating to Kanbaru's attacks. That seemed, if anything, untenable given its dull movements.

Yet, just ten or so minutes after its appearance—the armored warrior had clearly grown stronger.

I'd grasped one side of what was going on, but only the one. At that point, I should've been paying attention to the other.

"A—" voiced Kanbaru.

Still clinging and pushing into the armor following her double-leg takedown.

"Araragi-senpai—" she said, clinging on tight.

No.

Even her gripping arms now fell in vain—it was Kanbaru, not the warrior, who collapsed *despite it having done nothing to her.*

"—Run."

It was the one order I couldn't obey.

004

The armored warrior grew tougher and tougher—but I hadn't noticed how Kanbaru was growing weaker and weaker in contrast.

She started by delivering a blow to its body.

Then another blow—she was on one knee when she punched its chin. I found it strange that she'd buckled then, but when I saw her collapse right after grasping onto it with her tackle, I knew.

I noticed at last, all but too late. I should have sooner, or rather, it's strange that I didn't. I'd witnessed the phenomenon time and again, and experienced it as often.

An energy drain.

The ability to suck away a target's strength, vitality, and will through sheer proximity or by touch—an aberrational phenomenon that *we* were very familiar with.

In other words, there were two sides to it.

The armored warrior grew tougher and tougher, Kanbaru weaker and weaker—her sleek movements and judgment had worked against her.

She'd gotten far too close and touched it far too much before she could notice; had I been in her shoes, it couldn't have drained more than one attack's worth of energy.

No, maybe it was inevitable—try as we might, neither of us would have connected an armored warrior to energy drain. Whether it was me or Kanbaru, we wouldn't have figured it out for sure until we collapsed.

Why?

Why would an old-fashioned, anachronistic armored warrior—*use an energy drain like it was some sort of vampire?*

What was going on here?

What was this thing?

There was no time for thinking, though—realizing that the armored warrior could drain energy didn't change what I had to do. I had to retrieve Kanbaru, collapsed at the feet she'd charged into—that was all.

I didn't know the precise type of energy drain the armor used, or the specific conditions needed to activate it, but couldn't concern myself with that.

Unlike Kanbaru, who had an aberration within her left hand, I wasn't even a mockery of a vampire now that my link to Shinobu had been severed. I could very well collapse in a humiliatingly instantaneous moment if I were hit by a powerful energy drain.

I could very well be sucked dry, but I'd use that moment for the sake of Suruga Kanbaru, who'd summoned her last bit of strength to squeeze out her final order—to run.

I still didn't know why the armored warrior was here, why it had appeared, or anything about its identity—but she had come here for one reason alone. I'd asked her to.

She'd gotten caught up in this because of me and no one else.

If the worst were to happen to her, I'd never be able to look Senjogahara in the eye for the rest of my life—and so I charged at the armored warrior.

I wouldn't say I had any, but if I had to pick one, the idea was to dash past its legs and gallantly scoop up the fallen Kanbaru over the course of the next three seconds. For the most part, though, my life hasn't gone the way I imagine.

As all of you know very well.

My maneuver wasn't all for naught—because the armored warrior, with Kanbaru right under its eyes, reacted. Not that it had any eyes at all in its helm—but I felt as though it glared at me.

Then it moved, too—seemingly having absorbed Kanbaru's energy, it attempted a tackle like she'd done, oddly enough.

Imagine an armored warrior that feels about twice your size tackling you head-on. It looked to be going for a double-leg takedown by the way it moved, but naturally there was our significant height difference.

What was essentially a shoulder tackle smashed into my abdomen, and the impact made me wonder if my internal organs had all been torn apart. It wouldn't have been surprising—who could find fault with this story's punch line being me, deprived of vampiric regeneration, dying on the spot?

But maybe my lack of any half-hearted power was a blessing—because even a merciless fist that breaks ten bricks is surprisingly ineffective at piercing a thin scrap of silk floating in the air. In other words, I flew backwards, utterly unable to stand my ground.

I rolled along the floor, making a mess of the room's desks and chairs and forming new bruises across my body, yet I wasn't torn in half like I repeatedly have been.

I could've been the one left scattered across the room this time—but damn, had I gotten used to my vampiric immortality at some point? The dull pain in every inch of my body, and the blood oozing from all my scrapes, finally made me feel human.

How selfish of me. After spending all that time during spring break desperately wanting to turn back into a human, I desired those vampiric powers.

To protect Kanbaru—I told myself. I couldn't even stand up. I'd get to Kanbaru even if it meant crawling my way to her, but to cut to the chase, there was no need. My pointless struggle truly had no point.

I say this because the armored warrior ignored Kanbaru's collapsed form and began walking toward me—step by step.

While its pace hadn't changed, it didn't seem as sluggish as before—its walk almost seemed nimble, in spite of the heavy armor.

Had it absorbed my energy too when we collided? Nope, now that I was human, my juice wouldn't even whet its appetite—I couldn't believe it. In my own amateurish way, I'd faced off against a number of aberrations in quick succession, but never had I confronted one that got stronger the more it fought.

It got stronger the more it fought?

That basically made it my natural predator.

"■■■■—"

The armor seemed to mutter something else—but before I could decipher the sounds, only a step and a half separated us.

I thought it might continue on and just trample me.

It probably could, as if I were an ant—but instead, the armored warrior bent over slightly and grabbed me by the collar, as if to help me as I struggled to get up, and lifted me up like a tablecloth it was getting ready to put away.

It lifted me up—then looked straight at me.

Again, not that the armored warrior had any eyes—

"Wh…"

My words were halting.

The blows across my body as I rolled through the classroom—and the more direct damage to my abdomen—might not have been fatal, but they seemed significant, because I could no longer even struggle. I couldn't so much as put my hands on the gauntlets on my collar.

"Wh-What's your deal? What're you trying to do? What's your grudge—why are you doing this?"

I was being overly talkative, since talking was all I could do. Even if it was only air reverberating in the armor to make those whistling noises, I couldn't deny the feeling that it spoke.

If it did.

If we could communicate—we'd be able to negotiate.

I didn't think I could converse with an aberration the way these ruins' former resident, Mèmè Oshino, could—but he might have said something like: *All riled up and ready to fight. Something good happen to you?*

Actually, we'd attacked first.

Sure, Kanbaru had acted in order to defend me, but you could also see this situation as us trying to bum-rush an armored warrior who politely knocked on the door before entering the room.

The shoulder tackle it gave me was just about its only explicit attack against us, and even now, you could say it helped me up—

"Gah!!"

Okay, you couldn't say that.

It opened its hands, released my collar, and let me fall as gravity dictated, just to grab me again—but now that I'd fallen, it grabbed not my collar but my neck.

With one hand.

Strangling me.

I could feel it holding back, but it still showed little mercy—its hand around my throat as if to snap my neck, let alone stop my breathing.

"Guh...gah...ghaah!"

No, that wasn't it.

And that's why it was holding back.

The armored warrior was grasping my throat—to shut me up. The one thing I could do... By strangling me, it was cutting off my jumbled questions and keeping me from speaking to it. A clear rejection of communication.

Yet I also felt a kind of consumption.

A draining of energy.

Leaving me—through my grasped neck.

Stealing from me.

My vision grew blurry—my consciousness dim.

"..."

And then.

Over the armored warrior's shoulders—I saw Kanbaru standing up again. Her feet were unsteady, but I could sense the will in her eyes as they met mine. Yes, Suruga Kanbaru was an experienced team player—indeed, but why was she making eye contact with me?

Don't come this way...

If you can move, then get out of here already.

Or so I wished to say, but that too was impossible while being strangled. Although I didn't know if I had it in me as a total non-athlete, I had no choice but to return her eye contact.

Run.

I'm not running, her eyes replied briskly.

I was a bit shocked that Kanbaru and I were at a place where we could converse with mere looks—but what was the point if she was going to shoot down whatever signs I sent her? Not that I had much ground to stand on, being the first one of us who refused to run...

You be the one to run. I'm gonna make its knees buckle from behind, so use that as an opportunity.

...She was stupid even when we were communicating through eye contact alone.

She wanted to pull a prank? There weren't any knees in that armor to begin with—but at that very moment, as decisive as it was stupid—even as I had what might be my final thought.

The floor of the classroom burst into flames.

It emitted a pillar of flame as though an anti-personnel mine buried under the floor had exploded—and this pillar burned the warrior's gauntlet grasping my neck.

The flame was unbelievably intense, to the point that I fully expected it to burn straight through the armor—to give a familiar example, it looked like a Chinese restaurant's kitchen burner turned all the way up.

The armored warrior's hand, which could have crushed my throat and Adam's apple in the blink of an eye if it felt so inclined, reflexively let go because of the flames—allowing me, now free, to slam to the ground on my butt.

I had no time to celebrate my newfound sense of liberation, though—while I wished the sudden pillar of flame erupting from the floor had conveniently aimed for the warrior's arm, that was not the case. The *first* pillar happened to scorch its gauntlet, that's all.

One after another.

Like a dam had burst.

Like a chain reaction—flames came from below, all across the floor, spouting like fountains. These pillars piercing through the floor did not then sputter out, but continued on to the ceiling—given their force, they must have passed through the third and fourth floor ceilings, too, all the way to the roof.

These flames seemed like physically destructive hammers pounding their way up from below—in an aggressive game of Whack-A-Mole, if you want to put it that way.

Now on my butt, I more rolled than crawled to avoid the successive erupting pillars to make my way to Kanbaru—not that I and my scrap-of-silk uselessness meeting back up with her would accomplish anything. In fact, I could even expose her to danger if the armored warrior chased after me.

Kanbaru being Kanbaru, she stepped her way around the flames— her evasion skill, the way her body could move on its own in spite of not understanding what was going on, proved what a top-notch athlete she was.

What *was* going on?

Obviously, I assumed these piercing lances of flame were yet another aberrational phenomenon brought on by the armored warrior—but given how I had the pillars to thank for being freed from its hold, maybe not.

Even now, the cage of flaming pillars, the fiery fence I'd crawled through without an inch to spare, separated me from the armored warrior. Almost as if the flames were a wall protecting us—still, I had a hard time believing things were that convenient. Our side of the flaming cage was fiery enough.

So then?

What were these pillars?

"...Miss Hanekawa."

Kanbaru muttered a name, but why—Hanekawa? Why bring her up all of a sudden?

Nothing about fire or flames said Hanekawa to me—if anyone, wouldn't it be the Fire Sisters, my two little sisters Karen Araragi and Tsukihi Araragi?

But I was in no position to ask—the flames continued to burst forth in one place after another.

So many columns rose up that I barely had anywhere to stand— when a fiery lance climbed as high as it could go, that wasn't the end of it. Naturally, the fire then spread from the opened holes.

Ruins are, in general, full of flammable objects—and the classroom we were in was already stained an irrevocable shade of red.

None of the earlier darkness was left, but even amidst the flames—the armor's red shade stood out.

This wasn't the kind of fire where you hoped the firefighters would make it in time.

I had to get to safety asap when it was bad as this—hadn't I taken part in yearly drills since elementary school for precisely this moment?

Even I couldn't joke around and claim that "R-A-C-E" stood for "Really Adorable Children in Elementary"—just as I'd learned, it was Rescue, Alert, Contain, and Extinguish.

But.

There was no hope of containing or extinguishing this.

Forget about rescue—but as the armored warrior and I glared at each other across the flaming fence between us—an *alert*.

"Time to give it up, alas!"

Clearly.

This time.

The armored warrior—spoke in a way I could understand.

"It appears as though a full-fledged nuisance hath introduced itself—perhaps we've tread on the tiger's tail? I've no hope of handling this *as I am now*! It seems I've come at a bad time—*my master* appears to be away as well… I shall try again! Ye too, do not dally and make thy way home at once!"

Its words suddenly grown fluent.

Fluent, lively, even refreshing.

As though all its earlier muffled, instrument-like noises were a lie.

I tried to accompany my surprise with a reaction.

As I am now?

A bad time? My master?

What was it talking about?

I wanted to bombard it with questions—but couldn't because my throat hurt.

…No, that's not it.

This wasn't about a sore throat or something.

When the armored warrior grasped my neck tight—it had absorbed *my voice*.

Energy drain.

Just as it reproduced Kanbaru's tackle.

It now reproduced—my voice.

The fluent delivery made some amount of sense in that case, and so did an aged manner of speech that matched its archaic, even anachronistic attire.

Still.

Although the armored warrior was free to speak in any manner it wished—there was no way I could turn a blind eye to what it said next.

Given its traditional Japanese trappings—uttering a Western name called the character's entire historical background into question.

"When ye meet *Kissshot* next, tell her this! I will be coming to retrieve my precious enchanted blade *Kokorowatari* after a little more recovery! *Yes, no armored warrior is complete without a blade!* Indeed, it has been four hundred years since I lent it to her, so tell her to be prepared for a late fee! Hahahaha!"

Hahahaha, the voice laughed—though the jaw of the helm maintained its expression of fury.

"Ha!"Ha!"Haha!"Hahaha!"Hahahaha!"Hahahahaha!"Hahahaha!" Hahahahaha!"Hahahahahaahhahahahahahahahahahahahaha—!"

005

With those attention-grabbing parting words and roaring laugh, the armored warrior seemed to blend into the fire's black smoke and to disappear, just as it had promised—while the chapter has changed, the danger Kanbaru and I faced was far from over.

As beings of mostly flesh and blood, Kanbaru and I couldn't escape from the swirling flames by turning into what seemed like mist the way the warrior had.

The fiery sea engulfing the classroom was so thick you could nearly swim in it. The route to every exit, whether door or window, had been shut off—the fact that there was still enough space for us to make if not our last stand, then our last sit, seemed like the miracle of the century.

Of course, these would simply be our last moments if we didn't do something...

"What was that, my dear senior? That armored warrior—I found it strange that it didn't carry a sword, but the enchanted blade Kokorowatari? Isn't that—and also, Kissshot..."

"That...can wait...until later," I let out a disjointed reply.

In part because my throat wouldn't heal and I was dealing with a scratchy voice—not to mention, barely any humidity remained in the room among the rising flames, making it hard to talk. But even apart from all that, I wanted to leave it for later.

Honestly, I didn't even want to think about it then.

It was enough to fill my brain past its bursting point—what I needed to think about first and foremost was how to get Kanbaru out of the burning building without any harm coming to her.

This cram school engulfed in roaring flames.

If I had any degree of vampirism left in me, I might've shielded her and gallantly plunged through the flames and out of the building to safety—but even someone as bad at thinking things through as yours truly could figure that one out. I doubted I could even make it to the door—maybe I could get to a window if I didn't mind burning my feet, but unfortunately, it was just too risky to dive out of a second-floor window with injured, beet-red feet.

Staying in the classroom would be worse—forget about risk, the chances of dying in there were sky high. They say suffocation is the cause of most fire-related deaths.

But our predicament seemed like one of the exceptions implied by that "most"—the lances of flame continued to pierce the floor below us with no signs of slowing or stopping. The raging flames were just making that hard to see, but it wasn't abating in any way.

You couldn't tell from inside.

From outside, though, the entire building must have looked like a single flaming lance—a shaft piercing the heavens.

I'd had hopes for a dramatic twist, like a column shooting from below providing an opening in the floor we could use to escape, but things are never that easy in the real world. While the flames left holes that a person could fit through, looking down them to the floor below revealed a hellfire I wish I'd never seen.

The steel and concrete had grown molten.

By that logic, the holes in the ceiling might offer a lucky escape route—but how could I reach it now that my body was back to its regular settings? The chairs I might've stacked up to stand on were already a blazing shade of red and looked like some sort of torture device.

"Wait, hold on. Kanbaru, what if you tried… You might not be able to get a running start, but maybe two steps or so of momentum…just might be enough…for you to reach the ceiling? Wouldn't you be able to scramble up there? And then...we could use the elevator shaft to go from the third floor to the first, and—"

"You're overestimating your junior. My legs aren't that strong," Kanbaru immediately rejected my scraggy-voiced proposal. She wanted me to know just how ridiculous it was. "Even I can't leap all the way to the ceiling, certainly not with an older boy in my arms."

"I see."

Well.

It's not like she'd escape alone even if I told her to—as loyal as my junior was, she never listened to me. I needed to assume there was no way to save her and her alone.

A high school girl who lived in total opposition to Mèmè Oshino's dictum that people just go and get saved on their own... Perhaps such a philosophy was understandable, given her background, but at the same time, the idea that the third floor would be any better than the first or second was nothing more than pure optimism...

We were caught between a rock and a hard place—what's the right expression when it's flames on all sides?

"Senpai."

"What is it, Kanbaru?"

"Will you be my first?"

"Don't give up yet!"

She had a scary way of accepting her fate!

A confession, now?

Stop trying to push how girly you are.

"I don't want to die a virgin."

"Don't make admissions like that, either. You know, this sort of thing is why people skipped the story where you were the main character."

She was more unafraid than me two, or even several times over. I couldn't keep up with her—at this rate, she might turn this into a lovers' suicide.

Couldn't she be a little more serious? In the middle of a fire, at least?

You're never going to be serious in your life if you can't act serious here... Then again, her life was going to end here if we didn't do something.

"Heh. Well, it's fine. This isn't a bad way to die—I'd be happy if I got to die with you."

"Um, Kanbaru? Sorry, but I don't feel that extreme a way about you."

"What? That hurts."

I had to make it clear to her, even if it hurt—in fact, I wouldn't even feel happy dying with Senjogahara, my girlfriend. In May, during Golden Week, I was consumed with the notion of dying for Hanekawa's sake, but it wasn't like I wanted to die with her.

The list of people I'd die with—was only one name long.

A lone, golden-haired aberration.

Who wasn't here...

Which was exactly why—we needed to escape from this flaming building alive.

"Fine," I said, "I'm just going to accept it."

"Hm? Oh, you're going to accept my first time?"

"No, I couldn't ever accept something so huge. I mean the risk—our only option is to jump out a window and pray for the best. It's better than burning to death here, right?"

"Yeah... I was thinking about how that was our only option, too."

Liar. You were thinking about something completely different.

"Who knows, there might even be a car parked below us, and we can land on its roof."

"I've never been that lucky in my life before..."

That was the sort of thing that happened to Tsukihi, maybe. It'd be very much like her to emerge alive from a sea of flames—like a phoenix.

But wasn't I her brother? Couldn't I get as lucky at least once in my life?

I wasn't sure if we could even make it to a window through these flames—but standing around and being indecisive was a far worse use of our time.

And wasting it on banter? Unthinkable.

The two of us stood, an arm around each other's shoulders as if we were getting ready to run a three-legged race—the flames and the shimmering heat made the path ahead of us anything but visible. We were trying to make sure not to get separated during our run, and also guarding against one of us stepping in the many holes opened in the floor. If either of us was about to fall, the other could immediately help.

"Okay," Kanbaru said. "In a 1, 1, 2, 3, 5, 8, 13 rhythm."

"Why are we using the Fibonacci sequence as our rhythm?"

"Just match my pace."

"Don't be ridiculous. The slower runner needs to set the pace."

"Remember. Right foot first."

"Wait, I know I likened it to a three-legged race, but our legs aren't tied together. It shouldn't matter which leg we step with first…"

"And when I say right, I mean my right."

"We're facing the same way."

"I'm a lefty, though, so I sometimes get right and left mixed up."

"You really expect me to match the finer points of how you process the world?"

We continued our banter as though we were in some sort of Hollywood movie, and maybe it was somehow appropriate given the daring escape we were about to attempt.

In any case, we took our first step.

Onward toward our desperate ploy, fully prepared for severe burns.

After everything she said, Kanbaru dared start with her left leg, while I took off with my right—however.

However, our first steps were the only one we took.

The window we saw as our way out—with neither frame nor glass, really more of a rectangular hole to begin with—instantaneously expanded in every direction.

The window…spread along the entire wall.

A large amount of oxygen gushing into a burning building through an open door or broken window magnifies the fire's scale as a natural chemical result—the phenomenon is known as a backdraft.

That's exactly what happened.

Earlier, I likened the vertical flaming spears rising from directly under us to mines, and if I were to continue the comparison—this backdraft was a plastic explosive.

The blast originated at the very spot we were hoping to rush through, which is to say right in front of us—inflicting an inordinate amount of damage.

Ah. The "Contain" in "Rescue, Alert, Contain, and Extinguish" wasn't there for show, and this was a head-on collision.

But Kanbaru and I weren't the only ones to be affected by this fresh blast of fire—the *flames themselves* were blown out.

For a moment.

Only temporarily, of course—but the backdraft quelled the flames in the classroom by force.

"This is like how they sometimes fight fire with dynamite…"

Then, sure enough.

As I said this—from beyond the broken wall came a violent sorcerer's doll *shikigami*, a *tsukumogami* of a human corpse used for a hundred years—Yotsugi Ononoki.

I know I'm repeating myself, but we were on the second floor.

Literally above ground level.

Didn't matter to her.

With her grip strength, impressive even among the inhuman beings I know, Ononoki supported herself by holding onto a flat wall—and spoke to me, expressionless and emotionless.

"Don't think you can die out here. I'm going to be the one to kill you, monstieur."

"…"

What kind of character was she this time around?

006

I of course didn't recall doing anything to make Ononoki hate me to the point of wanting to kill me, and she rescued Kanbaru and me from inside the blazing building in a fairly normal way. My junior had flopped on the floor unconscious due to the impact of the backdraft and its explosive fire-fighting effects, so I put her on my back before clinging onto Ononoki. The energy drain had already brought Kanbaru close to her limit—despite her messing around, she'd been forcing herself to hold on, so I had no reservations at all as her senior about carrying her.

True, I nearly screamed something out in exasperation.

Why was she seriously not wearing a bra?!

Given the scale of the fire, it was a miracle that we made it out of there without serious burns—but I wasn't exactly heaving a sigh of relief, either.

If I had to find a silver lining, it was that the fire wasn't spreading beyond the building. These ruins were isolated, so perhaps I should say it's a good thing there were no nearby structures.

And then, without the help of any fire trucks rushing to the scene, the abandoned cram school, filled with memories both good and bad ever since spring break, burned itself out—fizzled out, you might say, like a candle's flame.

Only cinders lacking any semblance of their original form were left behind—and all I could do was look up with vacant eyes as I crouched near Kanbaru's prone form, unable to so much as stand.

A sense of loss.

No, I wasn't so attached to those ruins that I felt a sense of loss—but something that had stood there so naturally was gone all of a sudden, and I couldn't hide my shock at the fact.

It was as if—yes.

My connection, not to the building itself so much as to the guy, the expert who'd taken up residence there—had vanished completely.

As if the place he might return to was no more—but that was ridiculous, how could that vagabond have any place to return to? He was only stopping by in this town too—he drifted through, and the abandoned building was just shelter from the rain to him.

Still, that said—for the place to disappear in mere minutes?

Razed to nothing.

That felt wrong.

"Sorry to interrupt your sentimentalizing, monstieur, but what exactly happened?"

Ononoki.

She said this from behind me, expressionless and emotionless—rushing a conclusion without any consideration for my complicated feelings.

"I can't blame you for brooding over that snail girl, but don't go attempting a murder-suicide with a random girl you found."

"Even your misunderstandings are excessive."

A random girl?

She meant my adorable junior.

"Her name is Suruga Kanbaru."

"Oh, really. So she's—"

Miss Gaen's niece, Ononoki said, not sounding particularly interested—and she probably wasn't.

"The former Suruga Gaen. Suruga Kanbaru after Miss Gaen's elder sister—"

"If anything, Ononoki, I should be asking you why you're here. As far as I remember, your role isn't to be some girl who's always ready to dash in and save me whenever I'm in a tight spot."

"It seems I'm the only one assigned to that task as of late. I wish they'd give me a break. I get called to do audio commentary all the time, too."

"I can't say that's my fault."

"Even if it isn't, I wish you'd take responsibility for it. That's why you're around, right? To take responsibility."

"You think whoever's responsible exists only to take responsibility? And don't make me responsible for everything in the world."

"Well, I just happened to be around, I wasn't planning on saving you or anything, monstieur."

Her words sounded cold, depending on how you interpreted them—but nothing about her was either hot or cold.

Yotsugi Ononoki has no will.

She was just stating the facts of the matter.

"I was only doing my job—when I found you dragging a woman I don't know into a murder-suicide. I thought, 'Boy, do I need to mess up your plans,' that's all."

"Sounds like you have a hell of a will to me..."

Please, it wasn't a murder-suicide.

And what's with this "need" to mess up my plans?

"Well, I need to toy with whatever your plans are, whether that's a murder-suicide or a pedo-suicide."

"Just how much do you hate me?"

"I don't hate you. I just want to Toys-R-Ound with you."

"What does that even mean? Stop inventing new phrases whenever you feel like it."

I also let it slide, but what's a pedo-suicide, anyway?

She wasn't talking about what happened with Hachikuji, was she?

"I like you if anything," the shikigami said. "Hm? Oh, did your heart just skip a beat there?"

"You've turned into a pretty annoying character in the short time since we last met..."

What happened in just a half-day or so...

In any case, I'd lost count of how many times Ononoki had rescued me. I wanted to show my gratitude to her somehow, but she wasn't making it easy, ruffling my feelings. Still, this time she'd saved not just me, but Kanbaru too—how could I not thank her?

"Well, Ononoki. Thank you. I know my debt to you keeps getting larger and larger, but I promise to return the favor someday."

"What are you scheming? Are you hoping to get another kiss out of me by being noble?"

Such was Ononoki's reaction—it felt like there was no point in thanking her, and uh, I guess that did happen...

"Sorry to dash your hopes, but I did that to harass you. You're not getting a kiss from me when you're hoping for one."

"Then you're not sorry about dashing my hopes at all."

It was harassment...

Now that she mentioned it, that case was far from settled.

"So, monsieur. If you want to repay me, I'd normally want you to do so by bringing me immense wealth. But I'll accept an answer to my question this time around. What exactly happened?"

"What happened?"

"I'll lend an ear, if you'd just open up to me."

"As if I'd ever come to you for life advice."

Whatever she said and however she said it, her words always sounded wooden. No matter what kind of retort or reaction I gave, it sounded like me getting worked up on my own, which I have to admit was depressing.

Still, my sorrow forced me to cool off—my heart had been pounding since those raging flames, but my pulse seemed to be returning to normal.

Usually, she'd be the last person I'd open up to, but if she was willing to listen to my troubles despite being on the job, maybe I just had to accept her kindness and—hm?

Hold on, no.

What was that again? She wasn't planning on saving me, she just happened to see a fire at her job site—and decided to lift a finger because that fire was engulfing us.

Then asking me "what exactly happened" and attempting to get my story was nothing more than part of her job, not any kind of kindness.

You certainly couldn't say it was out of goodwill.

"Phew...that was close, Ononoki. I nearly got the mistaken impression that you like me or something. I was beginning to think, *Is she into me or what?*"

"I just told you that I like you. Stop running from the kindness of others. You cowardly little chicken."

"..."

She was awfully insulting for someone who liked me.

I couldn't tell how serious she was being, at all.

"If you can't bring yourself to accept my kindness, I wouldn't mind if you just accepted my body. Of course, me being a corpse, I doubt you'd be able to show it on TV. That's fine, right? The anime's basically over at this point."

"What did you talk about with whom in the past half-day to turn into your current character?"

Such a blasé character, too... Clawing at my teenage heartstrings like that...

Even if I couldn't accept anything of hers, I might at least answer her and explain what happened—but as far as nonsensical experiences went, nothing could outdo the one I'd just gone through.

No matter how cogent my explanation, the listener would think I'd gone crazy: a warrior in a full set of armor appearing after I met up with someone in an abandoned building; countless shafts of flame shooting up from below; getting trapped in a fiery cage; and the armored warrior then making a leisurely exit?

I was only able to tell Ononoki without worrying because she was an expert and an aberrational phenomenon herself, a familiar.

"Hmm. I don't understand at all. I think you've gone crazy, monstieur."

"Hey..."

"Don't worry, I'm kidding. You can laugh, you know. I can't completely deny that it doesn't make sense, though. Hm, an armored warrior?" As if to make absolutely sure, Ononoki said, "And it automatically rebuilds itself even if it gets scattered to pieces and can use an energy drain?"

"Yeah."

Hearing its abilities shortened down to a list of bullet points made it sound suspicious even to me, who'd not only witnessed the thing but been attacked by it. Still, being too strange to be real wasn't grounds to deny its existence in this case.

Aberrations are aberrant by nature.

I hadn't told Ononoki everything, though. Not that I was trying to hide anything from someone who'd saved my life—in fact, supplying her with the whole truth was the smart thing to do.

Why not fully rely on this shikigami, who surely knew far more about the subject than I did? Any weird sense of pride or vanity on my part would only get in the way.

Yet I couldn't disclose it all to her, couldn't but hesitate when it came to passing off something that I still hadn't fully processed myself. I hadn't—which isn't to say I couldn't tell her because it *made no sense whatsoever*. Rather, I couldn't tell Ononoki because she *just might make sense* of it.

The armored warrior's parting words.

The unthinkable, un-Japanese syllables—Kissshot.

The name that even I no longer called her—he used it.

The enchanted blade, Kokorowatari...

"..."

Ononoki gazed down at me, silent.

You couldn't call her tall. If anything, with her tween-girl design, she's short, but even then, her eyes were above mine as I hunched over, close to the ground. For some reason I found it a pretty significant strain on my psyche to be looked down on by the expressionless, emotionless girl.

I'd done nothing wrong, but I almost felt like apologizing.

"I'd say it's a bad thing to keep secrets from your savior, wouldn't you?"

"No... It's just..."

How was she so sensitive to my emotions when she had none?

Savior, though?

I wondered again if I should tell her, but still had my misgivings.

Maybe it was because telling her would feel like lying to her.

I mean—*there's no way it could be true.*

If that armored warrior's identity was who I thought it was, the exact existence I already knew about—but there was no way that could be true.

He—couldn't possibly exist in this world.

The thought, the line of reasoning had to be wrong—so I couldn't give voice to it carelessly. It had to be a mistake on my part.

If I was going to, I at least needed to check with Shinobu first—so I tried to distract Ononoki by changing the subject.

Actually, I guess it was more like moving our conversation along than changing its subject.

"Do you have any ideas, Ononoki? About this armored warrior—does it have anything to do with your current task?"

I did feel like I was late to asking this question—how could I not? Thanks to her task, she'd gotten me out of my tight spot.

From what I'd heard so far, though, she didn't seem to be chasing an aberrational phenomenon that dangerous all on her own...

"Well, true," Ononoki nodded.

Expressionless.

"Yes—you're right. While it's within the range of my official duties, according to what you're saying it's an almost entirely different phenomenon from my fieldwork target."

"?"

"Remember what I just told you? I wasn't lying when I said it didn't make sense to me. It seems to have grown far more ferocious than when I was looking for it. What could have happened over the course of these few days?"

It wasn't even an armored warrior when I was after it—Ononoki remarked, tilting her head this time, but her expressionlessness made it seem like she didn't find it all that strange.

Then again, she herself had undergone quite a change in character over the course of just half a day. It didn't seem that strange for an aberrational phenomenon she was after to change, too—but still.

Yeah, that wasn't it.

That armored warrior had to be special—not even a special case, but a special exception. Take how strong it had gotten in the mere minutes that we fought. The armor was nothing more than a heavy, dull object at first but roared with laughter by the time it left.

Its energy drain...

Then—it grew strong enough to confuse Ononoki thanks to no one but me and Kanbaru...

How could I not feel responsible in that case—it really made me the responsible party here. But...

"Hey, Ononoki?"

"What is it, monstieur?"

I replied without giving any pushback to the ridiculous nickname she'd managed to establish for me. "Do you think we could call this one off?"

"..."

"Er, wait, no—I'm fine with it. I don't mind, but...her," I said, pointing at Kanbaru's form lying on the ground.

I guess it's true that top-class athletes know how to rest for real when they need to? It felt really off to be concerned for her when she was happily (just look at that smug face) snoring away.

"It's okay if Kanbaru leaves, right?"

Ononoki stayed quiet for a moment, then asked, "What's that mean?" Her flat tone made her sound angry, but she didn't possess that emotion—she was asking because she simply didn't understand. "Monstieur, are you going to renege on your promise to Miss Gaen?"

"Renege?"

"You leaned on Miss Gaen and promised in return that you'd introduce this girl to her. Even if it was something you absolutely had to do to save Mayoi Hachikuji and you had no choice, a promise is still a promise—you've really got some guts, monstieur. Trying to break a promise with Miss Gaen? You're going to make me fall for you."

"That's...not what I'm trying to do."

I would be, in effect—but honestly, hadn't I already lived up to my promise? I thought I had.

"You've really got some abs on you."

"Don't touch on the subject of my abs."

"Oh, I'd love to touch them."

"Stop showing such unusual interest in my muscles."

"I'm a corpse, you know. My interest in flesh is almost instinctual—your reason?"

"Hm?"

"Your reason for trying to break your promise with Miss Gaen."

"I'm not unwilling to introduce Kanbaru to her, even now. But that's not all the promise was, right? She was trying to get Kanbaru to help her with a job."

That was the full picture of the promise I made with Miss Gaen—with Izuko Gaen, head boss of the experts on the supernatural and senior to Mèmè Oshino, Deishu Kaiki, and Yozuru Kagenui.

In return for leaning on the wisdom of a woman who boasted that she knew everything, I'd bring Kanbaru with me to follow up on Ononoki's job, which I'd interrupted regardless of the circumstances.

Miss Gaen had said—she needed Kanbaru's left hand, her left arm.

By no means had she asked me to introduce her to Kanbaru out of some desire to be reunited at long last with her niece.

I was the one who'd leaned on Miss Gaen's wisdom, of course, and Kanbaru had nothing to do with it. Hence, I'd made the promise on the condition that I'd only do it if Kanbaru agreed—but I'd messed up from the start.

I knew full well that Kanbaru would never turn down a request from me—and as a result, I'd exposed her to unthinkable danger.

I'd gotten her, a complete bystander, involved.

As her senior, I ought to have declined on her behalf.

"Yes. It's as if Miss Gaen tricked you there, monsieur. She told you it's a simple task anyone could do, didn't she?"

"No, not like she was recruiting someone for a little gig."

"A simple job that even you could do."

"Can it."

"Still, and I have no duty to cover for Miss Gaen, I doubt she expected an entire building to end up burning down right then."

No duty to cover for her... Why exactly was Ononoki acting as an extension of Miss Gaen, then? This was Izuko Gaen, the self-described woman who knows everything—how could anyone be certain that she hadn't predicted it? Or was I being too paranoid?

"As someone involved in this case from the start, monstieur, the fire seems particularly unusual—you're even making it sound like it saved you."

"..."

That did seem true.

Sure, we nearly ended up burning to death, but if a pillar of flame hadn't erupted from below when the armored warrior had me by the neck—wouldn't the life have been choked out of me right then and there?

It managed to take my voice.

But it might've taken a lot more.

What did it say again—the tiger's tail?

"Well, I guess it doesn't explain anything," Ononoki retracted her point. "After all, your junior did get killed."

"She's not dead."

"Um, her condition took a sudden turn. It looks like she's dead?"

"What?!"

I checked Kanbaru's breathing and pulse in a panic. I even opened her eyelids to check her pupils.

She was just as alive as ever.

"Whoopsie, I lied. Wow, you really fell for that one."

"Don't make me kick your ass."

I grabbed my tween-girl savior's head with both hands. A bystander might have thought I was getting ready to kiss her, but I wanted to straight-up headbutt her.

"To be fair, monstieur, whenever you and I chat, someone usually ends up dead nearby."

"Stop inventing creepy rules that are incredibly close to the truth."

"I understand how you feel. But I think you ought to give up. I can't recommend it," Ononoki suddenly returned to the matter at hand even though I was still gripping her head. "I'm warning you as a friend."

"I don't recall us ever becoming friends..."

"I've thought of you as a friend for a long time now."

"…"

In the right time, the right place, and from the right person, I'd be happy to hear those words…but I wasn't so sure this was it.

Well, fine, it did make me glad. I can't deny that it cast a glaring light on the small size of my circle of friends.

"I'm of course grateful to Miss Gaen, and I'd like to pay her back in any way I can, but like you've said, Ononoki, the conditions have changed—this isn't a safe job anymore. If she weren't Kanbaru, she'd be dead a few times over by now."

"And now she's died yet another time."

"That joke didn't land the first time, so stop playing off of it."

"Consider the fact that a corpse is telling it."

"That makes it even less funny."

"It's far too late to turn back now," Ononoki said, her voice composed.

Nothing was harder to get out of her than coherence. Otherwise, she wouldn't have saved us for no logical reason like some superhero.

"It's too late, monsieur. Don't get me wrong, it's up to you whether you want to break your promise to Miss Gaen. You have the freedom to ruin the rest of your life that way."

"What… Breaking a promise to her is tantamount to ruining my entire life?" To be honest, I wasn't prepared for that—I just wanted to get Kanbaru back home safely. "I-I was planning on working hard to make up for her absence, but that wouldn't do?"

"How incredibly conceited of you. How vein-poppingly vain. Do you really think you could take the place of Miss Gaen's niece?"

"That's how strong her bloodline is?"

"Even if you could—it wouldn't accomplish your goal."

"My goal?"

"You want to protect your junior now that you've gotten her wrapped up in your mess. I understand, I once felt the same way myself."

"Don't say things just because they sound cool."

You don't have any juniors.

Stop drawing the drama vs. comedy borderline within the same set of quotation marks.

"I will admit," Ononoki said, "that you make the situation sound worse than Miss Gaen's rundown of it—but why can't you see that having the girl go home after all of this'd do nothing to protect her?"

"Hm? Wait, what do you mean by that?"

"Merely seeing an aberration can get you afflicted—merely meeting one can get you cursed. Yet you say the girl touched the armored warrior."

"..."

More than touched... She punched it.

Even if she couldn't pull it off, she fearlessly tried to give it a double-leg takedown too... If all aberrations are indeed divine in a way, you'd be lucky to get off with nothing more than a curse.

Right.

Suruga Kanbaru—*was already involved.*

Not due to any promise of mine to Miss Gaen. You could call it a promise with the world—a contract that can't be broken, whose terms are non-negotiable.

"Please kneel, monstieur."

"Hm?"

"Kneel. Hurry up."

"..."

"At once. Expeditiously."

How might I explain this to you?

I had no reason to obey any sudden command, unless it was a rare one like a tween girl demanding that I kneel, but this was precisely such an instance...so I took my hands off of Ononoki's head and kneeled as she directed.

Both shins to the ground, my hands atop my thighs.

"Wait just a second. It won't be long," Ononoki said. Raising one leg, she began taking off her boot and tights. Why was she baring her foot now? I was about to find out.

Because she took her foot, fresh out of her boot, and stepped on my face.

At a perpendicular angle.

She grinded it into my cheek.

"Um, Ononoki?"

"You'd damn well better not think you can turn back now," she said, but not in a violent tone. In the same wooden voice as always: "Whether it's this or what happened with Mayoi Hachikuji—what you lack is resolve. I bet you think that you could start your life over from the beginning whenever you feel like it."

" . . . "

"You think it's never too late to start anything, don't you? Even if you fail or slip up, you think you can always come back from it, don't you? Even if you mess up, you think you can always make up for it, don't you?"

" . . . "

Grind, grind.

Ononoki shoved her heel into my face as I kneeled, her knee at a deft angle as she daintily held the edge of her skirt between her fingers.

She was stepping on the same spot that Kanbaru had kneed earlier... Was my cheek a rest area for girls' legs or something?

It was strange. Having a bare foot step on my face felt nothing at all like having the back of my head stepped on... I reflexively closed my eyes, but when I forced them open, I was so close to seeing up Ononoki's skirt—in between her big toe and second toe.

She was standing on one leg, proof that this warrior-girl's sheer strength was nothing to make light of.

"Everything evens out by the time you reach the end of your life—is that what you think? Hah. 'Course it does. Once you die, you're left with nothing. Zero."

As wooden as ever—but her tone didn't suggest a lack of thoughts or ideas behind her words. Something that I said must have poked at a tender spot somewhere in her heart.

If dolls had hearts.

"Umm, what were we talking about again?" she asked.

"Beats me..."

"Was it about you getting excited that my feet are all sweaty from wearing boots in the summer?"

"Could you not be so direct? Let's keep it dreamy."

"Don't worry. I'm a corpse, so my feet can't get sweaty."

"Oh…"

"You sound so disappointed… Come on, it hurts to see you look that way. Okay, so as far as what you should be doing next—"

"Hey! Don't just move on like it's a given that I'm disappointed!"

"Let's move on to another time."

"No! Take it easy, whether they're subjects or time!"

"Learn to keep up with me. I can't slow down to your pace if you're going to be such a sloth."

Apparently satisfied, Ononoki took her foot off my face… I'd like to think I showed you just how big of a man I am by not showing any signs of resistance the entire time.

I did have an excellent reason not to: if she'd used her foot there to activate her Unlimited Rulebook, she could've vaporized my head.

"I personally think you showed how deep your sins run, not how big of a man you are. So, monstieur, if you really do care about this girl, that's all the more reason for you to take her to Miss Gaen and not do something as irresponsible as send her home. From there, you could have Miss Gaen keep her safe."

"Have Miss Gaen…"

"That's right. You could keep your promise and her safe," Ononoki restated in a half-clever manner. Despite the forcedness and artificiality, the message itself was revelatory.

She was right.

Sending Kanbaru home might be the far more irresponsible thing to do. I'd gotten her wrapped up in what you could call my own selfish circumstances, and now I wanted to shutter up and throw her back to her home just because things hadn't gone exactly as I'd planned. How could I be so sure that was the right thing to do?

Kanbaru had crossed paths with it.

Though a total bystander—she'd crossed paths with that armored warrior and gotten herself involved in whatever phenomenon it was. In some ways, even more than me.

In which case sending her home, to be on her own, might be far more dangerous as Ononoki said—if we were talking about responsibility, wasn't working alongside Kanbaru until the end the responsible thing to do?

Well, the best move might've been to ditch this job whose details I didn't even know and go home with Kanbaru, but I, a student studying for college exams, couldn't afford my freedom to break my promise with Miss Gaen and ruin the rest of my life.

Aside from that, I wanted to keep my promises.

Promises should be kept.

…No, I'll be honest with you.

Of course I didn't want to get Kanbaru involved with that dangerous armored warrior—but that isn't to say that I didn't want to get involved with it.

If anything.

I had to get involved with it.

That thing—had entrusted me with a message.

A message to "my master."

So at the very least, I couldn't abandon my role until I'd delivered it. If the armored warrior was who I thought it was—as impossible as that seemed, if there was so much as the slightest possibility of it being true.

I couldn't throw it away.

I couldn't go home—not until I knew.

"…"

"It seems you've reached a conclusion."

My goodness, having friends can be such a hassle, muttered Ononoki, putting her tights and boot back on. Frankly, even if her feet didn't get sweaty, wearing boots in the summer did sound uncomfortable, but I wasn't dispensing any unsolicited advice about other people's life choices.

Though I guess they'd be un-life choices in Ononoki's case.

…What kind of girl had she been when she was still alive?

According to what I'd heard, she'd acquired her current demeanor and temperament after being born as an aberration…

Still, whether she was a familiar or just an animated object, if she was capable of doing this much on her own, why hadn't her master, the diviner Yozuru Kagenui, given her just one more feature, the ability to make facial expressions? It seemed strange.

Personally, I just wanted to see Ononoki smile...

"I'm going to try to chase down this armored warrior you say you saw—I doubt I'll be able to find it, given the way it disappeared, but my job is to tread forth on fools' errands."

"..."

"My job is to tread forth on fools' errands and your face."

"Don't bother correcting yourself, or making it your job to step on my face."

"Carry this niece of yours in your arms like you're a newlywed couple, all the way to Miss Gaen. Then explain what's going on to her."

"You're making it sound like Kanbaru's my niece..."

Not to mention, few people would seem more out of place on the receiving end of a bridal carry than Kanbaru... Just let me carry her on my back like before.

"*My Neighbor Totoro* had a niece too—"

"If you're talking about Mei, her name meant *May* rather than *niece*."

"Let me finish my jokes before quipping off of them. Anyway, I'm sure that if you give a wholehearted and sincere explanation to Miss Gaen, she wouldn't try to get you to help her with a dangerous job. My hunch is that you'll satisfy her expectations just by bringing her info about this armored warrior."

"..."

"Whatever the case, it's about time for us to part ways—you can stew in your emotions by these fire-ravaged remains, but the fire department and police will be showing up soon. If you want to avoid having any groundless suspicions placed on you, you ought to beat it."

Part of being an expert is knowing when to retreat—Ononoki said as she finished putting her boot back on. She seemed to have worn it slowly on purpose so that we could talk for as long as possible.

She was expressionless the whole time.

...With both of my hands, I reached out towards Ononoki's face once more—not out of anger, nor seeking revenge for having my cheek trampled—but to somehow see her smile.

I was just plotting to see if forcing her facial muscles into the right positions could create something resembling a smile even on Ononoki's expressionless face.

It was the least I could do to pay back this friend, who'd saved both my life and Kanbaru's, and moreover given me valuable advice when I felt so faint of heart.

"Fwuh-fwye. Muhhn-suhhhr."

"..."

Creepy.

007

Fighting fires with dynamite reminded me that the Nobel Prize, established based on the will of the inventor of none other than the explosive material, seems to be awarded in the six fields of physics, chemistry, physiology or medicine, literature, peace, and economics, but not in math for some reason. It would seem like a natural fit among that lineup, but one story says that Nobel once had a rival in love who was a mathematician, which is why no prize in math was established—just an urban legend, of course, whose authenticity can't be verified, but the idea that love affairs can influence even something with global recognition like the Nobel Prize does make you think a bit. I don't know if I'm qualified to say this, as someone who's only ever experienced teenage love, but are those the kinds of feelings you end up carrying around with you beyond the grave? Do feelings of love for another—really never disappear, no matter how many years pass? Instead of turning them into memories or funny stories, or forgetting or idealizing them—do we let them linger on forever and ever in our hearts and minds, across world history?

When you think about it, anecdotes about great historical figures do tend to involve romance at one point or another. Heroes are known for their conquests, including in love—perhaps not a single tale could be told apart from that kind of thing, in reality.

Putting that aside, after having my way for a while with Ononoki, playing with her cheeks as I saw fit, she at last put on a serious (expressionless) face. "Lehh ahh lehh maah (Lay off, layman)," she said, angrily swatting me away like a pest, and stormed off—to get back to work.

To go after the armored warrior, probably.

You couldn't get the first idea which way it headed or where it was going based on my intel, but perhaps having the tools needed to make that judgment was what made her a pro.

I wasn't certain what she meant by "lay off, layman" (was my handling of her cheeks inexpert, or was I an amateur when it came to aberrations?), but either way, I had to heed her warning. Even if I wasn't to blame for the fire at the abandoned cram school, I'd be tied up all night if I ended up getting interrogated as an involved party. They'd probably call my family too.

Please, I didn't want them knowing. My parents or my sisters.

I'd be burned alive. Sentenced to immolation.

In addition to this self-serving reason, to interpret Ononoki's warning broadly, I myself could spell trouble if I did get taken in (to the fire station? the police station?)—Kanbaru wasn't the only one who'd encountered the mysterious armored warrior, I had too.

Without any solid plan in mind, I piggybacked Kanbaru and started in the opposite direction from Ononoki—a course of action based on the shallow assumption that if she was following after him, we could avoid another encounter by traveling in the opposite direction.

Lacking my vampiric powers, I couldn't move at a fast pace with Kanbaru on my back. She was a girl but also a muscular athlete. I wanted to travel along the safest possible route until we reached our meeting spot with Miss Gaen.

I'd originally planned to meet Kanbaru at the abandoned cram school, explain the situation to her, and head on to this meeting spot together. In a circuitous or even convoluted way, my plan was back on track—but piggybacking someone your age is different from carrying a little sister or a tween girl.

It makes you strangely tense.

I'd have started to worry if she was out for too long, but once I walked for a good bit and the ruins were fully out of sight, my junior,

Suruga Kanbaru, seemed to regain consciousness.

"Mmmmgh..."

"Oh. Up now?"

"Mmmmgh, no, senpai, I can't... That's too freaky for me..."

"Wake up! What's that supposed to mean? How extreme of a personality do I have in your dreams?!"

What kind of act could possibly make Suruga Kanbaru hesitate?

Her head jerked up with an "Ah!" at my quip, and she glanced all around her—she was having trouble taking in the situation.

Since it was the backdraft that had knocked her out, it made no sense for her now to be on my back as we escaped through town—in fact, they say you forget what happened to you right before you went unconscious, so maybe she was surprised she wasn't in the middle of her fight with the armored warrior. That made our close contact even worse... She might take me out with a rear naked choke.

Rear naked choke.

What a fitting technique name for Kanbaru.

"Oh—my dear senior! You're okay!"

But there was no need for me to worry. The first words to come out of Kanbaru's mouth (aside from the inappropriate things she said in her sleep) expressed concern for my wellbeing—what a shining example of a junior.

"Wh-What about that thing?! What happened to it?! That guy with the helmet with the character for 'love' on it?!"

"Um, it's not like we were fighting Kanetsugu Naoe."

Her memories were cloudy after all.

Still, they'd surely come back to her if that was as bad as it got—I stopped for a moment to let the now-conscious Kanbaru off my back.

She didn't get off.

In fact, she started clinging to me.

I'd let go of her legs, but she wrapped them around me and stuck to me like she really was going to give me a rear naked choke, refusing to get off of me. I was a eucalyptus tree, and she was a koala.

"What're you trying to do?"

"I don't know what's going on, but my instincts are telling me that

I shouldn't let this opportunity get away."

"Some kind of instinct..."

Precisely what was it saying?

It needed to learn when to shut up.

"I don't think I can walk yet. You're gonna carry me on your back for now, we've decided," she informed me of their consensus.

Now her instincts were telling me things too?

Someone who couldn't walk had my torso in a leg scissors and wouldn't let go? Her legs had enough strength to split my body in two.

Plus, one of her arms was an aberration.

Don't act so spoiled, get down, walk on your own—rather than any of these things, what I said was, "Oh, fine. Just a little more, though. Don't expect me to baby you like this next time," doing my best to put on senior-like airs. Even I could tell how nervous and hollow I sounded... The airs I had put on were pretty hot ones.

"Whoa, I'm so close to the back of your head... I never knew life could get this good."

"Could you please not get excited over the back of my head?"

"Your hair whorl is so cool."

"Don't get worked up over parts of me that I don't even know about, please."

"You know, compared to when we first met, both you and I have grown our hair out."

"Hm? Well, yeah."

We were as friendly as could be now, to the point that I was carrying her on my back through the street at night, but come to think of it, we'd only started interacting a few months ago—Kanbaru still kept her hair short then, and mine wasn't as long around the back then either.

"I'd really like to get my hair all in yours. Once we both have hair that's a little longer, I'd like our locks to get joined together. Then maybe we could find a good bridge?"

"That's something you do with padlocks, not locks of hair."

Her level of perversion had gotten so extreme that it wasn't even smut anymore.

Joining our locks together would just be painful.

"You think?" she asked. "But pain is a very important factor."

"If it's pain you want, you know I could just fall on my back right now."

"No! Not right now. I might be okay physically, but mentally, I feel so fatigued—I kind of don't feel good."

"You don't feel good…"

I couldn't stop a shiver from going down my spine if she was this peppy even when she wasn't feeling good—but since she said she was unwell, I had to respect that. I asked her for details.

"It kind of reminds me of Kita-Shirahebi Shrine," she said.

Kita-Shirahebi Shrine—a forgotten shrine in our town located at the peak of a small mountain. It was in such rundown shape that you could describe it as a ruin. Kanbaru and I had visited it together, in June, I think.

Right.

Her condition was poor then—the strength had been sapped out of her, as if she'd been poisoned by the air surrounding the shrine. The same as then…

Hm.

What was the exact situation and reason that she felt unwell back then? My mind was a bit cloudy too if I couldn't recall why on the spot.

More than anything, though, I wanted to get as far away as possible from the abandoned cram school, and meet with Miss Gaen as soon as possible. This desire bordered on mild panic, so normally I'd be trying to temper it.

"It really takes me back… You and I kissed for the very first time under that shrine's trees, senpai."

"Okay, you're the one who's forgetting things."

"Huh? Oh, was it the second time? Or the third time?"

"You're assuming there was a first time. Also, when we went there together, we found hacked-up snakes pinned to those trees, all right?"

I remembered now.

That's right, I went there with Kanbaru on a job for the expert Mèmè Oshino, regarding an aberrational phenomenon that had yet to turn into a full-blown aberration. We'd visited the shrine to cleanse the grounds of a place where "bad things" gathered.

Kanbaru felt ill then because of the effect these bad things had on her—but thanks to Shinobu's protection, I was able to complete the job Oshino had given me without any serious problems.

…I'd been carrying out a request from him then, and now I was carrying out a request from his senior, Miss Izuko Gaen. Though the circumstances themselves only looked similar on a surface level, maybe Kanbaru and I were destined as a pair to do these kinds of things.

But if that was true, I couldn't turn a blind eye to Kanbaru comparing her poor condition to how she felt back then. She wouldn't tell such a lie just to have me piggyback her a little longer, would she?

"That's right, that's right. That was when I first met Sengoku—yes, it was Sengoku whom I first kissed under those trees, with tons of hacked-up snakes pinned to them."

"Your memories aren't just clouded if you're gonna go that far. The word would be altered."

"Which is why some people call me…the conductor of memories."

"What conductor of memories? You're saying you can make your memories play out however you like with the wave of a baton?" The probability that she was just lying to have me piggyback her for a little longer was spiking.

"But if I said it, they might add a kiss scene between me and Sengoku as an illustration once this part finally gets an anime adaptation."

"They're not making one of the final season. Or actually, of you. Of any stories involving you. Just for reference, Kanbaru. I don't really get it, but do you like them? Piggyback rides, I mean?"

"Well, I had an image to uphold as the star of the basketball team. It makes me happy to have a senior openly spoil me like this. I don't think I've ridden on anyone's back since my senior Senjogahara's in middle school."

"…"

I could only imagine how much work Senjogahara must have once put in.

What kind of side stories existed between the Valhalla Duo during their middle school years? In any case, as cool and stately as she could be, Kanbaru was surprisingly good at being spoiled.

On the other hand, I was pretty awful at it.

"Hm," Kanbaru said, "I've started to remember quite a bit as the conductor of memories—did you say we were on the way to meet someone you wanted to introduce me to?"

"Oh... Yeah, that's what we're doing. I need to apologize to you about that, though."

Right.

I'd forgotten to apologize because of how idiotic Kanbaru was being.

Whether it was the armored warrior or the fire, it was clear that my thoughtless invitation had put her life in serious danger.

"Heh. No need to apologize. In fact, I'd rather you didn't. It'd be a blot on my name if I ever allowed you to bow your head to me, dear senior."

"I feel like it's a way bigger blot on your name to have me carrying you on my back... So big that it'd look like a puddle. But no, listen, you might want to go home already, but it might be dangerous if you did. I want you to tag alongside me until we know what's going on at least."

"If you also want me to sleep alongside you, I wouldn't turn you down."

"Tag, not sleep."

"Well, that's not to say that some tag-team action couldn't be arranged for."

"No, let's say exactly that. What are you, one of those heroines-in-heat all over the place in YA novels about twenty years ago?"

"Heroine-in-heat... Talk about a new turn of phrase that gets the heart pounding."

"Please, let's not."

"Actually, it's literary fiction that's full of heroines-in-heat."

"Now isn't the time for satire."

I thought—having heard her lampoonery, I thought I should at least present her with the info I had at the moment—and tell her everything I could just as I'd done with Ononoki.

But I wanted to meet with Miss Gaen as soon as possible—not to mention an even more basic problem, namely that I didn't understand our current situation. I had as close to zero confidence as imaginable when it came to explaining the situation to Kanbaru.

I might as well have known nothing.

I should've seen this coming and asked Miss Gaen about the specifics of the job—the circumstances may not have permitted it, but now it felt like I was walking through a maze blindfolded.

"I promise I'll make it up to you, so please," I begged, "put up with it for this one night."

"This one night? Don't say such depressing things. I'm waiting for you to invite me over each and every night."

"In that case, you could also wait for me during the day..."

"You know there's only one thing I'll ever say to your orders." Kanbaru's voice dropped and she whispered, "Bon appétit ♪"

"Shut up! But that was kinda cute?!"

What the hell did I order?!

If she was taking any, my order was for her to stop saying all these things that made me want to just leave her there and walk off. I wasn't supposed to be climbing a mountain to ditch a granny like in feudal times.

"I do at least want to ask you where we're heading, though. Haven't we gone a little far if we're just trying to escape the fire? Don't we need to call the authorities?"

A rather mature suggestion, coming from someone who needed to have the authorities called on her. "It's fine. The fire is already out, and there weren't any victims, either... We're heading toward that meeting spot I mentioned. Um...maybe you know the place?" Back at the old cram school, there must be a commotion by now—actually, no, it was away from any homes, in an obscure area, and had burned down in the blink of an eye. Maybe nobody had contacted the authorities... "It's called Rohaku Park."

"Rohaku Park?"

"Or maybe it's Namishiro Park."

I still didn't know the correct reading—but in any case, it was one of the larger parks in town. I'd met Mayoi Hachikuji for the first time there, and come to think of it, it was also where Hitagi Senjogahara had told me that she had feelings for me.

In that sense, I didn't really want to make it a place to meet and talk about work, but I had no choice. Miss Gaen had chosen the spot. Speaking of her, since she knew everything, did she also know the correct reading?

"Rohaku Park... Namishiro Park... Hm. Does it have a basketball court?"

"No, I'm pretty sure it doesn't."

"Then I don't know it."

"Is that really your standard for parks? Oh, but maybe you've just forgotten? This neighborhood should have been Senjogahara's turf back in middle school."

Turf might not be the right term, but that's how she'd described it—in any case, it seemed like there might be a side story from the Valhalla Duo days when the two played in the park.

I'm ignorant on the subject of whether middle school girls play in parks, but Karen Araragi, my little sister, does at least. She gets on the swings and builds up enough speed to send her shoes flying far, far away.

...I'm concerned about my little sister's future.

"Hmm, then maybe I'll remember once I see it. Senjogahara-senpai's old home—heheh."

Kanbaru let out a soft chuckle behind me.

Depending on how you interpreted this, she was feeling warm and fuzzy, having recalled a time when she was closer to Senjogahara than she was now. I didn't know much about Senjogahara's old home, and wanted to learn more.

"She must have invited you over," I said.

"Yeah. She did. To a cozy li'l mansion."

"..."

God, what a rude junior.

Then again, the Japanese estate Kanbaru lived in went beyond being a mansion. Maybe her upbringing solidified her personality into what it was now.

"No, my senior. I lived a pretty impoverished life as a young child.

My parents eloped, after all. We were in real-deal poverty."

"That doesn't land as hard when you sound so cheerful about it…"

What a life of peaks and valleys.

I assumed this also lay at the root of Suruga Kanbaru's personality—her parents' elopement.

The Kanbarus' only son married the Gaens' eldest daughter without their families' blessing—was that how the story went? And this daughter was Miss Gaen's older sister…

Suruga Kanbaru's parents then died in a traffic accident, leaving her all on her own, which is where the Kanbarus took her in.

"Whatever the case, Araragi-senpai, I'm all set. We're heading to that park now, right? And this person you want me to meet is there?"

"Well, yeah."

To be honest, at this point, I didn't really want Kanbaru to meet her—considering the rift between the Kanbaru and Gaen families, and given our current situation.

I, personally, did want to meet up with Miss Gaen—and even more with Shinobu. We'd constantly been together for a while, so I felt uneasy being cut off from her. Take even the abandoned cram school just now, if Shinobu had been there—no, it was probably better that she wasn't… Either way, I had to see Miss Gaen to restore my link with Shinobu.

"But in that case," Kanbaru said. "Aren't we going in the total opposite direction?"

008

The opposite direction.

The words stopped me in my tracks—Kanbaru might not have known the park's name, but as we discussed earlier, she at least had some familiarity with the area. Given that they went to the same middle school, Kanbaru's home was geographically close to it, anyway.

That must have been why she could tell if we were going in the right direction—had I parted ways with her at the abandoned cram school, now the burned-out ruins, I probably wouldn't have noticed until later. Maybe not until dawn, in the worst case.

The fact that I was lost—

"Huh...what? But..."

—puzzled me.

True, my one and only concern at first was getting away from the scene of the fire. I wasn't particularly trying to head toward the park— but I thought I'd course-corrected once we were far enough away.

Straying a bit was to be expected, but...it'd been a while since I corrected course.

Speaking of turfs, the area around the park certainly wasn't mine, nor was it a place I frequented. Still, it stood out in my memories—and not only did it have a strong link to my memories, my fate was connected to it.

Was it really okay for Koyomi Araragi to get lost on his way there?

"Maybe you had a hard time navigating there on foot because you're always going around on your bike? I was seriously starting to wonder where you were trying to take me."

"Oh…"

"Hold on a second, I thought, there aren't any popular date spots in that direction."

"I have zero reason to take you to a popular date spot."

Well, if she was going to say I got lost because I always rode a bike, I didn't have a counterargument—of the two bikes I owned, one was destroyed by Kanbaru in May, and the other I'd lost just a few days ago. I'd be living a pedestrian life for some time, so this wouldn't do.

"I guess we'll turn around and figure out the best route… Sorry, Kanbaru. I feel bad for making us late."

"Oh, it's nothing serious. I'll leave it up to you. Do as you see fit."

"…"

I was glad that she was being generous, but she sounded so arrogant when she was trying to be humble. I wondered how she spoke to her teachers.

She acted like she expected others to do things for her—or maybe I should say to carry her through life, given her current perch.

In any case, as a senior who'd been entrusted with the reins, I'd do everything I could to turn around, change course, clear my name, and regain my honor.

My cell phone didn't have any map or navigational features (maybe it did, but I didn't know how to use them), so we'd march along checking whatever road signs and street maps we found. I may have wasted some time by failing to do so until now, but we wouldn't get lost again, we'd hurry and make up for it, I thought—but.

No.

"Hm?"

Ononoki's words came to mind—those cutting words.

You think you can always make up for it, don't you?

Even if I mess up.

An hour later… Naturally, an hour spent chatting about all kinds of stupid things with Kanbaru—a conversation I have no choice but to edit out whole...

I found myself in a completely unfamiliar location—not that we'd wandered into a jungle or a wasteland, it still had to be the town we lived in, but you could call it bizarre.

You could call it inexplicable—the degree to which we were lost.

"Do you have a bad sense of direction?" asked Kanbaru. "Or are you taking me on the scenic route because you want to spend as much time with me as possible?"

"I'd never go about it in that inconvenient of a way..."

My stamina wouldn't last.

I didn't think I could keep walking around like this for much longer. I did have an entire person on my back—it was past midnight at this point, too.

The date had changed.

August twenty-fourth.

Four days since the end of summer break. Was I ever going back to school? Of course, when I thought about the scolding from Senjogahara and Hanekawa that awaited me over my unexcused absences, I wasn't eager to go even if I could.

That said, it wasn't as if I could tell them what was up. I'd gotten Kanbaru mixed up in this already. How could I allow myself to add Senjogahara and Hanekawa to the mix?

Talking with Kanbaru was fun enough that the fact nearly slipped my mind, but we were knee-deep in a crisis—still, lost?

What was I doing? How could I so carelessly take the wrong streets in this emergency?

It was such an unbecoming mistake, idyllic in a way, and it aggravated me—but it was none other than Suruga Kanbaru who managed to calm me down.

"Now that you mention it, didn't you say something about maybe, or maybe not, or maybe getting more lost than not before? You know, with Hachikuji?"

"Hm? Oh."

I didn't recall ever saying *getting more lost than not*, but everything fell into place when I heard those words—they should have sooner.

Right. That's what it was.

This was the second time I was experiencing this phenomenon.

Three months ago.

In May, on Mother's Day, I, along with Mayoi Hachikuji and Hitagi Senjogahara—*got lost.*

The Lost Cow.

That was the name—of the aberration.

"*An aberration that makes people lose their way*—hm. But why would the Lost Cow show up now…"

No, hold on. Don't jump so quickly to conclusions—it made sense that I wanted a logical explanation for getting lost at this precise and extremely inconvenient moment, but there was a far more likely possibility. I'd simply lost track of where I was going because I felt shaken.

The Lost Cow was gone by now.

That day, Mèmè Oshino—resolved it for us.

The aberration that had been making people lose their way in this town for eleven years would never lead another on these streets astray—I should know that better than anyone.

I keenly felt it more than anyone.

So it couldn't be right—Kanbaru's point was nothing more than a irrelevant memory.

Still, I couldn't help but recall it.

The armored warrior's message as it howled with laughter in the fire.

Ye too, do not dally and make thy way home at once!

That's what it said.

No, strictly speaking, the "message" came later—which is why I hadn't paid attention to the preceding bit, assuming it was just a setup… but come to think of it, wasn't it odd?

Why would it warn me about my trip home, in that situation? Even if those flames were irregular and not caused by the warrior, why would someone who'd been choking me say that?

The thing wasn't some principal warning the student body that they represented their school while in public—if there was any hidden meaning to the statement, those words it pronounced.

If it had an opposite meaning.

"…"

Hm?

Wait, no… Wouldn't that be a pretty lame thing for the armored warrior to do?

It would contradict its dynamic image so far—its boldness as a phenomenon, if that's the right term. It revived itself despite shattering to pieces, withstood all our attacks, absorbed our energy, stole my voice—then turned to mist and disappeared.

Roaring with laughter.

It'd be a mean-spirited prank, not even bullying. Would something like that really do this to us? If that armored warrior was the opponent I thought it was—that went doubly so.

It didn't line up at all with my image of a heroic warrior.

Even if it was responsible for us being lost, what could its goal be? What good would it do to make Kanbaru and me lose our way—and not know where we were? Or did it have some sort of deeper plot in mind that the likes of me could never hope to fathom? Assuming the armor had a mind, of course—

"Kanbaru. I'm putting you down for a second."

"You're going to insult me?"

"On the ground," I said, making us both sound like idiots, as I got Kanbaru off my back at last—even she wasn't going to cling to me in resistance this time.

Maybe it was thanks to the *for a second*, promising her a next time, than Kanbaru understanding the gravity of the situation—but in any case, she stretched, jumped, and otherwise checked her physical condition now that she stood on solid ground with both feet. It seemed that being carried on my back involved a bit of work on her part as well.

It's not easy being good at being spoiled.

Meanwhile, I took out my cell phone.

It lacked both map apps and navigation features, so taking it out now was faint-hearted, an act of giving up early.

Giving up very early.

But whether you want to call me faint-hearted or lacking in self-reliance, my only choice seemed to be to call Miss Gaen.

She'd given me her phone number when we parted ways.

I'd also sought help in May when a snail led me astray, but it ended up being a pretty roundabout affair because I was trying to contact Oshino then, someone without any communication devices. This time, though, I was getting in touch with Miss Gaen, who walked around with five of them. The act of contacting her itself would be easy.

At the same time, I found myself in my troublesome situation precisely because I needed to pay her back for helping me. Contacting her was easy, but asking her for help wasn't. That's why I hadn't tried until now, but I needed to nip this situation in the bud.

Of course, it was already too late for Koyomi Araragi, if you believed Ononoki…

"What's this, my senior? Sending a goodnight text message to Senjogahara-senpai, are you? What a couple of fools in love you are."

"You're the only fool here. Hey, Kanbaru…" I began, but decided not to finish.

It was a small detail, but the armored warrior had said *make thy way home at once*, seeming to refer only to my home, not our homes—if it was causing us to stray, maybe its effect was limited to me.

In other words, if Kanbaru and I moved separately, at least she might be able to escape this strange situation that felt like being locked inside of being lost—the thought almost got me to encourage her to go ahead, but I couldn't see any way my junior would agree.

Her heart was so astonishingly loyal to me that she wouldn't even leave me behind in a burning building to save herself. I couldn't imagine her leaving my side to act on her own just because we got lost on the road.

Hmm.

Maybe I shouldn't say this, but loyalty taken too far doesn't seem that different from dependence… Senjogahara sometimes complained about my relationship with Kanbaru, and now I felt like I understood why.

The problem here, though, was that Suruga Kanbaru possessed a strength of character generally greater than mine or Senjogahara's.

"Hm? What's wrong, Araragi-senpai?"

"Oh, it's nothing... Could you be quiet for a second? I'm about to make a call."

"Fine with me. I'll do anything for you, no matter how unreasonable."

"Um, this is one of the few times I feel like I'm not making an unreasonable request..."

But to be fair, Kanbaru spent pretty much every waking moment talking, so perhaps asking her to shut up was a big deal.

"Phew..."

I calmed my breathing to refresh my mind, summoned up my courage, and selected Izuko Gaen's name from my phone's address book.

Just as I thought.

Before the phone could finish ringing a single time.

"Hey there, Koyomin—I'd been waiting, and I could barely wait anymore. I thought it was about time you called."

A voice.

From the other side—came a reply.

Brimming with boundless cheer, like it wasn't the middle of the night.

Nothing about the voice sounded serious, which made me think: *Yeah, I guess she'd be Kanbaru's aunt.*

009

Izuko Gaen.

The lady who knows everything.

Senior to Mèmè Oshino, Yozuru Kagenui, and Deishu Kaiki, as well as something like the big boss when it comes to aberrations—I'd heard of her existence here and there, but only met her for the first time a few days ago.

She was mature but not by any means old, wearing an outfit that made her seem younger than her real age. I never would have imagined her to be Oshino's senior. I suppose you could describe her as oddly or overly familiar; her chumminess was something she had in common with Kanbaru, a natural communicator.

At the same time, there was a clear line between her niece's sociable and engaging personality and her own. At the risk of being misunderstood, I'd say she wasn't the type I really wanted to befriend or get too involved with. In that sense, she definitely was a kind of senior figure to Oshino, Kagenui, and Kaiki...

I should've been celebrating my good fortune, having managed to contact the outside world with a cell phone amidst this new aberrational phenomenon—but I felt so strongly about her that part of me wished my phone had ended up being jammed and out of service in the middle of town.

While the location of our meeting had been decided, we hadn't set a specific hour—since I didn't know how long I'd need to talk (chat) with Kanbaru.

Miss Gaen shouldn't have been able to figure out when we'd arrive at the park, let alone whether I'd call her—but she seemed totally un-flapped when she picked up.

As if she'd been waiting, like she said.

"C'mon, Koyomin. Don't talk about me like I've got superpowers or something—I'm no big deal. Yotsugi gave me a progress report on the details, that's all. That, and I assumed you must have a phone with you."

" . . ."

"Seems like you've been through a lot—but I'm glad you're okay."

"Okay? I'm not sure if I could say that."

I somehow resisted the urge to complain—ranting at Miss Gaen wouldn't do me any good.

Ononoki was right, even she couldn't have predicted what happened back there... And how could I raise my voice at someone I was about to ask for advice?

As a matter of courtesy, of course, but also in terms of simple self-interest.

"You're okay," Miss Gaen said, her tone as assertive as ever. "People are okay so long as they're alive—and isn't it great? You're not dead. No, I'm being serious—if I'd let you get yourself killed, even I wouldn't be able to hold my head up to Mèmè with a smile on my face."

" . . ."

Something about her seemed so frivolous. Every little thing she said.

So she always smiled around him? Insincerely or something? Then again, her frivolity did make this easier for me...

"And? What's going on now? Go ahead, you can tell your friend Miss Gaen all about it."

"Well..."

"Is it a crab? A snail? A monkey? A snake? A cat?"

"Huh?"

I couldn't help but be disoriented at her attempt to anticipate what I was about to say—it felt like getting stabbed in the back right as I called to ask her for help.

A snail—a lost cow.

"Wh-What do you know?"

"I know everything."

As you know, she reminded me.

I went silent—I wouldn't have been able to hold the words back otherwise. Not complaints this time, but doubts.

What I'd started to doubt was Ononoki's claim that the current turn of events was far from what Miss Gaen could have predicted. Whatever report Ononoki might have given, how could Miss Gaen know that we were now lost—lost as though we'd been led astray on these streets by a lost cow—when she should be in a distant park?

But perhaps she could glean something even from my silence.

"Ahaha," she laughed. "C'mon, it's just a joke—what're you acting all serious for, Koyomin? It's all a trick to make myself seem more impressive. If I give five examples, one of them would have to be right. It's a dirty trick that adults pull."

"..."

"So, which is it? Wouldn't you please tell your friend Miss Gaen, she doesn't have the first clue—though my personal guess would be the snail."

She had it right after all.

Her explanation that one of her five examples had to be right did have some merit to it, but her afterthought ruined her own argument. Did she want to clear herself of any doubts, or only deepen them?

The simple answer would be that she was just toying around with me—but that's not to say it felt pleasant to be toyed around with.

"Oh, please. I just thought that if you were in a place to call for help, it must be the snail—it's called reasoning. So, what's the matter?"

"You're exactly right... Yes. Kanbaru and I are together—and we were heading toward the park to meet you, but we've spent over an hour and—"

"Hahaha," Miss Gaen laughed again.

Just like earlier, it felt like the gravity of my situation wasn't getting across at all.

"I was thinking of all the people it could be—but it looks like it's the smallest one of the bunch."

"...?"

Miss Gaen's inexplicable statement left me at a loss for words, but it did seem as though one of her points of concern had been addressed. Her already-clear voice grew even brighter.

"Koyomin," she said. "That to me is great news, if anything—and it just might be for you, too. Yes, how auspicious. I almost feel like getting a cake ready for you with candles and all."

"A cake..."

"That's a joke, don't worry about it. Anyway, hurry up. I'm starting to want to hear the details about this face-to-face. To be honest, I thought we might be in a little bit of trouble when I got that report from Yotsugi, but your intel is like a shining beam of hope."

"N-No, like I was saying, the issue is that we're having trouble hurrying up—I think we're going to be lost out here forever if we don't do something, which is why I was hoping to get some advice from you—"

"There's no need for me to give you advice. *That's nothing more than a little bit of meddling*—if you can't overcome a hassle like that on your own, then we've got a problem."

Her tone was neither cold nor harsh, but the words were a clear rejection—a clear rejection in a clear tone.

A problem? Sure, we had a problem. But it was she who dragged us into this situation.

"Oh, no, Koyomin. That's exactly why—you already know what it means to ask me for advice, don't you? You're in this predicament because you got yourself saved by me—the longer you want this endless cycle of assistance to continue, the worse of a light you paint yourself in. Find yourself a good distance from me. Fortunately, Koyomin, this isn't your first time getting lost. So why don't you follow Mèmè's principle and go and get saved on your own?"

Wait, no—Miss Gaen paused. Then continued insinuatingly:

"I guess you're not alone. You have your reliable junior there with you, don't you? Why not just rely on her?"

"J-Just rely on her?"

On Kanbaru?

When I'd already gotten her this involved?

This went beyond the armored warrior. I could look at everything that happened to me starting on the last day of summer break, and she still had nothing to do with any of it whatsoever. There wasn't a single reason for her to be lost on the street with me—and Miss Gaen wanted me to rely even more on Kanbaru, a complete bystander?

"Wh-Who exactly do you think Kanbaru is? Kanbaru is—"

"Suruga Kanbaru is the daughter of my sister," Miss Gaen replied cheerfully. "It'd be a waste to allow her talents to remain slumbering."

010

I'd actually gotten a call through, only for her to hang up on me—
I considered calling back, but there didn't seem to be much point in that.
I doubted she'd go so far as to ignore me, but she'd probably give me the
same answer—and she surely wouldn't give us any details about this job
that I'd apparently shined a beam of hope or whatever on.

I mean, of course I'd have preferred to discuss it face-to-face too...
Anyway, I shut my phone and turned to Kanbaru.

Her stretching, or possibly her warming up, had turned into some
yoga-like pose during the time I'd turned away from her. It left me
speechless. I never knew the human body could stretch to those kinds
of angles.

"Oh, finish your call?"

It seemed she hadn't listened to our conversation, out of politeness—
though it could also have been a lack of interest. When something didn't
interest Kanbaru, she really wasn't interested.

"That expression, too. I can tell you have a task for your slave."

"I don't own any slaves..."

"Then there's no need for my opinion? How encouraging."

"Wait, there is—"

Miss Gaen hadn't given me any advice.

However, if you interpreted her words favorably, Kanbaru held the key to escaping this crisis (or at least, this mysterious situation where we were lost). Even if I couldn't stop us from going in circles, Kanbaru could—well, true.

To repeat myself, it isn't as if Miss Gaen wanted me to introduce Kanbaru to her because she had a particular interest in meeting her niece after their many years apart. She'd gotten Kanbaru mixed up in exchange for helping us because her niece's arm was required to complete a job.

When Miss Gaen mentioned Kanbaru's arm, I'd taken her words at face value. In other words, she needed Kanbaru's left arm, or her monster's paw—but if you took it less literally, as a helping hand from Kanbaru, then relying on her to deal with an aberrational phenomenon made sense.

After all, she hadn't even hesitated to stand up against the phenomenon that was the armored warrior—the question was whether that showed her recklessness or her caliber.

Whatever the case, there was no longer any point in me keeping up appearances as her senior. I needed to look at Kanbaru as neither my junior nor my slave but as my partner and work with her to move forward.

"—I do need it. If you have any opinions, Kanbaru, I'd like them."

"Ohh? Is that all you'd like from me? Opinions?" Kanbaru smirked. "I wouldn't mind showing you my boobs if you so desire."

"I don't desire so. Why are you saying that with a smirk on your face? I know it's late at night, but could you stop it with this after-dark mood?"

"That's not it. I had a feeling tonight would be a late one from the moment I got that invitation from you. I made sure to get a lot of sleep at school today."

"So you aren't running on fumes, this is you on a full tank?"

That would be tough on me in its own way... But in any case.

I changed the subject and asked Kanbaru if she had any good ideas for beating this situation.

"You do hear it said that the best thing to do when you get lost is to stop moving," Kanbaru said, exiting her yoga pose to walk behind me. I thought the effect she was going for was a detective walking in circles, but she stopped once she got behind me—and tried to jump onto my back.

I dodged her.

"Huh? Why'd you move?"

"Why are *you* acting like piggyback is the new normal?"

"Well, it looked like you finished your call."

"Carrying on my back someone who's capable of leaping onto it? Even if I hypothetically did agree, can we at least figure out what we're doing first? You don't have a reserved seat on my back, okay?"

"Right. It's coach class." Kanbaru gave up on my back with those possibly fighting words—before continuing, "The rule about staying put doesn't necessarily hold if you have a destination... I'm going to ask this just to make sure there aren't any misunderstandings here, but is it okay for me to assume that this is similar to the experience you had of being lost before? You aren't just lost, right? This is some kind of aberrational phenomenon."

"Yeah...that's what I think." I didn't have proof yet, but it seemed like we could say that given Miss Gaen's reaction. "That said, I don't think it's the exact same as my past experience... I guess you could say the details are different?"

"Hmm. Out of curiosity, how did you handle the situation in May?"

"Umm..."

For someone preparing to take college entrance exams, I had very little confidence in my memory. The answer didn't come to me on the spot, but eventually I remembered how. The only problem was that we couldn't use the method this time around.

For a number of reasons, but the biggest being: *having to be on Senjogahara's level at the very least when it comes to making use of a cell phone (a map app).* Both Kanbaru and I were hopeless when it came to digital devices—unlike me, Kanbaru did now have a smartphone (she likes new things), but that didn't matter unless she was proficient in its use.

I explained to Kanbaru the way I dealt with the Lost Cow, thinking it might come in handy.

She heard me out, a grave expression on her face.

"Hmm," she looked to the side.

103

Could she have thought of something? No, that would be far too much to expect from her this early. Miss Gaen may have built her up in my mind, but at the end of the day, Kanbaru was a basketball player, not an expert on aberrations.

Regardless of who her mother or relatives were...

Regardless of her left arm.

Just as I decided that I, with my greater experience regarding aberrational phenomena, needed to take the lead in coming up with a solution and opened my mouth—

"My senior Araragi," she said. "Have you heard this story before?"

Still looking to the side.

"You know those bicycles that the police ride? It's about those."

"Umm...no, I don't know what you're talking about. I haven't heard any interesting stories about police bicycles."

"They don't have locks on them."

"What? Really? Not on either of the wheels?"

"Not one or the other. They're kept unlocked so that they can go on the move as soon as something happens—and it's possible because there's no need to lock them. No one would dare steal a police bicycle."

"Huh..."

I didn't know.

But now that she mentioned it, it made perfect sense.

What a neat story—but a moment after I found myself convinced...

"Of course, that's just a lie," Kanbaru continued.

"A lie?! So it really is just a neat story?!"

"Of course it's a lie. Think of how bad it'd be if someone stole a police bicycle and used it for something bad. Those bikes need to be protected more than anything."

"..."

I was the one who'd been conned, so why did it feel like *I* was being scolded? What a fine lie, though. If it were about police cars or motorcycles, no one would believe it.

"Okay, but why bring that up now? You're not going to suggest that we find a police station and ask for directions, are you?"

"Oh, no. Something completely unrelated just popped into my

mind. I thought I wouldn't forget it if I went ahead and told you about it."

"Don't use me as your personal scratchpad!"

Nor be thinking of completely unrelated things—we were just lost, but it was also an emergency!

"Sorry, sorry," Kanbaru casually apologized, her smile betraying no signs of guilt whatsoever. "I was bored because I came up with an easy way to claw our way out of this fix."

"Bored or not—wait, what? A way to claw our way out?"

"Yeah," she nodded.

Then Kanbaru moved—to an electric pole.

One nearby, the kind you found anywhere in town—then she reached a hand out to it. No, not just a hand—all four of her limbs.

Truly looking like a monkey as she made use of her arms and legs to glide up the pole.

"You know, this isn't an electric pole. It's a telephone pole."

"It doesn't matter!"

"It does. I could get electrocuted if it was an electric pole."

Kanbaru climbed all the way to the top of the electric, sorry, telephone pole like it was something you might find in a playground, all while talking (which is to say with ease)—then climbed down just as quickly after looking around.

It all happened in the blink of an eye.

Once complete, the purpose of these actions was clear as day—she must have gotten a look at the lay of the land from her high vantage point up at the top of the pole. That, or perhaps she'd even seen the park we were trying to get to—in either case, a full-grown high schooler climbing a telephone pole was bizarre enough of an act to have the police called on you. It was dangerous whether or not there was any risk of being electrocuted.

You only look cool climbing high and scowling down on the landscape below if it's an anime.

"Okay, I got it. This way."

Having landed, Kanbaru pointed in the direction she seemed to have just confirmed.

"I don't know where the park is, but if it's near where Senjoga-hara-senpai's home used to be, my nose should be able to point me most of the way there—let's go."

"Not your eyes but your nose... And can we really?"

While I hadn't gotten the idea to climb a telephone pole, confirming the direction we needed to travel in was no different from using road signs and residential maps—which hadn't kept us from getting lost. No matter how accurate maps or GPS might be, we'd never reach our destination if our basic sense of direction was off—but.

Just as I thought to inform Kanbaru of this fact that went without saying, she was already doing something else—there was no need to scramble up anything this time around.

All she needed was a small running start and a leap to jump onto the concrete block wall behind the pole—and once there, she turned to offer me her hand.

"Here, senpai."

"Wh-What are you, a ninja?"

How could anyone be so agile?

Okay, I knew quite well just how agile Kanbaru could be—the question was why she'd jumped on top of a wall.

And why she was offering me a hand.

Did she want me to climb up there, or what?

"Hm? Well, you said this Lost Cow aberration leads people on the street astray, right?"

Kanbaru spoke as though she was giving me a simple, unshakable answer, and the look on her face also said that it was obvious.

"All we have to do in that case is not walk on the street."

011

Taking the streets means taking the wrong streets.

Take not a street but a path less traveled—Kanbaru's proposal could be made to sound like some old-fashioned saying if you worded it the right way, but it wasn't as simple as that.

Really, I'd have felt more worried if we made our way through the crisis with what seemed like the answer to a trick question. I nearly breathed a sigh of relief when it didn't go well—but to cut to the chase, we did reach the park where we'd agreed to meet Miss Gaen.

It only took more time than we expected—no, I should be honest and say that I slowed Kanbaru down. I didn't have the balance needed to walk atop a concrete wall. Though my lovable little sister, Mlle. Karen Araragi, possessed the unique ability to travel any path upside-down on her hands, more fortunately than unfortunately, I did not—especially now that I was back to default settings, having lost my vampiric skills. In the end, Kanbaru had to help me along, not only in getting up to the wall but all the way, as I staggered and trembled like I was on a balance beam.

I had to walk while a younger girl led me by the hand.

I didn't have a shred of my dignity as a senior left.

My lack of dignity was boundless.

Even apart from that, it's not as if privately owned walls stretch on forever. We couldn't expect them to go in a straight line to the park in question.

Ononoki's master, the violent *onmyoji* known as Yozuru Kagenui, had an odd rule of never walking on the ground, moving by hopping from one wall or mailbox or fence or, in fact, electric pole to the next, and the two of us now found ourselves in a similar situation. Well, Miss Kagenui would laugh if she heard me call our situations similar, given how many times I fell to the ground.

We were forcing it, or powering through, via a method that was a far cry from the neat and tidy plan once proposed by Oshino and executed by Senjogahara—but not walking on the street did prove to be a valid way of escaping this labyrinth. It did feel like we were cheating, as if we'd completed a two-dimensional maze by going along its lines instead of the white space between them, but as someone who hadn't come up with a solution back in May or now, all I could really do was admire Kanbaru. Not to mention, the plan sounded fairly viable if you likened it to avoiding the center of a Shinto shrine's main path, a lane reserved for the gods.

Of course, we could only do this because it was the middle of the night. There's no way we could have used the method back in May, this was textbook suspicious behavior... Hachikuji was one thing, but I could harness the full powers of my imagination and still fail to picture Senjogahara walking atop a concrete wall.

To go into more detail, it seemed that gutters and empty lots didn't count as streets, just as the top of walls didn't. Even crossing a road was fine, as long as you didn't go down it. Learning these lessons, which would probably never be of use again, the two of us arrived at the park at last at around three in the morning.

Frankly, I wasn't sure if Kanbaru had done the kind of work that Miss Gaen had in mind, but it certainly wouldn't have worked without my junior's athleticism, even if we didn't need to be quite at Miss Kagenui's level—I fell again and again, in fact. But in the end, we did arrive at our destination without any help from the woman waiting there for us.

Naturally, I wasn't entirely happy about it.

No, not because I hurt my arm falling from the wall or anything (I got off with just a few scratches)—there were two separate reasons.

First, while we'd escaped our nonsensical situation thanks to Kanbaru, we never figured out exactly why we'd gotten lost in the first place—we'd pulled through, but nothing more. If it was the doing of that armored warrior, we had no idea why it had done such a thing. Its very identity and goals were still unclear to us...and we'd only gotten out of the way of a ball thrown in our direction. It's not as if we'd caught it or analyzed it. Yes, we solved it as a simple problem, but we barely touched it as a complex one—so I couldn't be just glad.

But the second reason I couldn't be was far more vital. Without it, I wouldn't be so greedy as to complain about the first, as though all I wanted was to analyze the situation, in spite of us being amateurs.

In other words—as long as a professional could enlighten us...

"..."

She wasn't there.

The all-important professional, Izuko Gaen, wasn't at the park where we'd promised to meet.

"Hm?"

Had she left because we'd taken forever? Did she just decide to go home? But where would she go home to? She was hardly rustic, and was a lady too—it's not as if she'd sleep rough like Oshino... But there weren't any hotels around here. Did she go to the town over?

There was of course a fairly good chance that she'd convinced a family in the area to let her stay the night, given her friendly demeanor...

"Hold on, no way," I fumed. "Am I really having the ladder pulled out from under me here?"

I looked over at Kanbaru to find her with burning eyes. Uh oh, Kanbaru's "senpai tricked me to take me to an empty park in the middle of the night" theory was starting to look realistic.

Miss Gaen needed to be here, for the sake of my honor...but a glance around the area showed it to be deserted.

No, stop. Calm down.

It did take time for us to get here, but it was a mere three hours since my earlier call—she wouldn't get impatient and leave over that. I didn't see Miss Gaen as someone that restless. Sure, I couldn't expect her to wait until the cows came home, but no, she was the type to wait and see things through.

She had to be hiding somewhere just to scare us. That was the kind of playful lady she was (, I hoped).

"My senior, normally people would just go home if you made them wait for three hours in the middle of the night."

"A fair point, but it's not as if we were coming here to meet her on a play date…"

It would be quite the late-night romp. A fisherman might even call this hour of the day the morning.

"Hmm…what kind of person could we be trying to meet? Oh, it's okay, don't tell me. My loyalty is being tested here."

"It's not, okay? If anything, what could I do to make you start doubting me a little more?"

One wrong turn and you'd be a stalker, I began to say before realizing that she'd been exactly that when she first appeared.

The girl rode a fine line in a whole lot of ways…

Anyhow, while I'd wanted Miss Gaen to explain the situation, if she wasn't here, maybe I needed to go ahead and tell Kanbaru that it was her aunt that we were trying to see—or rather, given this outcome, if Miss Gaen wasn't going to protect Kanbaru, I needed to see my junior home as I'd originally planned.

Ugh, as unreliable as you'd expect Oshino's senior to be, I thought, dumbfounded, only to arrive at another possibility.

Right.

It's not as if I had a monopoly on getting wrapped up in aberrational phenomena—could Miss Gaen have been visited by some sort of phenomenon, just as I'd gotten lost on the streets, leading to her absence?

If the phrase *wrapped up* sounds paranoid, so be it. Unlike Kanbaru and me, who'd been summoned as helpers, Miss Gaen was in town this time as part of her day job, her profession as an expert. In that sense, the probability that she'd encounter an aberration was higher for her than it was for us.

And just because she's an expert doesn't mean she can't be the victim of aberrations. It's not as if she can skate straight through every situation, no matter how serious, and come out unharmed—even Oshino was in awful shape after taking on Black Hanekawa, right?

True, I couldn't lump in Miss Gaen, the big boss, with Oshino. But what if, while we were playing walk the balance beam on top of some walls and fences, Miss Gaen had gotten attacked in this park by that armored warrior, who forced her to retreat to a location where she now awaited my help?

The hypothetical lost all traces of reality around the time I got to the *where she now awaited my help* bit, but even apart from that, she was someone you had to worry so little about. The thought of something happening to her seemed so improbable, I might as well worry about a meteor falling from the sky and hitting her square in the head.

Still, having envisioned this, I couldn't turn around and go home just because I couldn't find her at first glance.

"Kanbaru. I want you to do something for me."

"Bon appétit ♪"

"No, not that. I know it might be pointless, but I want us to split up and search every inch of the park."

"Oh. You're serious about your theory where this person waiting for us is hiding and trying to surprise us?"

"No."

"The hide-and-seek theory, then."

"Don't put forward any new theories. Look for anyone who might have collapsed in the shade or a bush, I want to check for that—if you find something, just holler."

"Okay. If I find something, I scream."

"Don't scream. You'll get me arrested."

"Well, you've captured my interest."

With that reply, mildly clever for being on the spur, Kanbaru ran off—it seemed she'd made a full recovery from her erstwhile malaise. I of course wasn't going to make my junior do all the work, and facing in the opposite direction—

"My senior! I found her!"

"…"

Was she trying to keep me from doing any of the work, or what?

I wasn't getting any chances at all to show off.

In fact, Kanbaru had managed to sweep three quarters of the park before I could take a single step—she was to the front of me.

I looked at her despondently, only to find a swing. By which Kanbaru stood.

Hm?

Uh… For as loud as she called to me, it didn't seem that Miss Gaen or anyone else was with her.

"No, no. See? Look closely," Kanbaru said as she pointed—at the ground.

More precisely, just under the swing—and of all things, there lay a person, face-up.

Sound asleep right under a swing.

The reason I didn't notice this figure playing with a swing in the most dangerous way on earth until Kanbaru pointed her finger was that it was far smaller than the one I was looking for—because it was about half of Miss Gaen's size, no, even smaller.

Tiny might be more apt than *small*—not that I'm making excuses.

I ought to be ashamed that I didn't notice at once. I should have noticed *the golden-haired, golden-eyed little girl* sooner than anyone, prior to all.

"Shi-Shinobu!"

"Zzz."

Asleep. Can you believe it?

In any case, here in the park where we were supposed to meet up with Miss Gaen, I was finally reunited with the former vampire whose link to me had been severed due to a mishap—my soulmate, Shinobu Oshino.

012

"Ah—so it's ye. How long it took. Thou hast grown quite haughty, I see, forcing me to stay wide awake, waiting here all night."

"You were sound asleep. What happened to you being nocturnal?"

"My sleep schedule's been turned around."

"If a vampire gets her sleep schedule turned around, that just means sleeping when a regular, healthy person does."

"Mnrrrgh."

Shinobu got up as she rubbed her eyes—but as she did, she bonked the top of her head against the swing. She fell back down with a "Gah!"

Just look at how cute she is...

While Kanbaru watched the little girl with a warm smile (now that I think about it, this would have been her first time meeting a speaking Shinobu), I of course had to do more.

We parted ways not knowing if we'd ever see the other alive again, so you could call this an emotional reunion—but the timing of it just wasn't right. It felt like getting a slow curve when you're expecting a fastball.

Like I might end up watching it go past me.

Whatever the case, I first needed to ask Shinobu why she was here— and I would also need to explain to her what had happened to me since our parting. I moved the swing to the side and helped Shinobu get up.

"Hey, Shinobu... Why are you here?"

"I know, I know—calm thyself, my master. I'll explain all in... zzz..."

"It looks to me the only thing you're interested in doing is sleeping... Hm?"

That's when I noticed—only once I'd taken her hand and approached her. Here and there on Shinobu's translucently white skin were what looked like scratch wounds.

Scratch wounds?

Wounds?

Don't tell me it's from playing on the swings, I thought, given her position and supine pose (she would seriously be getting lectured if it was)—but no, you didn't get scratches like hers from playing on a swing.

In that case, what could it be? The marks almost made it look like she'd been through a small skirmish before I arrived at the park. In that case, was she sleeping despite it being the middle of the night to restore her energy after a battle?

"Kakak!"

Shinobu laughed—then faced Kanbaru.

A pretty intrepid laugh, given that her entire body was covered in scratches.

Seeing her made me think. Maybe we'd remained connected in a sense despite our link being cut, considering the way I'd been subject to countless blows and scrapes.

"So—a monkey. Hmph. What a handful that was."

"...?"

I tilted my head in confusion at the words that accompanied her laugh—okay, well, Shinobu may have been living at the abandoned cram school with Oshino and not in my shadow when that stuff happened with Kanbaru's left hand, but I did draw on her strength. It still didn't explain why Shinobu herself described Kanbaru as a "handful," though...

"Heh. Yeah, this kitty really is a lot to handle," Kanbaru returned, her words coming from some strange fantasy unknown to me—please,

Kanbaru, just stay quiet for a while. I'm sorry, but you're only going to make things harder to deal with.

What was she going to do if Shinobu snapped at being calling a kitty? She knew that this little girl was also a vampire, right?

But.

"A cat, eh..."

Shinobu's smile only grew wider as she showed no signs of anger.

Of course, she showed close to zero interest in any humans other than myself—nothing had fundamentally changed about her in that sense since the days when she sat silently in a corner of the abandoned cram school, her arms around her knees.

Even this exchange that seemed like a conversation with Kanbaru was in fact nothing more than Shinobu talking to herself—she casually looked away from my junior and back to me.

You could say she only had herself to blame, but Kanbaru's body shook and jolted, having been ignored—but let's not get into the perverted stuff right now.

"Oh, no—when I say a monkey, I speak not of this girl. It wore a rain coat and long boots, but 'twas a different person."

"A different person?"

"A different aberration, I should perhaps say. Whatever the case, the aberration I fought elsewhere just now. Alongside a cat."

"Huh? Wha... What are you talking about?"

Could Shinobu, too, have encountered some kind of aberrational phenomenon while I was being led astray by mine? In fact, I was just thinking about how I don't have a monopoly on getting attacked by aberrations, but—a cat?

What did she mean, a cat?

What was going on in this town?

"Oh... Are those scratches all over your body from this...monkey you're talking about?"

So this monkey had nothing to do with Kanbaru's left hand—an evil I could neither hear, see, nor speak of.

It was similar to the way I'd gotten lost, in that it wasn't strictly the same as the snail I encountered in May—but what could it mean if we were coming across all of these aberrations that were close to but not the same as the ones before, like some sort of *rehash of the past*?

"Close but not the same? I'd be far more succinct and call it a cheap knockoff. Though to go into detail, about half of these scratches are collateral damage from the cat's attacks."

"Collateral damage... I'm having trouble understanding anything you're saying, but did you also fight this cat you're talking about while you were off elsewhere or whatever?"

"No, no... I was with the cat—aye, a contest for the ages in so many ways. But these are mere scrapes. Nothing to fret about. What about thee? Art thou unharmed?"

"Oh—yeah. So, um, about that Darkness after you and I split up..."

I still didn't want to be too specific about the topic in front of Kanbaru—so I tried to choose my words carefully, but my concerns were apparently unnecessary.

"Nay," Shinobu said. *"I've already heard a small bit about that*—it seems that I myself had been confused about many a thing for over four hundred years. What an utter fool I've shown myself to be."

"..."

Four hundred years.

Hearing about this time span made me recall something entirely different—the message for Shinobu that I'd been entrusted with by the armored warrior.

The enchanted blade it had lent her for over four hundred years...

What I should have been paying attention to, however, was the fact that she'd *heard a small bit* about it—heard it? From whom? Miss Gaen?

No, she and Shinobu hadn't been put in contact with each other yet—my link to Shinobu was already severed by the time I met Miss Gaen.

Of course, she'd promised to reconnect our link, but—right, I needed to ask Shinobu why she, and not Miss Gaen, was here at this park.

"Hmph. I should think that goes without saying," she said, glowering as she looked up from her position—looking up at me like she was looking down on me. She beamed with a sadistic smile. "I heard it from

116

the tween girl who trampled all over ye."

"A tween girl who trampled all over me? ? ? ? What could you possibly be talking about? You know you're the only one who's ever stepped on me with bare feet, Shinobu."

"I never spoke of bare feet."

"Ah! Oh no! This is what they mean by 'loose lips sink ships'!"

"It seems it's thy loose morals that have brought thee low in this case..." Shinobu said, shaking her head in disbelief. "In fact, thy face is still marked clearly by an adorable little footprint."

"What?!"

I looked at Kanbaru, as if to ask for confirmation.

Kanbaru awkwardly nodded with an *Um, yeah*. "I kept my questions about what could have gone on while I was passed out to myself this whole time."

"Come out and say them! Especially if you noticed something! And you enjoyed getting carried on the back of a senior who looked like that?!"

"Even if you're my most respected senior, I don't have the right to give you my unsolicited opinions about your sexual tastes..."

"Why is that the one thing you'd be modest about?! This kind of thing is your wheelhouse, you should be rolling up your sleeves and getting to work! I'd welcome it! The one time I'd want you to stomp your way into my business with muddy boots and leave no stone unturned!"

"But you'd prefer me to be barefoot, right?"

"It's not like that!"

This couldn't be real... Was I really wandering around town with a footprint on my face the entire time? How could anything I did be taken as remotely serious?

And just how hard did Ononoki step on me?

"But in a sense, it's the kind of stamp ye could only find in the world of the printed word."

"Lay off this 'printed word' stuff."

"Hmph... Well, normally I'd be so enraged by such marks that I'd feel compelled to flay thee alive, but that doll-girl did save me, however unwillingly—so I shall show thee generosity this one time."

While Shinobu said something unignorably violent, she also said something that was even harder to ignore. Saved.

Saved by Ononoki? On top of hearing about what happened?

"Hold on... Now I really need you to tell me what happened, Shinobu."

"Again, 'tis I who would ask that question more than thee... What exactly happened in that short time we were apart that led thee to have a tween girl's footprint impressed upon thy face?"

"Well, look at the time. I've got to head back to my room to listen to some paper-jacketed CDs on my vacuum-tube amp."

"Don't ye try to act cool in some unfathomable way. Vacuum-tube amps and paper-jacketed CDs? The only vacuum here is the one in thy skull, the depth of thy seedy character paper-thin. I'm asking thee about the reason for that footprint."

"If I'm being honest with you, I don't know either."

Try as she might, with her uncomfortably real remarks, to hound me and my attempts to gloss over the subject, I didn't understand much about anything that was going on, let alone the footprint—which is why I wanted to know what happened to Shinobu, at least.

"Oh, nothing worthy of mention—the cat and I were attacked by a monkey... And just as we struggled in our fight, the doll-girl appeared from nowhere to join us most admirably. What was that girl's secret technique again, the Unlimited Rulebook? Well, she used it to blow the right side of the monkey's body right off."

"..."

Ononoki was putting in good work.

All over the place.

In other words, after she heard from us at the abandoned cram school—or its burnt ruins, Ononoki went after the armored warrior only to come across Shinobu, whether by chance or by fate, just as the former vampire came across this aberrational phenomenon of her own.

Thinking about this, you could say that Shinobu and Ononoki had a strange kind of bond tying their lives together—despite the two getting into a serious fight during their first encounter.

Shinobu may have won an overwhelming victory then, but her

powers had been enhanced to a level close to their limit—my link with Shinobu was severed now, so her abilities in a fight wouldn't be too different from an average little girl's. It was also pretty rare for someone as obstinate and ostentatious as her to admit that she struggled to fight this monkey she herself dismissed as a cheap knockoff...

"And then you were saved by Ononoki—which is when she told you everything. In that case..."

If she'd heard about the Darkness, then could she have also heard about the armored warrior that came after it? No—that seemed unlikely. She wouldn't be asking me about what happened if she had.

Ononoki had no duty to explain that much to Shinobu, someone she generally wasn't on good terms with—she must have told her about where I'd be meeting Miss Gaen, which is to say this park, and gone back to tailing the armored warrior, looking for it and scurrying away.

God, what a hard worker.

While part of me was amazed, another part of me didn't know how to feel about Shinobu still not knowing about the armored warrior.

While it would've been easier for me if Ononoki had told her, I felt some sort of inchoate pride over being the one to deliver the news—and I'd been tasked with a message.

"Well, so long as the two of us are fine," Shinobu said. "No, I suppose it isn't as if we're fine."

"..."

If you're alive, you're fine—no, that's what Miss Gaen would say.

"It seems that our link will be restored by the Hawaiian-shirted boy's mentor or some such? Thus the doll-girl said I ought to convene with her, but when I arrived, I found neither thee or this mentor. And so."

"'And so' you fell asleep under a swing? What kind of idea is that? Where would it even come from? Even if you did get tired out by your unexpected battle, there have to be better places to sleep. Ononoki went out of her way to save you and your fight was finally over, so why go and do something as risky as—"

"Listen, ye," Shinobu interrupted me. Her sadistic smile had disappeared, replaced with an unexpected solemnity. "We shall talk about that later. Alas, it seems my battle has yet to end—the fight was not over."

"Hm?"

"Our battle is only beginning."

Then, when I looked.

In the direction Shinobu pointed with her chin—*it* stood there in the dead center of the park.

Kanbaru had her eyes trained on it as well.

Her gaze sharp.

Now I saw that Shinobu's description was accurate—a monkey in long boots wearing a raincoat. A large monkey that was both familiar and strange.

But only its left half.

As for its right half, blown away by Ononoki's Unlimited Rulebook—it was a massive crustacean.

There in its place—a *crab*.

013

The left half a monkey, and the right half a crab.

There's a Japanese folktale about the crab and the monkey, but this wasn't how that went.

If anything was only possible in the world of the printed word, this seemed to be it—I didn't have the first clue how the two halves were connected.

It seemed false, even when it actually stood there before my eyes.

I couldn't accept what they saw.

I only got a sense, nothing else.

Of a hostility or malice toward us coming from the crab-monkey—like a well-honed impulse of aggression.

It conveyed that, and nothing else.

When I say *us*, though, it seemed to be limited to me and Shinobu—the high school girl known as Suruga Kanbaru seemed to be spared its consideration.

You could say it disregarded her, or that it ignored her. It was one thing when a golden-haired, golden-eyed little girl did it, but my junior wasn't so perverted that she took joy in being ostracized by a monster this evidently dangerous.

Of course, she wasn't the type to celebrate her good luck because it didn't bother with her, either—if anything, she was the type to be infuriated. Readying her left arm to take a fighting stance before Shinobu or I did was proof enough.

Thinking back to everything that happened at the park that night, Kanbaru's immediate battle-readiness might've been far scarier than even this aberrational phenomenon that had come chasing after Shinobu.

She showed none of the pacifism you expect from kids these days.

Well, it's not like I was expecting some kind of generic reaction out of Suruga Kanbaru, a girl who heroically stood up even to the armored warrior, just because she was confronted with a monster out of a creature feature. But did she just not feel scared or hesitant in the face of danger?

She had to—national-level star athlete or not, she was only a high school student, and it's not as if she was an expert on aberrations.

But this junior of mine lived her life ready to overcome those nerves—it's how she's survived.

Since back in elementary school.

When she made a wish to a monkey and received her reward.

"I'll go from the right. You go from the left, senpai."

"Uh, yeah..."

She even gave precise instructions.

It kind of felt like I was the junior now. Maybe I should be glad she was counting on me in a fight?

"Let's go!"

"Y-Yes!"

Reduced to replying with a polite *yes*—but that aside, while Kanbaru attempted to make the first move just as she had with the armored warrior, her plans this time were thwarted.

This was foreshadowed.

When we attempted to escape from the fire, Kanbaru noted that she often mixed up her left and right because she was a lefty—and in fact mixed up her right foot with her left as we tried to get going.

Since it was her feet she mixed up, it wasn't a serious error then, but this time it was direction—Kanbaru and I started moving simultaneously on her signal, but we crashed into each other after one step. I tried to attack it from the right, and so did Kanbaru, causing a traffic accident.

Because of her ability to reach top speed after one step thanks to her powerful legs, she created what you might stylishly call a jackknife—I fell as well, caught up in the crash. While Kanbaru's natural athleticism allowed her to do a somersault and get right back up, my body slammed to the ground in an unsightly display. Despite smacking the dirt with my left arm in a sort of judo front fall, the only effect was my hand hurting from some pebbles.

A judo fall?

Who was I trying to impress here?

Kanbaru, who had mixed up her left and right, was entirely to blame, but it felt as a whole like we'd just proven how amateur and inexperienced we were when it came to fighting together—I suppose tag-team matches do require a lot of technique.

Even Suruga Kanbaru, who exerted her captaincy on the basketball court, was no exception... It made me realize again just how important my link to Shinobu was when it came to fighting as a pair.

Speaking of Shinobu, I looked back to find her sitting on the swing for some reason. There was nothing ordinary about Kanbaru, who readied herself for a fight as soon as she encountered danger, but why would someone start amusing herself on a plaything the moment an aberration chasing after her appeared? That wasn't just out of the ordinary, it was lacking in common sense.

She wasn't thinking of acting like a little girl to get out of this, was she? It might not be on the level of a monkey-crab, but a golden-haired, golden-eyed little girl creaking back and forth on a swing in a park in the middle of the night easily qualified as horror.

As I let myself be distracted by Shinobu playing on a swing, Kanbaru went back on the move—not waiting for me to return to my feet. I felt abandoned, but what happened in reality was that Kanbaru went to face this creature on her own. In fact, you could say she was defending my prostrate figure—because the fused monkey-crab aberration wasn't just standing there absentmindedly while we tripped over each other.

It wasn't going to provide us with an easy target. It began moving as well, and toward us—but as half of it was a crab, it couldn't go that fast the way it walked sideways. Its movements were so bizarre that I wanted to avert my eyes the moment they landed on it, though. Even if it didn't have speed, it moved in an unpredictable way that left me mentally shaken.

Nevertheless, its form didn't seem to produce a single ripple in Suruga Kanbaru's iron-clad mind—she entered straight into the pocket of this aberration I hesitated to so much as approach. In what seemed like her next movement, she sent her wrapped left hand flying in a fist, the same fist that had scattered the armored warrior to pieces.

Though a jock, Kanbaru wasn't learning karate like Karen. She didn't let out a *kiai* shout as she swung, but I could tell even from a distance that she put everything she had into the blow.

But.

The thing blocked her fist.

With the right side of its monkey-crab body, the crab part—with its pincer.

"Mgh!"

If this were a game of rock-paper-scissors, it was a unique case of rock losing to scissors—but when you think about it, punching the exoskeleton of a crab wouldn't have much effect.

Kanbaru had failed to think it through—if she was going to launch a solo attack, she should have aimed for its monkey side.

In any case, compared to the way it walked, the crab's pincer was strangely agile—it seemed to *have no weight at all* as it blocked Kanbaru's fist like a shield.

Then, the left side of the creature, the monkey half that Kanbaru should have aimed for, began to counter.

The monkey's hand—went to scratch Kanbaru.

The claw that covered Shinobu's body in wounds—missed Kanbaru by less than an inch as she twisted her body to let it by.

Less than an inch from her skin, not her clothes.

Her track jacket ripped.

Uh oh, Kanbaru wasn't wearing a bra!

I forced my wounded body to stand—and it creaked. Not only did I suffer from the pain of getting twisted up and falling, I carried the damage from the blows I suffered while getting unlost, and from the armored warrior's shoulder tackle.

I was reminded again that I'd been relying heavily on my vampiric immortality in my recent fights—but I could reflect on that later.

Regardless of what I was—undying or not, I had to help Kanbaru!

"Hold on, ye."

A voice from the swings behind me—Shinobu, who for some reason was in spectator mode.

Hold on? At least half of that monkey-crab is after you. What're you doing out there in the audience, I tried to get out all in one quick quip, but then...

"Use this."

With that, Shinobu—tossed it my way.

Whatever might have been thrown my way, my reflex was to catch it—but at the last second I saw what it was...

"Waaaagh!"

I barely dodged it—without Kanbaru's elegance, of course. I'd bothered to stand up, but now I was crawling on the ground again. If Kanbaru had evaded the monkey-crab's claw attack by only a layer's worth of clothes, this was only by my skin.

I evaded it.

Namely, a Japanese sword—a great katana.

Whose naked blade stuck out from the ground.

"Wh-What're you doing?! Were you serious about flaying me?!"

"Are ye only able to handle things thrown thy way when 'tis remarks?" sneered Shinobu, shamelessly, still holding her follow-through there on the swing. Then...

"Use it," she repeated.

That's when—I recognized the katana.

The enchanted blade that Shinobu Oshino normally kept sheathed inside her small frame. Kokorowatari. An item used to eradicate monsters.

Also known as—the Aberration Slayer.

" ..."

"No need for hesitation. *It* both is and is not an aberration—one of those 'bad things' that are not yet an aberration. No punishment will come to thee for cutting it down."

True—that went without saying.

This was no time for me to hesitate. I grabbed the hilt of the great katana sticking straight out of the ground and pulled it out like the holy sword Excalibur.

It wasn't that precious, of course.

In truth, the sword wasn't the original, but said to be created from the flesh and blood of a certain individual…

—Yes, no armored warrior is complete—

—Without a blade—

—Indeed, it has been four hundred years since I lent it to her—

"Aaaaaaaaaaagh!"

Rousing myself with a scream, as if to shake off any uncertainty, I wielded the sword and ran—but I doubt as fast as I imagined.

It was heavy, after all.

And it was hard to use because of its length.

No wonder Shinobu was abandoning the front lines to play on a swing—how could she ever make good use of something this long with her little girl's body?

"…"

Okay, no. I still couldn't accept it.

Help out a little, dammit. Borrow a page from Ononoki.

It took about ten seconds to go from my position by Shinobu, someone used to using others in a different sense than Kanbaru, and arrive at the monkey-crab—all while Kanbaru continued to fight it.

Her track jacket was already in tatters.

The tears were so perfect, she might have been dodging by a layer's worth on purpose, but no, even our pervert couldn't pull off something that skilled—she showed no signs of noticing me as I came running from behind, great katana in hand.

The enchanted blade was meant to cut aberrations, not humans. Kanbaru wouldn't suffer a scratch if I sliced straight through both her and the monkey-crab, but just because I knew this as a fact didn't mean I could execute it.

I was like a dog-lover who doesn't eat chocolate just because it's poison to dogs.

The circumstances were different from that time a little while ago with the cat—wait, now that I mention it, wasn't Shinobu's earlier explanation about the "cat" missing something?

"Kanbaru, move!" I yelled as I swung—with the technique of a complete amateur, but despite what you might expect, katanas are made so that even noobs can use them well enough. They cut using their weight.

I worried that Kanbaru, absorbed in her battle, hadn't heard me, but I needn't have. There's a move in basketball called the no-look pass, where you toss the ball without looking at your teammate, and in this case she pulled off the incredible feat of avoiding me as I came from behind with a sword without so much as turning around.

She couldn't have known that I held a katana since she didn't look back at me, but she'd have moved in the exact same way if she did. That's how well she discerned the path of the enchanted blade Kokorowatari as it cut through the air.

Then, surely enough, the blade I swung—traced a line down the center of the monkey-crab's body, slicing its body vertically.

The monkey-crab divided in two without any resistance, as if its body contained a perforated line—into left and right.

The left, monkey half.

And the right, crab half.

Quite literally split down the middle—I'd swung the blade a number of times before, but this outcome was the most decisive of them all. I'd split a whole in two in a hole in one.

Naturally, the complete lack of resistance, as if I had cut through a block of tofu, did come back to bite me as I met dirt for a third time—that part wasn't a hole in one at all. I had to admit, falling over three times in a fight and still being alive was a bit of a miracle.

The sword stuck deep in the ground once more, as if I'd tried to split Earth itself. My muscles must have gotten stiff from gripping too hard, because I couldn't pull my hands from the hilt. I sat there on my butt like I'd just tried to hit a pinata and failed.

"Ha... Haah... Haah..."

Perhaps the fight ending in a somewhat disappointing way was a given when I'd come to it with a cheat code of an item... Still, I couldn't help but breathe a sigh of relief, coward that I am.

Being visited by a succession of aberrational phenomena over the course of one night was rare—and we may have been far from finished.

Far from finished—

"Watch out, my senior!"

—indeed.

Despite being split in two, the monkey-crab wasn't finished—okay, the monkey-crab was. What wasn't finished was *its tail*.

Its tail that I hadn't seen until now.

A snake.

A twin-headed snake—bifurcated from the start, no need for anyone to split it—bared its fangs at both me and Kanbaru.

The yokai known as the Nue is said to have the head of a monkey and the tail of a snake... So this aberration wasn't just a combination of a monkey and a crab, it had a snake stuck on too?

A snake.

Jagirinawa.

The venomous snake that attacked Nadeko Sengoku, friend to my little sister, Tsukihi Araragi—a cursed serpent whose poison nullified even the regenerative abilities of a vampire...

Kanbaru, who alerted me despite the snake's fangs heading for her as well, didn't avoid the attack this time.

The same went for me, of course. Or should that be *as usual* instead of *this time*?

With the trusty enchanted blade Kokorowatari almost entirely below ground—I wouldn't be pulling it out swiftly the way I had moments earlier.

The snake's beady eyes had us in their sights.

Then, a pair of fangs buried—

"Kakak. Not so bad."

—no, got buried.

The monkey-crab, now monkey-crab-snake, was finished for good.

128

Shinobu Oshino had moved to stand in my shadow without me noticing. Grabbing, with her darling little hands, the head aimed at my neck as well as the one going for Kanbaru's left arm, she mercilessly crushed the life out of them.

Then scored me:

"Sixty-two."

014

Sixty-two out of a hundred.

A harsh score that tormented an entrance-exam taker like me, but it was a perfectly fair evaluation of someone who'd fallen over not just twice but thrice in a park. In other words, Shinobu had sat there on the swing and fancied herself a spectator because she wanted to see how much I could do on my own.

See, or maybe ascertain.

No wonder she was so quick to lend me an enchanted sword that I once had to beg on all fours for days to borrow.

"Just about perfect for a test of thy strength, no?"

This was her excuse.

I wanted to let loose on her—this isn't the time for such notions, didn't you just get saved by Ononoki, and so on, but according to Shinobu, that too was a matter of perspective.

From my ignorant, amateur point of view, a monkey-crab chimera was visibly frightening and appalling, but from Shinobu's, it was a patchwork of ready-made aberrational phenomena.

Alone, she'd struggled against the monkey, coming away from it covered in scratches, but Ononoki had blown away half of its body. The "bad things" that compensated for the missing half with other aberrational phenomena were nothing to fear—an uneven hodgepodge that could barely move, after one cheap rip-off was stuck to a broken rip-off.

"Its specs seemed to have been lowered as well," she said. "When it came upon me as a whole monkey, it could make use of rain. What a bothersome skill that was."

Rain?

Now that she mentioned it, the crab half, for its part, seemed to be unfettered by gravity—by weight.

Specs that did make me think—similar but not the same as what I knew.

Likewise with the snail earlier—in any case, the half-monkey had lost even this ability to "use rain."

Ononoki's Unlimited Rulebook had left it weakened.

In other words, Shinobu had left it to us to handle the persistent aftermath of a bothersome phenomenon—no, the real aftermath *started here*. And it was Shinobu's turn.

I say that because she started chomping away at the divided monkey and crab, as well as the snake's crushed heads. Nutrition for a vampire, the king of aberrations, but it was still a hard sight to bear...

Even Suruga Kanbaru, grand pervert, looked away—I guess it was like accidentally seeing a kitten toying with and eating a mouse?

They say it's impolite to stare at a vampire taking her meal, so to distract Kanbaru I asked, "Everything okay? Are you hurt?"

She'd avoided every swipe of the monkey's claws from the looks of it, but the damage to her track jacket was evident. You could tell how much of a healthy and beautiful sportswoman she was from the curious fact that all her exposed skin didn't come across as erotic.

Even so, I couldn't leave my junior in such a state, so I took off my sweater and lent it to her. Originally, of course, this was a hoodie that Shinobu had manifested for me.

"Yeah, I'm not hurt—heh. It's warm. It smells like you."

"Um, could you not say things that make this feel like a rom-com?"

"More specifically, it smells like your sweat stains."

"Don't be specific, either."

Well, it had been days since Shinobu created it for me, and I hadn't changed yet... Kanbaru would just have to put up with that.

"Are you sure, though? You'd be topless."

"No, I won't be. Don't think everything you say will be automatically true just because it's the printed word."

I was wearing a T-shirt.

That said, it might have been a little chilly for summer, now that it was the middle of the night.

"Hmph. Hold on a second," Kanbaru said, zipping the front of the hoodie before wriggling around for some reason. She pulled her arms out of the sleeves—it looked like she was preparing a magic trick or something.

After a moment, she extracted the track jacket she wore under the hoodie straight out from around her chest—she'd skillfully taken it off.

"A must-have skill for any girl jock," she noted, handing me her jacket with a "Wear this." Ah, so we were trading tops. "Since you're not braless, it shouldn't be an issue if you wore a torn-up-feeling jacket."

"I'm not sure *not braless* is the best way to describe me."

A *torn-up-feeling* jacket didn't seem right either, but that was more of a vocabulary problem so I wouldn't nitpick.

I'd never worn a girls' track jacket before, but then again, I'd half-forced her to wear my clothes first... I couldn't simply reject her kind offer.

It did feel a little embarrassing, but trading uniforms might have been a more common occurrence for an athlete like Kanbaru than I imagined.

A very small-minded senior who didn't want his junior to sense the sort of inexperience that getting flustered over indirect kisses or eating off of the same plate suggested, I tried to show zero resistance to the idea whatsoever as I passed my arms through the girls' track jacket.

"Whoa, you look," Kanbaru said, "like a rock star."

"Rock stars don't wear track jackets."

"Whaaat? It's expensive, though."

If Kanbaru called it expensive, it had to be.

I felt bad all over again that this expensive jacket was feeling all torn up.

"I'm sorry for dragging you into this, Kanbaru. I know fighting is the last thing a basketball player is supposed to do, too."

"Enough already. Apologize that many times and I'm going to start wondering if you're being sincere." She sounded broad-minded but was in fact being quite stern. "You don't need to worry. I may be a basketball player, but before that I'm the top general of Araragistan."

"Hold on, when did you form a bizarre nation like that? As far as I know, you're the only person who's stanning me."

Not even Senjogahara was.

If I had to name someone else, it'd be Ononoki these last few days.

"No, don't worry. Every member of my fan club has automatically been drafted into Araragistan."

"What a terrifying system. And we're talking about your own fan club, then. You're your own boss fan?"

I did feel like joining them after she'd been such a stud all night. Yes, that organization that my little sister Karen Araragi apparently belonged to...but wait, wasn't it unofficial?

"True, I need to avoid violence, but I don't know if you'd call that a fight," Kanbaru muttered, glancing in Shinobu's direction—just as she finished her meal. No trace left of the monkey-crab-snake that stood at three to four times Shinobu's size.

"I just hope the rare meat doesn't give her a tummy-ache," Kanbaru voiced a needless concern. "Oh, and by that, I don't mean how uncommon a catch a monster is."

"Yeah, that clarification really was needless... Hey, Shinobu."

"Hmm?"

When Shinobu turned around, the scratches on her body had disappeared—the energy she'd drained from the aberration by eating it must have healed them. Getting better thanks to a hearty meal seemed like a pretty healthy system to me... Still, energy drain.

Pulling the enchanted blade Kokorowatari, plunged into the ground like a large turnip, Shinobu stored it in her body as if for dessert.

Gulping down a great katana that was longer than she was tall—this too seemed like a magic trick but was by no means a must-have skill for little girls.

No.

It wasn't even a must for vampires—because originally, the enchanted blade didn't belong to her iron-blooded, hot-blooded, yet cold-blooded self.

It was a weapon wielded by an expert exterminator of monsters.

Shinobu Oshino originally belonged to the side of those the sword was meant to cut.

"Many thanks for waiting. I'm stuffed."

"Well, I'm sure it was filling."

"Now then. Let us continue our conversation."

"Continue our conversation... Um, what were we talking about again?"

"Weren't we talking about why she was sleeping under the swings?" my junior butted in to enlighten me.

Now that she mentioned it, we were.

"By the way, *swing* in Esperanto is *balancilo*," she added.

"No need to enlighten me on that point."

"By the way, *park swing set* is an anagram of *twinks pagers*. That's why my heart always starts singing when I see skinny young men playing on a swing."

"You really didn't need to enlighten me on that point."

"'Wait, might those guys actually be...'"

"No, they aren't."

"My heart's singing!"

"Me, I'm screaming on the inside. You've got so many hearts in your eyes that you just can't see straight."

"Who needs to see straight when they're doing a number on my heart rate?!"

"You know, maybe you're the one who needs a pounding."

She was making me question in the worst ways the fact that Karen still loved to play on the swings.

Shinobu sat there, waiting for our conversation to end.

She seemed just as uninterested in speaking with Kanbaru, a human, as before, but apparently had enough consideration to wait for us to finish our banter.

After experiencing a battle that dangerous (for me at least, regardless of how Shinobu saw it), part of me didn't care why she was sleeping under the swings… But it's awkward telling someone, *Never mind, I don't give a damn now.*

"Again, 'tis our link. We spoke of how my pairing to thee must be restored, did we not? Else we will be forced to struggle against even poor excuses for aberrations such as those."

"Hm? But what does that have to do with you sleeping under a swing? As far as restoring our link—that's something we need to ask this expert to do."

"Listen, ye. Practice makes perfect—why not try laying thyself a-sprawl, over there."

"What?"

"Thou ought to see something. Come now." Shinobu trotted over to the swings—now unbound from my shadow, she could move freely.

Still, just because she went over there ahead of me didn't mean I'd follow. I wasn't doing this. Lying under a swing? Not something you do past second grade.

Sorry, but I'm eighteen.

That's what I thought as I followed Shinobu, who hopped on top of the swing again. I say *again*, but instead of sitting, as she'd done like a conceited spectator during my battle alongside Kanbaru, this time she stood on the plank.

She stood and swung back and forth.

This might be somewhat of a tangent, but just for reference, Shinobu wore a one-piece dress.

A skirt bottom.

She stood on the swing and swung attired thus—creaking back and forth at a significant height.

"I'll handle this, my senior."

"I could never force a precious junior to. You're not ready for a mission like this. Let me take care of it."

We were fighting for the spot under the swing.

The number of bidders for this plot of land with zero interest until moments ago had shot up—though the competition wasn't too fierce, with just the two of us, it still represented a shocking increase.

Zero multiplied by anything is still zero, yet Shinobu had turned zero into not one, but even two. Yes, only a vampire from feudal times was capable of such unfathomable alchemy.

"No, my senior, if you really feel bad about getting me wrapped up in nonsensical battles all because I accepted your ridiculous invitation, let me handle this."

"Why suddenly so assertive? Where did the unselfish stance you've been taking this whole time go?"

"I demand a barter. I seek a memorable experience."

"See? You're just a bunch of desires on legs. I'm a year older than you, though. How about respecting seniority here, eh?"

"Respect seniority, when we're fighting over a little girl? This, senpai, is about juniority."

"Is that even a word? Whatever, we'll settle this with rock-paper-scissors."

"Oh? The version where it's okay to hit each other?"

"When has there ever been a version like that?"

"You know, like Goku early on in *Dragon Ball.*"

"I admit that takes me back, but no." Too bad Goku never used that move as a Super Saiyan...

"Fine, rock-paper-scissors it is."

"Okay. No shoot."

"That might be tough."

"Are you planning on shooting me with something?"

"Rock, paper—"

Scissors.

Kanbaru put out scissors, and I put out rock—since she wasn't that crab, it meant she'd lost. Scurrying over to the swings before any shooting could take place, I slipped under them like a runner on second sliding to third on a delayed steal.

Agh... Terrifying!

Scarier than any aberration! What was going on?!

Shinobu wasn't swinging that quickly, but even then, a solid pendulum swinging back and forth only a few inches from your face had such a mental impact on you!

The speed of a pendulum is determined by its length, not its weight, so in the case of a swing, you can control it based on where you hold onto the chain—Shinobu seemed to be shifting tempos on purpose, keeping my eyes from focusing.

The angle was off by ninety degrees, but it made me think of that contraption where an executioner's sickle is attached to a pendulum—I couldn't even see no little girl!

What exactly did Shinobu want here, what did she want me to understand? Now that I thought about it, she probably meant *seeing is believing*, not *practice makes perfect*, but—hm?

That was when.

I noticed—even as I fought the terror of a heavy object coming and going in front of my face, it struck me, when I used my dynamic vision to its fullest. Impressive, considering that my eyesight was now just an average human's—I may have only scored a sixty-two on brawn, but my vision was 20/20.

Stuck there under the swing was a picture from a photo booth. It showed Miss Izuko Gaen, the expert we were to meet, making a cute pose (how youthful of her).

The following words were written by hand on the sticker:

"Change → Kita-Shirahebi Shrine."

015

Kita-Shirahebi Shrine—a ruined Shinto shrine at the top of a small mountain in our town that has already come up many times before. Its crumbling structures and decaying front *torii* gate must have paradoxically meant that it was still being managed by someone somewhere, as it was allowed to sit abandoned instead of being cleared out. As far as I could tell, though, it was a forgotten place, with not so much as a single worshipper.

I doubt I'd have ever known about it, either, if I hadn't gone there on a job for Oshino—so Miss Gaen choosing it made her seem all the more like the lady who knows everything.

In fact, Shinobu and I had visited it quite recently—on the last day of summer break, meaning we'd be returning after not much time at all.

A mountain at night, a shrine at night.

The kinds of places you'd dare your friends to go, or at least places you wouldn't be too excited about visiting, but our ship had already sailed—and it seemed like day would break as we headed there, anyway.

Such were my thoughts as I, Koyomi Araragi, a little girl, Shinobu Oshino, and a pervert, Suruga Kanbaru, moved from a park whose name I couldn't read to our next stage.

I wondered what I'd do if Kanbaru demanded I carry her on my back again, but whether out of consideration for Shinobu, the fact that she'd made a full recovery, or unexpected but simple forgetfulness, she didn't. As for Shinobu, she neither asked to ride on my shoulders nor sank into my shadow as usual.

She didn't do the latter because our link had yet to be restored, but her not asking to ride on my shoulders wasn't because she felt particularly reserved around Kanbaru. Shinobu barely acknowledged her despite us traveling as a group and wouldn't have minded her seeing.

It was because of what I said as we left the park—well, she'd deny it, but at least that's what I think.

What I said—in other words, the message I delivered.

Honestly, I wasn't sure if I should tell her, right until the moment I did—but I had to, given that something about all this seemed to go beyond just my relationship with Shinobu.

I felt a twinge of annoyance over possibly playing into that armored warrior's hands, but after seeing the abandoned cram school burn down, getting lost, and being attacked by a monkey and a crab and a snake—I couldn't continue hiding his existence and his message from Shinobu.

"'I will be coming to retrieve my precious enchanted blade *Kokorowatari* after a little more recovery'—'It has been four hundred years since I lent it to her, so tell her to be prepared for a late fee.'"

Shinobu heard the words, then looked pensive as she repeated them.

"That is what this samurai said?"

"Yeah... Then he left, howling with laughter."

"In what manner?"

"Hm?"

"I asked ye the manner in which he laughed. Reenact it."

"..."

Reenact it?

That was a lot to ask...

"Ha!"Ha!"Haha!"Hahaha!"Hahahaha!"Hahahahaha!"Hahahaha!" Hahahahahaha!"Hahahahahaahhahahahahahahahahahahahaha—like that."

"Hm."

It felt like an excellent reenactment, if I do say so myself, but

Shinobu didn't so much as smile. If anything, she scowled. And then said nothing. I started to feel responsible, having brought it up.

Unable to take any more of the silence, I spoke.

"Shinobu. I'm just throwing this out there," I attempted to refer to the leading, if improbable possibility, but Shinobu stopped me.

"'Tis of no concern. That is an impossibility. Nothing more than a falsehood."

"A...falsehood? But—"

"*That man died four hundred years ago*—I witnessed it myself, with these very eyes. Earth and heaven could be turned on their head, night and day could trade places, and this alone would be set in stone. 'Tis an absurdity, unworthy of discussion."

"Wait, but Shinobu—"

"Balderdash. Malarkey, even."

"Okay, I get that you're willing to use every word you can think of, but...I still don't understand why you're ready to go that far."

"If this samurai *were feigning to be him*, it must be part of some plot."

"..."

"Perhaps it means to agitate us—so we shall pay it no mind. It merits no comment. Whatever its intention, that enchanted blade..."

The Aberration Slayer, Shinobu said—then smiled.

She smiled at last.

"I cede it to no one. Were this figure the force behind the monkey and such, I shall slice it in two myself upon our meeting—'tis all there is to be said."

And with this, our conversation was over.

I for one wanted to dig a little deeper, but Shinobu implicitly refused.

To be specific, she did so by drawing my attention to another subject—her ribs... By the time I realized it, we were engrossed in debate on the topic, and I couldn't blatantly go back to the armored warrior.

Still, Shinobu wasn't really so unconcerned that she was on the level when she told me not to be concerned. Or so I thought, not just because she didn't demand a shoulder ride, but in general. It wasn't as if she spoke less than usual or was acting strange, but I felt it in the air thanks to all the time, the half-year or so since spring break, that I'd spent as her soulmate.

But if I was going to say that…

Didn't the armored warrior have the right to feel the same way? The right to feel that way for no particular reason—a much stronger right than me, at that…

Fortunately, no more aberrational phenomena attacked us as we traveled from the park and climbed the mountain to Kita-Shirahebi Shrine.

A snail. A monkey. A crab. A snake.

Given what we'd seen, I was prepared to find a bee or a phoenix getting in our way next, and was a little let down when they didn't—but in any case, nothing of the sort obstructed our path.

This made the rules that much more confusing, about whatever was going on, and what Miss Gaen was trying to make us do.

Going back even further.

I didn't have a full picture of the job Ononoki was handling on her own—as time passed, the story expanded, and the cast grew, the number of mysteries only multiplied, making everything less and less clear.

But—I didn't have to think about that now.

All we had to do was climb this mountain and finally, this time, we should be able to meet with Miss Gaen and get an explanation— and I'd have my link to Shinobu restored after the few days we'd been apart.

The morning, the time when these mysteries would be solved, would come at last.

Or so I optimistically thought, but maybe my lot this night was to run into yet another inconvenience, Miss Gaen missing once more…

Thankfully, however, she was at least present within Kita-Shirahebi Shrine's derelict premises.

Izuko Gaen.

Luminary in her field.

The big boss of her experts, senior to Mèmè Oshino, Deishu Kaiki, and Yozuru Kagenui, aunt to Suruga Kanbaru, and a lady who knew everything.

142

Izuko Gaen—was there.

Although she'd changed clothes since I met her in a village the other day, her unique fashion choices, like her baggy, XXL clothes and her low-worn cap, told me at first sight that it was her.

She sat by the steps in front of the ruined shrine's offering box, fiddling with her smartphone as she met the three of us—I suppose it was a tablet and not a smartphone, given its size. She noticed us and raised a hand with a bright smile.

"Hey there, Koyomin. I was waiting for you," she said. "Good evening—or maybe it's dawning enough to say good morning? Welcome, I'm glad we could finally meet. Hold on just a second so I can come to a good stopping place."

I approached Miss Gaen to find that she wasn't doing any kind of work.

She was playing a mobile game.

...Don't play games when we're facing a crisis.

Still, her skillful playstyle and finger speed captivated me before I knew what was happening, keeping me from speaking a word of boilerplate complaint.

"Phew. Okay, all done."

Miss Gaen closed the app before I could figure out what was going on or how things ended—and just as she placed the tablet to her side, she pulled another device from her pants.

This time she started texting.

"Just a work-related message to Yotsugi—to let her know I managed to meet up with you. This is why I gave her a kids' phone. Heh, that doll seems to be uncharacteristically interested in you—your face is all the proof anyone needs."

"My face?"

What're you talking about, I almost asked, then remembered. I'd carelessly forgotten, but Ononoki's foot was still stamped across my face.

Did Miss Gaen see it and mistakenly think that Ononoki and I were off having fun or something? In reality, the shikigami had just mocked me and given me a lecture.

"'Koyomin's doing well'... Okay. Send. Alrighty, thanks for waiting.

Hello, Miss Shinobu Oshino, Miss Suruga Kanbaru."

Done with her text message, she put away her cell phone and faced us at last—placing her hands on her hips, and bowing deeply.

It seemed a little late for her to be greeting us in such a proper and polite way... I found myself at a loss for words, but the preposterous words that she spoke next truly silenced me.

"I'm *Izuko Oshino*. Little sister to Mèmè Oshino, whom you know well."

016

This falsehood was so blatant that it left me dumbstruck—it's not as if I'm so honest that I deserve the title *truth-teller*, but I was at a loss to learn that anyone could tell such a bold, bald-faced lie.

What?

Now that I thought about it, she'd told me in so many words to keep it secret. Still, wasn't she afraid I might have shared her background with Kanbaru, having asked her to come all this way?

I could even have let her name slip out of my mouth by accident. But then, she was a senior of that ominous swindler Deishu Kaiki, wasn't she?

Boss to a great liar who perpetrated an unimaginably large con game on this town, a man who once tricked even Hitagi Senjogahara—to hope for sincerity from her way of life was a mistake from the start.

Still, her dirty trick, which made me an accomplice to her lie, seemed even meaner in a way than anything Kaiki would do—but that's how it was. I just had to play along.

I didn't have the mental fortitude to speak up here and say: *No, we both know that's not true. Your last name is Gaen, isn't it?*

Miss Gaen must have discerned this fact in advance, of course—she looked at me with a sunny smile that seemed to contain a wordless message: *You get it, don't you?*

"Ah…so the Hawaiian-shirted boy had a younger sister. Now that ye mention it, I see the resemblance."

"…"

She'd fooled Shinobu too.

Of course, as another species, Shinobu wasn't able to distinguish between individual humans very well to begin with. Forget any resemblance, I sometimes doubted whether she could tell the difference between men and women.

She never remembered any names or faces—and didn't even try.

"Ha ha ha. I get that a lot. Yes, I feel like I need to apologize for all the trouble my older brother seems to have caused you—"

Miss Gaen kept the act up perfectly.

Her tone was so natural that it made me, who knew the truth, wonder if there was something wrong with her head—the only explanation seemed to be that she sincerely believed she was Oshino's little sister.

…The truth was that she was Oshino's senior. If she was going to lie, shouldn't she be calling herself his older sister?

Why little sister?

Why lie about her age for no good reason on top of it all?

"I'm Suruga Kanbaru."

Whatever the case or the truth.

Kanbaru reciprocated after hearing Miss Gaen's self-introduction.

"I'm employed as my senior Araragi's sex slave."

"Have you seriously been saying that to everyone you meet?!"

I managed to counter a lie this time—call it one of the benefits of being friends. But you could say Kanbaru's problem was far more deeply rooted.

"Ha ha ha. Is that so, a sex slave? So nice to be young and free," Miss Gaen showed understanding.

Her own niece was going down an awful path, but I guess you couldn't act accordingly if you were claiming not to be her aunt…

Speaking of resemblances, though, Kanbaru and Miss Gaen, separated by fewer than three degrees of blood, looked nothing alike. Perhaps it was because I was so tight with my junior that I made a clear distinction, but at the very least, they didn't seem to share a single part in common. I didn't know what Kanbaru's mother looked like, but maybe she just took more after her father?

Hold on, hold on… I was being too hostile.

I needed to give Miss Gaen the benefit of the doubt.

Shinobu and I, as well as Kanbaru herself, were seeking a full explanation of our current situation from this woman—it'd be a big problem if she was simply a pathological liar of a fabulist.

There had to be some reason (I needed there to be one).

A reason she had to hide her identity—thinking about this rationally, Kanbaru's mother, Toé Gaen, had been estranged from the Kanbarus for whatever various reasons, so maybe she couldn't use the Gaen family name?

Right, and it wasn't as if Miss Gaen wanted to meet her long-lost niece. She just needed Kanbaru's arm for some job… Calling herself Oshino's relative enhanced her authority on the subject of aberrations, at least among us.

In that case, I couldn't expose her lie after all… I needed to wait and see.

But if that was true, I had to be wary of Miss Gaen, this kind and cheerful lady—there was no telling when she might lie.

She presented herself as crisp and clear, but in reality, she was a total mess.

She was too much for naive high schoolers.

"In that case, everyone, let's get straight to the matter at hand. Let's talk business," Izuko Gaen—Izuko Oshino said, with her arms outstretched. She may have done this to show how open she was being, but it only made me want to close myself off.

"First, let me hear about the adventure you three had on your way here—give me your tale in full. I love hearing about people's lives, you see."

"Um… Well, it'll probably overlap a lot with the report you got from Ononoki."

"That doesn't bother me. The same story told from a different perspective is still a different tale—and that aside, there's no emotion breathed into the stories that Yotsugi tells me. You can't run through a list of facts and call that a tale."

She seemed to be fixated on that term, *tale*—something she had in common with her junior Oshino, whose little sister she claimed to be.

Urban legends.

Whispers on the street.

Secondhand gossip.

I didn't know if what we experienced that night lived up to any of those labels, but I did know our situation was already at a deadlock. It'd be pointless to try to gloss over things, so I told her about the night's events, just as they happened.

I did conceal matters that needed to be concealed, given that Kanbaru was right behind me—but just as things happened whenever I could.

The armored warrior that appeared in the classroom of the abandoned cram school.

The ruins going up in flames. The message left to me.

Getting lost and being unable to arrive anywhere.

The chimerical monkey-crab-snake aberration.

Like with Kanbaru, Shinobu never tried to speak to Miss Gaen. An expert or Oshino's senior (little sister in Shinobu's understanding), she was a human all the same. This meant I also had to relate Shinobu's story about her fight with a rain-controlling monkey.

I hadn't learned the details about this battle but figured an outline would suffice if she'd already received a report from Ononoki, who was party to it.

Shinobu acting like royalty and not caring to speak to any humans other than me didn't seem to bother Miss Gaen at all.

She seemed to enjoy listening to all thirty-or-so minutes of my story—all the way until the end.

"You really are used to telling stories, aren't you, Koyomin? That was interesting. A real fine narrator of a man. A real fine man, too."

Miss Gaen smiled and nodded.

I, with my simple personality, felt happy to be praised, but it wasn't as if I'd told her in order to be praised. While I may have finished the tale of my adventures, I wasn't ready to step down from the stage to her applause.

As I spoke, I was reminded of first term—the way I pedaled over to that abandoned cram school every time I encountered some new aberrational story, in order to consult with the expert Mèmè Oshino. It made me feel just a little sentimental, but it wasn't as if I'd come here to consult with Miss Gaen about the night's events.

No, I needed her to restore my link to Shinobu, and I needed to negotiate with her about protecting Kanbaru, but if you went all the way back to the start, I'd come to help Miss Gaen with her work.

I was here at her request.

We'd encountered so much trouble along our way, and even had our meeting spot changed at the last second—I wanted her to take responsibility for the mess.

"Ha ha ha. Don't be so petty, Koyomin—does friendship not mean a thing to you? You're going to lose friends acting that way, you know."

"I don't have enough friends to lose any," I said, thinking at first that I'd spoken a cool line, before realizing it was kind of sad—the sky was starting to grow bright as I spoke.

At this rate, I wouldn't be able to make it to school yet again—I was one thing, but as Kanbaru's senior, I'd be ashamed if I forced her to skip school too.

Meanwhile, Shinobu looked sleepy.

She hadn't lost all traces of being nocturnal, it seemed. She may have gotten some sleep under the swings, but maybe she felt drowsy again now that her tummy was full.

But then.

Miss Gaen went and said something—that pried her eyes open.

"Let me cut to the chase," she began, her tone unconcerned, like this was unimportant. "That armored warrior is the first thrall created by Shinobu's previous incarnation—Kissshot Acerolaorion Heartunderblade, the legendary and high-born, iron-blooded, hot-blooded, yet cold-blooded vampire, aberration slayer and king of aberrations—when she sucked his blood. In other words, Koyomi Araragi, as someone Shinobu turned into her second thrall when she drank your blood over spring break, he's sort of your senpai. And in the sense that he was the first Aberration Slayer, I guess that makes him Shinobu's senpai too?"

"…"

"…"

"…"

Of course.

Even if she'd put on airs and made a big, atmospheric show out of her explanation, I doubt any of us would have been the least bit surprised. Even Kanbaru, neither connected to this matter nor too familiar with it, seemed to have fathomed as much.

I thought so.

That's all you could say.

Nothing but *yeah, that's what I figured*—yet at the same time, an urge to contradict her welled up in me.

I thought so and figured as much but still wanted to say: *No, it can't be, there's no way.*

That wasn't the explanation I'd wanted to hear. I hadn't climbed up a mountain in the night to be treated to commentary that a clueless outsider could give. I wanted an expert's sharp insights to open our eyes.

Well.

I guess what she said—did accomplish that task.

"Um. Ye…" Out of all of us, Shinobu was the first to react—but she still spoke to me and not directly to Miss Gaen. "What an utter amateur she is. Is she truly that Hawaiian-shirted boy's little sister?"

That was a lie.

It wasn't true.

But Shinobu had to know what Miss Gaen was going to say—and she must have prepared a line for when she heard it.

Yet she didn't argue directly with Miss Gaen—maybe this wasn't a high-born vampire refusing to deal with humans so much as fear that her argument would be countered and defeated.

"Go and tell her, won't ye? Smack her with the truth sadistically. Thou ought to right this utter amateur's misunderstandings."

"Uh… Right."

Sadistically was asking for too much, but if Shinobu wouldn't say it, that meant I had to—it wasn't as if I could hand this off to Kanbaru.

I turned back to Miss Gaen.

"B-But Miss G—" I stammered, almost using her real name.

"Izuko is fine," she beat me to the punch.

First-name basis? Well, fine.

"Miss Izuko."

"Didn't I just say Izuko is fine?"

Drop the honorific? She wasn't Oshino or anything.

"Miss Izuko. Shinobu's first thrall should be dead—he should have died four hundred years ago. Shinobu herself saw it with her own eyes."

"Yes, m-hm."

"He leapt out into the sun as a vampire, *throwing himself to his own death*—"

Lamenting his misfortune as an expert exterminator of aberrations who found himself turned into a bloodsucker—opposing his own master despite being enthralled by her—bathing his entire body in the rays of the sun, nemesis of all vampires...

He burned up.

And turned to ashes—so.

"So he's gone now—there's no way he's around. It's impossible for that armored warrior to be Shinobu's first thrall."

"Why?"

"Huh? No, like I said—"

"Why? Why is that impossible?"

"..."

Getting asked this point-blank put me at a loss for an answer— I didn't know how to reply, as if I'd been asked *Why does one plus one equal two?*

In my confusion, I gave a few replies that weren't answers at all, like "Well, because he died," and "Because that's how it is, those are the rules"—but then from behind me.

Just as candidly.

Kanbaru spoke up.

"But if you're going to say that, wasn't he an undying vampire *because he doesn't die?*"

"Huh?"

He doesn't die, and because he doesn't die—he's undying?

No wait, that can't be right... That's not it, I mean, sunlight is a vampire's absolute weakness... Just like garlic, or crosses, or silver bullets, so...

He burned...and turned to ashes, and...

Hm?

If we're going to talk about characteristics, though...

Just like I discussed with Ononoki as we ate ice cream that day—a vampire's immortality is on a different order from a ghost's or a *tsukumogami*'s.

It's not that they don't die.

They're undying because there is no death for them.

In other words—they're not immortal because they come back to life.

They're immortal—because they continue to live no matter what happens.

Vampires.

"Ah...could that mean..."

"That's right, Miss Suruga Kanbaru—just the kind of brilliance I'd expect from someone who *made the monkey's paw work for her,*" Miss Gaen said. "In other words, *four hundred years after throwing himself to his death*—after scorching his body, turning to ashes, and returning to nothing, the vampire has made an amazing return."

He'd come back despite becoming nothing but ashes and bone.

No wonder the legendary vampire Kissshot Acerolaorion Heartunderblade chose him to be her first thrall, Miss Gaen remarked bluntly.

017

"All right, now gather 'round.

"Now that I'm done cutting to the chase, why don't we do things in order. I suppose I'll give a chronological explanation of what happened while using this tablet's dazzling screen to provide some illustrations—yes, vampires are of course weak to the sun.

"Even an elementary schooler knows that—and not even the iron-blooded, hot-blooded, yet cold-blooded vampire Kissshot Acerolaorion Heartunderblade is an exception.

"Neither are her thralls, of course.

"But while the king of aberrations whose name spread, without exaggeration, around the world is no exception, she is beyond the pale—her weakness does not function as a weakness.

"In fact, Koyomin, didn't you get set ablaze under the sun's rays over spring break yourself? But you recovered after that, right?

"Yes, I know.

"The same thing happened to the body of the First.

"That's what this is—of course, since he threw himself under the sun on purpose in order to die, and not by mistake like you, I guess you could call it a would-be, or rather, a would-never-be suicide.

"It does seem like it took a bit of time for him to return, though.

"A brief four hundred years or so.

"Or to be more precise, even now, four hundred years after his would-never-be suicide, the First has still not managed to fully return.

"You faced off against this armored warrior yourselves, so you must know, right? I bet you felt that the armored warrior was getting stronger and stronger—but if we're being accurate, it's not that he got stronger.

"He's recovering.

"He's on the road to rehabilitation.

"He's trying to return to his *full self*—so yes, he used that energy drain on you and Miss Suruga Kanbaru to feed and restore himself. Just as Shinobu recovered from the scratches she suffered from that mockery of an aberration by eating another mockery of an aberration.

"Maybe I ought to call you a sterling example of a successor, Koyomin, because you ended up aiding the First in his speedy recovery—no, no.

"I'm not just talking about tonight—I'm pointing to your personality, to the entire way you've been acting lately.

"You don't understand what I'm saying? Don't worry, you will soon.

"To put it another way, I personally wanted to put an end to all this before it got to this point.

"My plan was to have Yotsugi handle it herself.

"I messed up a whole lot of my calculations—just because I know everything doesn't mean that everything goes the way I think it will.

"Especially, Koyomin.

"Especially when I'm faced with reckless, impossible-to-predict youngsters like you who don't operate according to logic—which is why I took responsibility for getting my calculations wrong and stepped out into the front lines myself, and it's why I asked you for help.

"You might think that some mean old lady is getting you wrapped up in one of her annoying jobs right now—but really, this lady's giving you an opportunity.

"The perfect opportunity to take responsibility for the very things you bungled—but I doubt you'd be quick to see it my way.

"You might never be able to see it my way.

"But Koyomin, has it really never crossed your mind? Why you've been encountering these troublesome aberrational phenomena over the last six months on what seems like a monthly basis?

"You don't find that strange?

"Why the legendary vampire—

"Why, out of all the places in the world, Kissshot Acerolaorion Heartunderblade visited the very town you live in over spring break.

"Was it just a coincidence?

"Why the crab girl, why the snail girl, why the monkey girl, why the snake girl were in this town.

"Why the aberration hunted by my junior who gives even me trouble, Kagenui…

"Why the phoenix lived here in this town too. Do you think that's just another coincidence?

"The cat—the circumstances may have been a little special in that one case.

"But that must be exactly why the armored warrior stepped so carelessly on the tiger's tail—when you look at it that way, fortune favored you.

"A tiger, huh. Heh.

"As someone who'd once gone up in flames himself, the First must have been traumatized by the fire and the blaze—no wonder he decided to make a temporary retreat.

"If you manage to survive long enough to see Tsubasa Hanekawa again, you'd better thank her—hm? You don't know what I mean by that, either? Then don't worry about it yet—I'm just saying that your friend is a tragic girl who defends you, intentionally or not.

"You seem to think that things that happen to you could naturally happen to others, and while I feel a sense of modesty coming from your rejection of miracles, your way of thinking has one large flaw.

"Which is that you're judging anyone who'd see you as special as wrong—I'm really sorry for saying all these vague things.

"I start to want to lecture about life whenever I see a spunky youngster like you—I bet Mèmè, my big brother, would just give you a 'You're so spirited, something good happen to you?' and leave it at that, but I regret to say I'm not as tolerant as that novice.

"Speaking of which, didn't I promise to explain things in chronological order? Then I'll keep my promise. In the end, keeping promises is the quickest way to get results.

"Let's start four hundred years ago—when the current Shinobu Oshino, Kissshot Acerolaorion Heartunderblade, made her first slave after not creating a single thrall until that day.

"She drank the blood of a human.

"The reason things came to this—that's something I can skip over, right? It's been told in another place, and it's in the past.

"For you and for him.

"From the perspective of an expert aberration exterminator, finding himself on the side of the exterminated was something he couldn't take—he couldn't face the fact that he'd become a monster. And so he chose death.

"He threw himself under the sun.

"He turned to ashes and vanished, swept away by the wind—or at least, that's what should have happened.

"To Heartunderblade he left all his rancor, as well as a replica of the enchanted, aberration-slaying sword, Kokorowatari—and they all lived happily ever after.

"Except they didn't, for reasons I explained above.

"Even if he turned to ashes or disappeared, he didn't die—he may have vanished, but he wasn't gone. He may have died, but he couldn't die out.

"He.

"Kept living.

"He turned to nothing, he turned to nothingness, and he kept living.

"Over the course of four hundred years—over the course of a dizzying, a depressing amount of time, he slowly but surely restored his body.

"Burned by the sun each time he recovered, broken each time he put himself back together, he didn't succumb, didn't grow discouraged—he recovered.

"I can't say this with any first-hand knowledge because I've never had the experience of being immortal, but I imagine those four hundred years were like hell—a Sisyphean ordeal.

"Of course, you can't even laugh at the idea of a vampire being tormented by demons.

"He would doggedly pile up little pebbles.

"He could pile them up and up, but one swing of a rod would ruin it all. One beam of sunlight would ruin everything.

"Sunlight on a clear day would force him to start rebuilding from zero whatever little bonds he'd formed—and so this fruitless process of trial-and-error went on for this dizzying amount of time as he tried to recover.

"Of course, it's not as if the First had any sort of firm will of his own now that he was ash. This recovery is more like a vampire's biological reaction, probably nothing more than a reflex…

"When you think of it that way, it wasn't fruitless so much as hapless.

"A sad case of unlimited continues in a game you can never beat.

"He couldn't even die, all because he'd inherited a legendary vampire's damned immortality.

"Eternal youth and life in the truest sense—I'm sure Yotsugi would have been able to put him out of his misery if she'd been there, but we're talking about four hundred years ago.

"In any case.

"His karma looped endlessly in this one-man transmigration—which he'd be forced to repeat forever.

"That was the first Aberration Slayer's fate—but.

"His persistence was something special—the legendary vampire had chosen him to be her thrall for a reason. So, with a will that he shouldn't have had.

"With what little will he had.

"He rode the wind—still as ash.

"He was scattered but reassembled.

"Persistently, one speck at a time.

"Through sheer determination—*he returned to this town*.

"And he did so fifteen years ago."

018

"H-He came back? To this town?"

While I'd stayed silent as Miss Gaen went on and on, thinking that I shouldn't interrupt her, I couldn't hold back any longer when I heard those words, and reflexively spoke up.

Came back to this town? Really?

She didn't mean to say—to this country?

"Oh, when the timeline says fifteen years ago, that's a rough chronological estimate. It might not be accurate, but the number is meaningful—because it was exactly fifteen years ago, when I was still in college, that I came up with the idea to create, by way of necromancy, an immortal shikigami aberration named Yotsugi Ononoki using a human corpse that had been used for a century. And then..."

Miss Gaen looked at me with what seemed like a meaningful stare this time.

"That's exactly when the phoenix came upon its next host—which is why your friendly Izuko thinks that the ashes making up the First must've gathered in this town right about then."

" ... "

Fifteen years ago.

That number wasn't what gave me pause, by any means—but hearing her say fifteen years ago did bring one more thing to mind.

When Tsubasa Hanekawa was given the name Tsubasa Hane-kawa—back when she was three, that was fifteen years ago, right? No, that couldn't have anything to do with this. Was I reading too much into things?

The tsukumogami. The phoenix. The cat—no, but if I was going to say that, why focus only on fifteen years ago? If that's what we're talking about, I should think not of a point in time but a span of it, from fifteen years ago to this very moment.

The snail—first lost eleven years ago.

The monkey—whose wish came true seven years ago.

The crab—who stole a girl's weight three years ago.

Even what happened with the snake just two months ago came into consideration.

"There's no way… Are you really saying that all these stories of aberrations are the fault of those ashes riding into town or whatever?"

"Of course not. Yozuru and company didn't make Yotsugi in this town, anyway." Miss Gaen easily replied in the negative—but the denial felt so light that I couldn't see it as total. "I'm just saying it's an underlying cause. Or maybe I should call it a sign that should make you think. Every aberration has a reason—but this is nothing more than part of that reason. The aberrations you encountered were your own fault, generally speaking—I'm not letting you off the hook here. But," she said, glancing at Shinobu with what somehow felt like sympathy. "Kissshot Acerolaorion Heartunderblade came to this town during spring break—because of those ashes, I have to assume."

"What foolishness."

At last, Shinobu—turned directly to Miss Gaen.

Either she couldn't allow me to handle her business anymore, or she couldn't keep her silence. Her eyes glinted with what could almost be called malice as she set them on Miss Gaen.

"And ye claim to be that Hawaiian-shirted boy's little sister?"

That wasn't who she was, of course.

"I visited this country then because I wished to see Mount Fuji."

"Haha. Our sacred mountain? True, the forest in its foothills is a famous suicide spot. But this mountain isn't Mount Fuji. We're not even in Shizuoka or Yamanashi, we're in the wrong prefecture altogether—did you get lost on your way there? All while three vampire hunters were after you? No, you didn't get lost. You were led—to this town."

"Led?"

"If you'd like me to give an example, take how that armored warrior happened to wander into the abandoned cram school where you and Miss Suruga Kanbaru were meeting. Though I'm sure the First had neither a consciousness or an unconsciousness when he so politely knocked on the door."

"…"

Silenced, Shinobu grated her sharp teeth. She wasn't even attempting to hide her anger, which suggested that Miss Gaen was right on the mark.

As for me, it wasn't anger that I felt. It was disgust.

How to put it—Miss Gaen made it sound like all the travails visited upon me converged on one man, and I found it disgusting.

No.

Maybe it was just displeasure.

But when I thought about it, that wasn't how I should be feeling. If I now had an answer to the nagging question "Why is this all happening to me"—shouldn't I be glad?

So why did I feel sucky?

If the First had laid the groundwork for everything Shinobu and I did together—that would be no reason to feel displeasure. Why should I feel inferior?

It almost seemed like—I was jealous or something.

Even though she'd told me not to be.

"Impossible," Shinobu said, after a long silence.

Her tone was direct, strong, and final.

"Impossible—'tis impossible. He died—that man died. Died a death. He was an utter fool who lent no ear to my persuasions, who chose to toss his life away. Thy words are nothing more than sophistry. Underestimate not my poor sense of direction."

"Well, I do think your poor sense of direction deserves to be made fun of—ha ha ha, you sound pretty insistent there, Shinobu. You almost make it sound like it'd be a problem if the First was still alive, you know?"

Miss Gaen was undaunted by Shinobu's intimidating demeanor—Shinobu's former self, Kissshot Acerolaorion Heartunderblade, was no easy figure to take on, even for an expert, but Miss Gaen showed no signs of fear.

She only continued to provoke her.

"If anything, you ought to be celebrating that your beloved slave is still alive and trying to restore himself as we speak. I wouldn't mind arranging for a party, you know?"

"Don't ye tread too far, expert."

Shinobu had allowed herself to be provoked, and her body shook with anger—even I found myself upset by Miss Gaen's tone, but seeing Shinobu so shaken actually helped calm me down.

"Don't ye tread too far into sensitive matters. What do ye claim to know about what took place four hundred years ago?"

"I know everything—there's nothing I don't know," Miss Gaen declared. Then she seemed to shift the topic to something completely unrelated. "There's even a reason I changed our meeting place from the park to this shrine."

Now that she mentioned it—why did she change our meeting place anyway?

"I kind of feel like I'm being kept out of the loop here."

Then...speaking of calmness, the calmest person present—though maybe she was simply confused by Miss Gaen's words—raised her hand and spoke. Kanbaru.

"Is it okay if I ask a question, Miss Izuko?"

"Go ahead, Miss Suruga Kanbaru."

"Um."

Since this was Kanbaru, I wondered if she might be trying to smooth things over with a ridiculous line. I worried for her as her senior, but she asked the smiling Miss Gaen a proper question, and a surprisingly on-the-nose one at that.

"For four hundred years, this guy kept repeating a cycle of coming back, then getting turned into ash again because of the sun, right? That would mean he was still basically just ash when he came floating into this town fifteen years ago, wouldn't it? Then what exactly caused the cycle to stop and let him present himself to Araragi-senpai as an armored warrior?"

Did this girl ever feel nervous? She was being talkative, even social with someone she was meeting for the first time. Maybe she unconsciously sensed their kinship? No, Miss Gaen was treating her niece the exact same way as me and Shinobu.

"Why do you think that was, Miss Suruga Kanbaru? Can you come up with a guess as to why the cycle ended—why the First was released from his barren karmic cycle?"

"I can't, but...does the reason have something to do with why you changed our meeting place?"

A weird way to connect the dots, I thought, but Miss Gaen replied, "You're a sharp one" with a quick lick of her lips. "Ah, what a waste of talent to let you roam free—but I'll respect that eccentric's wish."

"What eccentric?" asked Kanbaru, confused.

"Don't worry," Miss Gaen said, "you're not out of the loop. In fact, you might just be at the center of it—I might only be saying this because of how often people refer to me as their senpai, but Miss Suruga Kanbaru, it'd be nice if you could support your own senior."

My juniors are all such good-for-nothings, the boss expert added, not in a half-joking manner but as a serious lament, shrugging her shoulders.

"Of course. Serving Araragi-senpai's person from the waist down is literally my job."

"Think you could serve me from the waist up too?"

Kanbaru looked surprised to hear this... Sheesh, like she didn't know what I meant.

"Fifteen years ago," Miss Gaen changed the topic, opening her timeline again. "The First returned to this town—his wanderings came to an end as he floated back into this, his hometown. What seemed to be his eternal trip through hell had reached its goal."

Hometown? Having tossed the word in casually, Miss Gaen continued without placing any importance on it.

"And each of those grains of ash floated in and gathered *in this town's air pocket of a spot...* Right here, in Kita-Shirahebi Shrine, built even then at the peak of this little mountain."

019

"As you can see, this shrine has fallen into ruin—with no one taking care of it, it's become an absolute mess. Of course, it wasn't always this way, but we're not here to talk about the founding and history of shrines, we'll discuss it another day if the opportunity presents itself.

"I do hope it does.

"In any case, this shrine was still being properly maintained fifteen years ago—seems like it was a nice and tidy little place. And I don't mean that as an insult, that's praise—it needs to be nice and tidy because this place is an air pocket.

"An aberrational air pocket.

"A place where it's easy for them to appear—easy for them to gather.

"A place where those 'bad things' gather before becoming aberrations.

"As well as a place where aberrations—come to an end.

"Geographic conditions have a lot to do with this kind of thing, you see. Like with locations that people call 'haunted highways' or 'suicide spots'—taken together, they're all places where 'that kind of thing' tends to happen. If you can pin down all of these points and all of these places, you can prevent accidents from ever happening—you can avoid them. Mèmè, my big brother, has the job of gathering stories of aberrations, but as far as my job goes, it's supposed to be more of this sort. Prevention, in other words, tidying up things before they happen—unless you clamp down on these spots, each of these hotbeds of scenes that dot everywhere you go…you can't prevent accidents.

"Hm? What? No, I said hotbeds of scenes, not hot beds obscene— what would that even mean? That sounds like a pretty awful accident, too. I don't want you and your junior going to any of those, okay? You two partner up in other ways. That's not what I mean by supporting your senior, Miss Suruga Kanbaru.

"Well, I'm just making things complicated by bringing up such specialized topics. To radically simplify, this is one of those kinds of places, which is why an onmyoji sorcerer so famous that I dare not speak my name in the same breath once built a shrine here, deified a god, and clamped down on it.

"It went well for the most part.

"The place functioned as a proper defense—those 'bad things' gathering here that could form into an aberration were properly scattered.

"The shrine had a good god, you see.

"But there is a limit to everything—um, Koyomin? You're studying for entrance exams, right? Do you carry a good-luck amulet, in that case?

"A good-luck amulet.

"Did you know those things have an expiration date? They expire when the paper charm inside of them rips—those wondrous and miraculous items aren't effective forever, and neither was this shrine or the god deified here.

"Fifteen years ago—that limit was reached.

"But it'd be too harsh to blame the shrine's managers, to say nothing of its god—how could they see it coming?

"The ashes of the *first thrall of a legendary vampire* gathering here from every direction—that's just too much.

"It was too much.

"It's not as if he came parading back home triumphant—but what did happen is that Kita-Shirahebi Shrine collapsed once, fifteen years ago.

"Both in spiritual and physical terms.

"Your thrall really is something, Shinobu. Destroying an entire shrine as nothing more than ash—though I'm sure his former life as an expert had something to do with it.

"Hm? What's the matter, Koyomin? It looks like something just clicked for you. Ah, it's suddenly making sense to you that Kita-Shira-hebi Shrine was even more ruined eleven years ago, when you time-traveled to a past world the other day.

"That's right, that—was the First's doing.

"The shrine that should have held this spot down—couldn't hold down a vampire thrall.

"Just for reference, they tried to renovate this shrine not once, not twice, but three times after that—but there's nothing shakier than repairing an empty shrine with no god.

"It collapsed each time they tried to renovate it—it broke down and withered away.

"The problem is Shinobu—or rather, Kissshot Acerolaorion Heartunderblade, or the First, her thrall, have such power that their very existence brings aberrations to them.

"So let's go back to eleven years ago.

"When you visited this shrine then, weren't these ruined grounds filled to the brim with 'bad things'? You thought it was strange for them to be here in such an intense concentration, but there was nothing strange about it. Those were the building blocks of aberrations that the First's ashes had gathered here.

"The building blocks of aberrations—and of his diet.

"After all that exposition, I assume that even someone without specialized knowledge such as yourself can guess what happens next, Koyomin—you can guess the reason why the First's ashes, gathered here, managed to escape his karmic cycle.

"That's right.

"If this shrine is a place where bad things easily gather, and if the First is an aberration that is easily gathered—that means *all the conditions were in place for an accident to occur.*

"Accidents—overlapped.

"The First, on the grounds of this very shrine.

"Here on the grounds of this godless shrine…he ate and ate, restoring his strength.

"It was barely anything at all, of course—I wouldn't call it drinking the mist, but maybe like eating plankton. As a thrall, and as a pile of ashes at that, he couldn't gather the massive amount of 'bad things' that Shinobu did. He couldn't gather food on a scale that could risk the breakout of a great yokai war in this town. He only made it a little easier for aberrational phenomena to take place here.

"Just the difference of a five-percent chance turning into six percent, or maybe seven percent at most.

"Of course, that's significant from an expert's point of view—life gets hard for us once you're past the five-percent mark, but we'll put that aside for now and just say that his environment changed.

"Just by a little, yes, but he could now feed—his existence of cycling between ashes and nothingness ended here.

"What began then unfolded over the next fifteen years—this tragic figure's dramatic return.

"A drama of return.

"Or just maybe—a drama of revenge."

0 2 0

A drama of revenge.

I couldn't stop myself from gulping when I heard those heavy words, but Miss Gaen's story made so many things make sense. I, at least, had a hard time dismissing it outright.

Did Kissshot Acerolaorion Heartunderblade come to this town during spring break not because she got lost, or because she was being chased by three experts, but because her thrall, the aberration-gathering First, drew her here? Is that what Izuko Gaen was saying?

He called aberrations to him—and one of them was a vampire.

He invited his master's presence.

He invited a suicidal vampire into the town he'd made his stronghold—no, according to what I'd just heard, the armored warrior only acquired a firm will of his own in that old cram school. It's not as if he'd consciously called Shinobu to him...

The hypothesis did suggest something, however.

After fifteen years, this existence that had floated into town as nothing more than ash—after fifteen years all but surviving on the morning dew, it would have at last returned to the level of *being able* to summon a legendary vampire. Though I'm not sure you could call it "summoning" given that she was the master and he the thrall...

And while he'd increased the probability of aberrational phenomena occurring in this town by a few percent for fifteen years now, at this point it seemed like I encountered aberrations almost monthly—or daily, depending on how you framed it. Didn't that have something to do with all this?

That worried me. It really worried me.

But at the same time…

When I think how it was here, in this deserted shrine forsaken by gods and worshippers alike, that the First kept on living for fifteen whole years—no, in that sense, four hundred years.

Four centuries.

An unimaginable span of time—for a mindbogglingly long period.

Kept on living didn't begin to cover it.

It was like he kept on dying.

It was—simply torture.

No more than five seconds under the sun as a vampire caused me a transcendental amount of pain—four hundred years of it? What do you have to multiply five seconds by to get four hundred years?

"No need to be on the lookout, Koyomin—the First has already left this shrine. He's not here," Miss Gaen said, taking out her cell phone.

A different one from the one she used a moment ago to contact Ononoki—I thought she might be texting someone else, but it seemed she was only checking the time. I realized it was morning already.

"Hm…good timing. I think I'm more or less done explaining, but Koyomin, Shinobu, Miss Suruga Kanbaru, anything else you don't get?"

"W-Well, there's still a ton of things I don't get," I said in a panic, practically clinging to her before she could bring this to an end.

"Whaaat. Can't you figure out most of the rest?"

"Wh-What should we even do after this? What kind of job did you want us helping out on?"

"Like I said, you need to take responsibility. You're going to pick it up. You're going to take in the responsibility. You, Koyomin—and Shinobu."

Miss Gaen didn't mention Kanbaru this time—and Kanbaru said nothing in return.

"You said the plan at first was for Ononoki to handle it herself, right?

That the situation now was beyond your calculations—so could you tell us what the original plan was?"

"Fine with me. There's no point in telling you about it, though. I don't see how it could possibly be carried out now—do you remember why Mèmè, my big brother, came to this town?"

"Because Shinobu came here, right? I want to say Kaiki gave the same reason. As for Miss Kagenui...I feel like she heard about it from Kaiki?"

"That's right. All of those experts, each with their own unique quirk or two, came to this town for similar reasons—and the results of their investigations came to me. I am important, believe it or not."

Miss Gaen continued.

"After scrutinizing these results—the intel I received from each of them, I came to know about the odd chain of events taking place in this town over the last fifteen years. *The way the wind was blowing here.* I came to know this—this friendly lady here who knows everything came to know the four-hundred-year-long tale of the First that I just finished explaining to you."

"..."

"That's why I sent Yotsugi here again. To lower the occurrence rate of aberrations that had risen by just a few percentage points. Her job was to *clean up the ashes*—to tidy up a shrine, to put it simply?"

Yotsugi Ononoki, one half of a two-man cell specializing in immortal aberrations. It seemed she still didn't know her mission when she encountered me on the last day of summer break—but she'd been given her Cinderella-like mission right afterwards.

Vampires are like the poster children for immortal aberrations, so cleaning up after one of their thralls does seem like her kind of job.

Okay, maybe I could have figured that much out without having to ask any questions—but why did she fail?

Did Ononoki ever fail when it came to her work?

We're talking about that workhorse who saved not just my life but Shinobu's over the course of one night here.

"Well, Ononoki does have an airheaded side to her...so maybe she fails now and then?"

"You're making it sound like it's someone else's problem, Koyomin. Yotsugi failed because of what you, plural, did."

"What we did?"

Who was included in this *you*?

A look at Miss Gaen's eyes answered this, though—she looked only at me and Shinobu.

"Just a guess, but does it have something to do with me and Shinobu using the...'bad things' gathered in the air pocket—which Oshino's talisman had sealed so they'd disperse over time?"

A blind guess.

I honestly didn't have the first idea about what we'd done, but that was about the only thing Shinobu and I did after we met Ononoki on the last day of summer break.

We used the "bad things," precursors to aberrations, left behind in this shrine to travel through time like we were in some sort of horror, or maybe more of an SF story. Had that backfired in some kind of way? No, those careless actions had already backfired plenty—but even more?

"If anything, if we came in and swiped the energy that could potentially serve the First's ashes. Wouldn't that delay his resurrection? I don't see it speeding things up, at lea—"

I looked back at Shinobu as I said this—to find her biting her nails.

Hey. Isn't that what you do when you're irritated?

Did you think of something?

We'd used the shrine's gathered energy to return from eleven years in the past to the present, too...if we'd messed up by doing that, what did it mean?

"Shinobu didn't do anything," Miss Gaen said. "Anything— *she didn't need to do anything.* Coming to this shrine was enough on its own."

"..."

"To correct you on one point you might be misunderstanding— when I say the First drew Shinobu here, that was only by way of their master-servant relationship formed four hundred years ago. It's not as if he asked her to show up the way you might ask someone with a text or call. In other words, he didn't know he was doing so until then. He had no idea—that his master had come close. He had no idea that the monster that had made him into a monster had come."

"…"

"To be honest, I don't know how much my dear older brother, Mèmè, had figured out—he doesn't say a whole lot, and even his reports only contain the bare minimum. All I really know is that he used that talisman to carry out first aid on this shrine—which you can say ended up starving the First out, but in his hungry state—"

Pushed once more to his breaking point.

Just then, in that state of mind.

"He found out. He—*saw her*. Kissshot Acerolaorion Heartunderblade. For the first time in four hundred years—he *witnessed her*."

A quiet gasp.

Shinobu stopped chewing her nails—and looked up.

Stunned, clear shock painted on her expression.

Right.

Right—when I visited this shrine with Kanbaru on an errand for Oshino, and again because of Sengoku, Shinobu Oshino had yet to start living in my shadow.

It wasn't until then that she first stepped into this air pocket—

"In other words," Kanbaru said pensively.

When we started talking about time travel, she could have lost the thread, as if I was talking about some dream from the night before. Commendably, she was keeping up.

"Seeing Shinobu for the first time in four hundred years gave the First strength, and this stimulation made him rouse himself despite being nothing more than ashes—resurrecting him despite his starved state?"

"Who ever said anything that romantic?" Despite Miss Gaen's high estimation of Kanbaru up until this point—she seemed to be unimpressed with this one opinion. "Why would ashes be roused back into life for a reason out of a teen rom-com? An existence close to his appeared in physical proximity, that's all, causing his aberrational nature to be rapidly excited. You know how putting a magnet against some iron for a while magnetizes it for a bit, so it can suck up iron sand? It's more or less like that."

"I see…" Kanbaru nodded. She seemed to want to press her point, but swallowed the words—an attitude you didn't see very often from someone as unreserved as her. "But it's true that Shinobu coming here had the effect of exciting…or booting up the First?"

"That's right, which is why Kita-Shirahebi Shrine was an empty husk by the time Yotsugi came here on her mission. A job that should've required little more than a duster got a little more difficult. She had to start by finding where the First had gone off to. While you two were out having fun time-traveling from this shrine gate, we were having all kinds of trouble."

" … "

We weren't having fun, but I couldn't blame her for thinking so.

"By now, you must've figured out my task for you. Hunt for the First—and it's not just that I want more hands on deck. Sheer manpower could result in casualties… Rather, as her second, you're suited to finding her first. The First and the Second, slave and slave, should end up attracting each other."

Don't worry. It's not like I want you to clean up the ashes, Miss Gaen assured.

"Though it's a little too perfect that you encountered the First before I gave you the deets, Koyomin—not to mention that you helped him grow."

"Grow…"

True—I'd helped him.

The armored warrior, sluggish and heavy when he first appeared, could even speak well after draining my energy and Kanbaru's.

If anything made us responsible, that would be it—right? Though it didn't seem like we could've avoided that outcome even if we'd known all this beforehand…

"Oh, sorry, did I make it sound like I was blaming you? You did make fairly irregular moves, but at this point, I'm almost grateful. You made the job easier for me in some ways—especially by endowing him with speech. That one's big. If he can understand words, that means we can negotiate—we can go carrot-and-stick."

"Carrot-and-stick…"

Miss Gaen was truly Kaiki's senior in that everything she said sounded like a lie, but this was the part that made her Oshino's. He did hate the idea of exterminating aberrations, for the most part.

But—I laid out in my mind the clear, the oh-so-clear profile of the armored warrior.

The vampire thrall who made use of *every* aberrational phenomenon that occurred in this town over fifteen years.

A legendary vampire's first slave.

The First—which made him my senior.

And Shinobu's as well, in terms of the title of Aberration Slayer, as the original wielder of the enchanted blade Kokorowatari.

Most of all.

Immortal.

"Isn't it Miss Kagenui you should've asked for? You know, Ononoki's master, the violent onmyoji who specializes in immortal aberrations?"

If Oshino was a pacifist, Miss Kagenui was a warmonger.

I never ended up having to face off against her directly, but she was skilled enough in combat that she could probably go toe-to-toe with Shinobu—however, Miss Gaen only shook her head.

"I can't control her," she said. "I'd prefer it if she has to spend the rest of her life complaining about never seeing action."

Getting Miss Gaen of all people to say this was kind of impressive.

Something about the onmyoji did strike me as unconventional, even among the various experts I knew, and I guess there really was something special about her.

"Will Ononoki be enough as far as combat reserves go?"

"No. When I got my status report from Yotsugi yesterday—which is to say when I heard that you and the First had come into contact, I already went ahead and called in another helper. Who's waiting to meet up with me."

So that's why she was concerned about the hour.

My being slow to understand must have eaten up more time than expected—so she was right, things don't always go exactly as planned, even for someone of Miss Gaen's level. Let alone for someone of mine…

"B-But a helper? Ononoki really isn't good enough on her own?"

"She's not, because I'd like to settle this before today is over," replied Miss Gaen, as unhurriedly as always—but for once, I sensed her determination as a professional. "Now that he has a will, and now that he's conscious, and now that he's able to use that energy drain as he wishes, the longer we leave him be, the stronger he'll get—doubling up and up and up and up and up and up. He'll make a full recovery if we aren't serious about tackling this. He'd be too much for me to handle at that point—that's when I really would have no choice but to call in Yozuru."

"..."

She spoke about Miss Kagenui as if she were some sort of inhumane weapon...

I nearly cracked a smile for the first time in a while, but the words that came from Miss Gaen's mouth next were more than enough to make me pull it back in.

Whatever the case.

"What I want—is to kill him before he eats a human."

021

Miss Gaen handed me a five-thousand-yen bill with an *All right, I'm going to get going so you go buy yourself some breakfast if you're hungry, Koyomin.* She then started to descend the mountain to go meet this helper, whoever it was. Shinobu and I were now left behind on the shrine's grounds. Miss Gaen never gave a clear explanation as to why she changed our meeting place from that park to Kita-Shirahebi Shrine, but her idea must have been to use this spot to explain something she originally had no intention of discussing with us. Her hand had been forced when the armored warrior began to move in earnest—and so she directed us here.

As for my link with Shinobu, it had yet to be restored. It seemed that Miss Gaen's original plan was to repair it as soon as we met—to *cram* Shinobu back into my shadow, but that'd have to wait until a little further down the line, now that the first Aberration Slayer had recovered to a level where he had an unmistakable ego of his own. It was safer to leave it until everything was settled.

Even if he didn't have a real consciousness when Shinobu and I time-traveled from this shrine, the fact that he entrusted me with a message to her, in that burning cram school, meant he already knew about her presence. We couldn't afford to let our location slip out to him by raising the level of Shinobu's vampirism.

To return to the magnet example, restoring our link and increasing

Shinobu's vampirism might raise the armored warrior's vampirism by way of their link—right, just as I'd been modulating my body's vampiric powers.

Don't worry, I'll keep my promise—I'd never be mean and not restore your link after dragging things out this long. In fact, it'd be a problem for me as an expert if I didn't—because all it takes for Kissshot Acerolaorion Heartunderblade to be considered harmless is for her to be sealed in your shadow, Miss Gaen had argued. Not that I didn't believe her, but I couldn't deny the feeling that she'd climbed down the mountain before this and a lot of other things could be resolved.

Yes, she might not have had any other choice, since she needed to pick up this helper—but speaking as someone who thought we'd be protected if we met up with Miss Gaen, part of me did feel let down when she went down the mountain.

Shinobu and I aside, I wanted to ask her to protect Kanbaru, a bystander I'd involved in this whole mess—but Miss Gaen had assured us that there was no need to worry.

The sun is starting to come up, after all. You're safe until night—your sense of this fact might be a little off because of Shinobu's free-spirited nature, but vampires are nocturnal. That's why you're safe during the day. You could even use this time to rest—because I'm going to put you to work at night. There's no real reason to hang around this shrine anymore, so why don't you go back home for now and put on a change of clothes?

That's what she'd said, but I couldn't possibly in our situation. I did feel bad about making Kanbaru skip school, but it seemed like the right choice was to make these shrine grounds our base for the day.

Oshino's holy of holies talisman, which Kanbaru and I had deployed here by his request, had purified this shrine, once an air pocket of sorts. To my amateur line of thinking, that vaguely meant the place was safe...

Upon consideration, it made perfect sense that Kanbaru had felt unwell that day and similarly fatigued this time around—the armored warrior's ashes were within these grounds back then.

If not a fleck of those ashes remained... Still, as her senior in both school and skipping it, I worried about her attendance record.

"Really? It's okay, you don't have to worry about that kind of thing."

"Oh… Well, you, I guess, can catch up after a day or two of classes, if you have good attendance for the most part."

"Yeah. Also, I wouldn't mind having to repeat a year if it was for your sake."

"Could you please not put that heavy of an emotional burden on me?"

I only felt more guilty now. She was too straightforward of a person.

I already felt like I'd never be able to atone for acting as a mediator and bringing this mild obstruction into her life.

"No, really, it's fine. I'm being serious when I say you don't have to worry. And anyway, *mild obstruction* almost sounds like *child abduction*."

"So what if it does? And why would your mind go to that?"

"Hm? Oh, you want me to explain my logical seduction?"

"You mean induction. Stop it, I don't want you putting the words *child* and *seduction* anywhere near each other. Aren't you supposed to be a wholesome young athlete? What kinds of workouts did you do to end up that way?"

"Child adduction."

"As in grabbing children's bodies and pulling them toward you…"

Speaking of which, Shinobu Oshino.

Once she'd finished hearing what Miss Gaen had to say, she watched her climb down the mountain but didn't offer any thoughts.

Her attitude standoffish.

Of course, it was true she couldn't dismiss everything with an "Impossible" after that thorough of an explanation…

I felt anxious seeing her like this, so I blurted out a cowardly, "So what're you going to do, Shinobu?" But.

"What is there to be done?" she asked back, sounding bored. "Though an irregularity may have occurred, we must act in accordance with that expert's plan. Whatever the case may be with him, he shall be finished this eve. 'Twould be one thing if he were in his full and true state, but just as I myself showed this spring break, he'll prove no match for multiple experts in his half-boiled condition. Despite what that expert said, I believe the doll-girl might be enough on her own."

"…"

"He will be eliminated, and that will be the end of it. Done. That is all—nothing left for us to do. If they say his power may increase when near me, then I ought not to meet him, though that may not be the case for thee. His end will come unknown to me... I must say this just in case, my master, but do not worry thyself when 'tis not called for." Her eyes alert, she continued as if to drive the point home. "While that woman spoke in ways to incite thee, in part to amuse herself—I have neither first nor second thrall. What use do orders and numberings have for me after five centuries alive? I was sure to preface my story to thee the other day, was I not?"

"Preface? Like what?"

"Occupy not thyself with foolish envy. Stem thy emotions at adorable jealousy. Do not worry."

Thou art the only one for me now, she said.

Having lived for five hundred years (almost six hundred, actually), she probably meant it with her advice, but it still seemed like she was trying to be considerate towards me—Kanbaru only listened quietly.

In any case.

A nonstop crisis that had begun at nine the previous night finally seemed to hit a short breather after the twelve-or-so-hour mark.

"Hit a short breather? So like spanking someone when they're panting," Kanbaru offered strange advice about how to deal with a hyperventilator. She continued to say idiotic things despite it being morning already (she did meet with me after napping, so maybe she was only now hitting a giddy, sleep-deprived high), but it eased the tension—and as it eased, my stomach growled.

And so, I decided to take the five-thousand-yen allowance given to me by Miss Gaen (I didn't want to think of it as payment for a job) and go buy some breakfast, just as she suggested.

I might not be able to go home yet, but that didn't mean I'd fast until nighttime—I wouldn't call myself resistant to hunger now that my link to Shinobu had been cut, nor could I allow my junior to starve.

"I desire donuts."

At least one thing about Shinobu was the same as ever.

Kanbaru, my overachieving junior, asked "Should I go run over and get some?" but I'd barely done any work yet and wanted her to let me do some shopping at least.

"Really? I want to make it up to you for kneeing you when you weren't able to heal."

"Oh, that... It's fine, you don't need to worry about it now."

"Hm. Okay, then I won't."

That was fast. Not that I minded.

"In that case, I'll look at Shinobu."

"Hm?"

"I'll look after Shinobu."

"..."

Was it really okay to leave Shinobu and Kanbaru alone? They were practically meeting for the first time. I couldn't bring Shinobu shopping with me, though. It might be safe during the day, but best to have her sit still.

In fact, Shinobu might be safer around someone as mobile as Kanbaru than with me, now that I'd lost my abilities...

Anyway, I was glad that Kanbaru was so quick to accept.

"In that case, my senior. I know I shouldn't be this brazen, but could I ask you for something while you're out shopping?"

"Hm? What is it, you can tell me anything."

"I want you to buy me a book. A new one coming out today."

"Out today? Huh. Fine with me, I'll go pick it up then. It looks like we'll have to wait around, so you can just read it until it's night."

"It's a light novel, is that okay?"

"Come on, Kanbaru. Really? Do you see me as someone who treats light novels as a decadent art? I'm the kind of high school boy who buys true-blue shojo manga with the front cover facing up at the cash register. Don't think of me as someone who'd ever be ashamed to buy a book."

"It's a relief to hear that."

"So, what's it called?"

"*The Savage Garçon Huffs and Puffs and Blows the Half-Boy Down!*"

"That's one of those light novels that's not light at all, isn't it?!"

What kind of books are you trying to get your senior to buy you?!

So it was boys' love after all...and what was with that title?

"Don't judge a book by its title. I know titles are getting more and more attention these days, even in the world of literature, but a lot of classics have pretty slapdash names."

"True, a novel is all about its content. Can I expect much out of the content of this one, though?"

"Oh, you can. Even experts have high hopes for this, the twenty-first book in the series."

"That's way too long of a series! And who are these 'experts,' anyway?!"

"The greatest mystery of the series, introduced in the very first volume, is going to be revealed at last: Is the savage garçon the one behind the carriage arson?"

"Probably?! The author dragged that out for twenty-one volumes?!"

"Oh, and when I said 'Bon appétit ♪' last night, that's actually a line I borrowed from the series' protagonist."

"So it was literally a line out of a boys' love novel?!"

And here I was thinking she sounded cute!

I'd never been more cheated in my life!

"Whaaat? You're not gonna buy it for me? Then maybe I'll just go home."

"I'll buy it, I'll buy it! Happy?!"

Don't try to threaten me.

What was she doing, pressuring me like that?

Was she going to leave over this, when she refused to after I explained again and again just how dangerous our situation was?

Even Miss Gaen couldn't have anticipated the allowance she gave us being used for BL…

"Oh, right. You don't have to, but if you can, could you also buy me a bra?"

"No, I can't. So I won't."

"Don't worry, I know you can do it."

"Your expectations of your senior are always too high, you know."

"I don't care about the design. Just pick one that you think looks good."

"Don't put it on my sense of fashion when it comes to bras."

"Listen, there's a million kinds of bra designs out there, but what really matters is what's on the inside."

"You think you're so clever."

"I can't go braless for much longer. I want to take care of what they're made to hold. I know I've supported you for all this time, but right now, I'm the one who needs some support."

"What you need are boundaries."

Of course, the main reason I went down the mountain, tasked with what seemed like some sort of punishment, was consideration for Shinobu and Kanbaru's safety. But it also had to do with just how awkward it'd be if Kanbaru went instead, thereby leaving me and Shinobu alone on those shrine grounds.

I felt a keen hatred for just how small I was as a man.

I was worrying myself over things that weren't serious at all—being alone and letting my head cool off seemed like a good idea.

I don't remember when she said it, but I recalled one of Hitagi Senjogahara's first-class aphorisms.

"It's wrong to think that the strong look down at the weak—in most cases, they aren't even looking at them in the first place."

She probably said it before she turned a new leaf, given how sharp-tongued it was, but it's probably true.

My thoughts and worries must have been incomprehensible to Miss Gaen for that reason—did the "nice lady who knows everything" even have a grasp on the concerns of someone of my level?

Don't feel envious.

Don't worry yourself over something stupid.

Shinobu was right—but why didn't she feel worried? Was there really nothing for her to worry about?

Her first thrall, who she thought had been separated from her in death four hundred years ago, had been resurrected after all that time—could she really stay unemotional about it?

And if I was going there, what about the armored warrior himself?

I didn't know how he felt about Shinobu—he may have hated her for turning him into a vampire, but until that the two were close, straddling the wall of human and aberration. Now that he had his will back, what

183

did he think of Shinobu, with whom he once fought side by side?

She'd return the enchanted blade Kokorowatari to him—that's what he said.

The sword was also a replica created in order to cut Shinobu down…

"…"

This too must have been a pointless concern.

Just as Shinobu said, Miss Gaen had no intention of allowing her to meet the first Aberration Slayer—whether the armored warrior plotted a drama of return or revenge.

Or of reunion. It wouldn't be realized.

The curtain would abruptly fall first.

The rate of aberrational stories occurring in this town would surely drop by a few percent if the experts dealt with the armored warrior— happily ever after, hip hip hooray. Whatever discomfort I felt barely meant a thing—something small, just like my concerns.

The object of my concerns would be eliminated while I was busy being concerned with it.

That's how it went.

This situation had grown out of me not finishing my homework over summer break—thus would my memories of my last summer as a high schooler be bookended.

I climbed down the mountain and returned to town as I wasted my time thinking these thoughts. On my mental shopping list were "Break-fast," "Book," "Donuts," and "Bra."

The most efficient itinerary would be: bookstore, supermarket, Mister Donut, then lingerie shop. It'd minimize the amount of time I had to carry a bra and allow me to return to the shrine without getting taken in by the police, considering the patrol routes and timetables of the officers in the area.

Fortunately, it was a weekday morning, so Senjogahara and Hanekawa would be at school. I wouldn't end up getting scolded by them.

I'd already sent a message to let them know I was safe, but maybe I should send one more, just to make sure they didn't worry? All while being absolutely sure not to get them involved, now that I had a better idea of the situation…

The thought went through my head as I started with the book-store—what was the name of the book Kanbaru wanted again? It felt like my brain refused to memorize it, but...something about a garçon?

Speaking of which, you often see butlers positioned in the world of subculture as antonyms to maids, but garçons were their real counterpart, I mused as I searched the shelves, only to find it. *The Savage Garçon Huffs and Puffs and Blows the Half-Boy Down!* And what a cover. It managed to keep up with the title... Forget freedom of expression, it expressed the full possibilities of human freedom.

They even released both parts on the same day.

The covers even connected to make a big picture.

I couldn't believe it. Even the copy on the bands around the covers connected—I know it's all the rage these days, but whoever made this was way too into connections.

While part of me was dumbstruck by the kind of junior who'd order her senior to go buy these for her, this was also what made it impossible to hate Suruga Kanbaru.

Given her national-level physical talent, her honest personality, and her incredible mental fortitude, just being close to her could make you feel inferior and suicidal, but she was also a pervert—when I thought of it that way, even these novels seemed lovable to me.

Still, I did feel a little embarrassed about buying just these two volumes...though I'd be opening up a huge can of worms if I started worrying about what bookstore employees thought of me.

It wasn't manly of me to buy a book as camouflage for another, but it actually seemed smart to avoid being too manly here. That kind of camouflage would be a kind of courtesy to the employee at the register, like thanking a bus driver when you get off. It wasn't as if I had a book I particularly wanted to buy for these deceptive purposes, but I was in a perfectly fine bookstore with a wide selection of titles. Not only had Sengoku looked up info about snake curses here, this is where I'd picked out some study aids myself.

I picked up the books in question for the time being, but another thought came to me.

It had been a while since my link to Shinobu had been established, but now that it had been severed by the Darkness, I was truly acting on my own for the first time in a long time.

I acted freely.

Freedom.

I was in the middle of running errands—but when I thought about how Miss Gaen would soon restore our link, my freedom struck me as being fleeting. Kaiki's senior though she may be, Miss Gaen surely wouldn't refuse to repair our bond...

In that case, shouldn't I at least make the most of this moment of freedom, this liminal space of extra time where I didn't have to concern myself with anyone's eyes, whether human or aberrational? The thought came to me in a flash, leading to an idea, and so as part of my search for literary camouflage, I headed for the first time in a while to the adult books section.

"Hmm..."

They didn't call this the town's only major bookstore for nothing.

Their lineup lived up to all my expectations.

Still, a rather discerning eye was necessary to pick out something that could neutralize the destructive power of the front covers of Kanbaru's BL.

It's not as if I didn't buy these kinds of publications in Shinobu's presence, but part of me always tries to show off around her—I wanted to choose without having to worry about how it looked in this rare moment roaming free.

It'd been so long that I didn't fully recall my way around these shelves, but I formulated a certain standard as I inspected them—a guiding ideology.

All of that earlier talk from Kanbaru of child abduction and whatnot reminded me: because I'd spent so much time having fun with Shinobu, Ononoki, and Hachikuji lately, people's suspicions that I was a pedophile were growing by the day.

I didn't think Kanbaru had been trying to humor me, but given the time and season I found myself in, the best thing to do would be to buck the trend and clear up these suspicions.

In other words, cougars.

Handing the volumes to Kanbaru, or taking them out of the bag, I'd nonchalantly show her a glimpse of a cougar mag, proof that her senior Araragi was by no means a pedophile—I'd have her know that when disinterested and true to himself, it was cougars that Koyomi Araragi desired. Something about this felt like I was only making the problem worse, but I put those concerns aside and began my investigation with this new guiding foundation.

I ended up agonizing for another hour, ultimately picking up two photo books with covers adorned by women whose clothing choices could be said to resemble Miss Gaen's. Much Introspection and Logical Formulation naturally led to cougars. I alternated these between Kanbaru's two volumes, creating a milf-euille of sorts, and brought it to the register with a sense of accomplishment.

3,850 yen.

That got pretty expensive…

I now had to cover breakfast for three, including donuts, as well as Kanbaru's bra with the remaining 1,150 yen—not to mention that it'd be the afternoon by the time I got back to the shrine.

Sheesh.

Could I not even shop right? How depressing.

If only I had half of Kanbaru's caliber as a person, or half of her guts, I surely wouldn't be worrying like this, I thought as I walked away from the cash register—and then.

I nearly knocked over a boy standing right behind me—that was close. Could he have been next in line to pay? No, he'd still be too close…

He was empty-handed anyway.

And wait, a boy who looked to be an elementary schooler being in a bookstore and not at school felt awfully strange.

Wearing long hair, a vertically striped sweater, and capri pants, he could almost be mistaken for a girl, but hah, did he really think he could hide the fact he was a boy from me? He was five years too late for that.

"…?"

What could it be?

Was he watching me making a captivating purchase out of boyish curiosity? I could understand if that was the case, but it was five years too soon for him. I tried to pass by him, but.

But then.

"Hello there, Second."

The boy spoke.

"Did ye give my message to Kissshot?"

His voice sounded like mine.

022

In the blink of an eye, the situation grew dramatically tense.

It was the middle of the day—the sun high, a blue-sky morning. Even if we were in a building, the encounter should have been impossible. The books I'd bought almost fell out of my hands.

I just barely held on, but—ridiculous.

How?

Hadn't Miss Gaen assured us that we'd be safe until night? And if *that*'s who this boy was.

If this child was—*him*.

Then why did he look like a boy?

I never asked exactly how old he was, but judging by the story Shinobu told that day, I assumed the first Aberration Slayer was a man in his prime.

Are you telling me this fresh-faced boy wore that empty armor?

However, I soon came to a hypothesis that answered both of my doubts at once—and not because I'm sharp or have any distinguished powers of deduction.

I'm not Miss Gaen, nor am I Hanekawa.

But I just knew.

I knew because of a *precedent*.

The dregs of a legendary vampire nearly indifferent about moving around at any hour, in the *form of a little girl*—while this couldn't be the same, had the armored warrior recovered to the point of taking human form, size aside?

In that case... In the time after he left that abandoned cram school in flames—just how much energy had he drained?

That armored warrior.

This boy.

"..."

"Hahahahaha."

The boy Aberration Slayer turned his back to me and briskly started to walk off.

Perhaps this was out of common sense, and he didn't want to cause a backup in front of the cash registers, but where had he learned that kind of common sense? Could it have been his energy drain? Absorbing not only physical energy and voice—but even knowledge?

"Let us leave. As First and Second—*as fellow beings whose blood was sucked by the same vampire,* let us two talk frankly. Ye must have something to say to me, no?"

Though I felt zero emotion coming from him the night before, whether he laughed or choked me during that appearance, he seemed different as a boy and I could see his expressions as he spoke.

Still, it seemed wrong to construe his relaxed attempt to invite me outside as innocence or guilelessness—just as Shinobu's true nature was that of a six-hundred-year-old vampire, however old she may appear to be.

The first Aberration Slayer was a man in his prime—no.

A vampire over four hundred years old.

I needed to think of him as someone with the ability to *absorb* every customer and employee in the bookstore in the blink of an eye if he felt like it.

I didn't say a word, but I didn't disobey or defy him. I followed behind the boy Aberration Slayer and left the store.

His steps lively, mine languid.

I did feel pathetic, but there was nothing else I could do here—no matter what happened next, I didn't want to involve any bystanders.

Calm down...

Don't feel shaken—and don't be too pessimistic, either.

I calmed my breathing.

True, the First appearing in the middle of the day, a time when Miss Gaen said it was safe, was a twist that I hadn't been emotionally prepared for at all, but I shouldn't despair.

Vampires are weak to the sun.

An absolute rule.

One that could not be broken, something set in stone—for him to be active like this under it, walking around on public streets, meant that the first Aberration Slayer, in his boyish form, should have nearly all of his abilities as a vampire unavailable to him.

Just as for Shinobu.

He should only have the kind of boyish strength that his appearance suggested—but was that really the case?

Even if it was, the first Aberration Slayer was no ordinary human— he'd been important enough to ride in on a palanquin.

A professional fighter of aberrations.

A warrior who donned armor and swung his great sword in battle. Could someone like me, an average high school student raised in a peaceful era who didn't even play sports properly, put up a fight against him? I doubted I could even move around if I wore armor.

The First and the Second.

Shinobu said there was no point in making that kind of comparison.

Thou art the only one for me now, she'd said, but to what extent could I believe those words? How seriously could I take them?

"'Tis nothing to look so worried over, Second."

And then.

The First spoke to me as if he saw through my concerns as he walked on, looking for a place suited to talking alone.

"'Tis not as if I'll bite."

"..."

"*I am an expert.* Though the age may have changed, I would not ignore another's *sign and seal*," the boy said, walking with both hands in his back pockets. True, I didn't feel any of the hostility I sensed from the chimeric monkey-crab-snake aberration in the park.

He may have been telling the truth about wanting to speak freely with me—but a sign and seal? What did he mean? As in signing my name in calligraphy then literally pressing a personal seal over it?

My expression might have betrayed these doubts, because the first Aberration Slayer turned around, took a hand out of his pocket, and pointed at his own face.

The left side of his face.

Then it struck me—or rather, I remembered.

My face had Ononoki's footprint on it—no, a whole night had passed. It must be gone by now, right? Or was it still there?

A stamp.

A mark.

That's how Shinobu described it.

"This is my prey, keep thy hands off—that is what the mark means. A sign among experts. Thou art inviolable to me so long as 'tis there."

Aye, as an expert. The boy Aberration Slayer turned back around—sticking his hand right back in his pocket as well.

"Without that mark…hah. As if I'd allow a vampire to remain alive for a single moment."

"…"

Ononoki had abused me verbally as she ground her foot into my face… So this was her hidden intention. She was protecting me from experts by imprinting a mark of her territory on me—as a shikigami, she may not have had any intent or will, but her footprint was keeping me safe.

Who could have imagined the line *I'm going to be the one to kill you, monstieur* was sincere? It seemed like getting stepped on by tween girls was worth it after all.

So that's what it was. Her lecture was also her way of being clever, shooing away any others with her shoe—could Miss Gaen have been talking about this mark when she said I was safe during the day? Thanks to Ononoki standing on my face? Had she predicted that the first Aberration Slayer, whose existence as an "expert" was strongest during the day, wouldn't lay a hand on my marked self? And is that what she meant when she said *that face of yours is all the proof anyone needs*? If that was the case, she could have said something.

Wait, so when I bought Kanbaru's books and my photo collections—having perfectly neutralized the two in my mind—there'd been a tween girl's footprint on my face the whole time? That really altered the situation from my original intentions... I wondered what the clerk thought about me as I paid. When I thought about it, the track jacket I had on was pretty avant-garde, the way it was shredded. On top of that, I left with a mysterious young boy... How was I ever going back to that bookstore? It was the only major one in town, too...

In any case, even if his earlier comment—*As if I would allow a vampire to remain alive for a single moment*—was just banter, it was potent.

Those vampire hunters during spring break were the same way... Did this mean I shouldn't see the first Aberration Slayer as an expert with a preventative approach like Miss Gaen, or with an investigatory focus like Oshino, but as being like that trio who specialized in exterminating aberrations?

But what about himself?

He was now one of those aberrations he needed to exterminate, a vampire.

He said he wouldn't allow one to remain alive for a single moment—but it's not as if finding fault with his words amounted to pointing out a contradiction.

Because this armored warrior who now took the form of a boy—*in fact killed himself*.

He committed suicide—and for four hundred years.

He continued to die.

"This place ought to be suitable for a relaxed conversation."

After a bit of a walk, the boy Aberration Slayer stopped in an odd open plot. I didn't know what it was for—experts really were skilled at finding these kinds of remote, inconspicuous places, whether it was the abandoned cram school or Kita-Shirahebi Shrine.

Maybe their eyes saw different things—Miss Gaen said something about geographic conditions earlier.

I followed him into the empty plot—thinking back on it, I may have been too careless. True, it was unlikely for any bystanders to get involved there, but it also meant no one would come to my rescue if push came to shove.

Maybe I felt emboldened by the sense that Ononoki was protecting me.

The boy Aberration Slayer plopped down on the ground in the utterly empty piece of land, a little too cramped to call a lot. He looked like nothing more than a scamp with no manners, but something about the way he acted made it seem like he was ready for anything. Maybe it was just my preconceived notions, but he reminded me of a martial artist prepared for a fight...

"Koyomi Araragi, was it?"

He spoke my name—just like that.

No surprise. He was the First, and he'd called Shinobu by the name Kissshot.

Calling me by name wasn't the issue here, though.

How did he know my full name?

Did Kanbaru call me that in the abandoned cram school? No, it was always *my senior* or *Araragi-senpai.*

Even if he'd heard her using my last name, he couldn't have learned my first name.

Did he do research on me? In just one night? No...

"Allow me to call thee Sir Araragi."

"Um...sure. That's fine with me."

"In that case, Sir Araragi."

I didn't know where it came from, but the boy Aberration Slayer offered me a plastic bottle of tea with an innocent smile on his face—his own in the other hand.

"Do not worry, these goods are not stolen. I paid for them properly and purchased them at the vending machine over yonder. An act of hospitality on my part. I am a fighter, not a master of the tea ceremony, but I do believe in the spirit of treating every encounter as precious. For this will likely be the last time the two of us speak under such peaceful conditions."

"..."

A plastic bottle of tea?

I mean, putting aside the stuff about tea ceremonies (my little sister is in a tea ceremony club, and even she hasn't learned anything about tea in plastic bottles), why was the first Aberration Slayer, who'd been dying for four hundred years until his consciousness was restored just yesterday, able to handle a polyethylene terephthalate bottle like it was the most normal thing in the world?

The theory that he could absorb knowledge with his energy drain suddenly started to seem a lot more credible... And what was up with his clothes? If he hadn't stolen the tea, he probably hadn't stolen his clothes either... Sure, he could have figured out the money part somehow, but a vertically striped sweater?

He was also wearing the kind of rubber sandals that were only getting popular in the last few years... How did a human from four hundred years ago have such a modern sense of fashion?

Shouldn't he be getting confused and mistaking cars for iron boars?

It was almost as if—he knew everything.

I took the bottle, though I felt anxious as I did so, and sat down to face him... So this would be the last time we spoke peacefully.

It could also be taken as his final attempt to negotiate—as an expert, at that.

That's what I thought, but I was wrong.

We spoke, but about nothing as simple as a negotiation.

In gentle terms, a request.

In harsh terms, an order.

In fact, it was a declaration of war.

"I shall cut straight to the point, Sir Araragi," he said.

Just like a blade.

"I would like ye to leave Kissshot."

023

"Surely thou must not object? In fact, thou must wish for this. Ye simply happened across Kissshot this spring break—and because ye happened across that fearsome vampire, ye had no choice but to enter into a partnered relationship. Restored to this current state, ye must have no desire to shoulder such a heavy burden—or am I mistaken?" asked the boy Aberration Slayer, staring at me.

Me, someone he'd consider his junior.

"*Kissshot needs not two thralls*—would ye not agree?"

"She shouldn't even need *one*," I answered—something like an attempt to steer the conversation off-topic, but I'd also thought so for a while. "Both you and me—we became her thralls by accident. She never planned on creating any."

"I do wonder about that." The boy Aberration Slayer gave a weak laugh. "Well, she is indeed aloof enough."

Though I couldn't help but feel annoyed that he was acting like he knew Shinobu, when I thought about it, he did know more about her than me.

My relationship with her had only lasted for the half-year or so since spring break, but the amount of time Kissshot Acerolaorion Heartunderblade spent with the first Aberration Slayer four hundred years earlier spanned years. From his perspective, I was greener than green.

"I do of course believe I understand the situation—I know ye and Kissshot are bound to one another in a relationship that can never be severed."

"You know…"

About my relationship with Shinobu.

A warped master-and-servant relationship between soulmates.

Right. In that sense, my stance regarding Shinobu was different from the first Aberration Slayer's—theirs was pretty warped itself, but probably not as much as ours.

My relationship with her was more irregular than his—which is why, according to him, I was the one who ought to step aside.

"But why do you know th—"

"*There is nothing I do not know about the stories of aberrations that take place in this town*—I am close to omnipotent as far as aberrations in this area."

For fifteen years now, he said.

Fifteen years ago—when the first Aberration Slayer, turned to ash after throwing his body under the sun, was assembled here after four hundred years of convergence, carried bit by bit by winds and waves.

Ever since, it became *just a little bit easier* for aberrational phenomena to occur in this town—making his existence an underlying cause of every such tale.

The crab. The snail. The monkey. The snake. The cat. The phoenix.

If he understood *everything* about it all—then that's where he got his knowledge, having regained consciousness.

He'd done all his fieldwork by way of his own ashes—which meant he could probably speak any Western name he wanted, not just Kissshot's.

He only grew stronger and stronger, and endlessly gained in knowledge. It felt like he was trying to show just how much greater the First was than the Second.

Shinobu may have called it pointless to compare us, but at this point, there was nothing to even compare.

He was incomparable.

Who was more suited to be the thrall and slave of the iron-blooded, hot-blooded, yet cold-blooded vampire? The question wasn't even worth asking. The answer was simple, a freebie.

But...

"I don't understand. Did you come back to form a partnership with Shinobu? What is it that you want? Why are you telling me to leave Shinobu?"

"Shinobu—Shinobu Oshino. Yes, so that is what ye have decided to call Kissshot," he took in my question without giving a direct reply. "Why do ye not call her by her name? Is that not an affront to a vampire?"

"You know why. You claim to be omnipotent. Why would you ask that if you're basically this town itself?"

"Calling me that goes a step too far—ah, I keenly see how distinct our personalities are. What a difference there is between the First and the Second."

I found it hard to believe he was being considerate as he spoke to me, but *disparity* might have been more apt—I bet he never expected his successor to be a youngster like me.

Of course, in his current form, he was far more of a youngster than me... But there had to be some kind of sly intent behind his delicate, all-but-girlish features.

"My goal is—Kissshot," he said with his pandering looks. "To *reconcile* with the one ye call Shinobu Oshino."

"R-Reckon?"

"Reconcile. Now that my physical form has been restored, I desire the same for our relationship. Thou must know, given thy demeanor. Kissshot and I separated after a quarrel—I said such heartless things to Kissshot in a *misguided moment*. I wish to apologize to her, and *to be forgiven.*"

"..."

"Then, just as we did before—*I would like for us to fight aberrations together.* I would like to defend the back of that spine-chillingly beautiful one with the looks of a goddess, fighting as her sword."

Ye may not understand—he said, as if to draw a line between us, and in fact, I didn't. Well, okay, I knew that Shinobu—the former Shinobu was a spine-chillingly beautiful demon, that I would never deny.

But fighting as her sword?

Is that—something he desired as an expert?

Or was it something he desired as a vampire thrall?

He was requesting the return of the Aberration Slayer's enchanted blade Kokorowatari—so that he himself could become a blade, his master's right arm?

Maybe he wasn't yet able to make his intentions clear back when he entrusted me with his message? No...how could I believe that?

Then Kanbaru had the right take on the situation.

As nothing more than ashes gathered in Kita-Shirahebi Shrine.

He sensed Shinobu's presence, which excited him into existence all to meet her again—his determination was singular. While Miss Gaen was dismissive, it did make some sense.

If we went with our magnetic theory to explain why he was roused, the same thing should have happened in the world of eleven years ago that we visited the other day, traveling through time. After all, if we went back and looked at the timeline, that was when Shinobu visited that spot for the "first" time.

It didn't happen in the world of eleven years ago because only four years had passed since the ashes arrived in the air pocket, and he couldn't even subconsciously recognize Shinobu... Shouldn't that be how I looked at it? Shinobu then used up all the aberrational materials in that location, which is why the First never returned in that timeline...

But would Miss Gaen overlook something that even I noticed?

"Surprised, Sir Araragi? That I wish to issue an apology to Kissshot?"

"Not surprised as much as it just sounds like a lie to me. In fact, you've already sent an assassin Shinobu's way—that mockery of a monkey aberration."

"That was an assassin sent thy way—just as the mockery of a snail aberration was. Just a bit of harassment of my junior... But do not worry. I shall dispatch no further mockeries now that I have seen the sign and seal on thy face. To thee, of course, or to Kissshot."

"It just sounds to me like you're trying to talk your way into getting close to Shinobu so you can get your revenge."

"Revenge? Revenge for what? What reason do I have to resent her? Ye who call her a name such as Shinobu?"

"Yes, you do have a reason. Don't try to gloss over it by calling it a *misguided moment*. You said some awful things to Shinobu."

"None more awful than calling her Shinobu, in my eyes—but such fruitless arguments aside, indeed, I cannot deny that. Thus I wish to apologize. I wish to meet her myself and apologize."

"Meet her yourself? Wait, so are you asking me to put you two in contact?"

"I shall say nothing of the sort. I do not expect thee to mediate between us. All I need from thee is thy separation from Kissshot."

She needs only one thrall, the boy Aberration Slayer said to me—with determination.

"I can become Kissshot's right arm—while ye could become nothing more than her shackles. Am I mistaken? Have ye once protected her?"

"What about you? You tried to kill her. And even that enchanted blade you said to return... If you go all the way back, you made that sword to kill her, didn't you?"

"Indeed I did. That imitation is a great sword created for the sole purpose of killing her—made with my flesh and blood, my body and bones. I cannot deny that either—but have ye never tried to kill her thyself? I was under the belief that we shared this one thing in common, but am I mistaken? Do ye wish for me not to treat us as similar?"

"You're surprisingly talkative," I said. "I imagined you to be more of the reserved type. Like the way you were in that armor."

"I could no longer keep my silence. Though for the time being, one may say I've been pulled into speaking by this tiny appearance of mine... Sir Araragi. Thou once tried to kill Kissshot thyself—but now ye have reconciled, have ye not? Do ye find it audacious that I wish to do the same?"

"..."

"She brought me back from the brink of death. Though I may have flipped out at the time, I am now grateful—are such words that strange to hear?"

I did find it strange to hear him say *flipped out,* but he wasn't wrong as a whole. It felt like we'd said and done the exact same things.

But while I couldn't deny his words, whether or not I could affirm them was a different question until I had a clearer view.

Yes, he might be right, we had that in common, but we could hardly contradict each other more regarding everything else.

Call me petty, a shortcoming I recognize myself, but I wouldn't be the only person to feel displeased, or as the boy Aberration Slayer might say, like flipping the hell out, upon being told to step aside.

I don't have the kind of integrity required to reply with a quick *is that so* and a nod.

Even if logically.

I thought he was right.

"Do ye not wish to leave her? Though anyone could replace thee, I could be replaced by none. For I am special. I am a chosen human."

"I love that. I wish I could say that kind of thing even once in my life—not that I'd ever be able to, given how flippant I'd sound."

"Hahaha. No, Second, I have not taken such offense," the boy Aberration Slayer said with lighthearted affectation.

I didn't understand what this reply meant for a moment, but then I realized he probably thought *flippant* was the adjective form of *flip out*.

…His self-claimed omnipotence had its limits.

I felt just a little more like I might be able to debate him on even ground—he may have been the first Aberration Slayer, but he wasn't faultless like Hanekawa.

If anything, the way he awkwardly tried to introduce modern words into our conversation felt like an attempt to vie against me, someone from four hundred years in the future.

That's right.

He was—just as serious about this as me.

On an edge just as sharp as a katana.

"Thou saved Kissshot—ye happened upon her in a time of crisis and saved her. But wouldn't anyone do the same and save a beautiful woman collapsed and on the brink of death?"

"…"

"'Tis something anyone could do, and something that could

happen to anyone—a common occurrence that could happen any-where in Japan. In that case, why not switch places with me? No…" He shook his head. "I suppose there is no point in confronting one another with our flaws and weaknesses so. What good would it serve for us to argue—'twould be nothing more than an unseemly civil war. For in the end, this is a case of two men fighting over a woman—I see everything about thee as flawed, while thou must see everything about me as flawed. They say that not even dogs dare to interrupt a quarrel between lovers. Not even an aberration would think to bother with a quarrel between slaves."

What good would it do to demonstrate to one another our slavishness, the boy Aberration Slayer said, before clapping and taking the cap off his plastic bottle.

He'd said something earlier along the lines of being more talkative because he had a boy's body, but knowing when to pause for breath at just the right time suggested that he was never a poor speaker to begin with.

"In that case, what should we do? Just start praising each other?" I asked as I waited for him to take the bottle away from his mouth.

"Now, that would be unseemly," he answered—sensibly. "So allow me to present the benefits. Sir Araragi, I shall inform thee of all the wonderful things that would befall thee were ye to leave Kissshot—as I do, think of what wonderful things would befall me if ye did not."

"B-Benefits? Wonderful things?"

The words felt completely out of place and ill-timed—like they ran counter to our situation. Was this that kind of negotiation?

"'Tis not a negotiation. I will merely explain to thee in a kind and meticulous manner those things thou must not understand. *That ye will be freed* were ye to leave Kissshot—that ye will be untied from those knots named Kissshot. That ye can be free from the way ye two are entwined and bound to one another. In other words, my proposal is nothing short of an offer to assume thy burdensome responsibility to her. I see the impressive settlement thou hast come to regarding Kissshot. It seems laudable from an expert's perspective—I know not who wrought it, but 'tis superb. Yet 'tis not as if ye pay no cost to maintain it. Thou must live a warped life—and I am offering to take over this distortion that has come to thee."

"Everything, then?" I answered cautiously—no matter what he said, I couldn't afford to speak thoughtlessly. The conversation between the First and the Second had indeed entered this sort of phase. "You're saying—you want to replace everything about me?"

"From my perspective, 'twas thee who replaced everything about me. Ye—took over my place. All I want is to have it back—my sword and my position. *I could become thee, but thou could never become me.*"

"…"

"Or do ye claim to be capable of better serving Kissshot? An amateur—better than I, an expert? Thou must realize I do not intend to slight thee, one who stayed by Kissshot's side while I was gone. Or to be more frank, I do not wish to hurt thee, one who must be important to her *in his own way.*"

"I gave her your message," I said in a low voice.

Her reply was the one piece of evidence that might allow me to stand against the boy Aberration Slayer.

"It sounds like—she has no interest in seeing you."

"Is that so. Well, surely 'tis so."

He didn't seem affected—as if he'd all but expected my response. As if he saw straight through anything Shinobu might say…

"But whatever Kissshot's intentions may be, I must have her return to me what I have lent her."

My sword, and my position.

He almost sounded like a bill collector.

"I wish to bloom a second time. I wish to shine once more after four hundred years. I do not see this as shameful—if anything, is not thy grasping at thy position of Second shameful?"

"Are you sure it's not as a human you want to bloom a second time? A thrall to Shinobu? Even if it isn't for revenge, aren't you trying to meet her so you could return to being a human?"

"I cannot return to being a human," the First shot me down. "It has been four hundred years, after all—too much time has passed. We two are different from that perspective as well. But…I no longer consider this a tragedy. 'Tis because 'tis too late for me that I wish to stay forever, semi-eternally with Kissshot."

"You might see that as true love or something, but these days...we call people like you stalkers."

Hm?

Something felt strange about this line coming from me—why? What felt unnatural just now? No, maybe not unnatural, but a strange concordance—

"As I said before, let us not give ourselves to disparaging one another. More importantly, did ye think of something? What great things will come to me if ye refuse to leave Kissshot?"

If I stayed with Kissshot.

Remained with Kissshot—

"..."

I of course couldn't come up with a thing—I couldn't come up with a single thing, and so to stall for time, I twisted the cap to the bottle of tea I'd been given. This was my relationship with Shinobu: something that made everyone unhappy, that brought despair to all with no survivors. I'd drink the tea—but I'd never come up with any idea. I just wanted to escape being chased down and cornered by the boy Aberration Slayer. I took the bottle, and as if I were dodging my right to answer him, I put it to my mouth.

My mouth.

I put it, put it—

"?!"

I couldn't put it anywhere.

It disintegrated.

I leapt back in surprise.

A *silver something* passed in front of my eyes at an incredible speed—and in the blink of an eye, smashed the bottle in my hands, contents and all.

It was crushed into dust—pulverized.

But neither a fragment of the bottle nor a drop of its contents fell on me. I'd lamely flopped over onto my butt before they could.

It wasn't that I'd reflexively bent backwards. I was more like...blown back by the violent wind pressure of an object passing before me at a terribly high speed.

Of course, the boy Aberration Slayer intentionally and immediately hopped up and back to avoid—it.

It—being a *massive silver cross.*

That's what he evaded.

The cross stood in the ground of the empty lot, buried deep like some sort of grave marker. This wasn't my first time seeing the impossibly large silver item. I recognized it.

This striking item that vampires would be weak to—

A vampire hunter's weapon.

"What the hell are you doing, drinking something an enemy gives you without a second thought? And I still saved you despite how much of an idiot you are—just how peaceful of a life do you lead, anyway? Even with your link cut the way it is now, you wouldn't last a second if you drank *holy water...*"

There he stood—golden hair and golden eyes.

A young man in a white traditional school uniform.

"Gotta love it."

024

Episode.

One of three vampire hunters who'd traveled to Japan during spring break to chase after the legendary vampire Kissshot Acerolaorion Heartunderblade and kill her.

A half-vampire youth with the characteristics of both a vampire and a human.

Opposed to both vampires and humans—he hated vampires and resented humans.

Neither vampire nor human, and moved not by duty or work.

A professional who had his private reasons.

This bellicose expert vampire slayer with his offensive fighting style had once battled me too, back when I became the thrall of the legendary vampire—or maybe you should just say he made a fool of me, but in the end, thanks both to Mèmè Oshino's wits and Tsubasa Hanekawa's tact, he returned to his motherland empty-handed, or at least he should have...so why was he here?

To save me?

Is that why he threw that cross?

At the plastic bottle containing—holy water?

"It appears as though an obstacle has presented itself, Sir Araragi," the boy Aberration Slayer said as he backed up—with only walls behind him and Episode standing at the entrance, we were in something like a dead end. "This issue would have been settled quickly had ye quaffed thy chalice more holy than poisoned—nor would I have ignored that sign and seal had ye purified thyself of your own volition."

I didn't understand what he was saying at first...but it seemed there was some sort of trick to the tea he'd handed me. So he lied about buying it at a vending machine?

Had I tasted its contents, unable to stand any more of our weighty conversation—something inconvenient would've happened to my body, though I wasn't sure exactly what.

Something the boy Aberration Slayer would find convenient—my parting ways with Shinobu, for example?

Had the boy been plotting to assassinate me, hiding every bit of his hostility?

The animosity this implied chilled my spine.

So the whole time we spoke—he was waiting with greedy eyes for me to fall into his trap? He was eagerly waiting for me to drink holy water?

No—maybe it was ardor, not animosity.

That—was the kind of fervor he held for Shinobu.

As I worried and shilly-shallied, he moved with purpose to accomplish his goal...

"Keheheheh—gotta love it. Don't be mad, thrall of Heartunderblade—anything goes when it comes to slaying aberrations. Sneak attacks, surprise attacks, they're all acceptable moves," Episode, the individual apparently responsible for saving me from this pinch, said—but no, I shouldn't use a word as uncertain as *apparently*. It was clear that he had saved me.

If he hadn't hurtled the massive object, itself purified—an oversized cross many times bigger than its wielder.

Surely I would have ingested that liquid, just as the boy Aberration Slayer wished—but I couldn't immediately accept the reality that I'd been saved by Episode. After all, he'd been such a pain to both me and Shinobu over spring break—wasn't his cross a weapon meant to kill, not save me?

The cross sticking out of the ground instilled far greater fear in me than any plastic bottle— despite having been told of its dangerous contents.

The cross's owner, too…

Anyone could see that I'd been rescued here, but I only felt like a new enemy had appeared.

Why was he here?

I couldn't stop myself from wondering.

My doubts may have been shared.

"Art thou a modern expert? So then, have ye come here to slay me?" the boy Aberration Slayer asked coolly.

"Hard to say. You seem more like an expert than a vampire to me right now, but I wonder if that's going to change once it's night," Episode replied. "In that case, I could always just kill you to the point that there's not even any fallout left."

Episode sounded far more heated talking to the boy Aberration Slayer, but his glare seemed to be pointed my way as well.

Of course.

From his point of view, the boy Aberration Slayer and I were birds of a feather.

"Allow me to clarify. I had no intent of a sneak or surprise attack— this too was an act of harassment delivered in place of a proper greeting. Anyone with the slightest amount of expert knowledge should have been able to notice it was holy water. How surprised I was to learn that an amateur ignorant to that degree stood close to Kissshot."

"Yeah, well, you look pretty amateurish to me yourself, trying to slay an aberration with a four-hundred-year-old move as pious as that—gotta love it."

"…"

I couldn't grasp what was going on here. Forget words, I was at a loss for letters. But then, as if to follow up—

"Well, good. Looks like I managed to make it in time. Nice to meet ya, little buddy First," the voice said, so cheerful it seemed out of place as it interrupted the three-way stalemate between me, Episode, and the boy Aberration Slayer—it belonged to Miss Gaen.

Fiddling with her cell phone, she made her appearance from behind Episode with light steps—I never thought I'd feel relieved to see her, of all people, but now it finally made sense.

Ah—so the "helper" Miss Gaen left the mountain to go and meet was Episode, the vampire hunter.

He did fight vampires, now that I thought about it.

Calling over an expert in vampire slaying was almost too by-the-book a move—and Episode?

He must've been the only one available…and hold on, did that mean she gave Miss Kagenui an even wider berth than him?

"You took forever, Miss Gaen," Episode said.

"Real sorry about that," she amiably apologized. "But you know, 'Sode, you're to blame here too. I wish you wouldn't put it all on me. You spent so much time having fun hitting on girls that you were almost late."

"Again, I wasn't hitting on anyone… Just how old do you think I am?"

This back-and-forth made it seem as though they'd met before. Well, if Miss Gaen was the big boss they said she was, maybe it wasn't so strange that she had international connections…

Unsurprised by the boy Aberration Slayer's appearance, Miss Gaen turned to him. "I am Izuko Gaen. I'm the lady who knows everything," she gave her full and proper name—or maybe not. There was no guarantee it was her real name, when I thought about it. "I'm here to negotiate with you," she said.

"I must admit, I am at a disadvantage."

'Tis still daytime, the boy Aberration Slayer laughed.

Not a comfortable laugh, but it did hint at his enthusiasm for the situation—perhaps it was far more of a real challenge than the one he was in until moments ago, when he faced off against a foolish, cowardly high school student.

"Sir Araragi. It appears as though our discussion ends here—so I ask for thy forgiveness. We could not discover a middle ground. As such, our relationship must move to the next stage."

"You call that a discussion?"

He had some nerve, after trying to trick me.

But wait, the next stage? What did that mean...

"What else? A duel," he said. Like it was part of a procedure. "Two men battling over a woman—a tradition that has stayed unchanged for four hundred years."

"..."

"Let us have a bloodbath this night," the boy Aberration Slayer declared. "I leave the detailed arrangements to thy camp of experts— Lady Izuko...was it? Do as ye wish. I shall visit thy location after having made my preparations. I shall do my best to make a full recovery by then—and be fully restored. Thou ought to erase that sign and seal on thy face, Sir Araragi. I shall neither run nor hide, but ye may do either if ye wish."

If ye will accept this duel, do not fail to say thy final farewell to Kiss-shot—he advised before turning his heels.

With Episode and Miss Gaen shutting down the entrance, he should've been trapped in the empty lot, but that was a two-dimensional way of looking at things.

He flew into the air—jumped.

As if he'd used Ononoki's Unlimited Rulebook. I've also heard that once upon a time, a certain legendary vampire needed to jump with only one leg to fly from Japan to the South Pole.

His feat was nowhere near that—but the boy Aberration Slayer, notwithstanding his incomplete recovery, jumped in a way that didn't seem possible with the sun still shining. He easily cleared any walls built to block humans.

"A—"

Are you going to run, you coward, I began to say, before swallowing the words—he said he wouldn't run or hide. I, relieved that he'd left this place and my sight, was the coward and the chicken here.

I wouldn't have to speak to him anymore.

I didn't have to face him—and that gave me peace of mind.

Even facing my smallness as a man felt easier in comparison—that's how much calmer I felt.

But forget about me. What about the two experts who'd just

appeared—why weren't Episode and Miss Gaen chasing after him? Unlike me, they had no reason to watch him run away—this was Miss Gaen's chance to get her hands on the first Aberration Slayer during the day, probably an unexpected twist.

Why didn't they give chase? And couldn't they have kept the boy Aberration Slayer from jumping in the first place? Taking away his ability to take to the skies—did they realize it almost looked like they wanted him to run away?

"Oh."

But once he was no longer visible in the sky, I turned around to Miss Gaen and Episode—which dispelled my doubts. It's not that they didn't chase after him, they couldn't—they had no choice but to stop.

When Episode threw his massive silver cross to shatter my plastic bottle, and the pressure of the wind pushed me back, I somehow dodged its destruction—but I'd ended up tossing the plastic bag I held in my hand opposite the one holding the bottle. Maybe the tape on it was weak, but the contents had spilled out onto the ground where it landed—down to even the receipt.

The situation called for Miss Gaen and Episode to give chase after the flying first Aberration Slayer, and their highly professional, instant judgment moved them to do so, but they'd been nailed to the ground by the items scattered at their would-be point of departure.

Nailed to the ground.

Nailed by the four volumes that had spilled from the plastic bag—each of them taking two and freezing as if they couldn't believe their own eyes.

Episode, the half-vampire expert, held both volumes of *The Savage Garçon Huffs and Puffs and Blows the Half-Boy Down!*—while Izuko Gaen held the two cougar photo books featuring a woman with a fashion sense obviously like hers.

They both stood there, frozen, a volume in each hand.

"N-No, you've got it all wrong!"

They were mostly right.

And thus, the Aberration Slayer—first thrall of Kissshot Acerolaorion Heartunderblade—eluded capture once again.

025

After I finished my exchange with the two pallid experts that was, in a sense, far more intense and arcane than my discussion with the boy Aberration Slayer ("Listen, Araragi (her name for me having gotten more distant), this freaks me out even more than you think it does, so please, just stop." "I don't love this at all."), I returned alone to Kita-Shirahebi Shrine—Miss Gaen and Episode went off on their own to "start on the formalities" (I hope it's not that they decided to avoid me).

Mentally and physically drained after my sudden succession of diverse ordeals, I held the plastic bag like a treasure as I arrived at the shrine—where I found yet another, a further ordeal.

"What…"

The little girl had pushed the athlete to the ground and was holding her there.

Within the shrine premises, of all the sacrilegious things you could do.

Shinobu Oshino straddled Suruga Kanbaru's supine torso—whaaaat?!

What happened? What's going on?!

What were they getting into there on the other side of the shrine gate?!

It'd be one thing if it was Kanbaru straddling Shinobu, but Shinobu straddling Kanbaru? Strike that—maybe she was just addled?!

Could that talk last night about beautiful girls taking the lead have been foreshadowing?!

I ran over to join in, sorry, no, to question them, but someone grabbed my arm and pulled me into the bushes—with enough strength that I could put up no resistance.

"Shh, monstieur," a voice said.

Just as I expected, Ononoki had been the one to tug on my hand— she was there in the bush, squatting. At first I was shocked that she'd managed to conceal her presence so close by, but then again, she was small to begin with, so I guess you wouldn't be able to find her if she crouched down with her hands around her knees...

Not to mention, she gave off no signs of life.

"O-Ononoki."

"Onthelowkey is fine."

"Who's that? No, really. You're Ononoki, I'm sure of it."

Could she please stop her character from changing every time we spent a half-day apart?

Still, I'd been reunited with an unexpected presence in an unexpected place—though she'd been protecting me indirectly ever since the fire through the stamp on my face.

How could I not be happy?

I leapt on her.

"Hugs!"

"Dodges."

She evaded me—it seemed she wasn't going to let me have my way with her.

Not only did she get out of the way of my beetle-horn hands with nimble movements while sitting, she used her back to scoop my legs out from under me, a beautiful trip—then made me sit, as if to fold me away.

Around the middle of that month, Miss Kagenui had folded my entire body up as if she were using some storage technique, and it seemed that her shikigami could do something similar, unsurprisingly enough— okay, maybe it was a surprise.

Considering how much power Ononoki, someone capable of literal death blows, had, how could I ever hope to manage her if she started using these kinds of aikido or judo-like moves?

I'd never be able to hug her again!

"Don't assume you can hug me to begin with. I'll prune you."

"Prune me? Oh god."

"I told you shh, didn't I? Shut your mouth, moron."

An order—I really couldn't get a grasp on what kind of character she was.

Knowing how she acted, she probably flew all around after we last met. Judging by the boy Aberration Slayer's words, her search was unfortunately fruitless, at least on an immediate level… Had she come here to Kita-Shirahebi Shrine to meet with Miss Gaen?

If I tried writing Ononoki's movements out on a timeline, I guess it would go in the order of "Saved me and Kanbaru (cram school ruins)" → "Gave report to Miss Gaen (via phone)" → "Fought the monkey with Shinobu (teaches her about that park)" → "Also goes to said park herself (learns that the meeting spot has changed)" → "Kita-Shirahebi Shrine (the present)"—I guess?

Really, what a hard-working shikigami…

I recalled how much of this busy, ever-moving girl's time I'd taken up, buying her nothing more than ice cream, and felt a little bad.

"It seems like you made your way out of a pretty tough battle yourself, monstieur—your clothes are in tatters."

"Oh, no, this is Kanbaru's…"

Well, the track jacket aside, I had indeed made it through a tough battle last night. I'd also experienced a fight with few parallels in history…

"If we're going to talk about tattered clothes, though, what about you, Ononoki?"

"These aren't in tatters. What are you trying to get by having me expose my skin? It seems like a lot has happened to you, monstieur, but I can ask you that later. More importantly, look over there."

Ononoki pointed.

At Shinobu and Kanbaru, tangled up on the shrine grounds—I

215

described Shinobu as straddling Kanbaru, but it looked more like a martial arts mount.

So Shinobu had Kanbaru locked down solid? Like beetle-horn legs, as opposed to my beetle-horn arms? But why was Shinobu doing it to Kanbaru? Were it the opposite, it'd feel amazing, like two puzzle pieces snapping right in.

"Let's go over and sneak a peep at that."

"Sneak a peep…"

Now that I thought about it, hadn't she done the same the other day when Shinobu and I were talking? Hadn't she been straining her ears to listen to Kissshot Acerolaorion Heartunderblade talk about the olden days?

I'd inadvertently convinced myself she was the fighting type, given how we first met, but maybe she was more of the type to run investigations, or rather, eavesdropping operations—though she wasn't running anything right now, sitting here.

"That's right. External affairs is my line of expertise."

"You might be able to run investigations, but you'd never be able to do external affairs."

"Why do you say that when I've forged such a strong relationship with you, monstieur?"

"No, I'm sorry, but the only reason we've forged a strong relationship is that I'm a pro when it comes to tween girls. Your communication skills are pretty rough, you know."

"What does that even mean, a pro when it comes to tween girls? Look."

The aberrational professional pointed at Shinobu and Kanbaru again.

For this girl, pointing was almost like setting a missile's targeting. Part of me felt nervous, knowing that two close friends were on the other side of it…

"They were like that when I got here."

"They were?"

That would mean Ononoki arrived at Kita-Shirahebi Shrine only a few moments ago. So she didn't know why they looked like that, either…

which is why she was watching them from afar?

"Wait, no. I can't agree with this, Ononoki. How are you ever going to move forward if you're always just watching people get it on like this? You've got to be assertive and climb to the next stage yourself."

"Speak for yourself, monsieur. I'm not spying on them for any vulgar reason. It seems there's some sort of affair going on."

"An affair…"

Like a romantic one?

But looking at them again, assuming that's not what she meant— there did seem to be some sort of intensity emanating from them.

Almost as if they were arguing…

Arguing?

Shinobu?

That didn't make sense—Shinobu barely acknowledged most other humans, nor did she speak to them, let alone get into a fight with them.

As far as I knew, there was spring break, when she spoke with Mèmè Oshino, an expert (it'd be hard to call her interaction with Tsubasa Hanekawa a proper conversation), the time the other day when she inserted herself between me and Miss Kagenui and spoke to her—and this time, when she spoke to Miss Gaen after being provoked. As far as I knew, that was it.

So why would she, a former noble vampire, dregs or not, an aberration with a lofty spirit and mind, be talking like that with Kanbaru?

And—arguing?

It almost seemed more like a verbal dispute than an argument, practically a verbal conflict—but a verbal conflict with someone you have in a front mount is about as far as a war of words could go, no?

Anything past that and you just have to scrap it out.

No, hold on. Don't make any panicked judgments, Kanbaru's involved here, should I just assume this is some sort of kink of hers? Still…

"It's no good. I can't make out anything they're saying. They're too far. If only they'd yell at each other louder," I said.

"They'd already be trading punches if they were yelling any louder."

"Can you hear them, Ononoki?"

"Of course. External affairs is my specialty."

"..."

Did she have an attachment to that title or something?

To be fair, it was some sort of affair, and it was taking place outside...

As a shikigami, Ononoki's sight and hearing must far surpass an average human's... Now that my link to Shinobu had been cut, I couldn't so much as read my partner's lips.

Dammit, unable to read her lips?

I was bringing dishonor to the name Koyomi Araragi!

"Can't we get a little closer to them, Ononoki? Close enough that I can hear a bit of what they're saying..."

"Oh, so you're all about this too, monsieur? Just look at you... You just love it when people fight, don't you?"

"Wait... What do you mean, look at me?"

If I was all about this, that made Ononoki too much about this.

Her staying expressionless the whole time made it that much better.

"No, I want to stop them. This looks like it's going in a bad direction... It's just."

It's just.

It was just too inscrutable, too bizarre a matchup on a fight card that it made me hesitate, if I'm being honest—if they were arguing, I wanted to know the circumstances before I tried to mediate... Not that I had the luxury of saying that if they were about to break into a brawl.

I would have to stop them at any cost if it were Kanbaru on top of Shinobu, but with the positions reversed...

With our link weakened along with Shinobu's lessened vampirism, Kanbaru was basically just romping around with a little girl, even if they were tangled up—but Kanbaru knew that Shinobu was the shadow of a vampire. Daring to argue with one was a keen reminder of Kanbaru's iron nerves—but what could they be arguing about?

What could get her that heated?

I couldn't imagine. Maybe they got into it over a BL ship or something... It wasn't too serious if it was for a stupid reason, but...I still wanted to get close enough to hear them so that I could know more.

"You want to move. Hm…" Ononoki nodded. "Using my Unlimited Rulebook?"

"Why would I want to use a method that'd attract as much attention as that one? We don't want them noticing."

"Maybe you should try a please."

"…Please."

"Hm. What should we do," Ononoki said, seeming to think as she crossed her arms—did she realize that Kanbaru and Shinobu's conversation was going to end before ours at this rate?

"Your request isn't very convincing. It feels like you're just saying that."

"What do you mean, not convincing…"

"I wouldn't mind moving you if you did something amusing."

"You're being ridiculous now."

"Also, don't you think it's about time for you to thank me for protecting me with that mark I put on you, monstieur?"

"…"

She now demanded my thanks.

Don't get me wrong, I felt grateful, but I thought this was one of those situations where you didn't have to say it out loud… Wasn't she planning on keeping quiet about it? She seemed like the kind of girl who'd go, "What are you even talking about?" if I thanked her in an awkward way, but no, she was apparently more assertive than that.

"Well, it doesn't have to be right now, monstieur. Promise me to do something amusing later, and I'll guide you to the best seat in the house."

"The best seat in the house?"

"Front-row tickets."

"They'd notice."

No matter how serious the problem fueling their quarrel, those two would stop if we went and watched them from that close.

"Okay, fine. I promise. I'll do something super amusing next time."

If there was a next time…

Ononoki took on a strange personality in response to my promise.

"Hmm, I dunno, your idea of amusing always involves the dirtiest jokes… You're the type who thinks all you have to do to amuse someone is take off your clothes." (Seriously, what happened to her over the last twelve hours?) Only her face stayed expressionless, but then she pulled my sleeve.

"This way."

I know I've been describing her as emotionless and expression-less this whole time, but at this point I started to wonder if maybe she was only expressionless, and in fact overflowing with emotion—but in any case, she continued to tug me while I followed her with stealthy steps.

She may not have been external affairs, but she must have surveyed all of Kita-Shirahebi Shrine. She led me straight to the best seat in the house as if we were walking through her backyard.

I could just barely hear their voices and just barely see their expressions, plus we were hidden in bushes, making it hard for them to notice—it must have been just as good as our previous spot for Ononoki, with her apparently sharp senses, but it was on another level for me in my current, human mode.

"…"

From the tone of the voices I now heard—and from the expressions I now saw, I was able to count out the possibility that they were fighting over something pointless and stupid.

The two were arguing.

Genuinely—and seriously.

"Monsieur, I've been wondering, what exactly is in those dirty books in that plastic bag you've been holding like some sort of treasure this whole time?"

"It sounds like you already know, you just said that they're dirty books."

"Well, the bag is strangely transparent. At least, to eyes like mine. Still, I never knew you were well-versed in the ways of boys' love. That seems a little too broad-minded to me."

"No, you don't understand. This isn't me trying to show how broad-minded I am. I bought these because Kanbaru asked me to…"

I recalled the earlier trouble this got me into—then realized something.

Kanbaru had asked me to pick something else up while I was out shopping—and hold on, why would she ask me, her senior, to pick up something extra while I was out shopping in her place to begin with? You could chalk it up to shamelessness, sure, and that's why I didn't find it odd until this moment, but...

What about that?

Was asking me to pick something else up a way of delaying my return? To give her more time to speak with Shinobu alone?

She couldn't have predicted that I'd encounter the boy Aberration Slayer at the bookstore, of course... But could Suruga Kanbaru have wanted to speak to Shinobu Oshino—in as frank of a manner as I spoke to the boy Aberration Slayer?

But the discussion, or rather, the argument the two girls were having seemed to be a fruitless one. Although I could hear them from my current distance, it was hard to pick out each exact thing they said—they both seemed to have gotten pretty emotional.

Ononoki was staring at the two, but could she really hear them?

"Hey, Ononoki... I have a request."

"Didn't I tell you to be quiet, you living interruption? If you're not going to be reasonable, I'm going to have to shut you up with a kiss."

Really?

Ononoki's character was changing from one moment to the next, but who ever taught her that one?

I'd wanted to ask her to translate the exchange for me, but that now seemed difficult—fieldwork may have been her job, but to me she just looked like a dedicated rubbernecker.

But then.

The heated argument between the two finally seemed to reach a stopping point—the conversation between Kanbaru and Shinobu paused for a moment.

It was like one of those fleeting silences that suddenly descend on a noisy classroom—we'd be liable to erupt in laughter next had this been a classroom, but of course, that didn't happen.

Kanbaru looked up at Shinobu, her lips firm—while Shinobu looked down at Kanbaru, baring her fangs as if to gnash her teeth.

They'd stopped trying to shout each other down—were they trying to stare each other down now?

I was prepared to jump in at any moment, expecting them to beat each other down next—but then.

Shinobu spoke.

"Listen."

Her voice deeper than before—calmer than before.

"I recognize thy courage—I see from thy recklessness, not ceding a single step to me, that thou art indeed my master's junior. So rather than grow emotional, I shall indulge this child before me, as an adult who has lived for five centuries—take back thy prior statement and I would be willing to act as though this interaction never occurred."

Apologize, and I shall forgive thee, Shinobu said.

She hadn't spoken in such a menacing voice in a while. It made me go from being prepared to leap out to cowering.

I was just trembling, but Ononoki seemed to overestimate me, thinking that I was getting ready to intervene.

"Calm down, monstieur," she said, taking my hand.

She really was quick to initiate physical contact with me. Maybe she's in love with me, I thought. She continued:

"A fight between girls isn't a boy's business."

A fight between girls?

This clearly went beyond that. The weak of heart could die on the spot if Shinobu pressured them in that manner. Couldn't Ononoki see it? That was what it meant for someone's gaze to pierce like a dagger—but the person in whose direction that dagger pointed.

Suruga Kanbaru.

Her mental fortitude could not be pierced that easily—as far as her spirit went, it could put some aberrations to shame, as far as I knew.

"I won't take it back. I won't apologize. I'll say it again and again."

Kanbaru sounded calmer, too—thanks to all the preceding, frenetic screaming and shouting? If this was how girls fought, Ononoki was right. No boy had any business trying to get in the way of that.

"Shinobu. You—ought to meet him."

A line that she'd most likely repeated over and over—Kanbaru said it again.

"You ought to meet the first Aberration Slayer."

026

Whap.

Shinobu's hand moved to grab Kanbaru's face.

It looked like she was using the Iron Claw—Shinobu seemed to launch another attack from the mount position upon the face-up girl she straddled, Kanbaru.

That said, it seemed the Iron Claw was only meant to threaten, with no strength put into her fingers—touching Kanbaru's face more than grabbing.

Still, how could anyone stay still with this sham of a vampire's hand on her face? Shinobu had enough grip strength to crush a snake aberration. Of course, a snake's head wasn't the same as a human head, but it was probably like having your head patted by a bear.

I thought I could hear Kanbaru gulp.

And yet she didn't retreat.

She didn't retreat.

"You're trying to avoid ever having to meet your former partner, who spent four hundred years coming back to life—that's not good. It's not good at all."

That's.

Not right—Kanbaru said.

"…"

I found myself gulping as well—so that's what Kanbaru wanted to talk to Shinobu about while I was gone? I had no way of knowing how she broached the topic, but given that she'd ended up pinned to the ground, she probably hadn't done so in a very good way.

No.

She absolutely hadn't broached the topic in a good way.

She would have been direct, her words loud, clear, and unconsidered when there may have been better ones to use.

You're wrong. It isn't right.

She must have said those kinds of things—and even if she did know what kind of explosion of anger those honest words would invite, she wouldn't have said it any other way.

Suruga Kanbaru.

She continued, still refusing to choose her words carefully.

"An adult for five centuries? Really? Seems to me you're nothing more than a coward who keeps running away, refusing to face her past." She said the words clearly. Her face still pressed down upon. "You told me to apologize—but don't you have someone you need to apologize to, if anything?"

"I haven't a clue as to what thou may speak of. I cannot make sense of it—'tis incomprehensible. I had seen from within my master's shadow that derangement is thy standard state of mind, but it seems thou hast exceeded even that."

So Shinobu agreed that there was something wrong with Kanbaru's head… That was plenty on its own, but right now I also shared Shinobu's inability to understand what Kanbaru was trying to say.

She needed to meet the first Aberration Slayer.

And—apologize to him?

Is that what she was saying? I recalled my conversation in the empty lot with the boy Aberration Slayer. He said something—about wanting to apologize to Shinobu.

He wanted to meet her in order to apologize.

I couldn't gauge just how much he meant it, and even if he was telling the truth, part of me felt it'd be a little selfish to want something like that after all this time—yet Kanbaru now said the total opposite to

Shinobu.

Meet him and apologize to him—what made Kanbaru feel like she needed to say that?

"I know better than anyone that I'm messed up in the head."

So she was aware of it...

"But that has nothing to do with this—I still know you're in the wrong, even with a messed-up head."

"And I've been asking thee all this time where I've gone wrong—I don't understand a lick of it. If a lowly human such as thee wishes to deliver a sermon to me, at least speak in a somewhat logical manner."

"To hell with logic!" Kanbaru screamed again.

It almost looked like she was eating Shinobu's palm when she screamed with her face pressed down—and Shinobu didn't move her hand away, either.

Depending on how you saw it, they painted a very surreal picture.

Ononoki might have smiled if she could form expressions—but this was as serious as could be for the two involved.

"Stop whining and just meet him! We're talking about a guy who spent four hundred years returning all in order to meet you—so why won't you do that for him?!"

"And again, that is where thy misunderstanding lies—'tis not as if he returned for any reason as trifling and emotional as that. 'Tis mere vitality, merely a natural phenomenon. No different from the arrival of the summer and the winter, the pouring of rain, the crashing of the waves, the day turning to night turning to day again. A natural phenomenon, where scattered ashes were gathered once more by the wind and excited in the way a magnet would be."

"Sure, but it's natural for someone to fall in love!" yelled Kanbaru. "Don't you dare deny someone's feelings of being in love with you!"

"Again... How incomprehensible ye are!" Low until now, Shinobu's voice also began to rise. "Just what kind of disposition doth thou possess? Stop trying to measure the world by thy own standards! That is not the nature of a vampire thrall—a vampire's relationship of master and servant! 'Tis not a matter of love and love not, ye—romantic rotbrain!"

Romantic rotbrain.

The words were strong enough to potentially end the argument, but Kanbaru still didn't fall back—she persisted in the same fraught tone.

"Your master and servant relationship isn't about love and love not? Is that—something you'd be able to say to Araragi-senpai's face?"

"..."

Shinobu fell silent.

She went from enraged to quiet.

While we weren't face to face, I was directly to the side of hers. But Shinobu couldn't have gone quiet because she knew that.

Had we been linked, I could never escape notice at this distance, no matter how expert a job I did at hiding...

How ironic. I'd come into contact with Shinobu's feelings like this precisely because our link had been severed.

"Hmph. And so ye created such an opportunity for the two of us to be alone? Ah, but now that I mention it, something about ye did appear strange when I said to my master I'd no intention of meeting that thrall... And so ye had him buy books and brassieres and whatnot?"

"No, that doesn't have anything to do with it."

...Apparently it didn't.

"I really just wanted him to buy those for me. If I'm being honest with you, I regret not putting more emphasis on the bra—I'm concerned now that he'll treat it as some kind of joke and not buy one. My chest really hurts after all that moving I did just now. My breasts can't keep up with my speed. I thought they might get torn off at the root."

"Thy movements were indeed dynamic..."

"By the way, back when I played basketball, there was this one team we used to face off against called the Commandos, but I could never quite focus during those games."

"Well, it seems thou art underprepared once more as far as underwear."

"Indeed. I'd never be down on the ground like this if I'd worn a bra... Though it's really easy to just have to lie here like this. It's like I've been freed from gravity."

"Hmph. A concern I do not share as I am now," Shinobu said,

seemingly annoyed.

As far as I could surmise, the beating-each-other-down portion of their conversation was behind them—you'd think the situation would start with them trying to talk each other down, then proceed to shouting each other down, then beating each other down, but it seemed that fights between girls followed the opposite path.

In other words, a beatdown, then the shouting down—and then, at last, they talked each other down.

Okay, it'd be disrespectful to girls around the country if I took anything Shinobu Oshino and Suruga Kanbaru did as representative, but still.

Just as I thought during our encounters with the armored warrior and the monkey-crab-snake, Kanbaru was so quick to act—she must have gone straight into this per usual, as soon as I started down the mountain to go shopping. An opportunity to get right into a fight, ending in Shinobu mounting her.

Ononoki and I had walked in on them as they tried to shout each other down.

Neither Ononoki nor I would be spying on them so easily without that battle at the start... Whether or not Kanbaru honestly didn't want anyone around, it was very much like her to have failed so spectacularly in the end.

That kind of inattention to detail was in character.

As was the fact that she didn't hesitate to face off against a vampire—if she had something she wanted to say, she said it, whether it was to a cute little girl with blond hair or her esteemed senior.

When she wouldn't compromise on something, she wouldn't compromise on it.

That stubbornness—could she have gotten it from her mother?

I mean, just think about her left hand...

Anyway, a side product of us learning about what led to this situation was the factoid that Kanbaru had moved around as fast and hard as she could while wearing my hoodie directly against her braless skin. This set my heart aflutter to no small degree. Shinobu made it for me, and I rather liked it, but how should I feel wearing it in the future?

Wait, why were they talking about breasts?

"Hold on a moment, why do we speak of breasts?"

"You're the one who brought it up, Shinobu."

"Um…"

Shinobu tried to get started again, her expression still annoyed—though Kanbaru may have thrown her off beat, that seemed to have calmed her mental state. Of course, just as Kanbaru pointed out, Shinobu called herself a five-hundred-year-old adult (actually five hundred ninety-eight years old) but had no choice but to take the form of a little girl.

In other words, nothing about her seemed mature.

It appeared as though they'd talked each other down, but she'd surely fly into another rage if Kanbaru said something else that bothered her—and in fact, her nails were still placed against Kanbaru's face.

"Fine, I understand what it is ye wish to say—but this is no mere misunderstanding, 'tis meddlesome as well. Just as I said to my master before, thy senior is the only one I could now call my thrall. As I am now—"

"You say you don't understand what I'm saying, but if anything, I don't understand you when you say that—that's exactly what I can't stand you saying."

"Hmm?"

"You're almost making it sound like you should only have one thrall—haven't you ever considered something like you, Araragi-senpai, and this first Aberration Slayer all getting along, the three of you together?"

"The three of us?"

Shinobu seemed confused by Kanbaru's opinion—as was I.

Because she was right.

I'd never considered it.

And—neither had the first Aberration Slayer, most likely.

She said she didn't need two thralls, but when I thought about it, she didn't have a reason for not having two, did she?

So then why had this idea never once come to any of us? That almost made it look like—the first Aberration Slayer and I knew we'd face off and fight over Shinobu from the start.

Fight over her?

Like some kind of love triangle?

Yes, almost as if—my brain had been rotted by romance.

"That man died out of resentment for me. He showered me in rancorous words—and I should forgive that? No—thou said I must apologize. Apologize? For making him a vampire out of my own feelings of solitude? And what—ye dare say I ought to make up with him?"

"It doesn't matter whether or not you make up with him."

You could hear in Kanbaru's words that she held nothing back. She mercilessly criticized Shinobu, who looked a little weaker after Kanbaru's earlier point—and it felt like she also criticized me as I listened.

"You don't have to. That'd involve the both of you, so maybe you can't—if you're going to say you want to pick Araragi-senpai over the first Aberration Slayer, that's fine. But you need to be the one to tell him that. You shouldn't leave it up to Miss Izuko or Araragi-senpai."

"And what do ye claim to know?" Shinobu said, disgusted. "This does not involve thee, so thou art able to say anything about it at all— thou knowest not. Not a single thing—not of my relation with him. Our history. Thou art nothing but a nuisance with thy arbitrary delusions. Nay, not only of what took place four hundred years ago—I dare say ye know nothing of even my current relationship with my master, or am I mistaken?"

"It's true, I don't know. But I can tell," Kanbaru insisted without denying Shinobu's words, her valid point.

She was serious—and sincere as she spoke.

"About how you feel about your first, and your second."

"…"

Shinobu gulped—as did I.

Ononoki was just silent—probably because she didn't understand what Kanbaru truly meant.

But I knew.

Given that the two didn't have too deep of a relationship, it was a bit strange that Kanbaru would get into it with Shinobu to this degree, her personality aside... But now it made sense.

I'd even thought that she, as my ever-caring junior, was inferring the way I felt and saying these difficult words to Shinobu in my place—but that wasn't it.

Kanbaru understood better than I did.

And better than Shinobu, of course.

She knew how the first Aberration Slayer felt.

Feelings of obsession—like some kind of true love.

"Enough of thy foolish empathy."

This seemed to come across even to Shinobu, someone who by no means was perceptive when it came to the subtleties of the human experience. She spoke to Kanbaru with a complicated expression on her face.

"That man, returned from four hundred years ago, may appear pitiful to thee—ye may feel sympathy. However."

"I'm not sympathizing with him. I don't feel bad for him, either. I even understand that no one could have stopped this from happening—but it'd just be so hopeless like this. Him coming back to life from four hundred years in the past is like a miracle that no one could have ever predicted, right? Not you, not Araragi-senpai, not Miss Izuko, probably not even Mister Oshino—and the miracle deserves a fitting reward. If you ignored this miracle, treated it like some sort of statistical phenomenon, pretended it never happened—it would just seem like you're leaving him so empty-handed."

"Which is what ye must find so pity-inducing... But what would satisfy thee? Why must ye raise such a fuss? Have ye not considered that my not meeting him is an act done for his own sake?"

Shinobu's replies grew weaker.

Something about them told me that.

It sounded like she was saying things to try to convince Kanbaru to come around to her side instead of making her own points—was she wavering?

The aberration who had lived for five hundred years?

Was she being defeated in an argument by a seventeen-year-old girl?

"Were I to meet him after all this time, I'd have no words for him—he was never a good thing for me from the start, nor was I for him. Face reality, monkey-girl. There is nothing to do to him now but eliminate him—his existence brings unrest to this town, and he is like the embodiment of those stories of aberrations that now infest this place. His role should be nothing more than that of prey to an expert. He could never be considered harmless the way I or my master have been—ironically, that man who once slew countless aberrations himself will now be defeated by a future colleague—and there is no way to prevent that."

"I know. And that's why."

"That is why? Why is it all the more reason for me to meet him? As I have said again and again, that man resents me—he may kill me if we were to meet. He may kill my master as well. It seems he says I must return his enchanted blade, but I may not be the only one to fall victim to it. So taking all this in consideration—"

"I've taken all that into consideration and I'm still saying you should meet him—like I said, forget about logic! Why does everyone refuse to meet people by saying things like that—it's such a non-starter! If people don't meet, it's game over from the start!"

There'd be nothing to tell!

Kanbaru raised her voice—before raising her torso, Shinobu's hand still around her face. Shinobu began to lose her balance—she couldn't have expected Kanbaru to get up from being mounted using her abs alone. Shinobu must have felt as though she had her opponent physically dominated, if not mentally—but Kanbaru tried to get up.

Without borrowing the strength of her aberrational left hand, either.

"Just come out and say it," Kanbaru urged. "You're scared. Say you're scared of meeting him."

" …"

"That you don't want to meet him and talk to him and get your emotions worked up—king of aberrations? Legendary vampire? Yeah, right. You're exactly what you look like—a little girl who's scared of monsters."

" …"

"You might feel like you're being faithful, or that you're showing how virtuous you are by not meeting him because you think you'd be betraying Araragi-senpai if you did—but that's not true. You're not betraying him, the only person you're betraying, the only person you're lying to, the only person you're being phony to is yourself. Your weak, phony self."

"…"

"What's wrong with saying it. Just say it. Say it. That the kind of love that brought him back over four hundred years is too heavy for you. That honestly, it creeps you out. That it's a problem if he comes back to life and into yours after all this time, just when you're getting along with Araragi-senpai. That it's a pain in the ass if he decides to rehash all these things that are just memories for you now. That the way he's being so pushy is gross. That you find his feelings annoying—just say that it would've been better if he stayed dead. If you can't, then don't ever go on about master this, lord that. There's nothing lofty or noble about you."

All you are is shy.

Kanbaru had now gotten all the way up.

"Don't give me that master and servant stuff—you don't deserve to have slaves or masters."

"Ka…"

"You don't deserve to form any relationships at all."

"Kakak!"

Shinobu—laughed.

A gruesome laugh—and I could tell there was strength in her hand now.

This would be my only chance to stop her—yes, there wasn't any logic left at this point, nor was it a discussion.

Right or wrong didn't exist now that it had gone this far.

This was no longer a Shinobu who could stay silent, in the face of that many hostile remarks—Ononoki had started to get up as well. While she probably didn't understand what they were saying, she could sense the disquiet in the air as a warrior.

But.

Just as Ononoki held me back earlier, I stopped her this time. I held her hand and kept her from trying to insert herself between the two.

"Why do you have your fingers wrapped around mine?"

"Oops, my mistake. I confused you with Senjogahara."

"You're disgusting."

I adjusted my grip.

"Wait just a little longer, Ononoki."

"Why? It's bad enough already."

"Even then."

I understood—this could go past the point of no return. Shinobu didn't discriminate between humans for the most part, and Kanbaru being my junior didn't mean a thing to her.

She couldn't suffer that much of an insult.

And not do a thing about it.

Even then…

"Kakak—kakak. So are those the dying words ye wish to leave behind? 'Tis I who should be asking thee—are ye satisfied after saying all ye wished to say?"

"I'm very dissatisfied. I still have a lot I want to say."

"I've not the space in my heart to hear it. I feel like crushing thy head right here, even if'twould ruin everything."

"Then go ahead, do it."

I'm not apologizing, Kanbaru said—still glaring at Shinobu from between the fingers clasped across her face.

"Do it, then you can feel awkward around Araragi-senpai next. I bet you'll start avoiding him, the way you're avoiding the first Aberration Slayer now. You know the way you've been talking about him like he's something from your past? Well—you can make everything about Araragi-senpai a story from your past too."

"What a fortunate girl—so many ways of killing thee have come to my mind that I hesitated to kill thee out of reflex just now," Shinobu said as she strengthened her grip—then blood.

She was already applying enough strength to Kanbaru's head that her skin tore and her blood ran—but I still didn't move.

I couldn't intervene—it felt wrong to.

If I were to jump in and settle everything down—it'd be such a farcical ending. It'd be wrong for me to end their conversation.

Even if—it went past the point of no return.

Even if it ruined everything.

"So I shall give thee one final chance."

"I don't need it. You're going to throw away your second someday, just like you threw away your first. How could you ever face who your second is when you can't face your first? And your third, and your fourth, and your fifth—just keep on splitting up with people forever."

"Forever?"

"You're immortal, aren't you? You know what Araragi-senpai said once? He said—that if you wanted to die tomorrow, he was ready for his own life to end tomorrow, too. But I bet you'd never say anything like that. Even if you did—you'd say it to your third, too. And to your fourth. And to your fifth—you'd keep on living, and you'd keep on saying it."

"…"

That…

The words were overpowering to Shinobu, someone who'd even tried to end her own life after she grew bored of immortality.

"Do not assume all are as social as thee. Ye summed me up as shy earlier—but 'tis natural to feel disinclined to meet someone, is it not?"

"No, it's unnatural. Even if you don't meet eye-to-eye with everyone, you still meet them."

"I am not a person."

"Maybe not, by the looks of you."

They were diametrically opposed.

My conversation with the boy Aberration Slayer had been pretty damn fruitless—but Shinobu and Kanbaru's was quite barren as well.

No, it even felt like the more they talked, the wider the disconnect—but.

It meant their roots were entwined.

Their roots were the same.

"'Tis not as if I could say something to him if we were to meet, thou must realize. Ours was a relationship defined by hate. We were brought together by mutual hate before we first separated, then hate brought us together once more before we were separated again, by death—I have no intention of reconciling with him, nor do I intend on the three of us all getting along. I do not intend on speaking of the first alongside the second. I consider the simple comparison between the two to be an affront to my master."

Something she said here surprised me.

No, not that Shinobu could consider anything to be an affront to me—it was what she said about mutual hate.

I'd heard that the first Aberration Slayer killed himself out of hatred—but this was my first time hearing that Shinobu hated him.

Of course it was.

It wasn't as if she'd told me everything, and there was the whole matter of her level of excitement when she spoke—but.

One thing was certain.

Suruga Kanbaru—had managed to pull out emotions from Shinobu that I never could.

Was this it?

Was this the real reason Miss Gaen gave this job to Kanbaru? She'd said she needed Kanbaru's left hand, and I'd assumed that Kanbaru's ties to the Gaen family was key. That's what I'd been telling myself, but here Kanbaru was an outsider, someone who stood distant from the situation—I'd seen her as nothing more than a bystander who'd been dragged in, but could Miss Gaen have actually "dragged her in" to put her up against Shinobu like this?

Whether Kanbaru had added an extra item to my shopping list on purpose, or if it was just another one of those miracles that happened around her... When I went back and thought about it, I went to go buy breakfast—I was encouraged to leave the scene—by Miss Gaen.

She could tell that I'd go shopping if she handed me a five-thousand-yen bill—and given that this was Miss Gaen, she could have known there'd be a chance, or was even sure that I'd encounter the first Aberration Slayer, were I to climb down the mountain.

Was I reading too much into this?

How could she predict something like the first Aberration Slayer returning with a will of his own when she first tried to drag Kanbaru into this job?

"..."

No, maybe she could.

I know everything.

The lady who knows everything.

Who knew, maybe she'd even predicted that I'd buy some cougar photo books...

"That's going a little too far," Ononoki jumped in, despite not knowing anything about that situation.

Really? She was going to zing me over a situation she didn't even know about?

"Please don't try to play stupid to provide comic relief here, monstieur. I think we're nearing the emotional climax."

"Emotional climax... This really is just a show to you, isn't it?"

"That's not true. You're about to see the tears start to really flow. From me."

"Yeah right. And that'd just be a cry-max, not a climax, anyway."

Whatever the case, Miss Gaen certainly had no desire to meet her long-lost niece—her older sister's daughter.

So—even if Miss Gaen knew everything, there were some things she didn't understand.

Wanting to meet someone.

The desire to meet someone—she didn't understand that.

Ah.

At that moment—after my eighteen years alive and many experiences, I understood for the first time.

Loving someone and wanting to meet them—are two different emotions.

"Nor is there anything I could do for the first, were I to meet him—I could not so much as give back the enchanted blade Kokorowatari, not now. It has integrated itself into my body," Shinobu said. In a subdued voice. "Listen close, for this is what I wish to say. It is not that I refuse to meet him because I derive no benefit from doing so—meeting would not be good for him, either. What meaning would there be in having him see me getting along well with my master? Having him see that I no longer have any feelings at all for him—what meaning is there in that? Ye would have me do something as cruel as that?"

"That's right. I'm telling you to do the cruel thing. It's your job to wound that man in your past," Kanbaru said. In a fierce voice. "Do you just want to be someone good and loved by all? Do you want to be loved and nothing else?"

"Thy words...are no different from saying that 'tis better to destroy what would otherwise grow weathered and faded—"

"Yeah, that's what I'm saying."

"And if he now wishes to kill me out of hatred, I have no choice but to kill him in turn—I would not allow myself to be killed for his sake. While I admit that I may owe him apologies, I do not expect him to forgive me. And still ye say I should?"

"You should. If that happens, just respond to those feelings of hate—just cut those feelings off. But if you apologize and he does forgive you—"

"The outcome would be no different. He would be eliminated by those experts the moment after he forgives me—still I should?"

"You still should."

You still should, Kanbaru repeated.

Shinobu seemed irritated—maybe she saw it as Kanbaru making fun of her, because her grip grew even tighter... It could barely be any stronger.

I thought I even heard the sound of Kanbaru's skull creaking.

"Even if thy foolish prediction is correct and that man did return out of his feelings for me—I would never respond to such feelings. Were I to meet him, the most I could ever do would be to mercilessly and unsparingly reject him. And still I should?"

"You still should."

"Say I met him—"

A gruesome smile reappeared on Shinobu's face.

More gruesome than I'd ever seen.

It was as grotesque as a smile could be.

"*What would ye do if I wanted to respond to those feelings?* If instead of thy senior—I chose the first Aberration Slayer, then what? *Still I should?*"

"*You still should.*"

And if that happens, Suruga Kanbaru declared—as her blood spilled.

"*Make a clean break from Araragi-senpai—and live by his side forever.*"

Dangle.

Shinobu's hand, the one wrapped tight around Kanbaru's head, dangled and fell—swinging back and forth, strengthless. Not just her hand. Shinobu's face and shoulders both slumped and drooped.

She didn't say it out loud.

Shinobu still had the far more dominant position. Though now off balance, she straddled Kanbaru—and Kanbaru was the one bleeding.

But it was so clear.

Yes.

Shinobu Oshino had admitted defeat.

The legendary vampire who had lived for over half a millennium, Kissshot Acerolaorion Heartunderblade, had just admitted that she lost—to a seventeen-year-old high school girl, at that.

It was my first time.

I'd never seen Shinobu Oshino lose one-on-one before.

"Ononoki," I said—at some point, I'd let go of her hand. "I have a request."

"Another one? Stop using me like some kind of convenient tool. Know your place, punk."

"Punk? Don't worry, this is my last request," I said, pointing at my face.

"Could you take this stamp off of me?"

"…?" Ononoki tilted her head like she didn't understand. "I can't guarantee your safety if I did that. I understand that my footprint is embarrassing, but you just have to put up for it this one night and everything will be okay."

She'd put her footprint on my face knowing that it'd be embarrassing? And you know, given the role it played, there didn't seem to be any particular need for it to be on my face, or even for it to be a footprint, so long as others could see it…

I spoke once more.

I spoke, looking straight forward—my eyes fixed on a bleeding Suruga Kanbaru and a defeated Shinobu Oshino.

"I feel like dueling someone."

027

Anyone looking back from the future and passing judgment on the situation would probably think that Kanbaru was right—but as someone living in the same time and the same place as her, Kanbaru's opinions were just too severe.

She'd been excessive, no matter how you look at it.

From the perspective of someone with a personality that's not particularly extroverted like myself, she, with her master's degree in sociability, acted in an utterly incomprehensible way.

It was as if she'd gone into a fairly settled situation and not just rocked the boat, she'd capsized it—I almost got a headache when I wondered why she would knowingly refuse to work everything out in a peaceful manner.

It made me want to throw everything I had at each of her sound arguments.

This was Suruga Kanbaru, after all. Someone with the distinguished record of having gone over to play at the homes of every girl in her class during her first month of school when she first entered Naoetsu High.

She approached her relationships with other people in a fundamentally different way from me, someone who couldn't even manage to join an extracurricular club or sports team—and when I thought about it,

Shinobu hadn't made a single thrall until four hundred years ago, living all on her own, and she'd only had a total of two thralls in her five hundred years alive (six hundred, really). That didn't mean she was chaste and well-behaved so much as it meant she showed a striking lack of communication abilities.

It wouldn't be right to speak of my solitude as being on the same level as Shinobu's, of course—but if you were to keep this in mind, both she and I would have a hard time understanding what Kanbaru was saying, nor would Kanbaru be able to understand how we felt.

We couldn't understand one another.

On a fundamental level.

But if I was going to say that—then maybe Kanbaru best understood how the first Aberration Slayer felt out of us all, or perhaps she was the only one who understood.

Middle school.

When Suruga Kanbaru had a pseudo-sisterly relationship with Hitagi Senjogahara—known then as the Valhalla Duo, she was one half of the best-known relationship in school, according to Hanekawa.

Kanbaru must have assumed that it'd last forever—but Senjogahara, one year older than her, proceeded to high school one step ahead of her.

And then she changed in high school.

Though Kanbaru had drawn on her inherent diligence to work hard and enter Naoetsu High despite her somewhat lacking academics, she found herself flatly rejected by a changed Senjogahara.

From what I hear, she said some awful things.

"I don't think of you as a friend or even as my junior—not now, nor did I ever." — "Being friends with a talented junior like you would boost my own reputation, and that was the only reason I was nice to you." — "I only acted like a caring senior."

And after that, the two didn't interact for over a year.

It wasn't all positive for Kanbaru when they started interacting again—because a hard-to-understand, thoughtless, stupid boy who lived a frivolous life appeared as well.

Me.

Koyomi Araragi.

I, this vague, nonsensical guy who could just as easily be replaced by anyone appeared as a partner of this changed Hitagi Senjogahara.

I can't imagine how Kanbaru must have felt then.

An average high schooler with no redeeming qualities actually stands out as its own strong personality, but I wasn't even that.

It was this person who seemed to have swept in and snatched away Senjogahara, her adored senior—and Suruga Kanbaru couldn't stand it.

She couldn't stand it, and so.

She made a wish to a monkey.

It was unlike a girl as honest and straightforward as her—but perhaps it was very much in character, since it was the only way she could keep herself from running away from how she lived her life.

That's the kind of girl she is.

Which is why she understood how the first Aberration Slayer felt.

How it felt to be someone's first—and how it felt to be the runner-up.

The scale was different, of course—equating the two situations might actually bother the first Aberration Slayer. It'd be like calling Shinobu's solitude and mine the same thing. Kanbaru's relationship with Senjogahara had been cut off for about the year it took for Kanbaru to finish middle school, two at most if you included the time after that—compared to that, what scale could there be for four hundred years?

Shinobu's relationship with the first Aberration Slayer couldn't have been anything like Senjogahara's relationship with Kanbaru—and if you were to say this, no one could understand the true relationship between the first Aberration Slayer and the second.

Not a single person existed who knew of that time.

Every one of them had been swallowed by the Darkness.

Still, Suruga Kanbaru sympathized.

She sympathized, but she didn't commiserate.

She empathized—and aligned with him.

That's why she hounded Shinobu—she couldn't stand there not saying a single word as Shinobu tried to avoid meeting him, to avoid facing him, and she couldn't keep herself to only a single word, either.

It wasn't something I could do.

I'd grown too close to Shinobu. I couldn't reject her way of thinking or way of life. I couldn't fight with her the way Kanbaru did, either—nor could I argue with her.

I couldn't confront her opinions with my own, nor could we engage in heated debate—that's just what it means to be soulmates, but maybe I should have been the one to say the kinds of things that Kanbaru said to Shinobu.

Not that I'd ever think about it, being so unsocial—honestly, just how much work was I going to pass off onto my junior?

Even here at Kita-Shirahebi Shrine, during Nadeko Sengoku's case, I had Kanbaru dirty her hands in facing the *Jagirinawa*.

To make matters worse, I'd handed most of the comic-relief duties off to her this time around, which is why I needed to face the first Aberration Slayer—at the very least to repay this girl who'd faced off against Shinobu alone.

That's what I thought.

That was my decision.

"It's not like you have to fight, you know."

Gotta love it, he added.

Episode, the half-vampire expert who had appeared at Kita-Shirahebi Shrine in the evening, smiled as he rested against the massive cross sticking out from the shrine grounds.

Apparently he wasn't able to keep this cross of his in some other dimension the way enchanted blades and the like were kept. It was a cross, after all, so maybe he couldn't use any vampiric abilities on it.

"All you had to do was get him to agree to a duel, and now Miss Gaen's plans have all fallen into place—now that we're able to summon the first Aberration Slayer to an established location, your role is basically done, thrall of Heartunderblade. Pretty sure Miss Gaen planned on me fighting him. Pretty sure that's why she wanted me."

"Maybe. But still."

"Oh, no, it's fine—I'm not gonna argue with you on that one. I'm a mercenary. I care less than anyone when it comes to who fights—

I'll gladly let you handle it, so long as it means one less vampire in this world. In fact, I'd even be happy if you, Heartunderblade, and the first Aberration Slayer all died."

I doubted this was a simple quip.

I was generally considered harmless—plus, he'd lost to me in the game set out by Oshino over spring break. He said he couldn't lay a hand on me and Shinobu, but inside, he saw all vampires as his enemies.

A half-vampire.

He hated humans and vampires alike.

"Are you done with whatever 'formalities' you had?" I asked, hesitantly.

He nodded. "Yes—of course. She's meticulous when it comes to that stuff. We tracked down the first Aberration Slayer and properly negotiated with him—just as Mèmè Oshino negotiated with me. Though I doubt Miss Gaen is as sincere as Mèmè Oshino."

"…"

I never imagined Oshino would ever be described as *sincere*, but to be fair, maybe he was in comparison to Miss Gaen—everything's relative, huh?

Should we be comparing everything, even the incomparable?

"Oh—Episode, I have to admit, I wondered what was going to happen after we let the first Aberration Slayer get away in that empty plot, but you tracked him down? You really are professionals."

"We really are professionals? That miracle you pulled off was no amateur feat."

At least, that was the first time I'd ever seen Miss Gaen let an opponent get away, Episode said—it didn't feel bad to hear that, though I felt sure it wasn't meant as a compliment.

"All that's left for us to do now is to wait for night, then you and the first Aberration Slayer can face off in a one-on-one duel—but just to help you relax a little, I'll tell you now. You can lose."

"…?"

"You losing would just mean me stepping in—and in the worst case, Miss Gaen will make a move. That's all. Sure, we're calling this a stage for a duel, but really, it's like the site of an exorcism. A real dead end this time, one he can't get away from. Do you see that as cowardly?" Episode asked as if to preempt me. "Didn't I tell you before? There's no such thing as cowardice when it comes to expelling aberrations—not to mention that we're up against another expert this time around. He knew that when he accepted this, and I'm sure he's doing everything he can to escape from the boundaries of our stage. Call it a battle of wits, if you want—it's not as much about strength as *duel* might make you think. So you don't have to win—all you have to do is not die."

"Not die?"

"Duh, because Heartunderblade will be completely freed if you did. Don't tell me you forgot."

"…"

It's not as if I'd forgotten.

But at the same time, I wouldn't have to worry even if something happened to me in the duel—as long as the first Aberration Slayer took on the role I now played.

"No, because I bet that's the one scenario Miss Gaen fears—Heartunderblade linking back up with her original thrall is the most worrying outcome of all. How could it not be bad? Two vampires out there like Heartunderblade? You need to be more conscious of the fact that you're holding back a monster that could destroy the world ten times over."

Being told that I'm Shinobu's safety valve didn't feel quite as good as what he said before, given how powerless and useless I was.

It almost made me feel like some guy whose special ability was to scatter adult magazines everywhere.

What kind of exorcist was I?

"There might not be any point in asking, since you don't seem to expect that much of me, but what happens to him if I do win this duel?"

"He'll be wiped out. He'll be so killed by either me or Miss Gaen that he'll leave no residual effects behind. It's too bad there's no bounty on his head, seeing that his existence as an aberration isn't recognized, but Miss Gaen will pay me a bonus. So don't worry about it—the result's gonna be the same whether you win or lose. Your duel with the first Aberration Slayer is, you know, like an opening act, a performance…

Like throwing out the first pitch."

Throwing out the first pitch.

I understood this was him trying in his own way to get me to relax, but it was deflating—well.

Even if it was the first pitch, I didn't know who was the pitcher, and who was the batter, not to mention that it'd be a weird opening ceremony if the batter was allowed to swing. Maybe you could call it a chance for me and the Aberration Slayer to show off.

"So, well…"

Finished with his explanation, Episode pulled up the cross he rested against and plopped it on his shoulder—he handled the silver cross, which could have weighed as much as a ton or so, with ease.

A half-vampire.

His powers as a vampire were halved, but so were his weaknesses— which meant this expert in a white traditional school uniform could use his powers even during the day.

"So, well, as you know, my mom and my dad were a vampire and a human, respectively."

"…?"

"But I don't want that example to lead the likes of you to think that humans can form bonds with aberrations, or get along with them, okay? If anything, I want you to think of my existence as a sad sort of failure."

Failure? It was unlike Episode to use such a word about himself. It couldn't have been modesty.

"I mean, my mom and my dad were killed afterwards—wiped out by humans and eaten by vampires not long at all after they got together."

Even I'd have been in trouble if I hadn't been taken in, he said, his tone unchanged. He spoke a truth so shocking that for a brief, fleeting moment, I forgot that I'd once been in a battle to the death with the guy.

"Gotta love it, right? But that's how it is—so don't get any weird hopes. Not about your relationship with Heartunderblade."

"But, that—"

Flustered, I turned to him.

I couldn't swallow that as the truth—wasn't his case a special exception? Though I saw why he'd become an expert with his private reasons.

If his father was sucked dry by vampires, and his mother was killed by humans, then of course—

"Hm? Oh, no, you've got it all mixed up. My human dad was *exorcised* by humans, and my vampire mom was *eaten* by vampires. Both of 'em were treated like traitors by their own kind. But I can't say I blame them. I'd think the same about a traitor."

"…"

His shocking truth…had only become more shocking.

How could I, with my peaceful upbringing, say anything to that? This youth in a white traditional school uniform who I once saw as nothing more than a hated enemy suddenly felt so familiar and distant at the same time.

"Who took you in? Who protected you when both humans and vampires were against you?"

"I dunno if I'd say protected—they probably had all kinds of plans for me…" Episode hesitated for a brief moment. "It was Guillotine Cutter's church."

Guillotine Cutter…

One of the three experts who'd visited this town over spring break to eliminate Shinobu…

"So…that makes you—"

"Oh, no way. That god freak wasn't some kind of parent to me. All I'm saying is that as someone with my own private reasons, I just can't take Heartunderblade's side here. I think she's getting what she deserves, stuck in the middle like this riding a fence. Gotta love it!"

Episode began to leave Kita-Shirahebi Shrine—to make his own preparations, no doubt. I nearly watched him walk off, but spoke out to his cross-bearing back at the last second.

"Hold on, I never heard the most important part."

Episode didn't care one way or another about whether I took part in this duel, so it must have slipped his mind… But I needed him to tell me.

"Where are these dueling grounds you set up? Where should I go tonight?"

"Oh, about that," he turned and said. He'd cheerfully told me about the way his parents were killed, but now he looked gloomy, as if he'd recalled something unpleasant. "We're following precedent here. A spot you're pretty familiar with—I'd call it fated."

"Fated?"

"Naoetsu Private High School's athletic field."

028

This is out of chronological order, but—

The fight between Suruga Kanbaru and Shinobu Oshino ended at around noon, so if you wanted to know what happened after that, it went in a direction that diverged a little from the "emotional climax" Ononoki expected.

First off, once Shinobu finished receiving all of Kanbaru's dressing-down and urging-on, her next act was to sulk and go to sleep—she stood up to get off of Kanbaru's body, then trudged to the rear of the shrine. Kanbaru didn't continue to follow her at that point. The nocturnal Shinobu was in part too sleepy to continue, but I'm sure being defeated in an argument by a high school girl hit her unexpectedly hard.

When I thought about it, going to sleep whenever anything annoying happens is a coping mechanism she's used for four hundred years now—in response, Ononoki, who'd seen their exchange from nearly the beginning, said by my side:

"Hah. Lame." (Again, what kind of character was she supposed to be?) The shikigami shrugged her shoulders, stood, and continued, "What a boring fight that was. I'm leaving, monstieur. I need to report to Miss Gaen about this. Once I'm done reporting to her, I think I'll delete my boring memories of this boring fight."

"What did you experience over the last twelve hours to make you like this? Also, were you listening to me? This sign and seal on me..."

"Sign and seal? Could you not use such old-fashioned terms? Please, call it *where others fear to tread.*"

"I'm not humoring your joke. What kind of bootlicker do you take me for? And you stepped on me with your bare feet, anyway, not your shoes."

"Okay, fine. I'll take it off tonight. I'll add that to my report, too."

"I'd appreciate it. Oh, and if you're going to meet Miss Gaen—"

"Your link, right? I guess you do have to restore it if you want a fighting chance," Ononoki said as she walked off and left Kita-Shira-hebi Shrine—walking straight down the mountain instead of using the stairs.

To be honest, I was at a loss as to what to do now that I was alone. I had so little idea about how I should face Kanbaru or Shinobu after seeing that exchange up close. I felt like climbing right back down the mountain, but it wasn't as if I could.

I did also want to take a look at Kanbaru's head. She was bleeding, though not severely—I may not have been able to treat her wounds now, but still.

I went back the way I came, passed through the torii gate once more, and with my best unconcerned look, tried to walk naturally (in truth probably a little faster than usual) before arriving at Kanbaru. I'd made a rather long detour.

"Hm? What's the matter, Kanbaru? What're you doing on the ground there? You're bleeding from your head, are you okay?"

"Huh? You know, don't you? You were watching from right over there until a second ago."

"You knew?!"

So she'd been having that conversation with Shinobu knowing I was close by?! Her heart was so tough that she actually needed to see a cardiologist!

Ononoki could hide her presence perfectly (or rather, she didn't have any presence to begin with), so it seemed as though Kanbaru hadn't no-ticed her, but she must have sensed me in the bushes, even if she couldn't see me.

You really shouldn't underestimate an athlete's sixth sense…

"Don't worry, Shinobu didn't notice you. So, did you buy me that book?"

"Hold on a second, you can't just brush that topic aside! You've gotta let us discuss what just happened a little more!"

"? But you already heard everything. More importantly, the book…"

"You're way too fixated on it. Just how important is it to you? At least let me look at your head wound."

Of course, what went on inside it worried me way more than any external injury…

"Mmf," Kanbaru thrust her head out toward me.

I didn't expect to find the gesture so adorable… Well, as long as I ignored the fact that it was a result of holding her novel's two volumes tightly in either hand.

I parted Kanbaru's hair, grown long ever since she quit the team, and took a look at the lacerations on her skin created by Shinobu's Iron Claw.

Hmm… Well, it seemed fine…

It looked bad, given how easy it is to bleed from your head, but when I wiped up the blood, I found the wounds minor enough. I could leave them be and not use any kind of vampiric ability…

"It'd be neat if you could play with my hair while I read this novel…"

"Could you please not amuse yourself with a novel while I'm concerned about you?"

"You don't need to worry, injuries like this come with the territory if you play sports. Anyway, could you keep touching my hair like that for a little longer?"

"What would be the point? Um…"

What was it again? I needed to talk to her about something…

"Eh, I guess it's fine."

"Hm? What is?"

"Nothing."

It'd be strange to thank her here, and things were fine for the time being now that I knew she wasn't seriously injured… That's all there was to say. I mussed Kanbaru's hair.

"Yup, nothing. C'mon, Kanbaru. Let's have lunch."

"Yeah, I'm starved. I'll just keep reading this book, so you feed me, okay? Aahh."

"Don't aahh me. No senior would ever spoil his junior that much."

"Hm? There doesn't seem to be much here."

"I ran into budget problems… I did buy some donuts, too, but Shinobu…" I looked over at the shrine, wondering what to do. It almost felt like I was going to have to wake a sleeping god. "What's next for her?"

"If she's sleeping, I say let her sleep. She's nocturnal, after all. Shouldn't she wake up once it's night?"

"Yeah, but… Um, are you not interested, Kanbaru? You laid it on that thick to her and yet you don't care about what she does next?"

"Whether I'm interested or not, it's up to her. I already said what I wanted to say, so I'm satisfied."

What I'm interested about right now is how the savage garçon is going to huff and puff and blow this half-boy down, Kanbaru said, engrossed in her book.

I wanted to let her know just how much trouble this savage garçon of hers had gotten me into, but this too was a part of who Kanbaru was—social people like her also have a solid line that divides them from others.

Meanwhile, people with as few friends as me have a tendency not to differentiate their own business with the business of others nearly as much as they should, which leads to trouble.

Something Shinobu and I may have in common.

"So, my senior? My bra?"

"Like that's what you really wanted me to buy. Yeah, I bought you one. Here."

"My bra?"

"Here!"

It was a cheap one from a discount store and not a lingerie shop due to my budget…but it's what's on the inside that counts.

Whether it comes to heads or chests.

"Okay, I'm going to keep on reading, so you put it on for me. Aahh."

"Stop trying to 'aahh' like it's some kind of double entendre. Anyway, Kanbaru. Don't you have anything for me?"

"Hm?"

"Some kind of advice you're willing to put your body on the line for?"

"What's that? You want me to put my body where?"

"Sorry, no. You can keep it right there. Just give it to me orally."

"I don't know about that one, either... But no, nothing really."

"Really? Nothing?"

"Oh, I could never be so forward as to dare give advice to my esteemed senior. I'm just a little girl," the little girl who'd unflinchingly argued with a five-hundred-plus-year-old vampire said as she kept her eyes laser-focused on her novel.

Readers like her were an author's blessing... I did wish she'd spare a little bit of her blessings for her senior, though.

"You just have to be the same senpai you always are. Don't try extra hard or anything, just be yourself. Treat practice like the real thing, and treat the real thing like practice. That's what athletes live by," Kanbaru said, almost like a captain speaking to a teammate the day before a big tournament. "If I gotta keep going, it's all about DIY."

"DIY?"

"Do your best."

"..."

That would be DYB, and not the term she'd used for amateur artisanship, but I decided not to make any quip.

Because—"do it yourself" was actually the exact advice I needed to hear.

After this, I took a nap in preparation for that night—Shinobu had monopolized the space inside the shrine proper, so I was basically sleeping rough. Lacking my physical enhancement, I needed to sleep, but had trouble getting any. Not just because I was outdoors though, I'm sure. Kanbaru kept reading her novel the entire time—did athletes never run out of stamina?

Episode visited the shrine in the evening and gave me the details about the duel Miss Gaen had set up.

Naoetsu Private High School's athletic field.

The school where both Kanbaru and I were enrolled.

Sure, Episode would see it as fate—it was where he fought a legendary vampire he'd chased after, as well as her thrall.

At the same time.

It was also where Shinobu and I, where Koyomi Araragi and Kissshot Acerolaorion Heartunderblade, fought to the death.

He was right. It did follow precedent, and it was a suitable location.

For a duel between the First and the Second.

For a schism between slaves.

For a conclusion—so suitable I could barely stomach it.

029

"Hi, Senjogahara?"

"Oh, Koyo."

"You've never once called me by that nickname before."

"What's the matter? If you're calling me like this, does that mean you've settled whatever problem you ran into this time around?"

"No…"

"Does it mean you've prepared yourself emotionally for the way Miss Hanekawa and I are going to rake you over the coals?"

"You're scaring me."

"You only have yourself to blame. You can't just skip school whenever the fancy strikes, you know… Not that I have any right to be saying that."

"Hm? Well…I'm not finished, anyway. My plan was to wait until this was over before contacting you, but I couldn't take it any longer. Sorry, I just got anxious."

"I see… Well, I'm happy to hear that. I'd thought you were off flirting with Kanbaru and had forgotten all about the likes of little old me."

"Of course not. Don't say that, you're going to make me mad. But, well—it'll all be settled tonight. Yeah, I can give you a proper explanation once I'm back."

"Is that so. Well, you can leave Miss Hanekawa to me."

"Hm? Did something happen with her?"

"…Kanbaru never told you?"

"? About what?"

"Oh, nothing… It seems we share a terrifying junior in common. If you haven't heard, though—just hear it straight from her once you're back. That should also motivate you to return safely, right? I know you must be acting as reckless as ever, Koyo."

"Could you please stop calling me Koyo?"

"Should I call you Koyote?"

"Oh, so I'm like your dog now?"

"If I'm being honest, I do wish you'd drop what you're doing and make your way back home like a faithful little boy… But I take it that's not something you can do."

"That's right. It's not… There's a lot I need to tell you once I'm back. A lot I want to apologize about, and a lot I want to say. We should talk about this face-to-face, though."

"Don't phrase things in a way that makes it sound like we're breaking up, please. You're scaring me."

"Oh, sorry. That came out wrong. Hey, Senjogahara?"

"What is it, Koyote?"

"I really hope you haven't decided on calling me that… Hey, there's something I wanted you to tell me."

"Chanel No. 5."

"That's not what I was going to ask, and that's a lie, anyway. When Kanbaru entered Naoetsu High a year ago and met you—how did you feel? I want you to be honest. When your junior whom you'd had no contact with for a full year, someone you saw as a friend from the past whom you'd left behind, came all the way into your today—how did you feel?"

"…"

"Oh, sorry. That was a weird question. My bad, just forget about it."

"No. Hearing that question, I see the problem you're in, Koncourse."

"Wow! Is that supposed to be a nickname for me?"

"Konsole works too."

"How do you even get to either of those from Koyomi?"

"To be honest, it felt like a lot—you know, the weight of her emotions."

"…"

"She'd always carried around too many fantasies about me—but if you'll allow me to correct you on just one point, I wouldn't say that I rejected Kanbaru unilaterally back then as she tried to cling onto me. She said some pretty rough things to me about the way I was going about my life."

"Yeah. I was starting to get that feeling."

"Of course, it didn't really resonate back then. She's special, someone chosen—which is why she could say those kinds of things, I thought. That she was a genius on another level compared to a phony like me."

"…"

"'Hard work doesn't always lead to success, but everyone successful has worked hard'—people who are successful always say that kind of thing, right? They try to convince you it wasn't luck that caused them to succeed, it was their own hard work. Well, I was at an age where I hated hearing that kind of thing."

"I'm pretty sure that's not something you age out of… In fact, I imagine you still hate it now."

"Well, I had another thought when you helped me reconcile with her. That's not how it is. Even geniuses struggle."

"…"

"Everyone struggles—I guess that's obvious. For so long, I wanted that feeling of 'I'm special' that special people have—but that's when I realized it doesn't mean anything."

"…"

"Did we get a little off track? I said the weight of her emotions was a lot—but I think part of that was me. I was too light then to endure all that weight. If I wanted to be with Kanbaru, though, I'd have to become someone capable of enduring it—which is something I'm still pursuing. Of course, I'm also doing it for you. I'm working at it, believe it or not. So that I can become your bride one day, Araragi."

"…"

"Was that too much?"

"No, not at all."

"Really, there's no such thing as special or normal. Those are just comparisons—right? Sure, people will think of you as special if you're born into a fabulously wealthy family, but if you're going to say that, everyone I know is special for being born during this age in such a peaceful country."

"This might be my last chance, so could I ask you something that might upset you?"

"I wouldn't mind answering as long as you redact that worrying lead-in."

"If someone who outclassed me in every way told you they loved you, what would you do?"

"Ugh, you're such a sissy! Oh my god, are you really asking that?"

"Er, um, yeah, I know, but."

"You're trying to get me to say something awful to you, aren't you? You're seeing how far you can push me before I get mad! Gross! That does it, we're breaking up tomorrow!"

"Um, you don't have to answer if you don't want to…and I think that reaction is enough of one on its own, but…please, could you not talk about breaking up tomorrow?"

"I get the feeling you're having to swallow your pride to ask me this, so I'll give you an honest answer. I'm a hundred percent certain I'd get over it."

"Wow, you're…amazing for being able to say that."

"I know that no bond between two people is absolute. Watching my parents taught me that."

"Senjogahara—no, that's—"

"And if you think about it, the idea of an unbreakable bond is pretty scary—which just means you need to hustle instead, so someone can't get over you. Even if you can't become a special person, you can still be special to someone, right?"

"Special to—someone."

"I'm working every day to be someone special to you and Kanbaru—so don't worry, Araragi. You're plenty special. To me, to Kanbaru—and to Shinobu. We've chosen you."

"So you really did understand... Wow."

"I'm your girlfriend. I'm very happy you called me. I love you."

"I love you too. Once I get back, why don't we...talk more about this kind of thing?"

"Let's. I'll be waiting for you in the nude."

"...You have a lot to do with why Kanbaru is such a pervert, don't you?"

030

From there, all the actors assembled at Naoetsu Private High School's athletic field on the night of August twenty-fourth—or so I wish I could say, but a number of them were still missing.

We can touch on this later, but it also marked my first time going to my high school in the four days since summer break ended. Now that I thought about it, my school didn't make us show up at any point during summer break like some others do (or maybe it does, but not to my knowledge), making this my first attendance in the thirty-seven or so days since first term ended. The fact that I'd come in the dead of night, when every student, teacher, administrator, and more had already left, was very much in character for me.

I still hadn't done my summer vacation homework, I realized only now. That had been the start of this whole string of incidents continuing on from the last day of summer break, but that homework would be so far in the past by the time I got back to school that I might dodge the bullet.

You know, I had some pretty serious guts on me too.

Anyway, now that a barrier had been constructed around the field, just like during spring break, intruders and third-party interventions were no longer a worry.

"All right, then. Let's get this started nice and quick, then ended nice and quick," Miss Gaen said.

It did feel like she was acting a little distant from me, but that had to be my imagination. Miss Gaen was an understanding adult.

Episode stood by her side.

His massive cross didn't stick out from the ground the way it did in Kita-Shirahebi Shrine (it'd have left an awful mark if it did), but rested instead on his shoulder—probably a sign that he was ready to fight at any moment.

It must have been because they were both that type of person at their core, but the two maintained a relaxed attitude—that, or they weren't too interested. Still, you could tell they took their job seriously.

I doubted either of them ever showed the kind of frivolity that Kaiki or Miss Kagenui wouldn't think twice about flaunting as they worked—perhaps it was understandable coming from Kaiki, a con artist, but Miss Kagenui being that way showed just how unusual she was.

Could that have been why Miss Gaen didn't get Miss Kagenui involved, even though this case involved immortal vampires? That was as much speculation as I could engage in as someone who'd fought and been spared by her.

In fact, the duel that would soon take place might not be that big of a deal, compared to how recklessly I'd gone to face off against Miss Kagenui—of course, one very big condition differed between that time and this one.

On that note, the tween doll girl and tsukumogami who acted as Miss Kagenui's shikigami, Yotsugi Ononoki—wasn't present.

Unbelievable! Ononoki, not here?!

No tween girls around?!

What did I bother coming here for, then?!

The fact made me want to scream all this and more (I'm joking here), but it seemed she'd been asked to handle another task after reporting to Miss Gaen about our interaction and was now off on a trip elsewhere.

Yet another task...

I'm not going to continue talking about the degree to which Ononoki is overworked, but where could she be going at this point and what would she be doing there? They said this job would come to a conclusion here no matter what. Curious, I asked Miss Gaen for details.

"She's tying up the loose ends now that we've set things straight with this job—a job's not over just because you set things straight, you know. Especially the way I do things. I make sure that things can never happen again by eliminating any potential reproducibility—I'm thorough about prevention. If an incident happens, I take it into account for the future. That's what she's doing."

Apparently, that's what Ononoki was doing.

I didn't quite understand, but in any case, Miss Gaen already had her eye on what would take place after tonight. Maybe that was natural from her perspective, but I did wish she'd stop pretending to act tough by folding her arms in front of her as she spoke when she really just wanted to block my view of her chest.

I did also wish she'd stop treating what I was about to attempt as garbage time—or wait, was it the first pitch?

"You're right. Don't worry, I'll undo Yotsugi's stamp—though it might not be possible to restore your link without the other party in question around," Miss Gaen said a bit cynically.

Yes.

That was right.

When I said there were missing actors, I meant Shinobu as much as Ononoki—Shinobu Oshino ended up not leaving the shrine.

I called out to her and knocked on the entrance once it was time to go, but she still didn't come out—this time it really was like me needing to wake a sleeping god, but no ritual I attempted had any effect.

She'd decided not to see the first Aberration Slayer, after all—in that case, I just had to respect her decision. Right. My determination didn't have to line up with Shinobu's resolution.

In that case, I just had to win the duel at any cost, so that Shinobu wouldn't have to see the first Aberration Slayer—not that any bald attempt to redouble my convictions mattered. Even if what seemed to be the predetermined outcome played out and I lost, Miss Gaen and Episode weren't going to let him see Shinobu anyway.

Even so, there was meaning in me doing this.

Just as she'd declared, Kanbaru hadn't tried to pull Shinobu out from the shrine proper where she'd confined herself—but as my junior, she did take part in some of my slapdash rituals, possibly because she just found it amusing.

"Why don't we get going already?" she urged nonchalantly—even adding, "Don't worry. If anything happens, I'll protect you."

What a reliable junior I had.

Not that I could stand to give her any more work after all she'd done—another reason I needed to give this my all.

I couldn't look lame in front of a junior like her.

And so, with the four of us, myself included, gathered—the last to appear was the man at the center of this series of affairs.

The first Aberration Slayer.

Kissshot Acerolaorion Heartunderblade's first thrall—a vampire who'd returned over the course of four hundred years.

An expert from olden times.

Out of nowhere—he appeared clad in armor.

"…"

The armored warrior—showing almost no trace of the boy I'd met this morning appeared, clad in equipment utterly foreign to our modern age.

The suit of armor somehow felt even bigger than before, possibly because he'd showed himself to me as a child—no, in fact, it must have been bigger.

He said he will have made a full recovery—that he'd be fully restored.

He'd have used his energy drain to further power himself up before appearing at this field—and he'd lost whatever talkative nature he had as a boy.

He appeared on time and said nothing.

He stood there in his thick suit of armor.

He wasn't the only one to grow quiet, either. So had Kanbaru to some degree once he appeared—before then, despite the feeling in the air, she'd managed to chatter on.

She must have felt the noxious force of all those "bad things" the first Aberration Slayer brought along with him—just as she felt ill before at

Kita-Shirahebi Shrine and during our last visit to the abandoned cram school.

No. Even worse than those times.

As someone who shared a common vampiric origin with him, it didn't affect me, nor did it affect the two professionals, Miss Gaen and Episode—but the amount of careful preparation he'd put into this moment was as clear as night.

As Kanbaru's senior, I worried about her body and her mind, but it wasn't as if she'd leave now even if I told her to... Just as I wondered what to do—

"All right, then. Let's get this started nice and quick, then ended nice and quick," Miss Gaen said to break the ice.

Nothing about her tone suggested any real concern for her niece's condition—you didn't have to be me to recognize that her interest in ending this *nice and quick* had nothing to do with any consideration for her.

"Araragi, and First—this friendly lady who knows everything right here is gonna be in charge of your duel. I'll make sure it's a fair fight—and you're going to let me act as judge."

"Our promise," the First spoke.

Not with the voice he'd taken from me.

It had turned into one of his own.

An elegant voice, profound and even entrancing.

"Thou shalt uphold our promise—Lady Izuko. As a fellow expert, I trust ye would not break such a promise."

Sad words to hear spoken to someone as willing and ready to break promises as Miss Gaen—but he couldn't have been serious when he said them, either.

He too was a sly and tested expert.

Someone not to be trusted, who wouldn't think twice about handing someone—not poisoned, but consecrated tea.

"Oh, of course. I've never broken a promise in my life before, and I've never lied, either. Miss Izuko right here is all about integrity."

I could tell by the way she refused to use her last name that she was being thorough when it came to hiding her identity from Kanbaru.

Was she really that set on keeping her in the dark, though? Maybe the reveal of the fact that Kanbaru was her long-separated niece deserved a little more gravity, but seeing her go this far started to make me suspicious…

It even felt like it wasn't about her relationship with Kanbaru so much as with Kanbaru's mother, which is to say, Miss Gaen's older sister.

Not that I needed to be thinking about that right now.

"Sir Araragi," the first Aberration Slayer then said to me. "It seems Kissshot is not here—am I right to think that I will meet her once I defeat thee in this duel?"

"Do whatever you want," I replied. The two of us were close enough that, looking at him with sober eyes, I was overwhelmed by his intense presence—still, I didn't drop my affectation. "I don't intend on surviving a loss to you, so go ahead, meet her as much as you feel like."

That is, I stopped myself from saying, *if you can*. Miss Gaen wouldn't have wanted me to say that, not to mention the first Aberration Slayer.

If you can.

Facing him now, I couldn't see him meeting Shinobu just to give her an honest apology—Kanbaru seemed mistaken when it came to that.

It wasn't love.

It wasn't gratitude.

It wasn't loyalty.

Yet it wasn't pure hate, resentment, or rebellion, either—as much as I hated to admit it, his feelings towards Shinobu were probably very close to mine.

To the point that they might be the same.

As my relationship to her—of love and hate.

I loved her, and I hated her.

So, in fact, the first Aberration Slayer wouldn't know himself until it came down to it—he probably wouldn't know until the moment he saw Shinobu.

How would he act then?

Would he love her, or would he kill her?

Was he being honest—or deceitful?

Wouldn't the answer to that question be decided in the moment?

...Not that the moment would ever come.

Even so, it was wrong to sympathize or empathize with him—perhaps I was complicit in the deception, but I only needed to win this duel to turn it into honesty and sincerity.

It was wrong.

To feel sorry for him.

You have to respect a being who spent four hundred years coming back to life, no matter who he is—Mèmè Oshino would surely say.

"You don't intend on surviving? Gotta love it. Don't say such alarming things, thrall of Heartunderblade...which is I guess both of you," Episode stumbled over his words—he must not have remembered my actual name. Miss Gaen now called me Araragi (not "Koyomin"), but he probably didn't remember names unless he had a specific interest in doing so... Not that I was any better, since I only knew him as Episode.

And what about the first Aberration Slayer's name?

This would probably end without me ever learning it.

"He's right, Araragi," Miss Gaen continued where Episode left off. "That is alarming. You shouldn't say that—haven't you been listening to us? What's about to take place is like a ceremony of sorts. You could call it a duel dedicated to a god—not something either of you will be dying from."

Come over here, she beckoned me with her hand.

I suppose enough time had passed since the accident in the open lot that she was finally allowing me to approach her. Miss Gaen touched my face.

"Okay. Now you're set," she said.

It didn't feel like anything had happened, but she must have *undone* Ononoki's footprint from the left half of my face.

The protection had been removed.

Now no footprint was there to defend me.

"The preparations are complete. And now you're ready to fight too, Araragi. Aren't you?"

"The preparations, complete? With that? Hold on one moment—

what of thy link, Sir Araragi?"

The first Aberration Slayer was the one to voice his doubts.

"Surely ye have no intention of dueling me—in such a weak state?"

"..."

"My word, it seems thy bond with Kissshot was nowhere as strong as I'd feared—I find it hard to believe she would dare send her servant to battle while so powerless."

I couldn't see because of his face guard, but he must have been sneering, not that I could blame him for thinking that.

Had I wanted to cover all my bases for this duel, I'd have restored my link to Shinobu, then had her drink my blood, strengthening my body to its limit before arriving here.

There lay the difference between this moment and my battle against Miss Kagenui—which actually made all the difference, but in any case, I'd be facing off against an aberration in an almost entirely human state.

This might have been my first time heading into battle at this much of a power disadvantage.

But there's a first time for everything.

Yes, Shinobu had holed up and refused to leave, but that wasn't the only reason our link hadn't been restored—this was, in its own way, something I wanted.

I didn't want to win using Shinobu's strength.

I wanted to win and become her strength.

Of course, it wasn't as if I'd shown up with neither prospects nor plans—even if my opponent claimed to have made a full recovery, he had to be far from fully restored.

And—even if I was wrong.

No matter what happened—win or lose, love or hate, I knew my opponent's intentions would never come to fruition. It was the least I could risk in a duel against such an adversary.

People should never get into fights they think they can't lose.

Of course, I wasn't sure if that held for vampires...

"Very well, then—however, Lady Izuko, in this case I would ask thee to compose a form for this duel that would properly handicap us.

And I'll have no objectionable excuses coming from thee."

"Of course not. My plan was to go with a universal dueling format that's existed throughout the ages—one that would allow you two to compete on pretty fair terms," Miss Gaen proposed as she walked toward the stand used for morning announcements—from which she took a cylindrical object that she must have placed there beforehand.

A bamboo sword. The kind the kendo club used.

"I guess you could call it an imaginary version of the enchanted blade Kokorowatari—though there is of course some spiritual energy flowing through it. Yeah, just think of it as a stun gun that you can use on each other," Miss Gaen said—plunging it into the ground.

As bamboo swords are built with round tips, she shouldn't have been able to do this, but she pierced the ground like it was a peg using only one hand.

I was surprised by the strength in her slender arms, but then realized it was thanks to the sword's spiritual energy.

"We're going to have you two stand on both sides of this bamboo sword, backs turned to each other. From there, you'll take ten steps forward on my count—and the battle will begin after the tenth. Run towards this bamboo blade, and whoever scores the first sword strike on his opponent wins. I guess you could call it a setup out of a Japanese-style Western," Miss Gaen explained, letting go of the sword. "Or maybe an unusual variation on beach flags. Of course, you shouldn't just give up if your opponent is the first to grab the hilt—you can still take the sword from him and score a strike. The match will only be judged by who can score the first sword strike—fair enough? First will have longer to travel because ten of his wide strides will take him farther than ten from someone as short, and short-legged, as Araragi. Not to mention that armor."

"Indeed, this armor is not light," the first Aberration Slayer responded.

Still, he was a vampire—even if you took the weight of his equipment into consideration, he'd have to be nimble... And also, it felt like Miss Gaen was kind of insulting me there with that comment about my short stature and legs...

Did I do something to make her dislike me?

"Allow me to confirm—a glancing blow from this bamboo blade will not count as a strike, will it? May I assume that this battle will be decided only by effective, decisive strikes?"

"Of course. I'm going by the standards of modern kendo when it comes to that—though the rules themselves are anything goes. A strike to the legs is still a strike."

"So you mean to say," the armored warrior continued with a shrug, "what ye've in fact set forth—are not rules to ensure a fair fight, but rather considerations so that Sir Araragi doth not perish in our duel. Quite astute."

"Well, I don't want my big brother Mèmè getting mad at me. He's scary when he's mad," Miss Gaen said, not explicitly denying the observation. "Any other questions?" she rushed to change the topic.

"No—what objections could I make to such a simple agreement? I do suppose 'tis preferable to a jumble of rules. Though I must say—in my hands, a glancing blow from any sword, even one made of bamboo, could bring Sir Araragi close to death. Would that then be considered an effective strike?"

"Sure, we can say that," Miss Gaen nodded without a moment's hesitation. "I guess that would be the more convenient arrangement for you—is that fine with you, Araragi?"

"Well, not really," I replied as she turned her attention to me, "but I have to say I am."

"Excellent—any questions from you, Araragi?"

"None about the rules… I'm an amateur when it comes to swords and fighting, though. Do you think I could get some expert instruction on at least this ten-pace run you're talking about?"

"Expert instruction?"

From me? On swords?

Miss Gaen tilted her head in confusion, but I wasn't referring here to any experts on the supernatural.

I wanted an expert when it came to full-tilt sprints.

An athlete who specialized in straight-line movement.

Japan's best short-distance runner—Suruga Kanbaru.

In other words, my junior, who was off to the side feeling sick.

"Okay. I think it'd be fair to add a handicap on that level. It's half past seven right now, so...the duel can begin at eight on the dot. Go and get warmed up, the both of you."

031

"Estimating based on your height, I'd say that your stride length is about seventy-two centimeters. In other words, ten steps would be seven meters and twenty centimeters. Just as you'd use one set of strategies to run a marathon and another to run a hundred-meter dash, you can use yet another set of strategies to run a seven-meter sprint—but in this case, the real issue might be how to ensure you have enough stamina left over."

Kanbaru explained this (using the metric system) as she touched and squished my legs—it felt more like a massage than some sort of warmup, but she was the expert here.

"What do you mean, the real issue?"

"It's not all over once you finish the race—you still have to grab the bamboo sword and get a strike in, don't you?"

"Oh. Right."

Even if I won our footrace and was the first to grab the hilt, that wouldn't matter if I then collapsed in exhaustion—similarly, if I focused only on speed and carried too much momentum, there was the strong possibility that I'd overshoot the sword sticking out of the ground. Then what would I do? It'd be like putting the cart before the horse, or rather, I'd just be making an ass of myself.

"So I'll have to accelerate and decelerate correctly in the space of just seven meters... Maybe I should practice?"

"No, I don't think you should."

"Because we'd be revealing our hand to the opponent?"

I glanced over at the first Aberration Slayer—he wasn't doing much of anything in particular. He just sat there on the stand for morning announcements where the bamboo sword had been until moments earlier, his arms crossed like a warrior preparing for battle. If you stood a flag and flew a banner behind him, it'd be a scene straight out of the Warring States period.

"It doesn't look to me like he's paying much attention to us," I said.

"It's not about our hand or anything. You wouldn't be able to do an all-out sprint when the time came if you also did some for practice."

"Oh, right."

"I know I just said your stride was seventy-two centimeters, but that's when you're walking. It'd probably go up to eighty running—which means you'd arrive at the seventy-two-centimeter mark in exactly nine steps. If you count your steps as you run, that should serve as a rough guide—though it'd only be a rough one."

"Okay. So I need to count."

"1, 1, 2, 3, 5, 8, 13."

"Why the Fibonacci Sequence again?"

"6, 0, 8, 6, 5, 5, 5, 6, 7, 0, 2, 3, 8, 3, 7, 8, 9, 8, 9, 6, 7, 0, 3, 7, 1, 7, 3, 4, 2, 4, 3, 1, 6, 9, 6, 2, 2, 6, 5, 7, 8, 3, 0, 7, 7, 3, 3, 5, 1, 8, 8, 9, 7, 0, 5, 2, 8, 3, 2, 4, 8, 6, 0, 5, 1, 2, 7, 9, 1, 6, 9, 1, 2, 6, 4."

"Why a sublime number?"

"How did you know that?"

"If anything, how did you say that?"

"I guessed about half of them. Did I get it right?"

"Yeah. Amazing."

Talk about luck.

Too much luck, in fact.

Forget any numbers, she was the sublime one here.

In any case, nine steps. I couldn't remember where I'd heard it, but nine steps was, coincidentally enough, the amount of space kendo practitioners opened between one another.

"So one rough standard could be to accelerate during the first three, go at full speed during the middle three, and slow down during the final three."

"Okay... By the way, he's not going to be 7.2 meters away, right? It's hard to tell because of the armor, but how far away do you think someone his size will be?"

Kanbaru must have estimated my stride based on my height—and while the first Aberration Slayer looked shorter than me when I saw him as a boy this morning, that of course was irrelevant now.

You'd think that the average height four centuries ago was lower, but he seemed pretty big to me given the size of his armor. That boy couldn't possibly be inside that armor as-is—though from the looks of it, the suit was easily seven feet tall...

Maybe about the size of Dramaturgy?

Now that I thought about it, I fought that vampire hunter on this field too...

"Umm." Kanbaru faced the stand and eyeballed him. "It's kinda hard to guess since he's sitting, but...I'd say about a one-meter stride, 1.1 meters running?"

"A one-meter stride—so ten meters in ten steps?"

Giving me a three-meter advantage. It sounded like a negligible distance but was pretty significant in an ultra-short sprint—not to mention my opponent's full suit of armor.

"Of course, that's not set in stone. He could waddle along with tiny little steps."

"Little steps... I think he has a little more dignity than that."

Then again, there was no real reason to go out of our way and take extra-long strides...

I guess our pride guaranteed our good behavior here.

"Oh, and another thing. Be careful not to twist your feet around when you turn after the ten steps. The trick is to turn around with your non-dominant foot as the axis, not your torso. Like this," Kanbaru said, demonstrating with a twirl.

This was a basketball move, not anything to do with running, but seeing it up close was indeed helpful—of course, the armored warrior by the stand got to see this move as well, but you couldn't pull off anything so light-footed while wearing heavy armor.

"Okay. That's about all I can teach you on the spot, but I think what's really important here is the swordplay after you grab that blade. Even if you get it, all your hard work will be for nothing if he dodges your attack and takes it from you, then uses it to smack you."

"You're right—but as far as that goes, what will be, will be. I'd be asking for too much from you otherwise."

"Oh? I'd even switch in for you if I could."

"You really are loyal, you know that?"

True, our chances of victory seemed like they'd be far higher if I let Kanbaru fight this duel for me—but of course I couldn't do that. I was happy to hear her say it, but...

I wanted a switch to flip inside of me.

"In that case, why don't I lend you my shoes? We wear the same size, right?"

"Oh, thanks..."

"It's normally risky to wear shoes you're not used to, but these have got to be better than those weird things you're wearing right now."

"Don't call them weird."

"Those shoes of yours that have to be tied in a unique way."

"I'm the only one to blame for how my shoes are tied."

"Here," she said, already handing me her shoes—well, whether or not my shoes were strange, hers did seem a lot easier to run in. I decided to take her up on her kind offer.

I was wearing Kanbaru's track jacket, and I was wearing her shoes. I must have seemed like a real Kanbaru freak right about now. Maybe I needed to ask Karen how to join the fan club.

"Ack, they're all warm on the inside..."

"I kept them warm for you."

"Who are you, Hideyoshi Toyotomi?"

"Ooh, Araragi-senpai's weird shoes..."

"Stop highlighting the fact they're weird." Especially if she was also highlighting that they were mine.

"My fatigue just melts away when I wear these. I feel so elevated that I might just level up."

"I'm pretty sure that my shoes aren't a Dragon Quest item... And hold on, do you actually wear a bigger shoe size than me?"

With this, I'd received my running instruction as well as a pair of shoes, and I'd had a good bit of fun on top. The time was now 7:55 p.m.—just five minutes until the duel.

It was at this moment that my cell phone rang—not because of an incoming call, but because a message had arrived.

"Really? What awful manners. You need to turn your phone off during a duel, you know," Episode grumbled from afar—I'd never heard anything about dueling manners, but I couldn't say anything back to him, either.

I was almost glad my phone rang now, because I'd have lost the duel for sure if it had gone off as I ran my ten paces. I went to check what it said before switching off the power, assuming either Karen or Tsukihi was warning me about the punishment awaiting me once I got back home.

Of all the people, it had been sent by Tsubasa Hanekawa.

032

"Huh... What is this?"

A message from Tsubasa Hanekawa.

Yet the body and subject were blank, with only a lone photograph attached. The e-mail seemed odd enough already—but the bizarre photo that appeared to be a selfie was truly beyond description.

That Tsubasa Hanekawa.

Had taken a selfie in my room, wearing my clothes.

That's what this one-of-a-kind photo showed (well, I guess it wasn't one of a kind since it was on both our phones as data).

"Wh-What's been going on at school while I've been away?"

My desire to see class president among class presidents Miss Hanekawa in street clothes had come true in an incomprehensible way, but I couldn't just sit there and enjoy the moment.

The clothes were mine in the first place, an outfit I was familiar with... While part of me felt like accepting the situation as it presented itself, the whole thing gave off such a strange vibe.

I was wearing Kanbaru's jacket and shoes and standing next to her as she wore my hoodie and weird shoes, and looking at a photo of Hanekawa wearing a full outfit belonging to me in my room? What a mess of a situation.

"What happened to Hanekawa... Kanbaru, do you know anything?"

"No, I don't have a clue… The only thing I could think of is that after her house burned down, she got introduced to Karen and Tsukihi through Senjogahara-senpai and asked them if she could stay at your home."

"That's probably it! …Wait, a fire? Her house burned down?! When did that happen?!"

"Oh, right. I guess you didn't know. In a nutshell, her home burned down on the first day of second term."

In a nutshell, indeed.

No way… I thought I'd been on a rough adventure since the last day of summer break, but it seemed like Hanekawa was having a tougher time…

Still, Kanbaru amazed me. She knew just how fanatical I was about Hanekawa, and yet she managed not to tell me for just about the whole day? Is this what Senjogahara meant when she described her as frightening? Oh, but Kanbaru and Hanekawa didn't have much of a relationship… Now that I thought about it, hadn't Kanbaru muttered something about Hanekawa while we were surrounded by flames at the abandoned cram school?

Hm? Could that fire have been—

"What's this? Looks like she's getting to the good stuff herself— what'll you do, Koyomin?"

Leaping in as if to sneak a peek at my cell phone, Miss Gaen called me Koyomin for the first time since that morning.

"Wait… The good stuff? Miss Ga—" Nope. "Miss Izuko, is there something you know? About Hanekawa—wait, do you know Hanekawa? And what do you mean, what'll I do?"

"I know everything—I'm trying to say it's a tiger, Koyomin. Ironically, it was also a tiger that saved you at the abandoned cram school. It seems that Tsubasa has made up her mind and decided to face that great tiger who wields its purgatorial flames. Heh, no wonder Mèmè was scared of her. I never expected her to make such a move. Still…it is convenient."

"Convenient… How?"

A tiger?

Wait, no—Shinobu had done all that talking about cats, too—what exactly was happening on Hanekawa's side right now? People said they knew, and even explained it to me, but I wasn't getting any kind of clear picture at all.

The only thing I knew—something pretty strange was taking place over there if Hanekawa had sent me a picture like this.

A distress signal—no, more like a cry for help.

"That's right, your precious Tsubasa is in trouble. So, what will you do, Koyomin?"

"What will I do? Again, like what?"

"If you'll allow your lady friend here who knows everything to give you a quick rundown, it's not actually just Tsubasa who's in trouble— your girlfriend, Senjogahara, is as well."

"What?"

It was Kanbaru who reacted first. You couldn't blame her, when Hitagi Senjogahara stood at the top of this ever-faithful junior's internal hierarchy, but it's not as if I wasn't surprised too. I mean, what about our phone call just now? It's not like she'd…shown any signs…or maybe she had, and…

…I hadn't noticed.

How could I be so negligent?

"Those girls just might be going up in flames as we speak—if you want to go rescue them, you should go as soon as humanly possible. Forget about this meaningless duel," Miss Gaen said, as if to lay it on me emotionally.

" …"

"That's what I mean when I say convenient. It makes things easier for me if you don't take part in this duel. Because it'd be an issue if you died—just as the First said, we've tried to set things up in a way that should keep you from dying, but it's not as if we can avoid it no matter what. I can't break the rules, which means I'd really appreciate it if you did instead. And this is good for you too, Koyomin. Now you have a perfect reason for calling the duel off."

Miss Gaen shut me down and silenced me completely.

I knew I was getting in a fight that no one wanted me in, but this made me keenly aware of just how little my involvement was desired—it made me realize there was no self-improvement involved in what I was doing, only self-satisfaction.

"It's time to choose, Koyomin," Miss Gaen said—in a nasty tone. "Stay here to fight in an idle duel, or run off to save Tsubasa and Senjogahara. Will you choose Shinobu, or will you choose Tsubasa, or will you choose Senjogahara?"

Choose.

Compare and choose.

A multiple-choice relationship problem.

Compare that which is important to me—and define which is more important.

Score them and differentiate them.

"Out of those three—whom do you love the most?" Miss Gaen seemed to joke. "Would a time limit of five minutes not be enough? Really, I think you could come up with an answer in five seconds. Shinobu hasn't even come here, while Tsubasa is your savior and Senjogahara is your girlfriend—oh?"

Still wordless, I handed the phone to Kanbaru—Miss Gaen was right. It took longer than an instant to come up with the answer, but five seconds was enough.

Just because an answer is simple to come up with, though, that doesn't mean it's an easy one.

Ah, so this is what it means to choose.

In that case, the right to decide—the final say—isn't really desirable.

But I had to choose.

And I had to decide.

"Kanbaru. Please handle this."

"I've got it," she answered at once.

I knew that *this answer* wasn't the one that Kanbaru, who treated Senjogahara like an older sister, wanted to hear—still, she nodded immediately.

Don't mistake who you're trying to save here, Kanbaru had said to me once—but she'd know better than anyone that there was no such thing as a right answer to such a question.

Not being able to make a mistake isn't necessarily right.

"I just need to go to your home?"

"Yeah. You're free to use that phone, so tell Karen to let you in— I doubt Hanekawa is still there, but there might be something left in my room. I'll be right behind you, so I want you to look into it until then."

Roger that.

Kanbaru was already off running by the time she signed off. It was hard to believe she had on my weird shoes as she sprinted away from Naoetsu High's athletic field at a speed faster than the eye could see, drilling into the earth with each step.

"Are you in your right mind?" asked Miss Gaen, appalled. Or maybe more like she couldn't begin to understand my decision. "That's unthinkable—do you really only consider whatever is in front of your eyes? How do you think Tsubasa and Senjogahara would feel if they learned about your decision here? Isn't chasing after that girl still the right thing to do?"

"..."

"True, Suruga Kanbaru is far more mobile than you, and she might be able to handle both situations with her running speed—and Tsubasa might be able to face her troubles on her own. You're the only one who can fight here, so it might be right for you to stay behind, but that's all logic—it's might this and might that. People have emotions. Don't you think she sent you that message believing in you? And you're going to betray her trust like this?"

Miss Gaen continued in her detached tone, but it also felt like the convenience she'd get out of me not taking the duel wasn't her only reason for saying all this.

The thought helped calm my mind to some small degree.

So she had a regular side to her, too—though maybe I didn't.

"After betraying them like this, those two might never trust you again," Miss Gaen said as if to hammer the point home.

"Maybe," I replied. Coolly, and without shame. "But I believe in them. From the bottom of my heart. In Hanekawa, and in Senjogahara."

I believed they'd understand.

Those two, who treated someone as un-special as me in such a special way—would never betray my trust.

Not those two special people in my life.

Not Tsubasa Hanekawa, not Hitagi Senjogahara.

"I believe they'll understand—that over any savior or any lover, the man known as Koyomi Araragi—is going to put a little girl first."

033

Perhaps the expression *little girl* was a bit too overpowering for the un-initiated, but whatever the case, Miss Gaen didn't say another word as she stepped away from me—no, to be exact, she did mutter something to herself, so low that I could barely make it out.

"It'd be nice if I could ever trust anyone enough to just hand them my phone."

Then, after one more actor went missing from the stage that was the Naoetsu High athletic field, eight o'clock came at last. Time came for the duel to begin—and a change occurred.

Something came raining down from the cloudy night sky—or maybe it would be better to say it came slashing down.

It was a blade—a great katana.

A Japanese sword is made to slash, not rain down—yet it clearly fell like a single bolt of lightning from high in the sky to the center of the field.

Its tip squarely hit the bamboo sword Miss Gaen had thrust into the ground earlier. She said spiritual energy or something had been used to strengthen it, to the point that you could stick it into the ground, yet it tore like a piece of vinyl tape, splitting exactly in two.

Of course it did.

What good was spiritual energy in the face of a great katana? Miss

Gaen's so-called imaginary version of the enchanted blade Kokorowatari was no match.

How could the imaginary ever rival the real thing?

What had come flying from the sky was the aberration-exterminating blade known before any other as the Aberration Slayer—the enchanted blade Kokorowatari.

It was as if the bamboo sword never existed in the first place.

Its presence was such that it seemed to always have been there, sticking out of the ground—and with that, the weapon signifying the start of our duel changed from a bamboo sword to an actual blade.

My head shot up to look at the sky at the same time as the armored warrior's—but there was nothing to be found there. Not the moon, not even a flying bat.

Even so, we knew. Who now owned this sword—and therefore who threw it between me and him.

A vampire known as the Aberration Slayer.

Whom I called Shinobu Oshino—and he, Kissshot.

Once an iron-blooded, hot-blooded, yet cold-blooded vampire—and now the dregs of one.

"Hah. Gotta love it," Episode said with an insincere laugh. Maybe he could see wherever she was. "So, the master has decided to provide the tool for this conflict between her slaves—or maybe the prize? Like she's saying she'd give the winner that enchanted blade."

"Maybe. Whatever the case, that bamboo sword I went to all the trouble of preparing just got split in half, so we're just going to have to use the real thing. Koyomin, First. We're running a little late, but why don't you get started—put your backs to one another around that sword, just as originally planned," Miss Gaen said, ordering us around as if nothing too unexpected had taken place—was she trying to say she'd accounted for even Shinobu's actions here?

In that case, I'd just have to play into her hands.

Yes, right.

I'd been thinking how dull this would be with a bamboo sword—not to mention, it changed nothing about what we needed to do.

I would run, grab the hilt, and score a strike.

It's all either of us had.

It's all there was, and yet it felt like our duel would now be fought under a completely different set of rules—and this seemed to go for the first Aberration Slayer as well, but not in the same way.

Because of his powerful sense of the enchanted blade Kokorowatari being his personal property, made of his own flesh and blood from the start, perhaps it didn't move him to see it presented as a tool or offered as a reward.

No.

I couldn't see his expression behind his face guard, but he seemed clearly displeased by this turn of events. In fact, as he faced me on the other side of the sword, he voiced his disappointment.

"She's come so close, so why doth my master—why doth our master, Kissshot, so stubbornly refuse to show herself?"

"..."

"Is she that loath to meet me, Sir Araragi? What say ye? Are my efforts meaningless? Is this turmoil between us nothing more than a nuisance to Kissshot?"

And ye—he asked.

"What about ye, Sir Araragi? What meaning do ye find in this duel?"

"You wouldn't understand what this means to me. I don't know if anyone would," I replied.

Maybe I shouldn't have been exchanging words with him like this right before our fight, from opposite sides of the blade—but I had to say something when I considered that this would be our last conversation regardless of what happened.

"You might be some kind of special, chosen person—I'm not special, and I might not even be chosen. It could be that no one can replace you, while anyone could replace me. But you see." I turned my back—to the first Aberration Slayer, standing there on the opposite side of the blade. "You can't become me. There might be an infinite amount of replacements for me, but only I am me."

"..."

"You're not me, and I'm not you. That's how it is, right?"

Though I phrased it as a question, I received no reply—I could only hear the sound of armor rattling.

He must have turned his back to me.

Yes, it was the position he needed to take to begin the duel, but it also seemed to symbolize how irreconcilable the two of us were.

Even if he was the first and I was the second.

Even if we were both servants and both slaves.

We weren't the same—and we wouldn't understand each other.

"One..."

Miss Gaen began the count once she saw us turn our backs—and I took a step forward. Behind me, I could sense the first Aberration Slayer moving as well.

"Two-o-o. Three-e-e."

The vague lack of energy in her voice must have been intentional—Miss Gaen was doing everything she could to scrub any deeper meaning from this duel. Just as Oshino had turned all my battles into games during spring break.

"Fo-o-our."

But not everything goes to plan, even if you are someone like Miss Gaen who knows everything—one person can't control other people that conveniently, to say nothing of aberrations. No matter how much of a farce she made this duel out to be, nothing guaranteed that its outcome would be a laughing matter.

"Fi-i-ive. Si-i-ix."

Even then—did the first Aberration Slayer really not know? Why Shinobu would come close enough to toss the sword at us but not make an appearance? No, even I didn't know why until now.

I'd assumed she'd holed herself up simply because she didn't want to meet the first Aberration Slayer, or because she didn't want to take on any more trouble—but maybe it wasn't that Shinobu didn't want to meet the First. Maybe she couldn't, I realized.

"Se-e-even."

Yes, that's where we differed.

Shinobu already hung on the edge of death when we met during spring break—and even after that, I'd only seen the true and full Kiss-shot Acerolaorion Heartunderblade in passing.

But four hundred years ago, when she interacted with the first Aberration Slayer...

She was in her prime.

At her most beautiful, her most splendid, her most radiant, her most sublime, her most powerful—that was the woman she was then.

Which is why—she couldn't stand it.

Showing her depleted, weakened, childish self to the first Aberration Slayer, both partner and fated rival to her in the past, would be—to come out and say it, embarrassing.

She felt embarrassed to be seen in her changed state.

She didn't want to be seen as the dregs of her former self.

As a part and cause of the aberrational phenomena occurring in this town, the First had to know about Shinobu turning into a child, but being seen by him was a different matter altogether.

I felt pathetic to have met this duel so unashamedly, not understanding feelings as obvious as these—but I also wasn't so magnanimous that I'd go out of my way to tell the First.

Even if I did, he probably wouldn't understand how she felt—to him, Shinobu, or rather, Kissshot Acerolaorion Heartunderblade, was *special*.

She was perfect.

A different person from the Shinobu I knew now.

I also felt like I understood why I always had such a hard time communicating with him—it was as if we'd been conversing across a mystery novel's narrative trick. We'd been talking about two entirely different people but acting as though they were one and the same.

Four hundred years.

It was so obvious that I actually didn't understand it at all—this once again taught me just how long that was.

"Ei-i-ight."

But who out there could laugh and call him old-fashioned or off the mark? The fact that Shinobu was now bound this way was unusual from the start—in her more than five hundred years, looking that way and being that weak was exceptional for her.

I knew what the First would think.

He'd want to return her to the way she was.

Not as her thrall—but as an expert.

To the way she was when they exterminated aberrations together.

What exactly would make Shinobu happy?

I'd bound her in unhappiness over spring break—and she'd put up with that unhappiness, but once reminded of her past, of four hundred years ago, could she still feel the same way?

"Ni-i-ine."

Kanbaru had told her.

If she met the first Aberration Slayer and found her mind siding with him—then she needed to leave me and spend her days by his side.

Kanbaru really was amazing for being able to say that.

She wasn't just able to say it, either. She could probably do it.

To make sure that didn't happen—I'd need to continue being someone special to Shinobu. That seemed to be my answer to this duel's meaning.

I wanted to keep being that special someone for Shinobu Oshino.

The girl who chose to live alongside me.

"Ten!"

I turned as I heard the word—spinning my body around my right foot as Kanbaru had taught me, so that I could sprint those seven meters.

I took my first step.

I accelerated toward the sword rising out of the field into which it had been plunged—and as I did, I saw a jarring and utterly unexpected scene.

The handicap for this duel consisted of two parts.

First, as ten of my steps created a distance different from ten of the first Aberration Slayer's, I would need to travel seven meters to reach the enchanted blade Kokorowatari, while he needed to go ten. I would have a three-meter advantage, and he would be three meters behind—a numerical gap that could not be closed.

But there was another part—the fact that this warrior in his armor should be at a disadvantage in a footrace. I hadn't realized just how easy it was for him to compensate for this point. I'd forgotten that my opponent was an expert who didn't care about appearances when it came to exterminating aberrations.

And so.

As he, the first Aberration Slayer, walked ten steps according to Miss Gaen's count with his back turned to me—*he'd been taking off the massive armor wrapped around his entire body.*

A tall, fit, and stunning young man with long, tied-back hair emerged from inside what had been empty in the abandoned cram school—and he dashed toward the enchanted blade Kokorowatari in order to cut me down.

That boy Aberration Slayer.

This is how he matured.

He even looked cool as he ran! Dammit!

What a figure he'd cut standing next to a legendary vampire—he wore Western clothing inappropriate for anyone in a Japanese suit of armor. The design of his clothes resembled that of a swallowtail coat, not something very suited to running, but it must have felt like athletic wear compared to being clad in armor.

He of course didn't step on any of the armor he scattered along the field during his ten steps, and he was already preparing to reach for the great katana.

I was now in a full sprint, keeping with the instruction I received from my sharp-eyed tutor, but god, this wasn't even going to be close! And I'd been conveniently ignoring the fact that a wider walking stride also meant a wider running stride. People with long legs are fast, I'm telling you!

Since he was running without the leg irons that was his armor, it was impossible for me to win this race in my current condition.

Naturally, his right hand grabbed the enchanted blade first.

I'd yet to run even half of my seven meters—was I just a slow runner or what?

The young Aberration Slayer, formerly the boy Aberration Slayer, grabbed the hilt of the enchanted blade but did not stop there—he continued sprinting forward at the exact same speed. This of course wasn't him over-shooting his mark. His intentions seemed to be to use his momentum to cut me down.

The fact that he didn't make use of the difference in strength between us to torture or bully me commended him as a genuine warrior—though from my perspective, it also meant he wouldn't be providing me with any openings.

The enchanted blade Kokorowatari.

The Aberration Slayer's sword—a sword that slew only aberrations.

I'd lost most of my vampiric abilities now that my link to Shinobu had been severed—though I only had the strength of an average human, that didn't mean I had lost all of my nature as a vampire.

The enchanted blade's sharp edge would cut well—the bamboo sword provided by Miss Gaen was one thing, but this sword created for the purpose of exterminating aberrations would have an immediate effect were it to so much as graze me.

At this point, I had in essence lost.

I guess you could say things were only progressing as they always do—but if there was ever a time when I couldn't lose, couldn't be cut down, and couldn't stop moving forward, it was now.

I took another step in Kanbaru's shoes.

The moment I did, one of them came off. Maybe they were the wrong size after all, but that didn't matter. I continued stepping forward, with the other foot.

Ahead—toward the armored warrior holding the great katana.

Well, no, he wasn't an armored warrior now that he'd tossed that armor off—this young man who held his sword ready even as he charged toward me was a berserker. What did that make me, empty-handed and hopeless? Cannon fodder?

The distance between us suddenly shrank.

For every one of my steps, the First took three—we were now in melee range. He held the sword high over his head, and—

"Ha!"

He laughed.

"Ha!"Haha!"Hahaha!"Hahahaha!"Hahahahaha!"Hahahahahaha—!"

Maybe something was *funny*.

Or maybe something was sad—as his laughter bellowed out.

He swung the sword, held high, down toward the tip of my shoulder—sparing no ounce of his physical strength as a vampire thrall.

Forget me.

He handled the sword as if he wanted to split the field itself in two—in fact, it'd be no surprise if he did.

It'd be a surprise if he didn't, in fact.

If there was a reason he didn't.

It's that he was a vampire.

And I a mockery of a vampire.

It was the difference between the first Aberration Slayer, who'd been a vampire ever since the day his blood was sucked four hundred years ago, and me, who'd been a vampire for no more than two weeks during spring break. The differences in our careers brought about a difference in results.

The inarguable pinnacle of immortality—which meant surviving being torn to pieces or turned to ashes, and continuing on and on and further on...

Something that Shinobu herself, the presence at both of our roots, once pointed out...

Vampires' defensive abilities aren't particularly high—because their immortality acts as a defense itself.

In other words, while I didn't know how he may have been back when he was a pure human, a pure warrior, a pure expert—right now.

He walked the night as a vampire.

He fought at night, and paid no attention whatsoever to *defense.*

He neglected himself.

Even at the abandoned cram school, he made no attempt to dodge Kanbaru's punches or tackles—and he was no different without his armor.

He held nothing back as he swung the lengthy great katana as if to split the field in half. Even though there was no need for that. He only needed to nick me with his enchanted blade to end the battle.

And I—found his torso, left wide open by his swing, and *slapped* it on.

I still carried all the momentum from my full sprint, which meant it looked like I countered his attack with a palm strike as I ran past—but in any case, the talisman I'd peeled from Kita-Shirahebi Shrine took to him.

It took ahold of him.

"Hah—ah, ha, ha, hahahaaaaaaaaaaaaaaaaaaaaaaAAAAAAAAAAAAAAA?!"

His roaring laughter turned to a shriek.

The sword he held aloft—promptly dropped to the ground.

Of course it did, the slip of wonder-working paper was mighty enough to write off my five-million-yen debt—and if you were to go all the way back, we'd used it to prevent the first Aberration Slayer's return to begin with.

I'd placed that *directly* on his body.

How could it not be effective? Especially now—when the armor protecting the First had been cast aside.

"That's Mèmè's... Oh, so that's what's going on."

Miss Gaen's voice.

An expert, she understood instantly.

"What a surprise—this, I'd really call unexpected. You took the duel I set up and turned it into a slap fight!"

No.

That's not what I did. Please stop.

Don't amuse yourself while I'm over here putting my life on the line.

Still, it was only natural for me to notice the talisman at Kita-Shirahebi Shrine as I awaited tonight's duel—as Kanbaru and I amused ourselves with ritualistic dances, trying to get Shinobu to come out. The two of us had come to that very shrine to place it there, after all.

Still—there was one thing.

In a *different timeline*—in a different history traveled by me and Shinobu, the talisman placed on the shrine was something else.

It affected the world in the same way, but its effects were different.

That talisman was a little too powerful, and neither Shinobu nor I, with our aberrational nature, could so much as touch it—which would have meant that Kanbaru's right hand placed it there.

I understood that to mean that in that timeline, Koyomi Araragi never built the same kind of relationship with Shinobu Oshino that I had with her in this one.

If that was the meaning of *that* history.

And if this history had a meaning too—it meant the talisman could be *reused*. It could be removed, then placed in another location.

Of course, no matter how much Mèmè Oshino acted like he saw it all coming, there's no way he could have imagined something like this duel—not to mention, it was Kanbaru who brought up the actual idea: *Couldn't you peel this thing off and take it with you to use somehow?*

It probably didn't count at all under Miss Gaen's rules, and I of course couldn't let this end after a mere touch from my palm.

So.

I reached for the katana he dropped—and picked it up.

The fearsome Aberration Slayer's enchanted blade, Kokorowatari— this duel wouldn't end until I delivered a strike with it.

"Guh, ah, ah, ahh... Ki—"

As he began to break apart.

As he crumbled, he screamed.

"—sshot, Kissshot, Kissshot, Kissshot, Kissshot, Kissshot—Ki-ki-ki-ki—"

He screamed—he screamed the name.

Of the one who met him four hundred years ago.

Who fought against him. Who fought with him.

The name of the monster—who turned him into a monster.

There was nothing I could say to the first Aberration Slayer and his rising voice. In fact, I couldn't so much as look at him.

But this dispelled my doubts. Any I might have had. My suspicion that reconciliation was nothing more than an excuse, and that he wanted to bring harm to Shinobu...

Now that I heard this voice, I finally believed it—what he wanted was to see her.

That didn't change anything, of course. He only continued to crumble.

Which isn't to say that he simply fell over—his form itself began to crumble—it broke apart.

Unable to maintain a human shape, unable to maintain his human form.

They began to pour out.

The tall, fit young man that was the first Aberration Slayer broke apart into *pieces* of the aberrations—he crumbled and sloshed into *every one of his accumulated things*, flooding forth like a cracked dam had finally burst.

Like a chipped blade—

The young Aberration Slayer's body lost its integrity, spilling all the aberrations it held.

A crab, a snail, a monkey, a snake, a cat, a bee, a phoenix, a tiger—a dog, a bear, a leopard, a zebra, a ladybug, a fox, a piece of coral, a camel, a sea slug, a cow, a lion, a giraffe, a crawfish, a shark, an ostrich, a wolf, a turtle, a deer, a goat, a chicken, a rabbit, a millipede, a slime mold, a tanuki, a lizard, a spider, a mole, a silkworm, a squirrel, a whale, an octopus, a dugong, a beetle, an otter, a crane, a turbo, an inchworm, a tadpole, an anteater, a flying squirrel, a narwhal, a scorpion, an earthworm, a stick-bug, a swan, an oyster, an elephant, a carp, a llama, a sea otter, a shiitake, a sheep, an alligator, a cicada, a rhino, a sea urchin, a mouse, a sea lion, a parrot, a porcupine fish, a reindeer, a flounder, a pangolin, a jellyfish, a peacock, a mantis—came spilling out, as if there was no end to them.

All in a confused mess.

Mixed, mingling, and muddled.

Impossible to tell one from another.

He *became* all those "bad things" themselves.

He returned—he regressed.

The talisman had enough power to purify an entire shrine with its touch—so maybe it was obvious that, placed directly on his body, this would happen.

That doesn't change the fact that the ghastly sight looked like madness itself.

Yet at the same time, it brought me relief.

I'll admit I knew it was a false and phony feeling—but it felt so incredibly stressful for someone with a spirit as weak as mine to swing a blade at an opponent who took a human form and spoke human words, even if I did know he was an aberration... Especially when he was once a human. Now that he crumbled, I had an easier time wielding it.

I had an easier time.

Of ending it.

"Kissshot—kissshot—kiss—"

His voice crumbled, too. So too did his self.

His senses crumbled, as did his memories.

At this rate, all of him would scatter, all would be dust, nothing would be left behind—adding a swing of this sword to his crumbling existence would change nothing.

I would win the duel.

It would have meaning for me.

But it would be all but meaningless to him—were he to return to ash, the first Aberration Slayer would only be engulfed in eternal recurrence again.

He would never die.

Not for eternity.

He was an immortal among immortals—and neither Miss Gaen nor Episode could do anything about that. What can be done about an opponent who can never die?

In this sense, it didn't matter whether it was me or the others—when would he return next?

Another four hundred years later?

Five hundred years later—a thousand years later?

Even if an expert did seal him away, he'd outlive them in the end—and if he was incapable of dying, he couldn't even commit suicide.

Immortality that even he could not break down.

"s, sh—ot, ototot—■■■■■■■■■■■■—■■■■—■■■—"

Now even his words held no meaning.

The whole of his body broke apart, spilled forth, and unraveled, leaving only his throat, still producing sounds—and it was to him that I spoke.

"Well... I don't know what age I'll live to—but if we can ever meet again."

If we can ever meet again.

Let's meet again.

I then readied the too-long sword, the Aberration Slayer's blade, made from his own flesh and blood, to this incomprehensible composite while it could still be called him, and—

"■■■■■—■■■■—■■■■■—■■■■■■■■—■■■■■■■■—■■■■■■■■■—■■■■■■■■■—■■■■"

"There is no need to apologize. I've forgiven thee," said the voice.

Before I could deliver my stroke, a voice responded to this voice that could no longer be called a voice—shoving aside the horde of aberrations that had flooded forth to cover most of the field, heading with singular purpose to his last remnant, his throat, and.

Biting deep into it.

"'Tis I who should apologize—Seishiro."

A little girl.

She appeared from wherever she'd watched this worthless duel, whether it was a roof or the shadows of the gym shed. A little girl with golden hair and golden eyes—a former vampire.

Shinobu Oshino had approached him from his back—which you could no longer call his back—wading through the horde of aberrations, covered in their fragments, to bite into his neck—baring her fangs as she called his name.

Seishiro.

This girl who shouldn't have distinguished between humans, who claimed she remembered nothing about him, that she never once called him by his name, called the name of her erstwhile thrall—she called the name of her erstwhile comrade-in-arms.

And ate.

Crying—she ate.

Gulping, gnashing, and gulping again.

She ate him—the shadow of her fist thrall, while he could still be called himself, turning him to her own flesh and blood. And by turning him to her flesh and blood, her prey and sustenance, her bone and body—she freed him from his eternal loop.

"I am glad we could meet. I believed we would never meet again. But never again shall we meet—for now I have one more important to me than thee. For now, I wish to be for him."

The mockeries of aberrations, spread across the field—now came together.

They came to an end.

The parts that had created the Aberration Slayer, the dust and ashes that briefly covered this entire town—entered her stomach, without a speck left behind. No matter how massive their volume, she finished them all herself.

I don't know how he heard her words, now that he had neither face nor expression—I don't even know if he heard them. At the very least, though, I didn't see my predecessor looking satisfied, or free of regret.

He'd been relieved of no burden, nor was he uplifted. Hearing the words spoken aloud did nothing to bring him comfort or any kind of salvation. Even so, after four hundred years—

His suicide had succeeded at last.

034

"Okay, then. So what happened after that, Araragi-senpai? C'mon, c'mon, c'mon! What's the epilogue, or maybe, the punch line of this story?"

I'm so, so curious, so curious to know what happened next—Ogi said, as if to rush me.

Not that I had anywhere to rush to—however much I wanted to meet her expectations when she pressed me this way.

"I already told you what happened next—as you know, or rather, as you were hoping, this connects everything together, right? I met up with Kanbaru, who'd gone ahead to my home—to deal with the case of Hanekawa's tiger. I headed to Hanekawa, while Kanbaru headed to Senjogahara."

"I see, I see. Yes, I had heard that before—so you made it in time for that, too. How wonderful. Again, I'm every bit as happy for you as I'd be if it happened to me. I do love Miss Hanekawa, you know," Ogi said as perfunctorily as ever.

She and Hanekawa got along horribly.

Their relationship was all sharp edges.

"Speaking of which, does that mean Miss Hanekawa ended up being right when she had the idea that the former Heartunderblade and the first Aberration Slayer might be lovers? She really does know everything, doesn't she."

"Um… Wait, did I say anything about that?"

"Why, of course you did. You'd never hide anything from me!"

"Hm… Now that you mention it, I guess you might be right."

"I suppose Miss Hanekawa wouldn't get mad just because you decided to put her off until later. You know, it's that chummy attitude of hers that I can't stand. Oh, so what about whatever Miss Ononoki had been sent to handle while you were fighting the First? What could Miss Gaen have asked her to do?"

"Oh… Like I mentioned, I guess you could say that had to do with Sengoku… Basically, she had to take a little trip to get that talisman. That tween girl really is full of surprises. Or maybe you could just call her a true jack of all trades…"

"Yes, such a surprise. To think that a tween girl would live under the same roof as you—that she'd come to cohabit with you."

You can kind of understand why Miss Gaen sees Miss Kagenui's existence as bothersome, huh, Ogi remarked as if she already knew about Miss Gaen, but it's not like they'd met, right?

Whatever the case, I was pretty sure that neither Miss Gaen nor Miss Kagenui had Ononoki staying at my home just so that I could cohabit with a tween girl.

"And while I'm sure that Miss Gaen was trying to further prevent things by using that talisman, it unfortunately didn't go as planned because of my own mistake…"

"That's right. Because Sengoku misused it, right?"

"*Misused* kind of paints her in a bad light…"

"Using a talisman to exorcise an immortal aberration almost sounds like something you'd do to a *jiangshi*… But would it be right to assume you went back and placed the talisman on the shrine once you were done?"

"Yeah… Only, reusing it that many times led to it being less effective, which might have led to what happened with Sengoku…"

"And it would be right to assume that this talisman was lost during the rebuilding of the shrine?"

"Um, well, probably…"

"What happened to li'l Episode after that?"

"Huh...?"

Li'l Episode? Why did she sound so pally? Not that it mattered.

"He took care of a little bit of the aftermath, then returned to his country—but I think he was really satisfied by the job. He hates vampires more than anything, and in the end, we managed to erase one from the world."

"Hm... I see, I see. Well, senpai, thank you very much," Ogi said, bowing her head. As she looked back up, her face was smiling. "Now all the pieces of the puzzle are in place. Well, some details do slightly contradict what I've heard until now, but we can overlook that. Tying up those kinds of paradoxical loose ends is part of the fun for the audience of all tales, which is to say me."

"Well, I'm glad to hear that... So much happened that I can't even keep it all straight. I don't know where I'd be if it wasn't for you explaining everything."

"Not at all. It's what any Koyomist would do."

"Koyomist? What's that supposed to mean? Is it like being a Sherlockian?"

"Ha haa. These seams form along the overall picture because you try to hide things for whatever reason. As far as unreliable narrators go, Deishu Kaiki is already more than enough—I wouldn't go so far as to say Sherlockian. I will be doing whatever I can for you, though."

"You know, I really don't understand why you're so interested in my stories."

If there is something you can do for me, I said to Ogi.

"I'd like to hear your tale—if there's anything I don't want you acting conceited about, it's that."

"It's not that I'm acting conceited. Just as there is a best time for all things, there is a best time for all tales—all the pieces need to be present. I'm a careful girl."

"Careful..."

"I do feel like I slipped up a bit at the very start—oh, that's it. I probably shouldn't call these replacements for my own tale, but I can provide an addendum or two to yours. You do have a lingering doubt, don't you?"

"Hm? About what?"

"Why you decided to meet Miss Kanbaru in the abandoned cram school to begin with—why you decided to wait for her in a deserted ruin, rather than at your own home. We still don't have an answer for that one, do we?"

"Oh—now that you mention it."

"Wasn't that probably part of Miss Gaen's plan?" Ogi said in a natural tone. Not as if she was solving any sort of mystery. "She probably made some kind of suggestion that worked on you—I assume it wouldn't be that difficult to lead you into doing something then, since your heart and mind had been weakened by what happened with Hachikuji."

"...Why? Even if that was true, why would Miss Gaen make a suggestion like that to me? Meeting there ended up aggravating all kinds of problems."

"What I'm saying is that she wanted them to be aggravated. Miss Gaen isn't at all a pacifist like my uncle—in other words, my guess is that everything might have gone according to her plans, all the way down to the very end, when Shinobu ate the first Aberration Slayer."

"..."

"Not that I have any grounds for saying that—it's just that I can't help but think that way when I see everything ending exactly the way it should in that final scene. It makes me feel like something's a little off."

Whatever the case, Ogi said.

That seemed to be as much as she wanted to touch on this topic, as she tried to hurry along to the next—something I didn't object to.

I wanted to avoid getting too deep into Miss Gaen's prevention strategy. I found it hard to believe I moved exactly as she'd planned, then or during Sengoku's case, but it probably would have been best if I had.

It really did make me wonder.

Why couldn't I just do things according to plan?

"So that's why you haven't encountered many aberrational tales since the start of second term, with the exception of Sengoku's—the ash once spread across town had vanished, lowering this percentage."

"Um... Well, I think it might be more complicated than just that."

Like Miss Gaen said.

The first Aberration Slayer disappearing did not at all mean peace going forward—which is exactly why she tried to install a new god at Kita-Shirahebi Shrine.

Rather than controlling the situation, Miss Gaen must have seen it as a necessary step from a risk management perspective, but…

"Well, I will say we managed to settle something once and for all. Both me and Shinobu."

"I do wonder, though. What about Miss Kanbaru?"

"Hm?"

"Miss Kanbaru—I may not be a member of her fan club, but I am a supporter of hers. Her position as far as this whole affair just wouldn't stop weighing on my mind. She ended up becoming so deeply involved in the tale, and she never played any role greater than that of a helper— ha haa, the questions just don't stop, do they? In the end, Miss Kanbaru never did end up learning that Miss Gaen is her aunt, right?"

"Yeah—she still thought she was Oshino's little sister when they parted ways…"

Parted ways, or rather, when she ran off Naoetsu High's athletic field, as the two never met back up after that.

I still felt guilt over being complicit in a lie told to a junior who'd done so much for me, but I guess you could say I kind of found it hard to believe it'd be a good thing for Kanbaru to learn she counted someone like Miss Gaen as a close relative…

"Not to mention, I never did figure out why Miss Gaen wanted Kanbaru for that job in the first place—she contributed a lot, but to say Miss Gaen planned for that to happen would be a little—"

"I think it was all in her plan. But," Ogi said, cracking a suggestive smile. "Her plan contained some miscalculations—in fact, I'm the result of just that."

"Huh?"

"No, we can talk about that next volume, which is to say next time. This was a lot to digest—I'd like to take a little recess first."

Though it might be more of the type you get in court than the one you get at school, Ogi added as she stood.

I probably should have mentioned this earlier, but we were talking in my room.

Koyomi's room, located on the second floor of the Araragi residence.

The date—March thirteenth.

The morning of my college exams.

My memory isn't entirely clear as to why my junior came to my room to play early in the morning the day of my exams, but I just about don't care at this point when it comes to Ogi.

See her as someone who came and went as she pleased.

If I were to wake up and find her sleeping in my bed, I wouldn't be surprised.

"A court case, huh? I wonder how many years I'm gonna get."

"Who knows. You might even get the death sentence," Ogi joked— wait, what about that is a joke? "Well, I'll be heading home for the day. Let's meet again if you're still alive."

"Yeah… Be careful on your way back, Ogi."

"You know I will be," she said and began to leave my room, but as she touched the doorknob, she turned back.

"One more thing," she said. "Did Miss Shinobu end up eating all of her first thrall?"

"Hm? Um… Didn't I already say she did?"

"No leftovers?"

"Yeah, no leftovers—"

"Not even the armor?"

"!"

"Not just all the 'bad things,' that aberrational kindling that came flooding forth—but each of those pieces of armor he took off in the midst of your duel… Did she remember to clean her plate and eat all that as well?"

"…She did."

*I think—or maybe not—but—*I gave a tapering reply.

I didn't remember.

It seemed impossible that she wouldn't, given the way everything went…and even then, that suit may have been one thing when it appeared on its own at the abandoned cram school, but it couldn't have been anything more than armor by the end, right?

I glanced at my own shadow before asking a question in return.

"Is that something we had to do?"

"Maybe you had to, or maybe you didn't. But I do think you should have," Ogi said with a grin.

As if we were discussing nothing of importance, and she was only chatting with a favorite senpai. She always kept up that stance.

"After all—wasn't that armor also the first Aberration Slayer's flesh and blood, his bone and body? If you melted it down and forged it anew, you might be able to make yet another one, right? A new—enchanted blade Kokorowatari."

Or, with luck, even better. The short sword Yumewatari as well—Ogi said.

...Yumewatari?

What was that again? I'd heard the name before.

The companion blade to Kokorowatari or something? But it too had been lost four hundred years ago...and Shinobu didn't keep it in her body, either... Hmm?

A replica?

"If I was Miss Gaen, I would have gathered the armor before Miss Shinobu could eat it—who knows, maybe that's why she called li'l Episode there. I wouldn't go so far as to compare it to *The North Wind and the Sun*, but you could kind of say that the rules of the duel were such that they'd nudge the first Aberration Slayer into taking off his armor... Anyway, I'm just saying there's room to imagine. What do you think, Araragi-senpai? I would like to hear your thoughts."

"Why would Miss Gaen do that? I think Shinobu just ate the armor, anyway. Yeah, I'm pretty certain she did."

"I see, I see. If you imagine she did, then I'm sure that's how it went—there's nothing more reliable than your imagination, after all. My goodness, I'm sorry for asking you so many questions. You must be feeling down after all of that."

"Of course not. I had fun talking to you. I feel like I'll be able to sit down with a good attitude as I take those exams."

"Is that so—well, hearing that makes me feel good too. Okay, then why don't I answer just one more of your questions. It's the least I could do."

"My questions? What—question do I have?"

"Seishiro Shishirui," Ogi said. "The full name of the first Aberration Slayer. Don't you want to know the name of your rival in love?"

Then she left my room. The gentlemanly thing to do was to follow her to the front door rather than ignore her, but *his* full name, tossed suddenly my way, robbed me of the opportunity to do so.

…

Seishiro Shishirui… He even had a cool name?

Forget being disgusted, I felt defeated…

Being able to face my exams with a good attitude wasn't at all an empty compliment, but she'd thrown one huge bombshell my way at the end there.

Good god…

And I mean that to the point that I felt like paying a visit to a shrine—while I thought I could at least skip out on the chore today of all days, Ogi's early morning, or rather, dawn visit left me with some time on my hands. Maybe I'd go up to Kita-Shirahebi Shrine before heading to the exam site… Even a godless shrine would at least be good for some luck, right?

With this in mind, I began getting ready to leave.

Shinobu had made a full recovery by now, which is to say she'd returned to being nocturnal, so she was sleeping in my shadow—though it did seem like Ogi had timed her visit to line up that way.

I finished getting dressed (I was in my pajamas until now. The ones Hanekawa wore in August) and stepped out into the hall, only to find Ononoki just standing there.

She was still in her nightclothes.

One of Tsukihi's yukatas, baggily draped over her body.

No, judging by the bath towel on her wet hair, it looked like she'd just finished her morning shower—the classic tween girl fresh out of the bath in her yukata. Her skin smooth and glossy despite being a corpse.

…Hold on, she was freeloading in our home under the pretense of being my little sisters' doll. Shouldn't she be acting a little more doll-like?

Why was she just living here out in the open?

"I just so happened to overhear you."

"Again?"

"Don't worry. I avoided contact with her. I clung to the ceiling and ran off when she passed by. Like Spider-man. Being a spy and all."

"I feel like that'd only make you stand out more if you did it in a regular home... Wait, what? Are you a spy hiding here in my home?"

"You act a little loose around her, monstieur—aren't you being too loose-lipped?"

"Really? I don't feel that way. If anything, I worry that I'm not getting across what I want to say because I'm always covering up the parts that need to be concealed."

"If it's fine with you, that's all that matters."

"I was thinking of heading to Kita-Shirahebi Shrine now, would you want to come along?"

"Where's that?"

"Don't forget something like that. You forget way too much, you know. The place where your master went missing."

"Ah...the temple in Asakusa."

"No, that's Sensoji. Just how bad is your memory?"

"I'm not going on an early morning date with you either way. Sensoji. Er, sen-sorry. There's something I'd like you to tell me, though."

"What is it?"

Her horrible memory, or rather, incredible forgetfulness aside, living in my home had seemed to bring some stability to her character and personality (I think it was Karen and Tsukihi's influence, unfortunately). I had zero objections to answering one of her questions, but not knowing what she might possibly ask, I did feel a sudden nervousness.

There wasn't much surprising about the question she asked, though—in fact, it felt similar to another one I remembered hearing before.

Of course, the target of that question was a lost young girl, Mayoi Hachikuji.

"Are you happy now that you're a vampire, monstieur?"

"..."

"Well, what I mean by that—the first Aberration Slayer said that, didn't he? He asked what good it did him for you to be together with Shinobu-sensei—and you weren't able to provide him a single positive. Do you still feel that way? Do you still think that you being with her makes no one happy?"

"…"

I had no clue what happened to turn her into the kind of person who called Shinobu *sensei*—but I did understand what she wanted to ask.

As someone created as an immortal aberration—as an artificial aberration, Ononoki wanted above all else to know how I approached being immortal, being an aberration. These were the few and unshakable elements of her identity.

And so I needed to give her a sincere answer.

"I still do."

"…"

"It's never going to make anyone happy, and we're never going to be happy. All it does is bring trouble to everyone for me to be a vampire, to be with Shinobu—and it brings the most misery of all to Shinobu."

But I.

Even if I make her more miserable than anyone.

Even if it makes me more miserable than anyone—still want to be with Shinobu.

"It does kind of sound like an excuse, though," Ononoki said, expressionless. "Like, give us a break because we won't be happy, find it in you to forgive us because we won't try to be happy, just overlook us, won't you. Like you're telling everyone, don't criticize us, just look at how miserable we are, don't you feel bad for us? Monsieur, isn't it possible that you think you're making the best of it when in reality you've only contented yourself with misery and misfortune?"

"Hm?"

"The rest of the world would call that *not doing anything*—constant indolence. You'd better not think that people will forgive you just because you're miserable. Just because it's over for you doesn't mean you should drop out. You need to try to make it to that happy end. Should I step on your face again?"

"You're pretty harsh, Ononoki."

314

Wasn't she going to give me her support as I readied myself to take these exams that my entire future rode on? Though maybe that's what she meant by hoping for people's forgiveness.

"Staying miserable is negligence, and not trying to become happy is cowardice. Are you really going to let your predecessor and his suicide be for naught?" asked Ononoki, before turning around and heading to my, or rather, my sisters' room.

"Yeah, I hear you," I said to her back.

No one is happy now.

Not me, not Shinobu, no one.

I still think that—I still think it.

But who knows? Maybe far off in the distant future, four hundred years from now, say, I may have changed my mind somewhat.

After all, even if we aren't happy, we're oh-so-lucky to have more time than we know what to do with. At least we have time. To think, to live—far more than enough of it, enough for corpses to rot and turn to dust.

But maybe it was only a matter of time before even that time was up.

Afterword

I've written a good number of books up to this point, and not just those in the *MONOGATARI* series, but when I went back to read my old work the other day, I started to wonder. What I noticed is that your author here seems to have an unusual attachment to guy-girl buddy stories that never turn into romantic relationships—maybe you'd think that after reading just one of my books, but hear me out. Guy-girl pairings are a story pattern about as universal as boy-meets-girl, but it's just that we're so liable to assume that opposite-sex combinations will turn into romances, or rather, that it feels fated for them to turn out that way before the story even begins to develop. I do of course like those kinds of stories too, and I do write them…I…think…? Have I? Anyway, whatever an author's preferences may be, the characters' lives and relationships ultimately depend on the characters themselves, and, what I wanted you to hear from me is that I got to depict the buddies Koyomi Araragi and Suruga Kanbaru from lots of different angles this time around while knowing their relationship would never turn romantic, and that I had a blast doing it.

Anyway, a middle volume of a three-part series. Can you believe it? Well, maybe you can, but I'd feel very fortunate as an author if you were at least a little surprised by it. Actually, now that the *MONOGATARI* series is already up to eighteen volumes, any readers who have made it to this point might not be surprised by anything, but maybe you'd be surprised if I told you this story was originally supposed to be settled within the pages of *ONIMONOGATARI* and *KABUKIMONOGATARI*? In other words, this isn't the middle volume of *OWARIMONOGATARI* as much as it was part of a trilogy with "Mayoi Jiangshi" and "Shinobu Time," structurally speaking. I'm selfishly filled with emotion as an author to be able to finish this volume that I'd fully given up on after more than three years. And so, this has been *OWARIMONOGATARI Part 02* "Chapter Four: Shinobu Mail."

Thank you very much, VOFAN, for drawing the illustration of Miss Gaen, her first appearance on a front cover. You might be able to call Koyomi Araragi and Ogi Oshino another pair of buddies whose relationship will never turn romantic, but guess what's coming next? The final part of *OWARIMONOGATARI*, "Ogi Dark." I'm going to have so much fun writing about them as a duo too! Anyway, while the *MONOGATARI* series is wrapping up with the next volume, *ZOKU-OWARIMONOGATARI* will still be coming out after that, so don't let that one catch you by surprise. It's not Ogi's fault.

NISIOISIN